A WORLD OF GREAT STORIES

Board of Editors

A WORLD OF

Great Stories

EDITED BY

Hiram Haydn
and
John Cournos

115 stories, the best of modern literature

GRAMERCY BOOKS
NEW YORK

This 2003 edition is published by Gramercy Books, an imprint of Random House Value Publishing, a division of Random House, Inc., New York.

Gramercy is a registered trademark and the colophon is a trademark of Random House, Inc.

Random House
New York • Toronto • London • Sydney • Auckland
www.randomhouse.com

Interior design by Robert Josephy.

Printed and bound in China.

A catalog record for this title is available from the Library of Congress.

ISBN 0-517-05049-8

10 9 8 7 6 5 4 3 2 1

ACKNOWLEDGMENT
LATIN AMERICAN SECTION

The adventurous task of choosing thirteen representative stories out of such a vast conglomerate of countries and authors was greatly aided by excellent advice. To the scholars listed below we owe a debt of sincere gratitude for courteous suggestions promptly given out of their own wealth of knowledge and experience in the field of Latin-American literature. They are: William Berrien, Harvard University; John E. Englekirk, Office of Inter-American Affairs, Rio de Janeiro; Angel Flores, Queens College; E. Herman Hespelt, New York University; Willis K. Jones, Miami University, who was also generous with his books; Sturgis E. Leavitt, Inter-American Institute, University of North Carolina; E. K. Mapes, State University of Iowa; E. Neale-Silva, University of Wisconsin; Federico de Onís, Columbia University; Donald D. Walsh, The Choate School; and Fernando Alegría and Concha Romero de James, Pan-American Union. If some readers miss certain authors, let it be remembered that the selection was arbitrarily spread to cover all the countries of South America as well as some of Central America.

CONTENTS

v

GERMANIC AND SCANDINAVIAN SECTION

RUSSIAN AND EAST EUROPEAN SECTION

ASIAN SECTION

LATIN AMERICAN SECTION

Foreword

THE SCOPE of this anthology is at once so large and so selective that some explanation of its editors' working procedure is needed.

In the first place, by making an honest attempt to choose at least one first-rate story from every country in the world with any appreciable literature, we have inevitably been forced to omissions we regret. An anthology of great stories of the twentieth century *world* will, by its very nature, fail to do justice to some significant writers.

Again, the matter of personal taste must enter the picture. With six editors and several assistants contributing their efforts to the collection, the problem becomes still more acute. However, we have, for the most part, followed a few simple rules in making our selections. With a literature such as the Anglo-American one, rich in short story writers, we have reluctantly but firmly left out writers who have been exclusively or even largely novelists. Hence, for example, the omission of such writers as John dos Passos, Theodore Dreiser, James T. Farrell, John Galsworthy, Thomas Hardy, H. G. Wells and Edith Wharton, among others. On the other hand, in a literature where the short story as such has not flourished in the twentieth century (France, for example), most of the selections are excerpts from novels, but excerpts that make complete and effective units in themselves.

Another problem was that of just where to begin, chronologically. With only one or two exceptions (unusually good stories written in the last decade of the nineteenth century) we have adhered strictly to the limits of the twentieth century. Hence, so great an influence upon English and American fiction as that of Dostoevsky, for example, lacks representation. Again, while Tolstoy lived well into the new century, his major work unquestionably belongs to the nineteenth.

We were confronted with still another problem in the cases of Joseph Conrad and Henry James. James, as Mr. Cournos points out in his introduction, has been a potent force upon twentieth century fiction; Conrad, certainly one of its ablest practitioners. Yet the best *stories* of both men run to such length that had we included one of each or even either, it would have meant sacrificing at the least three other stories of ordinary length. It was a hard choice to make (particularly, for me, in the case of Conrad's *Heart of Darkness*), but we did what seemed to us wisest and fairest under the circumstances.

These were the simple rules we followed in the main. Yet we have probably not been wholly consistent even in the practice of these rules. Let any man who has been in a like situation, be the first to cast a stone. Our final collection we do sincerely believe to be the most remarkable anthology of twentieth century fiction in existence.

An exhaustive effort has been made to locate all persons having any rights or interests in the stories appearing in this book, and to clear permissions with them. If any required acknowledgments have been omitted or any rights overlooked, it is by accident, and forgiveness is requested.

Before closing this brief foreword, special acknowledgment should be made of the help of two people not listed on the board of editors. Robert S. Rosen rendered valuable service in bringing his extremely comprehensive knowledge and sensitive judgment to bear on the selection of items for the Germanic and Scandinavian section. Sylvia Freeman, in her editorial capacity with the publishers, contributed so many kinds of help that it would be impossible to single out one particular sort.

Hiram Haydn

AMERICAN AND BRITISH SECTION

Introduction

What Is a Short Story?

MY LATE FRIEND AND COLLEAGUE, Edward J. O'Brien, well-known authority on the short story, who encouraged the art as no other man in our time, once wrote in an unguarded moment:

"A short story is a story which is short."

Now this, though a perfectly accurate statement, is at best a half-truth. It does not answer the question: how short must a story be to be called short? Is *The Turn of the Screw*? Or *The Heart of Darkness*? Or *The Red Badge of Courage*? Or *Ethan Frome*? Scarcely anyone would venture to call any of these a novel, even a short novel, least of all a novellete, which suggests something frothily light; or even a novella, which Mr. Whit Burnett, the best living authority on the short story prefers—though actually the Oxford Dictionary, by the fact of omission, fails to give sanction to the word and frankly applies the word "novel" even to any short story of the *Decameron* or *Heptameron* type.

In modern usage, to be sure (a usage which dates from about the middle of the seventeenth century) a novel—we owe the definition again to the Oxford Dictionary—is "a fictitious prose narrative of considerable length, in which characters and actions representative of real life are portrayed in a plot of more or less complexity." The same immense tome provides no definition whatsoever for the "short story."

To return to O'Brien's assertion: "A short story is a story which is short." It is, let me say, a statement subject to a significant modification in a very specific, technical sense, of which O'Brien himself could not have been unaware. Witness, for example, that in a treatise * on the short story, O'Brien includes among his illustrative selections both Maupassant's *The Little Soldiers* and Chekhov's *The Black Monk*—stories of roughly 2,500 and 12,000 words respectively. O'Brien might have explained that by "short" he had implied short, shorter, shortest. But actually, and oddly enough, if it sound like a paradox, a short story by no means wholly depends on its shortness. The decision as to its being short or long depends rather on the nature of its technique. A short story may, indeed, be long, even quite long, if conceptionally and

---

* *The Short Story Case Book*, by Edward J. O'Brien. 1935.

3

structurally it creates a concentratedness of mood and singlemindedness of purpose which permit of no digression or deviation, no over-running of the frame.

The greatness of a short story shines by the very reason of its limitation. I am, of course, speaking in a purely technical sense. What I wish to convey is that every detail in a short story must add to its oneness, its wholeness. A great short story is so conceived that it could not be thought of in terms of any other narrative art, least of all a novel. It is not, to use imagery, a necklace made up of many separate gems, but is a single resplendent pearl set in a ring and maintaining an existence independent of sister jewels.

For one thing, the novel is dependent on development of character; the short story has no time for these slow processes. In a short story, the characters are already formed; they are there, on the stage set before the eyes of the reader, waiting to accomplish something that is, perhaps, a culmination to much, or everything, that went before. There are no lapses of time in the ideal short story; the lapses of time have already occurred. They belong somewhere in the near or remote past; to the short story belongs the ultimate action. It is, in a sense, like the unfolding of a final chapter containing within it responses of a past made eloquent by mere implication, by the way the character or characters of a short story act.

In short, whereas in a novel we plod along with the author in a prolonged journey of life, straying if need be into side roads—for life's journey is like that—and observe character unfold in all the variety of inner and outer occurrences, in a short story we cannot brook any interference with a mood which comes, or should come, with the first sentence. At the risk of repetition, I will say what I have said elsewhere in a comparison of the two arts:

"A novel is, or should be, a development of plot, character or atmosphere, or, in the case of great art, of all three concurrently; but the short story is rarely development, and nearly always culmination. It is always a dramatic, an emotional highlight, a cumulative, a concentric moment, which may suggest but never state the dragging progression that led up to it. It may, indeed, be a series of such moments, as when the bud bursts into blossom, and the blossom into full flower. It is at such moments that the reader of the short story bursts in upon the garden, but the reader of the novel watches its slow, gradual growth from seed to the flower." *

If this sound like a parable, the truth is that nothing better than a parable will illustrate the precise meaning I wish to convey. Consider, for example, the parable of the Prodigal Son. Can you think of a more superb short story in any language? I am not referring now to its qualities of love, pity, irony, or any of those qualities which pass under

---

* *Introduction to the Best Short Stories of 1924* (English) edited by Edward J. O'Brien and John Cournos.

the general term of "a criticism of life." I am referring to its specific qualities as a short story.

Here it is, a story which deals with three characters, with three different reactions: the Prodigal's repentance, the father's forgiveness, the brother's anger. We know the sort of people they are from the start, but their three different reactions merge in a single impression eloquently conveyed by the final sentence.

This five-hundred-word story might be stretched by a modern writer to five thousand words to suit the requirements of the time. Such a story might exploit the shades, gradations and nuances of the situation, the half-feelings and in-between-emotions of the three persons concerned. None the less, the author would have to maintain the unbroken unity of the mood invoked, from the first sentence to the last.

On the other hand, a modern novelist might conceivably stretch the theme into a hundred-thousand-word novel; but he would have to change the whole technical essense of the story as well as its pace. He would possibly begin by drawing portraits of the Prodigal's forebears; he would certainly tell of the early influences of his life, of tendencies in his character, of his repressions and consequent complexes, and all the rest of the domestic set-up which inevitably led him to leave home and waste his substance. The novelist would, moreover, describe the father, the virtuous stay-at-home son; he would fill in the background with numerous minor characters and their minor emotions, possibly contributing to the main action, and possibly not. He might also describe the father's house and the objects in it. He would also go into considerable detail about the Prodigal's life away from home, about his travels and escapades and love affairs. He would go to great lengths to describe the detailed workings of his mind and the acts and motives which led up to his repentance. For contrast, perhaps, he would use many pages to picturing the life at home, where the father and the virtuous son are busily employed in looking after their calves, fatted and otherwise, and domestic arrangements.

It might be argued that the denouement will remain the same. Undoubtedly. But the effect would be cumulative, not instantaneous. The gaps will have been filled in; little would be left to the reader's imagination. The element of speed, surprise, and sting would be gone.

There is the story of Joseph and his brethren elaborated into a three-decker novel by Thomas Mann. Each reading of the story in its original form made Tolstoy weep. I doubt if anyone would weep over the encyclopedic Mannine version. None the less, it is true that even in the original, this story, in spite of its primitive brevity, has the elements of a modern serial in it. And, indeed, in the Bible the first episodes, those of Joseph's provocative dream of the future and of the abandoning of Joseph by his jealous brothers, occur separately and long before the story has a culmination in a whole series of episodes. It is, perhaps, one of the earliest examples we have of the form we call the novel. Its translation into the form of the short story might be accomplished, but only by doing violence to the sequence of episodes, perhaps by resorting to some device like beginning with the final episode and seeing the rest through a series of unobtrusive flashbacks passing through Joseph's mind, merging in the end in a single image vibrant with a sense of drama, which has never been other than climactic from the start but which at this point, its conclusion, has reached the ultimate grandeur resident in its beginning.

Only the greatest esthetic skill can weave a single impression out of a series of episodes and confer on it that sense of wholeness, of integrity, which belongs to the short story. The earliest example of this that comes to this writer's mind is that marvelous story of the widow of Ephesus, recorded in the *Satyricon* of Petronius.

This memorable widow, while her husband was still alive, was "so noted for her chastity that she even drew women from the neighboring states to come and gaze upon her!" This is from the first sentence of the story, the mood of which is thus promptly set. When the husband died, what a fuss the good lady did make! It was not enough that she should follow the corpse to the tomb. For days and nights she remained in the vault, weeping and wailing all the while, and astounding the city by such a spectacle of ultimate devotion.

It so fell out that at this time the governor of the province had ordered some robbers to be crucified within sight of the tomb in which the virtuous lady kept vigil. The soldier, guarding the crucified bodies, saw the lady weep and he approached to console her. On learning the depth of her bereavement and on seeing how beautiful she was, he set about to make every effort to comfort her.

In the end he persuaded her to eat. Strengthened by food and drink, the lady's eyes were opened to the soldier's good looks. He talked to her, to convince her that life did not end for her with her husband's death. And so strong were his arguments that in the end he prevailed on her to surrender her virtue in the very tomb in which she mourned.

The story might have ended here. But there is "a sting in the tail," that device so assiduously, and for no good reason, avoided by the writing gentry today. And, in a sense, the sting in this particular story is everything—for it makes the story.

Just as the lady's real nature was established by the author, it so happened that the soldier looked about him and, to his horror, discovered that during his dalliance with the lady, the parents of one of the crucified criminals had dragged the corpse down from the cross and had made away with it. It meant death to the soldier, whose duty it now was to put an end to himself. But at this moment the resourceful lady came to the rescue. Why, indeed, first lose her husband, then her lover? Why, indeed, gaze upon the two men she had loved most and behold both as corpses? She came forth with the fruitful suggestion: why not hang the dead husband in place of the corpse which had been removed from the cross? Which was done, to the satisfaction of lady and lover.

"Situation is the main concern of the short story, character of the novel," * wrote Edith Wharton in a charming essay over twenty years ago, and see how well the rule applies here. Here is a story that is wholly one of situation. That the lady's character had seemed to change from what it was in the first sentence to something wholly contrary in the last is a tribute to the artist's employment of situation in revealing the true nature of things. Men will call this a cynical story, but then it must be remembered that Petronius wrote in a day when the empire of Rome was falling; just as our writers are scarcely less cynical in a day in which the old culture of centuries is going, and nothing has yet been found to take its place. Incidentally, it is a story profoundly concerned with the analysis of human motives, which brings me inevitably to the short fiction of our time.

Importance of the Moment. The Scientific Motive in Fiction

Analysis always comes with increased knowledge, with the pre-ponderance of this knowledge over esthetic values; it comes with in-crease in science, with its dictatorship over the heart's impulses, it comes when civilizations and cultures are in their decline. The cynicism of Petronius in the twilight of Rome, the pessimism and analysis of Webster in *The Duchess of Malfi* and *The White Devil,* the swan songs of the Elizabethans—these are symptoms of age: the mind thinks, but the heart has ceased to sing. Or if it still sings, its songs are pitched in a somber key.

Volumes might be written on the influence of the sciences on the arts of an age. Here I shall have to limit myself to the presentation of a bare outline of certain scientific facts which in our time have made trends in the arts, and, more specifically, in the art of short fiction. Within the past generation, in particular, the spirit of science has im-posed on fiction a new consciousness, for the most part alien to it, and the strain of which we are not yet certain that it can bear without losing its own nature. For who will gainsay that, first and foremost, the function of the short story, as of the novel, is to tell a story for the sake of the story? As Somerset Maugham caustically observes, there are many among the intelligentsia who regard pure story-telling as a debased form of art. He does not insist that the novelist should limit himself to pure story-telling, but he does emphatically stipulate that he make not too obvious a display of his extracurricular knowledge in his fiction, lest the fiction be swamped by it.

We are coming to the microscope. What has the microscope to do with the art of fictional narrative? Clearly nothing. Yet I think we may use the microscope to describe a tendency in the art, use it as a symbol of the analytical and psycho-analytical age in which we are living. We have come to a time when we count the worms in a piece

---

* *Writing of Fiction,* by Edith Wharton, 1925.

of cheese. What made the cheese? Worms, of course. No longer do we
see men as good or bad. We are turning the microscope on fragments
of human consciousness in order to see the chemical or psychological
processes which dictate this or that action, or a whole series of actions.
The extreme naturalists and the psychoanalysts are the new realists, and
these can't see the soul for the cogs and the worms. There are no longer
noble or ignoble actions, but only actions and reactions dictated by
purely material processes. The processes themselves interest some
writers to the exclusion of all else. In place of tales of the imagination
which used to lift us out of ourselves, we too often have case histories,
exhibitionisms of latent feelings, which attempt to throw us back into
ourselves. The trends in the arts induced by the scientific spirit require
investigation; they should not be taken on trust.

An almost mystic significance has been attached by some modern
writers to microscopic phenomena. They see fragments of life, to be
sure, as under a microscopic glass; yet each fragment assumes the vastness of a universe, and a significance not less than that of the whole
universe. Pin-point fragments of life have been increasingly used by our
short story writers, and, indeed, they have Goethe's sanction for this:
"The particular is ever subordinate to the universal, and the universal
must ever adapt itself to the particular."

A striking example of this new consciousness is one of Katherine
Mansfield's more famous stories, *The Fly*. No tale could give you a
better idea of "infinitude lurking in smallness." It tells the story of a
man who begins by thinking of his son, who had been killed six years
before in France, and ends by killing a fly he had rescued from the ink-
pot. To understand this story the reader must realize the intimate connection between the two tragedies. One critic has aptly said of it: "It
uses the sense of universal cruelty to typify the eternal injustice of fate;
there is an atmosphere about it of sheer and terrible fatalism; it wrings
the heart without the least concession to sentiment." Which, even if
true, still leaves the question open: will this story stand re-telling by word
of mouth; will it even arouse excitement, some measure of eagerness and
suspense, in the reading of it? I think not. And if I am right, it surely
has failed to stand the test of a good short story, whether from Ford
Madox Ford's or Somerset Maugham's point of view, a point of view
easy to substantiate.

What a fragment is in space, a moment is in time. The moment has
been greatly exploited in fiction, more particularly in short fiction.
Chekhov, perhaps, was the first to exploit the moment in the short
story. At any rate (quite apart from the fact that Mansfield's *The Fly*
provides an excellent illustration for the moment as well as for the fragment), it would be easy to find ample examples of this tendency in
Chekhov. There's his story which tells of a man going out to post a
letter. He stands by the post box, wondering if he should send it. At
last, after a great deal of hesitation, he looks down and observes that he
has his bedroom slippers on, which is a violation of bourgeois decorum.

This discovery is decisive. Promptly the letter is dropped into the box, though heaven knows it may change the whole course of his life.

There is another Chekhov story, which tells about a man who contemplates suicide. He enters a shop which sells firearms, with the idea of buying a revolver. The shopkeeper, expansive in the way of a salesman bent on making a sale, dwells on the merits of this or that weapon, describing its particular function and virtue, until the self-destructive mood of the prospective buyer becomes dissipated and he leaves the shop after making the purchase of a bird-cage or some such article.

Note the ephemeral nature of the persons in these two stories; they are persons of the moment who live for the moment. Durability—that is, character—is absent. Chance, accident, moves them to make decisions of import; it is equally possible that another kind of moment would reverse their decision. This is peculiarly of our time; since the day that Chekhov wrote the tendency here described has increased rather than diminished; it has influenced our fiction. It is highly symptomatic of the malady of the age: absence of faith and deterioration of character. If art is a reflection of the time—and that may be accepted as an axiom —if it is a faithful mirror of what goes on in the human psyche, then, for better or for worse, the fact must be accepted, and we must make the most of it.

It is claimed, with some logic, that this trend makes for objectivity— scientific objectivity, if you please. Indeed, Chekhov himself, the first modern short story writer, perhaps, to catch the moment on the wing, was also the first to acknowledge his indebtedness to science. Not only did he frankly repudiate any intimation that he might "belong to the class of literary men who take up a skeptical attitude toward science, and to the class of those who rush into anything with only their imaginations to go upon," but he also boldly proclaimed that to this class he "should not like to belong." Again and again he reiterates: "Familiarity with the natural sciences and with the scientific method has always kept me on my guard, and I have always tried where it was possible to be consistent with the facts of science, and where it was impossible, not to write at all."

Chekhov suffered an almost psychopathic fear of being "over-pretentious," an adjective he indiscreetly applied to Dostoevsky. He could not abide the role of the visionary and the prophet in the artist. Lacking the faith of the author of *The Idiot* and *The Brothers Karamazov*, and bored with life, of whose tedium he speaks again and again in his letters, his own ambition was modest. "An artist," he says somewhere, "must only judge of what he understands; his field is just as limited as that of any other specialist."

Chekhov, it seems, was proud of being a physician. Implored by a friend to drop his medical pretensions, he piquantly replied: "Medicine is my lawful wife and literature is my mistress. When I get tired of one, I spend the night with the other."

For a man who claimed a loyalty to science, this is a curious statement, full of implications and contradictions. Art has been described as "a jealous mistress," and every fool knows that you can't treat your mistress as you would your wife. No mistress would put up with it. The truth is, Chekhov was a poet and a man of imagination in spite of himself, and what attracts us in his stories is not that they are in any way consistent with science—many of them are not—but that they are emotional statements fully consistent with poetry. Truth is not necessarily "scientific," nor is it a monopoly of science, since it proceeds from the heart as well as from the mind. Dostoevsky loathed science, as did also Tolstoy, who admired *The Darling* and wept every time he read it, not because it was "consistent with the facts of science," but because it sprang from a great heart.

Apotheosis of the Moment

It must be remembered—since the fact applies even more relevantly to the Anglo-Saxon civilization, which should account for Chekhov's peculiar appeal to us—that he was the first great artist of a newly industrialized Russia, whose prophet, in a sense, he was. So sudden was Russia's transformation from an agrarian into an industrial country that it has literally been possible for us to see (in a way not provided by the slower gradations of Anglo-Saxon historical experience) how such tremendous changes can affect literature. The new life not merely changed the writer's vision; it also changed his mode of expression, his technique. Mechanization was a force that was disintegrating the old Russian life, which henceforth lost its wholeness and was slowly yet inevitably dissolving into fragments—and its time equivalent, moments —calling upon specialists to give them voice. The writer ceased to see life broadly, in panoramic sweeps, expressed in immense novels teeming with indigenous life. As the pace of living was accelerated, the writer began to see life as a series of swift impressions rather than as a coherent whole. A group of poets sprang up, singing the joy of the instant, as did Balmont: *

> "With every instant, I am consumed.
> In every change I am reborn."

In a sense, life became richer. It lost in breadth and depth, it gained in its multiplicity of impressions. A contemporary critic of the post-Chekhov era thus summed up the essence of the new vision: "You walk in the street. You reflect for a moment. A pretty face flashes by. You fall in love with it for a moment. Someone jostles you. You are angry for a moment. Someone smiles at you. You are glad for a moment. Such are the daily feelings of the town person. . . . And how

---

* Constantine Dmitrievich Balmont, famous as one of the Symbolist group which included Bryusov, Sologub, Blok, etc.

unlike they are to the lingering, precise, ductile feelings of the late villager lost in the contemplation of three firs." *

The really extraordinary fact about the new vision is that the short story, which hitherto had been a secondary form in Russian fiction, replaced the novel as a form created by necessity. New conditions created new needs; the short story answered the purpose admirably. It was no accident, perhaps, that the new trio who replaced Turgenev, Tolstoy, and Dostoevsky were all primarily short story writers. They were Chekhov, Gorky and Andreyev. In reaction to these "realists" arose the Symbolists, Blok, Biely and Sologub, etc., who introduced sophistication and stylism; they provided the literature of "escape." Both schools had one essential feature in common: they both thought life damned tedious, and regarded not merely small town life, but all life, as "provinciality." We would apply the term "Main Street" to the same thing. And it's not such a far cry from Chekhov's *Gloomy Folk* to Sherwood Anderson's *Winesburg, Ohio*.

Possibly, on the other hand, our American writers are more preoccupied with sex than were the Russians. In the quest for their respective social freedoms, the Russians sought for a solution in Marx, the Americans in Freud.

Freud in the Clinic, Fraud in Art

Freud is new, Freudism is old. For the truth of this assertion, we must go again to the Russians. Is there a writer—and we do not exclude Freud himself—who did more psychoanalyzing than Dostoevsky? But there is a difference between a creative writer's analysis of human motives, and a scientist's. In the former case, the nature of the human psyche is evoked by the imagination combined with powers of observation and innate shrewdness—call it intuition. In the latter, the results are the product of deliberate and calculated study: something which may be accurate as science, but dead as mutton as art. Unconscious symbols make poetry, just as conscious symbols kill it. Freshness and spontaneity and surprise are the very soul and life of art. But fiction, long or short, which is built wholly on meticulous analyses of human behavior, without recourse to the creative imagination, remains sterile, and devoid of all the qualities that communicate inspirational warmth to the reader, who would do far better to read those textbooks upon which the author drew for the texts of his fictional sermons. Such is the reward of artists who have wholly surrendered to science, to complete objectivity and detachment. We used to speak of the personality inherent in a man's work—and, certainly, the great artist always retained some measure of his personality in his work—but those who have dabbled in Freud have paid the just penalty of losing their identity. They have reached an artistic dead-end.

---

* From *Chekhov's Days to Ours*, by Korney Chukovsky, published before the First World War.

Croce, in *Poetry and Non-Poetry*,* dwells at length on the poetical distinction which makes a work of art, and on the lack of it which at best fails to deprive a work of significance as a "cultural landmark." In true poetry, he says (and by poetry he does not necessarily mean rhyme or even rhythm or any kind of external decoration, but something as inherent and integral to the work as blood is to the body) "there is discovery, penetration by the imagination of a world previously unknown; here the simplest expressions fill us with surprise and with joy, because they reveal us to ourselves."

In a recent essay, Mr. Henry Seidel Canby said that the only hope for the technologically-minded world driving in its airplanes fast to disaster was for the public mind to be warmed once again by the imagination. But we live in a "factual" world, and our editors demand "factual" stories, whose other name is "slices of life"—a characteristic enough phrase of and for our time, definitely implying absence of wholeness, and stressing the fragmentary nature of an age gone to pieces and capable, in the esthetic sense, only of contemplating these pieces of itself. It has not needed the atom bomb to produce that social disintegration, reflected in the arts as in other contemporary human activities. For the artist, however, to accept this state, is to yield his birthright. Bits of color put together do not in themselves make a picture, dissonances do not make music, and "slices of life" do not make life.

In fictional practice, "slices of life" are novels or short stories which take a piece of life out of its context. In a short story we are too often confronted with a spectacle of inner motivations too briefly glimpsed to offer significant meaning. As often as not, there is neither beginning nor end, but only an indeterminate middle. Sometimes there is a beginning, but no middle or end; in rare instances, there is an end, but nothing of what led up to it. So we arrive again at the conception of the microscope, through which are examined bacilli of disease; competent writing alone provides the esthetic camouflage.

Good story-telling is not at all like that. It has a beginning, a middle, and an end. A good short story is not a "slice of life." Call it a "roll," if you must—but, at any rate, a whole roll. Concurrently, you may call a good novel a "loaf"—and, again, a whole loaf.

To be charitable, one might call the ultra-modern short story a form of experimentation, perhaps inevitable in our time, and, possibly, serving some purpose having no real end in itself but whose results still await incorporation in the short story of the future. This studied effort to view life in disintegrating particles, this refusal to see the beauty which scientific inhibitions have so fatally obscured, might ultimately, in the reaction, help to produce an art which shall take cognizance of all dimensions and bring about a coordination of all factors—even as in modern warfare there must be a coordination of sea and below sea, of land and the air. Or to use another image: a single chemical ingredient

---

* In the English translation this work appears under the less relevant title of *European Literature in the Nineteenth Century*.

may conceivably be a poison, several in combination may well prove a beneficent medicine. All beauty is a matter of proportion, of balance. A good short story is no exception to this esthetic rule. The good short story of the future must make science its bondswoman; it must incorporate it within itself and not allow itself to be incorporated by it, as in the common trend today.

As for Freud, Freud is for the clinic. In art, through no fault of his own but rather that of his indiscreet disciples, the letter "e" in the famous psychoanalyst's name curiously assumes the shape of the letter "a."

The hope of the short story of the future lies precisely in the imaginative writer's capacity for making use of every ingredient of modern life and absorbing it into his art, whose main function can never change. This function is to tell a story. It does not preclude the writer from utilizing any theme, grandiose or drab, since, as Desmond MacCarthy so graciously puts it, "we are always glad genuinely to live through some experience not our own—it is one of the functions of fiction to satisfy that need—provided we have not been swindled emotionally or intellectually." Yet even Mr. MacCarthy tempers his statement with another to the effect that the short story "is dependent to a much greater degree than other forms of fiction upon the value of its theme." He emphasizes something that I had been discussing earlier:

"A novelist may disguise, and even make palatable, the thinness of his story by brilliant descriptions, incidental portraiture, acute reflections, and he may add to its interest by linking it up with extraneous matters occupying his readers' minds (social questions, etc.). But in the short story there is no time for this; it has to go straight to the end, and if that is disappointing, the whole thing is a failure."

Thus, we may conclude that while social problems are the legitimate material of all fiction writers, the short story writer is limited by the fact that he cannot stop to discuss the problem itself but is forced to present it in terse episodic form; its effect on the reader must be visual. He must be made to see the thing happening before his eyes. It may awaken him to thought, but never present the thought itself. Any fragment of experience lucidly arranged, interpreted with detached yet penetrating sympathy, and presented with respect for truth, should produce conviction in the reader. The readers, in Mr. MacCarthy's words, "feel they have understood some fellow-creature's predicament, though they be as puzzled about it as they might be about anything that had happened to themselves."

Yet no general rule may be described. The personality of the writer plays an important part; it may color any experience to the extent of giving the reader the illusion that he is in the company of the writer, who is narrating his story by word of mouth. I exaggerate deliberately, to make my meaning clear.

Always, there is a coming back to first principles. At the root of things the sense of life is strongest; the sap of life comes shooting up from the root. Any art changes and evolves only in externals; its essential laws never alter. The art of the short story, let me repeat, still remains—regardless of a thousand and one things which have sought to crowd it out—the art of telling a story: to hold the listener breathless, excited, stimulated, in a state of curiosity and suspense. This should hold good even in the purely psychological sphere.

The Modern Short Story in English

We have so far tried to define the nature of the short story. There still remains the question of the specific evolution of the modern short story.

The short story has not always been a form so dominant among the literary arts as it is today. Indeed, in England, since Defoe, Fielding, Smollett, and straight down the line to Dickens and Thackeray, the short story scarcely prevailed at all as a form. Great fiction writers, when they had a short story to tell, usually incorporated it into their novels, which, now and again, were threedeckers. It was not until Kipling that there was any large public recognition of the short story as an independent form, having a legitimate life of its own.

On the other hand, the short story in this country came into its own much earlier, much earlier indeed than the novel. Whatever explanation is given, it comes down to the same thing: the Law of Supply and Demand, which operates in literature as it does in other human activities. It must be remembered: literature lives on audiences; without audiences there would be no literature, unless it is poetry, which alone, at least in some measure, seems to be above the laws of supply and demand.

The hurry and scurry of American life, the preoccupation with practical matters, has been one explanation given for the preference shown the short story at the beginning of our fictional history. A far more plausible reason was offered by one of our earliest short story writers. In his later years, Bret Harte contended that a certain type of native humor had given the American short story both its particular incentive and its particular form:

. . . While the American literary imagination was still under the influence of English tradition, an unexpected factor was developing to diminish its power. It was *humor,* of a quality as distinct and original as the country and civilization in which it was developed. It was noticeable in the anecdote or "story," and, after the fashion of such beginnings, was orally transmitted. It was common in the bar-rooms, the gatherings in the country store, and finally at public meetings in the mouths of "stump orators." Arguments were clinched and political principles illustrated by a "funny story." It invaded even the camp meeting and pulpit. It at last received the currency of the public press. But wherever met it was so distinctively original and novel, so individual and characteristic, that it was at once known and appreciated abroad as an American story. Crude at first, it received a literary polish in the press, but its dominant quality remained. It was concise and condensed, yet suggestive. It was delightfully extravagant, or a miracle of under-statement. It voiced not only the dialect, but the habits of thought of a people or locality. It gave a new interest to slang. From a paragraph of a dozen lines it grew into half a column, but always retaining its conciseness and felicity of statement. It was a foe to prolixity of any kind; it admitted no fine writing nor was burdened by no conscientiousness; it was often irreverent; it was devoid of all moral responsibility, but it was original. By degrees it developed character with its incident, often, in a few lines, giving a striking photograph of a community or a section, but always reached its conclusion without an unnecessary word. It became—and still exists as—an essential feature of newspaper literature. It was the parent of the American "short story."

Leaving elements of humor aside, this statement is extraordinary, because it does sum up in a very lucid fashion the natural history of the American short story, and, moreover, stamps its basic character as something arising out of democracy, whose implicit interpreter it has remained to this day. From the beginning our great community had utilized the periodicals and the newspapers to voice its needs and aspirations. Is it any wonder then that our first short story writers, journalists of the first order, used them as vehicles in which they found expression? These periodicals paid for contributions; there was little market for novels, which were an imported English commodity, whose quality our writers, with a few exceptions, could not hope to rival. Poe, for whom literature was poetry, and poetry "not a pursuit, but a passion," confessed in his correspondence that he condescended to popular taste in his prose pieces; even so, a publishing firm of his time would not publish his tales unless he consented to "lower himself a little to the ordinary comprehension of the generality."

It was Hawthorne and Melville, as later Henry James, who wrote as if oblivious of economics. *The Scarlet Letter,* because of its sexy element, was a lucky accident; but Melville's metaphysics and daemon-ism could not surmount the democratic hurdle. Yet the journalist, Bret Harte, made a real sensation with *The Luck of Roaring Camp,* published in 1868 in *The Overland Monthly,* of which he was the editor. He was, perhaps, the first of a line of American writers who knew what the public wanted and proceeded to supply it. A still greater sensation was created by the publication in the *Atlantic Monthly,* five years later, of *Marjorie Daw,* by Thomas Bailey Aldrich, likewise an editor, mark you. Essentially a short story writer, his success with *Marjorie Daw* impelled him to write a long novel. But he could write a fine long novel no more than could Chekhov, who once exclaimed in a sort of despair, "I wish I could write a novel a thousand versts long!" and then proceeded to write *The Steppe,* a series of separate episodes strung together, without an organic structure.

Lacking private means and the system of patronage which prevailed at various times and places in Europe, the American writers found a means of livelihood in the periodicals of their day, and periodicals, obviously, ran to the short story form. Ambrose Bierce, a practiced news-paper columnist of his day, dared to transgress the law of supply and demand when he ventured into the popular short story field. His stories, however good, were too pessimistic for the taste of the current market. Writing for posterity, as it were, the penalty he paid was to have only posterity read him.

As late as 1902, a novelist of the stature of Frank Norris could bluntly declare that the writer of fiction must imitate the journalist and main-tain the closest touch with "the American people." It was his duty, he further asserted, to respond to the public's demand, because "in the final analysis the people are always right." Finally, "a literature which cannot be vulgarised is no literature at all and will perish." If there is any validity to this astounding statement, then the formula stories of the big circulation magazines must inevitably be recognized as master-pieces of the short story art, which, of course, is the sheerest nonsense. Yet it cannot be denied that some of our best short story writers were journalists. You have but to recall the names of Stephen Crane, Richard Harding Davis and O. Henry, and, in our day, Ernest Hemingway, to grasp the importance of journalism in the development of the Amer-ican short story and the significance of men who have been able to respond to the law of supply and demand.

A big book might be written on the influence of economics on liter-ature. This much, however, may be taken for granted: that America owes its preeminence in the short story chiefly to economic conditions which made the form feasible. In turn, the American short story in-fluenced both the form of the art and its increased production elsewhere. Poe, who derived from de Quincey, was taken to heart by France, where he gave stimulation to the art of the short story; just so, in paint-ing, Constable, who learned something from the Dutch, helped the Barbizon School come into being. Such inter-relations are a matter of cultural history. At the same time, the American periodicals became a market for the English fiction writers, who found the short story profitable, perhaps more profitable than the longer form; they had the English market as well, for in England too the periodicals gained a new impetus. Short stories never sold well in book form; there have been notable exceptions, of course—Kipling, to mention one. Often enough, a well-known writer received more for a single story from a magazine than from an entire book of short stories which, incidentally, might have contained that very story.

A case in point is that excellent English short story writer, Stacy Aumonier. Meeting that charming man in the Strand, London, one day, I happened to ask him how well a new volume of his tales pub-lished in this country was doing. "Four hundred copies!" he shrugged. That probably meant a hundred dollars in royalty; yet he was known to receive as much as five hundred, and possibly more, from an Amer-ican magazine for a single story. The English periodicals scarcely paid so well—often enough only a quarter, or even a fifth, of the amount.

Hence, it is not too much to say that America gave a substantial impetus to the British short story.

It would be difficult to tell offhand the ways in which the short stories of America and England differ. It is obvious that the readers of each country, on the whole, prefer their own. Roughly, I should say, the English stories are, for the most part, better written. They are more quiet—underwritten if you like. The English are famous for understatement; they leave much to implication, things to be read between the lines. The English do not believe, on principle, in raising the voice. They are brilliant in what has come to be called "the comedy of manners." It was Edith Wharton who said that "the comedy of manners" was England's chief contribution to the world's fiction. The American short stories, if not always so well written as the English, are racier, less hidebound as to style and theme; they reveal greater originality, a greater flair for the unusual.

In this selection of stories from the United States and the British Commonwealth, I have sought to avail myself of the most representative examples of short fiction, which are distinguished not only for their writing but equally for their story-telling gift. So great has been the output of fine stories during the half century covered—oddly enough, the early 'twenties were particularly fecund in this art—that the process of selection was in itself a task which involved some heartbreaks. To leave out a favorite story now and again is a painful business which every anthologist must sooner or later face. A single judgment being what it is—that is, always an individual judgment—I have availed myself of every opportunity for consultations with others, not disdaining the advice of unprofessionals or the man in the street. (I was amazed, by the way, at the number of people who mentioned one or another story by "Saki" as their favorite!) I wish to express my appreciation for these many valuable suggestions. Above all, I want to express my indebtedness to my wife Helen for her constant and willing help and unfailing counsel.

Except where it was pertinent to the discussion of the short story in this essay, I have not touched on the great world short stories outside those of this country and the British Commonwealth. The art of short fiction of Russia and the Slav countries, of Scandinavia, of Germany, of France, of China, etc., will be discussed in each case in its own proper place by editors especially equipped for their respective tasks.

JOHN COURNOS

THE SELECTIONS

UNITED STATES

Neither the American nor the English section could be discussed without reference to Henry James. A novelist of two worlds, he wrote with suave subtlety of men and women of both, but whose essential character and culture differed but little in aspiration and social behavior. They are held together by class and self-interest, by finding themselves, except for slight differences, in the same blind-alley of manner and custom and mental stratification. No one could write about these worlds as well as he could; for he had said the last word about them. His circumlocutional method was singularly apt for describing the social dilemmas and states of mind of persons whose conditions had reached an attenuation we associate with the ultimate flowering, verging on disintegration. He was a master of the comedy of manners, in which the English have excelled; and the English themselves paid him the compliment of acknowledging his influence.

If Joseph Conrad (in his later work) was the greatest writer strongly influenced by James, his most distinguished American disciple was Edith Wharton. She hardly attained the stature of her master, however. Indeed, it is a question if she were not best in a genre alien to Henry James, and that she will survive for posterity less by her longer works than by such a native masterpiece as *Ethan Frome,* which has been called a short novel, but which as legitimately may be called a long short story. It is odd, by the way, that *Ethan Frome* does not deal with the elite society which both Henry James and Edith Wharton treated for the most part, but with a more humble class which could still afford to indulge in cruder passions denied to English "county" folk and their American equivalents.

No greater leap could be made than from James to O. Henry, superficially a more indigenous writer, one who through the depiction of "the four millions" has paid his tribute to democracy, hence to the common man. O. Henry, an American who wrote about and for Americans, has been one of the most widely read readers abroad, notably in Russia, where his popularity at one time reached extraordinary heights. There is nothing suave or subtle about him, but he could write stories to touch the hearts of men and women, both common and uncommon. He has been accused of artificial plots and trick endings. It must be remembered that he lived in an age when these things were considered desirable; he but responded, in the way of writers, to the law of supply and demand. Not exactly realistic is *The Love-Philtre of Ikey Schoenstein,* but a story written for pure entertainment, which it provides in good measure. And, pray, what's wrong with entertainment?

Of a different temper is Sherwood Anderson, the first of his kind, a fine story teller, and an influence on those who came after. Anderson revealed in his art a tolerance, a love for human beings, an understanding of their essential problems, and a revolt, implicit, against puritanism. There is something tender about his conceptions, and a powerful sympathy for the lonely and the misunderstood. *Hands* is a fine story, which also offers an eloquent glimpse of the mind and heart of Anderson himself; those who were fortunate enough to know Anderson the man will testify to the fiber of both.

If there had been no Sherwood Anderson, there possibly wouldn't have been any Ernest Hemingway either. There is no actual resemblance btween the two writers, one outwardly soft, the other hardboiled; nonetheless, Anderson taught many writers to find themes. An aggressive maleness is in everything Hemingway writes. A strongly naturalistic writer, he has captured the spoken word as perhaps no other writer has. If a photographic realism be a merit, his dialogue has a distinction unrivaled; other writers have sought to learn the lesson from him, but mostly with less success. We have a brilliant example of his method in *Ten Indians,* the story chosen to represent him in this book.

If Hemingway has helped to encourage writers away from the traditional literary prose in favor of what may be called a spoken prose, this cannot be said of William Faulkner, who is almost as suave and subtle as Henry James in the particular tale included in this anthology. There is something of the languor and indolence of the South in *A Rose For Emily,* something haunting as in a poem by Edgar Allan Poe. There is atmosphere here aplenty, and a story too, singularly well told.

For pure story-telling, Wilbur Daniel Steele is one of the best this country has produced; one need hardly say more than direct the reader to his *The Man Who Saw Through Heaven.* Mr. Steele has never done anything better than this story, which opens as vast an horizon, physical and psychological, as any ever written, and yet tells a melodramatically exciting yarn.

The twenties produced a good many first-rate writers. Among them was F. Scott Fitzgerald, whose first novels about the Jazz Age exploded on the literary scene like a Fourth of July celebration. After some years of relative obscurity, Fitzgerald has again become very popular. Most of his most effective tales are about the lost generation of the twenties—here and abroad. While this is not true of *The Baby Party,* this story has many of his characteristic touches.

An equally American writer of a very different sort was Ring Lardner, one of our most truly indigenous humorists. His sports stories, especially his *You Know Me, Al* baseball yarns, have had a devoutly enthusiastic following. But his range was wider than that. His true skill lay in extracting the universal human elements from the peculiarly American scene. *Ex Parte* is a notable example of this quality, one which raises the fine old American custom of irrational squabbles between husband and wife from the comic-page level to that of genuine art. His work was also increasingly permeated by a sardonic quality that seeps through the humorous surface.

With space limited, it was difficult to choose between Lardner and Dorothy Parker, another expert in the general field of humorous, satiric and ironic literature. Hers is a somewhat different temper. As acid as Lardner, her talent is at once more sharply focused and more brittle.

It is a long journey from Dorothy Parker to Thomas Wolfe. Wolfe's peculiar genius is too familiar to American readers to need much comment here. In *Circus Dawn* all his extracrdinary merits and faults are evident. The almost superhuman vitality and sensitiveness that enabled him to encompass in a few pages the full sweep of a comprehensive scene and yet squeeze out of it the last drop of its most delicate and elusive odor, taste, texture—these are here. Here is also that torrential Wolfian flood of words that renders some readers ecstatic and others indignant.

John Steinbeck's work is as familiar to most American readers as that of Wolfe, although he has probably not acquired so large a number of devout disciples. Steinbeck has more of the story teller's gift—indeed, in *The Grapes of Wrath,* the extent of this gift rivals that of Ernest Hemingway. Possibly his best work has been done in his regional stories of the West and the Southwest. The story in this collection, *Flight,* and *The Red Pony* are among the finest of these.

Another first-rate story teller is Ben Hecht. Of late he has done much of his best work for the motion pictures, but it is probably true that his long short stories will remain the most enduring contribution of a varied writing career. Such narrations as *The Adventures of Professor Emmett* and *The Death of Eleazer* are among the finest stories in American literature. The shorter one presented here, *Snowfall in Childhood,* is Mr. Hecht's own favorite. It combines the account of a great storm with a sensitive study of a boy's awakening to romantic love—to make a rarely beautiful story.

Two of the American women represented in this collection, Katharine Anne Porter and Eudora Welty, have perhaps the most discriminating short story following in the country. Each is an extraordinary craftsman; each satisfies the highest artistic requirements without sacrifice of substance or vitality. Each has, as well, a considerable range: it would be difficult to select a single story from either that would do full justice to all her attributes.

A Day's Work, by Katharine Anne Porter, is an inimitable saga of Irish-Americans—the Hallorans and the McCorkerys. There is Gerald McCorkery, who made his own merry way without too much concern for the niceties of a conventional code. There is Michael Halloran, who wishes that his had been a like fortune. And there are their wives: respectively, Rosie, a fine woman "to snuggle down with at night," and Lacey Mahaffy, who "had legs and hair and eyes and a complexion fit for a chorus girl," but didn't "do anything with them." From the relations of this quartet, Katharine Anne Porter has written a story informed with tenderness, humor and irony—a story of genuinely universal appeal.

Eudora Welty's *Petrified Man* is an equally remarkable story. To capture as she does the authentic flavor of that representative American institution, the beauty parlor; to reproduce with a faithfulness that is almost painful the banal conversation between the beautician and her customer; and still to insert the genuinely macabre effect she does into the story of the tired "petrified man" who is wanted for rape; to produce so richly satisfying a story out of this strange combination of elements without straining the reader's credulity—this is an extraordinary triumph in story telling.

Outstanding among stories by our younger writers is *Act of Faith,* by Irwin Shaw, which throws a light on the feelings of a Jew in the army who, sensitive to possibilities of inter-racial unfriendliness, resolves his dilemma with a courage which depends upon the faith that wills rather than upon the reason that doubts.

ENGLAND

Rudyard Kipling has been called the Laureate of Empire. It would take an historian, rather than a literary critic, to evaluate Kipling's political significance; his paean to Empire may or may not be explained on the ground that he was the inevitable product of his time and that he came at the zenith of England's political glory in order to sing the not less inevitable swan song. In any event, Kipling's propaganda will be forgotten when his writing and story-telling skill is still remembered. *The Eye of Allah* is representative of a side of his work too little known, a side that may possibly eventually be valued more than his popular Indian tales, *Jungle Book* and *Just So Stories*—delightful as hundreds of thousands of people have found these.

A scarcely less original genius is that of G. K. Chesterton, who in his way may be said to express the commonsensical gift of the English people. He has this gift in an abundance only rivaled by his eighteenth-century predecessor, Dr. Johnson, with whom on occasion he has been compared. Chesterton made no pretense of being pure artist. He had a philosophy of life which gradually led him to the acceptance of the Catholic faith. He expressed much of this philosophy in the typical English essay form; when he wrote his fiction he incorporated his ideas without violating the spirit of his story-telling art, which was considerable. It required consummate skill to give voice to his faith—call it propaganda if you will—without doing violence to his fiction. He did it best through the medium of a new kind of detective story and a new kind of detective. Father Brown, a quiet and humble Catholic priest, is the vehicle he devised for telling a story as well as for speaking his mind. The blend is startlingly successful. Of these famous Father Brown stories, which have fascinated Catholic and non-Catholic alike, the story selected for inclusion in this volume, *The Blue Cross,* is perhaps the most famous. In any case, it is typical of Chesterton's peculiar gifts, which bear little resemblance to the gifts of any other contemporary writer.

Somerset Maugham does not pretend to any desire to instruct. In a recent manifesto he frankly proclaimed himself first and foremost a storyteller whose function it is to entertain the reader, without compromise with the intellectual who demands other things with his fiction. He has been accused of malice and cynicism. He has both admirers and enemies. You must give him his due: he can tell a story, the sort of story which by his own confession he has set out to write, a story "with a beginning, a middle and an end." Typical of his ingenuity and skill is *Red*, the story included in this volume. The action in *Red* takes place in one of Maugham's favorite settings—an island in the South Seas. The technique—that of having one character tell the story to another, who has just met him—is also characteristic. And, as so often with Maugham, a good yarn is combined with romantic interest.

Another master of the short story is Saki (H. H. Munro), whose gifts lie in the direction of fantasy. His stories are delightfully original: it would be difficult to make comparisons, for there is no one quite like him. It was a toss-up whether *Tobermory,* a story of a cat that talked—truthfully rather than discreetly—or *The Open Window* should be chosen for inclusion here, but the editors—wisely, I think—have chosen the latter, which is replete with Saki's amazing powers of invention.

D. H. Lawrence has been the subject of much controversy, chiefly because of his preoccupation with sexual themes and the flouting of Victorian traditions. This is not the place, however, to dwell on his manifold genius—which handled the novel, the essay, the play, the poems and the short story with an unquestioned felicity of craftsmanship. In all these forms he weighed contemporary social values, and found them wanting. *The Rocking-Horse Winner* is a representative example of his effort in the short story form, though unusual in its preoccupation with a child. In it, as in much of his work, he combines realism with fantasy.

Edith Sitwell is another English genius who has revealed superb craftsmanship in several genres, including the novel, the poem and the essay. In *Fanfare For Elizabeth,* she offers a glimpse of Shakespeare's England, whose poor lived in wretchedness while their country was producing a literary art of transcendent beauty.

It is of another kind of England that Elizabeth Bowen has appointed herself the spokesman. In the period immediately preceding World War II she reflected a certain section of the complacent bourgeoisie going to seed and resigned to the futility of existence. In her recent book of short stories this mood is translated into a stoical mood of endurance and resistant courage. This is particularly well expressed in *Sunday Afternoon,* reproduced in this book, a story which grips you by its very matter-of-factness and understatement, so characteristic of the best contemporary English writing.

IRELAND

It would seem impossible wholly to dissociate the works of Irish writers from their English contemporaries. We do not think of George Moore as Irish, nor of Lawrence as Welsh. Their books are inevitably considered as a part of and in the stream of English literature. James Stephens, James Joyce and Liam O'Flaherty are Irish, but you cannot write of present-day English literature and exclude them from the record.

James Stephens, best known for his novel, *The Crock of Gold,* which won the Polignac Prize in 1912, has written many short stories which reveal a humor not without a touch of the grim and sardonic. He has a fine creative imagination which shines in a story like *Desire,* here reproduced. Lyrical and fanciful, Stephens found prompt acceptance with a wide audience.

On the other hand, his contemporary, James Joyce, world-famous for *Ulysses,* a revolutionary piece of creative literature which conquered the opposition of the squeamish and a censorship which sought to suppress it both here and in England, did not find his path strewn with roses. His *Dubliners,* a collection of short stories completed in 1905, encountered such difficulties, because of the Edwardian disapproval, that the work was not published until 1914. Before this happened two publishers broke contracts rather than risk sponsoring his work. Joyce never saw Ireland after 1912, so disgusted was he with his treatment there.

In general, the significance of Joyce's creation extends beyond Ireland. He is the major literary figure of the veritable revolution in language which has taken place in our time. Again, no one has more clearly noted the symptoms of prevalent moral disintegration and foreseen the collapse of western civilization than he did.

The Boarding House (from *Dubliners*) has none of the difficulty for the average reader that his later forays into the subconscious and the unconscious do. It is the strong but quiet story of a young man caught in a trap by two formidable women, and conveys wonderfully a sense of the dreariness of this sort of boarding house life in Dublin.

Of the three writers here included, Liam O'Flaherty is the most exclusively Irish. He took an active part in the Irish civil war, whose scenes he depicted in many of his novels and short stories. There is always drama in his stories, and it has been said that his writings particularly lend themselves to translation on the screen. His story, *The Sniper,* is thoroughly characteristic.

Scotland

Morley Jamieson is practically an unknown writer; the editors of this anthology take pride in the fact of discovery. *The Old Wife* reveals a fine talent of plot and characterization reminiscent of Maupassant, but in a Scottish setting and in the native vernacular. Only in this sense is it regional; actually, as a piece of story-telling, it has a universal appeal.

Wales

The pleasure of discovery was also granted the editors in the story *Keep Up Appearances* by Rhian Roberts—a new name in the short story field. The author is only twenty-four years old, yet this story might have been written by a veteran master of the craft. There is a grim but enjoyable humor in her account of how a ne'er-do-well old man tricks a whole town into celebrating his generosity at his death.

NEW ZEALAND

Katherine Mansfield has made New Zealand's most famous contribution to creative literature, though England has always considered her one of her own. A disciple of Chekhov, without apishly copying, she has used the Russian's method in describing the moods of the English bourgeoisie. Her talent is on the fragile side, but within limitations she has managed to convey with restraint and delicate skill the emotions of moments, caught as it were on the wing and held while in a state of flutter for the reader to glimpse before passing on. *Miss Brill* presents brilliantly such an experience in the life of an unremarkable spinster—the elements that comprise such a moment, and the shattering of it.

AUSTRALIA

Australia has been developing an impressive literature of its own. In its older generation of writers, Henry Lawson's tales achieved perhaps the widest following. Many of these dealt with the hard conditions of pioneer life.

Katharine Susannah Prichard, whose *The Gray Horse* appears in this collection, is outstanding among the writers of the following generation. Winner of the Hodder and Stoughton award for the best book on Australia with her novel, *The Pioneers,* she is a first-rate and subtle craftsman.

CANADA

The art of Morley Callaghan must be familiar to every short story lover in this country, which has long welcomed it through the medium of highbrow and popular periodicals and books. Never, in the opinion of this writer, has Callaghan shown greater power and pathos and tenderness than in *A Sick Call,* reprinted in this anthology.

JOHN COURNOS

O. HENRY

The Love-Philtre of Ikey Schoenstein

O. Henry (William Sydney Porter, 1862–1910), the most popular of all American short story writers, was born in Greensboro, N. C. He left school at fifteen. Five years later he went to Texas, where he lived for twelve years. He served three years in jail for alleged embezzlement of bank funds—a charge of which he might have been acquitted if he had not fled to Honduras. He spent his later years in New York, where he died of tuberculosis. Many of his most famous stories record the diverse daily lives of New Yorkers. [From *The Four Million* by O. Henry; copyright 1904 by Doubleday & Co., Inc.]

THE BLUE LIGHT DRUG STORE is downtown, between the Bowery and First Avenue, where the distance between the two streets is the shortest. The Blue Light does not consider that pharmacy is a thing of bric-à-brac, scent and ice-cream soda. If you ask it for pain-killer it will not give you a bon-bon.

The Blue Light scorns the labor-saving arts of modern pharmacy. It macerates its opium and percolates its own laudanum and paregoric. To this day pills are made behind its tall prescription desk—pills rolled out on its own pill-tile, divided with a spatula, rolled with the finger and thumb, dusted with calcined magnesia and delivered in little round pasteboard pill-boxes. The store is on a corner about which coveys of ragged-plumed, hilarious children play and become candidates for the cough drops and soothing syrups that wait for them inside.

Ikey Schoenstein was the night clerk of the Blue Light and the friend of his customers. Thus it is on the East Side, where the heart of pharmacy is not glacé. There, as it should be, the druggist is a counselor, a confessor, an adviser, an able and willing missionary and mentor whose learning is respected, whose occult wisdom is venerated and whose medicine is often poured, untasted, into the gutter. Therefore Ikey's corniform, be-spectacled nose and narrow, knowledge-bowed figure was well known in the vicinity of the Blue Light, and his advice and notice were much desired.

Ikey roomed and breakfasted at Mrs. Riddle's two squares away. Mrs. Riddle had a daughter named Rosy. The circumlocution has been in vain—you must have guessed it—Ikey adored Rosy. She tinctured all his thoughts; she was the compound extract of all that was chemically pure and officinal—the dispensatory contained nothing equal to her. But Ikey was timid, and his hopes remained insoluble in the menstruum of his backwardness and fears. Behind his counter he was a superior being, calmly conscious of special knowledge and worth; outside he was a weak-kneed, purblind, motorman-cursed rambler, with ill-fitting clothes stained with chemicals and smelling of socotrine aloes and valerinate of ammonia.

The fly in Ikey's ointment (thrice welcome, pat trope!) was Chunk McGowan.

Mr. McGowan was also striving to catch the bright smiles tossed about by Rosy. But he was no out-fielder as Ikey was; he picked them off the bat. At the same time he was Ikey's friend and customer, and often dropped in at the Blue Light Drug Store to have a bruise painted with iodine or get a cut rubber-plastered after a pleasant evening spent along the Bowery.

One afternoon McGowan drifted in in his silent, easy way, and sat, comely, smooth-faced, hard, indomitable, good-natured, upon a stool.

"Ikey," said he, when his friend had fetched his mortar and sat opposite, grinding gum benzoin to a powder, "get busy with your ear. It's drugs for me if you've got the line I need."

Ikey scanned the countenance of Mr. McGowan for the usual evidence of conflict, but found none.

"Take your coat off," he ordered. "I guess already that you have been stuck in the ribs with a knife. I have many times told you those Dagoes would do you up."

Mr. McGowan smiled. "Not them," he said. "Not any Dagoes. But you've located the diagnosis all right enough—it's under my coat, near the ribs. Say! Ikey—Rosy and me are goin' to run away and get married tonight."

Ikey's left forefinger was doubled over the edge of the mortar, holding it steady. He gave it a wild rap with the pestle, but felt it not. Meanwhile Mr. McGowan's smile faded to a look of perplexed gloom.

"That is," he continued, "if she keeps in the notion until the time comes. We've been layin' pipes for the getaway for two weeks. One day she says she will; the same evenin' she says nixy. We've agreed on tonight, and Rosy's stuck to the affirmative this time for two whole days. But it's five hours yet till the time, and I'm afraid she'll stand me up when it comes to the scratch."

"You said you wanted drugs," remarked Ikey.

Mr. McGowan looked ill at ease and harassed—a condition opposed to his usual line of demeanor. He made a patent-medicine almanac into a roll and fitted it with unprofitable carefulness about his finger.

"I wouldn't have this double handicap make a false start tonight for a million," he said. "I've got a little flat up in Harlem all ready, with chrysanthemums on the table and a kettle ready to boil. And I've engaged a pulpit pounder to be ready at his house for us at 9:30. It's got to come off. And if Rosy don't change her mind again!"—Mr. McGowan ceased, a prey to his doubts.

"I don't see then yet," said Ikey, shortly, "what makes it that you talk of drugs, or what I can be doing about it."

"Old man Riddle don't like me a little bit," went on the uneasy suitor, bent upon marshaling his arguments. "For a week he hasn't let Rosy step outside the door with me. If it wasn't for losin' a boarder they'd have bounced me long ago. I'm makin' $20 a week and she'll never regret flyin' the coop with Chunk McGowan."

"You will excuse me, Chunk," said Ikey. "I must make a prescription that is to be called for soon."

"Say," said McGowan, looking up suddenly, "say, Ikey, ain't there a drug of some kind—some kind of powders that'll make a girl like you better if you give 'em to her?"

Ikey's lip beneath his nose curled with the scorn of superior enlightenment; but before he could answer, McGowan continued:

"Tim Lacy told me he got some once from a croaker uptown and fed 'em to his girl in soda water. From the very first dose he was ace-high and everybody else looked like thirty cents to her. They was married in less than two weeks."

Strong and simple was Chunk McGowan. A better reader of men than Ikey was could have seen that his tough frame was strung upon fine wires. Like a good general who was about to invade the enemy's territory he was seeking to guard every point against possible failure.

"I thought," went on Chunk, hopefully, "that if I had one of them powders to give Rosy when I see her at supper tonight it might brace her up and keep her from reneging on the proposition to skip. I guess she don't need a mule team to drag her away, but women are better at coaching than they are at running bases. If the stuff'll work just for a couple of hours it'll do the trick."

"When is this foolishness of running away to be happening?" asked Ikey.

"Nine o'clock," said Mr. McGowan. "Supper's at seven. At eight Rosy goes to bed with a headache, at nine old Parvenzano lets me through to his backyard, where there's a board off Riddle's fence, next door. I go under her window and help her down the fire escape. We've got to make it early on the preacher's account. It's all dead easy if Rosy don't balk when the flag drops. Can you fix me one of them powders, Ikey?"

Ikey Schoenstein rubbed his nose slowly.

"Chunk," said he, "it is of drugs of that nature that pharmaceutists must have much carefulness. To you alone of my acquaintance would I entrust a powder like that. But for you I shall make it, and you shall see how it makes Rosy to think of you."

Ikey went behind the prescription desk. There he crushed to a powder two soluble tablets, each containing a quarter of a grain of morphia. To them he added a little sugar of milk to increase the bulk, and folded the mixture neatly in a white paper. Taken by an adult this powder would insure several hours of heavy slumber without danger to the sleeper. This he handed to Chunk McGowan, telling him to administer it in a liquid if possible, and received the hearty thanks of the backyard Lochinvar.

The subtlety of Ikey's action becomes apparent upon recital of his subsequent move. He sent a messenger for Mr. Riddle and disclosed the plans of Mr. McGowan for eloping with Rosy. Mr. Riddle was a stout man, brick-dusty of complexion and sudden in action.

"Much obliged," he said, briefly, to Ikey. "The lazy Irish loafer! My own room's just above Rosy's. I'll just go up there myself after supper and load the shot-gun and wait. If he comes in my backyard he'll go away in a ambulance instead of a bridal chaise."

With Rosy held in the clutches of Morpheus for a many-hours deep slumber, and the blood-thirsty parent waiting, armed and forewarned, Ikey felt that his rival was close, indeed, upon discomfiture.

All night in the Blue Light Drug Store he waited at his duties for chance news of the tragedy, but none came.

At eight o'clock in the morning the day clerk arrived and Ikey started hurriedly for Mrs. Riddle's to learn the outcome. And, lo! as he stepped out of the store who but Chunk McGowan sprang from a passing street car and grasped his hand—Chunk McGowan with a victor's smile and flushed with joy.

"Pulled it off," said Chunk with Elysium in his grin. "Rosy hit the fire escape on time to a second, and we was under the wire at the Reverend's at 9:30¼. She's up at the flat—she cooked eggs this mornin' in a blue kimono—Lord! how lucky I am! You must pace up some day, Ikey, and feed with us. I've got a job down near the bridge, and that's where I'm heading for now."

"The—the—powder?" stammered Ikey.

"Oh, that stuff you gave me!" said Chunk, broadening his grin; "well, it was this way. I sat down at the supper table last night at Riddle's, and I looked at Rosy, and I says to myself, 'Chunk, if you get the girl get her on the square—don't try any hocus-pocus with a thoroughbred like her.' And I keeps the paper you give me in my pocket. And then my lamps fall on another party present, who, I says to myself, is failin' in a proper affection toward his comin' son-in-law, so I watches my chance and dumps that powder in old man Riddle's coffee—see?"

SHERWOOD
ANDERSON

Hands

Born in Camden, Ohio, Sherwood Anderson (1876–1941) had but little schooling. During the Spanish-American War he served in Cuba. Later he became, in turn, manager of a paint factory and advertising copywriter. *Winesburg, Ohio* brought him into wide public notice, but only one of his poorest books, *Dark Laughter,* ever achieved a large sale. He died while on a trip to South America. [From *Winesburg, Ohio* by Sherwood Anderson; copyright 1919 by B. W. Huebsch, 1947 by Eleanor Copenhaver Anderson; used by permission of The Viking Press, Inc., New York.]

UPON THE HALF DECAYED VERANDA of a small frame house that stood near the edge of a ravine near the town of Winesburg, Ohio, a fat little old man walked nervously up and down. Across a long field that has been seeded for clover but that had produced only a dense crop of yellow mustard weeds, he could see the public highway along which went a wagon filled with berry pickers returning from the fields. The berry pickers, youths and maidens, laughed and shouted boisterously. A boy clad in a blue shirt leaped from the wagon and attempted to drag after him one of the maidens who screamed and protested shrilly. The feet of the boy in the road kicked up a cloud of dust that floated across the face of the departing sun. Over the long field came a thin girlish voice. "Oh, you Wing Biddlebaum, comb your hair, it's falling into your eyes," commanded the voice to the man, who was bald and whose nervous little hands fiddled about the bare white forehead as though arranging a mass of tangled locks.

Wing Biddlebaum, forever frightened and beset by a ghostly band of doubts, did not think of himself as in any way a part of the life of the town where he had lived for twenty years. Among all the people ot Winesburg but one had come close to him. With George Willard, son of Tom Willard, the proprietor of the new Willard House, he had formed something like a friendship. George Willard was the reporter on the *Winesburg Eagle* and sometimes in the evenings he walked out along the highway to Wing Biddlebaum's house. Now as the old man walked up and down on the veranda, his hands moving nervously about, he was hoping that George Willard would come and spend the evening with him. After the wagon containing the berry pickers had passed, he went across the field through the tall mustard weeds and climbing a rail fence peered anxiously along the road to the town. For a moment he stood thus, rubbing his hands together and looking up and down the road, and then, fear overcoming him, ran back to walk again upon the porch on his own house.

In the presence of George Willard, Wing Biddlebaum, who for twenty years had been the town mystery, lost something of his timidity,

29

and his shadowy personality, submerged in a sea of doubts, came forth to look at the world. With the young reporter at his side, he ventured in the light of day into Main Street or strode up and down on the rickety front porch of his own house, talking excitedly. The voice that had been low and trembling became shrill and loud. The bent figure straightened. With a kind of wriggle, like a fish returned to the brook by the fisherman, Biddlebaum the silent began to talk, striving to put into words the ideas that had been accumulated by his mind during long years of silence.

Wing Biddlebaum talked much with his hands. The slender expressive fingers, forever active, forever striving to conceal themselves in his pockets or behind his back, came forth and became the piston rods of his machinery of expression.

The story of Wing Biddlebaum is a story of hands. Their restless activity, like unto the beating of the wings of an imprisoned bird, had given him his name. Some obscure poet of the town had thought of it. The hands alarmed their owner. He wanted to keep them hidden away and looked with amazement at the quiet inexpressive hands of other men who worked beside him in the fields, or passed, driving sleepy teams on country roads.

When he talked to George Willard, Wing Biddlebaum closed his fists and beat with them upon a table or on the walls of his house. The action made him more comfortable. If the desire to talk came to him when the two were walking in the fields, he sought out a stump or the top board of a fence and with his hands pounding busily talked with renewed ease.

The story of Wing Biddlebaum's hands is worth a book in itself. Sympathetically set forth it would tap many strange, beautiful qualities in obscure men. It is a job for a poet. In Winesburg the hands had attracted attention merely because of their activity. With them Wing Biddlebaum had picked as high as a hundred and forty quarts of strawberries in a day. They became his distinguishing feature, the source of his fame. Also they made more grotesque an already grotesque and elusive individuality. Winesburg was proud of the hands of Wing Biddlebaum in the same spirit in which it was proud of Banker White's new stone house and Wesley Moyer's bay stallion, Tony Tip, that had won the two-fifteen trot at the fall races in Cleveland.

As for George Willard, he had many times wanted to ask about the hands. At times an almost overwhelming curiosity had taken hold of him. He felt that there must be a reason for their strange activity and their inclination to keep hidden away and only a growing respect for Wing Biddlebaum kept him from blurting out the questions that were often in his mind.

Once he had been on the point of asking. The two were walking in the fields on a summer afternoon and had stopped to sit upon a grassy bank. All afternoon Wing Biddlebaum had talked as one inspired.

By a fence he had stopped and beating like a giant woodpecker upon the top board had shouted at George Willard, condemning his tendency to be too much influenced by the people about him. "You are destroying yourself," he cried. "You have the inclination to be alone and to dream and you are afraid of dreams. You want to be like others in town here. You hear them talk and you try to imitate them."

On the grassy bank Wing Biddlebaum had tried again to drive his point home. His voice became soft and reminiscent, and with a sigh of contentment he launched into a long rambling talk, speaking as one lost in a dream.

Out of the dream Wing Biddlebaum made a picture for George Willard. In the picture men lived again in a kind of pastoral golden age. Across a green open country came clean-limbed young men, some afoot, some mounted upon horses. In crowds the young men came to gather about the feet of an old man who sat beneath a tree in a tiny garden and who talked to them.

Wing Biddlebaum became wholly inspired. For once he forgot the hands. Slowly they stole forth and lay upon George Willard's shoulders. Something new and bold came into the voice that talked. "You must try to forget all you have learned," said the old man. "You must begin to dream. From this time on you must shut your ears to the roaring of the voices."

Pausing in his speech, Wing Biddlebaum looked long and earnestly at George Willard. His eyes glowed. Again he raised the hands to caress the boy and then a look of horror swept over his face.

With a convulsive movement of his body, Wing Biddlebaum sprang to his feet and thrust his hands deep into his trousers pockets. Tears came to his eyes. "I must be getting along home. I can talk no more with you," he said nervously.

Without looking back, the old man had hurried down the hillside and across a meadow, leaving George Willard perplexed and frightened upon the grassy slope. With a shiver of dread the boy arose and went along the road toward town. "I'll not ask him about his hands," he thought, touched by the memory of the terror he had seen in the man's eyes. "There's something wrong, but I don't want to know what it is. His hands have something to do with his fear of me and of everyone."

And George Willard was right. Let us look briefly into the story of the hands. Perhaps our talking of them will arouse the poet who will tell the hidden wonder story of the influence for which the hands were but fluttering pennants of promise.

In his youth Wing Biddlebaum had been a schoolteacher in a town in Pennsylvania. He was not then known as Wing Biddlebaum, but went by the less euphonic name of Adolph Myers. As Adolph Myers he was much loved by the boys of his school.

Adolph Myers was meant by nature to be a teacher of youth. He was one of those rare, little-understood men who rule by a power so gentle that it passes as a lovable weakness. In their feeling for the boys under their charge such men are not unlike the finer sort of women in their love of men.

And yet that is but crudely stated. It needs the poet there. With the boys of his school, Adolph Myers had walked in the evening or had sat talking until dusk upon the schoolhouse steps lost in a kind of dream. Here and there went his hands, caressing the shoulders of the boys, playing about the tousled heads. As he talked his voice became soft and musical. There was a caress in that also. In a way the voice and the hands, the stroking of the shoulders and the touching of the hair was a part of the schoolmaster's effort to carry a dream into the young minds. By the caress that was in his fingers he expressed himself. He was one of those men in whom the force that creates life is diffused, not centralized. Under the caress of his hands doubt and disbelief went out of the minds of the boys and they began also to dream.

And then the tragedy. A half-witted boy of the school became enamored of the young master. In his bed at night he imagined unspeakable things and in the morning went forth to tell his dreams as facts. Strange, hideous accusations fell from his loose-hung lips. Through the Pennsylvania town went a shiver. Hidden, shadowy doubts that had been in men's minds concerning Adolph Myers were galvanized into beliefs.

The tragedy did not linger. Trembling lads were jerked out of bed and questioned. "He put his arms about me," said one. "His fingers were always playing in my hair," said another.

One afternoon a man of the town, Henry Bradford, who kept a saloon, came to the schoolhouse door. Calling Adolph Myers into the school yard he began to beat him with his fists. As his hard knuckles beat down into the frightened face of the schoolmaster, his wrath became more and more terrible. Screaming with dismay, the children ran here and there like disturbed insects. "I'll teach you to put your hands on my boy, you beast," roared the saloon keeper, who, tired of beating the master, had begun to kick him about the yard.

Adolph Myers was driven from the Pennsylvania town in the night. With lanterns in their hands a dozen men came to the door of the house where he lived alone and commanded that he dress and come forth. It was raining and one of the men had a rope in his hands. They had intended to hang the schoolmaster, but something in his figure, so small, white, and pitiful, touched their hearts and they let him escape. As he ran away into the darkness they repented of their weakness and ran after him, swearing and throwing sticks and great balls of soft mud at the figure that screamed and ran faster and faster into the darkness.

For twenty years Adolph Myers had lived alone in Winesburg. He was but forty but looked sixty-five. The name of Biddlebaum he got from a box of goods seen at a freight station as he hurried through an eastern Ohio town. He had an aunt in Winesburg, a black-toothed old woman who raised chickens, and with her he lived until she died. He had been ill for a year after the experience in Pennsylvania, and after his recovery worked as a day laborer in the fields, going timidly about and striving to conceal his hands. Although he did not understand what had happened he felt that the hands must be to blame. Again and again the fathers of the boys had talked of the hands. "Keep your hands to yourself," the saloon keeper had roared, dancing with fury in the schoolhouse yard.

Upon the veranda of his house by the ravine Wing Biddlebaum continued to walk up and down until the sun had disappeared and the road beyond the field was lost in the gray shadows. Going into his house he cut slices of bread and spread honey upon them. When the rumble of the evening train that took away the express cars loaded with the day's harvest of berries had passed and restored the silence of the summer night, he went again to walk upon the veranda. In the darkness he could not see the hands and they became quiet. Although he still hungered for the presence of the boy, who was the medium through which he expressed his love of man, the hunger became again a part of his loneliness and his waiting. Lighting a lamp, Wing Biddlebaum washed the few dishes soiled by his simple meal and, setting up a folding cot by the screen door that led to the porch, prepared to undress for the night. A few stray white bread crumbs lay on the cleanly washed floor by the table; putting the lamp upon a low stool he began to pick up the crumbs, carrying them to his mouth one by one with unbelievable rapidity. In the dense blotch of light beneath the table, the kneeling figure looked like a priest in some service of his church. The nervous expressive fingers, flashing in and out of the light, might well have been mistaken for the fingers of the devotee going swiftly through decade after decade of his rosary.

ERNEST HEMINGWAY

Ten Indians

Born in 1898 in Oak Park, Illinois, Ernest Hemingway first studied in public schools, then in France. As roving correspondent, ambulance driver and infantryman in the First World War, amateur bull-fighter and big-game hunter, he has captured the imaginations of two continents. His best known novels are *Farewell to Arms, The Sun Also Rises* and *For Whom the Bell Tolls*. [From *Men Without Women* by Ernest Hemingway; copyright 1927 by Charles Scribner's Sons; used by permission of the publishers.]

AFTER ONE FOURTH OF JULY, Nick, driving home late from town in the big wagon with Joe Garner and his family, passed nine drunken Indians along the road. He remembered there were nine because Joe Garner, driving along in the dusk, pulled up the horses, jumped down into the road and dragged an Indian out of the wheel rut. The Indian had been asleep, face down in the sand. Joe dragged him into the bushes and got back up on the wagon-box.

"That makes nine of them," Joe said, "just between here and the edge of town."

"Them Indians," said Mrs. Garner.

Nick was on the back seat with the two Garner boys. He was looking out from the back seat to see the Indian where Joe had dragged him alongside of the road.

"Was it Billy Tabeshaw?" Carl asked.

"No."

"His pants looked mighty like Billy."

"All Indians wear the same kind of pants."

"I didn't see him at all," Frank said. "Pa was down into the road and back up again before I seen a thing. I thought he was killing a snake."

"Plenty of Indians'll kill snakes tonight, I guess," Joe Garner said.

"Them Indians," said Mrs. Garner.

They drove along. The road turned off from the main highway and went up into the hills. It was hard pulling for the horses and the boys got down and walked. The road was sandy. Nick looked back from the top of the hill by the schoolhouse. He saw the lights of Petoskey and, off across Little Traverse Bay, the lights of Harbour Springs. They climbed back in the wagon again.

"They ought to put some gravel on that stretch," Joe Garner said. The wagon went along the road through the woods. Joe and Mrs. Garner sat close together on the front seat. Nick sat between the two boys. The road came out into a clearing.

"Right here was where Pa ran over the skunk."

"It was further on."

"It don't make no difference where it was," Joe said without turning his head. "One place is just as good as another to run over a skunk."

"I saw two skunks last night," Nick said.

"Where?"

"Down by the lake. They were looking for dead fish along the beach."

"They were coons probably," Carl said.

"They were skunks. I guess I know skunks."

"You ought to," Carl said. "You got an Indian girl."

"Stop talking that way, Carl," said Mrs. Garner.

"Well, they smell about the same."

Joe Garner laughed.

"You stop laughing, Joe," Mrs. Garner said. "I won't have Carl talk that way."

"Have you got an Indian girl, Nickie?" Joe asked.

"No."

"He has too, Pa," Frank said. "Prudence Mitchell's his girl."

"She's not."

"He goes to see her every day."

"I don't." Nick, sitting between the two boys in the dark, felt hollow and happy inside himself to be teased about Prudence Mitchell. "She ain't my girl," he said.

"Listen to him," said Carl. "I see them together every day."

"Carl can't get a girl," his mother said, "not even a squaw."

Carl was quiet.

"Carl ain't no good with girls," Frank said.

"You shut up."

"You're all right, Carl," Joe Garner said. "Girls never got a man anywhere. Look at your pa."

"Yes, that's what you would say," Mrs. Garner moved close to Joe as the wagon jolted. "Well, you had plenty of girls in your time."

"I'll bet Pa wouldn't ever have had a squaw for a girl."

"Don't you think it," Joe said. "You better watch out to keep Prudie, Nick."

His wife whispered to him and Joe laughed.

"What you laughing at?" asked Frank.

"Don't you say it, Garner," his wife warned. Joe laughed again.

"Nickie can have Prudence," Joe Garner said. "I got a good girl."

"That's the way to talk," Mrs. Garner said.

The horses were pulling heavily in the sand. Joe reached out in the dark with the whip.

"Come on, pull into it. You'll have to pull harder than this to-morrow."

They trotted down the long hill, the wagon jolting. At the farm-house everybody got down. Mrs. Garner unlocked the door, went inside, and came out with a lamp in her hand. Carl and Nick unloaded the things from the back of the wagon. Frank sat on the front seat to drive to the barn and put up the horses. Nick went up the steps and opened the kitchen door. Mrs. Garner was building a fire in the stove. She turned from pouring kerosene on the wood.

"Good-by, Mrs. Garner," Nick said. "Thanks for taking me."

"Oh shucks, Nickie."

"I had a wonderful time."

"We like to have you. Won't you stay and eat some supper?"

"I better go. I think Dad probably waited for me."

"Well, get along then. Send Carl up to the house, will you?"

"All right."

"Good night, Nickie."

"Good night, Mrs. Garner."

Nick went out the farmyard and down to the barn. Joe and Frank were milking.

"Good night," Nick said. "I had a swell time."

"Good night, Nick," Joe Garner called. "Aren't you going to stay and eat?"

"No, I can't. Will you tell Carl his mother wants him?"

"All right. Good night, Nickie."

Nick walked barefoot along the path through the meadow below the barn. The path was smooth and the dew was cool on his bare feet. He climbed a fence at the end of the meadow, went down through a ravine, his feet wet in the swamp mud, and then climbed up through the dry beech woods until he saw the lights of the cottage. He climbed over the fence and walked around to the front porch. Through the window he saw his father sitting by the table, reading in the light from the big lamp. Nick opened the door and went in.

"Well, Nickie," his father said, "was it a good day?"

"I had a swell time, Dad. It was a swell Fourth of July."

"Are you hungry?"

"You bet."

"What did you do with your shoes?"

"I left them in the wagon at Garner's."

"Come on out to the kitchen."

Nick's father went ahead with the lamp. He stopped and lifted the lid of the ice-box. Nick went on into the kitchen. His father brought in a piece of cold chicken on a plate and a pitcher of milk and put them on the table before Nick. He put down the lamp.

"There's some pie too," he said. "Will that hold you?"

"It's grand."

His father sat down in a chair beside the oil-cloth-covered table. He made a big shadow on the kitchen wall.

"Who won the ball game?"

"Petoskey. Five to three."

His father sat watching him eat and filled his glass from the milk-pitcher. Nick drank and wiped his mouth on his napkin. His father reached over to the shelf for the pie. He cut Nick a big piece. It was huckleberry pie.

"What did you do, Dad?"

"I went out fishing in the morning."

"What did you get?"

"Only perch."

His father sat watching Nick eat the pie.

"What did you do this afternoon?" Nick asked.

"I went for a walk up by the Indian camp."

"Did you see anybody?"

"The Indians were all in town getting drunk."

"Didn't you see anybody at all?"

"I saw your friend, Prudie."

"Where was she?"

"She was in the woods with Frank Washburn. I ran onto them. They were having quite a time."

His father was not looking at him.

"What were they doing?"

"I didn't stay to find out."

"Tell me what they were doing."

"I don't know," his father said. "I just heard them threshing around."

"How did you know it was them?"

"I saw them."

"I thought you said you didn't see them."

"Oh, yes, I saw them."

"Who was it with her?" Nick asked.

"Frank Washburn."

"Were they—were they——"

"Were they what?"

"Were they happy?"

"I guess so."

His father got up from the table and went out the kitchen screen door. When he came back Nick was looking at his plate. He had been crying.

"Have some more?" His father picked up the knife to cut the pie.

"No," said Nick.

"You better have another piece."

"No, I don't want any."

His father cleared off the table.

"Where were they in the woods?" Nick asked.

"Up back of the camp." Nick looked at his plate. His father said, "You better go to bed, Nick."

"All right."

Nick went into his room, undressed, and got into bed. He heard his father moving around in the living room. Nick lay in the bed with his face in the pillow.

"My heart's broken," he thought. "If I feel this way my heart must be broken."

After a while he heard his father blow out the lamp and go into his own room. He heard a wind come up in the trees outside and felt it come in cool through the screen. He lay for a long time with his face in the pillow, and after a while he forgot to think about Prudence and finally he went to sleep. When he awoke in the night he heard the wind in the hemlock trees outside the cottage and the waves of the lake coming in on the shore, and he went back to sleep. In the morning there was a big wind blowing and the waves were running high up on the beach and he was awake a long time before he remembered that his heart was broken.

WILLIAM FAULKNER

A Rose for Emily

William Faulkner was born in Oxford, Mississippi in 1897, where his father owned a livery stable and was treasurer of the University. Faulkner took special courses at the University and joined the Canadian Air Force during the First World War. His first novel was published in 1924; with *The Sound and the Fury*, in 1929, he attracted notice. *Sanctuary* was by far his biggest seller, but it is likely that his permanent reputation will rest on *The Sound and the Fury, As I Lay Dying, Light In August*, and the best of his short stories. [Copyright 1931 by William Faulkner.]

WHEN MISS EMILY GRIERSON DIED, our whole town went to her funeral: the men through a sort of respectful affection for a fallen monument, the women mostly out of curiosity to see the inside of her house, which no one save an old man-servant—a combined gardener and cook—had seen in at least ten years.

It was a big, squarish frame house that had once been white, decorated with cupolas and spires and scrolled balconies in the heavily lightsome style of the Seventies, set on what had once been our most select street. But garages and cotton gins had encroached and obliterated even the august names of that neighborhood; only Miss Emily's house was left, lifting its stubborn and coquettish decay above the cotton wagons and the gasoline pumps—an eyesore among eyesores. And now Miss Emily had gone to join the representatives of those august names where they lay in the cedar-bemused cemetery among the ranked and anonymous graves of Union and Confederate soldiers who fell at the battle of Jefferson.

Alive, Miss Emily had been a tradition, a duty, and a care; a sort of hereditary obligation upon the town, dating from that day in 1894 when Colonel Sartoris, the mayor—he who fathered the edict that no Negro woman should appear on the streets without an apron—remitted her taxes, the dispensation dating from the death of her father on into perpetuity. Not that Miss Emily would have accepted charity. Colonel Sartoris invented an involved tale to the effect that Miss Emily's father had loaned money to the town, which the town, as a matter of business, preferred this way of repaying. Only a man of Colonel Sartoris' generation and thought could have invented it, and only a woman could have believed it.

When the next generation, with its more modern ideas, became mayors and aldermen, this arrangement created some little dissatisfaction. On the first of the year they mailed her a tax notice. February came, and there was no reply. They wrote her a formal letter, asking her to call at the sheriff's office at her convenience. A week later the mayor wrote her himself, offering to call or to send his car for her, and received

38

in reply a note on paper of an archaic shape, in a thin, flowing calligraphy in faded ink, to the effect that she no longer went out at all. The tax notice was also enclosed, without comment.

They called a special meeting of the Board of Aldermen. A deputation waited upon her, knocked at the door through which no visitor had passed since she ceased giving china-painting lessons eight or ten years earlier. They were admitted by the old Negro into a dim hall from which a stairway mounted into still more shadow. It smelled of dust and disuse—a close, dank smell. The Negro led them into the parlor. It was furnished in heavy, leather-covered furniture. When the Negro opened the blinds of one window, they could see that the leather was cracked; and when they sat down, a faint dust rose sluggishly about their thighs, spinning with slow motes in the single sun-ray. On a tarnished gilt easel before the fireplace stood a crayon portrait of Miss Emily's father.

They rose when she entered—a small, fat woman in black, with a thin gold chain descending to her waist and vanishing into her belt, leaning on an ebony cane with a tarnished gold head. Her skeleton was small and spare; perhaps that was why what would have been merely plumpness in another was obesity in her. She looked bloated, like a body long submerged in motionless water, and of that pallid hue. Her eyes, lost in the fatty ridges of her face, looked like two small pieces of coal pressed into a lump of dough as they moved from one face to another while the visitors stated their errand.

She did not ask them to sit. She just stood in the door and listened quietly until the spokesman came to a stumbling halt. Then they could hear the invisible watch ticking at the end of the gold chain.

Her voice was dry and cold. "I have no taxes in Jefferson. Colonel Sartoris explained it to me. Perhaps one of you can gain access to the city records and satisfy yourselves."

"But we have. We are the city authorities, Miss Emily. Didn't you get a notice from the sheriff, signed by him?"

"I received a paper, yes," Miss Emily said. "Perhaps he considers himself the sheriff . . . I have no taxes in Jefferson."

"But there is nothing on the books to show that, you see. We must go by the—"

"See Colonel Sartoris. I have no taxes in Jefferson."

"But, Miss Emily—"

"See Colonel Sartoris." (Colonel Sartoris had been dead almost ten years.) "I have no taxes in Jefferson. Tobe!" The Negro appeared. "Show these gentlemen out."

So she vanquished them, horse and foot, just as she had vanquished their fathers thirty years before about the smell. That was two years after her father's death and a short time after her sweetheart—the one we believed would marry her—had deserted her. After her father's death she went out very little; after her sweetheart went away, people hardly saw her at all. A few of the ladies had the temerity to call, but were not received, and the only sign of life about the place was the Negro man—a young man then—going in and out with a market basket.

"Just as if a man—any man—could keep a kitchen properly," the ladies said; so they were not surprised when the smell developed. It was another link between the gross, teeming world and the high and mighty Griersons.

A neighbor, a woman, complained to the mayor, Judge Stevens, eighty years old.

"But what will you have me do about it, madam?" he said.

"Why, send her word to stop it," the woman said. "Isn't there a law?"

"I'm sure that won't be necessary," Judge Stevens said. "It's probably just a snake or a rat that nigger of hers killed in the yard. I'll speak to him about it."

The next day he received two more complaints, one from a man who came in diffident deprecation. "We really must do something about it, Judge. I'd be the last one in the world to bother Miss Emily, but we've got to do something." That night the Board of Aldermen met—three graybeards and one younger man, a member of the rising generation.

"It's simple enough," he said. "Send her word to have her place cleaned up. Give her a certain time to do it in, and if she don't . . ."

"Dammit, sir," Judge Stevens said, "will you accuse a lady to her face of smelling bad?"

So the next night, after midnight, four men crossed Miss Emily's lawn and slunk about the house like burglars, sniffing along the base of the brickwork and at the cellar openings while one of them performed a regular sowing motion with his hand out of a sack slung from his shoulder. They broke open the cellar door and sprinkled lime there, and in all the outbuildings. As they recrossed the lawn, a window that had been dark was lighted and Miss Emily sat in it, the light behind her, and her upright torso motionless as that of an idol. They crept quietly across the lawn and into the shadow of the locusts that lined the street. After a week or two the smell went away.

That was when people had begun to feel really sorry for her. People in our town, remembering how Old Lady Wyatt, her great-aunt, had gone completely crazy at last, believed that the Griersons held themselves a little too high for what they really were. None of the young men was quite good enough to Miss Emily and such. We had long thought of them as a tableau: Miss Emily a slender figure in white in the background, her father a spraddled silhouette in the foreground, his back to her and clutching a horse-whip, the two of them framed by the back-flung front door. So when she got to be thirty and was still single, we were not pleased exactly, but vindicated; even with insanity in the family she wouldn't have turned down all of her chances if they had really materialized.

When her father died, it got about that the house was all that was left to her; and in a way, people were glad. At last they could pity Miss

Emily. Being left alone, and a pauper, she had become humanized. Now she too would know the old thrill and the old despair of a penny more or less.

The day after his death all the ladies prepared to call at the house and offer condolence and aid, as is our custom. Miss Emily met them at the door, dressed as usual and with no trace of grief on her face. She told them that her father was not dead. She did that for three days, with the ministers calling on her, and the doctors, trying to persuade her to let them dispose of the body. Just as they were about to resort to law and force, she broke down, and they buried her father quickly.

We did not say she was crazy then. We believed she had to do that. We remembered all the young men her father had driven away, and we knew that with nothing left, she would have to cling to that which had robbed her, as people will.

She was sick for a long time. When we saw her again, her hair was cut short, making her look like a girl, with a vague resemblance to those angels in colored church windows—sort of tragic and serene.

The town had just let the contracts for paving the sidewalks, and in the summer after her father's death they began the work. The construction company came with niggers and mules and machinery, and a foreman named Homer Barron, a Yankee—a big, dark, ready man, with a big voice and eyes lighter than his face. The little boys would follow in groups to hear him cuss the niggers, and the niggers singing in time to the rise and fall of picks. Pretty soon he knew everybody in town. Whenever you heard a lot of laughing anywhere about the square, Homer Barron would be in the center of the group. Presently we began to see him and Miss Emily on Sunday afternoons driving in the yellow-wheeled buggy and the matched team of bays from the livery stable.

At first we were glad that Miss Emily would have an interest, because the ladies all said, "Of course a Grierson would not think seriously of a Northerner, a day laborer." But there were still others, older people, who said that even grief could not cause a real lady to forget *noblesse oblige*—without calling it *noblesse oblige*. They just said, "Poor Emily. Her kinsfolk should come to her." She had some kin in Alabama; but years ago her father had fallen out with them over the estate of Old Lady Wyatt, the crazy woman, and there was no communication between the two families. They had not even been represented at the funeral.

And as soon as the old people said, "Poor Emily," the whispering began. "Do you suppose it's really so?" they said to one another. "Of course it is. What else could . . ." This behind their hands; rustling of craned silk and satin behind jalousies closed upon the sun of Sunday afternoon as the thin, swift clop-clop-clop of the matched team passed: "Poor Emily."

She carried her head high enough—even when we believed that she was fallen. It was as if she demanded more than ever the recognition of her dignity as the last Grierson; as if it had wanted that touch of earthiness to reaffirm her imperviousness. Like when she bought the rat poison, the arsenic. That was over a year after they had begun to say "Poor Emily," and while the two female cousins were visiting her.

"I want some poison," she said to the druggist. She was over thirty then, still a slight woman, though thinner than usual, with cold, haughty black eyes in a face the flesh of which was strained across the temples and about the eye-sockets as you imagine a lighthouse-keeper's face ought to look. "I want some poison," she said.

"Yes, Miss Emily. What kind? For rats and such? I'd recom—"

"I want the best you have. I don't care what kind."

The druggist named several. "They'll kill anything up to an elephant. But what you want is—"

"Arsenic," Miss Emily said. "Is that a good one?"

"Is . . . arsenic? Yes, ma'am. But what you want—"

"I want arsenic."

The druggist looked down at her. She looked back at him, erect, her face like a strained flag. "Why, of course," the druggist said. "If that's what you want. But the law requires you to tell what you are going to use it for."

Miss Emily just stared at him, her head tilted back in order to look him eye for eye, until he looked away and went and got the arsenic and wrapped it up. The Negro delivery boy brought her the package; the druggist didn't come back. When she opened the package at home there was written on the box, under the skull and bones: "For rats."

So the next day we all said, "She will kill herself"; and we said it would be the best thing. When she had first begun to be seen with Homer Barron, we had said, "She will marry him." Then we said, "She will persuade him yet," because Homer himself had remarked—he liked men, and it was known that he drank with the younger men in the Elks' Club—that he was not a marrying man. Later we said, "Poor Emily" behind the jalousies as they passed on Sunday afternoon in the glittering buggy, Miss Emily with her head high and Homer Barron with his hat cocked and a cigar in his teeth, reins and whip in a yellow glove.

Then some of the ladies began to say that it was a disgrace to the town and a bad example to the young people. The men did not want to interfere, but at last the ladies forced the Baptist minister—Miss Emily's people were Episcopal—to call upon her. He would never divulge what happened during that interview, but he refused to go back again. The next Sunday they again drove about the streets, and the following day the minister's wife wrote to Miss Emily's relations in Alabama.

So she had blood-kin under her roof again and we sat back to watch developments. At first nothing happened. Then we were sure that they were to be married. We learned that Miss Emily had been to the jeweler's and ordered a man's toilet set in silver, with the letters H. B. on each piece. Two days later we learned that she had bought a complete outfit of men's clothing, including a nightshirt, and we said, "They are married." We were really glad. We were glad because the two female cousins were even more Grierson than Miss Emily had ever been.

So we were not surprised when Homer Barron—the streets had been finished some time since—was gone. We were a little disappointed that there was not a public blowing-off, but we believed that he had gone on to prepare for Miss Emily's coming, or to give her a chance to get rid of the cousins. (By that time it was a cabal, and we were all Miss Emily's allies to help circumvent the cousins.) Sure enough, after another week they departed. And, as we had expected all along, within three days Homer Barron was back in town. A neighbor saw the Negro man admit him at the kitchen door at dusk one evening.

And that was the last we saw of Homer Barron. And of Miss Emily for some time. The Negro man went in and out with the market basket, but the front door remained closed. Now and then we would see her at a window for a moment, as the men did that night when they sprinkled the lime, but for almost six months she did not appear on the streets. Then we knew that this was to be expected too; as if that quality of her father which had thwarted her woman's life so many times had been too virulent and too furious to die.

When we next saw Miss Emily, she had grown fat and her hair was turning gray. During the next few years it grew grayer and grayer until it attained an even pepper-and-salt iron-gray, when it ceased turning. Up to the day of her death at seventy-four it was still that vigorous iron-gray, like the hair of an active man.

From that time on her front door remained closed, save for a period of six or seven years, when she was about forty, during which she gave lessons in china-painting. She fitted up a studio in one of the downstairs rooms, where the daughters and granddaughters of Colonel Sartoris' contemporaries were sent to her with the same regularity and in the same spirit that they were sent to church on Sundays with a twenty-five-cent piece for the collection plate. Meanwhile her taxes had been remitted.

Then the newer generation became the backbone and the spirit of the town, and the painting pupils grew up and fell away and did not send their children to her with boxes of color and tedious brushes and pictures cut from the ladies' magazines. The front door closed upon the last one and remained closed for good. When the town got free postal delivery, Miss Emily alone refused to let them fasten the metal numbers above her door and attach a mailbox to it. She would not listen to them.

Daily, monthly, yearly we watched the Negro grow grayer and more stooped, going in and out with the market basket. Each December we sent her a tax notice, which would be returned by the post office a week later, unclaimed. Now and then we would see her in one of the downstairs windows—she had evidently shut up the top floor of the house—

like the carven torso of an idol in a niche, looking or not looking at us, we could never tell which. Thus she passed from generation to generation—dear, inescapable, impervious, tranquil, and perverse.

And so she died. Fell ill in the house filled with dust and shadows, with only a doddering Negro man to wait on her. We did not even know she was sick; we had long since given up trying to get any information from the Negro. He talked to no one, probably not even to her, for his voice had grown harsh and rusty, as if from disuse.

She died in one of the downstairs rooms, in a heavy walnut bed with a curtain, her gray head propped on a pillow yellow and moldy with age and lack of sunlight.

The Negro met the first of the ladies at the front door and let them in, with their hushed, sibilant voices and their quick, curious glances, and then he disappeared. He walked right through the house and out the back and was not seen again.

The two female cousins came at once. They held the funeral on the second day, with the town coming to look at Miss Emily beneath a mass of bought flowers, with the crayon face of her father musing profoundly above the bier and the ladies sibilant and macabre; and the very old men—some in their brushed Confederate uniforms—on the porch and the lawn, talking of Miss Emily as if she had been a contemporary of theirs, believing that they had danced with her and courted her perhaps, confusing time with its mathematical progression, as the old do, to whom all the past is not a diminishing road but, instead, a huge meadow which no winter ever quite touches, divided from them now by the narrow bottle-neck of the most recent decade of years.

Already we knew that there was one room in that region above stairs which no one had seen in forty years, and which would have to be forced. They waited until Miss Emily was decently in the ground before they opened it.

The violence of breaking down the door seemed to fill this room with pervading dust. A thin, acrid pall as of the tomb seemed to lie everywhere upon this room decked and furnished as for a bridal: upon the valance curtains of faded rose color, upon the rose-shaded lights, upon the dressing table, upon the delicate array of crystal and the man's toilet things backed with tarnished silver, silver so tarnished that the monogram was obscured. Among them lay a collar and tie, as if they had just been removed, which, lifted, left upon the surface a pale crescent in the dust. Upon a chair hung the suit, carefully folded; beneath it the two mute shoes and the discarded socks.

The man himself lay in the bed.

For a long while we just stood there, looking down at the profound and fleshless grin. The body had apparently once lain in the attitude of an embrace, but now the long sleep that outlasts love, that conquers even the grimace of love, had cuckolded him. What was left of him, rotted beneath what was left of the nightshirt, had become inextricable from the bed in which he lay; and upon him and upon the pillow beside him lay that even coating of the patient and biding dust.

Then we noticed that in the second pillow was the indentation of a head. One of us lifted something from it, and leaning forward, that faint and invisible dust dry and acrid in the nostrils, we saw a long strand of iron-gray hair.

WILBUR DANIEL

STEELE

The Man Who

Saw Through

Heaven

Born in 1886 in Greensboro, North Carolina, Wilbur Daniel Steele studied at the University of Denver. It was at Provincetown that he first tried his hand by writing a Cape Cod story. *A White Horse in Winter* was published in the *Atlantic Monthly* in 1912. Later he was a correspondent in the First World War. He has received O. Henry Memorial Prizes for his stories. [Copyright 1919, 1924, 1925, 1926, 1927 by Wilbur Daniel Steele.]

PEOPLE HAVE WONDERED (there being obviously no question of romance involved) how I could ever have allowed myself to be let in for the East African adventure of Mrs. Diana in search of her husband. There were several reasons. To begin with; the time and effort and money weren't mine; they were the property of the wheel of which I was but a cog, the Society through which Diana's life had been insured, along with the rest of that job lot of missionaries. The "letting in" was the firm's. In the second place, the wonderers have not counted on Mrs. Diana's capacity for getting things done for her. Meek and helpless. Yes, but God was on her side. Too meek, too helpless to move mountains herself, if those who happened to be handy didn't move them for her then her God would know the reason why. Having dedicated her all to making straight the Way, why should her neighbor cavil at giving a little? The writer for one, a colonial governor-general for another, railway magnates, insurance managers, *safari* leaders, the ostrich farmer of Ndua, all these and a dozen others in their turns have felt the hundred-ton weight of her thin-lipped meekness—have seen her in metaphor sitting grimly on the doorsteps of their souls.

A third reason lay in my own troubled conscience. Though I did it in innocence, I can never forget that it was I who personally conducted Diana's party to the Observatory on that fatal night in Boston before it sailed. Had it not been for that kindly intentioned "hunch" of mine, the astonished eye of the Reverend Hubert Diana would never have gazed through the floor of Heaven, and he would never have undertaken to measure the Infinite with the foot rule of his mind.

It all started so simply. My boss at the shipping-and-insurance office gave me the word in the morning. "Bunch of missionaries for the *Platonic* tomorrow. They're on our hands in a way. Show 'em the town." It wasn't so easy when you think of it: one male and seven females on their way to the heathen; though it was easier in Boston than it might have been in some other towns. The evening looked the simplest. My friend Krum was at the Observatory that semester; there at least I was sure their sensibilities would come to no harm.

On the way out in the street car, seated opposite to Diana and having to make conversation, I talked of Krum and of what I knew of his work with the spiral nebulæ. Having to appear to listen, Diana did so (as all day long) with a vaguely indulgent smile. He really hadn't time for me. That night his life was exalted as it had never been, and would perhaps never be again. Tomorrow's sailing, the actual fact of leaving all to follow Him, held his imagination in thrall. Moreover, he was a bridegroom of three days with his bride beside him, his nerves at once assuaged and thrilled. No, but more. As if a bride were not enough, arrived in Boston, he had found himself surrounded by a very galaxy of womanhood gathered from the four corners; already within hours one felt the chaste tentacles of their feminine dependence curling about the party's unique man; already their contacts with the world of their new lives began to be made through him; already they saw in part through his eyes. I wonder what he would have said if I had told him he was a little drunk.

In the course of the day I think I had got him fairly well. As concerned his Church he was at once an asset and a liability. He believed its dogma as few still did, with a simplicity, "the old-time religion." He was born that kind. Of the stuff of the fanatic, the reason he was not a fanatic was that, curiously impervious to little questionings, he had never been aware that his faith was anywhere attacked. A self-educated man, he had accepted the necessary smattering facts of science with a serene indulgence, as simply so much further proof of what the Creator could do when He put His Hand to it. Nor was he conscious of any conflict between these facts and the fact that there existed a substantial Heaven, geographically up, and a substantial Hot Place, geographically down.

So, for his Church, he was an asset in these days. And so, and for the same reason, he was a liability. The Church must after all keep abreast of the times. For home consumption, with modern congregations, especially urban ones, a certain streak of "healthy" skepticism is no longer amiss in the pulpit; it makes people who read at all more comfortable in their pews. A man like Hubert Diana is more for the cause than a hundred. But what to do with him? Well, such things arrange themselves. There's the Foreign Field. The blacker the heathen the whiter the light they'll want, and the solider the conception of a God the Father enthroned in a Heaven of which the sky above them is the visible floor.

And that, at bottom, was what Hubert Diana believed. Accept as he

would with the top of his brain the fact of a spherical earth zooming
through space, deep in his heart he knew that the world lay flat from
modern Illinois to ancient Palestine, and that the sky above it, blue by
day and by night festooned with guiding stars for wise men, was the
nether side of a floor on which the resurrected trod.

I shall never forget the expression of his face when he realized he
was looking straight through it that night. In the quiet dark of the
dome I saw him remove his eye from the eyepiece of the telescope up
there on the staging and turn it, in the ray of a hooded bulb, on the demon's keeper, Krum.

"What's that, Mr. Krum? I didn't get you!"

"I say, that particular cluster you're looking at——"

"This star, you mean?"

"You'd have to count awhile to count the stars describing their orbits
in that 'star,' Mr. Diana. But what I was saying—have you ever had the
wish I used to have as a boy—that you could actually look back into the
past? With your own two eyes?"

Diana spoke slowly. He didn't know it, but it had already begun to
happen; he was already caught. "I have often wished, Mr. Krum, that
I might actually look back into the time of our Lord. Actually. Yes."

Krum grunted. He was young. "We'd have to pick a nearer neighbor than *Messier 79* then. The event you see when you put your eye
to that lens is happening much too far in the past. The lightwaves
thrown off by that particular cluster on the day, say, of the Crucifixion
—*you* won't live to see them. They've hardly started yet—a mere twenty
centuries on their way—leaving them something like eight hundred
and thirty centuries yet to come before they reach the earth."

Diana laughed the queerest catch of a laugh. "And—and there—
there won't be any earth here, then, to welcome them."

"*What?*" It was Krum's turn to look startled. So for a moment the
two faces remained in confrontation, the one, as I say, startled, the
other exuding visibly little sea-green globules of sweat. It was Diana
that caved in first, his voice hardly louder than a whisper.

"W-w-will there?"

None of us suspected the enormousness of the thing that had happened in Diana's brain. Krum shrugged his shoulders and snapped his
fingers. Deliberately. *Snap!* "What's a thousand centuries or so in the
cosmic reckoning?" He chuckled. "We're just beginning to get out
among 'em with *Messier,* you know. In the print room, Mr. Diana, I can
show you photographs of clusters to which, if you cared to go, traveling
at the speed of light——"

The voice ran on; but Diana's eye had gone back to the eyepiece, and
his affrighted soul had re-entered the big black tube sticking its snout
out of the slit in the iron hemisphere. . . . "At the speed of light!"
. . . That unsuspected, that wildly chance-found chink in the armor
of his philosophy! The body is resurrected and it ascends to Heaven
instantaneously. At what speed must it be borne to reach instan-

taneously that city beyond the ceiling of the sky? At a speed inconceivable, mystical. At, say (as he had often said to himself), *the speed of light.* . . . And now, hunched there in the trap that had caught him, black rods, infernal levers and wheels, he was aware of his own eye passing vividly through unpartitioned emptiness, *eight hundred and fifty centuries at the speed of light!*

"And still beyond these," Krum was heard, "we begin to come into the regions of the spiral nebulæ. We've some interesting photographs in the print room, if you've the time."

The ladies below were tired of waiting. One had "lots of packing to do." The bride said, "Yes, I do think we should be getting along, Hubert, dear; if you're ready——"

The fellow actually jumped. It's lucky he didn't break anything. His face looked greener and dewier than ever amid the contraptions above. "If you—you and the ladies, Cora—wouldn't mind—if Mr.—Mr.— (he'd mislaid my name) would see you back to the hotel——" Meeting silence, he began to expostulate. "I feel that this is a rich experience. I'll follow shortly; I know the way."

In the car going back into the city Mrs. Diana set at rest the flutterings of six hearts. Being unmarried they couldn't understand men as she did. When I think of that face of hers, to which I was destined to grow only too accustomed in the weary, itchy days of the trek into Kavirondoland, with its slightly tilted nose, its irregular pigmentation, its easily inflamed lids, and long moist cheeks, like those of a hunting dog, glorying in weariness, it seems incredible that a light of coyness could have found lodgment there. But that night it did. She sat serene among her virgins.

"You don't know Bert. You wait; he'll get a perfectly wonderful sermon out of all that tonight, Bert will."

Krum was having a grand time with his neophyte. He would have stayed up all night. Immured in the little print room crowded with files and redolent of acids, he conducted his disciple "glassy-eyed" through the dim frontiers of space, holding before him one after another the likenesses of universes sister to our own, islanded in immeasurable vacancy, curled like glimmering crullers on their private Milky Ways, and hiding in their wombs their myriad "coal-pockets," star-dust fœtuses of which—their quadrillion years accomplished—their litters of new suns would be born, to bear their planets, to bear their moons in turn.

"And beyond these?"

Always, after each new feat of distance, it was the same. "And beyond?" Given an ell, Diana surrendered to a pop-eyed lust for nothing less than light-years. "And still beyond?"

"Who knows?"

"The mind quits For if there's no end to these nebulæ——"

"But supposing there is?"

"An end? But, Mr. Krum, in the very idea of an ending——"

"An end to what we might call this particular category of magnitudes. Eh?"

"I don't get that."

"Well, take this—take the opal in your ring there. The numbers and distances inside that stone may conceivably be to themselves as staggering as ours to us in our own system. Come! that's not so far-fetched. What are we learning about the structure of the atom? A nucleus (call it a sun) revolved about in eternal orbits by electrons (call them planets, worlds). Infinitesimal; but after all what are bigness and littleness but matters of comparison? To eyes on one of those electrons (don't be too sure there aren't any) its tutelary sun may flame its way across a heaven a comparative ninety million miles away. Impossible for them to conceive of a boundary to their billions of atomic systems, molecular universes. In that category of magnitudes its diameter is infinity; once it has made the leap into our category and become an opal it is merely a quarter of an inch. That's right, Mr. Diana, you may well stare at it: between *now* and *now* ten thousand histories may have come and gone down there. . . . And just so the diameter of our own cluster of universes, going over into another category, may be——"

"May be a—a ring—a little stone—in a—a—a—ring."

Krum was tickled by the way the man's imagination jumped and engulfed it.

"Why not? That's as good a guess as the next. A ring, let's say, worn carelessly on the—well, say the tentacle—of some vast organism—some inchoate creature hobnobbing with its cloudy kind in another system of universes—which in turn——"

It is curious that none of them realized next day that they were dealing with a stranger, a changed man. Why he carried on, why he capped that night of cosmic debauch by shaving, eating an unremarkable breakfast, packing his terrestrial toothbrush and collars, and going up the gangplank in tow of his excited convoy to sail away, is beyond explanation—unless it was simply that he was in a daze.

It wasn't until four years later that I was allowed to know what had happened on that ship, and even then the tale was so disjointed, warped, and opinionated, so darkly seen in the mirror of Mrs. Diana's orthodoxy, that I had almost to guess what it was *really* all about.

"When Hubert turned irreligious . . ." That phrase, recurrent on her tongue in the meanderings of the East African quest to which we were by then committed, will serve to measure her understanding. Irreligious! Good Lord! But from that sort of thing I had to reconstruct the drama. Evening after evening beside her camp fire (appended to the Mineral Survey Expedition Toward Uganda through the kindness —actually the worn-down surrender—of the Protectorate government) I lingered a while before joining the merrier engineers, watched with fascination the bumps growing under the mosquitoes on her forehead, and listened to the jargon of her mortified meekness and her scandalized faith.

There had been a fatal circumstance, it seems, at the very outset. If Diana could but have been seasick, as the rest of them were (horribly), all might still have been well. In the misery of desired death, along with the other contents of a heaving midriff, he might have brought up the assorted universes of which he had been led too rashly to partake. But he wasn't. As if his wife's theory was right, as if Satan was looking out for him, he was spared to prowl the swooping decks immune. Four days and nights alone. Time enough to digest and assimilate into his being beyond remedy that lump of whirling magnitudes and to feel himself surrendering with a strange new ecstasy to the drunkenness of liberty.

Such liberty! Given Diana's type, it is hard to imagine it adequately. The abrupt, complete removal of the toils of reward and punishment; the withdrawal of the surveillance of an all-seeing, all-knowing Eye; the windy assurance of being responsible for nothing, important to no one, no longer (as the police say) "wanted"! It must have been beautiful in those few days of its first purity, before it began to be discolored by his contemptuous pity for others, the mask of his inevitable loneliness and his growing fright.

The first any of them knew of it—even his wife—was in mid-voyage, the day the sea went down and the seven who had been sick came up. There seemed an especial Providence in the calming of the waters; it was Sunday morning and Diana had been asked to conduct the services.

He preached on the text: "For of such is the kingdom of Heaven."

"If our concept of God means anything it means a God *all*-mighty, Creator of *all* that exists, Director of the *infinite,* cherishing in His Heaven the saved souls of *all space and all time*."

Of course; amen. And wasn't it nice to feel like humans again, and real sunshine pouring up through the lounge ports from an ocean suddenly grown kind? . . . But—then—*what* was Diana *saying?*

Mrs. Diana couldn't tell about it coherently even after a lapse of fifty months. Even in a setting as remote from that steamer's lounge as the equatorial bush, the ember-reddened canopy of thorn trees, the meandering camp fires, the chant and tramp somewhere away of Kikuyu porters dancing in honor of an especial largesse of fat zebra meat—even here her memory of that impious outburst was too vivid, too aghast.

"It was Hubert's look! The way he stared at us! As if you'd said he was licking his chops! . . . That '*Heaven*' of his!"

It seems they hadn't waked up to what he was about until he had the dimensions of his sardonic Paradise irreparably drawn in. The final haven of all right souls. Not alone the souls released from this our own tiny earth. In the millions of solar systems we see as stars how many millions of satellites must there be upon which at some time in their histories conditions suited to organic life subsist? Uncounted hordes of wheeling populations! Of men? God's creatures at all events, a portion of them reasoning. Weirdly shaped perhaps, but what of that? And that's only to speak of our own inconsiderable cluster of universes.

That's to say nothing of other systems of magnitudes, where God's creatures are to our world what we are to the worlds in the atoms in our finger rings. (He had shaken *his,* here, in their astounded faces.) And all these, all the generations of these enormous and microscopic beings harvested through a time beside which the life span of our earth is as a second in a million centuries: all these brought to rest for an eternity to which time itself is a watch tick—all crowded to rest pellmell, thronged, serried, packed, packed to suffocation in layers unnumbered light-years deep. This must needs be our concept of Heaven if God is the God of the Whole. If, on the other hand——

The other hand was the hand of the second officer, the captain's delegate at divine worship that Sabbath day. He at last had "come to."

I don't know whether it was the same day or the next; Mrs. Diana was too vague. But here's the picture. Seven women huddled in the large stateroom on B-deck, conferring in whispers, aghast, searching one another's eye obliquely even as they bowed their heads in prayer for some light—and of a sudden the putting back of the door and the in-marching of the Reverend Hubert. . . .

As Mrs. Diana tried to tell me, "You understand, don't you, he had just taken a bath? And he hadn't—he had forgotten to——"

Adam-innocent there he stood. Not a stitch. But I don't believe for a minute it was a matter of forgetting. In the high intoxication of his soul release, already crossed (by the second officer) and beginning to show his zealot claws, he needed some gesture stunning enough to witness to his separation, his unique rightness, his contempt of match-flare civilizations and infinitesimal taboos.

But I can imagine that stateroom scene: the gasps, the heads colliding in aversion, and Diana's six weedy feet of birthday suit towering in the shadows, and ready to sink through the deck I'll warrant, now the act was irrevocable, but still grimly carrying it off.

"And if, on the other hand, you ask me to bow down before a God peculiar to this one earth, this one grain of dust lost among the giants of space, watching its sparrows fall, profoundly interested in a speck called Palestine no bigger than the quadrillionth part of one of the atoms in the ring here on my finger——"

Really scared by this time, one of the virgins shrieked. It was altogether too close quarters with a madman.

Mad? Of course there was the presumption: "Crazy as a loon." Even legally it was so adjudged at the *Platonic's* first port of call, Algiers, where, when Diana escaped ashore and wouldn't come back again, he had to be given over to the workings of the French Law. I talked with the magistrate myself some forty months later, when, "let in" for the business as I have told, I stopped there on my way out.

"But what would you?" were his words. "We must live in the world as the world lives, is it not? Sanity? Sanity is what? Is it, for example, an intellectual clarity, a balanced perception of the realities? Naturally, speaking out of court, your friend was of a sanity—of a sanity, sir——"

Here the magistrate made with thumb and fingers the gesture only the French can make for a thing that is matchless, a beauty, a transcendent instance of any kind. He himself was Gallic, rational. Then, with a lift of shoulder: "But what would you? We must live in the world that seems."

Diana, impounded in Algiers for deportation, escaped. What after all are the locks and keys of this pinchbeck category of magnitudes? More remarkable still, there in Arab Africa, he succeeded in vanishing from the knowledge and pursuit of men. And of women. His bride, now that their particular mission had fallen through, was left to decide whether to return to America or to go on with two of the company, the Misses Brookhart and Smutts, who were bound for a school in Smyrna. In the end she followed the latter course. It was there, nearly four years later, that I was sent to join her by an exasperated and worn-out Firm.

By that time she knew again where her husband-errant was—or where at least, from time to time in his starry dartings over this our mote of dust, he had been heard of, spoken to, seen.

Could we but have a written history of those years of his apostolic vagabondage, a record of the towns in which he was jailed or from which he was kicked out, of the ports in which he starved, of the ships on which he stowed away, presently to reveal himself in proselyting ardor, denouncing the earthlings, the fatelings, the dupes of bugaboo, meeting scoff with scoff, preaching the new revelation red-eyed, like an angry prophet. Or was it, more simply, like a man afraid?

Was that the secret, after all, of his prodigious restlessness? Had it anything in common with the swarming of those pale worms that flee the Eye of the Infinite around the curves of the stone you pick up in a field? Talk of the man without a country! What of the man without a universe?

It is curious that I never suspected his soul's dilemma until I saw the first of his mud-sculptures in the native village of Ndua in the province of Kasuma in British East. Here it was, our objective attained, we parted company with the government *safari* and shifted the burden of Way-straightening to the shoulders of Major Wyeside, the ostrich farmer of the neighborhood.

While still on the *safari* I had put to Mrs. Diana a question that had bothered me: "Why on earth should your husband ever have chosen this particular neck of the woods to land up in? Why Kavirondoland?"

"It was here we were coming at the time Hubert turned irreligious, to found a mission. It's a coincidence, isn't it?"

And yet I would have sworn Diana hadn't a sense of humor about him anywhere. But perhaps it *wasn't* an ironic act. Perhaps it was simply that, giving up the struggle with a society blinded by "a little learning" and casting about for a virgin field, he had remembered this.

"I supposed he was a missionary," Major Wyeside told us with a flavor of indignation. "I went on that. I let him live here—six or seven months of it—while he was learning the tongue. I was a bit nonplussed, to put it mildly, when I discovered what he was up to."

What things Diana had been up to the Major showed us in one of the huts in the native kraal—a round dozen of them, modeled in mud and baked. Blackened blobs of mud, that's all. Likenesses of nothing under the sun, fortuitous masses sprouting haphazard tentacles, only two among them showing postules that might have been experimental heads. . . . The ostrich farmer saw our faces.

"Rum, eh? Of course I realized the chap was anything but fit. A walking skeleton. Nevertheless, whatever it is about these beasties, there's not a nigger in the village has dared set foot inside this hut since Diana left. You can see for yourselves it's about to crash. There's another like it he left at Suki, above here. Taboo, no end!"

So Diana's "hunch" had been right. He had found his virgin field, indeed, fit soil for his cosmic fright. A religion in the making, here before our eyes.

"This was at the very last before he left," Wyeside explained. "He took to making these mud pies quite of a sudden; the whole lot within a fortnight's time. Before that he had simply talked, harangued. He would sit here in the doorway of an evening with the niggers squatted around and harangue 'em by the hour. I knew something of it through my house-boys. The most amazing rot. All about the stars to begin with, as if these black baboons could half grasp *astronomy!* But that seemed all proper. Then there was talk about something a hundred times as big and powerful as the world, sun, moon, and stars put to-gether—some perfectly enormous stupendous awful being—but know-ing how mixed the boys can get, it still seemed all regular—simply the parson's way of getting at the notion of an Almighty God. But no, they insisted, there wasn't any God. That's the point, they said; there *is no* God. . . . Well, that impressed me as a go. That's when I decided to come down and get the rights of this star-swallowing monstrosity the beggar was feeding my labor on. And here he sat in the doorway with one of these beasties—here it is, this one—waving it furiously in the niggers' benighted faces. And do you know what he'd done?—you can see the mark here still on this wabble-leg, this tentacle-business—he had taken off a ring he had and screwed it on just here. His finger ring, my word of honor! And still, if you'll believe it, I didn't realize he was just daft. Not until he spoke to me. 'I find,' he was good enough to en-lighten me, 'I find I have to make it somehow concrete.' . . . 'Make what?' . . . 'Our wearer.' 'Our *what, where?*' . . . 'In the following category.' . . . His actual words, honor bright. I was going to have him sent down-country where he could be looked after. He got ahead of me though. He cleared out. When I heard he'd turned up at Suki I ought, I suppose, to have attended to it. But I was having trouble with leopards. And you know how things go."

From there we went to Suki, the Major accompanying. It was as like Ndua as one flea to its brother, a stockade inclosing round houses of

mud, wattles, and thatch, and full of naked heathen. The Kavirondo
are the nakedest of all African peoples and, it is said, the most moral.
It put a great strain on Mrs. Diana; all that whole difficult anxious time,
as it were detachedly, I could see her itching to get them into Mother
Hubbard and cast-off Iowa pants.

Here too, as the Major had promised, we found a holy of holies,
rather a dreadful of dreadfuls, "taboo no end," its shadows cluttered
with the hurlothrumbos of Diana's artistry. What puzzled me was their
number. Why this appetite for experimentation? There was an uncertainty; one would think its effect on potential converts would be
bad. Here, as in Ndua, Diana had contented himself at first with words
and skyward gesticulations. Not for so long however. Feeling the need
of giving his concept of the cosmic "wearer" a substance much earlier,
he had shut himself in with the work, literally—a fever of creation. We
counted seventeen of the nameless "blobs," all done, we were told, in
the seven days and nights before their maker had again cleared out.
The villagers would hardly speak of him; only after spitting to protect
themselves, their eyes averted, and in an undertone, would they mention
him: "He of the Ring." Thereafter we were to hear of him only as "He
of the Ring."

Leaving Suki, Major Wyeside turned us over (thankfully, I warrant)
to a native who told us his name was Charlie Kamba. He had spent
some years in Nairobi, running for an Indian outfitter, and spoke English remarkably well. It was from him we learned, quite casually, when
our modest eight-load *safari* was some miles on its way, that the primary
object of our coming was nonexistent. Hubert Diana was dead.

Dead nearly five weeks—a moon and a little—and buried in the mission church at Tara Hill.

Mission church! There was a poser for us. *Mission church?*

Well then, Charlie Kamba gave us to know that he was paraphrasing
in a large way suitable to our habits of thought. We wouldn't have
understood *his* informant's "wizard house" or "house of the effigy."

I will say for Mrs. Diana that in the course of our halt of lugubrious
amazement she shed tears. That some of them were not tears of un-
realized relief it would be hardly natural to believe. She had desired
loyally to find her husband, but when she should have found him—
what? This problem, sturdily ignored so long, was now removed.

Turn back? Never! Now it would seem the necessity for pressing
forward was doubled. In the scrub-fringed ravine of our halt the porters
resumed their loads, the dust stood up again, the same caravan moved
on. But how far it was now from being the same.

From that moment it took on, for me at least, a new character. It
wasn't the news especially; the fact that Diana was dead had little to do
with it. Perhaps it was simply that the new sense of something aimfully
and cumulatively dramatic in our progress had to have a beginning, and
that moment would do as well as the next.

Six villages: M'nann, Leika, Leikapo, Shamba, Little Tara, and Tara, culminating in the apotheosis of Tara Hill. Six stops for the night on the road it had cost Diana as many months to cover in his singular pilgrimage to his inevitable goal. Or in his flight to it. Yes, his stampede. Now the pipers at that four-day orgy of liberty on the *Platonic's* decks were at his heels for their pay. Now that his strength was failing, the hosts of loneliness were after him, creeping out of their dreadful magnitudes, the hounds of space. Over all that ground it seemed to me we were following him not by the word of hearsay but, as one follows a wounded animal making for its earth, by the droppings of his blood.

Our progress had taken on a pattern; it built itself with a dramatic artistry; it gathered suspense. As though it were a story at its most breathless places "continued in our next," and I a reader forgetting the road's weariness, the dust, the torment of insects never escaped, the inadequate food, I found myself hardly able to keep from running on ahead to reach the evening's village, to search out the inevitable repository of images left by the white stranger who had come and tarried there awhile and gone again.

More concrete and ever more concrete. The immemorial compromise with the human hunger for a symbol to see with the eyes, touch with the hands. Hierarchy after hierarchy of little mud effigies—one could see the necessity pushing the man. Out of the protoplasmic blobs of Ndua, Suki, even M'nann, at Leikapo Diana's concept of infinity (so pure in that halcyon epoch at sea), of categories nested within categories like Japanese boxes, of an over-creature wearing our cosmos like a trinket, unawares, had become a mass with legs to stand on and a real head. The shards scattered about in the filth of the hut there (as if in violence of despair) were still monstrosities, but with a sudden stride of concession their monstrousness was the monstrousness of lizard and turtle and crocodile. At Shamba there were dozens of huge-footed birds.

It is hard to be sure in retrospect, but I do believe that by the time we reached Little Tara I began to see the thing as a whole—the fœtus, working out slowly, blindly, but surely, its evolution in the womb of fright. At Little Tara there was a change in the character of the exhibits; their numbers had diminished, their size had grown. There was a boar with tusks and a bull the size of a dog with horns, and on a tusk and on a horn an indentation left by a ring.

I don't believe Mrs. Diana got the thing at all. Toward the last she wasn't interested in the huts of relics; at Little Tara she wouldn't go near the place; she was "too tired." It must have been pretty awful, when you think of it, even if all she saw in them was the mud-pie play of a man reverted to a child.

There was another thing at Little Tara quite as momentous as the jump to boar and bull. Here at last a mask had been thrown aside. Here there had been no pretense of proselyting, no astronomical lectures, no doorway harangues. Straightway he had arrived (a fabulous figure already, long heralded), he had commandeered a house and shut himself up in it and there, mysterious, assiduous, he had remained three days and nights, eating nothing, but drinking gallons of the foul water they left in gourds outside his curtain of reeds. No one in the village had ever seen what he had done and left there. Now, candidly, those labors were for himself alone.

Here at last in Tara the moment of that confession had overtaken the fugitive. It was he, ill with fever and dying of nostalgia—not these naked black baboon men seen now as little more than blurs—who had to give the Beast of the Infinite a name and a shape. And more and more, not only a shape, but a *shapliness*. From the instant when, no longer able to live alone with nothingness, he had given it a likeness in Ndua mud, and perceived that it was intolerable and fled its face, the turtles and distorted crocodiles of Leikapo and the birds of Shamba had become inevitable, and no less inevitable the Little Tara boar and bull. Another thing grows plain in restrospect: the reason why, done to death (as all the way they reported him) he couldn't die. He didn't dare to. Didn't dare to close his eyes.

It was at Little Tara we first heard of him as "Father Witch," a name come back, we were told, from Tara, where he had gone. I had heard it pronounced several times before it suddenly obtruded from the native context as actually two English words. That was what made it queer. It was something they must have picked up by rote, uncomprehending; something then they could have had from no lips but his own. When I repeated it after them with a better accent they pointed up toward the north, saying "Tara! Tara!"—their eagerness mingled with awe.

I shall never forget Tara as we saw it, after our last blistering scramble up a gorge, situated in the clear air on a slope belted with cedars. A mid-African stockade left by some blunder in an honest Colorado landscape, or a newer and bigger Vermont. Here at the top of our journey, black savages, their untidy *shambas,* the very Equator, all these seemed as incongruous as a Gothic cathedral in a Congo marsh. I wonder if Hubert Diana knew whither his instinct was guiding him on the long road of his journey here to die. . . .

He had died and he was buried, not in the village, but about half a mile distant, on the ridge; this we were given to know almost before we had arrived. There was no need to announce ourselves, the word of our coming had outrun us; the populace was at the gates.

"Our Father Witch! Our Father Witch!" They knew what we were after; the funny parrot-wise English stood out from the clack and clatter of their excited speech. "Our Father Witch! Ay! Ay!" With a common eagerness they gesticulated at the hilltop beyond the cedars.

Certainly here was a change. No longer the propitiatory spitting, the averted eyes, the uneasy whispering allusion to him who had passed that way: here in Tara they would shout him from the housetops, with a kind of civic pride.

We learned the reason for this on our way up the hill. It was because they were his chosen, the initiate.

We made the ascent immediately, against the village's advice. It **was** near evening; the return would be in the dark; it was a bad country for goblins; wouldn't tomorrow morning do? . . . No, it wouldn't do the widow. Her face was set. . . . And so, since we were resolved to go, the village went with us, armed with rattles and drums. Charlie Kamba walked beside us, sifting the information a hundred were eager to give.

These people were proud, he said, because their wizard was more powerful than all the wizards of all the other villages "in the everywhere together." If he cared to he could easily knock down all the other villages in the "everywhere," destroying all the people and all the cattle. If he cared to he could open his mouth and swallow the sky and the stars. But Tara he had chosen. Tara he would protect. He made their mealies to grow and their cattle to multiply.

I protested, "But he is *dead* now!"

Charlie Kamba made signs of deprecation. I discerned that he was far from being clear about the thing himself.

Yes, he temporized, this Father Witch was dead, quite dead. On the other hand he was up there. On the other hand he would never die. He was longer than forever. Yes, quite true, he was dead and buried under the pot.

I gave it up. "How did he die?"

Well, he came to this village of Tara very suffering, very sick. The dead man who walked. His face was very sad. Very eaten. Very frightened. He came to this hill. So he lived here for two full moons, very hot, very eaten, very dead. These men made him a house as he commanded them, also a stockade. In the house he was very quiet, very dead, making magic two full moons. Then he came out and they that were waiting saw him. He had made the magic, and the magic had made him well. His face was kind. He was happy. He was full fed. He was full fed, these men said, without any eating. Yes, they carried up to him very fine food, because they were full of wonder and some fear, but he did not eat any of it. Some water he drank. So, for two days and the night between them, he continued sitting in the gate of the stockade, very happy, very full fed. He told these people very much about their wizard, who is bigger than everywhere and longer than forever and can, if he cares to, swallow the sky and stars. From time to time however, ceasing to talk to these people, he got to his knees and talked in his own strange tongue to Our Father Witch, his eyes held shut. When he had done this just at sunset of the second day he fell forward on his face. So he remained that night. The next day these men took him into the house and buried him under the pot. On the other hand Our Father Witch is longer than forever. He remains there still. . . .

The first thing I saw in the hut's interior was the earthen pot at the northern end, wrong-side-up on the ground. I was glad I had preceded Mrs. Diana. I walked across and sat down on it carelessly, hoping so that her afflicted curiosity might be led astray. It gave me the oddest feeling, though, to think of what was there beneath my nonchalant sitting-portion—aware as I was of the Kavirondo burial of a great man—up to the neck in mother earth, and the rest of him left out in the dark of the pot for the undertakings of the ants. I hoped his widow wouldn't wonder about that inverted vessel of clay.

I needn't have worried. Her attention was arrested otherwheres. I shall not forget the look of her face, caught above me in the red shaft of sundown entering the western door, as she gazed at the last and the largest of the Reverend Hubert Diana's gods. That long, long cheek of hers, buffeted by sorrow, startled now and mortified. Not till that moment, I believe, had she comprehended the steps of mud-images she had been following for what they were, the steps of idolatry.

For my part, I wasn't startled. Even before we started up the hill, knowing that her husband had dared to die here, I could have told her pretty much what she would find.

This overlord of the cosmic categories that he had fashioned (at last) in his own image sat at the other end of the red-streaked house upon a bench—a throne?—of mud. Diana had been no artist. An ovoid two-eyed head, a cylindrical trunk, two arms, two legs, that's all. But indubitably man, man-size. Only one finger of one of the hands had been done with much care. It wore an opal, a two-dollar stone from Mexico, set in a silver ring. This was the hand that was lifted, and over it the head was bent.

I've said Diana was no artist. I'll take back the words. The figure was crudeness itself, but in the relation between that bent head and that lifted hand there was something which was something else. A sense of scrutiny one would have said no genius of mud could ever have conveyed. An attitude of interest centered in that bauble, intense and static, breathless and eternal all in one—penetrating to its bottom atom, to the last electron, to a hill upon it, and to a two-legged mite about to die. Marking (yes, I'll swear to the incredible) the sparrow's fall.

The magic was made. The road that had commenced with the blobs of Ndua—the same that commenced with our hairy ancestors listening to the night-wind in their caves—was run.

And from here Diana, of a sudden happy, of a sudden looked after, "full fed," had walked out——

But no; I couldn't stand that mortified sorrow on the widow's face any longer. She had to be made to see what she wanted to see. I said it aloud:

"From here, Mrs. Diana, your husband walked out——"

"He had sunk to idolatry. *Idolatry!*"

"To the bottom, yes. And come up its whole history again. And from here he walked out into the sunshine to kneel and talk with 'Our Father Which——' "

She got it. She caught it. I wish you could have seen the light going up those long, long cheeks as she got it:

"Our Father which art in Heaven, Hallowed be Thy Name!"

We went downhill in the darkness, protected against goblins by a vast rattling of gourds and beating of goat-hide drums.

F. SCOTT FITZGERALD

The Baby Party

Francis Scott Key Fitzgerald (1896–1940) was born in Minnesota and attended Princeton University before serving in the First World War. His first novels brought him immediate attention in the 1920's. They include *This Side of Paradise, The Beautiful and the Damned, The Great Gatsby, Tender Is the Night* and *The Tycoon.* These and his short stories deal with both the American scene and expatriate life in Paris and elsewhere in Europe, where he spent much of his time. [From *All the Sad Young Men* by F. Scott Fitzgerald; copyright 1926 by Charles Scribner's Sons; used by permission of the publishers.]

WHEN JOHN ANDROS FELT OLD he found solace in the thought of life continuing through his child. The dark trumpets of oblivion were less loud at the patter of his child's feet or at the sound of his child's voice babbling mad non sequiturs to him over the telephone. The latter incident occurred every afternoon at three when his wife called the office from the country, and he came to look forward to it as one of the vivid minutes of his day.

He was not physically old, but his life had been a series of struggles up a series of rugged hills, and here at thirty-eight having won his battles against ill-health and poverty he cherished less than the usual number of illusions. Even his feeling about his little girl was qualified. She had interrupted his rather intense love-affair with his wife, and she was the reason for their living in a suburban town, where they paid for country air with endless servant troubles and the weary merry-go-round of the commuting train.

It was little Ede as a definite piece of youth that chiefly interested him. He liked to take her on his lap and examine minutely her fragrant, downy scalp and her eyes with their irises of morning blue. Having paid this homage John was content that the nurse should take her away. After ten minutes the very vitality of the child irritated him; he was inclined to lose his temper when things were broken, and one Sunday afternoon when she had disrupted a bridge game by permanently hiding up the ace of spades, he had made a scene that had reduced his wife to tears.

This was absurd and John was ashamed of himself. It was inevitable that such things would happen, and it was impossible that little Ede should spend all her indoor hours in the nursery upstairs when she was becoming, as her mother said, more nearly a "real person" every day.

She was two and a half, and this afternoon, for instance, she was going to a baby party. Grown-up Edith, her mother, had telephoned the information to the office, and little Ede had confirmed the business

59

by shouting "I yam going to a *pantry!*" into John's unsuspecting left ear.

"Drop in at the Markeys' when you get home, won't you, dear?" resumed her mother. "It'll be funny. Ede's going to be all dressed up in her new pink dress——"

The conversation terminated abruptly with a squawk which indicated that the telephone had been pulled violently to the floor. John laughed and decided to get an early train out; the prospect of a baby party in someone else's house amused him.

"What a peach of a mess!" he thought humorously. "A dozen mothers, and each one looking at nothing but her own child. All the babies breaking things and grabbing at the cake, and each mamma going home thinking about the subtle superiority of her own child to every other child there."

He was in a good humor today—all the things in his life were going better than they had ever gone before. When he got off the train at his station he shook his head at an importunate taxi man, and began to walk up the long hill toward his house through the crisp December twilight. It was only six o'clock but the moon was out, shining with proud brilliance on the thin sugary snow that lay over the lawns.

As he walked along drawing his lungs full of cold air his happiness increased, and the idea of a baby party appealed to him more and more. He began to wonder how Ede compared to other children of her own age, and if the pink dress she was to wear was something radical and mature. Increasing his gait he came in sight of his own house, where the lights of a defunct Christmas tree still blossomed in the window, but he continued on past the walk. The party was at the Markeys' next door.

As he mounted the brick step and rang the bell he became aware of voices inside, and he was glad he was not too late. Then he raised his head and listened—the voices were not children's voices, but they were loud and pitched high with anger; there were at least three of them and one, which rose as he listened to a hysterical sob, he recognized immediately as his wife's.

"There's been some trouble," he thought quickly.

Trying the door, he found it unlocked and pushed it open.

The baby party began at half past four, but Edith Andros, calculating shrewdly that the new dress would stand out more sensationally against vestments already rumpled, planned the arrival of herself and little Ede for five. When they appeared it was already a flourishing affair. Four baby girls and nine baby boys, each one curled and washed and dressed with all the care of a proud and jealous heart, were dancing to the music of a phonograph. Never more than two or three were dancing at once, but as all were continually in motion running to and from their mothers for encouragement, the general effect was the same.

As Edith and her daughter entered, the music was temporarily drowned out by a sustained chorus, consisting largely of the word *cute* and directed toward little Ede, who stood looking timidly about and fingering the edges of her pink dress. She was not kissed—this is the sanitary age—but she was passed along a row of mammas each one of whom said "cu-u-ute" to her and held her pink little hand before passing her on to the next. After some encouragement and a few mild pushes she was absorbed into the dance, and became an active member of the party.

Edith stood near the door talking to Mrs. Markey, and keeping one eye on the tiny figure in the pink dress. She did not care for Mrs. Markey; she considered her both snippy and common, but John and Joe Markey were congenial and went in together on the commuting train every morning, so the two women kept up an elaborate pretense of warm amity. They were always reproaching each other for "not coming to see me," and they were always planning the kind of parties that began with "You'll have to come to dinner with us soon, and we'll go in to the theater," but never matured further.

"Little Ede looks perfectly darling," said Mrs. Markey, smiling and moistening her lips in a way that Edith found particularly repulsive. "So *grown-up*—I can't *believe* it!"

Edith wondered if "little Ede" referred to the fact that Billy Markey, though several months younger, weighed almost five pounds more. Accepting a cup of tea she took a seat with two other ladies on a divan and launched into the real business of the afternoon, which of course lay in relating the recent accomplishments and insouciances of her child.

An hour passed. Dancing palled and the babies took to sterner sport. They ran into the dining-room, rounded the big table, and essayed the kitchen door, from which they were rescued by an expeditionary force of mothers. Having been rounded up they immediately broke loose, and rushing back to the dining-room tried the familiar swinging door again. The word "overheated" began to be used, and small white brows were dried with small white handkerchiefs. A general attempt to make the babies sit down began, but the babies squirmed off laps with peremptory cries of "Down! Down!" and the rush into the fascinating dining-room began anew.

This phase of the party came to an end with the arrival of refreshments, a large cake with two candles, and saucers of vanilla ice cream. Billy Markey, a stout laughing baby with red hair and legs somewhat bowed, blew out the candles, and placed an experimental thumb on the white frosting. The refreshments were distributed, and the children ate, greedily but without confusion—they had behaved remarkably well all afternoon. They were modern babies who ate and slept at regular hours, so their dispositions were good, and their faces healthy and pink —such a peaceful party would not have been possible thirty years ago.

After the refreshments a gradual exodus began. Edith glanced anxiously at her watch—it was almost six, and John had not arrived. She wanted him to see Ede with the other children—to see how dignified and polite and intelligent she was, and how the only ice-cream spot on her dress was some that had dropped from her chin when she was joggled from behind.

"You're a darling," she whispered to her child, drawing her suddenly against her knee. "Do you know you're a darling? Do you *know* you're a darling?"

Ede laughed. "Bow-wow," she said suddenly.

"Bow-wow?" Edith looked around. "There isn't any bow-wow."

"Bow-wow," repeated Ede. "I want a bow-wow."

Edith followed the small pointing finger.

"That isn't a bow-wow, dearest, that's a teddy-bear."

"Bear?"

"Yes, that s a teddy-bear, and it belongs to Billy Markey. You don't want Billy Markey's teddy-bear, do you?"

Ede did want it.

She broke away from her mother and approached Billy Markey, who held the toy closely in his arms. Ede stood regarding him with inscrutable eyes, and Billy laughed.

Grown-up Edith looked at her watch again, this time impatiently.

The party had dwindled until, besides Ede and Billy, there were only two babies remaining—and one of the two remained only by virtue of having hidden himself under the dining-room table. It was selfish of John not to come. It showed so little pride in the child. Other fathers had come, half a dozen of them, to call for their wives, and they had stayed for a while and looked on.

There was a sudden wail. Ede had obtained Billy's teddy-bear by pulling it forcibly from his arms, and on Billy's attempt to recover it, she had pushed him casually to the floor.

"Why, Ede!" cried her mother, repressing an inclination to laugh.

Joe Markey, a handsome, broad-shouldered man of thirty-five, picked up his son and set him on his feet. "You're a fine fellow," he said jovially. "Let a girl knock you over! You're a fine fellow."

"Did he bump his head?" Mrs. Markey returned anxiously from bowing the next to last remaining mother out the door.

"No-o-o-o," exclaimed Markey. "He bumped something else, didn't you, Billy? He bumped something else."

Billy had so far forgotten the bump that he was already making an attempt to recover his property. He seized a leg of the bear which projected from Ede's enveloping arms and tugged at it but without success.

"No," said Ede emphatically.

Suddenly, encouraged by the success of her former half-accidental manoeuver, Ede dropped the teddy-bear, placed her hands on Billy's shoulders and pushed him backward off his feet.

This time he landed less harmlessly; his head hit the bare floor just off the rug with a dull hollow sound, whereupon he drew in his breath and delivered an agonized yell.

Immediately the room was in confusion. With an exclamation Markey hurried to his son, but his wife was first to reach the injured baby and catch him up into her arms.

"Oh, *Billy,*" she cried, "what a terrible bump! She ought to be spanked."

Edith, who had rushed immediately to her daughter, heard this remark, and her lips came sharply together.

"Why, Ede," she whispered perfunctorily, "you bad girl!"

Ede put back her little head suddenly and laughed. It was a loud laugh, a triumphant laugh with victory in it and challenge and contempt. Unfortunately it was also an infectious laugh. Before her mother realized the delicacy of the situation, she too had laughed, an audible, distinct laugh not unlike the baby's, and partaking of the same overtones.

Then, as suddenly, she stopped.

Mrs. Markey's face had grown red with anger, and Markey, who had been feeling the back of the baby's head with one finger, looked at her, frowning.

"It's swollen already," he said with a note of reproof in his voice. "I'll get some witch-hazel."

But Mrs. Markey had lost her temper. "I don't see anything funny about a child being hurt!" she said in a trembling voice.

Little Ede meanwhile had been looking at her mother curiously. She noted that her own laugh had produced her mother's, and she wondered if the same cause would always produce the same effect. So she chose this moment to throw back her head and laugh again.

To her mother the additional mirth added the final touch of hysteria to the situation. Pressing her handkerchief to her mouth she giggled irrepressibly. It was more than nervousness—she felt that in a peculiar way she was laughing with her child—they were laughing together.

It was in a way a defiance—those two against the world.

While Markey rushed upstairs to the bathroom for ointment, his wife was walking up and down rocking the yelling boy in her arms.

"Please go home!" she broke out suddenly. "The child's badly hurt, and if you haven't the decency to be quiet, you'd better go home."

"Very well," said Edith, her own temper rising. "I've never seen any one make such a mountain out of——"

"Get out!" cried Mrs. Markey frantically. "There's the door, get out —I never want to see you in our house again. You or your brat either!"

Edith had taken her daughter's hand and was moving quickly toward the door, but at this remark she stopped and turned around, her face contracting with indignation.

"Don't you dare call her that!"

Mrs. Markey did not answer but continued walking up and down, muttering to herself and to Billy in an inaudible voice.

Edith began to cry.

"I will get out!" she sobbed, "I've never heard anybody so rude and c-common in my life. I'm glad your baby did get pushed down—he's nothing but a f-fat little fool anyhow."

Joe Markey reached the foot of the stairs just in time to hear this remark.

"Why, Mrs. Andros," he said sharply, "can't you see the child's hurt? You really ought to control yourself."

"Control m-myself!" exclaimed Edith brokenly. "You better ask her to c-control herself. I've never heard anybody so c-common in my life."

"She's insulting me!" Mrs. Markey was now livid with rage. "Did you hear what she said, Joe? I wish you'd put her out. If she won't go, just take her by the shoulders and put her out!"

"Don't you dare touch me!" cried Edith. "I'm going just as quick as I can find my c-coat!"

Blind with tears she took a step toward the hall. It was just at this moment that the door opened and John Andros walked anxiously in.

"John!" cried Edith, and fled to him wildly.

"What's the matter? Why, what's the matter?"

"They're—they're putting me out!" she wailed, collapsing against him. "He'd just started to take me by the shoulders and put me out. I want my coat!"

"That's not true," objected Markey hurriedly. "Nobody's going to put you out." He turned to John. "Nobody's going to put her out," he repeated. "She's——"

"What do you mean 'put her out'?" demanded John abruptly. "What's all this talk, anyhow?"

"Oh, let's go!" cried Edith. "I want to go. They're so *common,* John!"

"Look here!" Markey's face darkened. "You've said that about enough. You're acting sort of crazy."

"They called Ede a brat!"

For the second time that afternoon little Ede expressed emotion at an inopportune moment. Confused and frightened at the shouting voices, she began to cry, and her tears had the effect of conveying that she felt the insult in her heart.

"What's the idea of this?" broke out John. "Do you insult your guests in your own house?"

"It seems to me it's your wife that's done the insulting!" answered Markey crisply. "In fact, your baby there started all the trouble."

John gave a contemptuous snort. "Are you calling names at a little baby?" he inquired. "That's a fine manly business!"

"Don't talk to him, John," insisted Edith. "Find my coat!"

"You must be in a bad way," went on John angrily, "if you have to take out your temper on a helpless little baby."

"I never heard anything so damn twisted in my life," shouted Markey. "If that wife of yours would shut her mouth for a minute——"

"Wait a minute! You're not talking to a woman and child now——"

There was an incidental interruption. Edith had been fumbling on a chair for her coat, and Mrs. Markey had been watching her with hot, angry eyes. Suddenly she laid Billy down on the sofa, where he immediately stopped crying and pulled himself upright, and coming into the hall she quickly found Edith's coat and handed it to her without a word. Then she went back to the sofa, picked up Billy, and rocking him in her arms looked again at Edith with hot, angry eyes. The interruption had taken less than half a minute.

"Your wife comes in here and begins shouting around about how common we are!" burst out Markey violently. "Well, if we're so damn common, you'd better stay away! And, what's more, you'd better get out now!"

Again John gave a short, contemptuous laugh.

"You're not only common," he returned, "you're evidently an awful bully—when there's any helpless women and children around." He felt for the knob and swung the door open. "Come on, Edith."

Taking up her daughter in her arms, his wife stepped outside and John, still looking contemptuously at Markey, started to follow.

"Wait a minute!" Markey took a step forward; he was trembling slightly, and two large veins on his temple were suddenly full of blood. "You don't think you can get away with that, do you? With me?"

Without a word John walked out the door, leaving it open.

Edith, still weeping, had started for home. After following her with his eyes until she reached her own walk, John turned back toward the lighted doorway where Markey was slowly coming down the slippery steps. He took off his overcoat and hat, tossed them off the path onto the snow. Then, sliding a little on the iced walk, he took a step forward.

At the first blow, they both slipped and fell heavily to the sidewalk, half rising then, and again pulling each other to the ground. They found a better foothold in the thin snow to the side of the walk and rushed at each other, both swinging wildly and pressing out the snow into a pasty mud underfoot.

The street was deserted, and except for their short tired gasps and the padded sound as one or the other slipped down into the slushy mud, they fought in silence, clearly defined to each other by the full moonlight as well as by the amber glow that shone out of the open door. Several times they both slipped down together, and then for a while the conflict threshed about wildly on the lawn.

For ten, fifteen, twenty minutes they fought there senselessly in the moonlight. They had both taken off coats and vests at some silently agreed upon interval and now their shirts dripped from their backs in wet pulpy shreds. Both were torn and bleeding and so exhausted that they could stand only when by their position they mutually supported each other—the impact, the mere effort of a blow, would send them both to their hands and knees.

But it was not weariness that ended the business, and the very meaninglessness of the fight was a reason for not stopping. They stopped because once when they were straining at each other on the ground, they heard a man's footsteps coming along the sidewalk. They had rolled somehow into the shadow, and when they heard these footsteps they stopped fighting, stopped moving, stopped breathing, lay huddled together like two boys playing Indian until the footsteps had passed. Then, staggering to their feet, they looked at each other like two drunken men.

"I'll be damned if I'm going on with this thing any more," cried Markey thickly.

"I'm not going on any more either," said John Andros. "I've had enough of this thing."

Again they looked at each other, sulkily this time, as if each suspected the other of urging him to a renewal of the fight. Markey spat out a mouthful of blood from a cut lip; then he cursed softly, and picking up his coat and vest, shook off the snow from them in a surprised way, as if their comparative dampness was his only worry in the world.

"Want to come in and wash up?" he asked suddenly.

"No, thanks," said John. "I ought to be going home—my wife'll be worried."

He too picked up his coat and vest and then his overcoat and hat. Soaking wet and dripping with perspiration, it seemed absurd that less than half an hour ago he had been wearing all these clothes.

"Well—good night," he said hesitantly.

Suddenly they both walked toward each other and shook hands. It was no perfunctory hand-shake: John Andros's arm went around Markey's shoulder, and he patted him softly on the back for a little while.

"No harm done," he said brokenly.

"No—you?"

"No, no harm done."

"Well," said John Andros after a minute, "I guess I'll say good night."

"Good night."

Limping slightly and with his clothes over his arm, John Andros turned away. The moonlight was still bright as he left the dark patch of trampled ground and walked over the intervening lawn. Down at the station, half a mile away, he could hear the rumble of the seven o'clock train.

"But you must have been crazy," cried Edith brokenly. "I thought you were going to fix it all up there and shake hands. That's why I went away."

"Did you want us to fix it up?"

"Of course not, I never want to see them again. But I thought of course that was what you were going to do." She was touching the bruises on his neck and back with iodine as he sat placidly in a hot bath. "I'm going to get the doctor," she said insistently. "You may be hurt internally."

He shook his head. "Not a chance," he answered. "I don't want this to get all over town."

"I don't understand yet how it all happened."

"Neither do I." He smiled grimly. "I guess these baby parties are pretty rough affairs."

"Well, one thing—" suggested Edith hopefully, "I'm certainly glad we have beefsteak in the house for tomorrow's dinner."

"Why?"

"For your eye, of course. Do you know I came within an ace of ordering veal? Wasn't that the luckiest thing?"

Half an hour later, dressed except that his neck would accommodate no collar, John moved his limbs experimentally before the glass. "I believe I'll get myself in better shape," he said thoughtfully. "I must be getting old."

"You mean so that next time you can beat him?"

"I did beat him," he announced. "At least, I beat him as much as he beat me. And there isn't going to be any next time. Don't you go calling people common any more. If you get in any trouble, you just take your coat and go home. Understand?"

"Yes, dear," she said meekly. "I was very foolish and now I understand."

Out in the hall, he paused abruptly by the baby's door.

"Is she asleep?"

"Sound asleep. But you can go in and peek at her—just to say good night."

They tiptoed in and bent together over the bed. Little Ede, her cheeks flushed with health, her pink hands clasped tight together, was sleeping soundly in the cool, dark room. John reached over the railing of the bed and passed his hand lightly over the silken hair.

"She's asleep," he murmured in a puzzled way.

"Naturally, after such an afternoon."

"Miz Andros," the colored maid's stage whisper floated in from the hall, "Mr. and Miz Markey downstairs an' want to see you. Mr. Markey he's all cut up in pieces, ma'am. His face look like a roast beef. An' Miz Markey she 'pear mighty mad."

"Why, what incomparable nerve!" exclaimed Edith. "Just tell them we're not home. I wouldn't go down for anything in the world."

"You most certainly will." John's voice was hard and set.

"What?"

"You'll go down right now, and, what's more, whatever that other woman does, you'll apologize for what you said this afternoon. After that you don't ever have to see her again."

"Why—John, I can't."

"You've got to. And just remember that she probably hated to come over here just twice as much as you hate to go downstairs."

"Aren't you coming? Do I have to go alone?"

"I'll be down—in just a minute."

John Andros waited until she had closed the door behind her; then he reached over into the bed, and picking up his daughter, blankets and all, sat down in the rocking-chair holding her tightly in his arms. She moved a little, and he held his breath, but she was sleeping soundly, and in a moment she was resting quietly in the hollow of his elbow. Slowly he bent his head until his cheek was against her bright hair. "Dear little girl," he whispered. "Dear little girl, dear little girl."

John Andros knew at length what it was he had fought for so savagely that evening. He had it now, he possessed it forever, and for some time he sat there rocking very slowly to and fro in the darkness.

RING LARDNER

Ex Parte

Born in Michigan, Ring Lardner (1885–1933) worked for Chicago newspapers and began publishing as early as 1915. His talent was undeniable, and his *You Know Me, Al* series caught on quickly. Not until 1924, when he published *How to Write Short Stories*, did the critics discover his satirical vein and the black melancholy implicit in his "humorous" stories. He died at forty-eight after four years of poor health. [From *Round Up* by Ring Lardner; copyright 1929 by Charles Scribner's Sons; used by permission of the publishers.]

MOST ALWAYS WHEN A MAN leaves his wife, there's no excuse in the world for him. She may have made whoop-whoop-whoopee with the whole ten commandments, but if he shows his disapproval to the extent of walking out on her, he will thereafter be a total stranger to all his friends excepting the two or three bums who will tour the night clubs with him so long as he sticks to his habits of paying for everything.

When a woman leaves her husband, she must have good and sufficient reasons. He drinks all the time, or he runs around, or he doesn't give her any money, or he uses her as the heavy bag in his home gymnasium work. No more is he invited to his former playmates' houses for dinner and bridge. He is an outcast just the same as if he had done the deserting. Whichever way it happens, it's his fault. He can state his side of the case if he wants to, but there is nobody around listening.

Now I claim to have a little chivalry in me, as well as a little pride. So in spite of the fact that Florence has broadcast her grievances over the red and blue network both, I intend to keep mine to myself till death do me part.

But after I'm gone, I want some of my old pals to know that this thing wasn't as lopsided as she has made out, so I will write the true story, put it in an envelope with my will and appoint Ed Osborne executor. He used to be my best friend and would be yet if his wife would let him. He'll have to read all my papers, including this, and he'll tell everybody else about it and maybe they'll be a little sorry that they treated me like an open manhole.

(Ed, please don't consider this an attempt to be literary. You know I haven't written for publication since our days on "The Crimson and White," and I wasn't so hot then. Just look on it as a statement of facts. If I were still alive, I'd take a bible oath that nothing herein is exaggerated. And whatever else may have been my imperfections, I never lied save to shield a woman or myself.)

Well, a year ago last May I had to go to New York. I called up Joe Paxton and he asked me out to dinner. I went, and met Florence. She and Marjorie Paxton had been at school together and she was there for a visit. We fell in love with each other and got engaged. I stopped off in Chicago on the way home, to see her people. They liked me all right, but they hated to have Florence marry a man who lived so far away. They wanted to postpone her leaving home as long as possible and they made us wait till April this year.

I had a room at the Belden and Florence and I agreed that when we were married, we would stay there awhile and take our time about picking out a house. But the last day of March, two weeks before the date of our wedding, I ran into Jeff Cooper and he told me his news, that the Standard Oil was sending him to China in some big job that looked permanent.

"I'm perfectly willing to go," he said. "So is Bess. It's a lot more money and we think it will be an interesting experience. But here I am with a brand-new place on my hands that cost me $45,000, including the furniture, and no chance to sell it in a hurry except at a loss. We were just beginning to feel settled. Otherwise we would have no regrets about leaving this town. Bess hasn't any real friends here and you're the only one I can claim."

"How much would you take for your house, furniture and all?" I asked him.

"I'd take a loss of $5,000," he said. "I'd take $40,000 with the buyer assuming my mortgage of $15,000, held by the Phillips Trust and Mortgage Company in Seattle."

I asked him if he would show me the place. They had only been living there a month and I hadn't had time to call. He said, what did I want to look at it for and I told him I would buy it if it looked o. k. Then I confessed that I was going to be married; you know I had kept it a secret around here.

Well, he took me home with him and he and Bess showed me everything, all new and shiny and a bargain if you ever saw one. In the first place, there's the location, on the best residential street in town, handy to my office and yet with a whole acre of ground, and a bed of cannas coming up in the front yard that Bess had planted when they bought the property last fall. As for the house, I always liked stucco, and this one is *built!* You could depend on old Jeff to see to that.

But the furniture was what decided me. Jeff had done the smart thing and ordered the whole works from Wolfe Brothers, taking their advice on most of the stuff, as neither he nor Bess knew much about it. Their total bill, furnishing the entire place, rugs, beds, tables, chairs, everything, was only $8,500, including a mahogany upright player-piano that they ordered from Seattle. I had my mother's old mahogany piano in storage and I kind of hoped Jeff wouldn't want me to buy this, but it was all or nothing, and with a bargain like that staring me in the face, I didn't stop to argue, not when I looked over the rest of the furniture and saw what I was getting.

The living-room had, and still has, three big easy chairs and a couch, all over-stuffed, as they call it, to say nothing of an Oriental rug that alone had cost $500. There was a long mahogany table behind the couch, with lamps at both ends in case you wanted to lie down and read. The dining-room set was solid mahogany—a table and eight chairs that had separated Jeff from $1,000.

The floors downstairs were all oak parquet. Also he had blown himself to an oak mantelpiece and oak woodwork that must have run into heavy dough. Jeff told me what it cost him extra, but I don't recall the amount.

The Coopers were strong for mahogany and wanted another set for their bedroom, but Jake Wolfe told them it would get monotonous if there was too much of it. So he sold them five pieces—a bed, two chairs, a chiffonier and a dresser—of some kind of wood tinted green, with flowers painted on it. This was $1,000 more, but it certainly was worth it. You never saw anything prettier than that bed when the lace spreads were on.

Well, we closed the deal and at first I thought I wouldn't tell Florence, but would let her believe we were going to live at the Belden and then give her a surprise by taking her right from the train to our own home. When I got to Chicago, though, I couldn't keep my mouth shut. I gave it away and it was I, not she, that had the surprise.

Instead of acting tickled to death, as I figured she would, she just looked kind of funny and said she hoped I had as good taste in houses as I had in clothes. She tried to make me describe the house and the furniture to her, but I wouldn't do it. To appreciate a layout like that, you have to see it for yourself.

We were married and stopped in Yellowstone for a week on our way here. That was the only really happy week we had together. From the minute we arrived home till she left for good, she was a different woman than the one I thought I knew. She never smiled and several times I caught her crying. She wouldn't tell me what ailed her and when I asked if she was just homesick, she said no and choked up and cried some more.

You can imagine that things were not as I expected they would be. In New York and in Chicago and Yellowstone, she had had more *life* than any girl I ever met. Now she acted all the while as if she were playing the title rôle at a funeral.

One night late in May the telephone rang. It was Mrs. Dwan and she wanted Florence. If I had known what this was going to mean, I would have slapped the receiver back on the hook and let her keep on wanting.

I had met Dwan a couple of times and had heard about their place out on the Turnpike. But I had never seen it or his wife either.

Well, it developed that Mildred Dwan had gone to school with Florence and Marjorie Paxton, and she had just learned from Marjorie that Florence was my wife and living here. She said she and her husband would be in town and call on us the next Sunday afternoon.

Florence didn't seem to like the idea and kind of discouraged it. She said we would drive out and call on them instead. Mrs. Dwan said no, that Florence was the newcomer and it was her (Mrs. Dwan's) first move. So Florence gave in.

They came and they hadn't been in the house more than a minute when Florence began to cry. Mrs. Dwan cried, too, and Dwan and I stood there first on one foot and then the other, trying to pretend we didn't know the girls were crying. Finally, to relieve the tension, I invited him to come and see the rest of the place. I showed him all over and he was quite enthusiastic. When we returned to the living-room, the girls had dried their eyes and were back in school together.

Florence accepted an invitation for one-o'clock dinner a week from that day. I told her, after they had left, that I would go along only on condition that she and our hostess would both control their tear-ducts. I was so accustomed to solo sobbing that I didn't mind it any more, but I couldn't stand a duet of it either in harmony or unison.

Well, when we got out there and had driven down their private lane through the trees and caught a glimpse of their house, which people around town had been talking about as something wonderful, I laughed harder than any time since I was single. It looked just like what it was, a reorganized barn. Florence asked me what was funny, and when I told her, she pulled even a longer face than usual.

"I think it's beautiful," she said.

Tie that!

I insisted on her going up the steps alone. I was afraid if the two of us stood on the porch at once, we'd fall through and maybe founder before help came. I warned her not to smack the knocker too hard or the door might crash in and frighten the horses.

"If you make jokes like that in front of the Dwans." she said, "I'll never speak to you again."

"I'd forgotten you ever did," said I.

I was expecting a hostler to let us in, but Mrs. Dwan came in person.

"Are we late?" said Florence.

"A little," said Mrs. Dwan, "but so is dinner. Helga didn't get home from church till half past twelve."

"I'm glad of it," said Florence. "I want you to take me all through this beautiful, beautiful house right this minute."

Mrs. Dwan called her husband and insisted that he stop in the middle of mixing a cocktail so he could join us in a tour of the beautiful, beautiful house.

"You wouldn't guess it," said Mrs. Dwan, "but it used to be a barn."

I was going to say I had guessed it. Florence gave me a look that changed my mind.

"When Jim and I first came here," said Mrs. Dwan, "we lived in an ugly little rented house on Oliver Street. It was only temporary, of course; we were just waiting till we found what we really wanted. We used to drive around the country Saturday afternoons and Sundays, hoping we would run across the right sort of thing. It was in the late fall when we first saw this place. The leaves were off the trees and it was visible from the Turnpike.

" 'Oh, Jim!' I exclaimed. 'Look at that simply gorgeous old barn! With those wide shingles! And I'll bet you it's got handhewn beams in that middle, main section.' Jim bet me I was wrong, so we left the car, walked up the driveway, found the door open and came brazenly in. I won my bet as you can see."

She pointed to some dirty old rotten beams that ran across the living-room ceiling and looked as if five or six generations of rats had used them for gnawing practice.

"They're beautiful!" said Florence.

"The instant I saw them," said Mrs. Dwan, "I knew this was going to be our home!"

"I can imagine!" said Florence.

"We made inquiries and learned that the place belonged to a family named Taylor," said Mrs. Dwan. "The house had burned down and they had moved away. It was suspected that they had started the fire themselves, as they were terribly hard up and it was insured. Jim wrote to old Mr. Taylor in Seattle and asked him to set a price on the barn and the land, which is about four acres. They exchanged several letters and finally Mr. Taylor accepted Jim's offer. We got it for a song."

"Wonderful!" said Florence.

"And then, of course," Mrs. Dwan continued, "we engaged a house-wrecking company to tear down the other four sections of the barn— the stalls, the cow-shed, the tool-shed, and so forth—and take them away, leaving us just this one room. We had a man from Seattle come and put in these old pine walls and the flooring, and plaster the ceiling. He was recommended by a friend of Jim's and he certainly knew his business."

"I can see he did," said Florence.

"He made the hay-loft over for us, too, and we got the wings built by day-labor, with Jim and me supervising. It was so much fun that I was honestly sorry when it was finished."

"I can imagine!" said Florence.

Well, I am not very well up in Early American, which was the name they had for pretty nearly everything in the place, but for the benefit of those who are not on terms with the Dwans I will try and describe from memory the *objets d'art* they bragged of the most and which brought forth the loudest squeals from Florence.

The living-room walls were brown bare boards without a picture or scrap of wall-paper. On the floor were two or three "hooked rugs," whatever that means, but they needed five or six more of them, or one big carpet, to cover up all the knots in the wood. There was a maple "low-boy"; a "dough-trough" table they didn't have space for in the kitchen; a pine "stretcher" table with sticks connecting the four legs near the bottom so you couldn't put your feet anywhere; a "Dutch" chest that looked as if it had been ordered from the undertaker by one of Singer's Midgets, but he got well; and some "Windsor" chairs in which the only position you could get comfortable was to stand up behind them and lean your elbows on their back.

Not one piece that matched another, and not one piece of mahogany anywhere. And the ceiling, between the beams, had apparently been plastered by a workman who was that way, too.

"Some day soon I hope to have a piano," said Mrs. Dwan. "I can't live much longer without one. But so far I haven't been able to find one that would fit in."

"Listen," I said. "I've got a piano in storage that belonged to my mother. It's a mahogany upright and not so big that it wouldn't fit in this room, especially when you get that 'trough' table out. It isn't doing me any good and I'll sell it to you for $250. Mother paid $1,250 for it new."

"Oh, I couldn't think of taking it!" said Mrs. Dwan.

"I'll make it $200 even just because you're a friend of Florence's," I said.

"Really, I couldn't!" said Mrs. Dwan.

"You wouldn't have to pay for it all at once," I said.

"Don't you see," said Florence, "that a mahogany upright piano would be a perfect horror in here? Mildred wouldn't have it as a gift, let alone buy it. It isn't in the period."

"She could get it tuned," I said.

The answer to this was, "I'll show you the up-stairs now and we can look at the dining-room later on."

We were led to the guest-chamber. The bed was a maple four-poster, with pineapple posts, and a "tester" running from pillar to post. You would think a "tester" might be a man that went around trying out beds, but's really a kind of frame that holds a canopy over the bed in case it rains and the roof leaks. There was a quilt made by Mrs. Dwan's great-grandmother, Mrs. Anthony Adams, in 1859, at Lowell, Mass. How is that for a memory?

"This used to be the hay-loft," said Mrs. Dwan.

"You ought to have left some of the hay so the guests could hit it," I said.

The dressers, or chests of drawers, and the chairs were all made of maple. And the same in the Dwans' own room; everything maple.

"If you had maple in one room and mahogany in the other," I said, "people wouldn't get confused when you told them that so and so was up in Maple's room."

Dwan laughed, but the women didn't.

The maid hollered up that dinner was ready.

"The cocktails aren't ready," said Dwan.

"You will have to go without them," said Mrs. Dwan. "The soup will be cold."

This put me in a great mood to admire the "sawbuck" table and the "slat back" chairs, which were evidently the *chef-d'oeuvre* and the *pièce de résistance* of the *chez Dwan*.

"It came all the way from Pennsylvania," said Mildred, when Florence's outcries, brought on by her first look at the table, had died down. "Mother picked it up at a little place near Stroudsburg and sent it to me. It only cost $550, and the chairs were $45 apiece."

"How reasonable!" exclaimed Florence.

That was before she had sat in one of them. Only one thing was more unreasonable than the chairs, and that was the table itself, consisting of big planks nailed together and laid onto a railroad tie, supported underneath by a whole forest of cross-pieces and beams. The surface was as smooth on top as the trip to Catalina Island and all around the edges, great big divots had been taken out with some blunt instrument, probably a bayonet. There were stains and scorch marks that Florence fairly crowed over, but when I tried to add to the general ensemble by laying a lighted cigaret right down beside my soup-plate, she and both the Dwans yelled murder and made me take it off.

They planted me in an end seat, a location just right for a man who had stretched himself across a railway track and had both legs cut off at the abdomen. Not being that kind of man, I had to sit so far back that very few of my comestibles carried more than half-way to their target.

After dinner I was all ready to go home and get something to eat, but it had been darkening up outdoors for half an hour and now such a storm broke that I knew it was useless trying to persuade Florence to make a start.

"We'll play some bridge," said Dwan, and to my surprise he produced a card-table that was nowhere near "in the period."

At my house there was a big center chandelier that lighted up a bridge game no matter in what part of the room the table was put. But here we had to waste forty minutes moving lamps and wires and stands and when they were all fixed, you could tell a red suit from a black suit, but not a spade from a club. Aside from that and the granite-bottomed "Windsor" chairs and the fact that we played "families" for a cent a point and Florence and I won $12 and didn't get paid, it was one of the pleasantest afternoons I ever spent gambling.

The rain stopped at five o'clock and as we splashed through the puddles of Dwan's driveway, I remarked to Florence that I had never known she was such a kidder.

"What do you mean?" she asked me.

"Why, your pretending to admire all that junk," I said.

"Junk!" said Florence. "That is one of the most beautifully furnished homes I have ever seen!"

And so far as I can recall, that was her last utterance in my presence for six nights and five days.

At lunch on Saturday I said: "You know I like the silent drama one evening a week, but not twenty-four hours a day every day. What's the matter with you? If it's laryngitis, you might write me notes."

"I'll tell you what's the matter!" she burst out. "I hate this house and everything in it! It's too new! Everything shines! I loathe new things! I want a home like Mildred's, with things in it that I can look at without blushing for shame. I can't invite anyone here. It's too hideous. And I'll never be happy here a single minute as long as I live!"

Well, I don't mind telling that this kind of got under my skin. As if I hadn't intended to give her a pleasant surprise! As if Wolfe Brothers, in business thirty years, didn't know how to furnish a home complete! I was pretty badly hurt, but I choked it down and said, as calmly as I could:

"If you'll be a little patient, I'll try to sell this house and its contents for what I paid for it and them. It oughtn't to be much trouble; there are plenty of people around who know a bargain. But it's too bad you didn't confess your barn complex to me long ago. Only last February, old Ken Garrett had to sell his establishment and the men who bought it turned it into a garage. It was a livery-stable which I could have got for the introduction of a song, or maybe just the vamp. And we wouldn't have had to spend a nickel to make it as nice and comfortable and homey as your friend Mildred's dump."

Florence was on her way upstairs before I had finished my speech.

I went down to Earl Benham's to see if my new suit was ready. It was and I put it on and left the old one to be cleaned and pressed.

On the street I met Harry Cross.

"Come up to my office," he said. "There's something in my desk that may interest you."

I accepted his invitation and from three different drawers he pulled out three different quart bottles of Early American rye.

Just before six o'clock I dropped in Kane's store and bought myself a pair of shears, a blow torch and an ax. I started home, but stopped among the trees inside my front gate and cut big holes in my coat and trousers. Alongside the path to the house was a sizable mud puddle. I waded in it. And I bathed my gray felt hat.

Florence was sitting on the floor of the living-room, reading. She seemed a little upset by my appearance.

"Good heavens! What's happened?"

"Nothing much," said I. "I just didn't want to look too new."

"What are those things you're carrying?"

"Just a pair of shears, a blow torch and an ax. I'm going to try and antique this place and I think I'll begin on the dining-room table."

Florence went into her scream, dashed upstairs and locked herself in. I went about my work and had the dinner-table looking pretty Early when the maid smelled fire and rushed in. She rushed out again and came back with a pitcher of water. But using my vest as a snuffer, I had had the flames under control all the while and there was nothing for her to do.

"I'll just nick it up a little with this ax," I told her, "and by the time I'm through, dinner ought to be ready."

"It will never be ready as far as I'm concerned," she said. "I'm leaving just as soon as I can pack."

And Florence had the same idea—vindicating the old adage about great minds.

I heard the front door slam and the back door slam, and I felt kind of tired and sleepy, so I knocked off work and went up to bed.

That's my side of the story, Eddie, and it's true so help me my bootlegger. Which reminds me that the man who sold Harry the rye makes this town once a week, or did when this was written. He's at the Belden every Tuesday from nine to six and his name is Mike Farrell.

THOMAS WOLFE

Circus at Dawn

Thomas Wolfe (1900–1938) was born in Asheville, North Carolina. After graduation from the University of North Carolina, he studied playwriting at Harvard and received his M.A. (1922). He spent some time abroad and then returned to teach English at New York University, but after the publication of his first novel, *Look Homeward, Angel*, he devoted all his time to writing, completing three additional novels—*Of Time and the River, The Web and the Rock*, and *You Can't Go Home Again*; a collection of short stories, *From Death to Morning*; and a critical examination of his own work, *The Story of a Novel*. [From *From Death To Morning* by Thomas Wolfe; copyright 1935 by Charles Scribner's Sons; used by permission of the publishers.]

THERE WERE TIMES IN EARLY AUTUMN—in September—when the greater circuses would come to town—the Ringling Brothers,

Robinson's, and Barnum and Bailey shows, and when I was a route-boy on the morning paper, on those mornings when the circus would be coming in I would rush madly through my route in the cool and thrilling darkness that comes just before break of day, and then I would go back home and get my brother out of bed.

Talking in low excited voices we would walk rapidly back toward town under the rustle of September leaves, in cool streets just grayed now with that still, that unearthly and magical first light of day which seems suddenly to re-discover the great earth out of darkness, so that the earth emerges with an awful, a glorious sculptural stillness, and one looks out with a feeling of joy and disbelief, as the first men on this earth must have done, for to see this happen is one of the things that men will remember out of life forever and think of as they die.

At the sculptural still square where at one corner, just emerging into light, my father's shabby little marble shop stood with a ghostly strangeness and familiarity, my brother and I would "catch" the first streetcar of the day bound for the "depot" where the circus was—or sometimes we would meet someone we knew, who would give us a lift in his automobile.

Then, having reached the dingy, grimy, and rickety depot section, we would get out, and walk rapidly across the tracks of the station yard, where we could see great flares and steamings from the engines, and hear the crash and bump of shifting freight cars, the swift sporadic thunders of a shifting engine, the tolling of bells, the sounds of great trains on the rails.

And to all these familiar sounds, filled with their exultant prophecies of flight, the voyage, morning, and the shining cities—to all the sharp and thrilling odors of the trains—the smell of cinders, acrid smoke, of musty, rusty freight cars, the clean pine-board of crated produce, and the smells of fresh stored food—oranges, coffee, tangerines and bacon, ham and flour and beef—there would be added now, with an unforgettable magic and familiarity, all the strange sounds and smells of the coming circus.

The gay yellow sumptuous-looking cars in which the star performers lived and slept, still dark and silent, heavily and powerfully still, would be drawn up in long strings upon the tracks. And all around them the sounds of the unloading circus would go on furiously in the darkness. The receding gulf of lilac and departing night would be filled with the savage roar of the lions, the murderously sudden snarling of great jungle cats, the trumpeting of the elephants, the stamp of the horses, and with the musty, pungent, unfamiliar odor of the jungle animals: the tawny camel smells, and the smells of panthers, zebras, tigers, elephants, and bears.

Then, along the tracks, beside the circus trains, there would be the sharp cries and oaths of the circus men, the magical swinging dance of lanterns in the darkness, the sudden heavy rumble of the loaded vans and wagons as they were pulled along the flats and gondolas, and down the runways to the ground. And everywhere, in the thrilling mystery of darkness and awakening light, there would be the tremendous conflict of a confused, hurried, and yet orderly movement.

The great iron-gray horses, four and six to a team, would be plodding along the road of thick white dust to a rattling of chains and traces and the harsh cries of their drivers. The men would drive the animals to the river which flowed by beyond the tracks, and water them; and as first light came one could see the elephants wallowing in the familiar river and the big horses going slowly and carefully down to drink.

Then, on the circus grounds, the tents were going up already with the magic speed of dreams. All over the place (which was near the tracks and the only space of flat land in the town that was big enough to hold a circus) there would be this fierce, savagely hurried, and yet orderly confusion. Great flares of gaseous circus light would blaze down on the seared and battered faces of the circus toughs as, with the rhythmic precision of a single animal—a human riveting machine—they swung their sledges at the stakes, driving a stake into the earth with the incredible instancy of accelerated figures in a motion picture. And everywhere, as light came, and the sun appeared, there would be a scene of magic, order, and of violence. The drivers would curse and talk their special language to their teams, there would be the loud, gasping and uneven labor of a gasoline engine, the shouts and curses of the bosses, the wooden riveting of driven stakes, and the rattle of heavy chains.

Already in an immense cleared space of dusty beaten earth, the stakes were being driven for the main exhibition tent. And an elephant would lurch ponderously to the field, slowly lower his great swinging head at the command of a man who sat perched upon his skull, flourish his gray wrinkled snout a time or two, and then solemnly wrap it around a tent pole big as the mast of a racing schooner. Then the elephant would back slowly away, dragging the great pole with him as if it were a stick of match-wood.

And when this happened, my brother would break into his great "whah-whah" of exuberant laughter, and prod me in the ribs with his clumsy fingers. And further on, two town darkeys, who had watched the elephant's performance with bulging eyes, would turn to each other with ape-like grins, bend double as they slapped their knees and howled with swart rich nigger-laughter, saying to each other in a kind of rhythmical chorus of question and reply:

"He don't play with it, do he?"

"No, *suh*! He don't send no boy!"

"He don't say 'Wait a minute,' do he?"

"No, suh! He say 'Come with me!' That's what he say!"

"He go boogety—boogety!" said one, suiting the words with a prowling movement of his black face toward the earth.

"He go rootin' faw it!" said the other, making a rooting movement with his head.

"He say 'Ar-rumpf'!" said one.

"He say 'Big boy, we is on ouah way'!" the other answered.

"Har! Har! Har! Har! Har!"—and they choked and screamed with their rich laughter, slapping their thighs with a solid smack as they described to each other the elephant's prowess.

Meanwhile, the circus food-tent—a huge canvas top without concealing sides—had already been put up, and now we could see the performers seated at long trestled tables underneath the tent, as they ate breakfast. And the savor of the food they ate—mixed as it was with our strong excitement, with the powerful but wholesome smells of the animals, and with all the joy, sweetness, mystery, jubilant magic and glory of the morning and the coming of the circus—seemed to us to be of the most maddening and appetizing succulence of any food that we had ever known or eaten.

We could see the circus performers eating tremendous breakfasts, with all the savage relish of their power and strength: they ate big fried steaks, pork chops, rashers of bacon, a half dozen eggs, great slabs of fried ham and great stacks of wheat-cakes which a cook kept flipping in the air with the skill of a juggler, and which a husky-looking waitress kept rushing to their tables on loaded trays held high and balanced marvelously on the fingers of a brawny hand. And above all the maddening odors of the wholesome and succulent food, there brooded forever the sultry and delicious fragrance—that somehow seemed to add a zest and sharpness to all the powerful and thrilling life of morning—of strong boiling coffee, which we could see sending off clouds of steam from an enormous polished urn, and which the circus performers gulped down, cup after cup.

And the circus men and women themselves—these star performers—were such fine-looking people, strong and handsome, yet speaking and moving with an almost stern dignity and decorum, that their lives seemed to us to be as splendid and wonderful as any lives on earth could be. There was never anything loose, rowdy, or tough in their comportment, nor did the circus women look like painted whores, or behave indecently with the men.

Rather, these people in an astonishing way seemed to have created an established community which lived an ordered existence on wheels, and to observe with a stern fidelity unknown in towns and cities the decencies of family life. There would be a powerful young man, a handsome and magnificent young woman with blonde hair and the figure of an Amazon, and a powerfully-built, thick-set man of middle age, who had a stern, lined, responsible-looking face and a bald head. They were probably the members of a trapeze team—the young man and woman would leap through space like projectiles, meeting the grip of the older man and hurling back again upon their narrow perches, catching the swing of their trapeze in mid-air, and whirling thrice before they caught it, in a perilous and beautiful exhibition of human balance and precision.

But when they came into the breakfast tent, they would speak gravely yet courteously to other performers, and seat themselves in a family group at one of the long tables, eating their tremendous breakfasts with an earnest concentration, seldom speaking to one another, and then gravely, seriously and briefly.

And my brother and I would look at them with fascinated eyes: my brother would watch the man with the bald head for a while and then turn toward me, whispering:

"D-d-do you see that f-f-fellow there with the bald head? W-w-well he's the heavy man," he whispered knowingly. "He's the one that c-c-c-catches them! That f-f-fellow's got to know his business! You know what happens if he m-m-misses, don't you?" said my brother.

"What?" I would say in a fascinated tone.

My brother snapped his fingers in the air.

"Over!" he said. "D-d-done for! W-w-why, they'd be d-d-d-dead before they knew what happened. Sure!" he said, nodding vigorously. "It's a f-f-f-fact! If he ever m-m-m-misses it's all over! That boy has g-g-g-got to know his s-s-s-stuff!" my brother said. "W-w-w-why," he went on in a low tone of solemn conviction, "it w-w-w-wouldn't surprise me at all if they p-p-p-pay him s-s-seventy-five or a hundred dollars a week! It's a fact!" my brother cried vigorously.

And we would turn our fascinated stares again upon these splendid and romantic creatures, whose lives were so different from our own, and whom we seemed to know with such familiar and affectionate intimacy. And at length, reluctantly, with full light come and the sun up, we would leave the circus grounds and start for home.

And somehow the memory of all we had seen and heard that glorious morning, and the memory of the food-tent with its wonderful smells, would waken in us the pangs of such a ravenous hunger that we could not wait until we got home to eat. We would stop off in town at lunch-rooms and, seated on tall stools before the counter, we would devour ham-and-egg sandwiches, hot hamburgers red and pungent at their cores with coarse spicy sanguinary beef, coffee, glasses of foaming milk and doughnuts, and then go home to eat up everything in sight upon the breakfast table.

JOHN STEINBECK

Flight

John Steinbeck, born in 1902, attended Stanford University and worked at various jobs before beginning his literary career. His books have particularly been concerned with the problems of the landless farm laborer. Among his best known novels are *Tortilla Flat, In Dubious Battle, Of Mice and Men, The Grapes of Wrath*—which won a vast audience—and *The Wayward Bus*. He has published several volumes of short stories: *The Pastures of Heaven* and *The Long Valley*. [From *The Portable Steinbeck;* copyright 1938, 1943 by John Steinbeck; used by permission of The Viking Press, Inc., New York.]

ABOUT FIFTEEN MILES below Monterey, on the wild coast, the Torres family had their farm, a few sloping acres above a cliff that dropped to the brown reefs and to the hissing white waters of the ocean. Behind the farm the stone mountains stood up against the sky. The farm buildings huddled like little clinging aphids on the mountain skirts, crouched low to the ground as though the wind might blow them into the sea. The little shack, the rattling, rotting barn were gray-bitten with sea salt, beaten by the damp wind until they had taken on the color of the granite hills. Two horses, a red cow and a red calf, half a dozen pigs and a flock of lean, multicolored chickens stocked the place. A little corn was raised on the sterile slope, and it grew short and thick under the wind, and all the cobs formed on the landward sides of the stalks.

Mama Torres, a lean, dry woman with ancient eyes, had ruled the farm for ten years, ever since her husband tripped over a stone in the field one day and fell full length on a rattlesnake. When one is bitten on the chest there is not much that can be done.

Mama Torres had three children, two undersized black ones of twelve and fourteen, Emilio and Rosy, whom Mama kept fishing on the rocks below the farm when the sea was kind and when the truant officer was in some distant part of Monterey County. And there was Pepé, the tall smiling son of nineteen, a gentle, affectionate boy, and very lazy. Pepé had a tall head, pointed at the top, and from its peak, coarse black hair grew down like a thatch all around. Over his smiling little eyes Mama cut a straight bang so he could see. Pepé had sharp Indian cheek bones and an eagle nose, but his mouth was as sweet and shapely as a girl's mouth, and his chin was fragile and chiseled. He was loose and gangling, all legs and feet and wrists, and he was very lazy. Mama thought him fine and brave, but she never told him so. She said, "Some lazy cow must have got into thy father's family, else how could I have a son like thee." And she said, "When I carried thee, a sneaking lazy

81

coyote came out of the brush and looked at me one day. That must have made thee so."

Pepé smiled sheepishly and stabbed at the ground with his knife to keep the blade sharp and free from rust. It was his inheritance, that knife, his father's knife. The long heavy blade folded back into the black handle. There was a button on the handle. When Pepé pressed the button, the blade leaped out ready for use. The knife was with Pepé always, for it had been his father's knife.

One sunny morning when the sea below the cliff was glinting and blue and the white surf creamed on the reef, when even the stone mountains looked kindly, Mama Torres called out the door of the shack, "Pepé, I have a labor for thee."

There was no answer. Mama listened. From behind the barn she heard a burst of laughter. She lifted her full long skirt and walked in the direction of the noise.

Pepé was sitting on the ground with his back against a box. His white teeth glistened. On either side of him stood the two black ones, tense and expectant. Fifteen feet away a redwood post was set in the ground. Pepé's right hand lay limply in his lap, and in the palm the big black knife rested. The blade was closed back into the handle. Pepé looked smiling at the sky.

Suddenly Emilio cried, "Ya!"

Pepé's wrist flicked like the head of a snake. The blade seemed to fly open in mid-air, and with a thump the point dug into the redwood post, and the black handle quivered. The three burst into excited laughter. Rosy ran to the post and pulled out the knife and brought it back to Pepé. He closed the blade and settled the knife carefully in his listless palm again. He grinned self-consciously at the sky.

"Ya!"

The heavy knife lanced out and sunk into the post again. Mama moved forward like a ship and scattered the play.

"All day you do foolish things with the knife, like a toy-baby," she stormed. "Get up on thy huge feet that eat up shoes. Get up!" She took him by one loose shoulder and hoisted at him. Pepé grinned sheepishly and came half-heartedly to his feet. "Look!" Mama cried. "Big lazy, you must catch the horse and put on him thy father's saddle. You must ride to Monterey. The medicine bottle is empty. There is no salt. Go thou now, Peanut! Catch the horse."

A revolution took place in the relaxed figure of Pepé. "To Monterey, me? Alone? Sí, Mama."

She scowled at him. "Do not think, big sheep, that you will buy candy. No, I will give you only enough for the medicine and the salt."

Pepé smiled. "Mama, you will put the hatband on the hat?"

She relented then. "Yes, Pepé. You may wear the hatband."

His voice grew insinuating, "And the green handkerchief, Mama?"

"Yes, if you go quickly and return with no trouble, the silk green handkerchief will go. If you make sure to take off the handkerchief when you eat so no spot may fall on it. . . ."

"*Sí*, Mama. I will be careful. I am a man."

"Thou? A man? Thou art a peanut."

He went into the rickety barn and brought out a rope, and he walked agilely enough up the hill to catch the horse.

When he was ready and mounted before the door, mounted on his father's saddle that was so old that the oaken frame showed through torn leather in many places, then Mama brought out the round black hat with the tooled leather band, and she reached up and knotted the green silk handkerchief about his neck. Pepé's blue denim coat was much darker than his jeans, for it had been washed much less often.

Mama handed up the big medicine bottle and the silver coins. "That for the medicine," she said, "and that for the salt. That for a candle to burn for the papa. That for *dulces* for the little ones. Our friend Mrs. Rodriguez will give you dinner and maybe a bed for the night. When you go to the church say only ten Paternosters and only twenty-five Ave Marias. Oh! I know, big coyote. You would sit there flapping your mouth over Aves all day while you looked at the candles and the holy pictures. That is not good devotion to stare at the pretty things."

The black hat, covering the high pointed head and black thatched hair of Pepé, gave him dignity and age. He sat the rangy horse well. Mama thought how handsome he was, dark and lean and tall. "I would not send thee now alone, thou little one, except for the medicine," she said softly. "It is not good to have no medicine, for who knows when the toothache will come, or the sadness of the stomach. These things are."

"Adios, Mama," Pepé cried. "I will come back soon. You may send me often alone. I am a man."

"Thou art a foolish chicken."

He straightened his shoulders, flipped the reins against the horse's shoulder and rode away. He turned once and saw that they still watched him, Emilio and Rosy and Mama. Pepé grinned with pride and gladness and lifted the tough buckskin horse to a trot.

When he had dropped out of sight over a little dip in the road, Mama turned to the black ones, but she spoke to herself. "He is nearly a man now," she said. "It will be a nice thing to have a man in the house again." Her eyes sharpened on the children. "Go to the rocks now. The tide is going out. There will be abalones to be found." She put the iron hooks into their hands and saw them down the steep trail to the reefs. She brought the smooth stone *metate* to the doorway and sat grinding her corn to flour and looked occasionally at the road over which Pepé had gone. The noonday came and then the afternoon, when the little ones beat the abalones on a rock to make them tender and Mama patted the tortillas to make them thin. They ate their dinner as the red sun was plunging down toward the ocean. They sat on the doorsteps and watched the big white moon come over the mountain tops.

Mama said, "He is now at the house of our friend Mrs. Rodriguez. She will give him nice things to eat and maybe a present."

Emilio said, "Some day I too will ride to Monterey for medicine. Did Pepé come to be a man today?"

Mama said wisely, "A boy gets to be a man when a man is needed. Remember this thing. I have known boys forty years old because there was no need for a man."

Soon afterward they retired, Mama in her big oak bed on one side of the room, Emilio and Rosy in their boxes full of straw and sheepskins on the other side of the room.

The moon went over the sky and the surf roared on the rocks. The roosters crowed the first call. The surf subsided to a whispering surge against the reef. The moon dropped toward the sea. The roosters crowed again.

The moon was near down to the water when Pepé rode on a winded horse to his home flat. His dog bounded out and circled the horse yelping with pleasure. Pepé slid off the saddle to the ground. The weathered little shack was silver in the moonlight and the square shadow of it was black to the north and east. Against the east the piling mountains were misty with light; their tops melted into the sky.

Pepé walked wearily up the three steps and into the house. It was dark inside. There was a rustle in the corner.

Mama cried out from her bed. "Who comes? Pepé, is it thou?"

"*Sí*, Mama."

"Did you get the medicine?"

"*Sí*, Mama."

"Well, go to sleep, then. I thought you would be sleeping at the house of Mrs. Rodriguez." Pepé stood silently in the dark room. "Why do you stand there, Pepé? Did you drink wine?"

"*Sí*, Mama."

"Well, go to bed then and sleep out the wine."

His voice was tired and patient, but very firm. "Light the candle, Mama. I must go away into the mountains."

"What is this, Pepé? You are crazy." Mama struck a sulphur match and held the little blue burr until the flame spread up the stick. She set light to the candle on the floor beside her bed. "Now, Pepé, what is this you say?" She looked anxiously into his face.

He was changed. The fragile quality seemed to have gone from his chin. His mouth was less full than it had been, the lines of the lips were straighter, but in his eyes the greatest change had taken place. There was no laughter in them any more, nor any bashfulness. They were sharp and bright and purposeful.

He told her in a tired monotone, told her everything just as it had happened. A few people came into the kitchen of Mrs. Rodriguez.

There was wine to drink. Pepé drank wine. The little quarrel—the man started toward Pepé and then the knife—it went almost by itself. It flew, it darted before Pepé knew it. As he talked, Mama's face grew stern, and it seemed to grow more lean. Pepé finished. "I am a man now, Mama. The man said names to me I could not allow."

Mama nodded. "Yes, thou art a man, my poor little Pepé. Thou art a man. I have seen it coming on thee. I have watched you throwing the knife into the post, and I have been afraid." For a moment her face had softened, but now it grew stern again. "Come! We must get you ready. Go. Awaken Emilio and Rosy. Go quickly."

Pepé stepped over to the corner where his brother and sister slept among the sheepskins. He leaned down and shook them gently. "Come, Rosy! Come, Emilio! The mama says you must arise."

The little black ones sat up and rubbed their eyes in the candlelight. Mama was out of bed now, her long black skirt over her nightgown. "Emilio," she cried. "Go up and catch the other horse for Pepé. Quickly, now! Quickly." Emilio put his legs in his overalls and stumbled sleepily out the door.

"You heard no one behind you on the road?" Mama demanded.

"No, Mama. I listened carefully. No one was on the road."

Mama darted like a bird about the room. From a nail on the wall she took a canvas water bag and threw it on the floor. She stripped a blanket from her bed and rolled it into a tight tube and tied the ends with a string. From a box beside the stove she lifted a flour sack half full of black stringy jerky. "Your father's black coat, Pepé. Here, put it on."

Pepé stood in the middle of the floor watching her activity. She reached behind the door and brought out the rifle, a long 38-56, worn shiny the whole length of the barrel. Pepé took it from her and held it in the crook of his elbow. Mama brought a little leather bag and counted the cartridges into his hand. "Only ten left," she warned. "You must not waste them."

Emilio put his head in the door. "'Qui 'st 'l caballo, Mama."

"Put on the saddle from the other horse. Tie on the blanket. Here, tie the jerky to the saddle horn."

Still Pepé stood silently watching his mother's frantic activity. His chin looked hard, and his sweet mouth was drawn and thin. His little eyes followed Mama about the room almost suspiciously.

Rosy asked softly, "Where goes Pepé?"

Mama's eyes were fierce. "Pepé goes on a journey. Pepé is a man now. He has a man's thing to do."

Pepé straightened his shoulders. His mouth changed until he looked very much like Mama.

At last the preparation was finished. The loaded horse stood outside the door. The water bag dripped a line of moisture down the bay shoulder.

The moonlight was being thinned by the dawn and the big white moon was near down to the sea. The family stood by the shack. Mama confronted Pepé. "Look, my son! Do not stop until it is dark again. Do not sleep even though you are tired. Take care of the horse in order that he may not stop of weariness. Remember to be careful with the bullets—there are only ten. Do not fill thy stomach with jerky or it will make thee sick. Eat a little jerky and fill thy stomach with grass. When thou comest to the high mountains, if thou seest any of the dark watching men, go not near to them nor try to speak to them. And forget not thy prayers." She put her lean hands on Pepé's shoulders, stood on her toes and kissed him formally on both cheeks, and Pepé kissed her on both cheeks. Then he went to Emilio and Rosy and kissed both of their cheeks.

Pepé turned back to Mama. He seemed to look for a little softness, a little weakness in her. His eyes were searching, but Mama's face remained fierce. "Go now," she said. "Do not wait to be caught like a chicken."

Pepé pulled himself into the saddle. "I am a man," he said.

It was the first dawn when he rode up the hill toward the little canyon which let a trail into the mountains. Moonlight and daylight fought with each other, and the two warring qualities made it difficult to see. Before Pepé had gone a hundred yards, the outlines of his figure were misty; and long before he entered the canyon, he had become a gray, indefinite shadow.

Mama stood stiffly in front of her doorstep, and on either side of her stood Emilio and Rosy. They cast furtive glances at Mama now and then.

When the gray shape of Pepé melted into the hillside and disappeared, Mama relaxed. She began the high, whining keen of the death wail. "Our beautiful—our brave," she cried. "Our protector, our son is gone." Emilio and Rosy moaned beside her. "Our beautiful—our brave, he is gone." It was the formal wail. It rose to a high piercing whine and subsided to a moan. Mama raised it three times and then she turned and went into the house and shut the door.

Emilio and Rosy stood wondering in the dawn. They heard Mama whimpering in the house. They went out to sit on the cliff above the ocean. They touched shoulders. "When did Pepé come to be a man?" Emilio asked.

"Last night," said Rosy. "Last night in Monterey." The ocean clouds turned red with the sun that was behind the mountains.

"We will have no breakfast," said Emilio. "Mama will not want to cook." Rosy did not answer him. "Where is Pepé gone?" he asked.

Rosy looked around at him. She drew her knowledge from the quiet air. "He has gone on a journey. He will never come back."

"Is he dead? Do you think he is dead?"

Rosy looked back at the ocean again. A little steamer, drawing a line of smoke sat on the edge of the horizon. "He is not dead," Rosy explained. "Not yet."

Pepé rested the big rifle across the saddle in front of him. He let the horse walk up the hill and he didn't look back. The stony slope took on a coat of short brush so that Pepé found the entrance to a trail and entered it.

When he came to the canyon opening, he swung once in his saddle and looked back, but the houses were swallowed in the misty light. Pepé jerked forward again. The high shoulder of the canyon closed in on him. His horse stretched out its neck and sighed and settled to the trail.

It was a well-worn path, dark soft leaf-mould earth strewn with broken pieces of sandstone. The trail rounded the shoulder of the canyon and dropped steeply into the bed of the stream. In the shallows the water ran smoothly, glinting in the first morning sun. Small round stones on the bottom were as brown as rust with sun moss. In the sand along the edges of the stream the tall, rich wild mint grew, while in the water itself the cress, old and tough, had gone to heavy seed.

The path went into the stream and emerged on the other side. The horse sloshed into the water and stopped. Pepé dropped his bridle and let the beast drink of the running water.

Soon the canyon sides became steep and the first giant sentinel redwoods guarded the trail, great round red trunks bearing foliage as green and lacy as ferns. Once Pepé was among the trees, the sun was lost. A perfumed and purple light lay in the pale green of the underbrush. Gooseberry bushes and blackberries and tall ferns lined the stream, and overhead the branches of the redwoods met and cut off the sky.

Pepé drank from the water bag, and he reached into the flour sack and brought out a black string of jerky. His white teeth gnawed at the string until the tough meat parted. He chewed slowly and drank occasionally from the water bag. His little eyes were slumberous and tired, but the muscles of his face were hard set. The earth of the trail was black now. It gave up a hollow sound under the walking hoof-beats.

The stream fell more sharply. Little waterfalls splashed on the stones. Five-fingered ferns hung over the water and dripped spray from their fingertips. Pepé rode half over in his saddle, dangling one leg loosely. He picked a bay leaf from a tree beside the way and put it into his mouth for a moment to flavor the dry jerky. He held the gun loosely across the pommel.

Suddenly he squared in his saddle, swung the horse from the trail and kicked it hurriedly up behind a big redwood tree. He pulled up the reins tight against the bit to keep the horse from whinnying. His face was intent and his nostrils quivered a little.

A hollow pounding came down the trail, and a horseman rode by, a fat man with red cheeks and a white stubble beard. His horse put down its head and blubbered at the trail when it came to the place where Pepé had turned off. "Hold up!" said the man and he pulled up his horse's head.

When the last sound of the hoofs died away, Pepé came back into the trail again. He did not relax in the saddle any more. He lifted the big rifle and swung the lever to throw a shell into the chamber, and then he let down the hammer to half cock.

The trail grew very steep. Now the redwood trees were smaller and their tops were dead, bitten dead where the wind reached them. The horse plodded on; the sun went slowly overhead and started down toward the afternoon.

Where the stream came out of a side canyon, the trail left it. Pepé dismounted and watered his horse and filled up his water bag. As soon as the trail had parted from the stream, the trees were gone and only the thick brittle sage and manzanita and chaparral edged the trail. And the soft black earth was gone, too, leaving only the light tan broken rock for the trail bed. Lizards scampered away into the brush as the horse rattled over the little stones.

Pepé turned in his saddle and looked back. He was in the open now: he could be seen from a distance. As he ascended the trail the country grew more rough and terrible and dry. The way wound about the bases of great square rocks. Little gray rabbits skittered in the brush. A bird made a monotonous high creaking. Eastward the bare rock mountaintops were pale and powder-dry under the dropping sun. The horse plodded up and up the trail toward a little V in the ridge which was the pass.

Pepé looked suspiciously back every minute or so, and his eyes sought the tops of the ridges ahead. Once, on a white barren spur, he saw a black figure for a moment, but he looked quickly away, for it was one of the dark watchers. No one knew who the watchers were, nor where they lived, but it was better to ignore them and never to show interest in them. They did not bother one who stayed on the trail and minded his own business.

The air was parched and full of light dust blown by the breeze from the eroding mountains. Pepé drank sparingly from his bag and corked it tightly and hung it on the horn again. The trail moved up the dry shale hillside, avoiding rocks, dropping under clefts, climbing in and out of old water scars. When he arrived at the little pass he stopped and looked back for a long time. No dark watchers were to be seen now. The trail behind was empty. Only the high tops of the redwoods indicated where the stream flowed.

Pepé rode on through the pass. His little eyes were nearly closed with weariness, but his face was stern, relentless and manly. The high mountain wind coasted sighing through the pass and whistled on the edges of the big blocks of broken granite. In the air, a red-tailed hawk sailed over close to the ridge and screamed angrily. Pepé went slowly through the broken jagged pass and looked down on the other side.

The trail dropped quickly, staggering among broken rock. At the bottom of the slope there was a dark crease, thick with brush, and on the other side of the crease a little flat, in which a grove of oak trees grew.

A scar of green grass cut across the flat. And behind the flat another mountain rose, desolate with dead rocks and starving little black bushes. Pepé drank from the bag again for the air was so dry that it encrusted his nostrils and burned his lips. He put the horse down the trail. The hooves slipped and struggled on the steep way, starting little stones that rolled off into the brush. The sun was gone behind the westward mountain now, but still it glowed brilliantly on the oaks and on the grassy flat. The rocks and the hillsides still sent up waves of the heat they had gathered from the day's sun.

Pepé looked up to the top of the next dry withered ridge. He saw a dark form against the sky, a man's figure standing on top of a rock, and he glanced away quickly not to appear curious. When a moment later he looked up again, the figure was gone.

Downward the trail was quickly covered. Sometimes the horse floundered for footing, sometimes set his feet and slid a little way. They came at last to the bottom where the dark chaparral was higher than Pepé's head. He held up his rifle on one side and his arm on the other to shield his face from the sharp brittle fingers of the brush.

Up and out of the crease he rode, and up a little cliff. The grassy flat was before him, and the round comfortable oaks. For a moment he studied the trail down which he had come, but there was no movement and no sound from it. Finally he rode over the flat, to the green streak, and at the upper end of the damp he found a little spring welling out of the earth and dropping into a dug basin before it seeped out over the flat.

Pepé filled his bag first, and then he let the thirsty horse drink out of the pool. He led the horse to the clump of oaks, and in the middle of the grove, fairly protected from sight on all sides, he took off the saddle and the bridle and laid them on the ground. The horse stretched his jaws sideways and yawned. Pepé knotted the lead rope about the horse's neck and tied him to a sapling among the oaks, where he could graze in a fairly large circle.

When the horse was gnawing hungrily at the dry grass, Pepé went to the saddle and took a black string of jerky from the sack and strolled to an oak tree on the edge of the grove, from under which he could watch the trail. He sat down in the crisp dry oak leaves and automatically felt for his big black knife to cut the jerky, but he had no knife. He leaned back on his elbow and gnawed at the tough strong meat. His face was blank, but it was a man's face.

The bright evening light washed the eastern ridge, but the valley was darkening. Doves flew down from the hills to the spring, and the quail came running out of the brush and joined them, calling clearly to one another.

Out of the corner of his eye Pepé saw a shadow grow out of the bushy crease. He turned his head slowly. A big spotted wildcat was creeping toward the spring, belly to the ground, moving like thought.

Pepé cocked his rifle and edged the muzzle slowly around. Then he looked apprehensively up the trail and dropped the hammer again.

From the ground beside him he picked an oak twig and threw it toward the spring. The quail flew up with a roar and the doves whistled away. The big cat stood up: for a long moment he looked at Pepé with cold yellow eyes, and then fearlessly walked back into the gulch.

The dusk gathered quickly in the deep valley. Pepé muttered his prayers, put his head down on his arm and went instantly to sleep.

The moon came up and filled the valley with cold blue light, and the wind swept rustling down from the peaks. The owls worked up and down the slopes looking for rabbits. Down in the brush of the gulch a coyote gabbled. The oak trees whispered softly in the night breeze.

Pepé started up, listening. His horse had whinnied. The moon was just slipping behind the western ridge, leaving the valley in darkness behind it. Pepé sat tensely gripping his rifle. From far up the trail he heard an answering whinny and the crash of shod hooves on the broken rock. He jumped to his feet, ran to his horse and led it under the trees. He threw on the saddle and cinched it tight for the steep trail, caught the unwilling head and forced the bit into the mouth. He felt the saddle to make sure the water bag and the sack of jerky were there. Then he mounted and turned up the hill.

It was velvet dark. The horse found the entrance to the trail where it left the flat, and started up, stumbling and slipping on the rocks. Pepé's hand rose up to his head. His hat was gone. He had left it under the oak tree.

The horse had struggled far up the trail when the first change of dawn came into the air, a steel grayness as light mixed thoroughly with dark. Gradually the sharp snaggled edge of the ridge stood out above them, rotten granite tortured and eaten by the winds of time. Pepé had dropped his reins on the horn, leaving direction to the horse. The brush grabbed at his legs in the dark until one knee of his jeans was ripped.

Gradually the light flowed down over the ridge. The starved brush and rocks stood out in the half light, strange and lonely in high perspective. Then there came warmth into the light. Pepé drew up and looked back, but he could see nothing in the darker valley below. The sky turned blue over the coming sun. In the waste of the mountainside, the poor dry brush grew only three feet high. Here and there, big outcroppings of unrotted granite stood up like mouldering houses. Pepé relaxed a little. He drank from his water bag and bit off a piece of jerky. A single eagle flew over, high in the light.

Without warning Pepé's horse screamed and fell on its side. He was almost down before the rifle crash echoed up from the valley. From a hole behind the struggling shoulder, a stream of bright crimson blood pumped and stopped and pumped and stopped. The hooves threshed on the ground. Pepé lay half stunned beside the horse. He looked slowly down the hill. A piece of sage clipped off beside his head and another crash echoed up from side to side of the canyon. Pepé flung himself frantically behind a bush.

He crawled up the hill on his knees and one hand. His right hand held the rifle up off the ground and pushed it ahead of him. He moved with the instinctive care of an animal. Rapidly he wormed his way toward one of the big outcroppings of granite on the hill above him. Where the brush was high he doubled up and ran, but where the cover was slight he wriggled forward on his stomach, pushing the rifle ahead of him. In the last little distance there was no cover at all. Pepé poised and then he darted across the space and flashed around the corner of the rock.

He leaned panting against the stone. When his breath came easier he moved along behind the big rock until he came to a narrow split that offered a thin section of vision down the hill. Pepé lay on his stomach and pushed the rifle barrel through the slit and waited.

The sun reddened the western ridges now. Already the buzzards were settling down toward the place where the horse lay. A small brown bird scratched in the dead sage leaves directly in front of the rifle muzzle. The coasting eagle flew back toward the rising sun.

Pepé saw a little movement in the brush far below. His grip tightened on the gun. A little brown doe stepped daintily out on the trail and crossed it and disappeared into the brush again. For a long time Pepé waited. Far below he could see the little flat and the oak trees and the slash of green. Suddenly his eyes flashed back at the trail again. A quarter of a mile down there had been a quick movement in the chaparral. The rifle swung over. The front sight nestled in the v of the rear sight. Pepé studied for a moment and then raised the rear sight a notch. The little movement in the brush came again. The sight settled on it. Pepé squeezed the trigger. The explosion crashed down the mountain and up the other side, and came rattling back. The whole side of the slope grew still. No more movement. And then a white streak cut into the granite of the slit and a bullet whined away and a crash sounded up from below. Pepé felt a sharp pain in his right hand. A sliver of granite was sticking out from between his first and second knuckles and the point protruded from his palm. Carefully he pulled out the sliver of stone. The wound bled evenly and gently. No vein nor artery was cut.

Pepé looked into a little dusty cave in the rock and gathered a handful of spider web, and he pressed the mass into the cut, plastering the soft web into the blood. The flow stopped almost at once.

The rifle was on the ground. Pepé picked it up, levered a new shell into the chamber. And then he slid into the brush on his stomach. Far to the right he crawled, and then up the hill, moving slowly and carefully, crawling to cover and resting and then crawling again.

In the mountains the sun is high in its arc before it penetrates the gorges. The hot face looked over the hill and brought instant heat with it. The white light beat on the rocks and reflected from them and rose up quivering from the earth again, and the rocks and bushes seemed to quiver behind the air.

Pepé crawled in the general direction of the ridge peak, zig-zagging for cover. The deep cut between his knuckles began to throb. He crawled close to a rattlesnake before he saw it, and when it raised its dry head and made a soft beginning whirr, he backed up and took another way. The quick gray lizards flashed in front of him, raising a tiny line of dust. He found another mass of spider web and pressed it against his throbbing hand.

Pepé was pushing the rifle with his left hand now. Little drops of sweat ran to the ends of his coarse black hair and rolled down his cheeks. His lips and tongue were growing thick and heavy. His lips writhed to draw saliva into his mouth. His little dark eyes were uneasy and suspicious. Once when a gray lizard paused in front of him on the parched ground and turned its head sideways he crushed it flat with a stone.

When the sun slid past noon he had not gone a mile. He crawled exhaustedly a last hundred yards to a patch of high sharp manzanita, crawled desperately, and when the patch was reached he wriggled in among the tough gnarly trunks and dropped his head on his left arm. There was little shade in the meager brush, but there was cover and safety. Pepé went to sleep as he lay and the sun beat on his back. A few little birds hopped close to him and peered and hopped away. Pepé squirmed in his sleep and he raised and dropped his wounded hand again and again.

The sun went down behind the peaks and the cool evening came, and then the dark. A coyote yelled from the hillside, Pepé started awake and looked about with misty eyes. His hand was swollen and heavy; a little thread of pain ran up the inside of his arm and settled in a pocket in his armpit. He peered about and then stood up, for the mountains were black and the moon had not yet risen. Pepé stood up in the dark. The coat of his father pressed on his arm. His tongue was swollen until it nearly filled his mouth. He wriggled out of the coat and dropped it in the brush, and then he struggled up the hill, falling over rocks and tearing his way through the brush. The rifle knocked against stones as he went. Little dry avalanches of gravel and shattered stone went whispering down the hill behind him.

After a while the old moon came up and showed the jagged ridge top ahead of him. By moonlight Pepé traveled more easily. He bent forward so that his throbbing arm hung away from his body. The journey uphill was made in dashes and rests, a frantic rush up a few yards and then a rest. The wind coasted down the slope rattling the dry stems of the bushes.

The moon was at meridian when Pepé came at last to the sharp backbone of the ridge top. On the last hundred yards of the rise no soil had clung under the wearing winds. The way was on solid rock. He clambered to the top and looked down on the other side. There was a draw like the last below him, misty with moonlight, brushed with dry struggling sage and chaparral. On the other side the hill rose up sharply and at the top the jagged rotten teeth of the mountain showed against the sky. At the bottom of the cut the brush was thick and dark.

Pepé stumbled down the hill. His throat was almost closed with thirst. At first he tried to run, but immediately he fell and rolled. After that he went more carefully. The moon was just disappearing behind the mountains when he came to the bottom. He crawled into the heavy brush feeling with his fingers for water. There was no water in the bed of the stream, only damp earth. Pepé laid his gun down and scooped up a handful of mud and put it in his mouth, and then he spluttered and scraped the earth from his tongue with his finger, for the mud drew at his mouth like a poultice. He dug a hole in the stream bed with his fingers, dug a little basin to catch water; but before it was very deep his head fell forward on the damp ground and he slept.

The dawn came and the heat of the day fell on the earth, and still Pepé slept. Late in the afternoon his head jerked up. He looked slowly around. His eyes were slits of wariness. Twenty feet away in the heavy brush a big tawny mountain lion stood looking at him. Its long thick tail waved gracefully, its ears were erect with interest, not laid back dangerously. The lion squatted down on its stomach and watched him.

Pepé looked at the hole he had dug in the earth. A half inch of muddy water had collected in the bottom. He tore the sleeve from his hurt arm, with his teeth ripped out a little square, soaked it in the water and put it in his mouth. Over and over he filled the cloth and sucked it.

Still the lion sat and watched him. The evening came down but there was no movement on the hills. No birds visited the dry bottom of the cut. Pepé looked occasionally at the lion. The eyes of the yellow beast dropped as though he were about to sleep. He yawned and his long thin red tongue curled out. Suddenly his head jerked around and his nostrils quivered. His big tail lashed. He stood up and slunk like a tawny shadow into the thick brush.

A moment later Pepé heard the sound, the faint far crash of horses' hooves on gravel. And he heard something else, a high whining yelp of a dog.

Pepé took his rifle in his left hand and he glided into the brush almost as quietly as the lion had. In the darkening evening he crouched up the hill toward the next ridge. Only when dark came did he stand up. His energy was short. Once it was dark he fell over the rocks and slipped to his knees on the steep slope, but he moved on and on up the hill, climbing and scrabbling over the broken hillside.

When he was far up toward the top, he lay down and slept for a little while. The withered moon, shining on his face, awakened him. He stood up and moved up the hill. Fifty yards away he stopped and turned back, for he had forgotten his rifle. He walked heavily down and poked about in the brush, but he could not find his gun. At last he lay down to rest. The pocket of pain in his armpit had grown more sharp. His arm seemed to swell out and fall with every heartbeat. There was no position lying down where the heavy arm did not press against his armpit.

With the effort of a hurt beast, Pepé got up and moved again toward the top of the ridge. He held his swollen arm away from his body with his left hand. Up the steep hill he dragged himself, a few steps and a rest, and a few more steps. At last he was nearing the top. The moon showed the uneven sharp back of it against the sky.

Pepé's brain spun in a big spiral up and away from him. He slumped to the ground and lay still. The rock ridge top was only a hundred feet above him.

The moon moved over the sky. Pepé half turned on his back. His tongue tried to make words, but only a thick hissing came from between his lips.

When the dawn came, Pepé pulled himself up. His eyes were sane again. He drew his great puffed arm in front of him and looked at the angry wound. The black line ran up from his wrist to his armpit. Automatically he reached in his pocket for the big black knife, but it was not there. His eyes searched the ground. He picked up a sharp blade of stone and scraped at the wound, sawed at the proud flesh and then squeezed the green juice out in big drops. Instantly he threw back his head and whined like a dog. His whole right side shuddered at the pain, but the pain cleared his head.

In the gray light he struggled up the last slope to the ridge and crawled over and lay down behind a line of rocks. Below him lay a deep canyon exactly like the last, waterless and desolate. There was no flat, no oak trees, not even heavy brush in the bottom of it. And on the other side a sharp ridge stood up, thinly brushed with starving sage, littered with broken granite. Strewn over the hill there were giant outcroppings, and on the top the granite teeth stood out against the sky.

The new day was light now. The flame of the sun came over the ridge and fell on Pepé where he lay on the ground. His coarse black hair was littered with twigs and bits of spider web. His eyes had retreated back into his head. Between his lips the tip of his black tongue showed.

He sat up and dragged his great arm into his lap and nursed it, rocking his body and moaning in his throat. He threw back his head and looked up into the pale sky. A big black bird circled nearly out of sight, and far to the left another was sailing near.

He lifted his head to listen, for a familiar sound had come to him from the valley he had climbed out of; it was the crying yelp of hounds, excited and feverish, on a trail.

Pepé bowed his head quickly. He tried to speak rapid words but only a thick hiss came from his lips. He drew a shaky cross on his breast with his left hand. It was a long struggle to get to his feet. He crawled slowly and mechanically to the top of a big rock on the ridge peak. Once there, he arose slowly, swaying to his feet, and stood erect. Far below he could see the dark brush where he had slept. He braced his feet and stood there, black against the morning sky.

There came a ripping sound at his feet. A piece of stone flew up and

a bullet droned off into the next gorge. The hollow crash echoed up
from below. Pepé looked down for a moment and then pulled himself
straight again.

His body jarred back. His left hand fluttered helplessly toward his
breast. The second crash sounded from below. Pepé swung forward
and toppled from the rock. His body struck and rolled over and over,
starting a little avalanche. And when at last he stopped against a bush,
the avalanche slid slowly down and covered up his head.

BEN HECHT

Snowfall in Childhood

Ben Hecht was born in New York in 1894.
He was brought up in Wisconsin and
became, in turn, an acrobat, a violinist and
a newspaper reporter. He has written
many plays with Charles MacArthur,
among which are *The Front Page, 20th
Century* and *Ladies and Gentlemen;* many
novels, including *Erik Dorn* and *The
Florentine Dagger;* and numerous short
stories, many of which are in his *Collected
Stories.* [From *Esquire,* November, 1934;
copyright by Ben Hecht.]

I GOT OUT OF BED to see what had happened in the night. I was
thirteen years old. I had fallen asleep watching the snow falling
through the half-frosted window.

But though the snow had promised to keep falling for a long time,
perhaps three or four days, on opening my eyes I was full of doubts.
Snowstorms usually ended too soon.

While getting out of bed I remembered how, as I was nearly asleep,
the night outside the frosted window had seemed to burst into a white
jungle. I had dreamed of streets and houses buried in snow.

I hurried barefooted to the window. It was scribbled with a thick
frost and I couldn't see through it. The room was cold and through
the open window came the fresh smell of snow like the moist nose of
an animal resting on the ledge and breathing into the room.

I knew from the smell and the darkness of the window that snow was
still falling. I melted a peephole on the glass with my palms. I saw
that this time the snow had not fooled me. There it was, still coming
down white and silent and too thick for the wind to move, and the
streets and houses were almost as I had dreamed. I watched, shivering
and happy. Then I dressed, pulling on my clothes as if the house were
on fire. I was finished with breakfast and out in the storm two hours
before school time.

The world had changed. All the houses, fences, and barren trees had
new shapes. Everything was round and white and unfamiliar.

I set out through these new streets on a voyage of discovery. The unknown surrounded me. Through the thick falling snow, the trees, houses and fences looked like ghost shapes that had floated down out of the sky during the night. The morning was without light, but the snowfall hung and swayed like a marvelous lantern over the streets. The snowbanks, already over my head in places, glowed mysteriously.

I was pleased with this new world. It seemed to belong to me more than that other world which lay hidden.

I headed for the school, jumping like a clumsy rabbit in and out of snowbanks. It seemed wrong to spoil the smooth outlines of these snowdrifts and I hoped that nobody else would pass this way after me. In that case the thick falling snow would soon restore the damage. Reassured by this hope I continued on my devastations like some wanton explorer. I began to feel that no one would dare the dangers of my wake. Then, as I became more aware of the noble proportions of this snowstorm I stopped worrying altogether about the marring of this new and glowing world. Other snows had melted and been shoveled away, but this snow would never disappear. The sun would never shine again and the little Wisconsin town through which I plunged and tumbled to school on this dark storm-filled morning was from now on an arctic land full of danger and adventure.

When eventually, encased in snow, I arrived at the school, I found scores of white-covered figures already there. The girls had taken shelter inside, but the boys stayed in the storm. They jumped in and out of the snowdrifts and tumbled through the deep unbroken white fields in front of the school.

Muffled cries filled the street. Someone had discovered how far-away our voices sounded in the snowfall and this started the screaming. We screamed for ten minutes, delighted with the fact that our voices no longer carried and that the snowstorm had made us nearly dumb.

Tired with two hours of such plunging and rolling, I joined a number of boys who like myself had been busy since dawn and who now stood for the last few minutes before the school bell with half-frozen faces staring at the heavily falling snow as if it were some game they couldn't bear to leave.

When we were finally seated in our grade room we continued to watch the snowstorm through the windows. The morning had grown darker as we had all hoped it would and it was necessary to turn on the electric lights in the room. This was almost as thrilling as the pale storm still floating outside the windows.

In this yellow light the school seemed to disappear and in its place a picnic spread around us. The teachers themselves seemed to change. Their eyes kept turning toward the windows and they kept looking at us behind our desks as if we were strangers. We grew excited and even the sound of our lessons—the sentences out of geography and arithmetic books—made us tremble.

Passing through the halls during recess we whispered to one another about the snowstorm, guessing at how deep the snowdrifts must be by this time. We looked nervously at our teachers who stood in the class-room doorways stiff and far removed from our secret whispers about the snow.

I felt sorry for these teachers, particularly for the one who had taught me several years ago when I was in the Fifth Grade. I saw her as I walked by the opened door of her room. She was younger than the other teachers, with two dark braids coiled around her head, a white starched shirtwaist and soft dark eyes that had always looked kindly at me when I was younger. I saw her now sitting behind her large desk looking over the heads of her class out of the window and paying no attention to the whispers and giggles of her pupils.

As for my own teacher, a tall, thin woman with a man's face, by afternoon I had become so happy I could no longer hear what she was saying. I sat looking at the large clock over her head. My feeling on the way to school that it would never be light again and that the snowstorm would keep on forever had increased so that it was something I now knew rather than hoped. My eagerness to get out into the world of wind, gloom, and perpetual snow, kept lifting me out of my seat.

At three o'clock we rushed into the storm. Our screams died as we reached the school entrance. What we saw silenced us. Under the dark sky the street lay piled in an unbroken bank of snow. And above it the snowfall still hung in a thick and moving cloud. Nothing was visible but snow. Everything else had disappeared. Even the sky was gone.

I saw the teachers come out and look around them, frowning. The children of the lower grades stood chattering and frightened near the teachers. I waited until the teacher with the two black braids saw me and then, paying no attention to her warning, spoken in a gentle voice, I plunged into the storm. I felt brave but slightly regretful that Miss Wheeler could no longer see me as I pushed into the head-high piles of snow and vanished fearlessly into the storm. But I was certain that she was still thinking of me and worrying about my safety. This thought added excitement to the snowstorm.

After an hour I found myself alone. My legs were tired with jumping and my face burned. It had grown darker and the friendliness seemed to have gone out of the storm. The wind bit with a sharper edge and I turned toward my home.

I arrived at the house that now looked like a snow drift and ploughed my way up to its front door. My heart was beating violently. I stopped to take a last look at the storm. It was hard to leave it. But for the first time in my life an adult logic instructed me. There would be even more snow tomorrow. And in this wind and snow-filled gloom and even in the marvelously buried street, there was something now unplayful.

I entered the house calling for something to eat, but as soon as I had taken my coat off and shaken myself clean, I was at the window again. The way this storm was keeping on was hard to believe.

At the table I was too excited to eat. I trembled and was unable to hear what was being said around me. In this room I could feel the night outside and the storm still blowing on my face. It seemed as if I were still in the street. My eyes kept seeing snow and my nose breathing it. The room and the people in it became far away. I left the table, taking a slice of bread and butter with me, and ran upstairs to my own room.

There were a lot of things to do, such as making my leather boots more waterproof by rubbing lard on them, putting my stamp collection in order, sharpening a deer's-foot knife I had recently acquired, winding tape on my new hockey stick, or reading one of the half dozen new books I had bought with my last birthday money. But none of these activities or even redrawing the plans for the ice-boat on which I was working was possible. I sat in a chair near the window unable to think. The pale storm in the night seemed to spin like a top and, keeping the window frost melted with my palms, I sat and watched it snowing for an hour. Then, becoming sleepy, I went to bed. I thought drowsily of how happy Miss Wheeler would be to see me alive on Monday after the way I had rushed into the storm.

There was no seeing through my window when I awoke. The furnace never got going until after seven and before that hour on a winter's morning the house creaked with cold and the windows were sheeted thick with ice. But I knew as I dressed that the snowfall was over. There was too much wind blowing outside and the breath that came in from the snow-banked window ledge was no longer as fresh as it had been.

It was still dark. The bleak and gusty dawn lay over the snow like a guttering candle. The sky had finished with its snowing but now the wind sent the snowbanks ballooning into the air and the roof tops burst into little snowstorms.

I went outside and explored for ten minutes. When I came back into the house I needed no warning against going out to play. My skin was almost frozen and the wind was too strong to stand up in. I settled down as a prisoner in front of the fireplace after breakfast, lying on my stomach and turning the pages of a familiar oversized edition of Dante's "Inferno." It was full of Doré's nightmarish pictures.

The house bustled with cooking and cleaning. But these were the dim activities of grown-ups. I felt alone and took care of the fire to keep it from going out and leaving me to freeze to death. I carried logs all morning from the cellar and lay perspiring and half-scorched on the hearthstone. Every half-hour I went to the window to have a look at the enemy. The sight of the whirling snowbanks and the sound of the brutal wind as it hit against the houses sent me back to the fireplace to scorch myself anew.

In this way I spent the day until late afternoon. It grew dark early. The snow turned leaden. The wind stopped. The dead storm lay in the street and as far as I could see from the window there were no inhabitants in the world. The dark snow was empty. I shivered and went back to the fireplace.

A half-hour later our door bell rang. Company had arrived for supper. They were the Joneses, who lived in the town of Corliss some eight miles away. They had brought their daughter Anna.

The lights went on in the house. Baked and dizzy with the fire's heat, I joined the two families in the larger parlor. They were talking excitedly about the damage done by the storm. Accounts of store windows blown in, roofs blown off, signs blown down, and wagons abandoned in the drifts, were exchanged and I listened happily. Later when the talk turned to duller topics I became aware of Anna.

She was sitting in a corner watching me. She was a blondish girl two years older than I was and she went to high school. I had known her for a long time but had never liked her because she was too calm, never laughing or running, but always looking at people with a sad smile or just a stare as if she had something important on her mind. But now that she was watching me that way I felt suddenly interested in her. I wondered what she could be thinking of me and what made her smile in that half-sad way at me.

I sat next to her at the table and after looking at her several times out of the side of my eyes and catching her eyes doing the same thing, my heart started beating faster. I lost interest in eating. I wanted to be alone with her so we could sit and look at each other without the others noticing.

After supper the two families let us go to the hall upstairs, where I kept most of my possessions, without asking us any questions. I found a deck of cards and a cribbage board for a table. Underneath the lapboard our knees touched.

She played cribbage better than I and smiled at me as I kept losing. But I was only half aware of the game. I kept looking at her, unable to talk, and the light pressure of her knees began to make me feel weak. Her face seemed to become brighter and more beautiful as we played. A mist appeared around her eyes and her smile became so close, as if it were moving swiftly toward me, that I began to tremble. I felt ashamed of being so tongue-tied and red-faced, but with a half-frightened blissful indifference to everything—even Anna—I kept on playing.

We hardly spoke. I grew too nervous to follow the game and I wanted to stop. But I thought if we stopped we could no longer sit this way with our knees touching. At moments when Anna withdrew her touch I trembled and waited as if I were hanging from somewhere. When finally her knees returned to their place against mine, I caught my breath and frowned at the cards as if I were completely taken up with them.

As the hour passed, my face began to feel swollen and lopsided and it seemed to me my features had grown ugly beyond words. I tried to distract Anna's attention from this phenomenon by twisting my mouth, screwing up my eyes and making popping noises with my cheeks as we played. But a new fear arrived to uncenter my attention. I became afraid now that Anna would notice her knees were touching mine and move them away. I began at once pretending a deeper excitement in the game, complaining against my bad luck and denouncing her for cheating. I was determined to keep her interested in the game at any cost, believing that her interest in what we were doing made her unaware of her knees touching mine.

Finally Anna said she was tired of the game. She pushed the cribbage board away. I waited, holding my breath, for her to realize where her knees were and to move them away. I tried not to look at her but I was so frightened of this happening that I found myself staring at her. She seemed to be paying no attention to me. She was leaning back in her chair and her eyes were half closed. Her face was unsmiling and I felt she was thinking of something. This startled me. My throat filled with questions but I was so afraid of breaking this hidden embrace of our knees under the lapboard that I said nothing.

The mist seemed to have spread from her eyes to her hair and over the rest of her face. Wherever I looked this same glow rested around her. I noticed then that her hand was lying on the lapboard. I thought desperately of touching it but there was something disillusioning in this thought. I watched her fingers begin to tap gently on the board as if she were playing the piano. There was something strange about her hand as if it did not belong to the way her knees were touching mine or to the mist that rose from her eyes.

The minutes passed in silence and then Anna's mother called her from downstairs.

"I guess they're going home," I said and Anna nodded. She pressed closer against me but in my confusion I couldn't figure out whether this was the accidental result of her starting to get out of her chair or on purpose.

"Why don't you ride out with us?" she said. She leaned over the lapboard toward me. "We've got the wagon sleigh and there's plenty of room."

Before I could answer she had stood up. My knees felt suddenly cold. I slid the lapboard to the floor, ashamed and sad. Anna, without looking back at me, had gone down the stairs. I kept myself from running after her. I was sure she was laughing at me and that she was saying to herself, "He's a big fool. He's a big fool."

The Joneses were ready to leave when I came into the parlor. Anna's mother smiled at me.

"Why don't you come and visit us over Sunday?" she said. "There's even more snow in Corliss than here."

"More snow than you can shake a stick at," said another member of the Jones family. They all laughed and while they were laughing my mother hustled me off for my wraps. I was to drive away with the Jones family in the sleigh drawn by the two strong horses that stood in front of our house.

I pulled on my leather boots, sweater, and overcoat while the goodbyes were being made. I kept trying to catch Anna's attention, but she was apparently unaware that I was in the room. This made me sad, and slowly my eagerness to go to Corliss left me. I wanted instead to go up to my room and slam the door forever on all the Joneses. Anna's gayety, the way she said goodbye over and over again and laughed and kissed all the members of my family as if nothing had happened to her, as if she hadn't sat with her eyes closed pressing against my knees in the hallway upstairs, made me almost ill. I felt abandoned and forgotten.

Finally I stood muffled and capped and scowling as my family offered some final instructions for my behavior. I heard nothing of what was said but turned over and over in my mind what I was going to do on the ride and after we got to Corliss. Chiefly I was going to ignore Anna, neither speak to her nor show her by a single look that I knew she was alive.

At this point Anna, having said goodbye to everybody several times, seized my arm unexpectedly and whispered against my ear.

"Come, hurry," she said. "We want to get a good place."

Without a word I rushed out of the house, slipping down the snow-caked steps and tumbling headlong into a snowdrift. I scrambled after Anna into the wagon sleigh. It was a low-sided farm wagon placed on wide, heavy wooden runners and piled with warm hay and horse blankets. There was room for only one on the seat. The rest of the Joneses, seven including me, would have to lie in the hay covered by the robes.

Anna was already in the wagon half-buried in the hay, a blanket over her. She gave me excited orders to brush the snow from my clothes, to cover myself well and not to get out and run alongside the horses when we were going up hill.

"It doesn't help any," she said. "They can pull just the same if you stay in here. And besides I don't want you to."

The rest of the Joneses came out and crowded into the wagon around us. Anna's father took his place on the driver's seat, assuring my mother, who had come out with a shawl over her head, that there was no danger because the State plow had cleared the road even to way beyond Corliss. I heard my mother ask where I was. Mrs. Jones answered that I was buried somewhere in the hay and Anna whispered close to me not to answer or say anything. I obeyed her.

The sleigh started off. I heard the horses thumping in the snow and the harness bells falling into a steady jingling. Lying on my back I looked into the night. Stars filled the sky and a white glare hung over the house tops. The street was silent. I could no longer see the snow-covered houses with their lighted windows. My nose filled with the fresh smell of snow and the barn smells of hay and horse blankets, I lay listening to the different sounds—the harness bells and the snow crunching under the runners.

The stillness of this winter's night was as intense as the storm that had raged for three days. I felt that all the wind and snow there was had blown themselves out forever and that the night as far as the highest star had been emptied by the storm. This emptiness as I lay looking into it was like being hypnotized. It was something to run out into, to fly up into, as the snowfall had been. I began to want to see further and the star-filled sky that had seemed so vast a few minutes ago now didn't seem vast enough.

I had almost forgotten about Anna when I felt a now familiar warmth press against me. She had moved closer as if joggled by the sleigh. I held my breath waiting for her to order me to move away and give her room but she was silent.

My hand at my side touched her fingers. Now I forgot the sky and the great sprinkle of stars that seemed like a thin, far-away snowfall that had stopped moving. The night, the glare of snow, the jingling harness bells died away; only my fingers were alive. When I had looked at her hand tapping gently on the lapboard, it had seemed strange and the thought of touching it somehow disillusioning. But now under the horse blankets, hidden in the hay, this hand seemed more breathing and mysterious and familiar than anything about her. I lay unable to move closer to it, our fingertips barely touching. I grew dizzy wishing to reach her hand but I felt as powerless to move toward it as to fly.

The minutes passed. Two of the Joneses started singing. The thump of the horses, the jingling of the sleighbells, and the crunching of the snow under the runners seemed part of this soft singing. I too wished to sing, to stand up suddenly in this sweeping-along sleigh and bellow at the silent night.

Then the fingers for which I had been wishing until I was dizzy, seemed to start walking under the horse blankets, seemed to be running toward me in the warm hay. They came as far as my hand, closed around it, and I felt the throb of their tips against my palm. The night turned into a dream. I opened my eyes to the wide sprinkle of stars and a mist seemed to have come over them. The snow-covered hills over which we were gliding sparkled behind a mist and suddenly the night into which I was looking lost its hours. It stretched away without time as if it were not something that was passing like our sleigh over the snow, but a star-filled winter's night that would never change and never move.

Lying beside Anna, her hand in mine, with the sleigh now flying in a whirl of snow down the white hill, I thought this night would never end.

KATHERINE ANNE PORTER

A Day's Work

Born in 1894 in Texas, Katherine Anne Porter is a great-great-great-granddaughter of Daniel Boone. She began to write stories at the age of three, but did not attempt to publish anything until she was thirty. In 1930, her *Flowering Judas* appeared, and in 1939, *Pale Horse, Pale Rider*. These have received wide critical acclaim. She now lives in Louisiana, where she is working on a biography of Cotton Mather. [From *The Leaning Tower and Other Stories* by Katherine Anne Porter; copyright 1944 by Katherine Anne Porter; used by permission of Harcourt, Brace & Co., Inc.]

THE DULL SCRAMBLING like a giant rat in the wall meant the dumb-waiter was on its way up, the janitress below hauling on the cable. Mrs. Halloran paused, thumped her iron on the board, and said, "There it is. Late. You could have put on your shoes and gone around the corner and brought the things an hour ago. I can't do everything."

Mr. Halloran pulled himself out of the chair, clutching the arms and heaving to his feet slowly, looking around as if he hoped to find crutches standing near. "Wearing out your socks, too," added Mrs. Halloran. "You ought either go barefoot outright or wear your shoes over your socks as God intended," she said. "Sock feet. What's the good of it, I'd like to know? Neither one thing nor the other."

She unrolled a salmon-colored chiffon nightgown with cream-colored lace and broad ribbons on it, gave it a light flirt in the air, and spread it on the board. "God's mercy, look at that indecent thing," she said. She thumped the iron again and pushed it back and forth over the rumpled cloth. "You might just set the things in the cupboard," she said, "and not leave them around on the floor. You might just."

Mr. Halloran took a sack of potatoes from the dumb-waiter and started for the cupboard in the corner next the icebox. "You might as well take a load," said Mrs. Halloran. "There's no need on earth making a half-dozen trips back and forth. I'd think the poorest sort of man could well carry more than five pounds of potatoes at one time. But maybe not."

Her voice tapped on Mr. Halloran's ears like wood on wood. "Mind your business, will you?" he asked, not speaking to her directly. He carried on the argument with himself. "Oh, I couldn't do that, Mister Honey," he answered in a dull falsetto. "Don't ever ask me to think ot such a thing, even. It wouldn't be right," he said, standing still with his knees bent, glaring bitterly over the potato sack at the scrawny strange woman he had never liked, that one standing there ironing clothes with a dirty look on her whole face like a suffering saint. "I

103

may not be much good any more," he told her in his own voice, "but I still have got wits enough to take groceries off a dumb-waiter, mind you."

"That's a miracle," said Mrs. Halloran. "I'm thankful for that much."

"There's the telephone," said Mr. Halloran, sitting in the armchair again and taking his pipe out of his shirt pocket.

"I heard it as well," said Mrs. Halloran, sliding the iron up and down over the salmon-colored chiffon.

"It's for you, I've no further business in this world," said Mr. Halloran. His little greenish eyes glittered; he exposed his two sharp dogteeth in a grin.

"You could answer it. It could be the wrong number again or for somebody downstairs," said Mrs. Halloran, her flat voice going flatter, even.

"Let it go in any case," decided Mr. Halloran, "for my own part, that is." He struck a match on the arm of his chair, touched off his pipe, and drew in his first puff while the telephone went on with its nagging.

"It might be Maggie again," said Mrs. Halloran.

"Let her ring, then," said Mr. Halloran, settling back and crossing his legs.

"God help a man who won't answer the telephone when his own daughter calls up for a word," commented Mrs. Halloran to the ceiling. "And she in deep trouble, too, with her husband treating her like a dog about the money, and sitting out late nights in saloons with that crowd from the Little Tammany Association. He's getting into politics now with the McCorkery gang. No good will come of it, and I told her as much."

"She's no troubles at all, her man's a sharp fellow who will get ahead if she'll let him alone," said Mr. Halloran. "She's nothing to complain of, I could tell her. But what's a father?" Mr. Halloran cocked his head toward the window that opened on the brick-paved areaway and crowed like a rooster, "What's a father these days and who would heed his advice?"

"You needn't tell the neighbors, there's disgrace enough already," said Mrs. Halloran. She set the iron back on the gas ring and stepped out to the telephone on the first stair landing. Mr. Halloran leaned forward, his thin, red-haired hands hanging loosely between his knees, his warm pipe sending up its good decent smell right into his nose. The woman hated the pipe and the smell; she was a woman born to make any man miserable. Before the depression, while he still had a good job and prospects of a raise, before he went on relief, before she took in fancy washing and ironing, in the Good Days Before, God's pity, she didn't exactly keep her mouth shut, there wasn't a word known to man she couldn't find an answer for, but she knew which side her bread was buttered on, and put up with it. Now she was, you might say, buttering her own bread and she never forgot it for a minute. And it's her own fault we're not riding round today in a limousine with ash trays and a speaking tube and a cut-glass vase for flowers in it. It's what a man gets for marrying one of these holy women. Gerald McCorkery had told him as much, in the beginning.

"There's a girl will spend her time holding you down," Gerald had told him. "You're putting your head in a noose will strangle the life out of you. Heed the advice of one who wishes you well," said Gerald McCorkery. This was after he had barely set eyes on Lacey Mahaffy one Sunday morning in Coney Island. It was like McCorkery to see that in a flash, born judge of human nature that he was. He could look a man over, size him up, and there was an end to it. And if the man didn't pass muster, McCorkery could ease him out in a way that man would never know how it happened. It was the secret of McCorkery's success in the world.

"This is Rosie, herself," said Gerald that Sunday in Coney Island. "Meet the future Mrs. Gerald J. McCorkery." Lacey Mahaffy's narrow face had gone sour as whey under her big straw hat. She barely nodded to Rosie, who gave Mr. Halloran a look that fairly undressed him right there. Mr. Halloran had thought, too, that McCorkery was picking a strange one; she was good-looking all right, but she had the smell of a regular little Fourteenth Street hustler if Halloran knew anything about women. "Come on," said McCorkery, his arm around Rosie's waist, "let's all go on the roller coaster." But Lacey would not. She said, "No, thank you. We didn't plan to stay, and we must go now." On the way home Mr. Halloran said, "Lacey, you judge too harshly. Maybe that's a nice girl at heart; hasn't had your opportunities." Lacey had turned upon him a face ugly as an angry cat's, and said, "She's a loose, low woman, and 'twas an insult to introduce her to me." It was a good while before the pretty fresh face that Mr. Halloran had fallen in love with returned to her.

Next day in Billy's Place, after three drinks each, McCorkery said, "Watch your step, Halloran; think of your future. There's a straight good girl I don't doubt, but she's no sort of mixer. A man getting into politics needs a wife who can meet all kinds. A man needs a woman who knows how to loosen her corsets and sit easy."

Mrs. Halloran's voice was going on in the hall, a steady dry rattle like old newspapers blowing on a park bench. "I told you before it's no good coming to me with your troubles now. I warned you in time but you wouldn't listen. . . . I told you just how it would be, I tried my best. . . . No, you couldn't listen, you always knew better than your mother. . . . So now all you've got to do is stand by your married vows and make the best of it. . . . Now listen to me, if you want himself to do right you have to do right first. The woman has to do right first, and then if the man won't do right in turn it's no fault of hers. You do right whether he does wrong or no, just because he does wrong is no excuse for you."

"Ah, will you hear that?" Mr. Halloran asked the areaway in an awed voice. "There's a holy terror of a saint for you."

". . . the woman has to do right first, I'm telling you," said Mrs. Halloran into the telephone, "and then if he's a devil in spite of it, why she has to do right without any help from him." Her voice rose so the neighbors could get an earful if they wanted. "I know you from old, you're just like your father. You must be doing something wrong yourself or you wouldn't be in this fix. You're doing wrong this minute, calling over the telephone when you ought to be getting your work done. I've got an iron on, working over the dirty nightgowns of a kind of woman I wouldn't soil my foot on if I'd had a man to take care of me. So now you do up your housework and dress yourself and take a walk in the fresh air. . . ."

"A little fresh air never hurt anybody," commented Mr. Halloran loudly through the open window. "It's the gas gets a man down."

"Now listen to me, Maggie, that's not the way to talk over the public wires. Now you stop that crying and go and do your duty and don't be worrying me any more. And stop saying you're going to leave your husband, because where will you go, for one thing? Do you want to walk the streets or set up a laundry in your kitchen? You can't come back here, you'll stay with your husband where you belong. Don't be a fool, Maggie. You've got your living, and that's more than many a woman better than you has got. Yes, your father's all right. No, he's just sitting here, the same. God knows what's to become of us. But you know how he is, little he cares. . . . Now remember this, Maggie, if anything goes wrong with your married life it's your own fault and you needn't come here for sympathy. . . . I can't waste any more time on it. Good by."

Mr. Halloran, his ears standing up for fear of missing a word, thought how Gerald J. McCorkery had gone straight on up the ladder with Rosie; and for every step the McCorkerys took upward, he, Michael Halloran, had taken a step downward with Lacey Mahaffy. They had started as greenhorns with the same chances at the same time and the same friends, but McCorkery had seized all his opportunities as they came, getting in steadily with the Big Shots in ward politics, one good thing leading to another. Rosie had known how to back him up and push him onward. The McCorkerys for years had invited him and Lacey to come over to the house and be sociable with the crowd, but Lacey would not.

"You can't run with that fast set and drink and stay out nights and hold your job," said Lacey, "and you should know better than to ask your wife to associate with that woman." Mr. Halloran had got into the habit of dropping around by himself, now and again, for McCorkery still liked him, was still willing to give him a foothold in the right places, still asked him for favors at election time. There was always a good lively crowd at the McCorkerys, wherever they were; for they moved ever so often to a better place, with more furniture. Rosie helped hand around the drinks, taking a few herself with a gay word for everybody.

The player piano or the victrola would be going full blast, with every-body dancing, all looking like ready money and a bright future. He would get home late these evenings, back to the same little cold-water walk-up flat, because Lacey would not spend a dollar for show. It must all go into savings against old age, she said. He would be full of good food and drink, and find Lacey, in a bungalow apron, warming up the fried potatoes once more, cross and bitterly silent, hanging her head and frowning at the smell of liquor on his breath. "You might at least eat the potatoes when I've fried them and waited all this time," she would say. "Ah, eat them yourself, they're none of mine," he would snarl in his disappointment with her, and with the life she was leading him.

He had believed with all his heart for years that he would one day be manager of one of the G. and I. chain grocery stores he worked for, and when that hope gave out there was still his pension when they retired him. But two years before it was due they fired him, on account of the depression, they said. Overnight he was on the sidewalk, with no place to go with the news but home. "Jesus," said Mr. Halloran, still remembering that day after nearly seven years of idleness.

The depression hadn't touched McCorkery. He went on and on up the ladder, giving beefsteaks and beanfests and beer parties for the boys in Billy's Place, standing in with the right men and never missing a trick. At last the Gerald J. McCorkery Club chartered a whole boat for the big excursion up the river. It was a great day, with Lacey sitting at home sulking. After election Rosie had her picture in the papers, smiling at McCorkery; not fat exactly, just a fine figure of a woman with flowers pinned on her spotted fur coat, her teeth as good as ever. Oh, God, there was a girl for any man's money. Mr. Halloran saw out of his eye-corner the bony stooped back of Lacey Mahaffy, standing on one foot to rest the other like a tired old horse, leaning on her hands waiting for the iron to heat.

"That was Maggie, with her woes," she said.

"I hope you gave her some good advice," said Mr. Halloran. "I hope you told her to take up her hat and walk out on him."

Mrs. Halloran suspended the iron over a pair of pink satin panties. "I told her to do right and leave wrong-doing to the men," she said, in her voice like a phonograph record running down. "I told her to bear with the trouble God sends as her mother did before her."

Mr. Halloran gave a loud groan and knocked out his pipe on the chair arm. "You would ruin the world, woman, if you could, with your wicked soul, treating a new-married girl as if she had no home and no parents to come to. But she's no daughter of mine if she sits there peeling potatoes, letting a man run over her. No daughter of mine and I'll tell her so if she—"

"You know well she's your daughter, so hold your tongue," said Mrs. Halloran, "and if she heeded you she'd be walking the streets this minute. I brought her up an honest girl, and an honest woman she's going to be or I'll take her over my knee as I did when she was little. So there you are, Halloran."

Mr. Halloran leaned far back in his chair and felt along the shelf above his head until his fingers touched a half-dollar he had noticed there. His hand closed over it, he got up instantly and looked about for his hat.

"Keep your daughter, Lacey Mahaffy," he said, "she's none of mine but the fruits of your long sinning with the Holy Ghost. And now I'm off for a little round and a couple of beers to keep my mind from dissolving entirely."

"You can't have that dollar you just now sneaked off the shelf," said Mrs. Halloran. "So you think I'm blind besides? Put it back where you found it. That's for our daily bread."

"I'm sick of bread daily," said Mr. Halloran, "I need beer. It was not a dollar, but a half-dollar as you know well."

"Whatever it was," said Mrs. Halloran, "it stands instead of a dollar to me. So just drop it."

"You've got tomorrow's potatoes sewed up in your pocket this minute, and God knows what sums in that black box wherever you hide it, besides the life savings," said Mr. Halloran. "I earned this half-dollar on relief, and it's going to be spent properly. And I'll not be back for supper, so you'll save on that, too. So long, Lacey Mahaffy, I'm off."

"If you never come back, it will be all the same," said Mrs. Halloran, not looking up.

"If I came back with a pocket full of money, you'd be glad to see me," said Mr. Halloran.

"It would want to be a great sum," said Mrs. Halloran.

Mr. Halloran shut the door behind him with a fine slam.

He strolled out into the clear fall weather, a late afternoon sun warming his neck and brightening the old red-brick, high-stooped houses of Perry Street. He would go after all these years to Billy's Place, he might find some luck there. He took his time, though, speaking to the neighbors as he went. "Good afternoon, Mr. Halloran." "Good afternoon to you, Missis Caffery." . . . "It's fine weather for the time of year, Mr. Gogarty." "It is indeed, Mr. Halloran." Mr. Halloran thrived on these civilities, he loved to flourish his hat and give a hearty good day like a man who has nothing on his mind. Ah, there was the young man from the G. and I. store around the corner. He knew what kind of job Mr. Halloran once held there. "Good day, Mr. Halloran." "Good day to you, Mr. McInerny, how's business holding up with you?" "Good for the times, Mr. Halloran, that's the best I can say." "Things are not getting any better, Mr. McInerny." "It's the truth we are all hanging on by the teeth now, Mr. Halloran."

Soothed by this acknowledgment of man's common misfortune Mr. Halloran greeted the young cop at the corner. The cop, with his quick eyesight, was snatching a read from a newspaper on the stand across the sidewalk. "How do you do, Young O'Fallon," asked Mr. Halloran, "is your business lively these days?"

"Quiet as the tomb itself on this block," said Young O'Fallon. "But that's a sad thing about Connolly, now." His eyes motioned toward the newspaper.

"Is he dead?" asked Mr. Halloran; "I haven't been out until now, I didn't see the papers."

"Ah, not yet," said Young O'Fallon, "but the G-men are after him, it looks they'll get him surely this time."

"Connolly in bad with the G-men? Holy Jesus," said Mr. Halloran, "who will they go after next? The meddlers."

"It's that numbers racket," said the cop. "What's the harm, I'd like to know? A man must get his money from somewhere when he's in politics. They oughta give him a chance."

"Connolly's a great fellow, God bless him, I hope he gives them the slip," said Mr. Halloran, "I hope he goes right through their hands like a greased pig."

"He's smart," said the cop. "That Connolly's a smooth one. He'll come out of it."

Ah, will he though? Mr. Halloran asked himself. Who is safe if Connolly goes under? Wait till I give Lacey Mahaffy the news about Connolly, I'll like seeing her face the first time in twenty years. Lacey kept saying, "A man is a downright fool must be a crook to get rich. Plenty of the best people get rich and do no harm by it. Look at the Connollys now, good practical Catholics with nine children and more to come if God sends them, and Mass every day, and they're rolling in wealth richer than your McCorkerys with all their wickedness." So there you are, Lacey Mahaffy, wrong again, and welcome to your pious Connollys. Still and all it was Connolly who had given Gerald Mc-Corkery his start in the world; McCorkery had been publicity man and then campaign manager for Connolly, in the days when Connolly had Tammany in the palm of his hand and the sky was the limit. And McCorkery had begun at the beginning, God knows. He was running a little basement place first, rent almost nothing, where the boys of the Connolly Club and the Little Tammany Association, just the mere fringe of the district, you might say, could drop in for quiet evenings for a game and a drink along with the talk. Nothing low, nothing but what was customary, with the house taking a cut on the winnings and a fine profit on the liquor, and holding the crowd together. Many was the big plan hatched there came out well for everybody. For everybody but myself, and why was that? And when McCorkery says to me, "You can take over now and run the place for the McCorkery Club," ah, there was my chance and Lacey Mahaffy wouldn't hear of it, and with Maggie coming on just then it wouldn't do to excite her.

Mr. Halloran went on, following his feet that knew the way to Billy's Place, head down, not speaking to passersby any more, but talking it out with himself again, again. What a track to go over seeing clearly one by one the crossroads where he might have taken a different turn that would have changed all his fortunes; but no, he had gone the other way and now it was too late. She wouldn't say a thing but "It's not right and you know it, Halloran," so what could a man do in all? Ah, you could have gone on with your rightful affairs like any other man, Halloran, it's not the woman's place to decide such things; she'd have come round once she saw the money, or a good whack on the backsides would have put her in her place. Never had mortal woman needed a good walloping worse than Lacey Mahaffy, but he could never find it in his heart to give it to her for her own good. That was just another of your many mistakes, Halloran. But there was always the life-long job with the G. and I. and peace in the house more or less. Many a man envied me in those days I remember, and I was resting easy on the savings and knowing with that and the pension I could finish out my life with some little business of my own. "What came of that?" Mr. Halloran inquired in a low voice, looking around him. Nobody answered. You know well what came of it, Halloran. You were fired out like a delivery boy, two years before your time was out. Why did you sit there watching the trick being played on others before you, knowing well it could happen to you and never quite believing what you saw with your own eyes? G. and I. gave me my start, when I was green in this country, and they were my own kind or I thought so. Well, it's done now. Yes, it's done now, but there was all the years you could have cashed in on the numbers game with the best of them, helping collect the protection money and taking your cut. You could have had a fortune by now in Lacey's name, safe in the bank. It was good quiet profit and none the wiser. But they're wiser now, Halloran, don't forget; still it's a lump of grief and disappointment to swallow all the same. The game's up with Connolly, maybe; Lacey Mahaffy had said, "Numbers is just another way of stealing from the poor, and you weren't born to be a thief like that McCorkery." Ah, God, no, Halloran, you were born to rot on relief and maybe that's honest enough for her. That Lacey— A fortune in her name would have been no good to me whatever. She's got all the savings tied up, such as they are, she'll pinch and she'll starve, she'll wash dirty clothes first, she won't give up a penny to live on. She has stood in my way, McCorkery, like a skeleton rattling its bones, and you were right about her, she has been my ruin. "Ah, it's not too late yet, Halloran," said McCorkery, appearing plain as day inside Halloran's head with the same old face and way with him. "Never say die, Halloran. Elections are coming on again, it's a busy time for all, there's work to be done and you're the very man I'm looking for. Why didn't you come to me sooner, you know I never forget an old friend. You don't deserve your ill fortune, Halloran," McCorkery told him; "I said so to others and I say it now to your face, never did man deserve more of the world than you, Halloran, but the truth is, there's not always enough good luck to go round; but it's your turn now, and I've got a job for you up to your abilities at last. For a man like you, there's nothing to it at all, you can toss it off with one hand tied, Halloran, and good money in it. Organization work, just among your own neighbors, where you're known and respected for a man of your word and an old friend of Gerald McCorkery. Now look, Hallo- ran," said Gerald McCorkery, tipping him the wink, "do I need to say more? It's voters in large numbers we're after, Halloran, and you're to bring them in, alive or dead. Keep your eye on the situation at all times and get in touch with me when necessary. And name your figure in the way of money. And come up to the house sometimes, Halloran, why don't you? Rosie has asked me a hundred times, 'Whatever went with Halloran, the life of the party?' That's the way you stand with Rosie, Halloran. We're in a two-story flat now with green velvet cur- tains and carpets you can sink to your shoetops in, and there's no reason at all why you shouldn't have the same kind of place if you want it. With your gifts, you were never meant to be a poor man."

Ah, but Lacey Mahaffy wouldn't have it, maybe. "Then get yourself another sort of woman, Halloran, you're a good man still, find yourself a woman like Rosie to snuggle down with at night." Yes, but McCork- ery, you forget that Lacey Mahaffy had legs and hair and eyes and a complexion fit for a chorus girl. But would she do anything with them? Never. Would you believe there was a woman wouldn't take off all her clothes at once even to bathe herself? What a hateful thing she was with her evil mind thinking everything was a sin, and never giving a man a chance to show himself a man in any way. But she's faded away now, her mean soul shows out all over her, she's ugly as sin itself now, McCorkery. "It's what I told you would happen," said McCorkery, "but now with the job and the money you can go your ways and let Lacey Mahaffy go hers." I'll do it, McCorkery. "And forget about Connolly. Just remember I'm my own man and always was. Connolly's finished, but I'm not. Stronger than ever, Halloran, with Connolly out of the way. I saw this coming long ever ago, Halloran, I got clear of it. They don't catch McCorkery with his pants down, Halloran. And I almost forgot . . . Here's something for the running expenses to start. Take this for the present, and there's more to come. . . ."

Mr. Halloran stopped short, a familiar smell floated under his nose: the warm beer-and-beefsteak smell of Billy's Place, sawdust and onions, like any other bar maybe, but with something of its own besides. The talk within him stopped also as if a hand had been laid on his mind. He drew his fist out of his pocket almost expecting to find green money in it. The half-dollar was in his palm. "I'll stay while it lasts and hope McCorkery will come in."

The moment he stepped inside his eye lighted on McCorkery standing at the bar pouring his own drink from the bottle before him. Billy was mopping the bar before him idly, and his eye, swimming toward Hal- loran, looked like an oyster in its own juice. McCorkery saw him too. "Well, blow me down," he said, in a voice that had almost lost its old County Mayo ring, "if it ain't my old sidekick from the G. and I. Step right up, Halloran," he said, his poker-face as good as ever, no man ever saw Gerald McCorkery surprised at anything. "Step up and name your choice."

Mr. Halloran glowed suddenly with the warmth around the heart he always had at the sight of McCorkery, he couldn't put a name on it, but there was something about the man. Ah, it was Gerald all right, the same, who never forgot a friend and never seemed to care whether a man was rich or poor, with his face of granite and his eyes like blue agates in his head, a rock of a man surely. There he was, saying "Step right up," as if they had parted only yesterday; portly and solid in his expensive-looking clothes, as always; his hat a darker gray than his suit, with a devil-may-care roll to the brim, but nothing sporting, mind you. All first-rate, well made, and the right thing for him, more power to him. Mr. Halloran said, "Ah, McCorkery, you're the one man on this round earth I hoped to see today, but I says to myself, maybe he doesn't come round to Billy's Place so much nowadays."

"And why not?" asked McCorkery, "I've been coming around to Billy's Place for twenty-five years now, it's still headquarters for the old guard of the McCorkery Club, Halloran." He took in Mr. Halloran from head to foot in a flash of a glance and turned toward the bottle.

"I was going to have a beer," said Mr. Halloran, "but the smell of that whiskey changes my mind for me." McCorkery poured a second glass, they lifted the drinks with an identical crook of the elbow, a flick of the wrist at each other.

"Here's to crime," said McCorkery, and "Here's looking at you," said Mr. Halloran, merrily. Ah, to hell with it, he was back where he belonged, in good company. He put his foot on the rail and snapped down his whiskey, and no sooner was his glass on the bar than McCorkery was filling it again. "Just time for a few quick ones," he said, "before the boys get here." Mr. Halloran downed that one, too, before he noticed that McCorkery hadn't filled his own glass. "I'm ahead of you," said McCorkery, "I'll skip this one."

There was a short pause, a silence fell around them that seemed to ooze like a fog from somewhere deep in McCorkery, it was suddenly as if he had not really been there at all, or hadn't uttered a word. Then he said outright: "Well, Halloran, let's have it. What's on your mind?" And he poured two more drinks. That was McCorkery all over, reading your thoughts and coming straight to the point.

Mr. Halloran closed his hand round his glass and peered into the little pool of whiskey. "Maybe we could sit down," he said, feeling weak-kneed all at once. McCorkery took the bottle and moved over to the nearest table. He sat facing the door, his look straying there now and then, but he had a set, listening face as if he was ready to hear anything.

"You know what I've had at home all these years," began Mr. Halloran, solemnly, and paused.

"Oh, God yes," said McCorkery with simple good-fellowship. "How is herself these days?"

"Worse than ever," said Mr. Halloran, "but that's not it."

"What is it, then, Halloran?" asked McCorkery, pouring drinks. "You know well you can speak out your mind to me. Is it a loan?"

"No," said Mr. Halloran. "It's a job."

"Now that's a different matter," said McCorkery. "What kind of a job?"

Mr. Halloran, his head sunk between his shoulders, saw McCorkery wave a hand and nod at half a dozen men who came in and ranged themselves along the bar. "Some of the boys," said McCorkery. "Go on." His face was tougher, and quieter, as if the drink gave him a firm hold on himself. Mr. Halloran said what he had planned to say, had said already on the way down, and it still sounded reasonable and right to him. McCorkery waited until he had finished, and got up, putting a hand on Mr. Halloran's shoulder. "Stay where you are, and help yourself," he said, giving the bottle a little push, "and anything else you want, Halloran, order it on me. I'll be back in a few minutes, and you know I'll help you out if I can."

Halloran understood everything but it was through a soft warm fog, and he hardly noticed when McCorkery passed him again with the men, all in that creepy quiet way like footpads on a dark street. They went into the back room, the door opened on a bright light and closed again, and Mr. Halloran reached for the bottle to help himself wait until McCorkery should come again bringing the good word. He felt comfortable and easy as if he hadn't a bone or muscle in him, but his elbow slipped off the table once or twice and he upset his drink on his sleeve. Ah, McCorkery, is it the whole family you're taking on with the jobs? For my Maggie's husband is in now with the Little Tammany Association. "There's a bright lad will go far and I've got my eye on him, Halloran," said the friendly voice of McCorkery in his mind, and the brown face, softer than he remembered it, came up clearly behind his closed eyes.

"Ah, well, it's like myself beginning all over again in him," said Mr. Halloran, aloud, "besides my own job that I might have had all this time if I'd just come to see you sooner."

"True for you," said McCorkery in a merry County Mayo voice, inside Mr. Halloran's head, "and now let's drink to the gay future for old times' sake and be damned to Lacey Mahaffy." Mr. Halloran reached for the bottle but it skipped sideways, rolled out of reach like a creature, and exploded at his feet. When he stood up the chair fell backward from under him. He leaned on the table and it folded up under his hands like cardboard.

"Wait now, take it easy," said McCorkery, and there he was, real enough, holding Mr. Halloran braced on the one side, motioning with his hand to the boys in the back room, who came out quietly and took hold of Mr. Halloran, some of them, on the other side. Their faces were all Irish, but not an Irishman Mr. Halloran knew in the lot, and he did not like any face he saw. "Let me be," he said with dignity, "I came here to see Gerald J. McCorkery, a friend of mine from old times, and let not a thug among you lay a finger upon me."

"Come on, Big Shot," said one of the younger men, in a voice like a file grating, "come on now, it's time to go."

"That's a fine low lot you've picked to run with, McCorkery," said Mr. Halloran, bracing his heels against the slow weight they put upon him toward the door, "I wouldn't trust one of them far as I could throw him by the tail."

"All right, all right, Halloran," said McCorkery. "Come on with me. Lay off him, Finnegan." He was leaning over Mr. Halloran and pressing something into his right hand. It was money, a neat little roll of it, good smooth thick money, no other feel like it in the world, you couldn't mistake it. Ah, he'd have an argument to show Lacey Mahaffy would knock her off her feet. Honest money with a job to back it up. "You'll stand by your given word, McCorkery, as ever?" he asked, peering into the rock-colored face above him, his feet weaving a dance under him, his heart ready to break with gratitude.

"Ah, sure, sure," said McCorkery in a loud hearty voice with a kind of curse in it. "Crisakes, get on with him, do." Mr. Halloran found himself eased into a taxicab at the curb, with McCorkery speaking to the driver and giving him money. "So long, Big Shot," said one of the thug faces, and the taxicab door thumped to. Mr. Halloran bobbed about on the seat for a while, trying to think. He leaned forward and spoke to the driver. "Take me to my friend Gerald J. McCorkery's house," he said, "I've got important business. Don't pay any attention to what he said. Take me to his house."

"Yeah?" said the driver, without turning his head. "Well, here's where you get out, see? Right here." He reached back and opened the door. And sure enough, Mr. Halloran was standing on the sidewalk in front of the flat in Perry Street, alone except for the rows of garbage cans, the taxicab hooting its way around the corner, and a cop coming toward him, plainly to be seen under the street light.

"You should cast your vote for McCorkery, the poor man's friend," Mr. Halloran told the cop, "McCorkery's the man who will get us all off the spot. Stands by his old friends like a maniac. Got a wife named Rosie. Vote for McCorkery," said Mr. Halloran, working hard at his job, "and you'll be Chief of the Force when Halloran says the word."

"To hell with McCorkery, that stooge," said the cop, his mouth square and sour with the things he said and the things he saw and did every night on that beat. "There you are drunk again, Halloran, shame to you, with Lacey Mahaffy working her heart out over the washboard to buy your beer."

"It wasn't beer and she didn't buy it, mind you," said Mr. Halloran, "and what do you know about Lacey Mahaffy?"

"I knew her from old when I used to run errands for St. Veronica's Altar Society," said the cop, "and she was a great one, even then. Nothing good enough."

"It's the same today," said Mr. Halloran, almost sober for a moment.

"Well, go on up now and stay up till you're fit to be seen," said the cop, censoriously.

"You're Johnny Maginnis," said Mr. Halloran, "I know you well."

"You should know me by now," said the cop.

Mr. Halloran worked his way upstairs partly on his hands and knees, but once at his own door he stood up, gave a great blow on the panel with his fist, turned the knob and surged in like a wave after the door itself, holding out the money toward Mrs. Halloran, who had finished ironing and was at her mending.

She got up very slowly, her bony hand over her mouth, her eyes starting out at what she saw. "Ah, did you steal it?" she asked. "Did you kill somebody for that?" the words grated up from her throat in a dark whisper. Mr. Halloran glared back at her in fear.

"Suffering Saints, Lacey Mahaffy," he shouted until the whole houseful could hear him, "haven't ye any mind at all that you can't see your husband has had a turn of fortune and a job and times are changed from tonight? Stealing, is it? That's for your great friends the Connollys with their religion. Connolly steals, but Halloran is an honest man with a job in the McCorkery Club, and money in pocket."

"McCorkery, is it?" said Mrs. Halloran, loudly too. "Ah, so there's the whole family, young and old, wicked and innocent, taking their bread from McCorkery, at last. Well, it's no bread of mine, I'll earn my own as I have, you can keep your dirty money to yourself, Halloran, mind you I mean it."

"Great God, woman," moaned Mr. Halloran, and he tottered from the door to the table, to the ironing board, and stood there, ready to weep with rage, "haven't you a soul even that you won't come along with your husband when he's riding to riches and glory on the Tiger's back itself, with everything for the taking and no questions asked?"

"Yes, I have a soul," cried Mrs. Halloran, clenching her fists, her hair flying. "Surely I have a soul and I'll save it yet in spite of you. . . ."

She was standing there before him in a kind of faded gingham winding sheet, with her dead hands upraised, her dead eyes blind but fixed upon him, her voice coming up hollow from the deep tomb, her throat thick with grave damp. The ghost of Lacey Mahaffy was threatening him, it came nearer, growing taller as it came, the face changing to a demon's face with a fixed glassy grin. "It's all that drink on an empty stomach," said the ghost, in a hoarse growl. Mr. Halloran fetched a yell of horror right out of his very boots, and seized the flatiron from the board. "Ah, God damn you, Lacey Mahaffy, you devil, keep away, keep away," he howled, but she advanced on air, grinning and growling. He raised the flatiron and hurled it without aiming, and the specter, whoever it was, whatever it was, sank and was gone. He did not look, but broke out of the room and was back on the sidewalk before he knew he had meant to go there. Maginnis came up at once. "Hey there now, Halloran," he said, "I mean business this time. You get back upstairs or I'll run you in. Come along now, I'll help you get there this time, and that's the last of it. On relief the way you are, and drinking your head off."

Mr. Halloran suddenly felt calm, collected; he would take Maginnis up and show him just what had happened, "I'm not on relief any more, and if you want any trouble, just call on my friend, McCorkery. He'll tell you who I am."

"McCorkery can't tell me anything about you I don't know already," said Maginnis. "Stand up there now." For Halloran wanted to go up again on his hands and knees.

"Let a man be," said Mr. Halloran, trying to sit on the cop's feet. "I killed Lacey Mahaffy at last, you'll be pleased to hear," he said, looking up into the cop's face. "It was high time and past. But I did not steal the money."

"Well, ain't that just too bad," said the cop, hauling him up under the arms. "Chees, why'n't you make a good job while you had the chance? Stand up now. Ah, hell with it, stand up or I'll sock you one."

Mr. Halloran said, "Well, you don't believe it so wait and see."

At that moment they both glanced upward and saw Mrs. Halloran coming downstairs. She was holding to the rail, and even in the speckled hall-light they could see a great lumpy clout of flesh standing out on her forehead, all colors. She stopped, and seemed not at all surprised.

"So there you are, Officer Maginnis," she said. "Bring him up."

"That's a fine welt you've got over your eye this time, Mrs. Halloran," commented Officer Maginnis, politely.

"I fell and hit my head on the ironing board," said Mrs. Halloran. "It comes of overwork and worry, day and night. A dead faint, Officer Maginnis. Watch your big feet there, you thriving, natural fool," she added to Mr. Halloran. "He's got a job now, you mightn't believe it, Officer Maginnis, but it's true. Bring him on up, and thank you."

She went ahead of them, opened the door, and led the way to the bedroom through the kitchen, turned back the covers, and Officer Maginnis dumped Mr. Halloran among the quilts and pillows. Mr. Halloran rolled over with a deep groan and shut his eyes.

"Many thanks to you, Officer Maginnis," said Mrs. Halloran.

"Don't mention it, Mrs. Halloran," said Officer Maginnis.

When the door was shut and locked, Mrs. Halloran went and dipped a large bath towel under the kitchen tap. She wrung it out and tied several good hard knots in one end and tried it out with a whack on the edge of the table. She walked in and stood over the bed and brought the knotted towel down in Mr. Halloran's face with all her might. He stirred and muttered, ill at ease. "That's for the flatiron, Halloran," she told him, in a cautious voice as if she were talking to herself, and whack, down came the towel again. "That's for the half-dollar," she said, and whack, "that's for your drunkenness—" Her arm swung around regularly, ending with a heavy thud on the face that was beginning to squirm, gasp, lift itself from the pillow and fall back again, in a puzzled kind of torment. "For your sock feet," Mrs. Halloran told him, whack, "and your laziness, and this is for missing Mass and"—here she swung half a dozen times—"that is for your daughter and your part in her. . . ."

She stood back breathless, the lump on her forehead burning in its furious colors. When Mr. Halloran attempted to rise, shielding his head with his arms, she gave him a push and he fell back again. "Stay there and don't give me a word," said Mrs. Halloran. He pulled the pillow over his face and subsided again, this time for good.

Mrs. Halloran moved about very deliberately. She tied the wet towel around her head, the knotted end hanging over her shoulder. Her hand ran into her apron pocket and came out again with the money. There was a five-dollar bill with three one-dollar bills rolled in it, and the half-dollar she had thought spent long since. "A poor start, but something," she said, and opened the cupboard door with a long key. Reaching in, she pulled a loosely fitted board out of the wall, and removed a black-painted metal box. She unlocked this, took out one five-cent piece from a welter of notes and coins. She then placed the new money in the box, locked it, put it away, replaced the board, shut the cupboard door and locked that. She went out to the telephone, dropped the nickel in the slot, asked for a number, and waited.

"Is that you, Maggie? Well, are things any better with you now? I'm glad to hear it. It's late to be calling, but there's news about your father. No, no, nothing of that kind, he's got a job. I said a *job*. Yes, at last, after all my urging him onward. . . . I've got him bedded down to sleep it off so he'll be ready for work tomorrow. . . . Yes, it's political work, toward the election time, with Gerald McCorkery. But that's no harm, getting votes and all, he'll be in the open air and it doesn't mean I'll have to associate with low people, now or ever. It's clean enough work, with good pay; if it's not just what I prayed for, still it beats nothing, Maggie. After all my trying . . . it's like a miracle. You see what can be done with patience and doing your duty, Maggie. Now mind you do as well by your own husband."

EUDORA WELTY

Petrified Man

Eudora Welty was born in 1909 in Jackson, Mississippi. She attended Mississippi State College for Women, received her A.B. at Wisconsin in 1929, and went to Columbia University to study advertising. For a time she did newspaper and radio work in Jackson, and then settled down to writing. Her first book of short stories was *A Curtain of Green,* and her next, *The Robber Bridegroom;* her latest publication, a novel, is *Delta Wedding.* [From *A Curtain of Green and Other Stories* by Eudora Welty; copyright 1941 by Eudora Welty; used by permission of Harcourt, Brace & Co., Inc.]

"REACH IN MY PURSE and git me a cigarette without no powder in it if you kin, Mrs. Fletcher, honey," said Leota to her ten o'clock shampoo-and-set customer. "I don't like no perfumed cigarettes."

Mrs. Fletcher gladly reached over to the lavender shelf under the lavender-framed mirror, shook a hair net loose from the clasp of the patent-leather bag, and slapped her hand down quickly on a powder puff which burst out when the purse was opened.

"Why, look at the peanuts, Leota!" said Mrs. Fletcher in her marveling voice.

"Honey, them goobers has been in my purse a week if they's been in it a day. Mrs. Pike bought them peanuts."

"Who's Mrs. Pike?" asked Mrs. Fletcher, settling back. Hidden in this den of curling fluid and henna packs, separated by a lavender swing door from the other customers, who were being gratified in other booths, she could give her curiosity its freedom. She looked expectantly at the black part in Leota's yellow curls as she bent to light the cigarette.

"Mrs. Pike is this lady from New Orleans," said Leota, puffing, and pressing into Mrs. Fletcher's scalp with strong red-nailed fingers. "A friend, not a customer. You see, like maybe I told you last time, me and Fred and Sal and Joe all had us a fuss, so Sal and Joe up and moved out, so we didn't do a thing but rent out their room. So we rented it to Mrs. Pike. And Mr. Pike." She flicked an ash into the basket of dirty towels. "Mrs. Pike is a very decided blonde. *She* bought me the peanuts."

"She must be cute," said Mrs. Fletcher.

"Honey, 'cute' ain't the word for what she is. I'm tellin' you, Mrs. Pike is attractive. She has her a good time. She's got a sharp eye out, Mrs. Pike has."

She dashed the comb through the air, and paused dramatically as a cloud of Mrs. Fletcher's hennaed hair floated out of the lavender teeth like a small storm cloud.

"Hair fallin'."

"Aw, Leota."

118

"Uh-huh, commencin' to fall out," said Leota, combing again, and letting fall another cloud.

"Is it any dandruff in it?" Mrs. Fletcher was frowning, her hair-line eyebrows diving down toward her nose, and her wrinkled, beady-lashed eyelids batting with concentration.

"Nope." She combed again. "Just fallin' out."

"Bet it was that last perm'nent you gave me that did it," Mrs. Fletcher said cruelly. "Remember you cooked me fourteen minutes."

"You had fourteen minutes comin' to you," said Leota with finality.

"Bound to be somethin'," persisted Mrs. Fletcher. "Dandruff, dandruff. I couldn't of caught a thing like that from Mr. Fletcher, could I?"

"Well," Leota answered at last, "you know what I heard in here yestiddy, one of Thelma's ladies was settin' over yonder in Thelma's booth gittin' a machineless, and I don't mean to insist or insinuate or anything, Mrs. Fletcher, but Thelma's lady just happ'med to throw out —I forgotten what she was talkin' about at the time—that you was p-r-e-g, and lots of times that'll make your hair do awful funny, fall out and God knows what all. It just ain't our fault, is the way I look at it."

There was a pause. The women stared at each other in the mirror.

"Who was it?" demanded Mrs. Fletcher.

"Honey, I really couldn't say," said Leota. "Not that you look it."

"Where's Thelma? I'll get it out of her," said Mrs. Fletcher.

"Now, honey, I wouldn't go and git mad over a little thing like that," Leota said, combing hastily, as though to hold Mrs. Fletcher down by the hair. "I'm sure it was somebody didn't mean no harm in the world. How far gone are you?"

"Just wait," said Mrs. Fletcher, and shrieked for Thelma, who came in and took a drag from Leota's cigarette.

"Thelma, honey, throw your mind back to yestiddy if you kin," said Leota, drenching Mrs. Fletcher's hair with a thick fluid and catching the overflow in a cold wet towel at her neck.

"Well, I got my lady half wound for a spiral," said Thelma doubtfully.

"This won't take but a minute," said Leota. "Who is it you got in there, old Horse Face? Just cast your mind back and try to remember who your lady was yestiddy who happ'm to mention that my customer was pregnant, that's all. She's dead to know."

Thelma drooped her blood-red lips and looked over Mrs. Fletcher's head into the mirror. "Why, honey, I ain't got the faintest," she breathed. "I really don't recollect the faintest. But I'm sure she meant no harm. I declare, I forgot my hair finally got combed and thought it was a stranger behind me."

"Was it that Mrs. Hutchinson?" Mrs. Fletcher was tensely polite.

"Mrs. Hutchinson? Oh, Mrs. Hutchinson." Thelma batted her eyes. "Naw, precious, she come on Thursday and didn't ev'm mention your name. I doubt if she ev'm knows you're on the way."

"Thelma!" cried Leota staunchly.

"All I know is, whoever it is 'll be sorry some day. Why, I just barely knew it myself!" cried Mrs. Fletcher. "Just let her wait!"

"Why? What're you gonna do to her?"

It was a child's voice, and the women looked down. A little boy was making tents with aluminum wave pinchers on the floor under the sink.

"Billy Boy, hon, musn't bother nice ladies," Leota smiled. She slapped him brightly and behind her back waved Thelma out of the booth. "Ain't Billy Boy a sight? Only three years old and already just nuts about the beauty-parlor business."

"I never saw him here before," said Mrs. Fletcher, still unmollified.

"He ain't been here before, that's how come," said Leota. "He belongs to Mrs. Pike. She got her a job but it was Fay's Millinery. He oughtn't to try on those ladies' hats, they come down over his eyes like I don't know what. They just git to look ridiculous, that's what, an' of course he's gonna put 'em on: hats. They tole Mrs. Pike they didn't appreciate him hangin' around there. Here, he couldn't hurt a thing."

"Well! I don't like children that much," said Mrs. Fletcher.

"Well!" said Leota moodily.

"Well! I'm almost tempted not to have this one," said Mrs. Fletcher. "That Mrs. Hutchinson! Just looks straight through you when she sees you on the street and then spits at you behind your back."

"Mr. Fletcher would beat you on the head if you didn't have it now," said Leota reasonably. "After going this far!"

Mrs. Fletcher sat up straight. "Mr. Fletcher can't do a thing with me."

"He can't!" Leota winked at herself in the mirror.

"No siree, he can't. If he so much as raises his voice against me, he knows good and well I'll have one of my sick headaches, and then I'm just not fit to live with. And if I really look that pregnant already——"

"Well, now, honey, I just want you to know—I habm't told any of my ladies and I ain't goin' to tell 'em—even that you're losin' your hair. You just get you one of those Stork-a-Lure dresses and stop worryin'. What people don't know don't hurt nobody, as Mrs. Pike says."

"Did you tell Mrs. Pike?" asked Mrs. Fletcher sulkily.

"Well, Mrs. Fletcher, look, you ain't ever goin' to lay eyes on Mrs. Pike or her lay eyes on you, so what diffunce does it make in the long run?"

"I knew it!" Mrs. Fletcher deliberately nodded her head so as to destroy a ringlet Leota was working on behind her ear. "Mrs. Pike!"

Leota sighed. "I reckon I might as well tell you. It wasn't any more Thelma's lady tole me you was pregnant than a bat."

"Not Mrs. Hutchinson?"

"Naw, Lord! It was Mrs. Pike."

"Mrs. Pike!" Mrs. Fletcher could only sputter and let curling fluid roll into her ear. "How could Mrs. Pike possibly know I was pregnant or otherwise, when she doesn't even know me? The nerve of some people!"

"Well, here's how it was. Remember Sunday?"

"Yes," said Mrs. Fletcher.

"Sunday, Mrs. Pike an' me was all by ourself. Mr. Pike and Fred had gone over to Eagle Lake, sayin' they was goin' to catch 'em some fish, but they didn't, a course. So we was settin' in Mrs. Pike's car, is a 1939 Dodge——"

"1939, eh," said Mrs. Fletcher.

"—An' we was gettin' us a Jax beer apiece—that's the beer that Mrs. Pike says is made right in N.O., so she won't drink no other kind. So I seen you drive up to the drugstore an' run in for just a secont, leavin' I reckon Mr. Fletcher in the car, an' come runnin' out with looked like a perscription. So I says to Mrs. Pike, just to be makin' talk, 'Right yonder's Mrs. Fletcher, and I reckon that's Mr. Fletcher—she's one of my regular customers,' I says."

"I had on a figured print," said Mrs. Fletcher tentatively.

"You sure did," agreed Leota. "So Mrs. Pike, she give you a good look—she's very observant, a good judge of character, cute as a minute, you know—and she says, 'I bet you another Jax that lady's three months on the way.' "

"What gall!" said Mrs. Fletcher. "Mrs. Pike!"

"Mrs. Pike ain't goin' to bite you," said Leota. "Mrs. Pike is a lovely girl, you'd be crazy about her, Mrs. Fletcher. But she can't sit still a minute. We went to the travelin' freak show yestiddy after work. I got through early—nine o'clock. In the vacant store next door? What, you ain't been?"

"No, I despise freaks," declared Mrs. Fletcher.

"Aw. Well, honey, talkin' about bein' pregnant an' all, you ought to see those twins in a bottle, you really owe it to yourself."

"What twins?" asked Mrs. Fletcher out of the side of her mouth.

"Well, honey, they got these two twins in a bottle, see? Born joined plumb together—dead a course." Leota dropped her voice into a soft lyrical hum. "They was about this long—pardon—must of been full time, all right, wouldn't you say?—an' they had these two heads an' two faces an' four arms an' four legs, all kind of joined *here*. See, this face looked this-a-way, and the other face looked that-a-way, over their shoulder, see. Kinda pathetic."

"Glah!" said Mrs. Fletcher disapprovingly.

"Well, ugly? Honey, I mean to tell you—their parents was first cousins and all like that. Bill Boy, git me a fresh towel from off Teeny's stack—this 'n's wringin' wet—an' quit ticklin' my ankles with that curler. I declare! He don't miss nothin'."

"Me and Mr. Fletcher aren't one speck of kin, or he could never of had me," said Mrs. Fletcher placidly.

"Of course not!" protested Leota. "Neither is me an' Fred, not that we know of. Well, honey, what Mrs. Pike liked was the pygmies. They've got these pygmies down there, too, an' Mrs. Pike was just wild about 'em. You know, the tee-niniest men in the universe? Well honey, they can just rest back on their little bohunkus an' roll around an' you can't hardly tell if they're sittin' or standin'. That'll give you some idea. They're about forty-two years old. Just suppose it was your husband!"

"Well, Mr. Fletcher is five foot nine and one half," said Mrs. Fletcher quickly.

"Fred's five foot ten," said Leota, "but I tell him he's still a shrimp, account of I'm so tall." She made a deep wave over Mrs. Fletcher's other temple with the comb. "Well, these pygmies are a kind of a dark brown, Mrs. Fletcher. Not bad lookin' for what they are, you know."

"I wouldn't care for them," said Mrs. Fletcher. "What does that Mrs. Pike see in them?"

"Aw, I don't know," said Leota. "She's just cute, that's all. But they got this man, this petrified man, that ever'thing ever since he was nine years old, when it goes through his digestion, see, somehow Mrs. Pike says it goes to his joints and has been turning to stone."

"How awful!" said Mrs. Fletcher.

"He's forty-two too. That looks like a bad age."

"Who said so, that Mrs. Pike? I bet she's forty-two," said Mrs. Fletcher.

"Naw," said Leota, "Mrs. Pike's thirty-three, born in January, an Aquarian. He could move his head—like this. A course his head and mind ain't a joint, so to speak, and I guess his stomach ain't, either—not yet anyways. But see—his food, he eats it, and it goes down, see, and then he digests it"—Leota rose on her toes for an instant—"and it goes out to his joints and before you can say 'Jack Robinson,' it's stone —pure stone. He's turning to stone. How'd you like to be married to a guy like that? All he can do, he can move his head just a quarter of an inch. A course he *looks* just *terrible*."

"I should think he would," said Mrs. Fletcher frostily. "Mr. Fletcher takes bending exercises every night of the world. I make him."

"All Fred does is lay around the house like a rug. I wouldn't be surprised if he woke up some day and couldn't move. The petrified man just sat there moving his quarter of an inch though," said Leota reminiscently.

"Did Mrs. Pike like the petrified man?" asked Mrs. Fletcher.

"Not as much as she did the others," said Leota deprecatingly. "And then she likes a man to be a good dresser, and all that."

"Is Mr. Pike a good dresser?" asked Mrs. Fletcher skeptically.

"Oh, well, yeah," said Leota, "but he's twelve- fourteen years older 'n her. She ast Lady Evangeline about him."

"Who's Lady Evangeline?" asked Mrs. Fletcher.

"Well, it's this mind reader they got in the freak show," said Leota. "Was real good. Lady Evangeline is her name, and if I had another dollar I wouldn't do a thing but have my other palm read. She had what Mrs. Pike said was the 'sixth mind' but she had the worst manicure I ever saw on a living person."

"What did she tell Mrs. Pike?" asked Mrs. Fletcher.

"She told her Mr. Pike was as true to her as he could be and besides, would come into some money."

"Humph!" said Mrs. Fletcher. "What does he do?"

"I can't tell," said Leota, "because he don't work. Lady Evangeline didn't tell me near enough about my nature or anything. And I would like to go back and find out some more about this boy. Used to go with this boy got married to this girl. Oh, shoot, that was about three and a half years ago, when you was still goin' to the Robert E. Lee Beauty Shop in Jackson. He married her for her money. Another fortune teller tole me that at the time. So I'm not in love with him any more, anyway, besides being married to Fred, but Mrs. Pike thought, just for the hell of it, see, to ask Lady Evangeline was he happy."

"Does Mrs. Pike know everything about you already?" asked Mrs. Fletcher unbelievingly. "Mercy!"

"Oh yeah, I tole her ever'thing about ever'thing, from now on back to I don't know when—to when I first started goin' out," said Leota. "So I ast Lady Evangeline for one of my questions, was he happily married, and she says, just like she was glad I ask her, 'Honey,' she says, 'naw, he idn't. You write down this day, March 8, 1941,' she says, 'and mock it down: three years from today him and her won't be occupyin' the same bed.' There it is, up on the wall with them other dates—see, Mrs. Fletcher? And she says, 'Child, you ought to be glad you didn't git him, because he's so mercenary.' So I'm glad I married Fred. He sure ain't mercenary, money don't mean a thing to him. But I sure would like to go back and have my other palm read."

"Did Mrs. Pike believe in what the fortune teller said?" asked Mrs. Fletcher in a superior tone of voice.

"Lord, yes, she's from New Orleans. Ever'body in New Orleans believes ever'thing spooky. One of 'em in New Orleans before it was raided says to Mrs. Pike one summer she was goin' to go from state to state and meet some gray-headed men, and, sure enough, she says she went on a beautician convention up to Chicago. . . ."

"Oh!" said Mrs. Fletcher. "Oh, is Mrs. Pike a beautician too?"

"Sure she is," protested Leota. "She's a beautician. I'm goin' to git her in here if I can. Before she married. But it don't leave you. She says sure enough, there was three men who was a very large part of making her trip what it was, and they all three had gray in their hair and they went in six states. Got Christmas cards from 'em. Billy Boy, go see if Thelma's got any dry cotton. Look how Mrs. Fletcher's a-drippin'."

"Where did Mrs. Pike meet Mr. Pike?" asked Mrs. Fletcher primly.

"On another train," said Leota.

"I met Mr. Fletcher, or rather he met me, in a rental library," said Mrs. Fletcher with dignity, as she watched the net come down over her head.

"Honey, me an' Fred, we met in a rumble seat eight months ago and we was practically on what you might call the way to the altar inside of a half an hour," said Leota in a guttural voice, and bit a bobby pin open. "Course it don't last. Mrs. Pike says nothin' like that ever lasts."

"Mr. Fletcher and myself are as much in love as the day we married," said Mrs. Fletcher belligerently as Leota stuffed cotton into her ears.

"Mrs. Pike says it don't last," repeated Leota in a louder voice. "Now go git under the dryer. You can turn yourself on, can't you? I'll be back to comb you out. Durin' lunch I promised to give Mrs. Pike a facial. You know—free. Her bein' in the business, so to speak."

"I bet she needs one," said Mrs. Fletcher, letting the swing door fly back against Leota. "Oh, pardon me."

A week later, on time for her appointment, Mrs. Fletcher sank heavily into Leota's chair after first removing a drugstore rental book, called *Life Is Like That,* from the seat. She stared in a discouraged way into the mirror.

"You can tell it when I'm sitting down, all right," she said.

Leota seemed preoccupied and stood shaking out a lavender cloth. She began to pin it around Mrs. Fletcher's neck in silence.

"I said you sure can tell it when I'm sitting straight on and coming at you this way," Mrs. Fletcher said.

"Why, honey, naw you can't," said Leota gloomily. "Why, I'd never know. If somebody was to come up to me on the street and say, 'Mrs. Fletcher is pregnant!' I'd say, 'Heck, she don't look it to me.'"

"If a certain party hadn't found it out and spread it around, it wouldn't be too late even now," said Mrs. Fletcher frostily, but Leota was almost choking her with the cloth, pinning it so tight, and she couldn't speak clearly. She paddled her hands in the air until Leota wearily loosened her.

"Listen, honey, you're just a virgin compared to Mrs. Montjoy," Leota was going on, still absent-minded. She bent Mrs. Fletcher back in the chair and, sighing, tossed liquid from a teacup onto her head and dug both hands into her scalp. "You know Mrs. Montjoy—her husband's that premature-gray-headed fella?"

"She's in the Trojan Garden Club, is all I know," said Mrs. Fletcher.

"Well, honey," said Leota, but in a weary voice, "she come in here not the week before and not the day before she had her baby—she come in here the very selfsame day, I mean to tell you. Child, we was all plumb scared to death. There she was! Come for her shampoo an' set. Why, Mrs. Fletcher, in a hour an' twenty minutes she was layin' up there in the Babtist Hospital with a seb'm-pound son. It was that close a shave. I declare, if I hadn't been so tired I would of drank up a bottle of gin that night."

"What gall," said Mrs. Fletcher. "I never knew her at all well."

"See, her husband was waitin' outside in the car, and her bags was all packed an' in the back seat, an' she was all ready, 'cept she wanted her shampoo an' set. An' havin' one pain right after another. Her husband kep' comin' in here, scared-like, but couldn't do nothin' with her a course. She yelled bloody murder, too, but she always yelled her head off when I give her a perm'nent."

"She must of been crazy," said Mrs. Fletcher. "How did she look?"

"Shoot!" said Leota.

"Well, I can guess," said Mrs. Fletcher. "Awful."

"Just wanted to look pretty while she was havin' her baby, is all," said Leota airily. "Course, we was glad to give the lady what she was after—that's our motto—but I bet a hour later she wasn't payin' no mind to them little end curls. I bet she wasn't thinkin' about she ought to have on a net. It wouldn't of done her no good if she had."

"No, I don't suppose it would," said Mrs. Fletcher.

"Yeah man! She was a-yellin'. Just like when I give her her perm'nent."

"Her husband ought to could make her behave. Don't it seem that way to you?" asked Mrs. Fletcher. "He ought to put his foot down."

"Ha," said Leota. "A lot he could do. Maybe some women is soft."

"Oh, you mistake me, I don't mean for her to get soft—far from it! Women have to stand up for themselves, or there's just no telling. But now you take me—I ask Mr. Fletcher's advice now and then, and he appreciates it, especially on something important, like is it time for a permanent—not that I've told him about the baby. He says, 'Why dear, go ahead!' Just ask their *advice*."

"Huh! If I ever ast Fred's advice we'd be floatin' down the Yazoo River on a houseboat or somethin' by this time," said Leota. "I'm sick of Fred. I tole him to go over to Vicksburg."

"Is he going?" demanded Mrs. Fletcher.

"Sure. See, the fortune teller—I went back and had my other palm read, since we've got to rent the room agin—said my lover was goin' to work in Vicksburg, so I don't know who she could mean, unless she meant Fred. And Fred ain't workin' here—that much is so."

"Is he going to work in Vicksburg?" asked Mrs. Fletcher. "And——"

"Sure, Lady Evangeline said so. Said the future is going to be brighter than the present. He don't want to go, but I ain't gonna put up with nothin' like that. Lays around the house an' bulls—did bull—with that good-for-nothin' Mr. Pike. He says if he goes who'll cook, but I says I never get to eat anyway—not meals. Billy Boy, take Mrs. Grover that *Screen Secrets* and leg it."

Mrs. Fletcher heard stamping feet go out the door.

"Is that Mrs. Pike's little boy here again?" she asked, sitting up gingerly.

"Yeah, that's still him." Leota stuck out her tongue.

Mrs. Fletcher could hardly believe her eyes. "Well! How's Mrs. Pike, your attractive new friend with the sharp eyes who spreads it around town that perfect strangers are pregnant?" she asked in a sweetened tone.

"Oh, Mizziz Pike." Leota combed Mrs. Fletcher's hair with heavy strokes.

"You act like you're tired," said Mrs. Fletcher.

"Tired? Feel like it's four o'clock in the afternoon already," said Leota. "I ain't told you the awful luck we had, me and Fred? It's the worst thing you ever heard of. Maybe *you* think Mrs. Pike's got sharp eyes. Shoot, there's a limit. Well, you know, we rented out our room to this Mr. and Mrs. Pike from New Orleans when Sal an' Joe Fentress got mad at us 'cause they drank up some home-brew we had in the closet—Sal an' Joe did. So, a week ago Sat'day Mr. and Mrs. Pike moved in. Well, I kinda fixed up the room, you know—put a sofa pillow on the couch and picked some ragged robbins and put in a vase, but they never did say they appreciated it. Anyway, then I put some old magazines on the table."

"I think that was lovely," said Mrs. Fletcher.

"Wait. So, come night 'fore last, Fred and this Mr. Pike, who Fred just took up with, was back from they said they was fishin', bein' as neither one of 'em has got a job to his name, and we was all settin' around in their room. So Mrs. Pike was settin' there, readin' a old *Startling G-Man Tales* that was mine, mind you, I'd bought it myself, and all of a sudden she jumps!—into the air—you'd 'a' thought she'd set on a spider—an' says, 'Canfield'—ain't that silly, that's Mr. Pike—'Canfield, my God A'mighty,' she says, 'honey,' she says, 'we're rich, and you won't have to work.' Not that he turned one hand anyway. Well, me and Fred rushes over to her, and Mr. Pike, too, and there she sets, pointin' her finger at a photo in my copy of *Startling G-Man*. 'See that man?' yells Mrs. Pike. 'Remember him, Canfield?' 'Never forget a face,' says Mr. Pike. 'It's Mr. Petrie, that we stayed with him in the apartment next to ours in Toulouse Street in N.O. for six weeks. Mr. Petrie.' 'Well,' says Mrs. Pike, like she can't hold out one secont longer, 'Mr. Petrie is wanted for five hunderd dollars cash, for rapin' four women in California, and I know where he is.'"

"Mercy!" said Mrs. Fletcher. "Where was he?"

At some time Leota had washed her hair and now she yanked her up by the back locks and sat her up.

"Know where he was?"

"I certainly don't," Mrs. Fletcher said. Her scalp hurt all over.

Leota flung a towel around the top of her customer's head. "Nowhere else but in that freak show! I saw him just as plain as Mrs. Pike. *He* was the petrified man!"

"Who would ever have thought that!" cried Mrs. Fletcher sympathetically.

"So Mr. Pike says, 'Well whatta you know about that,' an' he looks real hard at the photo and whistles. And she starts dancin' and singin' about their good luck. She meant our bad luck! I made a point of tellin' that fortune teller the next time I saw her. I said, 'Listen, that magazine was layin' around the house for a month, and there was five hundred dollars in it for somebody. An' there was the freak show runnin' night an' day, not two steps away from my own beauty parlor, with Mr. Petrie just settin' there waitin'. An' it had to be Mr. and Mrs. Pike, almost perfect strangers.'"

"What gall," said Mrs. Fletcher. She was only sitting there, wrapped in a turban, but she did not mind.

"Fortune tellers don't care. And Mrs. Pike, she goes around actin' like she thinks she was Mrs. God," said Leota. "So they're goin' to leave tomorrow, Mr. and Mrs. Pike. And in the meantime I got to keep that mean, bad little ole kid here, gettin' under my feet ever' minute of the day an' talkin' back too."

"Have they gotten the five hundred dollars' reward already?" asked Mrs. Fletcher.

"Well," said Leota, "at first Mr. Pike didn't want to do anything about it. Can you feature that? Said he kinda liked that ole bird and said he was real nice to 'em, lent 'em money or somethin'. But Mrs. Pike simply tole him he could just go to hell, and I can see her point. She says, 'You ain't worked a lick in six months, and here I make five hunderd dollars in two seconts, and what thanks do I get for it? You go to hell, Canfield,' she says. So," Leota went on in a despondent voice, "they called up the cops and they caught the ole bird, all right, right there in the freak show where I saw him with my own eyes, thinkin' he was petrified. He's the one. Did it under his real name—Mr. Petrie. Four women in California, all in the month of August. So Mrs. Pike gits five hundred dollars. And my magazine, and right next door to my beauty parlor. I cried all night, but Fred said it wasn't a bit of use and to go to sleep, because the whole thing was just a sort of coincidence—you know: can't do nothin' about it. He says it put him clean out of the notion of goin' to Vicksburg for a few days till we rent out the room agin—no tellin' who we'll git this time."

"But can you imagine anybody knowing this old man, that's raped four women?" persisted Mrs. Fletcher, and she shuddered audibly. "Did Mrs. Pike *speak* to him when she met him in the freak show?"

Leota had begun to comb Mrs. Fletcher's hair. "I says to her, I says, 'I didn't notice you fallin' on his neck when he was the petrified man—don't tell me you didn't recognize your fine friend?' And she says, 'I didn't recognize him with that white powder all over his face. He just looked familiar,' Mrs. Pike says, 'and lots of people look familiar.' But she says that ole petrified man did put her in mind of somebody. She wondered who it was! Kep' her awake, which man she'd ever knew it reminded her of. So when she seen the photo, it all come to her. Like a flash. Mr. Petrie. The way he'd turn his head and look at her when she took him in his breakfast."

"Took him in his breakfast!" shrieked Mrs. Fletcher. "Listen—don't tell me. I'd 'a' felt something."

"Four women. I guess those women didn't have the faintest notion at the time they'd be worth a hundred an' twenty-five bucks apiece someday to Mrs. Pike. We ast her how old the fella was then, an' she says he musta had one foot in the grave, at least. Can you beat it?"

"Not really petrified at all, of course," said Mrs. Fletcher meditatively. She drew herself up. "I'd 'a' felt something," she said proudly.

"Shoot! I did feel somethin'," said Leota. "I tole Fred when I got home I felt so funny. I said, 'Fred, that ole petrified man sure did leave me with a funny feelin'.' He says, 'Funny-haha or funny-peculiar?' and I says, 'Funny-peculiar.'" She pointed her comb into the air emphatically.

"I'll bet you did," said Mrs. Fletcher.

They both heard a crackling noise.

Leota screamed, "Billy Boy! What you doin' in my purse?"

"Aw, I'm just eatin' these ole stale peanuts up," said Billy Boy.

"You come here to me!" screamed Leota, recklessly flinging down the comb, which scattered a whole ash tray full of bobby pins and knocked down a row of Coca-Cola bottles. "This is the last straw!"

"I caught him! I caught him!" giggled Mrs. Fletcher. "I'll hold him on my lap. You bad, bad boy, you! I guess I better learn how to spank little old bad boys," she said.

Leota's eleven o'clock customer pushed open the swing door upon Leota paddling him heartily with the brush, while he gave angry but belittling screams which penetrated beyond the booth and filled the whole curious beauty parlor. From everywhere ladies began to gather round to watch the paddling. Billy Boy kicked both Leota and Mrs. Fletcher as hard as he could, Mrs. Fletcher with her new fixed smile.

"There, my little man!" gasped Leota. "You won't be able to set down for a week if I knew what I was doin'."

Billy Boy stomped through the group of wild-haired ladies and went out the door, but flung back the words, "If you're so smart, why ain't you rich?"

IRWIN SHAW

Act of Faith

Born in 1913 in New York City, Irwin Shaw was educated in the Brooklyn public schools and at Brooklyn College. Once out of school, he wrote radio scripts and serials. He finished *Bury the Dead,* his first play, while still writing for the radio. Among his other plays are *The Gentle People* and *Quiet City.* His short story volumes include *Welcome to the City* and *Act of Faith.* [From *Act of Faith* by Irwin Shaw; copyright 1946 by Irwin Shaw; used by permission of Random House; originally published in *The New Yorker.*]

"PRESENT IT TO HIM in a pitiful light," Olson was saying as they picked their way through the almost frozen mud toward the orderly-room tent. "Three combat-scarred veterans, who fought their way from Omaha Beach to . . . What was the name of the town we fought our way to?"

"Königstein," Seeger said.

"Königstein." Olson lifted his right foot heavily out of a puddle and stared admiringly at the three pounds of mud clinging to his overshoe. "The backbone of the Army. The noncommissioned officer. We deserve better of our country. Mention our decorations, in passing."

"What decorations should I mention?" Seeger asked. "The Marksman's Medal?"

"Never quite made it," Olson said. "I had a cross-eyed scorer at the butts. Mention the Bronze Star, the Silver Star, the Croix de Guerre with palms, the Unit Citation, the Congressional Medal of Honor."

"I'll mention them all." Seeger grinned. "You don't think the C.O.'ll notice that we haven't won most of them, do you?"

"Gad, sir," Olson said with dignity, "do you think that one Southern military gentleman will dare doubt the word of another Southern military gentleman in the hour of victory?"

"I come from Ohio," Seeger said.

"Welch comes from Kansas," Olson said, coolly staring down a second lieutenant who was passing. The lieutenant made a nervous little jerk with his hand, as though he expected a salute, then kept it rigid, as a slight, superior smile of scorn twisted at the corner of Olson's mouth. The lieutenant dropped his eyes and splashed on through the mud. "You've heard of Kansas," Olson said. "Magnolia-scented Kansas."

"Of course," said Seeger. "I'm no fool."

"Do your duty by your men, Sergeant." Olson stopped to wipe the cold rain off his face and lectured him. "Highest-ranking noncom present took the initiative and saved his comrades, at great personal risk, above and beyond the call of you-know-what, in the best traditions of the American Army."

"I will throw myself in the breach," Seeger said.

"Welch and I can't ask more," said Olson.

They walked heavily through the mud on the streets between the rows of tents. The camp stretched drearily over the Reims plain, with the rain beating on the sagging tents. The division had been there over three weeks, waiting to be shipped home, and all the meager diversions of the neighborhood had been sampled and exhausted, and there was an air of watchful suspicion and impatience with the military life hanging over the camp now, and there was even reputed to be a staff sergeant in C Company who was laying odds they would not get back to America before July 4th.

"I'm redeployable," Olson sang. "It's so enjoyable." It was a jingle he had composed, to no recognizable melody, in the early days after the victory in Europe, when he had added up his points and found they came to only sixty-three, but he persisted in singing it. He was a short, round boy who had been flunked out of air cadets' school and transferred to the infantry but whose spirits had not been damaged in the process. He had a high, childish voice and a pretty, baby face. He was very good-natured, and had a girl waiting for him at the University of California, where he intended to finish his course at government expense when he got out of the Army, and he was just the type who is killed off early and predictably and sadly in moving pictures about the war, but he had gone through four campaigns and six major battles without a scratch.

Seeger was a large, lanky boy, with a big nose, who had been wounded at St.-Lô but had come back to his outfit in the Siegfried Line quite unchanged. He was cheerful and dependable and he knew his business. He had broken in five or six second lieutenants, who had later been killed or wounded, and the C.O. had tried to get him commissioned in the field, but the war had ended while the paperwork was being fumbled over at headquarters.

They reached the door of the orderly tent and stopped. "Be brave, Sergeant," Olson said. "Welch and I are depending on you."

"O.K.," Seeger said, and went in.

The tent had the dank, Army-canvas smell that had been so much a part of Seeger's life in the past three years. The company clerk was reading an October, 1945, issue of the Buffalo *Courier-Express,* which had just reached him, and Captain Taney, the company C.O., was seated at a sawbuck table which he used as a desk, writing a letter to his wife, his lips pursed with effort. He was a small, fussy man, with sandy hair that was falling out. While the fighting had been going on, he had been lean and tense and his small voice had been cold and full of authority. But now he had relaxed, and a little pot belly was creeping up under his belt and he kept the top button of his trousers open when he could do it without too public loss of dignity. During the war, Seeger had thought of him as a natural soldier—tireless, fanatic about detail, aggressive, severely anxious to kill Germans. But in the last few months, Seeger had seen him relapsing gradually and pleasantly into the small-town hardware merchant he had been before the war, sedentary and a little shy, and, as he had once told Seeger, worried, here in the bleak champagne fields of France, about his daughter, who had just turned twelve and had a tendency to go after the boys and had been caught by her mother kissing a fifteen-year-old neighbor in the hammock after school.

"Hello, Seeger," he said, returning the salute with a mild, offhand gesture. "What's on your mind?"

"Am I disturbing you, sir?"

"Oh, no. Just writing a letter to my wife. You married, Seeger?" He peered at the tall boy standing before him.

"No, sir."

"It's very difficult," Taney sighed, pushing dissatisfiedly at the letter before him. "My wife complains I don't tell her I love her often enough.

Been married fifteen years. You'd think she'd know by now." He smiled at Seeger. "I thought you were going to Paris," he said. "I signed the passes yesterday."

"That's what I came to see you about, sir."

"I suppose something's wrong with the passes." Taney spoke resignedly, like a man who has never quite got the hang of Army regulations and has had requisitions, furloughs, and requests for courts-martial returned for correction in a baffling flood.

"No, sir," Seeger said. "The passes're fine. They start tomorrow. Well, it's just—" He looked around at the company clerk, who was on the sports page.

"This confidential?" Taney asked.

"If you don't mind, sir."

"Johnny," Taney said to the clerk, "go stand in the rain someplace."

"Yes, sir," the clerk said, and slowly got up and walked out.

Taney looked shrewdly at Seeger and spoke in a secret whisper. "You pick up anything?" he asked.

Seeger grinned. "No, sir, haven't had my hands on a girl since Strasbourg."

"Ah, that's good." Taney leaned back, relieved, happy that he didn't have to cope with the disapproval of the Medical Corps.

"It's—well," said Seeger, embarrassed, "it's hard to say—but it's money."

Taney shook his head sadly. "I know."

"We haven't been paid for three months, sir, and—"

"Damn it!" Taney stood up and shouted furiously. "I would like to take every bloody, chair-warming old lady in the Finance Department and wring their necks."

The clerk stuck his head into the tent. "Anything wrong? You call for me, sir?"

"No!" Taney shouted. "Get out of here!"

The clerk ducked out.

Taney sat down again. "I suppose," he said, in a more normal voice, "they have their problems. Outfits being broken up, being moved all over the place. But it's rugged."

"It wouldn't be so bad," Seeger said, "but we're going to Paris tomorrow. Olson, Welch, and myself. And you need money in Paris."

"Don't I know it?" Taney wagged his head. "Do you know what I paid for a bottle of champagne on the Place Pigalle in September?" He paused significantly. "I won't tell you. You wouldn't have any respect for me the rest of your life."

Seeger laughed. "Hanging is too good for the guy who thought up the rate of exchange," he said.

"I don't care if I never see another franc as long as I live." Taney waved his letter in the air, although it had been dry for a long time.

There was silence in the tent, and Seeger swallowed a little embarrassedly. "Sir," he said, "the truth is, I've come to borrow some money for Welch, Olson, and myself. We'll pay it back out of the first pay we get, and that can't be too long from now. If you don't want to give it to us, just tell me and I'll understand and get the hell out of here. We don't like to ask, but you might just as well be dead as be in Paris broke."

Taney stopped waving his letter and put it down thoughtfully. He peered at it, wrinkling his brow, looking like an aged bookkeeper in the single, gloomy light that hung in the middle of the tent.

"Just say the word, Captain," Seeger said, "and I'll blow."

"Stay where you are, son," said Taney. He dug in his shirt pocket and took out a worn, sweat-stained wallet. He looked at it for a moment. "Alligator," he said, with automatic, absent pride. "My wife sent it to me when we were in England. Pounds don't fit in it. However . . ." He opened it and took out all the contents. There was a small pile of francs on the table in front of him when he finished. He counted them. "Four hundred francs," he said. "Eight bucks."

"Excuse me," Seeger said humbly. "I shouldn't've asked."

"Delighted," Taney said vigorously. "Absolutely delighted." He started dividing the francs into two piles. "Truth is, Seeger, most of my money goes home in allotments. And the truth is, I lost eleven hundred francs in a poker game three nights ago, and I ought to be ashamed of myself. Here." He shoved one pile toward Seeger. "Two hundred francs."

Seeger looked down at the frayed, meretricious paper, which always seemed to him like stage money anyway. "No, sir," he said. "I can't take it."

"Take it," Taney said. "That's a direct order."

Seeger slowly picked up the money, not looking at Taney. "Sometime, sir," he said, "after we get out, you have to come over to my house, and you and my father and my brother and I'll go on a real drunk."

"I regard that," Taney said gravely, "as a solemn commitment."

They smiled at each other, and Seeger started out.

"Have a drink for me," said Taney, "at the Café de la Paix. A small drink." He was sitting down to tell his wife he loved her when Seeger went out of the tent.

Olson fell into step with Seeger and they walked silently through the mud between the tents.

"Well, *mon vieux?*" Olson said finally.

"Two hundred francs," said Seeger.

Olson groaned. "Two hundred francs! We won't be able to pinch a whore's behind on the Boulevard des Capucines for two hundred francs. That miserable, penny-loving Yankee!"

"He only had four hundred," Seeger said.

"I revise my opinion," said Olson.

They walked disconsolately and heavily back toward their tent.

Olson spoke only once before they got there. "These raincoats," he said, patting his. "Most ingenious invention of the war. Highest saturation point of any modern fabric. Collect more water per square inch, and hold it, than any material known to man. All hail the quartermaster!"

Welch was waiting at the entrance of their tent. He was standing there peering excitedly and shortsightedly out at the rain through his glasses, looking angry and tough, like a big-city hack driver, individual and incorruptible even in the ten-million colored uniform. Every time Seeger came upon Welch unexpectedly, he couldn't help smiling at the belligerent stance, the harsh stare through the steel-rimmed G.I. glasses, which had nothing at all to do with the way Welch really was. "It's a family inheritance," Welch had once explained. "My whole family stands as though we were getting ready to rap a drunk with a beer glass. Even my old lady." Welch had six brothers, all devout, according to Welch, and Seeger from time to time idly pictured them standing in a row, on Sunday mornings in church, seemingly on the verge of general violence, amid the hushed Latin and the Sabbath millinery.

"How much?" Welch asked loudly.

"Don't make us laugh," Olson said, pushing past him into the tent.

"What do you think I could get from the French for my combat jacket?" Seeger said. He went into the tent and lay down on his cot.

Welch followed them in and stood between the two of them. "Boys," he said, "on a man's errand."

"I can just see us now," Olson murmured, lying on his cot with his hands clasped behind his head, "painting Montmartre red. Please bring on the naked dancing girls. Four bucks' worth."

"I am not worried," Welch announced.

"Get out of here." Olson turned over on his stomach.

"I know where we can put our hands on sixty-five bucks." Welch looked triumphantly first at Olson, then at Seeger.

Olson turned over slowly and sat up. "I'll kill you," he said, "if you're kidding."

"While you guys are wasting your time fooling around with the infantry," Welch said, "I used my head. I went into Reems and used my head."

"Rance," Olson said automatically. He had had two years of French in college and he felt, now that the war was over, that he had to introduce his friends to some of his culture.

"I got to talking to a captain in the Air Force," Welch said eagerly. "A little, fat old paddle-footed captain that never got higher off the ground than the second floor of Com Z headquarters, and he told me that what he would admire to do more than anything else is take home a nice shiny German Luger pistol with him to show to the boys back in Pacific Grove, California."

Silence fell on the tent, and Welch and Olson looked at Seeger.

"Sixty-five bucks for a Luger, these days," Olson said, "is a very good figure."

"They've been sellin' for as low as thirty-five," said Welch hesitantly.

"I'll bet," he said to Seeger, "you could sell yours now and buy another one back when you got some dough, and make a clear twenty-five on the deal."

Seeger didn t say anything. He had killed the owner of the Luger, an enormous S.S. major, in Coblenz, behind some bales of paper in a warehouse, and the major had fired at Seeger three times with it, once nicking his helmet, before Seeger hit him in the face at twenty feet. Seeger had kept the Luger, a heavy, well-balanced gun, lugging it with him, hiding it at the bottom of his bedroll, oiling it three times a week, avoiding all opportunities of selling it, although he had once been offered a hundred dollars for it and several times eighty and ninety, while the war was still on, before German weapons became a glut on the market.

"Well," said Welch, "there's no hurry. I told the captain I'd see him tonight around eight o'clock in front of the Lion d'Or Hotel. You got five hours to make up your mind. Plenty of time."

"Me," said Olson, after a pause, "I won't say anything."

Seeger looked reflectively at his feet, and the two other men avoided looking at him.

Welch dug in his pocket. "I forgot," he said. "I picked up a letter for you." He handed it to Seeger.

"Thanks," Seeger said. He opened it absently, thinking about the Luger.

"Me," said Olson. "I won't say a bloody word. I'm just going to lie here and think about that nice, fat Air Force captain."

Seeger grinned a little at him and went to the tent opening to read the letter in the light. The letter was from his father, and even from one glance at the handwriting, scrawly and hurried and spotted, so different from his father's usual steady, handsome, professorial script, he knew that something was wrong.

"Dear Norman," it read, "sometime in the future, you must forgive me for writing this letter. But I have been holding this in so long, and there is no one here I can talk to, and because of your brother's condition I must pretend to be cheerful and optimistic all the time at home, both with him and your mother, who has never been the same since Leonard was killed. You're the oldest now, and although I know we've never talked very seriously about anything before, you have been through a great deal by now, and I imagine you must have matured considerably, and you've seen so many different places and people. Norman, I need help. While the war was on and you were fighting, I kept this to myself. It wouldn't have been fair to burden you with this. But now the war is over, and I no longer feel I can stand up under this alone. And you will have to face it sometime when you get home, if you haven't faced it already, and perhaps we can help each other by facing it together."

"I'm redeployable. It's so enjoyable," Olson was singing softly, on his cot. He fell silent after his burst of song.

Seeger blinked his eyes in the gray, wintry, rainy light, and went on reading his father's letter, on the stiff white stationery with the university letterhead in polite engraving at the top of each page.

"I've been feeling this coming on for a long time," the letter continued, "but it wasn't until last Sunday morning that something happened to make me feel it in its full force. I don't know how much you've guessed about the reason for Jacob's discharge from the Army. It's true he was pretty badly wounded in the leg at Metz, but I've asked around, and I know that men with worse wounds were returned to duty after hospitalization. Jacob got a medical discharge, but I don't think it was for the shrapnel wound in his thigh. He is suffering now from what I suppose you call combat fatigue, and he is subject to fits of depression and hallucinations. Your mother and I thought that as time went by and the war and the Army receded, he would grow better. Instead, he is growing worse. Last Sunday morning when I came down into the living room from upstairs he was crouched in his old uniform, next to the window, peering out."

"What the hell," Olson was saying. "If we don't get the sixty-five bucks we can always go to the Louvre. I understand the Mona Lisa is back."

"I asked Jacob what he was doing," the letter went on. "He didn't turn around. 'I'm observing,' he said. 'V-1s and V-2s. Buzz bombs and rockets. They're coming in by the hundred.' I tried to reason with him and he told me to crouch and save myself from flying glass. To humor him I got down on the floor beside him and tried to tell him the war was over, that we were in Ohio, 4,000 miles away from the nearest spot where bombs had fallen, that America had never been touched. He wouldn't listen. 'These're the new rocket bombs,' he said, 'for the Jews.'"

"Did you ever hear of the Panthéon?" Olson asked loudly.

"No," said Welch.

"It's free."

"I'll go," said Welch.

Seeger shook his head a little and blinked his eyes before he went back to the letter.

"After that," his father went on, "Jacob seemed to forget about the bombs from time to time, but he kept saying that the mobs were coming up the street armed with bazookas and Browning automatic rifles. He mumbled incoherently a good deal of the time and kept walking back and forth saying, 'What's the situation? Do you know what the situation is?' And once he told me he wasn't worried about himself, he was a soldier and he expected to be killed, but he was worried about Mother and myself and Leonard and you. He seemed to forget that Leonard was dead. I tried to calm him and get him back to bed before your mother came down, but he refused and wanted to set out immediately to rejoin his division. It was all terribly disjointed, and at one time he took the ribbon he got for winning the Bronze Star and threw it in the fireplace, then he got down on his hands and knees and picked it out of the ashes and made me pin it on him again, and he kept repeating, 'This is when they are coming for the Jews.' "

"The next war I'm in," said Olson, "they don't get me under the rank of colonel."

It had stopped raining by now, and Seeger folded the unfinished letter and went outside. He walked slowly down to the end of the company street, and, facing out across the empty, soaked French fields, scarred and neglected by various armies, he stopped and opened the letter again.

"I don't know what Jacob went through in the Army," his father wrote, "that has done this to him. He never talks to me about the war and he refuses to go to a psychoanalyst, and from time to time he is his own bouncing, cheerful self, playing handball in the afternoons and going around with a large group of girls. But he has devoured all the concentration-camp reports, and I found him weeping when the newspapers reported that a hundred Jews were killed in Tripoli some time ago.

"The terrible thing is, Norman, that I find myself coming to believe that it is not neurotic for a Jew to behave like this today. Perhaps Jacob is the normal one, and I, going about my business, teaching economics in a quiet classroom, pretending to understand that the world is comprehensible and orderly, am really the mad one. I ask you once more to forgive me for writing you a letter like this, so different from any letter or any conversation I've ever had with you. But it is crowding me, too. I do not see rockets and bombs, but I see other things.

"Wherever you go these days—restaurants, hotels, clubs, trains—you seem to hear talk about the Jews, mean, hateful, murderous talk. Whatever page you turn to in the newspapers, you seem to find an article about Jews being killed somewhere on the face of the globe. And there are large, influential newspapers and well-known columnists who each day are growing more and more outspoken and more popular. The day that Roosevelt died I heard a drunken man yelling outside a bar, 'Finally they got the Jew out of the White House.' And some of the people who heard him merely laughed, and nobody stopped him. And on V-J Day, in celebration, hoodlums in Los Angeles savagely beat a Jewish writer. It's difficult to know what to do, whom to fight, where to look for allies.

"Three months ago, for example, I stopped my Thursday-night poker game, after playing with the same men for over ten years. John Reilly happened to say that the Jews got rich out of the war, and when I demanded an apology, he refused, and when I looked around at the faces of the men who had been my friends for so long, I could see they were not with me. And when I left the house, no one said good night to me. I know the poison was spreading from Germany before the war and during it, but I had not realized it had come so close.

"And in my economics class, I find myself idiotically hedging in my lectures. I discover that I am loath to praise any liberal writer or any liberal act, and find myself somehow annoyed and frightened to see an article of criticism of existing abuses signed by a Jewish name. And I hate to see Jewish names on important committees, and hate to read of Jews fighting for the poor, the oppressed, the cheated and hungry. Somehow, even in a country where my family has lived a hundred years, the enemy has won this subtle victory over me—he has made me disfranchise myself from honest causes by calling them foreign, Communist, using Jewish names connected with them as ammunition against them.

"Most hateful of all, I found myself looking for Jewish names in the casualty lists and secretly being glad when I saw them there, to prove that there, at least, among the dead and wounded, we belonged. Three times, thanks to you and your brothers, I found our name there, and, may God forgive me, at the expense of your blood and your brother's life, through my tears, I felt that same twitch of satisfaction.

"When I read the newspapers and see another story that Jews are still being killed in Poland, or Jews are requesting that they be given back their homes in France or that they be allowed to enter some country where they will not be murdered, I am annoyed with them. I feel that they are boring the rest of the world with their problems, that they are making demands upon the rest of the world by being killed, that they are disturbing everyone by being hungry and asking for the return of their property. If we could all fall in through the crust of the earth and vanish in one hour, with our heroes and poets and prophets and martyrs, perhaps we would be doing the memory of the Jewish race a service.

"This is how I feel today, son. I need some help. You've been to the war, you've fought and killed men, you've seen the people of other countries. Maybe you understand things that I don't understand. Maybe you see some hope somewhere. Help me. Your loving Father."

Seeger folded the letter slowly, not seeing what he was doing, because the tears were burning his eyes. He walked slowly and aimlessly across the dead, sodden grass of the empty field, away from the camp. He tried to wipe away his tears, because, with his eyes full and dark, he kept seeing his father and brother crouched in the old-fashioned living room in Ohio, and hearing his brother, dressed in the old, discarded uniform, saying, "These're the new rocket bombs. For the Jews."

He sighed, looking out over the bleak, wasted land. Now, he thought, now I have to think about it. He felt a slight, unreasonable twinge of anger at his father for presenting him with the necessity of thinking about it. The Army was good about serious problems. While you were fighting, you were too busy and frightened and weary to think about anything, and at other times you were relaxing, putting your brain on a shelf, postponing everything to that impossible time of clarity and beauty after the war. Well, now, here was the impossible, clear, beautiful time, and here was his father, demanding that he think. There are all sorts of Jews, he thought: there are the sort whose every waking moment is ridden by the knowledge of Jewishness; who see signs against the Jew in every smile on a streetcar, every whisper; who see pogroms in every newspaper article, threats in every change of the weather, scorn in every handshake, death behind each closed door. He had not been like that. He was young, he was big and healthy and easygoing, and people of all kinds had liked him all his life, in the Army and out. In America, especially, what was going on in Europe had been remote, unreal, unrelated to him. The chanting, bearded old men burning in the Nazi furnaces, and the dark-eyed women screaming prayers in Polish and Russian and German as they were pushed naked into the gas chambers, had seemed as shadowy and almost as unrelated to him, as he trotted out onto the stadium field for a football game, as they must have been to the men named O'Dwyer and Wickersham and Poole who played in the line beside him.

These tortured people had seemed more related to him in Europe. Again and again, in the towns that had been taken back from the Germans, gaunt, gray-faced men had stopped him humbly, looking searchingly at him, and had asked, peering at his long, lined, grimy face under the anonymous helmet, "Are you a Jew?" Sometimes they asked it in English, sometimes French, sometimes Yiddish. He didn't know French or Yiddish, but he learned to recognize that question. He had never understood exactly why they asked the question, since they never demanded anything of him, rarely even could speak to him. Then, one day in Strasbourg, a little, bent old man and a small, shapeless woman had stopped him and asked, in English, if he was Jewish. "Yes," he'd said, smiling at them. The two old people had smiled widely, like children. "Look," the old man had said to his wife. "A young American soldier. A Jew. And so large and strong." He had touched Seeger's arm reverently with the tips of his fingers, then had touched the Garand Seeger was carrying. "And such a beautiful rifle."

And there, for a moment, although he was not particularly sensitive, Seeger had got an inkling of why he had been stopped and questioned by so many before. Here, to these bent, exhausted old people, ravaged of their families, familiar with flight and death for so many years, was a symbol of continuing life. A large young man in the uniform of the liberator, blood, as they thought, of their blood, but not in hiding, not quivering in fear and helplessness, but striding secure and victorious down the street, armed and capable of inflicting terrible destruction on his enemies.

Seeger had kissed the old lady on the cheek and she had wept, and the old man had scolded her for it while shaking Seeger's hand fervently and thankfully before saying goodbye.

Thinking back on it, he knew that it was silly to pretend that, even before his father's letter, he had been like any other American soldier going through the war. When he had stood over the huge, dead S.S.

major with the face blown in by his bullets in the warehouse in Coblenz, and taken the pistol from the dead hand, he had tasted a strange little extra flavor of triumph. How many Jews, he'd thought, has this man killed? How fitting it is that I've killed him. Neither Olson nor Welch, who were like his brothers, would have felt that in picking up the Luger, its barrel still hot from the last shots its owner had fired before dying. And he had resolved that he was going to make sure to take this gun back with him to America, and plug it and keep it on his desk at home, as a kind of vague, half-understood sign to himself that justice had once been done and he had been its instrument.

Maybe, he thought, maybe I'd better take it back with me, but not as a memento. Not plugged, but loaded. America by now was a strange country for him. He had been away a long time and he wasn't sure what was waiting for him when he got home. If the mobs were coming down the street toward his house, he was not going to die singing and praying.

When he had been taking basic training, he'd heard a scrawny, clerkish soldier from Boston talking at the other end of the PX bar, over the watered beer. "The boys at the office," the scratchy voice was saying, "gave me a party before I left. And they told me one thing. 'Charlie,' they said, 'hold onto your bayonet. We're going to be able to use it when you get back. On the Yids.'"

He hadn't said anything then, because he'd felt it was neither possible nor desirable to fight against every random overheard voice raised against the Jews from one end of the world to the other. But again and again, at odd moments, lying on a barracks cot, or stretched out trying to sleep on the floor of a ruined French farmhouse, he had heard that voice, harsh, satisfied, heavy with hate and ignorance, saying above the beery grumble of apprentice soldiers at the bar, "Hold onto your bayonet."

And the other stories. Jews collected stories of hatred and injustice and inklings of doom like a special, lunatic kind of miser. The story of the Navy officer, commander of a small vessel off the Aleutians, who in the officers' wardroom had complained that he hated the Jews because it was the Jews who had demanded that the Germans be beaten first, and the forces in the Pacific had been starved in consequence. And when one of his junior officers, who had just come aboard, had objected and told the commander that he was a Jew, the commander had risen from the table and said, "Mister, the Constitution of the United States says I have to serve in the same Navy with Jews, but it doesn't say I have to eat at the same table with them." In the fogs and the cold, swelling Arctic seas off the Aleutians, in a small boat, subject to sudden, mortal attack at any moment. . . . And the million other stories. Jews, even the most normal and best adjusted, became living treasuries of them, scraps of malice and bloodthirstiness, clever and confusing and cunningly twisted so that every act by every Jew became suspect and blameworthy and hateful. Seeger had heard the stories and had made an almost conscious effort to forget them. Now, holding his father's letter in his hand, he remembered them all.

He stared unseeingly out in front of him. Maybe, he thought, maybe it would've been better to have been killed in the war, like Leonard. Simpler. Leonard would never have to face a crowd coming for his mother and father. Leonard would not have to listen and collect these hideous, fascinating little stories that made of every Jew a stranger in any town, on any field, on the face of the earth. He had come so close to being killed so many times; it would have been so easy, so neat and final. Seeger shook his head. It was ridiculous to feel like that, and he was ashamed of himself for the weak moment. At the age of twenty-one, death was not an answer.

"Seeger!" It was Olson's voice. He and Welch had sloshed silently up behind Seeger, standing in the open field. "Seeger, *mon vieux*, what're you doing—grazing?"

Seeger turned slowly to them. "I wanted to read my letter," he said.

Olson looked closely at him. They had been together so long, through so many things, that flickers and hints of expression on each other's faces were recognized and acted upon. "Anything wrong?" Olson asked.

"No," said Seeger. "Nothing much."

"Norman," Welch said, his voice young and solemn. "Norman, we've been talking, Olson and me. We decided—you're pretty attached to that Luger, and maybe, if you—well—"

"What he's trying to say," said Olson, "is we withdraw the request. If you want to sell it, O.K. If you don't, don't do it for our sake. Honest."

Seeger looked at them standing there, disreputable and tough and familiar. "I haven't made up my mind yet," he said.

"Anything you decide," Welch said oratorically, "is perfectly all right with us. Perfectly."

The three of them walked aimlessly and silently across the field, away from camp. As they walked, their shoes making a wet, sliding sound in the damp, dead grass, Seeger thought of the time Olson had covered him in the little town outside Cherbourg, when Seeger had been caught, going down the side of a street, by four Germans with a machine gun in the second story of a house on the corner and Olson had had to stand out in the middle of the street with no cover at all for more than a minute, firing continuously, so that Seeger could get away alive. And he thought of the time outside St.-Lô when he had been wounded and had lain in a minefield for three hours and Welch and Captain Taney had come looking for him in the darkness and had found him and picked him up and run for it, all of them expecting to get blown up any second. And he thought of all the drinks they'd had together, and the long marches and the cold winter together, and all the girls they'd gone out with together, and he thought of his father and brother crouching behind the window in Ohio waiting for the rockets and the crowds armed with Browning automatic rifles.

"Say." He stopped and stood facing them. "Say, what do you guys think of the Jews?"

Welch and Olson looked at each other, and Olson glanced down at the letter in Seeger's hand.

"Jews?" Olson said finally. "What're they? Welch, you ever hear of the Jews?"

Welch looked thoughtfully at the gray sky. "No," he said. "But remember, I'm an uneducated fellow."

"Sorry, bud," Olson said, turning to Seeger. "We can't help you. Ask us another question. Maybe we'll do better."

Seeger peered at the faces of his friends. He would have to rely upon them, later on, out of uniform, on their native streets, more than he had ever relied on them on the bullet-swept street and in the dark minefield in France. Welch and Olson stared back at him, troubled, their faces candid and tough and dependable.

"What time," Seeger asked, "did you tell that captain you'd meet him?"

"Eight o'clock," Welch said. "But we don't have to go. If you have any feeling about that gun—"

"We'll meet him," Seeger said. "We can use that sixty-five bucks."

"Listen," Olson said, "I know how much you like that gun, and I'll feel like a heel if you sell it."

"Forget it," Seeger said, starting to walk again. "What could I use it for in America?"

GILBERT KEITH CHESTERTON

The Blue Cross

Gilbert Keith Chesterton (1874–1936), educated in London, began his writing career as a book reviewer, producing many essays which were later published in book form. He also wrote novels and books of literary criticism, history, biography and poetry. Among his most popular writings have been his Father Brown stories. [From *The Innocence of Father Brown* by G. K. Chesterton; copyright 1911, 1938 by Frances Chesterton; used by permission of Dodd, Mead & Co., the estate of G. K. Chesterton, and Messrs. Cassell & Co.]

BETWEEN THE SILVER RIBBON of morning and the green glittering ribbon of sea, the boat touched Harwich and let loose a swarm of folk like flies, among whom the man we must follow was by no means conspicuous—nor wished to be. There was nothing notable about him, except a slight contrast between the holiday gaiety of his clothes and the official gravity of his face. His clothes included a slight, pale-gray jacket, a white waistcoat, and a silver straw hat with a gray-blue ribbon. His lean face was dark by contrast, and ended in a curt black beard that looked Spanish and suggested an Elizabethan ruff. He was smoking a cigarette with the seriousness of an idler. There was nothing about him to indicate the fact that the gray jacket covered a loaded revolver, that the white waistcoat covered a police card, or that the straw hat covered one of the most powerful intellects in Europe. For this was Valentin himself, the head of the Paris police and the most famous investigator of the world; and he was coming from Brussels to London to make the greatest arrest of the century.

Flambeau was in England. The police of three countries had tracked the great criminal at last from Ghent to Brussels, from Brussels to the Hook of Holland; and it was conjectured that he would take some advantage of the unfamiliarity and confusion of the Eucharistic Congress, then taking place in London. Probably he would travel as some minor clerk or secretary connected with it, but, of course, Valentin could not be certain; nobody could be certain about Flambeau.

It is many years now since this colossus of crime suddenly ceased keeping the world in a turmoil, and when he ceased, as they said after the death of Roland, there was a great quiet upon the earth. But in his best days (I mean, of course, his worst) Flambeau was a figure as statuesque and international as the Kaiser. Almost every morning the daily paper announced that he had escaped the consequences of one extraordinary crime by committing another. He was a Gascon of gigantic stature and bodily daring; and the wildest tales were told of his outbursts of athletic humor; how he turned the *juge d'instruction* upside down and stood him on his head, "to clear his mind"; how he ran down the Rue de Rivoli with a policeman under each arm. It is due to him to say that his fantastic physical strength was generally employed in such bloodless though undignified scenes; his real crimes were chiefly those of ingenious and wholesale robbery. But each of his thefts was almost a new sin, and would make a story by itself. It was he who ran the great Tyrolean Dairy Company in London, with no dairies, no cows, no carts, no milk, but with some thousand subscribers. These he served by the simple operation of moving the little milk cans outside people's doors to the doors of his own customers. It was he who had kept up an unaccountable and close correspondence with a young lady whose whole letter-bag was intercepted, by the extraordinary trick of photographing his messages infinitesimally small upon the slides of a microscope. A sweeping simplicity, however, marked many of his experiments. It is said that he once repainted all the numbers in a street in the dead of night merely to divert one traveler into a trap. It is quite certain that he invented a portable pillar-box, which he put up at corners in quiet suburbs on the chance of strangers dropping postal orders into it. Lastly, he was known to be a startling acrobat; despite his huge figure, he could leap like a grasshopper and melt into the tree-tops like a monkey. Hence the great Valentin, when he set out to find Flambeau, was perfectly aware that his adventures would not end when he had found him.

But how was he to find him? On this the great Valentin's ideas were still in process of settlement.

There was one thing which Flambeau, with all his dexterity of disguise, could not cover, and that was his singular height. If Valentin's quick eye had caught a tall apple-woman, a tall grenadier, or even a tolerably tall duchess, he might have arrested them on the spot. But all along his train there was nobody that could be a disguised Flambeau, any more than a cat could be a disguised giraffe. About the people on the boat he had already satisfied himself; and the people picked up at Harwich or on the journey limited themselves with certainty to six. There was a short railway official traveling up to the terminus, three fairly short market gardeners picked up two stations afterwards, one very short widow lady going up from a small Essex town, and a very short Roman Catholic priest going up from a small Essex village. When it came to the last case, Valentin gave it up and almost laughed. The little priest was so much the essence of those Eastern flats; he had a face as round and dull as a Norfolk dumpling; he had eyes as empty as the North Sea; he had several brown parcels, which he was quite incapable of collecting. The Eucharistic Congress had doubtless sucked out of their local stagnation many such creatures, blind and helpless, like moles disinterred. Valentin was a skeptic in the severe style of France, and could have no love for priests. But he could have pity for them, and this one might have provoked pity in anybody. He had a large, shabby umbrella, which constantly fell on the floor. He did not seem to know which was the right end of his return ticket. He explained with a moon-calf simplicity to everybody in the carriage that he had to be careful, because he had something made of real silver "with blue stones" in one of his brown-paper parcels. His quaint blending of Essex flatness with saintly simplicity continuously amused the Frenchman till the priest arrived (somehow) at Tottenham with all his parcels, and came back for his umbrella. When he did the last, Valentin even had the good nature to warn him not to take care of the silver by telling everybody about it. But to whomever he talked, Valentin kept his eye open for someone else; he looked out steadily for anyone, rich or poor, male or female, who was well up to six feet; for Flambeau was four inches above it.

He alighted at Liverpool Street, however, quite conscientiously secure that he had not missed the criminal so far. He then went to Scotland Yard to regularize his position and arrange for help in case of need; he then lit another cigarette and went for a long stroll in the streets of London. As he was walking in the streets and squares beyond Victoria, he paused suddenly and stood. It was a quaint, quiet square, very typical of London, full of an accidental stillness. The tall, flat houses round looked at once prosperous and uninhabited; the square of shrubbery in the center looked as deserted as a green Pacific islet. One of the four sides was much higher than the rest, like a dais; and the line of this side was broken by one of London's admirable accidents—a restaurant that looked as if it had strayed from Soho. It was an unreasonably attractive object, with dwarf plants in pots and long, striped blinds of lemon yellow and white. It stood specially high above the street and in the usual patchwork way of London, a flight of steps from the street ran up to meet the front door almost as a fire-escape might run up to a first-floor window. Valentin stood and smoked in front of the yellow-white blinds and considered them long.

The most incredible thing about miracles is that they happen. A few clouds in heaven do come together into the staring shape of one human eye. A tree does stand up in the landscape of a doubtful journey in the exact and elaborate shape of a note of interrogation. I have seen both these things myself within the last few days. Nelson does die in the instant of victory; and a man named Williams does quite accidentally murder a man named Williamson; it sounds like a sort of infanticide. In short, there is in life an element of elfin coincidence which people reckoning on the prosaic may perpetually miss. As it has been well expressed in the paradox of Poe, wisdom should reckon on the unforeseen.

Aristide Valentin was unfathomably French; and the French intelligence is intelligence specially and solely. He was not "a thinking machine"; for that is a brainless phrase of modern fatalism and materialism. A machine only *is* a machine because it cannot think. But he was a thinking man, and a plain man at the same time. All his wonderful successes, that looked like conjuring, had been gained by plodding logic, by clear and commonplace French thought. The French electrify the world not by starting any paradox, they electrify it by carrying out a truism. They carry a truism so far—as in the French Revolution. But exactly because Valentin understood reason, he understood the limits of reason. Only a man who knows nothing of motors talks of motoring without petrol; only a man who knows nothing of reason talks of reasoning without strong, undisputed first principles. Here he had no strong first principles. Flambeau had been missed at Harwich; and if he was in London at all, he might be anything from a tall tramp on Wimbledon Common to a tall toastmaster at the Hotel Métropole. In such a naked state of nescience, Valentin had a view and a method of his own.

In such cases he reckoned on the unforeseen. In such cases, when he could not follow the train of the reasonable, he coldly and carefully followed the train of the unreasonable. Instead of going to the right places—banks, police stations, rendezvous—he systematically went to the wrong places; knocked at every empty house, turned down every *cul de sac,* went up every lane blocked with rubbish, went round every crescent that led him uselessly out of the way. He defended this crazy course quite logically. He said that if one had a clue this was the worst way; but if one had no clue at all it was the best, because there was just the chance that any oddity that caught the eye of the pursuer might be the same that had caught the eye of the pursued. Somewhere a man must begin, and it had better be just where another man might stop. Something about that flight of steps up to the shop, something about the quietude and quaintness of the restaurant, roused all the detective's rare romantic fancy and made him resolve to strike at random. He went up the steps, and sitting down at a table by the window, asked for a cup of black coffee.

It was half-way through the morning, and he had not breakfasted; the slight litter of other breakfasts stood about on the table to remind him of his hunger; and adding a poached egg to his order, he proceeded musingly to shake some white sugar into his coffee, thinking all the time about Flambeau. He remembered how Flambeau had escaped, once by a pair of nail scissors, and once by a house on fire; once by having to pay for an unstamped letter, and once by getting people to look through a telescope at a comet that might destroy the world. He thought his detective brain as good as the criminal's, which was true. But he fully realized the disadvantage. "The criminal is the creative artist; the detective only the critic," he said with a sour smile, and lifted his coffee cup to his lips slowly, and put it down very quickly. He had put salt in it.

He looked at the vessel from which the silvery powder had come; it was certainly a sugar-basin; as unmistakably meant for sugar as a champagne-bottle for champagne. He wondered why they should keep salt in it. He looked to see if there were any more orthodox vessels. Yes; there were two salt-cellars quite full. Perhaps there was some specialty in the condiment in the salt-cellars. He tasted it; it was sugar. Then he looked round at the restaurant with a refreshed air of interest, to see if there were any other traces of that singular artistic taste which puts the sugar in the salt-cellars and the salt in the sugar-basin. Except for an odd splash of some dark fluid on one of the white-papered walls, the whole place appeared neat, cheerful and ordinary. He rang the bell for the waiter.

When that official hurried up, fuzzy-haired and somewhat bleary-eyed at that early hour, the detective (who was not without an appreciation of the simpler forms of humor) asked him to taste the sugar and see if it was up to the high reputation of the hotel. The result was that the waiter yawned suddenly and woke up.

"Do you play this delicate joke on your customers every morning?" inquired Valentin. "Does changing the salt and sugar never pall on you as a jest?"

The waiter, when this irony grew clearer, stammeringly assured him that the establishment had certainly no such intention; it must be a most curious mistake. He picked up the sugar-basin and looked at it; he picked up the salt-cellar and looked at that, his face growing more and more bewildered. At last he abruptly excused himself, and hurrying away, returned in a few seconds with the proprietor. The proprietor also examined the sugar-basin and then the salt-cellar; the proprietor also looked bewildered.

Suddenly the waiter seemed to grow inarticulate with a rush of words.

"I zink," he stuttered eagerly, "I zink it is those two clergymen."

"What two clergymen?"

"The two clergymen," said the waiter, "that threw soup at the wall."

"Threw soup at the wall?" repeated Valentin, feeling sure this must be some singular Italian metaphor.

"Yes, yes," said the attendant excitedly, and pointing at the dark splash on the white paper; "threw it over there on the wall."

Valentin looked his query at the proprietor, who came to his rescue with fuller reports.

"Yes, sir," he said, "it's quite true, though I don't suppose it has anything to do with the sugar and salt. Two clergymen came in and drank soup here very early, as soon as the shutters were taken down. They were both very quiet, respectable people; one of them paid the bill and went out; the other, who seemed a slower coach altogether, was some minutes longer getting his things together. But he went at last. Only, the instant before he stepped into the street he deliberately picked up his cup, which he had only half emptied, and threw the soup slap on the wall. I was in the back room myself, and so was the waiter; so I could only rush out in time to find the wall splashed and the shop empty. It don't do any particular damage, but it was confounded cheek; and I tried to catch the men in the street. They were too far off though; I only noticed they went round the next corner into Carstairs Street."

The detective was on his feet, hat settled and stick in hand. He had already decided that in the universal darkness of his mind he could only follow the first odd finger that pointed; and this finger was odd enough. Paying his bill and clashing the glass doors behind him, he was soon swinging round into the other street.

It was fortunate that even in such fevered moments his eye was cool and quick. Something in a shop-front went by him like a mere flash; yet he went back to look at it. The shop was a popular greengrocer and fruiterer's, an array of goods set out in the open air and plainly ticketed with the names and prices. In the two most prominent compartments were two heaps, of oranges and of nuts respectively. On the heap of nuts lay a scrap of cardboard, on which was written in bold, blue chalk, "Best tangerine oranges, two a penny." On the oranges was the equally clear and exact description, "Finest Brazil nuts, 4d. a lb." M. Valentin looked at these two placards and fancied he had met this highly subtle form of humor before, and that somewhat recently. He drew the attention of the red-faced fruiterer, who was looking rather sullenly up and down the street, to this inaccuracy in his advertisements. The fruiterer said nothing, but sharply put each card into its proper place. The detective, leaning elegantly on his walking-cane, continued to scrutinize the shop. At last he said, "Pray excuse my apparent irrelevance, my good sir, but I should like to ask you a question in experimental psychology and the association of ideas."

The red-faced shopman regarded him with an eye of menace; but he continued gaily, swinging his cane. "Why," he pursued, "why are two tickets wrongly placed in a greengrocer's shop like a shovel hat that has come to London for a holiday? Or, in case I do not make myself clear, what is the mystical association which connects the idea of nuts marked as oranges with the idea of two clergymen, one tall and the other short?"

The eyes of the tradesman stood out of his head like a snail's; he really seemed for an instant likely to fling himself upon the stranger. At last he stammered angrily: "I don't know what you 'ave to do with it, but if you're one of their friends, you can tell 'em from me that I'll knock their silly 'eads off, parsons or no parsons, if they upset my apples again."

"Indeed?" asked the detective, with great sympathy. "Did they upset your apples?"

"One of 'em did," said the heated shopman; "rolled 'em all over the street. I'd 'ave caught the fool but for havin' to pick 'em up."

"Which way did these parsons go?" asked Valentin.

"Up that second road on the left-hand side, and then across the square," said the other promptly.

"Thanks," replied Valentin, and vanished like a fairy. On the other side of the second square he found a policeman, and said: "This is urgent, constable; have you seen two clergymen in shovel hats?"

The policeman began to chuckle heavily. "I 'ave, sir; and if you arst me, one of 'em was drunk. He stood in the middle of the road that bewildered that——"

"Which way did they go?" snapped Valentin.

"They took one of them yellow buses over there," answered the man; "them that go to Hampstead."

Valentin produced his official card and said very rapidly: "Call up two of your men to come with me in pursuit," and crossed the road with such contagious energy that the ponderous policeman was moved to almost agile obedience. In a minute and a half the French detective was joined on the opposite pavement by an inspector and a man in plain clothes.

"Well, sir," began the former, with smiling importance, "and what may——?"

Valentin pointed suddenly with his cane. "I'll tell you on the top of the omnibus," he said, and was darting and dodging across the tangle of the traffic. When all three sank panting on the top seats of the yellow vehicle, the inspector said: "We could go four times as quick in a taxi."

"Quite true," replied their leader placidly, "if we only had an idea of where we were going."

"Well, where *are* you going?" asked the other, staring.

Valentin smoked frowningly for a few seconds; then, removing his cigarette, he said: "If you *know* what a man's doing, get in front of him; but if you want to guess what he's doing, keep behind him. Stray when he strays; stop when he stops; travel as slowly as he. Then you may see what he saw and may act as he acted. All we can do is to keep our eyes skinned for a queer thing."

"What sort of queer thing do you mean?" asked the inspector.

"Any sort of queer thing," answered Valentin, and relapsed into obstinate silence.

The yellow omnibus crawled up the northern roads for what seemed like hours on end; the great detective would not explain further, and perhaps his assistants felt a silent and growing doubt of his errand. Perhaps, also, they felt a silent and growing desire for lunch, for the hours crept long past the normal luncheon hour, and the long roads of the North London suburbs seemed to shoot out into length after length like an infernal telescope. It was one of those journeys on which a man perpetually feels that now at last he must have come to the end of the universe, and then finds he has only come to the beginning of Tufnell Park. London died away in draggled taverns and dreary scrubs, and then was unaccountably born again in blazing high streets and blatant hotels. It was like passing through thirteen separate vulgar cities all just touching each other. But though the winter twilight was already threatening the road ahead of them, the Parisian detective still sat silent and watchful, eyeing the frontage of the streets that slid by on either side. By the time they had left Camden Town behind, the policemen were nearly asleep; at least, they gave something like a jump as Valentin leapt erect, struck a hand on each man's shoulder, and shouted to the driver to stop.

They tumbled down the steps into the road without realizing why they had been dislodged; when they looked round for enlightenment they found Valentin triumphantly pointing his finger toward a window on the left side of the road. It was a large window, forming part of the long façade of a gilt and palatial public-house; it was the part reserved for respectable dining, and labeled "Restaurant." The window, like all the rest along the frontage of the hotel, was of frosted and figured glass; but in the middle of it was a big, black smash, like a star in the ice.

"Our cue at last," cried Valentin, waving his stick; "the place with the broken window."

"What window? What cue?" asked his principal assistant. "Why, what proof is there that this has anything to do with them?"

Valentin almost broke his bamboo stick with rage.

"Proof!" he cried. "Good God! the man is looking for proof! Why, of course, the chances are twenty to one that it has *nothing* to do with them. But what else can we do? Don't you see we must either follow one wild possibility or else go home to bed?" He banged his way into the restaurant, followed by his companions, and they were soon seated at a late luncheon at a little table, and looking at the star of smashed glass from the inside. Not that it was very informative to them even then.

"Got your window broken, I see," said Valentin to the waiter as he paid the bill.

"Yes, sir," answered the attendant, bending busily over the change, to which Valentin silently added an enormous tip. The waiter straightened himself with mild but unmistakable animation.

"Ah, yes, sir," he said. "Very odd thing, that sir."

"Indeed? Tell us about it," said the detective with careless curiosity.

"Well, two gents in black came in," said the waiter; "two of those foreign parsons that are running about. They had a cheap and quiet little lunch, and one of them paid for it and went out. The other was just going out to join him when I looked at my change again and found he'd paid me more than three times too much. 'Here,' I says to the chap who was nearly out of the door, 'you've paid too much.' 'Oh,' he says, very cool, 'have we?' 'Yes,' I says, and picks up the bill to show him. Well, that was a knockout."

"What do you mean?" asked his interlocutor.

"Well, I'd have sworn on seven Bibles that I'd put 4s. on that bill. But now I saw I'd put 14s., as plain as paint."

"Well?" cried Valentin, moving slowly, but with burning eyes, "and then?"

"The parson at the door he says all serene, 'Sorry to confuse your accounts, but it'll pay for the window.' 'What window?' I says. 'The one I'm going to break,' he says, and smashed that blessed pane with his umbrella."

All three inquirers made an exclamation; and the inspector said under his breath, "Are we after escaped lunatics?" The waiter went on with some relish for the ridiculous story:

"I was so knocked silly for a second, I couldn't do anything. The man marched out of the place and joined his friend just round the corner. Then they went so quick up Bullock Street that I couldn't catch them, though I ran round the bars to do it."

"Bullock Street," said the detective, and shot up that thoroughfare as quickly as the strange couple he pursued.

Their journey now took them through bare brick ways like tunnels; streets with few lights and even with few windows; streets that seemed built out of the blank backs of everything and everywhere. Dusk was deepening, and it was not easy even for the London policemen to guess in what exact direction they were treading. The inspector, however, was pretty certain that they would eventually strike some part of Hampstead Heath. Abruptly one bulging gas-lit window broke the blue twilight like a bull's-eye lantern; and Valentin stopped an instant before a little garish sweetstuff shop. After an instant's hesitation he went in; he stood amid the gaudy colors of the confectionery with entire gravity and bought thirteen chocolate cigars with a certain care.

He was clearly preparing an opening; but he did not need one.

An angular, elderly young woman in the shop had regarded his elegant appearance with a merely automatic inquiry; but when she saw the door behind him blocked with the blue uniform of the inspector, her eyes seemed to wake up.

"Oh," she said, "if you've come about that parcel, I've sent it off already."

"Parcel!" repeated Valentin; and it was his turn to look inquiring.

"I mean the parcel the gentleman left—the clergyman gentleman."

"For goodness' sake," said Valentin, leaning forward with his first real confession of eagerness, "for Heaven's sake tell us what happened exactly."

"Well," said the woman a little doubtfully, "the clergymen came in about half an hour ago and bought some peppermints and talked a bit, and then went off toward the Heath. But a second after, one of them runs back into the shop and says, 'Have I left a parcel?' Well, I looked everywhere and couldn't see one; so he says, 'Never mind; but if it should turn up, please post it to this address,' and he left me the address and a shilling for my trouble. And sure enough, though I thought I'd looked everywhere, I found he'd left a brown paper parcel, so I posted it to the place he said. I can't remember the address now; it was somewhere in Westminster. But as the thing seemed so important, I thought perhaps the police had come about it."

"So they have," said Valentin shortly. "Is Hampstead Heath near here?"

"Straight on for fifteen minutes," said the woman, "and you'll come right out on the open." Valentin sprang out of the shop and began to run. The other detectives followed him at a reluctant trot.

The street they threaded was so narrow and shut in by shadows that when they came out unexpectedly into the void common and vast sky they were startled to find the evening still so light and clear. A perfect dome of peacock-green sank into gold amid the blackening trees and the dark violet distances. The glowing green tint was just deep enough to pick out in points of crystal one or two stars. All that was left of the daylight lay in a golden glitter across the edge of Hampstead and that popular hollow which is called the Vale of Health. The holiday makers who roam this region had not wholly dispersed; a few couples sat shapelessly on benches; and here and there a distant girl still shrieked in one of the swings. The glory of heaven deepened and darkened around the sublime vulgarity of man; and standing on the slope and looking across the valley, Valentin beheld the thing which he sought.

Among the black and breaking groups in that distance was one especially black which did not break—a group of two figures clerically clad. Though they seemed as small as insects, Valentin could see that one of them was much smaller than the other. Though the other had a student's stoop and an inconspicuous manner, he could see that the man was well over six feet high. He shut his teeth and went forward, whirling his stick impatiently. By the time he had substantially diminished the distance and magnified the two black figures as in a vast microscope, he had perceived something else; something which startled him, and yet which he had somehow expected. Whoever was the tall priest, there could be no doubt about the identity of the short one. It was his friend of the Harwich train, the stumpy little *curé* of Essex whom he had warned about his brown paper parcels.

Now, so far as this went, everything fitted in finally and rationally enough. Valentin had learned by his inquiries that morning that a Father Brown from Essex was bringing up a silver cross with sapphires, a relic of considerable value, to show some of the foreign priests at the congress. This undoubtedly was the "silver with blue stones"; and Father Brown undoubtedly was the little greenhorn in the train. Now there was nothing wonderful about the fact that what Valentin had found out Flambeau had also found out; Flambeau found out everything. Also there was nothing wonderful in the fact that when Flambeau heard of a sapphire cross he should try to steal it; that was the most natural thing in all natural history. And most certainly there was nothing wonderful about the fact that Flambeau should have it all his own way with such a silly sheep as the man with the umbrella and the parcels. He was the sort of man whom anybody could lead on a string to the North Pole; it was not surprising that an actor like Flambeau, dressed as another priest, could lead him to Hampstead Heath. So far the crime seemed clear enough; and while the detective pitied the priest for his helplessness, he almost despised Flambeau for condescending to so gullible a victim. But when Valentin thought of all that had happened in between, of all that had led him to his triumph, he racked his brains for the smallest rhyme or reason in it. What had the stealing of a blue-and-silver cross from a priest from Essex to do with chucking soup at wall paper? What had it to do with calling nuts oranges, or with paying for windows first and breaking them afterwards? He had come to the end of his chase; yet somehow he had missed the middle of it. When he failed (which was seldom), he had usually grasped the clue, but nevertheless missed the criminal. Here he had grasped the criminal, but still he could not grasp the clue.

The two figures that they followed were crawling like black flies across the huge green contour of a hill. They were evidently sunk in conversation, and perhaps did not notice where they were going; but they were certainly going to the wilder and more silent heights of the Heath. As their pursuers gained on them, the latter had to use the undignified attitudes of the deer-stalker, to crouch behind clumps of trees and even to crawl prostrate in deep grass. By these ungainly ingenuities the hunters even came close enough to the quarry to hear the murmur of the discussion, but no word could be distinguished except the word "reason" recurring frequently in a high and almost childish voice. Once over an abrupt dip of land and a dense tangle of thickets, the detectives actually lost the two figures they were following. They did not find the trail again for an agonizing ten minutes, and then it led round the brow of a great dome of hill overlooking an amphitheatre of rich and desolate sunset scenery. Under a tree in this commanding yet neglected spot was an old ramshackle wooden seat. On this seat sat the two priests still in serious speech together. The gorgeous green and gold still clung to the darkening horizon; but the dome above was turning slowly from peacock-green to peacock-blue, and the stars detached themselves more and more like solid jewels. Mutely motioning to his followers, Valentin contrived to creep up behind the big branching tree, and, standing there in deathly silence, heard the words of the strange priests for the first time.

After he had listened for a minute and a half, he was gripped by a devilish doubt. Perhaps he had dragged the two English policemen to the wastes of a nocturnal heath on an errand no saner than seeking figs on its thistles. For the two priests were talking exactly like priests, piously, with learning and leisure, about the most aerial enigmas of theology. The little Essex priest spoke the more simply, with his round face turned to the strengthening stars; the other talked with his head bowed, as if he were not even worthy to look at them. But no more innocently clerical conversation could have been heard in any white Italian cloister or black Spanish cathedral.

The first he heard was the tail of one of Father Brown's sentences, which ended: ". . . what they really meant in the Middle Ages by the heavens being incorruptible."

The taller priest nodded his bowed head and said:

"Ah, yes, these modern infidels appeal to their reason; but who can look at those millions of worlds and not feel that there may well be wonderful universes above us where reason is utterly unreasonable?"

"No," said the other priest; "reason is always reasonable, even in the last limbo, in the lost borderland of things. I know that people charge the Church with lowering reason, but it is just the other way. Alone on earth, the Church makes reason really supreme. Alone on earth, the Church affirms that God himself is bound by reason."

The other priest raised his austere face to the spangled sky and said:

"Yet who knows if in that infinite universe——?"

"Only infinite physically," said the little priest, turning sharply in his seat, "not infinite in the sense of escaping from the laws of truth."

Valentin behind his tree was tearing his fingernails with silent fury. He seemed almost to hear the sniggers of the English detectives whom he had brought so far on a fantastic guess only to listen to the metaphysical gossip of two mild old parsons. In his impatience he lost the equally elaborate answer of the tall cleric, and when he listened again it was again Father Brown who was speaking:

"Reason and justice grip the remotest and the loneliest star. Look at those stars. Don't they look as if they were single diamonds and sapphires? Well, you can imagine any mad botany or geology you please. Think of forests of adamant with leaves of brilliants. Think the moon is a blue moon, a single elephantine sapphire. But don'- far.y that all that frantic astronomy would make the smallest difference to the reason and justice of conduct. On plains of opal, under cliffs cut out of pearl, you would still find a notice-board, 'Thou shalt not steal.' "

Valentin was just in the act of rising from his rigid and crouching attitude and creeping away as softly as might be, felled by the one great folly of his life. But something in the very silence of the tall priest made him stop until the latter spoke. When at last he did speak, he said simply, his head bowed and his hands on his knees:

"Well, I still think that other worlds may perhaps rise higher than our reason. The mystery of heaven is unfathomable, and I for one can only bow my head."

Then, with brow yet bent and without changing by the faintest shade his attitude or voice, he added:

"Just hand over that sapphire cross of yours, will you? We're all alone here, and I could pull you to pieces like a straw doll."

The utterly unaltered voice and attitude added a strange violence to that shocking change of speech. But the guarder of the relic only seemed to turn his head by the smallest section of the compass. He seemed still to have a somewhat foolish face turned to the stars. Perhaps he had not understood. Or, perhaps, he had understood and sat rigid with terror.

"Yes," said the tall priest, in the same low voice and in the same still posture, "yes, I am Flambeau."

Then, after a pause, he said:

"Come, will you give me that cross?"

"No," said the other, and the monosyllable had an odd sound.

Flambeau suddenly flung off all his pontifical pretensions. The great robber leaned back in his seat and laughed low but long.

"No," he cried, "you won't give it me, you proud prelate. You won't give it me, you little celibate simpleton. Shall I tell you why you won't give it me? Because I've got it already in my breast-pocket."

The small man from Essex turned what seemed to be a dazed face in the dusk, and said, with the timid eagerness of "The Private Secretary":

"Are—are you sure?"

Flambeau yelled with delight.

"Really, you're as good as a three-act farce," he cried. "Yes, you turnip, I am quite sure. I had the sense to make a duplicate of the right parcel, and now, my friend, you've got the duplicate and I've got the jewels. An old dodge, Father Brown—a very old dodge."

"Yes," said Father Brown, and passed his hand through his hair with the same strange vagueness of manner. "Yes, I've heard of it before."

The colossus of crime leaned over to the little rustic priest with a sort of sudden interest.

"*You* have heard of it?" he asked. "Where have *you* heard of it?"

"Well, I mustn't tell you his name, of course," said the little man simply. "He was a penitent, you know. He had lived prosperously for about twenty years entirely on duplicate brown-paper parcels. And so, you see, when I began to suspect you, I thought of this poor chap's way of doing it at once."

"Began to suspect me?" repeated the outlaw with increased intensity. "Did you really have the gumption to suspect me just because I brought you up to this bare part of the heath?"

"No, no," said Brown with an air of apology. "You see, I suspected you when we first met. It's that little bulge up the sleeve where you people have the spiked bracelet."

"How in Tartarus," cried Flambeau, "did you ever hear of the spiked bracelet?"

"Oh, one's little flock, you know!" said Father Brown, arching his eyebrows rather blankly. "When I was a curate in Hartlepool, there were three of them with spiked bracelets. So, as I suspected you from the first, don't you see, I made sure that the cross should go safe, anyhow. I'm afraid I watched you, you know. So at last I saw you change the parcels. Then, don't you see, I changed them back again. And then I left the right one behind."

"Left it behind?" repeated Flambeau, and for the first time there was another note in his voice beside his triumph.

"Well, it was like this," said the little priest, speaking in the same unaffected way, "I went back to that sweet-shop and asked if I'd left a parcel, and gave them a particular address if it turned up. Well, I knew I hadn't; but when I went away again I did. So, instead of running after me with that valuable parcel, they have sent it flying to a friend of mine in Westminster." Then he added rather sadly: "I learnt that, too, from a poor fellow in Hartlepool. He used to do it with handbags he stole at railway stations, but he's in a monastery now. Oh, one gets to know, you know," he added, rubbing his head again with the same sort of desperate apology. "We can't help being priests. People come and tell us these things."

Flambeau tore a brown-paper parcel out of his inner pocket and rent it in pieces. There was nothing but paper and sticks of lead inside it. He sprang to his feet with a gigantic gesture, and cried:

"I don't believe you. I don't believe a bumpkin like you could manage all that. I believe you've still got the stuff on you, and if you don't give it up—why, we're all alone, and I'll take it by force!"

"No," said Father Brown simply, and stood up also, "you won't take it by force. First, because I really haven't still got it. And, second, because we are not alone."

Flambeau stopped in his stride forward.

"Behind that tree," said Father Brown, pointing, "are two strong policemen and the greatest detective alive. How did they come here, do you ask? Why, I brought them, of course! How did I do it? Why, I'll tell you if you like! Lord bless you, we have to know twenty such things when we work among the criminal classes! Well, I wasn't sure you were a thief, and it would never do to make a scandal against one of our own clergy. So I just tested you to see if anything would make you show yourself. A man generally makes a small scene if he finds salt in his coffee; if he doesn't, he has some reason for keeping quiet. I changed the salt and sugar, and *you* kept quiet. A man generally objects if his bill is three times too big. If he pays it, he has some motive for passing unnoticed. I altered your bill, and *you* paid it."

The world seemed waiting for Flambeau to leap like a tiger. But he was held back as by a spell; he was stunned with the utmost curiosity.

"Well," went on Father Brown, with lumbering lucidity, "as you wouldn't leave any tracks for the police, of course somebody had to. At every place we went to, I took care to do something that would get us talked about for the rest of the day. I didn't do much harm—a splashed wall, spilt apples, a broken window; but I saved the cross, as the cross will always be saved. It is at Westminster by now. I rather wonder you didn't stop it with the Donkey's Whistle."

"With the what?" asked Flambeau.

"I'm glad you've never heard of it," said the priest, making a face. "It's a foul thing. I'm sure you're too good a man for a Whistler. I couldn't have countered it even with the Spots myself; I'm not strong enough in the legs."

"What on earth are you talking about?" asked the other.

"Well, I did think you'd know the Spots," said Father Brown, agreeably surprised. "Oh, you can't have gone so very wrong yet!"

"How in blazes do you know all these horrors?" cried Flambeau.

The shadow of a smile crossed the round, simple face of his clerical opponent.

"Oh, by being a celibate simpleton, I suppose," he said. "Has it never struck you that a man who does next to nothing but hear men's real sins is not likely to be wholly unaware of human evil? But, as a matter of fact, another part of my trade, too, made me sure you weren't a priest."

"What?" asked the thief, almost gaping.

"You attacked reason," said Father Brown. "It's bad theology."

And even as he turned away to collect his property, the three policemen came out from under the twilight trees. Flambeau was an artist and a sportsman. He stepped back and swept Valentin a great bow.

"Do not bow to me, *mon ami*," said Valentin with silver clearness. "Let us both bow to our master."

And they both stood an instant uncovered while the little Essex priest blinked about for his umbrella.

RUDYARD KIPLING

The Eye of Allah

Rudyard Kipling (1865–1936) was born in Bombay, the son of a well-known illustrator, and was educated at the United Services College, Westward Ho. From 1882 to 1889 he did journalistic work in India. His fame rests principally on his short stories, dealing with India, the sea, the jungle and the army, and to a lesser extent, on his verse. His works include *Departmental Ditties, Plain Tales from the Hills, The Jungle Book, Kim, The Light that Failed,* and *Captains Courageous.* [From *Debits and Credits* by Rudyard Kipling; copyright 1919 by Rudyard Kipling; used by permission of Mrs. George Baimbridge, Doubleday & Company, Inc., and the Macmillan Co. of Canada, Inc.]

THE CANTOR OF ST. ILLOD'S being far too enthusiastic a musician to concern himself with its Library, the Sub-Cantor, who idolized every detail of the work, was tidying up, after two hours' writing and dictation in the Scriptorium. The copying-monks handed him in their sheets—it was a plain Four Gospels ordered by an Abbot at Evesham—and filed out to vespers. John Otho, better known as John of Burgos, took no heed. He was burnishing a tiny boss of gold in his miniature of the Annunciation for his Gospel of St. Luke, which it was hoped that Cardinal Falcodi, the Papal Legate, might later be pleased to accept.

"Break off, John," said the Sub-Cantor in an undertone.

"Eh? Gone, have they? I never heard. Hold a minute, Clement."

The Sub-Cantor waited patiently. He had known John more than a dozen years, coming and going at St. Illod's, to which monastery John, when abroad, always said he belonged. The claim was gladly allowed for, more even than other Fitz Otho's, he seemed to carry all the Arts under his hand, and most of their practical receipts under his hood.

The Sub-Cantor looked over his shoulder at the pinned-down sheet where the first words of the Magnificat were built up in gold washed with red-lac for a background to the Virgin's hardly yet fired halo. She was shown, hands joined in wonder, at a lattice of infinitely intricate arabesque, round the edges of which sprays of orange-bloom seemed to load the blue hot air that carried back over the minute parched landscape in the middle distance.

"You've made her all Jewess," said the Sub-Cantor, studying the olive-flushed cheek and the eyes charged with foreknowledge.

"What else was Our Lady?" John slipped out the pins. "Listen, Clement. If I do not come back, this goes into my Great Luke, whoever finishes it." He slid the drawing between its guard-papers.

156

"Then you're for Burgos again—as I heard?"

"In two days. The new Cathedral yonder—but they're slower than the Wrath of God, those masons—is good for the soul."

"*Thy* soul?" The Sub-Cantor seemed doubtful.

"Even mine, by your permission. And down south—on the edge of the Conquered Countries—Granada way—there's some Moorish diaper-work that's wholesome. It allays vain thought and draws it toward the picture—as you felt, just now, in my Annunciation."

"She—it was very beautiful. No wonder you go. But you'll not forget your absolution, John?"

"Surely." This was a precaution John no more omitted on the eve of his travels than he did the recutting of the tonsure which he had provided himself with in his youth, somewhere near Ghent. The mark gave him privilege of clergy at a pinch, and a certain consideration on the roads always.

"You'll not forget, either, what we need in the Scriptorium. There's no more true ultramarine in this world now. They mix it with that German blue. And as for vermilion——"

"I'll do my best always."

"And Brother Thomas (this was the Infirmarian in charge of the monastery hospital) he needs——"

"He'll do his own asking. I'll go over his side now, and get me re-tonsured."

John went down the stairs to the lane that divides the hospital and cook-house from the back-cloisters. While he was being barbered, Brother Thomas (St. Illod's meek but deadly persistent Infirmarian) gave him a list of drugs that he was to bring back from Spain by hook, crook, or lawful purchase. Here they were surprised by the lame, dark Abbot Stephen, in his fur-lined night-boots. Not that Stephen de Sautré was any spy; but as a young man he had shared an unlucky Crusade, which had ended, after a battle at Mansura, in two years' captivity among the Saracens at Cairo where men learn to walk softly. A fair huntsman and hawker, a reasonable disciplinarian but a man of science above all, and a Doctor of Medicine under one Ranulphus, Canon of St. Paul's, his heart was more in the monastery's hospital work than its religious. He checked their list interestedly, adding items of his own. After the Infirmarian had withdrawn he gave John generous absolution, to cover lapses by the way; for he did not hold with chance-bought Indulgences.

"And what seek you *this* journey?" he demanded, sitting on the bench beside the mortar and scales in the little warm cell for stored drugs.

"Devils, mostly," said John, grinning.

"In Spain? Are not Abana and Pharphar——?"

John, to whom men were but matter for drawings, and well-born to boot (since he was a de Sanford on his mother's side), looked the Abbot full in the face and—"Did *you* find it so?" said he.

"No. They were in Cairo too. But what's your special need of 'em?"

"For my Great Luke. He's the master-hand of all Four when it comes to devils."

"No wonder. He was a physician. You're not."

"Heaven forbid! But I'm weary of our Church-pattern devils. They're only apes and goats and poultry conjoined. 'Good enough for plain red-and-black Hells and Judgment Days—but not for me."

"What makes you so choice in them?"

"Because it stands to reason and Art that there are all musters of devils in Hell's dealings. Those Seven, for example, that were haled out of the Magdalene. They'd be she-devils—no kin at all to the beaked and horned and bearded devils-general."

The Abbot laughed.

"And see again! The devil that came out of the dumb man. What use is snout or bill to *him*? He'd be faceless as a leper. Above all—God send I live to do it!—the devils that entered the Gadarene swine. They'd be—they'd be—I know not yet what they'd be, but they'd be surpassing devils. I'd have 'em diverse as the Saints themselves. But now, they're all one pattern, for wall, window, or picture-work."

"Go on, John. You're deeper in this mystery than I."

"Heaven forbid! But I say there's respect due to devils, damned tho' they be."

"Dangerous doctrine."

"My meaning is that if the shape of anything be worth man's thought to picture to man, it's worth his best thought."

"That's safer. But I'm glad I've given you Absolution."

"There's less risk for a craftsman who deals with the outside shapes of things—for Mother Church's glory."

"Maybe so, but John"—the Abbot's hand almost touched John's sleeve—"tell me, now, is—is she Moorish or—or Hebrew?"

"She's mine," John returned.

"Is that enough?"

"I have found it so."

"Well—ah well! It's out of my jurisdiction but—how do they look at it down yonder?"

"Oh, they drive nothing to a head in Spain—neither Church nor King, bless them! There's too many Moors and Jews to kill them all, and if they chased 'em away there'd be no trade nor farming. Trust me, in the Conquered Countries, from Seville to Granada, we live lovingly enough together—Spaniard, Moor, and Jew. Ye see, *we* ask no questions."

"Yes—yes," Stephen sighed. "And always there's the hope, she may be converted."

"Oh, yes, there's always hope."

The Abbot went on into the hospital. It was an easy age before Rome tightened the screw as to clerical connections. If the lady were not too forward, or the son too much his father's beneficiary in ecclesiastical preferments and levies, a good deal was overlooked. But, as the

Abbot had reason to recall, unions between Christian and Infidel led to sorrow. None the less, when John with mule, mails, and man, clattered off down the lane for Southampton and the sea, Stephen envied him.

He was back, twenty months later, in good hard case, and loaded down with fairings. A lump of richest lazuli, a bar of orange-hearted vermilion, and a small packet of dried beetles which make most glorious scarlet, for the Sub-Cantor. Besides that, a few cubes of milky marble, with yet a pink flush in them, which could be slaked and ground down to incomparable background-stuff. There were quite half the drugs that the Abbot and Thomas had demanded, and there was a long deep-red cornelian necklace for the Abbot's Lady—Anne of Norton. She received it graciously, and asked where John had come by it.

"Near Granada," he said.

"You left all well there?" Anne asked. (Maybe the Abbot had told her something of John's confession.)

"I left all in the hands of God."

"Ah me! How long since?"

"Four months less eleven days."

"Were you—with her?"

"In my arms. Childbed."

"And?"

"The boy too. There is nothing now."

Anne of Norton caught her breath.

"I think you'll be glad of that," she said after a while.

"Give me time, and maybe I'll compass it. But not now."

"You have your handwork and your art and—John—remember there's no jealousy in the grave."

"Ye-es! I have my Art, and Heaven knows I'm jealous of none."

"Thank God for that at least," said Anne of Norton, the always ailing woman who followed the Abbot with her sunk eyes. "And be sure I shall treasure this," she touched the beads, "as long as I shall live."

"I brought—trusted—it to you for that," he replied, and took leave. When she told the Abbot how she had come by it, he said nothing, but as he and Thomas were storing the drugs that John handed over in the cell which backs onto the hospital kitchen-chimney, he observed, of a cake of dried poppy-juice: "This has power to cut off all pain from a man's body."

"I have seen it," said John.

"But for pain of the soul there is, outside God's Grace, but one drug; and that is a man's craft, learning, or other helpful motion of his own mind."

"That is coming to me, too," was the answer.

John spent the next fair May day out in the woods with the monastery swineherd and all the porkers; and returned loaded with flowers and sprays of spring, to his own carefully kept place in the north bay of the Scriptorium. There with his traveling sketch-books under his left elbow, he sunk himself past all recollections in his Great Luke.

Brother Martin, Senior Copyist (who spoke about once a fortnight) ventured to ask, later, how the work was going.

"All here!" John tapped his forehead with his pencil. "It has been only waiting these months to—ah God!—be born. Are ye free of your plain-copying, Martin?"

Brother Martin nodded. It was his pride that John of Burgos turned to him, in spite of his seventy years, for really good page-work.

"Then see!" John laid out a new vellum—thin but flawless. "There's no better than this sheet from here to Paris. Yes! Smell it if you choose. Wherefore—give me the compasses and I'll set it out for you—if ye make one letter lighter or darker than its next, I'll stick ye like a pig."

"Never, John!" the old man beamed happily.

"But I will! Now, fellow! Here and here, as I prick, and in script of just this height to the hair's-breadth, ye'll scribe the thirty-first and thirty-second verses of Eighth Luke."

"Yes, the Gadarene Swine! '*And they besought him that he would not command them to go out into the abyss. And there was a herd of many swine'*"——Brother Martin naturally knew all the Gospels by heart.

"Just so! Down to '*and he suffered them.*' Take your time to do it. My Magdalene has to come off my heart first."

Brother Martin achieved the work so perfectly that John stole some soft sweetmeats from the Abbot's kitchen for his reward. The old man ate them; then repented; then confessed and insisted on penance. At which the Abbot, knowing there was but one way to reach the real sinner, set him a book called *De Virtutibus Herbarum* to fair-copy. St. Illod's had borrowed it from the gloomy Cistercians, who do not hold with pretty things, and the crabbed text kept Martin busy just when John wanted him for some rather specially spaced letterings.

"See now," said the Sub-Cantor reprovingly. "You should not do such things, John. Here's Brother Martin on penance for your sake——"

"No—for my Great Luke. But I've paid the Abbot's cook. I've drawn him till his own scullions cannot keep straight-faced. *He'*ll not tell again."

"Unkindly done! And you're out of favor with the Abbot too. He's made no sign to you since you came back—never asked you to high table."

"I've been busy. Having eyes in his head, Stephen knew it. Clement, there's no Librarian from Durham to Torre fit to clean up after you."

The Sub-Cantor stood on guard; he knew where John's compliments generally ended.

"But outside the Scriptorium——"

"Where I never go." The Sub-Cantor had been excused even digging in the garden, lest it should mar his wonderful book-binding hands.

"In all things outside the Scriptorium you are the master-fool of Christendie. Take it from me, Clement. I've met many."

"I take everything from you," Clement smiled beningly. "You use me worse than a singing-boy."

They could hear one of that suffering breed in the cloister below, squalling as the Cantor pulled his hair.

"God love you! So I do! But have you ever thought how I lie and steal daily on my travels—yes, and for aught you know, murder—to fetch you colors and earths?"

"True," said just and conscience-stricken Clement. "I have often thought that were I in the world—which God forbid!—I might be a strong thief in some matters."

Even Brother Martin, bent above his loathed *De Virtutibus,* laughed.

But about mid-summer, Thomas the Infirmarian conveyed to John the Abbot's invitation to supper in his house that night, with the request that he would bring with him anything that he had done for his Great Luke.

"What's toward?" said John, who had been wholly shut up in his work.

"Only one of his 'wisdom' dinners. You've sat at a few since you were a man."

"True: and mostly good. How would Stephen have us——?"

"Gown and hood over all. There will be a doctor from Salerno—one Roger, an Italian. Wise and famous with the knife on the body. He's been in the Infirmary some ten days, helping me—even me!"

" 'Never heard the name. But our Steven's *physicus* before *sacerdos,* always."

"And his Lady has a sickness of some time. Roger came hither in chief because of her."

"Did he? Now I think of it, I have not seen the Lady Anne for a while."

"Ye've seen nothing for a long while. She has been housed near a month—they have to carry her abroad now."

"So bad as that, then?"

"Roger of Salerno will not yet say what he thinks. But——"

"God pity Stephen! . . . Who else at table, beside thee?"

"An Oxford friar. Roger is his name also. A learned and famous philosopher. And he holds his liquor too, valiantly."

"Three doctors—counting Stephen. I've always found that means two atheists."

Thomas looked uneasily down his nose. "That's a wicked proverb," he stammered. "You should not use it."

"Hoh! Never come you the monk over me, Thomas! You've been Infirmarian at St. Illod's eleven years—and a lay-brother still. Why have you never taken orders, all this while?"

"I—I am not worthy."

"Ten times worthier than that new fat swine—Henry Who's-his-name—that takes the Infirmary Masses. He bullocks in with the Viaticum, under your nose, when a sick man's only faint from being bled. So the man dies—of pure fear. Ye know it! I've watched your face at such times. Take Orders, Didymus. You'll have a little more medicine and a little less Mass with your sick then; and they'll live longer."

"I am unworthy—unworthy," Thomas repeated pitifully.

"Not you—but—to your own master you stand or fall. And now that my work releases me for a while, I'll drink with any philosopher out of any school. And Thomas," he coaxed, "a hot bath for me in the Infirmary before vespers."

When the Abbot's perfectly cooked and served meal had ended, and the deep-fringed naperies were removed, and the Prior had sent in the keys with word that all was fast in the Monastery, and the keys had been duly returned with the word: "Make it so till Prime," the Abbot and his guests went out to cool themselves in an upper cloister that took them, by way of the leads, to the South Choir side of the Triforium. The summer sun was still strong, for it was barely six o'clock, but the Abbey Church, of course, lay in her wonted darkness. Lights were being lit for choir-practice thirty feet below.

"Our Cantor gives them no rest," the Abbot whispered. "Stand by this pillar and we'll hear what he's driving them at now."

"Remember all!" the Cantor's hard voice came up. "This is the soul of Bernard himself, attacking our evil world. Take it quicker than yesterday, and throw all your words clean-bitten from you. In the loft there! Begin!"

The organ broke out for an instant, alone and raging. Then the voices crashed together into that first fierce line of the *"De Contemptu Mundi."* *

"Hora novissima—tempora pessima"—a dead pause till, the assenting *sunt* broke, like a sob, out of the darkness, and one boy's voice, clearer than silver trumpets, returned the long-drawn *vigilemus.*

"Ecce minaciter, imminet Arbiter" (organ and voices were leashed together in terror and warning, breaking away liquidly to the *"ille supremus"*). Then the tone-colors shifted for the prelude to—*"Imminet, imminet, ut mala terminet——"*

"Stop! Again!" cried the Cantor; and gave his reasons a little more roundly than was natural at choir-practice.

"Ah! Pity o' man's vanity! He's guessed we are here. Come away!" said the Abbot. Anne of Norton, in her carried chair, had been listening too further along the dark Triforium, with Roger of Salerno. John heard her sob. On the way back, he asked Thomas how her health stood. Before Thomas could reply the sharp-featured Italian doctor pushed between them. "Following on our talk together, I judged it best to tell her," said he to Thomas.

"What?" John asked simply enough.

---

* Hymn No. 226, A. and M., "The world is very evil."

"What she knew already." Roger of Salerno launched into a Greek quotation to the effect that every woman knows all about everything.

"I have no Greek," said John stiffly. Roger of Salerno had been giving them a good deal of it, at dinner.

"Then I'll come to you in Latin. Ovid hath it neatly. *'Utque malum late solet immedicabile cancer*——' but doubtless you know the rest, worthy Sir."

"Alas! My school-Latin's but what I've gathered by the way from fools professing to heal sick women. *'Hocus-pocus*——' but doubtless you know the rest, worthy Sir."

Roger of Salerno was quite quiet till they regained the dining-room, where the fire had been comforted and the dates, raisins, ginger, figs, and cinnamon-scented sweetmeats set out, with the choicer wines, on the after-table. The Abbot seated himself, drew off his ring, dropped it, that all might hear the tinkle, into an empty silver cup, stretched his feet toward the hearth, and looked at the great gilt and carved rose in the barrel-roof. The silence that keeps from Compline to Matins had closed on their world. The bull-necked Friar watched a ray of sunlight split itself into colors on the rim of a crystal salt-cellar; Roger of Salerno had re-opened some discussion with Brother Thomas on a type of spotted fever that was baffling them both in England and abroad; John took note of the keen profile, and—it might serve as a note for the Great Luke—his hand moved to his bosom. The Abbot saw, and nodded permission. John whipped out silver-point and sketch-book.

"Na—modesty is good enough—but deliver your own opinion," the Italian was urging the Infirmarian. Out of courtesy to the foreigner nearly all the talk was in table-Latin; more formal and more copious than monk's patter. Thomas began with his meek stammer.

"I confess myself at a loss for the cause of the fever unless—as Varro saith in his *De Re Rustica*—certain small animals which the eye cannot follow enter the body by the nose and mouth, and set up grave diseases. On the other hand, this is not in Scripture."

Roger of Salerno hunched head and shoulders like an angry cat. "Always *that*!" he said, and John snatched down the twist of the thin lips.

"Never at rest, John," the Abbot smiled at the artist. "You should break off every two hours for prayers, as we do. St. Benedict was no fool. Two hours is all that a man can carry the edge of his eye or hand."

"For copyists—yes. Brother Martin is not sure after one hour. But when a man's work takes him, he must go on till it lets him go."

"Yes, that is the Demon of Socrates," the Friar from Oxford rumbled above his cup.

"The doctrine leans toward presumption," said the Abbot. "Remember, 'Shall mortal man be more just than his Maker?'"

"There is no danger of justice"; the Friar spoke bitterly. "But at least Man might be suffered to go forward in his Art or his thought.

Yet if Mother Church sees or hears him move anyward, what says she? 'No!' Always 'No.' "

"But if the little animals of Varro be invisible"—this was Roger of Salerno to Thomas—"how are we any nearer to a cure?"

"By experiment"—the Friar wheeled round on them suddenly. "By reason and experiment. The one is useless without the other. But Mother Church——"

"Ay!" Roger de Salerno dashed at the fresh bait like a pike. "Listen, Sirs. Her bishops—our Princes—strew our roads in Italy with carcasses that they make for their pleasure or wrath. Beautiful corpses! Yet if I—if we doctors—so much as raise the skin of one of them to look at God's fabric beneath, what says Mother Church? 'Sacrilege! Stick to your pigs and dogs, or you burn!' "

"And not Mother Church only!" the Friar chimed in. "*Every* way we are barred—barred by the words of some man, dead a thousand years, which are held final. Who is any son of Adam that his one say-so should close a door toward truth? I would not except even Peter Peregrinus, my own great teacher."

"Nor I Paul of Aegina," Roger of Salerno cried. "Listen Sirs! Here is a case to the very point. Apuleius affirmeth, if a man eat fasting of the juice of the cut-leaved buttercup—*sceleratus* we call it, which means 'rascally' "—this with a condescending nod toward John —"his soul will leave his body laughing. Now this is the lie more dangerous than truth, since truth of a sort is in it."

"He's away!" whispered the Abbot despairingly.

"For the juice of that herb, I know by experiment, burns, blisters, and wries the mouth. I know also the *rictus,* or pseudo-laughter on the face of such as have perished by the strong poisons of herbs allied to this ranunculus. Certainly that spasm resembles laughter. It seems then, in my judgment, that Apuleius, having seen the body of one thus poisoned, went off at score and wrote that the man died laughing."

"Neither staying to observe, nor to confirm observation by experiment," added the Friar, frowning.

Stephen the Abbot cocked an eyebrow toward John.

"How think *you?*" said he.

"I'm no doctor," John returned, "but I'd say Apuleius in all these years might have been betrayed by his copyists. They take shortcuts to save 'emselves trouble. Put case that Apuleius wrote the soul *seems to* leave the body laughing, after this poison. There's not three copyists in five (*my* judgment) would not leave out the 'seems to.' For who'd question Apuleius? If it seemed so to him, so it must be. Otherwise any child knows cut-leaved buttercup."

"Have you knowledge of herbs?" Roger of Salerno asked curtly.

"Only, that when I was a boy in convent, I've made tetters round my mouth and on my neck with buttercup-juice, to save going to prayer o' cold nights."

"Ah!" said Roger. "I profess no knowledge of tricks." He turned aside, stiffly.

"No matter! Now for your own tricks, John," the tactful Abbot broke in. "You shall show the doctors your Magdalene and your Gadarene Swine and the devils."

"Devils? Devils? I have produced devils by means of drugs; and have abolished them by the same means. Whether devils be external to mankind or immanent, I have not yet pronounced." Roger of Salerno was still angry.

"Ye dare not," snapped the Friar from Oxford. "Mother Church makes Her own devils."

"Not wholly! Our John has come back from Spain with brand-new ones." Abbot Stephen took the vellum handed to him, and laid it tenderly on the table. They gathered to look. The Magdalene was drawn in palest, almost transparent, grisaille, against a raging, swaying background of woman-faced devils, each broke to and by her special sin, and each, one could see, frenziedly straining against the Power that compelled her.

"I've never seen the like of this gray shadow-work," said the Abbot. "How came you by it?"

"*Non nobis!* It came to me," said John, not knowing he was a generation or so ahead of his time in the use of that medium.

"Why is she so pale?" the Friar demanded.

"Evil has all come out of her—she'd take any color now."

"Ay, like light through glass. *I* see."

Roger of Salerno was looking in silence—his nose nearer and nearer the page. "It is so," he pronounced finally. "Thus it is in epilepsy—mouth, eyes, and forehead—even to the droop of her wrist there. Every sign of it! She will need restoratives, that woman, and, afterward, sleep natural. No poppy-juice, or she will vomit on her waking. And thereafter—but I am not in my Schools." He drew himself up. "Sir," said he, "you should be of Our calling. For, by the Snakes of Aesculapius, you *see*!"

The two struck hands as equals.

"And how think you of the Seven Devils?" the Abbot went on.

These melted into convoluted flower- or flame-like bodies, ranging in color from phosphorescent green to the black purple of outworn iniquity, whose hearts could be traced beating through their substance. But, for sign of hope and the sane workings of life, to be regained, the deep border was of conventionalized spring flowers and birds, all crowned by a kingfisher in haste, atilt through a clump of yellow iris.

Roger of Salerno identified the herbs and spoke largely of their virtues.

"And now, the Gadarene Swine," said Stephen. John laid the picture on the table.

Here were devils dishoused, in dread of being abolished to the Void, huddling and hurtling together to force lodgment by every opening into the brute bodies offered. Some of the swine fought the invasion, foaming and jerking; some were surrendering to it, sleepily, as to a luxurious back-scratching; others, wholly possessed, whirled off in bucking droves for the lake beneath. In one corner the freed man stretched out his limbs all restored to his control, and Our Lord, seated, looked at him as questioning what he would make of his deliverance.

"Devils indeed!" was the Friar's comment. "But wholly a new sort."

Some devils were mere lumps, with lobes ana protuberances—a hint of a fiend's face peering through jelly-like walls. And there was a family of impatient, globular devillings who had burst open the belly of their smirking parent, and were revolving desperately toward their prey. Others patterned themselves into rods, chains and ladders, single or conjoined, round the throat and jaws of a shrieking sow, from whose ear emerged the lashing, glassy tail of a devil that had made good his refuge. And there were granulated and conglomerate devils, mixed up with the foam and slaver where the attack was fiercest. Thence the eye carried on to the insanely active backs of the downward-racing swine, the swineherd's aghast face, and his dog's terror.

Said Roger of Salerno, "I pronounce that these were begotten of drugs. They stand outside the rational mind."

"Not these," said Thomas the Infirmarian, who as a servant of the Monastery should have asked his Abbot's leave to speak. "Not *these*— look!—in the bordure."

The border to the picture was a diaper of irregular but balanced compartments or cellules, where sat, swam, or weltered, devils in blank, so to say—things as yet uninspired by Evil—indifferent, but lawlessly outside imagination. Their shapes resembled, again, ladders, chains, scourges, diamonds, aborted buds, or gravid phosphorescent globes— some well-nigh star-like.

Roger of Salerno compared them to the obsessions of a Churchman's mind.

"Malignant?" the Friar from Oxford questioned.

"'Count everything unknown for horrible,'" Roger quoted with scorn.

"Not I. But they are marvelous—marvelous. I think——"

The Friar drew back. Thomas edged in to see better, and half opened his mouth.

"Speak," said Stephen, who had been watching him. "We are all in a sort doctors here."

"I would say then"—Thomas rushed at it as one putting out his life's belief at the stake—"that these lower shapes in the bordure may not be so much hellish and malignant as models and patterns upon which John has tricked out and embellished his proper devils among the swine above there!"

"And that would signify?" said Roger of Salerno sharply.

"In my poor judgment, that he may have seen such shapes—without help of drugs."

"Now who—*who*"—said John of Burgos, after a round and unregarded oath—"has made thee so wise of a sudden, my Doubter?"

"I wise? God forbid! Only John, remember—one winter six years ago—the snowflakes melting on your sleeve at the cookhouse-door. You showed me them through a little crystal, that made small things larger."

"Yes. The Moors call such a glass the Eye of Allah," John confirmed.

"You showed me them melting—six-sided. You called them, then, your patterns."

"True. Snow-flakes melt six-sided. I have used them for diaper-work often."

"Melting snow-flakes as seen through a glass? By art optical?" the Friar asked.

"Art optical? *I* have never heard!" Roger of Salerno cried.

"John," said the Abbot of St. Illod's commandingly, "was it—is it so?"

"In some sort," John replied, "Thomas has the right of it. Those shapes in the bordure were my workshop-patterns for the devils above. In *my* craft, Salerno, we dare not drug. It kills hand and eye. My shapes are to be seen honestly, in nature."

The Abbot drew a bowl of rose-water toward him. "When I was a prisoner with—with the Saracens after Mansura," he began, turning up the fold of his long sleeve, "there were certain magicians—physicians—who could show—" he dipped his third finger delicately in the water—"all the firmament of Hell, as it were, in—" he shook off one drop from his polished nail on to the polished table—"even such a supernaculum as this."

"But it must be foul water—not clean," said John.

"Show us then—all—all," said Stephen. "I would make sure—once more." The Abbot's voice was official.

John drew from his bosom a stamped leather box, some six or eight inches long, wherein, bedded on faded velvet, lay what looked like silver-bound compasses of old box-wood, with a screw at the head which opened or closed the legs to minute fractions. The legs termined, not in points, but spoon-shapedly, one spatula pierced with a metal-lined hole less than a quarter of an inch across, the other with a half-inch hole. Into this latter John, after carefully wiping with a silk rag, slipped a metal cylinder that carried glass or crystal, it seemed, at each end.

"Ah! Art optic!" said the Friar. "But what is that beneath it?"

It was a small swivelling sheet of polished silver no bigger than a florin, which caught the light and concentrated it on the lesser hole. John adjusted it without the Friar's proffered help.

"And now to find a drop of water," said he, picking up a small brush.

"Come to my upper cloister. The sun is on the leads still," said the Abbot, rising.

They followed him there. Halfway along, a drip from a gutter had made a greenish puddle in a worn stone. Very carefully, John dropped a drop of it into the smaller hole of the compass-leg, and, steadying the apparatus on a coping, worked the screw in the compass-joint, screwed the cylinder, and swung the swivel of the mirror till he was satisfied.

"Good!" He peered through the thing. "My Shapes are all here. Now look, Father! If they do not meet your eye at first, turn this nicked edge here, left or right-handed."

"I have not forgotten," said the Abbot, taking his place. "Yes! They are here—as they were in my time—my time past. There is no end to them, I was told. . . . There *is* no end!"

"The light will go. Oh, let me look! Suffer me to see, also!" the Friar pleaded, almost shouldering Stephen from the eye-piece. The Abbot gave way. His eyes were on time past. But the Friar, instead of looking, turned the apparatus in his capable hands.

"Nay, nay," John interrupted, for the man was already fiddling at the screws. "Let the Doctor see."

Roger of Salerno looked, minute after minute. John saw his blue-veined cheek-bones turn white. He stepped back at last, as though stricken.

"It is a new world—a new world and—Oh, God Unjust!—I am old!"

"And now Thomas," Stephen ordered.

John manipulated the tube for the Infirmarian, whose hands shook, and he too looked long. "It is Life," he said presently in a breaking voice. "No Hell! Life created and rejoicing—the work of the Creator. They live, even as I have dreamed. Then it was no sin for me to dream. No sin—O God—no sin!"

He flung himself on his knees and began hysterically the *Benedicite omnia Opera.*

"And now I will see how it is actuated," said the Friar from Oxford, thrusting forward again.

"Bring it within. The place is all eyes and ears," said Stephen.

They walked quietly back along the leads, three English counties laid out in evening sunshine around them; church upon church, monastery upon monastery, cell after cell, and the bulk of a vast cathedral moored on the edge of the banked shoals of sunset.

When they were at the after-table once more they sat down, all except the Friar who went to the window and huddled bat-like over the thing. "I see! I see!" he was repeating to himself.

"He'll not hurt it," said John. But the Abbot, staring in front of him, like Roger of Salerno, did not hear. The Infirmarian's head was on the table between his shaking arms.

John reached for a cup of wine.

"It was shown to me," the Abbot was speaking to himself, "in Cairo, that man stands ever between two Infinities—of greatness and littleness. Therefore, there is no end—either to life—or——"

"And *I* stand on the edge of the grave," snarled Roger of Salerno. "Who pities *me?*"

"Hush!" said Thomas the Infirmarian. "The little creatures shall be sanctified—sanctified to the service of His sick."

"What need?" John of Burgos wiped his lips. "It shows no more than the shapes of things. It gives good pictures. I had it at Granada. It was brought from the East, they told me."

Roger of Salerno laughed with an old man's malice. "What of Mother Church? Most Holy Mother Church? If it comes to Her ears that we have spied into Her Hell without Her leave, where do we stand?"

"At the stake," said the Abbot of St. Illod's, and, raising his voice a trifle. "You hear that? Roger Bacon, heard you that?"

The Friar turned from the window, clutching the compasses tighter.

"No, no!" he appealed. "Not with Falcodi—not with our English-hearted Foulkes made Pope. He's wise—he's learned. He reads what I have put forth. Foulkes would never suffer it."

" 'Holy Pope is one thing, Holy Church another,' " Roger quoted.

"But I—*I* can bear witness it is no Art Magic," the Friar went on. "Nothing is it, except Art optical—wisdom after trial and experiment, mark you. I can prove it, and—my name weighs with men who dare think."

"Find them!" croaked Roger of Salerno. "Five or six in all the world. That makes less than fifty pounds by weight of ashes at the stake. I have watched such men—reduced."

"I will not give this up!" The Friar's voice cracked in passion and despair. "It would be to sin against the Light."

"No, no! Let us—let us sanctify the little animals of Varro," said Thomas.

Stephen leaned forward, fished his ring out of the cup, and slipped it on his finger. "My sons," said he, "we have seen what we have seen."

"That it is no magic but simple Art," the Friar persisted.

" 'Avails nothing. In the eyes of Mother Church we have seen more than is permitted to man."

"But it was Life—created and rejoicing," said Thomas.

"To look into Hell as we shall be judged—as we shall be proved—to have looked, is for priests only."

"Or green-sick virgins on the road to sainthood who, for cause any mid-wife could give you——"

The Abbot's half-lifted hand checked Roger of Salerno's outpouring.

"Nor may even priests see more in Hell than Church knows to be there. John, there is respect due to Church as well as to Devils."

"My trade's the outside of things," said John quietly. "I have my patterns."

"But you may need to look again for more," the Friar said.

"In my craft, a thing done is done with. We go on to new shapes after that."

"And if we trespass beyond bounds, even in thought, we lie open to the judgment of the Church," the Abbot continued.

"But thou knowest—*knowest!*" Roger of Salerno had returned to the attack. "Here's all the world in darkness concerning the causes of things—from the fever across the lane to thy Lady's—eating malady. Think!"

"I have thought upon it, Salerno! I have thought indeed."

Thomas the Infirmarian lifted his head again; and this time he did not stammer at all. "As in the water, so in the blood must they rage and war with each other! I have dreamed these ten years—I thought it was a sin—but my dreams and Varro's are true! Think on it again! Here's the Light under our very hand!"

"Quench it! You'd no more stand to roasting than—any other. I'll give you the case as Church—as I myself—would frame it. Our John here returns from the Moors, and shows us a hell of devils contending in the compass of one drop of water. Magic past clearance! You can hear the faggots crackle."

"But thou knowest! Thou hast seen it all before! For man's poor sake! For old friendship's sake—Stephen!" The Friar was trying to stuff the compasses into his bosom as he appealed.

"What Stephen de Sautré knows, you his friends know also. I would have you, now, obey the Abbot of St. Illod's. Give to me!" He held out his ringed hand.

"May I—may John here—not even make a drawing of one—one screw?" said the broken Friar, in spite of himself.

"Nowise!" Stephen took it over. "Your dagger, John. Sheathed will serve."

He unscrewed the metal cylinder, laid it on the table, and with the dagger's hilt smashed some crystal to sparkling dust which he swept into a scooped hand and cast behind the hearth.

"It would seem," said he, "the choice lies between two sins. To deny the world a Light which is under our hand, or to enlighten the world before her time. What you have seen, I saw long since among the physicians at Cairo. And I know what doctrine they drew from it. Hast *thou* dreamed, Thomas? I also—with fuller knowledge. But this birth, my sons, is untimely. It will be but the mother of more death, more torture, more division, and greater darkness in this dark age. Therefore I, who know both my world and the Church, take this Choice on my conscience. Go! It is finished."

He thrust the wooden part of the compasses deep among the beech logs till all was burned.

SOMERSET MAUGHAM

Red

William Somerset Maugham, born in 1874, was educated at King's School, Canterbury, Heidelberg University and St. Thomas's Hospital. He served in the Secret Service during the First World War. His best known novels are *Of Human Bondage, The Moon and Sixpence* and *Cakes and Ale*. Among his plays are *Our Betters* and *The Circle*. He has published many famous short stories. [From *The Trembling of a Leaf* by W. Somerset Maugham; copyright 1921 by Doubleday & Company, Inc.; used by permission of Doubleday & Company, Inc.]

THE SKIPPER THRUST HIS HAND into one of his trouser pockets and with difficulty, for they were not at the sides but in front and he was a portly man, pulled out a large silver watch. He looked at it and then looked again at the declining sun. The Kanaka at the wheel gave him a glance, but did not speak. The skipper's eyes rested on the island they were approaching. A white line of foam marked the reef. He knew there was an opening large enough to get his ship through, and when they came a little nearer he counted on seeing it. They had nearly an hour of daylight still before them. In the lagoon the water was deep and they could anchor comfortably. The chief of the village which he could already see among the coconut trees was a friend of the mate's, and it would be pleasant to go ashore for the night. The mate came forward at that minute and the skipper turned to him.

"We'll take a bottle of booze along with us and get some girls in to dance," he said.

"I don't see the opening," said the mate.

He was a Kanaka, a handsome, swarthy fellow, with somewhat the look of a later Roman emperor, inclined to stoutness; but his face was fine and clean-cut.

"I'm dead sure there's one right here," said the captain, looking through his glasses. "I can't understand why I can't pick it up. Send one of the boys up the mast to have a look."

The mate called one of the crew and gave him the order. The captain watched the Kanaka climb and waited for him to speak. But the Kanaka shouted down that he could see nothing but the unbroken line of foam. The captain spoke Samoan like a native, and he cursed him freely.

"Shall he stay up there?" asked the mate.

"What the hell good does that do?" answered the captain. "The blame fool can't see worth a cent. You bet your sweet life I'd find the opening if I was up there."

He looked at the slender mast with anger. It was all very well for a

171

native who had been used to climbing up coconut trees all his life. He
was fat and heavy.

"Come down," he shouted. "You're no more use than a dead dog.
We'll just have to go along the reef till we find the opening."

It was a seventy-ton schooner with paraffin auxiliary, and it ran, when
there was no head wind, between four and five knots an hour. It was a
bedraggled object; it had been painted white a very long time ago, but
it was now dirty, dingy, and mottled. It smelt strongly of paraffin and
of the copra which was its usual cargo. They were within a hundred
feet of the reef now and the captain told the steersman to run along it
till they came to the opening. But when they had gone a couple of
miles he realized that they had missed it. He went about and slowly
worked back again. The white foam of the reef continued without
interruption and now the sun was setting. With a curse at the stupidity
of the crew the skipper resigned himself to waiting till next morning.

"Put her about," he said. "I can't anchor here."

They went out to sea a little and presently it was quite dark. They
anchored. When the sail was furled the ship began to roll a good deal.
They said in Apia that one day she would roll right over; and the
owner, a German-American who managed one of the largest stores,
said that no money was big enough to induce him to go out in her.
The cook, a Chinese in white trousers, very dirty and ragged, and a
thin white tunic, came to say that supper was ready, and when the
skipper went into the cabin he found the engineer already seated at
table. The engineer was a long, lean man with a scraggy neck. He was
dressed in blue overalls and a sleeveless jersey which showed his thin
arms tatooed from elbow to wrist.

"Hell, having to spend the night outside," said the skipper.

The engineer did not answer, and they ate their supper in silence.
The cabin was lit by a dim oil lamp. When they had eaten the canned
apricots with which the meal finished the Chink brought them a cup of
tea. The skipper lit a cigar and went on the upper deck. The island
now was only a darker mass against the night. The stars were very
bright. The only sound was the ceaseless breaking of the surf. The
skipper sank into a deck-chair and smoked idly. Presently three or
four members of the crew came up and sat down. One of them had a
banjo and another a concertina. They began to play, and one of them
sang. The native song sounded strange on these instruments. Then
to the singing a couple began to dance. It was a barbaric dance, savage
and primeval, rapid, with quick movements of the hands and feet and
contortions of the body; it was sensual, sexual even, but sexual without
passion. It was very animal, direct, weird without mystery, natural in
short, and one might almost say childlike. At last they grew tired.
They stretched themselves on the deck and slept, and all was silent.
The skipper lifted himself heavily out of his chair and clambered down
the companion. He went into his cabin and got out of his clothes. He

climbed into his bunk and lay there. He panted a little in the heat of the night.

But next morning, when the dawn crept over the tranquil sea, the opening in the reef which had eluded them the night before was seen a little to the east of where they lay. The schooner entered the lagoon. There was not a ripple on the surface of the water. Deep down among the coral rocks you saw little colored fish swim. When he had anchored his ship the skipper ate his breakfast and went on deck. The sun shone from an unclouded sky, but in the early morning the air was grateful and cool. It was Sunday, and there was a feeling of quietness, a silence as though nature were at rest, which gave him a peculiar sense of comfort. He sat, looking at the wooded coast, and felt lazy and well at ease. Presently a slow smile moved his lips and he threw the stump of his cigar into the water.

"I guess I'll go ashore," he said. "Get the boat out."

He climbed stiffly down the ladder and was rowed to a little cove. The coconut trees came down to the water's edge, not in rows, but spaced out with an ordered formality. They were like a ballet of spinsters, elderly but flippant, standing in affected attitudes with the simpering graces of a bygone age. He sauntered idly through them, along a path that could be just seen winding its tortuous way, and it led him presently to a broad creek. There was a bridge across it, but a bridge constructed of single trunks of coconut trees, a dozen of them, placed end to end and supported where they met by a forked branch driven into the bed of the creek. You walked on a smooth, round surface, narrow and slippery, and there was no support for the hand. To cross such a bridge required sure feet and a stout heart. The skipper hesitated. But he saw on the other side, nestling among the trees, a white man's house; he made up his mind and, rather gingerly, began to walk. He watched his feet carefully, and where one trunk joined on to the next and there was a difference of level, he tottered a little. It was with a gasp of relief that he reached the last tree and finally set his feet on the firm ground of the other side. He had been so intent on the difficult crossing that he never noticed anyone was watching him, and it was with surprise that he heard himself spoken to.

"It takes a bit of nerve to cross these bridges when you're not used to them."

He looked up and saw a man standing in front of him. He had evidently come out of the house which he had seen.

"I saw you hesitate," the man continued, with a smile on his lips, "and I was watching to see you fall in."

"Not on your life," said the captain, who had now recovered his confidence.

"I've fallen in myself before now. I remember, one evening I came back from shooting, and I fell in, gun and all. Now I get a boy to carry my gun for me."

He was a man no longer young, with a small beard, now somewhat gray, and a thin face. He was dressed in a singlet, without arms, and a pair of duck trousers. He wore neither shoes nor socks. He spoke English with a slight accent.

"Are you Neilson?" asked the skipper.

"I am."

"I've heard about you. I thought you lived somewhere round here."

The skipper followed his host into the little bungalow and sat down heavily in the chair which the other motioned him to take. While Neilson went out to fetch whisky and glasses he took a look round the room. It filled him with amazement. He had never seen so many books. The shelves reached from floor to ceiling on all four walls, and they were closely packed. There was a grand piano littered with music, and a large table on which books and magazines lay in disorder. The room made him feel embarrassed. He remembered that Neilson was a queer fellow. No one knew very much about him, although he had been in the islands for so many years, but those who knew him agreed that he was queer. He was a Swede.

"You've got one big heap of books here," he said, when Neilson returned.

"They do no narm," answered Neilson with a smile.

"Have you read them all?" asked the skipper.

"Most of them."

"I'm a bit of a reader myself. I have the *Saturday Evening Post* sent me regler."

Neilson poured his visitor a good stiff glass of whisky and gave him a cigar. The skipper volunteered a little information.

"I got in last night, but I couldn't find the opening, so I had to anchor outside. I never been this run before, but my people had some stuff they wanted to bring over here. Gray, d'you know him?"

"Yes, he's got a store a little way along."

"Well, there was a lot of canned stuff that he wanted over, an' he's got some copra. They thought I might just as well come over as lie idle at Apia. I run between Apia and Pago-Pago mostly, but they've got smallpox there just now, and there's nothing stirring."

He took a drink of his whisky and lit a cigar. He was a taciturn man, but there was something in Neilson that made him nervous, and his nervousness made him talk. The Swede was looking at him with large dark eyes in which there was an expression of faint amusement.

"This is a tidy little place you've got here."

"I've done my best with it."

"You must do pretty well with your trees. They look fine. With copra at the price it is now. I had a bit of a plantation myself once, in Upolu it was, but I had to sell it."

He looked round the room again, where all those books gave him a feeling of something incomprehensible and hostile.

"I guess you must find it a bit lonesome here though," he said.

"I've got used to it. I've been here for twenty-five years."

Now the captain could think of nothing more to say, and he smoked in silence. Neilson had apparently no wish to break it. He looked at his guest with a meditative eye. He was a tall man, more than six feet high, and very stout. His face was red and blotchy, with a network of little purple veins on the cheeks, and his features were sunk into its fatness. His eyes were bloodshot. His neck was buried in rolls of fat. But for a fringe of long curly hair, nearly white, at the back of his head he was quite bald; and that immense, shiny surface of forehead, which might have given him a false look of intelligence, on the contrary gave him one of peculiar imbecility. He wore a blue flannel shirt, open at the neck and showing his fat chest covered with a mat of reddish hair, and a very old pair of blue serge trousers. He sat in his chair in a heavy ungainly attitude, his great belly thrust forward and his fat legs uncrossed. All elasticity had gone from his limbs. Neilson wondered idly what sort of man he had been in his youth. It was almost impossible to imagine that this creature of vast bulk had ever been a boy who ran about. The skipper finished his whisky, and Neilson pushed the bottle toward him.

"Help yourself."

The skipper leaned forward and with his great hand seized it.

"And how come you in these parts anyways?" he said.

"Oh, I came out to the islands for my health. My lungs were bad and they said I hadn't a year to live. You see they were wrong."

"I meant, how come you to settle down right here?"

"I am a sentimentalist."

"Oh!"

Neilson knew that the skipper had not an idea what he meant, and he looked at him with an ironical twinkle in his dark eyes. Perhaps just because the skipper was so gross and dull a man the whim seized him to talk further.

"You were too busy keeping your balance to notice, when you crossed the bridge, but this spot is generally considered rather pretty."

"It's a cute little house you've got here."

"Ah, that wasn't here when I first came. There was a native hut, with its beehive roof and its pillars, overshadowed by a great tree with red flowers; and the croton bushes, their leaves yellow and red and golden, made a pied fence around it. And then all about were the coconut trees, as fanciful as women, and as vain. They stood at the water's edge and spent all day looking at their reflections. I was a young man then—Good Heavens, it's a quarter of a century ago—and I wanted to enjoy all the loveliness of the world in the short time allotted to me before I passed into the darkness. I thought it was the most beautiful spot I had ever seen. The first time I saw it I had a catch at my heart, and I was afraid I was going to cry. I wasn't more than twenty-five, and though I put the best face I could on it, I didn't want to die. And somehow it seemed to me that the very beauty of this place made it easier for me to accept my fate. I felt when I came here that all my past life had fallen away, Stockholm and its University, and then Bonn: it all seemed the life of somebody else, as though now at last I had achieved the reality which our doctors of philosophy—I am one myself, you know—had discussed so much. 'A year,' I cried to myself, 'I have a year. I will spend it here and then I am content to die.'

"We are foolish and sentimental and melodramatic at twenty-five, but if we weren't perhaps we should be less wise at fifty.

"Now drink, my friend. Don't let the nonsense I talk interfere with you."

He waved his thin hand toward the bottle, and the skipper finished what remained in his glass.

"You ain't drinking nothin'," he said, reaching for the whisky.

"I am of a sober habit," smiled the Swede. "I intoxicate myself in ways which I fancy are more subtle. But perhaps that is only vanity. Anyhow, the effects are more lasting and the results less deleterious."

"They say there's a deal of cocaine taken in the States now," said the captain.

Neilson chuckled.

"But I do not see a white man often," he continued, "and for once I don't think a drop of whisky can do me any harm."

He poured himself out a little, added some soda, and took a sip.

"And presently I found out why the spot had such an unearthly loveliness. Here love had tarried for a moment like a migrant bird that happens on a ship in mid-ocean and for a little while folds its tired wings. The fragrance of a beautiful passion hovered over it like the fragrance of hawthorn in May in the meadows of my home. It seems to me that the places where men have loved or suffered keep about them always some faint aroma of something that has not wholly died. It is as though they had acquired a spiritual significance which mysteriously affects those who pass. I wish I could make myself clear." He smiled a little. "Though I cannot imagine that if I did you would understand."

He paused.

"I think this place was beautiful because here had been loved beautifully." And now he shrugged his shoulders. "But perhaps it is only that my aesthetic sense is gratified by the happy conjunction of young love and a suitable setting."

Even a man less thick-witted than the skipper might have been forgiven if he were bewildered by Neilson's words. For he seemed faintly to laugh at what he said. It was as though he spoke from emotion which his intellect found ridiculous. He had said himself that he was a sentimentalist, and when sentimentality is joined with skepticism there is often the devil to pay.

He was silent for an instant and looked at the captain with eyes in which there was a sudden perplexity.

"You know, I can't help thinking that I've seen you before somewhere or other," he said.

"I couldn't say as I remember you," returned the skipper.

"I have a curious feeling as though your face were familiar to me. It's been puzzling me for some time. But I can't situate my recollection in any place or at any time."

The skipper massively shrugged his heavy shoulders.

"It's thirty years since I first come to the islands. A man can't figure on remembering all the folk he meets in a while like that."

The Swede shook his head.

"You know how one sometimes has the feeling that a place one has never been to before is strangely familiar. That's how I seem to see you." He gave a whimsical smile. "Perhaps I knew you in some past existence. Perhaps, perhaps you were the master of a galley in ancient Rome and I was a slave at the oar. Thirty years have you been here?"

"Every bit of thirty years."

"I wonder if you knew a man called Red?"

"Red?"

"That is the only name I've ever known him by. I never knew him personally. I never even set eyes on him. And yet I seem to see him more clearly than many men, my brothers, for instance, with whom I passed my daily life for many years. He lives in my imagination with the distinctness of a Paolo Malatesta or a Romeo. But I daresay you have never read Dante or Shakespeare?"

"I can't say as I have," said the captain.

Neilson, smoking a cigar, leaned back in his chair and looked vacantly at the ring of smoke which floated in the still air. A smile played on his lips, but his eyes were grave. Then he looked at the captain. There was in his gross obesity something extraordinarily repellent. He had the plethoric self-satisfaction of the very fat. It was an outrage. It set Neilson's nerves on edge. But the contrast between the man before him and man he had in mind was pleasant.

"It appears that Red was the most comely thing you ever saw. I've talked to quite a number of people who knew him in those days, white men, and they all agree that the first time you saw him his beauty just took your breath away. They called him Red on account of his flaming hair. It had a natural wave and he wore it long. It must have been of that wonderful color that the pre-Raphaelites raved over. I don't think he was vain of it, he was much too ingenuous for that, but no one could have blamed him if he had been. He was tall, six feet and an inch or two—in the native house that used to stand here was the mark of his height cut with a knife on the central trunk that supported the roof—and he was made like a Greek god, broad in the shoulders and thin in the flanks; he was like Apollo, with just that soft roundness which Praxiteles gave him, and that suave, feminine grace which has in it something troubling and mysterious. His skin was dazzling white, milky, like satin; his skin was like a woman's."

"I had kind of a white skin myself when I was a kiddie," said the skipper, with a twinkle in his bloodshot eyes.

But Neilson paid no attention to him. He was telling his story now and interruption made him impatient.

"And his face was just as beautiful as his body. He had large blue eyes, very dark, so that some say they were black, and unlike most red-haired people he had dark eyebrows and long dark lashes. His features were perfectly regular and his mouth was like a scarlet wound. He was twenty."

On these words the Swede stopped with a certain sense of the dramatic. He took a sip of whisky.

"He was unique. There never was anyone more beautiful. There was no more reason for him than for a wonderful blossom to flower on a wild plant. He was a happy accident of nature.

"One day he landed at that cove into which you must have put this morning. He was an American sailor, and he had deserted from a man-of-war in Apia. He had induced some good-humored native to give him a passage on a cutter that happened to be sailing from Apia to Safoto, and he had been put ashore here in a dugout. I do not know why he deserted. Perhaps life on a man-of-war with its restrictions irked him, perhaps he was in trouble, and perhaps it was the South Seas and these romantic islands that got into his bones. Every now and then they take a man strangely, and he finds himself like a fly in a spider's web. It may be that there was a softness of fiber in him, and these green hills with their soft airs, this blue sea, took the northern strength from him as Delilah took the Nazarite's. Anyhow, he wanted to hide himself, and he thought he would be safe in this secluded nook till his ship had sailed from Samoa.

"There was a native hut at the cove and as he stood there, wondering where exactly he should turn his steps, a young girl came out and invited him to enter. He knew scarcely two words of the native tongue and she as little English. But he understood well enough what her smiles meant, and her pretty gestures, and he followed her. He sat down on a mat and she gave him slices of pineapple to eat. I can speak of Red only from hearsay, but I saw the girl three years after he first met her, and she was scarcely nineteen then. You cannot imagine how exquisite she was. She had the passionate grace of the hibiscus and the rich color. She was rather tall, slim, with the delicate features of her race, and large eyes like pools of still water under the palm trees; her hair, black and curling, fell down her back, and she wore a wreath of scented flowers. Her hands were lovely. They were so small, so exquisitely formed, they gave your heart-strings a wrench. And in those days she laughed easily. Her smile was so delightful that it made your knees shake. Her skin was like a field of ripe corn on a summer day.

Good Heavens, how can I describe her? She was too beautiful to be real.

"And these two young things, she was sixteen and he was twenty, fell in love with one another at first sight. That is the real love, not the love that comes from sympathy, common interests, or intellectual community, but love pure and simple. That is the love that Adam felt for Eve when he awoke and found her in the garden gazing at him with dewy eyes. That is the love that draws the beasts to one another, and the Gods. That is the love that makes the world a miracle. That is the love which gives life its pregnant meaning. You have never heard of the wise, cynical French duke who said that with two lovers there is always one who loves and one who lets himself be loved; it is a bitter truth to which most of us have to resign ourselves; but now and then there are two who love and two who let themselves be loved. Then one might fancy that the sun stands still as it stood when Joshua prayed to the God of Israel.

"And even now after all these years, when I think of these two, so young, so fair, so simple, and of their love, I feel a pang. It tears my heart just as my heart is torn when on certain nights I watch the full moon shining on the lagoon from an unclouded sky. There is always pain in the contemplation of perfect beauty.

"They were children. She was good and sweet and kind. I know nothing of him, and I like to think that then at all events he was ingenuous and frank. I like to think that his soul was as comely as his body. But I daresay he had no more soul than the creatures of the woods and forests who made pipes from reeds and bathed in the mountain streams when the world was young, and you might catch sight of little fawns galloping through the glade on the back of a bearded centaur. A soul is a troublesome possession and when man developed it he lost the Garden of Eden.

"Well, when Red came to the island it had recently been visited by one of those epidemics which the white man has brought to the South Seas, and one third of the inhabitants had died. It seems that the girl had lost all her near kin and she lived now in the house of distant cousins. The household consisted of two ancient crones, bowed and wrinkled, two younger women, and a man and a boy. For a few days he stayed there. But perhaps he felt himself too near the shore, with the possibility that he might fall in with white men who would reveal his hiding-place; perhaps the lovers could not bear that the company of others should rob them for an instant of the delight of being together. One morning they set out, the pair of them, with the few things that belonged to the girl, and walked along a grassy path under the coco-nuts, till they came to the creek you see. They had to cross the bridge you crossed, and the girl laughed gleefully because he was afraid. She held his hand till they came to the end of the first tree, and then his courage failed him and he had to go back. He was obliged to take off all his clothes before he could risk it, and she carried them over for him on her head. They settled down in the empty hut that stood here. Whether she had any rights over it (land tenure is a complicated business in the islands), or whether the owner had died during the epidemic, I do not know, but anyhow no one questioned them, and they took possession. Their furniture consisted of a couple of grass mats on which they slept, a fragment of looking-glass, and a bowl or two. In this pleasant land that is enough to start housekeeping on.

"They say that happy people have no history, and certainly a happy love has none. They did nothing all day long and yet the days seemed all too short. The girl had a native name, but Red called her Sally. He picked up the easy language very quickly, and he used to lie on the mat for hours while she chattered gaily to him. He was a silent fellow, and perhaps his mind was lethargic. He smoked incessantly the cigarettes which she made him out of the native tobacco and pandanus leaf, and he watched her while with deft fingers she made grass mats. Often natives would come in and tell long stories of the old days when the island was disturbed by tribal wars. Sometimes he would go fishing on the reef, and bring home a basket full of colored fish. Sometimes at night he would go out with a lantern to catch lobster. There were plantains round the hut and Sally would roast them for their frugal meal. She knew how to make delicious messes from coconuts, and the breadfruit tree by the side of the creek gave them its fruit. On feast-days they killed a little pig and cooked it on hot stones. They bathed together in the creek; and in the evening they went down to the lagoon and paddled about in a dugout, with its great outrigger. The sea was deep blue, wine-colored at sundown, like the sea of Homeric Greece; but in the lagoon the color had an infinite variety, aquamarine and amethyst and emerald; and the setting sun turned it for a short moment to liquid gold. Then there was the color of the coral, brown, white, pink, red, purple; and the shapes it took were marvelous. It was like a magic garden, and the hurrying fish were like butterflies. It strangely lacked reality. Among the coral were pools with a floor of white sand and here, where the water was dazzling clear, it was very good to bathe. Then, cool and happy, they wandered back in the gloaming over the soft grass road to the creek, walking hand in hand, and now the mynah birds filled the coconut trees with their clamor. And then the night, with that great sky shining with gold, that seemed to stretch more widely than the skies of Europe, and the soft airs that blew gently through the open hut, the long night again was all too short. She was sixteen and he was barely twenty. The dawn crept in among the wooden pillars of the hut and looked at those lovely children sleeping in one another's arms. The sun hid behind the great tattered leaves of the plantains so that it might not disturb them, and then, with playful malice, shot a golden ray, like the outstretched paw of a Persian cat, on their faces. They opened their sleepy eyes and they smiled to welcome another day. The weeks lengthened into months, and a year passed. They seemed to love one another as—I hesitate to say passionately, for passion has in it always a shade of sadness, a touch of bitterness or anguish, but as wholeheartedly, as simply and naturally as on that first day on which, meeting, they had recognized that a god was in them.

"If you had asked them I have no doubt that they would have thought it impossible to suppose their love could ever cease. Do we not know that the essential element of love is a belief in its own eternity? And yet perhaps in Red there was already a very little seed, unknown to himself and unsuspected by the girl, which would in time have grown to weariness. For one day one of the natives from the cove told them that some way down the coast at the anchorage was a British whalingship.

"'Gee,' he said, 'I wonder if I could make a trade of some nuts and plantains for a pound or two of tobacco.'

"The pandanus cigarettes that Sally made him with untiring hands were strong and pleasant enough to smoke, but they left him unsatisfied; and he yearned on a sudden for real tobacco, hard, rank, and pungent. He had not smoked a pipe for many months. His mouth watered at the thought of it. One would have thought some premonition of harm would have made Sally seek to dissuade him, but love possessed her so completely that it never occurred to her any power on earth could take him from her. They went up into the hills together and gathered a great basket of wild oranges, green, but sweet and juicy; and they picked plantains from around the hut, and coconuts from their trees, and breadfruit and mangoes; and they carried them down to the cove. They loaded the unstable canoe with them, and Red and the native boy who had brought them the news of the ship paddled along outside the reef.

"It was the last time she ever saw him.

"Next day the boy came back alone. He was all in tears. This is the story he told. When after their long paddle they reached the ship and Red hailed it, a white man looked over the side and told them to come on board. They took the fruit they had brought with them and Red piled it up on the deck. The white man and he began to talk, and they seemed to come to some agreement. One of them went below and brought up tobacco. Red took some at once and lit a pipe. The boy imitated the zest with which he blew a great cloud of smoke from his mouth. Then they said something to him and he went into the cabin. Through the open door the boy, watching curiously, saw a bottle brought out and glasses. Red drank and smoked. They seemed to ask him something, for he shook his head and laughed. The man, the first man who had spoken to them, laughed too, and he filled Red's glass once more. They went on talking and drinking, and presently, growing tired of watching a sight that meant nothing to him, the boy curled himself up on the deck and slept. He was awakened by a kick; and, jumping to his feet, he saw that the ship was slowly sailing out of the lagoon. He caught sight of Red seated at the table, with his head resting heavily on his arms, fast asleep. He made a movement toward him, intending to wake him, but a rough hand seized his arm, and a man, with a scowl and words which he did not understand, pointed to the side. He shouted to Red, but in a moment he was seized and flung overboard. Helpless, he swam round to his canoe which was drifting a little way off, and pushed it on to the reef. He climbed in and, sobbing all the way, paddled back to shore.

"What had happened was obvious enough. The whaler, by desertion or sickness, was short of hands, and the captain when Red came aboard had asked him to sign on; on his refusal he had made him drunk and kidnaped him.

"Sally was beside herself with grief. For three days she screamed and cried. The natives did what they could to comfort her, but she would not be comforted. She would not eat. And then, exhausted, she sank into a sullen apathy. She spent long days at the cove, watching the lagoon, in the vain hope that Red somehow or other would manage to escape. She sat on the white sand, hour after hour, with the tears running down her cheeks, and at night dragged herself wearily back across the creek to the little hut where she had been happy. The people with whom she had lived before Red came to the island wished her to return to them, but she would not; she was convinced that Red would come back, and she wanted him to find her where he had left her. Four months later she was delivered of a still-born child, and the old woman who had come to help her through her confinement remained with her in the hut. All joy was taken from her life. If her anguish with time became less intolerable it was replaced by a settled melancholy. You would not have thought that among these people, whose emotions, though so violent, are very transient, a woman could be found capable of so enduring a passion. She never lost the profound conviction that sooner or later Red would come back. She watched for him, and every time someone crossed this slender little bridge of coconut trees she looked. It might at last be he."

Neilson stopped talking and gave a faint sigh.

"And what happened to her in the end?" asked the skipper.

Neilson smiled bitterly.

"Oh, three years afterward she took up with another white man."

The skipper gave a fat, cynical chuckle.

"That's generally what happens to them," he said.

The Swede shot him a look of hatred. He did not know why that gross, obese man excited in him so violent a repulsion. But his thoughts wandered and he found his mind filled with memories of the past. He went back five and twenty years. It was when he first came to the island, weary of Apia, with its heavy drinking, its gambling and coarse sensuality, a sick man, trying to resign himself to the loss of the career which had fired his imagination with ambitious thoughts. He set behind him resolutely all his hopes of making a great name for himself and strove to content himself with the few poor months of careful life which was all that he could count on. He was boarding with a half-caste trader who had a store a couple of miles along the coast at the edge of a native village; and one day, wandering aimlessly along the grassy paths of the coconut groves, he had come upon the hut in which Sally lived. The beauty of the spot had filled him with a rapture so great that it was almost painful, and then he had seen Sally. She was the loveliest creature he had ever seen, and the sadness in those dark, magnificent eyes of hers affected him strangely. The Kanakas were a handsome race, and beauty was not rare among them, but it was the beauty of shapely animals. It was empty. But those tragic eyes were dark with mystery, and you felt in them the bitter complexity of the groping, human soul. The trader told him the story and it moved him.

"Do you think he'll ever come back?" asked Neilson.

"No fear. Why, it'll be a couple of years before the ship is paid off, and by then he'll have forgotten all about her. I bet he was pretty mad when he woke up and found he'd been shanghaied, and I shouldn't wonder but he wanted to fight somebody. But he'd got to grin and bear it, and I guess in a month he was thinking it the best thing that had ever happened to him that he got away from the island."

But Neilson could not get the story out of his head. Perhaps because he was sick and weakly, the radiant health of Red appealed to his imagination. Himself an ugly man, insignificant of appearance, he prized very highly comeliness in others. He had never been passionately in love, and certainly he had never been passionately loved. The mutual attraction of those two young things gave him a singular delight. It had the ineffable beauty of the Absolute. He went again to the little hut by the creek. He had a gift for languages and an energetic mind, accustomed to work, and he had already given much time to the study of the local tongue. Old habit was strong in him and he was gathering together material for a paper on the Samoan speech. The old crone who shared the hut with Sally invited him to come in and sit down. She gave him *kava* to drink and cigarettes to smoke. She was glad to have someone to chat with and while she talked he looked at Sally. She reminded him of the Psyche in the museum at Naples. Her features had the same clear purity of line, and though she had borne a child she had still a virginal aspect.

It was not till he had seen her two or three times that he induced her to speak. Then it was only to ask him if he had seen in Apia a man called Red. Two years had passed since his disappearance, but it was plain that she still thought of him incessantly.

It did not take Neilson long to discover that he was in love with her. It was only by an effort of will now that he prevented himself from going every day to the creek, and when he was not with Sally his thoughts were. At first, looking upon himself as a dying man, he asked only to look at her, and occasionally hear her speak, and his love gave him a wonderful happiness. He exulted in its purity. He wanted noth-

ing from her but the opportunity to weave around her graceful person
a web of beautiful fancies. But the open air, the equable temperature,
the rest, the simple fare, began to have an unexpected effect on his
health. His temperature did not soar at night to such alarming heights,
he coughed less and began to put on weight; six months passed without
his having a hemorrhage; and on a sudden he saw the possibility that
he might live. He had studied his disease carefully, and the hope
dawned upon him that with great care he might arrest its course. It
exhilarated him to look forward once more to the future. He made
plans. It was evident that any active life was out of the question, but
he could live on the islands, and the small income he had, insufficient
elsewhere, would be ample to keep him. He could grow coconuts; that
would give him an occupation; and he would send for his books and
a piano; but his quick mind saw that in all this he was merely trying
to conceal from himself the desire which obsessed him.

He wanted Sally. He loved not only her beauty, but that dim soul
which he divined behind her suffering eyes. He would intoxicate her
with his passion. In the end he would make her forget. And in an
ecstasy of surrender he fancied himself giving her too the happiness
which he had thought never to know again, but had now so miraculously achieved.

He asked her to live with him. She refused. He had expected that
and did not let it depress him, for he was sure that sooner or later she
would yield. His love was irresistible. He told the old woman of his
wishes, and found somewhat to his surprise that she and the neighbors,
long aware of them, were strongly urging Sally to accept his offer.
After all, every native was glad to keep house for a white man, and
Neilson according to the standards of the island was a rich one. The
trader with whom he boarded went to her and told her not to be a fool;
such an opportunity would not come again, and after so long she could
not still believe that Red would ever return. The girl's resistance only
increased Neilson's desire, and what had been a very pure love now
became an agonizing passion. He was determined that nothing should
stand in his way. He gave Sally no peace. At last, worn out by his
persistence and the persuasions, by turns pleading and angry, of everyone around her, she consented. But the day after when, exultant, he
went to see her he found that in the night she had burnt down the hut
in which she and Red had lived together. The old crone ran toward
him full of angry abuse of Sally, but he waved her aside; it did not
matter; they would build a bungalow on the place where the hut had
stood. A European house would really be more convenient if he
wanted to bring out a piano and a vast number of books.

And so the little wooden house was built in which he had now lived
for many years, and Sally became his wife. But after the first few weeks
of rapture, during which he was satisfied with what she gave him, he
had known little happiness. She had yielded to him, through weariness,
but she had only yielded what she set no store on. The soul which he

had dimly glimpsed escaped him. He knew that she cared nothing for him. She still loved Red, and all the time she was waiting for his return. At a sign from him, Neilson knew that, notwithstanding his love, his tenderness, his sympathy, his generosity, she would leave him without a moment's hesitation. She would never give a thought to his distress. Anguish seized him and he battered at that impenetrable self of hers which sullenly resisted him. His love became bitter. He tried to melt her heart with kindness, but it remained as hard as before; he feigned indifference, but she did not notice it. Sometimes he lost his temper and abused her, and then she wept silently. Sometimes he thought she was nothing but a fraud, and that soul simply an invention of his own, and that he could not get into the sanctuary of her heart because there was no sanctuary there. His love became a prison from which he longed to escape, but he had not the strength merely to open the door—that was all it needed—and walk out into the open air. It was torture and at last he became numb and hopeless. In the end the fire burnt itself out and, when he saw her eyes rest for an instant on the slender bridge, it was no longer rage that filled his heart but impatience. For many years now they had lived together bound by the ties of habit and convenience, and it was with a smile that he looked back on his old passion. She was an old woman, for the women on the islands age quickly, and if he had no love for her any more he had tolerance. She left him alone. He was contented with his piano and his books.

His thoughts led him to a desire for words.

"When I look back now and reflect on that brief passionate love of Red and Sally, I think that perhaps they should thank the ruthless fate that separated them when their love seemed still to be at its height. They suffered, but they suffered in beauty. They were spared the real tragedy of love."

"I don't know exactly as I get you," said the skipper.

"The tragedy of love is not death or separation. How long do you think it would have been before one or other of them ceased to care? Oh, it is dreadfully bitter to look at a woman whom you have loved with all your heart and soul, so that you felt you could not bear to let her out of your sight, and realize that you would not mind if you never saw her again. The tragedy of love is indifference."

But while he was speaking a very extraordinary thing happened. Though he had been addressing the skipper he had not been talking to him, he had been putting his thoughts into words for himself, and with his eyes fixed on the man in front of him he had not seen him. But now an image presented itself to them, an image not of the man he saw, but of another man. It was as though he were looking into one of those distorting mirrors that make you extraordinarily squat or out-rageously elongate, but here exactly the opposite took place, and in the obese, ugly old man he caught the shadowy glimpse of a stripling. He gave him now a quick, searching scrutiny. Why had a haphazard stroll brought him just to this place? A sudden tremor of his heart made him

slightly breathless. An absurd suspicion seized him. What had occurred
to him was impossible, and yet it might be a fact.

"What is your name?" he asked abruptly.

The skipper's face puckered and he gave a cunning chuckle. He
looked then malicious and horribly vulgar.

"It's such a damned long time since I heard it that I almost forget
it myself. But for thirty years now in the islands they've always called
me Red."

His huge form shook as he gave a low, almost silent laugh. It was
obscene. Neilson shuddered. Red was hugely amused, and from his
bloodshot eyes tears ran down his cheeks.

Neilson gave a gasp, for at that moment a woman came in. She was
a native, a woman of somewhat commanding presence, stout without
being corpulent, dark, for the natives grow darker with age, with very
gray hair. She wore a black Mother Hubbard, and its thinness showed
her heavy breasts. The moment had come.

She made an observation to Neilson about some household matter
and he answered. He wondered if his voice sounded as unnatural to her
as it did to himself. She gave the man who was sitting in the chair by
the window an indifferent glance, and went out of the room. The
moment had come and gone.

Neilson for a moment could not speak. He was strangely shaken.
Then he said:

"I'd be very glad if you'd stay and have a bit of dinner with me.
Pot luck."

"I don't think I will," said Red. "I must go after this fellow Gray.
I'll give him his stuff and then I'll get away. I want to be back in
Apia tomorrow."

"I'll send a boy along with you to show you the way."

"That'll be fine."

Red heaved himself out of his chair, while the Swede called one of
the boys who worked on the plantation. He told him where the skipper
wanted to go, and the boy stepped along the bridge. Red prepared
to follow him.

"Don't fall in," said Neilson.

"Not on your life."

Neilson watched him make his way across and when he had disappeared among the coconuts he looked still. Then he sank heavily in his
chair. Was that the man who had prevented him from being happy?
Was that the man whom Sally had loved all these years and for whom
she had waited so desperately? It was grotesque. A sudden fury seized
him so that he had an instinct to spring up and smash everything around
him. He had been cheated. They had seen each other at last and had
not known it. He began to laugh, mirthlessly, and his laughter grew
till it became hysterical. The Gods had played him a cruel trick. And
he was old now.

At last Sally came in to tell him dinner was ready. He sat down in

front of her and tried to eat. He wondered what she would say if he
told her now that the fat old man sitting in the chair was the lover
whom she remembered still with the passionate abandonment of her
youth. Years ago, when he hated her because she made him so unhappy, he would have been glad to tell her. He wanted to hurt her
then as she hurt him, because his hatred was only love. But now he did
not care. He shrugged his shoulders listlessly.

"What did that man want?" she asked presently.

He did not answer at once. She was old too, a fat old native woman.
He wondered why he had ever loved her so madly. He had laid at her
feet all the treasures of his soul, and she had cared nothing for them.
Waste, what waste! And now, when he looked at her, he felt only
contempt. His patience was at last exhausted. He answered her question.

"He's the captain of a schooner. He's come from Apia."

"Yes."

"He brought me news from home. My eldest brother is very ill and
I must go back."

"Will you be gone long?"

He shrugged his shoulders.

SAKI

The Open Window

Hector Hugh Munro (Saki, 1870–1916)
was born in Burma, the son of an inspec-
tor-general of the Burma police. He began
his writing career in London journalism,
and his first short stories appeared in the
Westminster Gazette. He has published
several volumes of short stories (*Reginald,
The Chronicles of Clovis, Beasts and Su-
perbeasts*) and a novel, *The Unbearable
Bassington.* [From *The Short Stories of
Saki* (H. H. Munro); copyright 1930 by
The Viking Press, Inc., New York; used
by permission of The Viking Press, Inc.,
and John Lane, The Bodley Head, Ltd.]

"MY AUNT WILL BE DOWN presently, Mr. Nuttel," said a very
self-possessed young lady of fifteen; "in the meantime you must try and
put up with me."

Framton Nuttel endeavored to say the correct something which
should duly flatter the niece of the moment without unduly discounting
the aunt that was to come. Privately he doubted more than ever whether
these formal visits on a succession of total strangers would do much
toward helping the nerve cure which he was supposed to be under-
going.

"I know how it will be," his sister had said when he was preparing to migrate to this rural retreat; "you will bury yourself down there and not speak to a living soul, and your nerves will be worse than ever from moping. I shall just give you letters of introduction to all the people I know there. Some of them, as far as I can remember, were quite nice."

Framton wondered whether Mrs. Sappleton, the lady to whom he was presenting one of the letters of introduction, came into the nice division.

"Do you know many of the people round here?" asked the niece, when she judged that they had had sufficient silent communion.

"Hardly a soul," said Framton. "My sister was staying here, at the rectory, you know, some four years ago and she gave me letters of introduction to some of the people here."

He made the last statement in a tone of distinct regret.

"Then you know practically nothing about my aunt?" pursued the self-possessed young lady.

"Only her name and address," admitted the caller. He was wondering whether Mrs. Sappleton was in the married or widowed state. An undefinable something about the room seemed to suggest masculine habitation.

"Her great tragedy happened just three years ago," said the child; "that would be since your sister's time."

"Her tragedy?" asked Framton; somehow in this restful country spot tragedies seemed out of place.

"You may wonder why we keep that window wide open on an October afternoon," said the niece, indicating a large French window that opened onto a lawn.

"It is quite warm for the time of the year," said Framton; "but has that window got anything to do with the tragedy?"

"Out through that window, three years ago to a day, her husband and her two young brothers went off for their day's shooting. They never came back. In crossing the moor to their favorite snipe-shooting ground they were all three engulfed in a treacherous piece of bog. It had been that dreadful wet summer, you know, and places that were safe in other years gave way suddenly without warning. Their bodies were never recovered. That was the dreadful part of it." Here the child's voice lost its self-possessed note and became falteringly human. "Poor aunt always thinks that they will come back some day, they and the little brown spaniel that was lost with them, and walk in at that window just as they used to do. That is why the window is kept open every evening till it is quite dusk. Poor dear aunt, she has often told me how they went out, her husband with his white waterproof coat over his arm, and Ronnie, her youngest brother, singing, 'Bertie, why do you bound?' as he always did to tease her, because she said it got on her nerves. Do you know, sometimes on still, quiet evenings like this, I almost get a creepy feeling that they will all walk in through that window—"

She broke off with a little shudder. It was a relief to Framton when the aunt bustled into the room with a whirl of apologies for being late in making her appearance.

"I hope Vera has been amusing you?" she said.

"She has been very interesting," said Framton.

"I hope you don't mind the open window," said Mrs. Sappleton briskly; "my husband and brothers will be home directly from shooting, and they always come in this way. They've been out for snipe in the marshes today, so they'll make a fine mess over my poor carpets. So like you men-folk, isn't it?"

She rattled on cheerfully about the shooting and the scarcity of birds, and the prospects for duck in the winter. To Framton it was all purely horrible. He made a desperate but only partially successful effort to turn the talk on to a less ghastly topic; he was conscious that his hostess was giving him only a fragment of her attention, and her eyes were constantly straying past him to the open window and the lawn beyond. It was certainly an unfortunate coincidence that he should have paid his visit on this tragic anniversary.

"The doctors agree in ordering me complete rest, an absence of mental excitement, and avoidance of anything in the nature of violent physical exercise," announced Framton, who labored under the tolerably widespread delusion that total strangers and chance acquaintances are hungry for the least detail of one's ailments and infirmities, their cause and cure. "On the matter of diet they are not so much in agreement," he continued.

"No?" said Mrs. Sappleton, in a voice which only replaced a yawn at the last moment. Then she suddenly brightened into alert attention—but not to what Framton was saying.

"Here they are at last!" she cried. "Just in time for tea, and don't they look as if they were muddy up to the eyes!"

Framton shivered slightly and turned toward the niece with a look intended to convey sympathetic comprehension. The child was staring out through the open window with dazed horror in her eyes. In a chill shock of nameless fear Framton swung round in his seat and looked in the same direction.

In the deepening twilight three figures were walking across the lawn toward the window; they all carried guns under their arms, and one of them was additionally burdened with a white coat hung over his shoulders. A tired brown spaniel kept close at their heels. Noiselessly they neared the house, and then a hoarse young voice chanted out of the dusk: "I said, Bertie, why do you bound?"

Framton grabbed wildly at his stick and hat; the halldoor, the gravel-drive, and the front gate were dimly noted stages in his headlong retreat. A cyclist coming along the road had to run into the hedge to avoid imminent collision.

"Here we are, my dear," said the bearer of the white mackintosh, coming in through the window; "fairly muddy, but most of it's dry. Who was that who bolted out as we came up?"

"A most extraordinary man, a Mr. Nuttel," said Mrs. Sappleton;

"could only talk about his illness, and dashed off without a word of good by or apology when you arrived. One would think he had seen a ghost."

"I expect it was the spaniel," said the niece calmly; "he told me he had a horror of dogs. He was once hunted into a cemetery somewhere on the banks of the Ganges by a pack of pariah dogs, and had to spend the night in a newly dug grave with the creatures snarling and grinning and foaming just above him. Enough to make anyone lose their nerve."

Romance at short notice was her specialty.

D. H. LAWRENCE

The Rocking-Horse Winner

David Herbert Lawrence (1885–1930) was born in Nottinghamshire. While teaching, he began to write. A novel, *The White Peacock,* was published in 1911. Two years later *Sons and Lovers,* the novel that secured his reputation, appeared. Then followed a series of novels and short stories, some of which caused considerable discussion. Among them were *The Rainbow, Women in Love, The Plumed Serpent* and *Lady Chatterley's Lover.* [From *The Portable D. H. Lawrence;* copyright 1933 by the Estate of D. H. Lawrence, 1947 by The Viking Press, Inc., New York.]

THERE WAS A WOMAN who was beautiful, who started with all the advantages, yet she had no luck. She married for love, and the love turned to dust. She had bonny children, yet she felt they had been thrust upon her, and she could not love them. They looked at her coldly, as if they were finding fault with her. And hurriedly she felt she must cover up some fault in herself. Yet what it was that she must cover up she never knew. Nevertheless, when her children were present, she always felt the center of her heart go hard. This troubled her, and in her manner she was all the more gentle and anxious for her children, as if she loved them very much. Only she herself knew that at the center of her heart was a hard little place that could not feel love, no, not for anybody. Everybody else said of her: "She is such a good mother. She adores her children." Only she herself, and her children themselves, knew it was not so. They read it in each other's eyes.

There were a boy and two little girls. They lived in a pleasant house, with a garden, and they had discreet servants, and felt themselves superior to anyone in the neighborhood.

Although they lived in style, they felt always an anxiety in the house. There was never enough money. The mother had a small income, and the father had a small income, but not nearly enough for the social position which they had to keep up. The father went in to town to some office. But though he had good prospects, these prospects never materialized. There was always the grinding sense of the shortage of money, though the style was always kept up.

At last the mother said: "I will see if *I* can't make something." But she did not know where to begin. She racked her brains, and tried this thing and the other, but could not find anything successful. The failure made deep lines come into her face. Her children were growing up, they would have to go to school. There must be more money, there must be more money. The father, who was always very handsome and expensive in his tastes, seemed as if he never *would* be able to do anything worth doing. And the mother, who had a great belief in herself, did not succeed any better, and her tastes were just as expensive.

And so the house came to be haunted by the unspoken phrase: *There must be more money! There must be more money!* The children could hear it all the time, though nobody said it aloud. They heard it at Christmas, when the expensive and splendid toys filled the nursery. Behind the shining modern rocking-horse, behind the smart doll's-house, a voice would start whispering: "There *must* be more money! There *must* be more money!" And the children would stop playing, to listen for a moment. They would look into each other's eyes, to see if they had all heard. And each one saw in the eyes of the other two that they too had heard. "There *must* be more money! There *must* be more money!"

It came whispering from the springs of the still-swaying rocking-horse, and even the horse, bending his wooden, champing head, heard it. The big doll, sitting so pink and smirking in her new pram, could hear it quite plainly, and seemed to be smirking all the more self-consciously because of it. The foolish puppy, too, that took the place of the teddy-bear, he was looking so extraordinarily foolish for no other reason but that he heard the secret whisper all over the house: "There *must* be more money!"

Yet nobody ever said it aloud. The whisper was everywhere, and therefore no one spoke it. Just as no one ever says: "We are breathing!" in spite of the fact that breath is coming and going all the time.

"Mother," said the boy Paul one day, "why don't we keep a car of our own? Why do we always use uncle's, or else a taxi?"

"Because we're the poor members of the family," said the mother.

"But why *are* we, mother?"

"Well—I suppose," she said slowly and bitterly, "it's because your father has no luck."

The boy was silent for some time.

"Is luck money, mother?" he asked, rather timidly.

"No, Paul. Not quite. It's what causes you to have money."

"Oh!" said Paul vaguely. "I thought when Uncle Oscar said *filthy lucker,* it meant money."

"*Filthy lucre* does mean money," said the mother. "But it's lucre, not luck."

"Oh!" said the boy. "Then what *is* luck, mother?"

"It's what causes you to have money. If you're lucky you have money. That's why it's better to be born lucky than rich. If you're rich, you may lose your money. But if you're lucky, you will always get more money."

"Oh! Will you? And is father not lucky?"

"Very unlucky, I should say," she said bitterly.

The boy watched her with unsure eyes.

"Why?" he asked.

"I don't know. Nobody ever knows why one person is lucky and another unlucky."

"Don't they? Nobody at all? Does *nobody* know?"

"Perhaps God. But he never tells."

"He ought to, then. And aren't you lucky either, mother?"

"I can't be, if I married an unlucky husband."

"But by yourself, aren't you?"

"I used to think I was, before I married. Now I think I am very unlucky indeed."

"Why?"

"Well—never mind! Perhaps I'm not really," she said.

The child looked at her, to see if she meant it. But he saw, by the lines of her mouth, that she was only trying to hide something from him.

"Well, anyhow," he said stoutly, "I'm a lucky person."

"Why?" said his mother, with a sudden laugh.

He stared at her. He didn't even know why he had said it.

"God told me," he asserted, brazening it out.

"I hope He did, dear!" she said, again with a laugh, but rather bitter.

"He did, mother!"

"Excellent!" said the mother, using one of her husband's exclamations.

The boy saw she did not believe him; or, rather, that she paid no attention to his assertion. This angered him somewhat, and made him want to compel her attention.

He went off by himself, vaguely, in a childish way, seeking for the clue to "luck." Absorbed, taking no heed of other people, he went about with a sort of stealth, seeking inwardly for luck. He wanted luck, he wanted it, he wanted it. When the two girls were playing dolls in the nursery, he would sit on his big rocking-horse, charging madly into space, with a frenzy that made the little girls peer at him uneasily. Wildly the horse careered, the waving dark hair of the boy tossed, his eyes had a strange glare in them. The little girls dared not speak to him.

When he had ridden to the end of his mad little journey, he climbed down and stood in front of his rocking-horse, staring fixedly into its lowered face. Its red mouth was slightly open, its big eye was wide and glassy-bright.

"Now!" he would silently command the snorting steed. "Now, take me to where there is luck! Now take me!"

And he would slash the horse on the neck with the little whip he had asked Uncle Oscar for. He *knew* the horse could take him to where there was luck, if only he forced it. So he would mount again, and start on his furious ride, hoping at last to get there. He knew he could get there.

"You'll break your horse, Paul!" said the nurse.

"He's always riding like that! I wish he'd leave off!" said his elder sister Joan.

But he only glared down on them in silence. Nurse gave him up. She could make nothing of him. Anyhow he was growing beyond her.

One day his mother and his Uncle Oscar came in when he was on one of his furious rides. He did not speak to them.

"Hallo, you young jockey! Riding a winner?" said his uncle.

"Aren't you growing too big for a rocking-horse? You're not a very little boy any longer, you know," said his mother.

But Paul only gave a blue glare from his big, rather close-set eyes. He would speak to nobody when he was in full tilt. His mother watched him with an anxious expression on her face.

At last he suddenly stopped forcing his horse into the mechanical gallop, and slid down.

"Well, I got there!" he announced fiercely, his blue eyes still flaring, and his sturdy long legs straddling apart.

"Where did you get to?" asked his mother.

"Where I wanted to go," he flared back at her.

"That's right, son!" said Uncle Oscar. "Don't you stop till you get there. What's the horse's name?"

"He doesn't have a name," said the boy.

"Gets on without all right?" asked the uncle.

"Well, he has different names. He was called Sansovino last week."

"Sansovino, eh? Won the Ascot. How did you know his name?"

"He always talks about horse-races with Bassett," said Joan.

The uncle was delighted to find that his small nephew was posted with all the racing news. Bassett, the young gardener, who had been wounded in the left foot in the war and had got his present job through Oscar Cresswell, whose batman he had been, was a perfect blade of the "turf." He lived in the racing events, and the small boy lived with him.

Oscar Cresswell got it all from Bassett.

"Master Paul comes and asks me, so I can't do more than tell him, sir," said Bassett, his face terribly serious, as if he were speaking of religious matters.

"And does he ever put anything on a horse he fancies?"

"Well—I don't want to give him away—he's a young sport, a fine sport, sir. Would you mind asking him himself? He sort of takes a pleasure in it, and perhaps he'd feel I was giving him away, sir, if you don't mind."

Bassett was serious as a church.

The uncle went back to his nephew, and took him off for a ride in the car.

"Say, Paul, old man, do you ever put anything on a horse?" the uncle asked.

The boy watched the handsome man closely.

"Why, do you think I oughtn't to?" he parried.

"Not a bit of it! I thought perhaps you might give me a tip for the Lincoln."

The car sped on into the country, going down to Uncle Oscar's place in Hampshire.

"Honor bright?" said the nephew.

"Honor bright, son!" said the uncle.

"Well, then, Daffodil."

"Daffodil! I doubt it, sonny. What about Mirza?"

"I only know the winner," said the boy. "That's Daffodil."

"Daffodil, eh?"

There was a pause. Daffodil was an obscure horse comparatively.

"Uncle!"

"Yes, son?"

"You won't let it go any further, will you? I promised Bassett."

"Bassett be damned, old man! What's he got to do with it?"

"We're partners. We've been partners from the first. Uncle, he lent me my first five shillings, which I lost. I promised him, honor bright, it was only between me and him; only you gave me that ten-shilling note I started winning with, so I thought you were lucky. You won't let it go any further, will you?"

The boy gazed at his uncle from those big, hot, blue eyes, set rather close together. The uncle stirred and laughed uneasily.

"Right you are, son! I'll keep your tip private. Daffodil, eh? How much are you putting on him?"

"All except twenty pounds," said the boy. "I keep that in reserve."

The uncle thought it a good joke.

"You keep twenty pounds in reserve, do you, you young romancer? What are you betting, then?"

"I'm betting three hundred," said the boy gravely. "But it's between you and me, Uncle Oscar! Honor bright?"

The uncle burst into a roar of laughter.

"It's between you and me all right, you young Nat Gould," he said, laughing. "But where's your three hundred?"

"Bassett keeps it for me. We're partners."

"You are, are you! And what is Bassett putting on Daffodil?"

"He won't go quite as high as I do, I expect. Perhaps he'll go a hundred and fifty."

"What, pennies?" laughed the uncle.

"Pounds," said the child, with a surprised look at his uncle. "Bassett keeps a bigger reserve than I do."

Between wonder and amusement Uncle Oscar was silent. He pursued the matter no further, but he determined to take his nephew with him to the Lincoln races.

"Now, son," he said, "I'm putting twenty on Mirza, and I'll put five for you on any horse you fancy. What's your pick?"

"Daffodil, uncle."

"No, not the fiver on Daffodil!"

"I should if it was my own fiver," said the child.

"Good! Good! Right you are! A fiver for me and a fiver for you on Daffodil."

The child had never been to a race-meeting before, and his eyes were blue fire. He pursed his mouth tight, and watched. A Frenchman just in front had put his money on Lancelot. Wild with excitement, he flayed his arms up and down, yelling *"Lancelot! Lancelot!"* in his French accent.

Daffodil came in first, Lancelot second, Mirza third. The child, flushed and with eyes blazing, was curiously serene. His uncle brought him four five-pound notes, four to one.

"What am I to do with these?" he cried, waving them before the boy's eyes.

"I suppose we'll talk to Bassett," said the boy. "I expect I have fifteen hundred now; and twenty in reserve; and this twenty."

His uncle studied him for some moments.

"Look here, son!" he said. "You're not serious about Bassett and that fifteen hundred, are you?"

"Yes, I am. But it's between you and me, uncle. Honor bright!"

"Honor bright all right, son! But I must talk to Bassett."

"If you'd like to be a partner, uncle, with Bassett and me, we could all be partners. Only, you'd have to promise, honor bright, uncle, not to let it go beyond us three. Bassett and I are lucky, and you must be lucky, because it was your ten shillings I started winning with. . . ."

Uncle Oscar took both Bassett and Paul into Richmond Park for an afternoon, and there they talked.

"It's like this, you see, sir," Bassett said. "Master Paul would get me talking about racing events, spinning yarns, you know, sir. And he was always keen on knowing if I'd made or if I'd lost. It's about a year since, now, that I put five shilling on Blush of Dawn for him—and we lost. Then the luck turned, with that ten shillings he had from you, that we put on Singhalese. And since that time, it's been pretty steady, all things considering. What do you say, Master Paul?"

"We're all right when we're sure," said Paul. "It's when we're not quite sure that we go down."

"Oh, but we're careful then," said Bassett.

"But when are you *sure*?" smiled Uncle Oscar.

"It's Master Paul, sir," said Bassett, in a secret, religious voice. "It's as if he had it from heaven. Like Daffodil, now, for the Lincoln. That was as sure as eggs."

"Did you put anything on Daffodil?" asked Oscar Cresswell.

"Yes, sir. I made my bit."

"And my nephew?"

Bassett was obstinately silent, looking at Paul.

"I made twelve hundred, didn't I, Bassett? I told uncle I was putting three hundred on Daffodil."

"That's right," said Bassett, nodding.

"But where's the money?" asked the uncle.

"I keep it safe locked up, sir. Master Paul he can have it any minute he likes to ask for it."

"What, fifteen hundred pounds?"

"And twenty! And *forty,* that is, with the twenty he made on the course."

"It's amazing!" said the uncle.

"If Master Paul offers you to be partners, sir, I would, if I were you; if you'll excuse me," said Bassett.

Oscar Cresswell thought about it.

"I'll see the money," he said.

They drove home again, and sure enough, Bassett came round to the garden-house with fifteen hundred pounds in notes. The twenty pounds reserve was left with Joe Glee, in the Turf Commission deposit.

"You see, it's all right, uncle, when I'm *sure!* Then we go strong, for all we're worth. Don't we, Bassett?"

"We do that, Master Paul."

"And when are you sure?" said the uncle, laughing.

"Oh, well, sometimes I'm *absolutely* sure, like about Daffodil," said the boy; "and sometimes I have an idea; and sometimes I haven't even an idea, have I, Bassett? Then we're careful, because we mostly go down."

"You do, do you! And when you're sure, like about Daffodil, what makes you sure, sonny?"

"Oh, well, I don't know," said the boy uneasily. "I'm sure, you know, uncle; that's all."

"It's as if he had it from heaven, sir," Bassett reiterated.

"I should say so!" said the uncle.

But he became a partner. And when the Leger was coming on, Paul was "sure" about Lively Spark, which was a quite inconsiderable horse. The boy insisted on putting a thousand on the horse, Bassett went for five hundred, and Oscar Cresswell two hundred. Lively Spark came in first, and the betting had been ten to one against him. Paul had made ten thousand.

"You see," he said, "I was absolutely sure of him."

Even Oscar Cresswell had cleared two thousand.

"Look here, son," he said, "this sort of thing makes me nervous."

"It needn't, uncle! Perhaps I shan't be sure again for a long time."

"But what are you going to do with your money?" asked the uncle

"Of course," said the boy, "I started it for mother. She said she had no luck, because father is unlucky, so I thought if *I* was lucky, it might stop whispering."

"What might stop whispering?"

"Our house. I *hate* our house for whispering."

"What does it whisper?"

"Why—why"—the boy fidgeted—"why, I don't know. But it's alway. short of money, you know, uncle."

"I know it, son, I know it."

"You know people send mother writs, don't you, uncle?"

"I'm afraid I do," said the uncle.

"And then the house whispers, like people laughing at you behind your back. It's awful, that is! I thought if I was lucky . . ."

"You might stop it," added the uncle.

The boy watched him with big blue eyes, that had an uncanny cold fire in them, and he said never a word.

"Well, then!" said the uncle. "What are we doing?"

"I shouldn't like mother to know I was lucky," said the boy.

"Why not, son?"

"She'd stop me"

"I don't think she would."

"Oh!"—and the boy writhed in an odd way—"I *don't* want her to know, uncle."

"All right, son! We'll manage it without her knowing."

They managed it very easily. Paul, at the other's suggestion, handed over five thousand pounds to his uncle, who deposited it with the family lawyer, who was then to inform Paul's mother that a relative had put five thousand pounds into his hands, which sum was to be paid out a thousand pounds at a time, on the mother's birthday, for the next five years.

"So she'll have a birthday present of a thousand pounds for five successive years," said Uncle Oscar. "I hope it won't make it all the harder for her later."

Paul's mother had her birthday in November. The house had been "whispering" worse than ever lately, and, even in spite of his luck, Paul could not bear up against it. He was very anxious to see the effect of the birthday letter, telling his mother about the thousand pounds.

When there were no visitors, Paul now took his meals with his parents, as he was beyond the nursery control. His mother went into town nearly every day. She had discovered that she had an odd knack of sketching furs and dress materials, so she worked secretly in the studio of a friend who was the chief "artist" for the leading drapers. She drew the figures of ladies in furs and ladies in silk and sequins for the newspaper advertisements. This young woman artist earned several thousand pounds a year, but Paul's mother only made several hundreds, and she was again dissatisfied. She so wanted to be first in something.

and she did not succeed, even in making sketches for drapery advertisements.

She was down to breakfast on the morning of her birthday. Paul watched her face as she read her letters. He knew the lawyer's letter. As his mother read it, her face hardened and became more expressionless. Then a cold, determined look came on her mouth. She hid the letter under the pile of others, and said not a word about it.

"Didn't you have anything nice in the post for your birthday, mother?" said Paul.

"Quite moderately nice," she said, her voice cold and absent.

She went away to town without saying more.

But in the afternoon Uncle Oscar appeared. He said Paul's mother had had a long interview with the lawyer, asking if the whole five thousand could not be advanced at once, as she was in debt.

"What do you think, uncle?" said the boy.

"I leave it to you, son."

"Oh, let her have it, then! We can get some more with the other," said the boy.

"A bird in the hand is worth two in the bush, laddie!" said Uncle Oscar.

"But I'm sure to *know* for the Grand National; or the Lincolnshire; or else the Derby. I'm sure to know for *one* of them," said Paul.

So Uncle Oscar signed the agreement, and Paul's mother touched the whole five thousand. Then something very curious happened. The voices in the house suddenly went mad, like a chorus of frogs on a spring evening. There were certain new furnishings, and Paul had a tutor. He was *really* going to Eton, his father's school, in the following autumn. There were flowers in the winter, and a blossoming of the luxury Paul's mother had been used to. And yet the voices in the house, behind the sprays of mimosa and almond blossom, and from under the piles of iridescent cushions, simply trilled and screamed in a sort of ecstasy: "There *must* be more money! Oh-h-h; there *must* be more money. Oh, now, now-w! Now-w-w—there *must* be more money!—more than ever! More than ever!"

It frightened Paul terribly. He studied away at his Latin and Greek with his tutors. But his intense hours were spent with Bassett. The Grand National had gone by: he had not "known," and had lost a hundred pounds. Summer was at hand. He was in agony for the Lincoln. But even for the Lincoln he didn't "know," and he lost fifty pounds. He became wild-eyed and strange, as if something were going to explode in him.

"Let it alone, son! Don't you bother about it!" urged Uncle Oscar. But it was as if the boy couldn't really hear what his uncle was saying.

"I've got to know for the Derby! I've got to know for the Derby!" the child reiterated, his big blue eyes blazing with a sort of madness.

His mother noticed how overwrought he was.

"You'd better go to the seaside. Wouldn't you like to go now to the seaside, instead of waiting? I think you'd better," she said, looking down at him anxiously, her heart curiously heavy because of him.

But the child lifted his uncanny blue eyes.

"I couldn't possibly go before the Derby, mother!" he said. "I couldn't possibly!"

"Why not?" she said, her voice becoming heavy when she was opposed. "Why not? You can still go from the seaside to see the Derby with your Uncle Oscar, if that's what you wish. No need for you to wait here. Besides, I think you care too much about these races. It's a bad sign. My family has been a gambling family, and you won't know till you grow up how much damage it has done. But it has done damage. I shall have to send Bassett away, and ask Uncle Oscar not to talk racing to you, unless you promise to be reasonable about it; go away to the seaside and forget it. You're all nerves!"

"I'll do what you like, mother, so long as you don't send me away till after the Derby," the boy said.

"Send you away from where? Just from this house?"

"Yes," he said, gazing at her.

"Why, you curious child, what makes you care about this house so much, suddenly? I never knew you loved it."

He gazed at her without speaking. He had a secret within a secret, something he had not divulged, even to Bassett or to his Uncle Oscar.

But his mother, after standing undecided and a little bit sullen for some moments, said:

"Very well, then! Don't go to the seaside till after the Derby, if you don't wish it. But promise me you won't let your nerves go to pieces. Promise you won't think so much about horse-racing and *events,* as you call them!"

"Oh, no," said the boy casually. "I won't think much about them, mother. You needn't worry. I wouldn't worry, mother, if I were you."

"If you were me and I were you," said his mother, "I wonder what we *should* do!"

"But you know you needn't worry, mother, don't you?" the boy repeated.

"I should be awfully glad to know it," she said wearily.

"Oh, well, you *can,* you know. I mean, you *ought* to know you needn't worry," he insisted.

"Ought I? Then I'll see about it," she said.

Paul's secret of secrets was his wooden horse, that which had no name. Since he was emancipated from a nurse and a nursery-governess, he had had his rocking-horse removed to his own bedroom at the top of the house.

"Surely, you're too big for a rocking-horse!" his mother had remonstrated.

"Well, you see, mother, till I can have a *real* horse, I like to have *some* sort of animal about," had been his quaint answer.

"Do you feel he keeps you company?" she laughed.

"Oh, yes! He's very good, he always keeps me company, when I'm there," said Paul.

So the horse, rather shabby, stood in an arrested prance in the boy's bedroom.

The Derby was drawing near, and the boy grew more and more tense. He hardly heard what was spoken to him, he was very frail, and his eyes were really uncanny. His mother had sudden strange seizures of uneasiness about him. Sometimes, for half-an-hour, she would feel a sudden anxiety about him that was almost anguish. She wanted to rush to him at once, and know he was safe.

Two nights before the Derby, she was at a big party in town, when one of her rushes of anxiety about her boy, her first-born, gripped her heart till she could hardly speak. She fought with the feeling, might and main, for she believed in commonsense. But it was too strong. She had to leave the dance and go downstairs to telephone to the country. The children's nursery-governess was terribly surprised and startled at being rung up in the night.

"Are the children all right, Miss Wilmot?"

"Oh, yes, they are quite all right."

"Master Paul? Is he all right?"

"He went to bed as right as a trivet. Shall I run up and look at him?"

"No," said Paul's mother reluctantly. "No! Don't trouble. It's all right. Don't sit up. We shall be home fairly soon." She did not want her son's privacy intruded upon.

"Very good," said the governess.

It was about one o'clock when Paul's mother and father drove up to their house. All was still. Paul's mother went to her room and slipped off her white fur cloak. She had told her maid not to wait up for her. She heard her husband downstairs, mixing a whisky-and-soda.

And then, because of the strange anxiety at her heart, she stole upstairs to her son's room. Noiselessly she went along the upper corridor. Was there a faint noise? What was it?

She stood, with arrested muscles, outside his door, listening. There was a strange, heavy, and yet not loud noise. Her heart stood still. It was a soundless noise, yet rushing and powerful. Something huge, in violent, hushed motion. What was it? What in God's name was it? She ought to know. She felt that she knew the noise. She knew what it was.

Yet she could not place it. She couldn't say what it was. And on and on it went, like a madness.

Softly, frozen with anxiety and fear, she turned the door-handle.

The room was dark. Yet in the space near the window, she heard and saw something plunging to and fro. She gazed in fear and amazement.

Then suddenly she switched on the light, and saw her son, in his green pajamas, madly surging on the rocking-horse. The blaze of light suddenly lit him up, as he urged the wooden horse, and lit her up, as she stood, blonde, in her dress of pale green and crystal, in the doorway.

"Paul!" she cried. "Whatever are you doing?"

"It's Malabar!" he screamed, in a powerful, strange voice. "It's Malabar!"

His eyes blazed at her for one strange and senseless second, as he ceased urging his wooden horse. Then he fell with a crash to the ground, and she, all her tormented motherhood flooding upon her, rushed to gather him up.

But he was unconscious, and unconscious he remained, with some brain-fever. He talked and tossed, and his mother sat stonily by his side.

"Malabar! It's Malabar! Bassett, Bassett, I *know*! It's Malabar!"

So the child cried, trying to get up and urge the rocking-horse that gave him his inspiration.

"What does he mean by Malabar?" asked the heart-frozen mother.

"I don't know," said the father stonily.

"What does he mean by Malabar?" she asked her brother Oscar.

"It's one of the horses running for the Derby," was the answer.

And, in spite of himself, Oscar Cresswell spoke to Bassett, and himself put a thousand on Malabar: at fourteen to one.

The third day of the illness was critical: they were waiting for a change. The boy, with his rather long, curly hair, was tossing ceaselessly on the pillow. He neither slept nor regained consciousness, and his eyes were like blue stones. His mother sat, feeling her heart had gone, turned actually into a stone.

In the evening, Oscar Cresswell did not come, but Bassett sent a message, saying could he come up for one moment, just one moment? Paul's mother was very angry at the intrusion, but on second thought she agreed. The boy was the same. Perhaps Bassett might bring him to consciousness.

The gardener, a shortish fellow with a little brown moustache, and sharp little brown eyes, tiptoed into the room, touched his imaginary cap to Paul's mother, and stole to the bedside, staring with glittering, smallish eyes, at the tossing, dying child.

"Master Paul!" he whispered. "Master Paul! Malabar came in first all right, a clean win. I did as you told me. You've made over seventy thousand pounds, you have; you've got over eighty thousand. Malabar came in all right, Master Paul."

"Malabar! Malabar! Did I say Malabar, mother? Did I say Malabar? Do you think I'm lucky, mother? I knew Malabar, didn't I? Over eighty thousand pounds! I call that lucky, don't you, mother? Over eighty thousand pounds! I knew, didn't I know I knew? Malabar came in all right. If I ride my horse till I'm sure, then I tell you, Bassett, you can go as high as you like. Did you go for all you were worth, Bassett?"

"I went a thousand on it, Master Paul."

"I never told you, mother, that if I can ride my horse, and *get there*, then I'm absolutely sure—oh, absolutely! Mother, did I ever tell you? I *am* lucky!"

"No, you never did," said the mother.

But the boy died in the night.

And even as he lay dead, his mother heard her brother's voice saying to her: "My God, Hester, you're eighty-odd thousand to the good, and a poor devil of a son to the bad. But, poor devil, poor devil, he's best gone out of a life where he rides his rocking-horse to find a winner."

EDITH SITWELL

Fanfare for Elizabeth

First and foremost a poet, Edith Sitwell, born in 1887, has written some distinguished works of prose, including a novel about Jonathan Swift called *I Live Under a Black Sun* and a biography of Queen Victoria. Her most recent work of prose was *Fanfare for Elizabeth.* She is the sister of the other two famous Sitwells— Sir Osbert and Sacheverell. [From *Fanfare for Elizabeth* by Edith Sitwell; used by permission of The Macmillan Company, publishers, and the author.]

THIS IS ENGLAND, this is the Happy Isle; it is the year 1533 and we are on our way to the country palace of the King—a giant with a beard of gold and a will of iron. Henry the Eighth was born to rule, and with all his lion's strength and ferocity he was in certain ways a great King. He was a man of great personal beauty: "His Majesty," wrote the Venetian, Sebastiano Guistiniani, "is as handsome as nature could form, above any Christian prince—handsomer far than the King of France. He is exceedingly fair, and as well proportioned as possible." Even in his later years Henry had still an appearance of great magnificence and power, like a sun running to seed. But he had grown heavier, the earth shook when he walked. And the prince with the face of an angel had fallen under the spell of his own princely will.

His temper had changed; but in earlier days he seemed a part of the English soil, of the English air, which were so mild that "laurel and rosemary flourish all winter, especially in the southern parts, and in summer time England yields apricots plentifully, muskmelons in good quantity, and figs in some places, all of which will ripen well; and by the same reason, all beasts bring forth their young in open fields, even in the time of winter. And England hath such an abundance of apples, pears, cherries and plums, such variety of them and so good in all respects, that no country yields more or better, for which the Italians would gladly exchange their citrons and oranges. But upon the sea coasts the winds many times blast the fruit in the very flower." All was fatness and plenty, until the nation of the beggars began with the destitution caused by the suppression of the Monasteries.

What is that rumbling noise we hear, resembling the beginning of an earthquake? It is the sound of the carts approaching London, bringing merchandise . . . But in the mornings to come, there will be less, and less travelers to London. The Plague is approaching London, slow wave by wave, and will soon overwhelm it like the sea.

Now we, and the carts, are coming nearer to "the noble city" (as Andrew Broorde, one of the King's physicians, called it), the "city which excelleth all others . . . for Constantinople, Venice, Rome, Florence, cannot be compared to London."

Presently we shall come to the heart of the City, the Tower, and see, fixed to one of the turrets by spears, the skulls "denuded of flesh," the signs of Henry's vengeance against traitors. But now we are only on the outskirts—the suburbs which were then the slums and the breeding places of the Plague, the dwelling places of the criminal population. "How happy," wrote Thomas Dekker, "were cities if they had no suburbes, sithence they serve but as caves, where monsters are tied up to devoure the Citties their-selves. Would the Divell hire a villain to spil blood? There we shall finde him. One to blaspheme? there he hath no choice. A Pandar that would court a nation at her praiers? hees there . . . a cheator that would turne his own father a-begging? Hees there too. A harlot that would murder her own new-borne Infant? She lies there."

Here, the "dores of notorious Carted Bawdes (like Hell-gates) stand night and day wide open, with a paire of Harlots in Taffeta gownes (like two painted posts) garnishing out those dores . . . when the dore of a poore Artificer (if his child had but died with one token of death about him) was close ramm'd up and guarded for feare others should have been infected. Yet the plague a whore-house lays upon a City is worse, yet is laughed at: if not laughed at, yet not look'd into, wincked at." And yet "Seriant Carbuncle, one of the Plague's chiefe officers, dare not venture within three yardes of an Harlot, because Mounseer Dry-Bone, the French-man, is a Ledger [lodger] before him." Mounseer Dry-Bone . . . or syphilis . . . the appalling disease which since the Siege of Naples had ravaged Europe, rivaling and eclipsing leprosy in its horror.

Now we are passing through the shamble-smelling, overhanging streets where the Plague breeds, onward through the streets haunted by Puffing Dick, King of the Beggars, he who "was a man crafty and bold; yet he died miserably. For, after he had commanded now fully eight years, he had the pyning of the Pox and the Neopolitan scurf, and there was an end of Puffing Dick." The company of the beggars, a nation within a nation, living by its own laws, even speaking its own language, was to become, in the reign of Elizabeth, one of the gravest menaces till there came a time when that nation bearded, and tried to browbeat, the great Queen in her own person.

By the year 1536, this nation had been joined by the "helpless, needy wretches, unused to dolour, and uninstructed in business" who were turned abroad following the overthrow of the Monasteries. Every day would see hordes of these poor creatures going to join the company of the ruffians. All the old Hospitals, St. Mary Bethlehem, St. Thomas of Southwark, St. Bartholomew, and that terrifying shadow of a nunnery, St. James-in-the-field, "an Hospitall for leprous virgins," were closed till the end of Henry the Eighth's reign, and their inmates were let loose in the streets, mingling their diseases and their miseries, hungry and naked, with wounds coalescing and decomposing under the enormous sun and the freezing moon, their stench offending the passers-by. If they begged without a written permission, they were rewarded by the pillory, the whip, branding, slavery, or the gallows.

Such was their destitution that they would defy even the Plague. A writer of thirty years later put these words in the mouths of the beggars: "If such plague do ensue, it is no great loss. We beggars reck nought of the carcass, but do defy it; we look for the cast coats, jackets, hose, caps, belts and shoes, by their deaths, which in their lives they would not depart from, and this is an hap. God send me one of them. . . ."

We have passed by these streets, and now move among the airs that drift from the gardens, until we come to a favorite palace of the King, Greenwich, "first builded by Humphrie of Gloucester, upon the Thames side foure miles east from London, in the time of Henrie the sixt, and called Pleasance. Afterward it was greatly enlarged by King Edward IV; garnished by King Henry VII, and finallie made perfect by King Hen. 8 the arche-Phenix of his time for fine and curious masonrie."

This palace of peach-red brick bore everywhere the daisy emblem of Marguerite of Anjou . . . the river ran past it, and the onelie Phenix could be rowed in his barge to the steps that led up to the palace. From the mullioned windows he, the father of the English navy, could watch his ships as they passed down the river.

As we come nearer, there is a sound of music, approaching us from the direction of the gardens.

The voice of trumpets approached—a dark and threatening sound, that seemed as if it heralded the birth of Fate, or told of some great event that would change the history of mankind. That sound told the story of a great King whose country was in danger because his male children did not live, of a wicked stepmother—a witch who through her enchantments became Queen—and of a young and disinherited Princess, who, through the spells of her stepmother, became a goose-girl, or a maid to her little sister. Then the sound changed once again, and told of a gigantic tragedy, of a spiritual upheaval in the history of mankind, a Sophoclan drama of an escape from an imagined or pretended incest cursed by heaven: the tale was of bloodshed and of huge lusts of the flesh and the spirit; of man's desire for spiritual freedom, and of a great Queen who sacrificed her heart and her life on the altar of her country.

The door that led out of the garden opened—and one saw that it was not the birth of Fate that the trumpets proclaimed, but the birth of a child: a little girl, the center of this procession.

"On Sunday last on the eve of Lady Day (September, the 7th. 1533), about three o'clock in the afternoon," the Imperial Ambassador told the Emperor Charles V, "the King's mistress was delivered of a girl, to the great disappointment and sorrow of the King, of the Lady herself, and of others of her party, and to the great shame and confusion of physicians, astrologers, witches and wizards, all of whom affirmed that it would be a boy. The people in general have rejoiced in the discomfiture of those who attach faith with such divinations . . . It must be concluded that God has entirely abandoned the King, and left him a prey to his own misfortune, and to his obstinate blindness, that he may be punished and completely ruined."

The King's voice was silent now, but since the birth of the child his fury had been terrifying to see and hear: it had raged for three days, breaking from the fires and darkness of his nature . . . The child a girl? Was it for this that he had put aside Catherine, his Queen, defied the Emperor and the Pope?

Thomas Dekker, after the death of this being whose christening we are about to witness, wrote—"She came in with the fall of the leafe, and went away in the spring: her life (which was dedicated to Virginitie) both beginning and closing in a miraculous Mayden circle: for she was born upon a Lady Eve, and died upon a Lady Eve: her Nativitie and Death being memorable for their wonder."

The room in which the Virgin Queen was born was named "The Chamber of the Virgins," because the tapestries with which it was hung represented the story of the Wise Virgins; and when the witch-Queen was told that the child was not the savior of England who had been expected, but only a useless girl, she said to the ladies: "They may now, with reason, call this room the chamber of Virgins, for a Virgin is born in it, on the Vigil of the auspicious day in which the Church commemorates the Nativity of the Virgin Mary."

ELIZABETH BOWEN

Sunday Afternoon

Elizabeth Bowen, born in Dublin in 1899 but most often classed as an English writer, published her first volume of short stories, *Encounters*, in 1923. She has several books to her credit, including a novel, *The Death of the Heart*, and her most recent collection of short stories, *Ivy Gripped the Steps*, which contains several dealing with the Second World War. [From *Ivy Gripped the Steps* by Elizabeth Bowen; copyright 1941, 1946 by Elizabeth Bowen; used by permission of Alfred A. Knopf, Inc.]

"SO HERE YOU ARE!" exclaimed Mrs. Vesey to the newcomer who joined the group on the lawn. She reposed for an instant her light, dry fingers on his. "Henry has come from London," she added. Acquiescent smiles from the others round her showed that the fact was already known—she was no more than indicating to Henry the role that he was to play. "What are your experiences?—Please tell us. But nothing dreadful: we are already feeling a little sad."

"I am sorry to hear that," said Henry Russel, with the air of one not anxious to speak of his own affairs. Drawing a cane chair into the circle, he looked from face to face with concern. His look traveled on to the screen of lilac, whose dark purple, pink-silver, and white plu..es sprayed out in the brilliance of the afternoon. The late May Sunday blazed, but was not warm: something less than a wind, a breath of coldness, fretted the edge of things. Where the lilac barrier ended, across the sun-polished meadows, the Dublin mountains continued to trace their hazy, today almost colorless line. The coldness had been admitted by none of the seven or eight people who, in degrees of elderly beauty, sat here full in the sun, at this sheltered edge of the lawn: they continued to master the coldness, or to deny it, as though with each it were some secret *malaise*. An air of fastidious, stylized melancholy, an air of being secluded behind glass, characterized for Henry these old friends in whose shadow he had grown up. To their pleasure at having him back among them was added, he felt, a taboo or warning—he was to tell a little, but not much. He could feel with a shock, as he sat down, how insensibly he had deserted, these last years, the æsthetic of living that he had got from them. As things were, he felt over him their suspended charm. The democratic smell of the Dublin bus, on which he had made the outward journey to join them, had evaporated from his person by the time he was half-way up Mrs. Vesey's chestnut avenue. Her house, with its fanlights and tall windows, was a villa in the Italian sense, just near enough to the city to make the country's sweetness particularly acute. Now, the sensations of wartime, that locked his inside being, began as surely to be dispelled —in the influence of this eternalized Sunday afternoon.

206

"Sad?" he said, "that is quite wrong."

"These days, our lives seem unreal," said Mrs. Vesey—with eyes that penetrated his point of view. "But, worse than that, this afternoon we discover that we all have friends who have died."

"Lately?" said Henry, tapping his fingers together.

"Yes, in all cases," said Ronald Cuffe—with just enough dryness to show how much the subject had been beginning to tire him. "Come, Henry, we look to you for distraction. To us, these days, you are quite a figure. In fact, from all we have heard of London, it is something that you should be alive. Are things there as shocking as they say— or are they more shocking?" he went on, with distaste.

"Henry's not sure," said someone, "he looks pontifical."

Henry, in fact, was just beginning to twiddle this far-off word "shocking" round in his mind, when a diversion caused some turning of heads. A young girl stepped out of a window and began to come their way across the lawn. She was Maria, Mrs. Vesey's niece. A rug hung over her bare arm: she spread out the rug and sat down at her aunt's feet. With folded arms, and her fingers on her thin pointed elbows, she immediately fixed her eyes on Henry Russel. "Good afternoon," she said to him, in a mocking but somehow intimate tone.

The girl, like some young difficult pet animal, seemed in a way to belong to everyone there. Miss Ria Store, the patroness of the arts, who had restlessly been refolding her fur cape, said: "And where have *you* been, Maria?"

"Indoors."

Someone said, "On this beautiful afternoon?"

"Is it?" said Maria, frowning impatiently at the grass.

"Instinct," said the retired judge, "now tells Maria it's time for tea."

"No, this does," said Maria, nonchalantly showing her wrist with the watch on it. "It keeps good time, thank you, Sir Isaac." She returned her eyes to Henry. "What have you been saying?"

"You interrupted Henry. He had been just going to speak."

"*Is* it so frightening?" Maria said.

"The bombing?" said Henry. "Yes. But as it does not connect with the rest of life, it is difficult, you know, to know what one feels. One's feelings seem to have no language for anything so preposterous. As for thoughts—"

"At that rate," said Maria, with a touch of contempt, "your thoughts would not be interesting."

"Maria," said somebody, "that is no way to persuade Henry to talk."

"About what is important," announced Maria, "it seems that no one can tell one anything. There is really nothing, till one knows it oneself."

"Henry is probably right," said Ronald Cuffe, "in considering that this—this outrage is *not* important. There is no place for it in human experience; it apparently cannot make a place of its own. It will have no literature."

"Literature!" said Maria. "One can see, Mr. Cuffe, that *you* have always been safe!"

"Maria," said Mrs. Vesey, "you're rather pert."

Sir Isaac said, "What does Maria expect to know?"

Maria pulled off a blade of grass and bit it. Something calculating and passionate appeared in her; she seemed to be crouched up inside herself. She said to Henry sharply: "But you'll go back, of course?"

"To London? Yes—this is only my holiday. Anyhow, one cannot stay long away."

Immediately he had spoken Henry realized how subtly this offended his old friends. Their position was, he saw, more difficult than his own, and he could not have said a more cruel thing. Mrs. Vesey, with her adept smile that was never entirely heartless, said: "Then we must hope your time here will be pleasant. Is it so very short?"

"And be careful, Henry," said Ria Store, "or you will find Maria stowed away in your baggage. And there would be an embarrassment, at an English port! We can feel her planning to leave us at any time."

Henry said, rather flatly: "Why should not Maria travel in the ordinary way?"

"Why should Maria travel at all? There is only one journey now—into danger. We cannot feel that that is necessary for her."

Sir Isaac added: "We fear, however, that that is the journey Maria wishes to make."

Maria, curled on the lawn with the nonchalance of a feline creature, through this kept her eyes cast down. Another cold puff came through the lilac, soundlessly knocking the blooms together. One woman, taken quite unawares, shivered—then changed this into a laugh. There was an aside about love from Miss Store, who spoke with a cold, abstracted knowledge—"Maria has no experience, none whatever; she hopes to meet heroes—she meets none. So now she hopes to find heroes across the sea. Why, Henry, she might make a hero of you."

"It is not that," said Maria, who had heard. Mrs. Vesey bent down and touched her shoulder; she sent the girl into the house to see if tea were ready. Presently they all rose and followed—in twos and threes, heads either erect composedly or else deliberately bowed in thought. Henry knew the idea of summer had been relinquished: they would not return to the lawn again. In the dining-room—where the white walls and the glass of the pictures held the reflections of summers—burned the log fire they were so glad to see. With her shoulder against the mantelpiece stood Maria, watching them take their places at the round table. Everything Henry had heard said had fallen off her—in these few minutes all by herself she had started in again on a fresh phase of living that was intact and pure. So much so, that Henry felt the ruthlessness of her disregard for the past, even the past of a few minutes ago. She came forward and put her hands on two chairs—to show she had been keeping a place for him.

Lady Ottery, leaning across the table, said: "I must ask you—we heard you had lost everything. But that cannot be true?"

Henry said, unwillingly: "It's true that I lost my flat, and everything in my flat."

"*Henry,*" said Mrs. Vesey, "all your beautiful things?"

"Oh dear," said Lady Ottery, overpowered, "I thought that could not be possible. I ought not to have asked."

Ria Store looked at Henry critically. "You take this too calmly. What has happened to you?"

"It was some time ago. And it happens to many people."

"But not to everyone," said Miss Store. "I should see no reason, for instance, why it should happen to me."

"One cannot help looking at you," said Sir Isaac. "You must forgive our amazement. But there was a time, Henry, when I think we all used to feel that we knew you well. If this is not a painful question, at this juncture, why did you not send your valuables out of town? You could have even shipped them over to us."

"I was attached to them. I wanted to live with them."

"And now," said Miss Store, "you live with nothing, forever. Can you really feel that that is life?"

"I do. I may be easily pleased. It was by chance I was out when the place was hit. You may feel—and I honor your point of view—that I should have preferred, at my age, to go into eternity with some pieces of glass and jade and a dozen pictures. But, in fact, I am very glad to remain. To exist."

"On what level?"

"On any level."

"Come, Henry," said Ronald Cuffe, "that is a cynicism one cannot like in you. You speak of your age: to us, of course that is nothing. You are at your maturity."

"Forty-three."

Maria gave Henry an askance look, as though, after all, he were not a friend. But she then said: "Why should he wish he was dead?" Her gesture upset some tea on the lace cloth, and she idly rubbed it up with her handkerchief. The tug her rubbing gave to the cloth shook a petal from a Chinese peony in the center bowl onto a plate of cucumber sandwiches. This little bit of destruction was watched by the older people with fascination, with a kind of appeasement, as though it were a guarantee against something worse.

"Henry is not young and savage, like you are. Henry's life is—or was —an affair of attachments," said Ria Store. She turned her eyes, under their lids, on Henry. "I wonder how much of you *has* been blown to blazes."

"I have no way of knowing," he said. "Perhaps you have?"

"Chocolate cake?" said Maria.

"Please."

For chocolate layer cake, the Vesey cook had been famous since Henry was a boy of seven or eight. The look, then the taste, of the brown segment linked him with Sunday afternoons when he had been brought here by his mother; then, with a phase of his adolescence when he had been unable to eat, but only to look round. Mrs. Vesey's beauty, at that time approaching its last lunar quarter, had swum on him when he was about nineteen. In Maria, child of her brother's late marriage, he now saw that beauty, or sort of physical genius, at the start. In Maria, this was without hesitation, without the halting influence that had bound Mrs. Vesey up—yes, and bound Henry up, from his boyhood, with her—in a circle of quizzical half-smiles. In revenge, he accused the young girl who moved him—who seemed framed, by some sort of anticipation, for the new catastrophic *outward* order of life—of brutality, of being without spirit. At his age, between two generations, he felt cast out. He felt Mrs. Vesey might not forgive him for having left her for a world at war.

Mrs. Vesey blew out the blue flame under the kettle, and let the silver trapdoor down with a snap. She then gave exactly one of those smiles—at the same time, it was the smile of his mother's friend. Ronald Cuffe picked the petal from the sandwiches and rolled it between his fingers, waiting for her to speak.

"It is cold, *indoors*," said Mrs. Vesey. "Maria, put another log on the fire—Ria, you say the most unfortunate things. We must remember Henry has had a shock—Henry, let us talk about something better. You work in an office, then, since the war?"

"In a Ministry—in an office, yes."

"Very hard?—Maria, that is all you would do if you went to England: work in an office. This is not like a war in history, you know."

Maria said: "It is not in history yet." She licked round her lips for the rest of the chocolate taste, then pushed her chair a little back from the table. She looked secretively at her wrist-watch. Henry wondered what the importance of time could be.

He learned what the importance of time was when, on his way down the avenue to the bus, he found Maria between two chestnut trees. She slanted up to him and put her hand on the inside of his elbow. Faded dark-pink stamen from the flowers above them had molted down onto her hair. "You have ten minutes more, really," she said. "They sent you off ten minutes before your time. They are frightened someone would miss the bus and come back; then everything would have to begin again. As it is always the same, you would not think it would be so difficult for my aunt."

"Don't talk like that; it's unfeeling; I don't like it," said Henry, stiffening his elbow inside Maria's grasp.

"Very well, then: walk to the gate, then back. I shall be able to hear your bus coming. It's true what they said—I'm intending to go away. They will have to make up something without me."

"Maria, I can't like you. Everything you say is destructive and horrible."

"Destructive?—I thought you didn't mind."

"I still want the past."

"Then how weak you are," said Maria. "At tea I admired you. The past—things done over and over again with more trouble than they were ever worth?—However, there's no time to talk about that. Listen, Henry: I must have your address. I suppose you *have* an address now?" She stopped him, just inside the white gate with the green drippings: here he blew stamen off a page of his notebook, wrote on the page and tore it out for her. "Thank you," said Maria, "I might turn up—if I wanted money, or anything. But there will be plenty to do: I can drive a car."

Henry said: "I want you to understand that I won't be party to this —*in any way*."

She shrugged and said: "You want *them* to understand"—and sent a look back to the house. Whereupon, on his entire being, the suspended charm of the afternoon worked. He protested against the return to the zone of death, and perhaps never ever seeing all this again. The cruciform lilac flowers, in all their purples, and the colorless mountains behind Mrs. Vesey's face besought him. The moment he had been dreading, returning desire, flooded him in this tunnel of avenue, with motors swishing along the road outside and Maria standing staring at him. He adored the stoicism of the group he had quitted—with their little fears and their great doubts—the grace of the thing done over again. He thought, with nothing left but our brute courage, we shall be nothing but brutes.

"What is the matter?" Maria said. Henry did not answer: they turned and walked to and fro inside the gates. Shadow played over her dress and hair: feeling the disenchantedness of his look at her she asked again, uneasily, "What's the matter?"

"You know," he said, "when you come away from here, no one will care any more that you are Maria. You will no longer be Maria, as a matter of fact. Those looks, those things that are said to you—they make you, you silly little girl. You are you only inside their spell. You may think action is better—but who will care for you when you only act? You will have an identity number, but no identity. Your whole existence has been in contradistinction. You may think you want an ordinary fate—but there is no ordinary fate. And that extraordinariness in the fate of each of us is only recognized by your aunt. I admit that her view of life is too much for me—that is why I was so stiff and touchy today. But where shall we be when nobody has a view of life?"

"You don't expect me to understand you, do you?"

"Even your being a savage, even being scornful—yes, even that you have got from them. Is that my bus?"

"At the other side of the river: it has still got to cross the bridge. Henry—" she put her face up. He touched it with kisses thoughtful and cold. "Good-by," he said, "Miranda."

"—Maria—"

"Miranda. This is the end of *you*. Perhaps it is just as well."

"I'll be seeing you—"

"You'll come round my door in London—with your little new number chained to your wrist."

"The trouble with you is, you're half old."

Maria ran out through the gates to stop the bus, and Henry got on to it and was quickly carried away.

JAMES

STEPHENS

Desire

James Stephens, born in 1882 in the Dublin slums, educated himself. He received recognition with *The Crock of Gold,* which won the Polignac Prize in 1912. A student of Gaelic, it has been his avowed purpose to give Ireland "a new mythology." He is assistant curator of the Dublin National Art Gallery. [From *Etched in Moonlight* by James Stephens; used by permission of The Macmillan Company, publishers.]

HE WAS EXCITED, and as he leaned forward in his chair and told this story to his wife he revealed to her a degree or a species of credulity of which she could not have believed him capable.

He was a level-headed man, and habitually conducted his affairs on hard-headed principles. He had conducted his courtship, his matrimonial and domestic affairs in a manner which she should not have termed reckless or romantic. When, therefore, she found him excited, and over such a story, she did not know how just to take the matter.

She compromised by agreeing with him, not because her reason was satisfied or even touched, but simply because he was excited, and a woman can welcome anything which varies the dull round and will bathe in exclamations if she gets the chance.

This was what he told her.

As he was walking to lunch a motor car came down the street at a speed much too dangerous for the narrow and congested thoroughfare. A man was walking in front of him, and, just as the car came behind, this man stepped off the path with a view to crossing the road. He did not even look behind as he stepped off. Her husband stretched a ready arm that swept the man back to the pavement one second before the car went blaring and buzzing by.

"If I had not been there," said her husband, who liked slang, "you would have got it where the chicken got the axe."

The two men grinned at each other; her husband smiling with good-fellowship, the other crinkling with amusement and gratitude.

They walked down the street and, on the strength of that adventure, they had lunch together.

They had sat for a long time after lunch, making each other's acquaintance, smoking innumerable cigarettes, and engaged in a conversation which she could never have believed her husband would have shared in for ten minutes; and they had parted with a wish, from her husband, that they should meet again on the following day, and a wordless smile from the man.

He had neither ratified nor negatived the arrangement.

"I hope he'll turn up," said her husband.

This conversation had excited her man, for it had drawn him into an atmosphere to which he was a stranger, and he had found himself moving there with such pleasure that he wished to get back to it with as little delay as possible.

Briefly, as he explained it to her, the atmosphere was religious; and while it was entirely intellectual it was more heady and exhilarating than the emotional religion to which he had been accustomed, and from which he had silently lapsed.

He tried to describe his companion; but had such ill success in the description that she could not remember afterward whether he was tall or short; fat or thin; fair or dark.

It was the man's eyes only that he succeeded in emphasizing; and these, it appeared, were eyes such as he had never before seen in a human face.

That also, he amended, was a wrong way of putting it, for his eyes were exactly like everybody else's. It was the way he looked through them that was different. Something, very steady, very ardent, very quiet and powerful, was using these eyes for purposes of vision. He had never met anyone who looked at him so . . . comprehendingly; so agreeably.

"You are in love," said she with a laugh.

After this her husband's explanations became more explanatory but not less confused, until she found that they were both, with curious unconsciousness, in the middle of a fairy-tale.

"He asked me," said her husband, "what was the thing I wished for beyond all things."

"That was the most difficult question I have ever been invited to answer," he went on; "and for nearly half an hour we sat thinking it out, and discussing magnificences and possibilities."

"I had all the usual thoughts; and, of course, the first of them was wealth. We are more dominated by proverbial phrases than we conceive of, and, such a question being posed, the words 'healthy, wealthy, and wise' will come, unbidden, to answer it. To be alive is to be acquisitive, and so I mentioned wealth, tentatively, as a possibility; and he agreed that it was worth considering. But after a while I knew that I did not want money."

"One always has need of money," said his wife.

"In a way, that is true," he replied, "but not in this way; for, as I thought it over, I remembered that we have no children; and that our relatively few desires, or fancies, can be readily satisfied by the money we already have. Also we are fairly well off; we have enough in the stocking to last our time even if I ceased from business, which I am not going to do; and, in short, I discovered that money or its purchasing power had not any particular advantages to offer."

"All the same!" she murmured; and halted with her eyes fixed on purchasings far away in time and space.

"All the same!" he agreed with a smile.

"I could not think of anything worth wishing for," he continued. "I mentioned health and wisdom, and we considered these; but, judging myself by the standard of the world in which we move, I concluded that both my health and knowledge were as good as the next man's; and I thought also that if I elected to become wiser than my contemporaries I might be a very lonely person for the rest of my days."

"Yes," said she thoughtfully, "I am glad you did not ask to be made wise, unless you could have asked it for both of us."

"I asked him in the end what he would advise me to demand, but he replied that he could not advise me at all. 'Behind everything stands desire,' said he, 'and you must find out your desire.'"

"I asked him then, if the conditions were reversed and if the opportunity had come to him instead of to me, what he should have asked for; not, as I explained to him, in order that I might copy his wish, but from sheer curiosity. He replied that he should not ask for anything. This reply astonished, almost alarmed me at first, but most curiously satisfied me on considering it, and I was about to adopt that attitude—"

"Oh," said his wife.

"When an idea came to me. 'Here I am,' I said to myself, 'forty-eight years of age: rich enough; sound enough in wind and limb; and as wise as I can afford to be. What is there now belonging to me, absolutely mine, but from which I must part, and which I should like to keep?' And I saw that the thing which was leaving me day by day; second by second; irretrievably and inevitably; was my forty-eighth year. I thought I should like to continue at the age of forty-eight until my time was up."

"I did not ask to live forever, or any of that nonsense, for I saw that to live forever is to be condemned to a misery of boredom more dreadful than anything else the mind can conceive of. But, while I do live, I wish to live competently, and so I asked to be allowed to stay at the age of forty-eight years with all the equipment of my present state unimpaired."

"You should not have asked for such a thing," said his wife, a little angrily. "It is not fair to me," she explained. "You are older than I am now, but in a few years this will mean that I shall be needlessly older than you. I think it was not a loyal wish."

"I thought of that objection," said he, "and I also thought that I was past the age at which certain things matter; and that both temperamentally and in the matter of years I am proof against sensual or suchlike attractions. It seemed to me to be right; so I just registered my wish with him."

"What did he say?" she queried.

"He did not say anything; he just nodded; and began to talk again of other matters—religion, life, death, mind; a host of things, which, for all the diversity they seem to have when I enumerate them, were yet one single theme."

"I feel a more contented man tonight than I have ever felt," he continued, "and I feel in some curious way a different person from the man I was yesterday."

Here his wife awakened from the conversation and began to laugh.

"You are a foolish man," said she, "and I am just as bad. If anyone were to hear us talking this solemn silliness they would have a right to mock at us."

He laughed heartily with her, and after a light supper they went to bed.

During the night his wife had a dream.

She dreamed that a ship set away for the Polar Seas on an expedition in which she was not sufficiently interested to find out its reason. The ship departed with her on board. All that she knew or cared was that she was greatly concerned with baggage, and with counting and going over the various articles that she had brought against arctic weather.

She had thick woolen stockings. She had skin boots all hairy inside, all pliable and wrinkled without. She had a great skin cap shaped like a helmet and fitting down in a cape over her shoulders. She had, and they did not astonish her, a pair of very baggy fur trousers. She had a sleeping sack.

She had an enormous quantity of things; and everybody in the expedition was equipped, if not with the same things, at least similarly.

These traps were a continuous subject of conversation aboard, and, although days and weeks passed, the talk of the ship hovered about and fell continually into the subject of warm clothing.

There came a day when the weather was perceptibly colder; so cold that she was tempted to draw on these wonderful breeches, and to fit her head into that most comfortable hat. But she did not do so; for, and everybody on the ship explained it to her, it was necessary that she should accustom herself to the feeling, the experience, of cold; and, she was further assured, that the chill which she was now resenting was nothing to the freezing she should presently have to bear.

It seemed good advice; and she decided that as long as she could bear the cold she would do so, and would not put on any protective covering; thus, when the cold became really intense, she would be in some measure inured to it, and would not suffer so much.

But steadily, and day by day, the weather grew colder.

For now they were in wild and whirling seas wherein great green and white icebergs went sailing by; and all about the ship little hummocks of ice bobbed and surged, and went under and came up; and the gray water slashed and hissed against and on top of these small hillocks.

Her hands were so cold that she had to put them under her armpits to keep any warmth in them; and her feet were in a worse condition. They had begun to pain her; so she decided that on the morrow she would put on her winter equipment, and would not mind what anybody said to the contrary.

"It is cold enough," said she, "for my arctic trousers, for my warm soft boots, and my great furry gloves. I will put them on in the morning," for it was then almost night and she meant to go to bed at once.

She did go to bed; and she lay there in a very misery of cold.

In the morning, she was yet colder; and immediately on rising she looked for the winter clothing which she had laid ready by the side of her bunk the night before; but she could not find them. She was forced to dress in her usual rather thin clothes; and, having done so, she went on deck.

When she got to the side of the vessel she found that the world about her had changed.

The sea had disappeared. Far as the eye could peer was a level plain of ice, not white, but dull gray; and over it there lowered a sky, gray as itself and of almost the same dullness.

Across this waste there blew a bitter, a piercing wind that her eyes winced from, and that caused her ears to tingle and sting.

Not a soul was moving on the ship, and the dead silence which brooded on the ice lay heavy and almost solid on the vessel.

She ran to the other side, and found that the whole ship's company had landed, and were staring at her from a little distance of the ship. And these people were as silent as the frozen air, as the frozen ship. They stared at her; they made no move; they made no sound.

She noticed that they were all dressed in their winter furs; and, while she stood, ice began to creep into her veins.

One of the ship's company strode forward a few paces and held up a bundle in his mittened hand. She was amazed to see that the bundle contained her clothes; her broad furry trousers; her great cozy helmet and gloves.

To get from the ship to the ice was painful but not impossible. A rope ladder was hanging against the side, and she went down this. The rungs felt hard as iron, for they were frozen stiff; and the touch of those glassy surfaces bit into her tender hand like fire. But she got to the ice and went across it toward her companions.

Then, to her dismay, to her terror, all these, suddenly, with one unexpressed accord, turned and began to run away from her; and she, with a heart that shook once and could scarcely beat again, took after them.

Every few paces she fell, for her shoes could not grip on the ice; and each time that she fell those monsters stood and turned and watched her, and the man who had her clothes waved the bundle at her and danced grotesquely, silently.

She continued running, sliding, falling, picking herself up, until her breath went, and she came to a halt, unable to move a limb further and scarcely able to breathe; and this time they did not stay to look at her.

They continued running, but now with great and greater speed, with the very speed of madmen; and she saw them become black specks away on the white distance; and she saw them disappear; and she saw that there was nothing where she stared but the long white miles, and the terrible silence, and the cold.

How cold it was!

And with that there arose a noiseless wind, keen as a razor.

It stung into her face; it swirled about her ankles like a lash; it stabbed under her armpits like a dagger.

"I am cold," she murmured.

She looked backward whence she had come, but the ship was no longer in sight, and she could not remember from what direction she had come.

Then she began to run in any direction.

Indeed she ran in every direction to find the ship; for when she had taken an hundred steps in one way she thought, frantically, "this is not the way," and at once she began to run on the opposite road. But run as she might she could not get warm; it was colder she got. And then, on a steel-gray plane, she slipped, and slipped again, and went sliding down a hollow, faster and faster; she came to the brink of a cleft, and swished over this, and down into a hole of ice and there she lay.

"I shall die!" she said. "I shall fall asleep here and die. . . ."

Then she awakened.

She opened her eyes directly on the window and saw the ghost of dawn struggling with the ghoul of darkness. A grayish perceptibility framed the window without, but could not daunt the obscurity within; and she lay for a moment terrified at that grotesque adventure, and thanking God that it had only been a dream.

In another second she felt that she was cold. She pulled the clothes more tightly about her, and she spoke to her husband.

"How miserably cold it is!" she said.

She turned in the bed and snuggled against him for warmth; and she found that an atrocity of cold came from him; that he was icy.

She leaped from the bed with a scream. She switched on the light, and bent over her husband—

He was stone dead. He was stone cold. And she stood by him, shivering and whimpering.

JAMES JOYCE

The Boarding House

James Joyce (1882–1941) was born in Dublin and educated at Clongowes Wood, Belvedere and University colleges in Dublin. His first published work was *Chamber Music,* a small volume of lyrics. Joyce left Ireland to live abroad in Rome, Zurich, Trieste and Paris. His principal works are *Dubliners,* a collection of short stories, *Portrait of the Artist as a Young Man, Ulysses* (frequently regarded as the most important novel of the twentieth century) and *Finnegan's Wake.* [From *Dubliners* in *The Portable James Joyce;* copyright 1946, 1947 by The Viking Press, Inc., New York.]

MRS. MOONEY WAS A BUTCHER'S DAUGHTER. She was a woman who was quite able to keep things to herself: a determined woman. She had married her father's foreman and opened a butcher's shop near Spring Gardens. But as soon as his father-in-law was dead Mr. Mooney began to go to the devil. He drank, plundered the till, ran headlong into debt. It was no use making him take the pledge: he was sure to break out again a few days after. By fighting his wife in the presence of customers and by buying bad meat he ruined his business. One night he went for his wife with the cleaver and she had to sleep in a neighbor's house.

After that they lived apart. She went to the priest and got a separation from him with care of the children. She would give him neither money nor food nor house-room; and so he was obliged to enlist himself as a sheriff's man. He was a shabby stooped little drunkard with a white face and a white mustache and white eyebrows, penciled above his little eyes, which were pink-veined and raw; and all day long he sat in the bailiff's room, waiting to be put on a job. Mrs. Mooney, who had taken what remained of her money out of the butcher business and set up a boarding house in Hardwicke Street, was a big imposing woman. Her house had a floating population made up of tourists from Liverpool and the Isle of Man and, occasionally, *artistes* from the music halls. Its resident population was made up of clerks from the city. She governed the house cunningly and firmly, knew when to give credit, when to be stern and when to let things pass. All the resident young men spoke of her as *The Madam.*

Mrs. Mooney's young men paid fifteen shillings a week for board and lodgings (beer or stout at dinner excluded). They shared in common tastes and occupations and for this reason they were very chummy with one another. They discussed with one another the chances of favorites and outsiders. Jack Mooney, the Madam's son, who was clerk to a commission agent in Fleet Street, had the reputation of being a hard case. He was fond of using soldiers' obscenities: usually he came home in the small hours. When he met his friends he had always a good one to tell them and he was always sure to be on to a good thing —that is to say, a likely horse or a likely *artiste*. He was also handy with the mits and sang comic songs. On Sunday nights there would often be a reunion in Mrs. Mooney's front drawing-room. The music-hall *artistes* would oblige; and Sheridan played waltzes and polkas and vamped accompaniments. Polly Mooney, the Madam's daughter, would also sing. She sang:

> *"I'm a . . . naughty girl.*
> *You needn't sham:*
> *You know I am."*

Polly was a slim girl of nineteen; she had light soft hair and a small full mouth. Her eyes, which were gray with a shade of green through them, had a habit of glancing upward when she spoke with anyone, which made her look like a little perverse madonna. Mrs. Mooney had first sent her daughter to be a typist in a corn-factor's office but, as a disreputable sheriff's man used to come every other day to the office, asking to be allowed to say a word to his daughter, she had taken her daughter home again and sent her to do housework. As Polly was very lively the intention was to give her the run of the young men. Besides, young men like to feel that there is a young woman not very far away. Polly, of course, flirted with the young men but Mrs. Mooney, who was a shrewd judge, knew that the young men were only passing the time away: none of them meant business. Things went on so for a long time and Mrs. Mooney began to think of sending Polly back to type-writing when she noticed that something was going on between Polly and one of the young men. She watched the pair and kept her own counsel.

Polly knew that she was being watched, but still her mother's persistent silence could not be misunderstood. There had been no open complicity between mother and daughter, no open understanding but, though people in the house began to talk of the affair, still Mrs. Mooney did not intervene. Polly began to grow a little strange in her manner and the young man was evidently perturbed. At last, when she judged it to be the right moment, Mrs. Mooney intervened. She dealt with moral problems as a cleaver deals with meat: and in this case she had made up her mind.

It was a bright Sunday morning of early summer, promising heat, but with a fresh breeze blowing. All the windows of the boarding house were open and the lace curtains ballooned gently toward the street beneath the raised sashes. The belfry of George's Church sent out constant peals and worshipers, singly or in groups, traversed the little circus before the church, revealing their purpose by their self-contained demeanor no less than by the little volumes in their gloved hands. Breakfast was over in the boarding house and the table of the breakfast-room was covered with plates on which lay yellow streaks of eggs with morsels of bacon-fat and bacon-rind. Mrs. Mooney sat in the straw arm-chair and watched the servant Mary remove the breakfast things. She made Mary collect the crusts and pieces of broken bread to help to make Tuesday's bread-pudding. When the table was cleared, the broken bread collected, the sugar and butter safe under lock and key, she began to reconstruct the interview which she had had the night before with Polly. Things were as she had suspected: she had been frank in her questions and Polly had been frank in her answers. Both had been somewhat awkward, of course. She had been made awkward by her not wishing to receive the news in too cavalier a fashion or to seem to have connived and Polly had been made awkward not merely because allusions of that kind always made her awkward but also because she did not wish it to be thought that in her wise innocence she had divined the intention behind her mother's tolerance.

Mrs. Mooney glanced instinctively at the little gilt clock on the mantelpiece as soon as she had become aware through her revery that the bells of George's Church had stopped ringing. It was seventeen minutes past eleven: she would have lots of time to have the matter out with Mr. Doran and then catch short twelve at Marlborough Street. She was sure she would win. To begin with she had all the weight of social opinion on her side: she was an outraged mother. She had allowed him to live beneath her roof, assuming that he was a man of honor, and he had simply abused her hospitality. He was thirty-four or thirty-five years of age, so that youth could not be pleaded as his excuse; nor could ignorance be his excuse since he was a man who had seen something of the world. He had simply taken advantage of Polly's youth and inexperience: that was evident. The question was: What reparation would he make?

There must be reparation made in such case. It is all very well for the man: he can go his ways as if nothing had happened, having had his moment of pleasure, but the girl has to bear the brunt. Some mothers would be content to patch up such an affair for a sum of money; she had known cases of it. But she would not do so. For her only one reparation could make up for the loss of her daughter's honor: marriage.

She counted all her cards again before sending Mary up to Mr. Doran's room to say that she wished to speak with him. She felt sure she would win. He was a serious young man, not rakish or loud-voiced like the others. If it had been Mr. Sheridan or Mr. Meade or Bantam Lyons her task would have been much harder. She did not think he would face publicity. All the lodgers in the house knew something of the affair; details had been invented by some. Besides, he had been employed for thirteen years in a great Catholic wine-merchant's office and publicity would mean for him, perhaps, the loss of his job. Whereas if he agreed all might be well. She knew he had a good screw for one thing and she suspected he had a bit of stuff put by.

Nearly the half-hour! She stood up and surveyed herself in the pier-glass. The decisive expression of her great florid face satisfied her and she thought of some mothers she knew who could not get their daughters off their hands.

Mr. Doran was very anxious indeed this Sunday morning. He had made two attempts to shave but his hand had been so unsteady that he had been obliged to desist. Three days' reddish beard fringed his jaws and every two or three minutes a mist gathered on his glasses so that he had to take them off and polish them with his pocket-handkerchief. The recollection of his confession of the night before was a cause of acute pain to him; the priest had drawn out every ridiculous detail of the affair and in the end had so magnified his sin that he was almost thankful at being afforded a loophole of reparation. The harm was done. What could he do now but marry her or run away? He could not brazen it out. The affair would be sure to be talked of and his employer would be certain to hear of it. Dublin is such a small city: everyone knows everyone else's business. He felt his heart leap warmly in his throat as he heard in his excited imagination old Mr. Leonard calling out in his rasping voice: "Send Mr. Doran here, please."

All his long years of service gone for nothing! All his industry and diligence thrown away! As a young man he had sown his wild oats, of course; he had boasted of his free-thinking and denied the existence of God to his companions in public-houses. But that was all passed and done with . . . nearly. He still bought a copy of *Reynolds's Newspaper* every week but he attended to his religious duties and for nine-tenths of the year lived a regular life. He had money enough to settle down on; it was not that. But the family would look down on her. First of all there was her disreputable father and then her mother's boarding house was beginning to get a certain fame. He had a notion that he was being had. He could imagine his friends talking of the affair and laughing. She *was* a little vulgar; some time she said "I seen" and "If I had've known." But what would grammar matter if he really loved her? He could not make up his mind whether to like her or despise her for what she had done. Of course he had done it too. His instinct urged him to remain free, not to marry. Once you are married you are done for, it said.

While he was sitting helplessly on the side of the bed in shirt and trousers she tapped lightly at his door and entered. She told him all, that she had made a clean breast of it to her mother and that her mother would speak with him that morning. She cried and threw her arms round his neck, saying:

"O Bob! Bob! What am I to do? What am I to do at all?"

She would put an end to herself, she said.

He comforted her feebly, telling her not to cry, that it would be all right, never fear. He felt against his shirt the agitation of her bosom.

It was not altogether his fault that it had happened. He remembered well, with the curious patient memory of the celibate, the first casual caresses her dress, her breath, her fingers had given him. Then late one night as he was undressing for bed she had tapped at his door, timidly. She wanted to relight her candle at his for hers had been blown out by a gust. It was her bath night. She wore a loose open combing jacket of printed flannel. Her white instep shone in the opening of her furry slippers and the blood glowed warmly behind her perfumed skin. From her hands and wrists too as she lit and steadied her candle a faint perfume arose.

On nights when he came in very late it was she who warmed up his dinner. He scarcely knew what he was eating feeling her beside him alone, at night, in the sleeping house. And her thoughtfulness! If the night was anyway cold or wet or windy there was sure to be a little tumbler of punch ready for him. Perhaps they could be happy together. . . .

They used to go upstairs together on tiptoe, each with a candle, and on the third landing exchange reluctant good nights. They used to kiss. He remembered well her eyes, the touch of her hand and his delirium. . . .

But delirium passes. He echoed her phrase, applying it to himself: "*What am I to do?*" The instinct of the celibate warned him to hold back. But the sin was there; even his sense of honor told him that reparation must be made for such a sin.

While he was sitting with her on the side of the bed Mary came to the door and said that the missus wanted to see him in the parlor. He stood up to put on his coat and waistcoat, more helpless than ever. When he was dressed he went over to her to comfort her. It would be all right, never fear. He left her crying on the bed and moaning softly: "*O my God!*"

Going down the stairs his glasses became so dimmed with moisture that he had to take them off and polish them. He longed to ascend through the roof and fly away to another country where he would never hear again of his trouble, and yet a force pushed him downstairs step by step. The implacable faces of his employer and of the Madam stared upon his discomfiture. On the last flight of stairs he passed Jack Mooney who was coming up from the pantry nursing two bottles of *Bass*. They saluted coldly; and the lover's eyes rested for a second or two on a thick bulldog face and a pair of thick short arms. When he reached the foot of the staircase he glanced up and saw Jack regarding him from the door of the return-room.

Suddenly he remembered the night when one of the music-hall *artistes*, a little blond Londoner, had made a rather free allusion to Polly. The reunion had been almost broken up on account of Jack's violence. Everyone tried to quiet him. The music-hall *artiste*, a little paler than usual, kept smiling and saying that there was no harm meant: but Jack kept shouting at him that if any fellow tried that sort of a game on with his sister he'd bloody well put his teeth down his throat, so he would.

Polly sat for a little time on the side of the bed, crying. Then she dried her eyes and went over to the looking-glass. She dipped the end of the towel in the water-jug and refreshed her eyes with the cool water. She looked at herself in profile and readjusted a hairpin above her ear. Then she went back to the bed again and sat at the foot. She regarded the pillows for a long time and the sight of them awakened in her mind secret, amiable memories. She rested the nape of her neck against the cool iron bed-rail and fell into a revery. There was no longer any perturbation visible on her face.

She waited on patiently, almost cheerfully, without alarm, her memories gradually giving place to hopes and visions of the future. Her hopes and visions were so intricate that she no longer saw the white pillows on which her gaze was fixed or remembered that she was waiting for anything.

At last she heard her mother calling. She started to her feet and ran to the banisters.

"Polly! Polly!"

"Yes, mamma?"

"Come down, dear. Mr. Doran wants to speak to you."

Then she remembered what she had been waiting for.

LIAM

O'FLAHERTY

The Sniper

Liam O'Flaherty was born in 1897 in the Aran Islands. After his discharge from the Irish Guards in 1917, he began writing novels and short stories. War, revolution and poverty are his chief themes. He took part in the Civil War in Ireland, upon which *The Informer,* familiar to American motion picture audiences, is based. [From *Spring Sowing* by Liam O'Flaherty; used by permission of Harcourt, Brace & Company, Inc., and Jonathan Cape, Ltd.]

THE LONG JUNE TWILIGHT faded into night. Dublin lay enveloped in darkness but for the dim light of the moon that shone through fleecy clouds, casting a pale light as of approaching dawn over the streets and the dark waters of the Liffey. Around the beleaguered Four Courts the heavy guns roared. Here and there through the city, machine-guns and rifles broke the silence of the night, spasmodically, like dogs barking on lone farms. Republicans and Free Staters were waging civil war.

On a roof-top near O'Connell Bridge, a Republican sniper lay watching. Beside him lay his rifle and over his shoulders were slung a pair of field glasses. His face was the face of a student, thin and ascetic, but his eyes had the cold gleam of the fanatic. They were deep and thoughtful, the eyes of a man who is used to look at death.

He was eating a sandwich hungrily. He had eaten nothing since morning. He had been too excited to eat. He finished the sandwich, and, taking a flask of whiskey from his pocket, he took a short draught. Then he returned the flask to his pocket. He paused for a moment, considering whether he should risk a smoke. It was dangerous. The flash might be seen in the darkness, and there were enemies watching. He decided to take the risk.

Placing a cigarette between his lips, he struck a match, inhaled the smoke hurriedly and put out the light. Almost immediately, a bullet flattened itself against the parapet of the roof. The sniper took another whiff and put out the cigarette. Then he swore softly and crawled away to the left.

Cautiously he raised himself and peered over the parapet. There was a flash and a bullet whizzed over his head. He dropped immediately. He had seen the flash. It came from the opposite side of the street.

He rolled over the roof to a chimney stack in the rear, and slowly drew himself up behind it, until his eyes were level with the top of the parapet. There was nothing to be seen—just the dim outline of the opposite housetop against the blue sky. His enemy was undercover.

Just then an armored car came across the bridge and advanced slowly up the street. It stopped on the opposite side of the street, fifty yards ahead. The sniper could hear the dull panting of the motor. His heart beat faster. It was an enemy car. He wanted to fire, but he knew it was useless. His bullets would never pierce the steel that covered the gray monster.

Then round the corner of a side street came an old woman, her head covered by a tattered shawl. She began to talk to the man in the turret of the car. She was pointing to the roof where the sniper lay. An informer.

The turret opened. A man's head and shoulders appeared, looking toward the sniper. The sniper raised his rifle and fired. The head fell heavily on the turret wall. The woman darted toward the side street. The sniper fired again. The woman whirled round and fell with a shriek into the gutter.

Suddenly from the opposite roof a shot rang out and the sniper dropped his rifle with a curse. The rifle clattered to the roof. The sniper thought the noise would wake the dead. He stopped to pick the rifle up. He couldn't lift it. His forearm was dead.

"Christ," he muttered, "I'm hit."

Dropping flat onto the roof, he crawled back to the parapet. With his left hand he felt the injured right forearm. The blood was oozing through the sleeve of his coat. There was no pain—just a deadened sensation, as if the arm had been cut off.

Quickly he drew his knife from his pocket, opened it on the breastwork of the parapet, and ripped open the sleeve. There was a small hole where the bullet had entered. On the other side there was no hole.

The bullet had lodged in the bone. It must have fractured it. He bent the arm below the wound. The arm bent back easily. He ground his teeth to overcome the pain.

Then taking out his field dressing, he ripped open the packet with his knife. He broke the neck of the iodine bottle and let the bitter fluid drip into the wound. A paroxysm of pain swept through him. He placed the cotton wadding over the wound and wrapped the dressing over it. He tied the ends with his teeth.

Then he lay still against the parapet, and, closing his eyes, he made an effort of will to overcome the pain.

In the street beneath all was still. The armored car had retired speedily over the bridge, with the machine gunner's head hanging lifeless over the turret. The woman's corpse lay still in the gutter.

The sniper lay still for a long time nursing his wounded arm and planning escape. Morning must not find him wounded on the roof. The enemy on the opposite roof covered his escape. He must kill that enemy and he could not use his rifle. He had only a revolver to do it. Then he thought of a plan.

Taking off his cap, he placed it over the muzzle of his rifle. Then he pushed the rifle slowly upward over the parapet, until the cap was visible from the opposite side of the street. Almost immediately there was a report, and a bullet pierced the center of the cap. The sniper slanted the rifle forward. The cap slipped down into the street. Then catching the rifle in the middle, the sniper dropped his left hand over the roof and let it hang, lifelessly. After a few moments he let the rifle drop to the street. Then he sank to the roof, dragging his hand with him.

Crawling quickly to the left, he peered up at the corner of the roof. His ruse had succeeded. The other sniper, seeing the cap and rifle fall, thought that he had killed his man. He was now standing before a row of chimney pots, looking across, with his head clearly silhouetted against the western sky.

The Republican sniper smiled and lifted his revolver above the edge of the parapet. The distance was about fifty yards—a hard shot in the dim light, and his right arm was paining him like a thousand devils. He took a steady aim. His hand trembled with eagerness. Pressing his lips together, he took a deep breath through his nostrils and fired. He was almost deafened with the report and his arm shook with the recoil.

Then when the smoke cleared he peered across and uttered a cry of joy. His enemy had been hit. He was reeling over the parapet in his death agony. He struggled to keep his feet, but he was slowly falling forward, as if in a dream. The rifle fell from his grasp, hit the parapet, fell over, bounded off the pole of a barber's shop beneath and then clattered on the pavement.

Then the dying man on the roof crumpled up and fell forward. The body turned over and over in space and hit the ground with a dull thud. Then it lay still.

The sniper looked at his enemy falling and he shuddered. The lust of battle died in him. He became bitten by remorse. The sweat stood out in beads on his forehead. Weakened by his wound and the long summer day of fasting and watching on the roof, he revolted from the sight of the shattered mass of his dead enemy. His teeth chattered, he began to gibber to himself, cursing the war, cursing himself, cursing everybody.

He looked at the smoking revolver in his hand, and with an oath he hurled it to the roof at his feet. The revolver went off with the concussion and the bullet whizzed past the sniper's head. He was frightened back to his senses by the shock. His nerves steadied. The cloud of fear scattered from his mind and he laughed.

Taking the whiskey flask from his pocket, he emptied it at a draught. He felt reckless under the influence of the spirit. He decided to leave the roof now and look for his company commander, to report. Everywhere around was quiet. There was not much danger in going through the streets. He picked up his revolver and put it in his pocket. Then he crawled down through the sky-light to the house underneath.

When the sniper reached the laneway on the street level, he felt a sudden curiosity as to the identity of the enemy sniper whom he had killed. He decided that he was a good shot, whoever he was. He wondered did he know him. Perhaps he had been in his own company before the split in the army. He decided to risk going over to have a look at him. He peered around the corner into O'Connell Street. In the upper part of the street there was heavy firing, but around here all was quiet.

The sniper darted across the street. A machine-gun tore up the ground around him with a hail of bullets, but he escaped. He threw himself face downward beside the corpse. The machine-gun stopped.

Then the sniper turned over the dead body and looked into his brother's face.

MORLEY

JAMIESON

*The Old Wife**

"JENNY," SAID THE OLD WIFE, her empty gums rubbing together, "Jenny, A doot A'm getting auld an' A'm no much longer for this warld. A'll hate to be leaving Dod." Jenny raised her grim visage to look at her, but said nothing. For the last ten years she had been accustomed to hearing the old wife talking like this. "Jenny," the croak-

---

* [Used by permission of the author.]

ing continued from the bed, "wud ye mairry Dod if he asked ye?" There was a pause since this part was unexpected. Jenny raised her awkward form from the fire-place where she had been polishing the grate. She looked at the old wife whose gray hair bounded her face which was worn with anxiety and age. Yes, the old wife was tired out: it was true she would soon be gone. "Aye," said Jenny in answer, and refolding the cloth in her hands she knelt abruptly to her work. The old wife lay quiet in her bed all day.

In the evening when Dod, her son, came in from the fields she eyed him, pleased with herself. Dod was about forty-seven; she felt pleased that at least she was seeing him right and gratified that he had stayed by her so long: kept her from the workhouse. She had arranged and settled his whole life hitherto, and was glad to have settled this last action, her desire to see him right. She never doubted that Jenny would marry him: women like Jenny couldn't be too pernickety. Nor did she doubt that Dod would marry his house-keeper.

She spoke to him about it later when Jenny was out for a moment. He was a little surprised, but there was a twist under his mustache. Of course he would marry Jenny if it would ease the old wife's mind: he told her that he had been thinking of it for some time. The thought had never entered his mind; this was Jenny in a new light: Jenny his wife? She might have been younger—but still. After Jenny came in the whole thing was settled; and the old wife said she would make them a present of all the money she had in the world which was five pounds: they could get married on it, she said.

Dod sat smoking his pipe for a long time by the fire after Jenny had gone to bed and the old wife was asleep. Out of his maze of thinking, which was really a kind of waking-dreaming preparing him for real sleep, he tried to consider sensibly this new idea. He felt somehow that his life was all pegs, and the pegs were things that kept him down to merely living as others did. He also felt vaguely that here was another peg. But then his mind wandered loosely to the other side: Jenny was all right and soon, sure enough, he would need somebody. Not that the old wife tended to his every need now, but she seemed to retain some moral hold on him, while at the same time she actively supported him in some way in his weakness and feebleness. He felt the need of a strong willed person behind him. Jenny was strong willed. Dod sighed and went to bed.

He felt embarrassed somewhat as he faced Jenny across the table at six o'clock the next morning. The old wife slept in the kitchen; and wheezes and little groans came from her bed in the corner; she was asthmatic. Dod regarded Jenny out of the corner of his eyes. She might've been a bit fatter, he thought, and wondered what she would look like on the mornings when they were married. They said nothing to each other beyond the usual remarks.

"Got your pipe and matches?"

"Aye."

"S'long then."

"S'long."

He unlocked the outer door and lifting the latch went out in the cutting winds of a November morning. He clumped through the farm steading and through the Close to the stables which he entered and began the day's work by lighting the lamps. Dod was first man on the farm: there was no grieve and the grieve's duties fell to him. The other three plowmen and the boy straggled in, and amid the jangle of the harness and clamping of horses they chaffed Dod about his unusual good humor. He had half a mind to tell them, but desisted. It would be wiser to wait a bit, he thought.

When it became lighter he took his horses out to the plow in the field; as he joggled along astride one broad back he felt complacent like the beasts he was driving. In the growing light he looked around at the hedges, and the bare trees that stood out against the sky: they seemed to ache, pitiably cold compared with the warmth of his thoughts. That morning his love of his horses increased, and he felt a clean delight as his plow passed through the earth. He noticed too, the dull shine of the forced clay of each furrow. Married, he thought; and the birds followed up the plow and the morning broke into forenoon. And so his thoughts went on in furrows: married, married, he thought; and sang all day into his mustache. His big body moved ponderously up and down the field like the horses, but he did not feel heavy. He felt picturesque like the plowman on the calendars that the Union distributed every year.

The chill evening came and he went home to Jenny and his mother. The house was brighter looking, his mother was more cheerful, and even Jenny was less dull. The three of them spent that night and the next night and the next, laying plans which were already laid.

In a week a striking change was seen in Jenny; she seemed to have lost three or four of her gaunt thirty-eight years, and the neighbors were noticing a change in the old wife; her cough was eased a bit. The day seemed to pass as quickly as Jenny's thin elbows flashed in front of the grate; and Jenny was tender with the old wife in all her caprices. The old body couldn't help being old. Dod in a clod-like manner even courted Jenny, and they went occasional jaunts to the cinema in the nearest village.

At the New Year Dod and Jenny were married on the strength of the old wife's five pounds. It didn't take all that of course, since it was a small celebration. Just the other plowmen and a few friends. They had an impromptu dance in the bothy which at that time had no occupants. After the bottle was empty and Dod had sung his last song with boisterous bucolic revelry and had become very short of breath and red in the face, he and Jenny went off to the house where they found the old wife tired out and fast asleep. They sat down on either side of the fire and said nothing. There seemed to be something tragic in the quietness which descended upon them, as if the cottage had known so many sorrows that the atmosphere was packed with sadness, which remained there, brooding. The two were in a way trying to fathom each other's thoughts, and after a long time Dod got to his feet. "Jenny," he said awkwardly, "will ye be using ma room?" She got up, her hair very straight like some doll's; her face was white; she said nothing. She nodded and turning went into his room. Dod followed lugubriously; it was queer being married.

At first, life didn't vary a great deal from the time when Jenny was only house-keeper. Of course she didn't work quite so hard at the beginning and she went about a bit more. It was the old wife who became aware of the change first. One might doubt if Jenny herself realized how much she changed. She just changed, that is all: it was an invisible process. The old wife would say to Jenny "Hand us ou'r a drink o' water, lassie," but Jenny always seemed to be doing something else, or she groused when she did it. Then the old wife would get annoyed and she took to snapping at Jenny, and Jenny took to snapping back at her.

Things were not so pleasant then. The old wife was weary and vexed. She could not understand why she hated everything so much; and she did not try to. She felt at a loss, as if she had given away some precious secret she had preserved for years: she was unsettled. No, it was not merely a secret, something more than that. It was not that she was jealous of Jenny and Dod, but it seemed as if life had done her out of something: had taken advantage of her age and done her. Was it Jenny who had so easily married a good man and a good home, Jenny who was safe now. Safe; safe from the Poorhouse.

The Poorhouse gave another line to the old wife's thoughts and she lay all day growing wearier and more cross. A terrible place the Poor-house; the things she had heard about it: she could have wept tears of joy over Dod for biding by her and keeping her out of it. At one time it was the fashion to sneer at paupers and the old wife herself had sneered at a few, with always the dread at the back of her mind that she might become one herself. The change went on and became gradually more and more unbearable to the old wife. Perhaps the trouble lay in the fact that Jenny was virtual mistress. She did not order or demand, but in a slow aggravating way obtained things and privileges which were not hers before. The old wife realized that her power was gone and she felt beaten, defeated.

The old wife watched everything in the house with a jealous eye; making a vague mental inventory of the articles around her from the padded armchair, to the china dog on the shelf which gazed at her with a bright impertinent look. Formerly, surrounded by these familiar sentimental objects, she had felt comfortable: at home in quiet back roads of her memory, enlivened on occasion with some whimsical melodies of long past years. Yet even that was all changed and now there was nothing but regret, regret for the mistakes. and regret for the joys of the past.

One evening Jenny lifted the tartan traveling rug off the old wife's bed and began folding it. "Ay its been a guid bit material that," said the old wife, "it maun be near haund twenty-three year syne Dod's feyther brocht it hame frae a big sale they had at Plenderleiths." Jenny stopped: "Dod's feyther never saw this rug, it came here wi me," she said.

"It did what, came wi you, well A never heard the like a' ma born days."

"Anywey its ma rug."

"Its nothing o' the kind."

"T'so."

"T'snut."

"T'so."

"T'snut."

"T'so."

Their voices rose unexpectedly. Then the old wife wept for vexation into her bedclothes and Jenny stood by white, and a little frightened by her own severity.

Dod sat stupidly regarding them, startled by this quarrel, yet unable to pacify or take sides with either of them. "A never thocht tae see the day A'd be spoken tae like that in ma ain hoose, yer feyther cud hardly see the wind blaw on me and he wadnae hae alloo'd it," the old wife snuffled. "But A suppose A maun tak a back sate noo A hae gotten nae mair'n a shaddy in this hoose." Dod became as angry as his wits would allow and even Jenny drew back from the glower on his face. But the old wife went on: could they not put her away somewhere: in a Poorhouse maybe, where she'd be out of the way: she couldn't help being old and helpless, but she'd go into the Poorhouse. Pay a little money every week she said: that would keep her: maybe she'd find people who would understand and care for her better. And so she went on: she angered Dod and wore him down with her moaning about her age, her frailty and her clean conscience, conceding issues with a martyred air before they were contended.

A week or so later Dod was harnessing his pair of horses, and Sandy the third plowman, a young talkative man with a small conceited mustache, asked, "Hoo's yer mother this weather, Dod?" There was a pause while Dod pulled on a strap. "Oh she's no sae bad either, but ay ailing ye ken. She went off tae the hospital yesterday." "Oh is that so," gossiped the young man, "well A suppose she'd be a haundfu for Jenny— Gee up Bess old yin," he went on, talking to the mare and slapping her large haunch. The mare moved awkwardly over in the stall. "Aye," he said, "yer fu' o rheumatiks, Bess, A doot ye'll be sune fur the knackerty." Then turning again to Dod, "Ah weel A suppose it's jist as weel, they hooses are nae place fur an invalid." "Aye," said Dod, taking the halter, "it's jist as weel," and the beasts made a clatter on the cobbled floor as they followed him out.

RHIAN ROBERTS

Keep Up

Appearances

Rhian Roberts was born in Abercynon in the heart of the Welsh mining valleys in 1923. She was bred on literature, Calvinism and song. Her first article was published in a school magazine in 1936. Her second venture, a prize-winning letter on Renaissance art, appeared about the same time in *The Children's Newspaper*. Between studies at London University, she wrote several stories which appeared in British magazines. [Used by permission of the author.]

SION WONDERED "How much longer does this goa on? Till Doomesday, p'raps. Never matter. It's a change."

Here he was, laid up with a fleabite of a cold but Eluned in her element, of course. There she was now like an old hen, clucking about the room arranging some smelly sweet peas in jam-jars. Well, it was kind of people to send flowers, indeed. He'd never had that happen to him before and it gave him a good feeling, a feeling of brotherhood and comradeship toward the old weasels.

"Now if you jus' hadn' a bin traipsin' about in the rain in next to nothin' this wouldn' a happened. You noa tha, doan you? Looka the work yore've put on my shoulders an me gettin' on an all. Havn' I toal you, time an' time again, 'Put on yore mack if yore goin' out in the rain?' But noa! You wouldn' listen an now look wass happened to you. In it enough to give anyone a headache?"

Go on you old fossil, Sion thought, isn't this just what you wanted? She didn't know the half of it, that one.

"Toal you, toal you, toal you, day in an day out . . ."

Sion lay back, head on pillow, thinking the Minister would be round soon, sanctimonious as an owl, his voice droning on about chapel and Sion's continued absence from the flock. The Parchedig was a good man but too old for the position. Authority and dignity after all were not articles of clothing you could wear automatically after the presentation of a diploma or a degree. Some had them, others hadn't. That was the only difference. Now he had had them in the old days. Chapel deacon, miner's representative, entertainments adviser at the Workmen's Hall. He hadn't bought his positions either. Had been a self-taught man with a way of getting round the people, a silver tongue, a gift of expression and a winning smile. A personality—that was it!—a personality.

Ah!—just for a moment of that former glory, what he'd give! The deferential greetings, the congratulations, the smiles and the tears.

Fate had been kind to him then but Fate is a fox with a bag of tricks at the back of every good deed. Had pushed him up to the top of the ladder, then pushed him down again. Well!—he'd like to walk hand in hand with Fate now, take along with him some tricks of his own.

231

"Day dreamin', day dreamin'," Eluned said. Jawch!—he was a handful. Hadn't she known it though when she'd first caught that fly-by-night expression in his eyes many years before!

"Yore lettin' yoreself in for somethin', you are," Maggie Ffatri had told her once upon a time. She knew it only too well now. Time had taught her quite a few lessons since. Consideration of the unfairness of a woman's lot had not helped either. The extra burdens, the added responsibilities of her later years, the excuses for Sion's recent wild and eccentric behavior had fallen entirely upon her shoulders. It was a hard life she'd chosen. But with experience had come wisdom and she was now able to review the situation, appreciate the inconsistencies and the hardships of this marriage with a greater calm and fortitude and patience than ever before. Still she'd like to put her feet up for a while, have a nap.

"Want some arrowroot?" she asked him.

"Aye! Might as well."

She went downstairs to prepare the meal. The difference in the old days! Sion had been a great man then, one who commanded respect wherever he went. Engaging, disarming. Ah well! it was no use looking back. Brought despair, regrets and misery. Now people laughed at him and no small wonder! The way he gadded around, getting himself drunk every Saturday night, preaching daft words on a box in the market, it was enough to put shame into the heart of a Delilah, and the Lord only knows!—there was plenty of that sort about nowadays. She sighed! Well, Eluned Parry you've done it well for yourself, slogging away bravely the way you've done all these years. You were the prettiest girl in the village once, yes indeed! And then who comes along but that silly baggage of nonsense and you got yourself saddled with him. And, Nezzie Evans, rich surveyor after you, forty-six and fat, but fine and secure. Isn't it funny the way things turn out, though? Duw, aye! That's life for you in this come-day, go-day world.

She remembered Sion that night in 1919 when they were sitting down beside the river. "Looka you, as lovely as the moon, honest to God! Yore like the river flowin' gently to the sea."

Tewch! What slop! Made you go red to think of it.

"You an me will make out fine, Eluned fach. I will be yore Llewellyn, indeed now, an you my princess. Aye!—important we'll be, mark you!"

Important? Look at it! Might as well help in a Teify fisherman's coracle as in this tumbledown little house. No room to move.

"You remember now, Eluned fach. I'm makin' no small promises. A self-taught man I am an noa my Bible from front to back, back to front. A prophet I am like to Isaiah. Watch me groa big!"

Duw!—hadn't she been soft, taking in all that rubbish and believing it. Experience had made her a wiser woman. Funny how love sours when things don't work out as expected.

She filled a small basin with the arrowroot and took it up to the bedroom. There he was, day-dreaming again.

"Oh, Eluned fach," he said, twisting his features into a monkey-like grimace, "Doan give me that awful arrowroot! I have a pain in my stomach like a lot of knives jabbin'."

"Come on all of a sudden, hasn't it?" she said angrily.

"Aye, hasn't it half!"

"You think I better get Doctor Price?"

"Poof, noa! Doan trust thoas doctors further than my noas. Get me the 'Hoam Doctor,' thess a good girl."

She set down the basin on the small table at the side of the bed and went in search of the book. This wasn't helping her rheumatism any either, this marching up and down the stairs all day! but men were inconsiderate creatures. Wanted to be served on, head and foot. Well! —all in a day's work.

She found the book in a box of rubbish in a corner of the parlor. It took her quite a time to find it and stooping over the box gave her a pain in the back. Where was the sense in slaving like this for him? That was what old John the Minister had told her when he had called after Chapel on Sunday evening.

"Mrs. Evans fach, you're working yourself to death. Take a rest!"

Weren't men funny! Didn't they know a housewife's work was never done?

"Sion can look after himself for a bit, I'm sure. I really didn't know he could be such a good-for-nothing."

There, of course, the Parchedig was right. Sion had become an idler, always harping on the wonders he had done, never dwelling on the future, not making any constructive effort to better their existence.

"Thass a good girl!" Sion smiled when she gave him the book. "Now less see what these pains are."

He began to turn over the pages. "It mus be somethin' finishing with an 'itis," he said thoughtfully. "Carn be nothin' less."

Eluned limped over to the dressing table, began to dust it. She had done it twice today, but dust settled so quickly in this dirty mining valley.

"Hullo," said Sion, "wass the matter with you, gruntin' and hoaldin' yoreself stiff like a poaker?"

"Rheumatics!" she snapped.

"Catom Pawb!" he laughed. "Two of us invalids, eh? Hop in here with me?"

She turned, glared. "Noa call for you to be indecent!" she retorted.

He grinned and looked at the book again. He ran his finger down a page, began to read, finally shook his head sadly.

"Thass awful," he said, "I've contracted somethin' bad."

Eluned wasn't in the least bit interested. He was putting it on, of course. Wasn't that just like him? Still, she'd better say something to keep up good relations.

"Do you think I should call the doctor?"

"Pah!"

Well, if that was the way he wanted it, let him be. He'd regret it sooner or later, treating her like a twopenny skivvy. One day he'd realize what a good wife she had been. Many would be the tears he'd shed when she'd passed away. She could just imagine him, weeping over her coffin.

"Eluned fach, what a bad husband I've been to you! If only we had our lives oaver, how different I'd be!"

Diwedd anwyl Dad! It nearly brought the tears into her eyes to think of it. But it was perfectly true. In the Minister's own words:

"One day, Eluned Evans fach, he will see the light like Saul at Damascus, and then the fruits of understanding and regret will come to him, but—too late, too late."

Everything was too late in this world. Never mind!—there would be a reckoning in the next and then Sion would embrace her and say, "Eluned fach, I've been a fool. How can you ever forgive me?"

That would be a great day. No longer would he linger on his past glory, flaunt his faded laurels and rest on his rusty spurs. That would be her day and they could meet the future together.

"Jawch!—am I really sufferin' from this terrible disease, Eluned?" came his voice from the bed. She saw he was smiling as if thrilled. Just as if he thought it wonderful to be ill. Now, if he had her rheumatics he would have something to complain about. Anyway, he'd probably get over it by tomorrow.

But the next day he was worse, pale faced and listless like a drooping lily, and on the following day she called in the doctor.

All that night she sat up in her rocking chair, knitting, worrying. Yes! He was very ill, the doctor had said. Plenty of care, warmth, and nourishing food and he might pull through to make his three-score years and ten. Might! She sighed. It was a cruel stroke of bad luck— this! Like a thunderbolt it was to her.

"He will get better, Eluned Evans fach," Mr. John had said to her only that afternoon, "for he has a strong foundation although he has been so inclined to a loose and sinful life in these last few years. Wherever there is a strong foundation, there is hope. Take our chapel, for instance. Debts keep pilin' up, funds are low, but are we disheartened? No! Of course not. For our chapel has a sound foundation and the backin' of good ordinary people. One day we shall be on our feet again, a flourishin' shrine of christianity. Same with Sion. He will get better and let us hope fervently, Eluned Evans fach, better in his ways, so that he will return to the fold."

Indeed, Mr. John was an inspiring speaker. Gave her hope, courage, and strength to meet this terrible obstacle. One needed a sympathetic adviser in times like these. Pity she hadn't listened to Mamgu years ago when she was about to plunge into marriage.

"Eluned," Mamgu had said, "doan you goa an marry tha marroaheaded softie. He's all talk and noa doin. I noa tha sort oanly too well. Marriage iss a great step, an thess noa getting out once yore in."

And wasn't it too true? Many had been the time when she'd considered the possibility of leaving him, starting a new life in new surroundings. But people behaved so cruelly in this community toward those who would break asunder the bonds that God had sanctified and blessed. Come to think of it, that would have been a dreadful blunder. No!—better to be badgered by a thousand power-loving, favor-seeking Sions than bring upon herself the wrath of God and the contempt of these people. What a life she would have had to lead if she had followed her impulses!—chased from pillar to post by the shadows of her shame and disgrace. Far better to stick it out with a stiff upper lip. Perhaps, too, as Mr. John had said, Sion would improve his ways after this trying illness and a realization would come to him of his neglect and disgusting conduct. She nodded with the satisfaction of a new hope, a hope that was too soon to be frustrated, for during the following week Sion was taken critically ill. He died on the Saturday. Yes! That was a dreadful blow, indeed, people said. Although he had been such a wretched rascal he had had his good points. Pity!

Eluned sat in her old rocking chair on that Saturday night. Mrs. Price the Tip, Sarah Lewis, and Lizzie Moel-y-glo were keeping her company. Mr. John had only just left. Wonder why Sion had wanted to see him so urgently that afternoon. Mr. John had not told her, just patted her on her head and remarked, "Perhaps you will be glad to know, Eluned fach, that he came back to the fold at last. For there is goodness in the heart of every man, and he was smilin' with new joy when I left him, his face lit up with glory and repentance God be with him and with you!"

And so he had left her, without as much as a word of what Sion had said. It was too bad! After all, she had been Sion's wife and it wasn't exactly nice to keep a thing like that to himself. Really!—these men had no tact.

"I think he coulda toald me," she grumbled.

"Aye! thass what I wass thinkin' too, Eluned Evans. But Mr. John iss a funny bloak sometimes, head in the clouds. Worryin' about Chapel Funds, no doubt."

Trust the Reverend! Naturally, that was it! No real sympathy for her in this bereavement, only high-sounding words and thoughts of funds and debts.

They finished their tea, laid their cups aside. Eluned smoothed the folds in her old black dress as if she had come to a decision.

"Now," she said calmly, "shall we go to see him."

Sadly, the four trooped up the stairs.

On Sunday evening, appropriately dressed, Eluned went to Chapel to pray. People inclined their heads toward her sympathetically. She sniffed throughout the service. Indeed, she had not wanted to come, but this was the best gesture she could make toward her late husband Sion at this time. It was only fitting that she should come here tonight to keep up appearances. Members of the congregation peered at her furtively, respectfully, and she bent her head.

"Aye, but it's a bloa to her, all the same," she heard someone whispering.

Knew what they were thinking. Well!—they were right. He had been a packet of trouble, but even so, she missed him. You can miss the load on your back, when it is lifted as much as the blessings of kindly Providence when they are taken from you. With all his funny ways Sion had not passed away without tears on her part. Granted she was free now; her time was her own. But freedom is strange at first to a caged bird. You need to get a solid footing, a kind and gentle launching. She was prepared, she'd be all right. No fear about that.

Service over, people coughed, sneezed. They smiled at her kindly! The Minister arose to speak. He looked grave and calm. Duw! My back aching so, and my lungs longing to get a few puffs of fresh air and he's going to jaw for the next half-hour probably, Eluned frowned.

Mr. John cleared his throat and began, "My friends, we all feel deeply the loss of a leading member of our community . . ."

Eluned looked up. What could be wrong with the man? Surely he knew that it was wrong to bring up such a painful topic before all these people, before Sion had been buried even. She felt bitterly the tactlessness of the Reverend William John, flushed. ". . . You know to whom I am referring, of course. Sion William Evans."

A low mumble of assent passed through the congregation.

"I shall be brief however and tell you the source of the inspiration for my sermon tonight, based as you will remember on the text "I am the good Shepherd." . . . Yes, my friends, all in connection with Sion Evans. With due apologies to Mrs. Evans, I bring up this subject of his death, but I am sure you will understand as she will understand that what I am about to say has a deep significance for the unenlightened, and also for the people gathered here. . . ."

Oh dear, dear! Eluned's brow was moist. It was so stuffy here and yet she was so curious. Fancy, though, the Minister bringing up such an intimate personal matter before these people. She was sure it must be that. She was resolved that she wouldn't take him into *her* confidence at any time. The man couldn't be trusted. She didn't want to listen, and yet—

"Yes, he asked to be taken back into the fold. . . ."

A soft surprised murmuring arose and passed. Jawch! Sion of all people! Eluned found it hard to believe. A confirmed chapel-hater, a man who jeered at her piety, asking to be forgiven? She became intent now.

". . . and let us give Sion the honor, the posthumous reward for his accomplishments, for the glory of his name . . ."

"Hear! hear!" piped up Twm Edwards from the Big Seat.

". . . and let us give him a worthy send off . . ."

Eluned produced her handkerchief, began to dab her eyes.

"We laughed at him, disdained him in recent days. An apology is due . . ."

The people nodded in agreement.

"I will tell you at this point, something which you may think confidential, but is not so, for Sion intimated that he wished you to know. He said that he had left two hundred pounds in his will toward the Chapel Funds . . ."

Eluned started. Will? What will? Sion had drawn up no will. The people gasped, whispered and looked wonderingly at the bereaved widow.

"It is therefore only right that we should all turn out to make our farewells. . . ."

Duw! Eluned trembled. What was this dreadful parting joke of Sion's? Trust him to get his finger into a pie even at the end. Men and women whispering "Good oal Sion," "Who'd have thought?" "Never knew he had it in him."

The Minister nodding, a sad little smile playing about his features. Everyone turning to look at Eluned, the widow of Sion. "Jawch!" she thought "and not a penny to Sion's name, never has been."

KATHERINE MANSFIELD

Miss Brill

Born in 1888 in Wellington, New Zealand, Katherine Mansfield came to London in 1903 to attend college. After a brief trip home, she returned to London, where she contributed to various newspapers and periodicals. Ill health pursued her for years, and she died in 1923. During her brief literary career she wrote several volumes of short stories, which received wide critical attention. [From *The Garden Party* by *Katherine Mansfield;* copyright 1922 by Alfred A. Knopf, Inc.; used by permission of Alfred A. Knopf, Inc.]

ALTHOUGH IT WAS SO BRILLIANTLY fine—the blue sky powdered with gold and great spots of light like white wine splashed over the Jardins Publiques—Miss Brill was glad that she had decided on her fur. The air was motionless, but when you opened your mouth there was just a faint chill, like a chill from a glass of iced water before you sip, and now and again a leaf came drifting—from nowhere, from the sky. Miss Brill put up her hand and touched her fur. Dear little thing! It was nice to feel it again. She had taken it out of its box that afternoon, shaken out the moth-powder, given it a good brush, and rubbed the life back into the dim little eyes. "What has been happening to me?" said the sad little eyes. Oh, how sweet it was to see them snap at her again from the red eiderdown! . . . But the nose, which was of some black composition, wasn't at all firm. It must have had a knock, somehow. Never mind—a little dab of black sealing-wax when the time came—when it was absolutely necessary. . . . Little rogue! Yes, she really felt like that about it. Little rogue biting its tail just by her left ear. She could have taken it off and laid it on her lap and stroked it. She felt a tingling in her hands and arms, but that came from walking, she supposed. And when she breathed, something light and sad—no, not sad, exactly—something gentle seemed to move in her bosom.

There were a number of people out this afternoon, far more than last Sunday. And the band sounded louder and gayer. That was because the Season had begun. For although the band played all the year round on Sundays, out of season it was never the same. It was like some one playing with only the family to listen; it didn't care how it played if there weren't any strangers present. Wasn't the conductor wearing a new coat, too? She was sure it was new. He scraped with his foot and flapped his arms like a rooster about to crow, and the bandsmen sitting in the green rotunda blew out their cheeks and glared at the music. Now there came a little "flutey" bit—very pretty!—a little chain of bright drops. She was sure it would be repeated. It was; she lifted her head and smiled.

Only two people shared her "special" seat: a fine old man in a velvet coat, his hands clasped over a huge carved walking-stick, and a big old woman, sitting upright, with a roll of knitting on her embroidered apron. They did not speak. This was disappointing, for Miss Brill always looked forward to the conversation. She had become really quite expert, she thought, at listening as though she didn't listen, at sitting in other people's lives just for a minute while they talked round her.

She glanced, sideways, at the old couple. Perhaps they would go soon. Last Sunday, too, hadn't been as interesting as usual. An Englishman and his wife, he wearing a dreadful Panama hat and she button boots. And she'd gone on the whole time about how she ought to wear spectacles; she knew she needed them; but that it was no good getting any; they'd be sure to break and they'd never keep on. And he'd been so patient. He'd suggested everything—gold rims, the kind that curved round your ears, little pads inside the bridge. No, nothing would please her. "They'll always be sliding down my nose!" Miss Brill had wanted to shake her.

The old people sat on the bench, still as statues. Never mind, there was always the crowd to watch. To and fro, in front of the flower-beds and the band rotunda, the couples and groups paraded, stopped to talk, to greet, to buy a handful of flowers from the old beggar who had his tray fixed to the railings. Little children ran among them, swooping and laughing; little boys with big white silk bows under their chins, little girls, little French dolls, dressed up in velvet and lace. And sometimes a tiny staggerer came suddenly rocking into the open from under the trees, stopped, stared, as suddenly sat down "flop," until its small high-stepping mother, like a young hen, rushed scolding to its rescue. Other people sat on the benches and green chairs, but they were nearly always the same, Sunday after Sunday, and—Miss Brill had often noticed—there was something funny about nearly all of them. They were odd, silent, nearly all old, and from the way they stared they looked as though they'd just come from dark little rooms or even—even cupboards!

Behind the rotunda the slender trees with yellow leaves down drooping, and through them just a line of sea, and beyond the blue sky with gold-veined clouds.

Tum-tum-tum tiddle-um! tiddle-um! tum tiddley-um tum ta! blew the band.

Two young girls in red came by and two young soldiers in blue met them, and they laughed and paired and went off arm-in-arm. Two peasant women with funny straw hats passed, gravely, leading beautiful smoke-colored donkeys. A cold, pale nun hurried by. A beautiful woman came along and dropped her bunch of violets, and a little boy ran after to hand them to her, and she took them and threw them away as if they'd been poisoned. Dear me! Miss Brill didn't know whether to admire that or not! And now an ermine toque and a gentleman in gray met just in front of her. He was tall, stiff, dignified, and she was wearing the ermine toque she'd bought when her hair was yellow. Now everything, her hair, her face, even her eyes, was the same color as the shabby ermine, and her hand, in its cleaned glove, lifted to dab her lips, was a tiny yellowish paw. Oh, she was so pleased to see him—delighted! She rather thought they were going to meet that afternoon. She described where she'd been—everywhere, here, there, along by the sea. The day was so charming—didn't he agree? And wouldn't he, perhaps? . . . But he shook his head, lighted a cigarette, slowly breathed a great deep puff into her face, and, even while she was still talking and laughing flicked the match away and walked on. The ermine toque was alone; she smiled more brightly than ever. But even the band seemed to know what she was feeling and played more softly, played tenderly, and the drum beat, "The Brute! The Brute!" over and over. What would she do? What was going to happen now? But as Miss Brill wondered, the ermine toque turned, raised her hand as though she'd seen someone else, much nicer, just over there, and pattered away. And the band changed again and played more quickly, more gayly than ever, and the old couple on Miss Brill's seat got up and marched away, and such a funny old man with long whiskers hobbled along in time to the music and was nearly knocked over by four girls walking abreast.

Oh, how fascinating it was! How she enjoyed it! How she loved sitting here, watching it all! It was like a play. It was exactly like a play. Who could believe the sky at the back wasn't painted? But it wasn't till a little brown dog trotted on solemn and then slowly trotted off, like a little "theater" dog, a little dog that had been drugged, that Miss Brill discovered what it was that made it so exciting. They were all on the stage. They weren't only the audience, not only looking on; they were acting. Even she had a part and came every Sunday. No doubt somebody would have noticed if she hadn't been there; she was part of the performance after all. How strange she'd never thought of it like that before! And yet it explained why she made such a point of starting from home at just the same time each week—so as not to be late for the performance—and it also explained why she had quite a queer, shy feeling at telling her English pupils how she spent her Sunday afternoons. No wonder! Miss Brill nearly laughed out loud. She was on the stage. She thought of the old invalid gentleman to whom she read the newspaper four afternoons a week while he slept in the garden. She had got quite used to the frail head on the cotton pillow, the hollowed eyes, the open mouth, and the high pinched nose. If he'd been dead she mighn't have noticed for weeks; she wouldn't have minded. But suddenly he knew he was having the paper read to him by an actress! "An actress!" The old head lifted; two points of light quivered in the old eyes. "An actress—are ye?" And Miss Brill smoothed the newspaper as though it were tne manuscript of her part and said gently: "Yes, I have been an actress for a long time."

The band had been having a rest. Now they started again. And what they played was warm, sunny, yet there was just a faint chill— a something, what was it?—not sadness—no, not sadness—a something that made you want to sing. The tune lifted, lifted, the light shone; and it seemed to Miss Brill that in another moment all of them, all the whole company, would begin singing. The young ones, the laughing ones who were moving together, they would begin, and the men's voices, very resolute and brave, would join them. And then she too, she too, and the others on the benches—they would come in with a kind of accompaniment—something low, that scarcely rose or fell, something so beautiful—moving. . . . And Miss Brill's eyes filled with tears and she looked smiling at all the other members of the company. Yes, we understand, we understand, she thought—though what they understood she didn't know.

Just at that moment a boy and a girl came and sat down where the old couple had been. They were beautifully dressed; they were in love. The hero and heroine, of course, just arrived from his father's yacht. And still soundlessly singing, still with that trembling smile, Miss Brill prepared to listen.

"No, not now," said the girl. "Not here, I can't."

"But why? Because of that stupid old thing at the end there?" asked the boy. "Why does she come here at all—who wants her? Why doesn't she keep her silly old mug at home?"

"It's her fu-fur which is so funny," giggled the girl. "It's exactly like a fried whiting."

"Ah, be off with you!" said the boy in an angry whisper. Then: "Tell me, ma petite chère—"

"No, not here," said the girl. "Not *yet*."

On her way home she usually bought a slice of honey-cake at the baker's. It was her Sunday treat. Sometimes there was an almond in her slice, sometimes not. It made a great difference. If there was an almond it was like carrying home a tiny present—a surprise—something that might very well not have been there. She hurried on the almond Sundays and struck the match for the kettle in quite a dashing way.

But today she passed the baker's by, climbed the stairs, went into the little dark room—her room like a cupboard—and sat down on the red eiderdown. She sat there for a long time. The box that the fur came out of was on the bed. She unclasped the necklet quickly; quickly, without looking, laid it inside. But when she put the lid on she thought she heard something crying.

KATHARINE
SUSANNAH
PRICHARD

*The Gray
Horse*

Katharine Susannah Prichard is an outstanding Australian novelist. She won the Hodder and Stoughton prize for the best book on Australia with her novel, *The Pioneers*. She has contributed many short stories to Australian magazines and has written a volume of verse, in addition to another novel, *Working Bullock*. [Copyright by Art in Australia, Ltd.]

HE WAS YOUNG, a draught stallion, gray, and Old Gourlay worked him on the roads.

Old Gourlay kept the road in order on the back of Black Swan and lived with his housekeeper in a bare-faced, wooden box of a house beside the road, where it loped over the mountain to Perth, by way of the river and half a dozen townships scattered across the plains. Gourlay was a dry stick of a man, and deaf; but Gray Ganger—the beauty of him took the breath like a blast of cold wind. There was nothing more beautiful in the ranges, not the wild flowers, yellow and blue, on the ledges of the road, nor the tall white gums gleaming through the dark of the bush from among thronging rough-barked red gums and jarrah.

A superb creature, broad and short of back, deep-barreled, with mighty quarters, the gray stallion carried Old Gourlay, on the floor of the tip-dray, uphill in the morning, curveting with kittenish grace, as though the tip-dray were a chariot; prancing and tossing his head so that silver threads glinted in the spume of his mane. He brought loads of gravel downhill, gaily, prancing still, with an air of curbing his pace to humor the queer, fussy insect of an old man who clung to the rope reins stretched out beside and behind him.

Wood-carters who worked on the Black Swan road envied the old man his horse. They wanted to buy him; but Gourlay would not sell the Ganger. Their great, rough-haired horses labored along the bush tracks and came slowly down the steep winding road, sitting back in the breaching, the roughly split jarrah for firewood stacked on the carts, jabbing their haunches.

O'Reilly had offered good money, cash down, for Gray Ganger; he had told Gourlay to name his own figure. But Old Gourlay shook his head. Nothing but cussedness, it was, O'Reilly declared. Gourlay had not enough work for the Ganger; a less powerful horse would suit him better, cost less, and be easier to manage. O'Reilly would have liked to mate the Ganger with his Lizzie when he found he could not buy the horse. Lizzie was a staunch enough working mare, shaggy and evil-smelling, with a roach back, and splay feet, but she had been "a good 'un in her day," he said.

Gourlay would have none of that either.

"Aw—aw," he stuttered; "she's rough stuff. He's only a baby. There'd be no holding him if——"

Old Gourlay had pride in his horse, enjoyed crying his measurements, the size of his collar. The Ganger was always in good condition, close knit and hard, his hide smooth and sheeny as the silk of a woman's dress. Not that Gourlay seemed to have any affection for him: rather was there hostility, a vague resentment in his bearing. He nagged at Gray Ganger as though he feared and had some secret grudge against him.

But no one envied Old Gourlay his horse more than Bill Moriarty, who, against the advice of every fruit-grower in the district, had taken up the block of land adjoining Gourlay's, and had planted vines and fruit-trees to make an orchard there, a few years before Gourlay, Mrs. Drouett and the gray stallion had come to live on the Black Swan road. As he cleared and grubbed, burnt off, and cultivated his land, Young Moriarty had watched Gourlay and Gray Ganger.

On the wildest, wettest nights, he had seen the flickering, loose golden star of Gourlay's lantern as he went to feed the Ganger and shut him into his stable for the night. He had been up when the old man pulled the board from across the stable door in the morning, and the Ganger, released, dashed round the small, muddy square of the yard, flinging up his heels, snorting and gamboling joyously, with such a clumsy, kittenish grace, that Moriarty himself would laugh and sing out to old Gourlay: "He's in great heart, this morning, all right."

Gourlay would mutter resentfully, and swear at the Ganger, clacking the gate of the stable-yard to, as he went up to breakfast. Nothing annoyed him more than to see Gray Ganger disporting himself.

When first he and his housekeeper had come to live at Black Swan, Old Gourlay had made those trips to feed and shut the Ganger in his stable for the night with zest, swinging his lantern religiously and whistling. And he had gone afterward into the shed beside the stable, where a bed was made up, put the light out there and slammed the door. But Young Moriarty had seen him stumble uphill in the starlight, or when he thought all Black Swan was sleeping, open the back door quietly, and go into his house.

Black Swan people did not appear to mind where Old Gourlay slept, really. They were too busy in their orchards or clearing and cultivating land for vines to bother much about what their neighbors were doing. Besides, Gourlay's and Mrs. Drouett's story had gone before them. Nobody expected Old Gourlay to sleep in the shed beside the stable. Even the children going along the road to school, as they passed Gourlay's, said mysteriously to each other: "He's got one mother up-country . . . and living here with another."

The neighbors were kind and friendly enough when they met either Gourlay or Mrs. Drouett. Their story had created a slightly romantic sympathy. It was said Old Gourlay had been a well-to-do farmer with a wife and family when Laura Drouett had come his way. He sold his farm and left his family to go away with her. They had wandered about for years and grown old together.

Mrs. Drouett had been a comely woman and still kept her figure tight at the waist. Her hips were thrust out from it, plump and heavy; she had a bosom and a fringe of brown, curly hair which she wore above the withered apple of her face when she was dressed for the afternoon, or going driving with Mr. Gourlay. She was older than he, perhaps; but better preserved; deaf also, and nervy, under the strain of living with Mr. Gourlay, "seeing how I am placed," as she explained to Young Moriarty when he hopped over the fence to talk to her, and cheer her up, sometimes.

Old Gourlay did not like Bill Moriarty hopping over the fence to talk to Mrs. Drouett.

"He's mad as a wet hen if he finds me having a yarn with the old girl," Bill explained to O'Reilly. "She's a decent sort . . . a bit lonely . . . and I've been trying to get round her to make the old man lend me his horse, now and then."

O'Reilly laughed. He thought he guessed what was at the back of Old Gourlay's mind. Bill was a good-looker, thick-set and swarthy, with crisp dark hair and blue eyes set in whites as hard as china, and so short-lashed that they stared at you unshaded from the bronze of his face. Though he was still more or less coltish, Young Moriarty, O'Reilly knew, was working too hard, and was too much in love with a girl who lived down on the flats, to be bold with any woman or give Tom Gourlay cause for doubting the fidelity of his Laura. But O'Reilly could not resist rubbing it in, when, a few days later, the old man stopped him on the road, not far from where Bill was pruning his vines.

"Good cut of a fellow, that," he shouted, waving an arm toward Moriarty. "Isn't a better man made in the ranges. Ever seen him stripped? By God, he's got good limbs on him."

In the evening, mean-spirited and vindictive, Gourlay gave Mrs. Drouett the benefit of that praise of Bill and the gall he had stewed in all day. The old woman cried; but she was coy and self-conscious with Young Moriarty next time she saw him. She put on her brown hair in the morning and pulled the strings of her corsets tighter. Old Gourlay guessed what he had done, and was madder than a wet hen, though Bill, for all Laura's youthful figure and hair, saw only her poor grandmother's face. He was soaked with the sight and shape of Rose Sharwood, her warm bosom; thirsty with desire for the sound and the smell of her. He was all a madness for Rose. So when he could not get a horse to do his spring plowing, he went again to Old Gourlay. He had asked before for the loan of his horse, and the old man had refused him, churlishly enough, but with excuses. And Bill had not pressed him. But this was different. It meant a great deal to him, getting that plowing done.

Black cockatoos had whirled about the clearing, shedding their wild cries high in the air that morning. A long spell of dry weather was breaking and Bill Moriarty needed a horse to cultivate between his vines after the rain.

"How's it for a loan of the Ganger to plow my orchard?" he asked Old Gourlay, leaning over the weather-worn saplings of the stallion's yard.

"Nothing doing," Old Gourlay growled.

Moriarty explained the difficulty he was in. He was hard up. He could not buy a horse: he could pay for the hire of one by the day. But every man in the district with working horses was waiting for the rain and required his horses to plow, and make the most of the ground while it was soft. Young Moriarty could not get the promise of a horse from anyone. And it meant everything to him, to have the earth turned and sweetened about his vines, this year; all the difference between a good, or a poor, yield of grapes. Bill let Old Gourlay know, with all the sentiment he could muster, that he was praying for a good harvest because he wanted to get married. He soft-pedaled about Rose, and the skinflint of an aunt who threatened to take her away to the Eastern States at the end of the autumn if Bill had not built a house and married the girl before then.

Old Gourlay pretended not to hear half of what he was saying.

"T-too busy to do any plowing," he said. "Rain'll w-wash away half the road up by The Beak. . . . Couldn' spare the Ganger . . . plenty of work for him to do on the road. . . . Too much for one man and one horse."

He stuttered away from the subject, irritably. Moriarty let him go, watching the stallion as he frisked and plunged about the yard where the gray sapling posts and rails, silvered by the early light, shook as he bumped against them.

"Ever mate him, Mr. Gourlay?" Young Moriarty yelled.

"No!" The old man's eyes leapt, sharp and startled in the weathered fallow of his face. "There'd be no holding him if ever I did."

So that was it, Bill thought. He and the Ganger were in the same boat. Old Gourlay would thwart them both if he could; defeat their instincts. Vaguely Bill understood that what Gourlay resented in the Ganger, and in himself, was their youth and virility, when the sap had dried in his old man's bones.

It was beginning to rain as Bill went back to his work.

"Mean old blighter," he muttered. "Had two women himself, and won't give a handsome animal like that his dues. Him breaking his neck . . . and me too."

Young Moriarty went out to the road to meet O'Reilly as the wood-carts came downhill that evening, looking top-heavy, the wood piled high on them red and umber with rain, the shaggy, brown-furred horses stepping warily for fear they might come down on the slippery roads beside which the feather-white torrents of rain-wash were flying.

Moriarty asked the wood-carter for the loan of his mare, Lizzie, some Sunday soon, when he was not using her. He told O'Reilly how Old Gourlay had refused to let him have the Ganger although the stallion spent most of his time on Sundays galloping up and down and cavorting about his yard beside the stable; and how he had explained to Gourlay what it meant to him to get his plowing and harrowing done just then.

O'Reilly knew about Rose Sharwood and that Bill wanted to marry her.

The rain beat around them as they talked, Bill hatless, hugging himself in the coat of his working clothes buttoned up to the throat; O'Reilly, his tarred overalls shining, his ruddy, unshaven face with dropped lip and lit eyes laughing from under his sodden hat. The rain-drops quivering on its brim ran and fell as he laughed, getting the gist of Young Moriarty's grievance, and the way he proposed to pay for the hire of old Lizzie.

Squalls swept up over the purple and green of the plains all the week, flung themselves against the ranges, scattering hailstones, and passed on inland. A film of fine, chill rain veiled the timbered hills about Black Swan for days. Then the sunshine of late spring leapt, shimmering on the water lying down on the flats, and drying the land in the hills quickly.

O'Reilly did not appear with Lizzie that Sunday. Moriarty was desperate. Rains had lashed the blossom from the almond-trees along the boundary of his fences. The tooth of green was everywhere; the flame of young leaves. Down near Gray Ganger's stable and yard, where Moriarty had put a row of nectarines below the vines, pink flowers were spraying widespread, varnished branches. It would soon be too late to conserve moisture for the vines. And the thought that Rose would go away with her aunt if he did not do well out of his grapes that year, overhung Young Moriarty like a doom.

But the next Sunday morning, while the Ganger was galloping about his yard, just from his stable, as fresh and beside himself as Bill had ever seen him, O'Reilly brought old Lizzie to cultivate the orchard.

O'Reilly and Bill stood watching the Ganger's gambolings for a moment, laughing and exclaiming their admiration. Then they got to work. O'Reilly drove the mare as they plowed, across the crest of the hillside, while Bill, stooping along before Lizzie, cleared stones and pruned branches out of the way. O'Reilly plowed well down the slope before he swung Lizzie from an upper to a lower furrow, uphill and along, downhill and along.

The Ganger came to the end of his yard as he sighted them. He watched Lizzie curiously, snorted as she passed, and galloped up and down, throwing himself about to attract her attention. When they had finished plowing that side of the hill, Moriarty and O'Reilly spelled Lizzie while they went up to the lean-to Bill lived in, for a meal.

They left her down near the fence where the young nectarines were in blossom. The gray stallion was trembling against his yard as they did so; taut, the breath blowing in gusty blasts from his nostrils. Lizzie swung her bland, white-splashed face toward him and blinked at him from behind her wide black winkers. Her tail moved gently. A hot, herby aroma reached the men. Young Moriarty went to lead her away, as if to avoid trouble and propitiate Old Gourlay. But it was too late. Gray Ganger rushed and broke his fences. He whirled round Lizzie, charging Moriarty. Bill got away from his plunging fury and flung heels. He picked up the dead branch of a fruit-tree as though to defend himself, or beat off the Ganger. O'Reilly ran away over the broken earth of the hillside.

The noise of the breaking fence and the stallion's whinnied blast brought Old Gourlay running from the house. Mrs. Druett jiggled marionette-wise on the back veranda for a moment; then when she saw what was happening at the bottom of the paddock, near Young Moriarty's flowering fruit-trees, she put her hands over her face and scuttered into the house again.

Old Gourlay writhed beside the fence, brandishing his whip and shrieking in a frenzy of rage. Moriarty tried to explain, but Gourlay would have no explanations. He was deaf to what Moriarty was saying, though he heard O'Reilly laughing up under the almond-trees. He knew well enough there was only one explanation—Old Gourlay—and Moriarty was not likely to give that.

"It's a put-up job," he spluttered; "a buddy put-up job. I'll have the law of ye for it. Taking the bread out of a man's mouth. There'll be no holding him now."

And there was not. Gourlay was right about that. At the sidings there was no keeping the Ganger from passing mares; and he was as flighty as a brumby on the roads. He dragged Gourlay, powerless at the end of his reins, behind the tip-dray as they came downhill, the old man looking more than ever like some dry, twiggy insect as he jogged there, shrilling fiercely. He was at his wits' end, and went in danger of his life, trying to manage the stallion. He could talk of nothing but the life the horse was leading him, and worry about each new incident in his career, as if an only son had kicked over the traces and was disgracing him in the district.

Mrs. Drouett got nerves with it all. She went about with her head in a shawl and said she was ill. She and Old Gourlay quarreled incessantly. Their voices could be heard cracking and rattling at each other in the evening. Nothing seemed left of their old passion except its animosities. But when Mrs. Drouett took to her bed, Old Gourlay became alarmed. He thought she might die, and he threw up his contract for mending the road to stay at home and nurse her.

Without telling anyone in Black Swan what he was going to do, or where the horse was going, he sold Gray Ganger then. O'Reilly called him by every name he could think of. But Gourlay would not have foregone his vengeance for a fiver. As it was, he had taken less for the horse than O'Reilly, and many another man round Black Swan, would have given. He sold his house and land too, and he and Mrs. Drouett went to live nearer town, where, if people were not as kind and friendly, at least they were less free with their neighbor's property.

Moriarty married Rose Sharwood soon after old Lizzie had foaled in O'Reilly's paddock beyond The Beak. At the end of the winter it was. His vines did well in that fifth year; he had expected so much from them. He dried currants, raisins, sultanas, and sold them at top prices on the London market. Even Rose's aunt was satisfied with the check he showed her from his agents.

It was not until the following season that "the bottom fell out of the market for dried fruit," as fruit-growers about Black Swan said. And about the same time Rose gave birth to a son.

Bill was not sorry when the baby died, a few months afterwards, during the summer. He believed it was better for a weakly child, as for a sick chicken or calf, to die. But the birth, brief screaming existence and death of the small puckered red creature, were a shock to him. He had not reckoned on a child from him being a weakling; and Death, like a hand out of the dark, had gripped, shaken, and squeezed life out of the youngster. There was something brutal and unfair about the whole business. If the thing was to die, why had it ever been born? Young Moriarty was dazed, numb and angry under the shock.

As he worked out of doors, milked the cows he had bought to make up for the falling price of dried fruit, fed pigs and fowls, plowed and harrowed the orchard, or cleared land for fodder crops, he still glanced often down to the Ganger's yard. Through his numbness and anger about the child, the cleaning of sties and cowyards, breaking of earth, slopping of milk into pig-troughs, thoughts of the stallion were fugitive.

Life with Rose was not what he imagined it would be. It was mostly a fitting-in of domestic jobs, talking about the cost of things, eating frugally, and sleeping without touching her. He had taken her as he wished, sometimes; and now she pushed him away, saying he was "low . . . a lustful brute."

Moriarty was depressed about it. He had not expected Rose to be like that; his joy in her to fade so soon. As he toiled, plowing, harrowing and pruning, he was conscious of belonging to the fecund earth and life, and yet of being apart from them.

Rose did not want any more children; she dreaded having another baby. It seemed simple and natural enough for a man and woman to have children. But not for Rose, or for him. . . . He snipped the shoots from a budding fruit-tree. . . . Perhaps they were burnt cats who feared the fire, he and Rose.

He noticed that grass had grown in the Ganger's yard and under his stable door.

Rose herself had no strong feelings, he was sure, except for the things that did not matter: dust in out-of-the-way corners, pennies spent unnecessarily. But she was keen on the scent of any hankering Bill might have for another woman, and so shrewish about it that for the sake of peace, at least, he had come to heel. He no longer sought other women.

But Lord, what was there to live for? His days tasted all the same to him, from dawn till dark, flat and dull. He worked hard but without the old zest. Couch had made its appearance in his orchard, his tilth was not what it had been. He invariably struck a bad day if he had cows to sell; and he missed the best price for eggs.

He was a fool, Moriarty told himself, as Rose had often said. He had been wrong about Rose; he had made a mistake about the orchard. There was no money in fruit, fresh or dried. He worked as hard as any of O'Reilly's draught horses for food and a roof over his head: and that was all there was to it. He was sick to death of pottering about pigsties, cowyards, fowl-houses, fruit-trees; and he supposed he would go on pottering among them, and being sick to death of them. It was the rut of life he had made and must stay in.

As he sprawled before the fire that evening, morose and weary, this was swarming over him, the thoughts crawling in and out of his brain and breeding, as fruit-fly had on rotting nectarines in his orchard.

O'Reilly swung into the kitchen.

"That draught stallion of Old Gourlay's," he said. "He's been bought by Purdies. Standing the season at The Beak farm and will travel the district. Be up at my place this day next week. . . . Thought you'd like to know."

Moriarty went to see the horse when he was at O'Reilly's stables.

As the groom led him out, the stallion came, arching his neck and tossing his head.

Gray Ganger was more beautiful than he had ever been; no longer skittish, but imperious, his quarters molded to perfection, the gray satin of his skin sheening under its dapples as he moved. Bill walked across and stood beside him, rubbing a hand over his shoulders, the anguish of his dissatisfaction with life breaking.

"I wish it was me, old man," he groaned. "I wish it was me. It's all I'm fit for really."

MORLEY

CALLAGHAN

A Sick Call

Morley Callaghan, born in Toronto in 1903, began his writing career as a journalist. During a visit to Paris in 1929 he met Ernest Hemingway, who encouraged him in his fiction writing. His first stories appeared in the "expatriate" periodicals abroad. He has written novels as well as short stories. Perhaps his best known work is *They Shall Inherit the Earth*. [From *Now That April's Here* by Morley Callaghan; copyright 1936 by Morley Callaghan.]

SOMETIMES FATHER MACDOWELL mumbled out loud and took a deep wheezy breath as he walked up and down the room and read his office. He was a huge old priest, white-headed except for a shiny baby-pink bald spot on the top of his head, and he was a bit deaf in one ear. His florid face had many fine red interlacing vein lines. For hours he had been hearing confessions and he was tired, for he always had to hear more confessions than any other priest at the cathedral; young girls who were in trouble, and wild but at times repentant young men, always wanted to tell their confessions to Father Macdowell, because nothing seemed to shock or excite him, or make him really angry, and he was even tender with those who thought they were most guilty.

While he was mumbling and reading and trying to keep his glasses on his nose, the house girl knocked on the door and said, "There's a young lady here to see you, Father. I think it's about a sick call."

"Did she ask for me especially?" he said in a deep but slightly cracked voice.

"Indeed she did, Father. She wanted Father Macdowell and nobody else."

So he went out to the waiting room, where a girl about thirty years of age, with fine brown eyes, fine cheek bones, and rather square shoulders, was sitting daubing her eyes with a handkerchief. She was wearing a dark coat with a gray wolf collar. "Good evening, Father," she said. "My sister is sick. I wanted you to come and see her. We think she's dying."

"Be easy, child; what's the matter with her? Speak louder. I can hardly hear you."

"My sister's had pneumonia. The doctor's coming back to see her in an hour. I wanted you to anoint her, Father."

"I see, I see. But she's not lost yet. I'll not give her extreme unction now. That may not be necessary. I'll go with you and hear her confession."

"Father, I ought to let you know, maybe. Her husband won't want to let you see her. He's not a Catholic, and my sister hasn't been to church in a long time."

"Oh, don't mind that. He'll let me see her," Father Macdowell said, and he left the room to put on his hat and coat.

When he returned, the girl explained that her name was Jane Stanhope, and her sister lived only a few blocks away. "We'll walk and you tell me about your sister," he said. He put his black hat square on the top of his head, and pieces of white hair stuck out awkwardly at the sides. They went to the avenue together.

The night was mild and clear. Miss Stanhope began to walk slowly, because Father Macdowell's rolling gait didn't get him along the street very quickly. He walked as if his feet hurt him, though he wore a pair of large, soft, specially constructed shapeless shoes. "Now, my child, you go ahead and tell me about your sister, he said, breathing with difficulty, yet giving the impression that nothing could have happened to the sister which would make him feel indignant.

There wasn't much to say, Miss Stanhope replied. Her sister had married John Williams two years ago, and he was a good, hard-working fellow, only he was very bigoted and hated all church people. "My family wouldn't have anything to do with Elsa after she married him, though I kept going to see her," she said. She was talking in a loud voice to Father Macdowell so he could hear her.

"Is she happy with her husband?"

"She's been very happy, Father. I must say that."

"Where is he now?"

"He was sitting beside her bed. I ran out because I thought he was going to cry. He said if I brought a priest near the place he'd break the priest's head."

"My goodness. Never mind, though. Does your sister want to see me?"

"She asked me to go and get a priest, but she doesn't want John to know she did it."

Turning into a side street, they stopped at the first apartment house, and the old priest followed Miss Stanhope up the stairs. His breath came with great difficulty. "Oh, dear, I'm not getting any younger, not one day younger. It's a caution how a man's legs go back on him," he said. As Miss Stanhope rapped on the door, she looked pleadingly at the old priest, trying to ask him not to be offended at anything that might happen, but he was smiling and looking huge in the narrow hallway. He wiped his head with his handkerchief.

The door was opened by a young man in a white shirt with no collar, with a head of thick black wavy hair. At first he looked dazed, then his eyes got bright with excitement when he saw the priest, as though he were glad to see someone he could destroy with pent-up energy. "What do you mean, Jane?" he said. "I told you not to bring a priest around here. My wife doesn't want to see a priest."

"What's that you're saying, young man?"

"No one wants you here."

"Speak up. Don't be afraid. I'm a bit hard of hearing." Father Macdowell smiled rosily. John Williams was confused by the unexpected deafness in the priest, but he stood there, blocking the door with sullen resolution as if waiting for the priest to try to launch a curse at him.

"Speak to him, Father," Miss Stanhope said, but the priest didn't seem to hear her; he was still smiling as he pushed past the young man, saying, "I'll go in and sit down, if you don't mind, son. I'm here on God's errand, but I don't mind saying I'm all out of breath from climbing those stairs."

John was dreadfully uneasy to see he had been brushed aside, and he followed the priest into the apartment and said loudly, "I don't want you here."

Father Macdowell said, "Eh, eh?" Then he smiled sadly. "Don't be angry with me, son," he said. "I'm too old to try and be fierce and threatening." Looking around, he said, "Where's your wife?" and he started to walk along the hall, looking for the bedroom.

John followed him and took hold of his arm. "There's no sense in your wasting your time talking to my wife, do you hear?" he said angrily.

Miss Stanhope called out suddenly, "Don't be rude, John."

"It's he that's being rude. You mind your business," John said.

"For the love of God let me sit down a moment with her, anyway. I'm tired," the priest said.

"What do you want to say to her? Say it to me, why don't you?"

Then they both heard someone moan softly in the adjoining room, as if the sick woman had heard them. Father Macdowell, forgetting that the young man had hold of his arm, said, "I'll go in and see her for a moment, if you don't mind," and he began to open the door.

"You're not going to be alone with her, that's all," John said, following him into the bedroom.

Lying on the bed was a white-faced, fair girl, whose skin was so delicate that her cheek bones stood out sharply. She was feverish, but her eyes rolled toward the door, and she watched them coming in.

Father Macdowell took off his coat, and as he mumbled to himself he looked around the room at the mauve-silk bed and the light wallpaper with the tiny birds in flight. It looked like a little girl's room. "Good evening, Father," Mrs. Williams whispered. She looked scared. She didn't glance at her husband. The notion of dying had made her afraid. She loved her husband and wanted to die loving him, but she was afraid, and she looked up at the priest.

"You're going to get well, child," Father Macdowell said, smiling and patting her hand gently.

John, who was standing stiffly by the door, suddenly moved around the big priest, and he bent down over the bed and took his wife's hand and began to caress her forehead.

"Now, if you don't mind, my son, I'll hear your wife's confession," the priest said.

"No, you won't," John said abruptly. "Her people didn't want her, and they left us together, and they're not going to separate us now. She's satisfied with me." He kept looking down at her face as if he could not bear to turn away.

Father Macdowell nodded his head up and down and sighed. "Poor boy," he said. "God bless you." Then he looked at Mrs. Williams, who had closed her eyes, and he saw a faint tear on her cheek. "Be sensible, my boy," he said. "You'll have to let me hear your wife's confession. Leave us alone awhile."

"I'm going to stay right here," John said, and he sat down on the end of the bed. He was working himself up and staring savagely at the priest. All of a sudden he noticed the tears on his wife's cheeks, and he muttered as though bewildered, "What's the matter, Elsa? What's the matter, darling? Are we bothering you? Just open your eyes and we'll go out of the room and leave you alone till the doctor comes." Then he turned and said to the priest, "I'm not going to leave you here with her, can't you see that? Why don't you go?"

"I could revile you, my son. I could threaten you; but I ask you, for the peace of your wife's soul, leave us alone." Father Macdowell spoke with patient tenderness. He looked very big and solid and immovable as he stood by the bed. "I liked your face as soon as I saw you," he said to John. "You're a good fellow."

John still held his wife's wrist, but he rubbed one hand through his thick hair and said angrily, "You don't get the point, sir. My wife and I were always left alone, and we merely want to be left alone now. Nothing is going to separate us. She's been content with me. I'm sorry, sir; you'll have to speak to her with me here, or you'll have to go."

"No; you'll have to go for a while," the priest said patiently.

Then Mrs. Williams moved her head on the pillow and said jerkily, "Pray for me, Father."

So the old priest knelt down by the bed, and with a sweet unruffled expression on his florid face he began to pray. At times his breath came with a whistling noise as though a rumbling were inside him, and at other times he sighed and was full of sorrow. He was praying that young Mrs. Williams might get better, and while he prayed he knew that her husband was more afraid of losing her to the Church than losing her to death.

All the time Father Macdowell was on his knees, with his heavy prayer book in his two hands, John kept staring at him. John couldn't understand the old priest's patience and tolerance. He wanted to quarrel with him, but he kept on watching the light from overhead shining on the one baby-pink bald spot on the smooth white head, and at last he burst out, "You don't understand, sir! We've been very happy together. Neither you nor her people came near her when she was in good health, so why should you bother her now? I don't want anything to separate us now; neither does she. She came with me. You see you'd be separating us, don't you?" He was trying to talk like a reasonable man who had no prejudices.

Father Macdowell got up clumsily. His knees hurt him, for the floor was hard. He said to Mrs. Williams in quite a loud voice, "Did you really intend to give up everything for this young fellow?" and he bent down close to her so he could hear.

"Yes, Father," she whispered.

"In Heaven's name, child, you couldn't have known what you were doing."

"We loved each other, Father. We've been very happy."

"All right. Supposing you were. What now? What about all eternity, child?"

"Oh, Father, I'm very sick and I'm afraid." She looked up to try to show him how scared she was, and how much she wanted him to give her peace.

He sighed and seemed distressed, and at last he said to John, "Were you married in the church?"

"No, we weren't. Look here, we're talking pretty loud and it upsets her."

"Ah, it's a crime that I'm hard of hearing, I know. Never mind, I'll go." Picking up his coat, he put it over his arm; then he sighed as if he were very tired, and he said, "I wonder if you'd just fetch me a glass of water. I'd thank you for it."

John hesitated, glancing at the tired old priest, who looked so pink and white and almost cherubic in his utter lack of guile.

"What's the matter?" Father Macdowell said.

John was ashamed of himself for appearing so sullen, so he said hastily, "Nothing's the matter. Just a moment. I won't be a moment." He hurried out of the room.

The old priest looked down at the floor and shook his head; and then, sighing and feeling uneasy, he bent over Mrs. Williams, with his good ear down to her, and he said, "I'll just ask you a few questions in a hurry, my child. You answer them quickly and I'll give you absolution." He made the sign of the cross over her and asked if she repented for having strayed from the Church, and if she had often been angry, and whether she had always been faithful, and if she had ever lied or stolen—all so casually and quickly as if it hadn't occurred to him that such a young woman could have serious sins. In the same breath he muttered, "Say a good act of contrition to yourself and that will be all, my dear." He had hardly taken a minute.

When John returned to the room with the glass of water in his hand, he saw the old priest making the sign of the cross. Father Macdowell went on praying without even looking up at John. When he had finished, he turned and said, "Oh, there you are. Thanks for the water. I needed it. Well, my boy, I'm sorry if I worried you."

John hardly said anything. He looked at his wife, who had closed her eyes, and he sat down on the end of the bed. He was too disappointed to speak.

Father Macdowell, who was expecting trouble, said, "Don't be harsh, lad."

"I'm not harsh," he said mildly, looking up at the priest. "But you weren't quite fair. And it's as though she turned away from me at the last moment. I didn't think she needed you."

"God bless you, bless the both of you. She'll get better," Father Macdowell said. But he felt ill at ease as he put on his coat, and he couldn't look directly at John.

Going along the hall, he spoke to Miss Stanhope, who wanted to apologize for her brother-in-law's attitude. "I'm sorry if it was unpleasant for you, Father," she said.

"It wasn't unpleasant," he said. "I was glad to meet John. He's a fine fellow. It's a great pity he isn't a Catholic. I don't know as I played fair with him."

As he went down the stairs, puffing and sighing, he pondered the question of whether he had played fair with the young man. But by the time he reached the street he was rejoicing amiably to think he had so successfully ministered to one who had strayed from the faith and had called out to him at the last moment. Walking along with the rolling motion as if his feet hurt him, he muttered, "Of course they were happy as they were . . . in a worldly way. I wonder if I did come between them?"

He shuffled along, feeling very tired, but he couldn't help thinking, "What beauty there was to his staunch love for her!" Then he added quickly, "But it was just a pagan beauty, of course."

As he began to wonder about the nature of this beauty, for some reason he felt inexpressibly sad.

ROMANCE LANGUAGE SECTION

Introduction

FRANCE

Of all the countries of Europe, France is the one whose literature has enjoyed the greatest prestige abroad in the twentieth century. French writers have carried on the tradition of their world famous predecessors of the eighteenth and nineteenth centuries. Just as formerly the writings and doings of Voltaire, Hugo, Zola, made news everywhere, so contemporary French authors are topics of the day throughout the world. An election to the French Academy, no matter how much criticism has been leveled at this venerable institution, the attribution of a *Goncourt Prize,* a *Femina Prize,* a *Renaudot Prize* or a *Grand Prix du Roman,* the jubilee or birth of a new literary school or coterie, all are international events.

Twentieth century French literature has been honored by the granting of the Nobel Prize to several of its celebrated representatives: Romain Rolland, Henri Bergson, Edouard Estaunié, Anatole France, Roger Martin du Gard. However, the prestige and influence of a national literature are not measured solely by the number of its laureates. What should be quoted here, and what we are unable to quote for want of space, are the innumerable works translated into all (or nearly all) foreign languages during the last thirty or forty years. As examples, we shall mention only some of the French writers whose works have been published in America in the course of the last decade: the list includes André Gide, Paul Claudel, Charles Péguy, Jules Romains, Georges Duhamel, André Maurois, André Malraux, Jean Giraudoux, Paul Valéry, Jean Giono, Antoine de Saint-Exupéry, Gontran de Poncins, Louis Aragon, Vercors, Jean-Paul Sartre, Albert Camus, detective-story writer Simenon and many others.

In the field of literary diffusion and exportation, France clearly takes the lead: no other literature has enriched the universal heritage to such an extent; no other has given so many works which have been considered worth translating, not only into English, but into all the principal European languages; no other has had more influence on young writers throughout the world.

The essential cause for this prestige lies in the human value of French literature, in its universal character, in its high conception of art. The

French writer has behind him a long tradition of freedom and humanism. From Rabelais and Montaigne to Gide and Sartre, he strives to free the mind, to fight against the material and moral restrictions which fetter liberty.

All French writers of the twentieth century have lived through the problems of the period: fear, hunger, misery, fascism, resistance to oppression. None has looked with indifference upon man struggling in the midst of ordeals that face him from all sides. These men have fought for the defense of Man. Their minds were preoccupied not only with France, but with man everywhere, and that is why they have exerted an influence in the whole world.

The career of the leading French writers reflects this interest in the human race. Anatole France and Romain Rolland are widely known and appreciated for their sympathetic approach to the problems of the common man. Their humanism was demonstrated by their attitude in the Dreyfus case and their hatred of war. France's *La Revolte des Anges,* the last great French satire, was a scathing tract on the uselessness of war. Rolland was, even more actively, opposed to militarism; during the First World War period, he retreated to neutral Switzerland. Both writers have been adopted by the whole world.

Proust, it is true, was not so directly interested in world affairs. Yet, in his brilliant and sensitive observations of the people and dying social order he knew so intimately, he has provided endless delight to an audience which, although more limited, is thoroughly international. In quite a different way, Colette's love stories have found a discriminating public outside of France. Her perennial theme is subject to no limitation through the crossing of national frontiers.

André Gide, the prophet and leader of French literature in the years between the two wars, has given to the period some of its main themes, symbols and slogans: *l'inquiète adolescence, l'acte gratuit* (as in "A Crime Without a Motive"), *la disponibilité.* Gide has come a long way since the short period when he was a timid symbolist poet. He has thrown himself into life, into the vital problems of mankind. He even entered politics, despite his scorn for politicians. He went to Russia, took to communism for a while, then dropped it after his return from the U.S.S.R. Always, he has been searching for solutions to the basic problems of the human race.

Jean Giraudoux, a delightful impressionist poet, original playwright, and delicate novelist, has meditated over the problems of war and revolution. During the second World War, he accepted responsibilities in politics and government. His last prose work before the war, *Pleins Pouvoirs,* was an essay on the political and moral problems of the citizens of tomorrow. During the occupation, he wrote another masterful essay on the same subject, *Sans Pouvoirs.* His very last work, written before his death, *La Folle de Chaillot,* is a satire against the so-called modern "civilization"—against plutocrats, speculators, and the black market.

Perhaps the most powerful of all twentieth-century French novelists is André Malraux. He has grappled with the brutal political realities of our time as few novelists have. His unswerving moral integrity, bare of sentimentalized idealism, is as apparent in his life as in his books. His record in the French Resistance is particularly impressive.

The name of Jean-Paul Sartre is connected with the philosophy which France is debating most eagerly following the liberation from the yoke of the Nazi occupation: *existentialisme.* The world of the *existentialiste* is not a pretty world. In it there are no values external to man, and if there is to be *meaning,* man must put it there. The *existentialiste* is acutely aware of this freedom to choose his values and make himself— a freedom at once exhilarative and terrifying in a world where man's consciousness is ironically alien to the otherwise unchanging order of *things.*

Like Malraux, Sartre and Aragon (a *maquisard* and soldier-poet of the Resistance) Albert Camus has led a very active life. During the two years preceding the Liberation of France, he worked extensively in the Resistance. He was one of the animators and editorialists of the underground newspaper *Combat* and wrote for the *Revue Libre* and *Cahiers de la Libération.* Born in 1913, Camus belongs to the generation that reached intellectual maturity after the rise of Fascism, after Munich, during the war and under the Occupation. He has become a strong symbol and spokesman of that "lost generation" of the Second World War.

The first chapter of his novel, *L'Etranger,* is one of our selections. The hero is a "condemned man"—a man who is a "stranger" to the world and to himself. Camus, pessimistic about the nature of man, still preaches a noble, courageous humanism. The conclusion of his *Mythe de Sisyphe* is that man must derive whatever happiness he can from the performance of an eternally meaningless task. "The struggle toward the height is enough to feel the heart of man."

A few words should be added here about the French short story. Maupassant is a brilliant but isolated representative of the modern French short story. In general, French writers have shown a marked preference for the novel, and they have somewhat neglected the other genre. Therefore, a good many excerpts included in this anthology are chapters or pages taken from novels, not independent short stories. An attempt has been made to select at once pieces of writing that make good independent units in themselves, that are characteristic of the writer, and that are not hackneyed through frequent re-publication.

BELGIUM

Belgium has two literatures—one in Flemish and one in French. Verhaeren, Rodenbach, Maeterlinck, Michaux—have written in French. Among the outstanding twentieth century writers of fiction are Georges Eekhoud and Hubert Krains.

Eekhoud was a man of broad cosmopolitan sympathies, but in much of his writing championed the underdogs and vagabonds of society. His contempt for the bourgeois was rooted in his trust in primitive impulse and individuality. In the story "Hiep-Hioup" the relationship between the model young men and the wild, unregenerate girl brings alive these sympathies and antipathies in vivid fashion.

SPAIN

Next to the French, Spanish literature is the most brilliant, the most varied, and the most interesting of Romance Language literatures of today. It has made the literary heritage of the twentieth century richer by several great works. Let us here name only Blasco Ibanez, whose work has been almost entirely translated into English, Eugenio d'Ors, Pio Baroja, Ramon de Valle Inclan, Perez de Ayala, Gabriel Miro, Ramon Gomez de la Cerna and Miguel de Unamuno.

The generation of the period between the two wars is much less well-known to the American public than the famous "generation of 1898." Nevertheless, it represents a great deal of talent. Some people have spoken of a Renaissance. Unfortunately, this Spanish Renaissance has, in a large measure, been scattered by the Civil War and the Franco regime. Federico Garcia Lorca and Antonio Machado were killed by fascist bullets. Others fled to America (Alberti, Jarnes, Ramon Sender, Jorge Guillen) or to the Soviet Union (Arconada). The Franco regime, less fortunate even than most fascist regimes, has contributed next to nothing to world literature.

We have tried to choose for this anthology a few stories by representative writers who, put together, may give an idea of Spanish character and soul. Azorin (José Martinez Ruiz) represents traditional Spain. In the first twenty years of the century, he exercised a tremendous influence on Spanish literature. He was the coiner of the phrase, the "generation of '98," and the leader of that generation.

Pio Baroja, considered by many the leading Spanish novelist of the twentieth century, might be said to deal with Goya's Spain. His favorite world is that of the adventurer, the rebel, the individualist; one of his most famous realistic trilogies deals with the underworld of Madrid.

Gabriel Miro reveals Spain's mystic features and her shocking realism. His novels are really a series of pictures or scenes which group themselves around an intrigue often lacking in unity. His characters escape you with their curious ambivalence of the mystery of passion and traditionalism. As Azorin praised the landscapes of Castille, so Miro, born and bred in Alicante, gives us ravishing descriptions of his native province. He speaks with love of nature; under his pen the rocks, the plants and the stars take on an extraordinary life.

ITALY

Italian literature is little known in the United States. However, some names have crossed the Ocean—particularly those of two Nobel Prize winners, Luigi Pirandello, the great Sicilian story-teller, playwright and author of ambiguous, paradoxical psychological fantasies, and Grazia Deledda.

Twentieth century Italian literature has suffered from fascism. The best authors have remained silent or escaped into narcissism or lyricism. Some writers have expressed themselves in exile; some have given their lives in fighting against fascism. Lauro de Bosis, the author of our selection, *The Story of My Death*, is a good example of the young Italy unable to express itself during the twenty years of Mussolini's tyranny.

The literature of the exile is, as a whole, decidedly militant. Emilio Lussu (*Sardinian Brigade*) has evoked his war memories. Ignazio Silone, who has written several novels (*Fontamara, Bread and Wine*), and, recently, a play *And He Hid Himself*, portrays the atmosphere of crisis, injustice and oppression which is characteristic of the fascist climate. He is a humanistic writer. In this connection, we should also name Leo Ferrero, the author of *Angelica*.

No major work has as yet come out of the new Italian Republic, but preparations are going on there for a magnificent rebirth, which will not fail to produce its fruit in time.

PORTUGAL

If Italian literature is little known in America, Portuguese literature is practically unknown. The greatest representative of naturalism, Eca de Queriroz, died in 1900. After him, the novel suffered an eclipse. However, a few names emerged, such as Fialho de Almeida (1852–1911), a prolific, bitter and sarcastic story-teller; Raul Brandao (1867–1930), the author of dramatic narratives, queer, hazy, and pathetic; Julio Dantas (born 1876), the most read of all Portuguese writers, author of love stories and historical novels. Aquilino Ribeiro (born 1885), the people's novelist, has most often represented the picturesque aspects of peasant life.

Unfortunately, there is no such thing as a great universal Portuguese fiction of the twentieth century. Socially significant novels are absent from contemporary Portuguese literature. Except for poetry, creative literature has been reduced to a rather commonplace level of expression.

PIERRE BRODIN

ANATOLE FRANCE

Madame de Luzy

Anatole France (Jacques Anatole Francois Thibault, 1844–1924) was educated at the Jesuit College Stanislas. He studied history and became literary editor of the *Temps*. In 1881, France won an Academy prize for his novel, *The Crime of Sylvestre Bonnard*. More novels and short stories followed: *Thais, Les Dieux Ont Soif, L'Etui de Nacre,* etc. He received the Nobel Prize in 1921. [From *Mother of Pearl* by Anatole France; used by permission of Dodd, Mead & Co. and John Lane, The Bodley Head, Ltd.; translated by Frederic Chapman.]

AS I ENTERED, Pauline de Luzy held out her hand to me. Then for a moment we remained silent. Her scarf and straw hat were thrown carelessly on an arm-chair.

The prayer from *Orpheus* was open on the spinet. Going toward the window, she watched the sun sinking to the blood-red horizon.

"Madame," I said at length, "do you remember the words you said two years ago this very day, at the foot of that hill on the bank of the river toward which at this moment your eyes are turned?

"Do you remember how, with your hand waving in a prophetic gesture, you called up before me, as in a vision, the coming days of trial, of crime and terror? On my very lips you arrested my confession of love, and bade me live and labor for justice and liberty. Madame, since your hand, which I could not anoint with kisses and tears enough, pointed out the way to me, I have pursued it unfaltering. I have obeyed you; I have written and spoken for the cause. For two years I have withstood the blunder-headed starvelings who are the source of dissension and hate, the demagogues who seduce the people by violent demonstrations of pretended sympathy, and the poltroons who do homage to the coming powers."

She stopped me with a motion of her hand, and made a sign to me to listen. Then we heard borne across the scented spaces of the garden, where birds were warbling, distant cries of "Death!" "To the gallows with the aristocrat!" "Set his head on a pike!"

Pale and motionless she held a finger to her lips.

"It is," I said, "some unhappy wretch being pursued. They are making domiciliary visits and effecting arrests in Paris night and day. It is possible they may force an entrance here. I ought to withdraw for fear of compromising you. Although I am but little known in this neighborhood, I am, as times go, a dangerous guest."

"Stay!" she adjured me.

For the second time cries rent the calm evening air. They were mingled now with the tramp of feet and the noise of fire-arms. They came nearer; then we heard a voice shout: "Close the approaches, so that he cannot escape, the scoundrel!"

Madame de Luzy seemed to grow calmer in proportion to the increasing nearness of the danger.

"Let us go up to the second floor," she said; "we shall be able to see through the sunblinds what is going on outside."

But scarcely had we opened the door when, on the landing, we beheld a half-dressed fugitive, his face blanched with terror, his teeth chattering and his knees knocking together. This apparition murmured in a strangled voice—

"Save me! Hide me! They are there. . . . They burst open my gate —overran my garden. They are coming. . . ."

Madame de Luzy, recognizing Planchonnet, the old philosopher who occupied the neighboring house, asked him in a whisper—

"Has my cook caught sight of you? She is a Jacobin!"

"Nobody has set eyes on me."

"God be praised, neighbor!"

She led him into her bedroom, whither I followed them. A consultation was necessary. Some hidingplace must be hit upon where she could keep Planchonnet concealed for several days, or at least for several hours, whatever time it might take to deceive and tire out the search party. It was agreed that I should keep the approaches under observation, and that when I gave the signal, the unfortunate man should make his escape by the little garden gate.

Whilst he waited, he was unable to remain standing. He was completely paralyzed with terror.

He endeavored to make us understand that he was being hounded down for having conspired with Monsieur de Cazotte against the Constitution, and for having on the 10th of August formed one of the defenders of the Tuileries—he, the enemy of priests and kings. It was an infamous calumny. The truth was that Lubin was venting his hate upon him—Lubin, hitherto his butcher, whom he had a hundred times had a mind to lay a stick about to teach him to give better weight, and who was now presiding over the section in which he had formerly been a mere stallholder.

As he uttered the name in strangled tones, he was persuaded that he actually saw Lubin, and hid his face in his hands. And of a truth there was the sound of footsteps on the stairs. Madame de Luzy shot the bolts and pushed the old man behind a screen. There was a hammering at the door, and Pauline recognized the voice of her cook, who called out to her to open, that the municipal officers were at the gate with the National Guard, and that they had come to make an inspection of the premises.

"They say," the woman added, "that Planchonnet is in the house. I know very well that it is not so, of course. I know you would never harbor a scoundrel of that sort; but they won't believe my word."

"Well, well, let them come up," replied Madame de Luzy through the door. "Let them go all over the house, from cellar to garret."

As he listened to this dialogue, the wretched Planchonnet fainted behind the screen, and I had a good deal of trouble in resuscitating him by sprinkling water on his temples. When I had succeeded—

"My friend," the young woman whispered to her old neighbor, "trust in me. Remember that women are resourceful."

Then, calmly, as though she had been engaged in some daily domestic duty, she drew her bedstead a little out from its alcove, took off the bedclothes, and with my assistance so arranged the three mattresses as to contrive a space next the wall between the highest and the lowest of them.

Whilst she was making these arrangements, a loud noise of shoes, sabots, gunstocks, and raucous voices broke out on the staircase. This was for all three of us a terrible moment; but the noise ascended by little and little to the floor above our heads. We realized that the searchers, under the guidance of the Jacobin cook, were ransacking the garrets first. The ceiling cracked; threats and coarse laughter were audible, and the sound of kicks and bayonet-thrusts against the wainscot. We breathed again, but there was not a second to lose. I helped Planchonnet to slip into the space contrived for him between the mattresses.

As she watched our efforts, Madame de Luzy shook her head. The bed thus disturbed had a suspicious appearance.

She endeavored to give it a finishing touch; but in vain, she could not make it look natural.

"I shall have to go to bed myself," she said.

She looked at the clock; it was exactly seven, and she felt that it would look extraordinary for her to be in bed so early. As to feigning illness, it was useless to think of it: the Jacobin cook would detect the ruse.

She remained thoughtful for some seconds; then calmly, simply, with royal unconcern, she undressed before me, got into bed, and ordered me to take off my shoes, my coat, and my cravat.

"There is nothing for it but for you to be my lover, and for them to surprise us together. When they arrive you will not have had time to rearrange your disordered clothes. You will open the door to them in your vest,[1] with your hair rumpled."

All our arrangements were made when the search party, with many exclamations of *"Sacré!"* and *"Peste!"* descended from the garrets.

The unfortunate Planchonnet was seized with such a paroxysm of trembling that he shook the whole bed.

Moreover, his breathing grew so stertorous that it must have been almost audible in the corridor.

---

[1] The vest was worn under the coat. It was a sort of waistcoat, longer than ours, and provided with sleeves of full length. (AUTHOR.)

"It's a pity," murmured Madame de Luzy. "I was so satisfied with my little artifice. But never mind: we won't despair. May God be our aid!"

A heavy fist shook the door.

"Who knocks?" Pauline inquired.

"The representatives of the Nation."

"Can't you wait a minute?"

"Open, or we shall break the door down!"

"Go and open the door, my friend."

Suddenly, by a sort of miracle, Planchonnet ceased to tremble and gasp.

Lubin was the first to enter. He had his scarf round him, and was followed by a dozen men armed with pikes. Casting his eyes first on Madame de Luzy and then on me—

"*Peste!*" he exclaimed. "It seems we are disturbing a pair of lovers. Excuse us, pretty one!"

Then turning to his followers, he remarked—

"The *sans-culottes* are the only folks who know how to behave."

But despite his theories this encounter had evidently put him in good spirits.

He sat down on the bed, and raising the chin of the lovely high-bred woman, said—

"It is plain that that pretty mouth wasn't made to mumble paternosters day and night. It would have been a pity if it were. But the Republic before all things. We are seeking the traitor, Planchonnet. He is here, I'm certain of it. I must have him. I shall get him guillotined. It will make my fortune."

"Search for him, then!"

They looked under the chairs and tables, in the cupboards, thrust their pikes under the bed, and probed the mattresses with their bayonets.

Lubin scratched his ear and looked at me slyly. Madame de Luzy, dreading that I might be subjected to an embarrassing catechism, said—

"Dear friend, you know the house as well as I do myself. Take the keys and show Monsieur Lubin all over it. I am sure you will be delighted to act as guide to such patriots."

I led them to the cellars, where they turned over the piles of faggots, and drank a fairly large number of bottles of wine; after which Lubin staved in the full casks with the butt end of his gun, and leaving the cellar flooded with wine, gave the signal of departure. I conducted them out as far as the gate, which I shut on their very heels, and then ran back to let Madame de Luzy know that we were out of danger.

When she heard this, she bent her head over the side of the bed next the wall, and called—

"Monsieur Planchonnet! Monsieur Planchonnet!"

A faint sigh was the response.

"God be praised!" she exclaimed. "Monsieur Planchonnet, you occasioned me the most appalling fear. I thought you were dead."

Then turning toward me—

"My poor friend, you used to take so much delight in declaring, from time to time, that you loved me; you will never tell me so again!"

ROMAIN ROLLAND

Deliverance

Romain Rolland (1866–1944) studied at the Ecole Normale Supérieure. After finishing his studies, he began to teach the history of art. In 1902 and 1905 his *Lives* of Beethoven and Michelangelo appeared. In 1904 he began to publish *Jean-Christophe*. During the First World War Rolland lived in Switzerland where, in 1914, he published *Au Dessus de la Mêlée*, a collection of articles in which he condemned the war. Some of his later works are *Colas Breugnon* and *Annette et Sylvie*. [From *Jean-Christophe* by Romain Rolland; copyright 1910 by Henry Holt & Co., 1938 by Gilbert Cannan; used by permission of the publishers; translated by Gilbert Cannan.]

HE HAD NO ONE. All his friends had disappeared. His dear Gottfried, who had come to his aid in times of difficulty, and whom now he so sorely needed, had gone some months before. This time forever. One evening in the summer of the last year a letter in large handwriting, bearing the address of a distant village, had informed Louisa that her brother had died upon one of his vagabond journeys which the little peddler had insisted on making, in spite of his ill health. He was buried there in the cemetery of the place. The last manly and serene friendship which could have supported Christophe had been swallowed up. He was left alone with his old mother, who cared nothing for his ideas—could only love him and not understand him. About him was the immense plain of Germany, the green ocean. At every attempt to climb out of it he only slipped back deeper than ever. The hostile town watched him drown. . . .

And as he was struggling a light flashed upon him in the middle of the night, the image of Hassler, the great musician whom he had loved so much when he was a child. His fame shone over all Germany now. He remembered the promises that Hassler had made him then. And he clung to this piece of wreckage in desperation. Hassler could save him! Hassler must save him! What was he asking? Not help, nor money, nor material assistance of any kind. Nothing but understanding. Hassler had been persecuted like him. Hassler was a free man. He

would understand a free man, whom German mediocrity was pursuing
with its spite and trying to crush. They were fighting the same battle.

He carried the idea into execution as soon as it occurred to him. He
told his mother that he would be away for a week, and that very evening he took the train for the great town in the north of Germany
where Hassler was *Kapellmeister*. He could not wait. It was a last
effort to breathe.

Hassler was famous. His enemies had not disarmed, but his friends
cried that he was the greatest musician, present, past and future. He was
surrounded by partisans and detractors who were equally absurd. As
he was not of a very firm character, he had been embittered by the last,
and mollified by the first. He devoted his energy to writing things to
annoy his critics and make them cry out. He was like an urchin playing pranks. These pranks were often in the most detestable taste. Not
only did he devote his prodigious talent to musical eccentricities which
made the hair of the pontiffs stand on end, but he showed a perverse
predilection for queer themes, bizarre subjects, and often for equivocal
and scabrous situations; in a word, for everything which could offend
ordinary good sense and decency. He was quite happy when the people
howled, and the people did not fail him. Even the Emperor, who
dabbled in art, as everyone knows, with the insolent presumption of
upstarts and princes, regarded Hassler's fame as a public scandal, and
let no opportunity slip of showing his contemptuous indifference to his
impudent works. Hassler was enraged and delighted by such august
opposition, which had almost become a consecration for the advanced
paths in German art, and went on smashing windows. At every new
folly his friends went into ecstasies and cried that he was a genius.

Hassler's coterie was chiefly composed of writers, painters, and
decadent critics who certainly had the merit of representing the party
of revolt against the reaction—always a menace in North Germany—
of the pietistic spirit and State morality; but in the struggle the independence had been carried to a pitch of absurdity of which they were
unconscious. For, if many of them were not lacking in a rude sort
of talent, they had little intelligence and less taste. They could not
rise above the fastidious atmosphere which they had created, and like all
cliques, they had ended by losing all sense of real life. They legislated
for themselves and hundreds of fools who read their reviews and gulped
down everything they were pleased to promulgate. Their adulation had
been fatal to Hassler, for it had made him too pleased with himself.
He accepted without examination every musical idea that came into his
head, and he had a private conviction, however he might fall below his
own level, he was still superior to that of all other musicians. And
though that idea was only too true in the majority of cases, it did not
follow that it was a very fit state of mind for the creation of great works.
At heart Hassler had a supreme contempt for everybody, friends and
enemies alike; and this bitter jeering contempt was extended to him-

self and life in general. He was all the more driven back into his ironic skepticism because he had once believed in a number of generous and simple things. As he had not been strong enough to ward off the slow destruction of the passing of the days, nor hypocritical enough to pretend to believe in the faith he had lost, he was forever gibing at the memory of it. He was of a Southern German nature, soft and indolent, not made to resist excess of fortune or misfortune, of heat or cold, needing a moderate temperature to preserve its balance. He had drifted insensibly into a lazy enjoyment of life. He loved good food, heavy drinking, idle lounging, and sensuous thoughts. His whole art smacked of these things, although he was too gifted for the flashes of his genius not still to shine forth from his lax music which drifted with the fashion. No one was more conscious than himself of his decay. In truth, he was the only one to be conscious of it—at rare moments which, naturally, he avoided. Besides, he was misanthropic, absorbed by his fearful moods, his egoistic preoccupations, his concern about his health—he was indifferent to everything which had formerly excited his enthusiasm or hatred.

Such was the man to whom Christophe came for assistance. With what joy and hope he arrived, one cold, wet morning, in the town wherein then lived the man who symbolized for him the spirit of independence in his art! He expected words of friendship and encouragement from him—words that he needed to help him to go on with the ungrateful, inevitable battle which every true artist has to wage against the world until he breathes his last, without even for one day laying down his arms; for, as Schiller has said, *"the only relation with the public of which a man never repents—is war."*

Christophe was so impatient that he just left his bag at the first hotel he came to near the station, and then ran to the theater to find out Hassler's address. Hassler lived some way from the center of the town, in one of the suburbs. Christophe took an electric train, and hungrily ate a roll. His heart thumped as he approached his goal.

The district in which Hassler had chosen his house was almost entirely built in that strange new architecture into which young Germany has thrown an erudite and deliberate barbarism struggling laboriously to have genius. In the middle of the commonplace town, with its straight, characterless streets, there suddenly appeared Egyptian hypogea, Norwegian chalets, cloisters, bastions, exhibition pavilions, pot-bellied houses, fakirs, buried in the ground, with expressionless faces, with only one enormous eye; dungeon gates, ponderous gates, iron hoops, golden cryptograms on the panes of grated windows, belching monsters over the front door, blue porcelain tiles plastered on in most unexpected places; variegated mosaics representing Adam and Eve; roofs covered with tiles of jarring colors; houses like citadels with castellated walls, deformed animals on the roofs, no windows on one side, and then suddenly, close to each other, gaping holes, square, red, angular, triangular, like wounds; great stretches of empty wall from which suddenly there would spring a massive balcony with one window —a balcony supported by Nibelungesque Caryatides, balconies from which there peered through the stone balustrade two pointed heads of old men, bearded and long-haired, mermen of Boecklin. On the front of one of these prisons—a Pharaohesque mansion, low and one-storied, with two naked giants at the gate—the architect had written:

> Let the artist show his universe,
> Which never was and yet will ever be.
>
> *Seine Welt zeige der Künstler,*
> *Die niemals war noch jemals sein wird.*

Christophe was absorbed by the idea of seeing Hassler, and looked with the eyes of amazement and under no attempt to understand. He reached the house he sought, one of the simplest—in a Carolingian style. Inside was rich luxury, commonplace enough. On the staircase was the heavy atmosphere of hot air. There was a small lift which Christophe did not use, as he wanted to gain time to prepare himself for his call by going up the four flights of stairs slowly, with his legs giving and his heart thumping with his excitement. During that short ascent his former interview with Hassler, his childish enthusiasm, the image of his grandfather were as clearly in his mind as though it had all been yesterday.

It was nearly eleven when he rang the bell. He was received by a sharp maid, with a *serva padrona* manner, who looked at him impertinently and began to say that "Herr Hassler could not see him, as Herr Hassler was tired." Then the naïve disappointment expressed in Christophe's face amused her; for after making an unabashed scrutiny of him from head to foot, she softened suddenly and introduced him to Hassler's study, and said she would go and see if Herr Hassler would receive him. Thereupon she gave him a little wink and closed the door.

On the walls were a few impressionist paintings and some gallant French engravings of the eighteenth century: for Hassler pretended to some knowledge of all the arts, and Manet and Watteau were joined together in his taste in accordance with the prescription of his coterie. The same mixture of styles appeared in the furniture, and a very fine Louis XV bureau was surrounded by new art armchairs and an oriental divan with a mountain of multi-colored cushions. The doors were ornamented with mirrors, and Japanese bric-a-brac covered the shelves and the mantelpiece, on which stood a bust of Hassler. In a bowl on a round table was a profusion of photographs of singers, female admirers and friends, with witty remarks and enthusiastic interjections. The bureau was incredibly untidy. The piano was open. The shelves were dusty, and half-smoked cigars were lying about everywhere.

In the next room Christophe heard a cross voice grumbling. It was

answered by the shrill tones of the little maid. It was clear that Hassler
was not very pleased at having to appear. It was clear, also, that the
young woman had decided that Hassler should appear; and she
answered him with extreme familiarity and her shrill voice penetrated
the walls. Christophe was rather upset at hearing some of the remarks
she made to her master. But Hassler did not seem to mind. On the
contrary, it rather seemed as though her impertinence amused him;
and while he went on growling, he chaffed the girl and took a delight in
exciting her. At last Christophe heard a door open, and, still growling
and chaffing, Hassler came shuffling.

He entered. Christophe's heart sank. He recognized him. Would to
God he had not! It was Hassler, and yet it was not he. He still had his
great smooth brow, his face as unwrinkled as that of a babe; but he
was bald, stout, yellowish, sleepy-looking; his lower lip drooped a little,
his mouth looked bored and sulky. He hunched his shoulders, buried
his hands in the pockets of his open waistcoat; old shoes flopped on his
feet; his shirt was bagged above his trousers, which he had not finished
buttoning. He looked at Christophe with his sleepy eyes, in which there
was no light as the young man murmured his name. He bowed automatically, said nothing, nodded toward a chair, and with a sigh, sank
down on the divan and piled the cushions about himself. Christophe
repeated:

"I have already had the honor . . . You were kind enough . . . My
name is Christophe Krafft. . . ."

Hassler lay back on the divan, with his legs crossed, his hands clasped
together on his right knee, which he held up to his chin as he replied:
"I don't remember."

Christophe's throat went dry, and he tried to remind him of their
former meeting. Under any circumstances it would have been difficult
for him to talk of memories so intimate; now it was torture for him. He
bungled his sentences, could not find words, said absurd things which
made him blush. Hassler let him flounder on and never ceased to look
at him with his vague, indifferent eyes. When Christophe had reached
the end of his story, Hassler went on rocking his knee in silence for a
moment, as though he were wating for Christophe to go on. Then he
said:

"Yes . . . That does not make us young again . . ." and stretched
his legs.

After a yawn he added:

"I beg pardon . . . Did not sleep . . . Supper at the theater last
night . . ." and yawned again.

Christophe hoped that Hassler would make some reference to what
he had just told him, but Hassler, whom the story had not interested
at all, said nothing about it, and he did not ask Christophe anything
about his life. When he had done yawning he asked:

"Have you been in Berlin long?"

"I arrived this morning," said Christophe.

"Ah!" said Hassler, without any surprise. "What hotel?"

He did not seem to listen to the reply, but got up lazily and pressed an electric bell.

"Allow me," he said.

The little maid appeared with her impertinent manner.

"Kitty," said he, "are you trying to make me go without breakfast this morning?"

"You don't think I am going to bring it here while you have some one with you?"

"Why not?" he said, with a wink and a nod in Christophe's direction. "He feeds my mind: I must feed my body."

"Aren't you ashamed to have someone watching you eat—like an animal in a menagerie?"

Instead of being angry, Hassler began to laugh and corrected her:

"Like a domestic animal," he went on. "But do bring it. I'll eat my shame with it."

Christophe saw that Hassler was making no attempt to find out what he was doing, and tried to lead the conversation back. He spoke of the difficulties of provincial life, of the mediocrity of the people, the narrow-mindedness, and of his own isolation. He tried to interest him in his moral distress. But Hassler was sunk deep in the divan, with his head lying back on a cushion and his eyes half closed, and let him go on talking without even seeming to listen; or he would raise his eyelids for a moment and pronounce a few coldly ironical words, some ponderous jest at the expense of provincial people, which cut short Christophe's attempts to talk more intimately. Kitty returned with the breakfast tray: coffee, butter, ham, etc. She put it down crossly on the desk in the middle of the untidy papers. Christophe waited until she had gone before he went on with his sad story which he had such difficulty in continuing. Hassler drew the tray toward himself. He poured himself out some coffee and sipped at it. Then in a familiar and cordial though rather contemptuous way he stopped Christophe in the middle of a sentence to ask if he would take a cup.

Christophe refused. He tried to pick up the thread of his sentence, but he was more and more nonplussed, and did not know what he was saying. He was distracted by the sight of Hassler with his plate under his chin, like a child, gorging pieces of bread and butter and slices of ham which he held in his fingers. However, he did succeed in saying that he composed, that he had had an overture in the *Judith* of Hebbel performed. Hassler listened absently.

"*Was?*" (What?) he asked.

Christophe repeated the title.

"*Ach! So, so!*" (Ah! Good, good!) said Hassler, dipping his bread and his fingers into his cup. That was all.

Christophe was discouraged and was on the point of getting up and going, but he thought of his long journey in vain, and summoning up all his courage he murmured a proposal that he should play some of his works to Hassler. At the first mention of it Hassler stopped him.

"No, no. I don't know anything about it," he said, with his chaffing and rather insulting irony. "Besides, I haven't the time."

Tears came to Christophe's eyes. But he had vowed not to leave until he had Hassler's opinion about his work. He said, with a mixture of confusion and anger:

"I beg your pardon, but you promised once to hear me. I came to see you for that from the other end of Germany. You shall hear me."

Hassler, who was not used to such ways, looked at the awkward young man, who was furious, blushing, and near tears. That amused him, and wearily shrugging his shoulders, he pointed to the piano, and said with an air of comic resignation:

"Well, then! . . . There you are!"

On that he lay back on his divan, like a man who is going to sleep, smoothed out his cushions, put them under his outstretched arms, half closed his eyes, opened them for a moment to take stock of the size of the roll of music which Christophe had brought from one of his pockets, gave a little sigh, and lay back to listen listlessly.

Christophe was intimidated and mortified, but he began to play. It was not long before Hassler opened his eyes and ears with the professional interest of the artist who is struck in spite of himself by a beautiful thing. At first he said nothing and lay still, but his eyes became less dim and his sulky lips moved. Then he suddenly woke up, growling his surprise and approbation. He only gave inarticulate interjections, but the form of them left no doubt as to his feelings, and they gave Christophe an inexpressible pleasure. Hassler forgot to count the number of pages that had been played and were left to be played. When Christophe had finished a piece, he said:

"Go on! . . . Go on! . . ."

He was beginning to use human language.

"That's good! Good!" he exclaimed to himself. Famous! . . . Awfully famous! (*Schrecklich famos!*) But, damme!" He growled in astonishment. "What is it?"

He had risen on his seat, was stretching for wind, making a trumpet with his hand, talking to himself, laughing with pleasure, or at certain odd harmonies, just putting out his tongue as though to moisten his lips. An unexpected modulation had such an effect on him that he got up suddenly with an exclamation, and came and sat at the piano by Christophe's side. He did not seem to notice that Christophe was there. He was only concerned with the music, and when the piece was finished he took the book and began to read the page again, then the following pages, and went on ejaculating his admiration and surprise as though he had been alone in the room.

"The devil!" he said. "Where did the little beast find that? . . ."

He pushed Christophe away with his shoulders and himself played certain passages. He had a charming touch on the piano, very soft, caressing and light. Christophe noticed his fine long, well-tended hands, which were a little morbidly aristocratic and out of keeping with the rest. Hassler stopped at certain chords and repeated them, winking, and clicking with his tongue. He hummed with his lips, imitating the sounds of the instruments, and went on interspersing the music with his apostrophes in which pleasure and annoyance were mingled. He could not help having a secret initiative, an unavowed jealousy, and at the same time he greedily enjoyed it all.

Although he went on talking to himself as though Christophe did not exist, Christophe, blushing with pleasure, could not help taking Hassler's exclamations to himself, and he explained what he had tried to do. At first Hassler seemed not to pay any attention to what the young man was saying, and went on thinking out loud; then something that Christophe said struck him and he was silent, with his eyes still fixed on the music, which he turned over as he listened without seeming to hear. Christophe grew more and more excited, and at last he plumped into confidence, and talked with naïve enthusiasm about his projects and his life.

Hassler was silent, and as he listened he slipped back into his irony. He had let Christophe take the book from his hands; with his elbow on the rack of the piano and his hand on his forehead, he looked at Christophe, who was explaining his work with youthful ardor and eagerness. And he smiled bitterly as he thought of his own beginning, his own hopes, and of Christophe's hopes, and all the disappointments that lay in wait for him.

Christophe spoke with his eyes cast down, fearful of losing the thread of what he had to say. Hassler's silence encouraged him. He felt that Hassler was watching him and not missing a word that he said, and he thought he had broken the ice between them, and he was glad at heart. When he had finished he shyly raised his head—confidently, too—and looked at Hassler. All the joy welling in him was frozen on the instant, like too early birds, when he saw the gloomy, mocking eyes that looked into his without kindness. He was silent.

After an icy moment, Hassler spoke dully. He had changed once more; he affected a sort of harshness toward the young man. He teased him cruelly about his plans, his hopes of success, as though he were trying to chaff himself, now that he had recovered himself. He set himself coldly to destroy his faith in life, his faith in art, his faith in himself. Bitterly he gave himself as an example, speaking of his actual works in an insulting fashion.

"Hog-waste!" he said. "That is what these swine want. Do you think there are ten people in the world who love music? Is there a single one?"

"There is myself!" said Christophe emphatically. Hassler looked at him, shrugged his shoulders, and said wearily:

"You will be like the rest. You will do as the rest have done. You will think of success, of amusing yourself, like the rest. . . . And you will be right. . . ."

Christophe tried to protest, but Hassler cut him short; he took the music and began bitterly to criticize the works which he had first been praising. Not only did he harshly pick out the real carelessness, the mistakes in writing, the faults of taste or of expression which had escaped the young man, but he made absurd criticisms, criticisms which might have been made by the most narrow and antiquated of musicians, from which he himself, Hassler, had had to suffer all his life. He asked what was the sense of it all. He did not even criticize: he denied; it was as though he were trying desperately to efface the impression that the music had made on him in spite of himself.

Christophe was horrified and made no attempt to reply. How could he reply to absurdities which he blushed to hear on the lips of a man whom he esteemed and loved? Besides, Hassler did not listen to him. He stopped at that, stopped dead, with the book in his hands, shut; no expression in his eyes and his lips drawn down in bitterness. At last he said, as though he had once more forgotten Christophe's presence:

"Ah! the worst misery of all is that there is not a single man who can understand you!"

Christophe was racked with emotion. He turned suddenly, laid his hand on Hassler's, and with love in his heart he repeated:

"There is myself!"

But Hassler did not move his hand, and if something stirred in his heart for a moment at that boyish cry, no light shone in his dull eyes, as they looked at Christophe. Irony and evasion were in the ascendant. He made a ceremonious and comic little bow in acknowledgment.

"Honored!" he said.

He was thinking:

"Do you, though? Do you think I have lost my life for you?"

He got up, threw the book on the piano, and went with his long spindle legs and sat on the divan again. Christophe had divined his thoughts and had felt the savage insult in them, and he tried proudly to reply that a man does not need to be understood by everybody; certain souls are worth a whole people; they think for it, and what they have thought the people have to think.—But Hassler did not listen to him. He had fallen back into his apathy, caused by the weakening of the life slumbering in him. Christophe, too sane to understand the sudden change, felt that he had lost. But he could not resign himself to losing after seeming to be so near victory. He made desperate efforts to excite Hassler's attention once more. He took up his music book and tried to explain the reason for the irregularities which Hassler had remarked. Hassler lay back on the sofa and preserved a gloomy silence. He neither agreed nor contradicted; he was only waiting for him to finish.

Christophe saw that there was nothing more to be done. He stopped short in the middle of a sentence. He rolled up his music and got up. Hassler got up, too. Christophe was shy and ashamed, and murmured excuses. Hassler bowed slightly, with a certain haughty and bored dis-

tinction, coldly held out his hand politely, and accompanied him to the
door without a word of suggestion that he should stay or come again.

Christophe found himself in the street once more, absolutely crushed.
He walked at random; he did not know where he was going. He
walked down several streets mechanically, and then found himself at a
station of the train by which he had come. He went back by it without
thinking of what he was doing. He sank down on the seat with his
arms and legs limp. It was impossible to think or to collect his ideas;
he thought of nothing, he did not try to think. He was afraid to envisage himself. He was utterly empty. It seemed to him that there was
emptiness everywhere about him in that town. He could not breathe
in it. The mists, the massive houses stifled him. He had only one idea,
to fly, to fly as quickly as possible—as if by escaping from the town he
would leave in it the bitter disillusion which he had found in it.

He returned to his hotel. It was half-past twelve. It was two hours
since he had entered it—with what a light shining in his heart! Now
it was dead.

He took no lunch. He did not go up to his room. To the astonishment of the people of the hotel, he asked for his bill, paid as though he
had spent the night there, and said that he was going. In vain did they
explain to him that there was no hurry, that the train he wanted to go
by did not leave for hours, and that he had much better wait in the
hotel. He insisted on going to the station at once. He was like a child.
He wanted to go by the first train, no matter which, and not to stay
another hour in the place. After the long journey and all the expense
he had incurred—although he had taken his holiday not only to see
Hassler, but the museums, and to hear concerts and to make certain
acquaintances—he had only one idea in his head: To go . . .

He went back to the station. As he had been told, his train did not
leave for three hours. And also the train was not express—(for
Christophe had to go by the cheapest class)—stopped on the way.
Christophe would have done better to go by the next train, which went
two hours later and caught up the first. But that meant spending two
more hours in the place, and Christophe could not bear it. He would
not even leave the station while he was waiting. A gloomy period of
waiting in those vast and empty halls, dark and noisy, where strange
shadows were going in and out, always busy, always hurrying; strange
shadows who meant nothing to him, all unknown to him, not one
friendly face. The misty day died down. The electric lamps, enveloped
in fog, flushed the night and made it darker than ever. Christophe grew
more and more depressed as time went on, waiting in agony for the
time to go. Ten times an hour he went to look at the train indicators
to make sure that he had not made a mistake. As he was reading them
once more from end to end to pass the time, the name of a place
caught his eye. He thought he knew it. It was only after a moment
that he remembered that it was where old Schulz lived, who had written

him such kind and enthusiastic letters. In his wretchedness the idea came to him of going to see his unknown friend. The town was not on the direct line on his way home, but a few hours away, by a little local line. It meant a whole night's journey, with two or three changes and interminable waits. Christophe never thought about it. He decided suddenly to go. He had an instinctive need of clinging to sympathy of some sort. He gave himself no time to think, and telegraphed to Schulz to say that he would arrive next morning. Hardly had he sent the telegram than he regretted it. He laughed bitterly at his eternal illusions. Why go to meet a new sorrow?—But it was done now. It was too late to change his mind.

These thoughts filled his last hour of waiting—his train at last was ready. He was the first to get into it, and he was so childish that he only began to breathe again when the train shook, and through the carriage window he could see the outlines of the town fading into the gray sky under the heavy downpour of the night. He thought he must have died if he had spent the night in it.

At the very hour—about six in the evening—a letter from Hassler came for Christophe at his hotel. Christophe's visit stirred many things in him. The whole afternoon he had been thinking of it bitterly, and not without sympathy for the poor boy who had come to him with such eager affection to be received so coldly. He was sorry for that reception and a little angry with himself. In truth, it had been only one of those fits of sulky whimsies to which he was subject. He thought to make it good by sending Christophe a ticket for the opera and a few words appointing a meeting after the performance. Christophe never knew anything about it. When he did not see him, Hassler thought:

"He is angry. So much the worse for him!"

He shrugged his shoulders and did not wait long for him.

Next day Christophe was far away—so far that all eternity would not have been enough to bring them together. And they were both separated forever.

MARCEL PROUST

Overture

Marcel Proust (1871–1922) was born in
Paris. He studied at the Lycée Condorcet
and at the Sorbonne. He was an intensely
observant young man, fascinated by the
society in which he lived. Due to ill health,
he retired in 1903 to lead a secluded life.
The best known of his works is the thir-
teen-volume cyclic novel, *Remembrance of
Things Past,* which depicts the crumbling
of class distinction under the Third Republic. [From *Remembrance of Things
Past* by Marcel Proust; copyright 1936 by
Random House, Inc.; used by permission
of the publishers and Chatto & Windus,
London, England; translated by C. Scott
Moncrieff.]

FOR A LONG TIME I used to go to bed early. Sometimes, when I
had put out my candle, my eyes would close so quickly that I had not
even time to say "I'm going to sleep." And half an hour later the
thought that it was time to go to sleep would awaken me; I would try
to put away the book which, I imagined, was still in my hands, and
to blow out the light; I had been thinking all the time, while I was
asleep, of what I had just been reading, but my thoughts had run into
a channel of their own, until I myself seemed actually to have become
the subject of my book: a church, a quartet, the rivalry between
François I and Charles V. This impression would persist for some
moments after I was awake; it did not disturb my mind, but it lay like
scales upon my eyes and prevented them from registering the fact that
the candle was no longer burning. Then it would begin to seem unintelligible, as the thoughts of a former existence must be to a reincarnate
spirit; the subject of my book would separate itself from me, leaving me
free to choose whether I would form part of it or no; and at the same
time my sight would return and I would be astonished to find myself
in a state of darkness, pleasant and restful enough for the eyes, and even
more, perhaps, for my mind, to which it appeared incomprehensible,
without a cause, a matter dark indeed.

I would ask myself what o'clock it could be; I could hear the whistling
of trains, which, now nearer and now farther off, punctuating the distance like the note of a bird in a forest, showed me in perspective the
deserted countryside through which a traveler would be hurrying
toward the nearest station: the path that he followed being fixed for
ever in his memory by the general excitement due to being in a strange
place, to doing unusual things, to the last words of conversation, to
farewells exchanged beneath an unfamiliar lamp which echoed still in
his ears amid the silence of the night; and to the delightful prospect of
being once again at home.

I would lay my cheeks gently against the comfortable cheeks of my pillow, as plump and blooming as the cheeks of babyhood. Or I would strike a match to look at my watch. Nearly midnight. The hour when an invalid, who has been obliged to start on a journey and to sleep in a strange hotel, awakens in a moment of illness and sees with glad relief a streak of daylight showing under his bedroom door. Oh, joy of joys! it is morning. The servants will be about in a minute: he can ring, and someone will come to look after him. The thought of being made comfortable gives him strength to endure his pain. He is certain he heard footsteps: they come nearer, and then die away. The ray of light beneath his door is extinguished. It is midnight; someone has turned out the gas; the last servant has gone to bed, and he must lie all night in agony with no one to bring him any help.

I would fall asleep, and often I would be awake again for short snatches only, just long enough to hear the regular creaking of the wainscot, or to open my eyes to settle the shifting kaleidoscope of the darkness, to savor, in an instantaneous flash of perception, the sleep which lay heavy upon the furniture, the room, the whole surroundings of which I formed but an insignificant part and whose unconsciousness I should very soon return to share. Or, perhaps, while I was asleep I had returned without the least effort to an earlier stage in my life, now for ever outgrown; and had come under the thrall of one of my childish terrors, such as that old terror of my great-uncle's pulling my curls, which was effectually dispelled on the day—the dawn of a new era to me—on which they were finally cropped from my head. I had forgotten that event during my sleep; I remembered it again immediately I had succeeded in making myself wake up to escape my great-uncle's fingers; still, as a measure of precaution, I would bury the whole of my head in the pillow before returning to the world of dreams.

Sometimes, too, just as Eve was created from a rib of Adam, so a woman would come into existence while I was sleeping, conceived from some strain in the position of my limbs. Formed by the appetite that I was on the point of gratifying, she it was, I imagined, who offered me that gratification. My body, conscious that its own warmth was permeating hers, would strive to become one with her, and I would awake. The rest of humanity seemed very remote in comparison with this woman whose company I had left but a moment ago: my cheek was still warm with her kiss, my body bent beneath the weight of hers. If, as would sometimes happen, she had the appearance of some woman whom I had known in waking hours, I would abandon myself altogether to the sole quest of her, like people who set out on a journey to see with their own eyes some city that they have always longed to visit, and imagine that they can taste in reality what has charmed their fancy. And then, gradually, the memory of her would dissolve and vanish, until I had forgotten the maiden of my dream.

When a man is asleep, he has in a circle round him the chain of the hours, the sequence of the years, the order of the heavenly host. Instinctively, when he awakes, he looks to these, and in an instant reads off his own position on the earth's surface and the amount of time that has elapsed during his slumbers; but this ordered procession is apt to grow confused, and to break its ranks. Suppose that, toward morning, after a night of insomnia, sleep descends upon him while he is reading, in quite a different position from that in which he normally goes to sleep, he has only to lift his arm to arrest the sun and turn it back in its course, and, at the moment of waking, he will have no idea of the time, but will conclude that he has just gone to bed. Or suppose that he gets drowsy in some even more abnormal position; sitting in an arm-chair, say, after dinner: then the world will fall topsy-turvy from its orbit, the magic chair will carry him at full speed through time and space, and when he opens his eyes again he will imagine that he went to sleep months earlier and in some far distant country. But for me it was enough if, in my own bed, my sleep was so heavy as completely to relax my consciousness; for then I lost all sense of the place in which I had gone to sleep, and when I awoke at midnight, not knowing where I was, I could not be sure at first who I was; I had only the most rudimentary sense of existence, such as may lurk and flicker in the depths of an animal's consciousness; I was more destitute of human qualities than the cave-dweller; but then the memory, not yet of the place in which I was, but of various other places where I had lived, and might now very possibly be, would come like a rope let down from heaven to draw me up out of the abyss of not-being, from which I could never have escaped by myself: in a flash I would traverse and sur-mount centuries of civilization, and out of a half-visualized succession of oil-lamps, followed by shirts with turned-down collars, would put together by degrees the component parts of my ego.

Perhaps the immobility of the things that surround us is forced upon them by our conviction that they are themselves, and not anything else, and by the immobility of our conceptions of them. For it always hap-pened that when I awoke like this, and my mind struggled in an unsuc-cessful attempt to discover where I was, everything would be moving round me through the darkness: things, places, years. My body, still too heavy with sleep to move, would make an effort to construe the form which its tiredness took as an orientation of its various members, so as to induce from that where the wall lay and the furniture stood, to piece together and to give a name to the house in which it must be living. Its memory, the composite memory of its ribs, knees, and shoulder-blades offered it a whole series of rooms in which it had at one time or another slept; while the unseen walls kept changing, adapting themselves to the shape of each successive room that it remembered, whirling madly through the darkness. And even before my brain, lingering in con-sideration of when things had happened and of what they had looked like, had collected sufficient impressions to enable it to identify the room, it, my body, would recall from each room in succession what the bed was like, where the doors were, how daylight came in at the windows, whether there was a passage outside, what I had had in my mind when

I went to sleep, and had found there when I awoke. The stiffened side underneath my body would, for instance, in trying to fix its position, imagine itself to be lying, face to the wall, in a big bed with a canopy; and at once I would say to myself, "Why, I must have gone to sleep after all, and Mamma never came to say good night!" for I was in the country with my grandfather, who died years ago; and my body, the side upon which I was lying, loyally preserving from the past an impression which my mind should never have forgotten brought back before my eyes the glimmering flame of the night-light in its bowl of Bohemian glass, shaped like an urn and hung by chains from the ceiling, and the chimney-piece of Siena marble in my bedroom at Combray, in my great-aunt's house, in those far distant days which, at the moment of waking, seemed present without being clearly defined, but would become plainer in a little while when I was properly awake.

Then would come up the memory of a fresh position; the wall slid away in another direction; I was in my room in Mme. de Saint-Loup's house in the country; good heavens, it must be ten o'clock, they will have finished dinner! I must have overslept myself, in the little nap which I always take when I come in from my walk with Mme. de Saint-Loup, before dressing for the evening. For many years have now elapsed since the Combray days, when, coming in from the longest and latest walks, I would still be in time to see the reflection of the sunset glowing in the panes of my bedroom window. It is a very different kind of existence at Tansonville now with Mme. de Saint-Loup, and a different kind of pleasure that I now derive from taking walks only in the evenings, from visiting by moonlight the roads on which I used to play, as a child, in the sunshine; while the bedroom, in which I shall presently fall asleep instead of dressing for dinner, from afar off I can see it, as we return from our walk, with its lamp shining through the window, a solitary beacon in the night.

These shifting and confused gusts of memory never lasted for more than a few seconds; it often happened that, in my spell of uncertainty as to where I was, I did not distinguish the successive theories of which that uncertainty was composed any more than, when we watch a horse running, we isolate the successive positions of its body as they appear upon a bioscope. But I had seen first one and then another of the rooms in which I had slept during my life, and in the end I would revisit them all in the long course of my waking dream: rooms in winter, where on going to bed I would at once bury my head in a nest, built up out of the most diverse materials, the corner of my pillow, the top of my blankets, a piece of a shawl, the edge of my bed, and a copy of an evening paper, all of which things I would contrive, with the infinite patience of birds building their nests, to cement into one whole; rooms where, in a keen frost, I would feel the satisfaction of being shut in from the outer world (like the sea-swallow which builds at the end of a dark tunnel and is kept warm by the surrounding earth), and where, the fire keeping in all night, I would sleep wrapped up, as it were, in

a great cloak of snug and savory air, shot with the glow of the logs
which would break out again in flame: in a sort of alcove without walls,
a cave of warmth dug out of the heart of the room itself, a zone of heat
whose boundaries were constantly shifting and altering in temperature
as gusts of air ran across them to strike freshly upon my face, from the
corners of the room, or from parts near the window or far from the fireplace which had therefore remained cold—or rooms in summer, where
I would delight to feel myself a part of the warm evening, where the
moonlight striking upon the half-opened shutters would throw down
to the foot of my bed its enchanted ladder; where I would fall asleep,
as it might be in the open air, like a titmouse which the breeze keeps
poised in the focus of a sunbeam—or sometimes the Louis XVI room,
so cheerful that I could never feel really unhappy, even on my first
night in it: that room where the slender columns which lightly supported its ceiling would part, ever so gracefully, to indicate where the
bed was and to keep it separate; sometimes again that little room with
the high ceiling, hollowed in the form of a pyramid out of two separate
stories, and partly walled with mahogany, in which from the first
moment my mind was drugged by the unfamiliar scent of flowering
grasses, convinced of the hostility of the violet curtains and of the insolent indifference of a clock that chattered on at the top of its voice
as though I were not there; while a strange and pitiless mirror with
square feet, which stood across one corner of the room, cleared for
itself a site I had not looked to find tenanted in the quiet surroundings
of my normal field of vision: that room in which my mind, forcing
itself for hours on end to leave its moorings, to elongate itself upward
so as to take on the exact shape of the room, and to reach to the summit
of that monstrous funnel, had passed so many anxious nights while
my body lay stretched out in bed, my eyes staring upward, my ears
straining, my nostrils sniffing uneasily, and my heart beating; until
custom had changed the color of the curtains, made the clock keep
quiet, brought an expression of pity to the cruel, slanting face of the
glass, disguised or even completely dispelled the scent of flowering
grasses, and distinctly reduced the apparent loftiness of the ceiling.
Custom! that skillful but unhurrying manager who begins by torturing
the mind for weeks on end with her provisional arrangements; whom
the mind, for all that, is fortunate in discovering, for without the help
of custom it would never contrive, by its own efforts, to make any room
seem habitable.

Certainly I was now well awake; my body had turned about for the
last time and the good angel of certainty had made all the surrounding
objects stand still, had set me down under my bedclothes, in my bedroom, and had fixed, approximately in their right places in the uncertain light, my chest of drawers, my writing-table, my fireplace, the
window overlooking the street, and both the doors. But it was no good
my knowing that I was not in any of those houses of which, in the
stupid moment of waking, if I had not caught sight exactly, I could

still believe in their possible presence; for memory was now set in motion; as a rule I did not attempt to go to sleep again at once, but used to spend the greater part of the night recalling our life in the old days at Combray with my great-aunt, at Balbec, Paris, Doncières, Venice, and the rest; remembering again all the places and people that I had known, what I had actually seen of them, and what others had told me.

COLETTE

The Gentle Libertine

Sidonie-Gabrielle Colette was born in Burgundy in 1873, and was educated in the local schools. In 1893 she married Henry Gautier-Villars, a writer known as "Willy" who discovered her literary talent. Her first book, *Claudine à L'Ecole,* based on childhood memories, was published in 1900. In 1905 Colette became an actress. She has also done newspaper work. Among her other books are *La Vagabonde, L'Envers du Music-Hall* and *Cheri.* [From *The Gentle Libertine* by Colette; copyright 1931 by Rinehart & Co., Inc.; used by permission of the publishers; translated by R. C. B.]

ARTHUR DUPIN, THE EDITORIAL WRITER OF THE *Journal,* had hammered out another chef-d'oeuvre.

MORE APACHES! IMPORTANT
CAPTURE—CURLY STILL MISSING

Our readers must remember our lugubrious but accurate account of what transpired last Tuesday night. The police have not remained inactive since that time. Ere twenty-four hours had elapsed Inspector Joyeux had his hand on Vandermeer, known as the Eel. Denounced by one of his wounded comrades who had been transported to the hospital, this criminal was taken into custody at a hotel room in Norvins Street. As to Copperhead, there is as yet no clue. Even her intimates seem in ignorance as to her whereabouts and it is said that anarchy reigns among gang circles, deprived as they are of their Queen. Up to a late hour last night, Curly had succeeded in also evading arrest.

Minne, going to her white bed, read the account again before throwing it into the wastebasket. She took a long time to drop off to sleep, roused herself to agitation and reflected:

"She is in hiding, their Queen! Probably in a den. The police don't even know how to go about looking for her. She has faithful friends who bring her cold meat and hard-boiled eggs by night. If they ever do discover her hiding place she'll always manage to kill a lot of policemen before they ever take her . . . But her people are in mutiny! And without Curly the Levallois-Perret gang will disperse. They really ought to have elected a vice-queen to reign in the absence of Copperhead."

To Minne, the above was enormously intriguing but no more than was to be expected of life as she had learned of it in old-fashioned novels. She knew beyond the shadow of a doubt that the rough ground of the fortifications was a strange land where swarmed a race of dangerous but attractive savages, quite different from us and easily recognizable by certain insignia, the bicyclist cap, the black jersey sweater striped in bright colors, a sweater that hugged the skin like tattooing. This race produces two distinct types:

1. The Squat. Swinging walk, large hands like raw beefsteaks, hair growing well down on the forehead and beetling eyebrows.

2. The Slim. Indolent, noiseless walk. Tennis sneakers, flowered socks, not always whole. Sometimes instead of socks, the delicate skin of an instep, bare, of a dubious white, veined with blue . . . Hair sweeping down over a well-shaved cheek, pasty white skin accentuating feverishly red lips.

According to Minne's classification, this latter individual was the incarnation of the most noble type of a mysterious race. The Squat type often sang voluntarily, arm in arm with rough-haired gay girls. The Slim one slipped his hands into the pockets of his wide trousers and smoked, his eyes half closed, while at his side some inferior feminine creature cried, wept and wailed. "She bores him," invented Minne, "with a lot of little domestic worries. He doesn't even listen to her, he dreams, watching the smoke of his Oriental cigarette . . ."

Minne admired the way this singular race remained patriarchal by daytime. On her way back from school at noon she perceived numbers of them on the slope of the embankment, their bodies stretched out, relaxed, dull, dozing. The females of the tribe, squatting on their heels, mended old clothes or lunched picnic fashion off greasy papers spread on their knees. The fine stalwart males slept. A few of them, more wakeful than the others, threw off their coats and wrestled with each other in friendly bouts to keep their muscles supple and in condition.

Minne compared them to cats who sleep or polish their coat by day, and sharpen their claws on the parquet flooring. The calm preparedness of cats. When night came they changed into screaming, sanguinary demons, whose cries like those of children being strangled, reached her ears even in sleep.

This mysterious race did not cry by night. But it whistled. Shrill, terrifying whistles echoed through the exterior boulevards carrying from outpost to outpost some incomprehensible telegraphic message. When Minne heard them, she shuddered from head to foot as if stabbed by a sharp needle.

"They whistled twice. A trembling *ui-ui-ui* answered from way over yonder. Does that mean 'Save yourself' or 'All done'? Perhaps just that they've finished a job, killed off some old woman? The old woman is even now at the foot of her bed, on the floor, in a 'pool of blood.' They have gone off to count the gold and the banknotes—and get drunk on red wine. Tomorrow on the enbankment, they'll tell their comrades all about the old lady and they'll split the booty . . . But alas! Their Queen is away and anarchy reigns! The *Journal* said so! How grand to be Queen, with a red ribbon and a revolver; to understand that code of whistles, to pat Curly's head and decide what crimes to commit. Queen Minne? Queen Minne. Why not? After all, isn't there a Queen Wilhelmine?"

And Minne fell asleep, her mind still rambling on.

Minne, all ready, agitatedly waited in her sunny room, nervous to the point of stamping with rage. Célénie, the fat housemaid, had made her late. Now what if *he* were gone!

Four days Minne had met *him* on the corner of the Avenue Gourgaud and the Boulevard Berthier. The first day he slept sitting up, his back leaning against a wall, sprawling and taking up half the sidewalk; but Minne—she was so absent-minded!—had already nearly stumbled on the feet of the sleeper, and he, he had opened his eyes. And what eyes! Minne had an electric shock when she saw them, a shiver of complete admiration. Black almond-shaped eyes, the white of which seemed bluish in the Italian-like pallor of the skin. His tiny mustache was fine as an ink drawing, his black hair curled with moisture. Before his nap he had thrown off his cap, a violet and black checked cap, and his right hand still held a dead cigarette, between thumb and index finger.

He stared at Minne, without moving, with such outrageously flattering effrontery that she almost stopped.

The day Minne got a *five* in history and, well, even at the Souhait school they say "a five is disgraceful!" Minne heard herself given a public reprimand, outwardly submissive, only her eyes straying, she cursed Mlle. Souhait to ignominious and complicated tortures.

Every day, at noon, Minne brushed past the vagrant and the vagrant stared back at Minne in her light summer dress and Minne return' his stare with serious eyes. She thought: "He is waiting for me. loves me. He understands me. How can I tell him that I am never If only I could slip him a piece of paper saying: 'I am held pr' Kill Célénie and we will flee together . . . Flee together . . life . . . toward a new life where I should never even rem' I am Minne.'"

She was a little surprised at the inertia of her "ravager" elegant and shirtless, at the foot of a sycamore. But ur found an explanation for this extenuated weaknes' pallor: "How many did he kill last night?" She looked with a furtive eye for blood which might stain the unknown's nails. But never a trace of blood! His slender fingers, all too pointed, never held anything but a cigarette lit or dead between the thumb and index finger. He was a fine Tom cat, whose eyes were watchful under sleepy lids! Might his leap be a terrible one when he slaughtered Célénie and carried Minne away!

Mama had also remarked the unknown loiterer in the noonday sun. She hurried her steps, blushed, and gave a deep sigh of relief once the peril was passed in the Avenue Gourgaud.

"Do you often see that man sitting there on the ground, Minne?"

"A man sitting on the ground?"

"No, don't turn around! A man sitting on the ground at the corner of the avenue. I'm always afraid those fellows can be up to no good in this neighborhood!"

Minne did not answer. All her secret being swelled with pride. "I'm the one he's looking for! It is for me alone that he's waiting there! Mama couldn't understand."

About the eighth day, Minne was struck by an idea that she considered no less than an inspiration: that clear pallor, the black hair that curled like lamb's wool . . . It's Curly. It's Curly himself. The newspapers had said "Curly's whereabouts are still unknown." And there he was at the corner of the Boulevard Berthier and Avenue Gourgaud, risking his life to see his great love pass twice a day.

Minne became so agitated she could not sleep. At night she would get up to look out of her window for Curly's shadow.

"It can't drag on this way much longer," she said to herself. "One evening he'll whistle under my window, I'll go down by a ladder or a knotted rope, and he will carry me away on a motorcycle, off to a den where his subjects will be assembled. He'll say: 'Here is your new Queen.' And . . . and . . . it will be terrible!"

One day Curly missed a rendezvous. Before the eyes of her worried Mama, Minne forgot to eat luncheon. But the next day and the next and all the following days still brought no Curly, no somnolent and supple Curly to open his eyes suddenly as Minne brushed past him.

Oh, these presentiments of Minne's! "I *knew* it was he, I knew that it was Curly. And now he's in prison. The guillotine perhaps!" Faced by Minne's inexplicable weeping, Minne's fever, Mama sent at once for Uncle Paul who prescribed bouillon, chicken, a light tonic wine—and immediate departure for the country.

While Mama packed trunks with the activity of an ant conscious of n approaching storm, Minne doleful and indolent, pressed her forehead ainst the window pane and dreamed. "He is in prison for me. He suffering for me, he is languishing and writes love poems in his : *To my unknown. . . .*"

ANDRE GIDE

A Crime

Without a

Motive

André Gide, born in Paris in 1869, studied under private tutors and traveled a great deal in Europe and North Africa. His many critical essays show his preoccupation with the problems of freedom and social justice. Among his best known works are *The Counterfeiters* and *Lafcadio's Adventures,* novels, and *Voyage au Congo,* a travel book. [From *Lafcadio's Adventures* by André Gide; copyright 1925, 1928 by Alfred A. Knopf, Inc.; used by permission of the publishers; translated by Dorothy Bussy.]

HE WAS SITTING ALL ALONE in a compartment of the train which was carrying him away from Rome, and contemplating—not without satisfaction—his hands in their gray doeskin gloves, as they lay on the rich fawn-colored plaid, which, in spite of the heat, he had spread negligently over his knees. Through the soft woolen material of his traveling-suit he breathed ease and comfort at every pore; his neck was unconfined in its collar which without being low was un-starched, and from beneath which the narrow line of a bronze neck-tie ran, slender as a grass-snake, over his pleated shirt. He was at ease in his skin, at ease in his clothes, at ease in his shoes, which were cut out of the same doeskin as his gloves; his foot in its elastic prison could stretch, could bend, could feel itself alive. His beaver hat was pulled down over his eyes and kept out the landscape; he was smoking dried juniper, after the Algerian fashion, in a little clay pipe and letting his thoughts wander at their will. He thought:

"—The old woman with the little white cloud above her head, who pointed to it and said: 'It won't rain today!' that poor, shriveled woman whose sack I carried on my shoulders" (he had followed his fancy of traveling on foot for four days across the Apennines, between Bologna and Florence, and had slept a night at Covigliajo) "and whom I kissed when we got to the top of the hill . . . one of what the curé of Covigliajo would have called my 'good actions.' I could just as easily have throttled her—my hand would have been steady—when I felt her dirty wrinkled skin beneath my fingers. . . . Ah! how caressingly she stroked and dusted my coat collar and said 'figlio mio! carino!' . . . I wonder what made my joy so intense when afterward—I was still in a sweat—I lay down on the moss—not smoking though—in the shade of that big chestnut-tree. I felt as though I could have clasped the whole of mankind to my heart in my single embrace—or strangled it, for that matter. Human life! What a paltry thing! And with what alacrity I'd risk mine if only some deed of gallantry would turn up—something really rather pleasantly rash and daring! . . . All the same, I can't turn alpinist or aviator. . . . I wonder what that hidebound old Julius

287

would advise. . . . It's a pity he's such a stick-in-the-mud! I should have liked to have a brother.

"Poor Julius! So many writers and so few readers! It's a fact. People read less and less nowadays . . . to judge by myself, as they say. It'll end by some catastrophe—some stupendous catastrophe, reeking with horror. Printing will be chucked overboard altogether; and it'll be a miracle if the best doesn't sink to the bottom with the worst.

"But the curious thing would be to know what the old woman would have said if I had begun to squeeze. One imagines what would happen if, but there's always a little hiatus through which the unexpected creeps in. Nothing ever happens exactly as one thinks it's going to. . . . That's what makes me want to act. . . . One does so little! . . . 'Let all that can be, be!' That's my explanation of the Creation. . . . In love with what might be, if I were the Government I should lock myself up.

"Nothing very exciting about the correspondence of that Monsieur Gaspard Flamand which I claimed as mine at the Poste Restante at Bologne. Nothing that would have been worth the trouble of returning to him.

"Heavens! how few people one meets whose portmanteau one would care to ransack! . . . And yet how few there are from whom one wouldn't get some queer reaction if one knew the right word—the right gesture! . . . A fine lot of puppets; but, by Jove, one sees the strings too plainly. One meets no one in the streets nowadays but jackanapes and blockheads. Is it possible for a decent person—I ask you, Lafcadio—to take such a farce seriously? No, no! Be off with you! It's high time! Off to a new world! Print your foot upon Europe's soil and take a flying leap. If in the depths of Borneo's forests there still remains a belated anthropopithex, go there and reckon thee chances of a future race of mankind. . . .

"I should have liked to see Protos again. No doubt he's made tracks for America. He used to make out that the barbarians of Chicago were the only persons he esteemed. . . . Not voluptuous enough for my taste—a pack of wolves! I'm feline by nature. . . . Well, enough of that!

"The padre of Covigliajo with his cheery face didn't look in the least inclined to deprave the little boy he was talking to. He was certainly in charge of him. I should have liked to make friends with him— not with the curé, my word!—but with the little boy.

"How beautiful his eyes were when he raised them to mine! He was as anxious and as afraid to meet my look as I his—but I looked away at once. He was barely five years younger than I. Yes, between fourteen and sixteen—not more. What was I at that age? A stripling full of covetousness, whom I should like to meet now; I think I should take a great fancy to myself. . . . Faby was quite abashed at first to feel that he had fallen in love with me; it was a good thing he made a clean breast of it to my mother; after that he felt lighter-hearted. But how irritated I was by his self-restraint! Later on in the Aures, when I told him about it under the tent, we had a good laugh together. . . . I should like to see him again; it's a pity he's dead. Well, enough of that!

"The truth is, I hoped the curé would dislike me. I tried to think of disagreeable things to say to him—I could hit on nothing that wasn't charming. It's wonderful how hard I find it not to be fascinating. Yet I really can't stain my face with walnut juice, as Carola recommended, or start eating garlic. . . . Ah! don't let me think of that poor creature any more. It's to her I owe the most mediocre of my pleasures. . . . Oh! What kind of ark can that strange old man have come out of?"

The sliding door into the corridor had just let in Amédée Fleurissoire. Fleurissoire had traveled in an empty compartment as far as Frosinone. At that station a middle-aged Italian had got into his carriage and had begun to stare at him with such glowering eyes that Fleurissoire had made haste to take himself off.

In the next compartment, Lafcadio's youthful grace, on the contrary, attracted him.

"Dear me! What a charming boy," thought he; "hardly more than a child! On his holidays, no doubt. How beautifully dressed he is! His eyes look so candid! Oh, what a relief it will be to be quit of my suspicions for once! If only he knew French, I should like to talk to him."

He sat down opposite to him in the corner next the door. Lafcadio turned up the brim of his hat and began to consider him with a lifeless and apparently indifferent eye.

"What is there in common between me and that squalid little rat?" reflected he. "He seems to fancy himself too. What is he smiling at me like that for? Does he imagine I'm going to embrace him? Is it possible that there exist women who fondle old men? No doubt he'd be exceedingly astonished to know that I can read writing or print with perfect fluency, upside down, or in transparency, or in a looking-glass, or on blotting-paper—a matter of three months' training and two years' practice—all for the love of art. Cadio, my dear boy, the problem is this: to impinge on that fellow's fate . . . but how? . . . Oh! I'll offer him a cachou. Whether he accepts or not, I shall at any rate hear in what language."

"Grazio! Grazio!" said Fleurissoire as he refused.

"Nothing doing with the old dromedary. Let's go to sleep," went on Lafcadio to himself, and pulling the brim of his hat down over his eyes, he tried to spin a dream out of one of his youthful memories.

He saw himself back at the time when he used to be called Cadio, in that remote castle in the Carpathians where his mother and he spent two summers in company with Baldi, the Italian, and Prince Wladimir Bielkowski. His room is at the end of passage. This is the first year he had not slept near his mother. . . . The bronze door-handle is

shaped like a lion's head and is held in place by a big nail. . . . Ah!
how clearly he remembers his sensations! . . . One night he is aroused
from a deep sleep to see Uncle Wladimir—or is it a dream?—standing
by his bedside, looking more gigantic even than usual—a very nightmare, draped in the fold of a huge rust-colored caftan, with his drooping mustache, and an outrageous night-cap stuck on his head like a
Persian bonnet, so that there seems no end to the length of him. He
is holding in his hand a dark lantern, which he sets down on the table
near the bed, beside Cadio's watch, pushing aside a bag of marbles to
make room for it. Cadio's first thought is that his mother is dead or
ill. He is on the point of asking, when Bielkowski puts his finger on
his lips and signs to him to get up. The boy hastily slips on his bath-
wrap, which his uncle takes from the back of a chair and hands to
him—all this with knitted brows and the look of a person who is not
to be trifled with. But Cadio had such immense faith in Wladi that
he hasn't a moment's fear. He pops on his slippers and follows him,
full of curiosity at these goings-on and, as usual, all athrill for amusement.

They step into the passage; Wladimir advances gravely—mysteriously, carrying the lantern well in front of him; they look as if they
are accomplishing a rite or walking in a procession; Cadio is a little
unsteady on his feet, for he is still dazed with dreaming; but curiosity
soon clears his brains. As they pass his mother's room, they both stop
for a moment and listen—not a sound! The whole house is fast asleep.
When they reach the landing they hear the snoring of a footman whose
room is in the attics. They go downstairs. Wladi's stockinged feet
drop on the steps as softly as cotton-wool; at the slightest creak he
turns round, looking so furious that Cadio can hardly keep from laughing. He points out one particular step and signs to him not to tread
on it, with as much seriousness as if they were really in danger. Cadio
takes care not to spoil his pleasure by asking himself whether their precautions are necessary, nor what can be the meaning of it all; he enters
into the spirit of the game and slides down the banister, past the step.
. . . He is so tremendously entertained by Wladi that he would go
through fire and water to follow him.

When they reach the ground floor, they both sit down on the bottom
step for a moment's breathing-space; Wladi nods his head and gives
vent to a little sigh through his nose, as much as to say: "My word!
we've had a narrow squeak!" They start off again. At the drawing-
room door, what redoubled precautions! The lantern, which it is now
Cadio's turn to hold, lights up the room so queerly that the boy hardly
recognizes it; it seems to him fantastically big; a ray of light steals
through a chink in the shutters; everything is plunged in a super-
natural calm; he is reminded of a pond the moment before the stealthy
casting of a net; and he recognizes all the familiar objects, each one
there in its place—but for the first time he realizes their strangeness.

Wladi goes up to the piano, half opens it and lightly touches two or three notes with his finger-tips, so as to draw from them the lightest of sounds. Suddenly the lid slips from his hand and falls with a terrific din. (The mere recollection of it made Lafcadio jump again.) Wladi makes a dash at the lantern, muffles it and then crumples up into an arm-chair; Cadio slips under the table; they stay endless minutes, waiting motionless, listening in the dark . . . but no—nothing stirs in the house; in the distance a dog bays the moon. Then gently, slowly, Wladi uncovers the lantern.

In the dining-room, with what an air he unlocks the sideboard! The boy knows well enough it is nothing but a game, but his uncle seems actually taken in by it himself. He sniffs about as though to scent out where the best things lie hid; pounces on a bottle of Tokay; pours out two small glasses full for them to dip their biscuits in; signs to Cadio to pledge him, with finger on lip; the glasses tinkle faintly as they touch. . . . When the midnight feast is over, Wladi sets to work to put the things straight again; he goes with Cadio to rinse the glasses in the pantry sink, wipes them, corks the bottle, shuts up the biscuit box, dusts away the crumbs with scrupulous care and gives one last glance to see that everything is tidy again in the cupboard. . . . Right you are! Not the ghost of a trace!

Wladi accompanies Cadio back to his bedroom door and takes leave of him with a low bow. Cadio picks up his slumbers again where he had left them, and wonders the next day whether the whole thing wasn't a dream.

An odd kind of entertainment for a little boy! What would Julius have thought of it? . . .

Lafcadio, though his eyes were shut, was not asleep; he could not sleep.

"The old boy over there believes I am asleep," thought he; "if I were to take a peek at him through my eyelids, I should see him looking at me. Protos used to make out that it was particularly difficult to pretend to be asleep while one is really watching; he claimed that he could always spot pretended sleep by just that slight quiver of the eyelids . . . I'm repressing now. Protos himself would be taken in. . . ."

The sun meanwhile had set, and Fleurissoire, in sentimental mood, was gazing at the last gleams of its splendor as they gradually faded from the sky. Suddenly the electric light that was set in the rounded ceiling of the railway carriage, blazed out with a vividness that contrasted brutally with the twilight's gentle melancholy. Fleurissoire was afraid too, that it might disturb his neighbor's slumbers, and turned the switch; the result was not total darkness but merely a shifting of the current from the center lamp to a dark blue night-light. To Fleurissoire's thinking, this was still too bright; he turned the switch again; the night-light went out, but two side brackets were immediately turned on, whose glare was even more disagreeable than the center

light's; another turn, and the night-light came on again; at this he
gave up.

"Will he never have done fiddling with the light?" thought Lafcadio
impatiently. "What's he up to now? (No! I'll not raise my eyelids.)
He is standing up. Can he have taken a fancy to my portmanteau?
Bravo! He has noticed that it isn't locked. It was a bright idea of
mine to have a complicated lock fitted to it at Milan and then lose
the key, so that I had to have it picked at Bologna! A padlock, at
any rate, is easy to replace. . . . God damn it! Is he taking off his coat?
Oh! all the same, let's have a look!"

Fleurissoire, with no eyes for Lafcadio's portmanteau, was struggling with his new collar and had taken his coat off, so as to be able
to put the stud in more easily; but the starched linen was as hard as
cardboard and he struggled in vain.

"He doesn't look happy," went on Lafcadio to himself. "He must be
suffering from a fistula or some unpleasant complaint of that kind.
Shall I go to his help? He'll never manage it by himself. . . ."

Yes, though! At last the collar yielded to the stud. Fleurissoire then
took up his tie, which he had placed on the seat beside his hat, his
coat and his cuffs, and going up to the door of the carriage, looked
at himself in the window-pane, endeavoring, like Narcissus in the
water to distinguish his reflection from the surrounding landscape.

"He can't see."

Lafcadio turned on the light. The train at that moment was running
alongside a bank, which could be seen through the window, illuminated
by the light cast upon it from one after another of the compartments
of the train; a procession of brilliant squares was thus formed which
danced alongside the railroad and suffered, each one in its turn, the
same distortions, according to the irregularities of the ground. In the
middle of one of these squares danced Fleurissoire's grotesque shadow;
the others were empty.

"Who could see?" thought Lafcadio. "There—just to my hand—
under my hand—this double fastening, which I can easily undo; the
door would suddenly give way and he would topple out; the slightest
push would do it; he would fall into the darkness like a stone; one
wouldn't even hear a scream. . . . And off tomorrow to the East! . . .
Who would know?"

The tie—a little ready-made sailor knot—was put on by now and
Fleurissoire had taken up one of the cuffs and was arranging it upon
his right wrist, examining, as he did so, the photograph above his seat,
which represented some palace by the sea, and was one of four that
adorned the compartment.

"A crime without a motive," went on Lafcadio, "what a puzzle for
the police! As to that, however, going along beside this blessed bank,
anybody in the next-door compartment might notice the door open and
the old blighter's shadow potch out. The corridor curtains, at any
rate, are drawn. . . . It's not so much about events that I'm curious,

as about myself. There's many a man thinks he's capable of anything, who draws back when it comes to the point. . . . What a gulf between the imagination and the deed! . . . And no more right to take back one's move than at chess. Pooh! If one could foresee all the risks, there'd be no interest in the game! . . . Between the imagination of a deed and . . . Hullo! the bank's come to an end. Here we are on a bridge, I think; a river . . ."

The window-pane had now turned black and the reflections in it became more distinct. Fleurissoire leant forward to straighten his tie.

"Here, just under my hand the double fastening—now that he's looking away and not paying attention—upon my soul, it's easier to undo than I thought. If I can count up to twelve, without hurrying, before I see a light in the country-side, the dromedary is saved. Here goes! One, two, three, four (slowly! slowly!), five, six, seven, eight, nine . . . a light! . . ."

Fleurissoire did not utter a single cry.

JEAN GIRAUDOUX

May on Lake Asquam

Jean Giraudoux (1892–1944) was born in Bellac and attended the Ecole Normale Supérieure. In 1909 he published his first book, *Provinciales*. Giraudoux in time became a high official of the French diplomatic service. He was equally famous as a playwright and a novelist (*Siegfried et le Limousin, Amphitryon 38*, plays; *La France Sentimentale, Bella, Juliette au Pays des Hommes, Choix des Elues* and *Eglantine*, prose). [From *Campaigns and Intervals* by Jean Giraudoux; used by permission of the publishers, Houghton Mifflin Co.; translated by Elizabeth S. Sargeant.]

I AM STRETCHED OUT in the middle of a great ring of mountains. When I get up onto my feet, I become their very pivot. I have put the sun on my left, as they taught me to do at school, and I am writing to you. The lake below me bears fragile islands on its surface, and pine logs, from the drifts broken up during the winter, wash vagrantly in its bays and coves. Humming-birds thrusting voraciously among the apple-blossoms, wound their swift bills on the hard wood and glance off again. To soothe the sore feet of the farm turkeys—a degenerate race—Mrs. Green is greasing the limbs of the tree where they come to roost. A thrush grazes me, a little breeze begins to stir. As when a bird alights by a dreaming poet and he is moved to see the very thought he was seeking within himself drop then, perfect—so a sweet and tender love, instead of stirring in my heart, lifts this page, fans me with its soft breath. In boat-houses hidden in the reeds the farmers are testing the motors of the boats which will be launched for their masters next month. Mrs. Green is beating a rose-colored puff for me, because my bed ends under the window, and when I wake in the morning I see my sunny feet under the spread—and yet feel cold. In the depths of the creeks where the new-cut pines are floating, the lumbermen jump from one log to the next, whistling as they go. I envy them their balance; I feel overweighted with a lake and a sun on my left, and nothing on my right.

Where am I? I am in a land which I instantly recognize to be enormous, because these wasps that are this second buzzing about my head are three times bigger than they are in Europe. I am in the middle of New Hampshire, which is having its first sight of the sky-blue uniform, and, supposing that I have chosen this color myself, imagines me to be sensitive and generous. The Harvard Regiment is having a week of examinations, and I am taking a rest.

The motor left Boston early on Monday, reaching the suburbs at the hour when the typewriters, perched on their high-heeled, pointed shoes, in their low-necked foulard dresses, and bent slant-wise to the wind, climb into the tramcars without touching the rail, anxious only for their hands; the stenographers following them rigidly erect, thinking only of their heads. On the door-steps Irish girls with brown braids looped over their ears passed on to us, through soft blue eyes, the holiest thoughts they had been pondering in the night. We were following the highway bordered with Washington elms, very old trees whose trunks had been repaired with the sort of cement of which they make statues in this country; and immortality—as sap was lacking—had already reached the topmost branches. Lakes that grew clearer and clearer the farther we went held the water of the richer and richer parts of Boston, and we came at last to the very round, very blue lake that supplies Beacon Street.

At noon we were at Portsmouth, where I presided at a meeting the children were holding on the beach to sell their pet animals, for the benefit of their French godchildren. There were at least a hundred of them, all grave, eager, or at least acquiescent, save Grace Henderson, who clung to her white calf and wept. They bought it of her quickly, and in pity gave it back to her; but her brother obliged her to sell it again, and so she had to struggle and suffer three times over. There were Cuban birds, that you bought with their cages; native birds that you bought so as to set them free; turtles which sold badly, as they wore the initials of their first master carved on their backs; goats; and there were animals which were also immolated for the cause—sad dogs, who had no resistance left in them, and sold themselves; a little elephant which clasped his mistress by a belt that gave, by a sleeve that tore, and so did not dare to take her by the pigtail. The governesses, to console their children, quickly bought these other animals, and took turns standing on a platform to read out letters from the godsons:

"*Venez chez moi, j'irai chez vous,*" wrote Jean Perrot, "*et si je meurs je veux vous voir.*" Some professors who were there were amazed to discover that all French children use rhythmic prose.

Then came green forests cut by tumbling brooks, where little boys, who were fishing for trout with both hands, hailed us with a wink, as they did not dare to move or call out. Then came the country of the field-mice, where the owls have such fat haunches that they have to perch sideways for fear of tumbling off their twigs head first. Then came Sandwich, where a Lithuanian was waving his national flag, protesting all by himself against conscription. Then came Lake Asquam, and this local hilltop where I have lain stretched out ever since, at the foot of a slim giant birch, which has only one tuft of verdure at its top, and will fall if it puts out a single other leaf.

My hostess is Mrs. Green, the farmer's wife, who wears her gray hair braided down her back, and a big striped shawl, and eyeglasses; but she twists the calves' tails, and fights with the rooster. When a word gets stuck in my fountain pen I shake it out into the lake from my steamer-chair. Sometimes, though, it is inside me that it hesitates, and then I have to get up myself, lean on my elbows, sometimes even stoop all the way over.

Who am I with? With two friends—a forester and an Australian poet. The morning belongs to Carnegie, the forester. By six o'clock he has me up and off on a dash to his district, straight across the islands where every owner keeps a different scheme of hours, according as he likes to see his children get up early or late. Silent beasts are waking in woods that still have their Indian names; the muskrat is taking his bath, the blue heron flies from an isthmus to an island, from an island to an islet, flying ever toward that little round point of noon. We land in haste, to avoid an upset—for a new-cut pine log is already sliding down the toboggan to the lake—and go to the sawmill by a path that was once covered with sawdust, but that my forester has had tarred since he lost his gold chain. He teaches me the secret sign by which one may recognize the red pine, the white pine, and the black pine; he gathers together his group of woodcutters, who are going off to France, and forces me to denounce our biggest trees in French—the oak, the elm; I saw my favorite beeches with difficulty. In the short cuts we walk through the briars stiffly, as people who do not speak the same tongue always do, and not one of these noble gestures is lost, my dear, for the forest is full of lynxes. In the clearings he shows me the remains of the wood fires he has kindled since his childhood, and twenty years of embers still blacken his fingers. He is moved and sits down, my love, to dream . . . and suddenly four little woodchucks, my sweet, hurry timidly out of the ground; real little woodchucks, my heart. We catch them—they bite us, and try to get away—we pet them, my dear love.

But the night belongs to Rogers, the Australian. The whole world is dark, invisible; only one red point to be seen, Carnegie's cigar—he is noiselessly paddling on the lake. But miles away the chosen tree that announces the moon suddenly twinkles down its whole length. That is because a whole moon is coming. Everything is radiant, everything shines. Rocks begin to show themselves, as white and polished as bleached bones. Far around the lake the reflection of the forest, just now cleft and jutting, becomes an even border. It is the hour when the Indians gave a name to all the things that surround us. The white mountains turn white, the yellow birches yellow, and blue, blue grow the owls. Every separate plane of the lake seems to lie on a different level, and the moon gnaws the water where it falls over the dams. A divine night, this, when the White Mountains are of silver and the birches of gold. At last the hour has come when I can find an epithet for my soul, and a name for my house. The bullfrog groans; the loon, black swan of the lake, utters cries, first piercing, then muffled, for he continually ducks his head under the water and pulls it out again. The true moon cautiously climbs farther and farther from the false moon. . . .

But Rogers insists on talking. He wants me to talk to him of Seeger, who is dead, of Blakely, who is dead—of all the American poets who were killed before the American war began. He persists in talking French, without allowing me to help him, and circles about the words he no longer knows: about the word "debonair," the word "ladder," the word "serenity." From my refuge in the very heart of the word I wait placidly for him, sometimes in the heart of a proper name, in the heart of Baudelaire—a stuffy place, his statue. Then he reads me his verses, which he wishes to adapt to Europe, because the Australian mouths are so different from our own.

"July has frozen the rivers," he says, "and the useless bridges are collected in the barn."

I shake my head; he understands, and corrects himself:

"Summer has frozen the rivers, and the bridges" . . .

The loon sings on. The lake suddenly bursts into flame, for Carnegie is lighting a second cigar. Rogers grows emotional, takes my hand and circles about a word which expresses both loons and friendships, a word which even we in France, alas, do not know.

When the storm breaks; when, by millions, the owners of the wooden houses bring their red-striped tents in from the rain: when a flash of lightning allows you to see—through the isinglass of the top of the car in front of you—the shadow of two gray heads; when the black bird with the red wings folds his wings; when the pro-German shuts his window and suddenly feels so lonely and beaten that he bursts into tears; when, in the public parks, the crowds swarm under the tents of the recruiting sergeants, and help them move their posters, and torpedoes, and mortars under shelter; when the mother astride the purple motor-cycle tries in vain to reach out a hand and feel the baby dozing in the side-car; when the golden stags, the dragons and the golden cows whirl madly on the clock-towers of the barns, but always in time; when

a Hannan shoe lies on the deserted avenue; when a blast of wind lifts
the page of the one-armed accountant, and he holds it down with the
point of his pen, calling for help; when one hears nothing on the sidewalks, on the sea, on the buildings, but the rain . . . then when a sunbeam comes down, and a sharp cloud cuts it, and it falls; when the rainbow shivers, its left on the solid city cement, its right on the sea; when
you gather the sun into a corner of the sky, as if it were your one last
match--and it finally burns; when a victorious sunbeam, falling on the
terrace beats by the fraction of an inch a rain-drop that has come from
thousands of miles less far away; when the baby in the side-car gets
the last drop of all, and begins to cry—then when the pond-lilies climb
up to the level of the new pond that has formed about them; when the
farmer in his rubber boots tramps out to empty his pitch cans and his
maple syrup cans of their water; when a child, for no reason at all,
wants to burn a joss-stick; when the traveler, at the turn of the Cañon,
gets down to pat his mule and all at once remounts quickly for the
storm is rumbling again, and he wants to keep his saddle dry; when
the rain begins to beat down once more, in a deluge, the very same rain,
as you can plainly recognize by its drops: then I think of him, of Seeger,
who loved storms, and I shudder.

"How did Seeger die?" asks Rogers.

In a month Rogers will be leaving for the war, and he loses no
opportunity of informing himself how the poets, his colleagues, were
killed. It would be very odd if two poets were killed in the same way,
the same identical way; each one of these deaths is death that fate will
deny him. He will not wander, like Rupert Brooke, repeating one
Christian name after another, and dying at the first woman's name. He
will not have him, as Dollero did, to write me three letters; the first
with a splinter and his blood saying good by; the second with his
nurse's pencil, hoping to see me; the last with the doctor's fountain pen
—confident, happy, unfinished. He will not drop dead like Hesslin, the
German poet, on the back of a mystical sergeant who rose slowly with
his load, and bore it to the hospital without casting a backward look. He
will need a whole grave to himself, since he is not to die like Blakely,
whose poor remains fitted into a Palmer's biscuit box. It will not be at
dark, as it was with Drouot, or at noon, as it was with Clermont. If
Seeger died at dawn, there is no time left for him but night. Bitter
night, running under the days like some infernal strawberry vine. Soft
night, with its lake, its loons. Night on the Sydney steamers, when the
world turns silent, and nothing stands in the way of a poet's thoughts
but the mute strain of a vessel. Night near some French spring where
you lie, scarcely aware of your wound, and nibble a leaf of water-cress.
Somber night, in whose very center, sharp cut against the velvet dark,
the sun suddenly appears. Happy he who dies at night!

"How did Seeger die? Did you know him?"

Rogers is astigmatic, wears heavy gold-rimmed spectacles with lenses
of different pattern, and always asks you two questions at a time. Yes,

I had seen him. Once it was in the Luxembourg, in summer; he was just coming into that unreal garden, with its world of fantastic and tender Parisians—those who felt themselves too heavy could buy little balloons at the gate. Another time it was at the house of a friend whom he had tried to find the two preceding evenings; on the first he left a couplet, on the second a sonnet. My friend allowed himself to be surprised in bed, the third day, and so did not get his poem.

"Did he suffer? Have you seen his last verses?"

For Rogers also collects the last poems of all the poets who have been killed. He even collects their last letters in prose, where sometimes two words clash into each other and rhyme—the same thing happens when a departing warrior is dressing in his apartment, with his friends standing about—and makes them tremble. It may be a last letter written to an aunt between the two last poems, when, in spite of himself, he uses the poetic epithet (as the other does not come)—talks of "steeds," and "blades," and "meads," and feels obliged to be somewhat ironic. Last poems where nearly all of them saw death as it was, in fact, to overtake them, Seeger like a mistress, longing for a rendezvous, Dollero like a storm with three stray birds, Blakely like a headless monster—and when only Brooke foresaw things all wrong. Poor Brooke who told us *"Si je meurs, dites vous que dans une terre étrangère il y aua toujours un coin de terre anglaise. Une poussière plus riche que la terre y sera contenue, un corps d'Angleterre lavé par les rivières anglaises, brûle par le soleil anglais,"* *"un corps horizontal tendu sur la ligne de tous les corps anglais,"* and in the end died on a boat, and was thrown into the sea with a cannon ball to keep his shroud upright. So that, for all one's pity one is put on one's guard, and when one turns over his other poems one no longer believes exactly what they say; no longer believes that love is *une rue ouverte où se precipite ce qui jamais ne voient, un traître qui livre au destin la citadelle du coeur, un enfant étendu.* One grows obstinate about it, insists on believing that love is a street, if you like, but a street with no outlet; a traitor perhaps, but in that case a friendly traitor; and sometimes one sees the charming fellow standing quite vertical, floating sadly in the air.

"How did Seeger die?"

It is summer. Everything that prevents one from breathing in summer—his cap, his gas-mask—he throws off. He holds his cigar behind him, because of the smoke; the company thief steals it away from him—thank heaven, for so his hands will not burn up after his death. Then he stretches himself, but without lifting his arms, crosswise. He has just one minute to live. There is your watch before you, with its second hand: one minute and he will be dead. In his pocket is the bottle of heliotrope perfume that he is to break as he falls. Now you have not even time, before he dies, to write that short sentence which he took for his motto, the one that he wrote at the head of every poem—about the poplars. If it is a shell, the cannon is being loaded. If it is a bullet, the German soldier is tapping his charge and slipping it in. Seeger raises his head. The sky is very blue. A poplar, yes, a poplar is outlined on the horizon. Seeger climbs the firing step—a bird, yes, a . . .

So my three days of rest have gone, and now it is noon. I think of you who wrote me every week from Europe, a letter of variable mood— Even the color of the paper is inconstant, and each one, like the flash of a revolving lighthouse, throws a new region into high relief. Love is a restive horse, a saddled antelope, a faithful traitor. The sun is just above me now. I was writing, to spare my eyes, in the shadow of my head; there is no shadow left; adieu, Madame, I write the last word, I write your name, full in the sun.

ANDRE

MALRAUX

Man's Fate

André Malraux, born in 1901, has lived an adventurous life. After doing archaeological research in Indo-China, he took part in an uprising in China. He then traveled in the East, before joining the Loyalists in the Spanish War. His most acclaimed novels are *Man's Fate* and *Man's Hope.* During the Second World War, he fought in the Maquis and was an executive committee officer of the National Liberation Movement. [From *Man's Fate* by Andre Malraux; copyright 1934 by Random House, Inc.; used by permission of the publishers; translated by Haakon M. Chevalier.]

Six o'clock in the evening IN THE LARGE HALL—formerly a schoolyard—two hundred wounded Communists were waiting to be taken out and shot. Katov, among the last ones brought in, was propped up on one elbow, looking. All were stretched out on the ground. Many were moaning, in an extraordinarily regular way; some were smoking, as had done those of the Post, and the wreaths of smoke vanished upward to the ceiling, already dark in spite of the large European windows, darkened by the evening and the fog. It seemed very high, above all those prostrate men. Although daylight had not yet disappeared, the atmosphere was one of night. "Is it because of the wounds," Katov wondered, "or because we are all lying down, as in a station? It is a station. We shall leave it for nowhere, and that's all. . . ."

Four Chinese sentries were pacing back and forth among the wounded, with fixed bayonets, and their bayonets reflected the weak light strangely, sharp and straight above all those formless bodies. Outside, deep in the fog, yellowish lights—street-lamps no doubt—also seemed to be watching them. As if it had come from them (because it also came from out there in the fog) a whistle rose and submerged the murmurs and groans: that of a locomotive; they were near the Chapei station. In that vast hall there was something atrociously tense, which was not the expectation of death. Katov was enlightened by his own throat: it was thirst—and hunger. With his back against the wall, he was looking from left to right: many faces that he knew, for a great number of the wounded were fighters of the *ch'ons*. Along one of the narrower walls, a free space, three meters wide, was reserved. "Why are the wounded lying on top of each other," he asked aloud, "instead of going over there?" He was among the last brought in. Leaning against the wall, he began to raise himself up; although he suffered from his wounds, it seemed to him that he would be able to hold himself upright; but he stopped, still bent over; although not a single word had been said, he sensed around him such a startling terror that it made him motionless. In the looks? He could scarcely make them out. In the attitudes? They were, above all, the attitudes of wounded men, absorbed in their own suffering. Yet, however it was transmitted, the dread was there—not fear, but terror, that of beasts, of men who are alone before the inhuman. Katov, without ceasing to lean against the wall, straddled the body of his neighbor.

"Are you crazy?" asked a voice from the level of the floor.

"Why?"

It was both a question and a command. But no one answered. And one of the guards, five meters away, instead of knocking him down, looked at him with stupefaction.

"Why?" he asked again, more fiercely.

"He doesn't know," said another voice, also from the ground, and at the same time, another, still lower: "He'll find out. . . ."

He had uttered the second question very loudly. The hesitancy of the crowd was terrifying—both in itself and because almost all these men knew him: the menace hanging over that wall weighed upon them all, but particularly upon him.

"Lie down again," said one of the wounded.

Why did no one call him by his name? And why did the sentry not interfere? He had seen him, awhile ago, knock down one of the wounded with the butt of his gun, when he had tried to change places. . . . He approached the last one who had spoken and lay down alongside of him.

"That's where they put those who are to be tortured," said the man in a low voice.

Katov understood. They all knew, but they had not dared to say it, either because they were afraid to speak of it, or because no one dared to speak to *him* about it. A voice had said: "He'll find out. . . ."

The door opened. Soldiers entered with lanterns, surrounding stretcher-bearers who deposited several wounded, like packages, close to Katov. Night was coming on, it rose from the ground where the groans seemed to run into one another like rats, mingled with a frightful stench; most of the men could not move. The door shut.

Time passed. Nothing but the pacing of the sentries and the last gleam of the bayonets above the thousand sounds of suffering. Suddenly, as if the darkness had made the fog more dense, the locomotive whistle sounded, more muffled, as if from a great distance. One of the new arrivals, lying on his belly, tightened his hands over his ears, and screamed. The others did not cry out, but terror was there again, close to the ground.

The man raised his head, lifted himself up on his elbows.

"Scoundrels," he screamed, "murderers!"

One of the sentries stepped forward, and with a kick in the ribs turned him over. He became silent. The sentry walked away. The wounded man began to mumble. It was too dark now for Katov to make out his features, but he heard his voice, he felt that he was becoming coherent. Yes—". . . don't shoot, they throw them alive into the boiler of the locomotive," he was saying. "And now, they're whistling. . . ." The sentry was approaching again. Silence, except for the pain.

The door opened again. More bayonets, now lighted up from below by a lantern, but no wounded. A Kuomintang officer entered alone. Although he could no longer see anything but the bulk of the bodies, Katov could feel each man stiffening. The officer, over there, incorporeal, a shadow between the flickering light of the lantern and the twilight behind him, was giving orders to a sentry. The latter approached, sought Katov, found him. Without touching him, without saying a word, with respect, he simply made Katov a sign to get up. He got to his feet with difficulty, faced the door, over there, where the officer continued to give orders. The soldier, with a gun on one arm, the lantern on the other, came and stood on his left. To his right, there was only the free space and the blank wall. The soldier pointed to the space with his gun. Katov smiled bitterly, with a despairing pride. But no one saw his face, and all those of the wounded who were not in the throes of death, followed him with their eyes. His shadow grew upon the wall of those who were to be tortured.

The officer went out. The door remained open.

The sentinels presented arms: a civilian entered. "Section A," shouted a voice from without, and thereupon the door was shut. One of the sentinels led the civilian toward the wall, grumbling as he went; when he was quite close, Katov, with stupefaction, recognized Kyo. As he was not wounded, the sentinels upon seeing him arrive between two officers had taken him for one of the foreign counselors of Chiang Kai-shek; now recognizing their mistake, they were abusing him from a distance. He lay down in the shadow beside Katov.

"You know what's ahead of us?" the latter asked.

"They've been careful to advise me—I don't care: I have my cyanide. Have you yours?"

"Yes."

"Are you wounded?"

"In the legs. But I can walk."

"Have you been here long?"

"No. When were you caught?"

"Last night. Any way of getting out of here?"

"Not a chance. Almost all are badly wounded. Soldiers everywhere outside. And you saw the machine-guns in front of the door?"

"Yes. Where did they get you?"

Both needed to get away from this death wake, to talk, to talk: Katov, of the taking of the Post; Kyo, of the prison, of his interview with König, of what he had learned since; even before he reached the temporary prison, he had found out that May had not been arrested.

Katov was lying on his side, right beside him, separated from him by the vast expanse of suffering—mouth half-open, lips swollen under his jovial nose, his eyes almost shut—but joined to him by that absolute friendship, without reticence, which death alone gives: a doomed life fallen next to his in the darkness full of menaces and wounds, among all those brothers in the mendicant order of the Revolution: each of these men had wildly seized as it stalked past him the only greatness that could be his.

The guards brought three Chinamen. Separated from the crowd of the wounded, but also from the men against the wall. They had been arrested before the fighting, summarily tried, and were now waiting to be shot.

"Katov!" one of them called.

It was Lu Yu Hsüan, Hemmelrich's associate.

"What?"

"Do you know if they're shooting us far from here, or near by?"

"I don't know. We can't hear it, in any case."

A voice said, a little beyond:

"Seems that the executioner, afterward, pilfers your gold teeth."

And another:

"I don't give a damn. I haven't any."

The three Chinamen were smoking cigarettes, puffing away stubbornly.

"Have you several boxes of matches?" asked one of the wounded, a little farther away.

"Yes."

"Throw me one."

Lu threw his.

"I wish someone could tell my son that I died bravely," he said in a low voice. And, even a little lower: "It is not easy to die."

Katov discovered in himself a lusterless joy: no wife, no children.

The door opened.

"Send one out!" shouted the sentry.

The three men were pressing close to one another.

"Come on, now," said the guard, "make up your minds . . ."

He did not dare to make a choice. Suddenly, one of the two unknown Chinamen took a step forward, threw down his scarcely burnt cigarette, lit another after breaking two matches and went off with a hurried step toward the door, buttoning as he went, one by one, all the buttons of his coat. The door again shut.

One of the wounded was picking up the broken matches. His neighbors had broken into small fragments those from the box Lu Yu Hsüan had given them, and were playing at drawing straws. In less than five minutes the door again opened:

"Another!"

Lu and his companion went forward together, holding each other by the arm. Lu was reciting in a loud voice, without resonance, the death of the hero in a famous play; but the old Chinese solidarity was indeed destroyed: no one was listening.

"Which one?" asked the soldier.

They did not answer.

"Well, is one of you going to come?"

With a blow of his rifle-butt he separated them. Lu was nearer to him than the other; he took him by the shoulder.

Lu freed his shoulder, stepped forward. His companion returned to his place and lay down.

Kyo felt how much more difficult it would be for this one to die than for those who had preceded him: he remained alone. As brave as Lu, since he had stood up with him. But now his manner of lying on the ground, like a hunting-dog, his arms held tight around his body, loudly proclaimed fear. In fact, when the guard touched him, he was seized with a nervous attack. Two soldiers took hold of him, one by his feet, and the other by his head, and carried him out.

Stretched out full length on his back, his arms resting on his chest, Kyo shut his eyes: it was precisely the posture of the dead. He imagined himself, stretched out, motionless, his eyes closed, his face composed in the serenity which death dispenses for a day to almost all corpses, as though the dignity of even the most wretched had to be asserted. He had seen much of death, and, helped by his Japanese education, he had always thought that it is fine to die by one's own hand, a death that resembles one's life. And to die is passivity, but to kill oneself is action. As soon as they came to fetch the first of their group, he would kill himself with full consciousness. He remembered—his heart stopped beating—the phonograph records. A time when hope still had meaning! He would not see May again, and the only grief that left him vulnerable was her grief, as if his own death were a fault. "The remorse of dying," he thought with a contracted irony. No such feeling with regard to his father, who had always given him the impression not of weakness, but of strength. For more than a year May had freed him from all solitude, if not from all bitterness. The memory of the poignant flight into the ecstasy of bodies linked for the first time burst forth, alas! as soon as he thought of her, already separated from the living. . . .

"Now she must forget me. . . ." To write her this would only have
heightened her grief and attached her all the more to him. "And it
would be telling her to love another."

O prison, place where time ceases—time, which continues elsewhere
. . . No! It was in this yard, separated from everyone by the machine-
guns, that the Revolution, no matter what its fate or the place of its
resurrection, was receiving its death-stroke; wherever men labor in
pain, in absurdity, in humiliation, they were thinking of doomed men
like these, as believers pray; and, in the city, they were beginning to
love these dying men as though they were already dead. . . . In all of
the earth that this last night covered over, this place of agony was
no doubt the most weighted with virile love. He could wail with this
crowd of prostrate men, join this sacrificed suffering even in its murmur
of complaint. . . .

And an inaudible chorus of lamentation prolonged this whispering
of pain into the depth of the night: like Hemmelrich, almost all these
men had children. Yet the fatality which they had accepted rose with
the murmur of these wounded men like the peace of evening, spread
over Kyo—his eyes shut, his hands crossed upon his abandoned body—
with the majesty of a funeral chant. He had fought for what in his
time was charged with the deepest meaning and the greatest hope; he
was dying among those with whom he would have wanted to live; he
was dying, like each of these men, because he had given a meaning to
his life. What would have been the value of a life for which he would
not have been willing to die? It is easy to die when one does not die
alone. A death saturated with this brotherly quavering, an assembly of
the vanquished in which multitudes would recognize their martyrs, a
bloody legend of which the golden legends are made! How, already
facing death, could he fail to hear this murmur of human sacrifice crying to him that the virile heart of men is for the dead as good a refuge
as the mind?

He had opened the buckle of his belt and was holding the cyanide
in his hand. He had often wondered if he would die easily. He knew
that if he made up his mind to kill himself, he would kill himself;
but knowing the savage indifference with which life unmasks us to
ourselves, he had not been without anxiety about the moment when
death would crush his mind with its whole weight and finality.

No, dying could be an exalted act, the supreme expression of a life
which this death so much resembled; and it was an escape from those
two soldiers who were approaching hesitantly. He crushed the poison
between his teeth as he would have given a command, heard Katov still
question him with anguish and touch him, and, at the moment when,
suffocating, he wanted to cling to him, he felt his whole strength go
outward, wrenched from him in an all-powerful convulsion.

The soldiers were coming to fetch two prisoners in the crowd who
could not get up. No doubt being burned alive entitled one to special,
although limited, honors: transported on a single stretcher, almost on

top of each other, they were laid down at Katov's left; Kyo, dead, was lying at his right. In the empty space which separated them from those who were only condemned to death, the soldiers crouched near their lantern. Little by little, heads and eyes fell back into the darkness, now emerging only rarely into this light which marked the place of the condemned.

Katov, since the death of Kyo—who had panted for at least a minute —felt himself thrown back into a solitude which was all the stronger and more painful as he was surrounded by his own people. The China-man whom they had had to carry out in order to kill, shaken by a nervous attack, obsessed him. And yet he felt in this complete desertion a sense of repose, as if for years he had been awaiting just this; a repose he had encountered, found again, in the worst moments of his life. Where had he read: "It was not the discoveries, but the sufferings of explorers which I envied, which attracted me. . . ."? As if in response to his thought, the distant whistle reached the hall for the third time. The two men on his left started. Very young Chinamen; one was Suan, whom he knew only through having fought by his side in the Post; the second, unknown. (It was not Pei.) Why were they not with the others?

"Organizing combat groups?" he asked.

"Atttempt at Chiang Kai-shek's life," Suan answered.

"With Ch'en?"

"No. He wanted to throw his bomb alone. Chiang was not in the car. I was waiting for the car much further on. They caught me with the bomb."

The voice which answered him was so choked that Katov scrutinized the two faces: the young men were weeping, without a sob. Suan tried to move his shoulder, and his face contracted with pain—he was wounded also in the arm.

"Burned," he said. "To be burned alive. The eyes, too, the eyes, you understand . . ."

His comrade was sobbing now.

"One can be burned by accident," said Katov.

It seemed as if they were speaking, not to each other, but to some invisible third person.

"It's not the same thing."

"No; it's not so good."

"The eyes too," the young man repeated in a lower voice, "the eyes . . . each finger, and the stomach, the stomach . . ."

"Shut up!" said the other with the voice of a deaf man.

He would have liked to cry out, but could not. His hands clutched Suan close to his wounds, causing the latter's muscles to contract.

"Human dignity," Katov murmured, thinking of Kyo's interview with König. The condemned men were no longer speaking. Beyond the lantern, in the darkness that was now complete, the murmur of the wounded continued. . . . He edged still closer to Suan and his companion. One of the guards was telling the others a story: their heads close together, they were between the lantern and the condemned: the latter could no longer even see one another. In spite of the hum, in spite of all these men who had fought as he had, Katov was alone, alone between the body of his dead friend and his two terror-stricken companions, alone between this wall and that whistle far off in the night. But a man could be stronger than this solitude and even, perhaps, than that atrocious whistle: fear struggled in him against the most terrible temptation in his life. In his turn he opened the buckle of his belt. Finally:

"Hey, there," he said in a very low voice. "Suan, put your hand on my chest, and close it as soon as I touch it: I'm going to give you my cyanide. There is abs'lutely enough only for two."

He had given up everything, except saying that there was only enough for two. Lying on his side, he broke the cyanide in two. The guards masked the light, which surrounded them with a dim halo; but would they not move? Impossible to see anything; Katov was making this gift of something that was more precious than his life not even to bodies, not even to voices, but to the warm hand resting upon him. It grew taut, like an animal, immediately separated from him. He waited, his whole body tense. And suddenly, he heard one of the two voices:

"It's lost. Fell."

A voice scarcely affected by anguish, as if such a catastrophe, so decisive, so tragic, were not possible, as if things were bound to arrange themselves. For Katov also it was impossible. A limitless anger rose in him, but fell again, defeated by this impossibility. And yet! To have given *that* only to have the idiot lose it!

"When?" he asked.

"Before my body. Could not hold it when Suan passed it: I'm wounded in the hand too."

"He dropped both of them," said Suan.

They were no doubt looking for it in the space between them. They next looked between Katov and Suan, on whom the other was probably almost lying, for Katov, without being able to see anything, could feel beside him the bulk of two bodies. He was looking too, trying to control his nervousness, to place his hand flat, at regular intervals, wherever he could reach. Their hands brushed his. And suddenly one of them took his, pressed it, held it.

"Even if we don't find it . . ." said one of the voices.

Katov also pressed his hand, on the verge of tears, held by that pitiful fraternity, without a face, almost without a real voice (all whispers resemble one another), which was being offered him in this darkness in return for the greatest gift he had ever made, and which perhaps was made in vain. Although Suan continued to look, the two hands remained united. The grasp suddenly became a tight clutch:

"Here!"

O resurrection! . . . But:

"Are you sure they are not pebbles?" asked the other.

There were many bits of plaster on the ground.

"Give it to me!" said Katov.

With his fingertips, he recognized the shapes.

He gave them back—gave them back—pressed more strongly the hand which again sought his, and waited, his shoulders trembling, his teeth chattering. "If only the cyanide has not decomposed, in spite of the silver paper," he thought. The hand he was holding suddenly twisted his, and, as though he were communicating through it with the body lost in the darkness, he felt that the latter was stiffening. He envied this convulsive suffocation. Almost at the same time, the other one: a choked cry which no one heeded. Then, nothing.

Katov felt himself deserted. He turned over on his belly and waited. The trembling of his shoulders did not cease.

In the middle of the night, the officer came back. In a clatter of rifles striking against one another, six soldiers were approaching the condemned men. All the prisoners had awakened. The new lantern, also, showed only long, vague forms—tombs in the earth already turned over—and a few reflections in the eyes. Katov managed to raise himself. The one who commanded the squad took Kyo's arm, felt its stiffness, immediately seized Suan's; that one also was stiff. A rumble was spreading, from the first rows of prisoners to the last. The chief of the squad lifted the foot of one of the men, then of the other: they fell back, stiff. He called the officer. The latter went through the same motions. Among the prisoners, the rumble was growing. The officer looked at Katov:

"Dead?"

Why answer?

"Isolate the six nearest prisoners!"

"Useless," answered Katov: "I gave them the cyanide."

"And you?" he finally asked.

"There was only enough for two," answered Katov with deep joy.

("I'm going to get a rifle-butt in my face," he thought to himself.)

The rumble of the prisoners had become almost a clamor.

"Come on, let's go," said the officer merely.

Katov did not forget that he had been condemned to death before this, that he had seen the machine-guns leveled at him, had heard them fire. . . . "As soon as I'm outside, I'm going to try to strangle one of them, and to hold my hands tightened to his throat long enough so they will be forced to kill me. They will burn me, but dead." At that very moment one of the soldiers seized him by the waist, while another brought his hands behind his back and tied them. "The little fellows were lucky," he said to himself. "Well! let's suppose I died in a fire." He began to walk. Silence fell, like a trap-door, in spite of the moans. The lantern threw Katov's shadow, now very black, across the great windows framing the night; he walked heavily, with uneven steps, hindered by his wounds; when the swinging of his body brought him closer to the lantern, the silhouette of his head vanished into the ceiling. The whole darkness of the vast hall was alive, and followed him with its eyes, step by step. The silence had become so great that the ground resounded each time his foot fell heavily upon it; all the heads, with a slight movement, followed the rhythm of his walk, with love, with dread, with resignation. All kept their heads raised: the door was being closed.

A sound of deep breathing, the same as that of sleep, began to rise from the ground: breathing through their noses, their jaws clenched with anguish, motionless now, all those who were not yet dead were waiting for the whistle.

JEAN-PAUL
SARTRE

The Wall

Jean-Paul Sartre, born in 1905, studied at the Ecole Normale Supérieure and became a professor of Philosophy. He was one of the leading underground writers of the Resistance during the occupation, and has achieved world-wide recognition as the originator and chief expositor of the philosophy of existentialism. His main works of fiction are *La Nausee, Le Mur* and *Les Chemins de la Liberté.* [Copyright 1945 by Random House, Inc.; used by permission of the publishers and the author; translated by Marie Jolas.]

THEY PUSHED US INTO a large white room and my eyes began to blink because the light hurt them. Then I saw a table and four fellows seated at the table, civilians, looking at some papers. The other prisoners were herded together at one end and we were obliged to cross the entire room to join them. There were several I knew, and others who must have been foreigners. The two in front of me were blond with round heads. They looked alike. I imagine they were French. The smaller one kept pulling at his trousers, out of nervousness.

This lasted about three hours. I was dog-tired and my head was empty. But the room was well-heated, which struck me as rather agreeable; we had not stopped shivering for twenty-four hours. The guards led the prisoners in one after the other in front of the table. Then the four fellows asked them their names and what they did. Most of the time that was all—or perhaps from time to time they would ask such questions as: "Did you help sabotage the munitions?" or, "Where were you on the morning of the ninth and what were you doing?" They didn't even listen to the replies, or at least they didn't seem to. They just remained silent for a moment and looked straight ahead, then they began to write. They asked Tom if it was true he had served in the International Brigade. Tom couldn't say he hadn't because of the papers they had found in his jacket. They didn't ask Juan anything, but after he told them his name, they wrote for a long while.

"It's my brother José who's the anarchist," Juan said. "You know perfectly well he's not here now. I don't belong to any party. I never did take part in politics." They didn't answer.

Then Juan said, "I didn't do anything. And I'm not going to pay for what the others did."

His lips were trembling. A guard told him to stop talking and led him away. It was my turn.

"Your name is Pablo Ibbieta?"

I said yes.

The fellow looked at his papers and said, "Where is Ramon Gris?"

"I don't know."

"You hid him in your house from the sixth to the nineteenth."

"I did not."

They continued to write for a moment and the guards led me away. In the hall, Tom and Juan were waiting between two guards. We started walking. Tom asked one of the guards, "What's the idea?" "How do you mean?" the guard said. "Was that just the preliminary questioning, or was that the trial?" "That was the trial," the guard said. "So now what? What are they going to do with us?" The guard answered drily, "The verdict will be told you in your cell."

In reality, our cell was one of the cellars of the hospital. It was terribly cold there because it was very drafty. We had been shivering all night long and it had hardly been any better during the day. I had spent the preceding five days in a cellar in the archbishop's palace, a sort of dungeon that must have dated back to the Middle Ages. There were lots of prisoners and not much room, so they housed them just anywhere. But I was not homesick for my dungeon. I hadn't been cold there, but I had been alone, and that gets to be irritating. In the cellar I had company. Juan didn't say a word; he was afraid, and besides, he was too young to have anything to say. But Tom was a good talker and knew Spanish well.

In the cellar there were a bench and four straw mattresses. When they led us back we sat down and waited in silence. After a while Tom said, "Our goose is cooked."

"I think so too," I said. "But I don't believe they'll do anything to the kid."

Tom said, "They haven't got anything on him. He's the brother of a fellow who's fighting, and that's all."

I looked at Juan. He didn't seem to have heard.

Tom continued, "You know what they do in Saragossa? They lay the guys across the road and then they drive over them with trucks. It was a Moroccan deserter who told us that. They say it's just to save ammunition."

I said, "Well, it doesn't save gasoline."

I was irritated with Tom; he shouldn't have said that.

He went on, "There are officers walking up and down the roads with their hands in their pockets, smoking, and they see that it's done right. Do you think they'd put 'em out of their misery? Like hell they do. They just let 'em holler. Sometimes as long as an hour. The Moroccan said the first time he almost puked."

"I don't believe they do that here," I said, "unless they really are short of ammunition."

The daylight came in through four air vents and a round opening that had been cut in the ceiling, to the left, and which opened directly onto the sky. It was through this hole, which was ordinarily closed by means of a trapdoor, that they unloaded coal into the cellar. Directly under the hole, there was a big pile of coal dust; it had been intended for heating the hospital, but at the beginning of the war they had evacuated the patients and the coal had stayed there unused; it even got rained on from time to time, when they forgot to close the trapdoor.

Tom started to shiver. "God damn it," he said, "I'm shivering. There, it is starting again."

He rose and began to do gymnastic exercises. At each movement, his shirt opened and showed his white, hairy chest. He lay down on his back, lifted his legs in the air and began to do the scissors movement. I watched his big buttocks tremble. Tom was tough, but he had too much fat on him. I kept thinking that soon bullets and bayonet points would sink into that mass of tender flesh as though it were a pat of butter.

I wasn't exactly cold, but I couldn't feel my shoulders or my arms. From time to time, I had the impression that something was missing and I began to look around for my jacket. Then I would suddenly remember they hadn't given me a jacket. It was rather awkward. They had taken our clothes to give them to their own soldiers and had left us only our shirts and these cotton trousers the hospital patients wore in midsummer. After a moment, Tom got up and sat down beside me, breathless.

"Did you get warmed up?"

"Damn it, no. But I'm all out of breath."

Around eight o'clock in the evening, a Major came in with two Falangists.

"What are the names of those three over there?" he asked the guard.

"Steinbock, Ibbieta and Mirbal," said the guard.

The Major put on his glasses and examined his list.

"Steinbock—Steinbock . . . Here it is. You are condemned to death. You'll be shot tomorrow morning."

He looked at his list again.

"The other two, also," he said.

"That's not possible," said Juan. "Not me."

The Major looked at him with surprise. "What's your name?"

"Juan Mirbal."

"Well, your name is here," said the Major, "and you're condemned to death."

"I didn't do anything," said Juan.

The Major shrugged his shoulders and turned toward Tom and me.

"You are both Basque?"

"No, nobody's Basque."

He appeared exasperated.

"I was told there were three Basques. I'm not going to waste my time running after them. I suppose you don't want a priest?"

We didn't even answer.

Then he said, "A Belgian doctor will be around in a little while. He has permission to stay with you all night."

He gave a military salute and left.

"What did I tell you?" Tom said. "We're in for something swell."

"Yes," I said. "It's a damned shame for the kid."

I said that to be fair, but I really didn't like the kid. His face was too refined and it was disfigured by fear and suffering, which had twisted all his features. Three days ago, he was just a kid with a kind of affected manner some people like. But now he looked like an aging fairy, and I thought to myself he would never be young again, even if they let him go. It wouldn't have been a bad thing to show him a little pity, but pity makes me sick, and besides, I couldn't stand him. He hadn't said anything more, but he had turned gray. His face and hands were gray. He sat down again and stared, round-eyed, at the ground. Tom was good-hearted and tried to take him by the arm, but the kid drew himself away violently and made an ugly face. "Leave him alone," I said quietly. "Can't you see he's going to start to bawl?" Tom obeyed regretfully. He would have liked to console the kid; that would have kept him occupied and he wouldn't have been tempted to think about himself. But it got on my nerves. I had never thought about death, for the reason that the question had never come up. But now it had come up, and there was nothing else to do but think about it.

Tom started talking. "Say, did you ever bump anybody off?" he asked me. I didn't answer. He started to explain to me that he had bumped off six fellows since August. He hadn't yet realized what we were in for, and I saw clearly he didn't *want* to realize it. I myself hadn't quite taken it in. I wondered if it hurt very much. I thought about the bullets; I imagined their fiery hail going through my body. All that was beside the real question; but I was calm, we had all night in which to realize it. After a while Tom stopped talking and I looked at him out of the corner of my eye. I saw that he, too, had turned gray and that he looked pretty miserable. I said to myself, "It's starting." It was almost dark, a dull light filtered through the air vents across the coal pile and made a big spot under the sky. Through the hole in the ceiling I could already see a star. The night was going to be clear and cold.

The door opened and two guards entered. They were followed by a blond man in a tan uniform. He greeted us.

"I'm the doctor," he said. "I've been authorized to give you any assistance you may require in these painful circumstances."

He had an agreeable, cultivated voice.

I said to him, "What are you going to do here?"

"Whatever you want me to do. I shall do everything in my power to lighten these few hours."

"Why did you come to us? There are lots of others: the hospital's full of them."

"I was sent here," he answered vaguely. "You'd probably like to smoke, wouldn't you?" he added suddenly. "I've got some cigarettes and even some cigars."

He passed around some English cigarettes and some *puros,* but we refused them. I looked him straight in the eye and he appeared uncomfortable.

"You didn't come here out of compassion," I said to him. "In fact, I know who you are. I saw you with some fascists in the barracks yard the day I was arrested."

I was about to continue, when all at once something happened to me which surprised me: the presence of this doctor had suddenly ceased to interest me. Usually, when I've got hold of a man I don't let go. But somehow the desire to speak had left me. I shrugged my shoulders and turned away. A little later, I looked up and saw he was watching me with an air of curiosity. The guards had sat down on one of the mattresses. Pedro, the tall thin one, was twiddling his thumbs, while the other one shook his head occasionally to keep from falling asleep.

"Do you want some light?" Pedro suddenly asked the doctor. The other fellow nodded, "Yes." I think he was not over-intelligent, but doubtless he was not malicious. As I looked at his big, cold, blue eyes, it seemed to me the worst thing about him was his lack of imagination. Pedro went out and came back with an oil lamp which he set on the corner of the bench. It gave a poor light, but it was better than nothing; the night before we had been left in the dark. For a long while I stared at the circle of light the lamp threw on the ceiling. I was fascinated. Then, suddenly, I came to, the light circle paled, and I felt as if I were being crushed under an enormous weight. It wasn't the thought of death, and it wasn't fear; it was something anonymous. My cheeks were burning hot and my head ached.

I roused myself and looked at my two companions. Tom had his head in his hands and only the fat, white nape of his neck was visible. Juan was by far the worst off; his mouth was wide open and his nostrils were trembling. The doctor came over to him and touched him on the shoulder, as though to comfort him; but his eyes remained cold. Then I saw the Belgian slide his hand furtively down Juan's arm to his wrist.

Indifferent, Juan let himself be handled. Then, as though absent-mindedly, the Belgian laid three fingers over his wrist; at the same time, he drew away somewhat and managed to turn his back to me. But I leaned over backward and saw him take out his watch and look at it a moment before relinquishing the boy's wrist. After a moment, he let the inert hand fall and went and leaned against the wall. Then, as if he had suddenly remembered something very important that had to be noted down immediately, he took a notebook from his pocket and wrote a few lines in it. "The son-of-a-bitch," I thought angrily. "He better not come and feel my pulse; I'll give him a punch in his dirty jaw."

He didn't come near me, but I felt he was looking at me. I raised my head and looked back at him. In an impersonal voice, he said, "Don't you think it's frightfully cold here?"

He looked purple with cold.

"I'm not cold," I answered him.

He kept looking at me with a hard expression. Suddenly I understood, and I lifted my hands to my face. I was covered with sweat. Here, in this cellar, in mid-winter, right in a draft, I was sweating. I ran my fingers through my hair, which was stiff with sweat; at the same time, I realized my shirt was damp and sticking to my skin. I had been streaming with perspiration for an hour, at least, and had felt nothing. But this fact hadn't escaped that Belgian swine. He had seen the drops rolling down my face and had said to himself that it showed an almost pathological terror; and he himself had felt normal and proud of it because he was cold. I wanted to get up and go punch his face in, but I had hardly started to make a move before my shame and anger had disappeared. I dropped back onto the bench with indifference.

I was content to rub my neck with my handkerchief because now I felt the sweat dripping from my hair onto the nape of my neck and that was disagreeable. I soon gave up rubbing myself, however, for it didn't do any good; my handkerchief was already wringing wet and I was still sweating. My buttocks, too, were sweating, and my damp trousers stuck to the bench.

Suddenly, Juan said, "You're a doctor, aren't you?"

"Yes," said the Belgian.

"Do people suffer—very long?"

"Oh! When . . . ? No, no," said the Belgian, in a paternal voice, "it's quickly over."

His manner was as reassuring as if he had been answering a paying patient.

"But I . . . Somebody told me—they often have to fire two volleys."

"Sometimes," said the Belgian, raising his head, "it just happens that the first volley doesn't hit any of the vital organs."

"So they have to reload their guns and aim all over again?" Juan thought for a moment, then added hoarsely, "But that takes time!"

He was terribly afraid of suffering. He couldn't think about anything else, but that went with his age. As for me, I hardly thought about it any more and it certainly was not fear of suffering that made me perspire.

I rose and walked toward the pile of coal dust. Tom gave a start and looked at me with a look of hate. I irritated him because my shoes squeaked. I wondered if my face was as putty-colored as his. Then I noticed that he, too, was sweating. The sky was magnificent; no light at all came into our dark corner and I had only to lift my head to see the Big Bear. But it didn't look the way it had looked before. Two days ago, from my cell in the archbishop's palace, I could see a big patch of sky and each time of day brought back a different memory. In the morning, when the sky was a deep blue, and light, I thought of beaches along the Atlantic; at noon, I could see the sun, and I remembered a bar in Seville where I used to drink manzanilla and eat anchovies and olives; in the afternoon, I was in the shade, and I thought of the deep shadow which covers half of the arena while the other half gleams in the sunlight: it really gave me a pang to see the whole earth reflected in the sky like that. Now, however, no matter how much I looked up in the air, the sky no longer recalled anything. I liked it better that way. I came back and sat down next to Tom. There was a long silence.

Then Tom began to talk in a low voice. He had to keep talking, otherwise he lost his way in his own thoughts. I believe he was talking to me, but he didn't look at me. No doubt he was afraid to look at me, because I was gray and sweating. We were both alike and worse than mirrors for each other. He looked at the Belgian, the only one who was alive.

"Say, do you understand? I don't."

Then I, too, began to talk in a low voice. I was watching the Belgian.

"Understand what? What's the matter?"

"Something's going to happen to us that I don't understand."

There was a strange odor about Tom. It seemed to me that I was more sensitive to odors than ordinarily. With a sneer, I said, "You'll understand, later."

"That's not so sure," he said stubbornly. "I'm willing to be courageous, but at least I ought to know . . . Listen, they're going to take us out into the courtyard. All right. The fellows will be standing in line in front of us. How many of them will there be?"

"Oh, I don't know. Five, or eight. Not more."

"That's enough. Let's say there'll be eight of them. Somebody will shout 'Shoulder arms!' and I'll see all eight rifles aimed at me. I'm sure I'm going to feel like going through the wall. I'll push against the wall as hard as I can with my back, and the wall won't give in. The way it is in a nightmare . . . I can imagine all that. Ah, if you only knew how well I can imagine it!"

"Skip it!" I said. "I can imagine it too."

"It must hurt like the devil. You know they aim at your eyes and mouth so as to disfigure you," he added maliciously. "I can feel the wounds already. For the last hour I've been having pains in my head and neck. Not real pains—it's worse still. They're the pains I'll feel tomorrow morning. And after that, then what?"

I understood perfectly well what he meant, but I didn't want to seem to understand. As for the pains, I, too, felt them all through my body, like a lot of little gashes. I couldn't get used to them, but I was like him, I didn't think they were very important.

"After that," I said roughly, "you'll be eating daisies."

He started talking to himself, not taking his eyes off the Belgian, who didn't seem to be listening to him. I knew what he had come for, and that what we were thinking didn't interest him. He had come to look at our bodies, our bodies which were dying alive.

"It's like in a nightmare," said Tom. "You want to think of something, you keep having the impression you've got it, that you're going to understand, and then it slips away from you, it eludes you and it's gone again. I say to myself, afterward, there won't be anything. But I don't really understand what that means. There were moments when I almost do—and then it's gone again. I start to think of the pains, the bullets, the noise of the shooting. I am a materialist, I swear it; and I'm not going crazy, either. But there's something wrong. I see my own corpse. That's not hard, but it's *I* who see it, with *my* eyes. I'll have to get to the point where I think—where I think I won't see anything more. I won't hear anything more, and the world will go on for the others. We're not made to think that way, Pablo. Believe me, I've already stayed awake all night waiting for something. But this is not the same thing. This will grab us from behind, Pablo, and we won't be ready for it."

"Shut up," I said. "Do you want me to call a father confessor?"

He didn't answer. I had already noticed that he had a tendency to prophesy and call me "Pablo" in a kind of pale voice. I didn't like that very much, but it seems all the Irish are like that. I had a vague impression that he smelled of urine. Actually, I didn't like Tom very much, and I didn't see why, just because we were going to die together, I should like him any better. There are certain fellows with whom it would be different—with Ramon Gris, for instance. But between Tom and Juan, I felt alone. In fact, I liked it better that way. With Ramon I might have grown soft. But I felt terribly hard at that moment, and I wanted to stay hard.

Tom kept on muttering, in a kind of absent-minded way. He was certainly talking to keep from thinking. Naturally, I agreed with him, and I could have said everything he was saying. It's not *natural* to die. And since I was going to die, nothing seemed natural any more: neither the coal pile, nor the bench, nor Pedro's dirty old face. Only it was disagreeable for me to think the same things Tom thought. And I knew perfectly well that all night long, within five minutes of each other, we would keep on thinking things at the same time, sweating or shivering at the same time. I looked at him sideways and, for the first time, he seemed strange to me. He had death written on his face. My pride was wounded. For twenty-four hours I had lived side by side with Tom, I had listened to him, I had talked to him, and I knew we had nothing in common. And now we were as alike as twin brothers, simply because we were going to die together. Tom took my hand without looking at me.

"Pablo, I wonder . . . I wonder if it's true that we just cease to exist."

I drew my hand away.

"Look between your feet, you dirty dog."

There was a puddle between his feet and water was dripping from his trousers.

"What's the matter?" he said, frightened.

"You're wetting your pants," I said to him.

"It's not true," he said furiously. "I can't be . . . I don't feel anything."

The Belgian had come closer to him. With an air of false concern, he asked, "Aren't you feeling well?"

Tom didn't answer. The Belgian looked at the puddle without comment.

"I don't know what that is," Tom said savagely, "but I'm not afraid. I swear to you, I'm not afraid."

The Belgian made no answer. Tom rose and went to the corner. He came back, buttoning his fly, and sat down, without a word. The Belgian was taking notes.

We were watching the doctor. Juan was watching him too. All three of us were watching him because he was alive. He had the gestures of a living person, the interests of a living person; he was shivering in this cellar the way living people shiver; he had an obedient, well-fed body. We, on the other hand, didn't feel our bodies any more—not the same way, in any case. I felt like touching my trousers, but I didn't dare to. I looked at the Belgian, well-planted on his two legs, master of his muscles—and able to plan for tomorrow. We were like three shadows deprived of blood; we were watching him and sucking his life like vampires.

Finally he came over to Juan. Was he going to lay his hand on the nape of Juan's neck for some professional reason, or had he obeyed a charitable impulse? If he had acted out of charity, it was the one and only time during the whole night. He fondled Juan's head and the nape of his neck. The kid let him do it, without taking his eyes off him. Then, suddenly, he took hold of the doctor's hand and looked at it in a funny way. He held the Belgian's hand between his own two hands and there was nothing pleasing about them, those two gray paws squeezing that fat red hand. I sensed what was going to happen and Tom must have sensed it, too. But all the Belgian saw was emotion, and he smiled paternally. After a moment, the kid lifted the big red paw to his mouth and started to bite it. The Belgian drew back quickly and stumbled toward the wall. For a second, he looked at us with horror. He must have suddenly understood that we were not men like himself. I began to laugh, and one of the guards started up. The other had fallen asleep with his eyes wide open, showing only the whites.

I felt tired and over-excited at the same time. I didn't want to think any more about what was going to happen at dawn—about death. It didn't make sense, and I never got beyond just words, or emptiness. But whenever I tried to think about something else I saw the barrels of rifles aimed at me. I must have lived through my execution twenty times in succession; one time I thought it was the real thing; I must have dozed off for a moment. They were dragging me toward the wall and I was resisting; I was imploring their pardon. I woke with a start and looked at the Belgian. I was afraid I had cried out in my sleep. But he was smoothing his mustache; he hadn't noticed anything. If I had wanted to, I believe I could have slept for a while. I had been awake for the last forty-eight hours, and I was worn out. But I didn't want to lose two hours of life. They would have had to come and wake me at dawn. I would have followed them, drunk with sleep, and I would have gone off without so much as "Gosh!" I didn't want it that way, I didn't want to die like an animal. I wanted to understand. Besides, I was afraid of having nightmares. I got up and began to walk up and down and, so as to think about something else, I began to think about my past life. Memories crowded in on me, helter-skelter. Some were good and some were bad—at least that was how I had thought of them *before.* There were faces and happenings. I saw the face of a little *nivolero* who had gotten himself horned during the *Feria,* in Valencia. I saw the face of one of my uncles, of Ramon Gris. I remembered all kinds of things that had happened: how I had been on strike for three months in 1926, and had almost died of hunger. I recalled a night I had spent on a bench in Granada; I hadn't eaten for three days. I was nearly wild, I didn't want to give up the sponge. I had to smile. With what eagerness I had run after happiness, and women, and liberty! And to what end? I had wanted to liberate Spain, I admired Py Margall, I had belonged to the anarchist movement, I had spoken at public meetings. I took everything as seriously as if I had been immortal.

At that time I had the impression that I had my whole life before me, and I thought to myself, "It's all a god-damned lie." Now it wasn't worth anything because it was finished. I wondered how I had ever been able to go out and have a good time with girls. I wouldn't have lifted my little finger if I had ever imagined that I would die like this. I saw my life before me, finished, closed, like a bag, and yet what was inside was not finished. For a moment I tried to appraise it. I would have liked to say to myself, "It's been a good life." But it couldn't be appraised, it was only an outline. I had spent my time writing checks on eternity, and had understood nothing. Now, I didn't miss anything. There were a lot of things I might have missed: the taste of manzanilla, for instance, or the swims I used to take in summer in a little creek near Cadiz. But death had taken the charm out of everything.

Suddenly the Belgian had a wonderful idea.

"My friends," he said to us, "if you want me to—and providing the military authorities give their consent—I could undertake to deliver a word or some token from you to your loved ones . . ."

Tom growled, "I haven't got anybody."

I didn't answer. Tom waited for a moment, then he looked at me with curiosity. "Aren't you going to send any message to Concha?"

"No."

I hated that sort of sentimental conspiracy. Of course, it was my fault, since I had mentioned Concha the night before, and I should have kept my mouth shut. I had been with her for a year. Even as late as last night, I would have cut my arm off with a hatchet just to see her again for five minutes. That was why I had mentioned her. I couldn't help it. Now I didn't care any more about seeing her. I hadn't anything more to say to her. I didn't even want to hold her in my arms. I loathed my body because it had turned gray and was sweating—and I wasn't even sure that I didn't loathe hers too. Concha would cry when she heard about my death; for months she would have no more interest in life. But still it was I who was going to die. I thought of her beautiful, loving eyes. When she looked at me something went from her to me. But I thought to myself that it was all over; if she looked at me *now* her gaze would not leave her eyes, it would not reach out to me. I was alone.

Tom, too, was alone, but not the same way. He was seated astride his chair and had begun to look at the bench with a sort of smile, with surprise, even. He reached out his hand and touched the wood cautiously, as though he were afraid of breaking something, then he drew his hand back hurriedly, and shivered. I wouldn't have amused myself touching that bench, if I had been Tom, that was just some more Irish play-acting. But somehow it seemed to me too that the different objects had something funny about them. They seemed to have grown paler, less massive than before. I had only to look at the bench, the lamp or the pile of coal dust to feel I was going to die. Naturally, I couldn't think clearly about my death, but I saw it everywhere, even on the different objects, the way they had withdrawn and kept their distance, tactfully, like people talking at the bedside of a dying person. It was *his own death* Tom had just touched on the bench.

In the state I was in, if they had come and told me I could go home quietly, that my life would be saved, it would have left me cold. A few hours, or a few years of waiting are all the same, when you've lost the illusion of being eternal. Nothing mattered to me any more. In a way, I was calm. But it was a horrible kind of calm—because of my body.

My body—I saw with its eyes and I heard with its ears, but it was no longer I. It sweat and trembled independently, and I didn't recognize it any longer. I was obliged to touch it and look at it to know what was happening to it, just as if it had been someone else's body. At times I still felt it, I felt a slipping, a sort of headlong plunging, as in a falling airplane, or else I heard my heart beating. But this didn't give me confidence. In fact, everything that came from my body had something damned dubious about it. Most of the time it was silent, it stayed put and I didn't feel anything other than a sort of heaviness, a loathsome presence against me. I had the impression of being bound to an enormous vermin.

The Belgian took out his watch and looked at it.

"It's half-past three," he said.

The son-of-a-bitch! He must have done it on purpose. Tom jumped up. We hadn't yet realized the time was passing. The night surrounded us like a formless, dark mass; I didn't even remember it had started.

Juan started to shout. Wringing his hands, he implored, "I don't want to die! I don't want to die!"

He ran the whole length of the cellar with his arms in the air, then he dropped down onto one of the mattresses, sobbing. Tom looked at him with dismal eyes and didn't even try to console him any more. The fact was, it was no use; the kid made more noise than we did, but he was less affected, really. He was like a sick person who defends himself against his malady with a high fever. When there's not even any fever left, it's much more serious.

He was crying. I could tell he felt sorry for himself; he was thinking about death. For one second, one single second, I too felt like crying, crying out of pity for myself. But just the contrary happened. I took one look at the kid, saw his thin, sobbing shoulders, and I felt I was inhuman. I couldn't feel pity either for these others or for myself. I said to myself, "I want to die decently."

Tom had gotten up and was standing just under the round opening looking out for the first signs of daylight. I was determined, I wanted to die decently, and I only thought about that. But underneath, ever since the doctor had told us the time, I felt time slipping, flowing by, one drop at a time.

It was still dark when I heard Tom's voice.

"Do you hear them?"

"Yes."

People were walking in the courtyard.

"What the hell are they doing? After all, they can't shoot in the dark."

After a moment, we didn't hear anything more. I said to Tom, "There's the daylight."

Pedro got up yawning, and came and blew out the lamp. He turned to the man beside him. "It's hellish cold."

The cellar had grown gray. We could hear shots at a distance.

"It's about to start," I said to Tom. "That must be in the back court-yard."

Tom asked the doctor to give him a cigarette. I didn't want any; I didn't want either cigarettes or alcohol. From that moment on, the shooting didn't stop.

"Can you take it in?" Tom said.

He started to add something, then he stopped and began to watch the door. The door opened and a lieutenant came in with four soldiers. Tom dropped his cigarette.

"Steinbock?"

Tom didn't answer. Pedro pointed him out.

"Juan Mirbal?"

"He's the one on the mattress."

"Stand up," said the Lieutenant.

Juan didn't move. Two soldiers took hold of him by the armpits and stood him up on his feet. But as soon as they let go of him he fell down.

The soldiers hesitated a moment.

"He's not the first one to get sick," said the Lieutenant. "You'll have to carry him, the two of you. We'll arrange things when we get there." He turned to Tom. "All right, come along."

Tom left between two soldiers. Two other soldiers followed, carrying the kid by his arms and legs. He was not unconscious; his eyes were wide open and tears were rolling down his cheeks. When I started to go out, the Lieutenant stopped me.

"Are you Ibbieta?"

"Yes."

"You wait here. They'll come and get you later on."

They left. The Belgian and the two jailers left too, and I was alone. I didn't understand what had happened to me, but I would have liked it better if they had ended it all right away. I heard the volleys at almost regular intervals; at each one, I shuddered. I felt like howling and tearing my hair. But instead, I gritted my teeth and pushed my hands deep into my pockets, because I wanted to stay decent.

An hour later, they came to fetch me and took me up to the first floor in a little room which smelt of cigar smoke and was so hot it seemed to me suffocating. Here there were two officers sitting in com-fortable chairs, smoking, with papers spread out on their knees.

"Your name is Ibbieta?"

"Yes."

"Where is Ramon Gris?"

"I don't know."

The man who questioned me was small and stocky. He had hard eyes behind his glasses.

"Come nearer," he said to me.

I went nearer. He rose and took me by the arms, looking at me in a way calculated to make me go through the floor. At the same time he pinched my arms with all his might. He didn't mean to hurt me; it was quite a game; he wanted to dominate me. He also seemed to think it was necessary to blow his fetid breath right into my face. We stood like that for a moment, only I felt more like laughing than anything else. It takes a lot more than that to intimidate a man who's about to die: it didn't work. He pushed me away violently and sat down again.

"It's your life or his," he said. "You'll be allowed to go free if you tell us where he is."

After all, these two bedizened fellows with their riding crops and boots were just men who were going to die one day. A little later than I, perhaps, but not a great deal. And there they were, looking for names among their papers, running after other men in order to put them in prison or do away with them entirely. They had their opinions on the future of Spain and on other subjects. Their petty activities seemed to me to be offensive and ludicrous. I could no longer put myself in their place. I had the impression they were crazy.

The little fat fellow kept looking at me, tapping his boots with his riding crop. All his gestures were calculated to make him appear like a spirited, ferocious animal.

"Well? Do you understand?"

"I don't know where Gris is," I said. "I thought he was in Madrid."

The other officer lifted his pale hand indolently. This indolence was also calculated. I saw through all their little tricks, and I was dumbfounded that men should still exist who took pleasure in that kind of thing.

"You have fifteen minutes to think it over," he said slowly. "Take him to the linen-room, and bring him back here in fifteen minutes. If he continues to refuse, he'll be executed at once."

They knew what they were doing. I had spent the night waiting. After that, they had made me wait another hour in the cellar, while they shot Tom and Juan, and now they locked me in the linen-room. They must have arranged the whole thing the night before. They figured that sooner or later people's nerves wear out and they hoped to get me that way.

They made a big mistake. In the linen-room I sat down on a ladder because I felt very weak, and I began to think things over. Not their proposition, however. Naturally I knew where Gris was. He was hiding in his cousins' house, about two miles outside of the city. I knew, too, that I would not reveal his hiding place, unless they tortured me (but they didn't seem to be considering that). All that was definitely settled and didn't interest me in the least. Only I would have liked to understand the reasons for my own conduct. I would rather die than betray Gris. Why? I no longer liked Ramon Gris. My friendship for him had died shortly before dawn along with my love for Concha, along with my own desire to live. Of course I still admired him—he was hard. But it was not for that reason that I was willing to die in his place; his life was no more valuable than mine. No life was of any value. A man was going to be stood up against a wall and fired at till he dropped dead. It didn't make any difference whether it was I or Gris or somebody else. I knew perfectly well he was more useful to the Spanish cause than I was, but I didn't give a God damn about Spain or anarchy, either; nothing had any importance now. And yet, there I was. I could save my skin by betraying Gris and I refused to do it. It seemed more ludicrous to me than anything else; it was stubbornness.

I thought to myself, "Am I hard-headed!" And I was seized with a strange sort of cheerfulness.

They came to fetch me and took me back to the two officers. A rat darted out under our feet and that amused me. I turned to one of the falangists and said to him, "Did you see that rat?"

He made no reply. He was gloomy, and took himself very seriously. As for me, I felt like laughing, but I restrained myself because I was afraid that if I started, I wouldn't be able to stop. The falangist wore mustaches. I kept after him, "You ought to cut off those mustaches, you fool."

I was amused by the fact that he let hair grow all over his face while he was still alive. He gave me a kind of half-hearted kick, and I shut up.

"Well," said the fat officer, "have you thought things over?"

I looked at them with curiosity, like insects of a very rare species.

"I know where he is," I said. "He's hiding in the cemetery. Either in one of the vaults, or in the gravediggers' shack."

I said that just to make fools of them. I wanted to see them get up and fasten their belts and bustle about giving orders.

They jumped to their feet.

"Fine. Moles, go ask Lieutenant Lopez for fifteen men. And as for you," the little fat fellow said to me, "if you've told the truth, I don't go back on my word. But you'll pay for this, if you're pulling our leg."

They left noisily and I waited in peace, still guarded by the falangists. From time to time I smiled at the thought of the face they were going to make. I felt dull and malicious. I could see them lifting up the grave stones, or opening the doors of the vaults one by one. I saw the whole situation as though I were another person: the prisoner determined to play the hero, the solemn falangists with their mustaches and the men in uniform running around among the graves. It was irresistibly funny.

After half an hour, the little fat fellow came back alone. I thought he had come to give the order to execute me. The others must have stayed in the cemetery.

The officer looked at me. He didn't look at all foolish.

"Take him out in the big courtyard with the others," he said. "When military operations are over, a regular tribunal will decide his case."

I thought I must have misunderstood.

"So they're not—they're not going to shoot me?" I asked.

"Not now, in any case. Afterward, that doesn't concern me."

I still didn't understand.

"But why?" I said to him.

He shrugged his shoulders without replying, and the soldiers led me away. In the big courtyard there was a hundred or so prisoners, women, children and a few old men. I started to walk around the grass plot in the middle. I felt absolutely idiotic. At noon we were fed in the dining hall. Two or three fellows spoke to me. I must have known them, but I didn't answer. I didn't even know where I was.

Toward evening, about ten new prisoners were pushed into the courtyard. I recognized Garcia, the baker.

He said to me, "Lucky dog! I didn't expect to find you alive."

"They condemned me to death," I said, "and then they changed their minds. I don't know why."

"I was arrested at two o'clock," Garcia said.

"What for?"

Garcia took no part in politics.

"I don't know," he said. "They arrest everybody who doesn't think the way they do."

He lowered his voice.

"They got Gris."

I began to tremble.

"When?"

"This morning. He acted like a damned fool. He left his cousins' house Tuesday because of a disagreement. There were any number of fellows who would have hidden him, but he didn't want to be indebted to anybody any more. He said, 'I would have hidden at Ibbieta's, but since they've got him, I'll go hide in the cemetery.'"

"In the cemetery?"

"Yes. It was the god-damnedest thing. Naturally they passed by there this morning; that had to happen. They found him in the gravediggers' shack. They opened fire at him and they finished him off."

"In the cemetery!"

Everything went around in circles, and when I came to I was sitting on the ground. I laughed so hard the tears came to my eyes.

ALBERT CAMUS

The Funeral

Albert Camus was born in Algiers in 1913. He was one of the most active writers of the Resistance and was an editorialist for the clandestine newspaper *Combat*. After the war, he emerged as one of the leading novelists and playwrights of his country. He has a fervent following among the younger generation. His principal works include *Caligula* and *Le Malentendu* (plays), *The Stranger* (novel) and *Le Mythe de Sisyphe* (essay). [From *The Stranger* by Albert Camus; copyright 1946 by Alfred A. Knopf, Inc.; used by permission of the publishers; translated by Stuart Gilbert.]

MOTHER DIED TODAY. Or, maybe, yesterday; I can't be sure. The telegram from the Home says: "Your Mother passed away. Funeral tomorrow. Deep sympathy." Which leaves the matter doubtful; it could have been yesterday.

The Home for Aged Persons is at Marengo, some fifty miles from Algiers. With the two-o'clock bus I should get there well before nightfall. Then I can spend the night there, keeping the usual vigil beside the body, and be back here by tomorrow evening. I have fixed up with my employer for two days' leave; obviously under the circumstances, he couldn't refuse. Still, I had an idea he looked annoyed, and I said, without thinking: "Sorry, sir, but it's not my fault you know."

Afterward it struck me I needn't have said that. I had no reason to excuse myself; it was up to him to express his sympathy and so forth. Probably he will do so the day after tomorrow, when he sees me in black. For the present, it's almost as if Mother weren't really dead. The funeral will bring it home to me, put an official seal on it, so to speak. . . .

I took the two-o'clock bus. It was a blazing hot afternoon. I'd lunched, as usual, at Celeste's restaurant. Everyone was most kind, and Celeste said to me, "There's no one like a mother." When I left they came with me to the door. It was something of a rush, getting away, as at the last moment I had to call in at Emmanuel's place to borrow his black tie and mourning band. He lost his uncle a few months ago.

I had to run to catch the bus. I suppose it was my hurrying like that, what with the glare off the road and from the sky, the reek of gasoline, and the jolts, that made me feel so drowsy. Anyhow, I slept most of the way. When I woke I was leaning against a soldier; he grinned and asked me if I'd come from a long way off, and I just nodded, to cut things short. I wasn't in a mood for talking.

The Home is a little over a mile from the village, I went there on foot. I asked to be allowed to see Mother at once, but the doorkeeper told me I must see the warden first. He wasn't free, and I had to wait a bit. The doorkeeper chatted with me while I waited; then he led me to the office. The warden was a very small man, with gray hair, and a Legion of Honor rosette in his buttonhole. He gave me a long look with his watery blue eyes. Then we shook hands, and he held mine so long that I began to feel embarrassed. After that he consulted a register on his table, and said:

"Madame Meursault entered the Home three years ago. She had no private means and depended entirely on you."

I had a feeling he was blaming me for something, and started to explain. But he cut me short.

"There's no need to excuse yourself, my boy. I've looked up the record and obviously you weren't in a position to see that she was properly cared for. She needed someone to be with her all the time, and young men in jobs like yours don't get too much pay. In any case, she was much happier in the Home."

I said, "Yes sir; I'm sure of that."

Then he added: "She had good friends here, you know, old folks like herself, and one gets on better with people of one's own generation. You're much too young; you couldn't have been much of a companion to her."

That was so. When we lived together, Mother was always watching me, but we hardly ever talked. During her first few weeks at the Home she used to cry a good deal. But that was only because she hadn't settled down. After a month or two she'd have cried if she'd been told to leave the Home. Because this, too, would have been a wrench. That was why, during the last year, I seldom went to see her. Also, it would have meant losing my Sunday—not to mention the trouble of going to the bus, getting my ticket, and spending two hours on the journey each way.

The warden went on talking, but I didn't pay much attention. Finally he said:

"Now I suppose you'd like to see your mother?"

I rose without replying, and he led the way to the door. As we were going down the stairs he explained:

"I've had the body moved to our little mortuary—so as not to upset the other old people, you understand. Every time there's a death here, they're in a nervous state for two or three days. Which means, of course, extra work and worry for our staff.

We crossed the courtyard where there were a number of old men, talking amongst themselves in little groups. They fell silent as we came up with them. Then, behind our backs, the chattering began again. Their voices reminded me of parakeets in a cage, only the sound wasn't quite so shrill. The warden stopped outside the entrance of a small, low building.

"So here I leave you, Monsieur Meursault. If you want me for anything, you'll find me in my office. We propose to have the funeral tomorrow morning. That will enable you to spend the night beside your mother's coffin, as no doubt you would wish to do. Just one more thing; I gathered from your mother's friends that she wished to be buried with the rites of the church. I've made arrangements for this; but I thought I should let you know."

I thanked him. So far as I knew, my mother, though not a professed atheist, had never given a thought to religion in her life.

I entered the mortuary. It was a bright, spotlessly clean room, with whitewashed walls and a big skylight. The furniture consisted of some chairs and trestles. Two of the latter stood open in the center of the room and the coffin rested on them. The lid was in place, but the screws had been given only a few turns and their nickeled heads stuck out above the wood, which was stained dark walnut. An Arab woman —a nurse, I supposed—was sitting beside the bier; she was wearing a blue smock and had a rather gaudy scarf wound round her hair.

Just then the keeper came up behind me. He'd evidently been running, as he was a little out of breath.

"We put the lid on, but I was told to unscrew it when you came in, so that you could see her.

While he was going up to the coffin I told him not to trouble.

"Eh? What's that?" he exclaimed. "You don't want me to . . .?"

"No," I said.

He put back the screwdriver in his pocket and stared at me. I realized then that I shouldn't have said, "No," and it made me rather embarrassed. After eying me for some moments he asked:

"Why not?" But he didn't sound reproachful; he simply wanted to know.

"Well, really I couldn't say," I answered.

He began twiddling his white mustache; then without looking at me, said gently:

"I understand."

He was a pleasant-looking man, with blue eyes and ruddy cheeks. He drew up a chair for me near the coffin, and seated himself just behind. The nurse got up and moved toward the door. As she was going by, the keeper whispered in my ear:

"It's a tumor she has, poor thing."

I looked at her more carefully and I noticed that she had a bandage around her head, just below her eyes. It lay quite flat across the bridge of her nose, and one saw hardly anything of her face except that strip of whiteness.

As soon as she had gone, the keeper rose.

"Now I'll leave you to yourself."

I don't know whether I made some gesture, but instead of going he halted behind my chair. The sensation of someone posted at my back made me uncomfortable. The sun was getting low and the whole room was flooded with a pleasant, mellow light. Two hornets were buzzing overhead, against the skylight. I was so sleepy I could hardly keep my eyes open. Without looking round, I asked the keeper how long he'd been at the Home. "Five years." The answer came so pat that one could have thought he'd been expecting my question.

That started him off, and he became quite chatty. If anyone had told him ten years ago that he'd end his days as doorkeeper at a home at Marengo, he'd never have believed it. He was sixty-four, he said, and hailed from Paris.

When he said that, I broke in. "Ah, you don't come from here?"

I remembered then that, before taking me to the warden, he'd told me something about Mother. He had said she'd have to be buried mighty quickly because of the heat in these parts, especially down in the plain. "At Paris they keep the body for three days, sometimes four." After that he had mentioned that he'd spent the best part of his life in Paris, and could never manage to forget it. "Here," he had said, "things have to go with a rush, like. You've hardly time to get used to the idea that someone's dead, before you're hauled off to the funeral." "That's enough," his wife had put in. "You didn't ought to say such things to the poor young gentleman." The old fellow had blushed and begun to apologize. I told him it was quite all right. As a matter of fact, I found it rather interesting, what he'd been telling me; I hadn't thought of that before.

Now he went on to say that he'd entered the Home as an ordinary inmate. But he was still quite hale and hearty, and when the keeper's job fell vacant, he offered to take it on.

I pointed out that, even so, he was really an inmate like the others, but he wouldn't hear of it. He was "an official, like." I'd been struck before by his habit of saying "they" or, less often, "them old folks," when referring to inmates no older than himself. Still, I could see his point of view. As doorkeeper he had a certain standing, and some authority over the rest of them.

Just then the nurse returned. Night had fallen very quickly; all of a sudden, it seemed, the sky went black above the skylight. The keeper switched on the lamps, and I was almost blinded by the blaze of light.

He suggested I should go to the refectory for dinner, but I wasn't hungry. Then he proposed bringing me a mug of "cafe au lait." As I am very partial to cafe au lait I said, "Thanks," and a few minutes later he came back with a tray. I drank the coffee, and then I wanted a cigarette. But I wasn't sure if I should smoke, under the circumstances—in Mother's presence. I thought it over; really, it didn't seem to matter, so I offered the keeper a cigarette, and we both smoked.

After a while he started talking again.

"You know, your mother's friends will be coming soon, to keep vigil with you beside the body. We always have a 'vigil' here, when anyone dies. I'd better go and get me some chairs and a pot of black coffee."

The glare off the white walls was making my eyes smart, and I asked him if he couldn't turn off one of the lamps. "Nothing doing," he said. They'd arranged the lights like that; either one had them all or none at all. After that I didn't pay much more attention to him. He went out, brought some chairs, and set them out round the coffin. On one he placed a coffeepot and ten or a dozen cups. Then he sat down facing me, on the far side of Mother. The nurse was at the other end of the room, with her back to me. I couldn't see what she was doing, but by the way her arms moved I guessed that she was knitting. I was feeling very comfortable; the coffee had warmed me up, and through the open door came scents of flowers, and breaths of cool air. I think I dozed off for a while.

I was wakened by an odd rustling in my ears. After having had my eyes closed, I had a feeling that the light had grown even stronger than before. There wasn't a trace of shadow anywhere, and every object, each curve or angle, seemed to score its outline on one's eyes. The old people, Mother's friends, were coming in. I counted ten in all, gliding almost soundlessly through the bleak white glare. None of the chairs creaked when they sat down. Never in my life had I seen anyone so clearly as I saw these people; not a detail of their clothes or features escaped me. And yet I couldn't hear them, and it was hard to believe they really existed.

Nearly all the women wore aprons, and the strings drawn tight round their waists made their big stomachs bulge more. I'd never yet noticed what big paunches old women usually have. Most of the men, however, were as thin as rakes, and they all carried sticks. What struck me most about their faces was that one couldn't see their eyes, only a dull glow in a sort of nest of wrinkles.

On sitting down, they looked at me, and wagged their heads awkwardly, their lips sucked in between their toothless gums. I couldn't decide if they were greeting me and trying to say something, or if it was due to some infirmity of age. I inclined to think that they were greeting me, after a fashion, but it had a queer effect, after seeing all those old fellows grouped round the keeper, solemnly eying me and dandling their heads from side to side. For a moment I had an absurd impression that they had come to sit in judgment on me.

A few minutes later one of the women started weeping. She was in the second row and I couldn't see her face because of another woman in front. At regular intervals she emitted a little choking sob; one had a feeling she would never stop. The others didn't seem to notice. They sat in silence, slumped in their chairs, staring at the coffin or at their walking sticks or any object just in front of them, and never took their eyes off it. And still the woman sobbed. I was rather surprised, as I didn't know who she was. I wanted her to stop crying, but dared not speak to her. After a while the keeper bent toward her and whispered in her ear; but she merely shook her head, mumbled something I couldn't catch, and went on sobbing as steadily as before.

The keeper got up and moved his chair beside mine. At first he kept silent; then without looking at me, he explained.

"She was devoted to your mother. She says your mother was her only friend in the world, and now she's all alone."

I had nothing to say, and the silence lasted quite a while. Presently the woman's sighs and sobs became less frequent, and after blowing her nose and snuffling for some minutes, she too, fell silent.

I'd ceased feeling sleepy, but I was very tired and my legs were aching badly. And now I realized that the silence of these people was telling on my nerves. The only sound was a rather queer one; it came only now and then, and at first I was puzzled by it. However after listening attentively, I guessed what it was; the old men were sucking at the insides of their cheeks, and this caused the odd, wheezing noises that had mystified me. They were so absorbed in their thoughts that they didn't know what they were up to. I even had an impression that the dead body in their midst meant nothing at all to them. But now I suspect that I was mistaken about this.

We all drank the coffee, which the keeper handed round. After that, I can't remember much; somehow the night went by. I can recall only one moment; I had opened my eyes and I saw the old men sleeping hunched up on their chairs, with one exception. Resting his chin on his hands clasped round his stick, he was staring at me, as if he had been waiting for me to wake up. Then I fell asleep again. I woke up after a bit, because the ache in my legs had developed into a sort of cramp.

There was a glimmer of dawn above the skylight. A moment or two later one of the men woke up and coughed repeatedly. He spat into a big check handkerchief, and each time he spat it sounded as if he were retching. This woke the others, and the keeper told them it was time to make a move. They got up at once. Their faces were ashen gray after the long night. To my surprise each of them shook hands with me, as though this night together, in which we hadn't exchanged a word, had created a kind of intimacy between us.

I was quite done in. The keeper took me to his room, and I tidied myself up a bit. He gave me some more "white" coffee, and it seemed to do me good. When I went out, the sun was up and the sky mottled red above the hills between Marengo and the sea. A morning breeze was blowing and it had a pleasant salty tang. There was the promise of a very fine day. I hadn't been in the country for ages, and I caught myself thinking what an agreeable walk I could have had, if it hadn't been for Mother.

As it was, I waited in the courtyard under a plane tree. I sniffed the smells of the cool earth and found I wasn't sleepy anymore. Then I thought of the other fellows in the office. At this hour they'd be getting up, preparing to go to work; for me this was always the worst hour of the day. I went on thinking, like this, for ten minutes or so; then the sound of a bell inside the building attracted my attention. I could see movements behind the windows; then all was calm again. The sun had risen a little higher and was beginning to warm my feet. The keeper came across the yard and said the warden wished to see me. I went to his office and he got me to sign some document. I noticed that he was in black, with pin-stripe trousers. He picked up the telephone receiver and looked at me.

"The undertaker's men arrived some moments ago, and they will be going to the mortuary to screw down the coffin. Shall I tell them to wait, for you to have a last glimpse of your mother?"

"No," I said.

He spoke into the receiver, lowering his voice.

"That's all right, Figeac. Tell the men to go there now."

He then informed me that he was going to attend the funeral, and I thanked him. Sitting down behind his desk, he crossed his short legs and leaned back. Besides the nurse on duty, he told me, he and I would be the only mourners at the funeral. It was a rule of the Home that inmates shouldn't be allowed to attend funerals, though there was no objection to letting some of them sit beside the coffin the night before.

"It's for their own sakes," he explained, "to spare their feelings. But in this particular instance I've given permission to an old friend of your mother to come with us. His name is Thomas Perez." The warden smiled. "It's a rather touching little story in its way. He and your mother had become almost inseparable. The other old people used to tease Perez about having a fiancée. 'When are you going to marry her?' they asked. He'd turn it with a laugh. It was a standing joke, in fact. So, as you can guess, he feels very badly about your mother's death. I thought I couldn't decently refuse him permission to attend the funeral. But, on our medical officer's advice, I forbade him to sit up beside the body last night."

For some time we sat there without speaking. Then the warden got up and went to the window. Presently he said:

"Ah, there's the padre from Marengo. He's a bit ahead of time."

He warned me that it would take us a good three quarters of an hour, walking to the church, which was in the village. Then we went downstairs.

The priest was waiting just outside the mortuary door. With him were two acolytes, one of them had a censer. The priest was stooping over him, adjusting the length of the silver chain on which it hung. When he saw us he straightened up and said a few words to me, addressing me as, "My son." Then he led the way into the mortuary.

I noticed at once that four men in black were standing behind the coffin and the screws in the lid had now been driven home. At the same moment I heard the warden remark that the hearse had arrived, and the priest started his prayers. Then everybody made a move. Holding a strip of black cloth, the four men approached the coffin, while the priest, the boys and myself filed out. A lady I hadn't seen before was standing by the door. "This is Monsieur Meursault," the warden said to her. I didn't catch her name, but I gathered she was a nursing sister attached to the Home. When I was introduced, she bowed, without the trace of a smile on her long, gaunt face. We stood by; then, following the bearers down a corridor, we came to the front entrance, where a hearse was waiting. Oblong, glossy, varnished black all over, it vaguely reminded me of the pen trays in the office.

Beside the hearse stood a quaintly dressed little man, whose duty it was, I understood, to supervise the funeral, as a sort of master of ceremonies. Near him, looking constrained, almost bashful, was old M. Perez, my mother's special friend. He wore a soft felt hat with a pudding-basin crown and a very wide brim—he whisked it off the moment the coffin emerged from the doorway—trousers that concertina'd on his shoes, a black tie much too small for his high white double collar. Under his bulbous, pimply nose, his lips were trembling. But what caught my attention most were his ears; pendulous, scarlet ears that showed up like blobs of sealing wax on the pallor of his cheeks and were framed in wisps of silky white hair.

The undertakers' factotum shepherded us to our places, with the priest in front of the hearse, and the four men in black on each side of it. The warden and myself came next, and bringing up the rear, old Perez himself and the nurse.

The sky was already a blaze of light, and the air stoking up rapidly. I felt the first waves of heat lapping my back, and my dark suit made things worse. I couldn't imagine why we waited so long for getting under way. Old Perez, who had put on his hat, took it off again. I had turned slightly in his direction and was looking at him when the warden started telling me more about him. I remember his saying that old Perez and my mother used often to have a longish stroll together in the cool of evening; sometimes they went as far as the village, accompanied by a nurse, of course.

I looked at the countryside, at the long lines of cypresses sloping up toward the skyline and the hills, the hot soil dappled with vivid green, and here and there a lonely house sharply outlined against the light—and I could understand Mother's feelings. Evenings in these parts must be a sort of mournful solace. Now, in the full glare of the morning sun, with everything shimmering in the heat haze, there was something inhuman, discouraging, about this landscape.

At last we made a move. Only then I noticed that Perez had a slight limp. The old chap steadily lost ground as the hearse gained speed. One of the men beside it, too, fell back and drew level with me. I was surprised to see how quickly the sun was climbing up the sky, and just then it struck me that the hum of insects and the rustle of grass warming up had been throbbing the air for quite a while. Sweat was running down my face. As I had no hat I tried to fan myself with my handkerchief.

The undertaker's man turned to me and said something that I didn't catch. At the same time he wiped the crown of his head with a handkerchief that he held in his left hand, while with his right he tilted up his hat. I asked him what he'd said. He pointed upward.

"Sun's pretty bad today, ain't it?"

"Yes," I said.

After a while he asked: "Is it your mother we're burying?"

"What was her age?"

"Well she was getting on." As a matter of fact, I didn't know exactly how old she was.

After that he kept silent. Looking back, I saw Perez limping along some fifty yards behind. He was swinging his felt hat at arm's length, trying to make the pace. I also had a look at the warden. He was walking with carefully measured steps, economizing every gesture. Beads of perspiration glistened on his forehead, but he didn't wipe them off.

I had an impression that our little procession was moving slightly faster. Wherever I looked I saw the same sun-drenched countryside, and the sky was so dazzling that I dared not raise my eyes. A shimmer of heat played over it and one's feet squelched at each step, leaving bright black gashes. In front, the coachman's glossy black hat looked like a lump of the same sticky substance, poised above the hearse. It gave one a queer, dreamlike impression, that blue-white glare overhead and all this blackness round one: the sleek black of the hearse, the dull black of the men's clothes, and the silvery-black gashes in the road. And then there were the smells, smells of hot leather and horse dung from the hearse, veined with whiffs of incense smoke. What with these and the hangover from a poor night's sleep, I found my eyes and thoughts growing blurred.

I looked back again. Perez seemed very far away now, almost hidden by the heat haze; then, abruptly, he disappeared altogether. After puzzling over it for a bit, I guessed that he had turned off the road into the fields. Then I noticed that there was a bend of the road a little way ahead. Obviously Perez, who knew this district so well, had taken a short cut, so as to catch up with us. He rejoined us soon after we were round the bend; then began to lose ground again. He took another short cut and met us again farther on; in fact, this happened several times during the next half-hour. But soon I lost interest in his movements; my temples were throbbing and I could hardly drag myself along.

After that everything went with a rush; and also with such precision and matter-of-factness that I remember hardly any details. Except that when we were on the outskirts of the village the nurse said something to me. Her voice took me by surprise; it didn't match her face at all; it was musical and slightly tremulous. What she said was: "If you go too slowly there's the risk of a heatstroke. But, if you go too fast, you perspire, and the cold air in the church gives you a chill." I saw her point; either way one was in for it.

Some other memories of the funeral have stuck in my mind. The old boy's face, for instance, when he caught up with us for the last time, just outside the village. His eyes were streaming with tears, of exhaustion or distress, or both together. But because of the wrinkles they couldn't flow down. They spread out, crisscrossed, and formed a smooth gloss on the old, worn face.

And I can remember the look of the church, the villagers in the street, the red geraniums on the graves, Perez's fainting fit—he crumpled up like a rag doll—the tawny-red earth pattering on Mother's coffin, the bits of white roots mixed up with it; then more people, voices, the wait outside a cafe for the bus, the rumble of the engine, and my little thrill of pleasure when we entered the first brightly lit streets of Algiers, and I pictured myself going straight to bed and sleeping twelve hours at a stretch.

GEORGES

EEKHOUD

Hiep-Hioup

Georges Eekhoud (1854–1927) was born in Antwerp. He worked for a while as a gentleman farmer near Antwerp, later as a journalist in Brussels. He began his literary career in 1877, and is best known for his short stories (*Kermesses*) and a novel (*The New Carthage*). [Translated by Edith Wingate Rinder.]

ON THE REMOTE TRACT OF LAND, which stretches between Wortel and Ippenroy, lies the farm of Boschhof, locally known as the "Maison Forestière."

It is a desolate country; though, as the landscapists are wont to say, full of character.

Russet heaths, spinneys of black-green fir, and stretches of the yellow flowering broom, alternate. Now and again clumps of juniper trees skirt the shallow waters of a green-discolored stagnant marsh, swampy tracts which our peasants call *Vennes*. Beyond these stand outlined dark copses of oak; at wide intervals a few spare patches of cultivated land; and, along the vanishing horizon, three or four spires, which appear to signal to one another across the leagues of lonely plain. Over all impends nearly always a vast cloudy sky, of an aspect the more changeable and stormy because of the quiet gloom of the moorland.

As with this environment, so with the remote inhabitants; there is the same contrast of placidity and unrest. Among the quiet industrious peasants the ferment of a vagrant and often ne'er-do-well element creates frequent disturbance. Poachers these, poachers and smugglers and often worse; attracted hither because of the contiguity of the Dutch frontier, and, for the tramps, of the haven of Hoogstraten workhouse.

The Overmaats, from father to son, occupants of Boschhof, were farmers and foresters for the Counts de Thyme, a great Dutch family now extinct, and were considered the most prosperous peasants in the neighborhood.

Jakkè Overmaat, the forester of the time of which I speak, was a fine fellow of twenty-five. "Firm as the oak, straight as the pine, healthy as the moorland!" is the saying down there for those of his build.

The sudden death of his father and of an elder brother, who would have succeeded to the paternal duties, recalled Jakkè from Malines college, where, like most of the younger sons of Flemish farmers, he was studying for the priesthood. He came back from college with polished manners. His imagination had been aroused by books, which, too, had stimulated in him that latent love of the marvelous which lies deep down in the soul of every Campinois.

With a reserved manner, older than the warrant of his years, he was regarded as the village oracle. The fact, too, that he would have become a priest added to his repute. Even those who were lawless acknowledged that he was at once just and humane. Though he permitted no familiarity, he made no enemies, and every mother dreamed of him as a son-in-law.

His mother greatly wished him to marry, but the young fellow, who was rather shy, fully convinced that he would never be happier than with her, was in no hurry.

Everything went well until one day, the vagabond section of the community was increased by the arrival of a poor woman and her daughter, exiled from country after country. These, through the charity of Count Thyme, enjoyed the right—if it can be called enjoyment— of a deserted hut, on the edge of the woods, opposite Boschhof.

Like others of the same calling, these strangers lived on occasional alms, a little work, and frequent thefts. Their acknowledged livelihood was gained by picking mushrooms, and beech-nuts, and by making mats. In addition they had opened a public-house in their hovel and the old woman told the fortunes of her wretched poverty-stricken customers.

The girl was a big ungainly, bony creature, her disheveled hair was black as coal, her long oval face was set with two stormy black eyes, her whole frame wrought by some consuming fever. Upon the whole she was a woman of little attraction for the honest farmers who admired fair buxom lassies of placid temperament. She picked up admirers only among passing laborers, peddlers, hawkers, the lower farm servants or among the poachers in whose pursuits she took part, either as receiver of stolen goods or as watchdog. Even then she had to court them openly, for however low they had sunk, these rapscallions had too much sense of shame to be proud of their unsought success.

Upon the whole the wench was good-natured. Like all her people she bore a grudge against those in authority, against the rural constable, the policeman, the judge, rich people and their dependents, in general; against all those fortunate people, in fact who possessed money or land, or who tracked, hunted down or annoyed in a thousand ways those with empty pockets and empty stomachs. These she truly hated with an unchristian hatred, and these she would at any time serve an ill turn. The villagers called her Hiep-Hioup! on account of this, her favorite

exclamation, which was invariably accompanied with a leap and a snap
of the fingers. In time she became known by this nickname only.

This girl had many a grievance against Jakkè Overmaat. The kind
of respect and sympathy which the keeper inspired, even among the
most incorrigible scamps, particularly irritated the hussy. She would
not admit this one braided cap should be singled out from among the
legion of those who tormented the poor.

One day, ax in hand, she was about, after a fashion of her own, to
prune some birches which were under the charge of the forester, when
young Overmaat came up to her. Instead of fleeing, she composedly
collected a good supply of branches. He reprimanded her quietly, suggesting that when she required wood she should rather come and ask
for it at the farm. The girl flashed her dark eyes at him, and when he
had stammered out his reproof, she laughed in his face with a laugh
that was as harsh as the trill of a fife, then turned on her heels, and,
brandishing her ax, disappeared with a bound: "Hiep-Hioup!"

This strident laugh gave the forester a sense of embarrassment and
discomfort such as he had never known before. For the remainder of
the day the laugh jarred on his ear. He was dissatisfied with himself and
for the first time doubted his worthiness for his office.

The feeling was still there, when, some time after, he found Hiep-
Hioup at dawn, squatted in the brushwood, stealing some pheasant's
eggs. He almost blessed this opportunity to make peace with his conscience. In a tone which did not brook reply, he ordered her to empty
the contents of her pockets, and to put the eggs back into the nest. As
she paid no attention, he gripped her arm. She cried out like a mole
bitten by a dog, let the eggs which she carried in her apron drop, and
smashed them on her sabot; she then escaped from his grasp, ran away
at full speed, and shouted in her most mocking way "Hiep-Hioup!"

Jakkè, amazed, saw her disappear, but made no effort to bring her
before the rural constable. He scarcely even muttered a threat about the
law. His eager zeal and desire for revenge were gone; he was even
more nonplussed and baffled by this strange personality than he had
been the first time. Such inexplicable impudence and aggression in a
woman were new to him. Those bright eyes, that shrill, hoarse voice,
caused him many sleepless nights.

Encouraged by the two first advantages which she had gained over
the Count de Thyme's keeper on his own ground, the malicious wench
had frequently tried to come across him in his beat. She no longer took
any trouble to hide her misdemeanors. She preferred to haunt the
vicinity of Boschhof and worked, so to stay, under Jakkè's very eyes.

He, on the contrary, had not yet recovered his serenity and peace of
mind, and the pitiful results of his encounters with this devil-dare
woman, far from encouraging him to face another meeting, made him
dread to measure his strength with her a third time.

He avoided her or turned his head away when she passed. It happened, however, that when at last they did meet, Jakkè looked so

strange, so shame-faced, and at once so sheepish and malicious, and replied so feebly to the impertinent greeting of the wastrel, that he might have been regarded as under the influence of gin, were it not for his reputation for sobriety.

"How stupid I am!" Hiep-Hioup said to herself at last. "This simpleton loves me!"

The discovery made her in a very good temper. Her rough mates thought she was joking when she told them, but they were delighted at the idea and gossiped about it to everyone. One Sunday, at the hour for early mass, Jakkè found Hiep-Hioup hunting a rabbit with a ferret in the fields near Boschhof. The incorrigible poacher, noticing the approach of the keeper, whistled to the little beast, far down a burrow, and having seized it and slowly hidden it in her bodice, she quietly awaited the spoil-sport.

Jakkè at once thrust his hand into her bodice, pulled out the ferret and wrung its neck. Then, having thrown the animal away and shaken his bleeding fingers, which had been sharply bitten, he prepared to take Hiep-Hioup before the rural constable at Wortel. All this took place in a moment.

Hiep-Hioup could not believe her eyes. Certainly something had happened to the accommodating Overmaat. It was still worse when she recovered from the shock of these sudden proceedings, and tried her usual wiles. Threats, challenges, capers, screams of rage, withering looks could not intimidate the guardian of justice. There was nothing for it; she was indeed to be locked up. As they went along, he reprimanded her very calmly, and thus added to her vexation at being made prisoner. The poacher's instinct did not here stand her in good stead. At that moment one kind word would have been enough to shake the keeper's resolution, to make him set her free again. For her former surmise was right: Jakkè loved Hiep-Hioup.

The honest fellow, rather apathetic by temperament, upon whom the gentle, blue-eyed girls of his own station had made no impression, had been pierced to the heart by the savage wiles of this creature. But the thing was so extraordinary, so odious that he would not have dared to own it to himself, and he would rather have died than confess it. Of late, moreover, when his mother, who was vaguely anxious, urged him to marry, he replied to her suggestions in a brusque, surly manner which he had never shown before. This also accounted for the mental struggles, the remorse, and above all for the unexpected energy which, in his desire to regain his independence at any cost, he had just displayed.

But, as it happened, the adventure which ought to have freed the fellow from Hiep-Hioup's toils, turned out to be the lure in which he was irretrievably trapped.

When the poacher was brought before the magistrate, and Jakkè was called as a witness, he withdrew his first statement and tried to clear the accused. He contradicted himself in his two depositions to such an extent, that he was on the point of compromising himself, and the judge was disposed to put him into the dock. The inhabitants of Ippenroy and Wortel who had come to take part in the case, affirmed that the keeper looked more like a defendant than a plaintiff.

Hiep-Hioup, who already had against her a too ample police record for offenses of this very kind, was, despite the retractions made by her accuser, sentenced to the full penalty of the law, that is to say, a fortnight's incarceration in Hoogstraten prison.

Jakkè did not know, until he heard them read out to the audience, the number or variety of convictions, for vagrancy, theft, loose conduct and other details, which had been passed upon this outcast. Such testimony ought to have cured an honest fellow of his perverted fancy; on the contrary, these drawbacks only stimulated his liking, and when the sentence was pronounced he blamed himself bitterly for having added another set-back to this *cavale de retour,* as the judge said.

Hiep-Hioup took the thing lightly. She had tasted enough of prison to have no fear of it. Jakkè's contrite and repentant manner had amused her even more than it had the others. Now she was sure he was under her power. This certainly compensated to a great extent for the disgrace of a fresh visit to Hoogstraten. Not that she was the least grateful to Jakkè for his feelings! She saw only a way to make him later pay dearly for his denunciation, and to gratify a hatred as inexplicable, but as violent, as was the keeper's love for her. On the return from the court the vagrants and law-breakers who had escorted their companion, were not slow to spread throughout the village an edifying report of the trial. These vagabonds, Hiep-Hioup's casual and indifferent lovers, now began to feel quite proud of their association with her. Up to now she had been passed backward and forward from one to another without jealousy, without rivalry; they shared her as the rest of the common booty. From the moment that a respectable fellow desired his share of this game, Hiep-Hioup, this *rebut*, this *pis-aller*, became a girl to be proud of. The result of this was that these *canaille* began to look upon Jakkè as their equal and associate. When Hiep-Hioup returned from serving her time at Hoogstraten, she encouraged this attitude of insubordination. If Jakkè interfered and threatened arraignment before the judge, they cried: "None o' that nonsense! The judge . . . you are more afraid of him than we are! We are Hiep-Hioup's servants only. You must find fault with her!"

Jakkè aware that he was in the wrong, and handicapped by his first fatal complaisance, could not insist.

Once, when he had merely threatened a professional poacher, four of the blackguards awaited him at night when he was on his road. Before he had time to ward them off, they sprang upon him, beat him like a dog, and stripped off all his clothes; then, with grim irony, leaving him his cap braided with the arms of the counts de Thyme, they tied him to a tree, with his loaded gun against his thighs. There they left him to the mercy of the night, of the December cold and fog. In the morning he had to parley for a long time with the suspicious and frightened peasants whom he descried on their way to market, before they would consent to set him free. To the great amazement of the entire village he lodged no complaint against his assailants, although he had recognized them through the soot with which they had smeared themselves; indeed he did his best to hush up the affair. Hiep-Hioup was not in any way grateful to him for his culpable forbearance, and as to his assailants, they laughed him in the face, and boasted of the excellent joke openly before him in the public house. He still continued to avoid the woman, but he could not drive her from his thoughts. Recollections of what he had read in his college books, in particular in the "Lives of the Saints," which had been read aloud in the refectory, troubled him more and more. He almost thought himself possessed by a demon.

Hiep-Hioup had sworn to reduce this fine, comely fellow, who was so sensible and so good, to despair. Though she had fully made up her mind not to belong to him, she was eager that he should throw himself at her feet. Knowing him well, she sought to further infatuate him, to stimulate his mad desire, by a frank surrender of herself to the first comer, preferably to the most rakish, the most wretched.

Whenever Jakkè met her, she was always hanging on to one of these lovers. Once, when the keeper came across her at the corner of a path, the thrasher, to whom she clung as the flame to a resinous branch, pushed her brutally away, weary of her maybe, or, perhaps, being a fellow with some faint remaining sense of decency, annoyed to be found in company with this wanton. Jakkè, who hastened on, heard the woman say to the churl:

"That fellow there won't tire of me so soon!" And in her hoarse strident voice, she called to the fugitive: "Hein, you will not deny it? eh! you! la Sainte-Nitouche?"

He passed quickly on, as reticent as his wont. All the same, a fierce rage seized him: he saw red, as the peasants say. Homicidal thoughts filled his brain. Should he kill Hiep-Hioup's lover? Which one? Yesterday's or tomorrow's? It was impossible to count them. It would be a battue, a massacre! Nearly all the male population of the village would be victims! He hid his passion as though it were an unmentionable thing: he would die rather than betray himself. No proof existed, it was true, of the mad folly attributed to him by the gossips of the place, and though the scandal-mongers and the envious declared they had sufficient warrant in the strange behavior of young Overmatt, the good souls had still their doubts about a thing trumpeted forth by Hiep-Hioup and those of her kind only.

Overmaat's mother, who had been told of what was happening by a charitable neighbor, although troubled by the change which had come over her son, was the first to refuse to attribute it to a dishonoring passion. She would even have blamed herself for questioning him on the subject. But she feared lest these tales invented by the keeper's rivals might come to the ears of the lord of the manor.

One Sunday, at the fair, Jakkè met Hiep-Hioup at a dance in the chief village inn.

Surrounded by a trio in blouses, plow-boys, and haymakers, she permitted the roughest familiarities. A quadrille was proposed. But since there was no woman in the crowd so forgetful of her good name as to make a vis-à-vis to Hiep-Hioup two of the men were obliged to dance together. More and more excited, the three fellows did not spare her, and she was made the mock of all there.

The other dancers, who did not care to come in contact with these mad fellows, left them a free field, formed in circle, and looked at them amused but contemptuous. When Hiep-Hioup noticed Jakkè in the room she encouraged her partners to emphasize their antics and herself doubled her abandon; she kicked about, she swooned, she threw herself into the arms of the galley-birds, then, after a wild whirl, she escaped brusquely, quivering all over and wriggling like a mad filly. Inflamed by several snacks of gin which he had imbibed one after another in order to drown his last scruples, Jakkè took advantage of a pause, pushed the onlookers aside, walked straight up to Hiep-Hioup and, in a tone which contradicted the assurance of his approach, asked for the first polka.

There was a flutter in the room; the scandal was greeted with ironic hurrahs. A fellow who respected himself would never have sought this outcast, at fair-time, in presence of the honest girls of the village. And here was Jakkè Overmaat, the Count de Thyme's keeper, coveted by more than one of these heiresses, who forgot himself, who demeaned himself to this point. Not one protest was raised. But what contempt in that stamping, in those coarse cheers in the gallery!

Jakkè did not hear the outcry. Already he was whirling round with Hiep-Hioup. He was panting, almost breathless with the thought that he was chosen in earnest; she was triumphant but implacable, happy at the idea of the scandal, enjoying the dismay of the honest people, the affront offered to the marriageable girls, delighted, above all, at the fall of those proud Overmaats.

She was, therefore, almost pleasant to her victim. When the dance was over, she consented to drink out of his glass. She chose him for the following waltz in preference to the most irresistible of her former partners. At the same time it was her malicious pleasure not to neglect these hangers-on of hers completely; she obliged Jakkè to get on well with them, they gave up their dances to him for some beer which they drank at the counter touching glasses in a friendly fashion. These fine fellows were no other than the devils who had managed things so well the winter before! "No ill-will," the miscreants said as they clinked their glasses against his.

He smothered his anger, and gave himself up to their buffoonry. Finally, after having made him suffer these heart-rending humiliations, the drab obliged him to beg and pray before she would permit him to take her home.

On the way back, as soon as they were some distance from the ballroom, he wished to kiss her. The warmth of the July evening wherein hay ricks exhaled their most pungent odors, further intoxicated him. Hiep-Hioup struck him, and as he still continued to annoy her, she boxed his ears.

"You allow yourself to be kissed by others, by any low tramp or dirty blackguard."

Jealously he enumerated them.

His pent-up rage, his suppressed feelings, broke loose. She, quite calmly, defied him and still further humiliated him.

"Very well my fine chap! Tramps, blackguards you say! Ah, if they could hear you! Are you not ashamed to rob these poor devils of their one possession. Ah! you despise them! They are worth as much as I am, all the same. You pretend to be proud, all the more reason for me to keep you at a distance. I comfort them, I am all that they have. You can have any girl; all those who despise these others and turn their backs on them. . . . Well, on the contrary, I like these fellows, and will have nothing to do with those who molest them, I will never yield to you, do you hear? I enjoy myself with these poor curs; as for you, their enemy, you disgust me!"

At this, he changed his tactics, demeaned himself to such an extent that he confounded sentiment with his madness. He promised always to love her. He would secure a more decent dwelling and provide for her. Why should she not try? The more tender he became, the more she chuckled.

Someone must have followed them, and now watched, unseen; for when he raised his voice against the hilarity of his companion half smothered laughter and mocking whispers re-echoed from the brushwood.

At last they neared Hiep-Hioup's hut. Jakkè, heavy at heart, his blood boiling, saw that his chance was becoming less at every step and that he was losing this long-awaited opportunity. He seized Hiep-Hioup violently and threw her down. She called for help, but did not seem much afraid. Her three partners at the ball emerged from the coppice, seized the gallant and held him while she scrambled to her feet. He struggled, they thrashed him; he foamed like an epileptic; finally they struck him on the head and he fell unconscious into the bottom of a ditch. Just then some peasants were approaching, otherwise the miscreants would have treated him as they did the first time. On this occasion they had not even taken the trouble to blacken their faces.

When he had recovered consciousness and succeeded in extricating himself from the mire, he heard dimly in the distance the mocking voices of the jade and her companions. They were going with Hiep-Hioup to her hovel, the red windows of which could be seen through the trees. One moment he thought of following them, of rejoining them in their den, but, exhausted, beaten about as he was, how could he renew this unequal strife? They would kill him.

He decided therefore to return home. At Boschhof there was also still a light. He pushed open the door of the large room. His mother was sitting in an arm-chair near the dead fire, chilly despite the stifling July evening. She had been warned of the scandal, but she did not expect such a terrible apparition. Jakkè hatless, with torn coat, trousers almost rent from him, wounded, bleeding, muddy, ignoble; the picture of dishonor and despair. She had been told that things were bad, but this was far worse. The guilty man read the agony, the reproach, the horror, in the poor woman's eyes. He did not dare to advance, but retired without saying a word and went to the hay-loft where he broke down and sobbed in rage and pain.

It was over. He would never be able to look up again. The avowal of his terrible trouble had cost him dearly, but he was almost happy now that the depth of his baseness was known, for there was no longer anything to hide.

His mother did not reproach him, and he did not urge any explanation, convinced that the most cogent reasons would stand him in no stead.

Once again the poor fool went to the woman who had almost caused his death; and once again received nothing from her but contumely and mockery. He ever returned to the charge, and importuned her with attentions; but, far from yielding, she became more and more inveterate.

Jakkè's ruin was so inexplicable to his mother that she could not bring herself to admit more than that this disgraceful affection which had caused it, had been provoked by witchcraft. Anxious, not only for her child's position, but also for his health, she made up her mind to a painful step. Unknown to her son, she, an honorable and respected farmer's wife, went to the house of those unfortunates, those thieves, those sorceresses, and implored both mother and daughter to break the spell cast over her poor boy. The two ribald women, who were always in accord feigned violent anger at being taken for associates of the devil, and dismissed Widow Overmaat, advising her to send her son to the madhouse. As she left the cottage, with bleeding heart, convinced more and more of the infernal dealings of these women, she thought for a moment of setting fire to them, and burning them in their den.

Some months later, the misfortune which the mother had dreaded, arrived. After several warnings, and acting on the repeated denunciations of the people of the neighborhood, Count de Thyme decided to dismiss the Overmaats, and to deprive Jakkè of the care of his property.

He allowed them until the next quarter to find another house. But this eviction was a secondary evil only. The Overmaats were not in danger of finding themselves penniless when their seigneur withdrew his confidence. The worthy woman was much more alarmed on account of her son's health! He became weaker daily, lost appetite, cared for no occupation, and was always plunged in morbid brooding. Then the mother, who had this one child only, had recourse to a supreme sacrifice:

"Well," she said to the sick man, "there is one way left to cure you and to disarm the woman who is slowly killing you. . . . Since we must leave this farm in a few months, this farm where all the Overmaats have been born and have died for so many years, it will be better for us to settle in another country. . . . You will get well, you are still young, you will work and will not even be obliged to break into your savings. If you must have this woman whatever happens, marry her. Perhaps she will amend her ways, besides which, they are not known away from here. . . . It will kill me; but you will live, my Jakkè, and you must live. . . ."

Jakkè barely thanked his mother, He fled at once in search of Hiep-Hioup. Ah! this time she would listen to him. He met her strolling about the country. She received the strange proposal unmoved. Her pale face scarcely expressed a doubtful pleasure. When the poor fellow ceased speaking, she looked at him for several seconds, then she burst into her laugh, her brutal laugh, snapped her fingers, and uttered her famous "Hiep-Hioup!"

When he implored her, she made a trumpet of her hands and cried: "Hallo, you others, come and hear what this fellow wants!"

The laborers, who were working some few yards away, left their harrows and spades, and ran up delighted.

"You do not know what Jakkè Overmaat seriously offers me. His hand! Do you hear? His hand! I have only to say yes, to become his wife. I, Hiep-Hioup, the vagabond, the daughter of the sorceress, the lost one, the village outcast, the sport of poachers and ne'er-do-wells."

And when the others questioned Jakkè with an air of pity, for the time to laugh at his folly was over except for the implacable Hiep-Hioup, he nodded his head sadly and confirmed all that this devil had just said.

"Well, is that enough, is that bad enough?" Hiep-Hioup continued. "Then, I'll be better than he is! And if he desides me for a wife, I persist in not desiring him, not even for a husband, not even for one single day, were he to die and set me free directly after the curé had pronounced his blessing."

All remained silent in dismay, divided between horror at the spitefulness of this demon, and admiration for her disinterestedness, not exactly knowing which in this moment was the madder of the two, the one who courted this lewd woman, or the good-for-nothing who refused the unexpected offer.

Then, to further emphasize her refusal, she fell upon the neck of a healthy lad among the group of astonished laborers, a little cowherd, a bad lot, in shirt sleeves, and patched trousers kept up by a shadow of a brace. She kissed him on the lips, and turning toward Jakkè cried: "Now, look. . . . Rather than be your wife! . . ."

Seeing Jakké reel, two of the workmen supported him on either side

and took him back to Boschhof. He submitted as one who is just recovering consciousness, as one in a dream.

They were obliged to put him to bed; he was shaking with fever
and was delirious. His mother watched over him for three days and
three nights. The fourth evening, as he was sleeping quietly, neither
crying nor struggling, the poor woman, overcome with fatigue, dozed
herself in the recess near. He awoke, looked at his watch. It was four
o'clock, the time he usually made his round; he dressed stealthily for
fear of awakening his mother, took down his loaded gun, and went out,
almost blithely, what had happened not leaving in his mind even the
confused memory of a nightmare.

However, as he passed through the pinewood and felt the fresh breeze
which precedes the dawn, the breeze which brings everything so clearly
back to the memory, the picture of Hiep-Hioup rose in the twilight of
his mind. This picture rose and increased as the red disc of the sun
behind the light clouds on the horizon. He remembered many phases
of his distrustful love, the early ones, not those of the latter days, not
those which had laid him by. The recent scenes were now beginning
to come back to him. Later he would remember the conversation with
his mother, the consent given to his marriage, his final appeal to Hiep-
Hioup.

His courage, revived by the fresh, life-giving morning air, diminished
now, at every step.

There was a prolonged rustle in the branches and briars. . . . Some
poacher doubtless. He raised his arm, cocked his gun and walked in
the direction of the noise.

Two shadowy figures emerged from a thicket and promptly fled. In
the badly dressed fellow the keeper recognized the little cowherd, Hiep-
Hioup's latest favorite. Before he saw her, he knew that she was the
second shadow.

Then he remembered everything.

"Stop!" he groaned.

Although the lad was some way in advance of his companion, she
cried, anxiously:

"Hurry up, little one!"

She exposed herself and leisurely fronted the keeper. As she did so,
she twisted up with one hand her long jet-black hair which hung
about her; and fastened her open bodice with the other. Jakké saw
her brown, seductive bosom. With her liquid eyes, but half awake, she
was cruel and desirable.

Jakké forgot the fugitive, who was now out of reach.

Hiep-Hioup, reassured, capable of affection for any low-scamp, but
persistently unmerciful to the keeper, burst out into the laugh which
Jakké knew only too well. He aimed.

She laughed as she fell wounded in the left breast "Hiep!" "Hioup!"
stuck in her throat.

AZORIN

An Unbeliever

Azorin (José Martinez Ruiz) was born in Monovar in 1873. He studied at the Valencia law school, but devoted much of his time to literature. He settled in Madrid in 1896, and became a member of the Spanish Academy in 1924. In 1930, Azorin declared himself for the Republic, and during the Civil War went to live in Paris. Some of his best known works are *Don Juan, The Syrens and Other Stories, Los Hidalgos, La Voluntad* and *Los Pueblos.* [From *The Syrens and Other Stories* by Azorin; translated by Warre B. Wells.]

"YOU DON'T BELIEVE in anything, Don Jenaro?"

"No, I don't believe in anything. Why do you ask?"

"Oh, for no special reason. I merely asked."

It was a question which was often asked by the friends and acquaintances of Don Jenaro. That gentleman's answer was always the same; everybody knew when they asked him that Don Jenaro would make the same reply. Sometimes, after having been questioned about his beliefs, Don Jenaro would add:

"You don't know what happened to the novelist, Eladio Peña?"

Everybody knew what had happened to the famous novelist; but—

"Has something happened to him, Don Jenaro?" they would ask, feigning anxiety.

"You don't know?" he repeated.

A smile ran around the circle of friends. The little scene had been repeated a hundred times, and it would go on being repeated as long as Don Jenaro lived.

"What has happened to Peña?" they insisted.

Slowly, scornfully, came Don Jenaro's answer: "His dog bit him!"

"Good Heavens!"

"You don't say so!"

"Well, I'll be damned!"

Everybody broke into his familiar, oft-repeated exclamation. And Don Jenaro would round off the incident with this master-sentence: "One cannot believe in anything at a time when dogs bite their masters."

Then—he was always doing this; it was his favorite gesture—he took out a little case with steel, flint, and tinder, and lit a cigarette, a cigarette which he rolled between his fingers, and then dusted the tobacco off his palms. Latterly, though before he had not dared to do so, Don Jenaro had used his steel, flint, and tinder in Madrid. Now, as his time was not long, "he had chosen the middle path," in his own words. It meant a great effort for him, who did not believe in anything, to do anything out of the way.

Don Jenaro left Madrid. He was old, and he wanted to live in peace. He betook himself to an old town of Castile. In Madrid he had already begun to use the old-fashioned tools of the smoker; but the watch-chain which was an heirloom from his grandfather, that long, narrow gold watch-chain which hung around his neck, fell across the breast of his black jacket, and after running through a buttonhole finally connected with the watch in his waistcoat pocket—that chain which, as a child, he had seen his paternal grandfather wear he had not dared to use in Madrid. But he wore it in the old town.

There Don Jenaro Pardales lived in a fine old house. The upper windows commanded a wide panorama over the fruit lands. On gray, melancholy days, when the sky was lowering, the whole landscape was a charming gradation of grays—pearl grays, silver gray, ashen gray, leaden gray. In the profoundly peaceful silence one's eyes could roam reposefully throughout that range of soft, fine shadings of color. Don Jenaro was an early riser, and he was familiar with the morning life of the whole town. In the morning the old town stirred itself a little. The fragrant smoke of chimneys went up into the blue sky. The pleasant smell of burning wood drifted through the narrow streets. Countrymen who came in with their wares uttered their long, plaintive, monotonous cries. Then silence and peace, profound tranquillity, returned to the streets, the squares, and the houses.

At the Club Don Jenaro was well-known. Everybody liked him; and when he came in, at two o'clock in the afternoon, they made room for him at the red plush table. And in the gatherings at the Club in the old town the same little scene as in Madrid had repeated itself for the past year.

"You don't believe in anything, Don Jenaro?"

"No, I don't believe in anything. Why do you ask?"

"Oh, for no special reason. I merely asked."

And then, when the cigarette was rolled and lit from the tinder, while he kept his thumb on the steel, he put the time-honored question:

"You don't know what happened to the novelist, Eladio Peña?"

"No, Don Jenaro, we don't know. What happened to him? Tell us, please."

And Don Jenaro smiled his ironical smile. "His dog bit him!"

"The deuce it did!"

"Well, I'll be damned!"

"You don't say so!"

Don Jenaro smiled his smile again, and let his sentence fall: "One cannot believe in anything at a time when dogs bite their masters."

Nowadays Don Jenaro wore round his neck that fine gold watch-chain. In the old town it did not seem so odd. Many old men could remember the time when their fathers or grandfathers wore chains like that. Don Jenaro went soberly clad in black. His low-cut waistcoat revealed his immaculate shirt. Across his black jacket the long chain gleamed like a flicker of fire-light. With the passing years, in this old town where he had lived five or six years as a child, Don Jenaro returned to the things of his childhood. Now, as he passed his hand from time to time along that fine watch-chain—with much the same gesture as a man who softly strokes his beard—as he felt the gold of the chain slip through his fingers, he experienced a deep sense of pleasure.

He had nothing to expect, nothing to desire. He could look back easily upon the past. There had been times in his youth, in the ardor of young manhood, when he had cherished ambitions to be somebody great and important. He had not succeeded in surpassing a decent mediocrity. But in this assured, deep-rooted, indestructible mediocrity he had the satisfaction of thinking about those who struggled, those who had a faith, an ideal, a political, social, or artistic belief for which they strove, for which they suffered privations and anxieties—and which perhaps they never saw realized.

Don Jenaro fought for nothing, believed in nothing. Believe? What was there in which to believe? There was no room for belief at a time of ingratitude, when life had gone mad, when people acted brutally and aggressively—a time when the very dogs bit their own masters.

At the Club they often talked about superstitions and beliefs. In old towns there are usually some believers in spiritualism and theosophy. They talked about such people as rarities. But the fact is that in the atmosphere of old towns everything has co-operated for centuries upon centuries to invest things with a deeper significance than they possess in the newer centers of life. For centuries upon centuries, while stones have grayed or mellowed and the old palaces have begun to crumble; for centuries upon centuries, while wood has warped, and roofs have rotted, and iron has rusted, how many sorrows and despairs, how many secret tragedies, have been known by those old houses, those silent rooms, those courtyards, those gardens, those narrow streets!

All this enormous, age-long accumulation of loves and longings, of anxiety and anguish, contained and concentrated within those old walls, has vanished for all there is to show; but it has left an elusive and mysterious crystallization. Even to the wayfarer, even to the stray sojourner in these towns if he is receptive, everything communicates to his spirit shudders for which he cannot find a name. At the fall of evening, in a silent room that looks upon the cypresses in a garden, while he listens to the slow tolling of the Angelus, there beat upon his brain the waves of a tide of melancholy and mystery that knows no telling.

Don Jenaro believed in nothing. In what should he believe? But, all unknown to himself, the atmosphere of the old town pervaded all his being. Don Jenaro walked abroad slowly through the streets. He laughed at those who made the conventional gestures when certain reptiles were mentioned, at those who threw a glass of water out of the window when a salt-cellar was upset on the table, at those who touched iron when they met a hump-back. Don Jenaro walked abroad slowly through the narrow streets of the old town. He was familiar with them all.

All? No, here was one with which he was not acquainted. It was a very narrow street, on a slope which must run down to the river. Don Jenaro walked slowly a little way down it: then suddenly he stopped. That seemed odd. What was that hanging from an iron bar over the door of a house? Our gentleman advanced a pace or two and stopped again. What was hanging from the iron bar was a miniature coffin—clearly, a coffin. Don Jenaro gazed at it a moment. Above the door of the house—a carpenter's shop—was a notice in big letters: BOX-MAKING. Box-making; what it meant was "Undertaking"; it was a workshop of boxes for the dead.

That day when he discovered the box-maker's shop in the Calle de Pellejeros Don Jenaro went no further. Nor did he ever pass through that street afterward. The street ran down to the river; it was the shortest way to the old Alameda; but Don Jenaro avoided using it. Our gentleman did even more than that. When he was with friends and they reached the entrance to the street, he invented some discreet but plausible reason why they should change their course.

Don Jenaro often reflected upon the absurdity of this apprehension of his. Was it possible that he, who believed in nothing, should have such a superstition? To be reluctant to pass through the street of the box-makers! The thing was really ridiculous. Was this he, Don Jenaro, the man who proclaimed every day in the Club that he believed in nothing?

"You don't believe in anything, Don Jenaro?"

"No, I don't believe in anything! Why should I?"

He was a coward, in short. Don Jenaro looked at himself, and found himself ridiculous. If he was reluctant to pass through the street of the box-makers, he had no right to say in the Club that he believed in nothing. It simply would not do. He must walk right down the street, slowly, with complete indifference.

One day Don Jenaro left his house fully decided to accomplish the great enterprise. He went his way serenely, looking about him as he went. There was the street: he could see in the distance the little coffin in front of the box-maker's shop. Don Jenaro started down the street; but suddenly he stopped. He could go no further. A mysterious force paralyzed his limbs. He went no further, halfway down the street Don Jenaro turned around and retraced his steps.

As he approached his house he found a friend waiting for him at the corner. The friend was accompanied by one of his own servants. Both of them had a serious, restrained air about them. They smiled as they met him; but their smiles were a little forced. Beating about the bush they finally broke the news to him . . . No, really it was nothing serious. The doctor said that there was no danger. Don Jenaro's wife had climbed up a ladder to wind a clock. She had fallen and cut her head badly. She was lucky not to have killed herself . . .

Yes, it was all his fault—the fault of Don Jenaro, the unbeliever. Thank Heaven that he had only gone halfway down the street! It was his fault; he was responsible for this all but fatal fall of his life's companion. He never forgave himself. He could think of nothing else; and he never went to the Club again. He took no further interest in his steel, his tinder, and his flint, nor in his gold watch-chain. One night when he went to bed he put the watch-chain in the drawer of his bedside table. There they found it. He never wore it again. . . .

PIO BAROJA

Blasa's Tavern

Pio y Nessi Baroja was born at San Sebastian in 1872. He received a medical degree from the University of Madrid, but after two years he gave up practice and devoted himself to writing. His best known novels are *The Quest, Weeds, Red Dawn, The Tree of Knowledge, Paradox* and *Caesar or Nothing.* [From *The Quest* by Pio Baroja; copyright 1922 by Alfred A. Knopf, Inc.; used by permission of the publishers; translated by Isaac Goldberg.]

SOME NIGHTS MANUEL WOULD HEAR Leandro tossing about in his bed and heaving sighs as deep as a bull's roar.

"Things are going rotten with him," thought Manuel.

The break between Milagros and Leandro was definitive. Lechuguino, on the other hand, was gaining ground: he had won over the girl's mother, would treat the proof-reader and wait for Milagros where she worked, accompanying her home.

One day, toward dusk, Manuel saw the pair near the foot of Embajadores Street; Lechuguino minced along with his cloak thrown back across his shoulder; she was huddled in her mantle; he was talking to her and she was laughing.

"What's Leandro going to do when he finds out?" Manuel asked himself. "No, I'm not going to tell him. Some witch of the neighborhood will see to it that he learns soon enough."

And thus it came about; before a month had passed, everybody in the house knew that Milagros and Lechuguino were keeping company, that he had given up the gay life in the dives of the city and was considering the continuation of his father's business—the sale of construction material; he was going to settle down and lead the life of a respectable member of the community.

While Leandro would be away working in the shoeshop, Lechuguino would visit the proof-reader's family; he now saw Milagros with the full consent of her parents.

Leandro was, or pretended to be, the only person unaware of Milagros' new beau. Some mornings as the boy passed Señor Zurro's apartment on the way down to the patio, he would encounter Encarna, who, catching sight of him, would ask maliciously after Milagros, or else sing him a tango which began:

> *Of all the crazy deeds a man commits in his life,*
> *The craziest is taking to himself a wife.*
> *(De las grandes locuras que el hombre hace,*
> *No comete ninguna como casarse.)*

Whereupon she would specify the madness and entering into details, would add at the top of her voice:

> *He's off to his office bright and early,*
> *While some neighborhood swell stays at home with his girlie.*
> *(Y por la mañana el va a la oficina,*
> *y ella queda en casa con algun vecino*
> *que es persona fina.)*

Leandro's bitterness corroded the very depths of his soul, and however much he tried to dominate his instincts, he could not succeed in calming himself. One Saturday night, as they were walking homewards along the Ronda, Leandro drew near to Manuel.

"Do you know whether Milagros talks to Lechuguino?"

"I?"

"Haven't you heard that they were going to get married?"

"Yes; so folks say."

"What would you do in my case?"

"I . . . I'd find out."

"And suppose it proved to be true?"

Manuel was silent. They walked along without a word. Soon Leandro came to an abrupt stop and placed his hand upon Manuel's shoulder.

"Do you believe," he asked, "that if a woman deceives a man, he has the right to kill her?"

"I don't believe he has," answered Manuel, staring into Leandro's eyes.

"Well, if a man has the guts he does it whether he has a right to or not.

"But, the deuce! Has Milagros deceived you? Were you married to her? You've had a quarrel; that's all."

"I'll wind up by doing something desperate. Take my word for it," muttered Leandro.

Neither spoke. They entered La Corrala, climbed up the stairways and walked into Leandro's house. They brought out supper, but Leandro didn't eat; he drank three glasses of water in succession and went out to the gallery.

Manuel was about to leave after supper, when he heard Leandro call him several times.

"What do you want?"

"Come on, let's be going."

Manuel ran out to the balcony; Milagros and her mother, from their door, were heaping insults upon Leandro.

"Outcast! Blackguard!" the proof-reader's wife was shouting. "If her father were here you wouldn't talk like that."

"I would, too, even if her grandfather were here," exclaimed Leandro, with a savage laugh. "Come on, let's be off," he added, turning to Manuel. "I'm sick and tired of these whores."

They left the gallery and were soon out of El Corralón.

"What was the matter?" asked Manuel.

"Nothing. It's all over now," answered Leandro. "I went in and said to her, nice enough, 'Listen Milagros, is it true that you're going to marry Lechuguino?' 'Yes, it is true. Is it any business of yours?' she says. 'Yes, it is,' I said to her. 'You know that I like you. Is it because he's richer than me?' 'Even if he were poorer than a church-mouse I'd marry him.' 'Bah!' 'You don't believe me?' 'All right.' Finally I got sore and I told her for all I cared she might marry a dog, and that she was a cheap street-walker. . . . It's all over now. Well, so much the better. Now we know just where we stand. Where shall we go? To Las Injurias again?"

"What for?"

"To see if that Valencia continues to put on airs when I'm around."

They crossed the wired-off surrounding path. Leandro, taking long strides, was very soon in Las Injurias. Manuel could hardly keep up with him.

They entered Blasa's tavern; the same men as on the previous night were playing cané near the stove. Of the women, only La Paloma and La Muerte were in. The latter, dead drunk, was asleep on the table. The light fell full upon her face which was swollen with erysipelas and covered with scabs; saliva drooled through the thick lips of her half-opened mouth; her tow-like hair—gray, filthy, matted—stuck out in tufts beneath the faded, greenish kerchief that was soiled with scurf; despite the shouts and the disputes of the gamblers she did not so much as blink; only from time to time she would give a prolonged snore, which, at the start was sibilant, but ended in a rasping snort. At her side Paloma, huddled on the floor near Valencia, held a tot of three or four in her arms—a pale, delicate creature who blinked incessantly—to whom she was giving whisky from a glass.

A gaunt, weak fellow wearing a small cap with a gilded number and a blue smock, passed moodily up and down before the counter; his arms hung beside his body as if they did not belong to him, and his legs were bent. Whenever it occurred to him, he took a sip from his glass; he wiped his lips with the back of his hand and would resume his languid pacing to and fro. He was the brother of the woman who owned the tavern.

Leandro and Manuel took a seat at the same table where the gamblers were playing. Leandro ordered wine, emptied a deep glass at a single gulp and heaved a few sighs.

"Christ!" muttered Leandro half under his breath. "Never let yourself go wild over a woman. The best of them is as poisonous as a toad."

Then he seemed to calm down. He gazed at the drawings scratched on the top of the table: there were hearts pierced by arrows, the names of women; he drew a knife from his pocket and began to cut letters into the wood.

When he wearied of this he invited one of the gamblers to drink with him.

"Thanks, friend," replied the gambler. "I'm playing."

"All right, leave the game. If you don't want to, nobody'll force you. Doesn't anybody want to drink with me? My treat."

"I'll have one," said a tall, bent fellow with a sickly air, who was called El Pastiri. He arose and came over to Leandro.

Leandro ordered more wine and amused himself by laughing loudly when anyone lost and in betting against Valencia.

Pastiri took advantage of the opportunity to empty one glass after the other. He was a sot, a crony of Tabuenca's and likewise dedicated himself to the deception of the unwary with ball-and-number tricks. Manuel knew him from having seen him often on la Ribera de Curtidores. He used to ply his trade in the suburbs, playing at three cards. He would place three cards upon a little table; one of these he would show, then slowly he would change the position of the other two, without touching the card he had shown; he would then place a little stick across the three cards and wager that nobody could pick out the one he had let them see. And so well was the game prepared that the card was never picked.

Pastiri had another trick on the same order, worked with three men from a game of checkers; underneath one of the men he would place a tiny ball of paper or a crumb of bread and then bet that nobody could tell under which of the three ball or crumb was to be found. If, by accident, anyone chanced upon the right man, Pastiri would conceal the crumb in his finger-nail as he turned the man up.

That night Pastiri was saturated with alcohol and had lost all power of speech.

Manuel, who had drunk a little too much, was beginning to feel sick and considered how he might manage to make his escape; but by the time he had made up his mind the tavern-keeper's brother was already locking the door.

Before he had quite done so there came in, through the space that was still left open, an undergrown fellow, shaved, dressed in black, with a visored woolen cap, curly hair and the repellant appearance of a hermaphrodite. He greeted Leandro affectionately. He was a lace-maker from Uncle Rilo's house, of dubious repute and called Besuguito (sea-bream) because his face suggested a fish; by way of more cruel sobriquet they had christened him the "Barrack hack."

The lacemaker took a sip from a glass, standing, and began to talk in a thick voice; yet it was a feminine voice, unctuous, disagreeable, and he emphasized his words with mimicked wonder, fright, and other mannerisms.

Nobody was bothered by his loquacity. Some fine day when they least expected, he informed them, the entire district of Las Injurias was going to be buried beneath the ruins of the Gas House.

"As far as I'm concerned," he went on, "this entire hollow ought to be filled in with earth. Of course, I'd feel sorry, for I have some good friends in this section."

"Ay! Pass!" said one of the gamblers.

"Yes, I'd be sorry," continued Besuguito, heedless of the interruption. "But the truth is that it would be a small loss, for, as Angelillo, the district watchman says, nobody lives here except outcasts, pickpockets and prostitutes."

"Shut up, you 'fairy'! You barrack hack!" shouted the proprietress. "This district is as good as yours."

"You're right, there," replied Besuguito, "for you ought to see the Portillo de Embajadores and las Peñuelas. I tell you. Why, the watchman can't get them to shut their doors at night. He closes them and the neighbors open them again. Because they're almost all denizens of the underworld. And they do give me such frights. . . ."

An uproar greeted the frights of Besuguito, who continued unabashed his meaningless, repetitious chatter, which was adorned with all manner of notions and involutions. Manuel rested an arm upon the table, and with his cheek upon it, he feel asleep.

"Hey you! Why aren't you drinking, Pastiri?" asked Leandro. "Do you mean to offend me? Me?"

"No, friend, I simply can't get any more down," answered the card-sharper in his insolent voice, raising his open hand to his throat. Then, in a voice that seemed to come from a broken organ, he shouted:

"Paloma!"

"Who's calling that woman?" demanded Valencia immediately, glaring at the group of gamblers.

"I," answered El Pastiri. "I want Paloma over here."

"Ah! . . . You? Well, there's nothing doing," declared Valencia.

"I said I want Paloma over here," repeated Pastiri, without looking at the bully.

The latter pretended not to have heard. The card-sharper, provoked by this discourtesy, got up and, slapping Valencia's sleeve with the back of his hand, he repeated his words, dwelling upon every syllable:

"I said that I wanted Paloma, and that these friends of mine want to talk with the lady."

"And I tell you that there's nothing doing," answered the other.

"Those gentlemen want to talk with her."

"All right. . . . Then let them ask my permission."

Pastiri thrust his face into the bully's, and looking him straight in the eye, croaked:

"Do you realize, Valencia, that you're getting altogether too damned high and mighty?"

"You don't say!" sneered Valencia, calmly continuing his game.

"Do you know that I'm going to let you have a couple with my fist?"

"You don't say!"

Pastiri drew back with drunken awkwardness and began to hunt in the inside pocket of his coat for his knife, amidst the derisive laughter of the bystanders. Then all at once, with a sudden resolve, Leandro jumped to his feet, his face as red as flame; he seized Valencia by the lapel of his coat, gave him a rude tug and sent him smashing against the wall.

The gamblers rushed into the fray; the table was overturned and there was a pandemonium of cries and curses. Manuel awoke with a frightened start. He found himself in the midst of an awful row; most of the gamblers, with the tavern-owner's brother at their head, wanted to throw Leandro out, but the raging youth, backed against the counter, was kicking off anybody that approached him.

"Leave us alone!" shouted Valencia, his lips slavering as he tried to work himself free of the men who were holding him.

"Yes, leave them alone," said one of the gamblers.

"I'll kill the first guy that touches me," warned El Valencia, displaying a long knife with black blades.

"That's the stuff," commented Leandro mockingly. "Let's see who are the red-blooded men."

"Olé!" shouted Pastiri enthusiastically, in his husky voice.

Leandro drew from the inside pocket of his sackcoat a long, narrow knife; the onlookers retreated to the walls so as to leave plenty of room for the duelists. Paloma began to bawl:

"You'll get killed! You'll get killed, I'm telling you!"

"Take that woman away," yelled Valencia in a tragic voice: "Ea!" he added, cleaving the air with his knife. "Now let's see who are the men with guts!"

The two rivals advanced to the center of the tavern, glaring furiously at each other. The spectators were enthralled by mingled interest and horror.

Valencia was the first to attack; he bent forward as if to seek out where to strike his opponent; he crouched, aimed at the groin and lunged forward upon Leandro; but seeing that Leandro awaited him calmly without retreating, he rapidly recoiled. Then he resumed his false attacks, trying to surprise his adversary with these feints, threatening his stomach yet all the while aiming to stab him in the face; but before the rigid arm of Leandro, who seemed to be sparing every motion until he should strike a sure blow, the bully grew disconcerted and once again drew back. Then Leandro advanced. The youth came on with such sangfroid that he struck terror into his opponent's heart; his face bespoke his determination to transfix Valencia. An oppressive silence weighed upon the tavern; only the sounds of Paloma's convulsive sobs were heard from the adjoining room.

Valencia, divining Leandro's resolve, grew so pale that his face turned a sickly blue, his eyes distended and his teeth began to chatter. At Leandro's first lunge he retreated, but remained on guard; then his fear overcame him and abandoning all thought of attack he took to flight, knocking over the chairs. Leandro, blind, smiling cruelly, gave implacable pursuit.

It was a sad, painful sight; all the partisans of the bully began to eye him with scorn.

"Now, you yellow-liver, you show the white feather!" shouted Pastiri. "You're flitting about like a grasshopper. Off with you, my boy! You're in for it! If you don't get out right away you'll be feeling a palm's length of steel in your ribs!"

One of Leandro's thrusts ripped the bully's jacket.

The thug, now possessed of the wildest panic, dashed behind the counter; his popping eyes reflected mad terror.

Leandro, insolently scornful, stood rigidly in the middle of the tavern; pulling the springs of his knife, he closed it. A murmur of admiration arose from the spectators.

Valencia uttered a cry of pain, as if he had been wounded; his honor, his repute as a bold man, had suffered a downfall. Desperately he made his way to the door of the back room, and looked at the panting proprietress. She must have understood him, for she passed him a key and Valencia sneaked out. But soon the door of the back room opened and the bully stood there anew; brandishing his long knife by the point he threw it furiously at Leandro's face. The weapon whizzed through the air like a terrible arrow and pierced the wall, where it stuck, quivering.

At once Leandro sprang up, but Valencia had disappeared. Then, having recovered from the surprise, the youth calmly dislodged the knife, closed it and handed it to the tavern-keeper.

"When a fellow don't know how to use these things," he said, petulantly, "he ought to keep away from them. Tell that gentleman so when you next see him."

The proprietress answered with a grunt, and Leandro sat down to receive general congratulations upon his courage and his coolness; everybody wanted to treat him.

"This Valencia was beginning to make too much trouble, anyway," said one of them. "Did as he pleased every night and he got away with it because it was Valencia; but he was getting too darned fresh."

"That's what," replied another of the players, a grim old jailbird who had escaped from the Ceuta penitentiary and who looked just like a fox. "When a guy has the nerve, he rakes in all the dough," and he made a gesture of scooping up all the coins on the table in his fingers—"and he skips."

"But this Valencia is a coward," said Pastiri in his thick voice. "A big mouth with a bark worse than his bite and not worth a slap."

"He was on his guard right away. In case of accident!" replied Besuguito in his queer voice, imitating the posture of one who is about to attack with a knife.

"I tell you," exclaimed El Pastiri, "he's a booby, and he's scared so stiff he can't stand."

"Yes, but he answered every thrust, just the same," added the lacemaker.

"Yah! Did you see him?"

"Certainly."

"Bah, you must be soused to the gills!"

"You only wish you were as sober as I. Bah!"

"What? You're so full you can't talk!"

"Go on; shut up. You're so drunk you can't stand; I tell you, if you run afoul of this guy"—and Besuguito pointed to Leandro—"you're in for a bad time."

"Hell, no!"

"That's my opinion, anyhow."

"You don't have any opinion here, or anything like it," exclaimed Leandro. "You're going to clear out and shut up. Valencia's liver is whiter than paper; it's as Pastiri says. Brave enough when it comes to exploiting boobs like you and the other tramps and low lives, . . . but when he bucks up against a chap that's all there, hey? Bah! He's a white-livered wretch, that's what."

"True," assented all.

"And maybe we won't let him hear a few things," said the escaped convict, "if he has the nerve to return here for his share of the winnings."

"I should say!" exclaimed Pastiri.

"Very well, gentlemen, it's my treat now," said Leandro, "for I've got the money and I happen to feel like it." He fished out a couple of coins from his pocket and slapped them down on the table. "Lady, let's have something to drink."

"Right away."

"Manuel! Manuel!" shouted Leandro several times. "Where in thunder has that kid disappeared?"

Manuel, following the example of the bully, had made his escape by the back door.

GABRIEL MIRO

The Woman of

Samaria

Gabriel Miro (1879–1930) was born in Alicante and studied law at the Universities of Valencia and Granada. He worked on a sacred encyclopedia in Barcelona and wrote many novels, the most famous of which are *Our Father San Daniel* and *El Obispo Leproso*. His most important book is *Figures of the Passion of Our Lord,* which portrays scenes from the life of Jesus. |From *Figures of the Passion of Our Lord;* translated by C. J. Hogarth. |

"There cometh a woman of Samaria to draw water. Jesus saith unto her: Give me to drink." *St. John* iv, 7.

FIELD-HANDS RETURNING from the plow, and craftsmen toiling in the workshop, and travelers resting in the shade of the *caravanserai,* with its turmoil of men and beasts, always turned their heads with a smile whenever the woman of Samaria, a fresh, graceful, rhythmical figure against the blue of the sky, set forth with her pitcher to the well.

The road which she followed from the compound of her homestead was the road which ran with twists and turns and undulations through the Valley of Sichem. About that road were plowed and fallow fields, and brilliant, green orchards of apple and mulberry and quince, and water-troughs fed from the slopes of Mount Gerizim, and masses of terebinth, and ancient gardens, and clumps of olive, and footpaths, and sheep-folds, and sluggish smoke-columns. For it was the region which Abraham had bought for the burial-place of his line, and Jacob afterward acquired for the price of "an hundred lambs," and held with sword and bow, and bequeathed to Joseph for a special patrimony. Also was it the region where the "Oak of the Pillar" had stood—a huge, dark, motionless, stately mass beneath whose branches Joshua had consecrated an altar in testimony to a new Covenant between Jehovah and the Chosen People, and the inhabitants of Sichem had anointed Abimelech to be their king, and Zebul deceived Gaal with a lie. And it was the region where, each afternoon, Jacob's Sepulcher threw its shadow upon a clump of palm-trees bending languidly over Jacob's Well. Hence all the countryside was great in story, and so poignantly charged with the footsteps and deaths of Patriarchs as always to seem to have quivering in its clear silences a cry, a throb, a Psalm.

And whenever the woman set forth with her pitcher to the palpitating, sparkling freshness men greeted her from their habitations, since they had long looked to see her beauty again exchange its marital bed, whilst, with the same thought, rich foreign merchants would fix upon her glistening eyes, and display for her benefit splendid packs of merchandise, and wines of delight, and many other luxuries which, but for her, would never have been seen in such a retired spot.

But always the woman replied:

"Prayer alone is become my meat and my salvation."

Wherefore the men of Sichem murmured:

"No longer is she our own Fatima. Aforetime she would listen unto our wooings, and smile unto us promises of love, and raise unto us her glorious breasts: but now she doth smile as though wearied, and as though saying in the words of the Book of Ruth: 'Call me not comely, but bitter.' Surely she is not bewailing the death of another husband, for five hath she had already, for love of, and for loathing of, their bodies. And she cannot have lost a child, for she is barren. And she cannot be fearing the loss of her possessions, seeing that never did she covet the same, but, after that they had been given to her, did use them but as an addition to the power of her grace."

So, as the woman trod Samaria's streets in solitary abstraction from love, she exhaled only a calm savor of chastity, and her eyes no longer flashed: they gleamed, rather, with the radiance of still water in moonlight.

And whenever a Samaritan returned from a journey to foreign parts she would seek him out, and say:

"Hast thou beheld yonder him who can read thoughts even the most secret, and, though a Jew, doth eat of the Samaritan's bread?"

But none had spoken but to Gentiles, or had had any dealings with dwellers in Israel save for usury.

For Deuteronomy had commanded that "thou shalt not lend money unto thine own brother."

No brotherly feeling for Samaria had the land of Judea. Had not Samaria prostituted herself to barbarous idols, and built herself a temple of Mount Gerizim, and instituted in it a ritual akin to the ritual of Jehovah, and sent unto Antioch, saying: "Come, consecrate my temple unto the Greek Zeus, seeing that my people are Sidonians, and desire not to have aught to do with Israel, who is altogether strange unto them, both in race and in habitude?"

Nor did the True Believer respect either the testaments or the marriage-bond or the charity or the hospitality or the amenities or the waters of the apostatized land. Only for gain of profit would he so much as admit the Samaritan within his boundaries. And even then he did so only under the regulations of a rigid and merciless tariff. Wherefore Samaria's resentment occasionally overflowed in forms of retaliation, and when Israel lighted beacon-fires upon his hills to proclaim the *neomenia* or entry of the Paschal season at the beginning of Nisan, Samaria similarly enflamed her heights, and, by passing the word of fire from summit to summit, induced certain devotees in Syria and Babylonia to believe that Jerusalem betimes had summoned them to the Festival of Unleavened Bread, so that eventually the *Sanhedrin* of Jerusalem had to exchange its signals of fire for proclamations by word of mouth. Similarly a Passover attended by particularly vast numbers, because the past year had been a year of plenty, was marred by men of Samaria penetrating into the Temple of God, defiling its Courts with filth and carrion, impeding the celebration of the holy rites, and turning rejoicing into woe.

Inasmuch as no returning traveler could give the woman tidings of the Lord, her anxiety increased. And when the Sichemites expressed surprise at this she retorted:

"Yet ye yourselves have both seen Him and heard Him. Surely ye have not forgotten how once He came walking over our hills and valleys like unto the bridegroom of the Psalms, and ye denied His Disciples lodging, and they did beseech the Lord with tears, saying: 'Wilt Thou that fire descend and consume them?' and He did reply: 'Not to destroy as I come, but to save'?"

And every evening the woman would descend to the Well of the Patriarch, and seat herself in the shade of its palm-trees, and sink her soul into the silence, that she might listen to every distant sound. For the place where she was waiting for the Lord was one where once His actual presence had rejoiced her, and left for ever unwinding themselves behind it memories of His aspect. It had been one noontide in the month of Sivan, when the valley had been lying ripe and ruddy and fragrant under mid-summer's breath, with cicalas chirping eagerly, and only the hum of a potter's wheel cleaving the heat.

And just beyond the village green she had been met by twelve travelers from whose worn mantles and cracked sandals there could have been shaken the mire of many days' journeying. And poor men they had been, with one who seemed to be a sort of steward to the rest, trudging with the heavy gait of a yoked bullock.

And she had cried to the travelers:

"Enter the hamlet without fear. And if no man shall give you succor, then take from my house whatsoever ye may find therein. It is open, is that house, and the whitest of all, with jasmine upon its walls."

And then she had continued upon her way, in all the gracious joyousness of her youth. And, arrived at the edge of the well enclosure, she had halted with the nervous blushes liable to befall any woman, even though a sinner, if she be beautiful.

For behold, there had been leaning upon the curb of the well, and inhaling the freshness and purity of the water, a Stranger. And in the sunlight, and as reflected against a circular patch of sky in the water, the Stranger's head had seemed to have around it a halo.

And He had raised His eyes, and looked upon her like a brother awaiting her coming. And then He had said: "Peace be unto thee!" and looked down into the blue mirror again, and added trustfully: "Give me to drink." And she had looked at Him, and thrilled with the weariness of His youthful face.

Likewise although other men always spoke to her with gallantry, as wooers, and with the sensual deference of those who see in a woman

merely feminine charm, this Stranger had looked upon her as though
she had been part of the spirit of the hour, and, even after straightening
His form to beg of her the innocent draught, and necessarily perceiving
her to be beautiful, had asked of her—only water! And the woman
had felt a subtle spell from the water come to her, and her heart seemingly share in His drinking, and once more hear the first speech addressed to her youthful beauty, and return to its first virginal condition.
And, smiling gently, timidly, she had murmured:

"How comest thou, who are a Jew, to ask water of me who am a
Samaritan?"

And the Stranger's eyes had flashed as with sudden glory, and His
form seemed to heighten, to become transfigured from that of a thirsty
youth into that of a father strong and mighty, or that of a noble come
on a visit to his estate. And He had replied:

"If thou hadst known who hath said unto thee: 'Give me to drink,'
thou wouldst have asked of him: 'Give me the water of my thirst, rather
than I thee.'"

And upon that the woman had felt re-arise in her her bad tendency
to malicious speech. And with the inclination of her gracious head
she had retorted to the Stranger's words: "The well is deep. How, therefore couldst thou have drawn water without me?" Whilst also she had
pointed to her bright, fresh pitcher of cedar-wood, and to the slender
cord around her waist.

And the Man had approached her as though with sorrowful compassion, and uttered the thrilling words:

"Whoso shall drink of the water which thou hast now taken from
the earth shall thirst again. But whoso shall drink of the water which
I do lighten shall thirst no more, but see the water of my giving remain
always within his breast, and spring to everlasting life."

Whereupon, heeding nor figure nor set of tunic nor tresses strewn
upon the herbage, but prostrating herself, the woman cried: "O Lord,
give me of Thy living water! I would fain thirst no more!"

And never since then had the water of the love of chastity which had
flowed from the grace of the Beloved failed to spring within her bosom,
and render her calm and restful after her restlessness as a sinner. Yet
still her soul was after a manner athirst, and though the thirst of a
year agone had been sated, she still would descend to the Well of Jacob,
and search the alley where hill and dale and grove and sky alike lay
charged with the Stranger's presence. But He was not there.

One evening when she was looking at her pale, repentant features in
the watery mirror, the mirror which had reflected the Lord Himself,
she heard behind her, voices and sandals coming along the road from
the Judean frontier.

And passing by she saw two strangers with neither scrip nor weapon,
but leaning upon staves, and wearing their mantles tucked up, wound
about their loins, for greater ease in walking.

And she darted forward, and hailed the men. But, though they turned their heads for a moment, they knew not who she was, and continued upon their way. And the woman overtook them, and cried:

"Surely ye are of those who once came hither with the Lord? For the likeness of you is the very likeness of His people. Yet, being of his people, how can ye pass this way without drinking of the water which that day He did ask of me, and in exchange for which He did grant unto me the living water of His grace?"

And when the men said: "Peace be to thee!" she fell down in an ecstasy of sobbing. For she said then:

"Your speech itself bringeth Him back unto my remembrance! Ye must indeed be His messengers! My soul doth bless you! But give me tidings of Him, now that I am pure throughout."

Gently the elder of the strangers, sunburnt, withered, beetling of brow, replied: "We are indeed Disciples and sowers of the word of Christ the Lord."

"Then give me such tidings as ye have! Tell me where He is lodging! Always I have borne Him within me, and keep seeking Him, yet find Him not. I wait for Him, and call upon His name, yet He never returneth. Where is He, I pray you?"

Gravely the elder man replied as he sought to detach himself and his companion:

"The peace of the Lord be upon thee!"

But she clung to their garments still, and cried: "For its peace my heart needeth more than just His name. It needeth also His eyes and His voice and His presence. I pray you bring me unto Him, that I may serve Him and anoint Him!"

A smile of sadness broke from the other Disciple as he said: "He is beside thee now, even as He is for ever beside all of us." But the woman failed to understand him, and clung to the twain.

Then there fell from the elder Apostle words which struck her heart as with flame and thunder.

For he said: "The Lord hath been put to death. He hath been put to death at Jerusalem. Yea, His Cross was raised beside her very walls. And go tell Samaria that one day the towers of the bloodthirsty city shall be trampled to the earth with the feet of men unclean."

Horror-stricken, the woman stood gazing at the lips which had loosed the blow upon her. And even when the men moved on again not a sob escaped her—her whole soul seemed, smitten to the earth, to be lying upon that road in speechlessness.

But again, suddenly, she darted forward, and said in hoarse, resolute accents: "I will yet go with you. Ye may drive me away like unto a dog, but I will follow you, and go with you until ye shall have brought me unto the land where lieth the Lord's body, that I may touch and kiss it, and, with that kiss, thrust into it my heart like unto a root seeking water."

But the elder Disciple looked at her coldly, and said:

"Woman, the Lord hath not a sepulcher. Foretold was it that He should rise again. And risen He hath."

"Then, if He be living yet, bring me unto His dwelling-place, that I may heal His wounds, or, if He hath a wife, tend Him as a servant."

"The Lord hath risen again, and ascended into Heaven, and is sitting upon the right hand of His Father. And thence hath He sent upon us the power of His Holy Spirit."

And with calm steadfastness the two Disciples continued upon their way: save that occasionally they halted to raise turbaned heads, and glance hither and thither, even as the Lord had done.

And the woman of Samaria, standing upon the road with the Tomb of Joseph casting its shadow upon her shoulders, felt in all her soul a chill desolation. And she ran to the curb of Jacob's Well, and, kissing its stones, sobbed: "O Rabbi, O Rabbi! Wherefore didst Thou rise again but to ascend into Heaven?"

LUIGI PIRANDELLO

Horse in the Moon

Luigi Pirandello (1867–1936) was born in Girigenti, Sicily. He was educated at the Universities of Rome and Bonn, where he received his Ph.D. For ten years he was a free-lance writer in Rome, gaining fame in the 1920's. Among his works are *Six Characters in Search of An Author* and *As You Desire Me* (plays) and *The Outcast, The Late Mattia Pascal* and *The Old and the Young* (novels). [From *Horse in the Moon* by Luigi Pirandello; copyright 1932 by E. P. Dutton & Co., Inc.; used by permission of the publishers; translated by Samuel Putnam.]

IN SEPTEMBER, upon that high and arid clayey plain, jutting perilously over the African sea, the melancholy countryside still lay parched from the merciless summer sun; it was still shaggy with blackened stubble, while a sprinkling of almond trees and a few aged olive trunks were to be seen here and there. Nevertheless, it had been decided that the bridal pair should spend at least the first few days of their honeymoon in this place, to oblige the bridegroom.

The wedding feast, which was held in a room of the deserted villa, was far from being a festive occasion for the invited guests. None of those present was able to overcome the embarrassment, or rather the feeling of dismay inspired in him by the aspect and bearing of that fleshy youth, barely twenty years of age, with purplish face and with the little darting black eyes, which were preternaturally bright, like a madman's. The latter no longer heard what was being said around him;

he did not eat, and he did not drink, but became, from moment to moment, redder and more purple of countenance.

Everyone knew that he had been madly in love with the one who now sat beside him as his bride, and that he had done perfectly mad things on her account, even to the point of attempting to kill himself. He was very rich, the sole heir to the Bernardi fortune, while she, after all, was only the daughter of an infantry colonel who had come there the year before, with the regiment from Sicily. But in spite of this, the colonel, who had been warned against the inhabitants of the island, had been reluctant about giving his consent to this match, for the reason that he had not wanted to leave his daughter there among people that were little better than savages.

The dismay which the bridegroom's aspect and actions inspired in the guests increased when the latter came to contrast him with his extremely young bride. She was really but a child, fresh, vivacious, and aloof; it seemed that she always shook off every unpleasant thought with a liveliness that was, at once, charming, ingenuous and roguish. Roguish as that of a little tomboy who as yet knows nothing of the world. A half-orphan, she had grown up without a mother's care; and indeed, it was all too evident that she was going into matrimony without any preparation whatsoever. Everyone smiles, but everyone felt a chill, when, at the end of the meal, she turned to the bridegroom and exclaimed:

"For goodness' sake, Nino, why so you make those tiny eyes? Let me —no, they burn! Why do your hands burn like that? Feel, Papa, feel how hot his hands are—Do you suppose he has a fever?"

The colonel, on pins and needles, did what he could to speed up the departure of the countryside guests. He wanted to put an end to a spectacle that impressed him as being indecent. They all piled into a half-dozen carriages. The one in which the colonel rode proceeded slowly down the lane and lagged a little behind, for the reason that the bridal couple, one on one side and one on the other, holding hands with the mother and father, had wanted to follow a short distance on foot, down to where the highway which led to the distant city began. At that point, the colonel leaned down and kissed his daughter on the head; he coughed and muttered: "Goodby, Nino."

"Goodby, Ida," said the bridegroom's mother with a laugh; and the carriage rattled away at a good pace, in order to overtake the others.

The two stood there for a moment gazing after it. But it was really only Ida who gazed; for Nino saw nothing, was conscious of nothing; his eyes were fastened upon his bride as she stood there, alone with him at last—his, all his—But what was this? Was she weeping?

"Daddy—" said Ida, as she waved her handkerchief in farewell. "There, do you see? He, too—"

"No, Ida—Ida dear—" and stammering, almost sobbing, trembling violently, Nino made an effort to embrace her.

"No, let me alone, please."

"I just wanted to dry your eyes—"

"Thanks, my dear; I'll dry them myself."

Nino stood there awkwardly. His face, as he looked at her, was pitiful to behold, and his mouth was half-open. Ida finished drying her eyes.

"But what's the matter?" she asked him. "You're trembling all over —No, no, Nino, for heaven's sake, no; don't stand there like that! You make me laugh. And if I once start laughing—you'll see—I'll never stop! Wait a minute; I'll wake you up."

She put her hands on his temples and blew in his eyes. At the touch of those fingers, at the breath from those lips, he felt his legs giving way beneath him; he was about to sink down on one knee, but she held him up and burst into a loud laugh:

"Upon the highway? Are you crazy? Come on, let's go! Look at that little hill over there! We shall be able to see the carriages still. Let's go look!"

And she impetuously dragged him away by one arm.

From all the countryside roundabout, where so many weeds and grasses, so many things dispersed by the hand of time lay withered, there mounted into the heat-ridden air something like a dense and ancient drought, mingling with the warm, heavy odor of the manure that lay fermenting in little piles upon the fallow fields, and with the sharper fragrance of sage and wildmint. Of that dense drought, those warm and heavy odors, that piercing fragrance, he alone was aware. She, as she ran, could hear how gaily the wood-larks sang up to the sun, from behind the thick hedges and from between the rugged yellowish tufts of burnt-over stubble; she could hear, too, in that impressive silence, the prophetic crow of cocks from distant barnyards; and she felt herself wrapped, every now and then, in the cool, keen breath that came up from the neighboring sea, to stir the few tired and yellowed leaves that were left on the almond trees, and the close-clustering, sharp-pointed, ashen-hued olive leaves.

It did not take them long to reach the hilltop; but he was so exhausted from running that he could no longer stand; he wanted to sit down, and tried to make her sit down also, there on the ground beside him, with his arm about her waist. But Ida put him off with "Let me have a look first."

She was beginning to feel restless inside, but she did not care to show it. Irritated by a certain strange and curious stubbornness on his part, she could not, she would not stand still, but longed to keep on fleeing, still farther away; she wanted to shake him up, to distract him, to distract herself as well, so long as the day lasted.

Down there, on the other side of the hill, there stretched away a devastated plain, a sea of stubble, amid which one could make out occasionally the black and meandering traces of wood-ashes that had been sprinkled there; now and again, too, the crude yellow gleam was broken by a few clumps of caper or of licorice. Away over there, as if on the other shore of that vast yellow sea, the roofs of a hamlet rose from the tall dark poplars.

And now Ida suggested to her husband that they go over there, all the way over to that hamlet. How long would it take? An hour or less. It was not more than five o'clock. Back home, in the villa, the servants must still be busy clearing away the things. They would be home before evening.

Nino made a feeble attempt at opposition, but she took him by the hands and dragged him to his feet; in a moment, she was running down the side of the hill and was off through that sea of stubble, as light and quick as a young doe. He was not fast enough to keep up with her, but, redder-faced than ever and seemingly stunned by it all, ran after her, pantingly and perspiringly, and kept calling to her to wait and give him her hand.

"Give me your hand, at least! At least, give me your hand!" he shouted.

All of a sudden, she uttered a cry and stopped short. A flock of cawing ravens had just flown up from in front of her, stretched out upon the earth, was a dead horse. Dead? No, no, it wasn't dead; it had its eyes open. Heavens, what eyes! What eyes! A skeleton, that was what it was. And those ribs! And those flanks!

Nino came up fuming and fretting:

"Come on, let's go—let's go back—at once!"

"It's alive, look!" cried Ida, shivering from compassion. "Lift its head—heavens, what eyes! Look, Nino!"

"Yes, yes," said he, panting still. "They've just put it out here—Leave it alone; let's go! What a sight! Don't you smell—?"

"And those ravens!" she exclaimed with a shudder. "Are those ravens going to eat it alive?"

"But Ida, for heaven's sake!" he implored her, clasping his hands.

"Nino that will do!" she cried. It was more than she could endure to see him so stupid and so contrite. "Answer me: what if they eat it alive?"

"What do I know about whether or not they'll eat it? They'll wait—"

"Until it dies here, of hunger, of thirst?" Her face was all drawn with horror and pity. "Just because it's old? Because it can't work any more? Ah, poor beast! What a shame! What a shame! Haven't they any heart, those peasants? Haven't you any heart, standing there like that?"

"Excuse me," he said, losing his temper, "but you feel so much sympathy for an animal—"

"And oughtn't I to?"

"But you don't feel any for me!"

"And are you an animal? Are you dying of hunger and thirst as you sit there in the stubble? You feel—Oh, look at the ravens, Nino, look, up there, circling around—Oh, what a horrible, shameful, monstrous thing!—Look—Oh, the poor beast—try to lift him up! Come, Nino,

get up; maybe he can still walk—Nino, get up, help me—shake yourself out of it!"

"But what do you expect me to do?" he burst out, exasperatedly.
"Do you expect me to drag him back? Put him on my shoulders?
What's a horse more or less? How do you think he is going to walk?
Can't you see he's half-dead?"

"And if we brought him something to eat?"

"And to drink, too?"

"Oh, Nino, you're wicked!" And the tears stood in Ida's eyes.

Overcoming her shudders, she bent over very gently to caress the
horse's head. The animal, with a great effort had managed to get to
its knees; and even in its last degrading agony, it showed the traces
of a noble beauty in head and neck.

Nino, owing possibly to the blood that was pounding in his veins,
possibly owing to the bitterness and contempt she had manifested, or
to the perspiration that was trickling from him, now suddenly felt his
breath failing him; he grew giddy, his teeth began chattering, and he
was conscious of a weird trembling all over his body. He instinctively
turned up his coat collar, and with his hands in his pockets, went over
and huddled down in gloomy despair upon a rock some distance away.

The sun had already set, and from the distant highway could be
heard the occasional sound of horses' bells.

Why were his teeth chattering like that? For his forehead was
burning up, the blood in his veins stung him, and there was a roaring
in his ears. It seemed to him that he could hear so many far-away bells.
All that anxiety, that spasm of expectation, her coldness and caprice,
that last foot-race, and that horse there, that cursed horse—Oh, God!
was it a dream? A nightmare within a dream? Did he have a fever?
Or perhaps, a worse illness? Ah! How dark it was, God—how dark!
And now, his sight was clouding over. And he could not speak, he
could not cry out. He tried to call "Ida, Ida!" but he could not get the
words out of his parched throat.

Where was Ida? What was she doing?

She had gone off to the distant hamlet, to seek aid for that horse;
she did not stop to think that the peasants had brought the animal
there to die.

He remained there, alone upon the rock, a prey to those growing
tremors; and as he sat there, huddled to himself like a great owl upon
a perch, he suddenly beheld a sight that seemed—Ah, yes—he could see
it plainly enough now—an atrocious sight, like a vision from another
world. The moon. A huge moon, coming slowly up from behind that
sea of stubble. And black against that enormous, vapory copper disk,
the headstrong head of that horse, waiting still with its neck stretched
out—it had, perhaps, been waiting like that always, darkly etched upon
that copper disk, while from far up in the sky could be heard the caw
of circling ravens.

When Ida, angry and disillusioned, came groping her way back over the plain, calling "Nino, Nino!" the moon had already risen; the horse had dropped down as if dead; and Nino—where was Nino? Oh, there he was over there; he was on the ground, too.

Had he fallen asleep there?

She ran up to him, and found him with a death-rattle in his throat. His face, also, was on the ground; it was almost black, and his eyes, nearly closed, were puffed and bloodshot.

"Oh, God!"

She looked about her, as if in a swoon. She opened her hands which held a few dried beans that she had brought from the hamlet over there to feed to the horse. She looked at the moon, then at the horse, and then at the man lying on the ground as if dead. She felt faint, assailed as she was by the sudden suspicion that everything she saw was unreal. Terrified, she fled back to the villa calling in a loud voice for her father, her father—to come and take her away. Oh, God! away from that man with the rattle in his throat—that rattle, the meaning of which she did not understand! away from under that mad moon, away from under those cawing ravens in the sky—away, away, away—

IGNAZIO SILONE

The Travelers

Ignazio Silone, born in 1900, is the pen name of Seconde Tranquilli. He early joined the Peasant League, dedicated to opposing the First World War and the Fascist Regime. He was imprisoned in Italy and Spain, then became an exile in Switzerland. He returned to Italy in 1945. His best known works are *Fontamara, Bread and Wine, The School for Dictators* and *The Seed Beneath the Snow*. [From *The Seed Beneath the Snow* by Ignazio Silone; copyright 1942 by Harper and Brothers; used by permission of the publishers; translated by Frances Frenaye.]

IN THE VALLEY BELOW there were no lights or other signs of human habitation; only in the distance, halfway up the enclosing mountains, shone the clustered lights of extensive villages, several hours away. All of a sudden Pietro was overcome by fatigue; the abrupt change of altitude and the emotion wrought in him by the landscape caused his heart to beat fast and irregularly. Faustina noticed his weariness; she took the reins from his hands and counseled him to close his eyes. But the gig bounced incessantly and there was no headpiece against which he could lean back; to fall asleep might mean falling out under the wheels. Pietro chose rather to slide down onto the floor and curl up on a suitcase, leaning his head against the seat. If only he could rest his aching back! The position was comfortable; he felt lucky to have discovered it. But his outlook was restricted; he could see no more than if he were shut up in a barrel. In front of him the only visible object was the rear end of the horse and, after a while, this dark, heavy, monstrous reality became a haunting vision, a self-sufficient reality, a bit of autonomous animal life consisting of two enormous buttocks, a short thick black tail and the shadowy opening of the intestines. Pietro was covered with cold perspiration; he tried to see the horse's head, mane, back or legs; he fought desperately to reconstruct before his eyes the whole horse in order to escape from the heart-rending vision of this detached mass of jet-black flesh which filled his whole horizon and shook continuously, involving his eyes in its up-and-down animal movement.

"What's the matter? Are you having a nightmare?" asked Faustina in a voice that was balsam to his heart.

He hid his face in a corner of her coat; she ran her hand over his head caressingly, but this was the limit of her daring; it seemed to be the very most that she could allow herself.

"Try to sleep," she said; "we've a long way to go."

Pietro closed his eyes. The valley was gradually filled with a constant, ever louder booming sound, perhaps from a river below. It must have seemed to Pietro the sound of Time which had once more begun to flow about him, the bouncing gig a frail bark on its waves. Much later, when he opened his eyes, a house appeared down the road, with a lamp hanging outside it; farther on was the entrance to a sizable village. The travelers' first impulse was one of relief, a hailing of "Land, land!" which wiped out the fatigue of the journey. But their second thought was one of embarrassment at the ambiguous situation in which they were about to find themselves and which neither one had dared to mention to the other along the way. Now it seemed to both of them too late to mention it at all and they avoided even looking at each other. Two carabinieri whom they saw on the main street of the village had the mournful air of prison guards making their rounds.

"Where's a decent hotel?" Pietro asked them.

"There's only one, where the road turns, down there in the square," answered one of the carabinieri, "but it's more of an inn than a hotel."

At the inn, after repeated loud knocks, a man answered and, before coming out to meet them, lit a lamp over the door which threw its light over the two travelers and a swinging sign: "Albergo Vittoria già del Commercio." Pietro noticed that Faustina was exceedingly pale.

"Faustina," he whispered hurriedly, "you have nothing to fear."

While the exaggeratedly voluble landlord looked after the horse and the gig, a sleepy half-dressed woman took their suitcases and escorted them up a dark smelly stairway to the only free room, on the third floor.

"Have you no other room?" Pietro insisted.

"No," the woman answered. "And what would you be wanting

with it? Did you bring your children with you? If you like I can put an extra mattress on the floor."

Then, as neither of them made answer, "Good night and a good rest to you," said the woman, anxious to go back to bed. With that she disappeared, closing the door behind her.

The room contained an immense double bed, a regular tournament ground, a bed of a ritual enormousness proper to an age of matriarchy. At either side were the customary smelly night-tables, ready to emit an odor of ammonia when they were opened. On one wall hung a portrait of the Black Virgin of Loreto, a holy-water font and a branch of olive. Faustina stood looking out the window; Pietro sat down on a suitcase.

"Faustina," he said, "I am sorry there was no way out of such a tiresome and ambiguous situation. I am very ill at ease, believe me."

"It's not your fault, Pietro," she said without turning around. "You needn't apologize. The circumstances are to blame, you know that."

"Faustina," he said, "if circumstances intended to play a trick on us, then it's up to us to turn the tables on them and laugh at their expense. I hope you'll help me do just that."

"How, Pietro?" she asked, turning toward him.

"No one can oblige us to act like the characters of a cheap novel, Faustina," explained Pietro, "simply because we are not such characters. If we are modestly and frankly ourselves, we can laugh at circumstances. Practically speaking, the main difficulty is resolved by my predilection for sleeping on the floor. Don't look as if you didn't believe me, Faustina; if you are in doubt, you can ask Simone tomorrow: there were no beds in his barn and yet I never slept better in my life. I'm going to take a pillow and a blanket and settle down on the floor. Good night, Faustina."

"But, Pietro, I've always wanted to sleep on the floor," answered Faustina indignantly. "I'm strong and I've never been ill; you can ask anyone you like about that; you've seen for yourself during our journey that I had not a single uncomfortable moment. That you can't deny! Don't be stubborn, Pietro; get into the bed and I'll take the floor."

"Faustina," said Pietro with all the firmness he could muster, "let me tell you that you can't be domineering with me. You are my guest and a woman into the bargain—let's forget that but, after all, you are a woman, undeniably—and there's an end to it: you go to bed and I'll lie here on the floor where I assure you I'll be perfectly comfortable because I'm used to sleeping there. Good night, Faustina, let's not discuss it any longer."

"Pietro, if you think you can win out by acting first and talking later, you are very much mistaken. Poor fellow, you haven't the slightest idea of my obstinacy. I'll take a pillow and a blanket and occupy this corner of the floor; you can do what you like but the wisest thing, since you are so tired, would be to go to bed. Good night, Pietro."

The floor was paved with dark red tiles with blue and yellow markings; it was uneven as if a river had been sweeping over it for years. Pietro's slender, curved body, wrapped in a yellow wool blanket, took on the shape of the keel of a boat half-buried in the sand and the pulsing irregular beat of his heart was like the vibration of a motor which refused to be put out of commission. Faustina had lain down near the door, her head resting on one open hand; she seemed to have gone to sleep and her motionless body under the blue blanket had the immobility of a figure on a sculptured tomb. It was the month of March and all night long two cats on a neighboring roof kept up a continuous stream of calls and invocations in a languorous and passionate key. Pietro, wrapped in deep sleep, only once opened his eyes. He saw Faustina at the other end of the room kneeling with her hands folded in prayer and her head against the wall. He closed his eyes again immediately so as not to disturb her. When he woke up in the morning, she had just finished washing her face in a tiny enameled basin which she had filled with water from a chipped earthenware pitcher. Pietro held his breath: in the early morning light she seemed even lovelier than before; from where he lay on the floor she appeared taller, more graceful, lighter and airier than her usual self, an enchanting, shady palm tree; if only he could climb up and gather its fragrant hidden fruits, sweeter than everything sweet, then greedily enjoy them, stretched out in the still shade. As she stood in front of a small mirror, precisely and gracefully piling up on her head the fragrant river of her chestnut hair, her beauty was revealed after the fashion of a flower in the morning sun; the molding of her breasts, the easy swing of her shoulders, the olive skin on either side of the pale blue shoulder-straps of her undershirt. She saw in the mirror that Pietro was awake.

"Oh, good morning! Did you sleep well?"

"Like a log. And you?"

Pietro summoned up his strength to get dressed: first he put his hat on his head and knotted his tie, then he lay back to rest. In order to reach his shoes, he would have to get up: what an absurd order of things. After he had got his shoes on, he snatched another moment of rest; then, when he had tied his shoelaces, he rested again.

"I have never been able to fathom, Faustina," he confessed solemnly, "why we have to take off our shoes every night, only to put them on again in the morning. Mind, it's not the effort that I find demoralizing but the senselessness and superfluousness of it."

"Your ancestors must have worn sandals, Pietro."

"All our ancestors wore sandals, Faustina, every single one of them. Shoes, like cigarettes, were inflicted upon us by the Piedmontese. Faustina, to whom do those suspicious-looking suitcases there in the corner belong?"

"The two big leather ones are yours, Pietro, as you very well know."

"Mine? Faustina, you are joking. I've not owned a suitcase since I left school; I get along very well with a few handkerchiefs and an extra pair of socks; I wash my shirt and hang it up to dry at night. Why should I burden myself with heavy and suspicious-looking baggage?"

"Donna Maria Vincenza gave them to Severino yesterday; I've told you that before, Pietro, don't you remember? Severino told me that your grandmother had worked for a whole month over your wardrobe; she filled the cases with fine linen and she was even going to embroider your initials, P.S., on the shirts when she realized that they were not quite suitable."

"P.S.? Oh, Public Safety, and *post scriptum;* what an idea! How could my grandmother, sensible as she is, think up anything of the kind? Faustina, I know that P.S. are my so-called initials but don't you think they are ridiculous? Can I be P.S.? Well, let's see; have you the keys to the suitcases?"

"The keys?"

Don Severino had forgotten to give them to her and Pietro was triumphant.

"You see what it is to travel with suitcases!" he observed.

While Pietro was washing, Faustina decided to go down to the kitchen to order breakfast.

"What would you like?" she asked Pietro.

"Some sweet dates and a fresh coconut," he answered vaguely. Then he realized that he was talking nonsense and he excused himself: "I was going through an attack of anthropophagy, yes, of pure cannibalism. Forgive me, Faustina, but it may happen to anyone; I'm really sorry. Just order black coffee for me, Faustina, some that's really strong."

Faustina understood not a word of what he was stammering and, slightly worried, she went down to the kitchen to order the coffee. The hostess, an easygoing soul, all sugar and honey, received her affably and, to establish her trustworthiness, said that her name was Sora Olimpia and that she had just taken a dose of salts, because her digestion was so delicate that she could stand no stronger laxative. It was clear that the purpose of this divagation was to inspire Faustina to confide in her.

"You two quarreled last night, didn't you?" added Sora Olimpia with an understanding smile. "Excuse me, I have no wish to be indiscreet, but while the girl was sweeping the hall outside your room this morning she put her eye to the keyhole and saw your husband sleeping on the floor. You musn't be embarrassed, you know; such things happen in the best of families and then it's easy to see that you've not been long married. Ah, the first days are always difficult. I need only tell you that for a while I quarreled with my husband regularly every night. Young husbands are either unbearably enthusiastic or else they are so inexperienced that they would try the nerves of a saint. May I venture to give you some advice, my lady?"

"For the love of heaven, please don't, I beg of you," Faustina managed to implore her.

By the light of day, the landlady's husband, too, seemed a good-natured sort: jovial, familiar and anxious to please. Whatever his guests might want, they had only to call on Sor Quintino. He met Pietro coming down the stairs and could not resist expressing regret that he had spent the night on the cold, hard floor.

"You don't need to apologize," he assured him, "there's no harm done and I'm not in the least shocked. An innkeeper sees a little of everything. When my wife was sweeping the stairs this morning, she happened to look through the keyhole and saw you lying on the floor. At first she was frightened, thinking you were dead, but then she called me and I reassured her. It's too bad to sleep on the floor when a man has a pretty little wife like yours, but don't be discouraged, my friend, it's always hard at the start. Persevere, that's the best advice I can give you; you may succeed tomorrow where you failed today. Young wives have the most exaggerated ideas of marriage, equaled only by their complete ignorance. It's enough to make even a hermit lose patience. You have no children? Very wrong, my friend; very, very, wrong. If I can give you some practical advice . . . Excuse me, I didn't mean to offend you."

LAURO DE BOSIS

The Story of My Death

Lauro de Bosis was born in Rome in 1901. He was first known as the author of a lyrical drama, *Icaro*. *The Story of My Death* was written on October 2, 1931 and sent to a friend with the request that it be published in case he failed to return from a flight over Rome, during which he dropped anti-fascist leaflets. He either was shot down or fell into the sea for lack of fuel. [From *The Story of My Death* by Lauro de Bosis; copyright 1934 by Oxford University Press; used by permission of the publishers and Ruth Draper.]

TOMORROW AT THREE O'CLOCK, in a meadow on the Côte d'Azur, I have a rendezvous with Pegasus.

Pegasus is the name of my airplane. It has a russet body and white wings; and though it is as strong as eighty horses, it is as slim as a swallow. Drunk with petrol, it leaps through the sky like its brother of old, but in the night it can glide at will through the air like a phantom. I found it in the Hercynian forest, and its old master will bring it to me on the shores of the Tyrrhenian Sea, believing in perfect sincerity that it will serve the pleasures of an idle young Englishman. My bad accent has not awakened his suspicions; I hope he will pardon my subterfuge.

And yet we are not going in search of chimeras, but to bear a message of liberty across the sea to a people that is in chains. To drop figures of speech (which I had to use in order to leave the origins of my airplane discreetly vague) we are going to Rome to scatter from the air these words of liberty which, for seven years, have been forbidden like a crime. And with reason, for if they had been allowed they would have shaken the Fascist tyranny to its foundation within a few hours.

Every régime in the world, even the Afghan and the Turkish, allows its subjects a certain amount of liberty. Fascism alone, in self-defense, is obliged to annihilate thought. It cannot be blamed for punishing faith in liberty, and fidelity to the Italian Constitution more severely than parricide: that is its only chance of existence. It cannot be blamed for deporting thousands of citizens without trial, or for meting out several thousand years of imprisonment in the space of four years. How could it dominate a free people if it did not terrorize them with its garrison of three hundred thousand mercenaries? Fascism has no choice. If one shares its point of view, one is obliged to declare with its apostle Mussolini: "Liberty is a rotten carcass." If one merely wishes it to last, one must approve the murder of Matteotti and the rewards meted out to his murderers, the destruction of all the newspapers of Italy, the sacking of the house of Croce, the millions spent on espionage and on *agents provocateurs,* in short, the sword of Damocles suspended over the head of every citizen.

I know that the Austrians in 1850, the Bourbons and the other tyrants of Italy never went thus far; they never deported people without trial; the total number of their condemnations never reached the figure of seven thousand years' imprisonment in four years. Above all, they never enrolled in their army of mercenaries the very sons of Liberals as Fascism does. It takes the children from all families (even if they be Liberal or Socialist) at the age of eight, imposing on them the uniform of executioners and giving them a barbarous and warlike education. "Love the rifle, worship the machine-gun, and do not forget the dagger," wrote Mussolini in an article for children.

One cannot both admire Fascism and deplore its excesses. It can only exist because of its excesses. Its excesses are its logic. For Fascism, the logic of its existence is to exalt violence and to strike Toscanini in the face. They say that the murder of Matteotti was a mistake; from the Fascist point of view, it was a stroke of genius. They say that Fascism is wrong to use torture to extort confessions from its prisoners; but if it wants to live it cannot do otherwise. The foreign press must understand this. One cannot expect Fascism to become peaceful and human without desiring its complete annihilation. Fascism has grasped this, and for several years Italy has been turned into a great prison where children are taught to adore their chains and to pity those who are free. The young people of twenty can remember no other atmosphere. The name of Matteotti is almost unknown to them. Since the age of thirteen, they have been taught that men have no rights except those which the State has the goodness to grant them, according to its whim. Many believe it. The myth that Mussolini has saved Italy from Bolshevism is accepted without discussion. But it must not be thought that Italy is deceived. The proof that she is by a very great majority profoundly anti-Fascist is given to us by the régime itself, through the fear it shows of all whispering, and the ferocity with which it punishes the slightest expression of free thought. A régime that knows its own strength does not need to resort to such measures.

In June 1930 I started to put in circulation bi-monthly letters, of a strictly constitutional character, explaining the necessity that all men of law and order should be in accord in preparation for the day when Fascism should fall. Since Fascism seems to have adopted the motto "after us the deluge," the initiative was most opportune, and as a matter of fact, the letters, according to the principle of the snowball, began to circulate by thousands. For five months I carried on the work alone, sending every fortnight six hundred letters signed "National Alliance," with the request that each recipient should send on six copies. Unfortunately, in December, during a short voyage which I was obliged to make abroad, the police arrested the two friends who had agreed to post the letters during my absence. They were subjected to torture and condemned to fifteen years' imprisonment. One of them, Mario Vinciguerra, one of the best-known writers of Italy, literary and art critic, although he was not well at the time, was left all night entirely naked (a night in December) on the roof of police headquarters in Rome. As a result of repeated blows on the head he has remained completely deaf in one ear. He was thrown into a cell six feet square, where there was not even a chair to sit on, and from which every morning his bed was removed. After the protest of foreign papers and of eminent political personages, both English and American, his conditions were bettered. Mussolini even went so far as to offer their liberty to both men if they would write a letter of submission, but this they refused to do.

The day on which I read of the arrest of my friends, I was on the point of crossing the frontier to return to Italy. My first instinct, naturally, was to go to Rome to share their fate, but I realized that the duty of a soldier is not to surrender, but to fight to the end. I decided immediately to go to Rome, not in order to surrender, but to carry on the work of the National Alliance by throwing four hundred thousand letters from the air, and then, either to fall in fighting or return to my base to make other plans. The sky of Rome had never been flown by enemy airplanes. I shall be the first—I said to myself—and I began at once to prepare the expedition. The venture was not an easy one, because for a poet it is always difficult even to earn his daily bread, and if he is exiled besides, and to cap the climax in a year of crisis, it is not surprising if he quickly descends to the lowest degrees of a Bohemian life. And then, I did not even know how to drive a motor-cycle, not to mention an airplane! I began by finding employment as a *concierge* at the Hotel Victor Emmanuel III, rue de Ponthieu. My Republican friends said that I was rightly punished there where I had sinned! To tell the truth I was not only *concierge* but also bookkeeper and telephone operator. Often three or four bells would ring at the same time, and I would cry up the stairs in a stentorian voice, "Irma, two portions of butter for number 35!" As a preparation for my raid over Rome it was not very effective. However, between the baker's bills and the clients' receipts, I was writing a message to the King of Italy and studying the map of the Tyrrhenian Sea. The rest of my preparation is the most interesting part of the story, but unfortunately it must remain secret.

In May I made my first solo flight in a Farman machine near Versailles. Then, having heard that my secret had reached the ears of the Fascists, I disappeared, and appeared again under another name in England. On July 13th I left Cannes in an English biplane, carrying with me eighty kilos of tracts. As I had only done five hours of solo flying I went alone so as not to risk the life of a friend. Unfortunately an accident on the coast of Corsica ended my venture, and I had to escape, leaving my airplane in a field. My secret was now revealed. In Italy they had no difficulty in realizing who the mysterious pilot was. The English and French police began a search for me with a diligence that flattered me; they even disputed my portrait. I ask their pardon for the trouble that I have caused them.

The worst of it was that I could now no more rely on the surprise, my greatest chance for success. None the less, Rome became for me as Cape Horn to the Flying Dutchman: dead or alive I swore to get there. My death—however undesired by me personally, who have so many things to achieve—could not but add to the success of my flight. As all the dangers lie on the return flight, I shall not die until after I have delivered my four hundred thousand letters, which will only be the better *recommandées*! After all, it is the question of giving a small example of civic spirit, and to draw the attention of my fellow citizens to their real situation. I am convinced that Fascism will not end until some twenty young people sacrifice their lives in order to awaken the spirit of the Italians. While during the Risorgimento there were thousands of young men who were ready to give their lives, today there are very few. Why? It is not that their courage and their faith are less than that of their fathers. It is because no one takes Fascism seriously. Beginning with its leaders, everyone counts on its speedy fall, and it seems out of proportion to give one's life to end something that will collapse by itself. That is a mistake. It is necessary to die. I hope that many others will follow me and will at last succeed in rousing public opinion.

It only remains for me to give the text of my three messages. In the first, to the King, I have sought to interpret the sentiment of the mass of my people in making a summary of my sentiment. I think that a Republican as well as a Monarchist can subscribe to it. We only put the question: for Liberty or against it? The King's grandfather, after the most terrible defeat in the history of Italy, resisted the Austrian marshal who wished to force him to abrogate the Constitution. Does the King after the greatest victory of Italian history (a victory of Liberals) really wish to let the last remnant of this Constitution perish without a single gesture?

Besides my letters, I shall throw down several copies of a splendid book by Bolton King, *Fascism in Italy*. As one throws bread on a starving city, one must throw history books on Rome.

After having flown over Corsica and the Island of Monte Cristo at a height of twelve thousand feet, I shall reach Rome about eight o'clock, having done the last twenty kilometers gliding. Though I have only done seven and a half hours of solo flying, if I fall it will not be through fault of pilotage. My airplane only flies at one hundred fifty kilometers an hour, whereas those of Mussolini can do three hundred. There are nine hundred of them, and they have all received the order to bring down at any cost, with machine-gun fire, any suspicious airplane. However little they may know me, they must realize that after my first attempt I have not given up. If my friend Balbo has done his duty, they are there waiting for me. So much the better; I shall be worth more dead than alive.

L. de B.

Here are the Texts:

I

THE NATIONAL ALLIANCE
TO THE KING OF ITALY

Your Majesty,

There is a sacred agreement between the King and the People to which You pledge Your oath. When You called us in the name of that agreement, to defend the freedom of Italy and the principles which You vowed to uphold, we joined, up to the number of six million, and six hundred thousand died at Your command. Today in the name of the same principles, trampled on as never before, in the name of Your honor as a King, and in the name of our dead, we must remind You of that agreement.

Six hundred thousand citizens have laid down their lives at Your bidding in order to set two cities free: is it Your will that an infinitely heavier yoke hangs over all Italy during these past years? Are You really willing, after Vittorio Veneto, to break that agreement which Your great ancestor kept after Novara?

Seven years ago we saw You sign the decrees of Radetzky with the pen of Charles Albert, but we do not want to lose faith in You. You led us to victory and for twenty-four years You have been the champion of liberty. We cannot forget it. We received a free Italy from our fathers. Is it to be You the victorious King, who will pass it on to our sons, enslaved? Your Majesty, we will not believe it.

Many have lost faith in the Monarchy. Do not allow their number to grow. Do not let the people of Italy follow the example of Spain and hold You responsible for their oppression. How can we go on having faith in

You if the best among us are punished for this faith as though it were the worst of crimes, and all this in Your name?

The Italian people who suffer the shame of being called a flock of servile sheep by the world, do not know whether You are on their side or with the garrison of their oppressors.

Your Majesty, choose. There is no third way.

From the depth of their despair forty million Italians are watching you.

THE DIRECTORATE.

II

THE NATIONAL ALLIANCE

Rome.   Year VIII after the Matteotti Murder.

Citizens,

You have set up an altar to the Unknown hero of Liberty, but you allow it to be desecrated daily by those who imprison everyone that still believes in Liberty. This Hapsburg in a black shirt has crept into his palace again and he is an outrage to all our dead. That Liberty for which they gave their life h . calls "a putrified corpse," and, unhampered, he tramples on it these past nine years.

Six hundred thousand citizens died that two cities might be liberated: how long will you bear with the man who holds all Italy enslaved?

For nine years you have been told that freedom of conscience must be sacrificed for the sake of a strong and capable government. After nine years you see that you have enjoyed not only the most tyrannical and corrupt but also the most bankrupt of all governments. You have given up Liberty only to find yourselves deprived also of bread!

Fascism, encamped among you like a foreign garrison, besides corrupting your very souls, destroys your substance; it paralyzes the economic life of the country, it wastes milliards to prepare for war and to hold you oppressed, it allows National expenditure to swell enormously because you no longer control it, and abandons the country to the rapacity of its starving hierarchy. While it boasts of its "world prestige," the world looks with horror at a régime which, in order to reduce you to slavery, is bound logically to strike Toscanini and to exalt the brutality of its henchmen.

Citizens, do not let yourselves be frightened by the gangs which you yourselves pay, nor by this "Radetzky of 1848": the second Risorgimento will triumph like the first. The National Alliance has launched its programme of a union of all forces against Fascism. The ferocious Bourbonism of the sentences passed on some of its leaders proves to you how much its programme frightens the régime. Gather in Alliance! The Spaniards have freed their country: do not betray yours!

THE DIRECTORATE.

III

THE NATIONAL ALLIANCE

Rome.   Year VIII after the Matteotti Murder.

Whoever you are, you are sure to be a severe critic of Fascism, and you must feel the servile shame. But even you are responsible for it by your inaction. Do not seek to justify yourself with the illusion that there is nothing to be done. That is not true. Every man of courage and honor is quietly working for a free Italy. Even if you do not want to join us, there are always TEN THINGS which you yourself can do. You can, and therefore you must.

1. Do not assist at any Fascist celebration.

2. Never buy a Fascist newspaper. They are all lies.

3. Do not smoke (the tobacco monopoly provides Fascism with three billion lires a year, enough to pay for its worst extravagances. Act toward the new Radetzky as the Milanese did toward the old. Thus the Five Days began).

4. Do no action and speak no word in praise of the régime.

5. Boycott all the servants of the régime in your personal and business relations. They are your exploiters.

6. Boycott or hamper every Fascist initiative by a policy of obstructionism. Even the best initiatives only serve to add another chain to your burden. (Bottai said: "The Corporative State is the finest police measure we have yet found.")

7. Accept nothing of Fascism. Whatever it offers you is the price of your slavery.

8. Circulate the leaflets of the National Alliance. Spread every piece of truthful news you may get hold of. The truth is always anti-Fascist.

9. Make a chain of trusted friends on whom you may rely whatever happens.

10. Believe in Italy and in Freedom. The defeatism of the Italian people is the real foundation of the Fascist régime. Tell others of your belief and fervor. We are in the fullness of the Risorgimento. The new oppressors are fiercer and more corrupt than the old, but they will also fall. They are only united by a conspiracy, and we are bound by the will to be free. The Spanish people have freed their country. Do not despair of yours.

THE DIRECTORATE.

AQUILINO RIBEIRO

The Last Faun

Aquilino Ribeiro was born in 1885 in the province of Beira, and studied at the Sorbonne. He returned to Portugal to teach school and lecture at the University of Lisbon. Many of his tales are about the Portuguese peasants. His best known books are *Garden of Storms, Lands of the Demon* and *Fauns Roam the Woods*. [From *Filhas de Babilonia;* used by permission of A. A. Wyn, Inc.; translated by Samuel Putnam.]

ON THAT BRIGHT SUNDAY, a Sunday given over to the glorious rites of Our Lady of Mercy, Padre Jesuino was about to rise from the confessional, after having absolved Ana Fusca of a hundred small sins, when there at his feet, trembling all over, eyes lowered, cheeks aflame, was the kneeling figure of Maria da Encarnaçao. Short of temper where the over-zealous devotions of pious ladies were concerned, and all the more so by reason of the fact that the candles for the mass were already lighted, while he still had a baptism to perform, Padre Jesuino received her none too graciously and with a *per signum crucis* that was hastier than the gesture he would have used in shooing a hen from the garden. Having quickly run through the preliminary prayers, he said to her, in an impatient tone of voice:

"Hurry, my daughter, tell me what it is. Have you a mortal sin on your conscience?"

"I went to confession and received communion one week ago today, at the mission of the Two Churches. I have no mortal sin to confess."

"Well, then!"

"Father," she said, with an air of firm resolve, "every night I hear a voice: 'Maria da Encarnaçao, thou shalt go up to the Mountain; without stick or stone, thou shalt do away with this fear!' Either I am greatly mistaken, or it is Our Lord who is giving me the task of putting an end to what is happening to the other girls."

The abbot gravely regarded this fair-haired girl of twenty, with the bright eyes and the simplicity of an angel, the only one in his congregation who followed the portions of the holy sacrifice in a prayer book. She had been a dainty, frolicsome little lass until Padre Baldomero came along, mounted on his black mule, as he went from place to place preaching his apostolic mission. He had filled her soul with a vehement contempt for the world and a fondness for all the practices of mystic devotion. Ever since she had listened to the missionary, her merry voice was no longer to be heard at corn-huskings and along the road on pilgrimages, nor was her gaze ever once lifted coquettishly to meet the glance of another. The charming voice which God had given her was now wholly reserved for God's use, in litanies and benedicites, and no one could steal those eyes away from their ineffable vistas of ecstasy and the contemplation of Jesus, the beloved bridegroom. The latter took on a delicate beauty as he hung there in effigy, in his vermilion-colored tunic, bordered in blue and spangled with gold; to the elect, he held out the promise of infinite joys beyond the grave. The short of the matter is, thanks to Maria da Encarnaçao's persevering efforts, the Society of the Sacred Heart of Jesus had been installed in the lukewarm town; and as a result, at that hour of the afternoon when tinkling cowbells were wont to be heard from the pasture-lands, the slumbering church-bells now rang out, summoning worshipers for the month of May, the month of St. Joseph, the Christ-Child's novena, and, during Holy Week, the Stations of the Cross. She went to confession every Sunday and received communion from Padre Jesuino's gnarled, tobacco-stained fingers; that is, providing she was not engaged in seeking sanctification elsewhere, at some solemn function in a neighboring church, from the long, pale fingers of a young priest. Padre Jesuino, a preceptor of boys, a huntsman, sower of grain rather than of souls, was repugnant to her taste for the spiritual; but he was her ordained pastor, and so she resigned herself to being the mistress of a house of worship that was very badly kept. Candlesticks, lamps, vases were now polished until they shone; and Maria da Encarnação's fingers were never more industrious and clever in fitting a dress than they were, of a Sunday morning, in decking the altars with flowers from the garden—from the first of the season to the last that were to be had.

This ascetic passion little by little laid hold of her, to such an extent that one night she was led to join a pilgrimage to Lamego, in the company of a group of young girls whom Padre Baldomero was conducting to Spain for a retreat. She left behind her, at home, an aged father and a paralyzed mother, and the foolish girl grew ashamed of what she had done and turned back; but this in no way diminished her fervor for the divine. She had the feeling that she was to be one of the Blessed, like St. Inez or St. Iria—and she proclaimed it in a voice for all to hear. Meanwhile, she continued to clutch at all the cassocks and to run about to all the feast-days. As a consequence of this activity, her fine rose-colored skin began to take on the mummified hue that is common to elderly virgins.

It was in one of her visionary moments that Pedro Jirigodes saw her and was smitten with her. In a young girl's eyes, he had certain drawbacks. He was forty years old, for one thing, with a reputation as a *matador*—which had enabled him to put by an enviable share of this world's goods—and an unprepossessing appearance, conferred upon him by his eyebrows bristling beneath a forehead to match and his heavy, very black and drooping mustache, which completely hid his mouth. But Pedro Jirigodes was somebody. His costume consisted of a dark-colored cashmere suit, a straw hat slouched down over his eyes, and a watchchain with big links and a piece of pottery as a charm. Such was the way in which he always appeared at fairs and other functions, kerchief waving, hand affably outstretched—How goes it, friend?—that was Sr. Jirigodes for you. His income was derived from certain church lands, bid in at Viseu behind closed doors, and from money loaned out at a high rate of interest. He did not do a stroke of work; when he was not taking a stroll, he was out hunting, and when he was not hunting, he was down at the river fishing. He was, above all, a great woodsman and an ingenious inventor of traps. He was blamed for heinous misdeeds and was highly respected. He had once creditably fulfilled the duties of administrator of the town of Moimenta, at election time. He was looked upon as an educated man, very well bred, and he subscribed to *O Seculo*. Though close to forty, he was hard as nails, and wanted—so he said—to found a family; and he accordingly proceeded to build a house along the highway, of good masonry and Pampilhosa brick, and, being mad about her, he then asked for the hand of Maria da Encarnação.

So many blemishes should have rendered him odious to her, especially as regarded his age and physique, which is always a matter of moment even to a girl who is saving her charms for a heavenly bridegroom, a bridegroom who is accustomed to plucking the most fragrant of virgin flowers. Nevertheless, she did not repulse him with aversion; no, nothing of the sort; with a melancholy manner, she reminded him of her vows of chastity, and gently sent him about his business.

But Pedro Jirigodes did not give up. Slowly and cleverly he worked his way into the good graces of those whose help he needed, bribing the pious neighbor women and winning the missionary father to his side with the gift of a few legs of veal and a mess of trout. As for the girl's parents, they urged her on to marry him, feeling certain that this would free her from the clutches of the bigots. And with a few maxims having to do with a life that was well provided for and well regulated and none the less virtuous for all of that, the apostle contributed his share by citing examples of holy wedlock—all of which had its due effect in time. Maria da Encarnaçao was thus left with no one to protect her. Pedro Jirigodes, meanwhile, stubbornly held on; and in the middle of May of that year, just as the fillies were beginning to neigh in the meadows and the feast of Our Lady the Mother of God and Men, of which he had been the major-domo, was drawing to a close, he finally obtained that Yes which he had stubbornly disputed with the Nazarene. It was at this time that the legal proceedings to establish Jirigodes' free status, which had been dragging along in foreign parts for more than a dozen years, were settled, so that he was in a position to go through with the marriage.

All this ran through Padre Jesuino's mind, which was not devoid of discernment, in the presence of that little blond head in front of him.

"So you heard a voice?" the abbot began, mildly. "And what was it the voice said? Tell me again."

" 'Maria da Encarnaçao, thou shalt go up to the Mountain; without stick or stone, thou shalt do away with this fear!' "

"Ah! And was that when you were asleep or when you were awake?"

"Asleep, Father; but I also heard it one night, just as I had finished saying my beads."

"One must not put too much faith in dreams. In authors who are worthy of all credence I have read that dreams may be the instrument either of angels or of the powers of darkness."

"That is all very well; but I am telling you, I also heard it when I was in possession of my five senses. It was as real as your voice now, Father, and I could hear it just as plainly."

"It would appear, then, that it is sending you up there, on Mount Nave, to put an end to the monster—"

"That is what I make of it."

"From where did the voice come?"

"I don't know; it sounded very distinctly in my ears, but it did not come from any definite direction. I even imagined that it came from above me—but I could not swear to it. And it was a very nice voice; I never heard anything like it before—"

The confessor asked her any number of other questions, all bearing upon the same point; for in his casuistry this case constituted a novelty, and his mind, trained to manual labor, to educating the young and to hunting rabbits, was hardly fitted to deal with so transcendental a problem. He avoided giving a decisive answer by saying:

"My daughter, with regard to something so mysterious as this, I cannot tell you what I think. I know that more than one person has received by such means as this a mandate from heaven to be carried out on earth. But if my memory serves me right, there have also been cases in which such voices proved to be false, having been sent by evil spirits. I shall consult the prelate—"

"The voice is so sweet and tender it could only come from heaven. When I hear it, my whole body is bathed in a joy so marvelous, so delicious, that I forget all about myself and the things of earth!" And as she said this, in a tone of great exaltation, she gave an upward arch to her brows, as if recalling the supreme delight she had experienced.

"Very well, but we cannot take too many precautions. The devil has arts of his own that he masters along with the learned in academies, and each trick of his is more subtle than the ones he has used before. Take my advice; be calm, and let us wait until this question has been settled by those above—"

"And in the meantime, the torture keeps up? Ah, Father—!"

"That is true enough; but the trouble is of so mysterious an origin that in order to be rid of it, the utmost prudence is to be recommended. Go, my daughter, and moderate your thirst for sacrifice, which for the matter of that is not becoming to you. Try to control yourself, and say three Hail Mary's to Our Lady of Good Counsel, that she may tell you what to do." And with these and similar words, he sought to break the spell which lay upon the young soul in his charge.

Two weeks went by, and more rapes were perpetrated in those desolate God-forsaken regions along the border of the old Roman roads, long fallen into disuse. At the monastery mass, Maria da Encarnação appeared once more to ask the abbot to hear her confession.

"Father," she murmured, "the voice still comes to me: 'To the Mountain thou shalt go; thou shalt do away with this fear.' I hear it five or six times a night. The bishop has not answered yet?"

"No, he has not had time."

"Very well, then, Father, I have made up my mind to go up the mountain, up to the very highest peaks, and Our Lord will take care of me."

"The mountain is big, my child; a good horse on the gallop could not make it in a day. It is full of caves—and dens—it will be your undoing!"

"Do not worry about that!"

"If at least you had company!"

"I do not want anyone. Judith went alone to the tent of Holofernes."

"Times are different now, little soul of the Lord! Times are different, and we are not the ancient Hebrews. In the matter of—of copulation, they were none too scrupulous. There was Sarah, wife of the great Abraham, in Egypt—"

"All that I may suffer will be well repaid, if tomorrow it can be said: young girls may now go without fear down those pathways of Christ. . . ."

"That may be. I do not say yes, and I do not say no. Just forget that I have said anything to you."

"The voice is from heaven—"

"Who can tell?"

"It is. I have conjured it night after night, putting my whole soul into the words: If you are divine, speak to me; if you are an angel of darkness, be gone, in the name of the Father, and of the Son, and of the Holy Ghost. And the voice did not stop; it was more melodious than ever—"

"I have observed that you have a tendency to mysticism. In the case of highly sensitive natures, there are sometimes phenomena of auditory, visual and other kinds of hallucination. What I mean to say is, your ears may be deciving you—"

"So often? God, Our Lord, would not permit a thing like that to happen."

The abbot had no reply to make to this argument of incontrovertible faith.

"My advice to you," he said once more, "was, and shall continue to be: wait!"

"And is *He* to wait, too?"

"You mean to go up in the mountains like that, just as you are?"

"Yes, Father, armed only with the sign of the cross."

"That is a powerful weapon, no doubt of it; but there are occasions when a good rifle is not to be spurned. Judith carried a cutlass—"

"Judith cut off the Philistine's head with the sword of the Philistine. I have read and reread the Book of Kings."

"Joan of Arc went armed—"

"But there was a war then—that was in time of war."

It was not feasible for the abbot to have recourse to his bishop; he felt that the help which the girl looked for from that quarter was a vain illusion. He did not have the heart to continue to deceive her any longer; and much less did he have the courage to keep a promise which called for so much tact and for such care in the matter of style and composition, not to speak of good paper, all of which were indispensable in a correspondence with My Lord, the Bishop, and which in this village monastery were as far removed from the padre as the padre was from his breviary. Years ago—when he still wore his lace rochet in the pulpit and spoke to God with the slow, solemn manner of a minister addressing his monarch—he had enjoyed wide fame as a preacher. Upon succeeding to the chaplaincy of Lama, Friar José had left him a well thumbed volume of sermons, in which he found enough and more than enough to provide a feast for a little rural congregation which hardly could be said to be hungering for spiritual things. And even aside from the book of sermons, inasmuch as the virtues are always exalted and sin irresistibly combated in the lives of the saints, any panegyric would be in order with a simple substitution of names. The major excellence of rhetoric lay in its adjustability to all the blessed, like kerchiefs to all heads. Padre Jesuino spent more time in the woods looking for a rabbit to tie to his belt than he did at his study table in transforming a sermon on St. Anthony into one on St. Blaise, or the tears of St. Peter into the thorns of Our Lord. The rest could be left to memory, and his memory was very good, thanks to a cerebral economy which afforded room only for the slow, larva-like passage and repassage of thoughts having to do with his duties at the altar.

With age and the vexations caused him by the prodigal sons intrusted to his care, his theological tools had grown rusty from lack of use; and to sit down now and compose a statement for the Bishop, laying before him the case of this visionary girl, was a task with which he was in no condition to cope. With scoldings and with maxims of plain common sense, he had done his best to counsel her, as one would a person bent upon butting down a door with his head; but all in vain. Maria da Encarnação, certain that her mission as a redeemer came from on high, was more determined than ever to go through with her plan.

At sunrise the next morning, after having milked the cows, Tomas Pateiro, surprised at not seeing his daughter up and stirring, went to the door of her room.

"Maria da Encarnaçao! Oh, lá! Get up! There's work to be done—"

Receiving no reply and not hearing so much as a sound, he began pounding on her door. Then it occurred to him that she might have had a bad night, addicted as she was to insomnia and nightmares, and he remembered that for some little while she had been given to dropping off into a heavy, death-like slumber shortly before daybreak. Outside, the cock had ceased crowing and the turtledoves were billing and cooing lasciviously and flying in rows over the pine-grove. As he set out with the hired man and his son to plant a field of beans, between a couple of mouthfuls of food he said to his paralyzed wife as she lay in bed:

"A plague on those padres who are putting notions in our lass's head! I called her and she didn't even answer."

The old woman went on saying the rosary of Our Lord, for this was her month, and estimating on her fingers the amount they owed in servant's wages. Time was slipping by; it was mid-morning and still no sign of her daughter.

"Maria da Encarnaçao!" the old woman shouted at last. "Hey! Maria da Encarnaçao!"

Frightened at hearing what she thought was a groan, she broke off, listening intently.

"Miaul! Miaul!"

"Plague take the cat! Scat!" she cried, "Scat!" And the puss, which had been foraging on top of the cupboard, gave a leap and scurried out of sight, as the paralytic once more called out:

"Maria da Encarnação! Get up, child; your father will be coming in starved for his breakfast—"

She called and called again, but there was nothing to disturb the deep well of silence that filled the house. It was a silence that seemed to come from the kitchen, from the street, from everywhere. Little by little, she became conscious of its presence about her bed, as hateful as that of certain individuals the very sight of whom filled her with loathing. Oppressed by a feeling of terror which she could not well define, her imagination more halting than a spavined horse, she lay for a time motionless, almost without breathing, withdrawn into herself, as at the bottom of a funnel. It seemed to her that all of human life was fleeing roundabout her, and that her own life, anguish-ridden, was following close after, to fill like a rising river the emptiness of space. Soon, however, her ear caught the sound, far away, very far away, of a creaking axle. Then, from the threshing-floor, came the merry fanfare of a cock, greeting the light of day with his *Orate, fratres;* and still more distant, like the closing of the missal when the priest has finished saying mass, she could make out the sound of the women beating clothes in the wash-houses. The world continued to revolve about her suspended by invisible cords, but stouter, stronger ones than any that could be fashioned from all the thread that there was.

In harmony with all of this, her anxiety of a moment ago returned to torment her; and once again she called:

"Daughter! Why don't you answer?"

Amid the universal immobility of things, the household utensils—the olive jar at the foot of the bed, the pots and the water jug over there on the shelf—took on the appearance of squatting bronzes, all of them, and seemed to be listening. The very silence itself was putting out unseen hands to stifle her. And then the sounds came back, infinitesimal sounds, the worm gnawing in the wood like a gimlet, the crackle and drip of melting tar on the roof in the heat of the day. And vaguer than the drone of a mosquito in the sun was the far-off rumble of a wagon on the Road of Our Lord.

"Maria da Encarnação! Oh, Maria da Encarnação!"

No answering voice, no sound of breathing was to be heard.

"Oh, Maria da Encarnação!" She was tearful now, like a child in pain. Everything then grew dark in front of her eyes, and the furniture of the room appeared to be doing a topsy-turvy dance, without making the slightest sound. Mad with fright, as if the mattress that she lay on were afire, she started screaming: "Help! Help!" For a long time the poor woman kept it up, in a voice which at first was as tremulous as tinkling bells, growing hoarser then until it could be heard all over the village, by those at work in their gardens.

They came running up in a swarm; and panting for breath, ever popping from her head, the paralytic with incoherent speech directed them to her daughter's room—"no sign of her—must be dead—"

The door was locked with a key; but Pedro Jirigodes with a shove had it off the hinges. And when they came back to tell the old lady that there was no Maria da Encarnação there, either dead or alive, her mother's heart was so relieved that she burst into tears upon finding that her immediate and darkest apprehensions were unfounded. As for Pedro Jirigodes, there was a look of amazement on his face and his manner was stern as he came down the stairs and asked all present to aid him in searching for his betrothed; and at his request, either out of sympathy or because they scented a possible scandal, whole groups of them now began hunting along the river banks and the mill-races, among the farms and hamlets, for a trace of the missing girl. Their search proved a fruitless one, and at the end of it, as they gathered to talk matters over, they were inclined in their discouragement to attribute this mysterious disappearance to the monster who had entered from the roof to rape Leopoldina Quaresma. At that very moment, however, just as the sun was tinging with purple the peaks of Caramula, they caught sight of Maria da Encarnação. She was coming along at an even stride, her head thrown back, as if her soul were inebriated with the holy peace of heaven.

Jirigodes bounded forward to meet her; but as she saw the anxious look on her lover's face, she drew herself erect with hieratic aplomb.

"Do not touch me, reprobate creature!" she said to him, in a tone of sovereign haughtiness, "do not touch me!"

"What's that?" he barked at her.

"Do not touch me! The Lord's elect has opened to me his amorous bosom and has sanctified me."

On her face was such a glow of light and in her bearing so serene a majesty that they hastened at once, in a body, to conduct her into the abbot's presence.

"Father," she said, "only in God's house is it permitted me to speak of the heavenly messenger."

The abbot was a bit put out by all this, for it was the time of day for him to be watering his onions; but throwing his cassock over his shoulders, he made for the church with Maria da Encarnação at his side. The latter's face was solemn, and she seemed to be walking on air as the two of them made their way through the silent throng. The nave of the church was filled to overflowing with people as she knelt in the confessional, and they all appeared to be deeply immersed in thought and waiting breathlessly, as if the Blessed Sacrament were being exposed on the high altar. Soon, however, Padre Jesuino rose from behind the grating with the gesture of one who had been undeceived.

"This is not a case for auricular confession!" he announced, describing spirals in the air with the palm of his hand, by way of emphasizing his remarks. "She has been seeing visions or something of the sort. I can't listen to it, I can't. If she wants to tell you about it, all right."

And without more ado, the folds of his cassock fluttering in his haste, he took his departure.

Maria da Encarnaçao, meanwhile, was standing on the first step of the high-altar, her back turned to the Blessed Sacrament; and after letting her gaze roam haughtily over the assembled multitude, she began speaking with the voice of one inspired:

"O people! Men and women, old and young, ye maidens above all, who with foolish tears bewail your maidenhood—I say unto you, rejoice! An angel of Heaven dwelleth among us. I have seen him, I have spoken with him, I have found repose in his arms, more trustingly than an innocent babe at its mother's breast. Oh, but he is beautiful! So beautiful that the beauty of Absalom is as nothing by comparison! And he is strong, stronger than the armies of David when they destroyed those of the six kings! His presence is more inebriating than the wine when it is sweet! He is the Ineffable of whom the Scriptures speak. Just as the Messiah saw the light in the desert of Judea, even so he has elected for the scene of his ministry these desolate backlands of Portugal. Rejoice! His mission it is to regenerate the race, to people the world with comely beings like himself, beings fashioned in the image and the likeness of God. Oh, ye mournful creatures, O piteous creatures, how little ye reckon of the divine Presence! Sin and toil have deformed your bodies, ye poor degenerate ones. But rejoice, for ye shall be exalted in your sons and those that are to come after you; for so hath he revealed it to me with his own sweet mouth. Those born of the Ineffable's embrace shall be beautiful and sound of limb and endowed with a wisdom from on high; but all those founts of life which he toucheth not shall wither and dry up. O ye of little faith, believe me, it is indeed an angel from Heaven that dwelleth among us. Ye maidens whom he shall touch, more lightly than the breeze stirring the canebrake, yet like the lightning's fire striking the earth—I say unto you: give thanks! Ye and your sons shall be of the elect! Let us kneel and pray to God, that God who giveth day and night, joy and sorrow, who one-thousand-nine-hundred years ago sent us a Redeemer for our souls, and who now, today, sends us a Redeemer for our bodies!"

In that great nave, the shadows of twilight appeared to stretch out into infinity, as all hearts felt the gentle wound of these mystic and transcendent words. Ejaculations burst forth from a thousand throats, in celebration of this epiphany of the flesh, a flesh now redeemed from its age-old anathema. And as night fell, it seemed that tongues of living flame, red and glowing from on high, were hovering over all the villages and door-sills, and the people had the feeling that something great was happening in the land.

From that hour forth, the news spread abroad: an angel from Heaven had come down to ransom the human race of all its sufferings and deformities, and had selected as the vessel for the divine seed those maidens who were young, virgin and marriageable. His ways were rude and mysterious, until the blind jealousy of man where woman is concerned should at last have been dissipated like the ocular cataract which it was. But nevertheless, the time would come when he would descend to the peoples, and each household would then harbor him as its guest, between the finest of sheets, proffering the embrace of the most sculpturesque of arms. Like a swelling river, spreading afar, the enthusiasm grew. On the trunk of the old religion a new religion of pleasure and delight had now been grafted. Even the old women spoke of the Ineffable with tenderness and deep-bosomed sighs: and few indeed were the men with the murky flames of jealousy still lingering in their eyes. Little by little, all gave in, the women out of passion, the men out of faith and humility.

Simultaneously, the brutal rapes in the silence of the woods and along the equally silent highways now ceased. Stealthily some and others boldly, under the seal of catechumens, the maidens voluntarily went up into the mountains to offer the voluptuous Messiah the flower of their virginity.

In the meantime, pregnancy among the elect was on the increase, and the hour of delivery was drawing near. Much good it did piously-sniffling mothers with their barbarous superstitions to invoke the intervention of the Virgin Saint Euphemia or to have recourse to witches and sorceresses; the pollen possessed the virtue of fecundity. Micas Olaia was the first to feel the pangs of parturition; whereupon all the old midwives came running up, prepared to make short work of the progeny, if it chanced to be a werewolf, and ready to conjure it back to hell if it proved to be a monster of Satan. For they were still doubtful, and Padre Jesuino himself spoke out clearly on the matter.

"If the child is not in our own image and likeness," he said, "Strangle it!" And so saying, he made the gesture which he used in wringing the necks of partridges brought down on the wing.

It was, however, a bouncing baby boy, perfect in every way, to whom Micas Olaia gave birth. It at once began to wail, as much as to say, Here I am; and in less than a jiffy, it was up and at its mother's well stocked breasts. After Micas, the others in turn were brought to bed, but without any more exorcisms or dread of monsters. All the offspring, without exception, were healthy, well formed and handsome; there was not a deformity or a cross-eye in the entire lot of them.

Compared to these young ones, those born within the bonds of wedlock were ill-favored indeed; they were, one would have said, the rejected of God. They possessed neither the complexion, the strength and natural hardihood, nor the delicate beauty of these sons of the Ineffable. Confounded by it all and smitten with compunction, the abbot could only shake his head and murmur with the apostles: Judicia divina dum nescintur, non audaci sermone discutienda sunt sed formidoloso silentio veneranda. (The ways of God being inscrutable, they are not to be the subject of frivolous conversation, but rather the object of a silent awe and veneration.)

GERMANIC AND
SCANDINAVIAN SECTION

Introduction

GERMANY AND AUSTRIA

Hitler's ascendance to power led to a repudiation of the immediate literary past. In the nineteenth and early twentieth century, political considerations rarely affected the recognition of German and Austrian writers. These writers might follow Emile Zola's realistic method, stressing the importance of heredity and environment. They might try to recapture the heroic fervor of Teutonic traditions. They might dissect man and society in a timely manner. There was—as in most cultures—room for all.

Realism was the prevailing literary school in fiction. Although this was less true in Austria than in Germany, some of the most outstanding Austrian writers were influenced by the realistic movement.

From late nineteenth century German realism to the pathological excesses of Nazism, the path of fiction and short story is rich in varied and contradictory elements. Germany and Austria went through a period of tragic and conflicting interests. It affected the quality of narrative art in manner and matter—for it subordinated art in fiction to its purely psychological, sociological and political ends. "Problem" stories developed into problems of the ends and means of literature. Frank Wedekind, the German author, accused realists and naturalists of being misguided recorders and detectives of the trivial. And, of course, individual writers were often unable to transfer their particular social and political sympathies or antipathies to the level of pure art.

There was much pessimism, much bewilderment expressed in this literature. The illusion of progress, so dear to the nineteenth century mind, seemed but a reflex to many German and Austrian authors. The anti-positivistic trends of philosophers, such as Dilthey, Heidegger, Jaspers, Rickert, Husserl; the psychoanalytical theories of Adler, Freud, and Jung—were indicative of an age in which human growth had lost its orientation, and was seeking forms for new experience. Oswald Spengler's pretentiously erudite interpretation of the decline of the West molded the attitude of those whose pessimism-ridden spirit discovered convincing arguments in Spengler's logic. Some writers were inclined to reject these sinister characteristics of the twentieth century by returning to the philosophical idealism of Schelling, the nineteenth century romanticist. Confusion itself intrigued many twentieth century German and Austrian writers.

391

Despite this climate, works of enduring merit have been produced. One could enumerate about a dozen writers besides those represented in this volum whose works possess permanent artistic value. The contribution of minor writers—especially of those who wrote during the Weimar Republic, and its attempt to democratize Germany, should not be minimized. And even throughout the Nazi dictatorship, despite the fact that the independent spirit was a prisoner of ruthless totalitarian forces, some writers continued to manifest artistic sensitivity. Nevertheless, those "impatient" with Hitlerian supremacy were soon silenced by their brutal adversaries.

Without exception the writers whose works appear in this anthology were either anti-Nazi by their active rejection of Hitlerism, or—as some were no longer alive when Hitler reached power—the purpose and quality of their works were antithetical to everything that Nazism stood for. However, most of these authors show no preference for timely problems—however timely some of them were and are. These stories are first of all narratives. They move in the world of psychological and imaginative dimensions; their source is the horror and pity of reality.

In his story, *Disorder and Early Sorrow,* having as a background the devastating inflation period of Germany, Thomas Mann, the famous novelist and Nobel prize winner, portrays the wide gulf in taste and temperament that separates the older generation from the younger one. Mann's proficiency in the multiform possibilities of contrasts—as a rule shown in the relationship of the artist to a non-artistic surrounding— is deftly revealed in this story.

Rainer Maria Rilke, one of the foremost twentieth century German-Austrian poets, is as sensitive in his prose as in his poetry. His spiritual curiosity is unworldly, but not in a primitive sense. *Hands of God,* which is an introduction to Rilke's *Stories of God,* has all the charm and ingenuity of his exquisite imagination. It is a mystic and childlike tale of God's hands, which affirms that "life is a glorious thing."

The Married Couple is quite typical of Franz Kafka's manner of writing, although it is not so illuminating of his unique ability as his longer pieces are. In Kafka's works a sense of guilt and a feeling that one is an alien in this world, play a prominent rôle. This tendency links his work with that of certain French "Existentialists." His novels, such as *The Trial, The Castle* and *America,* have pathos and satire, and register a new intonation in the eternal conflict between man's awareness and the enigmatic universe.

Stefan Zweig, the Austrian writer, is best known for his biographies. He was a *litterateur* in the best sense of the word; a highly civilized writer with a humane outlook. As a novelist and short story writer, parts of his works show virtuosity and well expressed understanding. *Moonbeam Alley,* which suggests the dreary atmosphere of a French coastal town, is a somewhat contrived story of a penurious German bourgeois and his dissipated wife, but the well developed plot and character delineation sustain the reader's interest. Arthur Schnitzler, another Austrian writer, whom critics like to compare with Guy de Maupassant, lacks the superb qualities of the French master. Nevertheless his stories and sketches possess an elegance of expression and a feeling for tender adventures, a comprehension of the interplay of significant and insignificant emotions, which explain his popularity with many readers. *The Dead Are Silent* is a smoothly told story of the unfaithful wife of a Viennese professor, the tragic death of her lover, her miraculous escape and her need to confess her guilt to her husband.

Humanitarianism and pacifism characterize Arnold Zweig. Zweig is best known for his novel, *The Case of Sergeant Grischa. Kong at the Seaside* is the effective story of loyalty, symbolized in the relationship of a boy to his dog.

One of the most audible voices of twentieth century German literature is that of Arthur Koestler, the Hungarian born writer who, however, writes in German. Koestler is primarily a political-minded, pamphleteering novelist—an uprooted, tireless and disquieting spirit. *Darkness at Noon,* from which the closing passage is published in this anthology, is related to the "liquidation" period of the Bolshevik revolution. It is usually regarded as the finest of his novels.

HOLLAND AND FLANDERS

The dominant traits of Dutch narrative art show definite kinship with the narrative art of Germany, the Scandinavian countries and Switzerland. Of course, one must reckon with local differences affecting the tone and allusions of Dutch authors, but human virtues and failings are expressed more or less in a similar narrative terminology. The best Dutch authors have been true to their regionalism of the nineteenth century, to Catholicism or Calvinism, or to their regionalistic traditions which include references to the Dutch East Indies; some authors were sociological, psychological or aesthetic experimentalists.

Louis Couperus of the older literary generation must be mentioned —the author of *The Book of Small Souls,* a prolific writer of family chronicles and portrayer of the Dutch landscape. *Bluebeard's Daughter,* included here, represents another side of his talent—a primarily satirical side.

In the post-bellum era of the first World War, Dutch authors found themselves at odds with the mental and moral climate of their age. Some were under the influence of Nazism. Most of them, however, deplored totalitarianism in any form. Macabre tales as well as humorous tales, pacifistic, social and historical stories, conservative and bold methods of writing characterized by a rigorous adherence to art as a criterion of creative writing indicate the variety of Dutch narrative expression. Herman de Man, Roel Houwink, Albert Holman, Arthur van Schendel are the literary leaders of this age.

The other writer represented in this anthology, also mirrors the taste and technique of the older generation of Dutch literature. Johannes L. Walch has a deep insight into the inconsistencies of human nature. *The Suspicion* is the story of a seemingly placid woman married to a "nice, fat husband"; the "other side" of her character is that of a Hedda Gabler-like restless woman.

In this chapter it is appropriate to refer briefly to the narrative literature of Flanders, which is politically a part of Belgium. Flemish, a low German dialect, is used by some of the most prominent writers of northern Belgium; there is, generally, a strong regionalistic character observable in Flemish stories. The most gifted forerunner of Flemish narrative art was Charles de Coster, the nineteenth century historical novelist; Felix Timmermans is the most talented twentieth century Flemish writer of stories.

SWITZERLAND

The perspective of Swiss-German literature transcends the boundaries of that country. Gottfried Keller and Conrad Ferdinand Meyer, the nineteenth century masters of the narrative art, hold a major position in Swiss and German literature. Carl Spitteler, the poet, is also the most distinguished twentieth century Swiss prose writer.

The Swiss are a mountain folk. Their ruggedness, their austere existence, the strength and weakness of their unsophisticated lives are recurrent themes of Swiss authors, often expressed in dialect. One finds such topics in the novels and stories of Ernest Zahn, or in the works of more recent writers, such as Jacob Bosshard and Alfred Huggenberger. The simplicity is indivisible from the moral and psychological intents of the writers. There are those who write about city life, but their writings are not the really significant note of Swiss literature.

Herman Hesse, the Nobel prize winner, is the author of novels, stories, poems. He is of Swabian origin, but considered Swiss by volition. There is nothing ethnically Swiss in the works of Herman Hesse, but there is nothing unalterably German either. His art is subjective, at times mysterious and exotic. It is timeless rather than timely, and it suggests the demonic forces of life, the indefinable perplexities of human destiny. *Steppenwolf* is considered Hesse's masterpiece, and *Harry's Loves,* a part of this novel, included in this anthology, is indicative of the main characteristics of his art.

SWEDEN

In the ceaseless effort to express life imaginatively on a narrative plane, Swedish literature is represented by writers as eminent as outstanding writers of greater nations. Naturalism, realism, neo-romanticism, expressionism, social and individual problems in the light of traditional and modern psychology, tragedy, religious faith, and simple and involved humor display the varied character of Swedish letters. Every generation has its regionalistic interests.

Since August Strindberg, no other Swedish writer has captured the attention of the world to such an extent as Selma Lagerlöf, the Nobel prize winner, the author of *Gösta Berling's Saga,* and of historical, religious, moral and legendary stories. Although not a master of form, one must recognize the striking psychological and ethical qualities of her work. *The Outlaws* aims to show that "the foundation of the world is justice." It tells of a peasant who kills a monk, and of a young fisherman accused of thievery.

The variety of Swedish narrative literature is shown by writers like Per Hallström, Ivan Oljelund, Hjalmar Bergmann, Per Lagerkvist, Harry Blomberg and others. Their taste and ideology are divergent with a range from social realism to folklore.

Of the two other writers chosen for this anthology, Sigfrid Siwertz is primarily interested in weary, disillusioned human destinies, in the confusing effects of sex upon human life, in the stealthy approach of old age. Siwertz is a subtle stylist. Moral idealism is emphasized in some of his works. *In Spite of Everything* is the love story of a "remorselessly beautiful woman" and a young man; it is a well drawn picture of "the human bondage." An impressionist, Hjalmar Söderberg likes to place his stories in the city of Stockholm. He seems to have an intimate understanding of the capital city of Sweden. He is also famous as the author of stories about children, of which *The Burning City* is an excellent example.

NORWAY

Considering the small population of Norway, her literature is rich, indeed. Social stories and folklore, virile and decadent expressions of the human spirit, exemplify the diverse, sometimes intensely conflicting standards of creativeness. Concern with the present and the future and a sincere attachment to nature illustrate the manifoldness of Norwegian creative imagination. Names like Jonas Lie, Knut Hamsun, Hans Ernst Kinck, Olav Dunn, Andreas Haukland represent a wealth of native ability which discredits the assertion that small nations cannot produce literary quality on a quantitative basis. It is pitiful that Knut Hamsun, the Nobel prize winner and author of such a universally acclaimed novel as *The Growth of the Soil,* succumbed to Nazism.

At present one of the most gifted Norwegian narrative artists, and their Nobel prize winner, is Sigrid Undset. Her conversion to Catholicism and the Catholic themes and implications of many of her stories are central to her work. So powerful a novel as *Kristin Lavransdatter,* from which a chapter appears in this anthology, could not have been written without Sigrid Undset's Roman Catholic belief.

Johan Bojer, outstanding novelist and dramatist, has won international acclaim for his realism and his robust style. He has grappled with almost all the problems dominating Norwegian life between 1890 and 1925. *The Shark,* although the first chapter of a novel, *The Great Hunger,* is an almost perfect short story in itself.

DENMARK

The school of narrative impressionism began with Jens Peter Jacobsen, the nineteenth century Danish author of *Niels Lyhne.* Much of late nineteenth century and early twentieth century Danish literature has romantic warmth and melancholy. But Danish tales are not exclusively subjective. Some writers portray social problems of modern times. There are those whose response to life is colored by regionalistic loyalties—for instance, Icelandic writers. There is naturally no single standard by which one could judge such Danish writers as Hermann Bang, Henrik Pontoppidan, Johannes Jensen, Johan Skjoldborg, Jacob Paludan, Johannes Anker-Larsen, Gunnar Gunnarsson.

Martin Anderson Nexö stresses the interrelation of work, human dignity and justice. Narration and description serve a social purpose. But it would be wrong to consider him a propagandist or didactic writer. His most ambitious work, *Pelle the Conqueror,* notwithstanding an inferior handling of construction, is a highly satisfactory novel. While almost formless, it has meticulously realized parts, and the final impression is that of a proletarian's heroic struggle. *Birds of Passage,* published in this volume, is the story of a shoemaker, "by nature a wandering journeyman," and his woman. It is poetic and humane—at once richly humorous and tender.

Isak Dinesen is the pen name of Baroness Karen Blixen of Rungstedlund. Although a member of an old Danish literary family, she writes in English, and it is in the United States that she is best known. Her stories are an exquisite blend of the fantastic and realistic, and *The Sailor-Boy's Tale* illustrates this quality admirably.

JOSEPH REMENYI

THOMAS MANN

Disorder and Early Sorrow

Thomas Mann, born in 1875 in Lubeck, attended the University of Munich. The years during and after the First World War caused Mann to be vitally concerned with the political and social issues of the day. He fled from the Nazis in 1933, living in Switzerland for a time and arriving in the United States in 1938, where he now lives. His most famous works are *Buddenbrooks, Death in Venice, The Magic Mountain, Mario and the Magician* and the *Joseph* series. [From *Stories of Three Decades* by Thomas Mann; copyright 1936 by Alfred A. Knopf, Inc.; used by permission of the publishers.]

THE PRINCIPAL DISH at dinner had been croquettes made of turnip greens. So there follows a trifle, concocted out of one of those dessert powders we use nowadays, that taste like almond soap. Xaver, the youthful manservant, in his outgrown striped jacket, white woolen gloves, and yellow sandals, hands it round, and the "big folk" take this opportunity to remind their father, tactfully, that company is coming today.

The "big folk" are two, Ingrid and Bert. Ingrid is brown-eyed, eighteen, and perfectly delightful. She is on the eve of her exams, and will probably pass them, if only because she knows how to wind masters, and even headmasters, round her finger. She does not, however, mean to use her certificate once she gets it; having leanings toward the stage, on the ground of her ingratiating smile, her equally ingratiating voice, and a marked and irresistible talent for burlesque. Bert is blond and seventeen. He intends to get done with school somehow, anyhow, and fling himself into the arms of life. He will be a dancer, or a cabaret actor, possibly even a waiter—but not a waiter anywhere else save at the Cairo, the nightclub, whither he has once already taken flight, at five in the morning, and been brought back crestfallen. Bert bears a strong resemblance to the youthful manservant Xaver Kleinsgutl, of about the same age as himself; not because he looks common—in features he is strikingly like his father, Professor Cornelius—but by reason of an approximation of types, due in its turn to far-reaching compromises in matters of dress and bearing generally. Both lads wear their heavy hair very long on top, with a cursory parting in the middle, and give their heads the same characteristic toss to throw it off the forehead. When one of them leaves the house, by the garden gate, bareheaded in all weathers, in a blouse rakishly girt with a leather strap, and sheers off bent well over with his head on one side; or else mounts his push-bike—Xaver makes free with his employers', of both sexes, or even, in acutely irresponsible mood, with the Professor's own—Dr. Cornelius from his bedroom window cannot, for the life of him, tell whether he is looking at his son or his servant. Both, he thinks, look like young moujiks. And both are impassioned cigarette-smokers, though Bert has not the means to compete with Xaver, who smokes as many as thirty a day, of a brand named after a popular cinema star. The big folk call their father and mother the "old folk"—not behind their backs, but as a form of address and in all affection: "Hullo, old folks," they will say; though Cornelius is only forty-seven years old and his wife eight years younger. And the Professor's parents, who lead in his household the humble and hesitant life of the really old, are on the big folk's lips the "ancients." As for the "little folk," Ellie and Snapper, who take their meals upstairs with blue-faced Ann—so-called because of her prevailing facial hue—Ellie and Snapper follow their mother's example and address their father by his first name, Abel. Unutterably comic it sounds, in its pert, confiding familiarity; particularly on the lips, in the sweet accents, of five-year-old Eleanor, who is the image of Frau Cornelius's baby pictures and whom the Professor loves above everything else in the world.

"Darling old thing," says Ingrid affably, laying her large but shapely hand on his, as he presides in proper middle-class style over the family table, with her on his left and the mother opposite: "Parent mine, may I ever so gently jog your memory, for you have probably forgotten: this is the afternoon we were to have our little jollification, our turkey-trot with eats to match. You haven't a thing to do but just bear up and not funk it; everything will be over by nine o'clock."

"Oh—ah!" says Cornelius, his face falling. "Good!" he goes on, and nods his head to show himself in harmony with the inevitable. "I only meant—is this really the day? Thursday, yes. How time flies! Well, what time are they coming?"

"Half past four they'll be dropping in, I should say," answers Ingrid, to whom her brother leaves the major rôle in all dealings with the father. Upstairs, while he is resting, he will hear scarcely anything, and from seven to eight he takes his walk. He can slip out by the terrace if he likes.

"Tut!" says Cornelius deprecatingly, as who should say: "You exaggerate." But Bert puts in: "It's the one evening in the week Wanja doesn't have to play. Any other night he'd have to leave by half past six, which would be painful for all concerned."

Wanja is Ivan Herzl, the celebrated young leading man at the Stadt-theater. Bert and Ingrid are on intimate terms with him, they often visit him in his dressing-room and have tea. He is an artist of the modern school, who stands on the stage in strange and, to the Professor's mind, utterly affected dancing attitudes, and shrieks lamentably. To a professor of history, all highly repugnant; but Bert has entirely suc-cumbed to Herzl's influence, blackens the lower rim of his eyelids—despite painful but fruitless scenes with the father—and with youthful

carelessness of the ancestral anguish declares that not only will he take
Herzl for his model if he becomes a dancer, but in case he turns out
to be a waiter at the Cairo he means to walk precisely thus.

Cornelius slightly raises his brows and makes his son a little bow—
indicative of the unassumingness and self-abnegation that befits his
age. You could not call it a mocking bow or suggestive in any special
sense. Bert may refer it to himself or equally to his so talented friend.

"Who else is coming?" next inquires the master of the house. They
mention various people, names all more or less familiar, from the city,
from the suburban colony, from Ingrid's school. They still have some
telephoning to do, they say. They have to phone Max. This is Max
Hergesell, an engineering student; Ingrid utters his name in the nasal
drawl which according to her is the traditional intonation of all the
Hergesells. She goes on to parody it in the most abandonedly funny and
lifelike way, and the parents laugh until they nearly choke over the
wretched trifle. For even in these times when something funny happens
people have to laugh.

From time to time the telephone bell rings in the Professor's study,
and the big folk run across, knowing it is their affair. Many people had
to give up their telephones the last time the price rose, but so far the
Corneliuses have been able to keep theirs, just as they have kept their
villa, which was built before the war, by dint of the salary Cornelius
draws as professor of history—a million marks, and more or less adequate to the chances and changes of post-war life. The house is comfortable, even elegant, though sadly in need of repairs that cannot be
made for lack of materials, and at present disfigured by iron stoves
with long pipes. Even so, it is still the proper setting of the upper
middle class, though they themselves look odd enough in it, with their
worn and turned clothing and altered way of life. The children, of
course, know nothing else; to them it is normal and regular, they belong
by birth to the "villa proletariat." The problem of clothing troubles
them not at all. They and their like have evolved a costume to fit the
time, by poverty out of taste for innovation: in summer it consists of
scarcely more than a belted linen smock and sandals. The middle-class
parents find things rather more difficult.

The big folk's table-napkins hang over their chair-backs, they talk
with their friends over the telephone. These friends are the invited
guests who have rung up to accept or decline or arrange; and the conversation is carried on in the jargon of the clan, full of slang and high
spirits, of which the old folk understand hardly a word. These consult
together meantime about the hospitality to be offered to the impending
guests. The Professor displays a middle-class ambitiousness: he wants
to serve a sweet—or something that looks like a sweet—after the
Italian salad and brown-bread sandwiches. But Frau Cornelius says
that would be going too far. The guests would not expect it, she is
sure—and the big folk, returning once more to their trifle, agree with
her.

The mother of the family is of the same general type as Ingrid, though not so tall. She is languid; the fantastic difficulties of the housekeeping have broken and worn her. She really ought to go and take a cure, but feels incapable; the floor is always swaying under her feet, and everything seems upside down. She speaks of what is uppermost in her mind: the eggs, they simply must be bought today. Six thousand marks apiece they are, and just so many are to be had on this one day of the week at one single shop fifteen minutes' journey away. Whatever else they do, the big folk must go and fetch them immediately after luncheon, with Danny, their neighbor's son, who will soon be calling for them; and Xaver Kleinsgutl will don civilian garb and attend his young master and mistress. For no single household is allowed more than five eggs a week; therefore the young people will enter the shop singly, one after another, under assumed names, and thus wring twenty eggs from the shopkeeper for the Cornelius family. This enterprise is the sporting event of the week for all participants, not excepting the moujik Kleinsgutl, and most of all for Ingrid and Bert, who delight in misleading and mystifying their fellowmen and would revel in the performance even if it did not achieve one single egg. They adore impersonating fictitious characters; they love to sit in a bus and carry on long lifelike conversations in a dialect which they otherwise never speak, the most commonplace dialogue about politics and people and the price of food, while the whole bus listens open-mouthed to this incredibly ordinary prattle, though with a dark suspicion all the while that something is wrong somewhere. The conversation waxes ever more shameless, it enters into revolting detail about these people who do not exist. Ingrid can make her voice sound ever so common and twittering and shrill as she impersonates a shop-girl with an illegitimate child, said child being a son with sadistic tendencies, who lately out in the country treated a cow with such unnatural cruelty that no Christian could have borne to see it. Bert nearly explodes at her twittering, but restrains himself and displays a grisly sympathy; he and the unhappy shop-girl entering into a long, stupid, depraved, and shuddery conversation over the particular morbid cruelty involved; until an old gentleman opposite, sitting with his ticket folded between his index finger and his seal ring, can bear it no more and makes public protest against the nature of the themes these young folk are discussing with such particularity. He uses the Greek plural: "themata." Whereat Ingrid pretends to be dissolving in tears, and Bert behaves as though his wrath against the old gentleman was with difficulty being held in check and would probably burst out before long. He clenches his fists, he gnashes his teeth, he shakes from head to foot; and the unhappy old gentleman, whose intentions had been of the best, hastily leaves the bus at the next stop.

Such are the diversions of the big folk. The telephone plays a prominent part in them: they ring up any and everybody—members of government, opera singers, dignitaries of the Church—in the character of

shop assistants, or perhaps as Lord or Lady Doolittle. They are only
with difficulty persuaded that they have the wrong number. Once they
emptied their parents' card-tray and distributed its contents among
the neighbors' letter-boxes, wantonly, yet not without impish sense of
the fitness of things to make it highly upsetting. God only knowing
why certain people should have called where they did.

Xaver comes to clear away, tossing the hair out of his eyes. Now that
he has taken off his gloves you can see the yellow chain-ring on his
left hand. And as the Professor finishes his watery eight-thousand-
mark beer and lights a cigarette, the little folk can be heard scrambling
down the stair, coming, by established custom, for their after-dinner
call on Father and Mother. They storm the dining-room, after a
struggle with the latch, clutched by both pairs of little hands at once;
their clumsy small feet twinkle over the carpet, in red felt slippers with
the socks falling down on them. With prattle and shoutings each makes
for his own place: Snapper to Mother, to climb on her lap, boast of all
he has eaten, and thump his fat little tum; Ellie to her Abel, so much
hers because she is so very much his; because she consciously luxuriates
in the deep tenderness—like all deep feeling, concealing a melancholy
strain—with which he holds her small form embraced; in the love in
his eyes as he kisses her little fairy hand or the sweet brow with its
delicate tracery of tiny blue veins.

The little folk look like each other, with the strong undefined likeness of brother and sister. In clothing and hair-cut they are twins. Yet
they are sharply distinguished after all, and quite on sex lines. It is a
little Adam and a little Eve. Not only is Snapper the sturdier and
more compact, he appears consciously to emphasize his four-year-old
masculinity in speech, manner, and carriage, lifting his shoulders and
letting the little arms hang down quite like a young American athlete,
drawing down his mouth when he talks and seeking to give his voice
a gruff and forthright ring. But all this masculinity is the result of
effort rather than natively his. Born and brought up in these desolate,
distracted times, he has been endowed by them with an unstable and
hypersensitive nervous system and suffers greatly under life's dis-
harmonies. He is prone to sudden anger and outbursts of bitter tears,
stamping his feet at every trifle; for this reason he is his mother's special
nursling and care. His round, round eyes are chestnut brown and already inclined to squint, so that he will need glasses in the near
future. His little nose is long, the mouth small—the father's nose and
mouth they are, more plainly than ever since the Professor shaved his
pointed beard and goes smooth-faced. The pointed beard had become
impossible—even professors must make some concession to the changing times.

But the little daughter sits on her father's knee, his Eleonorchen, his
little Eve, so much more gracious a little being, so much sweeter-faced
than her brother—and he holds his cigarette away from her while she
fingers his glasses with her dainty wee hands. The lenses are divided

for reading and distance, and each day they tease her curiosity afresh.

At bottom he suspects that his wife's partiality may have a firmer basis than his own: that Snapper's refractory masculinity perhaps is solider stuff than his own little girl's more explicit charm and grace. But the heart will not be commanded, that he knows; and once and for all his heart belongs to the little one, as it has since the day she came, since the first time he saw her. Almost always when he holds her in his arms he remembers that first time: remembers the sunny room in the Women's Hospital, where Ellie first saw the light, twelve years after Bert was born. He remembers how he drew near, the mother smiling the while, and cautiously put aside the canopy of the diminutive bed that stood beside the large one. There lay the little miracle among the pillows: so well formed, so encompassed, as it were, with the harmony of sweet proportions, with little hands that even then, though so much tinier, were beautiful as now; with wide-open eyes blue as the sky and brighter than the sunshine—and almost in that very second he felt himself captured and held fast. This was love at first sight, love everlasting: a feeling unknown, unhoped for, unexpected—in so far as it could be a matter of conscious awareness; it took entire possession of him, and he understood, with joyous amazement, that this was for life.

But he understood more. He knows, does Dr. Cornelius, that there is something not quite right about this feeling, so unaware, so undreamed of, so involuntary. He has a shrewd suspicion that it is not by accident it has so utterly mastered him and bound itself up with his existence; that he had—even subconsciously—been preparing for it, or, more precisely, been prepared for it. There is, in short, something in him which at a given moment was ready to issue in such a feeling; and this something, highly extraordinary to relate, is his essence and quality as a professor of history. Dr. Cornelius, however, does not actually say this, even to himself; he merely realizes it, at odd times, and smiles a private smile. He knows that history professors do not love history because it is something that comes to pass, but only because it is something that *has* come to pass; that they hate a revolution like the present one because they feel it is lawless, incoherent, irrelevant—in a word, unhistoric; that their hearts belong to the coherent, disciplined, historic past. For the temper of timelessness, the temper of eternity—thus the scholar communes with himself when he takes his walk by the river before supper—that temper broods over the past; and it is a temper much better suited to the nervous system of a history professor than are the excesses of the present. The past is immortalized; that is to say, it is dead; and death is the root of all godliness and all abiding significance. Dr. Cornelius, walking alone in the dark, has a profound insight into this truth. It is this conservative instinct of his, his sense of the eternal, that has found in his love for his little daughter a way to save itself from the wounding inflicted by the times. For father love, and a little child on its mother's breast—are not these timeless, and thus very, very holy and beautiful? Yet Cornelius, pondering there in the dark, descries something not perfectly right and good in his love. Theoretically, in the interests of science, he admits it to himself. There is something ulterior about it, in the nature of it; that something is hostility, hostility against the history of today, which is still in the making, and thus not history at all, in behalf of the genuine history that has already happened—that is to say, death. Yes, passing strange though all this is, yet it is true; true in a sense, that is. His devotion to this priceless little morsel of life and new growth has something to do with death, it clings to death as against life; and that is neither right nor beautiful—in a sense. Though only the most fanatical asceticism could be capable, on no other ground than such casual scientific perception, of tearing this purest and most precious of feelings out of his heart.

He holds his darling on his lap and her slim rosy legs hang down. He raises his brows as he talks to her, tenderly, with a half-teasing note of respect, and listens enchanted to her high, sweet little voice calling him Abel. He exchanges a look with the mother, who is caressing her Snapper and reading him a gentle lecture. He must be more reasonable, he must learn self-control; today again, under the manifold exasperations of life, he has given way to rage and behaved like a howling dervish. Cornelius casts a mistrustful glance at the big folk now and then, too; he thinks it not unlikely they are not unaware of those scientific preoccupations of his evening walks. If such be the case they do not show it. They stand there leaning their arms on their chairbacks and with a benevolence not untinctured with irony look on at the parental happiness.

The children's frocks are of a heavy, brick-red stuff, embroidered in modern "arty" style. They once belonged to Ingrid and Bert and are precisely alike, save that little knickers come out beneath Snapper's smock. And both have their hair bobbed. Snapper's is a streaky blond, inclined to turn dark. It is bristly and sticky and looks for all the world like a droll, badly fitting wig. But Ellie's is chestnut brown, glossy and fine as silk, as pleasing as her whole little personality. It covers her ears—and these ears are not a pair, one of them being the right size, the other distinctly too large. Her father will sometimes uncover this little abnormality and exclaim over it as though he had never noticed it before, which both makes Ellie giggle and covers her with shame. Her eyes are now golden brown, set far apart and with sweet gleams in them —such a clear and lovely look! The brows above are blond; the nose still unformed, with thick nostrils and almost circular holes; the mouth large and expressive, with a beautifully arching and mobile upper lip. When she laughs, dimples come in her cheeks and she shows her teeth like loosely strung pearls. So far she has lost but one tooth, which her father gently twisted out with his handkerchief after it had grown very wobbling. During this small operation she had paled and trembled very much. Her cheeks have the softness proper to her years, but they are not chubby; indeed, they are rather concave, due to her facial structure, with its somewhat prominent jaw. On one, close to the soft fall of her hair, is a downy freckle.

Ellie is not too well pleased with her looks—a sign that already she troubles about such things. Sadly she thinks it is best to admit it once for all, her face is "homely"; though the rest of her, "on the other hand," is not bad at all. She loves expressions like "on the other hand"; they sound choice and grown-up to her, and she likes to string them together, one after the other: "very likely," "probably," "after all." Snapper is self-critical too, though more in the moral sphere: he suffers from remorse for his attacks of rage and considers himself a tremendous sinner. He is quite certain that heaven is not for such as he; he is sure to go to "the bad place" when he dies, and no persuasions will convince him to the contrary—as that God sees the heart and gladly makes allowances. Obstinately he shakes his head, with the comic, crooked little peruke, and vows there is no place for him in heaven. When he has a cold he is immediately quite choked with mucus; rattles and rumbles from top to toe if you even look at him; his temperature flies up at once and he simply puffs. Nursy is pessimistic on the score of his constitution: such fat-blooded children as he might get a stroke any minute. Once she even thought she saw the moment at hand: Snapper had been in one of his berserker rages, and in the ensuing fit of penitence stood himself in the corner with his back to the room. Suddenly Nursy noticed that his face had gone all blue, far bluer, even, than her own. She raised the alarm, crying out that the child's all too rich blood had at length brought him to his final hour; and Snapper, to his vast astonishment, found himself, so far from being rebuked for evil-doing, encompassed in tenderness and anxiety—until it turned out that his color was not caused by apoplexy but by the distempering on the nursery wall, which had come off on his tear-wet face.

Nursy had come downstairs too, and stands by the door, sleek-haired, owl-eyed, with her hands folded over her white apron, and a severely dignified manner born of her limited intelligence. She is very proud of the care and training she gives her nurslings and declares that they are "enveloping wonderfully." She has had seven suppurated teeth lately removed from her jaws and been measured for a set of symmetrical yellow ones in dark rubber gums; these now embellish her peasant face. She is obsessed with the strange conviction that these teeth of hers are the subject of general conversation, that, as it were, the sparrows on the housetops chatter of them. "Everybody knows I've had a false set put in," she will say; "there has been a great deal of foolish talk about them." She is much given to dark hints and veiled innuendo: speaks, for instance, of a certain Dr. Bleifuss, whom every child knows, and "there are even some in the house who pretend to be him." All one can do with talk like this is charitably to pass it over in silence. But she teaches the children nursery rhymes: gems like:

Puff, puff, here comes the train!
Puff, puff, toot, toot,
Away it goes again.

Or that gastronomical jingle, so suited, in its sparseness, to the times, and yet seemingly with a blitheness of its own:

Monday we begin the week,
Tuesday there's a bone to pick.
Wednesday we're half way through,
Thursday what a great do-do!
Friday we eat what fish we're able,
Saturday we dance round the table.
Sunday brings us pork and greens—
Here's a feast for kings and queens!

Also a certain four-line stanza with a romantic appeal, unutterable and unuttered:

Open the gate, open the gate
And let the carriage drive in.
Who is it in the carriage sits?
A lordly sir with golden hair.

Or, finally that ballad about golden-haired Marianne who sat on a, sat on a, sat on a stone, and combed out her, combed out her, combed out her hair; and about blood-thirsty Rudolph, who pulled out a, pulled out a, pulled out a knife—and his ensuing direful end. Ellie enunciates all these ballads charmingly, with her mobile little lips, and sings them in her sweet little voice—much better than Snapper. She does everything better than he does, and he pays her honest admiration and homage and obeys her in all things except when visited by one of his attacks. Sometimes she teaches him, instructs him upon the birds in the picture-book and tells him their proper names: "This is a chaffinch, Buddy, this is a bullfinch, this is a cowfinch." He has to repeat them after her. She gives him medical instruction too, teaches him the names of diseases, such as inflammation of the lungs, inflammation of the blood, inflammation of the air. If he does not pay attention and cannot say the words after her, she stands him in the corner. Once she even boxed his ears, but was so ashamed that she stood herself in the corner for a long time. Yes, they are fast friends, two souls with but a single thought, and have all their adventures in common. They come home from a walk and relate as with one voice that they have seen two moollies and a teenty-weenty baby calf. They are on familiar terms with the kitchen, which consists of Xaver and the ladies Hinterhofer, two sisters once of the lower middle class who, in these evil days, are reduced to living *"au pair"* as the phrase goes and officiating as cook and housemaid for their board and keep. The little ones have a feeling that Xaver and the Hinterhofers are on much the same footing with their father and mother as they are themselves. At least sometimes, when they have been scolded, they go downstairs and announce that the master and mistress are cross. But playing with the servants lacks charm compared with the joys of playing upstairs. The kitchen could never rise to the height of the games their father can invent. For instance, there is "four gentlemen taking a walk." When they play it Abel will crook his knees until he is the same height with themselves and go walking with them, hand in hand. They never get enough of this sport; they could walk round and round the dining-room a whole day on end, five gentlemen in all, counting the diminished Abel.

Then there is the thrilling cushion game. One of the children, usually Ellie, seats herself, unbeknownst to Abel, in his seat at table. Still as a mouse she awaits his coming. He draws near with his head in the air, descanting in loud, clear tones upon the surpassing comfort of his chair; and sits down on top of Ellie. "What's this, what's this?" says he. And bounces about, deaf to the smothered giggles exploding behind him. "Why have they put a cushion in my chair? And what a queer, hard, awkward-shaped cushion it is!" he goes on. "Frightfully uncomfortable to sit on!" And keeps pushing and bouncing about more and more on the astonishing cushion and clutching behind him into the rapturous giggling and squeaking, until at last he turns round, and the game ends with a magnificent climax of discovery and recognition. They might go through all this a hundred times without diminishing by an iota its power to thrill.

Today is no time for such joys. The imminent festivity disturbs the atmosphere, and besides there is work to be done, and, above all, the eggs to be got. Ellie has just time to recite "Puff, puff," and Cornelius to discover that her ears are not mates, when they are interrupted by the arrival of Danny, come to fetch Bert and Ingrid. Xaver, meantime, has exchanged his striped livery for an ordinary coat, in which he looks rather rough-and-ready, though as brisk and attractive as ever. So then Nursy and the children ascend to the upper regions, the Professor withdraws to his study to read, as always after dinner, and his wife bends her energies upon the sandwiches and salad that must be prepared. And she has another errand as well. Before the young people arrive she has to take her shopping-basket and dash into town on her bicycle, to turn into provisions a sum of money she has in hand, which she dares not keep lest it lose all value.

Cornelius reads, leaning back in his chair, with his cigar between his middle and index fingers. First he reads Macaulay on the origin of the English public debt at the end of the seventeenth century; then an article in a French periodical on the rapid increase in the Spanish debt toward the end of the sixteenth. Both these for his lecture on the morrow. He intends to compare the astonishing prosperity which accompanied the phenomenon in England with its fatal effects a hundred years earlier in Spain, and to analyze the ethical and psychological grounds of the difference in results. For that will give him a chance to refer back from the England of William III, which is the actual subject in hand, to the time of Philip II and the Counter-Reformation, which is his own special field. He has already written a valuable work on this period; it is much cited and got him his professorship. While his cigar burns down and gets strong, he excogitates a few pensive sentences in a key of gentle melancholy, to be delivered before his class next day: about the practically hopeless struggle carried on by the belated Philip against the whole trend of history: against the new, the kingdom-disrupting power of the Germanic ideal of freedom and individual liberty. And about the persistent, futile struggle of the aristocracy, condemned by God and rejected of man, against the forces of progress and change. He savors his sentences; keeps on polishing them while he puts back the books he has been using; then goes upstairs for the usual pause in his day's work, the hour with drawn blinds and closed eyes, which he so imperatively needs. But today, he recalls, he will rest under disturbed conditions, amid the bustle of preparations for the feast. He smiles to find his heart giving a mild flutter at the thought. Disjointed phrases on the theme of black-clad Philip and his times mingle with a confused consciousness that they will soon be dancing down below. For five minutes or so he falls asleep.

As he lies and rests he can hear the sound of the garden gate and the repeated ringing at the bell. Each time a little pang goes through him, of excitement and suspense, at the thought that the young people have begun to fill the floor below. And each time he smiles at himself again —though even his smile is slightly nervous, is tinged with the pleasurable anticipations people always feel before a party. At half past four— it is already dark—he gets up and washes at the wash-stand. The basin has been out of repair for two years. It is supposed to tip, but has broken away from its socket on one side and cannot be mended because there is nobody to mend it; neither replaced because no shop can supply another. So it has to be hung up above the vent and emptied by lifting in both hands and pouring out the water. Cornelius shakes his head over this basin, as he does several times a day—whenever, in fact, he has occasion to use it. He finishes his toilet with care, standing under the ceiling light to polish his glasses till they shine. Then he goes downstairs.

On his way to the dining-room he hears the gramophone already going, and the sound of voices. He puts on a polite, society air; at his tongue's end is the phrase he means to utter: "Pray don't let me disturb you," as he passes directly into the dining-room for his tea. "Pray don't let me disturb you"—it seems to him precisely the *mot juste;* toward the guests cordial and considerate, for himself a very bulwark.

The lower floor is lighted up, all the bulbs in the chandelier are burning save one that has burned out. Cornelius pauses on a lower step and surveys the entrance hall. It looks pleasant and cozy in the bright light, with its copy of Marées over the brick chimney-piece, its wain-

scoted walls—wainscoted in soft wood—and red-carpeted floor, where
the guests stand in groups, chatting, each with his tea-cup and slice of
bread-and-butter spread with anchovy paste. There is a festal haze,
faint scents of hair and clothing and human breath come to him across
the room, it is all characteristic and familiar and highly evocative. The
door into the dressing-room is open, guests are still arriving.

A large group of people is rather bewildering at first sight. The
Professor takes in only the general scene. He does not see Ingrid, who
is standing just at the foot of the steps, in a dark silk frock with a
pleated collar falling softly over the shoulders, and bare arms. She
smiles up at him, nodding and showing her lovely teeth.

"Rested?" she asks, for his private ear. With a quite unwarranted
start he recognizes her, and she presents some of her friends.

"May I introduce Herr Zuber?" she says. "And this is Fräulein
Plaichinger."

Herr Zuber is insignificant. But Fräulein Plaichinger is a perfect
Germania, blond and voluptuous, arrayed in floating draperies. She has
a snub nose, and answers the Professor's salutation in the high, shrill
pipe so many stout women have.

"Delighted to meet you," he says. "How nice of you to come! A
classmate of Ingrid's I suppose?"

And Herr Zuber is a golfing partner of Ingrid's. He is in business;
he works in his uncle's brewery. Cornelius makes a few jokes about
the thinness of the beer and professes to believe that Herr Zuber could
easily do something about the quality if he would. "But pray don't let
me disturb you," he goes on, and turns toward the dining-room.

"There comes Max," says Ingrid. "Max, you sweep, what do you
mean by rolling up at this time of day?" For such is the way they
talk to each other, offensively to an older ear; of social forms, of hos-
pitable warmth, there is no faintest trace. They all call each other by
their first names.

A young man comes up to them out of the dressing-room and makes
his bow; he has an expanse of white shirt-front and a little black string
tie. He is as pretty as a picture, dark, with rosy cheeks, clean-shaven of
course, but with just a sketch of side-whisker. Not a ridiculous or flashy
beauty, not like a gypsy fiddler, but just charming to look at, in a
winning, well-bred way, with kind dark eyes. He even wears his
dinner-jacket a little awkwardly.

"Please don't scold me, Cornelia," he says; "it's the idiotic lectures."
And Ingrid presents him to her father as Herr Hergesell.

Well, and so this is Herr Hergesell. He knows his manners, does Herr
Hergesell, and thanks the master of the house quite ingratiatingly for
his invitation as they shake hands. "I certainly seem to have missed
the bus," says he jocosely. "Of course I have lectures today up to four
o'clock; I would have; and after that I had to go home to change."
Then he talks about his pumps, with which he has just been struggling
in the dressing-room.

"I brought them with me in a bag," he goes on. "Mustn't tramp all over the carpet in our brogues—it's not done. Well, I was ass enough not to fetch along a shoe-horn, and I find I simply can't get in! What a sell! They are the tightest I've ever had, the numbers don't tell you a thing, and all the leather today is just cast iron. It's not leather at all. My poor finger"—he confidingly displays a reddened digit and once more characterizes the whole thing as a "sell," and a putrid sell into the bargain. He really does talk just as Ingrid said he did, with a peculiar nasal drawl, not affectedly in the least, but merely because that is the way of all the Hergesells.

Dr. Cornelius says it is very careless of them not to keep a shoe-horn in the cloak-room and displays proper sympathy with the mangled finger. "But now you *really* must not let me disturb you any longer," he goes on. *"Auf wiedersehen!"* And he crosses the hall into the dining-room.

There are guests there too, drinking tea; the family table is pulled out. But the Professor goes at once to his own little upholstered corner with the electric light bulb above it—the nook where he usually drinks his tea. His wife is sitting there talking with Bert and two other young men, one of them Herzl, whom Cornelius knows and greets; the other a typical "Wandervogel" named Möller, a youth who obviously neither owns nor cares to own the correct evening dress of the middle classes (in fact, there is no such thing any more), nor to ape the manners of a gentleman (and, in fact, there is no such thing any more either). He has a wilderness of hair, horn spectacles, and a long neck, and wears golf stockings and a belted blouse. His regular occupation, the Professor learns, is banking, but he is by way of being an amateur folk-lorist and collects folk-songs from all localities and in all languages. He sings them, too, and at Ingrid's command has brought his guitar; it is hanging in the dressing-room in an oilcloth case. Herzl, the actor, is small and slight, but he has a strong growth of black beard, as you can tell by the thick coat of powder on his cheeks. His eyes are larger than life, with a deep and melancholy glow. He has put on rouge besides the powder —those dull carmine high-lights on the cheeks can be nothing but a cosmetic. "Queer," thinks the Professor. "You would think a man would be one thing or the other—not melancholic and use face paint at the same time. It's a psychological contradiction. How can a melancholy man rouge? But here we have a perfect illustration of the abnormality of the artist soul-form. It can make possible a contradiction like this— perhaps it even consists in the contradiction. All very interesting—and no reason whatever for not being polite to him. Politeness is a primitive convention—and legitimate. . . . Do take some lemon, Herr Hofschauspieler!"

Court actors and court theaters—there are no such things any more, really. But Herzl relishes the sound of the title, notwithstanding he is a revolutionary artist. This must be another contradiction inherent in his soul-form; so, at least, the Professor assumes, and he is probably

right. The flattery he is guilty of is a sort of atonement for his previous
hard thoughts about the rouge.

"Thank you so much—it's really too good of you, sir," says Herzl,
quite embarrassed. He is so overcome that he almost stammers; only
his perfect enunciation saves him. His whole bearing toward his hostess
and the master of the house is exaggeratedly polite. It is almost as
though he had a bad conscience in respect of his rouge; as though
an inward compulsion had driven him to put it on, but now, seeing it
through the Professor's eyes, he disapproves of it himself, and thinks,
by an air of humility toward the whole of unrouged society, to mitigate
its effect.

They drink their tea and chat: about Möller's folk-songs, about
Basque folk-songs and Spanish folk-songs; from which they pass to
the new production of *Don Carlos* at the Stadttheater, in which Herzl
plays the title-rôle. He talks about his own rendering of the part and
says he hopes his conception of the character has unity. They go on to
criticize the rest of the cast, the setting, and the production as a whole;
and Cornelius is struck, rather painfully, to find the conversation trend-
ing toward his own special province, back to Spain and the Counter-
Reformation. He has done nothing at all to give it this turn, he is perfectly innocent, and hopes it does not look as though he had sought
an occasion to play the professor. He wonders, and falls silent, feeling
relieved when the little folk come up to the table. Ellie and Snapper
have on their blue velvet Sunday frocks; they are permitted to partake
in the festivities up to bedtime. They look shy and large-eyed as they
say how-do-you-do to the strangers and, under pressure, repeat their
names and ages. Herr Möller does nothing but gaze at them solemnly,
but Herzl is simply ravished. He rolls his eyes up to heaven and puts
his hands over his mouth; he positively blesses them. It all, no doubt,
comes from his heart, but he is so addicted to theatrical methods of
making an impression and getting an effect that both words and behavior ring frightfully false. And even his enthusiasm for the little
folk looks too much like part of his general craving to make up for
the rouge on his cheeks.

The tea-table has meanwhile emptied of guests, and dancing is going
on in the hall. The children run off, the Professor prepares to retire.
"Go and enjoy yourselves," he says to Möller and Herzl, who have
sprung from their chairs as he rises from his. They shake hands and
he withdraws into his study, his peaceful kingdom, where he lets down
the blinds, turns on the desk lamp, and sits down to work.

It is work which can be done, if necessary, under disturbed conditions:
nothing but a few letters and a few notes. Of course, Cornelius's mind
wanders. Vague impressions float through it: Herr Hergesell's refractory pumps, the high pipe in that plump body of the Plaichinger female.
As he writes, or leans back in his chair and stares into space, his thoughts
go back to Herr Möller's collection of Basque folk-songs, to Herzl's pos-
ings and humility, to "his" Carlos and the court of Philip II. There is

something strange, he thinks, about conversations. They are so ductile, they will flow of their own accord in the direction of one's dominating interest. Often and often he has seen this happen. And while he is thinking, he is listening to the sounds next door—rather subdued, he finds them. He hears only voices, no sound of footsteps. The dancers do not glide or circle round the room; they merely walk about over the carpet, which does not hamper their movements in the least. Their way of holding each other is quite different and strange, and they move to the strains of the gramophone, to the weird music of the new world. He concentrates on the music and makes out that it is a jazz-band record, with various percussion instruments and the clack and clatter of castanets, which, however, are not even faintly suggestive of Spain, but merely jazz like the rest. No, not Spain. . . . His thoughts are back at the old round.

Half an hour goes by. It occurs to him it would be no more than friendly to go and contribute a box of cigarettes to the festivities next door. Too bad to ask the young people to smoke their own—though they have probably never thought of it. He goes into the empty dining-room and takes a box from his supply in the cupboard: not the best ones, nor yet the brand he himself prefers, but a certain long, thin kind he is not averse to getting rid of—after all, they are nothing but young-sters. He takes the box into the hall, holds it up with a smile, and deposits it on the mantel-shelf. After which he gives a look round and returns to his own room.

There comes a lull in dance and music. The guests stand about the room in groups or round the table at the window or are seated in a circle by the fireplace. Even the built-in stairs, with their worn velvet carpet, are crowded with young folk as in an amphitheater: Max Hergesell is there, leaning back with one elbow on the step above and gesticulating with his free hand as he talks to the shrill, voluptuous Plaichinger. The floor of the hall is nearly empty, save just in the center: there, directly beneath the chandelier, the two little ones in their blue velvet frocks clutch each other in an awkward embrace and twirl silently round and round, oblivious of all else. Cornelius, as he passes, strokes their hair, with a friendly word; it does not distract them from their small solemn preoccupation. But at his own door he turns to glance round and sees young Hergesell push himself off the stair by his elbow—probably because he noticed the Professor. He comes down into the arena, takes Ellie out of her brother's arms, and dances with her himself. It looks very comic, without the music, and he crouches down just as Cornelius does when he goes walking with the four gentlemen, holding the fluttered Ellie as though she were grown up and taking little "shimmying" steps. Everybody watches with huge enjoyment, the gramophone is put on again, dancing becomes general. The Professor stands and looks, with his hand on the door-knob. He nods and laughs; when he finally shuts himself into his study the mechanical smile still lingers on his lips.

Again he turns over pages by his desk lamp, takes notes, attends to a few simple matters. After a while he notices that the guests have forsaken the entrance hall for his wife's drawing-room, into which there is a door from his own study as well. He hears their voices and the sounds of a guitar being tuned. Herr Möller, it seems, is to sing— and does so. He twangs the strings of his instrument and sings in a powerful bass a ballad in a strange tongue, possibly Swedish. The Professor does not succeed in identifying it, though he listens attentively to the end, after which there is great applause. The sound is deadened by the portière that hangs over the dividing door. The young bank-clerk begins another song. Cornelius goes softly in.

It is half-dark in the drawing-room; the only light is from the shaded standard lamp, beneath which Möller sits, on the divan, with his legs crossed, picking his strings. His audience is grouped easily about; as there are not enough seats, some stand, and more, among them many young ladies, are simply sitting on the floor with their hands clasped round their knees or even with their legs stretched out before them. Hergesell sits thus, in his dinner jacket, next the piano, with Fräulein Plaichinger beside him. Frau Cornelius is holding both children on her lap as she sits in her easy-chair opposite the singer. Snapper, the Boeotian, begins to talk loud and clear in the middle of the song and has to be intimidated with hushings and finger-shakings. Never, never would Ellie allow herself to be guilty of such conduct. She sits there daintily erect and still on her mother's knee. The Professor tries to catch her eye and exchange a private signal with his little girl; but she does not see him. Neither does she seem to be looking at the singer. Her gaze is directed lower down.

Möller sings the "joli tambour":

"*Sire, mon roi, donnez-moi votre fille—*"

They are all enchanted. "How good!" Hergesell is heard to say, in the odd, nasally condescending Hergesell tone. The next one is a beggar ballad, to a tune composed by young Möller himself; it elicits a storm of applause:

Gypsy lassie a-goin' to the fair, Huzza!
Gypsy laddie a-goin' to be there—
Huzza, diddlety umpty dido!

Laughter and high spirits, sheer reckless hilarity, reigns after this jovial ballad. "Frightfully good!" Hergesell comments again, as before. Follows another popular song, this time a Hungarian one; Möller sings it in its own outlandish tongue, and most effectively. The Professor applauds with ostentation. It warms his heart and does him good, this outcropping of artistic, historic, and cultural elements all amongst the shimmying. He goes up to young Möller and congratulates him, talks about the songs and their sources, and Möller promises to lend him a certain annotated book of folk-songs. Cornelius is the more cordial because all the time, as fathers do, he has been comparing the parts and achievements of this young stranger with those of his own son, and being gnawed by envy and chagrin. This young Möller, he is thinking, is a capable bank-clerk (though about Möller's capacity he knows nothing whatever) and has this special gift besides, which must have taken talent and energy to cultivate. "And here is my poor Bert, who knows nothing and can do nothing and thinks of nothing except playing the clown, without even talent for that!" He tries to be just; he tells himself that, after all, Bert has innate refinement; that probably there is a good deal more to him than there is to the successful Möller; that perhaps he has even something of the poet in him, and his dancing and table-waiting are due to mere boyish folly and the distraught times. But paternal envy and pessimism win the upper hand; when Möller begins another song, Dr. Cornelius goes back to his room.

He works as before, with divided attention, at this and that, while it gets on for seven o'clock. Then he remembers a letter he may just as well write, a short letter and not very important, but letter-writing is wonderful for the way it takes up the time, and it is almost half past when he has finished. At half past eight the Italian salad will be served; so now is the prescribed moment for the Professor to go out into the wintry darkness to post his letters and take his daily quantum of fresh air and exercise. They are dancing again, and he will have to pass through the hall to get his hat and coat; but they are used to him now, he need not stop and beg them not to be disturbed. He lays away his papers, takes up the letters he has written, and goes out. But he sees his wife sitting near the door of his room and pauses a little by her easy-chair.

She is watching the dancing. Now and then the big folk or some of their guests stop to speak to her; the party is at its height, and there are more onlookers than these two: blue-faced Ann is standing at the bottom of the stairs, in all the dignity of her limitations. She is waiting for the children, who simply cannot get their fill of these unwonted festivities, and watching over Snapper, lest his all too rich blood be churned to the danger-point by too much twirling round. And not only the nursery but the kitchen takes an interest: Xaver and the two ladies Hinterhofer are standing by the pantry door looking on with relish. Fräulein Walburga, the elder of the two sunken sisters (the culinary section—she objects to being called a cook), is a whimsical, good-natured sort, brown-eyed, wearing glasses with thick circular lenses; the nose-piece is wound with a bit of rag to keep it from pressing on her nose. Fräulein Cecilia is younger, though not so precisely young either. Her bearing is as self-assertive as usual, this being her way of sustaining her dignity as a former member of the middle class. For Fräulein Cecilia feels acutely her descent into the ranks of domestic service. She positively declines to wear a cap or other badge of servitude, and her hardest trial is on the Wednesday evening when she has to serve the dinner while Xaver has his afternoon out. She hands the dishes with averted face and elevated nose—a fallen queen; and so distressing is it to behold her degradation that one evening when the little folk happened to be at table and saw her they both with one accord burst into tears. Such anguish is unknown to young Xaver. He enjoys serving and does it with an ease born of practice as well as talent, for he was once a "piccolo." But otherwise he is a thorough-paced good-for-nothing and windbag—with quite distinct traits of character of his own, as his long-suffering employers are always ready to concede, but perfectly impossible and a bag of wind for all that. One must just take him as he is, they think, and not expect figs from thistles. He is the child and product of the disrupted times, a perfect specimen of his generation, follower of the revolution, Bolshevist sympathizer. The Professor's name for him is the "minute-man," because he is always to be counted on in any sudden crisis, if only it address his sense of humor or love of novelty, and will display therein amazing readiness and resource. But he utterly lacks a sense of duty and can as little be trained to the performance of the daily round and common task as some kinds of dog can be taught to jump over a stick. It goes so plainly against the grain that criticism is disarmed. One becomes resigned. On grounds that appealed to him as unusual and amusing he would be ready to turn out of his bed at any hour of the night. But he simply cannot get up before eight in the morning, he cannot do it, he will not jump over the stick. Yet all day long the evidence of this free and untrammeled existence, the sound of his mouth-organ, his joyous whistle, or his raucous but expressive voice lifted in song, rises to the hearing of the world above-stairs; and the smoke of his cigarette fills the pantry. While the Hinterhofer ladies work he stands and looks on. Of a morning while the Professor is breakfasting, he tears the leaf off the study calendar—but does not lift a finger to dust the room. Dr. Cornelius has often told him to leave the calendar alone, for he tends to tear off two leaves at a time and thus to add to the general confusion. But young Xaver appears to find joy in this activity, and will not be deprived of it.

Again, he is fond of children, a winning trait. He will throw himself into games with the little folk in the garden, make and mend their toys with great ingenuity, even read aloud from their books—and very droll it sounds in his thick-lipped pronunciation. With his whole soul he loves the cinema; after an evening spent there he inclines to melancholy and yearning and talking to himself. Vague hopes stir in him that some day he may make his fortune in that gay world and belong to it by rights—hopes based on his shock of hair and his physical agility and daring. He likes to climb the ash tree in the front garden, mounting branch by branch to the very top and frightening everybody to death who sees him. Once there he lights a cigarette and smokes it as he sways to and fro, keeping a look-out for a cinema director who might chance to come along and engage him.

If he changed his striped jacket for mufti, he might easily dance with the others and no one would notice the difference. For the big folk's friends are rather anomalous in their clothing: evening dress is worn by a few, but it is by no means the rule. There is quite a sprinkling of guests, both male and female, in the same general style as Möller the ballad-singer. The Professor is familiar with the circumstances of most of this young generation he is watching as he stands beside his wife's chair; he has heard them spoken of by name. They are students at the high school or at the School of Applied Art; they lead, at least the masculine portion, that precarious and scrambling existence which is purely the product of the time. There is a tall, pale, spindling youth, the son of a dentist, who lives by speculation. From all the Professor hears, he is a perfect Aladdin. He keeps a car, treats his friends to champagne suppers, and showers presents upon them on every occasion, costly little trifles in mother-of-pearl and gold. So today he has brought gifts to the young givers of the feast: for Bert a gold lead-pencil, and for Ingrid a pair of ear-rings of barbaric size, great gold circlets that fortunately do not have to go through the little ear-lobe, but are fastened over it by means of a clip. The big folk come laughing to their parents to display these trophies; and the parents shake their heads even while they admire—Aladdin bowing over and over from afar.

The young people appear to be absorbed in their dancing—if the performance they are carrying out with so much still concentration can be called dancing. They stride across the carpet, slowly, according to some unfathomable prescript, strangely embraced; in the newest attitude, tummy advanced and shoulders high, waggling the hips. They do not get tired, because nobody could. There is no such thing as heightened color or heaving bosoms. Two girls may dance together or two young men—it is all the same. They move to the exotic strains of the gramophone, played with the loudest needles to procure the maximum of sound: shimmies, foxtrots, one-steps, double foxes, African shimmies, Java dances, and Creole polkas, the wild musky melodies follow one another, now furious, now languishing, a monotonous Negro program in unfamiliar rhythm, to a clacking, clashing, and strumming orchestral accompaniment.

"What is that record?" Cornelius inquires of Ingrid, as she passes him by in the arms of the pale young speculator, with reference to the piece then playing, whose alternate languors and furies he finds comparatively pleasing and showing a certain resourcefulness in detail.

"*Prince of Pappenheim:* 'Console thee, dearest child,' " she answers, and smiles pleasantly back at him with her white teeth.

The cigarette smoke wreathes beneath the chandelier. The air is blue with a festal haze compact of sweet and thrilling ingredients that stir the blood with memories of green-sick pains and are particularly poignant to those whose youth—like the Professor's own—has been over-sensitive. . . . The little folk are still on the floor. They are allowed to stop up until eight, so great is their delight in the party. The guests have got used to their presence; in their own way, they have their place in the doings of the evening. They have separated, anyhow: Snapper revolves all alone in the middle of the carpet, in his little blue velvet smock, while Ellie is running after one of the dancing couples, trying to hold the man fast by his coat. It is Max Hergesell and Fräulein Plaichinger. They dance well, it is a pleasure to watch them. One has to admit that these mad modern dances, when the right people dance them, are not so bad after all—they have something quite taking. Young Hergesell is a capital leader, dances according to rule, yet with individuality. So it looks. With what aplomb can he walk backward —when space permits! And he knows how to be graceful standing still in a crowd. And his partner supports him well, being unsuspectedly lithe and buoyant, as fat people often are. They look at each other, they are talking, paying no heed to Ellie, though others are smiling to see the child's persistence. Dr. Cornelius tries to catch up his little sweetheart as she passes and draw her to him. But Ellie eludes him, almost peevishly; her dear Abel is nothing to her now. She braces her little arms against his chest and turns her face away with a persecuted look. Then escapes to follow her fancy once more.

The Professor feels an involuntary twinge. Uppermost in his heart is hatred for this party, with its power to intoxicate and estrange his darling child. His love for her—that not quite disinterested, not quite unexceptionable love of his—is easily wounded. He wears a mechanical smile, but his eyes have clouded, and he stares fixedly at a point in the carpet, between the dancers' feet.

"The children ought to go to bed," he tells his wife. But she pleads for another quarter of an hour; she has promised already, and they do love it so! He smiles again and shakes his head, stands so a moment and then goes across to the cloak-room, which is full of coats and hats and scarves and overshoes. He has trouble in rummaging out his own coat, and Max Hergesell comes out of the hall, wiping his brow.

"Going out, sir?" he asks, in Hergesellian accents, dutifully helping the older man on with his coat. "Silly business this, with my pumps," he says. "They pinch like hell. The brutes are simply too tight for me, quite apart from the bad leather. They press just here on the ball of my great toe"—he stands on one foot and holds the other in his hand— "it's simply unbearable. There's nothing for it but to take them off; my brogues will have to do the business. . . . Oh, let me help you, sir."

"Thanks," says Cornelius. "Don't trouble. Get rid of your own tormentors. . . . Oh, thanks very much!" For Hergesell has gone on one knee to snap the fasteners of his snowboots.

Once more the Professor expresses his gratitude; he is pleased and touched by so much sincere respect and youthful readiness to serve. "Go and enjoy yourself," he counsels. "Change your shoes and make up for what you have been suffering. Nobody can dance in shoes that pinch. Good-by, I must be off to get a breath of fresh air."

"I'm going to dance with Ellie now," calls Hergesell after him. "She'll be a first-rate dancer when she grows up, and that I'll swear to."

"Think so?" Cornelius answers, already half out. "Well, you are a connoisseur, I'm sure. Don't get curvature of the spine with stooping."

He nods again and goes. "Fine lad," he thinks as he shuts the door. "Student of engineering. Knows what he's bound for, got a good clear head, and so well set up and pleasant too." And again paternal envy rises as he compares his poor Bert's status with this young man's, which he puts in the rosiest light that his son's may look the darker. Thus he sets out on his evening walk.

He goes up the avenue, crosses the bridge, and walks along the bank on the other side as far as the next bridge but one. The air is wet and cold, with a little snow now and then. He turns up his coat-collar and slips the crook of his cane over the arm behind his back. Now and then he ventilates his lungs with a long deep breath of the night air. As usual when he walks, his mind reverts to his professional preoccupations, he thinks about his lectures and the things he means to say tomorrow about Philip's struggle against the Germanic revolution, things steeped in melancholy and penetratingly just. Above all just, he thinks. For in one's dealings with the young it behooves one to display the scientific spirit, to exhibit the principles of enlightenment—not only for purposes of mental discipline, but on the human and individual side, in order not to wound them or indirectly offend their political sensibilities; particularly in these days, when there is so much tinder in the air, opinions are so frightfully split up and chaotic, and you may so easily incur attacks from one party or the other, or even give rise to scandal, by taking sides on a point of history. "And taking sides is unhistoric anyhow," so he muses. "Only justice, only impartiality is historic." And could not, properly considered, be otherwise. . . . For justice can have nothing of youthful fire and blithe, fresh, loyal conviction. It is by nature melancholy. And, being so, has secret affinity with the lost cause and the forlorn hope rather than with the fresh and blithe and loyal—perhaps this affinity is its very essence and without it it would not exist at all! . . . "And is there then no such thing as justice?" the Professor asks himself, and ponders the question so deeply that he absently posts his letters in the next box and turns round to go home. This thought of his is unsettling and disturbing to the scientific mind—but is it not after all itself scientific, psychological, conscientious, and therefore to be accepted without prejudice, no matter how upsetting? In the midst of which musings Dr. Cornelius finds himself back at his own door.

On the outer threshold stands Xaver, and seems to be looking for him.

"Herr Professor," says Xaver, tossing back his hair, "go upstairs to Ellie straight off. She's in a bad way."

"What's the matter?" asks Cornelius in alarm. "Is she ill?"

"No-o, not to say ill," answers Xaver. "She's just in a bad way and crying fit to bust her little heart. It's along o' that chap with the shirt-front that danced with her—Herr Hergesell. She couldn't be got to go upstairs peaceably, not at no price at all, and she's b'en crying bucketfuls."

"Nonsense," says the Professor, who has entered and is tossing off his things in the cloak-room. He says no more; opens the glass door and without a glance at the guests turns swiftly to the stairs. Takes them two at a time, crosses the upper hall and the small room leading into the nursery. Xaver follows at his heels, but stops at the nursery door.

A bright light still burns within, showing the gay frieze that runs all round the room, the large row of shelves heaped with a confusion of toys, the rocking-horse on his swaying platform, with red-varnished nostrils and raised hoofs. On the linoleum lie other toys—building blocks, railway trains, a little trumpet. The two white cribs stand not far apart, Ellie's in the window corner, Snapper's out in the room.

Snapper is asleep. He has said his prayers in loud, ringing tones, prompted by Nurse, and gone off at once into vehement, profound, and rosy slumber—from which a cannonball fired at close range could not rouse him. He lies with both fists flung back on the pillows on either side of the tousled head with its funny crooked little slumber-tossed wig.

A circle of females surrounds Ellie's bed: not only blue-faced Ann is there, but the Hinterhofer ladies too, talking to each other and to her. They make way as the Professor comes up and reveal the child sitting all pale among her pillows, sobbing and weeping more bitterly than he has ever seen her sob and weep in her life. Her lovely little hands lie on the coverlet in front of her, the nightgown with its narrow lace border has slipped down from her shoulder—such a thin, birdlike little shoulder—and the sweet head Cornelius loves so well, set on the neck like a flower on its stalk, her head is on one side, with the eyes rolled up to the corner between wall and ceiling above her head. For there she seems to envisage the anguish of her heart and even to nod to it—either on purpose or because her head wobbles as her body is shaken with the violence of her sobs. Her eyes rain down tears. The bow-shaped lips are parted, like a little *mater dolorosa's,* and from them issue long, low wails that in nothing resemble the unnecessary and exasperating shrieks of a naughty child, but rise from the deep extremity of her heart and wake in the Professor's own a sympathy that is well-nigh intolerable. He has never seen his darling so before. His feelings find immediate vent in an attack on the ladies Hinterhofer.

"What about the supper?" he asks sharply. "There must be a great deal to do. Is my wife being left to do it alone?"

For the acute sensibilities of the former middle class this is quite enough. The ladies withdraw in righteous indignation, and Xaver Kleinsgutl jeers at them as they pass out. Having been born to low life instead of achieving it, he never loses a chance to mock at their fallen state.

"Childie, childie," murmurs Cornelius, and sitting down by the crib enfolds the anguished Ellie in his arms. "What is the trouble with my darling?"

She bedews his face with her tears.

"Abel . . . Abel . . ." she stammers between sobs. "Why—isn't Max —my brother? Max ought to be—my brother!"

Alas, alas! What mischance is this? Is this what the party has wrought, with its fatal atmosphere? Cornelius glances helplessly up at blue-faced Ann standing there in all the dignity of her limitations with her hands before her on her apron. She purses up her mouth and makes a long face. "It's pretty young," she says, "for the female instincts to be showing up."

"Hold your tongue," snaps Cornelius, in his agony. He has this much to be thankful for, that Ellie does not turn from him now; she does not push him away as she did downstairs, but clings to him in her need, while she reiterates her absurd, bewildered prayer that Max might be her brother, or with a fresh burst of desire demands to be taken downstairs so that he can dance with her again. But Max, of course, is dancing with Fräulein Plaichinger, that behemoth who is his rightful partner and has every claim upon him; whereas Ellie—never, thinks the Professor, his heart torn with the violence of his pity, never has she looked so tiny and birdlike as now, when she nestles to him shaken with sobs and all unaware of what is happening in her little soul. No, she does not know. She does not comprehend that her suffering is on account of Fräulein Plaichinger, fat, overgrown, and utterly within her rights in dancing with Max Hergesell, whereas Ellie may only do it once, by way of a joke, although she is incomparably the more charming of the two. Yet it would be quite mad to reproach young Hergesell with the state of affairs or to make fantastic demands upon him. No, Ellie's suffering is without help or healing and must be covered up. Yet just as it is without understanding, so it is also without restraint— and that is what makes it so horribly painful. Xaver and blue-faced Ann do not feel this pain, it does not affect them—either because of native callousness or because they accept it as the way of nature. But the Professor's fatherly heart is quite torn by it, and by a distressful horror of this passion, so hopeless and so absurd.

Of no avail to hold forth to poor Ellie on the subject of the perfectly good little brother she already has. She only casts a distraught and scornful glance over at the other crib, where Snapper lies vehemently slumbering, and with fresh tears calls again for Max. Of no avail either the promise of a long, long walk tomorrow, all five gentlemen, round and round the dining-room table; or a dramatic description of the thrilling cushion games they will play. No, she will listen to none of all this, nor to lying down and going to sleep. She will not sleep, she will sit bolt upright and suffer. . . . But on a sudden they stop and listen, Abel and Ellie; listen to something miraculous that is coming to pass, that is approaching by strides, two strides, to the nursery door, that now overwhelmingly appears. . . .

It is Xaver's work, not a doubt of that. He has not remained by the door where he stood to gloat over the ejection of the Hinterhofers. No, he has bestirred himself, taken a notion; likewise steps to carry it out. Downstairs he has gone, twitched Herr Hergesell's sleeve, and made a thick-lipped request. So here they both are. Xaver, having done his part, remains by the door; but Max Hergesell comes up to Ellie's crib; in his dinner-jacket, with his sketchy side-whisker and charming black eyes; obviously quite pleased with his rôle of swan knight and fairy prince, as one who should say: "See, here am I, now all losses are restored and sorrows end."

Cornelius is almost as much overcome as Ellie herself.

"Just look," he says feebly, "look who's here. This is uncommonly good of you, Herr Hergesell."

"Not a bit of it," says Hergesell. "Why shouldn't I come to say good night to my fair partner?"

And he approaches the bars of the crib, behind which Ellie sits struck mute. She smiles blissfully through her tears. A funny, high little note that is half a sigh of relief comes from her lips, then she looks dumbly up at her swan knight with her golden-brown eyes—tear-swollen though they are, so much more beautiful than the fat Plaichinger's. She does not put up her arms. Her joy, like her grief, is without understanding; but she does not do that. The lovely little hands lie quiet on the coverlet, and Max Hergesell stands with his arms leaning over the rail as on a balcony.

"And now," he says smartly, "she need not 'sit the livelong night and weep upon her bed'!" He looks at the Professor to make sure he is receiving due credit for the quotation. "Ha ha!" he laughs, "she's beginning young. 'Console thee, dearest child!' Never mind, you're all right! Just as you are you'll be wonderful! You've only got to grow up. . . . And you'll lie down and go to sleep like a good girl, now I've come to say good night? And not cry any more, little Lorelei?"

Ellie looks up at him, transfigured. One birdlike shoulder is bare; the Professor draws the lace-trimmed nighty over it. There comes into his mind a sentimental story he once read about a dying child who longs to see a clown he had once, with unforgettable ecstasy, beheld in a circus. And they bring the clown to the bedside marvelously arrayed embroidered before and behind with silver butterflies; and the child dies happy. Max Hergesell is not embroidered, and Ellie, thank God, is not going to die, she has only "been in a bad way." But, after all, the effect is the same. Young Hergesell leans over the bars of the crib and rattles on, more for the father's ear than the child's, but Ellie does not know that—and the father's feelings toward him are a most singular mixture of thankfulness, embarrassment, and hatred.

"Good night, little Lorelei," says Hergesell, and gives her his hand through the bars. Her pretty, soft, white little hand is swallowed up in the grasp of his big, strong, red one. "Sleep well," he says, "and sweet dreams! But don't dream about me—God forbid! Not at your age—

ha ha!" And then the fairy clown's visit is at an end. Cornelius accompanies him to the door. "No, no, positively, no thanks called for, don't mention it," he large-heartedly protests; and Xaver goes downstairs with him, to help serve the Italian salad.

But Dr. Cornelius returns to Ellie, who is now lying down, with her cheek pressed into her flat little pillow.

"Well, wasn't that lovely?" he says as he smooths the covers. She nods, with one last little sob. For a quarter of an hour he sits beside her and watches while she falls asleep in her turn, beside the little brother who found the right way so much earlier than she. Her silky brown hair takes the enchanting fall it always does when she sleeps; deep, deep lie the lashes over the eyes that late so abundantly poured forth their sorrow; the angelic mouth with its bowed upper lip is peacefully relaxed and a little open. Only now and then comes a belated catch in her slow breathing.

And her small hands, like pink and white flowers, lie so quietly, one on the coverlet, the other on the pillow by her face—Dr. Cornelius, gazing, feels his heart melt with tenderness as with strong wine.

"How good," he thinks, "that she breathes in oblivion with every breath she draws! That in childhood each night is a deep, wide gulf between one day and the next. Tomorrow, beyond all doubt, young Hergesell will be a pale shadow, powerless to darken her little heart. Tomorrow, forgetful of all but present joy, she will walk with Abel and Snapper, all five gentlemen, round and round the table, will play the ever-thrilling cushion game."

Heaven be praised for that!

RAINER MARIA RILKE

The Tale of the Hands of God

Rainer Maria Rilke (1875–1926) was born in Prague. He completed his first volume of poetry at 19. Volume after volume of verse followed, and in 1899, Rilke began to wander restlessly all over Europe, finally settling in Paris, where he associated with the French sculptor, Auguste Rodin. Some of Rilke's best known works are *Poems from the Book of Hours, Duino Elegies, Sonnets to Orpheus, Stories of God* and *Journal of My Other Self*. [From *Stories of God* by Rainer Maria Rilke; copyright 1932 by W. W. Norton & Co., Inc.; used by permission of the publishers; translated by M. D. Herter Norton and Nora Purtscher-Wydenbruck.]

RECENTLY, ONE MORNING, I met the lady who lives next door. We exchanged greetings.

"What an autumn!" she exclaimed after a pause, and looked up at the sky. I did the same. The morning was indeed very clear and exquisite for October.

Suddenly I had an idea. "What an autumn!" I cried, waving about a little with my hands. And my neighbor nodded approvingly. I watched her thus for a moment. Her good, healthy face bobbed up and down so amiably. It was very bright, only around the lips and at the temples there were little shadowy wrinkles. How could she have got them? And then I asked, all unexpectedly: "And your little girls?"

The wrinkles in her face vanished for a second, but gathered again at once, darker than before. "Well, thank God; but—"; my neighbor began to walk on, and I now strode along at her left, as is proper.

"You know, they have both reached the age, those children, when they ask questions all day long. 'What'—all day long, and even into the night."

"Yes," I murmured, "there is a time . . ."

But she took no notice.

"And not just questions such as: Where does this street-car go? How many stars are there? And is ten thousand more than many? Quite different things! For example: Does God speak Chinese too? What does God look like? Always everything about God! But that's something we ourselves don't know—"

"No, of course—" I agreed, "though we can have our guesses . . ."

"Or about God's hands—what is one to—"

I looked my neighbor in the eyes. "Pardon me," said I very politely, "you just said the hands of God, did you not?"

She nodded. I think she was a little surprised.

"Well," I hastened to add, "I happen to know something about his hands. By chance," I remarked quickly, as I saw her eyes grow round, "quite by chance—I—well," I finished with considerable decision, "I will tell you what I know. If you have a moment, I will accompany you to your house; that will just give me time."

"Gladly," she said, when at last I let her speak, still much astonished, "but wouldn't you like . . . ?"

"To tell the children myself? No, dear lady, that wouldn't do, that wouldn't do at all. You see, I promptly get embarrassed when I have to talk with children. That in itself is not bad. But the children might think I was embarrassed because I felt myself telling lies. . . . And as the veracity of my story is very important to me . . . You can repeat it to the children; you will surely do it much better. You can put it together and embellish it; I will just give you the simple facts in the shortest form. Shall I?"

"Very well, very well," said my neighbor absently.

I reflected: "In the beginning—," but I broke off at once. "I may assume that you, my dear neighbor, already know many of the things that I would first have to tell the children. For example, about the creation . . ."

There was a considerable pause.

"Yes—and on the seventh day . . ." The good woman's voice was high and sharp.

"Stop!" said I. "We must think of the earlier days too; for indeed it is they that concern us. Well, God, as we know, began his work by making the earth, dividing it from the waters, and decreeing light. Then he fashioned, with amazing rapidity, things—I mean the big real things that are: rocks, mountains, a tree and after this pattern many trees."

Now I had for some time been hearing footsteps behind us, which, neither caught up to us nor fell back. That bothered me, and I became entangled in my story of the creation as I went on in the following manner: "One can only arrive at an understanding of this swift and fruitful activity if one assumes that after long and deep reflection everything must have been all ready in his head before he . . ."

Now at last the footsteps were beside us, and a not exactly pleasant voice fastened itself upon us: "Oh, surely you are speaking of Herr Schmidt, pardon me . . ."

I looked at the newcomer with annoyance, but my companion became very much embarrassed. "Hm," she coughed, "no—that is—yes—we were just speaking, in a way . . ."

"What an autumn!" said the other woman suddenly, as though nothing had happened, and her red little face beamed.

"Yes," I heard my neighbor reply, "you are right, Frau Hüpfer, an exceptionally fine autumn."

Then the ladies parted. Frau Hüpfer tittered on: "And give the little children my love." My good neighbor took no more notice; she was so curious to hear my story. I, however, declared with incomprehensible asperity: "Yes, but now I've forgotten where we stopped."

"You were just saying something about his head—that is—" My neighbor turned scarlet.

I was truly sorry for her, so I quickly went on: "Well, you see as long as only things had been created, God did not need to look down on the earth continually. Nothing could happen there. The wind was, indeed, already moving among the mountains, which were so like the clouds it had long known, but it still shunned the trees with a certain mistrust. And that was quite right with God. The things he had fashioned almost in his sleep, but when he came to the animals, the work began to interest him; he bent over them and only seldom lifted his broad brows to cast a glance down at the earth. He forgot it completely when he began to create man. I don't know which complicated part of the body he had arrived at, when there was a rush of wings about him. An angel hurried by, singing: 'Thou who seest all . . .'

"God started. He had caused that angel to sin, for it was a lie he had just sung. Quickly God-the-Father peered down. And sure enough, something had already happened that was hardly to be remedied. A little bird was fluttering hither and yon over the earth, as though it were frightened, and God was not in a position to help it home, for he had not seen out of which forest the poor creature had come. He grew very vexed and said: 'The birds are to sit still where I put them.' But then he remembered that at the request of the angels he had lent them wings, and this circumstance annoyed him even more. Now in such a state of mind nothing is so salutary as work. And busied with the construction of man, God quickly grew happy again. He had the eyes of the angels before him as mirrors, measured his own features in them, and slowly and carefully modeled the first face on a ball in his lap. He had succeeded with the forehead. But it was much more difficult for him to make the two nostrils symmetrical. He stooped lower and lower over the work, when a wind passed over him again; he looked up. The same angel was circling around him; no hymn was to be heard this time, for with the lie the boy's voice had been extinguished, but God could see by his mouth that he was still singing: 'Thou who seest all . . .'

"At that moment St. Nicholas, who stood high in God's favor, came up to him and said through his big beard: 'Your lions are sitting quite still, and very haughty beasts they are, I must say. But a little dog is running round on the very edge of the world, a terrier, see, he will fall off in a moment.'

"And indeed, God noticed a little bright speck, white, like a tiny light, dancing about in the neighborhood of Scandinavia, where the earth is already so fearfully round. And he was exceedingly angry and reproachfully told St. Nicholas, if he didn't like his lions, he should try and make some himself. Whereupon St. Nicholas walked out of heaven and slammed the door so hard that a star fell down, right on the terrier's head. Now the mischief was done, and God had to admit to himself that it was all his own fault; and he determined not to take his eyes off the earth any more. And so it was. He left the work to his hands, which of course are very wise themselves, and although he was extremely curious to see what man might look like, he continued to gaze fixedly down at the earth, where now, as if out of spite, not a leaflet would stir. In order to have at least a little pleasure after all this trouble, he had bidden his hands to show him man first before they handed him over to life. Repeatedly he asked, as children ask when they play hide-and-seek, 'Ready?' But in answer he heard the kneading of his hands and he waited. It seemed very long to him.

"Then suddenly he saw something falling through space, something dark and apparently coming from quite near him. Filled with evil foreboding, he called to his hands. They appeared, all blotched with clay, hot and trembling.

"'Where is man?' God thundered at them.

"The right hand flew at the left: 'You dropped him!'

"'Excuse me,' countered the left, provoked, 'you insisted on doing it all by yourself, you wouldn't even let me have anything to say.'

"'But you ought to have held him.' And the right hand drew back as if to strike, but then thought better of it, and both hands said together, drowning each other's voices:

"'He was so impatient, man. He was in such a hurry to live. It is not our fault; really, we are both innocent.'

"But God was seriously angry. He pushed both hands away, for they blocked the earth from his sight. 'I have finished with you from now on; go and do as you like!'

"And that is what his hands have been trying to do ever since, but whatever they start, they can only make a beginning. Without God there is no perfection. And so at last they grew tired of it. Now they are on their knees all day long, doing penance—at least, so it is said. To us, however, it appears as though God were resting, because he is angry with his hands. It is still the seventh day."

I was silent for a moment. My companion used that moment very sensibly: "And do you think they will never again be reconciled?"

"Oh, yes," I said. "At least I hope so."

"And when might that be?"

"Not until God knows what man, whom his hands dropped against his will, looks like."

My neighbor reflected, then said with a laugh: "But all he needs do is to look down . . ."

"Pardon me," said I politely, "your remark shows acumen, but my story is not yet done. You see, when the hands had got out of the way and God looked over the earth again, another instant—or, rather, a thousand years, which is of course the same thing—had gone by. Instead of one man, there were a million. But they were all already wearing clothes. And as the fashion was very unbecoming at that time and even distorted people's faces, God received an entirely false and (I will not conceal the fact) a very bad impression of mankind."

"Hm," said my neighbor, about to make some remark. I took no notice, but concluded with great emphasis:

"And that is why it is urgently necessary that God should learn what man really is like. Let us rejoice that there are those who tell him . . ."

But she did not yet rejoice.

"And who might they be, if you please?"

"Simply the children, and now and again the people too who paint, write poems, build . . ."

"Build what, churches?"

"Yes, churches too, and everything . . ."

My neighbor slowly shook her head. Parts of my story seemed to her very remarkable. We had already gone past her house and now turned slowly about. Suddenly she exclaimed with a merry laugh:

"But what nonsense, since God is omniscient! He must have known exactly where, for example, the little bird had come from." She looked at me triumphantly.

I must confess I was rather taken aback, but when I had recovered my composure, I succeeded in assuming a very serious expression. "My dear lady," I informed her, "that is really a story in itself. But lest you think that is merely an excuse on my part" [naturally, she protested warmly], "I will briefly explain. God has all the attributes, of course. But before he was in a position to exercise these faculties—as it were— upon the world, they all seemed to him like a single great force. I don't know whether I make myself clear. But in the face of things, his powers grew specialized and became, to a certain degree, duties. It was hard for him to remember everything. There are always conflicts. (Incidentally, all this I am telling to you alone, and you must on no account repeat it to the children.)"

"Oh, I wouldn't dream of it," my listener declared.

"You see, if an angel had flown by him singing: 'Thou who knowest all,' everything would have come right . . ."

"And there would have been no need for this story?"

"Exactly," I confirmed, and prepared to take my leave.

"But are you absolutely certain about all this?"

"I am absolutely certain," I replied almost solemnly.

"Then, I shall have plenty to tell the children today!"

"I should love to be able to listen. Good by."

"Good by," answered my neighbor.

Then she turned back again. "But why did that particular angel . . ."

"My dear neighbor," said I, interrupting, "I now see that your two dear little girls ask so many questions not because they are children . . ."

"But—?" she asked inquisitively.

"Well, the doctors say there are certain hereditary traits . . ."

My neighbor shook her finger at me. But we parted, nevertheless, the best of friends.

When I met my good neighbor again later (after a considerable interval, indeed), she was not alone, so I could not ask her whether she had told her little girls my story, and with what success. But my doubts upon that matter were dispelled by a letter I received soon afterward. As I have not the writer's permission to publish it, I must confine myself to telling how it ended, whence without further ado you will see who wrote it. It closed with the words: "I and still five other children, to wit, because I am one of them."

I answered, by return of post, as follows:

"My dear children, I well understand your liking the tale of the hands of God; I like it too. But all the same, I cannot come to see you. Do not take it amiss. Who knows whether you would like me? I have an ugly nose, and if, as sometimes happens, it also has a tiny red pimple at the tip, you would stare at that little point the whole time and be astonished and would not even hear what I was saying a little lower down. And you would probably dream of that little pimple. All this wouldn't suit me at all. Therefore I suggest another way out of the difficulty. We have (even without your mother) a lot of friends and acquaintances in common who are not children. You will soon find out who they are. To these intermediaries I will tell a story from time to time, and they will tell it to you much more beautifully than I could. For there are some very great poets among these our friends. I will not tell you what my stories will be about. But as I know that nothing is closer to your minds and hearts than God, I shall bring in at every suitable opportunity whatever I know about him. If anything isn't correct, write me another nice letter or let me know through your mother. For it is possible my memory might fail me at many points, because it is already so long since I have heard the nicest stories, and because since then I have had to remember a lot that are not so nice. That is the way it happens in life. But all the same, life is a glorious thing: and of that my stories will often speak. With love—I, who am one too, but only because I am one of you."

FRANZ KAFKA

The Married Couple

Franz Kafka (1883–1924) was born in Prague and took his law degree in 1906. He then worked for the workmen's compensation division of the Austrian Government. He suffered greatly from tuberculosis. Kafka's major works, all of which are concerned with the problem of man's guilt and his search for God, are *Metamorphosis, The Trial, The Castle,* and *Amerika.* [From *The Great Wall of China* by Franz Kafka; copyright 1946 by Schocken Books Inc.; used by permission of the publishers; translated by Willa and Edwin Muir.]

BUSINESS IN GENERAL is so bad that sometimes, when my work in the office leaves me a little time, I myself pick up the case of samples and call on my customers personally. Long since I had intended to visit some time, among others, N., with whom once I had constant business relations, which, however, during the last year have almost completely lapsed for some reason unknown to me. Besides, there need not always be real reasons for such misfortunes; in the present unstable state of affairs often a mere nothing, a word, will turn the scale, and in the same way a mere nothing, a word, can put things right again. To gain admittance to N., however, is a somewhat ticklish business; he is an old man, grown somewhat infirm too of late, and though he still insists on attending to business matters himself, he is hardly ever to be seen in his office; if you want to speak to him you have to go to his house, and one gladly puts off a business call of that kind.

Last evening after six I nevertheless set out for his house; it was really no time for paying calls, but my visit after all was a business, not a social, one, and might be regarded accordingly. I was in luck. N. was

in; he had just come back with his wife from a walk, the servant told
me, and was now in the bedroom of his son, who was unwell and confined to his bed. I was requested to go there; at first I hesitated, but
then the desire to get my disagreeable visit over as quickly as possible
turned the scale, and I allowed myself to be conducted as I was, in my
overcoat and hat with my case of samples, through a dark room into
a faintly lit one, where a small company was gathered.

My first glance fell, probably by instinct, on an agent only too well
known to me, a trade rival of myself in some respects. So he had stolen
a march on me, it seemed. He was sitting comfortably by the bed of the
sick man, just as if he were a doctor; he sat brazenly there in his
beautiful ample overcoat, which was unbuttoned; the sick man too
probably had his own thoughts as he lay there with his cheeks faintly
flushed with fever, now and then glancing at his visitor. He was no
longer young either, N.'s son, a man of about my own age with a short
beard, somewhat unkempt on account of his illness. Old N., a tall,
broad-shouldered man, but to my astonishment grown very thin because
of some creeping malady, bent and infirm, was still wearing the fur
coat in which he had entered, and mumbling something to his son. His
wife, small and frail, but immensely vivacious, yet only when she spoke
to him—us others she scarcely noticed—was occupied in helping him to
take off his overcoat, which, considering the great difference in their
height, was a matter of some difficulty, but at last was achieved. Perhaps, indeed, the real difficulty was caused by N.'s impatience, for
with restless hands he kept on feeling for the easy chair, which his
wife, after the overcoat was off, quickly pushed forward for him. She
herself then took up the fur coat, beneath which she almost vanished,
and carried it out.

Now at last, it seemed to me, my moment had come, or rather it had
not come and probably would never come; yet if I was to attempt anything it must be done at once, for I felt that here the conditions for
a business interview could only become increasingly unfavorable; and
to plant myself down here for all time, as the agent apparently intended,
was not my way: besides, I did not want to take the slightest notice of
him. So I began without ceremony to state my business, although I saw
that N. would have liked at that moment to have a chat with his son.
Unfortunately I have a habit when I have worked myself up—and that
takes a very short time, and on this occasion took a shorter time than
usual—of getting up and walking about while I am talking. Though a
very good arrangement in one's own office, in a strange house it may
be somewhat burdensome. But I could not restrain myself, particularly as I was feeling the lack of my usual cigarette. Well, every man
has his bad habits, yet I can congratulate myself on mine when I think
of the agent's. For what is to be said of his behavior, of the fact, for
instance, that every now and then he would suddenly and quite unexpectedly clap his hat on his head; he had been holding it on his knee
until then, slowly pushing it up and down there. True, he took it off

again immediately, as if he had made a blunder, but he had had it on his head nevertheless for a second or two, and besides he repeated this performance again and again every few minutes. Surely such conduct must be called unpardonable. It did not disturb me, however, I walked up and down, completely absorbed in my own proposals, and ignored him; but there are people whom that trick with the hat might have put off completely. However, when I am thoroughly worked up I disregard not only such annoyances as these, but everything. I see, it is true, all that is going on, but do not admit it, so to speak, to my consciousness until I am finished, or until some objection has been raised. Thus I noticed quite well, for instance, that N. was by no means in a receptive state; holding onto the arms of his chair, he twisted about uncomfortably, never even glanced up at me, but gazed blankly, as if searching for something, into vacancy, and his face was so impassive that one might have thought no syllable of what I was saying, indeed no awareness of my presence, had penetrated to him. Yes, his whole bearing, the bearing of a sick man, in itself inauspicious for me, I took in quite well; nevertheless I talked on as if I had still some prospect of putting everything right again by my talk, by the advantageous offers I made—I was myself alarmed by the concessions I granted, concessions that had not even been asked for. It gave me a certain satisfaction also to notice that the agent, as I verified by a fleeting glance, had at last left his hat in peace and folded his arms across his chest; my performance, which was partly, I must confess, intended for him, seemed to have given a severe blow to his designs. And in the elation produced by this result I might perhaps have gone on talking for a long time still, if the son, whom until now I had regarded as a secondary factor in my plans, had not suddenly raised himself in his bed and pulled me up by shaking his fist. Obviously he wanted to say something, to point out something, but he had not strength enough. At first I thought that his mind was wandering, but when I involuntarily glanced at old N. I understood better.

N. sat with wide-open, glassy, bulging eyes, which seemed on the point of failing; he was trembling and his body was bent forward as if someone were holding him down or striking him on the shoulders; his lower lip, indeed the lower jaw itself with the exposed gums, hung down helplessly; his whole face seemed out of drawing; he still breathed, though with difficulty; but then, as if delivered, he fell back against the back of his chair, closed his eyes, the mark of some great strain passed over his face and vanished, and all was over. I sprang to him and seized his lifeless hand, which was so cold that it sent a chill through me; no pulse beat there now. So it was all over. Still, he was a very old man. We would be fortunate if we all had such an easy death. But how much there was to be done! And what should one do first? I looked round for help; but the son had drawn the bedclothes over his head, and I could hear his wild sobbing; the agent, cold as a fish, sat immovably on his chair, two steps from N., and was obviously resolved to do nothing, to wait for what time would bring; so I, only I was left to do something, and the hardest thing that anyone could be asked to do, that was to tell the news to his wife in some bearable form, in a form that did not exist, in other words. And already I could hear her eager shuffling steps in the next room.

Still wearing her outdoor clothes—she had not found time to change —she bore in a night-shirt that she had warmed before the fire for her husband to put on. "He's fallen asleep," she said, smiling and shaking her head, when she found us sitting so still. And with the infinite trust-fulness of the innocent she took up the same hand that I had held a moment before with such fear and repugnance, kissed it playfully, and —how could we three others have borne the sight?—N. moved, yawned loudly, allowed his night-shirt to be put on, endured with a mixture of annoyance and irony his wife's tender reproaches for having over-strained himself by taking such a long walk, and strangely enough said in reply, to provide no doubt a different explanation for his having fallen asleep, something about feeling bored. Then, so as not to catch cold by going through the draughty passage into a different room, he lay down for the time being in his son's bed; a pillow was made beside his son's feet with two cushions hastily brought by his wife. After all that had gone before I found nothing particularly odd in that. Then he asked for the evening paper, opened it without paying any attention to his guests, but did not read it, only glancing through it here and there, and made several very unpleasant observations on our offers, observations which showed astonishing shrewdness, while he waved his free hand disdainfully, and by clicking his tongue indicated that our business methods had left a bad taste in his mouth. The agent could not refrain from making one or two untimely remarks, no doubt he felt in his insensitive way that some compensation was due to him after what had happened, but his way of securing it was the worst he could have chosen. I said good-by as soon as I could, I felt almost grateful to the agent; if he had not been there I would not have had the resolution to leave so soon.

In the lobby I met Frau N. again. At the sight of that pathetic figure I said impulsively that she reminded me a little of my mother. And as she remained silent I added: "Whatever people say, she could do wonders. Things that we destroyed she could make whole again. I lost her when I was still a child." I had spoken with deliberate slowness and distinctness, for I assumed the old lady was hard of hearing. But she must have been quite deaf, for she asked without transition: "And what does my husband intend to do about your offer?" From a few parting words I noticed, moreover, that she confused me with the agent; I like to think that otherwise she would have been more forthcoming.

Then I descended the stairs. The descent was more tiring than the ascent had been, and not even that had been easy. Oh, how many busi-ness calls come to nothing, and yet one must keep going.

STEFAN ZWEIG

Moonbeam Alley

Stefan Zweig, born in 1881 of a well-to-do family, grew up in Vienna. He began to write at 19, completing many biographies, stories and essays, among which are *Master Builders, Marie Antoinette* and *The Royal Game*. He fled from Austria in 1933 because of the Nazis, settling in Brazil. He and his young wife were suicides in 1942. [From *Kaleidoscope* by Stefan Zweig; copyright 1934 by The Viking Press, Inc.; used by permission of the publishers.]

STORMY WEATHER had delayed the ship, so that the evening was far advanced before she came to port on the French coast. Having missed the train which was to have carried me farther on my journey, I had a whole twenty-four hours on my hands. How could I best while away the time, marooned as I was in this unknown coast-town? There did not seem to be much doing. Melancholy strains of dance music issued from a dubious-looking haunt—not particularly attractive, I thought. The alternative would be to spend the interlude in desultory converse with my fellow-passengers. In the dining-room of the third-rate hotel where we put up, the air was thick with the smell of burned fat and tobacco smoke. Besides, it was an ill-kept and dirty place, its filthiness rendered all the more intolerable since for many days now I had enjoyed the pure ocean breezes and felt the salt, sweet taste of sea-spume upon my lips. I decided to go for a stroll along the broad main street leading to a square where the local band was giving a concert. It was pleasant to allow oneself to be carried gently along by the stream of idlers who, having done their work for the day, were taking the air after a wash and brush-up followed by a cozy meal at a provincial fireside. After a while, however, the jostling of the crowd and its empty laughter vexed me sorely; I found it exasperating to be gaped at because I happened to be a stranger in their midst; the physical proximity of so many unknown human beings was nauseating in the extreme.

The voyage had been far from calm, and the movement of swelling waters was still in my veins. Underfoot, the earth seemed to be heaving and rolling, the whole street and the skies swayed like a see-saw. I felt giddy and, in order to escape, I ducked my head and plunged down a side street without taking the trouble to decipher its name. This led me into an even narrower thoroughfare, where the din of music and mob was muffled almost to extinction. One street opened out of another like the anastomoses of arteries and veins. They were less well lighted the farther I withdrew from the central square, which was brightly illuminated with arc-lamps. Overhead the stars could be distinguished, now that my eyes were no longer dazzled by the glare. How dark the intervening spaces of heaven appeared as I gazed upward!

This must be "sailor-town," quite near the the harbor, for my nostrils were tickled with the stench of rotting fish and seaweed and tar, with the indescribable odor issuing from badly ventilated houses wherein the air remains stagnant until it is swept away by a health-bringing gale. Such twilight as hung over these alley-ways was healing to my mind. It was delightful to be alone. I slackened my pace, studied the narrow streets, each of which was different from the others, being here coquettish or amorous, there wrapped in inviolable peace. All, however, were dark, and filled with the soft murmur of voices and music which arose from nowhere in particular, but from unseen springs deep within the houses. Doors and windows were tightly shut, and the only lights were red or yellow lanterns hanging from a porch at rare intervals.

I have a special predilection for such quarters in unknown towns, these foul market-places of the passions, filled with temptations for men who sail the seas and who turn in here for a night of pleasure, hoping to realize their dreams in one short hour on land. These places are obliged to tuck themselves away out of sight in the less "respectable" areas of the town, because they tell a plain tale which the smug and well-built houses of the elect hide behind a hundred veils. Tiny rooms are crowded with dancing couples; glaring placards lure into the picture-houses, square-faced lanterns twinkle in doorways and beckon unambiguously to the passer-by. Drunken voices clamor from behind the red-curtained windows of drinking booths. Sailors grin at one another when they meet, their eyes are greedy with expectation, for here they may find women and gambling, drink and display, adventure that is sordid or worth the risk. But these allurements are discreetly housed behind drawn blinds. You have to go inside to find them out, and the mystery only serves to enhance the lure. Similar streets and alleys exist in Hamburg and Colombo and Havana and Liverpool, just as in these cities the broad avenues and boulevards where the wealthy forgather are likewise to be found, for the upper stratum of life and the lower bear a close resemblance everywhere in the matter of form. These disorderly streets are strange vestiges of an unregulated world of the senses, where impulses continue to discharge themselves brutally and without rein; they are a gloomy forest of the passions, a covert full of manifestations of our instinctive and animal existence; they stimulate by what they disclose, and allure by the suggestion of what they hide. They haunt our dreams.

A sensation of being trapped in this maze overwhelmed me. I had chanced to follow a couple of cuirassiers who, with swords clanking along the uneven pavement, were taking a stroll. Some women on the booze in a bar shouted coarse jokes as the pair sauntered by; shrieks of laughter, a finger knocking on the window, an oath from within—and then the men went on. Soon the ribald mirth grew so faint that I could barely catch the sound. Silence closed round me, a few windows were dimly lighted, the watery moon shone through the mist. I breathed my fill of the stillness, which was almost uncanny, seeing that behind it lurked a universe of mystery, sensuousness, and peril. The silence was a lie, for it covered the accumulated filth of a whole world. I stood listening, and peering into the void. All sense of the town, the street, its name, and even my own name vanished; I was cut adrift, my body in some miraculous way had been taken possession of by a stranger, I had no activity in view, no reason for being where I was, no relationship to my surroundings—and yet I was acutely conscious of the seething life that beset me on all sides; it flowed through my veins as if it were my own blood. Nothing that was happening was doing so on my account, though everything was germane to myself. An inexpressibly delightful feeling that I was not a participator was accompanied by the conviction that I was in for an experience which would bore down into the deepest springs of my being—a feeling which, whenever it comes to me, suffuses me with a pleasure that emanates from communion with the unconscious.

As I stood thus expectant, listening into the void, a voice came to me from a distance, muffled by intervening walls, but unmistakably singing in German. A simple melody, indeed; the "Schöner, grüner Jungfern-kranz" from Weber's *Freischütz*. A woman's voice, badly trained, but German, yes indeed, German. Strange to hear one's own tongue in so out-of-the-way a corner; and friendly, homely, at the same time. Poorly as the air was sung, it held a greeting from the land of my birth. Who can speak German here, who can be moved to hum this innocent refrain? Straining my ears against house after house, I reached one where there was a glimmer in one of the windows, and the shadow of a hand silhouetted against the blind. All doors were shut, and yet invitation to enter was to be deciphered on every brick and lintel. Nearer and nearer I approached the sound. This was the house! I hesitated a moment, and then pushed my shoulder against the door, having drawn aside a curtain which shielded the interior from draughts. On the threshold I encountered a man whose face was reddened by the hanging lamp, and was livid with fury. He scowled at me, murmured an apology, and thrust past me into the alley. "Queer customer," thought I, gazing after him. Meanwhile the voice continued singing; clearer than before, it seemed to me. I boldly entered.

The song was cut off sharp, as with a knife. A terrible silence compassed me about, giving me the impression that I had destroyed something. Gradually my eyes grew accustomed to the dim lighting, and I found that the room was scantily furnished with a little bar at one end, a table, a couple of chairs—obviously a mere waiting-room for the true business of the establishment which went on in the background. Nor was it difficult to guess what the real business was, for along a passage there were many doors, some of them ajar, leading into bedrooms in which beneath deeply shaded lamps double beds were to be discerned. A girl was seated on a bench leaning her elbows on the table; she was heavily made up, and appeared extremely tired. Behind the bar was a blowzy woman, slatternly and fat, with a second girl, a rather pretty lass, at her side. My good evening fell flat, and was not echoed back to me for a considerable time. It was eerie to have stepped into this silence of the desert, and I wished to get clear away. Yet, since there did not seem to be adequate reason for absconding, I took a place at the table and resigned myself to the inevitable.

Suddenly remembering her business in life, the girl got up and asked me what I wished to drink, and I recognized at once by her guttural pronunciation of the French words that she hailed from Germany. I ordered beer, which she fetched and brought to me, shuffling her feet in slovenly fashion, thus betraying even greater indifference than did her lack-luster eyes. Following the custom of such haunts, she placed another glass next mine and sat down before it. She raised her glass with a nod of greeting in my direction, but she gazed through and beyond me. I had a good look at her. A beautiful face still, with regular features; but it had grown like a mask, since the inner fires were quenched. There was a touch of coarseness about it, the skin and muscles were lax, the lids heavy, the hair unkempt, and two furrows had already formed on either side of the mouth. Her dress was disorderly, her voice husky from too much smoking and beer-drinking. Here undubitably was a fellow-mortal who was weary unto death, and who only continued living out of long-established habit. Embarrassed and horrified, I asked her a question. She answered without looking at me and scarcely moving her lips. I guessed that my coming was unwelcome. The elder woman behind the bar yawned prodigiously, the younger girl slouched in a corner, as if waiting for me to call her. If I could have got away, I should have done so precipitately. But my limbs were like lead and I sat on, inert, chained by disgust and curiosity, for, to speak frankly, this indifference stirred me strangely.

The girl next me suddenly burst into a fit of shrill laughter. Simultaneously, the flame of the lamp flickered in a draught of cold air coming through the open doorway.

"So you've come back," said the girl in German. "Creeping round the house again, you mean skunk. Oh, come along in—I shan't do you any harm."

I turned first to the speaker whose mouth seemed to be spewing forth fire, and then to the door. Slinking in was the individual who had scuttled away on my entry. He was a cringing creature, holding his hat in his hand like a beggar, trembling under the douche of words that had greeted him, writhing beneath the torrential flow of mirthless laughter, and rendered even more uneasy by the way in which, from behind the bar, the hostess was whispering to the girl.

"Go and sit down beside Françoise, the young woman said hectoringly. "Can't you see I've got a gentleman customer?"

She spoke to him exclusively in the German tongue, while the hostess and the younger girl split their sides with laughter though they could not understand a word she said. The man was evidently a habitué.

"Give him a bottle of champagne, Françoise, the most expensive brand," she yelled mockingly. "And if it's too dear for you, my man, you've only got to stay outside and not come bothering us. You'd like to have me for nothing, I know, and anything else you could get without paying you'd grab. Ugh, you filthy beast."

The tall figure crumpled under the lash of this tongue. Like a whipped cur, he sidled up to the counter and with a trembling hand he poured the wine into a glass. He evidently wanted to look at the slattern who was abusing him, and yet he was unable to lift his gaze from the floor. The lamplight caught his face, and I saw before me an emaciated visage, with damp locks of hair sticking in wisps on the brow. His limbs were slack, as if broken at the joints. He was a pitiable object, devoid of strength and yet not wholly lacking in a kind of vicious courage. Everything about him was askew; and the eyes he raised for a flash did not look straight, but were shifty and full of a wicked light.

"Don't bother about him," said the girl to me in her ponderous French and seizing me roughly by the arm as though she wanted me to turn away from my contemplation. "It's an old story between him and me. Doesn't date from yesterday!" She bared her teeth like a vixen ready to bite, and snarled: "You just listen to what I tell you, old fox. I'd rather fling myself into the sea than go with you. Got it?"

Again the sally was applauded by shouts of laughter from behind the bar. The pleasantry seemed to be a joy which was daily renewed. Then a horrible thing happened. The younger wench put her arms round the man in simulated affection and caressed him tenderly. He winced under her touch, and glanced at me, anxious and cringing. At the same moment the woman next me threw off her inertia as if she had just awakened from profound sleep, and her countenance was so contorted with malevolence, her hands trembled so violently, that I could bear the scene no longer. Throwing some coins upon the table, I rose to go. But she detained me, saying:

"If he's bothering you, I'll chuck him out, the swine. He's jolly well got to do what he's told. Come, let's drink another glass together."

She pressed up against me with assumed ardor, and I knew at once that she was playing a game in order to torment the man, for she kept on glancing in his direction out of the corner of her eyes. Disgust filled me when I saw how, with every endearment she lavished upon me, the poor wretch shrank together as if branded with a red-hot iron. I could not take my eyes off him, and I shivered when it became evident what a storm of rage, jealousy, and desire was brewing within him. Yet every time the girl looked toward him, he ducked his head in fear. She sidled closer, and I could feel her body quivering with pleasure as she pursued her wicked game. The scent of cheap powder and unwashed skin was sickening, and in order to keep her at a distance I took a cigar out of my case. Before I had time to light it, the girl was screaming.

"Here, you, bring a light, and be quick about it."

It was horrible to make myself a party to her machinations by allowing the man to serve me, and I made what haste I could to find a match for myself. But her orders had already whipped the poor devil into activity, and he shuffled up to the table with the necessary kindling material. Our eyes crossed, and in his I read abysmal shame mingled with pusillanimous bitterness. This look touched a brotherly chord in me and made me vibrate in sympathy with his humiliation. I said in German:

"Thank you, Sir; but you should not have bothered."

I offered him my hand. He hesitated for a moment, then my fingers were squeezed between his bony fists. Gratitude shone from his eyes during the second he fixed me, but soon he lowered his puffy lids. Defiance made me want to invite him to sit with us, and I had probably made a gesture of invitation for, ere the words dropped from my lips, the woman had said harshly:

"Back to your place, at once, and don't come bothering round here again."

I was nauseated by her strident voice and her whole demeanor. Why should I worry my head about this repulsive harlot, this weak-minded wench, this sewer of beer and cheap scent and tobacco-smoke? I longed for a breath of fresh air. I pushed the money toward her, stood up, and, when she tried to detain me with her endearments, I moved resolutely toward the exit. I could not participate in the humiliation of a fellow-creature, and I made it clear to the girl that her charms had no attraction for me. An angry flush spread over her face and neck, fierce words trembled on her lips; but she did not speak. She merely turned to the man and looked at him so meaningly that with the utmost speed he sought to do her unspoken bidding. His fingers shot down into his pocket, and he drew forth a purse. He was evidently frightened at being left alone with her, and in his excitement fumbled with the opening. I guessed that he was not accustomed to spending money freely, he had none of the generous way of a sailor who flings his coins carelessly about. This man was used to counting his money carefully, and to testing the pieces between his fingers before paying them away —as he now paid for his champagne.

"Look how he's trembling because he has to part with some of his beloved pence," she cried tauntingly, stepping nearer to him. "Too slow, I tell you. Just wait till I . . ."

He shrank back in fear. When she saw how frightened he was, she shrugged her shoulders and said jeeringly, and with an indescribable expression of disgust on her face:

"I'm not going to take anything away from you. I spit on your money. It is all counted beforehand, I know; never a farthing too much must be allowed to leave your purse. But," and she tapped him on the chest, "what about the bit of paper you've so carefully stitched into your waistcoat lining?"

His hand went to his side as if he were seized with a spasm of the heart. Having felt the place, his face, which had gone ashen pale, resumed its normal hue and his hand dropped away again.

"Miser," she screamed.

At this the martyr turned, flung the purse and its contents into the younger girl's lap, and rushed out as if the place were on fire. At first the girl gave a shriek of alarm, then, realizing what the man had done, she broke into peal upon peal of piercing laughter.

The woman stood for a moment rigid, her eyes sparkling with wrath. Then her lids closed, and her body went limp. She looked old and tired. A forlorn and drooping figure swayed before me.

"He'll be weeping over his lost money, out there. May even go to the police-station and tell them we've stolen it. Tomorrow he'll be here again. But he won't get me, no, that he won't. I'll give myself to anyone who offers, but never to him."

She stepped up to the bar and gulped down a glass of neat brandy. The wickedness still glinted in her eyes but it was misty now as if shining from behind a veil of tears. My gorge rose as I looked at her, so that I could find no compassion in my heart.

"Good evening," I said as I took my leave.

"Bon soir," answered the hostess, without a glance in my direction. Shrill and mocking laughter followed me into the street.

As I stepped forth into the alley, it seemed to me darker than ever, closed in by the starless sky and the night; but soon the pale moon shone down again, bringing me infinite alleviation. I took a deep breath, and the horror left me. Now I could once more relish the amazing tangle of human destinies; and a feeling of beatitude, akin to tears, filled me at the thought that behind every window fate was waiting, that at the opening of every door an experience was ready for the taking, that the multitudinous happenings of this world are ever present for those who choose to observe them, that even the foulest hovel is bursting with newly generated life like dung filled with the larvae that will become shining beetles. The unsavory encounter was no longer repulsive to me. On the contrary, the suspense it had produced in my mind now relaxed into an agreeable sensation of lassitude, and my sole desire was to convert my adventure into beautiful dreams. I cast a searching eye up and down the narrow street, wondering which direction would lead back to the hotel. A shadow fell across my path.

"Beg pardon, Sir," said a familiar whining voice in my native tongue, "but I'm afraid you will have some difficulty in finding your way out of the maze. May I act as guide, Sir? Your hotèl, Sir?"

I gave him the name.

"Yes, Sir, I know it, Sir. Will you allow me to accompany you, Sir?" he asked apologetically.

A shudder crept over me. It was horrible to have this slouching, ghostlike creature walking by my side, noiselessly, as if on stockinged feet. My perception of the gloom in the alley-ways of the sailors' quarter, the memory of my recent experience, were spontaneously replaced by a state of confused reverie. I knew that my companion's eyes still held the same meek expression, that his lips still twitched nervously, that he wanted to talk. But I did not wish to rouse myself from the inertia of mind which enfolded me, in order to take any active interest in the fellow. He hemmed, words choked in his throat, and I felt a cruel pleasure in not coming to his aid. Repulsion at the recollection of that dreadful woman spread through me like a miasma, and I was glad the man's shame should be wrestling with his spiritual need for explanation. No, I did not help him; but allowed a heavy curtain of silence to hang black and awesome between us. My footsteps rang out clear and youthful in contrast to his muffled and aged tread. The tension between his soul and mine grew stronger every minute. The silence became strident with unspoken words. At last the string, stretched to breaking-point, snapped, and he blurted out:

"You have . . . you have just witnessed a strange scene, Sir. I beg you to forgive me, Sir, if I refer to it . . . but it must have appeared very peculiar to you, Sir, and you must think me a ludicrous fellow, but you see, Sir, that woman . . . well, she is . . ."

He had got stuck again. His throat worked. Then, in a very small voice, he said hastily:

"She's my wife, Sir."

I must have shown surprise, for he hurriedly continued as if wishing to excuse himself.

"That is to say, Sir, she was my wife, five, no four years ago, at Geratz-heim in Hesse where I have my home. Please, Sir, you really must not think badly of her. It's probably my fault that she has become what she is. She was not always thus. But I . . . I teased and plagued her. You see, Sir, I married her in spite of her abject poverty. Why, she had hardly a chemise to her back, nothing, nothing at all. Whereas I am well-to-do, or, rather, I am comfortably off . . . at least I had a pretty competence in those days . . . and I was, perhaps—she is right—I was thrifty . . . yes, I was thrifty even before our great misfortune. But you see, Sir, my father and mother were so, and the whole family a bit on the stingy side. Besides, I worked hard for every penny I earned. She was fond of pretty things, and, being poor, she had nothing but what I gave her. I was constantly reminding her of this. Oh, I know it was wrong of me—I've had time to learn that since the catastrophe —for she was proud, very proud. Please don't run away with the idea that she is naturally of such a disposition as you witnessed this evening. Far from it, Sir; that's all make-believe. She hurts herself in order to make me suffer, in order to torture me, and because she is ashamed of her own doings, of her present mode of life. Maybe she has gone to the bad, but I . . . I refuse to accept such a notion . . . for I remember how good, how very good she used to be, Sir."

His excitement made him pause, both in speech and walk, while he wiped his eyes. I looked at him in spite of myself. He no longer appeared to be a figure of fun, and I was no longer annoyed by his constant repetition of the obsequious "Sir." The energy he had put into

phrasing his explanation had transfigured his countenance. We started
forward again, and he kept his eyes downcast as if reading his story
printed upon the pavement. He sighed heavily, and his voice took on a
sonorous tone very different from the querulous sound I had come to
expect from him.

"Yes, Sir, she was good—good, and kind to me as well—she was
grateful for having been raised out of her misery. I knew how thankful
she was . . . but I wanted to hear her say so . . . always and always
again . . . I could not listen too often to the verbal expression of her
gratitude. You see, Sir, it is so wonderful to feel that someone considers you to be better than you really are. I would willingly have parted
with all my money just to hear her say those few words, everlastingly
renewed . . . but she had her proper pride, and she found it increasingly difficult to acknowledge her debt to me, especially when I made
a claim upon her in the matter and almost ordered her point-blank to
pronounce the words I longed to hear. . . . And so, Sir, I insisted that
she ask me for everything she wanted, for every dress, for every scrap
of ribbon. . . . Three years I tortured her thus, and her martyrdom
grew worse as the time went by. And believe me, Sir, it was all because
I loved her so desperately. I loved her proud bearing, and yet I wished
to humiliate her. Oh, fool that I was! I pretended to be vexed when
she asked for a hat, or any other trifle she took a fancy for; while all the
time I was in the seventh heaven of delight at being given an opportunity to gratify her—and at the same time to make her eat humble-pie.
In those days, Sir, I did not realize how dear she was to me. . . ."

Again he stopped, and reeled in his gait. He had forgotten my existence, and spoke henceforward as if in a hypnotic trance.

"I only discovered how greatly I loved her on the day—the accursed
day—when she begged me to give her something to help her mother
out of a difficulty, and I refused. It was an insignificant sum. . . . I
had actually put the money aside for the purpose . . . but I longed for
her to ask me again . . . and then, when I came home I found a letter
on the table and learned that she had gone. . . . All she wrote was:
'Keep your damned money. I'll never ask you for another penny.'
That's all. Nothing more. I was like one demented for three days
and three nights. I had the river dragged and the forest scoured; indeed
I paid hundreds over to the authorities in the hope of discovering her
whereabouts. I even confided my troubles to the neighbors—but they
merely laughed me to scorn. No trace, no trace at all. Months later,
I learned that someone had seen her in the train, accompanied by a
soldier . . . a train going to Berlin. That very day I went to the capital,
leaving my business to take care of itself. Thousands did I lose in the
process. My farm laborers, my manager, my . . . oh, everyone profited
by my absence to line his pockets. But I assure you, Sir, I remained
indifferent to these losses . . . I stayed a week in Berlin . . . and, at
last, I found her. . . ."

He panted slightly, and then continued:

"I assure you, Sir, I never said a harsh word to her . . . I wept . . .
I knelt before her . . . I offered her anything she pleased. . . . She
would henceforward be the mistress of all I possessed—for I had come to
realize that life without her was impossible. . . . I loved every hair on
her head, her mouth, her body, every part and particle of her being. I
bribed the landlady (she was, in fact, a procuress, what they call a
'white-slave trader') generously and thus managed to see poor Lise
alone. Her face was like chalk; but she listened to me, oh, Sir, I believe
she really listened to me as if pleased, pleased to see me. But when I
began to speak of the money it was necessary to pay—and after all, Sir,
you will agree that we were obliged to discuss such practical issues—
she merely called her fancy-man onto the scene, and the two of them
laughed me out of countenance. I did not lose sight of her, Sir, but
returned to the charge day after day. The other lodgers told me that the
cur had left her, utterly unprovided for. So I sought her out yet again;
but she tore up the notes I gave her, and the next time I came—she
was gone. Oh, Sir, you can have no idea of what I did to trace her. I
followed her for a year, paying agents here and agents there. At last
I discovered that she had gone to Argentina . . . and . . . and . . .
that she was in . . . a house . . . of ill-fame. . . ."

Again he hesitated, and the last two words seemed to stick in his
throat. His voice became somber as he went on:

"At first I could hardly believe my ears . . . then I reflected that I
was to blame, I, only I, because I had humiliated her. And I thought
how terribly she must be suffering, she so proud, as I well knew her
to be. I got my solicitor to write to the consul out there, and I sent
money. But she was not to be told from whom it came. The sum was
more than sufficient to bring her home again. Soon I got a cable that
the scheme had worked, and that the boat would reach Amsterdam on
such a date. Well, so great was my impatience that I got there three
days too soon. When I saw the smoke in the distance, it seemed to me
I could not wait till the ship slowly entered port and came alongside the
quay. At last I caught a glimpse of her at the tail of the other passengers,
hardly recognizable at first, so heavily was she made up. When she
saw me waiting for her, she blanched even under her paint, and tottered
so that two sailors had to support her. No sooner had she stepped onto
land than I was at her side. I could not speak, my throat felt so dry.
She, too, said nothing, and did not look at me. I motioned to a porter
to carry the luggage, and we started for the hotel. Suddenly she turned
to me and said . . . oh, Sir, if you could have heard her voice, so sad,
I thought my heart would break . . . 'Do you want me still as your
wife, after . . . ?' I could only clasp her hand. . . . She trembled
violently, but spoke no more. I felt that now all would be well. . . . Ah,
Sir, how happy I was. When we got to our room, I danced for joy, I
knelt at her feet babbling out the most absurd things—at least I fancy
my words must have been rather funny, for she smiled through her
tears and stroked my hair—hesitatingly, of course. Her endearments

did me good, my heart overflowed. I rushed up and down stairs ordering dinner—I called it our wedding feast. I helped her to change her dress, and then we went down and ate and drank, a merry meal I assure you, Sir. She was like a child, so warm and affectionate, speaking of our home and how everything would start fresh. . . . Then . . ."

The man's voice became rasping, and he made a gesture as if he were strangling someone.

"Then . . . the waiter . . . a mean and vulgar cur . . . believed me to be the worse for drink because I laughed so much and had carried on in such a boyish fashion—and all because I was so happy, oh, so happy. . . . Well, I paid the bill and he, as I said, thinking me drunk, cheated me out of twenty francs in giving me the change. I called the fellow back, and demanded my due. He looked sheepish, and laid the money by my plate. . . . Then . . . quite suddenly . . . Lise began to laugh. I stared at her perplexed . . . and her face was completely changed . . . mocking, hard, angry. 'The same as ever . . . even after our wedding feast,' she said coldly—and yet her voice was full of pity. I cursed myself for having been so particular . . . but I tried to laugh the matter off. . . . Her gaiety had disappeared . . . it was dead and gone. . . . She insisted upon being given a separate room. . . . I was in a mood to grant every request . . . and lay alone, open-eyed, through the night, thinking what I should get her on the morrow . . . a handsome gift, that would show her I was no longer stingy . . . at least where she was concerned. Early next morning I was abroad . . . I bought a bracelet . . . and took it to her in her room . . . but she was no longer there . . . she had gone . . . as she had gone before. I looked round for a note . . . praying it would not be there, yet knowing that it would inevitably be awaiting me . . . and there it was, sure enough, on the dressing-table . . . and on it was scribbled . . ."

He hesitated. I stood still, looking into his martyred face. The man bowed his head, and whispered hoarsely:

"She had written . . . 'Leave me in peace. You are utterly repulsive to me.'"

Our walk had led us to the harbor; and, in the distance, the silence was broken by the roar of the Atlantic breakers on the coast. The vessels, their lights shining like the eyes of huge animals, swung at their anchors. A song floated to me from afar. Nothing was very clear. I seemed to feel presences rather than see them. The town was sleeping and dreaming an immense dream. By my side I distinguished the ghostly shadow of the man growing uncannily large and then dwindling to dwarfed proportions in the flickering lamplight. I was not inclined to speak, or to offer consolation, or to ask questions. The silence stuck to me, heavy and oppressive. Suddenly he seized my arm, and said quaveringly:

"But I'm determined not to leave this town without her. . . . After many months of search I found her. . . . I am invulnerable to the martyrdom she is putting me through. . . . I beseech you, Sir, to have a word with her . . . she refuses to listen if I speak . . . I must get her to come back. . . . Oh, won't you tell her she ought to? Please, Sir, have a try. . . . I can't go on living like this. I can't bear any longer to see other men go in there, knowing she is giving herself to them, while I wait in the street till they come down again, laughing and tipsy. The whole neighborhood knows me by now, and the people make mock of me when they see me waiting out on the pavement. . . . I shall go mad, but I must keep my vigil without fail. . . . Oh, Sir, I do beg of you to speak to her. . . . You are a stranger, I know, but for God's sake, Sir, have a word with her. Someone from her own country might influence her in this foreign land."

I wished to free my arm from the man's convulsive grip. Loathing and disgust alienated my sympathies. When he felt that I was trying to get away, he flung himself onto his knees in the middle of the street and clasped my legs.

"I conjure you, Sir, to speak to her; you must, you must—or something terrible will happen. All my money's gone in tracing her, and I'm not going to leave her here . . . not alive. I've bought a knife. Yes, Sir, I've got a knife. I won't let her stay here; at least not alive; I could not bear it. Oh, speak to her, Sir, I beg and pray you to have a talk with her. . . ."

He crouched like a maniac before me. At that moment two policemen turned into the street. I dragged him violently to his feet. He looked at me blankly for a moment, and then said in an utterly changed voice:

"Take the first turning on your right, and the hotel is about half-way down."

Once more he stared at me with eyes wherein the pupils seemed to have melted away into a bleak, white void. Then he vanished.

I hugged myself in my coat, for I was shivering. I was tired; and sleep, a kind of drunken sleep, black and feelingless, claimed me. I wanted to think, to turn these things over in my mind, but sleep was ruthless and would not be put off. I got to my hotel, fell onto the bed, and slept like an animal.

In the morning it was hard to disentangle dream from reality, and something within me urged me not to try and find out. I woke late, a stranger in a strange city, and visited a church far-famed for its mosaics. But my eyes were blind to such sights. The night's adventure rose vividly before my mind, and unconsciously my feet sought that alley-way and that house. But such thoroughfares do not become alive until after dark. During the daytime they wear cold, gray masks, and it is only those who know them well who are able to recognize one from another. Search as I might, I did not find the street I wanted. Weary and disappointed I returned to the hotel, followed by pictures that were either the figment of a disordered brain, or the remembrance of reality.

The train was scheduled to leave at nine o'clock that evening. I felt sorry to quit. A porter carried my bags to the station. Then, at a crossing, I recognized the street leading to that house. Telling the man to wait a minute, I went to cast a final glance at the site of my adventure, leaving the fellow smirking in a knowing way.

Yes, here it was, dark as last night, with the moonlight shining on the window-panes, and outlining the door. I was drawing nearer, when a figure emerged from the shadows. I recognized the German cowering on the threshold. He beckoned for me to approach. But mingled horror and fear made me take to my heels. I did not wish to be delayed, and to miss my train.

At the corner I turned for another look. As my eyes fell upon the poor devil, he sprang up and made for the entry. He pushed the door open, and a piece of metal shone in his hand. Was it money or a knife-blade that glittered so treacherously in the moonbeams?

ARNOLD ZWEIG

Kong at the Seaside

Arnold Zweig was born in Silesia in 1887. He wrote many short stories and after the First World War came his famous novel, *The Case of Sergeant Grischa.* When Zweig was driven out of Germany, he went to Palestine, where he now lives as an active Zionist. He has also written *Education Before Verdun* and *The Crowning of a King;* his latest novel, *The Axe of Wandsbeck,* deals with the Third Reich. [From *Playthings of Time* by Arnold Zweig; copyright 1935 by The Viking Press, Inc.; used by permission of the publishers; translated by Emma D. Ashton.]

KONG GOT HIS FIRST GLIMPSE of the sea as he ran on the beach, which stretched like a white arc along the edge of the cove. He barked vociferously with extravagant enthusiasm. Again and again, the bluish-white spray came dashing up at him and he was forbidden to hurl himself into it! A tall order for an Airedale terrier with a wiry brown coat and shaggy forelegs. However, Willie, his young god, would not permit it; but at any rate he could race at top speed across the firm sand, which was still damp from the ebbing waters, Willie following with lusty shouts. Engineer Groll, strolling after, noticed that the dog and his tanned, light-haired, eight-year-old master were attracting considerable attention among the beach-chairs and gaily striped bathing-houses. At the end of the row, where the sky was pale and dipped into the infinite—whereas it was vividly blue overhead and shed relaxation, happiness, and vigor on all these city people and their games in the sand—some controversy seemed to be in progress. Willie was standing there, slim and defiant, holding his dog by the collar. Groll hurried over. People in bathing-suits looked pretty much alike, social castes and classes intermingled. Heads showed more character and expression, though the bodies which supported them were still flabby and colorless, unaccustomed to exposure and pale after a long winter's imprisonment within the darkness of heavy clothing. A stoutish man was sitting in the shade of a striped orange tent stretched over a blue framework; he was bending slightly forward, holding a cigar.

"Is that your dog?" he asked quietly.

A little miss, about ten years old, was with him; she was biting her underlip, and a look of hatred for the boy and the dog flashed between her tear-filled narrow lids.

"No," said Groll with his pleasant voice, which seemed to rumble deep down in his chest, "the dog belongs to the boy, who, to be sure, is mine."

"You know dogs aren't allowed off the leash," the quiet voice continued. "He frightened my daughter a bit, has trampled her canals, and is standing on her spade."

"Pull him back, Willie," laughed Groll. "You're quite right, sir, but the dog broke away and, after all, nothing serious has happened."

Willie pushed Kong aside, picked up the spade and, bowing slightly, held it out to the group. Its third member was a slender, remarkably pretty young lady, sitting in the rear of the tent; Groll decided she was too young to be the mother of the girl and too attractive to be her governess. Well gotten up, he reflected; she looks like Irish with those auburn eyebrows.

No one took the spade from the boy, and Willie, with a frown, stuck the toy into the sand in front of the girl.

"I think that squares it, especially on such a beautiful day," Groll smiled and lay down. His legs behind him, his elbows on the sand, and his face resting on his hands, he looked over at the hostile three. Willie has behaved nicely and politely; how well he looks with his Kong. The dog, evidently not as ready to make peace, growled softly, his fur bristling at the neck; then he sat down.

"I want to shoot his dog, Father," the girl suddenly remarked in a determined voice; "he frightened me so." Groll noticed a gold bracelet of antique workmanship about her wrist—three strands of pale green-gold braided into the semblance of a snake. . . . These people need a lesson. I shall give it to them.

Groll nodded reassuringly at his boy, who was indignantly drawing his dog closer to him. Those grown-ups seemed to know that the girl had the upper hand of them, or, as Groll told himself, had the right to give orders. So he quietly waited for the sequel of this charming conversation; after all, he was still there to reprimand the brat if the gentleman with the fine cigar lacked the courage to do so because the sweet darling was not accustomed to proper discipline.

"No one is going to shoot my dog," threatened Willie, clenching his fists; but, without deigning to look at him, the girl continued:

"Buy him from the people, Father; here is my check-book." She actually took the thin booklet and a fountain-pen with a gold clasp from a zipper-bag inside the tent.

"If you won't buy him for me, I'll throw a soup-plate right off the table at dinner; you know I will, Father." She spoke almost in a whisper and was as white as chalk under her tan; her blue eyes, over which the sea had cast a greenish glint, flashed threateningly.

The gentleman said: "Ten pounds for the dog."

Groll sat up on the sand and crossed his legs. He was awaiting developments with curiosity.

"The dog is not mine; you must deal with my boy. He's trained him."

"I don't deal with boys. I offer fifteen pounds, a pretty neat sum for the cur."

Groll realized that this was an opportunity of really getting to know his eldest. "Willie," he began, "this gentleman offers you fifteen pounds for Kong so he may shoot him. For the money, you could buy the bicycle you have been wanting since last year. I won't be able to give it to you for a long time, we're not rich enough for that."

Willie looked at his father, wondering whether he could be in earnest. But the familiar face showed no sign of jesting. In answer he put an arm about Kong's neck, smiled up at Groll, and said: "I won't sell him to you, Father."

The gentleman in the bathing-suit with his still untanned, pale skin turned to Groll. Apparently the argument began to interest him. "Persuade him, I offer twenty pounds."

"Twenty pounds," Groll remarked to Willie, "that would buy you the bicycle and the canoe, which you admired so much this morning, Willie. A green canoe with double paddles for the water, and for the land a fine nickel-plated bicycle with a headlight, storage battery, and new tires. There might even be money left over for a watch. You only have to give up this old dog by handing the leash to the gentleman."

Willie said scornfully: "If I went ten steps away, Kong would pull him over and be with me again."

The beautiful and unusual young lady spoke for the first time. "He would hardly be able to do that," she said in a clear, sweet, mocking voice—a charming little person, thought Groll—and took a small Browning, gleaming with silver filigree work, out of her handbag. "This would prevent him from running very far."

Foolish of her, thought Groll. "You see, sir, the dog is a thoroughbred, pedigreed, and splendidly trained."

"We've noticed that!"

"Offer fifty pounds, Father, and settle it."

"Fifty pounds," repeated Groll, and his voice shook slightly. That would pay for this trip, and if I handled the money for him, his mother could at last regain her strength. The sanatorium is too expensive, we can't afford it. "Fifty pounds, Willie! The bicycle, the watch, the tent —you remember the brown tent with the cords and tassels—and you would have money left to help me send mother to a sanatorium. Imagine, all that for a dog! Later on, we can go to the animal welfare society, pay three shillings, and get another Kong."

Willie said softly: "There is only one Kong. I will not sell him."

"Offer a hundred pounds, Father. I want to shoot that dog. I shouldn't have to stand such boorishness."

The stoutish gentleman hesitated a moment, then made the offer. "A hundred pounds, sir," he said huskily. "You don't look as though you could afford to reject a small fortune."

"Indeed, sir, I can't," said Groll, and turned to Willie. "My boy," he continued earnestly, "a hundred pounds safely invested will within ten years assure you of a university education. Or, if you prefer, you can buy a small car to ride to school in. What eyes the other boys would make! And you could drive mother to market; that's a great deal of money, a hundred pounds for nothing but a dog."

Willie, frightened by the earnestness of the words, puckered up his face as though to cry. After all, he was just a small boy of eight and he was being asked to give up his beloved dog. "But I love Kong, and Kong loves me," he said, fighting down the tears in his voice. "I don't want to give him up."

"A hundred pounds—do persuade him, sir! Otherwise my daughter will make life miserable for me. You have no idea"—he sighed—"what a row such a little lady can kick up."

If she were mine, thought Groll, I'd leave the marks of a good lesson on each of her dainty cheeks; and after glancing at his boy, who, with furrowed brow, was striving to hold back his tears, he said it aloud, quietly, clearly, looking sternly into the eyes of the girl. "And now, I think, the incident is closed."

Then a most astounding thing happened. The little girl began to laugh. Evidently the tall, brown man pleased her, and the idea that anyone could dare to slap her, the little lady, for one of her whims fascinated her by its very roughness.

"All right, Father," she cried; "he's behaved well. Now we'll put the check-book back in the bag. Of course, Father, you knew it was all in fun!"

The stoutish gentleman smiled with relief and said that, of course, he had known it and added that such a fine day was just made to have fun. Fun! Groll didn't believe it. He knew too much about people.

Willie breathed more freely and, pretending to blow his nose, wiped away two furtive tears. He threw himself down in the sand next to Kong, happily pulled the dog on top of himself, and began to wrestle with him; the shaggy brown paws of the terrier and the slim tanned arms of the boy mingled in joyful confusion.

However, Groll, while he somewhat reluctantly accepted a cigar and a light from the strange gentleman and silently looked out into the blue-green sea, which lay spread before him like shimmering folds of silk with highlights and shadows—Groll thought: Alas for the poor! If this offer had come to me two years ago when my invention was not yet completed and when we lived in a damp flat dreaming of the little house we now have, then—poor Willie!—this argument might have had a different outcome, this struggle for nothing more than a dog, the love, loyalty, courage, and generosity in the soul of an animal and a boy. Yet, speaking in terms of economics, a little financial security was necessary before one could indulge in the luxury of human decency. Without it—he reflected—no one should be asked to make a decision similar to the one which has just confronted Willie and me; everyone was entitled to that much material safety, especially in an era which was so full of glittering temptations.

The little girl with the spade put her slim bare feet into the sand outside of the tent and called to Willie: "Help me dig new ones." But her eyes invited the man Groll, for whose approval she was striving.

She pointed to the ruined canals. Then, tossing her head, she indicated Kong, who lay panting and lazy in the warm sunshine, and called merrily: "For all I care, he can trample them again."

The whistle of an incoming steamboat sounded from the pier.

ARTHUR SCHNITZLER

The Dead Are Silent

Arthur Schnitzler (1862–1931) was born in Vienna and began his career as a physician, editing a medical journal. During this time he wrote non-medical plays and short stories, finally heading a literary movement which dominated Austrian letters until the First World War. His best known plays are *The Reckoning, The Lonely Way* and *The Vast Domain*. He has also written an autobiographical novel, *The Road to the Open*. [From *Viennese Idylls* by Arthur Schnitzler; used by permission of John W. Luce & Co., publishers; translated by F. Eisemann.]

HE COULD NOT BEAR SITTING in the carriage any longer; he got out and walked up and down. It was already dark; the few street lamps in this quiet side street flickered in the wind. It had stopped raining, and the sidewalks were almost dry; but the streets were still wet, and here and there a puddle had formed.

It's strange, thought Franz, how here, but a hundred feet away from the Praterstrasse, one can imagine oneself in a little Hungarian town. In any case, it was safe here; for in this street she would not be liable to meet any of her acquaintances.

He looked at his watch. Seven o'clock, and night had already fallen. An early autumn this year! And the cursed rain!

He pulled up his collar and walked up and down more quickly. The panes in the street lamps rattled. "A half hour more," he murmured to himself, "and if she's not here then, I can go. Ah, I almost wish that that half hour were up." He remained standing at the corner; for here he had a commanding view of the two streets, on either of which she might come.

Yes, today she'll come, he thought, as he held onto his hat, which threatened to blow away. Friday—Faculty meeting—then she'll dare come, and will even stay longer. He heard the ringing of the horse cars; and now the church bells began to ring. The street became more lively. More people passed and it seemed to him that they were mostly shopgirls and clerks. All of them walked quickly, and seemed to be fighting the storm. No one paid any attention to him; only two shopgirls gazed curiously up at him. Suddenly he saw a familiar figure hurrying toward him. He went quickly to meet her. Not in a carriage? Was it she?

It was; and as she became aware of him, she walked more slowly. "You come on foot?" he asked.

"I discharged my carriage before we reached this street, because I think I've had the same coachman before."

A man walked past and gave her a cursory glance. The young man stared at him, almost threateningly. He hurried on. The woman followed him with her eyes.

"Who was it?" she asked, frightened.

"I don't know him. You'll meet none of your acquaintances here, so you can rest easy. But come more quickly, and get into the carriage."

"Is it yours?"

"Yes."

"Is it open?"

"An hour ago the weather was ideal."

They hurried to the waiting carriage, and got in.

"Driver!" called the young man.

"Where has he gone to?" the young woman asked.

Franz looked all about. "It's unbelievable," he cried, "I don't see the fellow anywhere."

"For heaven's sake!" she cried softly.

"Wait a minute, dear; he must be here."

He opened the door of the little inn; the driver was sitting at a table with some other people. Now he rose quickly.

"Right here, sir!" he cried, and finished his glass of grog standing up.

"What in the deuce has got into you, to keep us waiting like this?"

"Excuse me, sir. But I'm right with ye now."

Swaying a little from side to side, he hurried to the carriage.

"Where d'ye want to drive, sir?"

"The Prater!"

The young man got in. His companion lay huddled up in the corner.

Franz took both of her hands in his. She remained immobile. "Well, won't you at least say good evening to me?"

"Please let me alone for just a few moments. I'm still quite out of breath."

He leaned back in his corner. Both were silent for a while. The carriage had turned into the Praterstrasse, had passed the Tegethoff Monument, and in a few seconds was flying down the dark Praterallee. Suddenly Emma threw her arms about her lover. He quickly raised the veil that separated her lips from his, and kissed her.

"At last I'm with you!" she said.

"Do you know how long it has been since we have seen one another?" he asked.

"Since Sunday."

"Yes, and then only from afar."

"Why, what do you mean? You were at our house."

"Well, yes—at your house. But this can't go on. I'm never going to your house again. But what's the matter with you?"

"A carriage just passed by."

"Dear child, the people who are driving in the Prater today aren't really going to bother about us."

"That I believe. But one of our friends might see us."

"That's impossible. It's too dark to recognize anyone."

"Please let us drive somewhere else."

"As you wish."

He called to the driver, but the latter did not seem to hear. Then he leaned forward and touched him with his hand. The coachman turned around.

"You're to turn back. . . . And why are you whipping your horses like that? We're in no hurry, do you hear! Drive to the—you know, the street that leads to the Reichs bridge."

"Yes, sir."

"And don't go driving like mad. There's no sense in that."

"Excuse me, sir, but it's the weather that makes them horses go so wild."

They turned back.

"Why didn't I see you yesterday?" she suddenly asked.

"How could you?"

"Why, I thought that my sister had invited you also."

"She did."

"And why didn't you come?"

"Because I cannot bear to be with you when others are around. No, never again!"

She shrugged her shoulders.

"Where are we?" she then asked.

They were driving under the railroad bridge into the Reichsstrasse.

"That's the road to the Danube," said Franz. "We're on the way to the Reichs bridge. You'll meet none of your friends here," he added in a jesting tone.

"The carriage is swaying terribly."

"That's because we're driving over cobblestones."

"But why does he drive in such zigzags?"

"You think he does!"

But he himself thought that they were being tossed about much more violently than was necessary. He did not, however, want to alarm her.

"I have some serious things to talk to you about today, Emma."

"Then you'll have to begin right away, because I have to be home by nine o'clock."

"All can be settled in two words."

"My God, what's that?" she suddenly cried. The carriage had been running in the car tracks, and now, as the coachman was trying to get out, it hung for a moment at such an angle that it almost overturned. Franz seized the driver by his cloak, and cried: "Will you stop! Why, you're drunk!"

With effort the horses were brought to a standstill.

"But, sir—"

"Come, Emma, let us get out here."

"Where are we?"

"At the bridge already. It's not so stormy now, so let us walk a bit. We can't really talk in a carriage."

Emma lowered her veil and followed.

"You don't call this stormy!" she exclaimed, as a gust of wind whirled about her.

He took her arm. "Follow us," he called to the driver.

They walked on ahead. When they heard the water rushing below them, they stopped. It was pitch dark. The broad river looked like a boundless expanse of gray. In the distance they saw red lights, which appeared to sway over the river and reflect themselves on its bosom. The lights on the bank which they had just left seemed to be dissolving themselves into the water. Now faint thunder, which came nearer and nearer, was audible. Both looked at the spot where the red lights shone. Trains with lighted windows came out of the night and disappeared again. The thunder gradually subsided, and, except for an occasional gust of wind, quiet reigned.

After a long silence, Franz said: "We ought to go away."

"Of course," Emma answered softly.

"We ought to go away," Franz repeated with animation. "I mean far away."

"It can't be done."

"Because we're cowards. That's why it can't be done."

"And my child?"

"I'm positive he'd let you take him."

"And how shall we do it?" she asked softly. "Steal away in the dead of night?"

"No, certainly not. All you have to do is simply tell him that you can't live with him any longer because you belong to another."

"Are you out of your mind, Franz?"

"If you prefer, I'll spare you that, too. I'll tell him myself."

"You'll not do that, Franz."

He tried to see her face, but all he noticed was that she had lifted her head and had turned it toward him.

He was silent for a while. Then he said quietly: "Don't be afraid. I'll not do it."

They were now approaching the other shore.

"Don't you hear something?" she asked. "What is it?"

"It comes from over there."

Slowly it came from out of the night, a small red light. Soon they saw it shone from a lantern tied to the front part of a peasant's cart. But they could not see whether anyone was in the wagon. Right in back of it lumbered two other carts. On the last they made out a man in peasant's dress, who was lighting his pipe. The wagons drove by. Then they heard nothing but the slow movement of the carriage, which kept about twenty paces ahead of them. Now the bridge gradually sank to the level of the other shore. They saw how the street ran on, between rows of trees, into the night. On both sides of them lay meadows, which looked like deep abysses.

After a long silence Franz suddenly said: "Well, this is the last time."

"What?" asked Emma in a worried tone.

"That we'll be together. Stay with him. I'll say good by to you."

"Are you in earnest?"

"Absolutely."

"Now you see that it is always you who spoil the few hours we spend together, and not I."

"Yes, yes; you're right," said Franz. "Come, let's drive back."

She held his arm more firmly. "No," she said tenderly, "not now. I'm not going to let you send me away like that."

She drew him down toward her and kissed him. "If we kept right on this road where should we get to?"

"Prague, my dear."

"Well, we won't go that far," she replied, smiling. "But let's go on a bit further, if you don't mind."

"Hey, driver!" called Franz.

The carriage rolled on. Franz ran after it. Now he saw that the driver had fallen asleep. By calling loudly enough, Franz finally succeeded in waking him.

"We're going to drive a little further along this straight road. Do you understand me?"

"Yes, sir; all right, sir."

They stepped in; the coachman whipped up the horses, and they raced down the muddy road. The couple in the carriage were folded in each other's arms while they were tossed from one side to the other.

"Isn't this glorious?" Emma whispered, with her lips almost touching his.

At this moment it seemed to her as if the carriage had shot up into the air. She felt herself hurled out; she tried to seize hold of something, and only clawed in the air. It seemed to her that she spun round and round in a circle at such a speed that she must close her eyes. Then she felt herself lying on the ground, and a terrible heavy quiet hung over her, as if she were all alone, far away from the world. Presently she heard noises: horses' hoofs pawing the ground near her, and a soft whinnying; but she could see nothing. A terrible fear gripped her; she cried out, and her fear became greater, for she could not hear her own voice. All of a sudden, she knew exactly what had happened: the carriage had hit something, probably a milestone, had overturned, and they had been thrown out. Where was Franz? She called his name. And she heard her voice—very vaguely—but she heard it. There was no answer. She tried to rise. She was able to sit up, and as she put forth her two hands she felt a human body next to her. And now, as her eyes had become accustomed to the darkness, she could see more clearly. Franz lay on the ground, motionless. She touched his face with her hand, and felt something warm and damp flowing over it. She caught her breath. Blood! Franz was wounded and unconscious. And the driver—where was he? She called to him. No answer. She was still sitting on the ground. Nothing had happened to her, she thought, although she felt pains in all parts of her body.

"Franz!" she called.

A voice close by answered:

"Where are ye, miss? And where's the gentleman? Nothing's happened, has it? Wait a minute, miss; I'll light one of the lamps so as we can see better. I don't know what's got into them horses today. It ain't my fault, as true's I'm living."

Emma had risen by this time in spite of her pains, and she was relieved to find that the coachman was not injured. She heard him open the lamp and strike a match. In terrible fear she waited for the light. She did not dare touch Franz again, who lay stretched out on the earth.

A ray of light came from the side. She saw the carriage, which, to her surprise, was not quite overturned, but was lying up against the main drain, as if one of the wheels had come off. The horses were standing stock-still. The light came nearer; she watched it as it crept over a milestone, over the stone heap, then on Franz's feet, on his body and, finally, on his face, where it remained. The driver had placed the lamp on the ground beside Franz's head. Emma knelt down, and when she saw his face, it seemed as if her heart stopped beating. His face was pale; his eyes were half open, and only the whites were visible. From the right temple trickled a small stream of blood, which, passing over the cheek, lost itself under the collar. His teeth had bitten into his lower lip.

"It isn't possible!" Emma murmured to herself.

The coachman was also on his knees, staring at the face. Then he took hold of the head with both of his hands and raised it.

"What are you doing?" screamed Emma, and recoiled from the head, which seemed to rise of its own accord.

"It looks to me, miss, like an awful accident."

"It isn't true," said Emma. "It can't be true. Did anything happen to you? And me—"

The driver slowly lowered the head of the unconscious man into Emma's lap. She trembled.

"If only somebody'd come . . . if only them peasants had come a quarter of an hour ago—"

"What shall we do?" Emma asked, her lips trembling.

"Yes, miss, if that there carriage only weren't broken— But now we've simply got to wait till someone comes."

He went on talking, but Emma was not listening. She regained control of her thoughts, and knew how to act.

"How far is it to the nearest house?" she asked.

"Not far, miss. We're almost in Franz Josefsland. We'd see the houses if it was light. It's only about five minutes away."

"Well, you go and get help. I'll stay here."

"Yes, miss. But I think it'd be better if I stayed here with you. It won't be long 'fore somebody is sure to turn up."

"Then it may be too late. We need a doctor."

The driver looked at the face of the motionless man; then he looked at Emma, shaking his head.

"That you can't know," cried Emma, "nor I either."

"Yes, miss . . . but where'll I find a doctor in Franz Josefsland?"

"From there someone can go to the city, and—"

"D'ye know what, miss: they've probably got telephones there, and I could call an ambulance."

"Yes, that's the best thing to do. But hurry up, for heaven's sake! And bring help and please go now this minute. Why, what are you doing?"

The driver was looking at the pale face in Emma's lap.

"Ambulance—doctor! It's too late for them to do any good!"

"Oh, please go now! For God's sake, go!"

"I'll go all right. Only, don't get scared here in the dark, miss."

He hurried off down the street and Emma was alone with the inanimate body in the dark street.

It wasn't possible—that thought kept going through her head. Of a sudden she seemed to feel someone breathing right next to her. She leaned over, and looked at the white lips. No, there was no breath coming from them. The blood on the temple and the cheek had dried. She looked at the eyes, and trembled. This was death! There was a dead man on her lap! And with shaking hands she raised the head and placed it on the ground. A terrible feeling of abandonment came over her. Why had she sent the driver away? How foolish of her! What should she do here on the highroad with a corpse? If anyone should come alone . . . What would she do if any people came along? She looked at the dead man again. The light of the lamp seemed to her kind and friendly, for which she ought to be thankful. She gazed at it so long that her eyes blinked, and everything began to dance before her. Suddenly she had the sensation of being awakened. She jumped up! She couldn't be found here with him! What was she waiting for?

Voices were now audible in the distance.

"Already?" she thought. She listened, fearfully. The voices came from the direction of the bridge. Those could not be the people whom the coachman had gone to get. But whoever they were, they would certainly notice the light—and that could not be, for then she would be discovered.

She kicked the lamp over. The light was extinguished. Now she was in total darkness. She did not see him any more. The voices came nearer. Only the white stone heap was visible now. She now began to tremble in her whole body. Not to be discovered there—that was the important thing! She was lost if anyone found out that she had had a liaison . . . But the people passed on. . . . And now . . . She would have to go to the police station, and everybody would find it out—and her husband—and her child!

Then she realized that she had been standing as if rooted to the ground, that she could go away, that by staying she would only bring unhappiness upon herself. She took a step. Soon she was in the middle of the street. She looked ahead and saw the outlines of the long, gray road. There—there was the city. She could not see it, but she knew the direction. Once more she turned around. She could see the horses and the carriage; and when she tried very hard, she could make out something that looked like the outline of a human body stretched out on the ground. . . . With all her might she tore herself away. The ground was wet, and the mud had sucked in her shoes. She walked faster . . . she ran back—into the light, the noise and the people! The street seemed to run toward her, and she held up her skirt in order to keep from falling. The wind was at her back, and it seemed to be driving her ahead. She remembered that she was fleeing from living people who must now be at the spot, and also looking for her. What would they think? But no one could possibly guess who the woman was with the man in the carriage. The driver did not know her, and he would never be able to recognize her if he saw her. It was very wise that she did not stay; and it was not wrong of her to have left. Franz himself would have said that she was in the right.

She hurried toward the city, whose lights she saw under the railroad bridge at the end of the street. Just this one lonely street and then she would be safe. She heard a shrill whistling in the distance; growing shriller, drawing nearer. A wagon flew past. Involuntarily she stopped and watched it. It was the ambulance, and she knew its destination. "How quick!" she thought. It was like magic. . . . For a moment she had the most terrible feeling of shame she had ever experienced. She knew that she had been cowardly. But as the whistling grew fainter, a wild joy seized her, and she rushed on. People came toward her; she was not afraid of them any more—the worst was over. The noise of the city became more audible, and there was more light; already she saw the rows of houses on the Praterstrasse, and it seemed to her as if she were being expected there by a crowd of people in which she could disappear without leaving a trace behind her. As she came under a street lamp she was calm enough to look at her watch. It was ten minutes of nine. It seemed to her as if she were entirely forgiven, as if none of the blame had been hers. She was a woman—and she had a child and a husband. She had done right: it was her duty. Had she stayed she would have been discovered. And the newspapers! She would have been ostracized forever! . . . There was the Tegethoff Monument where many streets meet. There were very few people abroad, but to her it seemed as if the whole life of the city were whirling about her. She had time. She knew that her husband would not be home till nearly ten—she even had time to change her clothes! She looked at her dress: it was covered with mud. What would she tell her maid? It went through her head that a full account of the accident would be in all the morning papers. And it would tell of the woman who was in the carriage at the time of the accident, and then could not be found. These thoughts made her tremble again—an imprudent thing, and all her cowardice had been for nought. But she had her key with her; she need not ring the bell. She would be quiet and no one would hear her. She got hurriedly into a carriage. She was about to give the coachman her address, when she thought that that would be unwise, and she gave him the name of the first street that came into her head. She had but one wish: to be safe at home. Nothing else made any difference. She was not heartless. Yet she was sure that days would come when she would doubt, and perhaps that doubt would ruin her; but now her only desire was to be at home, dry-eyed, at the table with her husband and child. The carriage was driving through the inner city. She stopped in a side street off the Ring, got out of the carriage, hurried round the corner, got into another carriage, and gave her right address to the driver. She was incapable of even thinking any more. She closed her eyes, and the carriage began to shake. She was afraid of being thrown out as before, and screamed. Then the carriage came to a stop in front of her home. She hurriedly got out, and quickly, with soft steps, passed the porter's window so that she would not be noticed. She ran up the stairs, softly opened the door . . . through the hall into her bedroom—it was done! She turned on the light, tore off her clothes and hid them in a closet. They would dry overnight—

tomorrow she would brush them herself. Then she washed her hands and face, and put on a dressing gown.

Then the doorbell rang. She heard the maid going to the door. She heard her husband's voice, and she heard his cane rattle in the umbrella jar. She felt that she must be strong or all would have been in vain. She hurried into the dining room so that she entered at the same moment that her husband did.

"You're at home already?" he asked.

"Surely," she answered. "I've been here quite a while."

"The maid didn't see you come in." She smiled without trying. But it tired her to smile. He kissed her on the brow.

Their little boy was already at the table. He had had to wait long and had fallen asleep. His book was on the plate, and his face rested on the open book. She sat down next to him, her husband opposite. He picked up a newspaper and glanced through it, then put it down and said:

"The others are still at the meeting, discussing things."

"What?" she asked.

And he started to tell her of the meeting. Emma pretended that she was listening, and kept nodding her head.

But she heard nothing; she did not know what he was speaking about. She felt as one who had wonderfully escaped from some terrible danger. As her husband talked, she moved her chair nearer to her son, and pressed his head against her breast. A feeling of great weariness crept over her. She could not control herself; she felt that sleep was overpowering her, and she closed her eyes.

Suddenly a thought flashed through her mind that had not occurred to her since she picked herself up out of the ditch. If he were not dead after all! If he should say to the doctors, "There was a woman with me, and she must have been thrown out also." What then?

"What is the matter?" asked the professor earnestly, as he looked up.

"Why . . . why—the matter!"

"Yes, what *is* the matter with you?"

"Nothing!" She pressed her boy close to her breast.

The professor looked at her for a long while, silently.

"Do you know that you began to doze, and suddenly cried out?"

". . . Really?"

"Yes, as if you had had a bad dream. Were you dreaming?"

"I really don't know. . . ."

She saw her image in the mirror, smiling horribly. Her face was all drawn. She knew that it was herself, but she shrank away from it. Her face had become fixed and she could not move her mouth. She tried to cry out. Then she felt two hands on her shoulders, and she noticed that the face of her husband had come between her and the mirror; his eyes, questioning, threatening, sank into hers. She knew that if she did not stand this last test, all was lost. She felt that she was regaining her strength; she had entire control of herself, and she knew that she must make use of this valuable moment. She took her husband's arms from her shoulders, drew him toward her, and gazed at him, gaily and tenderly.

As she felt her husband's lips on her brow she thought: "Surely . . . a bad dream. He must be dead . . . *and the dead are silent.*"

"Why did you say that?" she suddenly heard her husband ask.

"What did I say?" And it seemed to her as if she had told the whole story aloud, and once more she asked, as she faltered under his stern gaze:

"What did I say?"

" 'The dead are silent,' " he repeated, very slowly.

"Yes . . ." she said. "Yes . . ." But she read in his eyes that she could not hide anything more from him.

They gazed at each other for a long time.

"Put the boy to bed," he said to her. "I think you have something more to tell me."

"Yes," she answered.

She knew that in a few minutes she was going to tell this man, whom she had deceived for years, the whole truth.

And, as she slowly went out through the door with her son and felt her husband's eyes upon her, a feeling of quiet stole over her, as if everything was going to be put to rights again. . . .

ARTHUR KOESTLER

Darkness at Noon

Arthur Koestler was born in Budapest in 1905. After living in the Near East for a time, he became a newspaper man, working in the Near East, Russia, Paris, Zurich and Spain during the Civil War. His works include *Dialogue With Death, Scum of the Earth, Darkness at Noon, Arrival and Departure, Thieves in the Night* and a play, *Twilight Bar.* [From *Darkness at Noon* by Arthur Koestler; used by permission of The Macmillan Co., publishers, and Jonathan Cape Ltd.; translated by Daphne Hardy.]

SO NOW IT WAS ALL OVER. Rubashov knew that before midnight he would have ceased to exist.

He wandered through his cell, to which he had returned after the uproar of the trial; six and a half steps to the window, six and a half steps back. When he stood still, listening, on the third black tile from the window, the silence between the whitewashed walls came to meet him, as from the depth of a well. He still did not understand why it had become so quiet, within and without. But he knew that now nothing could disturb this peace any more.

Looking back, he could even remember the moment when this blessed quietness had sunk over him. It had been at the trial, before he had started his last speech. He had believed that he had burnt out the last vestiges of egotism and vanity from his consciousness, but in that moment, when his eyes had searched the faces of the audience and found only indifference and derision, he had been for a last time carried away by his hunger for a bone of pity; freezing, he had wanted to warm himself by his own words. The temptation had gripped him to talk of his past, to rear up just once and tear the net in which Ivanov and Gletkin had entangled him, to shout at his accusers like Danton: "You have laid hands on my whole life. May it rise and challenge you. . . ." Oh, how well he knew Danton's speech before the Revolutionary Tribunal. He could repeat it word for word. He had as a boy learnt it by heart: "You want to stifle the Republic in blood. How long must the footsteps of freedom be gravestones? Tyranny is afoot; she has torn her veil, she carries her head high, she strides over our dead bodies."

The words had burnt on his tongue. But the temptation had only lasted a moment; then, when he started to pronounce his final speech, the bell of silence had sunk down over him. He had recognized that it was too late.

Too late to go back again the same way, to step once more in the graves of his own footprints. Words could undo nothing.

Too late for all of them. When the hour came to make their last appearance before the world, none of them could turn the dock into a rostrum, none of them could unveil the truth to the world and hurl back the accusation at his judges, like Danton.

Some were silenced by physical fear, like Hare-lip; some hoped to save their heads; others at least to save their wives or sons from the clutches of the Gletkins. The best of them kept silent in order to do a last service to the Party, by letting themselves be sacrificed as scape-goats—and, besides, even the best had each an Arlova on his conscience. They were too deeply entangled in their own past, caught in the web they had spun themselves, according to the laws of their own twisted ethics and twisted logic; they were all guilty, although not of those deeds of which they accused themselves. There was no way back for them. Their exit from the stage happened strictly according to the rules of their strange game. The public expected no swan-songs of them. They had to act according to the text-book, and their part was the howling of wolves in the night. . . .

So now it was over. He had nothing more to do with it. He no longer had to howl with the wolves. He had paid, his account was settled. He was a man who had lost his shadow, released from every bond. He had followed every thought to its last conclusion and acted in accordance with it to the very end; the hours which remained to him belonged to that silent partner, whose realm started just where logical thought ended. He had christened it the "grammatical fiction" with that shamefacedness about the first person singular which the Party had inculcated in its disciples.

Rubashov stopped by the wall which separated him from No. 406. The cell was empty since the departure of Rip Van Winkle. He took off his pince-nez, looked round furtively and tapped:

2—4 . . .

He listened with a feeling of childlike shame and then knocked again:

2—4 . . .

He listened, and again repeated the same sequence of signs. The wall remained mute. He had never yet consciously tapped the word "I." Probably never at all. He listened. The knocking died without resonance.

He continued pacing through his cell. Since the bell of silence had sunk over him, he was puzzling over certain questions to which he would have liked to find an answer before it was too late. They were rather naïve questions; they concerned the meaning of suffering, or, more exactly, the difference between suffering which made sense and senseless suffering. Obviously only such suffering made sense as was inevitable; that is, as was rooted in biological fatality. On the other hand, all suffering with a social origin was accidental, hence pointless and senseless. The sole object of revolution was the abolition of senseless suffering. But it had turned out that the removal of this second kind of suffering was only possible at the price of a temporary enormous increase in the sum total of the first. So the question now ran: Was such an operation justified? Obviously it was, if one spoke in the abstract of "mankind"; but, applied to "man" in the singular, to the cipher 2—4, the real human being of bone and flesh and blood and skin, the principle led to absurdity. As a boy, he had believed that in working for the Party he would find an answer to all questions of this sort. The work had lasted forty years, and right at the start he had forgotten the question for whose sake he had embarked on it. Now the forty years were over, and he returned to the boy's original perplexity. The Party had taken all he had to give and never supplied him with the answer. And neither did the silent partner, whose magic name he had tapped on the wall of the empty cell. He was deaf to direct questions, however urgent and desperate they might be.

And yet there were ways of approach to him. Sometimes he would respond unexpectedly to a tune, or even the memory of a tune, or of the folded hands of the *Pietà,* or of certain scenes of his childhood. As if a tuning-fork had been struck, there would be answering vibrations, and once this had started a state would be produced which the mystics called "ecstasy" and saints "contemplation"; the greatest and soberest of modern psychologists had recognized this state as a fact and called it the "oceanic sense." And, indeed, one's personality dissolved as a grain of salt in the sea; but at the same time the infinite sea seemed to be contained in the grain of salt. The grain could no longer be localized in time and space. It was a state in which thought lost its direction and started to circle, like the compass needle at the magnetic pole; until finally it cut loose from its axis and traveled freely in space, like a bunch of light in the night; and until it seemed that all thoughts and all sensations, even pain and joy itself, were only the spectrum lines of the same ray of light, disintegrating in the prisma of consciousness.

Rubashov wandered through his cell. In old days he would have shamefacedly denied himself this sort of childish musing. Now he was not ashamed. In death the metaphysical became real. He stopped at the window and leaned his forehead against the pane. Over the machine-gun tower one could see a patch of blue. It was pale, and reminded him of that particular blue which he had seen overhead when as a boy he lay on the grass in his father's park, watching the poplar branches slowly moving against the sky. Apparently even a patch of blue sky was enough to cause the "oceanic state." He had read that, according to the latest discoveries of astrophysics, the volume of the world was finite—though space had no boundaries, it was self-contained, like the surface of a sphere. He had never been able to understand that; but now he felt an urgent desire to understand. He now also remembered where he had read about it: during his first arrest in Germany, comrades had smuggled a sheet of the illegally printed Party organ into his cell; at the top were three columns about a strike in a spinning-mill; at the bottom of a column, as a stop-gap, was printed in tiny letters the discovery that the universe was finite, and halfway through it the page was torn off. He had never found out what had been in the torn-off part.

Rubashov stood by the window and tapped on the empty wall with his pince-nez. As a boy he had really meant to study astronomy, and now for forty years he had been doing something else. Why had not the Public Prosecutor asked him: "Defendant Rubashov, what about the infinite?" He would not have been able to answer—and there, there lay the real source of his guilt. . . . Could there be a greater?

When he had read that newspaper notice, then also alone in his cell, with joints still sore from the last bout of torturing, he had fallen into a queer state of exaltation—the "oceanic sense" had swept him away. Afterward he had been ashamed of himself. The Party disapproved of such states. It called them *petit-bourgeois* mysticism, refuge in the ivory tower. It called them "escape from the task," "desertion of the class struggle." The "oceanic sense" was counter-revolutionary.

For in a struggle one must have both legs firmly planted on the earth. The Party taught one how to do it. The infinite was a politically suspect quantity, the "I" a suspect quality. The Party did not recognize its existence. The definition of the individual was: a multitude of one million divided by one million.

The Party denied the free will of the individual—and at the same time it exacted his willing self-sacrifice. It denied his capacity to choose between two alternatives—and at the same time it demanded that he should constantly choose the right one. It denied his power to distinguish good and evil—and at the same time it spoke pathetically of guilt and treachery. The individual stood under the sign of economic fatality, a wheel in a clockwork which had been wound up for all eternity and could not be stopped or influenced—and the Party demanded that the wheel should revolt against the clockwork and change its course. There was somewhere an error in the calculation; the equation did not work out.

For forty years he had fought against economic fatality. It was the central ill of humanity, the cancer which was eating into its entrails. It was there that one must operate; the rest of the healing process would follow. All else was dilettantism, romanticism, charlatanism. One cannot heal a person mortally ill by pious exhortations. The only solution was the surgeon's knife and his cool calculation. But wherever the knife had been applied, a new sore had appeared in place of the old. And again the equation did not work out.

For forty years he had lived strictly in accordance with the vows of his order, the Party. He had held to the rules of logical calculation. He had burnt the remains of the old, illogical morality from his consciousness with the acid of reason. He had turned away from the temptations of the silent partner, and had fought against the "oceanic sense" with all his might. And where had it landed him? Premises of unimpeachable truth had led to a result which was completely absurd; Ivanov's and Gletkin's irrefutable deductions had taken him straight into the weird and ghostly game of the public trial. Perhaps it was not suitable for a man to think every thought to its logical conclusion.

Rubashov stared through the bars of the window at the patch of the blue above the machine-gun tower. Looking back over his past, it seemed to him now that for forty years he had been running amuck—the running-amuck of pure reason. Perhaps it did not suit man to be completely freed from old bonds, from the steadying brakes of "Thou shalt not" and "Thou mayst not," and to be allowed to tear along straight toward the goal.

The blue had begun to turn pink, dusk was falling; round the tower a flock of dark birds was circling with slow, deliberate wing-beats. No, the equation did not work out. It was obviously not enough to direct man's eyes toward a goal and put a knife in his hand; it was unsuitable for him to experiment with a knife. Perhaps later, one day. For the moment he was still too young and awkward. How he had raged in the great field of experiment, the Fatherland of the Revolution, the Bastion of Freedom! Gletkin justified everything that happened with the principle that the bastion must be preserved. But what did it look like inside? No, one cannot build Paradise with concrete. The bastion would be preserved, but it no longer had a message, nor an example to give the world. No. 1's régime had besmirched the ideal of the Social State even as some Mediaeval Popes had besmirched the ideal of a Christian Empire. The flag of the Revolution was at half-mast.

Rubashov wandered through his cell. It was quiet and nearly dark. It could not be long before they came to fetch him. There was an error somewhere in the equation—no, in the whole mathematical system of thought. He had had an inkling of it for a long time already, since the story of Richard and the *Pietà*, but had never dared to admit it to himself fully. Perhaps the Revolution had come too early, an abortion with monstrous, deformed limbs. Perhaps the whole thing had been a bad mistake in timing. The Roman civilization, too, had seemed to be doomed as early as the first century b.c.; had seemed as rotten to the marrow as our own; then, too, the best had believed that the time was ripe for a great change; and yet the old worn-out world had held out for another five hundred years. History had a slow pulse; man counted in years, history in generations. Perhaps it was still only the second day of creation. How he would have liked to live and build up the theory of the relative maturity of the masses! . . .

It was quiet in the cell. Rubashov heard only the creaking of his steps on the tiles. Six and a half steps to the door, whence they must come to fetch him, six and a half steps to the window, behind which night was falling. Soon it would be over. But when he asked himself, For what actually are you dying? he found no answer.

It was a mistake in the system; perhaps it lay in the precept which until now he had held to be uncontestable, in whose name he had sacrificed others and was himself being sacrificed: in the precept, that the end justifies the means. It was this sentence which had killed the great fraternity of the Revolution and made them all run amuck. What had he once written in his diary? "We have thrown overboard all conventions, our sole guiding principle is that of consequent logic; we are sailing without ethical ballast."

Perhaps the heart of the evil lay there. Perhaps it did not suit mankind to sail without ballast. And perhaps reason alone was a defective compass, which led one on such a winding, twisted course that the goal finally disappeared in the mist.

Perhaps now would come the time of great darkness.

Perhaps later, much later, the new movement would arise—with new flags, a new spirit knowing of both: of economic fatality *and* the "oceanic sense." Perhaps the members of the new party will wear monks' cowls, and preach that only purity of means can justify the ends. Perhaps they will teach that the tenet is wrong which says that a man is the quotient of one million divided by one million, and will introduce a new kind of arithmetic based on multiplication: on the joining of a million individuals to form a new entity which, no longer an amorphous mass, will develop a consciousness and an individuality of its own, with an "oceanic feeling" increased a millionfold, in unlimited yet self-contained space.

Rubashov broke off his pacing and listened. The sound of muffled drumming came down the corridor.

The drumming sounded as though it were brought from the distance by the wind; it was still far, it was coming closer. Rubashov did not stir. His legs on the tiles were no longer subject to his will; he felt the earth's force of gravity slowly mounting in them. He took three steps backward to the window, without taking his eye off the spy-hole. He breathed deeply and lit a cigarette. He heard a ticking in the wall next to the bunk:

THEY ARE FETCHING HARE-LIP. HE SENDS YOU HIS GREETINGS.

The heaviness vanished from his legs. He went to the door and started to beat against the metal quickly and rhythmically with the flat of both hands. To pass the news on to No. 406 was no use now. The cell stood empty; the chain broke off there. He drummed and pressed his eye to the spy-hole.

In the corridor the dim electric light was burning as always. He saw the iron doors of No. 401 to No. 407, as always. The drumming swelled. Steps approached, slow and dragging, one heard them distinctly on the tiles. Suddenly Hare-lip was standing in the spy-hole's range of vision. He stood there, with trembling lips, as he had stood in the light of the reflector in Gletkin's room; his hands in handcuffs hung down behind his back in a peculiarly twisted position. He could not see Rubashov's eye behind the judas and looked at the door with blind, searching pupils, as though the last hope of salvation lay behind it. Then an order was spoken, and Hare-lip obediently turned to go. Behind him came the giant in uniform with his revolver-belt. They disappeared from Rubashov's field of vision, one behind the other.

The drumming faded; all was quiet again. From the wall next to the bunk came the sound of ticking:

HE BEHAVED QUITE WELL. . . .

Since the day when Rubashov had informed No. 402 of his capitulation, they had not spoken to each other. No. 402 went on:

YOU STILL HAVE ABOUT TEN MINUTES. HOW DO YOU FEEL?

Rubashov understood that No. 402 had started the conversation in order to make waiting easier for him. He was grateful for it. He sat down on the bunk and tapped back:

I WISH IT WERE OVER ALREADY. . . .

YOU WON'T SHOW THE WHITE FEATHER, tapped No. 402. WE KNOW YOU'RE THE DEVIL OF A FELLOW. . . . He paused, then, quickly, repeated his last words: THE DEVIL OF A FELLOW. . . . He was obviously anxious to prevent the conversation coming to a standstill. DO YOU STILL REMEMBER: "BREASTS LIKE CHAMPAGNE GLASSES"? HA-HA! THE DEVIL OF A FELLOW. . . .

Rubashov listened for a sound in the corridor. One heard nothing. No. 402 seemed to guess his thoughts, for he at once tapped again:

DON'T LISTEN. I WILL TELL YOU IN TIME WHEN

THEY ARE COMING. . . . WHAT WOULD YOU DO IF YOU
WERE PARDONED?

Rubashov thought it over. Then he tapped:

STUDY ASTRONOMY.

HA-HA! expressed No. 402. I, TOO, PERHAPS. PEOPLE SAY
OTHER STARS ARE PERHAPS ALSO INHABITED. PERMIT
ME TO GIVE YOU SOME ADVICE.

CERTAINLY, answered Rubashov, surprised.

BUT DON'T TAKE IT ILL. TECHNICAL SUGGESTION OF
A SOLDIER. EMPTY YOUR BLADDER. IS ALWAYS BETTER
IN SUCH CASES. THE SPIRIT IS WILLING BUT THE FLESH
IS WEAK. HA-HA!

Rubashov smiled and went obediently to the bucket. Then he sat
down again on the bunk and tapped:

THANKS. EXCELLENT IDEA. AND WHAT ARE YOUR
PROSPECTS?

No. 402 was silent for a few seconds. Then he tapped, rather slower
than he had before:

EIGHTEEN YEARS MORE. NOT QUITE, ONLY 6,530 DAYS.
. . . He paused. Then he added:

I ENVY YOU REALLY. And then, after another pause: THINK
OF IT—ANOTHER 6,530 NIGHTS WITHOUT A WOMAN.

Rubashov said nothing. Then he tapped:

BUT YOU CAN READ, STUDY. . . .

HAVEN'T GOT THE HEAD FOR IT, tapped No. 402. And
then, loud and hurriedly: THEY'RE COMING. . . .

He stopped, but a few seconds later, added:

A PITY. WE WERE JUST HAVING SUCH A PLEASANT
CHAT. . . .

Rubashov stood up from the bunk. He thought a moment and then
tapped:

YOU HELPED ME A LOT. THANKS.

The key ground in the lock. The door flew open. Outside stood the
giant in uniform and a civilian. The civilian called Rubashov by name
and reeled off a text from a document. While they twisted his arms
behind his back and put on the handcuffs, he heard No. 402 hastily
tapping:

I ENVY YOU. I ENVY YOU. FAREWELL.

In the corridor outside, the drumming had started again. It accompanied them till they reached the barber's room. Rubashov knew that
from behind each iron door an eye was looking at him through the spy-
hole, but he turned his head neither to the left nor to the right. The
handcuffs grazed his wrists; the giant had screwed them too tightly
and had strained his arms while twisting them behind his back; they
were hurting.

The cellar steps came in sight. Rubashov slowed down his pace. The civilian stopped at the top of the steps. He was small and had slightly protuberant eyes. He asked:

"Have you another wish?"

"None," said Rubashov, and started to climb down the cellar steps. The civilian remained standing above and looked down at him with his protuberant eyes.

The stairs were narrow and badly lit. Rubashov had to be careful not to stumble, as he could not hold on to the stair rail. The drumming had ceased. He heard the man in uniform descending three steps behind him.

The stairs turned in a spiral. Rubashov bent forward to see better; his pince-nez detached itself from his face and fell to the ground two steps below him; splintering, it rebounded lower down and remained lying on the bottom step. Rubashov stopped a second, hesitatingly; then he felt his way down the rest of the steps. He heard the man behind him bend down and put the broken pince-nez in his pocket, but did not turn his head.

He was now nearly blind, but he had solid ground under his feet again. A long corridor received him; its walls were blurred and he could not see the end of it. The man in uniform kept always three steps behind him. Rubashov felt his gaze in the back of his neck, but did not turn his head. Cautiously he put one foot before the other.

It seemed to him that they had been walking along this corridor for several minutes already. Still nothing happened. Probably he would hear when the man in uniform took the revolver out of its case. So until then there was time, he was still in safety. Or did the man behind him proceed like the dentist, who hid his instruments in his sleeve while bending over his patient? Rubashov tried to think of something else, but had to concentrate his whole attention to prevent himself from turning his head.

Strange that his toothache had ceased in the minute when that blessed silence had closed round him, during the trial. Perhaps the abscess had opened just in that minute. What had he said to them? "I bow my knees before the country, before the masses, before the whole people. . . ." And what then? What happened to these masses, to this people? For forty years it had been driven through the desert, with threats and promises, with imaginary terrors and imaginary rewards. But where was the Promised Land?

Did there really exist any such goal for this wandering mankind? That was a question to which he would have liked an answer before it was too late. Moses had not been allowed to enter the land of promise either. But he had been allowed to see it, from the top of the mountain, spread at his feet. Thus, it was easy to die, with the visible certainty of one's goal before one's eyes. He, Nicolas Salmanovitch Rubashov, had not been taken to the top of a mountain; and wherever his eye looked, he saw nothing but desert and the darkness of night.

A dull blow struck the back of his head. He had long expected it

and yet it took him unawares. He felt, wondering, his knees give way
and his body whirl round in a half-turn. How theatrical, he thought
as he fell, and yet I feel nothing. He lay crumpled up on the ground,
with his cheek on the cool flagstones. It got dark, the sea carried him
rocking on its nocturnal surface. Memories passed through him, like
streaks of mist over the water.

Outside, someone was knocking on the front door, he dreamed that
they were coming to arrest him; but in what country was he?

He made an effort to slip his arm into his dressing-gown sleeve. But
whose color-print portrait was hanging over his bed and looking at
him?

Was it No. 1 or was it the other—he with the ironic smile or he with
the glassy gaze?

A shapeless figure bent over him, he smelt the fresh leather of the
revolver belt; but what insignia did the figure wear on the sleeves and
shoulder-straps of its uniform—and in whose name did it raise the dark
pistol barrel?

A second, smashing blow hit him on the ear. Then all became quiet.
There was the sea again with its sounds. A wave slowly lifted him up.
It came from afar and traveled sedately on, a shrug of eternity.

HERMAN HESSE

Harry's Loves

Herman Hesse, Nobel Prize winner in
1946 for his novel *Steppenwolf*, was born
in 1877, the son of missionaries. His early
works glorified nature and childhood as
the period when man can enjoy a full life.
After the First World War, Hesse studied
his contemporaries and his culture to try
to find himself. His best known works
are *Demain, Siddhartha* and *Death and
the Lover*. [From *Steppenwolf* by Herman
Hesse; copyright 1929 by Henry Holt &
Co.; used by permission of the publishers;
translated by Basil Creighton.]

WITH AN IMMENSE RELIEF I remembered the notice I had seen
on first entering the theater, the one that the nice boy had stormed so
furiously—

ALL GIRLS ARE YOURS

and it seemed to me, all in all, that there was really nothing else so
desirable as this. I was greatly cheered at finding that I could escape
from that cursed wolf-world, and went in.

The fragrance of spring-time met me. The very atmosphere of boyhood and youth, so deeply familiar and yet so legendary, was around me

and in my veins flowed the blood of those days. All that I had done and thought and been since, fell away from me and I was young again. An hour, a few minutes before, I had prided myself on knowing what love was and desire and longing, but it had been the love and the longing of an old man. Now I was young again and this glowing current of fire that I felt in me, this mighty impulse, this unloosening passion like that wind in March that brings the thaw, was young and new and genuine. How the flame that I had forgotten leaped up again, how darkly stole on my ears the tones of long ago! My blood was on fire, and blossomed forth as my soul cried aloud and sang. I was a boy of fifteen or sixteen with my head full of Latin and Greek and poetry. I was all ardor and ambition and my fancy was laden with the artist's dreams. But far deeper and stronger and more awful than all there burned and leapt in me the flame of love, the hunger of sex, the fever and the foreboding of desire.

I was standing on a spur of the hills above the little town where I lived. The wind wafted the smell of spring and violets through my long hair. Below in the town I saw the gleam of the river and the windows of my home, and all that I saw and heard and smelt overwhelmed me, as fresh and reeling from creation, as radiant in depth of color, swayed by the wind of spring in as magical a transfiguration, as when once I looked on the world with the eyes of youth—first youth and poetry. With wandering hand I pulled a half-open leaf-bud from a bush that was newly green. I looked at it and smelt it (with the smell everything of those days came back in a glow) and then I put it between my lips, lips that no girl had ever kissed, and began playfully to bite it. At the sour and aromatically bitter taste I knew at once and exactly what it was that I was living over again. It all came back. I was living again an hour of the last years of my boyhood, a Sunday afternoon in early spring, the day that on a lonely walk I met Rosa Kreisler and greeted her so shyly and fell in love with her so madly.

She came, that day, alone and dreamingly up the hill toward me. She had not seen me and the sight of her approaching filled me with apprehension and suspense. I saw her hair, tied in two thick plaits, with loose strands on either side, her cheeks blown by the wind. I saw for the first time in my life how beautiful she was, and how beautiful and dreamlike the play of the wind in her delicate hair, how beautiful and provocative the fall of her thin blue dress over her young limbs; and just as the bitter spice of the chewed bud coursed through me with the whole dread pleasure and pain of spring, so the sight of the girl filled me with the whole deadly foreboding of love, the foreboding of woman. In that moment was contained the shock and the forewarning of enormous possibilities and promises, nameless delight, unthinkable bewilderments, anguish, suffering, release to the innermost and deepest guilt. Oh, how sharp was the bitter taste of spring on my tongue! And how the wind streamed playfully through the loose hair beside her rosy cheeks! She was close now. She looked up and recognized me.

For a moment she blushed a little and looked aside; but when I took off my schoolcap, she was self-possessed at once and, raising her head, returned my greeting with a smile that was quite grown-up. Then, entirely mistress of the situation, she went slowly on, in a halo of the thousand wishes, hopes and adorations that I sent after her.

So it had once been on a Sunday thirty-five years before and all that had been then came back to me in this moment. Hill and town, March wind and buddy taste, Rosa and her brown hair, the welling-up of desire and the sweet suffocation of anguish. All was as it was then, and it seemed to me that I had never in my life loved as I loved Rosa that day. But this time it was given me to greet her otherwise than on that occasion. I saw her blush when she recognized me, and the pains she took to conceal it, and I knew at once that she had a liking for me and that this encounter meant the same for her as for me. And this time instead of standing ceremoniously cap in hand till she had gone by, I did, in spite of anguish bordering on obsession, what my blood bade me do. I cried: "Rosa! Thank God, you've come, you beautiful, beautiful girl. I love you so dearly." It was not perhaps the most brilliant of all the things that might have been said at this moment, but there was no need for brilliance, and it was enough and more. Rosa did not put on her grown-up air, and she did not go on. She stopped and looked at me and, growing even redder than before, she said: "Heaven be praised, Harry—do you really like me?" Her brown eyes lit up her strong face, and they showed me that my past life and loves had all been false and perplexed and full of stupid unhappiness from that very moment on a Sunday afternoon when I had let Rosa pass me by. Now, however, the blunder was put right. Everything went differently and everything was good.

We clasped hands, and hand in hand walked slowly on as happy as we were embarrassed. We did not know what to do or to say, so we began to walk faster from embarrassment and then broke into a run, and ran till we lost our breath and had to stand still. But we did not let go our hands. We were both still children and did not know quite what to do with each other. That Sunday we did not even kiss, but we were immeasurably happy. We stood to get our breath. We sat on the grass and I stroked her hand while she passed the other one shyly over my hair. And then we got up again and tried to measure which of us was the taller. In reality, I was the taller by a finger's breadth, but I would not have it so. I maintained that we were of exactly the same height and that God had designed us for each other and that later on we would marry. Then Rosa said that she smelt violets and we knelt in the short spring grass and looked for them and found a few with short stalks and I gave her mine and she gave me hers, and as it was getting chill and the sun slanted low over the cliffs, Rosa said she must go home. At this we both became very sad, for I dared not accompany her. But now we shared a secret and it was our dearest possession. I stayed behind on the cliffs and lying down with my face over the edge of the sheer descent, I looked down over the town and watched for her sweet little figure to appear far below and saw it pass the spring and over the bridge. And now I knew that she had reached her home and was going from room to room, and I lay up there far away from her; but there was a bond between her and me. The same current ran in both of us and a secret passed to and fro.

We saw each other again here and there all through this spring, sometimes on the cliffs, sometimes over the garden hedge; and when the elder began to bloom we gave each other the first shy kiss. It was little that children like us had to give each other and our kiss lacked warmth and fullness. I scarcely ventured to touch the strands of her hair about her ears. But all the love and all the joy that was in us were ours. It was a shy emotion and the troth we plighted was still unripe, but this timid waiting on each other taught us a new happiness. We climbed one little step up on the ladder of love. And thus, beginning from Rosa and the violets, I lived again through all the loves of my life— but under happier stars. Rosa I lost, and Irmgard appeared; and the sun was warmer and the stars less steady, but Irmgard no more than Rosa was mine. Step by step I had to climb. There was much to live through and much to learn; and I had to lose Irmgard and Anna too. Every girl that I had once loved in youth, I loved again, but now I was able to inspire each with love. There was something I could give to each, something each could give to me. Wishes, dreams and possibilities that had once had no other life than my own imagination were lived now in reality. They passed before me like beautiful flowers, Ida and Laura and all whom I had loved for a summer, a month, or a day.

I was now, as I perceived, that good looking and ardent boy whom I had seen making so eagerly for love's door. I was living a bit of myself only—a bit that in my actual life and being had not been expressed to a tenth or a thousandth part, and I was living it to the full. I was watching it grow unmolested by any other part of me. It was not perturbed by the thinker, nor tortured by the Steppenwolf, nor dwarfed by the poet, the visionary or the moralist. No—I was nothing now but the lover and I breathed no other happiness and no other suffering than love. Irmgard had already taught me to dance and Ida to kiss, and it was Emma first, the most beautiful of them all, who on an autumn evening beneath a swaying elm gave me her brown breasts to kiss and the cup of passion to drink.

I lived through much in Pablo's little theater and not a thousandth part can be told in words. All the girls I had ever loved were mine. Each gave me what she alone had to give and to each I gave what she alone knew how to take. Much love, much happiness, much indulgence, and much bewilderment, too, and suffering fell to my share. All the love that I had missed in my life bloomed magically in my garden during this hour of dreams. There were chaste and tender blooms, garish ones that blazed, dark ones swiftly fading. There were flaring lust, inward reverie, glowing melancholy, anguished dying, radiant birth. I found women who were only to be taken by storm and those whom it was a joy to woo and win by degrees. Every twilit corner of my life where, if but for a moment the voice of sex had called me, a woman's glance kindled me or the gleam of a girl's white skin allured me, merged again and all that had been missed was made good. All were mine, each in her own way. The woman with the remarkable dark brown eyes beneath flaxen hair was there. I had stood beside her for a quarter of an hour in the corridor of an express and afterward she often appeared in my dreams. She did not speak a word, but what she taught me of the art of love was unimaginable, frightful, deathly. And the sleek, still Chinese, from the harbor of Marseilles, with her glassy smile, her smooth dead-black hair and swimming eyes—she too knew undreamed-of things. Each had her secret and the bouquet of her soil. Each kissed and laughed in a fashion of her own, and in her own peculiar way was shameful and in her own peculiar way shameless. They came and went. The stream carried them toward me and washed me up to them and away. I was a child in the stream of sex at play in the midst of all its charm, its danger and surprise. And it astonished me to find how rich my life—the seemingly so poor and loveless life of the Steppenwolf—had been in the opportunities and allurements of love. I had missed them. I had fled before them. I had stumbled on over them. I had made haste to forget them. But here they all were stored up in their hundreds, and not one missing. And now that I saw them I gave myself up to them without defense and sank down into the rosy twilight of their underworld. Even that seduction to which Pablo had once invited me came again, and other earlier ones, none of which at the time I had even fully grasped, fantastic games for three or four, caught me into their gambols with a laugh. Many things happened and many games were played not to be said in words.

When I rose once more to the surface of the unending stream of allurement and vice and entanglement, I was calm and silent.

LOUIS COUPERUS

Bluebeard's Daughter

Louis Couperus (1863–1923) was born at The Hague but spent his childhood in Java. He studied to be a teacher, but never taught. His first novel, *Eline Vere*, was immediately successful, and thereafter he produced many more, among them *Fate, Metamorphosis, World Peace* and *The Book of the Small Souls*, on the scale of *The Forsyte Saga*. [From *Eighteen Tales*; used by permission of Link House Publications, publishers; translated by J. Kooistra.]

HER NAME WAS FATMA, and she lived at one of her country-seats near Bagdad. She was the daughter of Bluebeard, by his first marriage, and she was a woman of marvelous beauty; about her moon-white face undulated her blue hair, falling down like a cloak over her frail shoulders. . . .

It is not generally known that Bluebeard had a daughter. Most people believe that he was killed, childless, by the brothers of his last wife, who inherited all his wealth. If they had, as I have, gone through the secret archives of the story, they would have found without much difficulty that Bluebeard died, his skull cleft in two, in the arms of his daughter, and left her all his possessions.

The young orphan, the charming Fatma, had loved her father very much, just as he had been very fond of her, although she had never been able to approve of the manner in which he rid himself of his many disobedient wives. She thought this method was not gentle, not noble, and psychologically monotonous. She understood perfectly that each new stepmother could not but yield to the temptation of her curiosity. She did not condone her father's course, and looked upon it as an inexcusable act of sadism.

The azure-locked Fatma remained a lonely young orphan, amidst her countless wealth and all her servants and slaves, who surrounded her like a royal court. The distinguished families at Bagdad, at the court of the Khalif, spoke often about the rich, young, blue-haired girl, but, in spite of her unbounded treasures, no one wished her to become the bride of son or nephew. Her locks were too reminiscent of horrors. So the beautiful Fatma remained alone, on her onyx terraces, which descended amidst groves of date trees and gardens of roses to crystal lakes. . . . And she wandered back alone between the onyx columns of the arcades to her summer palace, which, paved with gold and silver flagstones, was also roofed with gold and silver tiles.

Until she could no longer bear her loneliness, and was kindled with maidenly love for the overseer of her gardeners. He was a very handsome boy, who came from the country, and the rusticity of his occupation lent him in Fatma's eyes, somewhat tired with over-refinement, an irresistible charm. So that she married him, without worrying about what people would say of her at the court of the Khalif, or in the distinguished circles of Bagdad.

Fatma seemed very happy. She appeared with her husband in full state and elegant splendor in the town and in the country, in tapestried gondolas on the lakes, in cushioned litters in the streets, with a retinue of slaves in the bazaars and even at the Court festivities to which her rank and riches gave her admission. She and her beloved Emin made a magically beautiful couple: he, strong and young, glorying in his new riches—the upstart type did not yet exist in those days—she, radiating with love and inestimable jewels, which sparkled on her gauze turban and the hem of her cloak, while wonderfully large pearls glowed in her azure locks. And the distinguished Bagdad families began to feel sorry that they had not taken pains to win Bluebeard's daughter for a son or a nephew. . . .

Suddenly, however, the report spread that Emin had died. . . . Only the day before all the inhabitants of Bagdad had seen him in the mosque, and look, now they heard that . . . he had died! A shiver went through the town, but the Grand Vizier and the Lord Chief Justice saw no reason for taking steps in the matter, as the very creditable rumor was given out that Emin had, on that hot day, eaten too much watermelon, and had expired after a violent colic.

But people at Bagdad stared when after three months they heard that the young, azure-haired widow was again about to marry, this time the lieutenant of her own bodyguard. Amongst so many servants and attendants, Fatma seemed to have too large a choice to take notice of the sons and nephews of the distinguished families of Bagdad. The marriage took place with fantastic splendor, and Fatma's new husband gloried as Emin had done, now that he saw himself raised so suddenly from a humble position to that of husband to his transcendentally rich and beautiful mistress.

But the young lieutenant—Fatma had made him general of her body-guard—died suddenly, as it was given out, of a fall from his horse. It was a vague report, and besides, no one had seen the young lieutenant-general of Fatma's bodyguard either on his horse, or falling from it, nay, no one had seen him on the day of his death, and a violent emotion spread through the Bagdad families and at the Court of Khalif, because it was remembered but too well that Fatma was blue-haired, as her father had once been blue-bearded.

The sorrowing widow Fatma, in her black mourning veils, starred with black diamonds, looked like a Queen of the Night, particularly as her blue hair shimmered through the mourning veils with such a suggestive nocturnal tint that she could, without any makeup, have appeared in Mozart's *"Magic Flute."* However, she did not sing the heavy and difficult coloratura, but preferred to take a third husband; this time simply one of the bearers of her palanquin. That the young Ali was a magnificent fellow, who now, as third husband, looked in his damask samaar like a young sultan, could not be doubted, but what *was* doubted by the distinguished Bagdad families at the Court of the Khalif, was, whether after three months of married life, he had died a natural death. What! such a strong, fine healthy fellow as Fatma's palanquin-bearing husband to die of malaria—so it was said—and be unobtrusively buried like that! Heads nodded to each other, eyes stared with horror, mouths twitched with secret suppositions, and the Grand Vizier consulted with the Lord Chief Justice whether they should not intervene in the Fatma case; the case in which one husband after another died and disappeared after three months of matrimony.

They consulted so long, however, that Fatma married a fourth, a fifth and sixth time. The fourth time it was a Persian merchant from Teheran, to whom a long life had been foretold from the lines of his hand; the fifth time one of her gondoliers; the sixth time a humble slave who worked in Fatma's emerald mine. Each time, after three months, the wretched husband died, and the sorrowing widow went through Bagdad like the Queen of the Night.

Then the cup seemed full. Grand Vizier and Lord Chief Justice repaired to Fatma's pleasure-house, but it appeared that she had removed to another residence. For she had several: the one with the onyx terraces, and the one with the mother-of-pearl ballroom, and that with the chrysolyte towers, not to mention the one with the agate bathroom, that with the quicksilver fountain, and that with the secret libraries full of occult knowledge. . . . So that the Grand Vizier and Lord Chief Justice, after having trudged from one pleasure-house to another, with no better fortune, at last found Fatma at home in her pleasure-house of science. . . .

She received them slightly annoyed. She was not like the Queen of the Night; the beautiful, azure-haired widow of six husbands seemed rather like a Peri from Paradise, in her transparent white veils, but in this case a slightly annoyed Peri.

"What do you wish?" she asked, haughtily.

"To know the cause of your sixth husband's death."

"Do you start your inquiries," asked Fatma, "with my sixth husband?"

"We shall ascend to your first!" threatened the dignitaries.

"Why not descend to my last?" said Fatma; "and I have only this to say to you—that I have not got much to say. My sixth husband died . . . of tertian ague. . . ."

The dignitaries were about to make an angry reply, but at this moment appeared suddenly the man of the emerald mines himself, the sixth husband of Fatma. He looked healthy, strong and amiable and carried a few folios under his arm.

"What is this?" exclaimed the noble gentlemen.

Fatma shrugged her frail shoulders.

"This means no more," she deigned to explain, "than that the dear boy is not dead. He is only rather stupid, and so, to improve his conversational powers, I took him to this Secret Library, that he might read a little at his ease. . . ."

"But"—the Grand Vizier suddenly had his eyes opened—"what about your other five husbands, then, O blue-bearded, I mean, blue-haired Fatma?"

"They live," she admitted, "like my miner-husband. But I sequestered my gondolier husband in the pleasure-house of the quicksilver fountains to teach him to be somewhat quicker in his occupation of gondolier-husband, for he was often very slow at rowing the matrimonial boat over the lake of love, and quicksilver, administered in small doses, sends the blood flowing through the veins; my Persian merchant still drags out his life, which will be a long one, in my villa with the agate bathroom, for he sometimes smelt unpleasantly of his camels; my palanquin-spouse I locked up in my chrysolyte tower because the wretch flirted with my women, and I wanted to keep him to myself. Then there is my lieutenant-general; with him, gentlemen, I dance every night in my mother-of-pearl ballroom; he waltzes gloriously and it is not proper that such an intimate joy should be indulged in the presence of all and everyone; so the darling quietly waits in the mother-of-pearl ballroom, till I unlock it. . . . And, to speak the truth, my first boy is dearest to me, you know, my gardener, and, honestly, he also is still alive, and dwells not far away from the onyx terraces, so that I can easily reach him whenever I long for him. You look astonished, gentlemen, but there it is. You see, I am Bluebeard's daughter and I take after him, in soul and locks. He felt a desire for many wives, I feel a desire for many husbands. But he killed his wives, on the pretext that they were disobedient to him. I never killed my husbands. I preferred to lock them up, to civilize them, and have power over them. If I am hysterical, I am also very much of a feminist; and in every respect I am a woman. What more do you want to know?"

And the proud Fatma stood haughtily before the two dignitaries of the Khalif. But these unexpectedly called for their menials and commanded:

"Seize this bad woman and bring her before the divan of the Most High."

Thus it happened. Fatma, Bluebeard's daughter, was dragged through all the streets and all the squares of Bagdad, to the Khalif's divan, who condemned her to lay her azure-locked head on the block.

It is strange, thought Fatma, when she was given up to the hands of the executioners, my father murdered his wives and was very much blamed for it. I myself objected to his course . . . I, his daughter, never murdered my husbands: I tended them lovingly, nurtured them, civilized them, developed their faculties, it is true in a somewhat secluded manner, in onyx gardens, chrysolite towers, mother-of-pearl ballrooms, and all the rest of it, and this conception of marriage, however well thought out, also meets with disapproval.

It is strange—continued her thoughts—but I believe, I almost know it for certain, that it is not possible to satisfy public opinion in the matter of love and marriage . . . when one has a blue beard or blue locks. . . .

And somewhat saddened by this irrefutable philosophy, she bent down her azure-haired head on the block. . . .

Tried to solve the problem in the last second.

But failed, for in a purple stream her last ideas flowed from her riven neck.

And the azure-haired head of Bluebeard's daughter lay in blood on the floor of the hall of justice.

After which the six husbands inherited her wealth.

JOHANNES
L. WALCH

The Suspicion

Johannes L. Walch (1879–1946) was born in The Hague and received his Ph.D. at the University of Leiden. He taught literature at the Sorbonne. His main works are *Studies in Literature, Supreme Law* and *Judas Iscariot.* [From *Best Continental Short Stories,* 1927.]

IN AN APRIL DUSK, I was returning from one of my spring-time strolls along the dikes and polders. As I descended at the central station, I found my friend de Rive, accompanied by a man and woman. A certain contrast showed between him and them; the couple had the appearance of really being far from fashionable. Not that they weren't dressed up. . . . That's just it: they were "dressed up" after the fashion of provincials who have put on their Sunday best because they are "going out."

De Rive made a sign in my direction, signifying, "Wait a minute. We'll go on together." I took a place in the café of the quay in order to shorten the wait by observing the farewell.

It wasn't long; the couple got into the train; the door slammed; once installed, the husband, with the good nature of fat men, directed all his smiles and winks at his host; as for her . . .

What was there in this visage which attracted me, which forced me to scrutinize it more closely?

In the first place, this woman was much younger than her husband. At any rate, she was infinitely more "alive." And then, less corpulent. Her visage, just like that of her husband, wore an expression of perfect benevolence. Her placid steel-blue eyes smiled, as did her slightly too-large mouth. And still . . . I couldn't help seeing something disagreeably hard under the engaging exterior. My look followed the outlines of her silhouette and that only fortified my impression.

The door was open for some laggard and, while the conductor punched his ticket, I observed how the feet of my subject of study were planted on the ground, straight, stiff, with a precision of attitude that was almost gymnastic. At the same time, I noticed a pair of heavy and badly kept shoes.

The train started. There was handshaking on the part of my friend de Rive to which the husband responded with many movements of his fat little arm, and the wife by a nod, a nod so dry, so vigorous, that it seemed to symbolize the rupture of their momentarily common life.

De Rive had already turned, but I, continuing my study, saw disappear gradually the friendliness from the features of the wife, as a sunny reflection is little by little absorbed by the gray of a mist; much more, I thought I even distinguished something sinister. As for her fat husband, he installed himself comfortably and, his back turned toward the capital that he was leaving, curled himself up with satisfaction in his corner.

"That's decent," said de Rive, "to have waited for me! You are a grand man!"

"Good friends of yours?" I demanded with a gesture toward the departing couple.

"Old acquaintances," answered de Rive after an almost perceptible silence. "Yes, yes . . . very good acquaintances. He is an excellent fellow. I have always liked him a lot. An old colleague of former times, when I was still teaching. Yes, indeed! fifteen years ago we were both professors in the academy of Meppel. . . . Funny existence in such a hole. When one struts about the streets of Amsterdam like this, it is difficult to imagine the life of those who vegetate down there."

"Just the same, it is fattening. Look at your friend!" I said jokingly.

"Yes," responded de Rive in a meditative tone. I could not say whether his voice expressed melancholy rather than self-satisfaction. "Yes, he has aged early, hasn't he? We are the same age; we have known each other now since the University of Leiden. He was a gay and agreeable sort of fellow. He studied literature and I, naturally, political economy. We started out as poor enthusiastic fools—but that calmed down at the end of a year or two. It becomes monotonous; and then the idea that your work is, at least partly, the occupation of nursemaids. Anyway, after a certain time I left the class and started in pettifogging, and from that into underhand politics, as you say. He—he stayed. All that is a question of a little more or a little less vitality, of adventurous spirit. . . . And then, he was already married; in those conditions one does not risk a fixed position. At least, that is the way it goes for the most part, among us."

"His wife," I started—if I remember well, we were walking on the "Damrak," not without feeling some satisfaction at the difference between this great artery and Meppel—"his wife has quite a different air; one would say that she had remained infinitely more lively."

"So," said de Rive, stopping a minute to light a cigarette. In the light of the street lamp he threw me a piercing glance. "So—you have noticed that."

"Thanks to my vagabondage," I answered. "A day in the polders makes you dead tired, but clears the ideas miraculously. One becomes even too lucid, perhaps. And, it seemed to me—I'd rather tell you frankly—that this woman had something . . . something somber and menacing. For that matter, it was probably nothing but an impression —an impression made on me by the station and its lugubrious, dusky wagons."

De Rive did not answer. Then, appearing to make a sudden decision, "Let's sit down a minute at the Oporto," he said to me.

So, we were at the Oporto. A little barrel circled with red served as a table, whose brilliantly varnished top held two delicate goblets in which irised the sweetly pernicious liquid.

About us was the solitude of a café at the beginning of the evening: atmosphere close, enveloping, with here and there in the silent shadow a little skirted lamp. One knows that outside, excluded and rendered mute by the thickness of the bay windows, is a powerful image of a great city, where mount somber architectural masses; where great, luminous balloons, in interminable lines, throw their cold light on the streets seething with pedestrians and vehicles, as well as on the enormous blocks of piled stones, of which certain parts relentlessly expose themselves to the crude, searching rays.

De Rive looked about him. In the back, near the buffet, the white spot of an idle waiter's apron; we were alone. My friend leaned toward me.

"I'm going to tell you something," he told me, lowering his voice; "something about this woman. And also about a suspicion—nothing more, you understand, than a suspicion."

The beginning created an atmosphere of "Thousand-and-One Nights" ... Ali-Baba? I threw a glance at de Rive, who responded with a smile. Having finished lighting his cigarette, he settled himself comfortably after the fashion of someone who prepares himself to relate a long-winded story.

"I was just speaking to you," he said, "about these old acquaintances, the Burmeyers—and I spoke especially about him. Without a doubt, he is an excellent fellow; a little sleepy, however. That also, I've already told you. As for her—it is quite different. It is a woman . . . rather complicated—yes—but before everything, a woman with a strong will. A woman who . . . in a word, a sort of Hedda Gabler. That species multiplies, for that matter. Maybe you'll think I'm absurd since it has to do with someone well in her thirties; who is no longer young from any point of view. . . ."

"And who wears worn-down shoes," I said.

"No, really?" he said. "Yes, I confess I hadn't noticed. Yesterday, however, I accompanied them; it was a matter of finding a hat for her. As soon as we entered the shop, I saw her regard fasten itself on a real masterpiece. Very ostensibly, she made no allusion to it and chose a simple little thing, with a bit of feather, cheap, and not positively ugly. She asked Burmeyer if he liked it. He answered with a little laugh, and she concluded the affair. As for me—she didn't deign to ask my advice."

"It isn't you she wants to please," I said lightly.

"Agreed," responded de Rive. "However, every time that we stopped before an exhibition of paintings, or even before a fashion shop where there was nothing to buy, she exchanged ideas with me, and I assure you that she showed excellent taste. And her simpleton of a husband remained quiet. He was terribly bored, poor fellow."

"I see nothing yet of Hedda Gabler," I said. "Please be more clear."

"Well," de Rive started, "here's the way the thing presents itself. I believe that two opposing penchants fight for the soul of this Betsy. There is in her a good housewife; for that matter, she is an excellent mother. Haven't I already told you? They have four children, who are beautifully brought up. Not in the sense of books of study; they are not paragons either. No, they are brought up with infinite patience, with *love.* Each time that I have passed several days in their home—eight years of that now—I have been in continual admiration. Never an impatient move from the parents; they always had time and a desire to play with the children. Also in their own relations, the parents give an unchanging example. And that without the least show of affection; no, all that with a little serious air, a gentle irony. For example, children often have little tricks to draw attention to themselves, especially the girls. You have surely noticed that, haven't you? Well, it was delicious, the manner in which the father put them in their place. Yes, seen in their *milieu,* these people are charming; and especially he doesn't leave you with the disagreeable impression of middle-class life.

De Rive stopped a minute to think.

"Hedda Gabler disappears more and more," I said.

"Yes, and not only in your eyes," answered de Rive with a smile. "As I remember these things, as I see that exquisite interior, I tell myself I must be mistaken . . . and yet . . . wait, even there, at Meppel, in their own surroundings, it has happened that I've received other impressions. . . . It came from that that . . . Well, I believe that I, most particularly, act on her as an irritant."

"It is true, in many ways I am the opposite of her husband. I have nothing of a home man about me. Quite other desires have guided my life. Among others, the need of space; then, the desire for a life more intensely colored, perhaps more vain also. And finally, there is ambition. Yes, I imagine that that is always an element in the existence of men like me."

"You can say like us," I added.

"If you wish. So then, I lived, to speak in the language of these fine people, in a manner more 'outside.' It is not a mistake that they use this term. However, it is like all classifications: it is not complete."

"Old man," I said, "useless to explain and amplify that. I am an individual just as little commendable as you."

"Perfect! Well, to go on. In Madame Burmeyer there is also a strong leaning toward this sort of life. That comes from her origin, which means that Betsy will never feel entirely at ease in the surroundings in which she evolves. Nevertheless, there is something in her which speaks infinitely louder, and which affirms that her present existence is the better . . . better from an essential point of view. . . . Now do you see Hedda Gabler reappearing on the horizon?"

"Yes . . ."

"At heart, Betsy is vain; not exactly coquettish, but vain . . . and yet, she puts all her will to honor more solid principles. Her dress is characteristic. You tell me that she wears worn-down shoes. Just the same, she had a tailored suit in good taste; simple, almost smart. You see, she buys something really good, and then does not complete her toilette. Because then the other side of her nature remounts to the surface. Do you understand?"

"I understand at least that her stop in your house must not have been altogether a time of pleasure."

"You might say that sometimes it was a veritable torture. She had had too much confidence in herself. When she planned this little trip down there in Meppel, she must have said to herself that she would manage somehow; the years had given her sufficient reassurance. Besides, her husband counted on it. I had often invited them; he would have come before but I felt that the objections came from Betsy's side. And this impression was strengthened by what happened last night."

"Something happened then?"

"Yes, indeed—and it was then that my suspicion was aroused. We had passed the evening at the 'Concertgebouw'; then we went to the Trianon for oysters, in order to finish their visit properly. The conversation was animated, even gay. However, Betsy fell little by little into silence. I tried in vain to pull her out of it; she seemed to be thinking about something. I saw her watching outside, absorbed in the contemplation of the movement of the metropolis. Then, her eyes turned toward the luxury which surrounded us . . . but her attitude showed no contentment.

"Suddenly her husband observed: 'Betsy is quiet; she is telling herself that the cake is almost eaten.' Immediately, and with a violence that startled me, she defended herself. And she began to speak with fervor of her fireside, for which she was homesick, and her children whom she missed. At first her voice sounded false, but little by little, one felt that she repressed one part of herself in order to show another. When she stopped I found nothing better to do than to agree. But all to myself, I felt a decided satisfaction at living as I live. I hadn't the slightest desire to change my life for hers. No doubt about it: she read my thoughts in my face; she believed she saw something of kindly pity in my verbosity . . . of disdain, maybe . . . And that exasperated her. Not because it had anything to do with *me*—she cared nothing about my likes or dislikes—no, it was only because in me she found a part of herself—a detested part, that I continually and unconsciously awakened.

"In effect, after a moment, her husband and myself having taken up our conversation, and she believing herself forgotten, I saw suddenly, reflected in the glass, her eyes fastened on me. This regard—impossible to mistake it—was filled with a ferocious hatred, with a burning desire for destruction. I felt that she could no longer endure me; that she could no longer stand me—and that, because I represent that other side of herself: the scoffing side.

"The rest, now. Once inside my house, we stopped to talk. It was she who continually prolonged the conversation, who would not retire. At last Burmeyer said, laughing: 'You know, I am going to bed. But if you want to stay a while longer . . .'

" 'I, also, am going to bed,' I said in my turn. We expected naturally that she would accompany her husband. Not so! She said: 'Go ahead, you two! But leave me another minute here. It will amuse me to be alone a little in the night—just as though I belonged to the house.'

"She laughed when she said it, but not whole-heartedly.

"'Fine!' I cried. 'Will you know how to turn out the gas?'

"'Yes, yes, I'll take care of it!' she answered calmly."

De Rive stopped a minute and then began, more slowly:

"Just the same, now that I think of it, I believe she started slightly when I spoke of gas. Anyway . . .

"You know that my room is right next to the parlor. Very properly, I closed the folding door. Above this door, there is a movable pane. You remember—my invention, that I had shown them with pride—a means of airing during the night, without having the noises of the street. But the windows of my room, which open on the garden, were not opened during their stay because I had a cold, and we did not smoke on account of Betsy. . . .

"Good. She knew all that. I had told her the first day of their visit.

"So, I went to bed. By the transom I saw the light. But it didn't last long. I heard Betsy walk up and down several times; she even bumped against the stove. . . . I remember having thought, 'There, she is looking in the mirror.' Then I must have dropped off.

"But, perhaps after fifteen minutes, I awakened with a jump. I couldn't say why. The occultists would affirm that it was my ethereal self which pulled me out of sleep. The transom above the door was no longer lighted. The air was heavy; that came surely from the fact that the windows were closed and that I had a cold. I had, besides, completely lost the sense of smell.

"Suddenly a thought came to my mind: 'See if she had turned off the gas well. . . .' And—strange thing—from the minute it was formulated, I was sure that this was not only a passing idea; no . . . it was simply and surely a suspicion. . . .

"I left my bed; softly, so as not to disturb them above, I opened the door, and at once I noticed a whistling. One of the jets was wide open."

"And then?"

"Then I closed it, of course! And immediately afterward I felt a terrible desire to sleep; I had only one great desire: my bed!"

"And this morning?"

"Oh, I said with an indifferent air: 'You made a fine mistake, you know . . . One of the gas jets was open . . . !"

"Did she seem disturbed?"

"Not at all. She was calm, intensely calm. But that didn't give one the impression of being exactly natural either—let's not forget that, in all events, she had almost asphyxiated me. . . . 'Really,' she answered me in the most placid manner in the world."

"Funny story, isn't it?" I said.

"Very funny," answered de Rive.

After a moment I took up the conversation: "Aren't you mistaken? A mother, a mother exceptionally tender, you said yourself—who has a never-ending patience with her children. . . . She possesses just the same something positive, in her home; a *happiness;* something which could satisfy a human being. . . ."

"Yes . . . a mother exceptionally tender," continued de Rive, meditatively. "Strong in her love . . . ferocious even . . . it's just for that. . . . In any case, this great love doesn't suffice to keep her steady. That is undeniable . . . and it is also undeniable that she felt it . . . and that made her furious. Why do you smile?"

"I am thinking of her nice fat husband," I responded.

MARTIN

ANDERSEN

NEXO

Birds of

Passage

Martin Andersen Nexo was born in 1869 in Copenhagen. His family was poor and Nexo was apprenticed to a shoemaker. He was nearly thirty years old before he began to write, and many of his works were based on the region in which he spent his childhood, the island of Bornholm. His best known novels are *Pelle the Conqueror, Ditte: Daughter of Man, Toward Dawn* and *Under the Open Sky.* [From *Denmark's Best Stories;* copyright 1928 by The American Scandinavian Foundation; used by permission of W. W. Norton & Co.; translated by Lida Siboni Hanson.]

PETER NIKOLAI FERDINAND BALTASAR RASMUSSEN KJÖNG, whose name—following inviolable phonetic laws not to be explained here—in the course of time took the form of Nebuchadnezzar, was a man who had seen the world and knew the human race.

By trade he was a shoemaker; by nature, a wandering journeyman. He was one of those people in whose blood the rotation of the earth has become an urge, and who therefore feel themselves compelled to rotate around our globe like so many satellites. The desire to set out for the unknown was the moving power of his life; and he knew nothing finer than to break away, no matter from what. Thus he broke away from happiness several times, and felt all the happier for it.

He had wandered through the greater part of the civilized world, clearly and firmly defining civilization as synonymous with the wearing of leather shoes. He knew all the ins and outs of the German hostelries and the French highways, had walked across the Pyrenees and Alps more than once, and had stood with one foot in Switzerland and the other in France, spitting far down the Italian slopes. He had been in Sicily, at Gibraltar, in Asia Minor.

On his travels he had become acquainted with all the mysteries of modern traffic. He knew where it was possible to hang between the wheels of a freight car, and where it was more advisable to pretend having lost a ticket or to appeal to the generosity of the conductor. He slipped to Sicily from Gibraltar, by hiding in the cable-hold of a big steamer. After a while his hunger drove him to the deck, where he received a sound thrashing and countless threats of being thrown overboard to the sharks. But, after all, he reached his destination.

From Sicily he was to go as a stoker on another steamer, thereby earning his passage to Greece. But as it was soon discovered that he knew nothing about stoking, he was put ashore in Brindisi. Here he rubbed his feet with tallow, and walked north through the country, around the Adriatic, and down on the other side. It took him months, but this time also he gained his end. And what better use could he make of his time? King Nebuchadnezzar possessed some of the patience of a planet: he wandered for the sake of wandering, without any other purpose and without seeking other distractions. In the Balkans he had the pleasure of being captured by brigands who, however, rejected him with the greatest contempt after discovering the condition of his clothes. Afterward he used to say, with a magnificent gesture, "A mouse saved the king of the animals, but a louse saved King Nebuchadnezzar."

He took a short trip to California to have a look at the gold; but there he quickly came to the conclusion that gold was too heavy an article for a wandering journeyman, and he hurried back to New York, hanging between the axles of a coal car. On this occasion he made the discovery that the Americans really were practical people. In Germany the railroad employees would go peering under the trains with lanterns in search of tramps, who were then pulled out and dragged to the police court. There they were questioned, and often solemnly expelled from the district because of their criminal use of the benefits of society. But in America a man would run back and forth with a hose, and simply squirt cold water under the train. That made one's clothes freeze when the train put on its hellish speed, and for the rest of his life a fellow would have rheumatism in his left shoulder.

In New York he tried to get a job, first as chief cook and then as deck hand, in order to earn his passage back to Copenhagen. As both plans failed, he had a stroke and fell over in the street. All he then had to do was to open his eyes a little at the right moment and whisper, "Dane." He was taken to the Danish consulate, and from there transported back to Denmark.

He had indeed seen life and mankind! His trade had carried him over half the earth. He had worked in all big cities, as short a time as possible in each so as to get around and see them all. He had, as it were in passing, wheedled every secret out of his trade. He did not spend much time working, but what he produced was masterly. His work stood out among that of thousands of others as long as there was one whit left of it.

He thought with a smile of the greasy little shop where he had learned his trade. Now he was going to make things hum. It was his plan to settle down in Denmark and profit by his experience in the great world, following the maxim that a man owes his best to his own country. He hung around for about a month, so as to accustom his digestive organs to home cooking, whereupon he went to work in a shoemaker's shop.

But King Nebuchadnezzar was used to moving in big spaces, according to great simple laws. On his wanderings he had learned to eliminate and discard. Life had taught him thoroughly that most of the accessories which were burdening the shops were unnecessary baggage—at least to him who had the unique talent of simplification. The big apparatus set in motion by a Danish shoemaker before beginning his work could not but seem comical to a man who more than once had turned out first-class products, sitting by the wayside and only equipped with an awl, a knife, a small amount of shoemaker's thread, and the broken leg of a chair for the final polishing.

The result was that he did not hesitate to sell the superfluous tools wherever he went. But although this did not impair his work, his bosses did not like it, and deducted the cost from his wages. They even fired him and threatened to turn him over to the police.

He began to work in his lodging, and extended his economy from tools to material. Moreover, he knew the value of cardboard, and thus was able to save a surprisingly big part of the leather delivered by the bosses according to exact measurement. He sold this, and used the money to stretch his Blue Monday to Wednesday evening.

His comrades considered him a genius, by which they meant a person who could turn out a marvelously neat piece of work with the speed of lightning and out of almost nothing, and who loved idleness and hunger and little drams above anything else in this world.

Doubtless King Nebuchadnezzar was a genius. When he worked, he worked—nobody could say that his fingers acted like thumbs. A howling blue flame—zip! Two pair of ladies' shoes done before five. Then he would drink up his double wages, sleep off his debauch on a pile of paving-stones or behind a fence, and at a pinch be ready to resume work next morning.

But he did not like to do this. He preferred to hustle three pair together in one day, instead of working two days in succession.

While at work, he was lost to the world. But when he would straighten his back to go on a spree, he would sometimes find that he had to go alone. Time after time the most ridiculous of all phenomena spoiled his plans: people had no time. The Lord help us, no time to carouse! He could not understand it, but it was a fact.

It was comical beyond words. It took him some time to have his laugh and finally discover that he was a lonely man. His comrades had simply gone back on him and his firm convictions, and had—perhaps a little sheepishly—continued their drudgery so as not to fall behind. They had become useful citizens, petty respectable members of society with stomachs and earnest political consciences. They jogged to work at seven in the morning and went home at six in the evening—he could have set his watch by them if he had had one. In the evening they went to political meetings. They even married and shuffled to the circus with wives and children on Sunday afternoons. They called that enjoying life—phew!

Those that went on sprees were no longer men of his kind who felt the need of hammering out the dents given them by drudgery. More and more the magnificent debauches passed into the hands of professional toughs. King Nebuchadnezzar was not a tough. He was simply a free man who happened to have moved around and seen the world while his colleagues continued being slaves.

Well, that was their own funeral—if they were willing to be drummed together in factories and big workshops at the stroke of the clock, all right! King Nebuchadnezzar went on working in his lodging, refusing to work in the shops. He was his own boss. He was not going to have a foreman standing around watching all his doings. And as to being a member of the Union and having to obey all its orders down to the very air one breathed—the devil, no!

King Nebuchadnezzar was quite able to look after his own affairs. He wanted the right to do three days' work in one and spend the next two days enjoying life. No need to worry about the prices. One day he learned that the Union had succeeded in prohibiting all home work. He was unspeakably scornful. "They can't touch *me*," he said, and continued working in his own way. Thanks to his efficiency, the bosses employed him whenever they needed an especially good man.

However, they could only employ him secretly, and ordinarily they preferred to follow the rules laid down by the Union. One never knew what to expect from King Nebuchadnezzar: right in the middle of a piece of pressing work ordered by some prominent person he might suddenly become possessed by the devil. Nor could he live on air while the few notabilities Denmark could boast were wearing the shoe leather that came from his hand.

Like all geniuses, he finally came to the conclusion that conditions in Denmark were too narrow. He would have to turn his back on his miserable country once more. He had kept the great world in mind, and always thought of it with gratitude and joy. Once more he broke away.

But he had lost the exhilaration of former days when his bones, like those of the birds, had been filled with air, and he felt that he must flit from one place to the other. The centrifugal force had left him; only gravity remained and bound him to the earth. He could not understand it; still it was so. It was an effort for him to set out on his flight, whereas it had formerly been an effort to remain quiet.

One no longer flew out at random—one sat down soberly and thought the matter over. The rotation of the earth no longer whirled mountains and rivers and unending white roads through one's brain. Now the question was whether or not one could stand the wear and tear. Certain things were required, especially strong feet; and it was advantageous to have a stomach that could crush stones. In the course of time he had lost these two assets. Then there was the general feeling of heaviness as if one were glued to the earth. The great world with its eternal restlessness and tension no longer tempted him. He had become afraid of it. A bit of a home with soft boiled food, warm clothes, a room with a clean bed, was all he aspired to now.

He tried to realize his wishes and keep the wolf from the door by allowing himself to be supported by a feeble-minded woman who lived on what the day might bring. They were always squabbling except when they were drunk. But a year or two of this life cured him thoroughly of all desire for a home and family. Let others enjoy domesticity as much as they wanted to; he knew now what it meant!

He tried to take up his trade again, but the door was irrevocably closed to a vagrant like him. Finally he resolved to accept what great men in antiquity had accepted before him: meals at the cost of the community. To this end he sought and received admittance to the prytaneum situated on Aaboulevard between Örstedsvej and Svineryggen—sometimes referred to as the public workhouse.

He was at once given awl and waxed end, and shown his seat among the shoemakers. But he had not entered the place in order to create any unfair competition with the outer world. Neither had he revolted against fixed working hours and workshop rules in order to sit as a slave with cropped hair in the workroom of the inmates and be granted one hour's liberty in the yard, dressed in the uniform of the institution and walking at the regulation pace. He loved liberty still more than his art, and, thanks to the rheumatism in his shoulder and his sadly trembling hands which were utterly unable to hold the point of the knife away from the vamps, he was declared impossible as an artisan.

The officials then tried him on the light brigade which every day swarms over the bridges and markets of Copenhagen, armed with brooms and shovels. He would saunter along and pass his broom indolently over the pavement, while the sparrows fluttered wildly in the sweepings, and life around him pulsated in a restless, feverish chase. He would watch the passionate hurry with a mild, sedate smile like one who knows the stakes but is safely out of the game. He had lived as deeply and fully as any of the rest, therefore it tempted him no longer. But when he saw a street-worker stride over piles of stone or gravel to his coat and take a clear, little bottle out of his pocket, he would feel a faint pang and a longing to lift it caressingly to his mouth. But otherwise he was quite satisfied and envied nobody—not a mother's soul!

One afternoon as he was sweeping Höjbroplads, lost in quiet, happy content, he saw something which robbed his philosophical heart of its calm and made it pound and flutter.

A woman came shuffling from Köbmagergade, crossed Höjbroplads, and walked toward the Bourse. She wore a black, shiny straw hat, the brim of which had become detached from the crown and was jolting on the bridge of her nose so that she was peering over it as through a visor. Besides this, she wore the remains of an old French shawl, a thin, scant skirt, and prunella shoes. Her cheeks and nose were protruding like three red pippins. She leaned forward and wriggled her hips coquettishly, not lifting her feet, but sliding them over the pavement. His expert eye saw at once that she did this so as not to lose her shoes: both vamps were split.

His wildly pounding heart told him that the woman was Malvina, his lady, his last and only great—but also unhappy—love, the woman who had shared her bed and her liquor with him, whom he had beaten and who had returned his blows, according to their relative states of drunkenness—the lady whom he had bidden a heart-rending farewell the day when they had knocked at the door of the workhouse, and had been admitted respectively to the female and male departments.

Evidently she had a free afternoon and was going out on a jaunt— Malvina who from the time of her confirmation to her eighteenth year had been the mistress of a decrepit count!—Malvina who with all her hoarseness could lisp so genteely, who smacked a bit of all strata, from court to gutter!—the only being he had ever met who, like him, had some of the rotation of the universe in her blood.

And now she was going on a jaunt!

An irrepressible impulse to go along once more, to have just one more fling, awakened in him. He was on the point of throwing his broom aside and calling to her to wait and take him with her. But a remnant of his old presence of mind shot up in him. He dropped the broom, became quite pale, and staggered over to the overseer, Petersen, whom he asked for permission to steal away quietly as he felt sick to his stomach.

Overseer Petersen knew that King Nebuchadnezzar had no greater wish than to spend the rest of his days in the workhouse. He looked doubtfully first at his watch, then at the policeman under "the Clock," and finally at the patient. Really the man looked alarmingly ill.

"Do you think you can manage to get home by yourself?" he asked.

"Oh yes! But, of course, if I had ten öre I could ride right to the door."

"Well, see that you catch that bus!"

But King Nebuchadnezzar did not catch the bus, he was too feeble to hurry. He staggered over to Thorvaldsen's Museum where the street car was standing, but it started before he reached it, whereupon he followed it at an anxious trot, beckoning sadly to the conductor.

Overseer Petersen shook his head with misgivings. Nebuchadnezzar must be sick indeed if he thought he could catch up with an electric car. Oh well, there would be another in a minute, there were enough of them.

When King Nebuchadnezzar's calculation told him that there were houses between him and the overseer, he slackened his pace and turned from the Stormbridge into the Palace yard. It was important not to be suspected and caught on account of his uniform. Behind the Bourse he bought a huge yellow envelope for three öre and a newspaper for two öre. The remaining money was spent for a quid of tobacco. He never chewed tobacco, but simply felt uncomfortable with money in his pocket. It occurred to him that he could give the quid to his comrades. Later he realized that he might have spent the money for a milk toddy, but he was not the man to deplore his actions. He stuffed the newspaper into the envelope, put it carefully under his arm, and left the Palace yard walking as straight as an orderly on a confidential mission. The policemen on Knippelsbro looked askance at him, but he went ahead with the assurance born of an easy conscience.

He sauntered around in the bystreets behind Christianshavn market until he caught sight of Malvina, who disappeared through the door of a many-windowed house in Dronningensgade. He knew her errand at once, and went straight up to the third floor where many one-room apartments opened into a long, pitch-dark corridor.

Upon hearing Malvina's clothes rustle in the dark, he said solemnly, "Good day, Lady," and took hold of both her ears and kissed her.

"Mercy, how you scared me, little Nezzar! It might have been a strange fellow for all one can see here," she said coquettishly.

"Are you looking for the Prince, dear Lady? I shouldn't wonder if he had been ditched."

"No, I heard him cry a minute ago. But there is no key in the door."

King Nebuchadnezzar examined the lock with expert fingers and peered through the keyhole. "That is as simple as they make 'em," he said in an undertone, "if one only had a bit of wire." He thought for a moment. Then he tiptoed a few steps down the corridor to a door behind which a woman was scolding and some children were yelling. He picked the key out of the door and returned. The key fitted exactly.

"You are a great fellow, Nezzar," Malvina simpered.

"No, the landlord is a stingy louse who has had one kind of key made for the whole shootingmatch," he answered modestly, and put the key back as noiselessly as he had taken it. "That's what he is."

"Oh, you," said Malvina, rapping his fingers with small, genteel blows, faintly suggestive of aristocracy. "You always want to joke about nasty things. In our department we change every week, I want you to know."

King Nebuchadnezzar did not understand her. When she was acting the countess, the meaning of her words was sometimes hazy to him. But he knew that the origin of her refinement was genuine enough.

"Lady—" he said, and solemnly held the door open for her.

They entered a small room with one and a half narrow windows. The other half of the second window belonged to the kitchen, which measured six feet each way, and was separated from the room by a partition. Through this arrangement an alcove was formed in a corner of the room, just big enough to hold an old wooden bed, which was covered with rags. The space under it was filled with bottles. Half a table stood on its two legs leaning against the opposite wall, and in a dirty wicker cradle under the window slept a six-months-old baby sucking a pacifier made of an old curtain. The curtain had been tied into many pacifiers, which had been sucked and discarded in their turn, and were now dragging on the floor. The baby slowly pulled its present pacifier in and out while sleeping. Each time the whole heavy row was lifted and lowered; it looked like a ball fringe. The unused end of the curtain was thrown over a nail.

On the only chair in the room sat a boy of two or three years. He was tied to the chair and was evidently supposed to be looking out of the near-by window. On the window-sill before him lay the gnawed-off crusts of some lard sandwiches. The boy was asleep, his heavy head hanging down inertly to one side. His feeble breathing sounded like soft whistling. He opened two big eyes and stared at them.

"My stars, Sonny, Sonny!" cried King Nebuchadnezzar in a delighted falsetto, and stretched out his hands with a stage gesture, "don't you know your own father, eh?"

Between them they untied him, and Malvina placed him on her knees and began to clean him a little. Meanwhile the happy father strode around, giving vent to his delight in short exclamations—"You look fine that way, girl! You look mighty fine being good to him! If you could only see for yourself how fine you look with him on your lap!"

The child let them fuss with him without showing any noticeable interest. He seemed strangely dull and apathetic, breathed heavily and audibly, and evidently was not in the least impressed by the course of events. It was as if he had once for all made the resolution to walk through life unaffected by its ups and downs. There was a certain drowsiness over him. He did not by any movement help Malvina in her work, but went on breathing with a heavy, snoring sound which might well be interpreted as a purring of content.

"He makes himself heavy," said Malvina, "he just wants to be petted. And do see how plump he is, Nezzar!"

"He doesn't jabber any too much, does he?" said Nebuchadnezzar musingly. "I wonder if he can talk at all? How old did you say he was?"

"Three years, Nezzar—three years and then some. Mercy, that you could forget that!"

"Why—a man has so many more important things to think of."

Three years—oh, well, then there was time enough for him to have his say, even if he should turn out to be a Rigsdag deputy.

"He may still learn to talk the leg off an iron pot. By the way, have you ever thought of what profession he is going to take up?"

"Lord, no," said Malvina in a frightened voice.

"Still that is as important as anything I know of! There are all kinds of possibilities in such a little body. He is a human seed, to express it nicely. Who knows, maybe some day he will sit astraddle of the whole cake!—It would be grand to see that day."

"Well, I think he is going to be a confectioner," said Malvina, in response to the word cake. Besides, she was fond of sweets.

King Nebuchadnezzar made a grimace of despair.

"I don't mean any offense, Lady, but you women have no imagination. No—the time of handicraft is over. Or did you ever know a finer craftsman than King Nebuchadnezzar? And what did he get for it? Nowadays you've got to have *head*—brains are what tell in our day, see? And his head is big enough, Lord knows!—The little brat!"

King Nebuchadnezzar had taken the child's head between his big hands. "Is the yeast working in there? Is it, Sonny?" he said, laughing through tears. The thought of the boy's great future stirred him and made his hands tremble. "He doesn't say a word, he doesn't even blink. I tell you, there is backbone in him. And do you know, Malvina, I can feel the workings up here in his blessed little dome. His mind is busy even now. He'll be a good one, I tell you! Just see how calm and cool he is! Small as he is, he acts like our Lord himself, knowing the ins and outs of the whole thing. I guess nothing will hang too high for *him!*"

King Nebuchadnezzar began to whistle softly, gazing into the unknown. With his thoughts in the far future he did not hear Malvina ask him for his handkerchief. Anyway, he could not have given her any. Out there in the future his own existence was being repeated in a bigger and more successful way. He himself had beaten the record, but only in a matter which already was doomed. He had won the race hundreds of times, but he did not feel victorious. But when Sonny grew up, things were going to hum. He could sense the turmoil and bustle, and had taken part in enough of it to feel dizzy for Sonny.

His thoughts were gradually released from the future, and with a sigh he came back to earth and discovered that his throat was dry. He took a few turns around the room and sent his restless eyes investigating in all corners. "I wonder how the wine cellar is getting on?" he said, pulling out the bottles from under the bed and holding them to the light. "Bone dry all along the line! Fine state of affairs! See here, don't you think your sister has an account somewhere around here?"

Malvina shook her head. She was busy cleaning the boy's nose with a corner of her handkerchief.

"But, my goodness, they live in style! Here she is supporting the family, and he has his sixteen crowns a week and can spend every öre of it! And you think they would have no account where one could charge a drop of liquor?" Such nonsense was incomprehensible. "Sonny, can you say 'Daddy'? My, now you look pretty! The Lord help us, I think he takes after both of us, Lady. That is what comes from agreeing in everything!"

He took a turn into the kitchen, which was the size of an ordinary table.

"They can afford running water, the spendthrifts!—Ah!"

He came back to Malvina and the child.

"Sonny, can you say 'Daddy'? Well, give me a smack, girl! You look fine with a little one on your knees! If you could only see yourself!"

But Malvina was pouting.

"You always find fault with my relatives. And yet they are grand to Sonny, keeping him here for nothing."

"Oh yes, they are good enough according to their lights," said King Nebuchadnezzar appeasingly. "Don't get on your hind legs, Mally!— Sonny!" He fumbled in his vest pocket for some gift for the boy and got hold of the tobacco quid. The deuce take it! Here he might have spent that darned five öre on something for the boy—cream, for instance. Cream was not a bit too grand for such a prince. He sauntered back to the kitchen and began to look over the plate rack, driven by some desperate hope.

Suddenly he gave a little surprised whistle: he had found a ten-öre piece under one of the cups.

He came back to Malvina with joyful, dancing steps.

"See here, Malvina, girl of my heart! run down and get five öre's worth of cream for the Prince, and brandy with the rest of the money. Tell them it is for a sick person, and they will give you better measure."

Nobody on earth, least of all Malvina herself, could help buying brandy with all the money. For one thing, the cream was sour at this time of day, also there was none to be had, and finally one could not buy brandy with less than ten öre. King Nebuchadnezzar was not the person to utter reproaches after hearing these altogether satisfactory reasons; and Sonny was already man enough to feel sufficiently compensated by a few drops of brandy on a crust of bread.

But after the drink it was as if the coziness of home life had vanished. King Nebuchanezzar no longer felt the quiet satisfaction of dwelling in the bosom of his assembled family. Every now and then he went to the window and looked out. Some of his old flourish had returned. He was still buoyant, and felt the need of some personal outlet—the need of one more bout with the world, to say it nicely.

It was an unusually beautiful day, one of the few days when the sun triumphantly pierces the veil of smoke generally hanging over the city, and pours a flood of light over the streets. The sky, a marvelous blue between the trees on the old rampart, seemed to be nothing but limitless, immaterial space, resting in lucidity and peace. It was like looking into limpid infinity.

King Nebuchadnezzar shook himself.

"Such a day ought to be celebrated," he said, "and not be spent sitting here moping. Besides, Sonny is sleepy. I think I'll go out and get a breath of air.—If one could only have raised a few coins."

He sighed and cast a searching glance at the bare room.

"You can't show yourself publicly in that outfit!" said Malvina.

"No, of course, it would be better to be in plain clothes, but there are clothes enough in the wardrobe—any amount of them."

They examined the contents of the bed, and unanimously chose the least ragged pair of trousers and the remnants of a brown overcoat. King Nebuchadnezzar donned the finery, and contemptuously threw the tell-tale garb of the workhouse inmate on the bed.

"Now when I take a stitch here and there, you will look fine," said Malvina, and stroked him caressingly.

"Yes, that isn't half bad," he said delighted, "but they'll nab me anyhow when they see my socks."

"You'll have to let down the pants, Nezzar."

"That won't be enough! But never mind, it'll be all right to go barefoot in wooden shoes this time of year."

"I shall certainly not go with you if you are barefoot. There are plenty of others I can go with!"

"Did you think I meant it?" he said hurriedly. "We are not that far gone yet." He spoke swaggeringly, yet remained irresolute.

"You might try the attic," suggested Malvina.

"That was just what I was thinking of," he answered calmly, anxious to maintain as much as possible of his superiority over his lady. He went out quickly, and returned soon after, carrying a shabby high silk hat and a pair of worn-out boots with side inserts of elastic. "Look at the mud boats," he said, showing them triumphantly. "Of course it's a bum piece of work—still they are always better than wooden shoes. I hate wooden shoes more than anything. They ruin the profession. And think of the club-footed walk they give!"

The clothes looked like crumped paper that had been unfolded. But the couple only heeded the actual holes, and Malvina searched in vain for needle and thread. The baby in the cradle now began to move and cry, and they realized that Malvina's sister would soon come back. With much petting, they again placed Sonny on the chair near the window, and tied him so that he would not tumble out.

"It's fine for Sonny to sit there and look at the sky," said King Nebuchadnezzar, patting him gently on his thin hair. But Sonny preferred to sleep. His head dropped heavily down to one side, and he began once more to whistle softly.

The baby was angry. She had lost her pacifier, and was crying furiously, raising her naked stomach till her little body formed a bridge resting on her head and feet.

"She is hungry, poor thing," said King Nebuchadnezzar and looked around for an inspiration, "look how she humps her stomach. Would you like something poured into your little tummy, eh?"

He shyly patted her tense little drum. Then he took the empty bottle and held it to the light for inspection, but not the least particle was left. The last drop had been poured on Sonny's crust.

"It does seem a shame," said Malvina, "of course, she's not ours, still it does seem a shame."

She found a few morsels of bread which she held under the faucet, to moisten them before tying the lump into the curtain above the other knots. The baby stopped crying and began to doze, moving the whole machinery up and down with her small pumping apparatus, without realizing that she had now one more ball to keep going.

For a while King Nebuchadnezzar stood and looked at her patient drudgery. "She goes at it like a regular steam engine," he said musingly. "She'll be great when she grows up! Whew—I should hate to be the man that crosses her way. But shan't we cut all that old stuff off? It's a pity for her to lie there working at the whole mess."

"No, we better not; perhaps Sister wants to use the curtain," answered Malvina.

They sauntered aimlessly down the street. Malvina took her Nezzar's arm and walked along mincingly. "You'll take us to a nice place, won't you? Not to anything low-down? There are good places enough where *you* can get in." She spoke with such conviction that King Nebuchadnezzar felt extremely poor and powerless.

She left all details about the choice of a place entirely to him. Now and then she threw a rapt glance at him, but otherwise kept her eye modestly to the ground. It was so long since she had gone out with a man that she felt as if it were the first time. She felt as bashful as a young girl, and that was a lovely sensation. This, however, did not prevent her from stealthily watching the stores from which people turned their heads to look after the couple. King Nebuchadnezzar looked fine in a silk hat, and she knew that they created admiration of all by their appearance.

"I know where you are going to take us," she said gaily and hung heavily on his arm. But she did not know, and did not care to know. She only said it to express her blind faith in him. She wanted most of all to hang on his arm and with closed eyes walk straight into the light. Then, when they were in the full illumination, she would open her eyes quickly, and let herself be hurt and dazzled by the sudden radiance which would make her cry out.

How beautiful life could be!

King Nebuchadnezzar felt a little uneasy. When they reached the bridge leading to the heart of the city, he turned, and a minute later he turned again. Certainly, there were places enough. The whole city, brimful of splendors, was offering itself. The difficulty was to be sure of choosing the right place, so as not to sit there and be sorry afterward. He himself would have preferred to begin at one end and "do" the whole town lengthwise and crosswise. But that was out of the question if one had a lady along. He was just waiting for an idea which might save the day, a "darned good little hunch," such as he had had hundreds of times before. Meanwhile one simply had to keep going, and King Nebuchadnezzar varied his maneuvers like a skipper who tries to kill time while tacking in wait for the pilot.

Malvina began to take notice. "It seems to me we are going in a circle," she said surprised.

"But really, the first thing is to get needle and thread," mumbled King Nebuchadnezzar offended. "A gentleman—"

Malvina hugged his arm and looked innocently up to him, astonished at his angry tone. And Nebuchadnezzar felt with a pang his responsibility toward this woman who walked by his side looking forward to a merry evening. She knew perfectly well that he had not a red öre, but she simply believed in him. And under normal conditions this would have been the right thing to do, for King Nebuchadnezzar was ordinarily not without resources when planning for a good time. But today his genius didn't seem to be at home. He did not feel a trace of that play of intelligence which in ways numerous and varied had supplied him with cash when he had needed it.

"We might go and dance in 'The Decanter,'" he said crestfallen, "only they won't let us in." He had the sad sensation that he was failing in the main issue. Sure, the world was chock full of excitement and fun, but what was the good if one no longer knew how to nab them? He had never quite realized the value of money, but now it began to dawn on him. Money was all right after all, when one was worn out and could think of nothing else.

Rather downcast, they sauntered up on the old rampart and sat down on a bench. The sun was setting. The dying day enveloped the city in a purple mist, which was wafted in and out among the trees on the rampart like voluptuous exhalations from a glowing, joy-sated world.

A short distance away some children were singing and dancing rounds under the trees, and at the end of the street the tower of Our Saviour's Church shone in its golden luster. It was impossible to be sad, and gradually they forgot their grudge against life and began to chat innocently about nothing and everything. The evening filled them with well-being and gentleness. With a tinge of melancholy they watched the sun take its leave, unhindered, as something too great to have its right disputed. Before it disappeared, it kissed their vapid faces and made them blush once more in giddy anticipation. Their eyes had perhaps never before shone so beautifully; far away over the city hovered the festive glow that was kindled again in them. For a short while ineffable joy—happiness unknown to the world—flowed into them and inflated their shriveled hearts.

Malvina had persuaded a little girl to go home for needle and thread. Eagerly she mended her big beautiful man here and there, surrounded by a crowd of open-mouthed children. King Nebuchadnezzar had to lie down on the bench to make the work go more quickly, and was told to turn round so as to be mended on all sides. He lay tossing about like a frolicsome puppy, overdoing everything, and making monstrous puns in order to amuse the children. In spite of the dying light, Malvina used her needle deftly and completed her work in the twinkling of an eye.

"There, Nezzar," she said, looking into his eyes elated. The last obstacle was overcome.

He gave her a humble and impotent look in return. Alas, the obstacles were overcome; there was no longer any hiding-place. Behind this careful mending, a secret hope had been lying in wait for him—for why make one's self so smart? Surely, there must be a reason! Now this hope failed before their very eyes, and revealed man's miserable poverty when deserted by his intelligence.

All his life King Nebuchadnezzar had kept his faith in himself. It had been present as a gigantic ruin in his dream of this very day, and had lured him into the attempt to revive his youth for one evening, to make a journey round the world on a small scale. That ought to be a mere trifle for a man who had tramped comfortably and easily through three continents without having a red öre in his pocket, and had partaken of all that life had to offer. And now the miserable end of it all was that he was sitting here, in the most self-evident place in the world, and had to admit his inability to pay fifty öre for admission to a dance-hall!

Of course one could always do something or other without money. Even the poorest bum must have connections enough to get a glad evening out of them without spending any money. Malvina hinted as much —after all, the women expected to hang on and get a good time out of the men. But King Nebuchadnezzar was not of the kind that sponged on his acquaintances. He much preferred to play the returned American. He had not gone out today to nibble a crumb here and there, but to visit once more the happy hunting grounds of his youth. If he found himself pushed out of the game—well, then he could call it square and return to the Institution if need be. But sit and lick the plates after the banquet—no, he couldn't do that. Leave that to those who had never been at the festive board themselves. "One has obligations toward the other fellows in the Institution," he argued aloud, thinking that even a woman would understand that. "One represents them all, so to say. But you go ahead, Lady! You will always find some guy—you with your face!"

But Malvina only clung still tighter to him and declared that she cared for nobody else in this world and wanted to stay with him. She could always find somebody else some day when he was not along.

"I expected as much of you," said King Nebuchadnezzar with emotion. "You answered as I should have done in your place."

Malvina accepted his praise with a brave smile, but suddenly burst out crying. She let herself go like a young girl, as if this were the first time her world had broken down around her. King Nebuchadnezzar did not try to console her with words, but put his arm gently round her. With her head on his shoulder she sobbed herself to sleep.

The evening had set in. Darkness was gathering under the trees of the rampart, and in the streets the lamps were lighted one by one, twinkling in the dusk. King Nebuchadnezzar's eyes had assumed a strange, far-away expression.

He was gazing into the distance, farther than anyone could see. He had not the heart to stir and possibly awake Malvina, and he felt frightfully lonesome—so lonesome that he had to let things take their course and confess to himself that it was all over. He was absolutely good for nothing. He had grown old. It was a relief to acknowledge this at last, instead of trying to prop up the impossible by putting a tired shoulder to it. Well, now it was over. Life could no longer be snatched in passing. It lurched by so swiftly that, if he tried to jump on board, he only split his skull against the pavement.

But he had had his day. He had been no common trash. Gosh almighty, how he had made things hum! What precious memories he had! He could not restrain himself any longer, but felt that he must have a partaker in his reminiscences. When Malvina awoke, however, and looked at him, his whole glory faded before the disillusion in her eyes. Perhaps she had dreamed that she was in the midst of splendor.

They sat huddled close together, neither feeling the need of words. King Nebuchadnezzar wondered that Malvina did not scold him. A while ago he would have wished her to do so. It would have led to a brawl, and he could have withdrawn from it with the air of a man who would have redeemed everything if, woman-like, she had not spoiled the game by her squabble. But now he had surrendered to decrepitude, and was grateful to her for not throwing it up to him.

There were thickets growing on the slopes of the rampart, in which children and tramps had made little paths. The darkness put a soft shroud over the foliage, and here and there through the bushes the glimmering of ripples and the rustling of reeds told of the near-by water in the moat.

Something about all this went softly to King Nebuchadnezzar's heart, like a greeting from his great and good days. Here he could still in his present poor condition taste the sweetness of our great earth. A night in the open was something which he could still afford, and at the same time the gist of the whole thing. All he had attained in his life, nay, Life itself was founded on the furtive thrill he had felt when sleeping under the stars and awaking drenched by the morning dew, in the center of the whole universe. Surely, he was yet equal to as much as that!

But Malvina jumped up offended. She wasn't going to make her bed in the open air like she wouldn't say what kind of a woman. They were not used to that in her department. "We have decent beds, with all comforts—but I can certainly take myself away if you are going to be vulgar."

King Nebuchadnezzar gave her a despairing look while she carried on. She needn't have put on her aristocratic airs for his sake. He had

felt the pain and loneliness of old age, and was not going to quarrel
with anybody.

"You are acting so Spanish this evening," he said with a bitter smile.
"One might think that one of the overseers had begun to make eyes
at you."

"Why, Nezzar, for shame!" she exclaimed, offended, "you know
very well that I am no scab."

Well, why not?—If that would lead to one or two small concessions.
He, too, began to realize the importance of concessions, and was already slowly adapting himself to his new and humbler existence. This
called to his mind the hayloft of Jensen, the livery man. He was now
tired and longed for a rest, and such a hayloft could be perfectly splendid
—the best thing next to a haystack in the open air.

He made his suggestion meekly, and to his surprise Malvina did not
object, but rose silently. For a short time they walked southward on
the rampart, then descended and crossed an empty lot where there was
quite an accumulation of old boilers, rusty iron plates, and heavy, half
corroded cables. Through an opening in the fence they entered a yard
surrounded on three sides by low buildings and wooden barns. A
black, factory-like building stood on the fourth side. King Nebuchadnezzar had taken Malvina's hand and was pulling her with him. They
walked in the shadow of wagons and lumber piles, and were steering
toward a low building from which was heard the steady sound of
champing horses.

King Nebuchadnezzar stuck his head through the open upper half of
the door and whistled softly. A youthful tension had come over his
movements. He stood there straining every sense, ready to light out or
change his tactics at the faintest sound. After all, this tasted mag-
nificently of old times and the outer world. He turned and signaled to
Malvina with his eyes while he stealthily unhooked the door. Then he
entered the stable on tiptoe, and Malvina shuffled after him.

"Here is the hotel," he whispered, and looked around in delight.
"Look, Malvina! Horses, and beautiful hay. No ordinary draught-
horses either—just notice the manure; you smell the difference at once.
The stable boy has gone out—fine fellow! Well, get up in the hay,
Lady!"

He climbed up the ladder to the hayloft, and Malvina followed him.
It was hard for her, and she held her dress together with unnecessary
tightness in order to show her disapproval of Nezzar's vulgar exclamations.

That night King Nebuchadnezzar dreamed of the big plains and
the starry skies: He had prepared for next day's hike by rubbing his
feet with tallow and lacing his stomach firmly. Now he was resting
in the finest haystack, gazing toward the distant mountains, and quietly
anticipating what was to be found on the other side of them. Overhead
the universe was moving to its eternal music. He sensed the unending

melody of the vast night, and knew from this that he was alone. But it did not make him sad.

Malvina, dreaming too, was in "The Decanter" and was dancing the old dance called "The Crested Hen." She daintily lifted her dress far up on one side, for her leg was covered in its whole length with yellow silk.

Overseer Petersen had returned with his light brigadge, and learned to his surprise that King Nebuchadnezzar had not yet arrived. It happened now and then that one or another of the inmates made themselves scarce for a couple of days, but they generally returned of their own accord. Even if not, they were always easy to trace, so the event did not arouse much concern.

Yet the authorities began to take a few leisurely steps to find Nezzar, and at a certain point his trail converged with Malvina's. She, too, was missed, and as their former relations were known, the matter began to look a bit more serious. Their connection with the family on Christianshavn was also known, and the investigations were started in Dronningensgade.

Here the man had come back and found the inmate's uniform in his bed. He saw at once how matters stood, and, knowing that they would be bothered by the police, he preferred to report his find at once to the station.

This double alarm stirred the police to action. Search was made, and all trails led to the Christianshavn rampart. But there they ended.

In some way or other the eloping of the indigent couple gradually changed its aspect and appeared romantic instead of comical. The beautiful summer night spun its mystic web around them. Perhaps the air was filled with love that night. Be this as it may, little by little their excursion took the shape of a love drama. The daily papers were notified, and the moat examined as far as possible during the night.

At dawn a policeman who knew all the ins and outs of the haunts of Christianshavn took it upon himself to investigate them one by one. A little later in the morning the sun rose over the distant mountains and tickled King Nebuchadnezzar's nose. He rubbed his eyes and awoke to the most odious of all sights, a red-haired policeman! However, he had by long experience learned to deal cordially with the archfiend, and said yawning—after having extricated himself from Malvina's arms— "Well, are we to beat it?"

The sergeant nodded.

"We would have come anyway by ourselves, but of course it's nicer to be sent for. You have a cab, I suppose?"

"There is one waiting in the square," said the sergeant laughing.

They found it, and all three stepped in. Malvina and King Nebuchadnezzar were equally delighted. They had received permission to have the top down, and were now leaning elegantly back in their seats. They were driving home from the banquet, a little dizzy from the splendor. The light and music were still pulsating through them and made them exuberant. King Nebuchadnezzar waved his hand condescendingly at the passers-by, and Malvina threw kisses at them with her fingers. Then they both laughed, and the policeman pretended not to notice.

"After all, that was a worthy ending," said King Nebuchadnezzar, as they swung up before the gate of the workhouse.

Malvina said nothing, but graciously put her finger to her closed lips and bowed slowly. King Nebuchadnezzar took this as it was meant— it was the high, aristocratic world's way of saying "Thanks for buns and chocolate," and he respected her silence. He lifted his old silk hat, made a deep bow to Madame, and entered his prison like a high-born guest from Bredgade who deigns to taste the food of the poor.

It turned out to be their last fling. Malvina had caught cold in the night and died shortly afterward, and King Nebuchadnezzar never again had the courage to compete by himself with the big world. Scenting future defeats, he preferred to live in his memories of the glorious days in which he had held his own so valiantly.

ISAK DINESEN

The Sailor-Boy's Tale

Isak Dinesen, the nom de plume of Baroness Karen Blixen of Rungstedlund, was born of an old Danish family. In 1914, she married a cousin, Baron Blixen, and went with him to British East Africa, where they established a successful coffee plantation. In 1931, the collapse of the coffee market forced her to return to Denmark, where she lives now. Her best known books are *Seven Gothic Tales, Out of Africa* and *Winter's Tales*. [From *Winter's Tales* by Isak Dinesen; copyright 1942 by Random House, Inc.; used by permission of the publishers, and Putnam & Co., Ltd.]

THE BARQUE *Charlotte* was on her way from Marseille to Athens, in gray weather, on a high sea, after three days' heavy gale. A small sailor-boy, named Simon, stood on the wet, swinging deck, held onto a shroud, and looked up toward the drifting clouds, and to the upper top-gallant yard of the main-mast.

A bird, that had sought refuge upon the mast, had got her feet entangled in some loose tackle-yarn of the halliard, and, high up there, struggled to get free. The boy on the deck could see her wings flapping and her head turning from side to side.

Through his own experience of life he had come to the conviction that in this world everyone must look after himself, and expect no help from others. But the mute, deadly fight kept him fascinated for more than an hour. He wondered what kind of bird it would be. These last days a number of birds had come to settle in the barque's rigging: swallows, quails, and a pair of peregrine falcons; he believed that this bird was a peregrine falcon. He remembered how, many years ago, in his own country and near his home, he had once seen a peregrine falcon quite close, sitting on a stone and flying straight up from it. Perhaps this was the same bird. He thought: "That bird is like me. Then she was there, and now she is here."

At that a fellow-feeling rose in him, a sense of common tragedy; he stood looking at the bird with his heart in his mouth. There were none of the sailors about to make fun of him; he began to think out how he might go up by the shrouds to help the falcon out. He brushed his hair back and pulled up his sleeves, gave the deck round him a great glance, and climbed up. He had to stop a couple of times in the swaying rigging.

It was indeed, he found when he got to the top of the mast, a peregrine falcon. As his head was on a level with hers, she gave up her struggle, and looked at him with a pair of angry, desperate yellow eyes. He had to take hold of her with one hand while he got his knife out, and cut off the tackle-yarn. He was scared as he looked down, but at the same time he felt that he had been ordered up by nobody, but that this was his own venture, and this gave him a proud, steadying sensation, as if the sea and the sky, the ship, the bird and himself were all one. Just as he had freed the falcon, she hacked him in the thumb, so that the blood ran, and he nearly let her go. He grew angry with her, and gave her a clout on the head, then he put her inside his jacket, and climbed down again.

When he reached the deck the mate and the cook were standing there, looking up; they roared to him to ask what he had had to do in the mast. He was so tired that the tears were in his eyes. He took the falcon out and showed her to them, and she kept still within his hands. They laughed and walked off. Simon set the falcon down, stood back and watched her. After a while he reflected that she might not be able to get up from the slippery deck, so he caught her once more, walked away with her and placed her upon a bolt of canvas. A little after she began to trim her feathers, made two or three sharp jerks forward, and then suddenly flew off. The boy could follow her flight above the troughs of the gray sea. He thought: "There flies my falcon."

When the *Charlotte* came home, Simon signed aboard another ship, and two years later he was a light hand on the schooner *Hebe* lying at Bodo, high up on the coast of Norway, to buy herrings.

To the great herring-markets of Bodo ships came together from all corners of the world; here were Swedish, Finnish and Russian boats, a forest of masts, and on shore a turbulent, irregular display of life, with many languages spoken, and mighty fights. On the shore booths had been set up, and the Lapps, small yellow people, noiseless in their movements, with watchful eyes, whom Simon had never seen before, came down to sell bead-embroidered leather-goods. It was April, the sky and the sea were so clear that it was difficult to hold one's eyes up against them—salt, infinitely wide, and filled with bird-shrieks—as if someone were incessantly whetting invisible knives, on all sides, high up in Heaven.

Simon was amazed at the lightness of these April evenings. He knew no geography, and did not assign it to the latitude, but he took it as a sign of an unwonted good-will in the Universe, a favor. Simon had been small for his age all his life, but this last winter he had grown, and had become strong of limb. That good luck, he felt, must spring from the very same source as the sweetness of the weather, from a new benevolence in the world. He had been in need of such encouragement, for he was timid by nature; now he asked for no more. The rest he felt to be his own affair. He went about slowly, and proudly.

One evening he was ashore with land-leave, and walked up to the booth of a small Russian trader, a Jew who sold gold watches. All the sailors knew that his watches were made from bad metal, and would not go, still they bought them, and paraded them about. Simon looked at these watches for a long time, but did not buy. The old Jew had divers goods in his shop, and amongst others a case of oranges. Simon had tasted oranges on his journeys; he bought one and took it with him. He meant to go up on a hill, from where he could see the sea, and suck it there.

As he walked on, and had got to the outskirts of the place, he saw a little girl in a blue frock, standing at the other side of a fence and looking at him. She was thirteen or fourteen years old, as slim as an eel, but with a round, clear, freckled face, and a pair of long plaits. The two looked at one another.

"Who are you looking out for?" Simon asked, to say something. The girl's face broke into an ecstatic, presumptuous smile. "For the man I am going to marry, of course," she said. Something in her countenance made the boy confident and happy; he grinned a little at her. "That will perhaps be me," he said. "Ha, ha," said the girl, "he is a few years older than you, I can tell you." "Why," said Simon, "you are not grown up yourself." The little girl shook her head solemnly. "Nay," she said, "but when I grow up I will be exceedingly beautiful, and wear brown shoes with heels, and a hat." "Will you have an orange?" asked Simon, who could give her none of the things she had named. She looked at the orange and at him. "They are very good to eat," said he. "Why do you not eat it yourself then?" she asked. "I have eaten so many already," said he, "when I was in Athens. Here I had to pay a mark for it." "What is your name?" asked she. "My name is Simon," said he. "What is yours?" "Nora," said the girl. "What do you want for your orange now, Simon?"

When he heard his name in her mouth Simon grew bold. "Will you give me a kiss for the orange?" he asked. Nora looked at him gravely for a moment. "Yes," she said, "I should not mind giving you a kiss." He grew as warm as if he had been running quickly. When she stretched out her hand for the orange he took hold of it. At that moment somebody in the house called out for her. "That is my father," said she, and tried to give him back the orange, but he would not take it. "Then come again tomorrow," she said quickly, "then I will give you a kiss." At that she slipped off. He stood and looked after her, and a little later went back to his ship.

Simon was not in the habit of making plans for the future, and now he did not know whether he would be going back to her or not.

The following evening he had to stay aboard, as the other sailors were going ashore, and he did not mind that either. He meant to sit on the deck with the ship's dog, Balthasar, and to practice upon a concertina that he had purchased some time ago. The pale evening was all round him, the sky was faintly roseate, the sea was quite calm, like milk-and-water, only in the wake of the boats going inshore it broke into streaks of vivid indigo. Simon sat and played; after a while his own music began to speak to him so strongly that he stopped, got up and looked upward. Then he saw that the full moon was sitting high on the sky.

The sky was so light that she hardly seemed needed there; it was as if she had turned up by a caprice of her own. She was round, demure and presumptuous. At that he knew that he must go ashore, whatever it was to cost him. But he did not know how to get away, since the others had taken the yawl with them. He stood on the deck for a long time, a small lonely figure of a sailor-boy on a boat, when he caught sight of a yawl coming in from a ship farther out, and hailed her. He found that it was the Russian crew from a boat named *Anna,* going ashore. When he could make himself understood to them, they took him with them; they first asked him for money for his fare, then, laughing, gave it back to him. He thought: "These people will be believing that I am going into town, wenching." And then he felt, with some pride, that they were right, although at the same time they were infinitely wrong, and knew nothing about anything.

When they came ashore they invited him to come in and drink in their company, and he would not refuse, because they had helped him. One of the Russians was a giant, as big as a bear; he told Simon that his name was Ivan. He got drunk at once, and then fell upon the boy with a bear-like affection, pawed him, smiled and laughed into his face, made him a present of a gold watch-chain, and kissed him on both cheeks. At that Simon reflected that he also ought to give Nora a present when they met again, and as soon as he could get away from the Russians he walked up to a booth that he knew of, and bought a small blue silk handkerchief, the same color as her eyes.

It was Saturday evening, and there were many people amongst the houses; they came in long rows, some of them singing, all keen to have some fun that night. Simon, in the midst of this rich, bawling life under the clear moon, felt his head light with the flight from the ship and the strong drinks. He crammed the handkerchief in his pocket; it was silk, which he had never touched before, a present for his girl.

He could not remember the path up to Nora's house, lost his way, and came back to where he had started. Then he grew deadly afraid that he should be too late, and began to run. In a small passage between two wooden huts he ran straight into a big man, and found that it was Ivan once more. The Russian folded his arms round him and held him. "Good! Good!" he cried in high glee, "I have found you, my little chicken. I have looked for you everywhere, and poor Ivan has wept because he lost his friend." "Let me go, Ivan," cried Simon. "Oho," said Ivan, "I shall go with you and get you what you want. My heart and my money are all yours, all yours; I have been seventeen years old myself, a little lamb of God, and I want to be so again tonight." "Let me go," cried Simon, "I am in a hurry." Ivan held him so that it hurt, and patted him with his other hand. "I feel it, I feel it," he said. "Now trust to me, my little friend. Nothing shall part you and me. I hear the others coming; we will have such a night together as you will remember when you are an old grandpapa."

Suddenly he crushed the boy to him, like a bear that carries off a sheep. The odious sensation of male bodily warmth and the bulk of a man close to him made the lean boy mad. He thought of Nora waiting, like a slender ship in the dim air, and of himself, here, in the hot embrace of a hairy animal. He struck Ivan with all his might. "I shall kill you, Ivan," he cried out, "if you do not let me go." "Oh, you will be thankful to me later on," said Ivan, and began to sing. Simon fumbled in his pocket for his knife, and got it opened. He could not lift his hand, but he drove the knife, furiously, in under the big man's arm. Almost immediately he felt the blood spouting out, and running down in his sleeve. Ivan stopped short in the song, let go his hold of the boy and gave two long deep grunts. The next second he tumbled down on his knees. "Poor Ivan, poor Ivan," he groaned. He fell straight on his face. At that moment Simon heard the other sailors coming along, singing, in the by-street.

He stood still for a minute, wiped his knife, and watched the blood spread into a dark pool underneath the big body. Then he ran. As he stopped for a second to choose his way, he heard the sailors behind him scream out over their dead comrade. He thought: "I must get down to the sea, where I can wash my hand." But at the same time he ran the other way. After a little while he found himself on the path that he had walked on the day before, and it seemed as familiar to him, as if he had walked it many hundred times in his life.

He slackened his pace to look round, and suddenly saw Nora standing on the other side of the fence; she was quite close to him when he caught sight of her in the moonlight. Wavering and out of breath he sank down on his knees. For a moment he could not speak. The little girl looked down at him. "Good evening, Simon," she said in her small coy voice. "I have waited for you a long time," and after a moment she added: "I have eaten your orange."

"Oh, Nora," cried the boy. "I have killed a man." She stared at him, but did not move. "Why did you kill a man?" she asked after a moment. "To get here," said Simon. "Because he tried to stop me. But he was my friend." Slowly he got onto his feet. "He loved me!" the boy cried out, and at that burst into tears. "Yes," said she slowly and thoughtfully. "Yes, because you must be here in time." "Can you hide me?" he asked. "For they are after me." "Nay," said Nora, "I cannot hide you. For my father is the parson here at Bodo, and he would be sure to hand you over to them, if he knew that you had killed a man." "Then," said Simon, "give me something to wipe my hands on." "What is the matter with your hands?" she asked, and took a little step forward. He stretched out his hands to her. "Is that your own blood?" she asked. "No," said he, "it is his." She took the step back again. "Do you hate me now?" he asked. "No, I do not hate you," said she. "But do put your hands at your back."

As he did so she came up close to him, at the other side of the fence, and clasped her arms round his neck. She pressed her young body to his, and kissed him tenderly. He felt her face, cool as the moonlight, upon his own, and when she released him, his head swam, and he did not know if the kiss had lasted a second or an hour. Nora stood up straight, her eyes wide open. "Now," she said slowly and proudly, "I promise you that I will never marry anybody, as long as I live." The boy kept standing with his hands on his back, as if she had tied them there. "And now," she said, "you must run, for they are coming." They looked at one another. "Do not forget Nora," said she. He turned and ran.

He leapt over a fence, and when he was down amongst the houses he walked. He did not know at all where to go. As he came to a house, from where music and noise streamed out, he slowly went through the door. The room was full of people; they were dancing in here. A lamp hung from the ceiling, and shone down on them; the air was thick and brown with the dust rising from the floor. There were some women in the room, but many of the men danced with each other, and gravely or laughingly stamped the floor. A moment after Simon had come in the crowd withdrew to the walls to clear the floor for two sailors, who were showing a dance from their own country.

Simon thought: "Now, very soon, the men from the boat will come round to look for their comrade's murderer, and from my hands they will know that I have done it." These five minutes during which he stood by the wall of the dancing-room, in the midst of the gay, sweating dancers, were of great significance to the boy. He himself felt it, as if during this time he grew up, and became like other people. He did not entreat his destiny, nor complain. Here he was, he had killed a man, and had kissed a girl. He did not demand any more from life, nor did life now demand more from him. He was Simon, a man like the men round him, and going to die, as all men are going to die.

He only became aware of what was going on outside him, when he saw that a woman had come in, and was standing in the midst of the cleared floor, looking round her. She was a short, broad old woman, in the clothes of the Lapps, and she took her stand with such majesty and fierceness as if she owned the whole place. It was obvious that most of the people knew her, and were a little afraid of her, although a few laughed; the din of the dancing-room stopped when she spoke.

"Where is my son?" she asked in a high shrill voice, like a bird's. The next moment her eyes fell on Simon himself, and she steered through the crowd, which opened up before her, stretched out her old skinny, dark hand, and took him by the elbow. "Come home with me now," she said. "You need not dance here tonight. You may be dancing a high enough dance soon."

Simon drew back, for he thought that she was drunk. But as she looked him straight in the face with her yellow eyes, it seemed to him that he had met her before, and that he might do well in listening to her. The old woman pulled him with her across the floor, and he followed her without a word. "Do not birch your boy too badly, Sunniva," one of the men in the room cried to her. "He has done no harm, he only wanted to look at the dance."

At the same moment as they came out through the door, there was an alarm in the street, a flock of people came running down it, and one of them, as he turned into the house, knocked against Simon, looked at him and the old woman, and ran on.

While the two walked along the street, the old woman lifted up her skirt, and put the hem of it into the boy's hand. "Wipe your hand on my skirt," she said. They had not gone far before they came to a small wooden house, and stopped; the door to it was so low that they must bend to get through it. As the Lapp-woman went in before Simon, still holding onto his arm, the boy looked up for a moment. The night had grown misty; there was a wide ring round the moon.

The old woman's room was narrow and dark, with but one small window to it; a lantern stood on the floor and lighted it up dimly. It was all filled with reindeer skins and wolf skins, and with reindeer horn, such as the Lapps use to make their carved buttons and knife-handles, and the air in here was rank and stifling. As soon as they were in, the woman turned to Simon, took hold of his head, and with her crooked fingers parted his hair and combed it down in Lapp fashion. She clapped a Lapp cap on him and stood back to glance at him. "Sit down on my stool, now," she said. "But first take out your knife." She was so commanding in voice and manner that the boy could not but choose to do as she told him; he sat down on the stool, and he could not take his eyes off her face, which was flat and brown, and as if smeared with dirt in its net of fine wrinkles. As he sat there he heard many people come along outside, and stop by the house; then someone knocked at the door, waited a moment and knocked again. The old woman stood and listened, as still as a mouse.

"Nay," said the boy and got up. "This is no good, for it is me that they are after. It will be better for you to let me go out to them." "Give me your knife," said she. When he handed it to her, she stuck it straight into her thumb, so that the blood spouted out, and she let it drip all over her skirt. "Come in, then," she cried.

The door opened, and two of the Russian sailors came and stood in the opening; there were more people outside. "Has anybody come in here?" they asked. "We are after a man who has killed our mate, but he has run away from us. Have you seen or heard anybody this way?" The old Lapp-woman turned upon them, and her eyes shone like gold in the lamplight. "Have I seen or heard anyone?" she cried, "I have heard you shriek murder all over the town. You frightened me, and my poor silly boy there, so that I cut my thumb as I was ripping the skin-rug that I sew. The boy is too scared to help me, and the rug is all ruined. I shall make you pay me for that. If you are looking for a murderer, come in and search my house for me, and I shall know you when we meet again." She was so furious that she danced where she stood, and jerked her head like an angry bird of prey.

The Russian came in, looked round the room, and at her and her blood-stained hand and skirt. "Do not put a curse on us now, Sunniva," he said timidly. "We know that you can do many things when you like. Here is a mark to pay you for the blood you have spilled." She stretched out her hand, and he placed a piece of money in it. She spat on it. "Then go, and there shall be no bad blood between us," said Sunniva, and shut the door after them. She stuck her thumb in her mouth, and chuckled a little.

The boy got up from his stool, stood straight up before her and stared into her face. He felt as if he were swaying high up in the air, with but a small hold. "Why have you helped me?" he asked her. "Do you not know?" she answered. "Have you not recognized me yet? But you will remember the peregrine falcon which was caught in the tackle-yarn of your boat, the *Charlotte,* as she sailed in the Mediterranean. That day you climbed up by the shrouds of the top-gallantmast to help her out, in a stiff wind, and with a high sea. That falcon was me. We Lapps often fly in such a manner, to see the world. When I first met you I was on my way to Africa, to see my younger sister and her children. She is a falcon too, when she chooses. By that time she was living at Takaunga, within an old ruined tower, which down there they call a minaret." She swathed a corner of her skirt round her thumb, and bit at it. "We do not forget," she said. "I hacked your thumb, when you took hold of me; it is only fair that I should cut my thumb for you tonight."

She came close to him, and gently rubbed her two brown, claw-like fingers against his forehead. "So you are a boy," she said, "who will kill a man rather than be late to meet your sweetheart? We hold together, the females of this earth. I shall mark your forehead now, so that the girls will know of that, when they look at you, and they will like you for it." She played with the boy's hair, and twisted it round her finger.

"Listen now, my little bird," said she. "My great grandson's brother-in-law is lying with his boat by the landing-place at this moment; he is to take a consignment of skins out to a Danish boat. He will bring you back to your boat, in time, before your mate comes. The *Hebe* is sailing tomorrow morning, is it not so? But when you are aboard, give him back my cap for me." She took up his knife, wiped it in her skirt and handed it to him. "Here is your knife," she said. "You will stick it into no more men; you will not need to, for from now you will sail the seas like a faithful seaman. We have enough trouble with our sons as it is."

The bewildered boy began to stammer his thanks to her. "Wait," said she, "I shall make you a cup of coffee, to bring back your wits, while I wash your jacket." She went and rattled an old copper kettle upon the fireplace. After a while she handed him a hot, strong, black drink in a cup without a handle to it. "You have drunk with Sunniva now," she said; "you have drunk down a little wisdom, so that in the future all your thoughts shall not fall like raindrops into the salt sea."

When he had finished and set down the cup, she led him to the door and opened it for him. He was surprised to see that it was almost clear morning. The house was so high up that the boy could see the sea from it, and a milky mist about it. He gave her his hand to say good by.

She stared into his face. "We do not forget," she said. "And you, you knocked me on the head there, high up in the mast. I shall give you that blow back." With that she smacked him on the ear as hard as she could, so that his head swam. "Now we are quits," she said, gave him a great, mischievous, shining glance, and a little push down the doorstep, and nodded to him.

In this way the sailor-boy got back to his ship, which was to sail the next morning, and lived to tell the story.

SIGRID UNDSET

The Death of Kristin Lavransdatter

Sigrid Undset, born in 1882, grew up in Christiania. Her father died when she was a young girl and she was forced to work in an office. This gave her material for her early tales (*The Happy Age, Jenny, Springtime*). She won the Nobel Prize in 1928, and came to visit in the United States in 1940. She is now living in Norway. Her two great historical novels are the trilogy, *Kristin Lavransdatter* and the tetralogy, *Olav Audunsson*. [From *Kristin Lavransdatter* by Sigrid Undset; copyright 1927 by Alfred A. Knopf, Inc.; used by permission of the publishers; translated by Charles Archer.]

THERE CAME AN EVENING when they were sitting round the chimney-place in the convent hall—the little flock of folk that were left alive in Rein cloister. Four nuns and two lay sisters, an old stable-man and a half-grown boy, two bedeswomen and some children, huddled together round the fire. On the high-seat bench, where a great crucifix gleamed in the dusk on the light-hued wall, lay the abbess and Sister Kristin and Sister Turid sat at her hands and feet.

It was nine days since the last death among the sisters, and five days since any had died in the cloister or the nearer houses. The pestilence seemed to be lessening throughout the parish, too, said Sira Eiliv. And for the first time for near three months something like a gleam of peace and hope and comfort fell upon the silent and weary folk that sat together there. Old Sister Torunn Marta let her rosary sink upon her lap, and took the hand of the little girl who stood at her knee:

"What can it be she means? Ay, child, now seems it as we should see that never for long does God's mother, Mary, turn away her loving-kindness from her children."

"Nay, 'tis not Mary Virgin, Sister Torunn, 'tis Hel. She will go from out this parish, with both rake and broom, when they offer up a man without blemish at the graveyard gate—tomorrow she'll be far away—"

"What means she?" asked the nun again, uneasily. "Fie upon you, Magnhild; what ugly heathenish talk is this? 'Twere fit you should taste the birch—"

"Tell us what it is, Magnhild—have no fear"—Sister Kristin was standing behind them; she asked the question breathlessly. She had remembered—she had heard in her youth from Lady Aashild—of dreadful, unnamably sinful devices that the Devil tempts desperate men to practice—

The children had been down in the grove by the parish church in the falling dusk, and some of the boys had strayed through the wood to a turf hut that stood there, and had eavesdropped and heard some men in it laying plans. It seemed from what they heard that these men had laid

507

hold on a little boy, Tore, the son of Steinunn, that lived by the strand, and tonight they were to offer him up to the pest-ogress, Hel. The children talked eagerly, proud that the grown-up folk were paying heed to what they said. They seemed not to think of pitying the hapless Tore— maybe because he was somewhat of an outcast. He wandered about the parish begging, but never came to the cloister, and if Sira Eiliv or any sent by the abbess sought out his mother, she ran away, or she kept a stubborn silence, whether they spoke lovingly or harshly to her. She had lived in the stews of Nidaros for ten years, but then a sickness took hold on her, and left her of so ill a favor that at last she could not win her livelihood as she had used to do; so she had forsaken the town for the Rein parish, and now dwelt in a hut down by the strand. It still befell at times that a chance beggar or some such stroller would take lodging with her for a while. Who was father to her boy she herself knew not.

"We must go thither," said Kristin. "Here we cannot sit, while christened souls sell themselves to the Devil at our very doors."

The nuns whimpered in fear. These were the worst men in the parish; rough, ungodly fellows; and uttermost need and despair must have turned them now into very devils. Had Sira Eiliv only been at home, they moaned. In this time of trial the priest had so won their trust, that they deemed he could do all things—

Kristin wrung her hands:

"Even if I must go alone—my mother, have I your leave to go thither?"

The abbess gripped her by the arm so hard that she cried out. The old, tongue-tied woman got upon her feet; by signs she made them understand that they should dress her to go out, and called for her golden cross, the badge of her office, and her staff. Then she took Kristin by the arm—for Kristin was the youngest and strongest of the women. All the nuns stood up and followed.

Through the door of the little room between the chapter-hall and the choir of the church, they went forth into the raw, cold winter night. Lady Ragnhild's teeth began to chatter and her whole frame to shiver— she still sweated without cease by reason of her sickness, and the pest-boil sores were not fully healed, so that it must have wrought her great agony to walk. But she muttered angrily and shook her head when the sisters prayed her to turn, clung the harder to Kristin's arm, and plodded on, shaking with cold, before them through the garden. As their eyes grew used to the darkness, the women made out the dim sheen of the withered leaves strewn on the path beneath their feet, and the faint light from the clouded sky above the naked tree-tops. Cold water-drops dripped from the branches, and puffs of wind went by with a faint soughing sound. The roll of the waves on the strand behind the high ground came to them in dull, heavy sighs.

At the bottom of the garden was a little wicket—the sisters shuddered when the bolt, fast rusted in its socket, shrieked as Kristin withdrew it by main force. Then they crept onward through the grove down toward the parish church. Now they could see dimly the black-tarred mass, darker against the darkness; and against the opening in the clouds above the low hills beyond the lake they saw the roof-top, and the ridge turret with its beasts' heads and cross over all.

Ay—there were folk in the graveyard—they felt rather than saw or heard it. And now a faint gleam of light was to be seen low down, as of a lanthorn set upon the ground. Close by it the darkness seemed moving.

The nuns pressed together, moaning almost soundlessly amid whispered prayers, went a few steps, halted and listened, and went on again. They were wellnigh come to the graveyard gate. Then they heard from out of the dark a thin child-voice crying:

"Oh, oh, my bannock; you've thrown dirt on it!"

Kristin let go the abbess's arm, and ran forward through the church-yard gate. She pushed aside some dark shapes of men's backs, stumbled over heaps of up-turned earth, and then was at the edge of the open grave. She went down to her knees, bent over, and lifted up the little boy who stood at the bottom, still whimpering because the dirt had spoiled the good bannock he had been given for staying quietly down there.

The men stood there frightened from their wits—ready to fly—some stamped about on the same spot—Kristin saw their feet in the light from the lanthorn on the ground. Then one, she made sure, would have sprung at her—at the same moment the gray-white nuns' dresses came into sight—and the knot of men hung wavering—

Kristin had the boy in her arms still; he was crying for his bannock; so she set him down, took the bread, and brushed it clean:

"There, eat it—your bannock is as good as ever now— And now go home, you men"—the shaking of her voice forced her to stop a little. "Go home and thank God you were saved from the doing of a deed 'twere hard to atone." She was speaking now as a mistress speaks to her serving-folk, mildly, but as if it could not cross her mind that they would not obey. Unwittingly some of the men turned toward the gate.

Then one of them shouted:

"Stay a little—see you not our lives at the least are forfeit—mayhap all we own—now that these full-fed monks' whores have stuck their noses into this! Never must they come away from here to spread the tidings of it—"

Not a man moved—but Sister Agnes broke into a shrill shriek, and cried in a wailing voice:

"O sweet Jesus, my bridegroom—I thank Thee that Thou sufferest Thy handmaidens to die for the glory of Thy name—!"

Lady Ragnhild pushed her roughly behind her, tottered forward, and took up the lanthorn from the ground—no one moved a hand to hinder her. When she lifted it up, the gold cross on her breast shone out. She stood propped on her staff, and slowly turned the light upon the ring about her, nodding a little at each man she looked on. Then she made a sign to Kristin to speak. Kristin said:

"Go home peaceably and quietly, dear brothers—be sure that the reverend mother and these good sisters will be as merciful as their duty to God and the honor of his Church will suffer. But stand aside now, that we may come forth with this child—and thereafter let each man go his way."

The men stood wavering. Then one cried out as though in direst need:

"Is it not better that *one* be offered up than that we should all perish—? This child here who is owned by none—"

"Christ owns him. 'Twere better we should perish one and all than to hurt one of His little ones—"

But the man who had spoken first shouted again:

"Hold your tongue—no more suchlike words, or I cram them back down your throat with this"—he shook his knife in the air. "Go you home, go to your beds and pray your priest to comfort you, and say naught of this—or I tell you, in Satan's name, you shall learn 'twas the worst thing you ever did to put your fingers into our affairs—"

"You need not to cry so loud for him you named to hear you, Arntor —be sure he is not far from here," said Kristin calmly, and some of the men seemed affrighted, and pressed unwittingly nearer to the abbess, who stood holding the lanthorn. "The worst had been, both for us and for you, had we sat quiet at home while you went about to make you a dwelling-place in hottest hell."

But the man Arntor swore and raved. Kristin knew that he hated the nuns; for his father had been forced to pledge his farm to them when he had to pay amends for man-slaying and incest with his wife's cousin. Now he went on casting up at the sisters all the Enemy's most hateful lies, charging them with sins so black and unnatural that only the Devil himself could prompt a man to think such thoughts.

The poor nuns bowed them terrified and weeping under the hail of his taunts, but they stood fast around their old mother, and she held the lanthorn high, throwing the light upon the man, and looking him calmly in the face while he raved.

But anger flamed up in Kristin like new-kindled fire:

"Silence! Have you lost your wits, or has God smitten you with blindness? Should we dare to murmur under His chastisement—we who have seen His consecrated brides go forth to meet the sword that has been drawn by reason of the world's sins? They watched and prayed while we sinned and each day forgot our Maker—shut them from the world within the citadel of prayer, while we scoured the world around, driven by greed of great and small possessions, of our own lusts and our own wrath. But they came forth to us when the angel of death was sent out amongst us—gathered in the sick and the defenseless and the hungry—twelve of our sisters have died in this plague—that you all know—not one turned aside, and not one gave over praying for us all in sisterly love, till the tongue dried in their mouths and their life's blood ebbed away—"

"Bravely speak you of yourself and your like—"

"*I* am *your* like," she cried, beside herself with anger. "I am not one of these holy sisters—I am one of you—"

"You have grown full humble, woman," said Arntor, scornfully; "you are frighted, I mark well. A little more and you will be fain to call her—the mother to this boy—your like."

"That must God judge—He died both for her and for me, and He knows us both.—Where is she—Steinunn?"

"Go down to her hut; you will find her there sure enough," answered Arntor.

"Ay, truly someone must send word to the poor woman that we have her boy," said Kristin to the nuns. "We must go out to her tomorrow."

Arntor gave a jeering laugh, but another man cried, uneasily:

"No, no—She is dead," he said to Kristin. "'Tis fourteen days since Bjarne left her and barred the door. She lay in the death-throes then—"

"She lay in—" Kristin gazed at the men, horror-struck. "Was there none to fetch a priest to her—? Is the—body—lying there—and no one has had so much compassion on her as to bring her to hallowed ground —and her child you would have—?"

At the sight of the woman's horror, it was as though the men went clean beside themselves with fear and shame; all were shouting at once; a voice louder than all the rest rang out:

"Fetch her yourself, sister!"

"Ay! Which of you will go with me?"

None answered. Arntor cried:

"You will have to go alone, I trow."

"Tomorrow—as soon as 'tis light—we will fetch her, Arntor—I myself will buy her a resting-place and masses for her soul—"

"Go thither now, go tonight—then will I believe you nuns are choke-full of holiness and pureness—"

Arntor had stuck his head forward close to hers. Kristin drove her clenched fist into his face, with a single loud sob of rage and horror—

Lady Ragnhild went forward and placed herself at Kristin's side; she strove to bring forth some words. The nuns cried out that tomorrow the dead woman should be brought to her grave. But the Devil seemed to have turned Arntor's brain; he went on shrieking:

"Go now—then will we believe on God's mercy—"

Kristin drew herself up, white and stiff:

"I will go."

She lifted the child and gave it into Sister Torunn's arms, pushed the men aside, and ran quickly, stumbling over grass tussocks and heaps of earth, toward the gate, while the nuns followed wailing, and Sister Agnes cried out that she would go with her. The abbess shook her

clenched hands toward Kristin, beckoning her to stop; but she seemed
quite beside herself and gave no heed—

Suddenly there was a great commotion in the dark over by the graveyard gate—next moment Sira Eiliv's voice asked: who was holding
Thing here. He came forward into the glimmer of the lanthorn—they
saw that he bore an ax in his hand. The nuns flocked around him; the
men made shift to steal away in the dark, but in the gateway they were
met by a man bearing a drawn sword in his hand. There was some
turmoil and the clash of arms, and Sira Eiliv shouted toward the gate:
woe to any who broke the churchyard peace. Kristin heard one say
'twas the strong smith from Credo Lane—the moment after, a tall,
broad-shouldered, white-haired man appeared at her side—'twas Ulf
Haldorssön.

The priest handed him the ax—he had borrowed it from Ulf—and
took the boy Tore from the nun, while he said:

" 'Tis past midnight already—none the less 'twere best you all came
with me to the church; I must get to the bottom of these doings this very
night."

None had any thought but to obey. But, when they were come out onto the road, one of the light-gray women's forms stepped aside from the
throng and turned off by the path through the wood. The priest called
out, bidding her come on with the others. Kristin's voice answered from
the darkness—she was some way along the track already:

"I cannot come, Sira Eiliv, till I have kept my promise—"

The priest and some others sprang after her. She was standing leaning against the fence when Sira Eiliv came up with her. He held up
the lanthorn—she was fearfully white of face, but, when he looked into
her eyes, he saw that she was not gone mad, as at first he had feared.

"Come home, Kristin," he said. "Tomorrow we will go thither with
you, some men—I myself will go with you—"

"I have given my word. I cannot go home, Sira Eiliv, till I have done
that which I vowed to do."

The priest stood silent a little. Then he said in a low voice:

"Mayhap you are right. Go then, sister, in God's name."

Like a shadow, Kristin melted away into the darkness, which swallowed up her gray form.

When Ulf Haldorssön came up by her side, she said—she spoke by
snatches, vehemently: "Go back—I asked not you to come with me—"

Ulf laughed low:

"Kristin, my lady—you have not learnt yet, I see, that some things
can be done without your asking or bidding—nor, though you have seen
it many a time, I ween—that you cannot always carry through alone all
that you take upon you. But this burden of yours *I* will help you to
carry."

The fir woods sighed above them, and the boom of the rollers away
on the beach came stronger or more faint as the gusts of wind rose or
died away. They walked in pitch darkness. After a while Ulf said:

"—I have borne you company before, Kristin, when you went out at night—methought 'twere but fitting I should go with you this time too—"

She breathed hard and heavily in the dark. Once she stumbled over somewhat, and Ulf caught her. After that he took her hand and led her. In a while the man heard that she was weeping as she went, and he asked her why she wept.

"I weep to think how good and faithful you have been to us, Ulf, all our days. What can I say—? I know well enough 'twas most for Erlend's sake, but almost I believe, kinsman—all our days you have judged of me more kindly than you had a right to, after what you first saw of my doings."

"I loved you, Kristin—no less than him." He was silent. Kristin felt that he was strongly stirred. Then he said:

"Therefore meseemed 'twas a hard errand, when I sailed out hither today—I came to bring you such tidings as I myself deemed it hard to utter. God strengthen you, Kristin!"

"Is it Skule?" asked Kristin softly in a little. "My son is dead?"

"No; Skule was well when I spoke with him yesterday—and now not many are dying in the town. But I had news from Tautra this morning—" He heard her sigh heavily once, but she said naught. A little after he said:

" 'Tis ten days now since they died. There are but four brothers left alive in the cloister, and the island is all but swept clean of folk."

They were come now where the wood ended. Over the flat stretch of land in front the roaring of the sea and the wind came to meet them. One spot out in the dark shone white—the surf in a little bay, by a steep, light-hued sand-hill.

"She dwells there," said Kristin. Ulf felt that long, convulsive shudders went through her frame. He gripped her hand hard:

"You took this on yourself. Remember that, and lose not your wits now."

Kristin said, in a strangely thin, clear voice, that the blast caught and bore away:

"Now will Björgulf's dream come true—I trust in God's and Mary's grace."

Ulf tried to see her face—but it was too dark. They were walking on the shore—in some places so narrow under the bluffs that now and then a wave washed right up to their feet. They tramped forward over tangled heaps of seaweed and great stones. After a while they were ware of a dark hump in against the sandy bank.

"Stay here," said Ulf, shortly. He went forward and thrust against the door—then she heard him hew at the withy bands and thrust at the door again. Then she was ware that the door had fallen inwards, and he had gone in through the black hole.

It was not a night of heavy storm. But it was so dark that Kristin could see naught, save the little flashes of foam that came and vanished

the same instant on the lifting sea, and the shining of the waves breaking along the shores of the bay—and against the sand-dune she could
make out that black hump. And it seemed to her that she was standing
in a cavern of night, and that it was the forecourt of death. The roll of
breaking waves and the hiss of their waters ebbing among the stones of
the beach kept time with the blood-waves surging through her, though
all the time it was as though her body must shiver in pieces, as a vessel
of wood falls apart in staves—her breast ached as if something-would
burst in it sunder from within; her head felt hollow and empty and as if
it were rifted, and the unceasing wind wrapped her round and swept
clean through her. She felt, with a strange listlessness, that she herself
had surely caught the sickness now—but 'twas as though she looked
that the darkness should be riven by a great light that would drown the
roar of the sea with its thunder, and that in the horror of this she should
perish. She drew up her hood, blown back from her head by the wind,
wrapped the black nun's cloak close about her, and stood with her hands
crossed beneath it—but it came not into her thought to pray; it was as
though her soul had more than enough to do to work a way forth from
its mansion trembling to its fall, and as though it tore at her breast with
every breath.

She saw a light flare up within the hut. A little after, Ulf Haldorssön
called out to her: "You must come hither and hold the light for me,
Kristin"—he was standing in the doorway—as she came, he reached her
a torch of some tarred wood.

A choking stench from the corpse met her, though the hut was so
draughty and the door was gone. With staring eyes and mouth half
open—and she felt her jaws and lips grow stiff the while and wooden—
she looked round for the dead. But there was naught to see but a long
bundle lying in the corner on the earthen floor, wrapped in Ulf's
cloak.

He had torn loose some long planks from somewhere and laid the
door upon them. Cursing his unhandy tools, he made notches and holes
with his light ax and dagger, and strove to lash the door fast to the
boards. Once or twice he looked up at her swiftly, and each time his
dark, gray-bearded face grew more hard set.

"I marvel much how you had thought to get through this piece of
work alone," he said as he wrought—then glanced up at her—but the
stiff, death-like face in the red gleam of the tar brand was set and unmoved as ever—'twas the face of a dead woman or of one distraught.
"Can you tell me that, Kristin?" he laughed harshly—but still 'twas of
no avail. "Methinks now were the time for you to say a prayer."

Stiff and lifeless as ever, she began to speak:

"*Pater noster qui es in cœlis. Adveniat regnum tuum. Fiat voluntas
tua sicut in cœlo et in terra—*" Then she came to a stop.

Ulf looked at her. Then he took up the prayer:

"*Panem nostrum quotidianum da nobis hodie—*" Swiftly and firmly
he said the Lord's prayer to the end, went over and made the sign of

the cross over the bundle—swiftly and firmly he took it up and bore it to the bier that he had fashioned.

"Go you in front," he said. "Maybe 'tis somewhat heavier, but you will smell the stench less there. Throw away the torch—we can see more surely without it—and see you miss not your footing, Kristin—for I had liefer not have to take a hold of this poor body any more."

The struggling pain in her breast seemed to rise in revolt when she got the bier poles set upon her shoulders; her chest *would* not bear up the weight. But she set her teeth hard. So long as they went along the beach, where the wind blew strong, but little of the corpse smell came to her.

"Here I must draw it up first, I trow, and the bier after," said Ulf, when they were come to the steep slope they had climbed down.

"We can go a little farther on," said Kristin; " 'tis there they come down with the seaweed sleighs—there 'tis not steep."

She spoke calmly, the man heard, and as in her right mind. And a fit of sweating and trembling took him, now it was over—he had deemed she must lose her wits that night.

They struggled forward along the sandy track that led across the flat toward the pine wood. The wind swept in freely here, but yet 'twas not as it had been down on the strand, and, as they drew farther and farther way from the roar of the beach, she felt it as a homefaring from the horror of utter darkness. Beside their path the ground showed lighter— 'twas a cornfield that there had been none to reap. The scent of it, and the sight of the beaten-down straw, welcomed her home again—and her eyes filled with tears of sisterly pity—out of her own desolate terror and woe she was coming home to fellowship with the living and the dead.

At times, when the wind was right behind, the fearful carrion stench enwrapped her wholly, but yet it was not so awful as when she stood in the hut—for the night was full of fresh, wet, cold, cleansing streams of air.

And much stronger than the feeling that she bore a thing of dread upon the bier behind her, was the thought that Ulf Haldorssön was there, guarding her back against the black and living horror they were leaving behind—and whose roar sounded fainter and more faint.

When they were come to the edge of the fir woods they were ware of lights: "They are coming to meet us," said Ulf.

Soon after, they were met by a whole throng of men bearing pine-root torches, a couple of lanthorns and a bier covered with a pall—Sira Eiliv was with them, and Kristin saw with wonder that in the troop were many of the men who had been that same night in the churchyard, and that many of them were weeping. When they lifted the burthen from her shoulders she was like to fall. Sira Eiliv would have caught a hold of her, but she said quickly:

"Touch me not—come not near me—I have the pest myself; I feel it—"

But none the less Sira Eiliv stayed her up with a hand below her arm: "Then be of good cheer, woman, remembering that our Lord has said:

'Inasmuch as ye have done it unto one of the least of these my brethren or sisters, ye have done it unto Me.'"

Kristin gazed at the priest. Then she looked across to where the men were shifting the body from the stretcher that Ulf had fashioned to the bier they had brought. Ulf's cloak slipped aside a little—the point of a worn-out shoe stuck out, dark wet in the light of the torches.

Kristin went across, kneeled between the poles of the bier, and kissed the shoe:

"God be gracious to you, sister—God give your soul joy in His light —God look in His mercy on us here in our darkness—"

Then it seemed to her as if it were life itself that tore its way from out of her—a grinding, inconceivable pain, as though something within her, rooted fast in every outermost fiber of her limbs, were riven loose. All that was within her breast was torn out—she felt her throat full of it, her mouth filled with blood that tasted of salt and foul copper—next moment her whole dress in front was a glistening wet blackness—Jesus! is there so much blood in an old woman? she thought.

Ulf Haldorssön lifted her in his arms and bore her away.

At the gate of the cloister the nuns, bearing lighted candles, came to meet the train of men. Already Kristin scarce had her full senses, but she felt that she was half borne, half helped, through the door, and was ware of the whitewashed, vaulted room, filled with the flickering light of yellow candle flames and red pine torches, and of the tramp of feet rolling like a sea—but to the dying woman the light was like the shimmer of her own dying life-flame, and the footfalls on the flags as the rushing of the rivers of death rising up to meet her.

Then the candlelight spread out into a wider space—she was once again under the open, murky sky—in the courtyard—the flickering light played upon a gray stone wall with heavy buttresses and high, tall windows—the church. She was borne in someone's arms—'twas Ulf again—but now he seemed to take on for her the semblance of all who had ever borne her up. When she laid her arms about his neck and pressed her cheek against his stubbly throat, it was as though she were a child again with her father, but also as though she were clasping a child to her own bosom— And behind his dark head there were red lights, and they seemed like the glow of the fire that nourishes all love.

—A little later she opened her eyes, and her mind was clear and calm. She was sitting, propped up, in a bed in the dormitory; a nun with a linen band over her lower face stood bending over her; she marked the smell of vinegar. It was Sister Agnes, she knew by her eyes and the little red wart she had on her forehead. And now 'twas day—clear, gray light was sifting into the room from the little glass window.

She had no great pain now—she was but wet through with sweat, woefully worn and weary, and her breast stung and smarted when she breathed. Greedily she drank down a soothing drink that Sister Agnes held to her mouth. But she was cold—

Kristin lay back on the pillows, and now she remembered all that had befallen the night before. The wild dream fantasies were wholly gone —her wits must have wandered a little, she understood—but it was good that she had gotten this thing done, had saved the little boy, and hindered these poor folk from burdening their souls with such a hideous deed. She knew she had need to be overjoyed—that *she* had been given grace to do this thing just before she was to die—and yet she could rejoice as it was meet she should; it was more a quiet content she felt, as when she lay in her bed at home at Jörundgaard, tired out after a day's work well done. And she must thank Ulf too—

—She had spoken his name, and he must have been sitting hidden, away by the door and have heard her, for here he came across the room and stood before her bed. She reached out her hand to him, and he took and pressed it in a firm clasp.

Suddenly the dying woman grew restless; her hands fumbled under the folds of linen about her throat.

"What is it, Kristin?" asked Ulf.

"The cross," she whispered, and painfully drew forth her father's gilded cross. It had come to her mind that yesterday she had promised to make a gift for the soul's weal of that poor Steinunn. She had not remembered then that she had no possessions on earth any more. She owned naught that she could give, saving this cross she had had of her father—and then her bridal ring. She wore that on her finger still.

She drew it off and gazed at it. It lay heavy in her hand; pure gold, set with great red stones. Erlend—she thought—and it came upon her now it were liker she should give this away—she knew not wherefore, but it seemed that she ought. She shut her eyes in pain and held it out to Ulf:

"To whom would you give this?" he asked, low, and as she did not answer: "Mean you I should give it to Skule—"

Kristin shook her head, her eyes tight closed.

"Steinunn—I promised—masses for her—"

She opened her eyes, and sought with them the ring where it lay in the smith's dusky palm. And her tears burst forth in a swift stream, for it seemed to her that never before had she understood to the full what it betokened. The life that ring had wed her to, that she had complained against, had murmured at, had raged at and defied—none the less she had loved it so, joyed in it so, both in good days and evil, that not one day had there been when 'twould not have seemed hard to give it back to God, nor one grief that she could have forgone without regret—

Ulf and the nun changed some words that she could not hear, and he went from the room. Kristin would have lifted her hand to dry her eyes, but she could not—the hand lay moveless on her breast. And now the pain within was sore; her hand felt so heavy, and it seemed as though the ring were on her finger still. Her head began to grow unclear again—she *must* see if it were true that the ring was gone, that she had not only dreamed she had given it away— And now too she began to grow uncertain—all that had befallen last night: the child in the

grave; the black sea with its swift little flashing waves; the corpse she
had borne—she knew not whether she had dreamed it all, or had been
awake. And she had no strength to open her eyes.

"Sister," said the nun, "you must not sleep now—Ulf has gone to fetch
a priest for you."

Kristin woke up fully again with a start, and fixed her eyes upon her
hand. The gold ring was gone, that was sure enough—but there was a
white, worn mark where it had been on her middle finger. It showed
forth quite clearly on the rough brown flesh—like a scar of thin, white
skin—she deemed she could make out two round spots on either side
where the rubies had been, and somewhat like a little mark, an M, where
the middle plate of gold had been pierced with the first letter of Mary
Virgin's holy name.

And the last clear thought that formed in her brain was that she
should die ere this mark had time to vanish—and she was glad. It
seemed to her to be a mystery that she could not fathom, but which she
knew most surely none the less, that God had held her fast in a covenant
made for her without her knowledge by a love poured out upon her
richly—and in despite of her self-will, in despite of her heavy, earth-
bound spirit, somewhat of this love had become *part* of her, had wrought
in her like sunlight in the earth, had brought forth increase which not
even the hottest flames of fleshly love nor its wildest bursts of wrath
could lay waste wholly. A handmaiden of God had she been—a wayward, unruly servant, oftenest an eye-servant in her prayers and faithless
in her heart, slothful and neglectful, impatient under correction, but
little constant in her deeds—yet had he held her fast in his service, and
under the glittering golden ring a mark had been set secretly upon her,
showing that she was his handmaid, owned by the Lord and King who
was now coming, borne by the priest's anointed hands, to give her freedom and salvation—

Soon after Sira Eiliv had given her the last oil and viaticum, Kristin
Lavransdatter again lost the knowledge of all around. She lay in the
sway of sore fits of blood-vomiting and burning fever, and the priest,
who stayed by her, told the nuns that 'twas like to go quickly with her.

—Once or twice the dying woman came so far to herself that she
knew this or the other face—Sira Eiliv's, the sister's—Lady Ragnhild
herself was there once, and Ulf too she saw. She strove to show she
knew them, and that she felt it was good they should be by her and
wished her well. But to those who stood around it seemed as she were
but fighting with her hands in the throes of death.

Once she saw Munan's face—her little son peeped in at her through a
half open door. Then he drew back his head, and the mother lay gazing
at the door—if perchance the boy might peep out again. But instead
came Lady Ragnhild and wiped her face with a wet cloth; and that too
was good—Then all things were lost in a dark red mist, and a roar, that
first grew fearsomely; but then it died away little by little, and the red

mist grew thinner and lighter, and at last it was like a fair morning mist ere the sun breaks through, and all sound ceased, and she knew that now she was dying—

Sira Eiliv and Ulf Haldorssön went out together from the room of death. In the doorway out to the cloister yard they stopped short—

Snow had fallen. None had marked it, of them who had sat by the woman while she fought with death. The white gleam from the steep church roof over against the two men was strangely dazzling; the tower shone white against the ash-gray sky. The snow lay so fine and white on all the window-moldings, and all buttresses and jutting points, against the church's walls of gray hewn stone. And it was as though the two men lingered because they were loth to break with their foot-prints the thin coverlid of new-fallen snow.

They drank in the air. After the noisome smell that ever fills the sick-room of one pest-stricken, it tasted sweet—cool, and as it were a little thin and empty; but it seemed as though this snow-fall must have washed the air clean of all poison and pestilence—it was as good as fresh spring water.

The bell in the tower began to ring again—the two looked up to where it swung behind the belfry bars. Small grains of snow loosened from the tower roof as it shook, rolled down, and grew to little balls—leaving spots where the black of the shingles showed through.

"This snow will scarce lie," said Ulf.

"No, 'twill melt, belike, before evening," answered the priest. There were pale golden rifts in the clouds, and a faint gleam of sunshine fell, as it were provingly, across the snow.

The men stood still. Then Ulf Haldorssön said low:

"I am thinking, Sira Eiliv—I will give some land to the church here—and a beaker of Lavrans Björgulfssön's that she gave me—to found a mass for her—and my foster-sons—and for him, Erlend, my kinsman—"

The priest answered as low, without looking at the man:

"—Meseems, too, you might think you had need to show your thank-fulness to Him who led you hither yestereven—you may be well content, I trow, that 'twas granted you to help her through this night."

"Ay, 'twas that I thought of," said Ulf Haldorssön. Then he laughed a little: "And now could I well-nigh repent me, priest, that I have been so meek a man—toward her!"

"Bootless to waste time in such vain regrets," answered the priest.

"What mean you—?"

"I mean, 'tis but a man's sins that it boots him to repent," said the priest.

"Why so?"

"For that none is good saving God only. And we can do no good save of Him. So it boots not to repent a good deed, Ulf, for the good you have done cannot be undone; though all the hills should crash in ruin, yet would it stand—"

"Ay, ay. These be things I understand not, my Sira. I am weary—"

"Ay—and hungry too you may well be—you must come with me to the kitchen-house, Ulf," said the priest.

"Thanks, but I have no stomach to meat," said Ulf Haldorssön.

"None the less must you go with me and eat," said Sira Eiliv—he laid his hand on Ulf's sleeve and led him along with him. They went out into the courtyard and down toward the kitchen-house. Unwittingly, both men trod as lightly and charily as they could upon the new-fallen snow.

JOHAN BOJER ·

The Shark

Johan Bojer was born in 1872 in Orkdal-soren. One of the most widely read Norwegian writers, Bojer has covered practically every major event and problem between 1890 and 1925 in his many novels, among which are *A Procession, The Power of a Lie, The Great Hunger, Last of the Vikings* and *The Prisoner Who Sang*. [From *The Great Hunger* by Johan Bojer; copyright 1918, 1919, 1947; used by permission of the author.]

FOR SHEER HAVOC, there is no gale like a good northwester, when it roars in, through the long winter evenings, driving the spindrift before it between the rocky walls of the fjord. It churns the water to a froth of rushing wave crests, while the boats along the beach are flung in somersaults up to the doors of the gray fisher huts, and solid old barn gangways are lifted and sent flying like unwieldy birds over the fields. "Mercy on us!" cry the maids, for it is milking-time, and they have to fight their way on hands and knees across the yard to the cowshed, dragging a lantern that *will* go out and a milk-pail that *won't* be held. And "Lord preserve us!" mutter the old wives seated round the stove within doors—and their thoughts are far away in the north with the Lofoten fishermen, out at sea, maybe, this very night.

But on a calm spring day, the fjord just steals in smooth and shining by ness and bay. And at low water there is a whole wonderland of strange little islands, sand-banks, and weed-fringed rocks left high and dry, with clear pools between, where bare-legged urchins splash about, and tiny flatfish as big as a halfpenny dart away to every side. The air is filled with a smell of salt sea-water and warm, wet beach-waste, and the sea-pie, see-sawing about on a big stone in the water, lifts his red beak cheerily sunwards and pipes: "Kluip, kluip! the spring has come!"

On just such a day, two boys of fourteen or thereabouts came hurrying out from one of the fishermen's huts down toward the beach. Boys are never so busy as when they are up to some piece of mischief, and evidently the pair had business of this sort in hand. Peer Tröen, fair-haired and sallow-faced, was pushing a wheelbarrow; his companion, Martin Bruvold, a dark youth with freckles, carried a tub. And both talked mysteriously in whispers, casting anxious glances out over the water.

Peer Tröen was, of course, the ringleader. That he always was: the forest fire of last year was laid at his door. And now he had made it clear to some of his friends that boys had just as much right to lay out deep-sea lines as men. All through the winter they had been kept at grown-up work, cutting peat and carrying wood; why should they be left now to fool about with the inshore fishing, and bring home nothing better than flounders and coal-fish and silly codlings? The big deep-sea line they were forbidden to touch—that was so—but the Lofoten fishery was at its height, and none of the men would be back till it was over. So the boys had baited up the line on the sly down at the boat-house the day before, and laid it out across the deepest part of the fjord.

Now the thing about a deep-sea line is that it may bring to the surface fish so big and so fearsome that the like has never been seen before. Yesterday, however, there had been trouble of a different sort. To their dismay, the boys had found that they had not sinkers enough to weight the shore end of the line; and it looked as if they might have to give up the whole thing. But Peer, ever ready, had hit on the novel idea of making one end fast to the trunk of a small fir growing at the outermost point of the ness, and carrying the line from there out over the open fjord. Then a stone at the farther end, and with the magic words, "Fie, fish!" it was paid out overboard, vanishing into the green depths. The deed was done. True, there were a couple of hooks dangling in mid-air at the shore end, between the tree and the water, and, while they might serve to catch an eider duck, or a guillemot, if anyone should chance to come rowing past in the dark and get hung up—why, the boys might find they had made a human catch. No wonder, then, that they whispered eagerly and hurried down to the boat.

"Here comes Peter Rönningen," cried Martin suddenly.

This was the third member of the crew, a lanky youth with whitish eyebrows and a foolish face. He stammered, and made a queer noise when he laughed: "Chee-hee-hee." Twice he had been turned down in the confirmation classes; after all, what was the use of learning lessons out of a book when nobody ever had patience to wait while he said them?

Together they ran the boat down to the water's edge, got it afloat, and scrambled in, with much waving of patched trouser legs. "Hi!" cried a voice up on the beach, "let me come too!"

"There's Klaus," said Martin. "Shall we take him along?"

"No," said Peter Rönningen.

"Oh yes, let's," said Peer.

Klaus Brock, the son of the district doctor, was a blue-eyed youngster in knickerbockers and a sailor blouse. He was playing truant, no doubt—Klaus had his lessons at home with a private tutor—and would certainly get a thrashing from his father when he got home.

"Hurry up," called Peer, getting out an oar. Klaus clambered in, and the white-straked four-oar surged across the bay, rocking a little as the boys pulled out of stroke. Martin was rowing at the bow, his eyes fixed on Peer, who sat in the stern in command with his eyes dancing, full of great things to be done. Martin, poor fellow, was half afraid already; he never could understand why Peer, who was to be a parson when he grew up, was always hitting upon things to do that were evidently sinful in the sight of the Lord.

Peer was a town boy, who had been put out to board with a fisherman in the village. His mother had been no better than she should be, so people said, but she was dead now, and the father at any rate must be a rich gentleman, for he sent the boy a present of ten whole crowns every Christmas, so that Peer always had money in his pocket. Naturally, then, he was looked up to by the other boys, and took the lead in all things as a chieftain by right.

The boat moved on past the gray rocks, the beach and the huts above it growing blue and faint in the distance. Up among the distant hills a red wooden farm-house on its white foundation wall stood out clear.

Here was the ness at last, and there stood the fir. Peer climbed up and loosed the end of the line, while the others leaned over the side, watching the cord where it vanished in the depths. What would it bring to light when it came up?

"Row!" ordered Peer, and began hauling in.

The boat was headed straight out across the fjord, and the long line with its trailing hooks hauled in and coiled up neatly in the bottom of a shallow tub. Peer's heart was beating. There came a tug—the first—and the faint shimmer of a fish deep down in the water. Pooh! only a big cod. Peer heaved it in with a careless swing over the gunwale. Next came a ling—a deep water fish at any rate this time. Then a tusk, and another, and another; these would please the women, being good eating, and perhaps make them hold their tongues when the men came home. Now the line jerks heavily; what is coming? A gray shadow comes in sight. "Here with the gaff!" cries Peer, and Peter throws it across to him. "What is it, what is it?" shriek the other three. "Steady! don't upset the boat; a catfish." A stroke of the gaff over the side, and a clumsy gray body is heaved into the boat, where it rolls about, hissing and biting at the bottom-boards and baler, the splinters crackling under its teeth. "Mind, mind!" cries Klaus—he was always nervous in a boat.

But Peer was hauling in again. They were nearly half-way across the fjord by now, and the line came up from mysterious depths, which no fisherman had ever sounded. The strain on Peer began to show in his looks; the others sat watching his face. "Is the line heavy?" asked Klaus. "Keep still, can't you?" put in Martin, glancing along the slanting line to where it vanished far below. Peer was still hauling. A sense of something uncanny seemed to be thrilling up into his hands from the deep sea. The feel of the line was strange. There was no great weight, not even the clean tug-tug of an ordinary fish; it was as if a giant hand were pulling gently, very gently, to draw him overboard and down into the depths. Then suddenly a violent jerk almost dragged him over the side.

"Look out! What is it?" cried the three together.

"Sit down in the boat," shouted Peer. And with the true fisherman's sense of discipline they obeyed.

Peer was gripping the line firmly with one hand, the other clutching one of the thwarts. "Have we another gaff?" he jerked out breathlessly.

"Here's one." Peter Rönningen pulled out a second iron-hooked cudgel.

"You take it, Martin, and stand by."

"But what—what is it?"

"Don't know what it is. But it's something big."

"Cut the line, and row for your lives!" wailed the doctor's son. Strange he should be such a coward at sea, a fellow who'd tackle a man twice his size on dry land.

Once more Peer was jerked almost overboard. He thought of the forest fire the year before—it would never do to have another such mishap on his shoulders. Suppose the great monster did come up and capsize them—they were ever so far from land. What a to-do there would be if they were all drowned, and it came out that it was his fault. Involuntarily he felt for his knife to cut the line—then thrust it back again, and went on hauling.

Here it comes—a great shadow heaving up through the water. The huge beast flings itself round, sending a flurry of bubbles to the surface. And there!—a gleam of white; a row of great white teeth on the underside. Aha! now he knows what it is! The Greenland shark is the fiercest monster of the northern seas, quite able to make short work of a few boys or so.

"Steady now, Martin—ready with the gaff."

The brute was wallowing on the surface now, the water boiling around him. His tail lashed the sea to foam, a big, pointed head showed up, squirming under the hook. "Now!" cried Peer, and two gaffs struck at the same moment, the boat heeled over, letting in a rush of water, and Klaus, dropping his oars, sprang into the bow, with a cry of "Jesus, save us!"

Next second a heavy body, big as a grown man, was heaved in over the gunwale, and two boys were all but shot out the other way. And now the fun began. The boys loosed their hold of the gaffs, and sprang apart to give the creature room. There it lay raging, the great black beast of prey, with its sharp threatening snout and wicked red eyes ablaze. The strong tail lashed out, hurling oars and balers overboard, the long teeth snapped at the bottom-boards and thwarts. Now and again it would leap high up in the air, only to fall back again, writhing furiously, hissing and spitting and frothing at the mouth, its red eyes glaring from one to another of the terrified captors, as if saying: "Come on—just a little nearer!"

Meanwhile, Martin Bruvold was in terror that the shark would smash the boat to pieces. He drew his knife and took a step forward—a flash in the air, and the steel went in deep between the back fins, sending up a spurt of blood. "Look out!" cried the others, but Martin had already sprung back out of reach of the black tail. And now the dance of death began anew. The knife was fixed to the grip in the creature's back; one gaff had buried its hook between the eyes, and another hung on the flank—the wooden shafts were flung this way and that at every bound, and the boat's frame shook and groaned under the blows.

"She'll smash the boat and we'll go to the bottom," cried Peer.

And now *his* knife flashed out and sent a stream of blood spouting from between the shoulders, but the blow cost him his foothold—and in a moment the two bodies were rolling over and over together in the bottom of the boat.

"Oh, Lord Jesus!" shrieked Klaus, clinging to the stempost. "She'll kill him! She'll kill him!"

Peer was half up now, on his knees, but as he reached out a hand to grasp the side, the brute's jaws seized on his arm. The boy's face was contorted with pain—another moment and the sharp teeth would have bitten through, when, swift as thought, Peter Rönningen dropped his oars and sent his knife straight in between the beast's eyes. The blade pierced through to the brain, and the grip of the teeth relaxed.

"C-c-cursed d-d-devil!" stammered Peter, as he scrambled back to his oars. Another moment, and Peer had dragged himself clear and was kneeling by the forward thwart, holding the ragged sleeve of his wounded arm, while the blood trickled through his fingers.

When at last they were pulling homeward, the little boat overloaded with the weight of the great carcase, all at once they stopped rowing.

"Where is Klaus?" asked Peer—for the doctor's son was gone from where he had sat, clinging to the stem.

"Why—there he is—in the bottom!"

There lay the big lout of fifteen, who already boasted of his love-affairs, learned German, and was to be a gentleman like his father—there he lay on the bottom-boards in the bow in a dead faint.

The others were frightened at first, but Peer, who was sitting washing his wounded arm, took a dipper full of water and flung it in the unconscious one's face. The next instant Klaus had started up sitting, caught wildly at the gunwale, and shrieked out:

"Cut the line, and row for your lives!"

A roar of laughter went up from the rest; they dropped their oars and sat doubled up and gasping. But on the beach, before going home, they agreed to say nothing about Klaus's fainting fit. And for weeks afterward the four scamps' exploit was the talk of the village, so that they felt there was not much fear of their getting the thrashing they deserved when the men came home.

SELMA LAGERLOF

The Outlaws

Selma Lagerlöf (1858–1940) was born in Varmland, the Swedish province with which most of her fiction deals. All of her tales and novels are based on the folk legends of Sweden. Among the most famous are *The Saga of Gosta Berling, The Wonderful Adventures of Nils, Marbacka* and *Memories of My Childhood*. [From *Invisible Links* by Selma Lagerlöf; copyright 1899 by Pauline Bancroft Flach; used by permission of Doubleday & Co., Inc.; translated by Pauline Bancroft Flach.]

A PEASANT WHO HAD murdered a monk took to the woods and was made an outlaw. He found there before him in the wilderness another outlaw, a fisherman from the outermost islands, who had been accused of stealing a herring net. They joined together, lived in a cave, set snares, sharpened darts, baked bread on a granite rock and guarded one another's lives. The peasant never left the woods, but the fisherman, who had not committed such an abominable crime, sometimes loaded game on his shoulders and stole down among men. There he got in exchange for black-cocks, for long-eared hares and fine-limbed red deer, milk and butter, arrowheads and clothes. These helped the outlaws to sustain life.

The cave where they lived was dug in the side of a hill. Broad stones and thorny sloe-bushes hid the entrance. Above it stood a thick growing pine-tree. At its roots was the vent-hole of the cave. The rising smoke filtered through the tree's thick branches and vanished into space. The men used to go to and from their dwelling-place, wading in the mountain stream, which ran down the hill. No one looked for their tracks under the merry, bubbling water.

At first they were hunted like wild beasts. The peasants gathered as if for a chase of bear or wolf. The wood was surrounded by men with bows and arrows. Men with spears went through it and left no dark crevice, no bushy thicket unexplored. While the noisy battue hunted through the wood, the outlaws lay in their dark hole, listening breathlessly, panting with terror. The fisherman held out a whole day, but he who had murdered was driven by unbearable fear out into the open, where he could see his enemy. He was seen and hunted, but it seemed to him seven times better than to lie still in helpless inactivity. He fled from his pursuers, slid down precipices, sprang over streams, climbed up perpendicular mountain walls. All latent strength and dexterity in him was called forth by the excitement of danger. His body became elastic like a steel spring, his foot made no false step, his hand never lost its hold, eye and ear were twice as sharp as usual. He understood what the leaves whispered and the rocks warned. When he had climbed up a precipice, he turned toward his pursuers, sending them gibes in biting rhyme. When the whistling darts whizzed by him, he caught them, swift as lightning, and hurled them down on his enemies. As he forced his way through whipping branches, something within him sang a song of triumph.

The bald mountain ridge ran through the wood and alone on its summit stood a lofty fir. The red-brown trunk was bare, but in the branching top rocked an eagle's nest. The fugitive was now so audaciously bold that he climbed up there, while his pursuers looked for him on the wooded slopes. There he sat twisting the young eaglets' necks, while the hunt passed by far below him. The male and female eagle, longing for revenge, swooped down on the ravisher. They fluttered before his face, they struck with their beaks at his eyes, they beat him with their wings and tore with their claws bleeding weals in his weather-beaten skin. Laughing, he fought with them. Standing upright in the shaking nest, he cut at them with his sharp knife and forgot in the pleasure of the play his danger and his pursuers. When he found time to look for them, they had gone by to some other part of the forest. No one had thought to look for their prey on the bald mountain-ridge. No one had raised his eyes to the clouds to see him practicing boyish tricks and sleep-walking feats while his life was in the greatest danger.

The man trembled when he found that he was saved. With shaking hands he caught at a support, giddy he measured the height to which he had climbed. And moaning with the fear of falling, afraid of the birds, afraid of being seen, afraid of everything, he slid down the trunk. He laid himself down on the ground, so as not to be seen, and dragged himself forward over the rocks until the underbrush covered him. There he hid himself under the young pine-tree's tangled branches. Weak and powerless, he sank down on the moss. A single man could have captured him.

Tord was the fisherman's name. He was not more than sixteen years old, but strong and bold. He had already lived a year in the woods.

The peasant's name was Berg, with the surname Rese. He was the tallest and the strongest man in the whole district, and moreover handsome and well-built. He was broad in the shoulders and slender in the waist. His hands were as well shaped as if he had never done any hard work. His hair was brown and his skin fair. After he had been some time in the woods he acquired in all ways a more formidable appearance. His eyes became piercing, his eyebrows grew bushy, and the muscles which knitted them lay finger thick above his nose. It showed now more plainly than before how the upper part of his athlete's brow projected over the lower. His lips closed more firmly than of old, his whole face was thinner, the hollows at the temples grew very deep, and his powerful jaw was much more prominent. His body was less well filled out but his muscles were as hard as steel. His hair grew suddenly gray.

Young Tord could never weary of looking at this man. He had

never before seen anything so beautiful and powerful. In his imagination he stood high as the forest, strong as the sea. He served him as a master and worshiped him as a god. It was a matter of course that Tord should carry the hunting spears, drag home the game, fetch the water and build the fire. Berg Rese accepted all his services, but almost never gave him a friendly word. He despised him because he was a thief.

The outlaws did not lead a robber's or brigand's life; they supported themselves by hunting and fishing. If Berg Rese had not murdered a holy man, the peasants would soon have ceased to pursue him and have left him in peace in the mountains. But they feared great disaster to the district, because he who had raised his hand against the servant of God was still unpunished. When Tord came down to the valley with game, they offered him riches and pardon for his own crime if he would show them the way to Berg Rese's hole, so that they might take him while he slept. But the boy always refused; and if anyone tried to sneak after him up to the wood, he led him so cleverly astray that he gave up the pursuit.

Once Berg asked him if the peasants had not tried to tempt him to betray him, and when he heard what they had offered him as a reward, he said scornfully that Tord had been foolish not to accept such a proposal.

Then Tord looked at him with a glance, the like of which Berg Rese had never before seen. Never had any beautiful woman in his youth, never had his wife or child looked so at him. "You are my lord, my elected master," said the glance. "Know that you may strike me and abuse me as you will, I am faithful notwithstanding."

After that Berg Rese paid more attention to the boy and noticed that he was bold to act but timid to speak. He had no fear of death. When the ponds were first frozen, or when the bogs were most dangerous in the spring, when the quagmires were hidden under richly flowering grasses and cloudberry, he took his way over them by choice. He seemed to feel the need of exposing himself to danger as a compensation for the storms and terrors of the ocean, which he had no longer to meet. At night he was afraid in the woods, and even in the middle of the day the darkest thickets or the wide-stretching roots of a fallen pine could frighten him. But when Berg Rese asked him about it, he was too shy to even answer.

Tord did not sleep near the fire, far in in the cave, on the bed which was made soft with moss and warm with skins, but every night, when Berg had fallen asleep, he crept out to the entrance and lay there on a rock. Berg discovered this, and although he well understood the reason, he asked what it meant. Tord would not explain. To escape any more questions, he did not lie at the door for two nights, but then he returned to his post.

One night, when the drifting snow whirled about the forest tops and drove into the thickest underbrush, the driving snowflakes found their way into the outlaws' cave. Tord, who lay just inside the entrance, was, when he waked in the morning, covered by a melting snowdrift. A few days later he fell ill. His lungs wheezed, and when they were expanded to take in air, he felt excruciating pain. He kept up as long as his strength held out, but when one evening he leaned down to blow the fire, he fell over and remained lying.

Berg Rese came to him and told him to go to his bed. Tord moaned with pain and could not raise himself. Berg then thrust his arms under him and carried him there. But he felt as if he had got hold of a slimy snake; he had a taste in the mouth as if he had eaten the unholy horse-flesh, it was so odious to him to touch the miserable thief.

He laid his own big bearskin over him and gave him water, more he could not do. Nor was it anything dangerous. Tord was soon well again. But through Berg's being obliged to do his tasks and to be his servant, they had come nearer to one another. Tord dared to talk to him when he sat in the cave in the evening and cut arrow shafts.

"You are of a good race, Berg," said Tord. "Your kinsmen are the richest in the valley. Your ancestors have served with kings and fought in their castles."

"They have oftener fought with bands of rebels and done the kings great injury," replied Berg Rese.

"Your ancestors gave great feasts at Christmas, and so did you, when you were at home. Hundreds of men and women could find a place to sit in your big house, which was already built before Saint Olof first gave the baptism here in Viken. You owned old silver vessels and great drinking-horns, which passed from man to man, filled with mead."

Again Berg Rese had to look at the boy. He sat up with his legs hanging out of the bed and his head resting on his hands, with which he at the same time held back the wild masses of hair which would fall over his eyes. His face had become pale and delicate from the ravages of sickness. In his eyes fever still burned. He smiled at the pictures he conjured up: at the adorned house, at the silver vessels, at the guests in gala array and at Berg Rese, sitting in the seat of honor in the hall of his ancestors. The peasant thought that no one had ever looked at him with such shining, admiring eyes, or thought him so magnificent, arrayed in his festival clothes, as that boy thought him in the torn skin dress.

He was both touched and provoked. That miserable thief had no right to admire him.

"Were there no feasts in your house?" he asked.

Tord laughed. "Out there on the rocks with father and mother! Father is a wrecker and mother is a witch. No one will come to us."

"Is your mother a witch?"

"She is," answered Tord, quite untroubled. "In stormy weather she rides out on a seal to meet the ships over which the waves are washing, and those who are carried overboard are hers."

"What does she do with them?" asked Berg.

"Oh, a witch always needs corpses. She makes ointments out of them, or perhaps she eats them. On moonlight nights she sits in the surf, where it is whitest, and the spray dashes over her. They say that she sits and searches for shipwrecked children's fingers and eyes."

"That is awful," said Berg.

The boy answered with infinite assurance: "That would be awful in others, but not in witches. They have to do so."

Berg Rese found that he had here come upon a new way of regarding the world and things.

"Do thieves have to steal, as witches have to use witchcraft?" he asked sharply.

"Yes, of course," answered the boy; "everyone has to do what he is destined to do." But then he added, with a cautious smile: "There are thieves also who have never stolen."

"Say out what you mean," said Berg.

The boy continued with his mysterious smile, proud at being an unsolvable riddle: "It is like speaking of birds who do not fly, to talk of thieves who do not steal."

Berg Rese pretended to be stupid in order to find out what he wanted. "No one can be called a thief without having stolen," he said.

"No; but," said the boy, and pressed his lips together as if to keep in the words, "but if someone had a father who stole," he hinted after a while.

"One inherits money and lands," replied Berg Rese, "but no one bears the name of thief if he has not himself earned it."

Tord laughed quietly. "But if somebody has a mother who begs and prays him to take his father's crime on him. But if such a one cheats the hangman and escapes to the woods. But if someone is made an outlaw for a fish-net which he has never seen."

Berg Rese struck the stone table with his clenched fist. He was angry. This fair young man had thrown away his whole life. He could never win love, nor riches, nor esteem after that. The wretched striving for food and clothes was all which was left him. And the fool had let him, Berg Rese, go on despising one who was innocent. He rebuked him with stern words, but Tord was not even as afraid as a sick child is of its mother, when she chides it because it has caught cold by wading in the spring brooks.

On one of the broad, wooded mountains lay a dark tarn. It was square, with as straight shores and as sharp corners as if it had been cut by the hand of man. On three sides it was surrounded by steep cliffs, on which pines clung with roots as thick as a man's arm. Down by the pool, where the earth had been gradually washed away, their roots stood up out of the water, bare and crooked and wonderfully twisted about one another. It was like an infinite number of serpents which had wanted all at the same time to crawl up out of the pool but had got entangled in one another and been held fast. Or it was like a mass of blackened skeletons of drowned giants which the pool wanted to throw up on the land. Arms and legs writhed about one another, the long fingers dug deep into the very cliff to get a hold, the mighty ribs formed arches, which held up primeval trees. It had happened, however, that the iron arms, the steel-like fingers with which the pines held themselves fast, had given way, and a pine had been borne by a mighty north wind from the top of the cliff down into the pool. It had burrowed deep down into the muddy bottom with its top and now stood there. The smaller fish had a good place of refuge among its branches, but the roots stuck up above the water like a many-armed monster and contributed to make the pool awful and terrifying.

On the tarn's fourth side the cliff sank down. There a little foaming stream carried away its waters. Before this stream could find the only possible way, it had tried to get out between stones and tufts, and had by so doing made a little world of islands, some no bigger than a little hillock, others covered with trees.

Here where the encircling cliffs did not shut out all the sun, leafy trees flourished. Here stood thirsty, gray-green alders and smooth-leaved willows. The birch-tree grew there as it does everywhere where it is trying to crowd out the pine woods, and the wild cherry and the mountain ash, those two which edge the forest pastures, filling them with fragrance and adorning them with beauty.

Here at the outlet there was a forest of reeds as high as a man, which made the sunlight fall green on the water just as it falls on the moss in the real forest. Among the reeds there were open places; small, round pools, and water-lilies were floating there. The tall stalks looked down with mild seriousness on those sensitive beauties, who discontentedly shut their white petals and yellow stamens in a hard, leather-like sheath as soon as the sun ceased to show itself.

One sunshiny day the outlaws came to this tarn to fish. They waded out to a couple of big stones in the midst of the reed forest and sat there and threw out bait for the big, green-striped pickerel that lay and slept near the surface of the water.

These men, who were always wandering in the woods and the mountains, had, without their knowing it themselves, come under nature's rule as much as the plants and the animals. When the sun shone, they were open-hearted and brave, but in the evening, as soon as the sun had disappeared, they became silent; and the night, which seemed to them much greater and more powerful than the day, made them anxious and helpless. Now the green light, which slanted in between the rushes and colored the water with brown and dark-green streaked with gold, affected their mood until they were ready for any miracle. Every outlook was shut off. Sometimes the reeds rocked in an imperceptible wind, their stalks rustled, and the long, ribbon-like leaves fluttered against their faces. They sat in gray skins on the gray stones. The shadows in the skins repeated the shadows of the weather-beaten, mossy stone. Each saw his companion in his silence and immovability change into a stone image. But in among the rushes swam mighty fishes with rainbow-colored backs. When the men threw out their hooks and saw the circles spreading among the reeds, it seemed as if the motion grew stronger and stronger, until they perceived that it was not caused only by their cast. A sea-nymph, half human, half a shining fish, lay and slept on the surface of the water. She lay on her back with her whole body under water. The waves so nearly covered her that they had not noticed her before. It was her breathing that caused the motion of the waves. But there was nothing strange in her lying there, and when the next instant she was gone, they were not sure that she had not been only an illusion.

The green light entered through the eyes into the brain like a gentle intoxication. The men sat and stared with dulled thoughts, seeing visions among the reeds, of which they did not dare to tell one another. Their catch was poor. The day was devoted to dreams and apparitions.

The stroke of oars was heard among the rushes, and they started up as from sleep. The next moment a flat-bottomed boat appeared, heavy, hollowed out with no skill and with oars as small as sticks. A young girl, who had been picking water-lilies, rowed it. She had dark-brown hair, gathered in great braids, and big dark eyes; otherwise she was strangely pale. But her paleness toned to pink and not to gray. Her cheeks had no higher color than the rest of her face, the lips had hardly enough. She wore a white linen shirt and a leather belt with a gold buckle. Her skirt was blue with a red hem. She rowed by the outlaws without seeing them. They kept breathlessly still, but not for fear of being seen, but only to be able to really see her. As soon as she had gone they were as if changed from stone images to living beings. Smiling, they looked at one another.

"She was white like the water-lilies," said one. "Her eyes were as dark as the water there under the pine-roots."

They were so excited that they wanted to laugh, really laugh as no one had ever laughed by that pool, till the cliffs thundered with echoes and the roots of the pines loosened with fright.

"Did you think she was pretty?" asked Berg Rese.

"Oh, I do not know, I saw her for such a short time. Perhaps she was."

"I do not believe you dared to look at her. You thought that it was a mermaid."

And they were again shaken by the same extravagant merriment.

Tord had once as a child seen a drowned man. He had found the body on the shore on a summer day and had not been at all afraid, but at night he had dreamed terrible dreams. He saw a sea, where every wave rolled a dead man to his feet. He saw, too, that all the islands were covered with drowned men, who were dead and belonged to the sea, but who still could speak and move and threaten him with withered white hands.

It was so with him now. The girl whom he had seen among the rushes came back in his dreams. He met her out in the open pool, where the sunlight fell even greener than among the rushes, and he had time to see that she was beautiful. He dreamed that he had crept up on the big pine-root in the middle of the dark tarn, but the pine swayed and rocked so that sometimes he was quite under water. Then she came forward on the little islands. She stood under the red mountain ashes and laughed at him. In the last dream-vision he had come so far that she kissed him. It was already morning, and he heard that Berg Rese had got up, but he obstinately shut his eyes to be able to go on with his dream. When he awoke, he was as though dizzy and stunned by what had happened to him in the night. He thought much more now of the girl than he had done the day before.

Toward night he happened to ask Berg Rese if he knew her name.

Berg looked at him inquiringly. "Perhaps it is best for you to hear it," he said. "She is Unn. We are cousins."

Tord then knew that it was for that pale girl's sake Berg Rese wandered an outlaw in forest and mountain. Tord tried to remember what he knew of her. Unn was the daughter of a rich peasant. Her mother was dead, so that she managed her father's house. This she liked, for she was fond of her own way and she had no wish to be married.

Unn and Berg Rese were the children of brothers, and it had long been said that Berg preferred to sit with Unn and her maids and jest with them than to work on his own lands. When the great Christmas feast was celebrated at his house, his wife had invited a monk from Draksmark, for she wanted him to remonstrate with Berg, because he was forgetting her for another woman. This monk was hateful to Berg and to many on account of his appearance. He was very fat and quite white. The ring of hair about his bald head, the eyebrows above his watery eyes, his face, his hands and his whole cloak, everything was white. Many found it hard to endure his looks.

At the banquet table, in the hearing of all the guests, this monk now said, for he was fearless and thought that his words would have more effect if they were heard by many, "People are in the habit of saying that the cuckoo is the worst of birds because he does not rear his young in his own nest, but here sits a man who does not provide for his home and his children, but seeks his pleasure with a strange woman. Him will I call the worst of men."—Unn then rose up. "That, Berg, is said to you and me," she said. "Never have I been so insulted, and my father is not here either." She had wished to go, but Berg sprang after her. "Do not move!" she said. "I will never see you again." He caught up with her in the hall and asked her what he should do to make her stay. She had answered with flashing eyes that he must know that best himself. Then Berg went in and killed the monk.

Berg and Tord were busy with the same thoughts, for after a while

Berg said: "You should have seen her, Unn, when the white monk fell. The mistress of the house gathered the small children about her and cursed her. She turned their faces toward her, that they might forever remember her who had made their father a murderer. But Unn stood calm and so beautiful that the men trembled. She thanked me for the deed and told me to fly to the woods. She bade me not to be robber, and not to use the knife until I could do it for an equally just cause."

"Your deed had been to her honor," said Tord.

Berg Rese noticed again what had astonished him before in the boy. He was like a heathen, worse than a heathen; he never condemned what was wrong. He felt no responsibility. That which must be, was. He knew of God and Christ and the saints, but only by name, as one knows the gods of foreign lands. The ghosts of the rocks were his gods. His mother, wise in witchcraft, had taught him to believe in the spirits of the dead.

Then Berg Rese undertook a task which was as foolish as to twist a rope about his own neck. He set before those ignorant eyes the great God, the Lord of justice, the Avenger of misdeeds, who casts the wicked into places of everlasting torment. And he taught him to love Christ and his mother and the holy men and women, who with lifted hands kneeled before God's throne to avert the wrath of the great Avenger from the hosts of sinners. He taught him all that men do to appease God's wrath. He showed him the crowds of pilgrims making pilgrimages to holy places, the flight of self-torturing penitents and monks from a worldly life.

As he spoke, the boy became more eager and more pale, his eyes grew large as if for terrible visions. Berg Rese wished to stop, but thoughts streamed to him, and he went on speaking. The night sank down over them, the black forest night, when the owls hoot. God came so near to them that they saw his throne darken the stars, and the chastising angels sank down to the tops of the trees. And under them the fires of Hell flamed up to the earth's crust, eagerly licking that shaking place of refuge for the sorrowing races of men.

The autumn had come with a heavy storm. Tord went alone in the woods to see after the snares and traps. Berg Rese sat at home to mend his clothes. Tord's way led in a broad path up a wooded height.

Every gust carried the dry leaves in a rustling whirl up the path. Time after time. Tord thought that someone went behind him. He often looked round. Sometimes he stopped to listen, but he understood that it was the leaves and the wind, and went on. As soon as he started on again, he heard someone come dancing on silken foot up the slope. Small feet came tripping. Elves and fairies played behind him. When he turned round, there was no one, always no one. He shook his fists at the rustling leaves and went on.

They did not grow silent for that, but they took another tone. They began to hiss and to pant behind him. A big viper came gliding. Its tongue dripping venom hung far out of its mouth, and its bright body shone against the withered leaves. Beside the snake pattered a wolf, a big, gaunt monster, who was ready to seize fast in his throat when the snake had twisted about his feet and bitten him in the heel. Sometimes they were both silent, as if to approach him unperceived, but they soon betrayed themselves by hissing and panting, and sometimes the wolf's claws rung against a stone. Involuntarily Tord walked quicker and quicker, but the creatures hastened after him. When he felt that they were only two steps distant and were preparing to strike, he turned. There was nothing there, and he had known it the whole time.

He sat down on a stone to rest. Then the dry leaves played about his feet as if to amuse him. All the leaves of the forest were there: small, light yellow birch leaves, red speckled mountain ash, the elm's dry, dark-brown leaves, the aspen's tough light red, and the willow's yellow green. Transformed and withered, scarred and torn were they, and much unlike the downy, light green, delicately shaped leaves, which a few months ago had rolled out of their buds.

"Sinners," said the boy, "sinners, nothing is pure in God's eyes. The flame of his wrath has already reached you."

When he resumed his wandering, he saw the forest under him bend before the storm like a heaving sea, but in the path it was calm. But he heard what he did not feel. The woods were full of voices.

He heard whisperings, wailing songs, coarse threats, thundering oaths. There was laughter and laments, there was the noise of many people. That which hounded and pursued, which rustled and hissed, which seemed to be something and still was nothing, gave him wild thoughts. He felt again the anguish of death, as when he lay on the floor in his den and the peasants hunted him through the wood. He heard again the crashing of branches, the people's heavy tread, the ring of weapons, the resounding cries, the wild, bloodthirsty noise, which followed the crowd.

But it was not only that which he heard in the storm. There was something else, something still more terrible, voices which he could not interpret, a confusion of voices, which seemed to him to speak in foreign tongues. He had heard mightier storms than this whistle through the rigging, but never before had he heard the wind play on such a many-voiced harp. Each tree had its own voice; the pine did not murmur like the aspen nor the poplar like the mountain ash. Every hole had its note, every cliff's sounding echo its own ring. And the noise of the brooks and the cry of foxes mingled with the marvelous forest storm. But all that he could interpret; there were other strange sounds. It was those which made him begin to scream and scoff and groan in emulation with the storm.

He had always been afraid when he was alone in the darkness of the forest. He liked the open sea and the bare rocks. Spirits and phantoms crept about among the trees.

Suddenly he heard who it was who spoke in the storm. It was God, the great Avenger, the God of justice. He was hunting him for the sake of his comrade. He demanded that he should deliver up the murderer to His vengeance.

Then Tord began to speak in the midst of the storm. He told God what he had wished to do, but had not been able. He had wished to speak to Berg Rese and to beg him to make his peace with God, but he had been too shy. Bashfulness had made him dumb. "When I heard that the earth was ruled by a just God," he cried, "I understood that he was a lost man. I have lain and wept for my friend many long nights. I knew that God would find him out, wherever he might hide. But I could not speak, nor teach him to understand. I was speechless, because I loved him so much. Ask not that I shall speak to him, ask not that the sea shall rise up against the mountain."

He was silent, and in the storm the deep voice, which had been the voice of God for him, ceased. It was suddenly calm, with a sharp sun and a splashing as of oars and a gentle rustle as of stiff rushes. These sounds brought Unn's image before him.—The outlaw cannot have anything, not riches, nor women, nor the esteem of men.—If he should betray Berg, he would be taken under the protection of the law.—But Unn must love Berg, after what he had done for her. There was no way out of it all.

When the storm increased, he heard again steps behind him and sometimes a breathless panting. Now he did not dare to look back, for he knew that the white monk went behind him. He came from the feast at Berg Rese's house, drenched with blood, with a gaping axe-wound in his forehead. And he whispered: "Denounce him, betray him, save his soul. Leave his body to the pyre, that his soul may be spared. Leave him to the slow torture of the rack, that his soul may have time to repent."

Tord ran. All this fright of what was nothing in itself grew, when it so continually played on the soul, to an unspeakable terror. He wished to escape from it all. As he began to run, again thundered that deep, terrible voice, which was God's. God himself hunted him with alarms, that he should give up the murderer. Berg Rese's crime seemed more detestable than ever to him. An unarmed man had been murdered, a man of God pierced with shining steel. It was like a defiance of the Lord of the world. And the murderer dared to live! He rejoiced in the sun's light and in the fruits of the earth as if the Almighty's arm were too short to reach him.

He stopped, clenched his fists and howled out a threat. Then he ran like a madman from the wood down to the valley.

Tord hardly needed to tell his errand; instantly ten peasants were ready to follow him. It was decided that Tord should go alone up to the cave, so that Berg's suspicions should not be aroused. But where he went he should scatter peas, so that the peasants could find the way.

When Tord came to the cave, the outlaw sat on the stone bench and sewed. The fire gave hardly any light, and the work seemed to go badly. The boy's heart swelled with pity. The splendid Berg Rese seemed to him poor and unhappy. And the only thing he possessed, his life, should be taken from him. Tord began to weep.

"What is it?" asked Berg. "Are you ill? Have you been frightened?"

Then for the first time Tord spoke of his fear. "It was terrible in the wood. I heard ghosts and saw specters. I saw white monks."

" 'Sdeath, boy!"

"They crowded round me all the way up Broad mountain. I ran, but they followed after and sang. Can I never be rid of the sound? What have I to do with them? I think that they could go to one who needed it more."

"Are you mad tonight, Tord?"

Tord talked, hardly knowing what words he used. He was free from all shyness. The words streamed from his lips.

"They are all white monks, white, pale as death. They all have blood on their cloaks. They drag their hoods down over their brows, but still the wound shines from under; the big, red, gaping wound from the blow of the axe."

"The big, red, gaping wound from the blow of the axe?"

"Is it I who perhaps have struck it? Why shall I see it?"

"The saints only know, Tord," said Berg Rese, pale and with terrible earnestness, "what it means that you see a wound from an axe. I killed the monk with a couple of knife-thrusts."

Tord stood trembling before Berg and wrung his hands. "They demand you of me! They want to force me to betray you!"

"Who? The monks?"

"They, yes, the monks. They show me visions. They show me her, Unn. They show me the shining, sunny sea. They show me the fishermen's camping-ground, where there is dancing and merry-making. I close my eyes, but still I see. 'Leave me in peace,' I say. 'My friend has murdered, but he is not bad. Let me be, and I will talk to him, so that he repents and atones. He shall confess his sin and go to Christ's grave. We will both go together to the places which are so holy that all sin is taken away from him who draws near them.' "

"What do the monks answer?" asked Berg. "They want to have me saved. They want to have me on the rack and wheel."

"Shall I betray my dearest friend, I ask them," continued Tord. "He is my world. He has saved me from the bear that had his paw on my throat. We have been cold together and suffered every want together. He has spread his bear-skin over me when I was sick. I have carried wood and water for him; I have watched over him while he slept; I have fooled his enemies. Why do they think that I am one who will betray a friend? My friend will soon of his own accord go to the priest and confess, then we will go together to the land of atonement."

Berg listened earnestly, his eyes sharply searching Tord's face. "You shall go to the priest and tell him the truth," he said. "You need to be among people."

"Does that help me if I go alone? For your sin, Death and all his specters follow me. Do you not see how I shudder at you? You have lifted your hand against God himself. No crime is like yours. I think that I must rejoice when I see you on rack and wheel. It is well for him who can receive his punishment in this world and escapes the wrath to come. Why did you tell me of the just God? You compel me to betray you. Save me from that sin. Go to the priest." And he fell on his knees before Berg.

The murderer laid his hand on his head and looked at him. He was measuring his sin against his friend's anguish, and it grew big and terrible before his soul. He saw himself at variance with the Will which rules the world. Repentance entered his heart.

"Woe to me that I have done what I have done," he said. "That which awaits me is too hard to meet voluntarily. If I give myself up to the priests, they will torture me for hours; they will roast me with slow fires. And is not this life of misery, which we lead in fear and want, penance enough? Have I not lost lands and home? Do I not live parted from friends and everything which makes a man's happiness? What more is required?"

When he spoke so, Tord sprang up wild with terror. "Can you repent?" he cried. "Can my words move your heart? Then come instantly! How could I believe that! Let us escape! There is still time."

Berg Rese sprang up, he too. "You have done it, then—"

"Yes, yes, yes! I have betrayed you! But come quickly! Come, as you can repent! They will let us go. We shall escape them!"

The murderer bent down to the floor, where the battle-axe of his ancestors lay at his feet. "You son of a thief!" he said, hissing out the words, "I have trusted you and loved you."

But when Tord saw him bend for the axe, he knew that it was now a question of his own life. He snatched his own axe from his belt and struck at Berg before he had time to raise himself. The edge cut through the whistling air and sank in the bent head. Berg Rese fell head foremost to the floor, his body rolled after. Blood and brains spouted out, the axe fell from the wound. In the matted hair Tord saw a big, red, gaping hole from the blow of an axe.

The peasants came rushing in. They rejoiced and praised the deed. "You will win by this," they said to Tord.

Tord looked down at his hands as if he saw there the fetters with which he had been dragged forward to kill him he loved. They were forged from nothing. Of the rushes' green light, of the play of the shadows, of the song of the storm, of the rustling of the leaves, of dreams were they created. And he said aloud: "God is great."

But again the old thought came to him. He fell on his knees beside the body and put his arm under his head.

"Do him no harm," he said. "He repents; he is going to the Holy

Sepulcher. He is not dead, he is not a prisoner. We were just ready to go when he fell. The white monk did not want him to repent, but God, the God of justice, loves repentance."

He lay beside the body, talked to it, wept and begged the dead man to awake. The peasants arranged a bier. They wished to carry the peasant's body down to his house. They had respect for the dead and spoke softly in his presence. When they lifted him up on the bier, Tord rose, shook the hair back from his face, and said with a voice which shook with sobs—

"Say to Unn, who made Berg Rese a murderer, that he was killed by Tord the fisherman, whose father is a wrecker and whose mother is a witch, because he taught him that the foundation of the world is justice."

SIGFRID SIWERTZ

In Spite of Everything

Sigfrid Siwertz, a member of the Swedish Academy, was born in 1882 in Stockholm. He has been most successful with short stories, many of which are based on his experiences in the city. His best known collections are *Old People* and *A Handful of Feathers*. He also won critical approval for his novel *Downstream*. [From *Sweden's Best Stories;* used by permission of The American Scandinavian Foundation.]

HE WAS TO BE A FATHER, he who could hardly look after himself. Down in the little railway park, where he had gone to meet her, she had suddenly told him. A locomotive had been staring at him with its red-and-yellow eye and had broken the brittle silence between their words with its panting groans. And he had stood dumbfounded before his first experience involving life and death. But behind his anxiety was a faint, tremulous intimation of days when the child should be his joy and consolation.

Now they were sitting in his student room in the Quarter. He spoke a long while in order to reassure her, but he himself noticed how vague and helpless were his words. Agda sat looking out of the window at the neighboring poplars and their shadows on the old mossy tile roof. A high gable which faced them obliquely was illuminated with a dead, unnatural light, and the reflection of the crescent moon gleamed pallidly up from a pool of water in the street. There was a deathly silence, and he drew nearer to her. Was she weeping? No. Suddenly her look seemed strange to him. She had become another being in the light of this new event. Yes, it was another woman who sat at his side, another woman whom he must seek to know and conquer.

He pulled down the curtains and lighted his lamp. How beautiful she was with the heavy mass of her bright hair knotted low and her neck slightly bent over the edge of her bodice. He stood before her and regarded her searchingly.

"Have you suffered much for my sake? I don't seem to recognize your eyes . . . Say something!"

She smiled absently.

"You are so young and nice, Erik, and this is such a warm, sad little room . . . I'm certainly a different sort from you . . . I don't feel a bit badly—here."

She began to loosen her bodice and shoe-laces. The strange woman began to loosen her bodice and shoe-laces in his room! Erik stole close to her and took possession of her with eyes and hands, and she caressed him in return. But there was pity in her caresses.

He kindled the fire to a big blaze and put out the lamp. She took off her last white garment and stood softly bowed with a warm restless light playing over her naked form. Erik caught his breath . . . he had never seen her before. She was remorselessly beautiful without a shadow of shame. No one could believe that this girl would be a mother.

She ran her hands gently up to her hair with a gesture that raised her breast and gave her body a prouder attitude. She let the loosened tresses glide through her fingers.

"Should you be vexed if I went away from you?"

There was something arrogant in her tone. Again he stole close to her. She accepted him in silence, her eyes closed, near yet remote. Her hands alone spoke.

In the following days Erik found in Agda a carelessness, a gaiety even, which he little expected. He felt that he was on uncertain ground, and had a dim foreboding that he was destined to suffer. He could not succeed in persuading himself that the change in her came from the fact that there were now two lives speaking through her mouth.

One evening he sought her at the office, but it was already closed, and her window was dark. Afraid of his solitary room, he dragged himself about, weary and helpless as a child.

Next morning Agda came up to his room, flushed and hurried. She stood in the middle of the floor with her hat and coat on, adventure gleaming in her eyes.

"I'm going to America!"

Erik did not understand.

"America? But the child—where will you—?"

"As soon as I guessed how it was with me, I wrote a letter to some relatives in Chicago. They are rich and childless. I told them everything and asked if I mightn't come to them; I thought they might adopt the child. The answer has made me so happy—both for your sake and for mine. They had been wanting to adopt a child. They made only one condition—that the child should never know anything of its real father and mother."

She had been talking in feverish haste, and now was suddenly silent with a great questioning look at him.

Erik felt no suffering as yet. He thought he knew what she wanted to hear.

"You mustn't go—you should have told me everything right away. We can manage somehow here at home, get married as soon as possible—"

She wasn't listening. He felt that his voice had begun to tremble.

"Because I have a right in the child too, don't you see?—a right—"

She stood there, hard, unconcerned.

"Are you so sure it's yours?"

It wasn't badness—she was only a child; she was confused by motherhood. She did not realize what she was saying!

He started forward, caught her behind the neck with both hands, and kissed her neck and lips.

"You mustn't go, you mustn't!"

She let him keep hold of her. "Everything is packed, but I'm not going till day after tomorrow. We can write."

Finally he understood and let go of her, his face pale with impotent grief.

Then the door shut behind her, and she was gone without his asking where they should meet to say good by.

She was going away with his child—there was no way to stop her. He was helpless, helpless.

Erik tried to stay where he was and reflect, but the room stifled him, and he rushed out. He went up one street and down another without seeing or hearing, while he fought a silent, bitter fight with his pride. At length he came to her stairs, but his heart thumped, and his breathing hurt so that he had to take hold of the door jamb so as not to fall. All the letters of her visiting card danced before his eyes. No, he couldn't ring.

On the way home he saw Agda's large black hat, but he shrank into a side street so as not to encounter her. He stopped at a cigar store window to see her go by . . . First came a boy with a basket on his arm, then an old woman, then a dog that cast a look up along the alley, sniffed at the corner, and slouched off with his tail between his legs. Now she would come. No, she did not come, she must have turned off.

In the evening he heard her step in the corridor. There was a knock; he did not stir. There was another knock.

"I know you're in—there was a light in your window. Open there!"

He sprang up and turned the key. She was quite calm, there was an atmosphere of coolness about her. She gave him her mouth to kiss, and smiled when he drew back.

"Think how it will be when I come back after it's all over!"

He knew she did not in the least expect to come back, but none the less felt a little comforted against his will. She drew him softly to her.

"Oh, how I long to see the ocean and the big cities over there!"

"But think a little of me and the child, the child . . . You're going to utter strangers!"

"Strangers, strangers—that's just what I want. I can't go around here with a child. And then it's so stifling in the old familiar surroundings. I hate this town . . . Though I'm still ever so fond of you, you and your quiet room."

"How can you go away like this then?"

"I have to!" Adventure glittered in her eyes. "It seems to be easier to go if one knows there's somebody at home who's sorry."

"I have never known you. I can't understand you." Erik had a sudden intimation of what it was like to go into oneself in order to comprehend another person.

Agda clasped her hands over her knee.

"We're so different . . . I often couldn't understand you at all. I remember one evening by the window here; the sky outside was gray and heavy . . . you said something about quietness, love for what is near, poverty—it sounded so strange—beautiful but strange."

A thought flitted across her countenance, but vanished before a smile. It seemed to him like a grimace. Understand, understand! What does a woman understand? If she understood, how could one draw down the curtains on the stars and luxuriate with hands and limbs in her softness, forgetting one's thoughts?

Erik felt himself for a moment cold, malicious, and a trifle emancipated; but as soon as she was gone, and he did not hear her speak, she regained her power over him.

Two days later he followed her down to the Stockholm Central Station. The train set off; he had a glimpse of her at the window waving her handkerchief slightly, and she was gone. He stood alone in the gray empty hall of the station till people began to stare at him. Then he sank down on a chair in the waiting-room. The loneliness was so thick and heavy about him that he could not so much as stir a hand.

It was but slowly Erik could teach himself to forgive and overcome.

Long months passed before he could remember without deep pain and oppression the tranquil charm of her gait and gestures, the bend of her neck, her smile as she let the black skirt glide down from her hips, all the thousand details which in mysterious combination fed his love and came to life within him when he whispered her name. There were times when he felt all the hot agony of life, when the strong imperative desire which awoke in him lay clutching helplessly at emptiness. There were other times when life shrank far away and spread great expanses of cold and darkness between him and her. Yes, everything seemed dead, sticky, loathsome now, since flower and fruit had been torn from him; and he could lose even the diffident pride in his own suffering which is our last resource in misfortune . . .

But one morning when he awoke from his degradation and found that the daylight and his books once more attracted him, he felt also that he had become another man.

He went out in the late winter dawn.

The heavens hung dark and gray above the spires of the cathedral, stillness lay and dreamed in the treetops, the air was as though filled with pitying kindness and cool, chaste caresses. Far away across the plain the sky was a mild and sad symphonic prelude in violet-gray and transparent blue-green, where the stars had just dissolved . . .

He walked on. The high, wing-shaped walls of the Carolina * seemed to freeze under their thin gray hue. The frozen berries on the wayside aspens burned a strange red against all this white and gray.

He was conscious of a silent thankfulness. There was something new in him, something which was above both happiness and grief; his days would now pass like a cool wind.

Yes, there was now something in him which was unassailable; in spite of all casual suffering, unrest, insensibility, a space deep within him would radiate with tranquil light. And he divined without fear that he would become yet more lonely, for from that time he was a force enclosed within himself; he was his own goal and his own meaning . . .

In that faith he lived on.

Evening had come.

The electric trains kindled their wandering lights, and the oily-smooth water between the Dam and the railroad bridge heaved slowly in dark violet. In the midst of a narrow red strip of light across the Malar the bronze signal lantern gleamed like a little green sparkling jewel. Above, no stars appeared.

The strip of light narrowed inexorably; night would soon shut its heavy iron-gray vault over the sorrowing waters out there.

Agda stopped a moment on the path around the Statue. She did not know what it was that welled up within her. Her thoughts fluttered hither and thither with restless wing-beats. She found no words, no outlet, she only felt an insufferable weight upon her limbs. If there was only someone who understood her, who could smile at her weakness, could speak terse and cool words to her. But she was alone.

She stood on the corner of a narrow side-street up in South Stockholm. Erik Vallenius lived there. She fought a silent battle with herself, as she had done so many times before, but it was impossible, she could not bring herself to go up to him.

So she took a carriage home.

In the deserted apartment out in Östermalm there was a dusty, stifling atmosphere, and all the windows were boarded up. The darkness of the great silent rooms frightened her. She lighted a lamp and two candles before the mirror in the bedroom and looked long into her own face. It was young, dangerous, without humility. She did not understand it; it was a mask that did not fit with her inner nature.

She undressed before the mirror, thinking all the while that she hated

---

* The main building of Upsala University.

her neck and shoulders because they were white and soft, and because they belonged to him she hated.

Next day Agda started out again to visit Erik Vallenius. She wandered long amid the old dark shanties far up above Fishers' Harbor before she finally stopped in front of his number.

Two pale and silent children, who were sailing egg-shells in the little iron trough under the yard-pump, ceased their play to look at her with their large eyes. In the low windows on the ground floor were crowded all the pretty flowers that poor people grow, and between the four brown pillars of the porch cresses were trained in festoons along a network of strings.

Agda tried to deaden the rustle of her skirts, which seemed out of place here.

She then proceeded slowly up the old harshly creaking wooden stairway with high shining newel-posts, and found herself up under the beams and laths of the roof. Erik's name was on the door, and she knocked hesitatingly several times.

"Go down a flight, if it's urgent."

His voice sounded strangely weak and far away. She dared not say who she was, but obeyed in silence.

Below, an old gray-clad woman opened the door and scanned her severely and searchingly.

"Who are you?"

Agda was bashful as a child at her own elegant costume.

"I've come from America. . . . I'm an old friend of Mr. Erik Vallenius."

"Doesn't the lady know he has been ill, poor man?"

"Ill?" Agda felt dizzy for a moment. "Can't I speak to him?"

The old woman went softly up the stairs and vanished into Erik's room. After a while she appeared again and signed to Agda that she might come.

She entered a largish low room with a deep white window recess where white azalea blossomed together with amaryllis and some dark myrtle plants. Directly opposite this Agda could discern through a gap in a large tottering bookcase a bed which seemed in need of a wall to prop it. In the ceiling above was a damp space like the outline map of a mountain range. Agda took in all this with a quick, restless glance, after which she stole forward to the bed without daring to look up.

"I heard you were sick, so I wanted to come to you."

She hardly realized she was lying.

Erik lay white against the white pillows. His eyes were bright as formerly, though more sunken and prone to dwell longer and more skeptically on all they saw. His face showed neither surprise nor joy, he merely smiled pallidly out at the sunlight.

"Have you seen the ocean and the big cities now?"

Agda did not remember her former words. She was shy and uncertain under his calm gaze.

"You are so pale, and your hands are thin. Have you suffered a great deal?"

"A little at first on account of you—you were mild and hard just as spring is—there was no merciful kindness in you. My illness—something with my heart—had only an external origin. I've just begun to succeed in making it something spiritual. There is in me a silent acquiescence toward everything—even toward death."

Agda sank down on a chair.

"I'm so unhappy too!"

He shut his eyes wearily.

"I don't know that it's a question of happiness."

She leaned gently down toward him with a hand on the bedpost.

"It would have been such a comfort to me to see you in different circumstances."

But he pursued his thoughts with something of the obstinate egoism peculiar to sick persons.

"Happiness—I dislike the word, I don't long for any happiness—but joy, that's different—joy is brief, but it's the deepest of all feelings."

Erik had long been living alone and self-absorbed. He continued, as though oblivious of her, to talk out toward the sunlight—about joy. It might come suddenly and upon slight occasions. It might be the expression of a face one met, the sunlight glittering on a gutter, a few tones of a piano from an open window, that transfigured the world. One walked with a lighter step, the heavens grew deep and radiant, the street resounded like a Wagner overture . . . Ah, joy—it was a kind of lightness, a kind of noble generosity toward the moment—one forgave life for being so barren and stupid.

Here he turned with a new smile to Agda:

"When I was young and unchastened, I spoke to you of sorrow, and you didn't understand. Now I'm speaking to you of joy, and assuredly you understand no better. But you've grown more beautiful than you were—yes, you are very beautiful—and so elegant."

When Agda had heard Erik was ill, she had not merely been sorry for him. She had then hoped to find in him someone she could help, someone upon whom to lavish little attentions. Now she stood there blushing, shy and at a loss.

"Have you been dangerously ill?"

"Oh, I shall soon be all right again, though I've never thought I should live to be old—now I know . . ."

He sank back on the pillow. "But I think you'd better go now; I'm tired."

Agda took his hand.

"Mayn't I come again? Won't you ask about the child?"

He did not answer. She went then, silent, submissive. When she was at the door, he called her back with an unsteady voice.

"I should be grateful if you'd write—write a little more of how things went with you and Edgar out there. I know most of what was in your old letters—that you'd married and that he's well and hearty. But write anyhow. I think it would be best for you not to come here any more—I'm not like this always."

"Mayn't I come and help you?" She pleaded with both eyes and hands.

He drew a deep breath.

"No, there's no need."

Agda went away with heavy steps.

She wandered back and forth on the streets, waiting for the boat which was to take her to her country house and her husband.

She wasn't to visit Erik Vallenius any more—Did he hate her? No, how could he do that? But he despised her; yes, despised. There was so much manly strength and firmness in his attitude, that she hadn't felt she was in the presence of an invalid. In the midst of her bloom she had become so small and humble before him, as he lay on the white pillow and looked out into far and silent realms which she could hardly guess at.

She wasn't to visit him any more—there was something in that which gnawed at her like self-contempt, which would some day become acute suffering, she divined. And she felt crushed and humiliated—like a servant. . . .

It was several days later, in Erik's room.

Agda had come silently slipping in through the open door.

She had to see him just once more; she had not been able to bring herself to write. He sat dressed at the open window with a book in his hand. The murmur of the streets and the harbor lived as a continuous grating note within the bright walls of the room. He laid the book gently aside.

Eager to find some excuse for her visit, she at once began to tell about her fortunes over there; she spoke rapidly, restlessly, with leaps over sudden digressions.

Being poor, she had been forced to travel as an emigrant, and she had strong and painful words for all the misery on board the great steamer out in the autumn gales. On their arrival they had been numbered on the back with chalk—her number was 38—and had been fenced off like cattle in various pens to be examined. She had had a horrible fear of being sent home again.

She had only had a glimpse of New York. In Chicago she had been cordially received by her cousin—he was a factory owner—but had been sent out almost immediately to a farm on the plains. And she had walked alone along the great billowing grain-fields, waiting with ever increasing anxiety for her child to come. When that was all over, she had been given a place in an office in New York; she wasn't allowed to stay with the child. There she had sat ten hours a day at her typewriter and rattled off letters direct from the dictaphone which sat like a helmet on her head and spoke the letters into her ears.

Agda was still a moment and turned away, tortured by what she was going to say.

"I saved as much as I could so as to come home . . . It was then I met Tom Ahrén . . . If it only hadn't been for that dreadful helmet it wouldn't have gone as it did . . . And then I knew so little about him. He had a good business, and I began to lead a life of indolence, far away from my real self, with his hard will around me like a wall.

"Two years went by. Then came a letter to say that my father was dead. I don't know what happened to me, but I felt ever so homesick and deserted in the midst of my luxury. The amusements I had longed for seemed as ridiculous as the billboards outside a vaudeville. And then I began to hate my husband—especially at table. We didn't talk much, but when he said anything, I compared his words with yours—I understood them now—and I could not answer.

"Well, so then we came back home here. We've been here a little less than a year. He buys houses and sells them at a profit. . . . You should see him when he takes out his pocketbook. For anything he can't take hold of with his hands he has a little dry laugh of derision; in that laugh is all his coldness and poverty of soul. He has surely never suffered, never had a gloomy dream. I didn't notice it so much over there, but now it's growing on him, growing at the expense of everything else; for me there will soon be nothing left of him but that laugh. When I don't hear it, I wait to hear it; and when I hear it, it cuts through me . . ."

Erik had risen from his chair and sunk down on a sofa, where it was darker. He now checked her wearily.

"Why do you tell me all this?"

"I don't know how to say it . . . it's such a comfort to be able to tell you about my life . . . it's as if it began to have a little meaning."

"Do you hate him really?"

"Yes."

"But you live together as man and wife?"

"No."

Erik felt to the tips of his fingers that she was lying. He shut his eyes and sat silent in the shadowy corner.

Agda glided to the window recess. In front of the house hung a little garden with bright red blossoms and lilac arbors rising above the narrow dark rows of broken-backed tile roofs. On the loosened moss-covered stones of the doorsteps below, a noisy crowd of children were scrambling, and two drunken workmen with carnations in their button-holes embraced each other on an empty packing-case in a little black hole of a yard. Beyond was the water and the city with the strong sun-light of late summer upon it . . .

This then had been constantly before his eyes for a long time. Agda divined how tranquilly his life slipped away, how different it had been from hers. Her eyes filled with tears; she glided down to him and took his hand forcibly.

"You mustn't despise me!"

Erik gazed searchingly into her face.

"Why have you come here, what do you really want with me?"

"My life has been so restless and confused . . . You must help me, talk with me. You know more about me than I do about myself."

"You've been reading, I think you said."

"Oh yes, I wrote for the books I saw on your shelves. There was so much I got a glimpse of there, but when the intoxication had passed, the old burden weighed me down again, and I couldn't see any escape. . . . . You must help me."

"How can I help you? You won't understand me."

"Tell me something about your life in the past years! You smile almost all the time, but your eyes are so sad. Hasn't it been hard to be all alone?—for I know you've been alone. Tell me!"

"My life?" Erik made a motion toward the bookcase and shook his head, as if she had asked for the impossible. But then he seemed to recollect.

"Alone, you said—Loneliness isn't so hard to bear for a man who has taught himself to love life in its entirety: people and things, perhaps most of all things. He who doesn't hear too many empty words, to him everything begins to speak: the light, clouds, lamps, trees. If you have ever listened to their mysterious whispers, you know they are not far off and indifferent. Out of the turmoil of a thousand contours gradually emerge one's own features—lost in the outer world; one rediscovers oneself and reposes there magnified in the certainty . . . It's like being borne on through a blue endlessness—I am inwardly one with all that is, all that was and is to be; I am all that in which I seem to move as an indistinguishable and evanescent part."

Erik rose and walked back and forth in the room with moist, radiant eyes and small feverish spots on his cheeks.

Agda followed him with her gaze, kindled by his emotion, but with her thoughts struggling in the depths, unable to rise to any clarity.

She then kissed him in farewell.

It was as if something of his soul had flowed into her. When she mounted the drawbridge, she felt a man's faculty of comprehending everything and feeling its nature in an instant. . . .

Across the shore of Kungsholm the evening brooded a menacing red, as it is only above a factory district, but around the church spires of Norrmalm the glow lingered more pallidly, as if in fear that no one had seen its beauty. Under her feet was the Old City with roof upon roof, chimney upon chimney out into a deep evening-blue perspective, where the star-seed of the lights was still thin and pale. Agda shivered at the thought that every stone, every beam, every tile, everything she now embraced in a swift glance, was formed with toil during long hours by human brains and human hands. Her thought labored painfully and helplessly to lift this to the light of an ultimate meaning, but it could not, and she passed on with an oppressive weight on her breast and limbs.

A month later Erik and Agda visited Upsala together.

They walked a long time in silence along the small streets up in the Quarter, whence they had glimpses of the plain in the background like a bright blue band. The air had an autumnal stillness above the asters of the garden terraces, the dahlias still defied the night frosts with their dusky glow. There was no wind in the hanging gold of the birches.

Agda stopped in front of the little yellow house where Erik had lived.

"Shan't we go in and see your old room?"

Erik went in to find out from the landlord whether it would be all right.

Oh yes, the student lodger hadn't come to Upsala yet.

Up in the room which used to be his the dust lay soft and gray on the old furniture, but the walls were covered with drawings from *Aphrodite* by Pierre Louys.

"Poor fellow!" laughed Agda, but Erik went to the window and looked out at the old poplars which raised their deep, still unfaded verdure above the roof opposite. Under his hands were the holes he had bored with his pen in the edge of the table when he was tired and could not think any longer.

Agda sat down silently. In her look was a prayer that he would come to her.

"No, come away—I can't stay in here any longer!" His voice sounded broken.

As the twilight came on, they went out from the town. The plain was a vast enfolding melancholy. In the distance an avenue of maples drew its dim streak of gold across the dark hill ridges.

He stood still and took her by the arm.

"It was my pride to rest myself without a hold on anyone else. I believed so firmly in my strength. 'Solitude' I said to myself, thinking of something great, deep—What have you done to me now, what will be the years I have left to live? . . . I know your failings, your deceit, your hardness when you think yourself secure, your heavy and helpless emptiness when you are alone; and yet I live only in you, all my dreams are in you. . . . I hate you."

He kissed her long with trembling lips.

And she gently lifted his hand to her breast.

HJALMAR SODERBERG

The Burning City

Hjalmar Söderberg (1869–1941) was born in Stockholm. He worked as a government clerk and then turned to writing, producing many short stories in the vein of Maupassant. In his later life he turned to studies of religion. His best known works are *Martin Birck's Youth*, a novel, and *Little Histories*, his first collection of stories. [From *Sweden's Best Stories;* used by permission of The American Scandinavian Foundation.]

THROUGH THE TWO WINDOWS with their bright lattice-figured curtains the level sunlight of the winter morning falls in two slanting oblong quadrilaterals on the soft green carpet, and in the warm sunny spaces a little boy skips and dances. He knows but little of the world as yet. He knows he is little and is going to be big, but he does not know either that he has been born or that he will die. He knows he is four and will soon be five, but he does not know what is meant by "a year"; he still measures time only into yesterday, today, and tomorrow.

"Papa," he suddenly exclaims to his father, who has just finished breakfast and lighted his first cigar of the day—he being a person to measure time with cigars—"papa, I dreamed so many things last night! I dreamed about the whole room! I dreamed about the chairs and the green carpet and the mirror and the clock and the stove and the shutters and the cupboards."

With that he skips forward to the stove, where the fire flames and crackles, and turns a somersault. He considers the stove and the place in front of it as the most important and dignified things in the room.

His father nods and laughs at him over the corner of his paper, and the boy laughs back, laughs away uncontrollably. He is at the age when laughter is still only an utterance of joy, not of appreciation for the ridiculous. When he stood at the window some days ago and laughed at the moon, it was not because he found the moon funny, but because it gave him joy with its round bright face.

When he has had his laugh out, he clambers up on a chair and points to one of the pictures on the wall.

"—And I dreamed most of all about that picture," he says.

The picture is a photograph of an old Dutch painting, *A Burning City*.

"Well, and what was it you dreamed?" his father asks.

"I don't know."

"Come, think!"

"Oh yes, I dreamed it was burning and that I patted a doggie."

"But generally you are afraid of doggies."

"Yes, but on pictures I can pat them nicely."

Then he laughs and skips and dances.

549

At last he comes up to his father and says, "Papa dear, take down the picture. I want papa to show me the picture again the way he did yesterday."

The picture is a new arrival in the room; it came the day before. With the other pictures around the walls the little boy has acquainted himself long ago: Uncle Strindberg and Uncle Schopaur (i.e., Schopenhauer) and Uncle Napoleon and ugly old Goethe and grandmother when she was young. But the Burning City is new, and is furthermore in itself a much more amusing picture than the others. The father humors the little boy, takes the picture down from the wall, and they enjoy it together. Over a broad estuary that winds toward the sea and is filled with sloops and rowboats runs an arched bridge with a fortified tower. On the left shore lies the burning city: rows of narrow houses with pointed gables, high roofs, churches, and towers; a throng of people running hither and thither, a sea of fire and flames, clouds of smoke, ladders raised against walls, horses running away with shaking loads, docks crowded with barrels and sacks and all manner of rubbish; on the river a mass of people in a rowboat that is almost ready to capsize, while across the bridge people are running for dear life, and away off in the foreground stand two dogs sniffing at each other. But far in the background, where the estuary widens toward the sea, a much too-small moon sits on the horizon in a mist of pale clouds, peeping wanly and sadly at all this misery.

"Papa," inquires the little boy, "why is the city burning?"

"Somebody was careless with fire," says the father.

"*Who* was it that was careless?"

"Ah, one can't be sure of that so long afterward."

"How long afterward?"

"It is many hundred years since that city was burned," says the father.

This is a bit puzzling to the little boy, as the father clearly realizes, but he had to answer something. The boy sits quiet a moment and ponders. New thoughts and impressions about things stir in his brain and mingle with the old. He points with his little finger on the glass over the burning city and says:

"Yes, but it was burning yesterday, and now today it's burning too."

The father ventures on an explanation of the difference between pictures and reality. "That is not a real city," he says, "that is only a picture. The real city was burned up long, long ago. It is gone. The people that run about there waving their arms are dead and don't exist any more. The houses have been burned up, the towers have fallen. The bridge is gone too."

"Have the towers burned down or tumbled down?" asks the boy.

"They have both burned and tumbled down."

"Are the steamboats dead too?"

"The boats too have been gone long ago," replied the father. "But those are not steamboats, they are sailing vessels. There were no steamboats in those days."

The little boy sticks out his lower lip with a dissatisfied expression.

"But I *see* that they're steamboats," he says. "Papa, what's that steamboat's name?"

He has a mind of his own, has the boy. The father is tired of the labor of instruction and holds his peace. The boy points with his finger to the old Dutch merchantmen and prattles to himself: "That steamer's name is *Bragë,* and that one's is *Hillersea,* and that is the *Princess Ingeborg.*"

"Papa," he cries all of a sudden, "is the moon gone too?"

"No, the moon still exists. It is the one thing of all there that still exists. It is the same moon you laughed at the other day in the nursery window."

Again the little boy sits still and ponders. Then comes yet another question:

"Papa, is it *very* long ago this city was burned? Is it as long ago as when we went away on the *Princess Ingeborg?*"

"It is much, much longer ago," answers the father. "When that city burned, neither you nor I nor mamma nor grandma was here."

The boy's face becomes very serious all at once. He looks positively troubled. He sits quiet a long while pondering. But it seems as if things would not work out for him.

"Tell me, papa," he finally asks, "where was I when that city was burned? Was it when I was at Grenna with mamma?"

"No, old fellow," replies the father, "when that city burned you didn't yet exist."

The boy sticks out his under lip again with an attitude as much as to say: no, I can't agree to such a thing as that. He then repeats with emphasis:

"Yes, but where was I then?"

His father answers, "You didn't exist at all."

The boy looks at his father with round eyes. Suddenly all the little face brightens, the boy tears himself away from his father, and begins to skip and dance again in the sunny spots on the green carpet, crying at the top of his lungs:

"Oho yes, I did just the same. I was somewhere, I was somewhere!"

He thought his father was only joking with him. Such an idea was clearly too ridiculous! The maids used sometimes to talk nonsense to him in jest, and he thought his father had done the same.

So he skips and dances in the sunlight.

RUSSIAN AND EAST
EUROPEAN SECTION

Introduction

Many critics and readers consider Russian novels and short stories gloomy. To be sure, there is much depressing material in the powerful novels of Gogol, Turgenev, Dostoevsky and Tolstoy, and in the stories of Chekhov and Gorky. Nonetheless, nineteenth century Russian storytellers—for example, Goncharov, the author of *Oblomov* and other novels—had abundant humor. Writers stifled by censorship enlivened their stories with the observation and presentation of life's humorous incongruities. Gogol and Chekhov took full advantage of the comical aspects of human existence. Aside from stirring the reader, they had the gift of amusing him.

However, there is a plausible reason why Russian tales should seem gloomy. The preoccupation with salvation as a path to man's individual and social improvement was perplexing in its intensity, and seemed alien or morbid to many readers and critics abroad. A westernized writer, like Turgenev, objected to the nationalistic and "provincial" ideas of his great contemporaries. Yet in his declining years, he returned to the "pure Russian spirit."

Twentieth century Russian authors, especially those in the Soviet orbit, deviated from the principles and taste of nineteenth century writers; many of them repudiated the narrative conventions of the past. The personal and collective aims of the non-Soviet and Soviet writers differ considerably; their artistic and ideological objectives are incompatible. Yet both groups have merits and links one must reckon with. Although Gorky, for example, is aptly called the most important pioneer of Soviet imaginative literature, he, like Chekhov, is linked to nineteenth century Russian literature.

At the turn of the century, Russia was prepared for a radical change in her social structure and literary taste. There was a marked shift in creative trends. The centralized government of Russia played havoc with creative freedom, but writers risking jail or exile remained scathing critics of Tsarism and of Russia's retrograde society. The bitter consequences of the Russo-Japanese war and the frustrated revolutionary upheaval of 1905 led to a pessimistic or fatalistic outlook, to an acceptance of emotional anarchy as an escape from defeat. Some writers of the period were antagonistic to the status quo; some judged all life as a futile pilgrimage or sought orientation in the irrational fog of existence. All revealed an underlying restlessness. Among the outstanding figures of the time were Leonid Andreyev, Mikhail Artsybashev, Ivan Bunin, Alexander Kuprin, Dmitri Merezhkovsky, Feodor Sologub and Alexey Tolstoy.

After the Revolution of 1917, writers opposed to Bolshevism had to seek refuge abroad. Some, however, made an about-face. Of these Alexey Tolstoy was the most successful; he became the most acclaimed historical novelist of the Soviet Union. The discontent expressed by émigré writers was, of course, symptomatic of their uprootedness; they felt impoverished as creators in an alien environment. Some were apologists of old Russia, others lonely individuals offering a sad spectacle of resignation. Even competent writers like Bunin and Merezhkovsky gave signs of artistic disintegration.

Literature in Soviet Russia is primarily a vehicle of propaganda; as a rule, art is but a marginal experience. This is considered not only legitimate, but necessary, in the light of dialectical materialism. At all events, the building of a new society inevitably stresses ideological communication at the expense of artistic form.

Nevertheless, talented Soviet authors—for example, Leonid Leonov or Mikhail Sholokov—are conscious of their literary responsibilities. Some of the Soviet writers, in spite of thematic and ideological differences, are appreciative of nineteenth century masters—of Gogol, for instance. Besides the above mentioned Soviet authors the following deserve mention: Isaac Babel, Ilya Ehrenburg, Feodor Gladkov, Valentin Kataev, Boris Pilniak, Konstantin Simonov, Mikhail Zozchenko.

To achieve a degree of authenticity in this book, writers had to be chosen who are presumably representative of certain common characteristics of twentieth century Russian literary taste and tendencies. Inevitably, in so rich a literature, there have been regrettable omissions.

Of the authors in this section it is more than fair to begin with Anton Chekhov. This master of compression, unity, moods and psychological insight, influenced many Russian and foreign writers—especially in the short story. Katharine Mansfield was one of his most faithful disciples. His usually plotless, though not static, stories and sketches are in definite contrast with the violence and activities that explode from the works of Soviet writers. Chekhov was not only a great short story writer, but an eminent playwright as well. A superior and delicate craftsmanship is evident in his portrayals of the pathetic, farcical or comic traits of the "little man," the inertia of the Russian gentry and the middle class, the perseverance of upstarts, the sly complexities of bureaucracy, the sweetness of children, the helplessness of parents. Nemirovich-Dauchenko, co-director of the Moscow Art Theatre, said that Chekhov was the great lyric poet of the bourgeoisie. And despite his genuinely sharp analyses of weakness, a nostalgic sympathy for the neurotic and the unsuccessful pervades Chekhov's work. This is apparent in the story included here, *In Exile*—a study of contrasting types and their reactions to the bleak hopelessness of Siberia.

There was a time when the prestige of Andreyev overshadowed that of Chekhov. In retrospect, this seems incomprehensible. Andreyev was the author of allegorical and symbolic plays, novels and stories, a protagonist of ideas and ideals which at first appear startlingly original, but often on longer thought, seem rather the manufactured hallucinations of a skillful writer. *Satan's Diary, The Red Laugh, The Seven That Were Hanged* are still read despite critical objections. *The Abyss,* perhaps Andreyev's best short story, starts out as a more or less conventional love story; but it has nightmarish psychological overtones which produce a powerful effect.

The artistic qualities of Ivan Bunin, the Nobel prize winner, surpass those of Andreyev. Influenced by Turgenev, he has words for the unsaid, images for pensive moods. His atmospherical reproduction of Russian manors, villages and landscapes, his irony developing steadily through the years, express an uncompromising loyalty to conservative style and taste. He represents the "lost generation" of pre-Soviet writers. Notwithstanding his cosmopolitanism—which the story in this anthology, the famous *Gentleman from San Francisco* amply demonstrates—he found no infallible remedy for the ills of the uprooted. *The Dreams of Chang, The Village, Grammar of Love,* are some of Bunin's major works translated into English.

Feodor Sologub (the pen name of Teternikov), the "demoniac" writer, was fascinated by the weird and the unattainable. Some of his stories seem like eruptions of the irrational. *The Little Demon* and *The Old House* are illustrative of Sologub's particular manner of story-telling. It has been said of him that he expressed a Manichean contempt for the actual world. Sologub's reputation as a superstition-ridden spirit is supported by such a "children" story as *Hide and Seek,* where the elements of innocence, mysteriousness and fear mingle.

Of the Soviet writers, Maxim Gorky (pen name of Pjeskov), is the best known. Gorky, the self-taught, the former vagabond, exercised a profound influence upon Russian writers. His early stories represent first-rate narrative art. He had a superb comprehension of the downtrodden, and of the emotional and social values of their existence. Like his plays, such as *The Lower Depths,* his stories, novels and autobiographies emphasize the principle of social justice. Such stories as *Twenty-Six Men and a Girl, Creatures That Once Were Men,* or such novels as *Mother,* leavened the revolutionary movement in the framework of Russian society. One of the most moving of his stories is *One Autumn Night,* included here.

Alexey Tolstoy, to whom we have already referred as one of the most successful of those writers who did a right-about-face after the Revolution, eventually became one of the most prominent exponents of the Soviet philosophy, and is read very widely in Russia. It is possible that his reputation has exceeded his ability as an artist. *Vasily Suchkov* is an exception to this generality; it is an effective and powerful story.

Konstantin Simonov, another Soviet writer who appears in this anthology, sees the world through Marxian spectacles. Like Ilya Ehrenburg—the well-known journalist—he does not consider the writing of stories an end in itself. His novel, *Days and Nights,* has nationalistic and communistic connotations. The theme is the defense of Stalingrad; plot and characterization have timely authenticity. However, compassion for his characters finds elemental expression in Simonov's war-story, *His Only Son,* which is less sharply propagandist than some of his other work.

NORTH-EASTERN EUROPE

Of the countries referred to as North-eastern Europe, Poland is the largest in population. Despite her present political affiliation with Soviet Russia, Polish culture is closely allied with the West of Europe. As Russian literature in the past has been conditioned by Byzantine taste and by the Greek Orthodox creed, Polish literature shows strong Roman Catholic influences. A good example of this influence is Henryk Sienkievicz, the author of historical novels and stories and Nobel prize winner.

Twentieth century Polish writers have also been affected considerably by Western literary movements. As elsewhere, some of them have bridged the gap between tradition and modernity; some have definitely been leftists. Among the realists, Wladyslaw Reymont is the most talented. He is a Nobel prize winner, and the author of a masterly narrative about Polish rural life entitled *The Peasants*. Several of Reymont's works are obtainable in English, as are some of the novels and stories of Julius Kaden Bandrowski, Ferdynand Goetel, Stefan Zeromski and others. Joseph Wittlin, who now lives in the United States, is primarily known as the author of the novel, *Salt of the Earth,* a story set against the background of the first World War. There is humaneness and irony in Wittlin's story *The Emperor and the Devil*.

Local color plays an important part in Polish fiction—for instance, in the stories of Jezimiers Tetmajer, in whose *Tales of the Tatras* Polish mountain folk are well presented. Local color is also noticeable in the tales of North-eastern European countries, in the works of Finnish, Estonian, Lithuanian, and Latvian writers. Finland's popular heroic epic, the *Kalevala,* and its Estonian version, the *Kalevipoeg,* contain poetic and psychological ingredients which are echoed in some of the recent folk tales. Without question, folk tales constitute one of the most valid contributions of Finland and the Baltic countries to world literature.

Other common features of Finnish writers are the mythical spirit and a keen awareness of reality. The road from serfdom to freedom, vigor and strength pitted against nature, the function of age-old customs in the life of modern Finland, are topics which determine the substance and manner of such twentieth century Finnish authors as Arvi Jarventaus, Aino Kallas, Jlamari Kianto and Unto Seppanen. However, it is F. E. Sillanpaa, the Nobel prize winner and author of *Maid Silja, Meek Heritage* and other novels, who occupies the most prominent position in twentieth century Finnish fiction. His splendid characterizations of maidservants, peasants and Finnish gentility reveal a writer of unusual ability. *Selma Koljas,* here included, is the story of a young woman's fulfillment and ripening into maturity through love.

Friedebert Tuglas, the Estonian writer, shows an equal talent for stories of the life of peasant families, of their perseverance and their sufferings, and for fantasies revealing a world of unreality and terror. Another Estonian writer who should be mentioned is Johannes Semper, whose work has been profoundly influenced by psychoanalysis.

Of the Lithuanian authors, Jieva Simonaityte, the regionalist, is outstanding, as are Juozas Paukstelis and Petronele Orientaite, social realists of rural and urban conditions. Janis Akiraters and Andrey Upitis, Latvian writers, are reliable craftsmen of the short story, and represent well the artistic maturity of Latvian fiction. Ukrainian (Carpatho-Russian) regionalism—independent of Soviet influences—is manifest in Ivan Franko and Vasil Stefanyk, two popular realists.

Sholom Aleichem occupies, with Isaac Loeb Perez, I. J. Singer, and Sholem Asch, a place among the four outstanding writers in Yiddish Literature—the product of Jewish writers born and raised in Russia, Poland, Lithuania and other sections of Eastern and North-eastern Europe. Singer and Asch have been translated into English much more widely than have the other two. In the case of Sholom Aleichem this has been due to his quality as a folk artist, highly colloquial, presenting more formidable translation difficulties than the conventional stylists.

"Sholom Aleichem" ("Peace to you") is the pseudonym of Solomon Rabinowitch, who was born in Pereyeslav in the Ukraine, but lived his later life in New York. He has been called "the Jewish Mark Twain." He wrote his stories, novels, and plays about simple people leading simple lives in the ghetto towns and among the Jewish peasantry of his region. His claim is strong to the title of the best-loved writer in Yiddish. His many plays are widely performed on the Yiddish stage.

Tevye Wins a Fortune represents him in a characteristic vein. Tevye the dairyman, poverty-ridden, cheerfully pious, blandly misinformed, and given to Talmudic misquotation, is one of his famous characterizations.

SOUTH-EASTERN EUROPE

To the American public, it does not seem important to distinguish between Central Europe, which includes Czechoslovakia and Hungary, and South-eastern Europe, which consists of Albania, Bulgaria, Greece, Romania, and Yugoslavia. None the less, weighed by objective consideration, a distinction must be made. Czechoslovakia and Hungary and, in fact, the western section of Yugoslavia—that of the Croatians and Slovenians—are manifestly closer to the traditions of scholasticism and the Renaissance than the Balkan countries. Hence it is rather a matter of editorial policy than of historical and cultural accuracy to discuss Czechoslovak and Hungarian writers under the heading of South-eastern Europe.. With reference to Czechoslovakia and Yugoslavia, the Slav relationship must be stressed; with reference to Hungary and Roumania the juxtaposition of Hungarian and Roumanian culture in Transylvania must be emphasized.

The Czechs lay claim to being the most westernized Slavs. Their literature is a proof of this. Much of Czech literature is actuated by racial and national pride; but the ideals and values, the provincial and universal attitudes that define the character of Czech novels and stories are, as a rule, parallel to a Western European cultural rhythm. No one denies that Czech writers were influenced by nineteenth century Russian literature and by Soviet literature, as were some of the North-eastern European authors. Nevertheless, the integrative elements of Czech stories are likely to meet the challenge of Western European literary postulates more successfully than those of Eastern Europe.

In Bohemia, for example, baroque traditions prevail—as exemplified in Jaroslav Durych, the twentieth century Czech author. Western ideologies, colored by a socialist attitude, are perceivable in the technological, moral and psychological problems of Karel Capek, the renowned playwright and storyteller, in such works of his as *Krakatit* and *Meteor*. The theme of Capek's realistic and moral story, *Money*, suggests money as the symbol of a spider's web in human relationships. Egon Hostovsky fuses innate idealism with analytical intelligence and contemporary interest in a Western European sense. *Vertigo* gives a convincing example of the combination forces in his work. Similar observations are more or less applicable to the following Czech writers: Bozena Benesova, Frantisek Hasek, Frantisek Sramek. Communist authors, such as Ivan Olbracht and Vladislav Vancura, despite their political orientation, remained organically tied to their own culture. The social and moral problem of their people are the concern of two outstanding Slovak realists, Jan Hrusovsky and Milo Urban. Peter Jilemnicky is a well-known Slovak didactic writer with a communistic bent.

The Hungarians (Magyars) are a Finno-Ugrian people, but in the course of centuries the blood of other western, eastern and southern races was blended with theirs. Except in folklore, in its Catholic and Protestant features and in its intellectual and aesthetic characteristics, Hungarian culture is a part of Western European culture. Photographic realism and the stream of consciousness method, candor and subtleties characterize the unorthodox tendencies of modern Hungarian fiction. A rejection of patriarchal habits and intensive social criticism shaped the expression of such writers as Mihaly Babits, Dezso Kosztolanyi, Dezso Szabo and Aron Tamasi. Kalman Mikszath wrote with affection and humor about his own class, the gentry; he also was a master of stories about children and simple folk. Mikszath was introduced to the English speaking world with his delightful novelette, *Saint Peter's Umbrella.* His story *The Green Fly* shows the qualities of the born narrator. The internationally recognized playwright, Ferenc Molnar, has written stimulating novels and sketches containing wit, sentimentality and urbanity. *The Silver Hilt,* while more fantastic than realistic, contains his characteristic irony.

French influence is evident in Roumanian literature, but its indigenous character is much stronger. Roumanian writers like to stress their historical affinity with Latin culture, despite the Greek Orthodox attributes of their religious and national life. Panait Istrati, the author of *Kyra Kyralina,* a tragic and vivid story, wrote in French, but the majority of Roumanian writers adhere to their native tongue and to the responsibilities of their environment. Historical, biographical, social, biological, pacifistic topics characterize the works of such writers as Ion Luca Caragiale, Jon Minulescu, Liviu Rebreanu, Mihail Sadoveanu. As a playwright, novelist and short story writer, Ion Luca Caragiale, the author represented in this anthology, was primarily a psychological satirist. The sorrow and savagery of his story, *The Easter Torch,* retain their force in translation.

In Bulgarian literature, folkish references predominate; there is real interest in Balkan legends. Experiences of the Balkan Wars and of the first and second World Wars are described with documentary faithfulness. Some have written about the brotherhood of man, others about modern shallowness and disillusionments. Problems of social and folkish significance are the regular topics of Svetoslav Minkov, Ellin-Pellin, Anton Strashimirov and Angel Karalitcheff. This last-named writer was fond of using folk tales as a background for his stories, and explored rather ingeniously their artistic possibilities. The story entitled *The Little Coin,* intense in imagery and sincerity, coincides with the general tone of Karalitcheff's works.

Greek writers, handicapped by the glories of antiquity, have drawn their inspiration partly from the past, partly from contemporary events. In the stories of Stratis Myrivilis, Gregory Xenopoulos, Elia Venezis and other writers, the following subjects appear with variations: the problems of the Greeks in Asia Minor, the conditions of Greece between the two World Wars, the conflict between leftist and rightist forces, the position of the oppressed and the emancipated woman. Lilika Nakos' *Maternity,* the story of a motherless baby and a fourteen-year-old Armenian refugee in Marseilles, shows the humane terms in which the author judges the world's cruelty.

Yugoslavia, a conglomerate of various Slav and non-Slavic nationalities—with, however, the Serbian, Croatian and Slovenian elements predominating—has writers who depict the picturesque, noble and brutal features of the country with fervor. In South-eastern Europe few authors indulge in artistic detachment. Notwithstanding certain primitive conditions, Yugoslav writers have not been isolated from the timely literary schools of the West of Europe and Russia. The composite picture of Yugoslav social and individual conditions is present in the work of such twentieth century storytellers as Grigorije Bozovic, Bora Stankovic and Miroslav Krleza. The social-mindedness of Ivan Cankar, the Slovenian, and the realism of Anton Gustav Matos, the Croatian writer, convey to the reader concepts of values which make an unfamiliar world familiar. Cankar's *Children and Old Folk* and Matos' *The Neighbor* are stories built intuitively, with the freedom of the artist, and didactically, with the self-imposed ethical restrictions of the reformer endowed with indignation.

Albanian fiction is still in the heroic epic stage, but the stories of Tajar Zavalini, influenced by Russian writers, show a growing interest in modern realism.

JOSEPH REMENYI

ANTON CHEKHOV

In Exile

Anton Chekhov (1860–1904), Russian dramatist and short story writer, was born the son of a former serf, attended the University of Moscow as a medical student, and then turned to literature. His first play, *Ivanov*, was produced in 1887, followed by *The Seagull, Uncle Vanya, The Three Sisters* and *The Cherry Orchard.* He also wrote many short stories and a few novels—*The Peasants, My Life, Ward Number 6.* [From *A Treasury of Russian Life and Humor;* copyright 1943 by Coward-McCann, Inc.; used by permission of the publishers; translated by John Cournos.]

OLD SIMEON, NICKNAMED WISEACRE, and a young Tartar, whose name no one knew, were sitting on the bank of the river by a wood fire. The other three ferrymen were in the hut. Simeon, who was an old man of about sixty, gaunt and toothless, but broad-shouldered and robust, was drunk. He would long ago have gone to bed, but he had a bottle in his pocket and feared lest his comrades ask him for vodka. The Tartar was ill and miserable, and, pulling his rags about him, he went on talking about the good things in the province of Simbirsk, and what a beautiful and clever wife he had left at home. He was not more than twenty-five, and now, by the light of the wood fire, with his pale, sorrowful, sickly face, he looked a mere boy.

"Of course, it's not a paradise here," said Wiseacre. "You see water, the bare bushes by the river, clay everywhere—nothing else. . . . It is long past Easter and there is still ice on the water and this morning there was snow. . . ."

"Wretched! Wretched!" said the Tartar with a haunted look.

A few yards away flowed the dark, cold river, muttering, dashing against the holes in the clayey bank as it tore along to the distant sea. By the bank on which they were sitting, loomed a great barge, which the ferrymen call a *karbass.* Far away and away, flashing out, flaring up, were fires crawling like snakes—last year's grass being burned. And behind the water again was darkness. Little banks of ice could be heard knocking against the barge. . . . It was very damp and cold.

The Tartar glanced at the sky. There were as many stars as at home, and the darkness was the same, but something was lacking. At home in the Simbirsk province the stars and the sky were quite different.

"Bad! Bad!" he repeated.

"You'll get used to it," said Wiseacre with a laugh. "You are young yet and foolish; the milk is hardly dry on your lips, and in your folly you imagine that there is no one unhappier than you, but there will come a time when you will say: 'God grant everyone such a life!' Just look at me. In a week's time the floods will be gone, and we will fix a ferry here, and all of you will go away into Siberia and I shall stay here, going to and fro. I have been living thus for the last two-and-twenty years, but, thank God, I want nothing. God grant everyone such a life."

The Tartar threw some branches onto the fire, crawled near to it, and said:

"My father is ill. When he dies, my mother and my wife have promised to come here."

"What do you want your mother and your wife for?" asked Wiseacre. "Just foolishness, my friend. It's the devil tempting you, plague take him. Don't listen to the Evil One. Don't give way to him. When he talks to you about women you should answer him sharply: 'I don't want them!' When he talks of freedom, you should stick to it and say: 'I don't want it. I want nothing. No father, no mother, no wife, no freedom, no home, no love! I want nothing.' Plague take 'em all."

Wiseacre took a swig at his bottle and went on:

"My brother, I am not an ordinary peasant. I don't come from the servile masses. I am the son of a deacon, and when I was a free man at Rursk, I used to wear a frock coat, and now I have brought myself to such a point that I can sleep naked on the ground and eat grass. God grant everyone such a life. I want nothing. I am afraid of nobody, and I think there is no man richer or freer than I. When they sent me here from Russia I set my teeth at once and said: 'I want nothing!' The devil whispers to me about my wife and my kindred, and about freedom, and I say to him: 'I want nothing!' I stuck to it, and, you see, I live happily and have nothing to grumble at. If a man gives the devil the least chance and listens to him just once, then he is lost and has no hope of salvation: he will be over ears in the mire and will never get out. Not only peasants the like of you are lost, but the well-born and the educated too. About fifteen years ago a certain nobleman was banished here from Russia. He had had some trouble with his brothers and had made a forgery in a will. People said he was a prince or a baron, but maybe he was only a high official—who knows? Well, he came here and at once bought a house and land in Moukhzyink. 'I want to live by my own work,' said he, 'in the sweat of my brow, because I am no longer a nobleman but an exile.' 'Why,' said I, 'God help you, for that is good.' He was a young man then, fiery and eager; he used to mow and go fishing, and he would ride sixty miles on horseback. Only one thing was wrong; from the very start he was always driving to the post office at Guyrin. He used to sit in my boat and sigh: 'Ah! Simeon, it is a long time since they sent me any money from home.' 'You are better without money, Vassily Andreich,' said I. 'What's the good of it? You just fling away the past, as if it had never happened, as if it were only a dream, and start life afresh. Don't listen to the devil,' I said, 'he won't do you any good, and he will only tighten the noose. You want money now, but in a little while you will want something else, and then again something else. If,' said I, 'you want to be happy you must want nothing. That's it. . . . If,' I said, 'fate has been hard on you and me, it is no good asking her for charity and falling at her feet. We must ignore her and make mock of her.' That's what I said to him. . . . Two years later I ferried him over, and he rubbed his hands and laughed. 'I'm going,' said he, 'to Guyrin to meet my wife. She has taken pity on me, she says, and she is coming here. She is very kind and good.' And he gave a gasp of joy. Then one day he came with his wife, a beautiful young lady with a little girl in her arms and a lot of luggage. And Vassily Andreich kept turning and looking at her and could not look at her or praise her enough. 'Yes, Simeon, my friend, even in Siberia people live.' Well, thought I, all right, it won't last. And from that time on, mark you, he used to go to Guyrin every week to find out if money had been sent from Russia. A big heap of money was wasted. 'She stays here,' said he, 'for my sake, and her youth and beauty wither away here in Siberia. She shares my bitter lot with me,' said he, 'and I must give her all the pleasure I can afford. . . .' To make his wife happier he took up with the officials and any kind of riff-raff. And they couldn't have company without giving food and drink, and they must have a piano and a fluffy little dog on the sofa. . . . Luxury, in a word, and all kinds of silliness. The lady did not stay with him long. How could she? Clay, water, cold, no vegetables, no fruit; uneducated people and drunkards, coarse as you make 'em, and she was a pretty pampered young lady from the big city. . . . To be sure, she got bored. And her husband was no longer a gentleman, but an exile—quite another thing. Three years later, I remember, on the eve of the Assumption, I heard shouts from the other bank. I went over in the ferry and saw the lady, all bundled up, with a young gentleman, a government official, in a troika. . . . I ferried them across, they got into the carriage and off they went, and I saw no more of them. Toward the morning Vassily Andreich came racing up in a coach and pair. 'Has my wife been across, Simeon, with a gentleman in spectacles?' 'She has,' said I, 'but you might as well look for the wind in the fields.' He chased after them and kept it up for five days and nights. When he came back he jumped onto the ferry and began to knock his head against the side and to cry aloud. 'You see,' said I, 'there you are.' And I laughed and reminded him: 'Even in Siberia people live.' But he went on beating his head all the harder. . . . Then he began to yearn for freedom. His wife had gone to Russia, and he longed to go there to see her and take her away from her lover. And he went to the post office every day, and then to the authorities of the town. He was always sending applications or personally handing them to the authorities, asking them to have his term remitted and to be allowed to go, and he told me that he had spent over two hundred roubles on telegrams. He sold his land and mortgaged his house to the money-lenders. His hair went gray, he grew round-shouldered, and his face got yellow and consumptive-looking. He used to cough whenever he spoke and tears would come into his eyes. He spent eight years on his applications, and at last he became cheerful again and lively: he had thought of a new consolation. His daughter, you see, had grown up. He doted on her and couldn't take his eyes off her. And, it's a fact, she was mighty pretty, dark and clever. Every Sunday he used to go to church with her at Guyrin. They would stand side by side on the ferry, and she would smile and he would devour her with his eyes. 'Yes, Simeon,' he would say. 'Even in Siberia people live. Even in Siberia there is happiness. Look what a fine daughter I have. You wouldn't find one like her in a thousand miles' journey.' 'She's a nice girl,' said I. 'Oh, yes.' . . . And I thought to myself: 'You wait. . . . She is young. Young blood will have its way; she wants to live, and what life is there here?' And she began to pine away. . . . Wasting, wasting away, she withered away, fell ill and had to keep to her bed. . . . Consumption. That's Siberian happiness, plague take it, that's Siberian life. . . . He rushed all over the place after the doctors and dragged them home with him. If he heard of a doctor or a quack three hundred miles off he would rush off after him. He spent a mighty big lot of money on doctors and, in my opinion, it would have been much better spent on drink. All the same she'll die. No help for it. Then it was all up with him. He thought of hanging himself, and of trying to escape to Russia. That would be the end of him. He would try to escape: he would be caught, tried, penal servitude, flogging."

"Good! Good!" muttered the Tartar with a shiver. "What is good?" asked Wiseacre.

"Wife and daughter. What does penal servitude and suffering matter? He saw his wife and his daughter. You say one should want nothing. But nothing—is evil! His wife spent three years with him. God granted him that. Nothing is evil, and three years is good. Can't you see it?"

Trembling and stammering as he groped for Russian words, of which he knew only a few, the Tartar began to say: "God forbid he should fall ill among strangers, and die and be buried in the cold sodden earth, and then, if his wife could come to him if only for one day or even for one hour, he would gladly endure any torture for such happiness, and would even thank God. Better one day of happiness than nothing."

Then once more he said what a beautiful, clever wife he had left at home, and with his head in his hands he began to cry, assuring Simeon that he was innocent, and had been falsely accused. His two brothers and his uncle had stolen some horses from a peasant and beaten the old man nearly to death, and the community never investigated the affair at all, and judgment was passed by which all three brothers were exiled to Siberia, while his uncle, a rich man, remained at home.

"You'll get used to it," said Simeon.

The Tartar relapsed into silence and stared into the fire with eyes red from weeping; he looked perplexed and frightened, as if he could not understand why he was in the cold and the darkness, among strangers, and not in the province of Simbirsk. Wiseacre lay down near the fire, smiled at something, and began to say in an undertone:

"But what a joy she must be to your father," he muttered after a pause. "He loves her and she is a comfort to him, eh? But, my man, don't tell me. He is a strict, harsh old man. And girls don't want strictness; they want kisses and laughter, scents and pomade. Yes. . . . Ah! What a life!" Simeon swore. "No vodka left! That means it's time to go to bed. I must be going!"

Left alone, the Tartar threw more branches on the fire, lay down, and, looking into the blaze, began to think of his native village and of his wife; if she could come if but for a month, or even a day, and then, if she liked, go back again! Better a month or even a day, than nothing. But even if his wife came, how could he provide for her? Where was she to live?

"If there is nothing to eat, how are we to live?" asked the Tartar aloud.

For working at the oars day and night he was paid two kopecks a day; the passengers gave tips, but the ferrymen shared them out and gave nothing to the Tartar, and only laughed at him. And he was poor, cold, hungry, and afraid. . . . With his whole body aching and shivering, he thought it would be good to go into the hut and sleep; but there was nothing to cover himself with, and it was colder there than on the bank. He had nothing to cover himself with there, but he could make up a fire. . . .

In a week's time, when the floods had subsided and the ferry would be fixed up, all the ferrymen except Simeon would not be wanted any longer and the Tartar would be forced to go from village to village, begging and looking for work. His wife was only seventeen; beautiful, soft, and shy. . . . Could she go unveiled begging through the villages? No. The idea of it was revolting.

It was already dawning. The barges, the bushy willows above the water, the swirling flood began to take shape, and up above in a clayey cliff a hut thatched with straw, and above that the straggling houses of the village, where the cocks had begun to crow.

The ginger-colored clay cliff, the barge, the river, the strange wild people, hunger, cold, illness—perhaps all these things did not really exist. Perhaps, thought the Tartar, it was only a dream. He felt that he must be asleep, and he heard his own snoring. . . . Of course: he was at home in the Simbirsk province; he had but to call his wife and she would reply; and his mother was in the next room. . . . What awful dreams there are! Why? The Tartar smiled and opened his eyes. What river was that? The Volga?

It was snowing.

"Hi! Ferry!" someone shouted from the opposite bank. "*Karba-a-ass!*"

The Tartar awoke and went to fetch his companions to row over to the other side. Hurrying into their sheepskins, swearing sleepily in hoarse voices, and shivering from the cold, the four men appeared on the bank. After their sleep, the river, from which there came a piercing blast, seemed to them horrible and loathsome. They stepped slowly into the barge. . . . The Tartar and the three ferrymen took the long, broad-bladed oars, which in the dim light looked like a crab's claw, and Simeon flung himself with his belly against the tiller. And on the other side the voice kept on shouting, and a revolver was fired twice, for the man probably thought the ferrymen were asleep or gone to the village inn.

"All right. Plenty of time!" said Wiseacre in the tone of one who was sure that there is no need for hurry in this world—and, indeed, there is no reason for it.

The heavy, clumsy barge left the bank and heaved through the willows, and by the willows slowly receding it was possible to tell that the barge was moving. The ferrymen plied the oars with a slow measured stroke; Wiseacre hung over the tiller with his stomach pressed against it and swung from side to side. In the dim light they looked like men sitting on some antediluvian animal with long limbs, swimming out to a cold dismal nightmare land.

They got clear of the willows and swung out into midstream. The thud of the oars and the splash could be heard on the other bank and shouts came: "Hurry! Hurry!" After another ten minutes the barge bumped clumsily against the landing-stage.

"And it is still snowing, always snowing," Simeon murmured, wiping the snow from his face. "God knows where it comes from!"

On the other side a tall, gaunt old man was waiting in a short fox-fur coat and white astrakhan hat. He stood stock-still some distance from his horses; he had a severe concentrated expression as if he were trying to remember something and were angry with his uncompliant memory. When Simeon went up to him and took off his hat with a smile he said:

"I'm in a hurry to get to Anastasievka. My daughter is worse again, and they tell me there's a new doctor at Anastasievka."

The coach was clamped onto the barge and they rowed back. All the while as they rowed the man, whom Simeon called Vassily Andreich, stood motionless, pressing his thin lips tight and staring in front of him. When the driver asked for leave to smoke in his presence, he did not reply, as if he did not hear. And Simeon hung over the rudder and looked at him mockingly and said:

"Even in Siberia people live. L-i-v-e!"

On Wiseacre's face was an expression of triumph as if he were proving something, as if pleased that things had happened just as he thought they would. The unhappy, helpless look of the man in the fox-fur coat seemed to give him considerable pleasure.

"The roads are now muddy, Vassily Andreich," he said, when the horses had been harnessed on the bank. "You'd better wait a couple of weeks, until it gets dryer. . . . If there were any point in going—but you know yourself that people are always on the move day and night and there's no point in it. Sure!"

Vassily Andreich said nothing, gave him a tip, took his seat in the coach, and drove away.

"Look! He's gone galloping after the doctor!" said Simeon, shivering in the cold. "Yes. To look for a real doctor, trying to overtake the wind in the fields, and catch the devil by the tail, plague take him! What strange fish there are! God forgive me, a miserable sinner."

The Tartar went up to Wiseacre and, peering at him with mingled hatred and disgust, and mixing Tartar words up with his broken Russian said with a quaver:

"He good . . . good. And you . . . bad! You are bad! The gentleman is a good soul, very good, and you are a beast, you are bad! The gentleman is alive and you are dead. . . . God made man that he should be alive, that he should have joy, sorrow, grief, and you want nothing, so you are not alive, but a stone! A stone wants nothing, and you want nothing. . . . You are a stone—and God does not love you, but the gentleman He loves."

They all laughed: the Tartar fiercely knit his brows, waved his hand, drew his rags round him, and went to the fire. The ferrymen and Simeon went slowly to the hut.

"It's cold," said one of the ferrymen hoarsely, as he lay down on the straw with which the damp clay floor was covered.

"Yes. It's not warm," another acquiesced. . . . "It's a hard life."

All of them lay down. The wind blew the door open. Snow drifted into the hut. No one could bring himself to get up and shut the door; it was cold, but they put up with it.

"And I am happy," muttered Simeon as he fell asleep. "God grant everyone such a life."

"You surely are the devil's own. Even the devil needn't bother to take you."

"Sounds like the barking of a dog came from outside.

"Who is that? Who is there?"

"It's the Tartar crying."

"Oh! he's an odd one."

"He'll get used to it!" said Simeon, and soon fell asleep. Soon the others slept too, and the door was left open.

MAXIM GORKY

One Autumn Night

Maxim Gorky (1868–1936) was self-educated and began working at the age of nine. He first became famous through his short, realistic stories published in the period from 1895 to 1900. His later work was mostly plays and novels, and his autobiography in three parts. Another important work was *Reminiscences of Tolstoy*, published in 1920. [From *Best Russian Short Stories*.]

ONCE IN THE AUTUMN I happened to be in a very unpleasant and inconvenient position. In the town where I had just arrived and where I knew not a soul, I found myself without a farthing in my pocket and without a night's lodging.

Having sold during the first few days every part of my costume without which it was still possible to go about, I passed from the town into the quarter called Yste, where were the steamship wharves—a quarter which during the navigation season fermented with boisterous, laborious life, but now was silent and deserted, for we were in the last days of October.

Dragging my feet along the moist sand, and obstinately scrutinizing it with the desire to discover in it any sort of fragment of food, I wandered alone among the deserted buildings and warehouses, and thought how good it would be to get a full meal.

In our present state of culture hunger of the mind is more quickly satisfied than hunger of the body. You wander about the streets, you are surrounded by buildings not bad-looking from the outside and—you may safely say it—not so badly furnished inside, and the sight of them may excite within you stimulating ideas about architecture, hygiene, and many other wise and high-flying subjects. You may meet warmly and neatly dressed folks—all very polite, and turning away from you tactfully, not wishing offensively to notice the lamentable fact of your existence. Well, well, the mind of a hungry man is always better nourished and healthier than the mind of the well-fed man; and there you have a situation from which you may draw a very ingenious conclusion in favor of the ill-fed.

The evening was approaching, the rain was falling, and the wind blew violently from the north. It whistled in the empty booths and shops, blew into the plastered windowpanes of the taverns, and whipped into foam the wavelets of the river which splashed noisily on the sandy shore, casting high their white crests, racing one after another into the dim distance, and leaping impetuously over one another's shoulders. It seemed as if the river felt the proximity of winter, and was running at random away from the fetters of ice which the north wind might well have flung upon her that very night. The sky was heavy and dark; down from it swept incessantly scarcely visible drops of rain, and the melancholy elegy in nature all around me was emphasized by a couple of battered and misshapen willow trees and a boat, bottom upwards, that was fastened to their roots.

The overturned canoe with its battered keel and the miserable old trees rifled by the cold wind—everything around me was bankrupt, barren, and dead, and the sky flowed with undryable tears. . . . Everything around was waste and gloomy . . . it seemed as if everything were dead, leaving me alone among the living, and for me also a cold death waited.

I was then eighteen years old—a good time!

I walked and walked along the cold wet sand, making my chattering teeth warble in honor of cold and hunger, when suddenly, as I was carefully searching for something to eat behind one of the empty crates, I perceived behind it, crouching on the ground, a figure in woman's clothes dank with the rain and clinging fast to her stooping shoulders. Standing over her, I watched to see what she was doing. It appeared that she was digging a trench in the sand with her hands—digging away under one of the crates.

"Why are you doing that?" I asked, crouching down on my heels quite close to her.

She gave a little scream and was quickly on her legs again. Now that she stood there staring at me, with her wide-open gray eyes full of terror, I perceived that it was a girl of my own age, with a very pleasant face embellished unfortunately by three large blue marks. This spoiled her, although these blue marks had been distributed with a remarkable sense of proportion, one at a time, and all were of equal size—two under the eyes, and one a little bigger on the forehead just over the bridge of the nose. This symmetry was evidently the work of an artist well inured to the business of spoiling the human physiognomy.

The girl looked at me, and the terror in her eyes gradually died out. . . . She shook the sand from her hands, adjusted her cotton headgear, cowered down, and said:

"I suppose you too want something to eat? Dig away then! My hands are tired. Over there"—she nodded her head in the direction of a booth—"there is bread for certain . . . and sausages too. . . . That booth is still carrying on business."

I began to dig. She, after waiting a little and looking at me, sat down beside me and began to help me.

We worked in silence. I cannot say now whether I thought at that moment of the criminal code, of morality, of proprietorship, and all the other things about which, in the opinion of many experienced persons, one ought to think every moment of one's life. Wishing to keep as close to the truth as possible, I must confess that apparently I was so deeply engaged in digging under the crate that I completely forgot about everything else except this one thing: What could be inside that crate?

The evening drew on. The gray, moldy, cold fog grew thicker and thicker around us. The waves roared with a hollower sound than before, and the rain pattered down on the boards of that crate more loudly and more frequently. Somewhere or other the night-watchman began springing his rattle.

"Has it got a bottom or not?" softly inquired my assistant. I did not understand what she was talking about, and I kept silence.

"I say, has the crate got a bottom? If it has we shall try in vain to break into it. Here we are digging a trench, and we may, after all, come upon nothing but solid boards. How shall we take them off? Better smash the lock; it is a wretched lock."

Good ideas rarely visit the heads of women, but, as you see, they do visit them sometimes. I have always valued good ideas, and have always tried to utilize them as far as possible.

Having found the lock, I tugged at it and wrenched off the whole thing. My accomplice immediately stooped down and wriggled like a serpent into the gaping-open, four-cornered cover of the crate whence she called to me approvingly, in a low tone:

"You're a brick!"

Nowadays a little crumb of praise from a woman is dearer to me than a whole dithyramb from a man, even though he be more eloquent than all the ancient and modern orators put together. Then, however, I was less amiably disposed than I am now, and, paying no attention to the compliment of my comrade, I asked her curtly and anxiously:

"Is there anything?"

In a monotonous tone she set about calculating our discoveries.

"A basketful of bottles—thick furs—a sunshade—an iron pail."

All this was uneatable. I felt that my hopes had vanished. . . . But suddenly she exclaimed vivaciously:

"Aha! here it is!"

"What?"

"Bread . . . a loaf . . . it's only wet . . . take it!"

A loaf flew to my feet and after it herself, my valiant comrade. I had already bitten off a morsel, stuffed it in my mouth, and was chewing it. . . .

"Come, give me some too! . . . And we mustn't stay here. . . . Where shall we go?" she looked inquiringly about on all sides. . . . It was dark, wet, and boisterous.

"Look! there's an upset canoe yonder . . . let us go there."

"Let us go then!" And off we set, demolishing our booty as we went, and filling our mouths with large portions of it. . . . The rain grew more violent, the river roared; from somewhere or other resounded a prolonged mocking whistle—just as if Someone great who feared no-body was whistling down all earthly institutions and along with them this horrid autumnal wind and us its heroes. This whistling made my heart throb painfully, in spite of which I greedily went on eating, and in this respect the girl, walking on my left hand, kept even pace with me.

"What do they call you?" I asked her—why I know not.

"Natasha," she answered shortly, munching loudly.

I stared at her. My heart ached within me; and then I stared into the mist before me, and it seemed to me as if the inimical countenance of my Destiny was smiling at me enigmatically and coldly.

The rain scourged the timbers of the skiff incessantly, and its soft patter induced melancholy thoughts, and the wind whistled as it flew down into the boat's battered bottom through a rift, where some loose splinters of wood were rattling together—a disquieting and depressing sound. The waves of the river were splashing on the shore, and sounded so monotonous and hopeless, just as if they were telling something unbearably dull and heavy, which was boring them into utter disgust, something from which they wanted to run away and yet were obliged to talk about all the same. The sound of the rain blended with their splashing, and a long-drawn sigh seemed to be floating above the overturned skiff—the endless, laboring sigh of the earth, injured and exhausted by the eternal changes from the bright and warm summer to the cold, misty and damp autumn. The wind blew continually over the desolate shore and the foaming river—blew and sang its melancholy songs. . . .

Our position beneath the shelter of the skiff was utterly devoid of comfort; it was narrow and damp; tiny cold drops of rain dribbled through the damaged bottom; gusts of wind penetrated it. We sat in silence and shivered with cold. I remembered that I wanted to go to sleep. Natasha leaned her back against the hull of the boat and curled herself up into a tiny ball. Embracing her knees with her hands, and resting her chin upon them, she stared doggedly at the river with wide-open eyes; on the pale patch of her face they seemed immense, because of the blue marks below them. She never moved, and this immobility and silence—I felt it—gradually produced within me a terror of my neighbor. I wanted to talk to her, but I knew not how to begin.

It was she herself who spoke.

"What a cursed thing life is!" she exclaimed plainly, abstractedly, and in a tone of deep conviction.

But this was no complaint. In these words there was too much of indifference for a complaint. This simple soul thought according to her understanding—thought and proceeded to form a certain conclusion which she expressed aloud, and which I could not confute for fear of contradicting myself. Therefore I was silent, and she, as if she had not noticed me, continued to sit there immovable.

"Even if we croaked . . . what then . . . ?" Natasha began again, this time quietly and reflectively, and still there was not one note of complaint in her words. It was plain that this person, in the course of her reflections on life, was regarding her own case, and had arrived at the conviction that, in order to preserve herself from the mockeries of life, she was not in a position to do anything else but simply "croak" —to use her own expression.

The clearness of this line of thought was inexpressibly sad and painful to me, and I felt that if I kept silence any longer I was really bound to weep. . . . And it would have been shameful to have done this before a woman, especially as she was not weeping herself. I resolved to speak to her.

"Who was it that knocked you about?" I asked. For the moment I could not think of anything more sensible or more delicate.

"Pashka did it all," she answered in a dull and level tone.

"And who is he?"

"My lover. . . . He was a baker."

"Did he beat you often?"

"Whenever he was drunk he beat me. . . . Often!"

And suddenly, turning toward me, she began to talk about herself, Pashka, and their mutual relations. He was a baker with red mustaches and played very well on the banjo. He came to see her and greatly pleased her, for he was a merry chap and wore nice clean clothes. He had a vest which cost fifteen roubles and boots with dress tops. For these reasons she had fallen in love with him, and he became her "creditor." And when he became her creditor, he made it his business to take away from her the money which her other friends gave to her for bonbons, and, getting drunk on this money, he would fall to beating her; but that would have been nothing if he hadn't also begun to "run after" other girls before her very eyes.

"Now, wasn't that an insult? I am not worse than the others. Of course, that meant that he was laughing at me, the blackguard. The day before yesterday I asked leave of my mistress to go out for a bit, went to him, and there I found Dimka sitting beside him drunk. And he, too, was half-seas over. I said, 'You scoundrel, you!' And he gave me a thorough hiding. He kicked me and dragged me by the hair. But that was nothing to what came after. He spoiled everything I had on—left me just as I am now! How could I appear before my mistress? He spoiled everything . . . my dress and my jacket too—it was quite a new one; I gave a fiver for it . . . and tore my kerchief from my head. . . . O Lord! What will become of me now?" she suddenly whined in a lamentable overstrained voice.

The wind howled, and became ever colder and more boisterous. . . . Again my teeth began to dance up and down, and she, huddled up to avoid the cold, pressed as closely to me as she could, so that I could see the gleam of her eyes through the darkness.

"What wretches all you men are! I'd burn you all in an oven; I'd cut you in pieces. If any one of you was dying I'd spit in his mouth, and not pity him a bit. Mean skunks! You wheedle and wheedle, you wag your tails like cringing dogs, and we fools give ourselves up to you, and it's all up with us! Immediately you trample us underfoot. . . . Miserable loafers!"

She cursed us up and down, but there was no vigor, no malice, no hatred of these "miserable loafers" in her cursing that I could hear.

The tone of her language by no means corresponded with its subject matter, for it was calm enough, and the gamut of her voice was terribly poor.

Yet all this made a stronger impression on me than the most eloquent and convincing pessimistic books and speeches, of which I had read a good many and which I still read to this day. And this, you see, was because the agony of a dying person is much more natural and violent than the most minute and picturesque descriptions of death.

I felt really wretched—more from cold than from the words of my neighbor. I groaned softly and ground my teeth.

Almost at the same moment I felt two little arms about me—one of them touched my neck and the other lay upon my face—and at the same time an anxious, gentle, friendly voice uttered this question:

"What ails you?"

I was ready to believe that someone else was asking me this and not Natasha, who had just declared that all men were scoundrels and expressed a wish for their destruction. But she it was, and now she began speaking quickly, hurriedly.

"What ails you, eh? Are you cold? Are you frozen? Ah, what a one you are, sitting there so silent like a little owl! Why, you should have told me long ago that you were cold. Come . . . lie on the ground . . . stretch yourself out and I will lie . . . there! How's that? Now put your arms around me. . . . Tighter! How's that? You shall be warm very soon now. . . . And then we'll lie back to back. . . . The night will pass so quickly, see if it won't. I say . . . have you too been drinking? . . . Turned out of your place, eh? . . . It doesn't matter."

And she comforted me. . . . She encouraged me.

May I be thrice accursed! What a world of irony was in this single fact for me! Just imagine! Here was I, seriously occupied at this very time with the destiny of humanity, thinking of the reorganization of the social system, of political revolutions, reading all sorts of devilishly wise books whose abysmal profundity was certainly unfathomable by their very authors—at this very time, I say, I was trying with all my might to make of myself "a potent active social force." It even seemed to me that I had partially accomplished my object; anyhow, at this time, in my ideas about myself, I had got so far as to recognize that I had an exclusive right to exist, that I had the necessary greatness to deserve to live my life, and that I was fully competent to play a great historical part therein. And a woman was now warming me with her body, a wretched, battered, hunted creature, who had no place and no value in life, and whom I had never thought of helping till she helped me herself, and whom I really would not have known how to help in any way even if the thought of it had occurred to me.

Ah! I was ready to think that all this was happening to me in a dream—in a disagreeable, an oppressive dream.

But, ugh! it was impossible for me to think that, for cold drops of rain were dripping down upon me, the woman was pressing close to me, her warm breath was fanning my face, and—despite a slight odor of vodka—it did me good. The wind howled and raged, the rain smote upon the skiff, the waves splashed, and both of us, embracing each other convulsively, nevertheless shivered with cold. All this was only too real, and I am certain that nobody ever dreamed such an oppressive and horrid dream as that reality.

But Natasha was talking all the time of something or other, talking kindly and sympathetically, as only women can talk. Beneath the influence of her voice and kindly words a little fire began to burn up within me, and something inside my heart thawed in consequence.

Then tears poured from my eyes like a hailstorm, washing away from my heart much that was evil, much that was stupid, much sorrow and dirt which had fastened upon it before that night. Natasha comforted me.

"Come, come, that will do, little one! Don't take on! That'll do! God will give you another chance . . . you will right yourself and stand in your proper place again . . . and it will be all right. . . ."

And she kept kissing me . . . many kisses did she give me . . . burning kisses . . . and all for nothing. . . .

Those were the first kisses from a woman that had ever been bestowed upon me, and they were the best kisses too, for all the subsequent kisses cost me frightfully dear, and really gave me nothing at all in exchange.

"Come, don't take on so, funny one! I'll manage for you tomorrow if you cannot find a place." Her quiet persuasive whispering sounded in my ears as if it came through a dream. . . .

There we lay till dawn. . . .

And when the dawn came, we crept from behind the skiff and went into the town. . . . Then we took friendly leave of each other and never met again, although for half a year I searched in every hole and corner for that kind Natasha, with whom I spent the autumn night just described.

If she be already dead—and well for her if it were so—may she rest in peace! And if she be alive . . . still I say, "Peace to her soul!" And may the consciousness of her fall never enter her soul . . . for that would be a superfluous and fruitless suffering if life is to be lived. . . .

SHOLOM ALEICHEM

Tevye Wins a Fortune

Sholom Aleichem (1859–1916) is the pen name of Solomon Rabinowitch, the best known modern Jewish writer. Born in the Ukraine, he wrote some 300 stories, five novels and many plays—all in Yiddish, his native tongue. He died in New York and his grave, in Brooklyn, has become a shrine which many Jews visit every year. Some of his short stories have been translated and collected under the title of *The Old Country*. [From *The Old Country* by Sholom Aleichem; copyright 1946 by Crown Publishers; translated by Julius and Frances Butwin.]

Who raiseth up the poor out of the dust,
And lifteth up the needy out of the dung-
hill.

—PSALMS, 113:7.

IF YOU ARE DESTINED to draw the winning ticket in the lottery, Mr. Sholom Aleichem, it will come right into your house without your asking for it. As King David says, "It never rains but it pours." You don't need wisdom or skill. And, on the contrary, if you are not inscribed as a winner in the Books of the Angels, you can talk yourself blue in the face—it won't help you. The *Talmud* is right: "You can lead a horse to water, but you cannot make him drink." A person slaves, wears himself to the bone, and gets nowhere. He might as well lie down and give up his ghost. Suddenly, no one knows how or for what reason, money rolls in from all sides. As the passage has it, "Relief and deliverance will come to the Jews." I don't have to explain that to you. It should be clear to both of us that so long as a Jew can still draw breath and feel the blood beating in his veins, he must never lose hope. I have seen it in my own experience, in the way the Lord dealt with me in providing me with my present livelihood. For how else should I happen to be selling cheese and butter all of a sudden? In my wildest dreams I had never seen myself as a dairyman.

Take my word for it, the story is worth hearing. I'll sit down for a little while here near you on the grass. Let the horse do a little nibbling meanwhile. After all, even a horse is one of God's living creatures.

Well, it was in the late spring, around *Shevuos* time. But I don't want to mislead you; it may have been a week or two before *Shevuos,* or—let's see—maybe a couple of weeks after *Shevuos*. Don't forget, this didn't happen yesterday. Wait! To be exact, it was nine or ten years ago to the day. And maybe a trifle more.

In those days I was not the man I am today. That is, I *was* the same Tevye, and yet not exactly the same. The same old woman, as they say, but in a different bonnet. How so? I was as poor as a man could be, com-

577

pletely penniless. If you want to know the truth I'm not a rich man now either, but compared with what I was then I can now really call myself a man of wealth. I have a horse and wagon of my own, a couple of cows that give milk, and a third that is about to calve. We can't complain. We have cheese and butter and fresh cream all the time. We make it ourselves; that is, our family does. We all work. No one is idle. My wife milks the cows; the children carry pitchers and pails, churn the butter. And I myself, as you see, drive to market every morning, go from *datcha* to *datcha* in Boiberik, visit with people, see this one and that one, all the important businessmen from Yehupetz who come there for the summer. Talking to them makes me feel that I am somebody, too; I amount to something in the world.

And when Saturday comes—then I really live like a king! I look into the Holy Books, read the weekly portion of the Bible, dip into the commentaries, Psalms, *Perek,* this, that, something else . . . Ah, you're surprised, Mr. Sholom Aleichem! No doubt you're thinking to yourself, "Ah, that Tevye—there's a man for you!"

Anyway, what did I start to tell you? That's right. Those days. Oh, was Tevye a pauper then! With God's help I starved to death—I and my wife and children—three times a day, not counting supper. I worked like a horse, pulling wagonloads of logs from the woods to the railroad station for—I am ashamed to admit it—half a *ruble* a day. And that not every day, either. And on such earnings just try to fill all those hungry mouths, not counting that boarder of mine, the poor horse, whom I can't put off with a quotation from the *Talmud.*

So what does the Lord do? He is a great, all-powerful God. He manages His little world wisely and well. Seeing how I was struggling for a hard crust of bread, He said to me: "Do you think, Tevye, that you have nothing more to live for, that the world has come to an end? If that's what you think, you're a big lummox. Soon you will see: if I will it, your luck can change in one turn of the wheel, and what was dark as the grave will be full of brightness." As we say on *Yom Kippur,* the Lord decides who will ride on horseback and who will crawl on foot. The main thing is—hope! A Jew must always hope, must never lose hope. And in the meantime, what if we waste away to a shadow? For that we are Jews—the Chosen People, the envy and admiration of the world.

Anyway, this is how it happened. As the Bible says, ".\nd there came the day . . ." One evening in summer I was driving through the woods on my way home with an empty wagon. My head was bent, my heart was heavy. The little horse, poor thing, was barely dragging its feet. "Ah," I said to it, "crawl along, *shlimazl*! If you are Tevye's horse you too must know the pangs of hunger . . ." All around was silence, every crack of the whip echoed through the woods. As the sun set the shadows of the trees stretched out and lengthened—like our Jewish exile. Darkness was creeping in and a sadness filled my heart. Strange, faraway thoughts filled my mind, and before my eyes passed the images of people a long time dead. And in the midst of it all I thought of my home and my family. And I thought, "Woe unto us all." The wretched dark little hut that was my home, and the children barefoot and in tatters waiting for their father, the *shlimazl*. Maybe he would bring them a loaf of bread or a few stale rolls. And my wife, grumbling as a wife will: "Children I had to bear him—seven of them. I might as well take them all and throw them into the river—may God not punish me for these words!"

You can imagine how I felt. We are only human. The stomach is empty and words won't fill it. If you swallow a piece of herring you want some tea, and for tea you need sugar. And sugar, I am told, is in the grocery store. "My stomach," says my wife, "can get along without a piece of bread, but if I don't take a glass of tea in the morning, I am a dead woman. All night long the baby sucks me dry."

But in spite of everything, we are still Jews. When evening comes we have to say our prayers. You can imagine what the prayers sounded like if I tell you that just as I was about to begin *Shmin-esra* my horse suddenly broke away as if possessed by the devil and ran wildly off through the woods. Have you ever tried standing on one spot facing the east while a horse was pulling you where *it* wanted to go? I had no choice but to run after him, holding onto the reins and chanting, "*God of Abraham, God of Isaac, and God of Jacob.*" A fine way to say *Shmin-esra*! And just my luck, at a moment when I was in the mood to pray with feeling, out of the depths of my heart, hoping it would lift my spirits . . .

So there I was, running after the wagon and chanting at the top of my voice, as if I were a cantor in a synagogue: "*Thou sustainest the living with loving kindness* (and sometimes with a little food) *and keepest thy faith with them that sleep in the dust.* (The dead are not the only ones who lie in the dust; Oh, how low we the living are laid, what hells we go through, and I don't mean the rich people of Yehupetz who spend their summers at the *datchas* of Boiberik, eating and drinking and living off the fat of the land . . . Oh, Heavenly Father, why does this happen to me? Am I not as good as others? Help me, dear God!) *Look upon our afflictions.* (Look down, dear God! See how we struggle and come to the aid of the poor, because who will look out for us if you don't?) *Heal us, O Lord, and we shall be healed.* (Send us the cure, we have the ailment already.) *Bless this year for us, O Lord, our God, with every kind of produce* (corn and wheat and every other grain, and if you do, will I get anything out of it, *shlimazl* that I am? For instance, what difference does it make to my poor horse whether oats are dear or cheap?)."

But that's enough. Of God you don't ask questions. If you're one of the Chosen People you must see the good in everything and say, "This too is for the best." God must have willed it so . . .

"*And for slanderers let there be no hope,*" I chant further. The slanderers and rich scoffers who say there is no God—a fine figure

they'll cut when they get *there*. They'll pay for their disbelief, and
with interest too, for He is one who "breaketh his enemies and humbleth
the arrogant." He pays you according to your deserts. You don't trifle
with Him; you approach Him humbly, pray to Him and beg His
mercy. *"O Merciful Father, hear our voice, pay heed to our lamentations. Spare us and have mercy upon us* (my wife and children too—
they are hungry). *Accept, O Lord, thy people Israel and their prayer,
even as you did in the days of the Holy Temple, when the priests and
the Levites . . ."*

Suddenly the horse stopped. In a hurry I finish *Shmin-esra*, lift up
my eyes, and behold two mysterious creatures coming toward me out
of the forest, disguised or at least dressed in the strangest fashion.
"Thieves," I thought, but corrected myself at once. "What is the
matter with you, Tevye? You've been driving through this forest for
so many years by day and by night; why should you suddenly begin to
worry about thieves?" And swinging my whip over my head, I yelled
at the horse, "Giddap!"

"Mister!" one of the two creatures called out to me. "Stop! Please
stop! Don't run away, Mister, we won't do you any harm!"

"An evil spirit!" I said to myself, and a second later, "You ox, Tevye,
you ass! Why should the evil spirits come to you all of a sudden?"
And I stop the horse. I look the creatures over from head to foot: they
are ordinary women. One elderly with a silk shawl on her head and
the other a younger one with a *sheitel*. Both flushed and out of
breath.

"Good evening," I cry out loud, trying to sound cheerful. "Look
who's here! What is it you want? If you want to buy something, all
I have is a gnawing stomach, a heart full of pain, a head full of worries,
and all the misery and wretchedness in the world."

"Listen to him going on," they say. "That's enough. You say one
word to a man and you get a lecture in return. There is nothing we
want to buy. We only want to ask: do you know where the road to
Boiberik is?"

"To Boiberik?" I say, and let out a laugh, still trying to sound
cheerful. "You might as well ask me if I know my name is Tevye."

"Oh? So that's what they call you—Tevye? Good evening, then,
Mr. Tevye. What is there to laugh at? We are strangers here. We
are from Yehupetz, and we are staying at a *datcha* in Boiberik. This
morning we went out for a short walk in the woods, and we've been
wandering ever since, going round and round in circles. A little while
ago we heard someone singing in the forest. At first we thought it
was a highwayman, but when we came closer and saw it was only you,
we felt relieved. Now do you understand?"

"Ha-ha!" I laughed. "A fine highwayman! Have you ever heard
the story about the Jewish highwayman who waylaid a traveler in the
forest and demanded—a pinch of snuff? If you'd like, I could tell it
to you . . ."

"Leave that for some other time," they said. "Right now, show us how to get back to Boiberik."

"To Boiberik?" I said again. "Why, this is the way to Boiberik. Even if you don't want to, you couldn't help getting there if you followed this path."

"Oh," said they. "Is it far?"

"No, not far. Only a few *versts*. That is, five or six. Maybe seven. But certainly not more than eight."

"Eight *versts*!" they both cried out, wringing their hands and all but bursting into tears. "Do you know what you're saying? Only eight *versts*!"

"What do you want me to do about it?" I asked. "If it were up to me, I'd have made it a little shorter. But people have to have all sorts of experiences. How would you like to be in a carriage crawling up a hill through mud in a heavy rain, late Friday afternoon and almost time to light the candles for the Sabbath? Your hands are numb, you're faint with hunger . . . And crash! The axle breaks!"

"You talk like a half-wit," they said. "You must be out of your head. Why do you tell us these old-wives' tales? We're too tired to take another step. We've had nothing to eat all day except for a glass of coffee and a butter roll in the morning, and you come bothering us with foolish tales."

"Well, that's different," I told them. "You can't expect a person to dance before he's eaten. The taste of hunger is something I understand very well. You don't have to explain it to me. It's quite possible that I haven't even seen a cup of coffee or butter roll for the past year . . ." And as I utter these words a glass of steaming coffee with milk in it appears before my eyes, with rich, fresh butter rolls and other good things besides. "Oh, *shlimazl*," I say to myself, "is that what you've been raised on—coffee and butter rolls? And a plain piece of bread with herring isn't good enough for you?" But there, just to spite me, the image of hot coffee remained; just to tempt me the vision of rolls hovered before my eyes. I smelled the odor of the coffee, I savored the taste of the butter roll on my tongue—fresh and rich and sweet . . .

"Do you know what, Reb Tevye?" the women said to me. "Since we are standing right here, maybe it would be a good idea if we jumped into your wagon and you took us home to Boiberik. What do you say?"

"A fine idea," I said. "Here am I, coming *from* Boiberik, and you're going *to* Boiberik. How can I go both ways at the same time?"

"Well," they said, "don't you know what you can do? A wise and learned man can figure it out for himself. He would turn the wagon around and go back again—that's all. Don't be afraid, Reb Tevye. You can be sure that when you and the Almighty get us back home again, we'll see to it that your kindness won't go unrewarded."

"They're talking Chaldaic," I told myself. "I don't understand them. What do they mean?" And the thought of witches and evil spirits

and goblins returned to me. "Dummy, what are you standing there
for?" I asked myself. "Jump into the wagon, show the horse your
whip, and get away from here!" But again, as if I were under a spell,
these words escaped me: "Well, get in."

The women did not wait to be asked again. Into the wagon they
climb, with me after them. I turn the wagon around, crack the whip
—one, two, three, let's go . . . Who? What? When? The horse
doesn't know what I'm talking about. He won't move an inch. "Ah-ha,"
I think to myself. "Now I can see what these women are. That's all
I had to do—stop in the middle of the woods to make conversation
with women!" You get the picture: on all sides the woods, silent,
melancholy, with night coming on, and here behind me these two
creatures in the guise of women. My imagination runs away with me. I
recall a story about a teamster who once was riding through the woods
by himself when he saw lying on the road a bag of oats. He jumped
down, heaved the heavy sack to his back and just managed to tip it
into the wagon, and went on. He rode a *verst* or two, looked around
at the sack—but there was neither sack nor oats. In the wagon was a
goat, a goat with a beard. The teamster tried to touch it with his
hand, but the goat stuck out his tongue—a yard long—and let out a
wild, piercing laugh and vanished into air . . .

"Well, what's keeping you?" ask the women.

"What's keeping me? Can't you see what's keeping me? The horse
doesn't want to play. He is not in the mood."

"Well, you've got a whip, haven't you? Then use it."

"Thanks for the advice," I say. "I'm glad you reminded me. The
only trouble with that is that my friend here is not afraid of such
things. He is as used to the whip as I am to poverty," I add, trying to
be flippant, though all the time I am shaking as if in a fever.

Well, what more can I tell you? I vented all my wrath on the poor
animal. I whipped him till with God's help the horse stirred from
his place, and we went on our way through the woods. And as we ride
along a new thought comes to plague me. "Ah, Tevye, what a dull ox
you are! You have always been good for nothing and you'll die good
for nothing. Think! Here something happens to you that won't happen
again in a hundred years. God Himself must have arranged it. So
why didn't you make sure in advance how much it is going to be
worth to you—how much you'll get for it? Even if you consider
righteousness and virtues, decency and helpfulness, justice and equity
and I don't know what else, there is still no harm in earning a little
something for yourself out of it. Why not lick a bone for once in your
life, since you have the chance? Stop your horse, you ox. Tell them
what you want. Either you get so much and so much for the trip, or
ask them to be so kind as to jump off the wagon at once! But then,
what good would that do? What if they promised you the whole world
on a platter? You have to catch a bear before you can skin it . . .

"Why don't you drive a little faster?" the women ask again, prodding me from behind.

"What's your hurry?" I say. "Nothing good can come from rushing too much." And I look around at my passengers. I'll swear they look like women, just plain ordinary women, one with a silk shawl, the other with a *sheitel*. They are looking at each other and whispering. Then one of them asks: "Are we getting closer?"

"Closer, yes. But not any closer than we really are. Pretty soon we'll go uphill and then downhill, then uphill and downhill again, and then after that we go up the steep hill and from then on it's straight ahead, right to Boiberik."

"Sounds like a *shlimazl*," says one to the other.

"A seven-year itch," the other answers.

"As if we haven't had troubles enough already," says the first.

"A little crazy too, I'm afraid," answers the other.

"I must be crazy," I tell myself, "if I let them pull me around by the nose like that."

And to them I say, "Where do you want to be dropped off, ladies?"

"Dropped off? What do you mean—dropped off? What kind of language is that?"

"It's only an expression. You hear it among coarse and impolite drovers," I tell them. "Among genteel people like us we'd say it like this: 'Where would you wish to be transported, dear ladies, when with God's help and the blessings of Providence we arrive at Boiberik?' Excuse me if I sound inquisitive, but as the saying goes, 'It's better to ask twice than to go wrong once.'"

"Oh, so that's what you mean?" said the women. "Go straight ahead through the woods until you come to the green *datcha* by the river. Do you know where that is?"

"How could I help knowing?" I say. "I know Boiberik as well as I know my own home. I wish I had a thousand *rubles* for every log I've carried there. Last summer I brought a couple of loads of wood to that *datcha* you mention. Somebody from Yehupetz was living there then, a rich man, a millionaire. He must have been worth at least a hundred thousand *rubles*."

"He still lives there," they tell me, looking at each other, whispering together and laughing.

"In that case," I said, "if you have some connections with the man, maybe it would be possible, if you wanted to, that is, if you could say a word or two in my behalf . . . Maybe you could get some sort of job for me, work of some kind. I know a man, a young fellow called Yisroel, who lived not far from our village—a worthless good-for-nothing. Well, he went off to the city, no one knows how it happened, and today, believe it or not, he is an important man somewhere. He makes at least twenty *rubles* a week, or maybe even forty. Who knows for sure? Some people are lucky, like our *shochet's* son-in-law. What

would he ever have amounted to if he hadn't gone to Yehupetz? It is
true, the first few years he starved to death. But now I wouldn't mind
being in his boots. Regularly he sends money home, and he would like
to bring his wife and children to Yehupetz to live with him, but he
can't do it, because by law he isn't allowed to live there himself. Then
how does he do it? Never mind. He has trouble aplenty, only if you
live long enough . . . Oh, here we are at the river, and there is the
green *datcha!*"

And I drive in smartly right up to the porch. You should have seen
the excitement when they saw us. Such cheering and shouting!
"Grandmother! Mother! Auntie! They've come home again! Congratulations! *Mazl-tov!* Heavens, where were you? We went crazy
all day! Sent messengers in all directions. . . . We thought—who can
tell? Maybe wolves, highwaymen—who knows? Tell us, what happened?"

"What happened? What should happen? We got lost in the woods,
wandered far away, till a man happened along. What kind of a man?
A *shlimazl* with a horse and wagon. It took a little coaxing, but here
we are."

"Of all horrible things! It's a dream, a nightmare! Just the two of
you—without a guide! Thank God you're safe!"

To make a long story short, they brought lamps out on the porch,
spread the table, and began bringing things out. Hot samovars, tea
glasses, sugar, preserves, and fresh pastry that I could smell even from
where I was standing; after that all kinds of food: rich fat soup, roast
beef, goose, the best of wines and salads. I stood at the edge of the
porch looking at them from a distance and thinking, "What a wonderful
life these people of Yehupetz must live, praise the Lord! I wouldn't
mind being one of them myself. What these people drop on the floor
would be enough to feed my starving children all week long. O God,
All-powerful and All-merciful, great and good, kind and just, how does
it happen that to some people you give everything and to others nothing? To some people butter rolls and to others the plague?" But then
I tell myself, "You big fool, Tevye! Are you trying to tell Him how
to rule His world? Apparently if He wants it that way, that's the way
it ought to be. Can't you see? If it should have been different it would
have been? And yet, what would have been wrong to have it different?
True! We were slaves in Pharaoh's day, too. That's why we are the
Chosen People. That's why we must have faith and hope. Faith, first
of all in a God, and hope that maybe in time, with His help, things
will become a little better . . ."

But then I hear someone say, "Wait! Where is he, this man you've
mentioned? Did he drive away already—the *shlimazl?*"

"God forbid!" I call out from the edge of the porch. "What do you
think? That I'd go away like this—without saying anything? Good
evening! Good evening to you all, and may the Lord bless you. Eat
well, and may your food agree with you!"

"Come here!" they said to me. "What are you standing there for in the dark? Let's take a look at you, see what you are like! Maybe you'd like a little whiskey?"

"A little whiskey?" said I. "Who ever refused a drink of whiskey? How does it say in the *Talmud?* 'God is God, but whiskey is something you can drink!' To your health, ladies and gentlemen."

And I turn up the first glass. "May God provide for you," I say. "May He keep you rich and happy. Jews," I say, "must always be Jews. And may God give them the health and the strength to live through all the troubles they're born to . . ."

The *nogid* himself, a fine looking man with a skullcap, interrupts me. "What's your name?" he asks. "Where do you hail from? Where do you live now? What do you do for a living? Do you have any children? How many?"

"Children?" I say. "Do I have children? Oh . . . if it is true that each child were really worth a million, as my Golde insists, then I should be richer than the richest man in Yehupetz. The only thing wrong with this argument is that we still go to bed hungry. What does the Bible say? 'The world belongs to him who has money.' It's the millionaires who have the money; all I have is daughters. And as my grandmother used to say, 'If you have enough girls, the whole world whirls.' But I'm not complaining. God is our Father. He has His own way. He sits on high, and we struggle down below. What do I struggle with? I haul logs, lumber. What else should I do? The *Talmud* is right, 'If you can't have chicken, herring will do.' That's the whole trouble. We still have to eat. As my old grandmother— may she rest in peace—used to say, 'If we didn't have to eat, we'd all be rich.' "

I realized that my tongue was going sideways. "Excuse me, please," I said. "Beware of the wisdom of a fool and the proverbs of a drunkard."

At this the *nogid* cries out, "Why doesn't somebody bring something to eat?" And at once the table is filled with every kind of food—fish and fowl and roasts, wings and giblets and livers galore.

"Won't you take something?" they say. "Come on!"

"A sick person you ask; a healthy person you give," I say. "Thanks, anyway. A little whiskey—granted. But don't expect me to sit down and eat a meal like this while there, at home, my wife and children . . ."

Well, they caught onto what I was driving at, and you should have seen them start packing things into my wagon. This one brought rolls, that one fish, another one a roast chicken, tea, a package of sugar, a pot of chicken fat, a jar of preserves.

"This," they say, "take home for your wife and children. And now tell us how much you'd want us to pay you for all you did for us."

"How do I know what it was worth?" I answer. "Whatever you think is right. If it's a penny more or a penny less I'll still be the same Tevye either way."

"No," they say. "We want you to tell us yourself, Reb Tevye. Don't be afraid. We won't chop your head off."

I think to myself, "What shall I do? This is bad. What if I say one *ruble* when they might be willing to give two? On the other hand, if I said two they might think I was crazy. What have I done to earn that much?" But my tongue slipped and before I knew what I was saying, I cried out, "Three *rubles!*"

At this the crowd began to laugh so hard that I wished I was dead and buried.

"Excue me if I said the wrong thing," I stammered. "A horse, which has four feet, stumbles once in a while too, so why shouldn't a man who has but one tongue?"

The merriment increased. They held their sides laughing.

"Stop laughing, all of you!" cried the man of the house, and from his pocket he took a large purse and from the purse pulled out—how much do you think? For instance, guess! A ten-*ruble* note, red as fire! As I live and breathe . . . And he says, "This is from me. And now, the rest of you, dig into your pockets and give what you think you should."

Well, what shall I tell you? Fives and threes and ones began to fly across the table. My arms and legs trembled. I was afraid I was going to faint.

"*Nu,* what are you standing there for?" said my host. "Gather up the few *rubles* and go home to your wife and children."

"May God give you everything you desire ten times over," I babble, sweeping up the money with both hands and stuffing it into my pockets. "May you have all that is good, may you have nothing but joy. And now," I said, "good night, and good luck, and God be with you. With you and your children and grandchildren and all your relatives."

But when I turn to go back to the wagon, the mistress of the house, the woman with the silk shawl, calls to me, "Wait a minute, Reb Tevye. I want to give you something, too. Come back tomorrow morning, if all is well. I have a cow—a milch cow. It was once a wonderful cow, used to give twenty-four glasses of milk a day. But some jealous person must have cast an evil eye on it: you can't milk it any more. That is, you can milk it all right, but nothing comes."

"Long may you live!" I answer. "Don't worry. If you give us the cow we'll not only milk it—we'll get milk too! My wife, Lord bless ner, is so resourceful that she makes noodles out of almost nothing, adds water and we have noodle soup. Every week she performs a miracle: we have food for the Sabbath! She has brought up seven children, though often she has nothing to give them for supper but a box on the ear! . . . Excuse me, please, if I've talked too much. Good night and good luck and God be with you," I say, and turn around to leave. I come out in the yard, reach for my horse—and stop dead! I look everywhere. Not a trace of a horse!

"Well, Tevye," I say to myself. "This time they really got you!"

And I recall a story I must have read somewhere, about a gang of thieves that once kidnaped a pious and holy man, lured him into a palace behind the town, dined him and wined him, and then suddenly vanished, leaving him all alone with a beautiful woman. But while he looked the woman changed into a tigress, and the tigress into a cat, the cat into an adder.

"Watch out, Tevye," I say to myself. "No telling what they'll do next!"

"What are you mumbling and grumbling about now?" they ask.

"What am I grumbling about? Woe is me! I'm ruined! My poor little horse!"

"Your horse," they tell me, "is in the stable."

I come into the stable, look around. As true as I'm alive, there's my bony little old nag right next to their aristocratic horses, deeply absorbed in feeding. His jaws work feverishly, as if this is the last meal he'll ever have.

"Look here, my friend," I say to him. "It's time to move along. It isn't wise to make a hog of yourself. An extra mouthful, and you may be sorry."

I finally persuaded him, coaxed him back to his harness, and in good spirits we started for home, singing one hymn after another. As for the old horse—you would never have known him! I didn't even have to whip him. He raced like the wind. We came home late, but I woke up my wife with a shout of joy.

"Good evening!" said I. "Congratulations! *Mazl-tov*, Golde!"

"A black and endless *mazl-tov* to you!" she answers me. "What are you so happy about, my beloved bread-winner? Are you coming from a wedding or a *bris*—a circumcision feast—my goldspinner?"

"A wedding and a *bris* rolled into one," I say. "Just wait, my wife, and you'll see the treasure I've brought you! But first wake up the children. Let them have a taste of the Yehupetz delicacies, too!"

"Are you crazy?" she asks. "Are you insane, or out of your head, or just delirious? You sound unbalanced—violent!" And she lets me have it—all the curses she knows—as only a woman can.

"Once a wife always a wife," I tell her. "No wonder King Solomon said that among his thousand wives there wasn't one that amounted to anything. It's lucky that it isn't the custom to have a lot of wives any more!"

And I go out to the wagon and come back with my arms full of all the good things that they had given me. I put it all on the table, and when my crew saw the fresh white rolls and smelled the meat and fish they fell on it like hungry wolves. You should have seen them grab and stuff and chew—like the Children of Israel in the desert. The Bible says, "And they did eat," and I could say it, too. Tears came to my eyes.

"Well," says my helpmate, "tell me—who has decided to feed the countryside? What makes you so gay? Who gave you the drinks?"

"Wait, my love," I say to her. "I'll tell you everything. But first heat up the samovar. Then we'll all sit around the table, as people should now and then, and have a little tea. We live but once, my dear. Let's celebrate. We are independent now. We have a cow that used to be good for twenty-four glasses a day. Tomorrow morning, if the Lord permits, I'll bring her home. And look at this, my Golde! Look at this!" And I pull out the green and red and yellow banknotes from my pockets. "Come, my Golde, show us how smart you are! Tell me how much there is here!"

I look across at my wife. She's dumfounded. She can't say a word.

"God protect you, my darling!" I say to her. "What are you scared of? Do you think I stole it? I am ashamed of you, Golde! You've been Tevye's wife so many years and you think that of me! Silly, this is *kosher* money, earned honestly with my own wit and my own labor. I rescued two women from a great misfortune. If it were not for me, I don't know what would have become of them."

So I told her everything, from *a* to *z*. The whole story of my wanderings. And we counted the money over and over. There were eighteen *rubles*—for good luck, you know—and another eighteen for more good luck, and one besides. In all—thirty-seven *rubles*!

My wife began to cry.

"What are you crying for, you foolish woman?" I ask.

"How can I help crying when my tears won't stop? When your heart is full your eyes run over. May God help me, Tevye, my heart told me that you would come with good news. I can't remember when I last saw my Grandmother Tzeitl—may she rest in peace—in a dream. But just before you came home I was asleep and suddenly I dreamed I saw a milkpail full to the brim. My Grandmother Tzeitl was carrying it under her apron to shield it from an evil eye, and the children were crying, 'Mama . . .' "

"Don't eat up all the noodles before the Sabbath!" I interrupt. "May your Grandmother Tzeitl be happy in Paradise—I don't know how much she can help us right now. Let's leave that to God. He saw to it that we should have a cow of our own, so no doubt He can also make her give milk. Better give me some advice, Golde. Tell me—what shall we do with the money?"

"That's right, Tevye," says she. "What do you plan to do with so much money?"

"Well, what do you think we can do with it?" I say. "Where shall we invest it?"

And we began to think of this and that, one thing after another. We racked our brains, thought of every kind of enterprise on earth. That night we were engaged in every type of business you could imagine. We bought a pair of horses and sold them at a profit; opened a grocery store in Boiberik, sold the stock and went into the drygoods business. We bought an option on some woodland and made something on that, too, then obtained the tax concession at Anatevka, and with our earnings began to loan out money on mortgages.

"Be careful! Don't be so reckless!" my wife warned me. "You'll throw it all away. Before you know it, you'll have nothing left but your whip!"

"What do you want me to do?" I ask. "Deal in grain and lose it all? Look what's happening right now in the wheat market. Go! See what's going on in Odessa!"

"What do I care about Odessa? My great-grandfather was never there, and so long as I'm alive and have my senses, my children will never be their, either!"

"Then what *do* you want?"

"What do I want? I want you to have some brains and not act like a fool."

"So you're the brainy one! You get a few *rubles* in your hand and suddenly you're wise. That's what always happens."

Well, we disagreed a few times, fell out, had some arguments, but in the end this is what we decided: to buy another cow—in addition to the one we were getting for nothing. A cow that would really give milk.

Maybe you'll say, "Why a cow?" And I'll answer, "Why not a cow?" Here we are, so close to Boiberik, where all the rich people of Yehupetz come to spend the summer at their *datchas*. They're so refined that they expect everything to be brought to them on a platter—meat and eggs, chickens, onions, peppers, parsnips—everything. Why shouldn't there be someone who would be willing to come right to their kitchen door every morning with cheese and butter and cream? Especially since the Yehupetzers believe in eating well and are ready to pay?

The main thing is that what you bring must be good—the cream must be thick, the butter golden. And where will you find cream and butter that's better than mine?

So we make a living . . . May the two of us be blessed by the Lord as often as I am stopped on the road by important people from Yehupetz —even Russians—who beg me to bring them what I can spare. "We have heard, Tevel, that you are an upright man, even if you are a Jewish dog . . ." Now, how often does a person get a compliment like that? Do our own people ever praise a man? No! All they do is envy him.

When they saw that Tevye had an extra cow, a new wagon, they began to rack their brains. "Where did he get it? How did he get it? Maybe he's a counterfeiter. Maybe he cooks alcohol in secret."

I let them worry. "Scratch your heads and rack your brains, my friends! Break your heads if you begrudge me my small living."

I don't know if you'll believe my story. You're almost the first person I've ever told it to.

But I'm afraid I've said too much already. If so, forgive me! I forgot that we all have work to do. As the Bible says, "Let the shoemaker stick to his last." You to your books, Mr. Sholom Aleichem, and I to my pots and jugs . . .

One thing I beg of you. Don't put me into one of your books, and if you do put me in, at least don't tell them my real name.

Be well and happy always.

FEODOR SOLOGUB

Hide and Seek

Feodor Sologub (1863–1927) was born in St. Petersburg and educated at St. Petersburg Teachers' Institute. In 1907 he retired from teaching to devote all his time to writing poetry and novels. Although he remained aloof from the revolutionary movement in 1917, he continued to live in Russia. His best known novels are *The Little Demon, The Created Legend, Phantom Charms* and *The Charmer of Snakes*. [Used by permission of the translator, John Cournos.]

EVERYTHING IN LELECHKA'S NURSERY WAS BRIGHT, pretty, and cheerful. Lelechka's sweet voice charmed her mother. Lelechka was a delightful child. There was no other such child, there never had been, and there never would be. Lelechka's mother, Serafima Alexandrovna, was sure of that. Lelechka's eyes were dark and large, her cheeks were rosy, her lips were made for kisses and for laughter. But it was not these charms in Lelechka that gave her mother the keenest joy. Lelechka was her mother's only child. That was why every movement of Lelechka's bewitched her mother. It was great bliss to hold Lelechka on her knees and to fondle her; to feel the little girl in her arms—a thing as lively and as chipper as a little bird.

To tell the truth, Serafima Alexandrovna felt happy only in the nursery. She felt cold with her husband.

Perhaps it was because he himself loved the cold—he loved to drink cold water, and to breathe cold air. He was always fresh and cool, with a frigid smile, and wherever he passed cold currents seemed to move in the air.

The Nesletyevs, Sergei Modestovich and Serafima Alexandrovna, had married without love or calculation, because it was the accepted thing. He was a young man of thirty-five, she a young woman of twenty-five; both were of the same circle and well brought up; he was expected to take a wife, and the time had come for her to take a husband.

It even seemed to Serafima Alexandrovna that she was in love with her future husband, and this made her happy. He looked handsome and well-bred; his intelligent gray eyes always preserved a dignified expression; and he fulfilled his obligations of a fiancé with irreproachable gentleness.

The bride was good-looking; she was a tall, dark-eyed, dark-haired girl, somewhat timid but very tactful. He was not after her dowry, though it pleased him to know that she had something. He had connections, and his wife came of good, influential people. This might, at the proper opportunity, prove useful. Always irreproachable and tactful, Nesletyev got on in his position not so fast that anyone should envy him, nor yet so slow that he should envy anyone else—everything came in the proper measure and at the proper time.

After their marriage there was nothing in the manner of Sergei Modestovich to suggest anything wrong to his wife. Later, however, when his wife was about to have a child, Sergei Modestovich established connections elsewhere of a light and temporary nature. Serafima Alexandrovna found this out, and, to her own astonishment, was not particularly hurt; she awaited her infant with a restless anticipation which swallowed every other feeling.

A little girl was born; Serafima Alexandrovna gave herself up to her. At the beginning she used to tell her husband, with rapture, of all the joyous details of Lelechka's existence. But she soon found that he listened to her without the slightest interest, and only from politeness. Serafima Alexandrovna drifted farther and farther away from him. She loved her little girl with the ungratified passion that other women, deceived in their husbands, show their chance young lovers.

"*Mamochka*, let's play *priatki*," (hide and seek), cried Lelechka, pronouncing the *r* like the *l*, so that the word sounded "pliatki."

This charming inability to speak always made Serafima Alexandrovna smile with tender rapture. Lelechka then ran away, stamping with her plump little legs over the carpets, and hid herself behind the curtains near her bed.

"*Tiu-tiu, mamochka!*" she cried out in her sweet, laughing voice, as she looked out with a single roguish eye.

"Where is my baby girl?" the mother asked, as she looked for Lelechka and made believe that she did not see her.

And Lelechka poured out her rippling laughter from her hiding place. Then she came out a little farther, and her mother, pretending that she had only just caught sight of her, seized her by her little shoulders and exclaimed joyously: "Here she is, my Lelechka!"

Lelechka laughed long and merrily, her head close to her mother's knees, and all of her cuddled up between her mother's white hands. Her mother's eyes glowed with passionate emotion.

"Now, *mamochka*, you hide," said Lelechka, as she ceased laughing.

Her mother went to hide. Lelechka turned away as if not to see, but watched her *mamochka* stealthily all the time. Mamma hid behind the cupboard, and exclaimed: "*Tiu-tiu*, baby girl!"

Lelechka ran round the room and looked into all the corners, making believe, as her mother had done before, that she was seeking—though she really knew all the time where her *mamochka* was standing.

"Where's my *mamochka*?" asked Lelechka. "She's not here, and she's not here," she kept on repeating, as she ran from corner to corner.

Her mother stood, with suppressed breathing, her head pressed against the wall, her hair somewhat disarranged. A smile of utter bliss played on her red lips.

The nurse, Fedosya, a good-natured and fine-looking, if somewhat stupid woman, smiled as she looked at her mistress with her characteristic expression, which seemed to say that it was not for her to object to gentlewomen's caprices. She thought to herself: "The mother is like a little child herself—look how excited she is."

Lelechka was getting nearer her mother's corner. Her mother was growing more absorbed every moment by her interest in the game; her heart beat with short quick strokes, and she pressed even closer to the wall, disarranging her hair still more. Lelechka suddenly glanced toward her mother's corner and screamed with joy.

"I've found 'oo," she cried out loudly and joyously, mispronouncing her words in a way that again made her mother happy.

She pulled her mother by her hands to the middle of the room, they were merry and they laughed; and Lelechka again hid her head against her mother's knees, and went on lisping and lisping, without end, her sweet little words, so fascinating yet so awkward.

Sergei Modestovich was approaching the nursery at this moment. Through the half-closed doors he heard the laughter, the joyous outcries, the sound of romping. He entered the nursery, smiling his genial cold smile; he was irreproachably dressed, and he looked fresh and erect, and he spread round him an atmosphere of cleanliness, freshness and coldness. He entered in the midst of the lively game, and distressed them all by his radiant coldness. Even Fedosya felt abashed, now for her mistress, now for herself. Serafima Alexandrovna at once became calm and apparently cold—and this mood communicated itself to the little girl, who ceased to laugh, but instead looked, silently and intently, at her father.

Sergei Modestovich gave a swift glance round the room. He liked coming here, where everything was beautifully arranged; this was done by Serafima Alexandrovna, who wished to surround her little girl, from her very infancy, only with the loveliest things. Serafima Alexandrovna dressed herself tastefully; this, too, she did for Lelechka, with the same end in view. One thing Sergei Modestovich had not become reconciled to, and this was his wife's almost continuous presence in the nursery.

"It's just as I thought. . . . I knew that I'd find you here," he said with a derisive and condescending smile.

They left the nursery together. As he followed his wife through the door Sergei Modestovich said rather indifferently, in an incidental way, laying no stress on his words: "Don't you think that it would be well for the little girl if she were sometimes without your company? Merely, you see, that the child should feel its own individuality," he explained in answer to Serafima Alexandrovna's perplexed glance.

"She's still so little," said Serafima Alexandrovna.

"In any case, this is but my humble opinion. I don't insist. It's your kingdom there."

"I'll think it over," his wife answered, smiling, as he did, coldly but genially.

Then they began to talk of something else.

Nurse Fedosya, sitting in the kitchen that evening, was telling the silent housemaid Darya and the talkative old cook Agathya about the young lady of the house, and how the child loved to play *priatki* with her mother—"She hides her little face, and cries *'tiu tiu'*!"

"And the *barinya* * herself is like a little one," added Fedosya, smiling.

Agathya listened and shook her head ominously; while her face became grave and reproachful.

"That the *barinya* does it, well, that's one thing; but that the young lady does it, that's bad."

"Why?" asked Fedosya with curiosity.

This expression of curiosity gave her face the look of a wooden, roughly-painted doll.

"Yes, that's bad," repeated Agathya with conviction. "Terribly bad!"

"Well?" said Fedosya, the ludicrous expression of curiosity on her face becoming more emphatic.

"She'll hide, and hide, and hide away," said Agathya, in a mysterious whisper, as she looked cautiously toward the door.

"What are you saying?" exclaimed Fedosya, frightened.

"It's the truth I'm saying, remember my words," Agathya went on with the same assurance and secrecy. "It's the surest sign."

The old woman had invented this sign, quite suddenly, herself; and she was evidently very proud of it.

Lelechka was asleep, and Serafima Alexandrovna was sitting in her own room, thinking with joy and tenderness of Lelechka. Lelechka was in her thoughts, first a sweet, tiny girl, then a sweet, big girl, then again a delightful little girl; and so until the end she remained mamma's little Lelechka.

Serafima Alexandrovna did not even notice that Fedosya had come up to her and paused. Fedosya had a worried, frightened look.

"*Barinya, barinya,*" she said quietly, in a trembling voice.

Serafima Alexandrovna gave a start. Fedosya's face made her anxious.

"What is it, Fedosya?" she asked with great concern. "Is there anything wrong with Lelechka?"

"No, *barinya,*" said Fedosya, as she gesticulated with her hands to reassure her mistress and to make her sit down. "Lelechka is asleep, may God be with her! Only I'd like to say something—you see—Lelechka is always hiding herself—that's not good."

---

* Gentlewoman.

Fedosya looked at her mistress with fixed eyes, which had grown round from fright.

"Why not good?" asked Serafima Alexandrovna, with vexation, succumbing involuntarily to vague fears.

"I can't tell you how bad it is," said Fedosya, and her face expressed the most decided confidence.

"Please speak in a sensible way," observed Serafima Alexandrovna dryly. "I understand nothing of what you are saying."

"You see, *barinya,* it's a kind of omen," explained Fedosya abruptly, in a shamefaced way.

"Nonsense!" said Serafima Alexandrovna.

She did not wish to hear any further as to the sort of omen it was, and what it foreboded. But, somehow, a sense of fear and sadness crept into her mood, and it was humiliating to feel that an absurd tale should disturb her beloved fancies, and should distress her so deeply.

"Of course I know that gentlefolk don't believe in omens, but it's a bad omen, *barinya,*" Fedosya went on in a doleful voice, "the young lady will hide, and hide . . ."

Suddenly she burst into tears, sobbing out loudly: "She'll hide, and hide, and hide away, angelic little soul, in a damp grave," she continued, as she wiped her tears with her apron and blew her nose.

"Who told you all this?" asked Serafima Alexandrovna in an austere low voice.

"Agathya says so, *barinya,*" answered Fedosya; "it's she that knows."

"Knows!" exclaimed Serafima Alexandrovna in irritation, as if she wished to protect herself somehow from this sudden anxiety. "What nonsense! Please don't come to me with any such notions in the future. Now you may go."

Fedosya, dejected, her feelings hurt, left her mistress.

"What nonsense! As if Lelechka could die!" thought Serafima Alexandrovna, trying to conquer the feeling of cold fear which took possession of her at the mere thought of Lelechka's death. Serafima Alexandrovna, upon reflection, attributed these women's beliefs in omens to ignorance. She saw clearly that there could be no possible connection between a child's quite normal diversion and the continuation of the child's life. She made a special effort that evening to occupy her mind with other matters, but her thoughts returned involuntarily to the fact that Lelechka loved to hide.

When Lelechka was still quite small, and had learned to distinguish between her mother and her nurse, she sometimes, sitting in her nurse's arms, made a sudden roguish grimace, and hid her laughing face in the nurse's shoulder. Then she would look out with a sly glance.

Of late, in those rare moments of the *barinya's* absence from the nursery, Fedosya had again taught Lelechka to hide; and when Lelechka's mother, on coming in, saw how lovely the child looked when she was hiding, she herself began to play hide and seek with her tiny daughter.

The next day Serafima Alexandrovna, absorbed in her happy cares for Lelechka, had forgotten Fedosya's words of the day before.

But when she returned to the nursery, after having ordered the dinner, and she heard Lelechka suddenly cry *"Tiu-tiu!"* from under the table, a feeling of fear suddenly took hold of her. Though she reproached herself at once for this unfounded, superstitious dread, nevertheless she could not enter wholeheartedly into the spirit of Lelechka's favorite game, and she tried to divert Lelechka's attention to something else.

Lelechka was a lovely and obedient child. She eagerly complied with her mother's new wishes. But as she had contracted the habit of hiding from her mother in some corner, and of crying out *"Tiu-tiu!"* so even that day she returned more than once to the game.

Serafima Alexandrovna tried desperately to amuse Lelechka. This was not so easy because restless, threatening thoughts obtruded themselves constantly.

"Why does Lelechka keep on recalling the *tiu-tiu?* Why does she not get tired of the same thing—of eternally closing her eyes, and of hiding her face? Perhaps," thought Serafima Alexandrovna, "she is not as strongly drawn to the world as other children, who are attracted by many things. If this is so, is it not a sign of organic weakness? Is it not a germ of the unconscious non-desire to live?"

Serafima Alexandrovna was tormented by presentiments. She felt ashamed of herself for ceasing to play hide and seek with Lelechka before Fedosya. But this game had become agonizing to her, all the more agonizing because she had a real desire to play it, and because something drew her very strongly to hide herself from Lelechka and to seek out the hiding child. Serafima Alexandrovna herself began the game once or twice, though she played it with a heavy heart. She suffered as if she were committing an evil deed with full consciousness.

It was a sad day for Serafima Alexandrovna.

Lelechka was about to fall asleep. No sooner had she climbed into her little bed, protected by a network on all sides, than her eyes began to close with fatigue. Her mother covered her with a blue blanket. Lelechka drew her sweet little hands from under the blanket and stretched them out to embrace her mother. Her mother bent down. Lelechka, with a tender expression on her sleepy face, kissed her mother and let her head fall on the pillow. As her hands hid themselves under the blanket Lelechka whispered: "The hands *tiu-tiu!*"

The mother's heart seemed to stop—Lelechka lay there so small, so frail, so quiet. Lelechka smiled gently, closed her eyes and said quietly: "The eyes *tiu-tiu!*"

Then even more quietly: "Lelechka *tiu-tiu!*"

With these words she fell asleep, her face pressing the pillow. She appeared so small and so frail under the blanket that covered her. Her mother looked at her with sad eyes.

Serafima Alexandrovna remained standing over Lelechka's bed a long while, and she kept looking at Lelechka with tenderness and fear.

"I'm a mother: is it possible that I shouldn't be able to protect her?" she thought, as she imagined the various ills which might befall Lelecha.

She prayed long that night, but the prayer did not relieve her sadness.

Several days passed. Lelechka caught cold. The fever came upon her at night. When Serafima Alexandrovna, awakened by Fedosya, came to Lelechka and saw her looking so hot, so restless, and so tormented, she instantly recalled the evil omen, and from the first moment a hopeless despair took possession of her.

A doctor was called, and everything was done that is usual on such occasions—but the inevitable happened. Serafima Alexandrovna tried to console herself with the hope that Lelechka would get well, and would again laugh and play—yet this seemed to her an unthinkable happiness! And Lelechka grew feebler from hour to hour.

All simulated calmness, so as not to frighten Serafima Alexandrovna, but their masked faces only made her sad.

Nothing made her so unhappy as the reiterations of Fedosya, uttered between sobs: "She hid herself and hid herself, our Lelechka!"

But the thoughts of Serafima Alexandrovna were confused, and she could not quite grasp what was happening.

Fever was consuming Lelechka, and there were times when she lost consciousness and spoke in delirium. But when she returned to herself she bore her pain and fatigue with gentle good nature; she smiled feebly at her *mamochka,* so that her *mamochka* should not see how much she suffered. Three days passed, as horrible as a nightmare. Lelechka grew quite feeble. She did not know that she was dying.

She glanced at her mother with her dimmed eyes, and lisped in a scarcely audible, hoarse voice: *"Tiu-tiu, mamochka!* Make *tiu-tiu, mamochka!"*

Serafima Alexandrovna hid her face behind the curtains near Lelechka's bed. How tragic!

"Mamochka!" called Lelechka in an almost inaudible voice.

Lelechka's mother bent over her, and Lelechka, her vision grown still more dim, saw her mother's pale, despairing face for the last time.

"A white *mamochka!"* whispered Lelechka.

Mamochka's white face became blurred, and everything grew dark before Lelechka. She caught the edge of the bed-cover feebly with her hands and whispered: *"Tiu-tiu!"*

Something rattled in her throat; Lelechka opened and again closed her rapidly paling lips, and died.

Serafima Alexandrovna was in dumb despair as she left Lelechka, and went out of the room. She met her husband.

"Lelechka is dead," she said in a quiet, dull voice.

Sergei Modestovich looked anxiously at her pale face. He was struck by the strange stupor in her formerly animated handsome features.

Lelechka was dressed, placed in a little coffin, and carried into the parlor. Serafima Alexandrovna was standing by the coffin and looking dully at her dead child. Sergei Modestovich went to his wife and, consoling her with cold, empty words, tried to draw her away from the coffin. Serafima Alexandrovna smiled.

"Go away," she said quietly. "Lelechka is playing. She'll be up in a minute."

"Sima, my dear, don't distress yourself," said Sergei Modestovich in a whisper. "You must resign yourself to your fate."

"She'll be up in a minute," persisted Serafima Alexandrovna, her eyes fixed on the dead little girl.

Sergei Modestovich looked round him cautiously: he was afraid of the unseemly and of the ridiculous.

"Sima, don't distress yourself," he repeated. "This would be a miracle, and miracles do not happen in the nineteenth century."

No sooner had he said these words than Sergei Modestovich felt their irrelevance to what had happened. He was confused and annoyed.

He took his wife by the arm, and cautiously led her away from the coffin. She did not oppose him.

Her face seemed calm and her eyes were dry. She went into the nursery and began to walk round the room, looking into those places where Lelechka used to hide herself. She walked all about the room, and bent now and then to look under the table or under the bed, and kept on repeating cheerfully: "Where is my little one? Where is my Lelechka?"

After she had walked round the room once she began to make her quest anew. Fedosya, motionless, with dejected face, sat in a corner, and looked frightened at her mistress; then she suddenly burst out sobbing, and she wailed loudly:

"She hid herself, and hid herself, our Lelechka, our angelic little soul!"

Serafima Alexandrovna trembled, paused, cast a perplexed look at Fedosya, began to weep, and left the nursery quietly.

Sergei Modestovich hurried the funeral. He saw that Serafima Alexandrovna was terribly shocked by her sudden misfortune, and as he feared for her reason he thought she would more readily be diverted and consoled when Lelechka was buried.

Next morning Serafima Alexandrovna dressed with particular care —for Lelechka. When she entered the parlor there were several people between her and Lelechka. The priest and deacon paced up and down the room; clouds of blue smoke drifted in the air, and there was a smell of incense. There was an oppressive feeling of heaviness in Serafima Alexandrovna's head as she approached Lelechka. Lelechka lay there still and pale, and smiled pathetically. Serafima Alexandrovna laid her cheek upon the edge of Lelechka's coffin, and whispered: "*Tiu-tiu*, little one!"

The little one did not reply. Then there was some kind of stir and confusion around Serafima Alexandrovna; strange, unnecessary faces bent over her, someone held her—and Lelechka was carried away somewhere.

Serafima Alexandrovna stood up erect, sighed in a lost way, smiled, and called loudly: "Lelechka!"

Lelechka was being carried out. The mother threw herself after the coffin with despairing sobs, but was held back. She sprang behind the door, through which Lelechka had passed, sat down there on the floor, and as she looked through the crevice, she cried out: "Lelechka, *tiu-tiu!*"

Then she put her head out from behind the door, and began to laugh.

Lelechka was quickly carried away from her mother, and those who carried her seemed to run rather than to walk.

LEONID ANDREYEV

The Abyss

Leonid Andreyev (1871–1919) was born in Orel and graduated as a lawyer from the University of Moscow. He lost his first case and turned to writing, first as a court reporter and then as a short story author. He bitterly opposed the Bolshevik Revolution and died in exile in Finland. His best known works include *The Little Angel and Other Stories, When the King Loses His Head and Other Stories, A Dilemma* and *The Red Laugh.* [From *A Treasury of Russian Life and Humor;* copyright 1943 by Coward-McCann, Inc.; used by permission of the publishers; translated by John Cournos.]

THE DAY WAS COMING to an end, but the young pair continued to walk and to talk, observing neither the time nor the way. Before them, in the shadow of a hillock, there loomed the dark mass of a small grove, and between the branches of the trees, like the glowing of coals, the sun blazed, igniting the air and transforming it into a flaming golden dust. So near and so luminous the sun appeared that everything seemed to vanish; it alone remained, and it painted the road with its own fiery tints. It hurt the eyes of the strollers; they turned back, and all at once everything within their vision was extinguished, became peaceful and clear, and small and intimate. Somewhere afar, barely a mile away, the red sunset seized the tall trunk of a fir, which blazed among the green like a candle in a dark room; the ruddy glow of the road stretched before them, and every stone cast its long black shadow; and the girl's hair, suffused with the sun's rays, now shone with a golden-red nimbus. A stray thin hair, wandering from the rest, wavered in the air like a golden spider's thread.

The newly fallen darkness did not break or change the course of their talk. It continued as before, intimately and quietly; it flowed along tranquilly on the same theme: on strength, beauty, and the immortality of love. They were both very young: the girl was no more than seventeen; Nemovetsky was four years older. They wore students' uniforms: she the modest brown dress of a pupil of a girls' school, he the handsome attire of a technological student. And, like their conversation, everything about them was young, beautiful, and pure. They had erect, flexible figures, permeated as it were with the clean air and borne along with a light, elastic gait; their fresh voices, sounding even the simplest words with a reflective tenderness, were like a rivulet in a calm spring night, when the snow had not yet wholly thawed from the dark meadows.

They walked on, turning the bend of the unfamiliar road, and their lengthening shadows, with absurdly small heads, now advanced separately, now merged into one long, narrow strip, like the shadow of a poplar. But they did not see the shadows, for they were too much absorbed in their talk. While talking, the young man kept his eyes fixed on the girl's handsome face, upon which the sunset had seemed to leave a measure of its delicate tints. As for her, she lowered her gaze on the footpath, brushed the tiny pebbles to one side with her umbrella, and watched now one foot, now the other as alternately, with a measured step, they emerged from under her dark dress.

The path was intersected by a ditch with edges of dust showing the impress of feet. For an instant they paused. Zinotchka raised her head, looked round her with a perplexed gaze, and asked:

"Do you know where we are? I've never been here before."

He made an attentive survey of their position.

"Yes, I know. There, behind the hill, is the town. Give me your hand. I'll help you across."

He stretched out his hand, white and slender like a woman's, and which did not know hard work. Zinotchka felt gay. She felt like jumping over the ditch all by herself, running away and shouting: "Catch me!" But she restrained herself, with decorous gratitude inclined her head, and timidly stretched out her hand, which still retained its childish plumpness. He had a desire to squeeze tightly this trembling little hand, but he also restrained himself, and with a half-bow he deferentially took it in his and modestly turned away when in crossing the girl slightly showed her leg.

And once more they walked and talked, but their thoughts were full of the momentary contact of their hands. She still felt the dry heat of his palms and his strong fingers; she felt pleasure and shame, while he was conscious of the submissive softness of her tiny hand and saw the black silhouette of her foot and the small slipper which tenderly embraced it. There was something sharp, something perturbing in this unfading appearance of the narrow hem of white skirts and of the slender foot; with an unconscious effort of will he crushed this feeling. Then he felt more cheerful, and his heart so abundant, so generous in its mood that he wanted to sing, to stretch out his hands to the sky, and to shout: "Run! I want to catch you!"—that ancient formula of primitive love among the woods and thundering waterfalls.

And from all these desires tears struggled to the throat.

The long, droll shadows vanished, and the dust of the footpath became gray and cold, but they did not observe this and went on chatting. Both of them had read many good books, and the radiant images of men and women who had loved, suffered, and perished for pure love were borne along before them. Their memories resurrected fragments of nearly forgotten verse, dressed in melodious harmony and the sweet sadness investing love.

"Do you remember where this comes from?" asked Nemovetsky, recalling: ". . . once more she is with me, she whom I love; from whom, having never spoken, I have hidden all my sadness, my tenderness, my love . . ."

"No," Zinotchka replied, and pensively repeated: "all my sadness, my tenderness, my love . . ."

"All my love," with an involuntary echo responded Nemovetsky.

Other memories returned to them. They remembered those girls, pure like the white lilies, who, attired in black nunnish garments, sat solitarily in the park, grieving among the dead leaves, yet happy in their grief. They also remembered the men, who, in the abundance of will and pride, yet suffered, and implored the love and the delicate compassion of women. The images thus evoked were sad, but the love which showed in this sadness was radiant and pure. As immense as the world, as bright as the sun, it arose fabulously beautiful before their eyes, and there was nothing mightier or more beautiful on the earth.

"Could you die for love?" Zinotchka asked, as she looked at her childish hand.

"Yes, I could," Nemovetsky replied, with conviction, and he glanced at her frankly. "And you?"

"Yes, I too." She grew pensive. "Why, it's happiness to die for one you love. I should want to."

Their eyes met. They were such clear, calm eyes, and there was much good in what they conveyed to the other. Their lips smiled. Zinotchka paused.

"Wait a moment," she said. "You have a thread on your coat."

And trustfully she raised her hand to his shoulder and carefully, with two fingers, removed the thread.

"There!" she said and, becoming serious, asked: "Why are you so thin and pale? You are studying too much, I fear. You musn't overdo it. you know."

"You have blue eyes; they have bright points like sparks," he replied, examining her eyes.

"And yours are black. No, brown. They seem to glow. There is in them . . ."

Zinotchka did not finish her sentence, but turned away. Her face slowly flushed, her eyes became timid and confused, while her lips involuntarily smiled. Without waiting for Nemovetsky, who smiled with secret pleasure, she moved forward, but soon paused.

"Look, the sun has set!" she exclaimed with grieved astonishment.

"Yes, it has set," he responded with a new sadness.

The light was gone, the shadows died, everything became pale, dumb, lifeless. At that point of the horizon where earlier the glowing sun had blazed, there now, in silence, crept dark masses of cloud, which step by step consumed the light blue spaces. The clouds gathered, jostled one another, slowly and reticently changed the contours of awakened monsters; they unwillingly advanced, driven, as it were, against their will by some terrible, implacable force. Tearing itself away from the rest, one tiny luminous cloud drifted on alone, a frail fugitive.

Zinotchka's cheeks grew pale, her lips turned red; the pupils of her eyes imperceptibly broadened, darkening the eyes. She whispered:

"I feel frightened. It is so quiet here. Have we lost our way?"

Nemovetsky contracted his heavy eyebrows and made a searching survey of the place.

Now that the sun was gone and the approaching night was breathing with fresh air, it seemed cold and uninviting. To all sides the gray field spread, with its scant grass, clay gullies, hillocks and holes. There were many of these holes; some were deep and sheer, others were small and overgrown with slippery grass; the silent dusk of night had already crept into them; and because there was evidence here of men's labors, the place appeared even more desolate. Here and there, like the coagulations of cold lilac mist, loomed groves and thickets and, as it were, hearkened to what the abandoned holes might have to say to them.

Nemovetsky crushed the heavy, uneasy feeling of perturbation which had arisen in him and said:

"No, we have not lost our way. I know the road. First to the left, then through that tiny wood. Are you afraid?"

She bravely smiled and answered:

"No. Not now. But we ought to be home soon and have some tea."

They increased their gait, but soon slowed down again. They did not glance aside, but felt the morose hostility of the dug-up field, which surrounded them with a thousand dim motionless eyes, and this feeling bound them together and evoked memories of childhood. These memories were luminous, full of sunlight, of green foliage, of

love and laughter. It was as if that had not been life at all, but an
immense, melodious song, and they themselves had been in it as
sounds, two slight notes: one clear and resonant like ringing crystal,
the other somewhat more dull yet more animated, like a small bell.

Signs of human life were beginning to appear. Two women were
sitting at the edge of a clay hole. One sat with crossed legs and looked
fixedly below. She raised her head with its kerchief, revealing tufts
of entangled hair. Her bent back threw upward a dirty blouse with
its pattern of flowers as big as apples; its strings were undone and
hung loosely. She did not look at the passers-by. The other woman
half reclined near by, her head thrown backward. She had a coarse,
broad face, with a peasant's features, and, under her eyes, the project-
ing cheekbones showed two brick-red spots, resembling fresh scratches.
She was even filthier than the first woman, and she bluntly stared
at the passers-by. When they had passed by, she began to sing in a
thick, masculine voice:

> For you alone, my adored one,
> Like a flower I did bloom . . .

"Varka, do you hear?" She turned to her silent companion and,
receiving no answer, broke into loud, coarse laughter.

Nemovetsky had known such women, who were filthy even when
they were attired in costly handsome dresses; he was used to them,
and now they glided away from his glance and vanished, leaving no
trace. But Zinotchka, who nearly brushed them with her modest brown
dress, felt something hostile, pitiful and evil, which for a moment
entered her soul. In a few minutes the impression was obliterated, like
the shadow of a cloud running fast across the golden meadow; and
when, going in the same direction, there had passed them by a barefoot
man, accompanied by the same kind of filthy woman, she saw them
but gave them no thought. . . .

And once more they walked on and talked, and behind them there
moved, reluctantly, a dark cloud, and cast a transparent shadow. . . .
The darkness imperceptibly and stealthily thickened, so that it bore the
impress of day, but day oppressed with illness and quietly dying.
Now they talked about those terrible feelings and thoughts which
visit man at night, when he cannot sleep, and neither sound nor
speech give hindrance; when darkness, immense and multiple-eyed,
that is life, closely presses to his very face.

"Can you imagine infinity?" Zinotchka asked him, putting her plump
hand to her forehead and tightly closing her eyes.

"No. Infinity . . . No . . ." answered Nemovetsky, also shutting his
eyes.

"I sometimes see it. I perceived it for the first time when I was yet
quite little. Imagine a great many carts. There stands one cart, then
another, a third, carts without end, an infinity of carts . . . It is terrible!" Zinotchka trembled.

"But why carts?" Nemovetsky smiled, though he felt uncomfortable.
"I don't know. But I did see carts. One, another . . . without end."

The darkness stealthily thickened. The cloud had already passed over their heads and, being before them, was now able to look into their lowered, paling faces. The dark figures of ragged, sluttish women appeared oftener; it was as if the deep ground holes, dug for some unknown purpose, cast them up to the surface. Now solitary, now in twos or threes, they appeared, and their voices sounded loud and strangely desolate in the stilled air.

"Who are these women? Where do they all come from?" Zinotchka asked in a low, timorous voice. Nemovetsky knew who these women were. He felt terrified at having fallen into this evil and dangerous neighborhood, but he answered calmly:

"I don't know. It's nothing. Let's not talk about them. It won't be long now. We only have to pass through this little wood, and we shall reach the gate and town. It's a pity that we started out so late."

She thought his words absurd. How could he call it late when they started out at four o'clock? She looked at him and smiled. But his eyebrows did not relax, and, in order to calm and comfort him, she suggested:

"Let's walk faster. I want tea. And the wood's quite near now."
"Yes, let's walk faster."

When they entered the wood and the silent trees joined in an arch above their heads, it became very dark but also very snug and quieting.

"Give me your hand," proposed Nemovetsky.

Irresolutely she gave him her hand, and the light contact seemed to lighten the darkness. Their hands were motionless and did not press each other. Zinotchka even slightly moved away from her companion. But their whole consciousness was concentrated in the perception of the tiny place of the body where the hands touched one another. And again the desire came to talk about the beauty and the mysterious power of love, but to talk without violating the silence, to talk by means not of words but of glances. And they thought that they ought to glance, and they wanted to, yet they didn't dare.

"And here are some more people!" said Zinotchka cheerfully.

In the glade, where there was more light, there sat near an empty bottle three men in silence, and expectantly looked at the newcomers. One of them, shaven like an actor, laughed and whistled in such a way as if to say:

"Oho!"

Nemovetsky's heart fell and froze in a trepidation of horror, but, as if pushed on from behind, he walked straight on the sitting trio, beside whom ran the footpath. These were waiting, and three pairs of eyes looked at the strollers, motionless and terrifying. And, desirous of gaining the good will of these morose, ragged men, in whose silence he scented a threat, and of winning their sympathy for his helplessness, he asked:

"Is this the way to the gate?"

They did not reply. The shaven one whistled something mocking and not quite definable, while the others remained silent and looked at them with a heavy, malignant intentness. They were drunken, and evil, and they were hungry for women and sensual diversion. One of the men, with a ruddy face, rose to his feet like a bear, and sighed heavily. His companions quickly glanced at him, then once more fixed an intent gaze on Zinotchka.

"I feel terribly afraid," she whispered with lips alone.

He did not hear her words, but Nemovetsky understood her from the weight of the arm which leaned on him. And, trying to preserve a demeanor of calm, yet feeling the fated irrevocableness of what was about to happen, he advanced on his way with a measured firmness. Three pairs of eyes approached nearer, gleamed, and were left behind one's back. "It's better to run," thought Nemovetsky and answered himself: "No, it's better not to run."

"He's a dead 'un! You ain't afraid of him?" said the third of the sitting trio, a bald-headed fellow with a scant red beard. "And the little girl is a fine one. May God grant everyone such a one!"

The trio gave a forced laugh.

"Mister, wait! I want to have a word with you!" said the tall man in a thick bass voice and glanced at his comrades.

They rose.

Nemovetsky walked on, without turning round.

"You ought to stop when you're asked," said the red-haired man. "An' if you don't, you're likely to get something you ain't counting on!"

"D'you hear?" growled the tall man, and in two jumps caught up with the strollers.

A massive hand descended on Nemovetsky's shoulder and made him reel. He turned and met very close to his face the round, bulgy, terrible eyes of his assailant. They were so near that it was as if he were looking at them through a magnifying glass, and he clearly distinguished the small red veins on the whites and the yellowish matter on the lids. He let fall Zinotchka's numb hand and, thrusting his hand into his pocket, he murmured:

"Do you want money? I'll give you some, with pleasure."

The bulgy eyes grew rounder and gleamed. And when Nemovetsky averted his gaze from them, the tall man stepped slightly back and, with a short blow, struck Nemovetsky's chin from below. Nemovetsky's head fell backward, his teeth clicked, his cap descended to his forehead and fell off; waving with his arms, he dropped to the ground. Silently, without a cry, Zinotchka turned and ran with all the speed of which she was capable. The man with the clean-shaven face gave a long-drawn shout which sounded strangely:

"Aa-a-ah! . . ."

And, still shouting, he gave pursuit.

Nemovetsky, reeling, jumped up, and before he could straighten himself he was again felled with a blow on the neck. There were two of them, and he one, and he was frail and unused to physical combat. Nevertheless, he fought for a long time, scratched with his fingernails like an obstreperous woman, bit with his teeth, and sobbed with an unconscious despair. When he was too weak to do more they lifted him and bore him away. He still resisted, but there was a din in his head; he ceased to understand what was being done with him and hung helplessly in the hands which bore him. The last thing he saw was a fragment of the red beard which almost touched his mouth, and beyond it the darkness of the wood and the light-colored blouse of the running girl. She ran silently and fast, as she had run but a few days before when they were playing tag; and behind her, with short strides, overtaking her, ran the clean-shaven one. Then Nemovetsky felt an emptiness around him, his heart stopped short as he experienced the sensation of falling, then he struck the earth and lost all consciousness.

The tall man and the red-haired man, having thrown Nemovetsky into a ditch, stopped for a few moments to listen to what was happening at the bottom of the ditch. But their faces and their eyes were turned to one side, in the direction taken by Zinotchka. From there arose the high stifled woman's cry which quickly died. The tall man muttered angrily:

"The pig!"

Then, making a straight line, breaking twigs on the way, like a bear, he began to run.

"And me! And me!" his red-haired comrade cried in a thin voice, running after him. He was weak and he panted; in the struggle his knee was hurt, and he felt badly because the idea about the girl had come to him first and he would get her last. He paused to rub his knee; then, putting a finger to his nose, he sneezed; and once more began to run and to cry his plaint:

"And me! And me!"

The dark cloud dissipated itself across the whole heavens, ushering in the calm, dark night. The darkness soon swallowed up the short figure of the red-haired man, but for some time there was audible the uneven fall of his feet, the rustle of the disturbed leaves, and the shrill, plaintive cry:

"And me! Brothers, and me!"

Earth got into Nemovetsky's mouth, and his teeth grated. On coming to himself, the first feeling he experienced was consciousness of the pungent, pleasant smell of the soil. His head felt dull, as if heavy lead had been poured into it; it was hard to turn it. His whole body ached, there was an intense pain in the shoulder, but no bones were broken. Nemovetsky sat up, and for a long time looked above him, neither thinking nor remembering. Directly over him, a bush lowered its broad leaves, and between them was visible the now clear sky. The cloud had passed over, without dropping a single drop of rain, and leaving the air dry and exhilarating. High up, in the middle of the heavens, appeared the carven moon, with a transparent border. It was living its last nights, and its light was cold, dejected, and solitary. Small tufts of cloud rapidly passed over in the heights where, it was clear, the wind was strong; they did not obscure the moon, but cautiously passed it by. In the solitariness of the moon, in the timorousness of the high bright clouds, in the blowing of the wind barely perceptible below, one felt the mysterious depth of night dominating over the earth.

Nemovetsky suddenly remembered everything that had happened, and he could not believe that it had happened. All that was so terrible and did not resemble truth. Could truth be so horrible? He, too, as he sat there in the night and looked up at the moon and the running clouds, appeared strange to himself and did not resemble reality. And he began to think that it was an ordinary if horrible nightmare. Those women, of whom they had met so many, had also become a part of this terrible and evil dream.

"It can't be!" he said with conviction, and weakly shook his heavy head. "It can't be!"

He stretched out his hand and began to look for his cap. His failure to find it made everything clear to him; and he understood that what had happened had not been a dream, but the horrible truth. Terror possessed him anew, as a few moments later he made violent exertions to scramble out of the ditch, again and again to fall back with handfuls of soil, only to clutch once more at the hanging shrubbery.

He scrambled out at last, and began to run, thoughtlessly, without choosing a direction. For a long time he went on running, circling among the trees. With equal suddenness, thoughtlessly, he ran in another direction. The branches of the trees scratched his face, and again everything began to resemble a dream. And it seemed to Nemovetsky that something like this had happened to him before: darkness, invisible branches of trees, while he had run with closed eyes, thinking that all this was a dream. Nemovetsky paused, then sat down in an uncomfortable posture on the ground, without any elevation. And again he thought of his cap, and he said:

"This is I. I ought to kill myself. Yes, I ought to kill myself, even if this is a dream."

He sprang to his feet, but remembered something and walked slowly, his confused brain trying to picture the place where they had been attacked. It was quite dark in the woods, but sometimes a stray ray of moonlight broke through and deceived him; it lighted up the white tree trunks, and the wood seemed as if it were full of motionless and mysteriously silent people. All this, too, seemed as if it had been, and it resembled a dream.

"Zinaida Nikolaevna!" called Nemovetsky, pronouncing the first word loudly, the second in a lower voice, as if with the loss of his voice he had also lost hope of any response.

And no one responded.

Then he found the footpath, and knew it at once. He reached the glade. Back where he had been, he fully understood that it all had actually happened. He ran about in his terror, and he cried:

"Zinaida Nikolaevna! It is I! I!"

No one answered his call. He turned in the direction where he thought the town lay, and shouted a prolonged shout:

"He-l-l-p!" . . .

And once more he ran about, whispering something while he swept the bushes, when before his eyes there appeared a dim white spot, which resembled a spot of congealed faint light. It was the prostrate body of Zinotchka.

"Oh, God! What's this!" said Nemovetsky, with dry eyes, but in a voice that sobbed. He got down on his knees and came in contact with the girl lying there.

His hand fell on the bared body, which was so smooth and firm and cold but by no means dead. Trembling, he passed his hand over her.

"Darling, sweetheart, it is I," he whispered, seeking her face in the darkness.

Then he stretched out a hand in another direction, and again came in contact with the naked body, and no matter where he put his hand it touched this woman's body, which was so smooth and firm and seemed to grow warm under the contact of his hand. Sometimes he snatched his hand away quickly, and again he let it rest; and just as, all tattered and without his cap, he did not appear real to himself, so it was with this bared body: he could not associate it with Zinotchka. All that had passed here, all that men had done with this mute woman's body, appeared to him in all its loathsome reality, and found a strange intensely eloquent response in his whole body. He stretched forward in a way that made his joints crackle, dully fixed his eyes on the white spot, and contracted his brows like a man thinking. Horror before what had happened congealed in him, and like a solid lay on his soul, as it were, something extraneous and impotent.

"Oh, God! What's this?" he repeated, but the sound of it ran untrue, like something deliberate.

He felt her heart: it beat faintly but evenly, and when he bent toward her face he became aware of its equally faint breathing. It was as if Zinotchka were not in a deep swoon, but simply sleeping. He quietly called to her:

"Zinotchka, it is I!"

But at once he felt that he would not like to see her awaken for a long time. He held his breath, quickly glanced round him, then he cautiously smoothed her cheek; first he kissed her closed eyes, then her lips, whose softness yielded under his strong kiss. Frightened lest she awaken, he drew back, and remained in a frozen attitude. But the body was motionless and mute, and in its helplessness and easy access there was something pitiful and exasperating, not to be resisted and attracting one to itself. With infinite tenderness and stealthy, timid caution, Nemovetsky tried to cover her with the fragments of her dress, and this double consciousness of the material and the naked body was as sharp as a knife and as incomprehensible as madness. . . . Here had been a banquet of wild beasts . . . he scented the burning passion diffused in the air, and dilated his nostrils.

"It is I! I!" he madly repeated, not understanding what surrounded him and still possessed of the memory of the white hem of the skirt, of the black silhouette of the foot and of the slipper which so tenderly embraced it. As he listened to Zinotchka's breathing, his eyes fixed on the spot where her face was, he moved a hand. He listened, and moved the hand again.

"What am I doing?" he cried out loudly, in despair, and sprang back, terrified of himself.

For a single instant Zinotchka's face flashed before him and vanished. He tried to understand that this body was Zinotchka, with whom he had lately walked, and who had spoken of infinity; and he could not understand. He tried to feel the horror of what had happened, but the horror was too great for comprehension, and it did not appear.

"Zinaida Nikolaevna!" he shouted, imploringly. "What does this mean? Zinaida Nikolaevna!"

But the tormented body remained mute, and, continuing his mad monologue, Nemovetsky descended on his knees. He implored, threatened, said that he would kill himself, and he grasped the prostrate body, pressing it to him. . . . The now warmed body softly yielded to his exertions, obediently following his motions, and all this was so terrible, incomprehensible and savage that Nemovetsky once more jumped to his feet and abruptly shouted:

"Help!"

But the sound was false, as if it were deliberate.

And once more he threw himself on the unresisting body, with kisses and tears, feeling the presence of some sort of abyss, a dark, terrible, drawing abyss. There was no Nemovetsky; Nemovetsky had remained somewhere behind, and he who had replaced him was now with passionate sternness mauling the hot, submissive body and was saying with the sly smile of a madman:

"Answer me! Or don't you want to? I love you! I love you!"

With the same sly smile he brought his dilated eyes to Zinotchka's very face and whispered:

"I love you! You don't want to speak, but you are smiling, I can see that. I love you! I love you! I love you!"

He more strongly pressed to him the soft, will-less body, whose lifeless submission awakened a savage passion. He wrung his hands, and hoarsely whispered:

"I love you! We will tell no one, and no one will know. I will marry you tomorrow, when you like. I love you. I will kiss you, and you will answer me—yes? Zinotchka . . ."

With some force he pressed his lips to hers, and felt conscious of his teeth's sharpness in her flesh; in the force and anguish of the kiss he lost the last sparks of reason. It seemed to him that the lips of the girl quivered. For a single instant flaming horror lighted up his mind, opening before him a black abyss.

And the black abyss swallowed him.

IVAN BUNIN

The Gentleman from San Francisco

Ivan Bunin was born in 1870 at Voronezh. His first poems were published in 1888. In 1919 he was exiled to France, where he is now living. Among his best known works are *The Gentleman From San Francisco, The Dreams of Chang, The Village, Mitya's Love* and *The Well of Days,* which was awarded the Nobel Prize in 1933. [Copyright 1923 by Alfred A. Knopf, Inc.; used by permission of the publishers.]

Alas, alas, that great city Babylon,
that mighty city!
—THE APOCALYPSE

THE GENTLEMAN FROM SAN FRANCISCO—neither at Naples nor at Capri had anyone remembered his name—was journeying to the Old World for two full years, with his wife and daughter, wholly for recreation.

He felt firmly assured that he had every right to take a rest, pleasure in a prolonged and comfortable journey, and other things besides. For such an assurance he had the good reason that, in the first place, he was rich; and that, in the second, in spite of his fifty-eight years, he was only just taking his first plunge into life. Before this he had not lived but merely existed—to be sure, not so badly, but none the less putting all his hopes in the future. He had labored diligently—the coolies, whom he had employed by the thousands, knew well what this meant!—and at last he saw that much had been achieved, that he was now equal to those he had at one time appointed as his models, and he decided to give himself a well-earned rest. It was a custom among his kind of people to begin the enjoyment of life with a journey to Europe, to India, to Egypt. He proposed to follow their example.

Before all, of course, he desired to reward himself for his years of hard toil; nevertheless, he was happy also for his wife's and daughter's sakes. His wife had never been distinguished for any particular susceptibility to fresh impressions, but then all elderly American women are ardent travelers. As for his daughter, a girl no longer young and somewhat ailing, the journey would do her positive good: to say nothing of the benefits her health would derive, was there not always the likelihood of happy encounters during journeys? While traveling, one may indeed, at times, sit at the same table with a multi-millionaire, or enjoy looking at frescoes in his company.

The itinerary planned by the gentleman from San Francisco was an extensive one. In December and January he hoped to enjoy the sun of southern Italy, the monuments of antiquity, the *tarantella,* the serenades of strolling singers, and another thing for which men of his age have a peculiar relish: the love of young Neapolitan women, conferred—let us admit—not with wholly disinterested motives; he planned to spend the Carnival in Nice, in Monte Carlo, toward which the most select society gravitated at this season—that society upon which all the blessings of civilization depend: not alone the cut of the smoking jacket, but also the stability of thrones, and the declaration of wars, and the welfare of hotels—where some devote themselves with ardor to automobile and sail races, others to roulette, while a third group engages in what is called flirting; a fourth in shooting pigeons which, emerging from their shelters, gracefully soar upward above emerald-green lawns, against the background of a sea of the color of forget-me-nots, only in the next instant to strike the ground as crumpled little shapes of whites. The beginning of March he wanted to devote to Florence; on the eve of the Passion of our Lord to arrive at Rome, in order to hear the *Misere* there; his plans also included Venice, and Paris, and bull-fights in Seville, and sea-bathing in the British Isles, and Athens, and Constantinople, and Palestine, and Egypt, and even Japan—naturally, on the return journey. . . . And everything went splendidly at first.

It was the end of November; almost to Gibraltar itself the ship proceeded now through an icy mist, now through a storm with wet snow; but it sailed on unperturbed and even without rolling; the passengers on the steamer were many, and all of them persons of consequence; the ship—the famous *Atlantis*—resembled the most expensive of European hotels, with all conveniences; an all-night bar, Turkish baths, a newpspaper of its own—and life upon it flowed in accordance with a splendid system of regulations: the passengers rose early, to the sound of bugles, sharply reverberating through the passages at the yet dark hour when day was so slowly and reluctantly dawning above the gray-green watery desert, ponderously restless in the mist. They put on their flannel pajamas, drank coffee, chocolate, cocoa; then they reclined in marble bathtubs, performed exercises, awakening an appetite and a sense of well-being, attended to their daily toilet, and went to breakfast. Until eleven they were supposed to promenade the decks lustily, breathing in the cool freshness of the ocean, or to play at shuffleboard and other games for a renewed stimulation of the appetite; and at eleven, to seek refreshment in bouillon and sandwiches; after which they read their newspaper with pleasure and calmly awaited lunch, a meal even more nourishing and varied than the breakfast; the following two hours were dedicated to repose; all the decks were then arranged with chaise longues, upon which the travelers reclined, covered up with plaid rugs, contemplating the cloudy sky and the foaming billows flashing by beyond the rail, or else gently drowsing. At five o'clock, enlivened and refreshed, they were served with strong fragrant tea and pastries; at seven, the bugle call announced dinner, consisting of nine courses. . . . At this point the gentleman from San Francisco, greatly cheered, would hurry to his magnificent cabin de luxe, to dress.

In the evening the tiers of the *Atlantis* gaped through the dusk as with fiery, countless eyes, and a great multitude of servants worked with especial feverishness in the kitchens, sculleries, and wine vaults. The ocean, heaving on the other side of the walls, was terrifying, but none gave it a thought, firmly believing it under the sway of the captain—a red-haired man of monstrous bulk and ponderousness, always seeming sleepy, resembling, in his uniform frock coat, with its golden chevrons, an enormous idol; it was only very rarely that he left his mysterious quarters to appear in public. A siren on the forecastle howled ceaselessly in hellish sullenness and whined in frenzied malice, but not many of the diners heard the siren—it was drowned by the strains of a splendid string orchestra, playing exquisitely and without pause in the two-tiered hall, decorated with marble, its floors covered with velvet rugs; festively flooded with the lights of crystal lusters and gilded *girandotes,* filled to capacity with diamond-bedecked ladies in *décolleté* and men in smoking jackets, graceful waiters and deferential maîtres d'hôtel—among whom one, who took orders for wines exclusively, even walked about with a chain around his neck, like a lord mayor. A smoking jacket and perfect linen made the gentleman from San Francisco appear very much younger. Spare, not tall, awkwardly but strongly built, groomed until he shone, moderately animated, he sat in the aureate-pearly refulgence of this palatial room, at a table with a bottle of amber Johannesberg, with countless goblets, small and large, of the thinnest glass, with a fragrant bouquet of curly hyacinths. There was something Mongolian about his yellowish face with clipped silvery mustache; his large teeth gleamed with gold fillings; his stalwart, bald head glistened like old ivory. Rich, yet in keeping with her years, was the attiture of his wife—a big, broad, calm woman; elaborate, yet light and diaphanous, with an innocent frankness, was that of his daughter—a girl innocently frank, tall, slender, with magnificent hair, exquisitely dressed, with breath aromatic from violet cachous and with the tenderest of tiny moles about her lips and between her shoulder blades, slightly powdered. . . .

The dinner went on for two whole hours; after dinner there was dancing in the ballroom, during which the men—the gentleman from San Francisco among their number, of course—with their feet cocked up, decided, upon the basis of the latest political and stock-exchange news, the destinies of nations, smoking Havana cigars and drinking liqueurs until their faces were flushed, while seated in the bar, where the waiters were Negroes in red jackets, the whites of their eyes resembling peeled, hard-boiled eggs. The ocean, with a dull roar, was moving in black mountains on the other side of the wall; the snow-gale whistled fiercely through the soaked rigging; the whole ship quivered as it mastered both the gale and the mountains, sundering to either side, as though with a plow, their shifting masses, which again and again boiled up and flung themselves high, with tails of foam; the siren, stifled by the fog, was moaning with a deathly anguish; the lookouts up in their crow's-nest froze with the cold and grew dazed from straining their attention beyond their strength. Akin to the grim sultry depths of the infernal regions, akin to their ultimate, their ninth circle, was the womb of the steamer, below the water line—that womb where dully gurgled the gigantic furnaces, devouring with their fiery maws mountains of hard coal, cast into them by men stripped to the waist, purple from the flames, and with smarting, filthy sweat pouring over them; while here, in the bar, men threw their legs over the arms of their chairs, with never a care, sipping cognac and liqueurs, and were wafted among clouds of spicy smoke as they indulged in refined conversation; in the ballroom everything was radiant with light and warmth and joy; couples were now whirling in waltzes, now swaying in the tango— and the music insistently, in some delectably shameless melancholy, supplicated always of one, always of the same thing. . . . There was an ambassador among this brilliant throng—a lean, modest little old man; there was a rich man—clean-shaven, lanky, of indeterminate years, and with the appearance of a prelate, in an old-fashioned frock coat; there was a well-known Spanish writer; there was a world-celebrated beauty, already just the very least trifle faded and of an unenviable morality; there was an exquisite couple in love with each other, whom all watched with curiosity and whose happiness was unconcealed: *he* danced only with *her;* sang—and with great ability—only to *her* accompaniment; everything they did was carried out so charmingly; and only the captain knew that this pair was hired by Lloyd's to play at love for good money, and that they had been sailing for a long time, now on one ship, now on another.

At Gibraltar everybody was gladdened by the sun—it seemed like early spring; a new passenger, whose person aroused the general interest, made his appearance on board the *Atlantis*—he was the hereditary prince of a certain Asiatic kingdom, traveling incognito; a little man who somehow seemed to be all made of wood, even though he was agile in his movements; broad of face, with narrow eyes, in gold-rimmed spectacles; a trifle unpleasant owing to the fact that his skin showed through his coarse black mustache like that of a corpse; on the whole, however, he was charming, simple, and modest. On the Mediterranean Sea there was a whiff of winter again; the billows ran high, were as multi-colored as the tail of a peacock, and had snowy-white crests, due, in spite of the sparklingly bright sun and perfectly clear sky, to a *tramontana,* a chill northern wind from beyond the mountains, that was joyously and madly rushing to meet the ship. . . . Then, on the second day, the sky began to pale, the horizon became covered with mist, land was nearing; Ischia, Capri appeared; through the binoculars, Naples—lumps of sugar strewn at the foot of some dove-colored mass —could be seen; while over it and this dove-colored object were visible the ridges of distant mountains, vaguely glimmering with the dead whiteness of snow. There was a great number of people on deck; many of the ladies and gentlemen had already put on short, light fur coats, with the fur outside; Chinese boys, patient and always speaking in a whisper, bow-legged striplings with pitch-black queues reaching to their heels and with eyelashes as long and thick as those of young girls, were already dragging, little by little, sundry plaids, canes, and portmanteaux and grips of alligator hide toward the companionways. . . . The daughter of the gentleman from San Francisco was standing beside the prince, who had been, by a happy chance, presented to her yesterday evening, and she pretended to be looking intently into the distance, in a direction he was pointing out to her, telling, explaining something or other to her, hurriedly and quietly. On account of his height he seemed a boy by contrast with others—he was odd and not at all prepossessing of person, with his spectacles, his bowler, his English greatcoat, while his scanty mustache looked just as if it were of horsehair, and the swarthy, thin skin seemed to be drawn tightly over his face, and somehow had the appearance of being lacquered—but the young girl was listening to him, without understanding, in her perturbation, what he was saying; her heart was thumping from an incomprehensible rapture in his presence and from pride that he was speaking with her, and not someone else; everything about him that was different from others—his lean hands, his clear skin, under which flowed the ancient blood of kings, even his wholly unpretentious, yet somehow singularly neat, European dress—everything held a secret, inexplicable charm, evoked a feeling of amorousness. As for the gentleman from San Francisco himself—he, in a high silk hat, in gray spats over patent-leather shoes, kept on glancing at the famous beauty, who was standing beside him—a tall blonde of striking figure, with eyes painted in the lastest Parisian fashion; she was holding a diminutive, hunched-up, mangy lap dog on a silver chain and was chattering to it without pause. And the daughter, in some vague embarrassment, tried not to notice her father.

Like all Americans of means, he was very generous while traveling, and, like all of them, believed in the full sincerity and good will of those who brought him food and drink with such solicitude, who served him from morn till night, anticipating his slightest wish; of those who guarded his cleanliness and rest, lugged his things around, summoned porters for him, delivered his trunks to hotels. Thus had it been everywhere, thus had it been on the ship, and thus it had to be in Naples as well. Naples grew, and drew nearer; the musicians, the brass of their instruments flashing, had already clustered upon the deck, and suddenly deafened everybody with the triumphant strains of a march; the gigantic captain, in his full-dress uniform, appeared upon his stage, and, like a gracious pagan god, waved his hand amiably to the passengers—and to the gentleman from San Francisco it seemed that it was for him alone that the march so beloved by proud America was thundering, that it was he whom the captain was felicitating upon a safe arrival. And every other passenger felt similarly about himself— or herself. And when the *Atlantis* finally entered the harbor, heaved to at the wharf with her many-tiered mass, black with people, and the gang-planks clattered down—what a multitude of porters and their helpers in caps with gold braid, what a multitude of different *commissionaires,* whistling gamins, and strapping ragamuffins with packets of colored postalcards in their hands, made a rush toward the gentleman from San Francisco with offers of their services! And he smiled, with a kindly contemptuousness, at these ragamuffins, as he went toward the automobile of precisely that hotel where there was a likelihood of the prince's stopping. He drawled through his teeth, now in English, now in Italian:

"Go away! *Via!*"

Life at Naples at once assumed its wonted, ordered routine: in the early morning, breakfast in the gloomy dining room with its damp draught from windows, opening on some sort of a stony little garden. The sky was overcast, holding out little promise, and there was the usual crowd of guides at the door of the vestibule; then came the first smiles of a warm, rosy sun. From the high hanging balcony Vesuvius came into view, enveloped to its foot by radiant morning mists, and the silver-and-pearl eddies on the surface of the Bay, and the delicate contour of Capri against the horizon. One could see tiny burros, harnessed in twos to little carts, running down below over the quay, sticky with mire, and detachments of diminutive soldiers, marching somewhere to lively and exhilarating music. Next came the procession to the waiting automobile and the slow progress through populous, narrow, and damp corridors of streets, between tall, many-windowed houses; the inspection of lifelessly clean museums, evenly and pleasantly, yet bleakly, lighted, seemingly illuminated by snow; or of cool churches, smelling of wax, which everywhere and always contain the same things: a majestic portal, screened by a heavy curtain of leather, and inside—empty vastness, silence, quiescent tiny flames of a seven-branched candlestick glowing redly in the distant depths, on an altar bedecked with laces; a solitary old woman among the dark wooden pews; slippery tombstones underfoot; and someone's "Descent from the Cross"—it goes without saying, a celebrated one. At one o'clock there was luncheon upon the mountain of San Martino, where, toward noon, not a few people of the very first quality gathered, and where the daughter of the gentleman from San Francisco had once almost fainted away for joy, because she thought she saw the prince sitting in the hall, although she already knew through the newspapers that he had left for a temporary stay at Rome. At five came tea at the hotel, in the showy salon, so cozy with its rugs and flaming fireplaces; and after that it was already time to prepare for dinner—and once more came the mighty clamor of the gong reverberating through the hotel; once more the moving queues of ladies in *décolleté,* rustling in their silks upon the staircases and reflected in all the mirrors; once more the palatial dining room, widely and hospitably opened, and the red jackets of the musicians upon their platform, and the black cluster of waiters about the maître d'hôtel, who, with inordinate skill, was ladling some sort of thick, reddish soup into plates. . . . The dinners, as everywhere else, were the crowning glory of each day; the guests dressed for them as for a party, and these dinners were so abundant in edibles, and wines, and mineral waters, and sweets, and fruits, that toward eleven o'clock at night the chambermaids were distributing through all the rooms rubber bags with hot water to warm the stomachs.

As it happened, the December of that year proved to be not a wholly successful one for Naples; the porters grew confused when one talked with them of the weather, and merely shrugged their shoulders guiltily, muttering that they could not recall such a year—although it was not the first year that they had been forced to mutter this, and to base their statement on that "something terrible is happening everywhere"; there were unheard-of storms and torrents of rain on the Riviera; there was snow in Athens; Etna was also all snowed over and was aglow at night; tourists were fleeing from Palermo in all directions, to escape from the cold. The morning sun deceived the Neapolitans every day that winter: toward noon the sky became gray and a fine rain began falling, but grew heavier and colder all the time; then the palms near the entrance of the hotel glistened as though they were of tin, the town seemed especially dirty and cramped, the museums curiously alike; the cigar stumps of the corpulent cabmen, whose rubber coats flapped in the wind like wings, seemed to have an insufferable stench, while the energetic snapping of their whips over their scrawny-necked nags was patently false; the footgear of the *signori* sweeping the rails of the tramways seemed horrible; the women, splashing through the mud, their black-haired heads bared to the rain, appeared hideously short-legged; as for the dampness, and the stench of putrid fish from the sea foaming at the quay—there was nothing to be said. The gentleman and the lady from San Francisco began quarreling in the morning; their daughter either walked about pale, with a headache, or, coming to life again, went into raptures over everything, and was, at such times, both charming and beautiful: beautiful were those tender and complex emotions which had been awakened within her by meeting that unsightly man through whose veins flowed uncommon blood; for, after all is said and done, perhaps it is of no actual importance just what it is, precisely, that awakens a maiden's soul—whether it be money, or fame, or illustrious ancestry. . . . Everybody asserted that things were quite different in Sorrento, in Capri—there it was both warmer and sunnier, and the lemons were in blossom, and the customs were more honest, and the wine was better. And so the family from San Francisco resolved to set out with all its trunks to Capri, and, after seeing it all, after treading the stones where the palace of Tiberius had once stood, after visiting the fairy-like caverns of the Blue Grotto, and hearing the bagpipers of Abruzzi, who for a whole month preceding Christmas wander over the island and sing the praises of the Virgin Mary, they meant to settle in Sorrento.

On the day of departure—a most memorable one for the family from San Francisco!—there was no early-morning sun. A heavy fog hid Vesuvius to the very base; this gray fog spread low over the leaden swell of the sea that was lost to the eye at a distance of a half a mile. Capri was quite invisible—as if there had never been such an island in the world. And the tiny steamer that set out for it was so tossed from side to side that the family from San Francisco was laid prostrate upon the divans in the sorry general cabin of this tiny steamer, their feet wrapped up in plaid rugs and their eyes closed. The mother suffered— so she thought—more than anybody; she was overcome by seasickness several times; it seemed to her that she was dying, while the stewardess, who always ran up to her with a small basin—she had been, for many years, day in and day out, rolling on these waves, in sultry weather and in cold, and yet was still tireless and kind to everybody— merely laughed. The daughter was dreadfully pale and held a slice of lemon between her teeth; now she could not have been comforted even by the hope of a chance meeting with the prince at Sorrento, where he intended to be about Christmas. The father, who was lying on his back, in roomy overcoat and large cap, never opened his jaws all the way over; his face had grown darker and his mustache whiter, and his head ached dreadfully: during the last days, thanks to the bad weather, he had been drinking too heavily of evenings, and had too much admired the "living pictures" in the haunts of manufactured libertinage. But the rain kept on lashing against the jarring windows, the water from them running down on the divans; the wind, howling, bent the masts, and at times, aided by the onslaught of a wave, careened the little steamer entirely to one side, and then something in the hold would roll with a rumble. During the stops at Castellamare, at Sorrento, things were a trifle more bearable, but even then the rocking was fearful—the shore, with all its cliffs, gardens, pine groves, its pink and white hotels and hazy mountains clad in wavy greenery, swayed up and down as if on a swing; boats bumped up against the sides of the ship; sailors and steerage passengers were shouting fiercely;

somewhere, as if it had been crushed, a baby was wailing and smothering; a raw wind was blowing in at the door; and, from a swaying boat with the flag of the Hotel Royal, a lisping gamin was screaming, luring travelers: "Kgoya-all! Hotel Kgoya-all! . . ." And the gentleman from San Francisco, feeling himself to be incredibly old—which was as it should be—was already thinking with sadness and loathing of all these Royals, Splendids, Excelsiors, and of these greedy, insignificant little men, reeking of garlic, called Italians. Once, having opened his eyes and raised himself from the divan, he saw underneath the craggy barrier on the shore a cluster of stone hovels, moldy through and through, stuck one on top of another near the very edge of the water, near boats, near all sorts of rags, tins, and brown nets—hovels so wretched that, at the recollection this was the very Italy he had come here to enjoy, he felt despair. . . . Finally, at twilight, the dark mass of the island began to draw near, seemingly bored through and through by little red lights near its base; the wind became softer, warmer, more fragrant; over the abating waves, as opalescent as black oil, golden serpents flowed from the lanterns on the wharf. . . . Then came the sudden rumble of the anchor, and it fell with a splash into the water; the savage shouts of the boatmen, vying with one another, floated in from all quarters—and at once the heart grew lighter, the lamps in the general cabin shone more brightly, a desire arose to eat, to drink, to smoke, to be stirring. . . . Ten minutes later the family from San Francisco had descended into a large boat; within fifteen minutes it had set foot upon the stones of the wharf, and had then got into a bright little railway car and to its buzzing started the ascent of the slope, amid the stakes of the vineyards, half-crumbled stone enclosures, and wet, gnarled orange trees, some of them under coverings of straw—trees with thick, glossy foliage, aglimmer with the orange fruits; all these objects were sliding downward, past the open windows of the little car, toward the base of the mountain. . . . Sweetly smells the earth of Italy after rain, and her every island has its own, its especial aroma!

On this evening the island of Capri was damp and dark. But now for an instant it came to life; lights sprang up here and there, as always on the steamer's arrival. At the top of the mountain, where stood the station of the *funicular,* there was another throng of those whose duty it was to receive fittingly the gentleman from San Francisco. There were other arrivals, but they merited no attention—several Russians who had settled in Capri—absent-minded because of their bookish meditations, unkempt, bearded, spectacled, the collars of their old frayed overcoats turned up; and a group of long-legged, long-necked, round-headed German youths in Tyrolean costumes, with canvas knapsacks slung over their shoulders; these stood in no need of anybody's services, feeling themselves at home everywhere, and knowing how to practice the strictest economies. The gentleman from San Francisco, on the other hand, who was calmly keeping aloof from both the one group and the other, was immediately observed. He and his ladies were promptly helped out, some men running ahead of him to show him the way. Again he was surrounded by urchins, and by those stalwart Caprian wives who bear on their heads the portmanteaux and trunks of respectable travelers. The wooden pattens of these women clattered over a little square, which seemed to belong to some opera, an electric globe swaying above it in the damp wind. The rabble of urchins burst into sharp, birdlike whistles—and, as if on a stage, the gentleman from San Francisco proceeded in their midst toward some medieval arch underneath houses that had become merged into one mass, beyond which a little echoing street—with the tuft of a palm above flat roofs on its left, and with blue stars in the black sky overhead—led slopingly to the now visible grand entrance of the hotel, all agleam with light. . . . And again it seemed that it was in honor of the guests from San Francisco that this damp little town of stone on a craggy little island of the Mediterranean Sea had come to life, that it was they who had made the proprietor of the hotel so happy and affable, that it was only for them that the Chinese gong began to sound the summons to dinner through all the stories of the hotel, the instant they had set foot in the vestibule.

The proprietor, a young man of courtly elegance, who had met them with a polite and exquisite bow, for a minute dumfounded the gentleman from San Francisco. After a glance at him, the gentleman from San Francisco suddenly remembered that just the night before, among the confusion of numerous images which had beset him in his sleep, he had seen precisely this gentleman—just like him, down to the least detail: in the same sort of frock with rounded skirts, and with the same pomaded and painstakingly combed head. Startled, he almost paused. But since, from long, long before, there was not even a mustard seed of any sort of so-called mystical emotions left in his soul, his astonishment was dimmed the same instant; as he proceeded through a corridor of the hotel, he spoke jestingly to his wife and daughter of this strange coincidence of dream and reality. And only his daughter glanced at him with alarm at that moment: her heart suddenly contracted from sadness, from a feeling of their loneliness upon this dark alien island—a feeling so strong that she almost burst into tears. Nevertheless, she said nothing of her feelings to her father—as always.

An exalted personage—Rais XVII—who had been visiting Capri, had just taken his departure. And now the guests from San Francisco were conducted to the same apartments that he had occupied. To them was assigned the ablest and handsomest chambermaid, a Belgian, whose waist was slenderly and firmly corseted, and whose tiny starched cap looked like a scalloped crown; also, the best-looking and most dignified of flunkeys a fiery-eyed Sicilian, black as coal; and the nimblest of bell-boys, the short and stout Luigi—a fellow who was very fond of a joke, and who had served many masters in his time. And a minute later there was a slight tap at the door of the room of the gentleman from San Francisco—the French maître d'hôtel had come to find out if the newly arrived guests would dine, and, in the event of an answer in the affirmative—of which, of course, there was no doubt—to inform them that the *carte de jour* consisted of crawfish, roast beef, asparagus, pheasants, and so forth. The floor was still rocking under the gentleman from San Francisco—so badly had the atrocious little Italian steamer tossed him about—but, without hurrying, with his own hands, although somewhat awkwardly from being unaccustomed to such things, he shut a window that had banged when the maître d'hôtel had entered and had let in the odors of the distant kitchen and of the wet flowers in the garden, and with a lingering deliberateness replied that they would dine, that their table must be placed as far as possible from the door, at the other end of the dining room, that they would drink local wine and champagne—moderately dry and only slightly chilled. The maître d'hôtel approved every word of his, in most varied intonations, having, in any case, but one significance—that there was never a doubt, nor could there possibly be any, about the correctness of the wishes of the gentleman from San Francisco, and that everything would be carried out with precision. In conclusion he inclined his head, and asked deferentially:

"Will that be all, sir?"

And, having received in answer a leisurely "Yes," he added that the *tarantella* would be danced in the vestibule tonight—the dancers would be Carmella and Giuseppe, known to all Italy and to "the entire world of tourists."

"I have seen her on postcards," said the gentleman from San Francisco in a wholly inexpressive voice. "As for this Giuseppe—is he her husband?"

"Her cousin, sir," answered the maître d'hôtel.

And, after a brief pause during which he appeared to be considering something, the gentleman from San Francisco dismissed him with a nod.

And then he once more began his preparations, as if for a wedding ceremony: he turned on all the electric lights, filling all the mirrors with reflections of light and glitter, of furniture and opened trunks; he began shaving and washing, ringing the bell every minute, while other impatient rings from his wife's and daughter's room sounded through the entire corridor and interrupted his. And Luigi, in his red apron, was rushing forward to answer the bell, with an agility peculiar to many stout men, not omitting grimaces of horror that made the chambermaids, running by with glazed porcelain pails in their hands, laugh till they cried. He knocked on the door with his knuckles, and asked with an assumed timidity, with a deference which verged on idiocy:

"*Ha sonato, signore?*"

And from the other side of the door came an unhurried, grating voice, humiliatingly polite:

"Yes, come in. . . ."

What were the thoughts, what were the emotions of the gentleman from San Francisco on this evening, that was to be of such significance to him? He felt nothing exceptional—for the trouble in this world is just that everything is apparently all too simple! And even if he had sensed within his soul that something was impending, he would, nevertheless, have thought that this thing would not occur for some time to come—in any case, not immediately. Besides that, like every-one who has experienced the rocking of a ship, he wanted very much to eat, was looking forward to the first spoonful of soup, the first mouthful of wine, and performed the usual routine of dressing, even with a certain degree of exhilaration that left no time for reflections.

After shaving and washing himself, after inserting several artificial teeth properly, he remained standing before a mirror, while he wetted the remnants of his thick, pearly-gray hair and plastered it down around his swarthy yellow skull, with brushes set in silver; drew a suit of cream-colored silk underwear over his strong old body, begin-ning to be full at the waist from excesses in food, and put silk socks and dancing slippers on his shriveled, splayed feet; sitting down, he put in order his black trousers, drawn high by black silk braces, as well as his snowy-white shirt, with the bosom bulging out; put the links through the glossy cuffs, and began the agonizing manipulation of the collar button underneath the stiffly starched collar. The floor was still swaying beneath him, the tips of his fingers pained him greatly, the collar buttom at times nipped hard the flabby skin in the hollow under his Adam's apple, but he was persistent; and at last, his eyes glittering from the exertion, his face all livid from the collar that was choking his throat—a collar far too tight—he did succeed in accomplishing his task, and sat down in exhaustion in front of the pier glass. He was reflected in it from head to foot, a reflection that was repeated in all the other mirrors.

"Oh, this is dreadful!" he muttered, lowering his strong bald head, and without trying to understand, without considering just what, pre-cisely, was dreadful; then, with an accustomed and attentive glance, he inspected his stubby fingers, with gouty hardenings at the joints, and his convex nails of an almond color, and repeated, with conviction: "This is dreadful. . . ."

At this point the second gong, sonorously, as in some pagan temple, dinned through the entire house. And, getting up quickly from his seat, the gentleman from San Francisco drew his collar still tighter with the necktie and his stomach by means of the low-cut vest, put on his smoking jacket, arranged his cuffs, surveyed himself once more in the mirror. . . . This Carmella, swarthy, with eyes which she knew well how to use tellingly, resembling a mulatto woman, clad in a dress of many colors, with the color of orange predominant, must dance ex-ceptionally, he imagined. And, stepping briskly out of his room and walking over the carpet to the next one—his wife's—he asked, loudly, if they would be ready soon?

"In five minutes, Dad!" a girl's voice, ringing and by now gay, responded from the other side of the door.

"Very well," said the gentleman from San Francisco.

And, leisurely, he walked through red-carpeted corridors and down staircases, in quest of the reading room. The servants he met stood aside and hugged the wall to let him pass, but he kept on his way as though he had never even noticed them. An old woman who was late for dinner, already stooping, with milky hair but *décolleté* in a light-gray gown of silk, was hurrying with all her might, but drolly, in a henlike manner, and he easily outstripped her. Near the glass doors of the dining room, where all the guests had already assembled and were beginning their dinner, he stopped before a little table piled with boxes of cigars and Egyptian cigarettes, took a large Manila cigar, and flung three *lire* upon the little table. Walking on the terrace, he glanced, in passing, through the open window; out of the darkness he felt a breath of the balmy air upon him, thought he saw the tip of an ancient palm. Its gigantic fronds seemed to reach out across the stars. He heard the distant, measured din of the sea. . . . In the reading room —snug, quiet, and illuminated only above the tables, some gray-haired German was standing, rustling the newspapers—unkempt, resembling Ibsen, in round silver spectacles and with mad, astonished eyes. After scrutinizing him coldly, the gentleman from San Francisco sat down in a deep leather chair in a corner near a green-shaded lamp, put on his pince-nez, twitching his head because his collar was choking him, and hid himself completely behind the newspaper. He rapidly ran through the headlines of certain items, read a few lines about the never-ceasing Balkan war, with an accustomed gesture turned the newspaper over—when suddenly the lines flared up before him with a glassy glare, his neck became taut, his eyes bulged out, the pince-nez flew off his nose. . . . He lunged forward, tried to swallow some air— and made a wild horse sound; his lower jaw sank, lighting up his entire mouth with the reflection of the gold fillings; his head dropped back on his shoulder and began to sway; the bosom of his shirt bulged out like a basket—and his whole body, squirming, his heels catching the carpet, slid downward to the floor, desperately struggling with someone.

Had the German not been in the reading room, the hotel attendants would have managed, quickly and adroitly, to hush up this dreadful occurrence; instantly, through back passages, seizing him by the head and feet, they would have rushed off the gentleman from San Francisco as far away as possible—and not a soul among the guests would have found out what he had been up to. But the German had dashed out of the reading room with a scream—he had aroused the entire house, the entire dining room. And many jumped up from

their meal, overturning their chairs; many, paling, ran toward the
reading room. "What—what has happened?" was heard in all languages—and no one gave a sensible answer, no one comprehended
anything, since even to this day men are amazed most of all by death,
and will not, in any circumstances, believe in it. The proprietor dashed
from one guest to another, trying to detain those who were running
away and to pacify them with hasty assurances that this was just a
trifling occurrence, a slight fainting spell of a certain gentleman from
San Francisco. . . . No one listened to him; many had seen the flunkeys
and corridor attendants tearing the necktie, the vest, and the rumpled
smoking jacket off this gentleman, and even, for some reason or
other, the dancing slippers off his splayed feet, clad in black silk. He
was still struggling. He was still obdurately wrestling with death;
he absolutely refused to yield to her, who had so unexpectedly and
inconsiderately fallen upon him. His head was swaying, he rattled
hoarsely, like one with his throat cut; his eyes had rolled up, like a
drunkard's. . . . When he was hurriedly carried in and laid upon a bed
in Room Number Forty-three—the smallest, the poorest, the dampest
and the coldest, situated at the end of the bottom corridor—his daughter ran in, with her hair down, in a little dressing-gown that had flown
open, her bosom, raised up by the corset, uncovered; then his wife,
big and ponderous, already dressed for dinner—her mouth rounded in
terror. . . . But by now he had ceased even wagging his head.

A quarter of an hour later everything in the hotel had assumed a
semblance of order. Nevertheless, the evening was irreparably spoiled.
Some guests, returning to the dining room, finished their dinner, but
in silence, with aggrieved faces, while the proprietor would approach
now one group, now another, shrugging his shoulders in polite yet
impotent irritation, feeling himself guilty without guilt, assuring
everybody that he understood very well "how unpleasant all this was,"
and pledging his word that he would take "all measures within his
power" to remove this unpleasantness. The *tarantella* had to be called
off, all superfluous electric lights were extinguished, the majority of
the guests withdrew into the bar, and it became so quiet that one
heard distinctly the ticking of the clock in the vestibule, whose sole
occupant was a parrot, dully muttering something, fussing in his cage
before going to sleep, contriving to doze off at last with one claw
ludicrously stretched up to the upper perch. . . . The gentleman from
San Francisco was lying upon a cheap iron bed, under coarse woolen
blankets, upon which the dull light of a single bulb beat down from
the ceiling. An ice-bag was askew on his moist and cold forehead. The
livid face, already dead, was gradually growing cold; the hoarse rattling, expelled from the open mouth, illuminated by the reflection of
gold, was growing fainter. This was no longer the gentleman from
San Francisco rattling—he no longer existed—but some other. His
wife, his daughter, the doctor, and the servants were standing, gazing
at him dully. Suddenly, that which they awaited and feared was con-

summated—the rattling ceased abruptly. And slowly, slowly, before the eyes of all, a pallor suffused the face of the man who had died, and his features seemed to grow finer, to become irradiated with a beauty which had been rightfully his in the long ago. . . .

The proprietor entered. *"Già è morto,"* said the doctor to him in a whisper. The proprietor, with dispassionate face, shrugged his shoulders. The wife, down whose cheeks the tears were quietly coursing, walked up to him and timidly said that the deceased ought now to be carried to his own room.

"Oh, no, madam," hastily, correctly, but now without any amiability and not in English, but in French, retorted the proprietor, who was not at all interested now in such trifling sums as the arrivals from San Francisco might leave in his coffers. "That is absolutely impossible, madam," he said, and added in explanation that he valued the apartments occupied by them very much; that, were he to carry out her wishes, everybody in Capri would know it and the tourists would shun those apartments.

The young woman, who had been all this time gazing at him strangely, sat down on a chair and, pressing a handkerchief to her mouth, burst into sobs. The wife dried her tears immediately, her face flaring up. She adopted a louder tone, making demands in her own language, and still incredulous of the fact that all respect for them had been completely lost. The proprietor, with polite dignity, cut her short: if madam was not pleased with the customs of the hotel, he would not venture to detain her; and he firmly announced that the body must be gotten away this very day, at dawn, that the police had already been notified, and one of the police officers would be here very soon and would carry out all the necessary formalities. Was it possible to secure even a common coffin in Capri?—madam asked. Regrettably, no—it was beyond possibility, and no one would be able to make one in time. It would be necessary to have recourse to something else. . . . He had a suggestion.—English soda water came in large and long boxes. . . . It was possible to knock the partitions out of such a box. . . .

At night the whole hotel slept. The window in Room Number Forty-three was opened—it gave out upon a corner of the garden where, near a high stone wall with broken glass upon its crest, a consumptive banana tree was growing; the electric light was switched off; the key was turned in the door; and everybody went away. The dead man remained in the darkness—the blue stars looked down upon him from the sky, a cricket with a pensive insouciance began his song in the wall. . . . In the dimly lit corridor two chambermaids were seated on a window sill, at some darning. Luigi, in slippers, entered with a pile of clothing in his arms.

"Pronto?" he asked solicitously, in an audible whisper, indicating with his eyes the fearsome door at the end of the corridor. And, he waved his hand airily in that direction. . . . *"Partenza!"* he called out

in a whisper, as though he were speeding a train, the usual phrase used in Italian depots at the departure of trains—and the chambermaids, choking with silent laughter, let their heads sink on each other's shoulder.

Thereupon, hopping softly, he ran up to the very door, gave it the merest tap, and, inclining his head to one side, in a low voice, asked with the utmost deference:

"*Ha sonato, signore?*"

And, squeezing his throat, thrusting out his lower jaw, in a grating voice, slowly and sadly, he answered his own question, in English, as though from the other side of the door:

"Yes, come in. . . ."

And at dawn, when it had become light beyond the window of Room Number Forty-three, and a humid wind had begun to rustle the tattered leaves of the banana tree; when the blue sky of morning had lifted and spread out over the island of Capri, and the pure and clear-cut summit of Monte Solaro had grown golden against the sun that was rising beyond the distant blue mountains of Italy; when the stone-masons, who were repairing the tourists' paths on the island, had set out to work—a long box that had formerly been used for soda water was brought to Room Number Forty-three. Soon it became very heavy, and was pressing hard against the knees of the junior porter, who bore it off briskly on a one-horse cab over the white paved highway that was sinuously winding over the slopes of Capri, among the stone walls and the vineyards, ever downwards, to the sea itself. The cabby, a puny little man with reddened eyes, in an old jacket with short sleeves and in much-worn shoes, was suffering the aftereffects of drink—he had spent the whole night long in playing with dice in a *tratoria*—and kept on lashing his sturdy little horse, rigged out in Sicilian fashion, with all sorts of little bells livelily jingling· upon the bridle with its tufts of colored wool, and upon the brass points of its high pad; with a yard-long feather stuck in its cropped forelock—a feather that shook as the horse ran. The cabby kept silent; he was oppressed by his shiftlessness, his vices—by the circumstance that he had, that night, lost to the last mite all those coppers with which his pockets had been filled. But the morning was fresh; in air such as this, with the sea all around, under the morning sky, the aftereffects of drink quickly evaporate, and a man is soon restored to a carefree mood, and the cabby was furthermore consoled by that unexpected windfall, con-ferred upon him by some gentleman from San Francisco, whose life-less head was bobbing from side to side in the box at his back. . . . The little steamer—a beetle lying far down below, against the tender and vivid deep blue with which the Bay of Naples is so densely and highly flooded—was already blowing its final whistles, that reverberated loudly all over the island, whose every bend, every ridge, every stone, was as distinctly visible from every point as if there were absolutely no such thing as atmosphere. Near the wharf the junior porter was joined by the senior, who was speeding with the daughter and wife of the gentleman from San Francisco in his automobile—they were pale, with eyes hollow from tears and a sleepless night. And ten minutes later the little steamer was again noisily making its way through the water, again running toward Sorrento, toward Castellamare, carrying away from Capri, for all time, the family from San Francisco. . . . And again peace and quiet reigned upon the island.

Upon this island, two thousand years ago, had lived a man who had become completely enmeshed in his cruel and foul deeds, who had for some reason seized the power over millions of people in his hands, and who, having himself lost his head at the senselessness of this power and from the fear of death by assassination by someone, lurking round the corner, had committed cruelties beyond all measure—and humankind has remembered him for all time; and those who, in their collusion, just as incomprehensively and, in substance, just as cruelly as he, reign at present in power over this world, gather from all over the earth to gaze upon the ruins of that stone villa where he had dwelt on one of the steepest ascents of the island. On this marvelous morning all those who had come to Capri for just this purpose were still sleeping in the hotels, although, toward the entrances, were already being led little mouse-gray burros with red saddles, upon which, after awaking and sating themselves with food, Americans and Germans, men and women, young and old, would again ponderously clamber up the steep paths this day, and after whom would again run the old Caprian beggar women, with sticks in their gnarled hands—would run over stony paths, and always uphill, up to the very summit of Mount Tiberio. Comforted by the knowledge that the dead old man from San Francisco, who had likewise been planning to go with them but instead of that had only frightened them with a reminder of death, had already been shipped off to Naples, the travelers slept on heavily, and the quiet of the island was still undisturbed, the shops in the town were still shut. The market place in the little square alone was carrying on traffic—in fish and greens; and the people there were all simple folk, among whom, without anything to do, as always, was standing Lorenzo, the boatman, famous all over Italy—a tall old man, a carefree rake and a handsome fellow, who had served more than once as a model to many artists; he had brought, and had already sold for a trifle, two lobsters that he had caught that night and which were already rustling in the apron of the cook of that very hotel where the family from San Francisco had passed the night, and now he could afford to stand in calm idleness even until the evening, looking about him with a kingly bearing, consciously and flauntingly picturesque with his tatters, clay pipe, and a red woolen *beretta* drooping over one ear.

And along the precipices of Monte Solaro, upon the ancient Phoenician road, hewn out of the crags, down its stone steps, two mountaineers of Abruzzi were descending from Anacapri. One had bag-

pipes under his leathern mantle—a large bag made from the skin of a
she-goat, with two pipes; the other had something in the nature of
wooden Pan's-reeds. They went on—and all the land, joyous, lovely,
sun-swept, spread out below them: the stony humps of the island,
which was lying almost in its entirety at their feet; and that fairy-
like deep blue in which it was afloat; and the shining morning vapors
over the sea, toward the east, under the blinding sun, that was now
beating down hotly, rising ever higher and higher; and, still in their
morning vagueness, the mistily blue massive outlines of Italy, of her
mountains near and far, whose beauty human speech is impotent to
express. . . . Halfway down, the pipers slackened their pace; over the
path, within a grotto in the craggy side of Monte Solaro, all bright in
the sun, all bathed in its warmth and glow, in snowy-white raiment
of gypsum, and in a royal crown, golden-rusty from inclement weathers,
stood the Mother of God, meek and gracious, Her orbs lifted up to
heaven, to the eternal and happy abodes of Her thrice-blessed Son.
The pipers bared their heads, put their reeds to their lips—and there
poured forth their naïve and humbly jubilant praises to the sun, to the
morning, to Her, the Immaculate Intercessor for all those who suffer
in this evil and beautiful world, and to Him Who had been born of
Her womb in a cavern at Bethlehem, in a poor shepherd's shelter in
the distant land of Judaea. . . .

Meanwhile, the body of the dead old man from San Francisco was
returning to its home, to a grave on the shores of the New World.
Having gone through many humiliations, through much human neglect, having wandered for a week from one port warehouse to another,
it had finally gotten once more on board that same famous ship upon
which but lately, with so much deference, he had been borne to the
Old World. But now he was already being concealed from the quick
—he was lowered in his tarred coffin deep into the black hold. And
once more the ship was sailing on and on upon its long sea voyage. By
night it sailed past the Island of Capri, and, to one watching them
from the island, there was something sad about the ship's lights, slowly
disappearing over the dark sea. But, upon the ship itself, in its brilliant
salons, resplendent with lusters and marble, there was, as usual, a
crowded ball that night.

There was a ball on the second night, and also on the third—again
in the midst of a raging snow gale, whirling over an ocean booming
like a burial mass, and rolling in mountains arrayed in mourning by
the silvery foam. The innumerable fiery eyes of the ship were barely
visible, because of the snow, to the devil watching from the crags of
Gibraltar, from the stony gateway of two worlds, the ship receding
into the night and the snow gale. The devil was as enormous as a
cliff, but even more enormous was the ship, many-tiered, many-
funneled, created by the pride of the New Man with an ancient heart.
The snow gale smote upon its rigging and wide-throated funnels,
white from the snow, but the ship was steadfast, firm, majestic—and

terrifying. Upon its topmost deck were reared, in their solitude among the snowy whirlwinds, those snug, dimly lighted chambers where, plunged in a light and uneasy slumber, was its ponderous guide who resembled a pagan idol, reigning over the whole ship. He heard the pained howlings and the ferocious squealings of the storm-stifled siren, but comforted himself by the proximity of that which, in the final summing up, was incomprehensible even to himself, that which was on the other side of his wall: that large cabin, which had the appearance of being armored, and was constantly filled by the mysterious rumbling, quivering, and crisp sputtering of blue flames, flaring up and exploding around the pale-faced operator with a metal half-hoop upon his head. In the very depths, in the submerged womb of the *Atlantis,* were the thirty-thousand-pound masses of boilers and of all sorts of other machinery—dully glittering with steel, hissing out steam and exuding oil and boiling water—of that kitchen, made red-hot from internal furnaces underneath, wherein was brewing the motion of the ship. Forces, fearful in their concentration, were bubbling, were being transmitted to its very keel, into an endlessly long dungeon, into a tunnel, illuminated by electricity, wherein slowly, with an inexorableness that was crushing to the human soul, was revolving within its oily couch the gigantic shaft, exactly like a living monster that had stretched itself out in this tunnel.

Meanwhile, amidship the *Atlantis,* its warm and luxurious cabins, its dining halls and ballrooms poured forth radiance and joyousness, were humming with the voices of a well-dressed gathering, were fragrant with fresh flowers, and the strains of the string orchestra were their song. And again excruciatingly coiled and at intervals feverishly came together among this throng, among this glitter of lights, silks, diamonds, and bared feminine shoulders, the pliant pair of hired lovers: the sinfully modest, very pretty young woman, with eyelashes cast down, with a chaste coiffure, and the well-built young man, with black hair that seemed to be pasted on, with his face pale from powder, shod in the most elegant of patent-leather footgear, clad in a tight-fitting dress coat with long tails—a handsome man who resembled a huge leech. And none knew that, already for a long time, this pair had grown weary of languishing dissemblingly in their blissful torment to the sounds of the shamelessly sad music—nor that far, far below, at the bottom of the black hold, stood a tarred coffin, neighboring on the gloomy, sultry depths of the ship that was ponderously overcoming the darkness, the ocean, the gale. . . .

ALEXEY
TOLSTOY

Vasily Suchkov

Alexey Tolstoy (1882–1945) was trained as an engineer, but experimented with poetry at an early age. He began writing prose in about 1901, and with the appearance of *Peter the Great* in 1932, he attained his full stature as the foremost contemporary Soviet writer. His other works include *The Sisters, Road to Calvary, The Revolt of the Machines, Bread* and a popular children's play, *The Golden Key.* [From *Bonfire;* used by permission of the publishers, Ernest Benn, Ltd.]

"I'LL PUT IT THIS WAY: *If only our children had some* understanding, like we old people have—even that would be something to praise the Lord for."

"Musn't praise the Lord nowadays, Timofey Ivanovich."

"Well then, praise labor . . . Don't pick holes—I am an old man . . . Look here—we did fight, didn't we?"

"We did, Timofey Ivanovich. Strictly speaking, mine is a quiet occupation, I didn't fight, but you fought, that's a fact."

"I like your way of answering, Ivan Ivanovich, you are a straightforward person. The kind of person we need. . . . Waiter, another couple of bottles and two salmon sandwiches. . . . Well, then, we suffered, didn't we Ivan Ivanovich?"

"No question about that. . . ."

"When the Putilovsky works produced nothing but cigarette-lighters, do you realize what it was for us, old skilled men, to look on. Who is to answer? Go on, blame the White Guards, the Allies. . . . Quite, they'll say, quite. . . . But who started? Did we overthrow everything just to see the biggest works in the Union grind cigarette-lighters? It is all right now they are building timber-carriers in the wharves. All the shops working to full capacity. . . . But in those days one lost hope. . . . Felt like lying down in the midst of all that destruction and giving up the ghost. . . . Isn't that suffering? And who set the works running again? See these hands? Even the bones are saturated with machine oil—see how black the fingers are. . . . It means that I've got the right to speak. . . . And I say this: our children are no damn good. . . . Did they fight? No. Did they suffer? No. They gather in the fruits. And we are an out-of-date lot for them. My Mishka is a 'Young Communist.' All right. Mustn't touch him. Say a word to him—you'll get back ten. All right, all right. Let him learn, let him try to get into the front ranks, follow the great humanitarian ideal. Though, it would be best to give him an occasional shaking, but he'll straighten out. . . . Barking impertinently at every word you say doesn't yet mean his father is a fool. All right, I say, all right. Mishka is an honest lad. But as for my Kolka . . . Well as for him . . . That's where I draw the line. He wears loose bags and a hunting knife. Works one day and spends the next by the sea with the girls . . . And mark you, Ivan Ivanovich, I mustn't touch him with a stick, or take him by the hair. . . . What's the matter with his hair? Is it sacred? But he straightway goes off to complain about me, and at the very best I get a reprimand for torturing the child. . . . And all the while Kolka's future is obvious—ten years, with solitary confinement. Do you know what he answers me? 'You've got to prove to me, old cock, why I should work when I want to go out? In what book is it written, cock, that I should neglect my pleasures? . . .' And that scamp, Kolka, says it all so confidently as if he's the ruling class. 'And if you hit me,' he says, 'I'll cut you a hole through the stomach.' And plays with his knife, his eyes burning. . . ."

"Desperate position you are in, Timofey Ivanovich."

"All right, I won't live to see the final triumph. I am an old man. But I want my children, my grandchildren to speak three languages, Ivan Ivanovich. I want them to fly about the earth in airships, as simple as sitting at home. . . . I want their hands to know fine and brainy work. . . . I weep, Ivan Ivanovich, because my mother gave me life at the wrong moment. I was born for knocking brick walls down with my head. . . . We are the heroic generation, Ivan Ivanovich. . . . Our children and grandchildren come after us. . . . We have done the dirty work. . . . But what are they like? That's the tormenting question. For instance. . . . Down our way, outside the Narva Gate, there are new blocks being built for working men—houses on foreign lines, with balconies and baths. Meaning that there is a hint that the workman won't have to live like a pig now. I come home from the wharf, I wash and sit down to dinner very orderly. My family is well groomed. We eat in a clean room and our conversation is about lofty matters, about human progress. That's right, isn't it? And now—what are the facts? This spring I move into a new house. Good. And here I am going home from the wharf; and before I get home—my overcoat is robbed off my shoulders in an alley, for one thing. . . . I am rushed by people with hunting knives and my belly is cut open for a bit of sport, for another thing. . . . And, if I escape these two accidents and come home safe and sound, my neat dining-table is already occupied by Kolka. . . . His ugly dial just about reeking with obscenity. No, Ivan Ivanovich, we have expected many misfortunes, but this misfortune is unexpected."

Timofey Ivanovich pushed the beer bottles to one side, leant over the little table close to Ivan Ivanovich's face and raised his finger.

"A secret. Haven't told anyone yet. Even my relations don't know. I am beginning to fear my son-in-law, Varvara's husband, Vasily Alekseyevich Suchkov. I don't trust him. He is a suspicious man."

"Chuck it, Timofey Ivanovich! Really you are beginning to see things. . . ."

"True. No foundation at all. But I get a bitter taste in my mouth whenever I think of him."

This conversation took place in June, in a beer-shop on the Peterburgsky Side. Two old friends chatted together: one was Zhavlin, Timofey Ivanovich, a workman on the Putilovsky wharf and the other Ivan Ivanovich Farafono, employed by the River Conservancy as keeper of the shallow riverbank by the Petrovsky Island.

It was a windless, sunny day: a Sunday. The beer-shop was almost empty and filled with a sour smell and stray whiffs of crayfish. The droning of flies against a plate glass window, which displayed the words "Stenka Razin Beer" written backwards, suggested a midday languidness.

The friends finished up their beer. Smoked for a while. Paid the bill and went out. The blue sky with its summer stillness was spread above the miserable streets of the Peterburgsky Side.

"And yet," said Timofey Ivanovich, "and yet, my son-in-law is an inscrutable person."

After that they walked side by side along the broken pavement strewn with the pods of sunflower-seeds. An airplane floated in the sky above. So did the clouds, white as the snow. Silence, the monotony of a Sunday. Flower-pots in the windows. Some children were playing ball on a vacant site among ruins of brick, and the smallest of them sat amongst pigweeds, weeping.

A girl in a light summer frock walked toward the two friends. Her youthful neck, her shoulders and her slender hands showed a golden sunburn. Fair, curly hair covered her pretty head like a cap.

Wider and wider grinned the friends as they looked at the approaching girl. The day was fair, the drink had warmed their hearts, and it was a pleasure to look at Youth browned by the sun.

"Your daughter is first class; meets my approval," said Timofey Ivanovich.

"Nastya, dear, where are you off to?" asked Ivan Ivanovich, pleased.

She raised her blue eyes and her face became sweeter still. She stopped, sighed slightly.

"I promised to call on Varvara Timofeyevna today."

"I have been over at the daughter's today."—Timofey Ivanovich, with a sudden frown, began to look down under his feet, "I have been there and could not stand it for an hour. . . . I shan't go again for six months. . . . You've got no business there, either, Nastya. . . . To listen to the discourses of citizen Suchkov? . . . No point. Yes. . . ."

Nastya raised a narrow eyebrow, shrugged a pretty shoulder. She could not see why Timofey Ivanovich had become angry. The three stood silent for a moment. Then Nastya smiled at her father and went her way, so upright that one could see at a glance there was nothing wrong with her.

"A clean girl she is," said Ivan Ivanovich looking after her. "That's just it . . . she'd better not visit Varvara; no good will come of it. . . ."

A Sunday afternoon is tedious enough on Peterburgsky Side, in streets where no occasional tram ever appears. It is deserted and miserable. And it seems as though behind the dusty little windows, behind

the dilapidated gateways, in little wooden houses built round courtyards overgrown with weeds, in little houses that through a single
attic window look through ruined buildings, "The Side" would like
to slumber forever—leave it alone—that's all.

Here's a pink house with three stories. It has just been painted; the
drain pipes have been repaired; the long blots of plaster have not yet
been washed off the windows; it has a blue sign Peterburgsky District
Workmen's Co-operative Society. And then right down to the river—
weather-beaten walls, fences, ruins; a tobacco stall by the war-cripple
who is bored to slumber; a woman with penny sweets; and sunflower-
seeds by the side of the drain pipe. . . . Seeds, seeds. . . . Surely the
earth and the sun have not given rise to men just in order that he might
crack these damned seeds, while shuffling without thought, without
passion, along the dreary pavement?

Here's a fence made of rusty corrugated iron. Behind it, on a vacant
site, there are a few beds with potatoes, and around them heaps of
broken stone overgrown with stinging-nettle. A goat wanders about.
A woman sits on a stone, with her chin on her fist, a baby on her lap,
and stares vacantly.

Here's another vacant site. By the side of the pavement there are
three steps—all that is left of the front entrance. And it seems as though
one can walk up these steps into an unseen house. Its outlines can
still be seen. On the right a triangle on the wall of the neighboring
house marks the roof that has disappeared; and lower down the remains
of blue wallpaper with flowers. On the left, a brick arch still exists, and
there is a door leading into the open air.

If you ask the old keeper, who sits by the gateway on the other side
of the street, he will tell you that the three steps did in fact lead to a
two-storied house. It was a good wooden house. Some of the tenants
have disappeared, some have died, others live on the Vasilevsky. And
the owner of the unseen house is the old man himself, now the keeper.

Thus he sits all day under the gateway opposite, looking back into
the past. Higher up a close-cropped girl is reading a book, and sitting
on the sill of an open window with her bony knees raised. A citizen
in brown knitted trousers crosses the road with a teapot in his hand
and leers at the maid in the window. At the sight of Nastya he turns
toward her.

"Begging your pardon . . . why are you walking alone?"

"Least of all your concern," retorts Nastya as she passes with a
haughty look at the knitted trousers.

"All matters of skirt are my concern. . . . What's the hurry? You'll
come to the same thing in the end, so why not take the bird-in-hand?"

Nastya rounds the corner and enters the courtyard of Varvara Timofeyevna's house. In one of the open windows of her flat, on the second
floor, she could see Suchkov's strong back clad in a gray shirt with a
cycling belt. He was playing a guitar and the strong nape of his neck
reflected the strain.

Varvara met Vasily Suchkov last year at the "Leshy" cinema. He struck her as an interesting man. He was very polite, cold, neatly dressed. Narrow, clean-shaven face, small eyes, a scar on one cheek, near the mouth. During the interval he fixed his eyes on Varvara (who was dark, round-faced, and somewhat stout) moved to the seat next to her and lent her the program. Then he said that he did not smoke from hygienic considerations and offered her some fruit drops. Varvara crushed the fruit drops with her ivory teeth and probably a merry, eager smile never left her face—Suchkov looked at her mouth with a cool avidity.

She liked the way he made haste to define his social position: he was an instructor in a school of surveying. His conversational approach indicated the seriousness of his intentions. Varvara told him that she worked as a packer in a chocolate factory; this seemed to please him—it was clean work, and it followed that the girl must also be clean. During the rest of the performance they exchanged impressions—the film shown was "The Bandits of Paris." Suchkov saw Varvara as far as the tram, and next Sunday they again met in a cinema on the Nevsky. After the performance he suggested going to a Caucasian restaurant. Varvara blushed and declined. She yielded to him only after the third visit to a cinema, being under the disturbing influence of the adventures of Mary Pickford.

Suchkov himself offered to have their union legalized at the Registry Office (he insisted on orderliness before everything else in life)—and Varvara moved to his house on the Peterburgsky Side. A year has passed since that time. Varvara told her relations that she lived well and could not wish for anything better. But people began to notice that she was getting thinner, fading, losing her happy disposition. It turned out that she was fiercely jealous because during the year she had lived with him she had not come to know him any better than during the first evening's acquaintance.

The table was laid. Through the open door one could see Varvara in the smoke of the kitchen, busy round a petrol-cooker. Suchkov was half-heartedly playing a guitar. Looking diligent, Andrey Matti, a Finnish subject, fair and well groomed, with bovine eyelashes, sat near him. He was dressed in a new gray suit and wore a pink tie. His straight thin mouth smiled good naturedly. He could sit like this for any length of time—discreetly silent.

Varvara cast piercing glances at her husband and Matti, as she hovered about the kitchen. What are they keeping silent about, I ask you, now? Matti wouldn't be hanging about the house just for a how-d'you-do, if it wasn't with an object; Suchkov wouldn't be playing him the guitar with a smile. That's the umpteenth Sunday the Finn has turned up with a flower or a packet of chocolate for Varvara, and Suchkov has immediately assumed this strange wry smile (it would be good to chuck this saucepan with hot cabbage-soup at his ugly face).

Varvara's raging heart knew that they were conspiring, that the Finn was urging her husband, enticing him, leading him away and the husband is willing. . . . No mistake. . . . Would he smile like this otherwise? . . .

Playing a polka with scoundrelly variations, the scoundrel. He's trimmed his nails this morning, so that they should not catch against the strings. Oh, dear, there's no doubt about it; the Finn has found a girl for him. . . .

"I say, Varya," quietly called Suchkov, "how are you getting on with the rissoles, or else we'd better sit down to some vodka?"

Varvara thunderously rattled the saucepans, choking with anger. But that was inopportune, because Matti took advantage of the noise in the kitchen to say weightily:

"It is a big inconvenience to be without a cook. Such a decent house should, of course, have a servant. A man with your tastes must have money."

Varvara lay in bed with the bedclothes pulled over her head. Such-kov undressed without hurrying, lay down on his back by her side and began to smoke cigarettes. The light of a Northern summer night crept through the dirty glass of the lime-splashed window. Varvara lay as still as a corpse. The clock was ticking on the chest of drawers. Something inside it tripped, groaned, as if existence had become unbearable in this silent bedroom filled with Suchkov's thoughts. It groaned, then recovered and again began to slice off life's seconds, sweeping away their little corpses into the unknown.

. . . Suchkov hopped out of bed, went to the dining-room, angrily treading on the loose strings of his underwear.

He produced out of a drawer in the writing desk a school copybook with the motto "Grind the granite rock of learning," and sat down near the window to make an entry:

"17th June. Left the Office this morning, under the pretext of an unendurable toothache. Went to Petrovsky Park. Bathed. Met N. Her constitution comes up to expectations. Spoke to her, very successfully prepared the ground for the next morning. In the evening made final arrangements with M., though I don't yet know what the work will turn out to be like. But I already feel I am spreading my wings. By the way, M. has proposed getting rid of Varvara. Nothing very definite. Perhaps she will understand herself that she should go. . . ."

Having locked the copybook in the drawer and hidden the key in his purse, Suchkov returned to his bedroom. Looking at the pendulum of the clock, he said:

"I am sleepless. Perhaps you will put the kettle on the oil cooker for me?"

Then Varvara tore off the sheet. She sat up in bed in an unbuttoned frock, dishevelled, her stocking dropping down. She did not care— let him look at her swollen, tear-stained face. . . .

"You didn't know I was on the lake today, did you? . . . You rotter," she nodded emphatically, "rotter. . . ."

"Don't get abusive," he said icily. "For your language, the way you have hit me in the face, and for the word 'rotter' you have just hurled at me, you might find yourself before the Magistrate in no time. . . . Besides, I made no promises that I would limit my requirements to one woman. . . ."

"I know . . . I know. . . . But there's one thing that's unfortunate for you—the fact that I've got you summed up, Alekseyevich. . . . My eyes are open once and for all. . . . You are a beast. . . . You clean-shaven brute. . . ."

"For the last time: stop it. . . ."

"I shan't stop it, even if you threaten to kill me. Do you think I've a pennyworth of fear for you? You are unclean. . . . Why don't you keep a she-goat instead of a woman? Or this same Nastya under whom you dived this morning! I haven't heard a human word from you during the whole year. You couldn't speak one, my dear, if you tried. . . . Curse these damned rags, your presents. . . ." (She tore open her dress down to the hem.) "I had known men before you. Three men. From our factory. Didn't you know that? Well then, I did. . . . They called me darling, sweetheart . . . dearest comrade. I gave up the third one just before you. He is still pining for me . . ."

"Full stop," said Suchkov disdainfully—"the details do not interest me."

Varvara lowered her head and kept silent for a moment. When she looked at her husband again, her face quivered violently.

"If you need more women than one, you'll have to use a different receptacle, my friend. . . . Take care, of course, not to catch any disease. But I must tell you about two secrets." (Suchkov threw a rapid sidelong glance at her. She noticed it and smiled.) "I am pregnant, Vasily Alekseyevich, the third month . . . I won't kill the child, I shall bring him into the world and you will pay maintenance. . . ."

"Oh," Suchkov pulled a wry face and began to pace the room. "As to that, we shall wait and see. If you really are pregnant it does not follow yet that I am the father. . . . The identity of the father is still an open question. . . ."

He succeeded at last in stepping on the strings, frenziedly jerked his leg, broke them, and shouted: "And I won't be blackmailed! . . . Don't rely too much on the maintenance . . ."

Then Varvara pulled the torn dress over her breast, covered herself up to the neck, gathered in her bare legs. She seemed now afraid to look at her husband, running about the bedroom in his underwear: she gazed at the window. Wetting her lips she said:

"Now—for the second secret, Vasily Alekseyevich. . . . Since this is the way you look at things . . . I will tell you also. I didn't want to . . . No, no, no . . . After all, you have been my husband . . . but, Vasily Alekseyevich, I am going to denounce you . . ."

Suchkov stopped dead. His long face, with the newly appearing shadows of unshaven cheeks, seemed deathly greenish through the sleeplessness of the twilight summer night. Quietly, sorrowfully Varvara said:

"Vasily Alekseyevich, you are a spy."

There the conversation ended. Varvara lay down again and covered her head. Suchkov went into the dining-room. Then he made tea for himself. Toward seven o'clock he went into the bathroom for his clothes. He went out soon afterwards.

"18th June—One o'clock at night. Been on the lake. . . . N. has not come to the rendezvous. Waited in vain until seven o'clock. Walked around the bungalow and saw a lock on the door. If that is a challenge on N.'s part, I am not one to give up before the aim is attained. Spoke with M. in the evening and frankly expressed my fears concerning Varya. M. insists. I promised to be a good comrade. Worked out the plan together. Yes, M. is right in saying that one must be modern; see the aim clearly and destroy everything that stands in the way."

That night Suchkov slept in the dining-room under an old military great-coat. He did not hear how Varvara came quietly near the door and looked at him for a long time. In the black narrow opening of the door her face seemed deathly pale.

On the 10th June, Suchkov returned home from work earlier than usual and grilled the pork chops himself. Varya usually came in from the chocolate factory at half-past five. He opened the front door for her and said with a pleasant smile:

"We must end our rowing, Varya. You have misunderstood me, I have misunderstood you. You have thrown an accusation at me and it has wounded me deeply. But now I understand that we are both guiltless. We must talk it over seriously. . . . Once and for all."

Varvara repeated, looking into the darkness of the passage: "Once and for all." Then Suchkov brought the chops from the kitchen and called out:

"Come and feed! I am the chef today."

He drank several glasses of vodka, groaning good-naturedly. Even told a funny story about a mother-in-law and an inspector of taxes from "The Rhinoceros." Varvara sat at the table somewhat on her guard. At last, rolling little balls of bread, he turned to the main theme.

"You have overheard my conversation with Matti. A cinema-like situation develops; the wife finds out that her husband is a spy. Ha, ha, ha! . . . I can understand your feelings . . . But, Varya, my dear. . . . The real explanation is much simpler. Matti is the representative of a certain big firm. And, you see, they tread very warily. They are just collecting preliminary information—to get their bearings, estimates, and so forth . . . But for the present, it is a strict secret . . . That's the sort of spy I am . . . Ha, ha! . . . Yesterday I at last softened Matti's heart and he has allowed me to tell you everything, and put your fears at rest." (He rubbed Varvara's hand.) "And as for that girl

Nastya, be reasonable, Varya. . . . It is not even a fleeting attraction
. . . Just playing with a kitten . . . I don't like the innocent."

Varvara had suffered so much during these last days that she was
glad to believe anything, and even against her will she believed her
husband. What if it really was just her imagination? With the palm
of her hand over her eyes, she said:

"But didn't you say yourself that you never promised me you would
limit your requirements to one woman? . . ."

"Chuck it, Varya . . . Worse things than that are said in anger."

"I shall never forget that talk last Sunday at table. . . . Especially
Nastya being there and that friend of yours. . . . And it was clear to
everybody you were tired of me, ready to throw yourself at the first
woman that came your way. . . ."

"Nerves, Varya, nerves. . . . Feminine imagination. . . . I was speaking theoretically, to keep up an interesting conversation at table . . .
But you are a fine one as well, aren't you? Slapping me in the face. . . ."

Varvara sighed deeply with her last breath of bitterness. She could
not bear to suffer any longer. Leaving the chop unfinished she went
into the bedroom. Put on a touch of powder, got her hair in order,
thought awhile, then changed her dress. And suddenly a great weight
seemed to be removed. No sooner had she left the room than Suchkov
seemed to crumple up, lowered his head and began to beat out a tune
on the oilcloth. Then he drank three glasses of vodka, one after the
other without a snack. Turned round on his chair and stared at the
wall behind which Varvara could be heard walking about.

"Varya," he called faintly and hoarsely; cleared his throat and then
loudly: "Varya, you know, I've got an idea. . . ." She returned to the
dining-room. "Let's go out into the air. We haven't had a walk together for a long time . . ." Varvara suddenly smiled trustingly and
readily, just as she did a year ago in the cinema. Suchkov glanced at
her and poured out some more vodka . . . "We'll have a walk and a
talk. . . . A man I know has a boat on the Goloday, not far from the
Smolensky Cemetery . . . Come on, dress . . . Don't put a hat on . . .
better take a shawl . . ."

In the ante-room he began to rub his forehead, waved his hand as
though vexed.

"Most vexing, I've quite forgotten. You go on to where No. 6 stops,
in the Bolshoy, and wait for me; I'll just call in at the house-committee
offices."

Varvara went away. Suchkov listened at the half-open door as she
walked downstairs. It seemed that she had not met or spoken to anyone.

Then he took a long time over putting his cap on in front of a mirror,
looked round to see that he had taken everything—cigarettes, matches.
On tip-toe, not knowing it—he went out of the flat, noiselessly closing
the door behind him. Creeping, he came down to the house-office, and
there said to the official very loudly:

"The wife's gone out somewhere, and didn't take the front door key. Please give her the key when she comes back. I am off to work overtime; won't be back until late probably. . . ."

Behind the Smolensky Cemetery, to the west of it, lay a deserted, barren, low-lying ground, called New Petersburg. Here it was once planned to build a town as beautiful as a dream, all in marble and granite, a new Palmira of the northern seas. But all they had time to build was a small number of five-story buildings, with their windows looking gloomily at the sea, at the muddy shores with here and there a boat pulled aground, at the abandoned villa of Gregory Gregorevich Ge (who had one night got the fright of his life sitting on the roof during a flood), at the dykes, the piles of broken stone and iron scattered about the island, at the remains of the fountain showing through the grass. The lonely houses are inhabited, but there are few people about, especially in the southwestern part of the island.

That was just where they were going to now: Suchkov, who walked ahead with his hands in his pockets, taking long strides, and Varvara who could not quite keep up with him. In the distance, low over the mirror-like sea, hung the clouds, already colored by the setting sun. The red, golden, watery-green light of the sunset spread peacefully behind the Kronstadt fortification, behind the woody shores of Lakhta, that hung as in a mirage over the bay.

"Don't run, Vasya, what's the hurry?" repeated Varvara, gasping for breath. All the way to the Cemetery, Suchkov had stood on the platform of the tram. On getting out he offered Varya his arm. He was walking fast, ever faster. His small eyes jumped about restlessly over the faces of occasional passers-by. Round the corner, when before them spread a mirror-like sea and above them the evening sky, and Varvara hugged close to her husband for a caress, he abruptly disengaged his arm and ran ahead. He stopped on the edge of a small cliff. Below, a thin sheet of water lazily licked the sand, the bits of broken bottles, the stones.

"Curse! there's no boat," said Suchkov looking at the sea toward the slumbering sails of the becalmed yachts. "We'll have to wait, curse it. . . ."

He jumped down on to the sand, and, without turning: "Come on . . . jump. . . . Let's sit down . . ."

Varvara's heart beat furiously. She jumped, sat down on the sand, threw herself back, and leaning on her hands, closed her eyes at the sunset. The action jerked her blue striped frock above her knees. She did not pull it down, left it as it was. She wanted happiness so much this summer evening, that from the moment when she ran off to the bedroom to powder her face and to the very end, she was deluded, guessed nothing.

Suchkov squatted down and smoked. He kept looking round and

repeating: "Presently, presently, wait a moment. . . ." In the distance, in the Goloday Island stadium, a band began to play, but that was a couple of miles away; here the shore was deserted.

"Vasya," said Varvara, with her eyes still screwed up, "I don't want a lot, you know. . . . I am not like the others, jealous, tyrannizing . . . So long as I know you pity me, love me . . . What else do I want?"

"Shut up, shut up," said Suchkov through his teeth. Steps creaked on the cliff above, and Matti's voice said hastily:

"Hurry up and get it over."

Varvara straightened out, opened her mouth for some air. Cried out. The most terrifying thing of all was her husband's ghastly pale long face. He looked at her with the fierce hatred of the devil incarnate . . . Varvara tried to jump up from the stand, but he grasped her leg, threw her down, briskly leapt on to her chest, put his icy fingers round her throat. He was strangling her, putting the weight of his shoulders into the work. Letting go with one hand, he picked up a brick from the sand and struck Varvara on the head with it several times—struck her till the brick broke. Then he got up from Varvara's chest, glanced back at her blood-covered face and walked away along the edge of the water. Matti was by that time far away, walking across the waste grounds toward the Cemetery.

KONSTANTIN SIMONOV

His Only Son

Konstantin Simonov, one of Russia's outstanding war correspondents, was born in Leningrad in 1915. He was graduated from the Literary Institute of the Writers' Union in 1937. Versatile, he has written short stories, plays, poetry and a novel entitled *Days and Nights,* based on his war experiences in Stalingrad. His play called *Russian People* won the Stalin Prize in 1942. [Used by permission of Miss Helen Black; translated by D. L. Fromberg.]

IT WAS FAR BEHIND the lines. Fierce gusts of wind drove the snow and sleet over the ground.

The scouts, who had been dropped by plane, trudged along in the direction of the bridge, weighed down by the heavy satchels filled with T.N.T.

Skirting the precipitous slopes of a high hill they suddenly ran into a German patrol.

Their only chance of success now lay in giving their pursuers the slip and reaching the bridge at least half an hour ahead of the Germans.

After the first thaw the barren hillsides had become coated with ice, making progress both difficult and slow. The Germans dogged their steps with the tenacity of a pack of wolves, at times falling behind and losing the trail in the hills only to pick it up again.

Everything would have gone off splendidly had not Lieutenant Yermolov been wounded at the very first encounter by a burst from a tommy gun fired at random—just that sheer bad luck which suddenly befalls people who have scores of times, smilingly, escaped death by a hair's breadth. Both the Lieutenant's legs were hit above the knees. Here, in the present circumstances, without expert medical aid rendered at once, the wounds were bound to prove fatal. It was only a question of a few hours.

He fell to the ground and then raised himself on his elbows and asked for a drink. A few drops were poured into his mouth from a flask. He looked at his crippled legs, at the dark pool of blood under him which was quickly staining the snow all around and said:

"Leave me here."

They all knew that he was right, but to leave him was simply beyond their power.

Captain Sergeyev, trying not to meet Yermolov's eyes, gave the order to lift him up and carry him.

The scouting party now consisted of only four men. They carried Yermolov in turn, two at a time. The other two carried the explosives.

Coming to a bit of steep ground they laid him down on the snow and then, while two of them scrambled to the top those down below raised him in their arms and handed him up. Careful as they tried to be, they could see that he was suffering great pain.

They were moving much slower now and the Germans were hard on their heels. The men in the rear would every now and then drop behind some boulder on the way and with a few telling shots from their light machine guns force the Germans to keep at a respectful distance. Some two hours later it began to lose all point. They were moving so much slower now than the Germans that there was a danger that the latter, by making a wide detour, would cut them off and intercept them before they reached the bridge.

While they were crossing a snow-covered valley Yermolov came to for a moment out of his stupor. He called to the Captain.

"Nearer. Come nearer," he said.

Sergeyev put his ear to the Lieutenant's burning lips.

"You can't do things like that," Yermolov said. Although his words were scarcely audible, the tone in which he spoke suddenly took on a hard and metallic sound. "You can't do things like that. You're jeopardizing the whole expedition. It's downright treachery."

He stopped speaking and closed his eyes. He did not want to talk.

Sergeyev understood that the word "treachery" had been used deliberately, in order to force his hand, to compel him to do what Yermolov wanted. The Lieutenant's thoughts were focused on the bridge. He was afraid that the German patrol would overtake them before they managed to blow it up. Yermolov's fears were well-founded, of course. What he insisted on was absolutely right, it was dreadful, but right.

Sergeyev straightened up and continued to walk alongside in silence. On the other side of the hollow, on the slope of a small hill strewn with rocks, he gave the order to put Yermolov down.

They spread a ground-sheet on the snow and propped him up on it against some boulders. He had lost an enormous amount of blood and was hovering on the verge of unconsciousness.

Sergeyev ordered the others to go on ahead. He wished to do the last services for his friend himself. He unbuckled Yermolov's flask from his belt, took a tin of canned food from his knapsack and opened it with his knife. He placed the tin and the flask near Yermolov, just within reach of his left hand. After that he opened Yermolov's holster, took out his revolver and this, too, he lay down on the ground-sheet in such a way that the wooden butt touched Yermolov's fingers.

Yermolov looked at him with calm, unblinking eyes, but said nothing. He was reclining as though in an armchair, his back resting against the angle made by two boulders.

Sergeyev could now meet his gaze frankly. He had done everything, everything that was required of him, just as the dying man had wished.

"That's all," Sergeyev said. "Good-by.

Yermolov took his hand and, without saying a word, shook it with a firmness entirely unexpected.

Sergeyev hurried after the others, not turning even once to take a last look at his friend. A second later his figure clad in white had disappeared behind a crag and Yermolov realized that this was the last man he was destined to see, barring of course, the Germans who were tracking them down.

He was suffering terribly. He wanted to put an end to the pain as quickly as possible, but the very thought of the Germans at once drove the idea of doing away with himself out of his mind.

He raised his revolver, cocked the hammer, and fired into the air. He did not want his comrades to undergo the torments of uncertainty: let them think that all was over, that this was the end. But he—he would still go on fighting.

He was overjoyed by the ease with which he had cocked the stiff hammer. He still had strength in his hands then—that was fine. He again raised the revolver and took aim at a bit of moss that showed from under the snow. He could sight it easily, his hand did not shake. He lowered the revolver.

Snow was still falling. Pale, snow-laden clouds overcast the sky. The Polar sun did not set but the northern twilight was darker than usual.

With the instinct of a veteran scout he felt certain that, sooner or later, the Germans would pass his way, following the trail. The one question was—how near would they come? At about thirty yards he would be able to score a hit. He glanced anxiously at the sky: if only the snowstorm held on.

He was alone, all alone, nobody could help him, neither his comrades, nor even his oldest friend—his father.

Closing his eyes, he recalled his father as he had seen him last, in his dugout at Army Headquarters. He had sat there, poring over his artillery schedules, chewing the butt of his cigarette and, without raising his head, had remarked in a gruff voice that the scouts weren't doing their jobs properly—that during the last month they had spotted only four batteries. But in spite of the gruff voice Yermolov had known that he had done his job well and that his father was satisfied with him, that he was only grumbling out of habit—that that was his way of hiding his affection for his only son.

And then Yermolov's mind was suddenly crowded with disjointed, fleeting memories of trifling episodes in his friendship with his father. How his father had once roundly abused him, had not felt at all sorry for him when, while still a youngster, he had been thrown from his horse; how they had fenced together in the gym in the artillery school in which his father had served at one time; how on one occasion he had forced his father into a corner and how pleased the old man had been and, how for the first time, he had told his wife at dinner to place two wine glasses on the table, "for the two men."

He recalled how strict his father had always been to him, how he had never outwardly shown him the slightest sign of affection, never once called him Alyosha but always the formal "Alexei," how he had always reprimanded him in front of others and praised him but rarely, and then never to his face.

And yet, with all that poignancy of feeling which a man experiences who has but a few hours more to live, he sensed the intense love, tenderness and pride behind that long-standing, tranquil, even slightly cold friendship with his father.

He loved his mother, of course, yes, but just then it was not her loving hands, her tired smile, or the fine wrinkles under her eyes when she cried that came into his mind. All that seemed to be very far away just then and had no bearing on what was happening to him at the moment.

But the odd memories of his father were of vital importance to him now: they had a direct bearing on his lying here, with a revolver near his hand, and although he had to muster all his will-power to suppress the desire to put an end to the frightful pain his legs were causing him, he would nevertheless wait, and go on waiting.

He had reached this decision to act as he was not only because this was the eleventh time he had gone out on an expedition like the present and was accustomed to the thought of a violent death, but because ever since a boy of four he had accompanied his father from barracks to barracks, from unit to unit, because his father had never expressed sympathy for him when he had been thrown from his horse, because his father had been so pleased when he had forced him into a corner that time when they were fencing, and because his father, as he knew beyond all doubt, could not imagine him dying in any other way than the way he wanted to just now.

He opened his eyes and glanced round. The snow was falling as heavily as before, his legs were entirely hidden under a white mound and the dark spots on the ground-sheet could no longer be seen. For an instant it seemed to him that he was a small boy again, in bed, and that this was not snow but a white blanket and that his mother would come and draw it over his shoulders and tuck him in.

Loss of blood was evidently the cause of his becoming drowsy. He felt himself falling into a coma which he had to overcome at all costs.

Clenching his teeth, mentally preparing himself for the inevitable pain, he mustered all his strength and suddenly jerked his leg. The frightful agony which for a moment had died down shot through his whole body: the pain was something awful, as if somebody had driven a stake right through him. But he had achieved his object—the pain had aroused him from his stupor.

He listened intently. He heard a rustling to the right, on the opposite slope of the hill.

"It's a good thing I won't have to wait long," he thought and with his left hand he overturned the tin can and placed it under his right arm. Then, cocking his revolver, he rested his right elbow on the tin—it was higher and steadier like that.

The rustling grew louder. The Germans were coming his way, moving carelessly, very carelessly. Well, so much the better. But why was he alone, all alone? If only he had a couple of his men here armed with tommy guns . . .

"It'll all be over in a minute and nobody will ever know how it happened, not a soul, not even Dad," he thought with sudden anguish.

He settled his elbow more comfortably on the tin can and once again took aim to see whether he could sight the same bit of moss which was now barely perceptible in the snow.

The tracks led somewhat away from him, to the right, and the first German passed him by at a distance of about fifteen yards without even glancing in his direction. The second one, with a dirty white tunic over his gray cavalry greatcoat and an automatic rifle slung round his neck, was moving forward with his eyes glued to the ground but, suddenly, glancing to the left in Yermolov's direction, he let out a yell.

Yermolov, his elbow pressing tightly against the tin can until the jagged edge almost cut his skin, fired. The kick of the gun caused his weakened arm to slip off the tin. With an effort he settled his elbow onto the tin again and took aim at the other German who, hearing the yell and the thud of the falling body, turned in his direction.

The German's automatic rifle got tangled in the tape of his overalls and Yermolov waited until he had wrenched it free.

He fired only at the very last instant when the German, throwing his automatic rifle across his arm, was about to press the trigger.

The rifle dropped from the German's hands; he staggered forward for several paces and then collapsed face down in the snow, right alongside, his hands almost touching Yermolov's legs.

Several shadows appeared simultaneously from the other side of the slope. Yes—mere shadows. And precisely because they were no longer human beings but specters which tended to merge into a single whole, Yermolov understood that he was losing consciousness and that if he did not want to fall into their hands alive he must fire the last shot.

In this last second he suddenly thought of his mother who had so often fondly caressed his face and hair, and he pressed the revolver not to his temple but under his unbuttoned jacket, about a couple of inches below the left pocket of his tunic. His fingers gripped the butt so tightly that when his right hand, in its final convulsive movement, fell onto the snow, the revolver was still clutched in it.

Day was already breaking when Colonel Yermolov returned to Army Headquarters. Owing to the spring snowdrifts he had had to cover the last twenty kilometers on foot and now, having pulled off his sodden boots, he was lying stretched out on his camp bed enjoying a smoke.

The snowstorm, unusual for this time of the year, had been raging for two days now. The gusts of wind drew all warmth out of the dugout and the Colonel, from time to time, got up in order to throw a log into the round iron stove.

He had already reported to his superior officers the situation at the forward positions. The Commissar's bed was empty; he had not yet returned from Divisional Headquarters and an unusual silence reigned in the dugout, broken only from time to time by the crackling of the logs and the dismal moaning of the wind outside.

What previously, in the days of peace, he had regarded as loneliness —being parted from his dear ones, his wife and son, and home—now during the war, had long since ceased to be regarded by him as such. The endless number of people who came to see him—Chief of Army Ordnance—at all hours of the day and night, his Commissar—a merry and shrewd Yaroslavite—with whom he had been sharing a common roof for nearly eleven months, the commanders of his regiments, all of whom he could recognize by their voices and called up every night, the thousand and one things which never left him a moment to spare the live-long day and was the breath of life to him, had long ago deprived him of any feeling of loneliness.

But today, when owing to the snowstorm it was impossible to see a thing from the observation posts, when suddenly, for an hour or two, there was no necessity to call anybody up over the phone, or even to talk things over here, at Headquarters, he—for some reason—could not sleep. A feeling of loneliness, keener than any he had ever experienced before, suddenly held him in its grip.

He tried to picture his wife to himself. But she was somewhere so far away just then, in Siberia, that all he could conjure up in his mind's eye was a fleeting vision of an endless line of envelopes addressed in her hand, some of them still there, in Siberia, lying in a mail box, others on their way, in a mail train, others already somewhere near at hand, being sorted out at the local post office by strange hands. They were all moving, coming toward him, but after all they were only letters, just letters.

But his son was there. And, perhaps, just because he was there all the time, closer at hand, the Colonel felt so poignantly this sensation of loneliness.

He very rarely saw his son. At one time he had made a request through some old friends that his son be assigned to the same Army Corps in which he himself was serving, and for the very reason that, contrary to his rule, he had once permitted himself to make such a request, he had never since gone out of his way to see his son more often than duty required. And duty required it rarely, very rarely. The last time he had seen him was a month ago, here—in this very dugout—when his son had reported the results of an artillery reconnoitering mission far behind the enemy's lines.

The Colonel had been delighted at the time to see that his son had such a firm and manly face, that he was calm, terse and even a little over-formal with him, his father. For the first time then he had felt that his dear, indulgent wife with whom he had argued so much on the subject of bringing up children had, nevertheless, not spoiled his only son, and that he had found his boy at twenty just as he had wanted him to be, yes, just as he recollected himself to have been when he was of the same age.

He was even pleased that his son had refused the invitation to have tea with him and, drawing up to attention, had requested leave to go. He had given him permission, but when his son had reached the door of the dugout had suddenly called to him:

"Alexei!"

And when his son turned round, he had given him a wink, one of those friendly winks full of fun he used to give him years ago when the youngster had been guilty of some prank revealing in him the traits of the future man.

His son had winked back and with a smile on his lips had repeated: "May I go, Sir?"

Such was their last meeting.

He had in fact a tender love for him and yearned for him as only fathers can yearn who have an only son, embodying their hopes, their pride, their faith that their child, their own youngster, will in the long run grow up to be a real man—like themselves, or even better.

And just because he was ashamed of what he secretly condemned as his overweening love, the Colonel never called his son anything but "Alexei," although, in his heart of hearts, he always thought of him as "Alyosha" or "Alyoska."

It seemed to him at times that his son guessed this tender love of his, sensed it, and precisely at those very moments when he was being particularly strict with him.

It was again cold in the dugout. The Colonel drew up a chair to the stove and began to throw some logs into it.

The iron stove brought back memories of his youth—days when he was in command of a light-horse battery under Budyonny.

Of late he had become accustomed to his staff duties and, on occasion, would laugh to scorn those of his subordinates who were overfond, without good reason, of poking into places where they had no right to be. But at times, at moments such as the present, he felt that he had been cheated of the direct feeling of coming to grips with the enemy, of the thrill of battle.

Fleeting memories passed through his mind of field-guns drawn by teams of horses tearing over the ground, swinging round into position and opening fire at short range, of gruff commands, the sweaty faces of gun crews, of men in enemy uniforms crashing to the ground. But now he had been deprived of all this. The only times during the war when he had experienced this feeling, so reminiscent of the past, had been yesterday and the day before yesterday. The Army Corps had taken the offensive and the chief observation post had been advanced much nearer to the front lines on to a high, rugged hill which dominated the whole sector.

On this occasion duty had not only permitted but demanded that he should be there, and so, for two days on end, he had personally directed the fire of several artillery units.

These were batteries of the Army Corps heavy artillery and they bombarded at a long range the enemy's fortifications, emplacements and batteries. But from the hill one could see for such a long distance that through his field-glasses he could make out, very faintly true, the scurrying figures of Germans, of horses going down and logs being blown sky-high.

His observation post had also come under the fire of first one and then another German battery; he had corrected the fire and fought them; and this feeling of a duel, of coming personally to grips with the enemy, had pervaded him and his voice, when he had snapped out an order, had been gruff not only because of his cold and of the sleepless nights, but because of the thrill of battle which had held him enraptured.

But what had been yesterday and the day before yesterday might not happen again very soon. In this respect his son was more fortunate than he.

The specialty of a scout which his only son had chosen was, looking at it from a personal standpoint, that of a father, one constantly fraught with danger and alarm. His son had not asked for his approval, and he had acted rightly. What could he have said to him? Of course he would have approved. Even more, had his son asked for a job under him, at Staff Headquarters, he would not only have been angry but he would have done everything in his power to prevent it.

No, he did not despise staff work in general—that was stupid—but his son had to travel the same road he himself had traveled, and under no circumstances must he skip a single stage of this road. To come through alive—that depended on himself alone, and as for his father, it was none of his business—just as those long sleepless hours which he, the father, had lived through at nights, when the scouting parties were stranded for days on end somewhere in the enemy rear and there was no news of them as was the case just now, were none of his son's business.

As a matter of fact, to be honest to himself, the real reason why he could not fall asleep today was after all his son. There had been no news of the scouting party for several days already, a snowstorm was raging and nobody could say when it would end.

The Colonel added the last log and, sitting on his bed, began to take off his belt in the vain hope of getting some sleep. Just then there was a knock on the door.

"Come in."

Captain Sergeyev, the commander of the scouting battalion, entered the dugout. He had evidently only just come back; he was still in his white overalls, his automatic rifle slung over his shoulder and he had no distinctive badges.

"Well? What is it?"

"All in good time," Sergeyev replied, bringing down his automatic rifle with a clatter to the floor and sitting down on the Commissar's bed.

A glance at Sergeyev's face showed that he was dead beat. Then again, on this last reconnoitering expedition he had had no special assignment from the artillery; consequently, there was something untoward and alarming in his dropping in to see him at this hour.

"Well, what is it?" the Colonel asked again and, lighting a cigarette, shifted along his bed so as to sit opposite Sergeyev, face to face.

"All in good time," Sergeyev repeated, and for some reason he slowly pushed his automatic rifle away as though it hindered him from saying what he wanted.

"Is he wounded?" the Colonel asked.

"No, Andrei Petrovitch," Sergeyev replied huskily.

It was not so much the way he pronounced the word "no" but the fact that for the first time during all the months of war he addressed him so compassionately, as though he were a sick man, by his name and patronymic, that the Colonel understood that it was only a question of learning the details.

When Sergeyev had gone the Colonel stretched himself out on his bed, his face to the ceiling, and tried to think. But his mind was a blank; one word kept boring into his brain, just one—"Alyosha," "Alyosha," "Alyosha"—the word he had never uttered aloud while his son was alive.

"Alyosha," he repeated, "Alyosha," and he again fell silent, closing his eyes, and again he opened them and endlessly repeated this one word. And still his mind was a blank. All he had now was his grief, for which it seemed to him he had so many times prepared himself during these long months of war—without apparently succeeding.

In a desperate effort to pull himself together he began to recall his conversation with Sergeyev. Why had he asked that pitiful and futile question:

"Is there a note for me?"

Of course there wasn't. Wouldn't Sergeyev have given it to him had there been one? But after all, why not? If only a couple of words.

And, suddenly, thinking of this note and the fact that there was no note, he pictured to himself in detail how it must have happened: the ground-sheet on the snow, his son's crippled legs, the butt of the revolver, and that last shot Sergeyev had heard when he left him all alone. No, no note was necessary. He, too, would not have written a note.

Again he saw in his mind's eye his son's last road—the cliffs over which the motionless body had been carried on the makeshift stretcher, the rocks on which he had been left lying alone, all alone, or no— together with his weapon, his revolver, the soldier's last mate in life. He saw his cold body, and the Germans coming up to him. Germans . . .

Half an hour ago Captain Sergeyev had deliberately, as though trying somewhat to soften the blow, recounted at length the scouting expeditions in which he had taken part, together with his son, the hand grenades sent flying into the enemy's bunkers, the bridges that had been blown up, the German officers they had wiped out.

But no, it had been cold comfort. It was his only son and, now that he was dead, nothing in the world could replace him. But the thought that his son had succeeded, had nevertheless succeeded in settling his score for himself, prevented his grief from turning into despair, although the grief remained.

Involuntarily he thought of himself during these last days, the scurrying soldiers he had observed through his field-glasses, the horses going down, the logs blown sky-high, and it seemed to him just then that in the ferocity of this battle in which he had taken part during these latter days there had been a foreboding, as it were, of the death of his son, a foreboding of the vengeance that was his, the bereaved father.

It seemed to him that at those moments, when he was snapping out orders in a gruff voice at the observation post, that he was next to his son and that together they were demolishing, destroying, killing these men whom he hated so intensely that he was ready to choke the lives out of them.

But he did not feel any the better for that. He realized just then that he could never give way to hopelessness, to despair, that just as before, in spite of the grief that he had to bear, he just as vehemently wanted to live and fight, yes, above all, to fight.

But his wife? What would she say . . . She could not choke the lives out of these murderers with her own hands, she could not, as he, train the long muzzles of death-dealing guns on them. To write to her, tell her that her boy had left his last bullet for himself—no, that was impossible. To tell her that his comrades had not been able to lower her boy's body into the grave—that was also impossible.

He realized that his grief would not pass, neither tomorrow nor the day after tomorrow—never, that he must write to her at once, right now, at this table, not putting it off till tomorrow, because tomorrow it would be still harder than today. He would write to her at once. May she forgive him for the lie he would tell her for, in telling her the most vital and terrible part of the truth, he had no option but to tell her a white lie as to the rest.

When he finished his letter the gray imperceptible spring night had already drawn to a close. He went out of his dugout. Above the snowstorm, above the hilltops, a cold sun was rising.

From the West came the heavy thunder of guns. He looked at his watch: yes, it was exactly eight. It was his guns firing, the artillery preparations for the offensive had begun—the very bombardment which he had timed yesterday evening for eight this morning when he had not yet known that he no longer had a son.

The guns opened fire at eight o'clock sharp—just as it should be. The war went on.

WLADYSLAW STANISLAW REYMONT

Death

Wladyslaw Stanislaw Reymont (1867–1925) spent a lonely, impoverished childhood on a farm in Russian Poland. He failed in school and became a vagabond, wandering all over Poland. In 1893 he settled down to writing stories, many of which were published in Polish journals. *The Peasants,* dealing with peasant life and customs, is his masterpiece. Among his other books are *The Comedienne, The Promised Land* and *The Dreamer.* He was awarded the Nobel Prize in 1924. [From *Polish Tales by Modern Authors;* used by permission of the publishers, Oxford University Press.]

"FATHER, EH, FATHER, GET UP, do you hear?— Eh, get a move on!"

"Oh God, oh Blessed Virgin! Aoh!" groaned the old man, who was being violently shaken. His face peeped out from under his sheepskin, a sunken, battered, and deeply-lined face, of the same color as the earth he had tilled for so many years; with a shock of hair, gray as the furrows of plowed fields in autumn. His eyes were closed; breathing heavily he dropped his tongue from his half-open bluish mouth with cracked lips.

"Get up! Hi!" shouted his daughter.

"Grandad!" whimpered a little girl who stood in her chemise and a cotton apron tied across her chest, and raised herself on tiptoe to look at the old man's face.

"Grandad!" There were tears in her blue eyes and sorrow in her grimy little face. "Grandad!" she called out once more, and plucked at the pillow.

"Shut up!" screamed her mother, took her by the nape of the neck and thrust her against the stove.

"Out with you, damned dog!" she roared, when she stumbled over the old half-blind bitch who was sniffing the bed. "Out you go! will you . . . you carrion!" and she kicked the animal so violently with her clog that it tumbled over, and, whining, crept toward the closed door. The little girl stood sobbing near the stove, and rubbed her nose and eyes with her small fists.

"Father, get up while I am still in a good humor!"

The sick man was silent, his head had fallen on one side, his breathing become more and more labored. He had not much longer to live.

"Get up. What's the idea? Do you think you are going to do your dying here? Not if I know it! Go to Julina, you old dog! You've given the property to Julina, let her look after you . . . come now . . . while I'm yet asking you!"

"Oh blessed Child Jesus! Oh Mary . . ."

649

A sudden spasm contracted his face, wet with anxiety and sweat. With a jerk his daughter tore away the feather-bed, and, taking the old man round the middle, she pulled him furiously half out of the bed, so that only his head and shoulders were resting on it; he lay motionless like a piece of wood, and, like a piece of wood, stiff and dried up.

"Priest . . . His Reverence . . ." he murmured under his heavy breathing.

"I'll give you your priest! You shall kick your bucket in the pigsty, you sinner . . . like a dog!" She seized him under the armpits, but dropped him again directly, and covered him entirely with the feather-bed, for she had noticed a shadow flitting past the window. Someone was coming up to the house.

She scarcely had time to push the old man's feet back into the bed. Blue in the face, she furiously banged the feather-bed and pushed the bedding about.

The wife of the peasant Dyziak came into the room.

"Christ be praised."

"In Eternity . . ." growled the other, and glanced suspiciously at her out of the corners of her eyes.

"How do you do? Are you well?"

"Thank God . . . so so . . ."

"How's the old man? Well?"

She was stamping the snow off her clogs near the door.

"Eh . . . how should he be well? He can hardly fetch his breath any more."

"Neighbor . . . you don't say so . . . neighbor . . ." She was bending down over the old man.

"Priest," he sighed.

"Dear me . . . just fancy . . . dear me, he doesn't know me! The poor man wants the priest. He's dying, that's certain, he's all but dead already . . . dear me! Well, and did you send for his Reverence?"

"Have I got anyone to send?"

"But you don't mean to let a Christian soul die without the sacrament?"

"I can't run off and leave him alone, and perhaps . . . he may recover."

"Don't you believe it . . . hoho . . . just listen to his breathing. That means that his inside is withering up. It's just as it was with my Walek last year when he was so ill."

"Well, dear, you'd better go for the priest, make haste . . . look!"

"All right, all right. Poor thing! He looks as if he couldn't last much longer. I must make haste . . . I'm off . . ." and she tied her apron more firmly over her head.

"Good-by, Antkowa."

"Go with God."

Dyziakowa went out, while the other woman began to put the room in order; she scraped the dirt off the floor, swept it up, strewed wood-ashes, scrubbed her pots and pans and put them in a row. From time to time she turned a look of hatred onto the bed, spat, clenched her fists, and held her head in helpless despair.

"Fifteen acres of land, the pigs, three cows, furniture, clothes—half of it, I'm sure, would come to six thousand . . . good God!"

And as though the thought of so large a sum was giving her fresh vigor, she scrubbed her saucepans with a fury that made the walls ring, and banged them down on the board.

"May you . . . may you!" She continued to count up: "Fowls, geese, calves, all the farm implements. And all left to that trull! May misery eat you up . . . may the worms devour you in the ditch for the wrong you have done me, and for leaving me no better off than an orphan!"

She sprang toward the bed in a towering rage and shouted:

"Get up!" And when the old man did not move, she threatened him with her fists and screamed into his face:

"That's what you've come here for, to do your dying here, and I am to pay for your funeral and buy you a hooded cloak . . . that's what he thinks. I don't think! You won't live to see me do it! If your Julina is so sweet, you'd better make haste and go to her. Was it I who was supposed to look after you in your dotage? She is the pet, and if you think . . ."

She did not finish, for she heard the tinkling of the bell, and the priest entered with the sacrament.

Antkowa bowed down to his feet, wiping tears of rage from her eyes, and after she had poured the holy water into a chipped basin and put the asperges-brush beside it, she went out into the passage, where a few people who had come with the priest were waiting already.

"Christ be praised."

"In Eternity."

"What is it?"

"Oh, nothing! Only that he's come here to give up . . . with us, whom he has wronged. And now he won't give up. Oh dear me . . . poor me!"

She began to cry.

"That's true! He will have to rot, and you will have to live," they all answered in unison and nodded their heads.

"One's own father," she began again. ". . . Have we, Antek and I, not taken care of him, worked for him, sweated for him, just as much as they? Not a single egg would I sell, not half a pound of butter, but put it all down his throat; the little drop of milk I have taken away from the baby and given it to him, because he was an old man and my father . . . and now he goes and gives it all to Tomek. Fifteen acres of land, the cottage, the cows, the pigs, the calf, and the farm-carts and all the furniture . . . is that nothing? Oh, pity me! There's no justice in this world, none . . . Oh, oh!"

She leant against the wall, sobbing loudly.

"Don't cry, neighbor, don't cry. God is full of mercy, but not always toward the poor. He will reward you some day."

"Idiot, what's the good of talking like that?" interrupted the speaker's husband. "What's wrong is wrong. The old man will go, and poverty will stay."

"It's hard to make an ox move when he won't lift up his feet," another man said thoughtfully.

"Eh . . . You can get used to everything in time, even to hell," murmured a third, and spat from between his teeth.

The little group relapsed into silence. The wind rattled the door and blew snow through the crevices onto the floor. The peasants stood thoughtfully, with bared heads, and stamped their feet to get warm. The women, with their hands under their cotton aprons, and huddled together, looked with patient resigned faces toward the door of the living-room.

At last the bell summoned them into the room; they entered one by one, pushing each other aside. The dying man was lying on his back, his head deeply buried in the pillows; his yellow chest, covered with white hair, showed under the open shirt. The priest bent over him and laid the wafer upon his outstretched tongue. All knelt down and, with their eyes raised to the ceiling, violently smote their chests, while they sighed and sniffled audibly. The women bent down to the ground and babbled: "Lamb of God that takest away the sins of the world."

The dog, worried by the frequent tinkling of the bell, growled ill-temperedly in the corner.

The priest had finished the last unction, and beckoned to the dying man's daughter.

"Where's yours, Antkowa?"

"Where should he be, your Reverence, if not at his daily job?"

For a moment the priest stood, hesitating, looked at the assembly, pulled his expensive fur tighter round his shoulders; but he could not think of anything suitable to say; so he only nodded to them and went out, giving them his white, aristocratic hand to kiss, while they bent toward his knees.

When he had gone they immediately dispersed. The short December day was drawing to its close. The wind had gone down, but the snow was now falling in large, thick flakes. The evening twilight crept into the room. Antkowa was sitting in front of the fire; she broke off twig after twig of the dry firewood, and carelessly threw them upon the fire.

She seemed to be purposing something, for she glanced again and again at the window, and then at the bed. The sick man had been lying quite still for a considerable time. She got very impatient, jumped up from her stool and stood still, eagerly listening and looking about; then she sat down again.

Night was falling fast. It was almost quite dark in the room. The little girl was dozing, curled up near the stove. The fire was flickering feebly with a reddish light which lighted up the woman's knees and a bit of the floor.

The dog started whining and scratched at the door. The chickens on the ladder cackled low and long.

Now a deep silence reigned in the room. A damp chill rose from the wet floor.

Antkowa suddenly got up to peer through the window at the village street; it was empty. The snow was falling thickly, blotting out everything at a few steps' distance. Undecided, she paused in front of the bed, but only for a moment; then she suddenly pulled away the feather-bed roughly and determinedly, and threw it onto the other bedstead. She took the dying man under the armpits and lifted him high up.

"Magda! Open the door."

Magda jumped up, frightened, and opened the door.

"Come here . . . take hold of his feet."

Magda clutched at her grandfather's feet with her small hands and looked up in expectation.

"Well, get on . . . help me to carry him! Don't stare about . . . carry him, that's what you've got to do!" she commanded again, severely.

The old man was heavy, perfectly helpless, and apparently unconscious; he did not seem to realize what was being done to him. She held him tight and carried, or rather dragged him along, for the little girl had stumbled over the threshold and dropped his feet, which were drawing two deep furrows in the snow.

The penetrating cold had restored the dying man to consciousness, for in the yard he began to moan and utter broken words:

"Julisha . . . oh God . . . Ju . . ."

"That's right, you scream . . . scream as much as you like, nobody will hear you, even if you shout your mouth off!"

She dragged him across the yard, opened the door of the pigsty with her foot, pulled him in, and dropped him close to the wall.

The sow came forward, grunting, followed by her piglets.

"Malusha! malu, malu, malu!"

The pigs came out of the sty and she banged the door, but returned almost immediately, tore the shirt open on the old man's chest, tore off his chaplet, and took it with her.

"Now die, you leper!"

She kicked his naked leg, which was lying across the opening, with her clog, and went out.

The pigs were running about in the yard; she looked back at them from the passage.

"Malusha! malu, malu, malu!"

The pigs came running up to her, squeaking; she brought out a bowlful of potatoes and emptied it. The mother-pig began to eat greedily, and the piglets poked their pink noses into her and pulled at her until nothing but their loud smacking could be heard.

Antkowa lighted a small lamp above the fireplace and tore open the chaplet, with her back turned toward the window. A sudden gleam came into her eyes, when a number of banknotes and two silver rubles fell out.

"It wasn't just talk then, his saying that he'd put by the money for the funeral." She wrapped the money up in a rag and put it into the chest.

"You Judas! May eternal blindness strike you!"

She put the pots and pans straight and tried to cheer the fire which was going out.

"Drat it! That plague of a boy has left me without a drop of water."

She stepped outside and called "Ignatz! Hi! Ignatz!"

A good half-hour passed, then the snow creaked under stealthy foot-steps and a shadow stole past the window. Antkowa seized a piece of wood and stood by the door which was flung wide open; a small boy of about nine entered the room.

"You stinking idler! Running about the village, are you? And not a drop of water in the house!"

Clutching him with one hand she beat the screaming child with the other.

"Mummy! I won't do it again. . . . Mummy, leave off. . . . Mumm . . ."

She beat him long and hard, giving vent to all her pent-up rage.

"Mother! Ow! All ye Saints! She's killing me!"

"You dog! You're loafing about, and not a drop of water do you fetch me, and there's no wood . . . am I to feed you for nothing, and you worrying me into the bargain?" She hit harder.

At last he tore himself away, jumped out by the window, and shouted back at her with a tear-choked voice:

"May your paws rot off to the elbows, you dog of a mother! May you be stricken down, you sow! . . . You may wait till you're manure before I fetch you any water!"

And he ran back to the village.

The room suddenly seemed strangely empty. The lamp above the fireplace trembled feebly. The little girl was sobbing to herself.

"What are you sniveling about?"

"Mummy . . . oh . . . oh . . . grandad . . ."

She leant, weeping, against her mother's knee.

"Leave off, idiot!"

She took the child on her lap, and pressing her close, she began to clean her head. The little thing babbled incoherently, she looked feverish; she rubbed her eyes with her small fists and presently went to sleep, still sobbing convulsively from time to time.

Soon afterward the husband returned home. He was a huge fellow in a sheepskin, and wore a muffler round his cap. His face was blue with cold; his moustache, covered with hoar-frost, looked like a brush. He knocked the snow off his boots, took muffler and cap off together, dusted the snow off his fur, clapped his stiff hands against his arms, pushed the bench toward the fire, and sat down heavily.

Antkowa took a saucepan full of cabbage off the fire and put it in front of her husband, cut a piece of bread and gave it him, together with the spoon. The peasant ate in silence, but when he had finished he undid his fur, stretched his legs, and said: "Is there any more?"

She gave him the remains of their midday porridge; he spooned it up after he had cut himself another piece of bread; then he took out his pouch, rolled a cigarette and lighted it, threw some sticks on the fire and drew closer to it. A good while later he looked round the room. "Where's the old man?"

"Where should he be? In the pigsty."

He looked questioningly at her.

"I should think so! What should he loll in the bed for, and dirty the bedclothes? If he's got to give up, he will give up all the quicker in there. . . . Has he given me a single thing? What should he come to me for? Am I to pay for his funeral and give him his food? If he doesn't give up now—and I tell you, he is a tough one—then he'll eat us out of house and home. If Julina is to have everything let her look after him—that's nothing to do with me."

"Isn't my father . . . and cheated us . . . he has. I don't care. . . . The old speculator!"

Antek swallowed the smoke of his cigarette and spat into the middle of the room.

"If he hadn't cheated us we should now have . . . wait a minute . . . we've got five . . . and seven and a half . . . makes . . . five and . . . seven . . ."

"Twelve and a half. I had counted that up long ago; we could have kept a horse and three cows . . . bah! . . . The carrion!"

Again he spat furiously.

The woman got up, laid the child down on the bed, took the little rag bundle from the chest and put it into her husband's hand.

"What's that?"

"Look at it."

He opened the linen rag. An expression of greed came into his face, he bent forward toward the fire with his whole frame, so as to hide the money, and counted it over twice.

"How much is it?"

She did not know the money values.

"Fifty-four rubles."

"Lord! So much?"

Her eyes shone; she stretched out her hand and fondled the money.

"How did you come by it?"

"Ah bah . . . how? Don't you remember the old man telling us last year that he had put by enough to pay for his funeral?"

"That's right, he did say that."

"He had stitched it into his chaplet and I took it from him; holy things shouldn't knock about in a pigsty, that would be sinful; then I felt the silver through the linen, so I tore that off and took the money. That is ours; hasn't he wronged us enough?"

"That's God's truth. It's ours; that little bit at least is coming back to us. Put it by with the other money, we can just do with it. Only yesterday Smoletz told me he wanted to borrow a thousand rubles from me; he will give his five acres of plowed fields near the forest as security."

"Have you got enough?"

"I think I have."

"And will you begin to sow the fields yourself in the spring?"

"Rather . . . if I shouldn't have quite enough now, I will sell the sow; even if I should have to sell the little ones as well I must lend him the money. For he won't be able to redeem it," he added, "I know what I know. We shall go to the lawyer and make a proper contract that the ground will be mine unless he repays the money within five years."

"Can you do that?"

"Of course I can. How did Dumin get hold of Dyziak's fields? . . . Put it away; you may keep the silver, buy what you like with it. Where's Ignatz?"

"He's run off somewhere. Ha! no water, it's all gone. . . ."

The peasant got up without a word, looked after the cattle, went in and out, fetched water and wood.

The supper was boiling in the saucepan. Ignatz cautiously crept into the room; no one spoke to him. They were all silent and strangely ill at ease. The old man was not mentioned; it was as if he had never been.

Antek thought of his five acres; he looked upon them as a certainty. Momentarily the old man came into his mind, and then again the sow he had meant to kill when she had finished with the sucking-pigs. Again and again he spat when his eyes fell on the empty bedstead, as if he wanted to get rid of an unpleasant thought. He was worried, did not finish his supper, and went to bed immediately after. He turned over from side to side; the potatoes and cabbage, groats and bread gave him indigestion, but he got over it and went to sleep.

When all was silent, Antkowa gently opened the door into the next room where the bundles of flax lay. From underneath these she fetched a packet of banknotes wrapped up in a linen rag, and added the money. She smoothed the notes many times over, opened them out, folded them up again, until she had gazed her fill; then she put out the light and went to bed beside her husband.

Meanwhile the old man had died. The pigsty, a miserable lean-to run up of planks and thatched with branches, gave no protection against wind and weather. No one heard the helpless old man entreating for mercy in a voice trembling with despair. No one saw him creep to the closed door and raise himself with a superhuman effort to try and open it. He felt death gaining upon him; from his heels it crept upwards to his chest, holding it as in a vice, and shaking him in terrible spasms; his jaws closed upon each other, tighter and tighter, until he was no longer able to open them and scream. His veins were hardening till they felt like wires. He reared up feebly, till at last he broke down on the threshold, with foam on his lips, and a look of horror at being left to die of cold, in his broken eyes; his face was distorted by an expression of anguish which was like a frozen cry. There he lay.

The next morning before dawn Antek and his wife got up. His first thought was to see what had happened to the old man.

He went to look, but could not get the door of the pigsty to open, the corpse was barring it from the inside like a beam. At last, after a great effort, he was able to open it far enough to slip in, but he came out again at once, terror-stricken. He could hardly get fast enough across the yard and into the house; he was almost senseless with fear. He could not understand what was happening to him; his whole frame shook as in a fever, and he stood by the door panting and unable to utter a word.

Antkowa was at that moment teaching little Magda her prayer. She turned her head toward her husband with questioning eyes.

"Thy will be done . . ." she babbled thoughtlessly.

"Thy will . . ."

". . . be done . . ."

". . . be done . . ." the kneeling child repeated like an echo.

"Well, is he dead?" she jerked out, ". . . on earth . . ."

". . . on earth . . ."

"To be sure, he's lying across the door," he answered under his breath.

". . . as it is in Heaven . . ."

". . . is in Heaven . . ."

"But we can't leave him there; people might say we took him there to get rid of him—we can't have that . . ."

"What do you want me to do with him?"

"How do I know? You must do something."

"Perhaps we can get him across here?" suggested Antek.

"Look at that now . . . let him rot! Bring him in here? Not if . . ."

"Idiot, he will have to be buried."

"Are we to pay for his funeral? . . . but deliver us from evil . . . what are you blinking your silly eyes for? . . . go on praying."

". . . deliver . . . us . . . from . . . evil . . ."

"I shouldn't think of paying for that, that's Tomek's business by law and right."

". . . Amen . . ."

"Amen."

She made the sign of the cross over the child, wiped its nose with her fingers and went up to her husband.

He whispered: "We must get him across."

"Into the house . . . here?"

"Where else?"

"Into the cowshed; we can lead the calf out and lay him down on the bench, let him lie in state there, if he likes . . . such a one as he has been!"

"Monika!"

"Eh?"

"We ought to get him out there."

"Well, fetch him out then."

"All right . . . but . . ."

"You're afraid, what?"

"Idiot . . . damned . . ."

"What else?"

"It's dark . . ."

"If you wait till it's day, people will see you."

"Let's go together."

"You go if you are so keen."

"Are you coming, you carrion, or are you not?" he shouted at her; "he's your father, not mine." And he flung out of the room in a rage.

The woman followed him without a word.

When they entered the pigsty, a breath of horror struck them, like the exhalation from a corpse. The old man was lying there, cold as ice; one half of his body had frozen onto the floor; they had to tear him off forcibly before they could drag him across the threshold and into the yard.

Antkowa began to tremble violently at the sight of him; he looked terrifying in the light of the gray dawn, on the white coverlet of snow, with his anguished face, wide-open eyes, and drooping tongue on which the teeth had closed firmly. There were blue patches on his skin, and he was covered with filth from head to foot.

"Take hold," whispered the man, bending over him. "How horribly cold he is!"

The icy wind which rises just before the sun, blew into their faces, and shook the snow off the swinging twigs with a dry crackle.

Here and there a star was still visible against the leaden background of the sky. From the village came the creaking noise of the hauling of water, and the cocks crew as if the weather were going to change.

Antkowa shut her eyes and covered her hands with her apron, before she took hold of the old man's feet; they could hardly lift him, he was so heavy. They had barely put him down on a bench when she fled back into the house, throwing out a linen-rag to her husband to cover the corpse.

The children were busy scraping potatoes; she waited impatiently at the door.

"Have done . . . come in! . . . Lord, how long you are!"

"We must get someone to come and wash him," she said, laying the breakfast, when he had come in.

"I will fetch the deaf-mute."

"Don't go to work today."

"Go . . . no, not I . . ."

They did not speak again, and ate their breakfast without appetite, although as a rule they finished their four quarts of soup between them.

When they went out into the yard they walked quickly, and did not turn their heads toward the other side. They were worried, but did not know why; they felt no remorse; it was perhaps more a vague fear of the corpse, or fear of death, that shook them and made them silent.

When it was broad day, Antek fetched the village deaf-mute, who washed and dressed the old man, laid him out, and put a consecrated candle at his head.

Antek then went to give notice to the priest and to the Soltys of his father-in-law's death and his own inability to pay for the funeral.

"Let Tomek bury him; he has got all the money."

The news of the old man's death spread rapidly throughout the village. People soon began to assemble in little groups to look at the corpse. They murmured a prayer, shook their heads, and went off to talk it over.

It was not till toward evening that Tomek, the other son-in-law, under pressure of public opinion, declared himself willing to pay for the funeral.

On the third day, shortly before this was to take place, Tomek's wife made her appearance at Antek's cottage.

In the passage she almost came nose to nose with her sister, who was just taking a pail of dishwater out to the cowshed.

"Blessed be Jesus Christ," she murmured, and kept her hand on the door-handle.

"Now: look at that . . . soul of a Judas!" Antkowa put the pail down hard. "She's come to spy about here. Got rid of the old one somehow, didn't you? Hasn't he given everything to you . . . and you dare show yourself here, you trull! Have you come for the rest of the rags he left here, what?"

"I bought him a new sukmana at Whitsuntide, he can keep that on, of course, but I must have the sheepskin back, because it has been bought with money I have earned in the sweat of my brow," Tomekowa replied calmly.

"Have it back, you mangy dog, have it back?" screamed Antkowa. "I'll give it you, you'll see what you will have . . ." and she looked round for an object that would serve her purpose. "Take it away? You dare! You have crawled to him and lickspittled till he became the idiot he was and made everything over to you and wronged me, and then . . ."

"Everybody knows that we bought the land from him, there are witnesses . . ."

"Bought it? Look at her! You mean to say you're not afraid to lie like that under God's living eyes? Bought it! Cheats, that's what you

are, thieves, dogs! You stole the money from him first, and then. . . .
Didn't you make him eat out of the pig-pail? Adam is a witness that he
had to pick the potatoes out of the pig-pail, ha! You've let him sleep
in the cowshed, because, you said, he stank so that you couldn't eat.
Fifteen acres of land and a dower-life like that . . . for so much property! And you've beaten him too, you swine, you monkey!"

"Hold your snout, or I'll shut it for you and make you remember,
you sow, you trull!"

"Come on then, come on, you destitute creature!"

"I . . . destitute?"

"Yes, you! You would have rotted in a ditch, the vermin would
have eaten you up, if Tomek hadn't married you."

"I destitute? Oh you carrion!"

They sprang at each other, clutching at each other's hair; they fought
in the narrow passage, screaming themselves hoarse all the time.

"You street-walker, you loafer . . . there! that's one for you! There's
one for my fifteen acres, and for all the wrong you have done me, you
dirty dog!"

"For the love of God, you women, leave off, leave off! It's a sin and
a shame!" cried the neighbors.

"Let me go, you leper, will you let go?"

"I'll beat you to death, I will tear you to pieces, you filth!"

They fell down, hitting each other indiscriminately, knocked over
the pail, and rolled about in the pigwash. At last, speechless with rage
and only breathing hard, they still banged away at each other. The
men were hardly able to separate them. Purple in the face, scratched
all over, and covered with filth, they looked like witches. Their fury
was boundless; they sprang at each other again, and had to be separated a second time.

At last Antkowa began to sob hysterically with rage and exhaustion,
tore her own hair and wailed: "Oh, Jesus! Oh little child Jesus! Oh
Mary! Look at this pestiferous woman . . . curse those heathen . . .
oh! oh! . . ." she was only able to roar, leaning against the wall.

Tomekowa, meanwhile, was cursing and shouting outside the house,
and banging her heels against the door.

The spectators stood in little groups, taking counsel with each other,
and stamping their feet in the snow. The women looked like red
spots dabbed onto the wall; they pressed their knees together, for the
wind was penetratingly cold. They murmured remarks to each other
from time to time, while they watched the road leading to the church,
the spires of which stood out clearly behind the branches of the bare
trees. Every minute someone or other wanted to have another look at
the corpse; it was a perpetual coming and going. The small yellow
flames of the candles could be seen through the half-open door, flaring
in the draught, and momentarily revealing a glimpse of the dead man's
sharp profile as he lay in the coffin. The smell of burning juniper floated

through the air, together with the murmurings of prayers and the grunts of the deaf-mute.

At last the priest arrived with the organist. The white pine coffin was carried out and put into the cart. The women began to sing the usual lamentations, while the procession started down the long village street toward the cemetery.

The priest intoned the first words of the Service for the Dead, walking at the head of the procession with his black biretta on his head; he had thrown a thick fur cloak over his surplice; the wind made the ends of his stole flutter; the words of the Latin hymn fell from his lips at intervals, dully, as though they had been frozen; he looked bored and impatient, and let his eyes wander into the distance. The wind tugged at the black banner, and the pictures of heaven and hell on it wobbled and fluttered to and fro, as though anxious to display themselves to the rows of cottages on either side, where women with shawls over their heads and bare-headed men were standing huddled together.

They bowed reverently, made the sign of the cross, and beat their breasts.

The dogs were barking furiously from behind the hedges, some jumped onto the stone walls and broke into long-drawn howls.

Eager little children peeped out from behind the closed windows, beside toothless used-up old people's faces, furrowed as fields in autumn.

A small crowd of boys in linen trousers and blue jackets with brass buttons, their bare feet stuck into wooden sandals, ran behind the priest, staring at the pictures of heaven and hell, and intoning the intervals of the chant with thin, shivering voices: a! o! . . . They kept it up as long as the organist did not change the chant.

Ignatz proudly walked in front, holding the banner with one hand and singing the loudest of all. He was flushed with exertion and cold, but he never relaxed, as though eager to show that he alone had a right to sing, because it was his grandfather who was being carried to the grave.

They left the village behind. The wind threw itself upon Antek, whose huge form towered above all the others, and ruffled his hair; but he did not notice the wind, he was entirely taken up with the horses and with steadying the coffin, which was tilting dangerously at every hole in the road.

The two sisters were walking close behind the coffin, murmuring prayers and eyeing each other with furious glances.

"Tsutsu! Go home! . . . Go home at once, you carrion!" One of the mourners pretended to pick up a stone. The dog, who had been following the cart, whined, put her tail between her legs, and fled behind a heap of stones by the roadside; when the procession had moved on a good bit, she ran after it in a semi-circle, and anxiously kept close to the horses, lest she should be prevented again from following.

The Latin chant had come to an end. The women, with shrill voices, began to sing the old hymn: "He who dwelleth under the protection of the Lord."

It sounded thin. The blizzard, which was getting up, did not allow the singing to come to much. Twilight was falling.

The wind drove clouds of snow across from the endless, steppe-like plains, dotted here and there with skeleton trees, and lashed the little crowd of human beings as with a whip.

". . . and loves and keeps with faithful heart His word . . .," they insisted through the whistling of the tempest and the frequent shouts of Antek, who was getting breathless with cold: "Woa! woa, my lads!"

Snowdrifts were beginning to form across the road like huge wedges, starting from behind trees and heaps of stones.

Again and again the singing was interrupted when the people looked round anxiously into the white void: it seemed to be moving when the wind struck it with dull thuds; now it towered in huge walls, now it dissolved like breakers, turned over, and furiously darted sprays of a thousand sharp needles into the faces of the mourners. Many of them returned half-way, fearing an increase of the blizzard, the others hurried onto the cemetery in the greatest haste, almost at a run. They got through the ceremony as fast as they could; the grave was ready, they quickly sang a little more, the priest sprinkled holy water on the coffin; frozen clods of earth and snow rolled down, and the people fled home.

Tomek invited everybody to his house, because "the reverend Father had said to him, that otherwise the ceremony would doubtless end in an ungodly way at the public-house."

Antek's answer to the invitation was a curse. The four of them, including Ignatz and the peasant Smoletz, turned into the inn.

They drank four quarts of spirits mixed with fat, ate three pounds of sausages, and talked about the money transaction.

The heat of the room and the spirits soon made Antek very drunk. He stumbled so on the way home that his wife took him firmly under the arm.

Smoletz remained at the inn to drink an extra glass in prospect of the loan, but Ignatz ran home ahead as fast as he could, for he was horribly cold.

"Look here, mother . . .," said Antek, "the five acres are mine! aha! mine, do you hear? In the autumn I shall sow wheat and barley, and in the spring we will plant potatoes . . . mine . . . they are mine! . . . God is my comfort, sayest thou . . .," he suddenly began to sing.

The storm was raging and howling.

"Shut up! You'll fall down, and that will be the end of it."

". . . His angel keepeth watch . . .," he stopped abruptly. The darkness was impenetrable, nothing could be seen at a distance of two feet. The blizzard had reached the highest degree of fury; whistling and howling on a gigantic scale filled the air, and mountains of snow hurled themselves upon them.

From Tomek's cottage came the sound of funeral chants and loud talking when they passed by.

"These heathen! These thieves! You wait, I'll show you my five acres! Then I shall have ten. You won't lord it over me! Dogs'-breed . . . aha! I'll work, I'll slave, but I shall get it, eh, mother? We will get it, what?" he hammered his chest with his fist, and rolled his drunken eyes.

He went on like this for a while, but as soon as they reached their home, the woman dragged him into bed, where he fell down like a dead man. But he did not go to sleep yet, for after a time he shouted: "Ignatz!"

The boy approached, but with caution, for fear of contact with the paternal foot.

"Ignatz, you dead dog! Ignatz, you shall be a first-class peasant, not a beggarly professional man," he bawled, and brought his fist down on the bedstead.

"The five acres are mine, mine! Foxy Germans,* you . . . da . . ."

JOSEPH

WITTLIN

The Emperor

and the Devil

Joseph Wittlin was born in 1896 in Austrian Poland and educated in Lwow. A passionate pacifist, Wittlin turned to the study of Greek classical civilization to escape the realities of war. He produced a new translation of the *Odyssey* in 1924. His principal contribution to Polish literature is the novel, *Salt of the Earth*. He now lives in Riverdale, New York. [From *Salt of the Earth* by Joseph Wittlin; used by permission of the author; translated by Pauline de Chary.]

PEACE REIGNED IN THE HEAVENS, and quiet on earth; not a dog barked, not a cock crowed, when the Emperor Francis Joseph called his soldiers. The Emperor's own voice could not reach to the Huzul land, but the Imperial Post could reach it, and where even the Post broke down, the gendarmes and district clerks took over the task.

Sergeant-majors sat in orderly-rooms, side by side with Suppaken;† and they delved into the oldest folios, and found there the lists of the annual conscript classes, back to the very earliest years. They copied out the names of all the men in each class; and they knew of these men one thing only: that they had names. So, to every name they addressed

---

*The term "German" is used for "foreigner" generally, whom the Polish peasant despises.

† *Suppaken.* The term applied to soldiers who remained in the service after their term had expired, in return for their keep (the soup).

a summons, and the summonses they sent to the municipality. Many of those so summoned had lain for years in the municipal cemetery, or were rotting in foreign soil. But names die less quickly than men, and death keeps his registers more carefully than sergeant-majors. So the Emperor summoned both the living and the dead.

Peter Neviadomski belonged to the class of 1873. He had no idea of that himself, having no head for figures; but the municipality knew it. The municipality knew everything. The municipality kept books and forms on which it wrote down, in ink, and for all times, who was born into the world, and when, and who had left it. Every year, in peace-time, the municipality draws up a list, and sets down every man who has completed his twenty-first year; and every man has to report himself to the Army. Blind, lame, deaf, or hunchbacked—it makes no difference. Once in his life every man must report for service. For the Army, as for the Kingdom of Heaven, all are called but not all are chosen.

In the days of peace Peter had been thrice exempted as being the sole support of his family, which, at the time, included his gray-haired mother and Parashka's illegitimate child. A little later both died, the bastard first and then the old woman. But what had Peter gained? He had gained this: that he was not taken by the Army. He believed they had forgotten him, but he was wrong. The Emperor had not forgotten Peter Neviadomski; he had reserved him for the dark hour.

And now the hour had come. Not dark, but light, being the hour before the night falls, the hour when the earth grows still, as though stroked by the hand of her for whom the bells of all the churches were ringing at that moment. A clear sky, blue as the robe of the Blessed Virgin, softly enfolded the earth where noise and strife were dying down. The very insects, weary of endless circling in the warm air, had muffled their buzzing wings. At that hour human hearts, full of turmoil, beat more quietly, and to the most brutal there was granted the blessing of peace.

And this great peace had laid hold of Peter. He had forgotten the war which was raging somewhere far off beyond the dimming horizon, outside the boundaries of his tired senses. Already in the cooling air the whir of the distant sawmill had died down, and smoke was climbing up over the green bank of bushes which hid the village from his view. All the housewives were preparing supper. Over the favored cottages that had real chimneys the smoke went up in straight, tall columns and melted into the blue sky; from the poor mud huts it swirled out, clinging close to the ground, and lay there like a broad and lazy mist. Peter fell to peeling potatoes; the last passenger train of the day had gone past signal-box 86. There was nothing to come now but a freight train due in two hours. Peter sat down in the doorway of his little house and removed his cap. Bass lay beside him, with his nose to the ground and one eye on the ants which were crawling all around him. Wrapped in peace, he would do them no harm. One could hear his placid, regular breathing.

But suddenly the dog threw up his head and pricked his ears. He had heard a suspicious sound below the embankment. A moment later he leaped up and stood on watch. Somebody must have stumbled against the wires connecting Peter's levers with the gates: they twanged softly. They were placed so low, almost touching the ground, that, in the silence, even their quivering was audible. Something was moving in the stillness, someone was coming to the box. Peter paid no attention to the dog's disquiet. He was industriously peeling the potatoes and throwing them into an earthen pot full of water. But Bass had smelled danger and began to growl; and when the noise came nearer, he could bear it no longer; he broke into a loud bark of fear and anger and protest, which nearly choked him. And the danger, like a poisonous snake, wound softly through the bushes, gleamed golden against the grass, disappeared again, and finally slid out into the open.

"Quiet, Bass!" exclaimed Peter Neviadomski, putting his potatoes aside. Intimidated, Bass stopped barking and only growled softly to himself. Down in the bushes a bayonet flashed and glinted, catching and mirroring the rays of the setting sun. Then the brass spike of a helmet appeared. And suddenly War came over the embankment. It strode along in black hobnailed boots; it climbed the steps with its sword and rifle, and presented itself to Peter Neviadomski in the guise of the corporal of the gendarmerie, Jan Durek.

Peter always felt that there was something sinister about a gendarme. Not that he had anything on his conscience, but because a gendarme always smells of jail and doubtless keeps a pair of handcuffs in his bag. Corporal Durek knew Peter well. He often talked with him at the station, and the railway-man was very proud of the acquaintanceship. In Peter's eyes the gendarme represented the very pinnacle of intelligence and good taste. The unusual smell of a certain shaving-soap that Corporal Durek used never failed to impress Neviadomski. But most of all he was impressed by the shining gold tooth which the gendarme displayed whenever he opened his mouth, whether on public or on private occasions. It was the tooth which set the barrier of class between Peter and the great Jan Durek far more than all the gold on his helmet and uniform, more than the ominous, black chin-strap, more even than his carbine and his sword. It inspired respect *ad personam,* so that even if Corporal Durek had undressed and revealed himself naked, even then the gold tooth would have protected him against familiarity.

This time, it was in his public capacity that Durek opened his mouth, but he condescended to ease the strain of the occasion by smiling like a private individual.

"I've got an invitation for you, Neviadomski!"

"For military service?"

"Oh, no! To a ball!"

The habit of irony was so uncommon in these parts that, just at first, Peter did not catch the point of the gendarme's words. For a moment, fragments of dance music lilted in his head, a Kolomyika * played by a concertina and a fiddle, and heavy, brightly colored skirts swayed before his eyes. Their lovely warmth beat against his face. But the gendarme soon called him back to earth. From the leather bag (the one where he kept the handcuffs) he extracted a paper, folded and sealed.

Gutenberg, Johann Gutenberg, was the name of that man whom the devil made drunk with Rhine wine in Mainz, and who, in the year 1450, invented a new torture for those who knew nothing of letters, for the meek in spirit. Possessed by the devil, Gutenberg, in league with a certain Faust, founded the first printing works. From that time on the devilish business spread like a cholera plague, to bewilder, bewitch, and poison, day and night, grasping souls imprisoned by the pride of knowledge. But also since then so much harmless paper has been blackened by the devil's marks that the whole globe might be wrapped in it, yet, in the year 1914, there were still many righteous souls, especially in the district of Snyatin, who had not yielded to temptation. They did not falter, even when confronted by compulsory school attendance, by fines and by imprisonment, preferring to pay, or to languish in jail, rather than to afflict the souls of their children with the Latin or Cyrillian alphabet. It is true that in this triumphant struggle they had a silent but powerful ally: the budget of the Imperial and Royal Ministry of Education. And so it came about that indirectly the Government itself fought against the devil who is present in all written words, even in those of the Holy Books. Wherefore, the righteous man never signs papers; he makes three crosses: $+++$. And these are three holy signs, which cast out the devil from all contracts, receipts, and promissory notes.

But the devil is vengeful: on all the ways of man's life—not only at crossroads, but on straight paths—he has set up sign-boards, and warnings, like scarecrows.

Here it is forbidden to spit. There it is forbidden to smoke. And ignorance of the law is no safeguard against punishment. "The use of this water for drinking purposes is forbidden," the devil proclaims from over the great barrel on Topory-Czernielitza station.

"Beware of the train."

"Strzez sie pociagu!"

"Sterehty sia pojizdu!"

"Sama la trenu!"

the devil shrieks from a board set up in the open field, not far from signal-box 86. He apes the devotion of a friend anxious to preserve a man's life, as though it were life he was concerned with, and not death. And death is everywhere, and everywhere, not only in war, one must

---

* Ukrainian folk dance.

needs be on guard against it. Wherever railways run, death lurks ready
to leap at any moment from the rails. Death lies in wait in the sunshine
and falls like sudden lightning onto the heads of the reapers. There is
death in the water. And often, in the summer, the bodies of the
drowned are taken from the Pruth and the Czeremosz. Death sits in
the mushrooms of the fields, it slips into men's bellies with the plums in
the sweetness of which lies mortal dysentery. The devil mocks at men's
death—the false friend! He talks in words to the dead, in signs to the
blind. But there are, of course, means to outwit the devil. For example,
the turnpike gates. Horses, and cows, and Huzuls cannot read; but,
none the less, God sent them an angel, who couldn't read either, yet preserved them from death on the rails. But for Peter Neviadomski, many
a cow, many a Huzul, would have been taken by the devil, and in war-
time particularly.

The Corporal knew quite well that Peter couldn't read, but all the
same he handed the calling-up order over to him, with an air of not
knowing anything of the kind. That Neviadomski should be compelled to ask him to read out the contents of the paper flattered his
vanity. In his relations with people who could read, Durek was no
more than the executor of a higher power, but in dealing with people
who couldn't read, he felt that he was not only the partner of that
Power, aware of its intentions, but also the representative of its culture.
To such people he personified not only the punishment of guilt, and
not only the key to prison cells, but also the key to all the secrets of the
written word. So Durek couldn't refrain from enjoying his superiority
over Neviadomski, although he hadn't the smallest intention of gloating
over the misfortune of the lowly. Quite the contrary. Not an hour ago
he had spoken with sympathy of this very misfortune in the hall of a
neighboring country house to which he had taken a preliminary notice
of a requisition for fodder, and where he had been welcomed with a
small glass of vodka, a piece of cake and cigarettes:

"Our people are still very uneducated, gracious Countess—the minimum of illiterates is 80 per cent."

The word "minimum" was intended to show that he himself belonged to the educated.

Neviadomski did not disappoint him. He cast a helpless look at the
paper and said:

"Will you do me the favor, Herr Korporal? . . ."

The Corporal was used to this procedure and enjoyed it. He quickly
broke the seal, glanced at the date and announced sternly:

"In five days' time, punctually at nine o'clock in the morning, before
the Draftboard in Snyatin."

He emphasized the word "punctually" in a tone suggesting that he,
Corporal Durek, quite agreed with those who had issued the order.
But Peter wanted to know what the blue paper contained, and entreated
Durek to read it from beginning to end. Durek beamed. He adopted

an even sterner expression than before and put on a special voice, like an actor reading the death-sentence in a play. He stressed particularly all words of Latin origin.

"Herr Peter Neviadomski," he intoned, "is to report before the Draft-board."

It can't be so bad if they address me as "Herr," thought Peter, and gave a sigh of relief. His ears took in every word and his imagination struggled to assimilate them. Some words, however, were indigestible. They were as sharp and cruel as bayonets. "The conscript is to appear in a sober and clean condition. . . ." I shall have to take a bath in the Pruth and Magda must wash a shirt. . . . "Non-appearance on the appointed day has as a consequence the taking of coercive measures to bring the culprit before the Draftboard and is punishable with imprison-ment and fine, according to Section 324, Clause 12, and Section 161, Clause 13, of the Landsturm Regulations of the year 1861."

What did it all mean? First they said "Herr" to a man, summoned him kindly, put confidence in him; but if he didn't obey them, then it was— "fix bayonets!", and off with him to prison! Already Peter pictured Corporal Durek taking the handcuffs out of his leather bag and holding a bayonet to Peter's throat. Had he not been there when Corporal Durek took the bandit Matwij, alias The Bull, away by train, in chains?

The gendarme, having read to the end, folded the paper carefully, handed it back, looking hard at the conscript to see what impression his recital had created. Peter was silent and seemed unconcerned. The gendarme was displeased, for the whole effect had miscarried. To emphasize the gravity of the situation, and at the same time to call attention to his own powers, he said curtly:

"And do you know how they treat deserters nowadays? Court-martial and a bullet in the head."

"That's as it should be," Neviadomski agreed.

Durek was taken aback. To hide his confusion he smiled, showing his gold tooth, and ostentatiously unslung his rifle. He examined the mushroom head, made sure that it was on the safety-catch, and leaned the weapon against the wall. He took off his helmet, damped his fore-head with his handkerchief and sat down in the doorway. Next, he took from his pocket a shining, imitation-silver cigarette case, a present that had been given him by the Countess herself. And with hands which, at any moment, could transform themselves into the hands of justice, he offered the well-filled case to Peter. Peter took a cigarette, and noted that inside the lid of the case there was an enameled picture of a softly pink female body leaning forward roguishly out of a foam of lacy underwear. He felt a sensation of heat creeping up his spine and remembered Magda was due with milk after sunset. For a time they smoked in silence. Suddenly the Emperor Francis Joseph looked down at Peter Neviadomski. He looked down from a little cross, a memento of the sixtieth anniversary of his accession, which hung from a red-

and-white ribbon on the gendarme's tunic. Just where the arms of the cross met, there glittered the golden bust of the Emperor, encircled by a wreath. For God and the Emperor are always together. The cold, metal eyes of Francis Joseph pierced through Peter's sweaty shirt and stabbed his soul and conscience. Whoever, in such an hour, failed to obey with his whole heart the Emperor who called from the cross would not be pardoned by Jesus Christ on the day of the Last Judgment. Twice Peter had appeared before a judge, but on each occasion as a witness. There had been thefts on the railway. He had taken the oath before a crucifix, placed between two lighted candles on the table. The judge, in a long, black robe and a cap like a priest's biretta, had pronounced judgment. "In the name of His Majesty." And at that everyone had to rise, as they do in church during Holy Mass. The judge stood up, and the accused and the witnesses, the just as well as the unjust. But they were not asked to kneel. And above the green table, exactly over the crucifix, hung an immense portrait of the Emperor.

Peter finished his cigarette; and as he threw down the fag end, it suddenly struck him that, with it, he had thrown the Imperial eagle onto the floor. The eagle was painted on the cigarette paper. The cigarette monopoly was the Emperor's.

Everything on this earth belongs either to the Emperor or to God, reflected Peter. Earth and sky, the Pruth, the Czeremosz, and the Carpathians, and cows and dogs, and man belong to God. All the railways, on the other hand, all the cars and engines, all the signal-boxes and gates, down to a rusty bit of wire, down to a rotten tie under the rails, belong to the Emperor. To steal a tie is to injure the Emperor, and for that an Imperial gendarme takes people to an Imperial prison. And quite right. And, of course, the chief thing on this earth is money. And to whom does money belong? It belongs to him whose head is engraved on it. The Emperor gives men money, just as God gives them life. Money and life are just loans. The Emperor is a partner of God. Therefore he has the right to a man's life, which is only lent to him by God.

"Very well, then, I'll go into the Army," Neviadomski said aloud.

The gendarme had again slung his rifle over his shoulder, clapped on his helmet, and settled the black chin-strap.

"Don't be frightened, Neviadomski. You're sure to be taken, there's no getting out of that; they're taking everybody now. If you ask me, the whole show will be over before Christmas."

He said "before Christmas"; but he was really convinced that the war would be over in a month. He saluted and went on his way. Peter forgot that he, too, was wearing an Imperial cap and lifted it civilianwise. Bass jumped up and began to bark, and Peter silenced him with a kick. The wires twanged again, but the gendarme had already crossed the line and his footsteps were soon lost in the silence. The blue paper lay in Peter's motionless hands, like a pictured saint clasped between the stiff fingers of the dead. And suddenly he grew frightened of the paper which he could not understand. As long as the gendarme had been there, the letters had been alive and human, but now the devil was in them and scared folk with his secrets. Peter's fate depended now on rounded black circles, and fine straight strokes. To be so at the mercy of all these letters, and not even to know what words they represented. He looked at the word "punctual," and it was as though he saw the word "arrest." A dark cell with iron bars across its little window. The written characters seemed to close round his hands like the links of an iron chain. Already he saw red welts around his wrists. There awoke in him some obscure sense of personal freedom, which was his to defend. He couldn't understand how it could be destroyed by a mere piece of blue paper. To be powerless in the face of an enemy he could crumple in his hands, if he would, or tear to pieces without resistance or opposition: it was this which filled him with despair.

Perhaps it was all untrue. Perhaps the gendarme had been lying. How could a lifeless bit of paper dominate a living person? Why are people so silly as to believe in a piece of paper? And then Peter remembered with a sudden shock of horror that railway tickets also were made of paper, and yet that money was paid for them. And, after all, money itself was paper also. Particularly big money, like the ten- and twenty-crown notes, and woe betide the poor wretch who lost one of them! He himself had labored all his life, merely to receive, on the first of each month, a bit of paper and five silver crowns. That was it! The devil had invented all this. And what good would it do if he, Peter Neviadomski, destroyed the calling-up order? At best he would be cheating himself, not the devil. Up till now Neviadomski had believed that man was only made a prisoner when another, stronger than himself, tied his hands, took him by the scruff of the neck and threw him to the ground. But this paper? He knew now that a man could be robbed of his strength and freedom by invisible powers. They dwelt somewhere far off, and they knew everything about a man, and could decide what was to be done with him; they could even send him to his death. Individual intelligence and will power were no longer any use. For invisible threads, like telephone wires, ended in these tiny black living letters, and they came from far, far away, from Vienna, even from the Emperor himself. That was obvious, for otherwise they would not be so powerful.

So this is how it works? The Emperor knows all about me. He knows that railway-man Peter Neviadomski, the son of Wasylina, lives in the municipality of Topory-Czernielitza, in the district of Snyatin, on the Lemberg-Czernowitz-Itzkàny line, and that he has served him faithfully for twenty years. So the Emperor knows me? He wants me, and so he writes to me and calls me "Herr." "Herr Peter Neviadomski!" How grand it sounds! And Peter pictured the Emperor seated at a great table with gold corners, in his Chancellery in Vienna, writing to all the Huzuls, to the *Herren* Huzuls.

Night was beginning to fall over the Huzul land. Over the two rivers, the Pruth and the Czeremosz, wisps of mist and swirling vapors were rising. Peter got up, straightened his back, sighed heavily, picked up the pot with the still-uncooked potatoes, and turned his back on the sky, the earth and the falling night. Bass he left outside. He went into his room and put the potatoes on the cold hearth. He lay down on his back, still with his boots on. His appetite was gone. Suddenly he got up hastily, strode to the door, and turned the key in the lock. It was a thing he had never done before. Then he threw himself down again on the bed. He lay on his back, trying to see nothing and think of nothing. But, all the same, he saw quite a lot. So he shut his eyes. But that also was useless. Reality stole into his mind through the shut lids and tortured him with pictures. He saw and felt the pawing hands of Corporal Jan Durek, the threatening hands of justice.

It was the hour when the cows, stuffed with green grass and meadow flowers, were returning from pasture. The grave procession halted on its way to the cow-sheds and stood still a while. The cows slid their horns along their backs, and the sound of their lowing was like the blaring call of river boats; they wanted to be rid of the intolerable burden which swelled their udders. In the hymn of the cows there sounded the primeval forces of life and vegetation, of milk and motherhood. There was a bitter break in their voices, as though in anticipation of the slaughterhouse. In this rending cry for relief, for rest, for sleep, Peter recognized the voice of his own soul. His soul, too, was heavy and burdened, and fed on grass. With difficulty it now digested its fate, as indigestible as raw meat.

Frogs began their nightly quarrels. The sharp, needle-like chirp of the crickets pierced the stillness. Bass remembered old sorrows, perhaps those of a former existence, but he was not barking at the war, he was only yowling sadly to the rising moon. Maybe a tooth was aching.

Peter lay with wide-open eyes, staring moodily into the dark.

Over the whole world gendarmes were spoiling people's appetites.

F. E. SILLANPAA

Selma Koljas

Frans Eemil Sillanpaa, Finnish Nobel Prize winner in 1939, was born in Haemeenkyroe in 1888. He has been closely associated with the free community of artists in Southern Finland, among them the composer Jan Sibelius. Sillanpaa's best known works are *Life and Sun*, *The Maid Silja*, *A Man's Road*, *People in a Summer Night* and *Meek Heritage*. [From *Best Continental Short Stories*, 1926.]

SELMA KOLJAS WAS LITTLE UNDERSTOOD by her associates, especially by young men in search of adventure. She created the impression of being an accomplished woman of the world, with her seductive, languishing eyes, of the sort which inspire poets to write sonnets.

People wondered why she had never married, nor had ever tempted the village gossips to chatter about her. She was most attractive in every way. She danced gracefully, and dressed in good taste. Added to these attributes the charm of her manner and the alluring expression of her limpid eyes won for her many hearts.

At a dance one evening which Selma attended a rather amusing incident happened. The young girls were chaperoned by their mother or by friends of their families. One of the chaperons, Madame Litukka, the wife of a rich merchant, was accompanied by her daughter Elma, and her prospective son-in-law, an impecunious student who lived from time to time in the family of the merchant, and in consequence was rather looked down upon by the community.

When Elma danced with her fiancé people began to whisper and knowing looks were exchanged with her mother. During the evening it became apparent that Elma was sitting in solitary grandeur and there was no sign of her fiancé about. After an embarrassing interval he suddenly reappeared, accompanied by Selma Koljas, and began dancing with her.

The merchant's wife, purple with indignation, rose and made her exit so hastily that she lost much of her finery en route to the door. Her daughter, Elma, knowing no more about love than her mother had told her, followed in her mother's wake with the meek simplicity of her eighteen years, listening to her mother's indignant remarks regarding the embarrassment of the situation.

In the meantime a kind friend whispered to the student quietly that Madame Litukka was about to go home.

Vainly the unfortunate youth endeavored to explain the situation to her, but she would accept no apology.

Selma, on the other hand, never gave the affair a second thought; a moment afterward she was dancing with Ilmari Salonen. Affairs of this sort worried her but little, and she danced calmly and happily until dawn, driving home, accompanied by her brother and younger sister, quite satisfied with the evening's pleasure.

The house of Koljas is very beautifully situated, and can be seen from many points of view from the surrounding countryside. Those who pass by know and admire its many points of attractiveness.

It forms, with its group of outbuildings, a most picturesque ensemble, especially after a summer rain. The glistening red roofs, in contrast with the white walls, stand out in strong relief against the wet foliage, with the blue sky above, and the disappearing rain clouds adding additional charm.

Once a student, not the one already mentioned, however, wandering aimlessly along on his bicycle, changed his course for the sake of coming nearer to the gates. He knew Selma Koljas and her younger sister, who still went to school, by sight, and as he peered through the gates of the fine old mansion he visualized them moving gently from room to room. He knew their brother Urho Koljas, a medical student, very slightly.

This particular day there seemed to be nobody about. Even the roses and vines, creeping up the balcony, looked unfriendly seen behind the railings.

As he gazed he could see, far away at the back of the house, clumps of giant elms stretching down to the borders of the lake. Plunged in daydreams he wandered into the grounds. It is just by such little incidents as these that a chain of events begins to develop, just as the cells expand in the flowers, filling the air with perfume and promise—the clover ripening for the scythe in the fields, adds its own harbinger to nature's fulfillment.

In one of the upper windows Selma appeared for a moment, just long enough for the student to recognize her pretty brown hair framing her silhouette against the light. She fastened back a blue-and-white curtain, which had been blowing in the breeze, pausing at the window to gaze thoughtfully on the peace and beauty spread beneath her.

It was just such an event which the student fondly hoped for when he paused before Koljas.

Two days had passed since Vieno Koljas' sixteenth birthday and the traces of the party in celebration of the event were still to be seen about the place.

Although everyday life had enveloped the house again Selma was still full of the impression that the festival had made upon her.

All the guests, including her brother, had gone, even the chef and his staff.

The kitchen had assumed its usual air, and the cook had resumed her daily routine again.

Vieno had betaken herself, as often for long hours at a time she was in the habit of doing, to hide away in an old doll's house, far away in the park.

Everything about the old house seemed to be sleeping on that warm July afternoon.

Time hung heavily, yet was passing silently by. Selma sat down upon the arm of a chair and thought: "Vieno is 16 years old now—quite a big girl, and I am 28. What does it all signify? That I have lived so many summers—in two more I shall be 30. How happy I am. Would it be possible to grow old here—no. I don't believe it would," she said to herself.

Thoughts such as these filled her mind as she sat there musing by herself. Thoughts becoming more and more vague as if her mind were hiding things away in its recesses. She appreciated the happiness of her life. She had everything she wanted. She was pretty and popular—and yet there was some little thing missing . . . she knew not what.

Although Vieno's birthday had passed, the elder sister was still expectant. She was vaguely looking for something to happen, some event of an unusual sort.

As mistress of the house she should have been satisfied with the success of the party. On the contrary, the days following she wandered aimlessly from room to room, seemingly neglecting all her household duties. She had the sensation of the party having been interrupted and something missing.

As Selma sat there she hummed an old waltz tune, one that had not been played at the party, however.

A dream took possession of her, seeming almost a reality in its vividness. She had the impression that it had transpired in the park toward midnight of a July evening.

Every event seemed real to her. The sensation held her as music holds one with its charms. Her mind became imbued with it—even the things of nature seemed to echo it.

July, with its abundance of natural gifts, is a beautiful month. This time of mid-summer is perhaps the richest of the year—rich in flowers and fruits and the ripening crops. The sun is at its warmest and the days at their longest. Yet it passes quickly just as our life slips by, the years roll away. Children grow into maturity as the crops ripen, each fulfilling its own destiny.

The spirit of this July day was nestling in Selma Koljas' heart with its limpid, tender perfection, and its mysterious promise.

She mused: "I shall never be stronger than I am today, but how can I too ripen into fulfillment. One day, alas, I shall die. . . ."

This thought of death drove all else from her mind for the moment. It was like the clouds obscuring the sun as it sinks in the west at evening-tide. All her happiness seemed to hang pendent, expectant, vaguely inquieted.

This beautiful afternoon, harbinger of a lovely evening to follow, seemed to portend some rare event in store for Selma. She felt this instinctively.

Since the party something out of the ordinary had been maturing. Her habitually calm spirit had been disturbed by a sweet inquietude as if an event which was to influence her life was developing that could no longer be stayed. Something surely was about to occur. Someone, a young man, a dear friend, was coming to the house. "Can it be he, the one I have always wished and yearned for? Who can say, What joy, if my longings are about to be realized, my most secret hopes come true."

Upon this July day a stranger came to Koljas. There was nobody about. The vast entrance halls were deserted, no one greeted him, yet the welcoming spirit of the old house was enough to satisfy him. He knew the house well and recalled happy memories of days gone by, within its walls.

He passed along, wandering from room to room until he reached the

drawing room. He stood, and admired the view before him, listening
to the tick of the clock, recalling the days of long ago. He touched the
needlework on the table, and the music on the piano. Everything was
quiet and the visitor felt his pulse beat in unison with this peaceful life.
It was this precious needlework which said to him that she whom he
sought was at home and that everything was just as he had pictured it.

He had not attended the recent party. The two days which had
elapsed since the event had left little else save a sad memory.

Suddenly the door opened, and there the two stood face to face, the
young man and the girl whom he longed for.

Love hung suspended for one short moment. They were alone together. Everyone else was away in the fields, everyone except this
young girl.

Standing upon the threshold of the half-open door Selma still held
Ilmari Salonen's hand, waiting unconsciously for him to kiss her.
Slowly he gathered her in his arms and kissed her here in the quiet
corner of the sweet old house. From that moment they belonged to
one another. The happiness of Selma's life was truly blossoming as
the flowers and crops of the summertime.

This moment was the realization of her dream.

Ilmari, too, was conscious of this fulfillment. His heart beat faster
. . . for a moment he felt almost suffocated.

He let the girl's hand slip away and in a preoccupied way tried to
go on by himself.

"Won't you sit down here," she asked him, "just for a moment?"

"No," he replied. "I should prefer to refresh myself."

"Then come with me to the guest room," and she led the way. The
young man seemed to be entering upon a new life, and the present
moment had brought him more than he had hoped for.

And love had full possession of Selma's heart. It pervaded her whole
being. It seemed to expand as a flower in full bloom, the epitome of
promise realized once only in a lifetime.

This was the supreme moment of Selma's life. As she attended to
her daily duties and occupations she walked as in a dream.

Before Ilmari had stood before her on the threshold, she felt herself
to be alone in the house, but in a pleasant sort of way under the protection of her father's roof. Now that she was no longer alone and
someone else was with her she felt no uneasiness.

As she set the tea things on the table she experienced a new sensation. What was this feeling—had the newcomer become less agreeable
to her? Quite the contrary. Selma did not realize the change that
had come over her. Her recent dreams were fading and merging into
others as they trailed away into the past without ever being consum-
mated. She liked Ilmari Salonen, but he still seemed a stranger to her.
He soon came back into the room, and as they took their coffee in the
drawing room together they chatted of many things best known to
lovers, until Selma's father came in from the fields. Later on in the

evening the conversation gradually developed into a dialogue between Monsieur Koljas and Ilmari, who told his hosts of his plans for the future and of his success, feeling that they were lending a sympathetic ear to his tale and shared his enthusiasm.

Selma heard much of what he said as she went about attending to her domestic duties. She realized with pleasure, that this man, become so dear to her a few short hours ago, was a man of affairs as well as a lover. . . .

As the days went by the twilight evenings in the old dining-room were passed in a simple manner. Soon after dinner the girls retired, and it was not long before the guest bade his host good night.

One evening Selma, leaving her door ajar, was looking out at the evening. As Ilmari passed the door, seeing it open, he looked in and quietly and cautiously advanced into the room.

"He is coming," she whispered to herself. "Now he will take me in his arms. What shall I do?" She knew the answer, and that she would let him. She knew he was the one man for her. She sensed something new and fragile being born within her heart that must not be crushed before it should be properly formed, something that would never be born anew.

Ilmari Salonen thought he understood women but this evening he realized he had much to learn concerning them. For long he had imagined Selma as his future companion. As he mounted the stairs this lovely evening he knew the sublime moment of his life had come. The air he breathed seemed to be permeated with the sense of it. He felt uplifted and exalted.

In this mood he took his love in his arms and kissed her, she yielding and smiling back at him. She returned his embraces, as he smilingly said, "For friendship and the spell this gorgeous evening is casting upon us."

Resting in his arms she murmured little snatches as she had done in the afternoon, sentences of no moment, the outpourings of a happy heart, enjoying the feast too long delayed.

The twilight, in its soft perfection, was as many another this old home had seen in past generations, succeeding one upon another. Generations that had been born, lived and died, leaving the invisible stamp of their dreams in these ancient walls, flitting in shadowy outlines across the faces of the windows, eddying with the swirls of leaves in the gardens and along the stately alleys stretching toward the horizon.

When Ilmari had left her, Selma sat long dreaming and reviewing the events of the last hours, so potent for her. She felt she had grown older in this short interval but as she fell asleep she was drowsily surprised how indifferent she felt about it.

KAREL CAPEK

Money

Karel Capek (1890–1938) was born in Bohemia, the son of a physician. He studied philosophy and wrote—in collaboration with his brother, Joseph—plays and short stories. He was a close friend of Masaryk, the first president of Czechoslovakia. His best known plays are *R U R*, *The Life of the Insects* and *The Power and the Glory*. [From *Best European Short Stories, 1928.*]

AGAIN, AGAIN IT HAD COME OVER HIM; he had scarcely swallowed a few mouthfuls of food when a painful heaviness seized him; a perspiration of faintness broke out on his forehead. He left his dinner untouched and leaned his head on his hand, suddenly indifferent to the landlady's officious solicitude. At length she went out sighing and he lay down on the sofa meaning to rest, but in reality to listen with alarm and attention to torturing sounds within him. The faintness did not pass off; his stomach seemed to have become a heavy stone, and his heart throbbed with rapid, irregular beats; from sheer exhaustion he perspired as he lay. Ah, if he could only sleep!

After an hour the landlady knocked; she handed him a telegram. He opened it in alarm and read "19.10. 7.34 Coming tonight. Rosa." What this might mean he simply could not grasp; bewildered, he stood up and read through the numbers and words, and at length understood— his married sister Rosa would arrive this evening and, of course, he must go and meet her. Probably she was coming to do some shopping, and he felt annoyed at the hasty, feminine thoughtlessness and disregard for others, which disturbed him for no reason at all. He paced up and down the room, irritated because his evening was spoiled. He was thinking how comfortably he would have rested on his old sofa, soothed by the humming of his faithful lamp, with a book in his hand; he had passed weary and tedious hours there, but now, for some unknown reason, they seemed to him especially attractive, full of wise musings and very peaceful. A wasted evening, an end to rest. Full of childish and resentful bitterness, he tore the luckless telegram to fragments.

But that evening, when he was waiting in the lofty, cold damp station for the belated train, a wider feeling of distress took possession of him—distress at the squalor and poverty around him, the weary folk who arrived, the disappointment of those who had been waiting in vain. With difficulty he found his fragile little slip of a sister in the thick of the hurrying crowd. Her eyes were frightened and she was dragging a heavy trunk along, and at once he saw that something serious had happened. He put her into a cab and took her straight home. During the journey it occurred to him that he had neglected to find a room for her. He asked her if she would like to go to a hotel, but this only evoked an outburst of tears. He really could do nothing with her in that state,

677

so he gave it up, took her thin, nervous hand in his, and was immensely cheered when she at length looked up at him with a smile.

Once at home he looked closely at her and was alarmed. Distressed, trembling, strangely excited, with flaming eyes and parched lips, she sat there on his sofa, supported by the cushions which he heaped round her and talked. He asked her to speak softly, for it was already night.

"I have run away from my husband," she burst out, talking quickly. "Ah, if you knew what I have had to bear! If you knew how hateful he is to me! I have come to you to advise me," and she burst into a flood of tears.

Gloomily George paced the room. One word after another called up before him a picture of her life with an overfed, money-grubbing, and vulgar husband, who insulted her before the servant, was ill-timed and immoderate in his affection, plagued her with endless scenes about nothing, foolishly squandered her dowry, was self-indulgent at home, and at the same time spent extravagantly on the silly whims of a hypochondriac. He heard the story of food doled out bite by bite, of reproaches, humiliations and cruelty, shabby generosity, frenzied and brutal quarrels, exacted love, stupid and overbearing taunts. George paced the room choking with disgust and sympathy: it was intolerable, he could not endure this endless torrent of shame and pain. And there sat the small, fragile, capricious girl whom he had never thoroughly known, his proud and violent little sister; she had always been combative, and refused to listen to reason, her eyes used to flash wickedly when she was a small girl. There she sat, her chin quivering with sobs and with the ceaseless torrent of words, exhausted and feverish. George wanted to soothe her, but was half afraid.

"Stop," he said roughly, "that will do, I know all about it." But he was powerless to restrain her.

"Don't," wept Rosa, "I have no one but you." Then the stream of complaints began again, more broken, at greater length, in calmer tones; details were repeated and incidents enlarged upon. Suddenly Rosa stopped and asked:

"And you, George, how are you getting on?"

"As for me," grumbled George, "I can't complain. But tell me, won't you go back to him?"

"Never," declared Rosa excitedly. "That is impossible. I'd rather die than— If you only knew what it was like!"

"Yes, but wait," observed George. "In that case, what do you think of doing?"

Rosa expected that question. "I made up my mind about it a long time ago," she said warmly. "I will give lessons or go somewhere as a governess, to an office or anywhere. You will see how I can work. I'll get my living all by myself, and be so happy doing anything. You must advise me. I will find a room somewhere, just a little one. . . . Tell me, something will turn up; won't it?" She could not sit still for excitement, but jumped up and paced the room beside her brother with an eager face. "I have thought it all out. I will take the furniture, the old furniture, you know, which belonged to our parents; wait till you see. I really want nothing, but to be left in peace. I don't mind if I am poor, if only I don't have to—I want nothing else, nothing more in life than that, so little will suffice! I shall be satisfied with anything only if I am right away from—from all that. I am looking forward to working. I will do all my own sewing and sing over it—I have not sung for years. Ah, Georgie, if you only knew!"

"Work," reflected George doubtfully. "I don't know if any can be found—and anyway you are not accustomed to that, Rosy, it will be hard for you, very hard."

"No," retorted Rosa with flashing eyes. "You don't know what it has been to be reproached for every mouthful, every rag, for everything. All the time to be told that you don't work but only spend. I should like to tear off all these things, it's all become so hateful to me. No, Georgie, you will see how glad I shall be to work, how happily I shall live. I shall enjoy every mouthful, even if it is only dry bread: I shall be proud of it. With pride I shall sleep, dress in calico, cook for myself. Tell me, I can be a working woman, can't I? if nothing else turns up I will go into a factory. I am looking forward to it all so much—!"

George gazed at her with delighted astonishment. Heavens, what radiance, what courage in such a downtrodden life! He was ashamed of his own effeminacy and weariness; he thought of his own work with sudden warmth and happiness, infected by the ardent vitality of this strange, feverish girl. She had really become a young girl again, blushing, animated, childishly naïve. Oh, it will turn out all right, how can it fail to?

"I shall manage, you'll see," said Rosa, "I want nothing from anyone, I will support myself, and I will really earn, at least enough to provide for myself, and have a few flowers on the table. And if I had no flowers there I would go into the street and just look at them. You cannot imagine how each thing has filled me with happiness since—I decided to run away. How beautifully, delightfully, different everything looks! A new life has begun for me. Till now I never understood how beautiful everything is. Ah, Georgie," she exclaimed with tears running down her face, "I am so happy."

"Little silly," Georgie smiled at her, delighted. "It will not be so easy. Well, we will try it. But now lie down, you musn't make yourself ill. Don't talk to me any more now, please. I have something to think over, and in the morning I will let you know. Go to sleep now and let me think."

Nothing that he could say would induce her to take his bed; she lay down fully dressed on the sofa, he covered her with everything warm he had and turned down the lamp. It was quiet; only her rapid, childish breathing seemed to appeal to heaven for sympathy. George gently opened the window to the cool October night. The peaceful, lofty sky was bright with stars. Once in their father's house they had stood by the open window, he and little Rosa; she, shivering with cold, pressed close to him, as they waited for falling stars. "When a star falls," whispered Rosa, "I shall ask to be changed into a boy, and do something glorious." Ah, father was asleep as soundly as a log; the bed could be heard creaking under his ponderous fatigue. And George, filled with a feeling of importance, meditated on something grand and with masculine gravity protected little Rosa, who was trembling with cold and excitement.

Over the garden a star shot across the sky.

"George," Rosa's voice called him softly from the room.

"All right, directly," answered George shivering with excitement and cold.

Yes, to do something great; there was no other way out. Poor, foolish creature, what great deed did you want to do? You have your burden to bear; if you want to do something fine carry a greater one, the greater your burden, the greater are you. Are you a weakling, sinking under your own burden? Rise and help to support one who is fainting: you cannot do otherwise unless you would fall yourself.

"George," called Rosa in a hushed voice.

George turned where he stood at the window. "Listen," he began hesitatingly. "I have thought it out. I think that—you will not find work to suit you. There is work enough but you will not earn enough to—oh, it's nonsense."

"I shall be satisfied with anything," said Rosa quietly.

"No, wait a moment. You really don't know what it means. You see, I have quite a fair salary now, I am glad to say, and I could get afternoon work, too. Sometimes I really do not know what to do. It is quite enough for me. And I could let you have money—"

"What money?" murmured Rosa.

"My share from our parents and the interest which has accumulated; that makes about five thousand a year. No, not five thousand, only four. It is only the interest, you understand? It has occurred to me that I could let you have that interest, so that you might have something."

Rosa bounded off the sofa. "That is not possible," she cried excitedly.

"Don't scream," growled George. "It's only the interest, I tell you. Whenever you don't want it you need not draw it out. But now, just for the beginning . . ."

Rosa stood like an amazed little girl. "But that will not do, what would you have?"

"Oh, don't trouble about that," he protested, "I have thought for a long time that I should like to get afternoon work, but—I was ashamed to take work away from my colleagues. However, you see how I live; I shall be glad to have something to do. That's how it is; you understand, don't you? That money only hindered me. So now, do you want it or not?"

"I do," sighed Rosa, approaching him on tiptoe, flinging her arms round his neck and pressing her moist little face to his. "George," she whispered, "I never dreamed of this; I swear to you that I wanted nothing from you, but since you are so good—"

"Never mind," he said, deeply stirred. "That's beside the point. That money really does not matter to me, Rosa; when a man is fed up with life, he must do something. . . . But what can one do all alone? In spite of all efforts one can only come face to face with oneself again in the end. You know, it is like living surrounded by nothing but mirrors, and whenever one looks in them there is only one's own face, one's own boredom, one's own loneliness. . . . If you knew what that means! No, Rosa, I do not want to tell you about myself, but I am so glad that you are here, so glad that this has happened. Look how many stars there are: do you remember how once at home we watched for falling stars?"

"No, I don't remember," said Rosa, turning a pale face to his; in the dim frosty light he saw her eyes shining like stars. "Why are you like this?"

He thrilled with pleasant excitement and stroked her hair. "Don't talk about the money. It is so dear of you to come to me. Heavens, how glad I am, as if a window had opened—among the mirrors. Can you imagine it? I really only cared for myself. I was sick of myself, tired of myself, but I had nothing else. . . . Oh! there was no sense in it at all. Do you remember, when the stars fell, what you asked for then? What would you ask for tonight if a star fell?"

"What should I ask?" Rosa smiled sweetly. "Something for myself. . . . No, something for you, for something to happen for you?"

"I have nothing to wish for, Rosa, I am so glad to have got rid . . . Now, how will you arrange? Wait, tomorrow I will find you a nice room with a pleasant outlook. From here, you only look onto the yard; in the daytime, when there are no stars shining, it is a trifle depressing."

Quite excited and enthusiastic, he strode about the room planning out the future, eagerly picturing each new detail, laughing, talking, promising all sorts of things. Of course, lodging, work, money, would all be forthcoming; the main thing was that this would be a new life. He felt how her eyes shone in the darkness, smiling, following him with their ardent brightness; his heart was so full that he could have laughed for joy; he did not think of resting till exhausted, worn out by sheer happiness and too much talking they fell into long pauses of weariness, in utter harmony.

At last, he made her lie down; she did not resist his quaint, motherly solicitude, and could not even thank him; but when he looked up from the piles of newspapers in which he was glancing through advertisements of lodgings and agencies, he found her eyes fixed on him with an ardent and strange brilliancy, and his heart was wrung with happiness. Thus morning found him.

Yes, it was a new life. His wretched lassitude was gone now as he swallowed a hasty dinner, then strode through countless houses in search of a room, coming home perspiring like a hunting dog and happy as a bridegroom, and settling down in the evening to plow through pieces of extra work, until he finally fell asleep, worn out and enthusiastic over a profitable day. But he had, alas! to put up with a room without a pleasant outlook, a detestable room, upholstered in plush and outrageously dear, where he placed Rosa, for the present. Sometimes, indeed, in the course of his work he was attacked by faintness and weakness, his eyelids would tremble, a sweat from giddiness breaking out on his suddenly livid brow; but he succeeded in mastering this, set his teeth and laid his hand on the cold slab of the table, saying resolutely: "Bear it—you must bear it—indeed, you are not living for yourself alone." In this way he did feel better and better as day followed day. This was a new life.

Suddenly one day he had an unexpected visitor. It was his other sister, Tylda. She was married to a manufacturer in a small way who was not doing well and lived some little distance out of town. She always called on him when she came to Prague for anything—on business trips—for she looked after everything herself. She used regularly to sit with eyes cast down and talk in brief, quiet phrases of her three children and her many worries as if there were nothing else in the world. Today, however, she alarmed him; she was breathing heavily, struggling in her cobweb of ceaseless cares, and her fingers, disfigured by writing and sewing, touched his heart and made it ache with sympathy. Thank heaven, she got out brokenly, the children were well and good, but the workshop was not going well, machines were worn out; she was just looking for a purchaser.

"And so Rosa is here?" she suddenly said in a half-questioning tone, vainly trying to raise her eyes. Strange to say, wherever her eyes rested there was a hole in the carpet, frayed furniture covers, something old, shabby, and neglected. Somehow or other neither he nor Rosa had paid any attention to such things. This vexed him, and he looked away; he was ashamed to meet her eyes, keen as needles and relentless as unceasing care.

"She has run away from her husband," she began indifferently. "Says that he plagued her. Perhaps he did, but everything has a cause."

"He had cause, too," she went on, failing to provoke questions. "You see, Rosa is—I don't know how to put it . . ." She was silent, stitching with heavy eyes at a large hole in the carpet. "Rosa isn't a housewife," she began after a time. "And of course, she has no children, need not work, has no cares, but—"

George looked gloomily out of the window.

"Rosa is a spendthrift," Tylda forced out of herself. "She has run him into debt, you see. . . . Have you noticed what her linen is like?"

"No."

Tylda sighed and made as if wiping something from her forehead.

"You have no idea what it costs. She buys, say, furs, for thousands, and then sells them for a few hundred to pay for boots. She used to hide the bills from him; then there came summonses. Do you know about this?"

"No. He and I are not on speaking terms."

Tylda nodded. "He is queer, of course, I don't dispute. But when she does not mend a scrap of linen for him, and when she herself goes about like a duchess—tells him lies—carries on with other men—"

"Stop," begged George in anguish.

Tylda's sad eyes mended a torn bed cover. "Perhaps she has offered you," she asked uncertainly, "to housekeep for you? Suggested your taking larger lodgings—and that she should cook for you?"

George's heart contracted painfully. This had never occurred to him. Nor had it to Rosa. Heavens, how happy he would be! "I should not want her to," he said sharply, controlling himself by main force.

Tylda succeeded in raising her eyes. "Perhaps she would not want it either. She has got him here—her officer. They transferred him to Prague. That's why she ran away—and has taken up with him—a married man. Of course, she has said nothing about it to you."

"Tylda," he said hoarsely, withering her with his glance, "you lie."

Her hands and face quivered, but she would not give in yet. "See for yourself," she stammered. "You are too kind-hearted. I would not have said this if—if I were not sorry for you. Rosa never cared for you. She said you were—"

"Go!" he cried, beside himself with rage. "For God's sake leave me in peace!"

Tylda rose slowly. "You should—you should get better lodgings, George," she said with dignified calm. "Look how dirty this place is. Would you like me to send you a little box of pears?"

"I don't want anything."

"I must be off. How dark it is here. Dear, dear, George; well, good-by, then."

The blood throbbed in his temples, his throat contracted; he tried to work, but he had only just sat down when he broke his pen in a rage, sprang to his feet and hurried round to see Rosa. He ran to her place in a sweat and rang; the landlady opened the door, and said that the young lady had been out since the morning: was there any message?

"It does not matter," growled George, and shuffled home as though carrying an immense load. There he sat down to his papers, leaned his head on his hand and began to study; but an hour went by and he had not turned over a page; dusk was followed by darkness, and he did not light up. Then the bell rang in a breezy, cheery way, there was a rustle of skirts in the passage and Rosa flew into the room. "You are asleep, Georgie?" She smiled tenderly. "Why, how dark it is here; where are you?"

"Eh? I have been busy," he remarked drily. There was an air of chilliness in the room and an exceedingly pleasant scent.

"Listen," she began cheerfully.

"I wanted to go round to you," he interrupted, "but I thought perhaps you would not be at home."

"Why, where should I have been?" she asked in genuine wonder. "Oh, how nice it is here. Georgie, I am so glad to be with you." Joy and youth breathed from her and she was radiant with happiness. "Come and sit by me," she said, and when he was seated beside her on the sofa she slipped her arm round his neck and repeated, "I am so happy, Georgie." He rested his face against her cold fur, bedewed with autumn mist, let himself be rocked gently, and thought: "Suppose she has been somewhere, what is that to me after all? At any rate, she has come back to me at once." But his heart grew faint and oppressed with a strange mixture of keen pain and a sweet odor.

"What is the matter, Georgie?" she cried in shrill alarm.

"Nothing," he said as though lulled. "Tylda has been here."

"Tylda," she repeated, dismayed. "Let go of me," she said, after awhile. "What did she say?"

"Nothing."

"Come now, she spoke of me, didn't she? Did she say anything horrid?"

"Well, yes—a few things."

Rosa burst into wrathful tears. "The nasty creature. She is always jealous of everything I have. How can I help it that things go badly with them? She must have come because—because she found out what you had been doing for me. If things went better with them, she would forget all about you. It is so disgusting. She wants everything for herself—for her children—those horrid children."

"Don't talk about it," entreated George.

But Rosa went on crying. "She wants to spoil everything for me. I have scarcely begun to have a happier life when she comes along, slandering me, wanting to take things from me. Tell me, do you believe what she has been saying?"

"No."

"I really want nothing more than to be free. Haven't I a right to be a little more happy? I want so little, and was so happy here, George, and then she comes along—"

"Don't worry about that," he said, and went to light the lamp. Rosa stopped crying at once. He looked at her closely, as though for the first time. She was looking at the floor, her lips were trembling. Ah, how pretty and youthful! She had on new clothes, small gloves, so close fitting that they seemed ready to burst; and silk stockings peeped from under her skirt. Her little nervous hands played with the threads of the worn sofa-covering.

"Excuse me," he said sighing. "I have some work to do just now."

She obeyed and rose. "Ah, Georgie," she began, and did not know how to go on. With hands clasped against her breast, she gave him a swift, agonized glance and stood there, white-lipped, like an image of fear. "Don't be anxious," he said briefly, and turned to his work.

Next day he was sitting over his papers until twilight. He compelled himself to work mechanically, smoothly and unheedingly, and forced himself to go quicker and quicker; but all the time he was working there grew and deepened within him a keen sense of pain. Presently Rosa came in. "Go on writing," she whispered. "I shall not disturb you." She sat down quietly on the sofa, but he felt that her passionate, sleep-robbed, vigilant eyes never left him.

"Why didn't you come to me?" she burst out suddenly. "I was at home today." He felt in this a confession which touched him. He laid down his pen and turned to her; she was dressed in black like a penitent, paler than usual, folded in her lap were her appealing little hands, which even from where he sat he felt must be cold.

"It is rather chilly there," he observed apologetically, and tried to talk as usual without making reference to the happenings of the previous day. She replied humbly and gently like a grateful child.

"About Tylda, you know," the words came all at once, "the reason things go so badly with them is that her husband is a duffer. He stood surety for someone and then had to pay. It is his own fault, and he ought to have thought of his children; but then, he doesn't understand anything. He had an agent who robbed him, and yet goes on trusting everyone. You know they are suing him for fraudulent bankruptcy?"

"I know nothing about it," George turned it off. He saw that she had been brooding over it all night, and felt somehow ashamed. Rosa was not aware of his quiet rebuff: she lost her temper, got excited, and immediately played her highest card: "They wanted my husband to help them, but he obtained information and simply laughed at them outright. To give them money, he said, would be to throw it away; they have three hundred thousand of liabilities. . . . A man would be a fool to put a single heller into that; he would lose it all."

"Why do you tell me this?"

"So that you might know," she forced herself to a gentle tone. "You know you are so kind-hearted, you would very likely let yourself be deprived of everything."

"You are very kind," he said without taking his eyes from her. She was highly strung, burning with desire to say something more, but his scrutiny made her uneasy; she began to be afraid that she had gone too far. She asked him to find some work so that she might be a burden to no one, no one at all; she could live with strictly limited expenditure; she felt she ought not to have such expensive lodgings. . . . Now at last perhaps she would offer to housekeep for him. He waited with beating heart, but she looked away toward the window and began on something else.

The next day he received the following letter from Tylda:

Dear George:

I am sorry we parted under such a misunderstanding. If you knew all, I am sure you would read this letter differently. We are in desperate position. If we succeeded in paying off that fifty thousand we should be saved, for our business has a future, and in two years it would begin to pay. We would give you every guarantee for the future if you would let us have the money now. You would be part proprietor of the works and take a share of the proceeds as soon as business began to pay. If you will come and look at our establishment, you will see for yourself that it has a future. You will also get to know our children better, and see how nice and good they are and so diligent, and you will not have the heart to ruin their whole future. Do it, at least, for the children, for they are of our blood, and Charles is already big and intelligent and gives promise of a great future. Forgive me for writing this, we are in a fine flutter and are quite sure that you will come to our rescue and become fond of our children, for you have a kind heart. Be sure and come. When little Tylda is grown up she will be glad to be housekeeper to her uncle, you will see what a darling she is. If you don't help us my husband will never get over it and these children will be beggars.

Kind love, dear George, from your unhappy sister,

TYLDA

P.S.—With regard to Rosa, you said that I told lies. When my husband comes to Prague he will bring you proofs. Rosa does not deserve your support and generosity, for she has brought shame on us. She had better go back to her husband; he will forgive her, and she ought not to rob innocent children of their bread.

George flung the letter aside. He felt bitter and disgusted, the unfinished work on his table presented an air of hopeless triviality. Disgust rose in a painful lump in his throat; he left everything and went round to Rosa. He was already on the steps before her doors when he changed his mind with a sudden jerk of his hand, came down again, and strolled aimlessly about the street. He saw in the distance a young woman in furs on an officer's arm; he started running after them like a jealous lover, but it was not Rosa. He saw a pair of bright eyes in a woman's face, heard a laugh on rosy lips, saw the woman radiating and exhaling happiness, full of trust and joy and beauty. Wearily he returned home at last. On his sofa lay Rosa in tears. Tylda's open letter fell to the floor.

"Miserly creature," she sobbed passionately, "and not ashamed of herself. She wants to rob you of everything, Georgie; don't give her anything, don't believe a word of it. You can't understand what a crafty, avaricious woman she is. Why does she pursue me like that? What have I done to her? For the sake of your money—to slander me in that way! It is only—only because of your money. It is really monstrous!"

"She has children, Rosa," George observed gently.

"That is her own lookout," she cried fiercely, choking with sobs.

"She has always robbed us and only cares for money. She married for money; even when she was little she boasted that she would be rich. She is absolutely disgusting, vulgar, stupid—tell me, Georgie, what is there in her? You know what she was like when things went better with them—fat, insolent, unfriendly. And now she wants—to rob me. George, would you let her? Would you get rid of me? I would rather drown myself than go back."

George listened with bowed head. Yes, this girl was fighting for everything, for her love and happiness; she wept with rage, she cried out in passionate hatred against everyone, against Tylda, and even against himself who could take everything from her. Money—the word stung George like a whip whenever she said it; it struck him as shameless, disgusting, offensive.

"It was like a miracle to me when you offered me money," wept Rosa. "It meant for me freedom—everything. You offered it yourself, Georgie, and you should not have offered it at all if you meant to take it away again. Now, when I am counting on it—"

George was no longer listening. Remotely he heard reproaches, lamentations, sobs. He felt humiliated beyond measure. Money, money, but was it only a question of money? O God, how had it come about? What had coarsened the careworn heart grown hard and indifferent? What had money to do with it at all? In a strange way he was aware of his power to hurt Rosa, and of an inexplicable desire to wound her by saying something cruel, humiliating, and masterful.

He rose with a certain lightness. "Wait," he said coldly. "It is my own money. And I," he concluded with a magnificent gesture of dismissal, "shall think it over."

Rosa sprang up with eyes full of alarm. "You—you—" she stammered. "But at all events—that's understood. Please, Georgie—perhaps you did not understand me—I didn't mean that—"

"All right," he broke in drily. "I say I shall think it over."

A gleam of hatred blazed in Rosa's eyes; but she bit her lip, and went out with bowed head.

Next day there was a new visitor waiting in his room: Tylda's husband, an awkward, blushing man, full of embarrassment and doglike submissiveness. George, choking with shame and fury, refrained from sitting down, so as to compel his visitor to stand.

"What is your business?" he said, in the impersonal tone of an official.

The awkward man shivered and forced out of himself: "I—I—that is, Tylda—has sent some documents—which you asked for—" and began to hunt feverishly in his pockets.

"I certainly did not ask for any papers," said George with a negative wave of his hand. There was a painful pause.

"Tylda wrote to you—brother-in-law," began the unfortunate tradesman, blushing more than ever, "that our business—to put it shortly, if you would like to be a partner—"

George purposely let him flounder.

"The fact is—things are not so bad, and if you were a partner, to put it shortly, our undertaking has a future, and as one who—shared—"

The door opened softly and there stood Rosa. She became petrified at the sight of Tylda's husband.

"What is the matter?" said George sharply.

"Georgie," gasped Rosa.

"I am engaged," George rebuffed her, and turned to his guest. "I beg your pardon."

Rosa did not stir.

Tylda's husband perspired with shame and terror. "Here are—please—these proofs, letters which her husband wrote us and other papers intercepted—"

Rosa clutched at the door for support. "Show me them," said George. He took the letters and feigned to read the first, but then crushed them all in his hand and gave them to Rosa. "There you are," he smiled malevolently. "And now excuse me. And don't go to the bank to draw anything out; you would go for nothing."

Rosa retreated without a word, her face ashen.

"Well now, your business," continued George hoarsely, closing the door.

"Yes, the prospects are—of the very best, and if there were capital—that is, of course, without interest—"

"Listen," George interrupted unceremoniously. "I know that you are to blame; I am informed that you are not provident or—business-like—"

"I would do my best," stammered Tylda's husband, gazing at him with pleading, doglike eyes, from which George turned away.

"How can I put any confidence in you?" he asked, shrugging his shoulders.

"I assure you—that I would value your confidence—and all that is possible—we have children, brother-in-law."

A terrible, intense, embarrassing feeling of sympathy wrung George's heart. "Come in a year's time," he finished, holding on to the last fragment of his shattered will.

"In a year's time— O God—" groaned Tylda's husband, and his pale eyes filled with tears.

"Good-by," said George, extending his hand.

Tylda's husband did not see the proffered hand. He made for the door and stumbled over a chair, groping vainly for the door-knob. "Good-by," he said in a broken voice at the door, "and—thank you."

George was alone. A sweat of intense weakness burst out on his forehead. He arranged the papers on his table once more and called the landlady; when she arrived he was pacing the room with both hands pressed to his heart; he forgot what he wanted her for.

"Stop," he cried, as she was going out, "if today, tomorrow, or at any time my sister Rosa comes, tell her that I am not well and that . . . I would rather not see anyone."

Then he stretched himself on his sofa, fixing his eyes on a new spider's web freshly spun in the corner above his head.

EGON

HOSTOVSKY

Vertigo

Egon Hostovsky was born in Northern
Bohemia, and became an editor in a publishing house in Prague. Later he joined
the Czech diplomatic service and went to
Brussels, Paris and New York, where he
worked in the foreign service of Czechoslovakia. The story *Vertigo* appears in his
Letters in Exile (1942), an English translation. [From *Letters in Exile;* copyright
1942 by Egon Hostovsky; used by permission of the author; translated by Ann
Krtil.]

28th March, 1940.

ALL OF US, MY DEAR FRIEND, are suffering so acutely from
vertigo that you could tell it at once by our eyes, which have seen so
many things that had hitherto seemed secure, crumble so quickly to
dust.

I was looking for Mr. Albe in the café yesterday.

"Mr. Albe?" pondered the waiter.

"He wears glasses; he is bald . . ."

"The one who always orders chocolate?"

"He wears a blue suit."

"I know whom you mean; he drinks mineral water with his coffee.
Or wait a minute, it must be the one who drinks no brandy but
Raphael."

Believe me, the waiter was not jesting; he really knows the guests by
what they eat or wear. Why do I feel uneasy? Because I don't know
how I can recognize people, and how they can recognize me. I just
don't know; I just don't know.

"You are Müller, of course," said an eccentrically dressed young man,
with a waxed moustache under an enormously large nose, who ac-
costed me in the street.

"I'm not Müller."

"Stop kidding, man, of course you are Müller! My name is Colt,
I want to work with you. Forty per cent for me and sixty for you. Shall
we shake on it?"

"Sorry, I'm not Müller!"

"Then seventy for you—all right? . . . Then who *are* you? It's as
plain as the nose on your face that you're not a native here. Keep
your incognito and take a chance on me. Surely you must have heard
of me? Colt—diamonds. Gentleman of the first water. Listen here,
Müller, I have a grand new system, sure to make eighty per cent
profit . . ."

He was one hundred per cent thief. It was a long while before he was
convinced that I was not Müller. That didn't worry him; it was enough
that I am an emigré. His offer was some crooked deal with stolen or
smuggled diamonds. I confessed regretfully that I had never been

guilty of any kind of fraud, and he said I was a mug. That we did not speak the same language. That he had been in prison here for three months, and that many emigrés were in jail. Not that they had ever stolen anything; but no one treats emigrés any better than thieves. What, they do treat them better? Everything in this world is one hundred per cent ramp. Useless to tell him that I earn my living in a respectable way, he knows I am an emigré, and emigrés are not allowed to earn a sensible living. Suppose I give him my address?—He will come to see me, and learn how his proposition has struck me.

How can we recognize the people we seek? By what they eat and drink? How distinguish a thief from an honest man when everything in this world is a ramp. No, everything is not a ramp. Mr. Thief, if only for the reason that you have held my arm for the past ten minutes and have stolen nothing from me! Mr. Albe, my good waiter, is an exceedingly good man; you would know that at once if you looked into his eyes. You may be up against it some day, waiter, and then you won't know to whom you can turn, if you cannot tell people by their faces.

I repeat, my dear friend, we all suffer from vertigo. So swift is time in its phantasmal flight that our senses reel; one rushes off somewhere, one collapses somewhere, and still one remains in the same place; one's hopes fly away and return with the coming of the birds; we grow old, we become gray, but we go on defying death and the devil. To them we refuse to yield. They circle and circle around us, they plague us with nightmares, but we do not give in to them. "We shall wake up when it comes to the worst," we whisper in a faint, small voice through the nightmare. Sometimes those two, the devil and death, all but hold us by the collar. "You poor fool," they grin, "from what do you expect to wake? You're not asleep, you *are* awake. This is no dream, this is the truth! All this is reality!"

No, no, we are not yet in their clutches, and please God we shan't be. You say we are not dreaming. Perhaps not; I don't know.

Now it's your turn, poets and bards; give ear to the tale of Jeronimo, the fiery Spaniard.

It was just before the end of their civil war. He was taken prisoner. For three days they let him starve in some sort of a hole, some deep cellar. He carried a small bag of gold slung round his neck. I forget how he had come by this gold. "Why suffer?" asked the grisly one, tenderly, "come, let's be betrothed!" He let himself be persuaded, although she was ugly, and her breath freezing. He began lustily, to shout awful obscenities, and to kick in the door. He was ready to hurl himself at the first guard who entered the dungeon, and to bite off his nose, so that he might be shot on the spot. And as he kicked and banged upon the door, he turned the knob—and behold, a miracle!— the door opened. Either it had not been closed, or it had been insecurely locked. He tottered out, stumbled up the stairs, and suddenly ran into a soldier who was armed to the teeth. He was about to grab the soldier by the throat and bite off his nose, but before he could raise his hands, the soldier asked, in a matter of fact way:

"Have you got the bowl already?"

"I haven't it," whispered Jeronimo, in astonishment.

"Then go quickly!"

Jeronimo will never know for whom the soldier mistook him, nor of what bowl he spoke. Perhaps the soldier was drunk, perhaps he was walking and talking in his sleep. It was night, Jeronimo walked out of the cellar and out of the prison and disappeared in the darkness. With the gold he had with him he bought people. They helped him to get to the frontier. In France he was imprisoned again. Then . . . Is all this true? Or is it a lie? . . .

My pale-faced countryman goes about like a somnambulist, whispering something unintelligible.

"What are you muttering about?"

He lifts his head and looks at me, stupidly, as if he were seeing me for the first time. He swallows, and then he says:

"I must go to France!"

"We must all of us go there; have patience!"

"But I want to get to the front right away!"

"Why?"

"Because . . . I saw them die . . ."

"Saw whom die?"

"Our people . . . Those five . . . Back home . . . I alone escaped!"

This is the incident of the six who were staying at a certain Italian nobleman's castle near Prague. A true incident? How can I tell! A kind-hearted stranger took pity upon the six; they were five men and one woman, and their names were on the German's black list. While the usurpers were marching upon Prague a small car brought the six, one by one, to the castle. The Italian saved them from torture. They stayed with him for four months and six days (exiles in their own country); they huddled together in the library, and were only allowed to go into the garden at night. From the adjoining rooms they could hear voices, music, the ring of glasses, and laughter, but that had nothing to do with them. They were underlings. The pale-faced youth wanted to run away; he begged the others to let him go; he declared that he could get to Poland. They would not let him go, since his capture might reveal their hiding-place. They were allowed to play cards, to eat and drink, to talk in whispers—they had permission to exist. One night the pale-faced youth succeeded in climbing over the fence, but they pulled him back, beat him, and imprisoned him in the empty attic. One of them, a red-bearded man, had brought a yellow box to the castle with him; he guarded it constantly, and kept it hidden. No one had the slightest inkling of what was in the box, until the evening when the Italian, pale as death, burst into the library and blurted out: "They're here; you must give yourselves up!"

Thereupon the red-bearded man is said to have pounded upon the

table until the windows rattled, while the others began to laugh boisterously and to sing some rollicking song. The Italian ran away from
them, weeping; the pale-faced youth clasped his hands, knelt, and
pleaded: "Let me go, please let me go! I can crawl through the drain
under the garden wall!"

"You can go to hell now, you coward!"

He was still able to see the red-bearded man open the box with hammer and pincers. The box held weapons. They pounced upon the
weapons as upon some prey; they were laughing no longer, only
smiling, they were no longer singing, no longer talking, they only
fondled the weapons. It was night when they ran out into the garden,
but there was a full moon. And it started immediately. The Germans
opened fire from three sides. The fourth side, that side of the garden
under which the drain ran, was unguarded; so the pale-faced youth
was able to escape. He got into Poland, and after a time, to us. But
before he ran away he saw the red-bearded man fall. He fell slowly,
holding himself erect, facing forward, and firing twice as he fell. He
saw the woman fall, too; she was barely twenty-three, and very
beautiful, just like a story-book princess. The Italian was said to be in
love with her (give ear, ye bards and poets!). The pale-faced boy saw
a strand of her golden hair blend in tender union with a stream of
living crimson on her brow. Shot in the forehead, she fell upon her
knees, and thus remained, as if in prayer.

Hearken, all ye poets and all ye bards, hearken well to the outlaws,
and then inscribe, on some eternal memorial, how our people died at
home, and how, of six who saw death in a castle garden, somewhere
near Prague, only one was afraid to die.

Vertigo is the disease in which we are writhing; vertigo, from the
dizzying whirl of too many deeds compressed within too short a time;
vertigo from the necromantic procession of facts and impressions.

Sometimes, at close of day, when I sit before my fire in the deepening
dusk and listen to the lamentations of the widows, the orphans, the
hungry, the lost and the wandering—familiar cries, which are akin to
the wailing lament of a lost soul—the door seems to open noiselessly,
and friends and kinsfolk from my home tiptoe in to see me. They seat
themselves round about me on the chairs, on the edge of the bed, and
even on the floor; they bow their heads and are silent. They have come
from prisons, from confiscated homes, from plundered estates, from
burned synagogues. When I fled from my native land I was not able
to clasp their hands in farewell. What shall I say to them now? What
shall I say? Why are they all silent? Are they reproaching me?

We sit in the dark. Outdoors the elements are ranging. Terrifying
stories flood the world; somewhere the bells are ringing an alarm; the
laws in all the statute-books are topsy-turvy; nobody understands them;
woe unto all men! A great storm is gathering, the most terrible storm
that has ever come to pass, a storm such as is only visited upon a sinful

land when the people thereof have burned and crucified the saints. My friends and relatives, my dearest ones, the hungry, the half frozen, the sick, the tortured, the demented, now lift their heads as in question and raise their eyes from the floor. The wind has ceased its wailing lament; it is I who am weeping now. What shall I say to them? What shall I say to my dearest ones?

When our frontier vanished they celebrated a shabby peace in this little country. When droves of humanity came flocking from our sunny hills into the weeping valleys they were dancing here and singing; our lamentations were shouted down by drunkards; there was no one to whom we could appeal, our desolate hearts found no confessor. And now this small country is hard hit; fear has beset it; the good fortune they sought to build upon our misfortune is passing away. The stuffed shirts are still sitting at laden tables, but the food sticks in their throats; the false prophets cry out in their sleep, the traitors seek alibis; who has given warning of the impending storm? Ah, those dissensions! Do you hear them, my dearest ones? They say the Ministers are to blame. The nations which did not defend themselves are to blame. Russia is to blame. They say England is to blame. The priests are to blame. Unfaithful wives, who broke the commandments, are to blame. Who is to blame? Who is guilty?

My dearest ones, why are you rising to your feet? Must you go? I know, you living dead, you are going forth to a battle in which poverty is your only weapon. You go without fear, without ignominy; I know, I know everything. See, I am no longer weeping, I am smiling now, for he who is your leader has never yet lost a battle.

Decay has hardly touched the fallen autumn leaves, and behold the spring is here again, with its blue sky. Now green whistles can be made of willow bark, and the primroses are in bloom. The silver snows of the worst winter known have at last melted away; forgotten is the silver in our hair, and spent, too, is the silver saved up for a final tip.

"You resemble my grandson, sir," says the old man who has been pushed into the doctor's waiting-room in a wheeled chair. "I am a Pole, sir; my grandson fell on the very first day of the war. My son died some time ago; I am the only man left of our whole family. I'm eighty-five; that's a good many years. I didn't want to leave my country, sir, but the women gave me no peace. There are too many women around me all the time. I find them a trial; they won't let me drink vodka; I mustn't eat this, I mustn't eat that; besides, they're always keeping things away from me. But now, sir, I'm glad I came away. I could never have survived what has happened back home, and I don't want to die yet; I still go on waiting, for it isn't possible that I left home never to see it again. Whatever should I say to Stanislaus then? That was my grandson's name. Do you think there's no reason for my outliving him? No, sir, there's reason for everything in this world; nothing happens by chance. I want to wait a little longer, perhaps a year or two, perhaps five. Since the good Lord has seen fit to visit me with so many afflictions, it is surely because I am to remember this and that, because I am to brood upon it, so that I may be able to say to Stanislaus: 'You had to go before your grandfather, my darling, so that you might not see the things that left the rest of us drained of tears. You see, my boy, I did not die of grief only because it has been decreed that I should live to see, like Job . . .' Well, sir, here they come to carry me to the doctor. This is my niece, sir, and this my daughter-in-law, both no longer chickens. Well, good-by. No, indeed, I'm going to wait a bit longer, I don't want to die yet! Good-by!"

His name is unknown to me. He did tell it to me, but I think he did not give me his right name. He comes from Vienna, and by the merest chance he left his country a few days before the occupation of Austria. I suspect that he is a poet, although he denied it. He has been ill for a long while here, and he was practically starving; and moreover, the police were always harassing him until recently. I think he has even been arrested. He volunteered for the Foreign Legion, but was turned down. I have shared my money with him, the money which you have sent me. He is getting along better now; he no longer goes about in rags, and even shaves occasionally.

We go walking along a country road not far from the city. Myriads of brooks are trickling all around us; the sky is one vast smile; our hearts are enamored of its heavenly azure. He walks with a stick, and has a habit of gazing far into the distance when he is telling one anything.

"I cannot understand how people can be so irresponsible. Have you met a single person who has been anxious and terrified, even for a moment, at the thought that he himself, he alone, is the accomplice of the catastrophe that has befallen the world?"

"I could not have met such a person, because I meet no dictators or other rulers of the world."

He stopped, thrusting his stick into the ground with a quick, angry jerk, but did not take his eyes off the horizon.

"You don't really think that dictators, ministers, and generals rule the world?"

"Who then?"

He pulled his stick out of the ground and strode on. Quietly, but seriously, he answered: "Perhaps you or I."

Now it was I who stopped abruptly. Poor fellow! Why hadn't I noticed it before? I ought to see about getting him home as quickly as possible. Obviously one would have to be very careful in talking to him. When could this have begun?

"That's really a very interesting idea of yours."

"Don't think I'm joking!"

"God forbid! Then you believe that you or I may be to blame for all that has befallen the world? H'm! wouldn't you like to elucidate that a little farther?"

"That is very difficult to explain to anyone who believes that he lives for and by himself alone. I have never believed that; ever since I was a child I have felt . . . Listen . . . No, I don't care to talk about this; there's no sense in doing so. I should only seem very ridiculous to you."

"Go ahead, and tell me about it. Nothing seems ridiculous or impossible to me any more. You evidently think—if I understand you correctly—that you are somehow to blame for the collapse of Europe."

"To tell you the truth . . . yes! Look at it this way: I am guilty too, and it may be that my guilt is the last link in a chain of casual events. At the same time, my whole personal history does not coincide with politics in the least. Now, consider this; you must be familiar enough with the myths of the religious fanatics, according to whom there are upon this earth, a very small number of apparently ordinary people for whom alone the world exists, and upon whose shoulders the whole arch of heaven is supported. If a single one of these chosen people should stumble on his allotted path, the results would be terrible. I don't in the least believe that it is possible to discover the tracks of these chosen ones in the events of which we read through which we are living. I am firmly convinced that the real causes of the appalling complex of events are concealed from us; that Napoleon and his wars need never have been, had it not been for some—well, let us say—some unknown barmaid in a tavern somewhere, and for some incident in her life, some incident even less known to the world than she herself. Do you understand?"

"Not a bit. About what barmaid are you talking?"

"It might not have been a barmaid; it might have been a chimney-sweep, or a miller; how do I know? Do you think that He who makes the world revolve and directs the fate of humanity cares about emperors and generals? Nonsense! He is more likely to be concerned about a country schoolteacher, the hunchbacked child of drunken parents, or some crazy poet. Believe me, the world still revolves upon its axis for the chosen unknown, and it is because of their sins that States are shattered and cities burned, and it will only be because of their repentance that in due time there will be peace upon earth once more to men of good will."

"Then you . . . If you'll forgive me . . . then you think of yourself as . . . you think you are one of the chosen ones?"

"Yes. You need not be afraid of me (and a sad smile flitted over his face). I'm otherwise perfectly harmless. My life has been a very happy one; whatever I have touched has prospered. I was dependent upon good fortune; I depended on luck as every spoiled darling depends upon the indulgence of his benefactors. I was forgiven much; far more than others, for my many little knaveries, lies, and deceptions were hard to prove. But I also committed a crime, and that likewise was hard to prove. Even while I was contemplating this crime I knew that I should be punished. I had been warned, I had been admonished; every time I opened a newspaper or a book the first words that met my eyes cautioned me. But I did it in spite of everything. I wanted to get rid of my wife and marry a younger and prettier woman. Weeks and months went by, and still my wife and I were living together, living together like a murderer and his chosen victim. Surely every time she looked into my eyes she must have seen that I wanted to kill her! Nevertheless, I managed to keep on friendly terms with her; I smiled at her now and then, I seemed to be anxious and attentive when she was ill. It would have been better if I had killed her and had atoned for the crime in jail. But I was too great a coward; besides, I knew that the world would come to an end if I touched even a hair of her head. I did not ask her to divorce me; I only hinted, half in jest and wholly in earnest, that she was standing in the way of my happiness. She was such a small, shy, good woman; she never lied, she was always pottering about in the kitchen, or straightening out the linen cupboard. Although we had a servant, she washed up the dishes, mended my socks, and never wanted to go to the theater; for, as she said, we are not out to squander our money. She used to help me on with my coat, poor thing; she did all that she could to hold me. As a girl she had had many admirers, and I had striven hard to win her for myself—why had I wronged her so? How did it happen? One day I came home drunk. I tripped over the rug in the hall; I switched on the light and looked into the mirror— my hat was on askew, my mouth twisted. How well I remember it; the white door of the bathroom was half open; the water from the shower was dripping into the bath. I went into our room; on the right was a bookcase, on the left a sofa, made up as a bed. My wife was sitting on the sofa, fully dressed; she was waiting for me. 'I'll tell her now,' flashed through my brain. She understood, and quietly said: 'Tell me!'

" 'See here, you must go away; I simply can't stand you. we can't go on like this . . .' "

"She rose and walked out of the room, like a mechanical doll. Her cheeks were bloodless, her mouth wide open, but she did not cry until she got into the bathroom. She forgot to close the door. I could hear her sobbing; I heard her strike her head against the wall. Something within me cried out, desperately: 'There is still time. Hurry after her, crush her in your arms, beg her forgiveness! There's still time!' But I didn't stir. She went away that night, and I have never seen her again; I have never known where or how she is living. I didn't ask the lawyer who arranged the divorce. She refused to accept alimony.

"I was very unhappy in my second marriage; my new wife deceived me from the very beginning. I said to myself: This is your punishment. But I had a premonition that something worse was coming, that the world would be shaken to its depths for what I had done.

"Just think, man! Three years later, chance brought me to this country, where I didn't know a soul. I came here to see a sick friend about something; his relatives here persuaded me to stay with them in their country house while I was here. They themselves lived on the ground floor; I was to have the first floor. Splendid! And now just listen to this! They gave me a key. I went upstairs, opened the door, tripped over the rug, and looked about me. Overcome with horror, my feet gave way under me, for I was standing in my former home, in the same rooms from which I had driven my wife. A round mirror, just like the one we had at home, hung in the hall. My eyes stared back at me from the mirror; I could see that my hat was askew, and my mouth twisted, just as then. I turned round—the white door of the bathroom was half open, and water from the shower was dripping into the bath. Still carrying my bag, I staggered across the threshold into the room; yes—a bookcase on the right, a sofa on the left, but no one was sitting on the sofa. I let my bag fall to the floor with a thud; I staggered on; I sat down on the bed; and at that moment the invisible radio announcer was shouting from somewhere: ALL TELEPHONE CONNECTIONS DOWN! GERMAN SOLDIERS ARE ENTERING VIENNA!

"My first thought was: I cannot go home!

"I got up; I was gasping, and pale as death, and I went, as she had gone, into the bathroom, not closing the door behind me. There I beat my head against the wall and wailed; but no one heard me, no one came to help me. I called my wife's name again and again, but in vain, a thousand times in vain. The world is collapsing, the world is tottering, and I know that I am a fellow accomplice."

The rain beating across the windows again. Here I sit, writing to you, my friend. This may be my last letter to you, or the last but one. I think I shall soon be leaving this country; and for that matter, you will soon be leaving your native land. Shall we still be able to write to each other? Shall we ever see each other again?

I looked out of the window a little while ago and watched the passers-by. I found them ugly. I did not like their ears. The ear is really a very ugly appendage, don't you think so? It seems to me, sometimes, that people are actually uglier than rats. No doubt this is because of the vertigo in which we are writhing, and because it is so long since I have kissed anyone, so long since anyone has embraced me. The distance between my dearest ones and myself is continually increasing. There are so many words in the vocabulary of love and beauty that we have never yet used in speaking to one another.

Shall we not forget these words before we meet again, before this vertigo passes? We must not forget them; we dare not . . . for these are the words that alone can redeem the world.

FERENC

MOLNAR

The Silver Hilt

Ferenc Molnar was born in Budapest in 1878 and was graduated from the Universities of Geneva and Budapest. He began his literary career as a journalist at the age of eighteen. Best known as a dramatist, he has written *Liliom, The Swan* and *The Guardsman,* among other plays. [Copyright by Ferenc Molnar.]

A NARROW RIBBON OF SMOKE wound its way lightly out of one of the many chimneys of the ancient feudal castle, and rose into the misty autumn dawn as the sun was just beginning to shine. Any well-informed serf, noticing the smoke from the valley below, would have known that the cooks were not preparing breakfast for Count Scarlet, or as they called him in the Valley, the Red Scoundrel. In the castle of Count Scarlet the cooks were gentlemen, and never rose before seven in the morning. Any well-informed self would know what the little ribbon of blue smoke meant. It was Maestro Conrad Superpollingerianus who rose so early. He was the Count's professional alchemist. He had come from Würzburg a year and a half before and had ever since been working at his alchemy without the least success.

Indeed, Maestro Conrad was already awake and up. He was standing by his fire in a long black coat. Over the fire boiled mysterious and strange-smelling concoctions. The man's long white beard reached to his knees, and whenever he wanted to stroke his beard (which was often) he had to bend down almost to the ground. Even then he could seldom reach the end of it.

He was surrounded by all sorts of mysterious instruments. On the walls hung mysterious charts showing the movements of the stars, and all the heavens were divided into those spheres by which one may read the whims of fate. Everywhere were ovens and smelting-furnaces built of brick, strong jars against which the fire of hell was futile, slabs of lead, shining quartz, enormous bellows which panted like the lungs of a fresh-killed dragon, and in a corner on a richly carved stand, under a glass cover on a small velvet pillow, was one tiny bit of gold about half the size of a grain of rice.

The Maestro looked at this bit of gold and scratched his head. Count Scarlet had flown into a violent temper the night before. He was tired of having had him on his back for the past year and a half. The Maestro ate, drank and lived well, besides spending enormous sums for experiments, and he had not been able to make more than this tiny bit of gold. Once last year, the Count had determined to throw the Maestro out, when luckily the Maestro had succeeded in creating the gold. It is true that he had been able to do so only by inserting the gold—which he had bought—into the lead which he was supposed to have transformed. But Count Scarlet, cunning rascal though he was, had not discovered this. With the weirdest and most impressive ceremonies, exactly at the stroke of midnight, the Maestro put the stick of lead into the fire in the

698

presence of the Count, and when they removed the jar from under the lead, the gold was discovered in the bottom of it.

And then the Maestro's trouble began. The Count demanded more gold.

"Until now," he said, "I believed that Superpollingerianus was the stupidest ox in the world. But now I am beginning to discover that he is not a fool, but an old scoundrel, who knows how to make gold but doesn't want to. If by tomorrow morning there is not a considerable lump of gold in the furnace, I will defy the coming generations, who will certainly brand me as a scoundrel for having done it, and will tear your whiskers out, Maestro, and have you dragged to the top of the highest tower of my castle and kicked off. *Quod dixi, dixi.*"

With that he turned on his heel, ate his supper, looked at his calendar to see in which of his villages there then was likely to be a little *jus primæ noctis,* and spreading some scented pomade on his scanty red mustache, he rode out of the castle.

I repeat, this happened at night. At dawn the next day, the Maestro was still scratching his head.

"Alas," sighed the Maestro, turning away from his strange-smelling concoction with disgust, "I cannot help myself. There can be no question about making gold, because I haven't even a worn copper. All the money I've been able to get out of Count Scarlet, I have sent to my illegitimate child. To think I have struggled through eighty-eight years of life by sheer deception, and now I cannot extricate myself from this predicament! That scoundrelly Scarlet will keep his promise. Only five years ago, for a similar offense, my honorable friend and colleague, Paphnucius Ratenowienis, was nailed to the gate of the castle by his ears, and made to look like a stray bat. Alas, how can I save myself?"

Thus wailed the Maestro, bending to the floor again and again to stroke his long whiskers.

Suddenly, in the midst of his distress, he heard footsteps in the corridor. In a moment the door opened, and in the middle of the diabolical kitchen stood Count Scarlet with threateningly puckered eyebrows. The Count was tall, lanky, freckled, with close-cropped red hair, and a wicked bony face. His hands were as large as beefsteaks. His knees stuck out from his tightly fitting trousers like two bunions. He lifted his aristocratic, hairy red hand, and his tiny pig eyes grinned searchingly:

"Well, Maestro!"

The Maestro suddenly grew limp and tried to sit down on the air. He gulped a big dry gulp, turned the color of onyx and faintingly whispered, "Well, what does that 'Well' mean?"

"It means what it means," said the Count coldly.

It was a terrible moment. The seriousness of the situation was accentuated by the fact that the Count had deviated from his usual custom, in rising at such an early hour. It was evident that he was in earnest about his threat. Deadly silence reigned in the room. Only the strange smelling concoction of herbs boiled impertinently in the stillness of the room.

"Count," said the Maestro at last, "there is no gold."

"Then give me your whiskers," shouted the Count, and leaped toward the Maestro, who quickly threw his whiskers across his left shoulder so that they hung down over his back.

"Stop, sire!" he yelled in despair.

The Count was startled.

"What is it?"

"There is no gold," moaned the Maestro, "but there is something better."

"What?"

At this moment Maestro Superpollingerianus made an awful gulp, but this time it was no longer dry. His mouth watered at the thought of the fine lie that had just occurred to him. He felt that he was saved.

"What?" repeated the Count sternly.

"Something that is better than gold."

"The philosopher's stone?"

"No."

"What then?"

"The happiness of eternal love!" said the Maestro, and gulped again.

The Count stroked his nose. This was a sign of skepticism.

"Must I swallow this?" he asked. "Must I swallow this lie, too, as I have swallowed for a year and a half all the deceptions with which you have contrived to prolong your stay here, you shameless blot upon the heaven of science?"

To be undecided is half of believing, thought the Maestro and went on developing his lie with the greatest tranquillity.

"In the course of my experiments I have discovered the way to conquer the feminine heart."

The Count opened his eyes wide. He was known as an admirer of feminine charms, but had never had any success with ladies of rank. His face was gleaming with joy.

"I have ground silver into dust," continued the Maestro, "and boiled it in the juice of Asperula Odorato and then in the juice of the root of Azarum Europæum. These are the ingredients. But the chemical proportion that yields the magic is my own secret. *Ecce* . . ."

And he raised the lid of one of the pots. There were indeed bits of silver balls boiling in the juice of something that smelled horribly strange. He had cooked the whole mess the night before as a last chance.

"And—?"

"And of this silver dust I shall mold a thin sheet of silver plate; with that silver plate you will graciously cover the hilt of your sword and while you are courting the ladies keep your left hand on the hilt of the sword. There is no great lady, baroness, countess, duchess, or even queen, who will be able to resist the charm of this wizardry. With this sword you will have success with any lady in the world."

"Hm," said the Count, "may I have complete confidence?"

"Not the slightest chance of failure, sir."

The silver hilt was ready that same night.

"I am gaining time," said the Maestro to himself, and to save himself the trouble of bending down, he lifted his beard up over his arm and stroked it musingly.

The rumor soon spread throughout the district. In the neighborhood castles and fortresses, the great ladies dressed in gold-embroidered gowns, whispered and exchanged meaning glances, and everywhere conversation centered on the silver-hilted sword of Count Scarlet. Not three days had passed before Maestro Conrad Superpollingerianus had received eighteen offers from various other lords, promising him lifelong positions, any amount of gold, together with board and lodging, if he would only communicate to them the secret of the chemical composition of the silver hilt. But the Scarlet Count bid more than any of them, and would not permit the Maestro to leave his castle.

On the fourth day he set out to conquer with his silver hilt. His first trip took him to the neighboring castle, whose lord was journeying in foreign lands. Only the beautiful Lady of the Castle was at home, in company with her thirty-three ladies-in-waiting. For a long time, this had been the unsuccessful hunting-ground of the Scarlet Count, but now the women were waiting for him with a strange excitement and expectancy. All thirty-three of them wanted to receive the Count, and they all insisted that they were not afraid of the silver hilt. But the Lady of the Castle dismissed them and she, the model of faithfulness and womanly virtue, received the Count alone.

She lay resting on a large sofa when the Red Bone (that was what they called the Scarlet Count among themselves) entered the room. She rose and went to meet him, offering him a seat. The Lord sat down on a footstool and, as was customary with knights, held his sword between his knees. The Lady, who until now had not dared to cast even a glance at the sword, looked at it shyly. She was taken aback by the sight. The sword, studded with diamonds and precious stones, ended at the hilt in a simple silver sheet. It had an uncanny faded look about it and gleamed in the dimness of the room with a ghostly light.

They could not see the thirty-three women peeping in from behind the heavy drapery and curtains. But these women agreed that the Count looked irresistibly powerful, though they always before considered him ridiculous.

"It's fine weather," said the Red Bone.

"Yes, very fine," said the Lady, and was greatly relieved when she saw that the Count had not placed his hand on the hilt of the sword.

"Neither too warm nor too cold," said the Count.

"Very pleasant, indeed," said the Lady.

"At noon it's warm, but the nights are cool," the Count went on, "but tonight the sunset is the most wonderful of all, more wonderful indeed if one spends the time in the company of a beautiful woman."

And so saying, he placed his large red hand upon the silver hilt.

The Lady, who had been watching it with staring eyes, began to tremble a little. The heavy curtains began to move and a pleasant tremor passed through the veins of the women.

"He placed his hand on it," said those in front to those standing behind.

"He placed his hand on it . . . he did indeed!" the whisper passed around.

The Lady of the Castle could not take her eyes off the hand resting upon the hilt. The Red Count was talking away foolishly, but the Lady paid no attention to what he said.

"Eh," she said to herself, "the whole thing is a stupid superstition; why should I look at it at all?"

But as soon as she looked away, something constrained her to look back immediately. The Count drew his footstool nearer to her, grasping at the hilt with all his might. The lady grew frightened.

"Why are you afraid of me?" asked the Count with a smile. "I do not wish to hurt you. On the contrary . . ."

"Perhaps it would be better," whispered one of the women behind the curtain, "if we left them alone."

A soft, creeping noise could be heard, as the ladies, with their fingers on their lips, slipped away from behind the curtains.

"I have loved you for a long time," said the Red Scoundrel in a melting tone.

Something seemed to choke the woman, but she told herself it was only imagination.

"I adore you."

The woman could not take her eyes off his hand. And she pleaded: "If you love me, let go the hilt of your sword."

"Never," shouted Scarlet in the heat of his passion, and drew his chair closer.

The Lady was trembling like a leaf in an evening breeze.

"You are beautiful!" howled the Scarlet Bone. "You are as beautiful as the morning star, and I tell you frankly I am going to make you my own love."

His grip on the sword tightened.

"He will not let go of it," thought the terrified woman. "He will not let go of it. I am lost."

She made an attempt to stand up, but at that moment she felt the prickly hairs of a thin mustache on her lips. She wanted to scream, but the Count had already imprisoned her shoulders in his long, strong arms. Her beautiful head dropped like a flower, and she felt that the Scarlet Bone was holding her wilting head in the palm of his enormous hand. Kisses were beating heavily against her lips like hot rain.

"You are mine," said the Count between two kisses, still tightly grasping his sword with his left hand.

"I am yours," panted the Lady.

"What is the formula?" asked the Dark Blue Baron of the dying Maestro ten years later, for he had bought the scientist from the Scarlet Count for a hundred thousand gold pieces. He was a great lover of women and had seen that for the past ten years the Scarlet Count had virtually made a harvest of beautiful women by the magic of the Silver Hilt. "What is the formula?"

"By the Fires of Hell, there is no formula!" moaned the Maestro from his bed. "A silver hilt, a brass button, a tin spur, a golden horse shoe nail, it makes no difference. The man's bearing must announce that he is sure of himself—that is the formula. There is no escape from one who is sure of himself. But you must believe in the silver hilt, because if you do not, the women will not believe in it either. Now then: whether you believe in a silver hilt, a brass button, a tin spur, a golden horseshoe nail, your good manners, your beauty, your self-confidence or your discretion, it all amounts to the same thing. But now that I have told you this, O Dark Blue Baron, you will go to the women in vain with your silver hilt, because you will not believe in it any more. And the women will feel that you no longer believe in your own powers. And you will be defeated everywhere, O Dark Blue Ba . . ."

He could not finish the sentence, because the Dark Blue Baron struck him a blow on the head. He would have died anyway within the next ten minutes, but the Baron found it better to assist him in this manner.

So died Maestro Conrad Superpollingerianus, the gray-haired swindler, with the truth on his lips.

KALMAN MIKSZATH

The Green Fly

Kalman Mikszath (1847–1910) studied law at the University of Budapest, served as a county official and then turned to journalism. He was a member of the Hungarian Parliament and the Hungarian Scientific Academy as well as president of the Society of Hungarian Journalists. He wrote many stories and novels, among which are *Saint Peter's Umbrella, Gentlemen and Peasants, The Old Scoundrel, A Ghost in Lublo* and *The Black City.* [From *Great Short Stories of the World;* translated by Joseph Szebenyei.]

THE OLD PEASANT, the richest man in the village, lay very ill at the point of death. God was holding judgment over him, pointing to him as an example for all mankind:

"Look at John Gal. What do you mortals imagine yourselves to be? You are nothing. Now, John Gal is really somebody. Even the county judge shakes his hand occasionally. The Countesses of the village come and visit him. He is the richest among you. Still, I could smite him. I did not have to send a hungry wolf to bite him, nor do I have to up-root a giant oak to fall upon and crush him. A tiny fly will do the work."

That is what actually happened. A fly bit his hand; it soon began to swell, becoming blacker and redder.

The priest and the lady of the Castle persuaded him to call a doctor.

He would have been willing to have the surgeon sent for, but they prevailed upon him to telegraph for a specialist to Budapest. Professor Birli was chosen. One visit would cost three hundred florins, but that was money well spent.

"Nonsense," said the peasant, "that tiny fly couldn't have caused three hundred florins' worth of damage in me."

The Countess insisted and offered to pay the doctor's bill herself. This did the trick. John Gal was a proud peasant. The telegram was dispatched and a young man, slim and bespectacled—not at all imposing—arrived in the carriage that had been sent to meet him at the station.

Mrs. Gal, the young wife of the elderly peasant, received him at the gate.

"Are you the famous Doctor from Budapest?" she asked. "You had better come and look at my husband. He's making as much fuss over a fly-bitten hand as if he'd been bitten by an elephant."

This was absolutely untrue. John Gal had never said a word; never even mentioned the bite unless he was asked, and even then he was extremely curt. He lay on his bed indifferent and stoical. His head rested on a sheepskin, his pipe in his mouth.

"What's the trouble, old man?" asked the Doctor. "I understand a fly bit you."

"That's it," answered the peasant between his teeth.

"What sort of a fly was it?"

"A green fly," he said curtly.

"You just question him, Doctor," interrupted the woman. "I shall have to look after my work. I have nine loaves in the oven."

"All right, *mother*," said the Doctor absent-mindedly.

She turned upon him immediately as if stung, her hands on her hips:

"Why, you're old enough to be my father!" she said, half offended and half flirting. "You don't seem to see well through those windows on your eyes."

She turned quickly about and the many starched skirts whirled like the wind as she walked out, erect with the sense of youth and strength.

The Doctor followed her with his eyes. She was devilish pretty, much younger than the Doctor, and of course very much younger than her husband. He wanted to mutter some sort of apology, but she was gone before he could say a word.

"Well, let's see that hand. Does it hurt?"

"Quite a good deal," was the answer.

The Doctor examined the swollen hand, and his face assumed a grave look.

"Bad enough. It must have been a poisonous insect."

"Maybe," said John without the least emotion. "I could tell it wasn't an ordinary kind."

"It was a fly that had come from a dead body."

A mute curse was all John Gal vouchsafed for this information.

"It was lucky I arrived in time. We can still do something. Tomorrow it would have been too late. You'd have been dead."

"That's strange," said the peasant, pressing the tobacco into his pipe with one thumb.

"Blood-poisoning works fast. We have no time to lose. You must harden your nerves, old man. Your arm will have to come off."

"My arm?" he asked with surprise and a touch of sarcasm, and a great deal of resignation.

"Yes. It has to be done."

John Gal did not say a word; he only shook his head and went on smoking.

"You see," the Doctor went on in his persuasive tone, "it will not hurt you. I shall put you to sleep and when you wake up you will be saved. Otherwise, tomorrow at this time you'll be as dead as a mouse. Not even God can save you."

"Oh, leave me alone," he said as though he were tired of so much talk; turned to the wall, and closed his eyes.

The Doctor was quite unprepared for such stubbornness. He left the room and went to have a word with the woman.

"How is my husband?" she asked with such indifference as she could muster, continuing her work at the same time in order to show her contempt for the Doctor.

"Bad enough. I just came to ask you to try and persuade him to let me amputate his arm."

"Good gracious!" she exclaimed, turning as white as the apron before her. "Must it be done?"

"He will die otherwise within twenty-four hours."

Her face turned red, as she took the Doctor by the arm. She dragged him into the sick-room and there, placing her hands on her hips, addressed him:

"Do I look like a woman who would be satisfied to be the wife of a cripple? I'd die of shame. There! Just look at him!" She turned to her husband and almost shouted: "Don't you let him cut your arm off, John. Don't you listen to him!"

The old peasant gave her a friendly look.

"Don't you worry, Kriska," he assured her. "There'll be no butchering here. I don't intend to die in pieces."

It was in vain that the Doctor spoke to the old man of the darkness of death and the beauties of life. It was to no purpose that he called the Countess from the Castle to plead his suit, and the priest and all the most eloquent and impressive talkers of the village. John Gal remained obdurate. He declined to be cut.

The resignation with which the peasant meets death, without bitterness, without reproach, and without vain tears, was expressed in the calm of his face and the tone of his voice. Death held no terrors for him. If his time was at hand, he was ready to go as his father and his grandfather had gone before him.

It was plain that nothing was to be gained through appeals to the old man to save himself. But at length the very real concern of the almost frantic Doctor began to touch the old man's heart. He pitied the fellow's agitation. He was sorry that this man should be so grieved and, half-ridiculously, half-pathetically, John began to console the physician.

Suddenly the Doctor remembered that considerations of money will work wonders where a peasant is concerned. So he said:

"You'll have to pay the three hundred, you know, whether I amputate your arm or not. It would be wasting money not to have the operation. It only takes five minutes."

"Well, you can prescribe some ointment, just to be earning your fee," said the old man, as calmly as if he were bargaining over a pair of boots.

It was no use. Disgusted and disappointed, the Doctor left the man and went out for a walk to think matters over and discuss the problem with some of the village wiseacres. He found little good advice, however, and it was equally in vain to bring the notary and the Justice of the Peace to the patient's bedside. The young woman was always there to offset any wicked plan on the part of the Doctor, and she never missed an opportunity for putting in a word or two to strengthen the obduracy of her husband. The Doctor gave her a wicked glance now and again, and even shouted at her:

"You hold your tongue when men are in conference!" he said.

"The hen is somebody on the cock's dunghill," she retorted, swinging her body.

John Gal hastened to prevent a quarrel.

"Don't get too noisy, Kriska. You'd better get a bottle of wine for the visitors."

"From which barrel!" she asked.

"From the two-hecto barrel. But for my funeral-feast you'd better tap the three-hecto barrel: it's getting sour."

He was quite resigned to the idea of death. The visitors drank and left him to make his peace with God.

In the courtyard Doctor Birli met the hired man, a young, powerful-looking fellow, a man-of-all-work.

"Get the carriage ready, I shall be off in half-an-hour," he said to the man. "And tell Mrs. Gal I shall not stay for supper."

Outside the gate he stopped, undecided as to what to do next. Through the crack of the gate-door he saw the man go up to Mrs. Gal, and could not help seeing the coquettish look she gave him and the self-important bearing of the young fellow as he approached her. It was evident that they were playing with fire and that there was some understanding between them. All he had to do now was to get a little further information on the subject. There must be an old witch in the village who knows all about the love-affairs of the villagers, and who deals in love potions. The notary would surely know. He did.

"Old witch Rebek," he said. "She lives two doors away from the Gals."

The Doctor handed her two silver florins.

"I am in love with a woman, and I'd like something that would make her love *me*," he said.

"Oh, that can't be, my boy. You look like a scarecrow, and they don't usually fall in love with men like you."

"True, mother, but I could give her all the silks she wants and all the money she could spend. . . ."

"And who be the woman?"

"Mrs. John Gal."

"You can pluck every rose, excepting those that are plucked."

That was just what the Doctor wanted to know.

"And who may the other man be?" he asked.

"Paul Nagy, the hired man. She must be in love with him, because she comes here often for potions. I gave her the last year's dust of three-year-old creepers to pour into his wine."

"And does John Gal suspect anything?"

"Smart as he may be, feminine wit beats him every time."

The Doctor returned to the Gal house and found the lovers still chatting, while the hired man wiped with a rag the backs of the horses that were now ready to take the Doctor to the station. She beckoned to him to approach. She dug her hand into her bosom as the city man approached, and drew out three hundred florins in bills.

"For your trouble, Doctor," she said, offering him the money.

"Right," said the Doctor, "but it will rest on your conscience, you pretty woman, that I did not deserve it more."

"My soul will bear it all right. Don't you worry."

"Very well. Just have my bag put into the carriage, while I say good-by to your husband."

John Gal was lying exactly where he had been left. His pipe was unlit, and his eyes were closed as if he were taking a nap.

He looked up and cocked one eye as the door opened.

"I just came to say good-by, Mr. Gal," said the Doctor.

"Are you going?" he asked with indifference.

"I have nothing to do here."

"Did the woman give you the money?"

"Yes. You've got a pretty wife, Mr. Gal. My, she's beautiful!"

The patient opened his other eye, and as he offered his good hand to the Doctor, he only said: "Ain't she?"

"Her lovely lips are like cherries."

"So they are." There was almost a happy smile on his face.

"That loafer Paul will have a fine time with her, I daresay."

The old peasant began to tremble, and looked up.

"What was it you said, Doctor?"

The Doctor closed his lips suddenly as if he had said something he had not intended to say.

"Nonsense. It's none of my business. One has eyes and brains and one sees things, and comprehends things. I was suspicious the moment she refused to let me cut your arm off. Didn't *you* suspect anything? But now I understand. Of course, of course."

John Gal began to shake both his fists, forgetting for the moment that one of them was swollen. He groaned with pain.

"Oh, my arm, my arm! Don't say another word, Doctor."

"Not another word," said the other.

A deep groan broke forth from the sick man's chest as he clutched the Doctor's arm with his right.

"Which Paul, Doctor? Which Paul do you mean? Who is he?"

"You really mean to say you don't know? Paul Nagy, your hired man." The old peasant turned white. His lips were trembling and the blood rushed to his heart. His hand didn't hurt him a bit now. He suddenly slapped his forehead and looked up. "What a stupid fool I was. I should have noticed long ago. . . . That snake of a woman!"

"No use swearing at the woman, Mr. Gal. She has her youth; she's full of health and life. That's what. She may *yet* be quite innocent, but after all she'll have to get married after you're gone. . . . And gone you'll be. . . ."

The old peasant moved with an effort and turned to the Doctor, who continued speaking:

"You have nothing to lose if she marries a younger man after you are gone. You wouldn't know anything about it after you're under the earth. And, besides, you ought to be glad she'll have a handsome fellow for a husband. Good-looking chap, Paul!"

The old fellow was crunching his teeth. It sounded as if two tusks had been ground against each other.

"You mustn't be greedy, Mr. Gal. It would be a pity to let that wonderful body of hers waste away without embraces. Paul isn't a fool. He wouldn't let a woman like her pass him by without taking a bite. Besides, she'll have all your money, and the farm. The woman, too, would like to live. The only fool among you three is you, Mr. Gal."

The peasant groaned again and the perspiration covered his forehead. In his heart was bitterness almost ready to overflow.

"You see, Mr. Gal, it would be better to hug her with one arm than with none at all."

This was too much for the old man. He jumped up and extended his swollen arm toward the Doctor.

"Get your knife, Doctor, and cut away!"

IVAN CANKAR

Children and

Old Folk

Ivan Cankar (1876–1918) grew up in dire poverty. He graduated from high school in 1896 and won a scholarship to a school of architecture in Vienna, but gave up his studies in a short time to devote himself to writing. He spent thirteen years in Vienna, after which time he went to Austria, where he died. His works include a volume of poetry, *Erotika;* collections of short stories, *Vignettes, Parables from My Dreams;* and an unfinished autobiography, *My Life.* [From *Parables from My Dreams;* translated by Helen Hlacha.]

EACH NIGHT, BEFORE THEY WENT TO BED, the children used to chat together. Seating themselves on the ledge of the broad oven, they uttered whatever came into their minds. Through the dim window the evening twilight peered into the room with dream-laden eyes. Out of every corner the silent shadows drifted upwards, carrying strange stories with them.

They spoke of whatever came to their minds, but to their minds came only pleasant stories of sunlight and warmth interwoven with love and hope. The whole future was one long bright holiday; no Lent, between Christmas and Eastertide. Over there, somewhere behind the flowered curtain, all life, blinking and throbbing, silently poured from the light into light. Words were whispered and only half understood. No story had any beginning, nor definite form. No story had an end. At times all four children spoke at once, yet none confused the other. All gazed enthralled into a beauteous heavenly light where each word was clear and true, where each story had a clear and living face, and each tale its glorious finish.

The children bore so marked a resemblance to one another that in the dim twilight the face of the youngest, four-year-old Tonchek, could not be distinguished from that of the ten-year-old Loizka, the eldest. All had thin, narrow faces and large, wide-open eyes—introspective eyes.

That evening, something unknown from an unknown place reached with violent hand into that heavenly light and struck pitilessly among the holidays, the stories, and legends. The post had brought tidings that the father "had fallen" on Italian soil. Something unknown, new, strange, entirely incomprehensible rose before them. It stood there, tall and broad, but had neither face, nor eyes, nor mouth. Nowhere did it belong, not to that clamorous life before the church and on the street, nor to that warm twilight around the oven, nor to the stories.

It was nothing joyful, but neither was it particularly sorrowful, for it was dead; because it had no eyes that it might by their look reveal wherefore and whence, and no mouth that it might explain by words. Thought stood humbly and timidly before that enormous apparition

709

as before a great black wall, motionless. It approached the wall, and stared dumb and ponderous.

"But when will he come back?" asked Tonchek, wonderingly.

Loizka nudged him with an angry look. "How can he come back if he has fallen?"

All lapsed into silence. They stood before that great black wall, and beyond it they could not see.

"I'm going to war, too!" unexpectedly announced seven-year-old Matiche, as if he had swiftly hit up the right thought. That was evidently all that it was necessary to say.

"You're too small," admonished four-year-old Tonchek, in a deep voice. Tonchek still wore dresses!

Milka, the thinnest and sickliest of them, who was wrapped in her mother's large shawl and resembled a wayfarer's pack, asked in her soft little voice from somewhere out of the shadows, "What is war like? Tell us, Matiche, tell us that story!"

Matiche explained, "Well, war is like this. People stab each other with knives, cut each other down with swords, and shoot each other with guns. The more you stab and cut down, the better it is. Nobody says anything to you, 'cause that's how it has to be. That's war."

"But why do they stab and cut each other down?" Milka insisted.

"For the Emperor!" said Matiche, and all were silent.

In the dim distance before their clouded eyes appeared something mighty, glistening with the radiance of glory. They sat motionless, their breath barely daring to escape their mouths, as in church at the benediction.

Then Matiche again swiftly gathered his thoughts; possibly just to dispel the silence which lay so heavy over them. "I'm going to war, too. Against the enemy."

"What is the enemy like? Has he horns?" suddenly inquired the thin voice of Milka.

" 'Course he has, else how could he be the enemy?" seriously, almost angrily replied Tonchek in emphatic tones. And now not even Matiche himself knew the correct answer.

"I don't think he—has them!" he said slowly, haltingly.

"How can he have horns? He's a person like us," voiced Loizka unwillingly. Then, reconsidering, she added, "Only he has no soul."

After a lengthy pause Tonchek inquired, "But how does a person fall in the war? Like this, backward?" And he illustrated the point.

"They kill him to death!" calmly explained Matiche.

"Father promised to bring me a gun."

"How can he bring you a gun if he has fallen?" Loizka roughly retorted.

"And they killed him—to death?"

"To death."

Through the youthful and wide-open eyes silence and sorrow stared into darkness, into something unknown, to heart and mind inconceivable.

At the same time on a bench before the cottage sat the grandfather and grandmother. The last red rays of the sun glowed through the dark foliage in the garden. The evening was silent except for a smothered, prolonged sob, already grown hoarse, which came from the stable. In all probability it was the wail of the young mother who had gone there to tend the livestock.

The two old people sat deeply bowed, close to one another, and held each other's hands as they had not done for a long time. They gazed into the heavenly afterglow with eyes devoid of tears, and did not speak.

ANTUN

GUSTAV MATOS

The Neighbor

Antun Gustav Matos (1873–1914) was the son of a village schoolmaster. He studied veterinary medicine in Vienna, but after serving in the army, he went to Zagreb, where he worked as a journalist and teacher. He did more than any other prose writer to develop a native Croatian literature. His main works are *Waste Wood, New Waste Wood, Tired Tales,* and *Perspectives and Paths.* [From *Great Short Stories of the World;* translated by Ivan Mladineo.]

HE WAS VERY TIRED. While cooling himself at a window of his apartment on the second floor, his thoughts wandered afar. He had had to leave his country on account of debts. His family had turned him away, not without giving him the necessary expenses for his journey to America. He stopped at Geneva and began gambling, winning at poker fom the Slavic, especially the Bulgarian, students. When one of the students committed suicide, because of his losses, by drowning himself in the lake, Tkalac stopped gambling and conceived a happy thought; he would rent a large apartment, buy a few mats and start giving lessons in fencing and later on in boxing (having learned this latter sport from a Parisian expert).

By means of the sword he made his way into the highest social circles, securing excellent recommendations, especially for Russia. After the wonderful match which placed him among the world champions, he made preparations to move to Paris. For the first time in his life he had managed to save money. The young, eccentric, cosmopolitan ladies, in particular, were paying him in a princely fashion. He started paying off his debts in his native country. Everyone was won over by his behavior, which was undeniably good, being a heritage from a long line of heroic borderland officers, noblemen of Laudon's time. Like most of our frivolous men, he remained good at heart—a childish, almost girlish,

soul shining from his yellowish, eagle-like eyes; and a black, manly
beard accentuated his rapacious profile, as it does in all our mountaineer
descendants of *hajduks* and *uskoks*. Though he loved much, not a
single woman did he really like, because at bottom he remained somewhat of a Don Quixote, dreaming of the ideal woman like all men who
are brought up on the ideals of chivalry.

From the huge yard, transformed into a garden, was wafted an agreeable breeze. A canary was heard singing from a nearby window, and
elsewhere a sweetly grieving strain from a Chopin ballad was audible.
Tkalac followed the curling smoke of his cigarette, dreaming, with eyes
open, like a savage. Suddenly he winced. On his bare, perspiring neck,
he felt some drops. He wiped them off with his handkerchief, but,
alas, rain again, and from a clear June sky. The young man turned his
head, and above, from the upper window among the flower-pots and
blossoms, there blushed a beautiful woman who lacked words to excuse herself and was powerless to turn her eyes from his confused
countenance.

"Along with your beautiful flowers, you are also watering nettle,
madame," he finally said in his foreign French which, reminding them
so much of a child's prattle, caused him to be well liked by the ladies.

"I am too far away to be hurt," she retorted, continuing to observe
him with childish surprise.

"But there is also nettle without thorns."

"I am quite poor in botany, but I am willing to accept what you say."

"Please do not go, madame; it is so wonderful to look up to heaven
and you in that blue sky surrounded by those beautiful flowers."

"You are a foreigner, I gather, fom your accent and manner of
speech."

"I am, to my sorrow. I am an army officer who has failed and, as
you doubtless know, I teach fencing and boxing."

"Yes, I have read about you in the newspapers. You are on the path
of glory."

"Miserable glory! But even that is better than stealing. What can one
do? A man must work. Should my plans succeed, I shall go to Paris
and, besides, teach horseback-riding. I am a passionate equestrian, and
you cannot understand how I feel here without my horse. At the sight
of a fine horse I become as sad as a Bedouin. We horsemen alone know
that a horse and a horseman may become one; not a horse's soul in a
human body—naturally!"

"You are a survival of extinct centaurs! And have you found an
Amazon?"

Tkalac noticed how suddenly she paled and then blushed, and his
eyes, darkening, filled with a surprising moisture, which confused her.
He wanted to reply with warmth and great affection, but among the
flowers there remained only a short greeting and a suppressed and
siren-like giggle.

Thus they became acquainted.

In the evening, Tkalac did not wish to go to the city for dinner. He felt ashamed about something. The presence of a stranger embarrassed him. In the evening, in the dark room, lying on a leather sofa which served also as a bed, he felt utterly unhappy and alone. He thought of his dead mother who had spoiled him—her only child; even as a cadet he had had to go to her bed every morning before she arose. His memories turned to his father, a colonel, the real "bruder Jovo," red of face with a white mustache, hard as a provost's stick, wearing his civilian clothes as though they were on a hanger, and those red, dilapidated morning slippers. Even as an officer he dared not light a cigarette in the presence of his father without first asking for permission. He remembered, when taking his departure, the sudden burst of tears which flowed like molten iron, the burning of which he still felt on his cheeks.

"Be righteous, Pero, not being successful as a soldier. Even be a laborer, but remain honest as all your ancestors. Here is a revolver which may be of use to you, even for yourself, in case of any shame you may commit, to yourself or to me. It is better to die honorably than to live in disgrace."

And Tkalac found, in the disorder of his luggage, which was like that of a gipsy's, a photograph, and although it was quite dark, a lady, somewhat gray-haired, stepped out of the picture—she was still of a girlish build, pale, attractive, dark-eyed, with a permanent, sad smile—and this foreigner, after two years of dissipation, pressed this dear, lifeless relic to his lips, weeping like a child before going to sleep, great big tears; and consoled by the shadow of his dead mother, he fell asleep without so much as removing his clothes.

He was abruptly awakened by a tapping on the window. Knowing every emotion except fear, he was greatly surprised and thought he was suffering from hallucination. The tapping on the window was repeated, once, twice, three times. He rose, approached, and noticed a key dangling from a string which had been lowered from the floor above. Fastened to the key was a gingerbread heart bought at a fair. It was then near midnight. Silence reigned everywhere with the exception of the sound of a passing automobile on the street and the singing, accompanied by a mandolin, of some Italian laborers in the distance.

"We were to a fair on the outskirts of France, and remembering that you were alone, I brought you this present. This is not my home. I am a Frenchwoman who considers loneliness a misfortune and really believe that you are very unhappy alone there in the darkness of your gloomy, empty rooms."

"Thank you, thank you," he said, untying the gift, and still under the sway of the memories that had lulled him to sleep. His voice trembled with restrained sobs. Leaning back over the window sill and untying the string, he looked up to her, transformed in the soft and tepid light of the gentle full moon.

"Oh, how beautiful you are, my charming neighbor! If you could only realize what a gift you have made and what happiness you have brought to me by this cake, you would, perhaps, have reconsidered your act, because, in holding this dry heart, I feel as though I had a part of your heart and your soul."

"Ah, speak quietly, lest the neighbors should hear."

"Do not fear! Below live people who are always traveling."

Tkalac then leaped up and with the hand of a gymnast, took hold of the ledge of the outer window, hanging with his back and his whole body over the deep, dark, and black yard as over an abyss.

"Ah, for God's sake! What are you doing, you maniac? Should this old rotted wood give, you would break your neck. I beg you, as a brother, a son, a god, I implore you, enter your room! Have mercy!"

Suddenly she began weeping and his grasp loosening, he almost fell from the window. He felt a warm moisture upon his forehead, like a tear.

"Oh, my dear, charming, kind neighbor, were I not afraid of grieving you, I would this instant dive into the abyss as into a pool of water, because something fell on my forehead like a dewdrop, from that beautiful, refreshing heaven of yours."

"Mercy, mercy! Have mercy on me and yourself, you madman," she proceeded to beg, hardly able, out of great fear and sympathy, to utter a sound. "I will allow you everything, everything, you understand, if you will enter your room and be sensible."

As the wood of the window creaked and broke, she uttered a suppressed screech, while he, with one great swing, fell into his room with a loud and cheerful laugh.

"Until now I hung between you and darkness, between life and death, and now life and happiness look upon me from your moonlit window, my dear beautiful neighbor!"

As before, he lay on the window-sill, looking at her, her shadow, interwoven in the moonlight, surrounded by warm and luminous stars, and she silently observed this new, unusual man. They conversed in silence, with their eyes, for a long time, until finally she said:

"I like you because you have not insisted upon my word and do not ask anything of me. Good night; it is necessary to save those minutes. Good night and thank you, my neighbor!"

"Ah, stay a little longer! Tell me, at least, how I should call you?"

"My Christian name is Valentina."

"Beautiful name! Once upon a time, if I remember correctly, a beautiful princess was thus called."

"Yes, Valentina of Milan. And what is your name?"

"Peter, vulgar Peter."

"Good night, dear Mr. Peter, and 'au revoir.' Soon my husband will come."

"Who?"

"My husband!"

"Eh! Good night!"

Husband! He had never thought of that. Suddenly a cold sweat appeared on his brow. He went out and roamed until dawn around the quiet, moonlit lake, filled with the reflection of bright stars which resembled greenish sparkling fireflies.

He was just about to lie down, when a tap, tap, tap, tap sounded on the window pane. His charming neighbor appeared, just like the dawn, golden and blushing, rose-like and white, in a lace morning gown, her lovely blue eyes still heavy with sleep. She held a little finger to her red, sinful lips, luscious and sanguine, as a sign of silence.

"I found no peace throughout the night," he whispered, pale and weary.

"Do not fear. I understand you. Do not fear, Peter; I am true to you alone!"

And only the trembling of a flower from her breath remained, as Tkalac extended his hungry arms toward the quiet, blooming window, lit by the first rays of the sun, while from above was heard the unpleasant voice of a man, severely rolling his r's.

This was repeated daily for two weeks.

Valentina was very much surprised when Tkalac disappeared without leaving a trace. She became ill from worry and torment. One rainy evening her husband told her in a puzzling way that he was awaiting a very important guest and that they would remain alone. She thought it would be some tiresome business matter, some tedious signing of papers; and while at supper, she almost fainted on hearing Peter's steps on the upper floor. Notwithstanding all her questioning, her husband refused to explain this unexpected visit.

Like a thunderbolt from a clear sky, the servant announced that "Monsieur Kalak" sends his card and wishes to enter.

She did not recognize him at first; so emaciated had he become in the few days. Her husband arose, changed the expression on his bloated, otherwise quite pleasing face adorned with spectacles and a blond mustache, wiped his bald head and wheezed harshly, like one suffering from asthma. The visitor bowed courteously and in military fashion, kissed with visible embarrassment the hand of his hostess, sat down, and, after a brief, unpleasant silence, addressed his host.

"I am very glad, Monsieur Colignon, that you received me so gallantly, and, as I see, you have not advised madame regarding my coming. If there still exists some knighthood these days, it consists in that honorable and sensible people eliminate every unpleasantness with as little trouble as possible."

"Very well, very well," broke in the host, breathing heavily. "I have thoroughly inquired and learned all about you today, and I know that your affairs are in good condition and that you have a glorious future before you, though, relatively, very difficult. As a man of affairs and business, I guess your intention and the cause for your presence. You have no acquaintance here nor any countrymen of yours; in your native country you have no reason, presumably, to look for help. Therefore,

as your neighbor, you wish to turn to me, offering no more security than
your energy and your indubitable honesty. You have begged me for the
presence of my wife to show me that in such a delicate matter you fear
not even such a—pardon!—embarassing witness. I have, sir, no children from heaven, and although a man of means, I sympathize with
everything young and fit for life."

"But pardon me."

"Allow me, allow me, my dear 'Kalak.' I am really not as wealthy as
they say, but I will always have enough to help you in your eventual establishment. It is known to me that your institution prospers excellently,
and I feel proud that you should, notwithstanding your great acquaintance with foreign, especially Slavic, aristocracy, turn to me, an ordinary
citizen and business man."

"You are absolutely wrong, my dear neighbor," the young man gasped
with difficulty, and paled as though he were going to fall from his chair.

Deep, asthmatic breathing. The ticking of a clock mingled with the
wild, loud throbbing of hearts. Valentina's eyes became glassy.

"From your words, dear neighbor, I see that you are better than I
ever dreamed, and my mission, therefore, is so much more painful and
distressing. If I had known this, I never would have determined to
undertake this step," came from Tkalac as from a tomb, and Colignon
began to look around fearfully, thinking that he must deal with a dangerous, gorilla-like lunatic.

"Well, what is it? What is it?" he breathed with great effort, meantime kicking his petrified wife under cover of the table to convey his
alarm. She did not feel his nudges, so paralyzed was her moral and
physical strength.

"No, sir, I have not come for money, but I came for her, for your
wife, for Valentina, for my dear——"

"Are you sane?" sighed the host, rushing toward the window as if
wanting to cry "Fire." Tkalac almost brought him back to his chair
with his burning, feverish gaze.

"Yes, sir, you have spoken correctly. I am an honest man, so honest
that I am unable to lie, and I would kill and I would die before stealing
another man's wife, robbing the love that belongs to another, especially
of such a sympathetic man as you. I love your wife, your wife loves
me, and I came tonight to tell you this honestly and openly, and to take
her with me," continued Tkalac, placing a revolver on the table. "Here,
sir, do not fear! I am not a lunatic, I am not a criminal, and you may,
if you find no other exit, take this gun and shoot me here like an ordinary vagabond and burglar."

And again there was a painful, grievous, fatal silence; difficult, asthmatic breathing, then the ticking of watches as of hearts, and the beating of hearts as of watches.

"Why, what do I hear? Is all this possible; tell me, tell me, Valentina?
Why, it is not, it is not, it cannot be true; say it isn't, Valentina, my dear
little Valentina," sobbed the husband.

"Peter Tkalac, peer of Zvečaj castle, is poor, has no more a uniform, but he remains an officer and never tells lies!" The young man, with his chest expanded, spoke energetically, as if commanding his troops. Valentina's glassy eyes revived; slowly, as if awakening, she arose and stepped toward Peter and said, looking at him from head to foot:

"Whether you are Austrian, Hungarian, Slovak, or what not, you should know that I am a Frenchwoman, and that in France it is not customary for lovers to denounce their sweethearts to their husbands. Monsieur Colignon, I have in fact liked his type, although I have not given myself to him; but from now on I hate him deeply and let that foreigner consider himself slapped. Good-by, gentlemen!"—and she swept from the room.

"Noble sir, Monsieur 'Kalak,' do you need any help? I am at your service," said Colignon to the young man, who staggered out of the room as though he were drunk and feeling like a whipped cur.

The servant ran after him into the hallway.

"Pardon, sir, you have forgotten your revolver!"

I. L. CARAGIALE

The Easter Torch

Ion Luca Caragiale (1853–1912) had no schooling and did newspaper and office work before he became director general of the Bucharest National Theatre. He inherited a fortune and spent his last years in Berlin, living comfortably and devoting himself to music. Some of his plays are *False Accusation, Carnival Adventures* and *Lost Letter*. [From *Roumanian Stories*; translated by Lucy Byng.]

LEIBA ZIBAL, MINE HOST OF PODENI, was sitting, lost in thought, by a table placed in the shadow in front of the inn; he was awaiting the arrival of the coach which should have come some time ago; it was already an hour behind time.

The story of Zibal's life is a long and cheerless one: when he is taken with one of his feverish attacks it is a diversion for him to analyze one by one the most important events in that life.

Huckster, seller of hardware, jobber, between whiles even rougher work perhaps, seller of old clothes, then tailor, and bootblack in a dingy alley in Jassy; all this had happened to him since the accident whereby he lost his situation as office boy in a big wine-shop. Two porters were carrying a barrel down to a cellar under the supervision of the lad Zibal. A difference arose between them as to the division of their earnings. One of them seized a piece of wood that lay at hand and struck his comrade on the forehead, who fell to the ground covered in blood. At the sight of the wild deed the boy gave a cry of alarm, but the wretch hurried through the yard, and in passing gave the lad a blow. Zibal fell to the ground fainting with fear. After several months in bed he returned to his master, only to find his place filled up. Then began a hard struggle for existence, which increased in difficulty after his marriage with Sura. Their hard lot was borne with patience. Sura's brother, the innkeeper of Podeni, died; the inn passed into Zibal's hands, and he carried on the business on his own account.

Here he had been for the last five years. He had saved a good bit of money and collected good wine—a commodity that will always be worth good money. Leiba had escaped from poverty, but they were all three sickly, himself, his wife, and his child, all victims of malaria, and men are rough and quarrelsome in Podeni—slanderous, scoffers, revilers, accused of vitriol throwing. And the threats! A threat is very terrible to a character that bends easily beneath every blow. The thought of a threat worked more upon Leiba's nerves than did his attacks of fever.

"Oh, wretched Gentile!" he thought, sighing.

This "wretched" referred to Gheorghe—wherever he might be!— a man between whom and himself a most unpleasant affair had arisen.

Gheorghe came to the inn one autumn morning, tired with his walk; he was just out of hospital—so he said—and was looking for work. The innkeeper took him into his service. But Gheorghe showed himself to be a brutal and a sullen man. He swore continually, and muttered to himself alone in the yard. He was a bad servant, lazy and insolent, and he stole. He threatened his mistress one day when she was pregnant, cursing her, and striking her on the stomach. Another time he set a dog on little Strul.

Leiba paid him his wages at once, and dismissed him. But Gheorghe would not go: he asserted with violence that he had been engaged for a year. Then the innkeeper sent to the town hall to get guards to remove him.

Gheorghe put his hand swiftly to his breast, crying:

"Jew!" and began to rail at his master. Unfortunately a cart full of customers arived at that moment. Gheorghe began to grin, saying: "What frightened you, Master Leiba? Look, I am going now." Then bending fiercely over the bar toward Leiba, who drew back as far as possible, he whispered: "Expect me on Easter Eve; we'll crack red eggs together, Jew! You will know then what I have done to you, and I will answer for it."

Just then, customers entered the inn.

"May we meet in good health at Easter, Master Leiba!" added Gheorghe as he left.

Leiba went to the town hall, then to the sub-prefecture to denounce the threatener, begging that he might be watched. The sub-prefect was a lively young man; he first accepted Leiba's humble offering, then he began to laugh at the timid Jew, and make fun of him. Leiba tried hard to make him realize the gravity of the situation, and pointed out how isolated the house stood from the village, and even from the high road. But the sub-prefect, with a more serious air, advised him to be prudent; he must not mention such things, for, truly, it would arouse the desire to do them in a village where men were rough and poor, ready to break the law.

A few days later an official with two riders came to see him about Gheorghe; he was "wanted" for some crime.

If only Leiba had been able to put up with him until the arrival of these men! In the meanwhile, no one knew the whereabouts of Gheorghe. Although this had happened some time ago, Gheorghe's appearance, the movement as though he would have drawn something from his breast, and the threatening words had all remained deeply impressed upon the mind of the terror-stricken man. How was it that that memory remained so clear?

It was Easter Eve.

From the top of the hill, from the village lying among the lakes about two miles away, came the sound of church bells. One hears in a strange way when one is feverish, now so loud, now so far away. The coming night was the night before Easter, the night of the fulfillment of Gheorghe's promise.

"But perhaps they have caught him by now!"

Moreover, Zibal only means to stay at Podeni till next quarter-day. With his capital he could open a good business in Jassy. In a town, Leiba would regain his health, he would go near the police station—he could treat the police, the commissionaires, the sergeants. Who pays well gets well guarded.

In a large village, the night brings noise and light, not darkness and silence as in the isolated valley of Podeni. There is an inn in Jassy— there in the corner, just the place for a shop! An inn where girls sing all night long, a Café Chantant. What a gay and rousing life! There, at all hours of the day and night, officials and their girls, and other dirty Christians will need entertainment.

What is the use of bothering oneself here where business keeps falling off, especially since the coming of the railway which only skirts the marshes at some distance?

"Leiba," calls Sura from within, "the coach is coming, one can hear the bells."

The Podeni valley is a ravine enclosed on all sides by wooded hills. In a hollow toward the south lie several deep pools caused by the springs which rise in the hills; above them lie some stretches of ground covered with bushes and rushes. Leiba's hotel stands in the center of the valley, between the pools and the more elevated ground to the north; it is an old stone building, strong as a small fortress: although the ground is marshy, the walls and cellars are very dry.

At Sura's voice Leiba raises himself painfully from his chair, stretching his tired limbs; he takes a long look toward the east; not a sign of the diligence.

"It is not coming; you imagined it," he replied to his wife, and sat down again.

Very tired, the man crossed his arms on the table, and laid his head upon them, for it was burning. The warmth of the spring sun began to strike the surface of the marshes and a pleasant lassitude enveloped his nerves, and his thoughts began to run riot as a sick man's will, gradually taking on strange forms and colors.

Gheorghe—Easter Eve—burglars—Jassy—the inn in the center of the town—a gay restaurant doing well—restored health.

And he dozed.

Sura and the child went without a great deal up here.

Leiba went to the door of the inn and looked out onto the road.

On the main road there was a good deal of traffic, an unceasing noise of wheels accompanied by the rhythmic sound of horses' hoofs trotting upon the smooth asphalt.

But suddenly the traffic stopped, and from Copou a group of people could be seen approaching, gesticulating and shouting excitedly.

The crowd appeared to be escorting somebody: soldiers, a guard and various members of the public. Curious onlookers appeared at every door of the inn.

"Ah," thought Leiba, "they have laid hands on a thief."

The procession drew nearer. Sura detached herself from the others, and joined Leiba on the steps of the inn.

"What is it, Sura?" he asked.

"A madman escaped from Golia."

"Let us close the inn so that he cannot get at us."

"He is bound now, but a while ago he escaped. He fought with all the soldiers. A rough Gentile in the crowd pushed a Jew against the madman and he bit him on the cheek."

Leiba could see well from the steps; from the stair below Sura watched with the child in her arms.

It was, in fact, a violent lunatic held on either side by two men: his wrists were tightly bound over each other by a thick cord. He was a man of gigantic stature with a head like a bull, thick black hair, and hard, grizzled beard and whiskers. Through his shirt, which had been torn in the struggle, his broad chest was visible, covered, like his head, with a mass of hair. His feet were bare; his mouth was full of blood, and he continually spat out hair which he had bitten from the Jew's beard.

Everyone stood still. Why? The guards unbound the lunatic's hands. The crowd drew to one side, leaving a large space around him. The madman looked about him, and his fierce glance rested upon Zibal's doorway; he gnashed his teeth, made a dash for the three steps, and in a flash, seizing the child's head in his right hand and Sura's in his left, he knocked them together with such force that they cracked like so many fresh eggs. A sound was heard, a scrunching impossible to describe, as the two skulls cracked together.

Leiba, with bursting heart, like a man who falls from an immense height, tried to cry out: "The whole world abandons me to the tender mercies of a madman!" But his voice refused to obey him.

"Get up, Jew!" cried someone, beating loudly upon the table with a stick.

"It's a bad joke," said Sura from the doorway of the inn, "thus to frighten the man out of his sleep, you stupid peasant!"

"What has scared you, Jew?" asked the wag, laughing. "You sleep in the afternoon, eh? Get up, customers are coming, the mail coach is arriving."

And, according to his silly habit which greatly irritated the Jew, he tried to take his arm and tickle him.

"Let me alone!" cried the innkeeper, drawing back and pushing him away with all his might. "Can you not see that I am ill? Leave me in peace."

The coach arrived at last, nearly three hours late. There were two passengers who seated themselves together with the driver, whom they had invited to share their table.

The conversation of the travelers threw a light upon recent events. At the highest posting station, a robbery with murder had been committed during the night in the inn of a Jew. The murdered innkeeper should have provided a change of horses. The thieves had taken them, and while other horses were being found in the village the curious travelers could examine the scene of the crime at their leisure. Five victims! But the details! From just seeing the ruined house one could believe it to have been some cruel vendetta or the work of some religious fanatic. In stories of sectarian fanaticism one heard occasionally of such extravagant crimes.

Leiba shook with a violent access of fever and listened aghast.

What followed must have undoubtedly filled the driver with respect. The young passengers were two students, one of philosophy, the other of medicine; they were returning to amuse themselves in their native town. They embarked upon a violent academic discussion upon crime and its causes, and, to give him his due, the medical student was better informed than the philosopher.

Atavism; alcoholism and its pathological consequences; defective birth; deformity; Paludism; then nervous disorders! Such and such conquest of modern science—but the case of reversion to type! Darwin, Häckel, Lombroso. At the case of reversion to type, the driver opened wide his eyes in which shone a profound admiration for the conquests of modern science.

"It is obvious," added the medical student. "The so-called criminal proper, taken as a type, has unusually long arms, and very short feet, a flat and narrow forehead, and a much developed occiput. To the experienced eye his face is characteristically coarse and bestial; he is rudimentary man: he is, as I say, a beast which has but lately got used to standing on its hind legs only, and to raising its head toward the sky, toward the light."

At the age of twenty, after so much excitement, and after a good repast with wine so well vinted and so well matured as Leiba's, a phrase with a lyrical touch came well even from a medical student.

Between his studies of Darwin and Lombroso, the enthusiastic youth had found time to imbibe a little Schopenhauer—"toward the sky, toward the light!"

Leiba was far from understanding these "illuminating" ideas. Perhaps for the first time did such grand words and fine subtleties of thought find expression in the damp atmosphere of Podeni. But that which he understood better than anything, much better even than the speaker, was the striking illustration of the theory: the case of reversion to type he knew in flesh and blood, it was the portrait of Gheorghe. This portrait, which had just been drawn in broad outline only, he could fill in perfectly in his own mind, down to the most minute details.

The coach had gone. Leiba followed it with his eyes until, turning to the left, it was lost to sight round the hill. The sun was setting behind the ridge to the west, and the twilight began to weave soft shapes in the Podeni valley.

The gloomy innkeeper began to turn over in his mind all that he had heard. In the dead of night, lost in the darkness, a man, two women and two young children, torn without warning from the gentle arms of sleep by the hands of beasts with human faces, and sacrificed one after the other, the agonized cries of the children cut short by the dagger ripping open their bodies, the neck slashed with a hatchet, the dull rattle in the throat with each gush of blood through the wound; and the last victim, half-distraught, in a corner, witness of the scene, and awaiting his turn. A condition far worse than execution was that of the Jew without protection in the hands of the Gentile— skulls too fragile for such fierce hands as those of the madman just now

Leiba's lips, parched with fever, trembled as they mechanically followed his thoughts. A violent shivering fit seized him; he entered the porch of the inn with tottering steps.

"There is no doubt," thought Sura, "Leiba is not at all well, he is really ill; Leiba has got 'ideas' into his head. Is not that easy to understand after all he has been doing these last days, and especially after what he has done today?"

He had had the inn closed before the lights were lit, to remain so until the Sabbath was ended. Three times had some customers knocked at the door, calling to him, in familiar voices, to undo it. He had trembled at each knock and had stood still, whispering softly and with terrified eyes:

"Do not move—I want no Gentiles here."

Then he had passed under the portico, and had listened at the top of the stone steps by the door which was secured with a bar of wood. He shook so that he could scarcely stand, but he would not rest. The most distressing thing of all was that he had answered Sura's persistent questions sharply, and had sent her to bed, ordering her to put out the light at once. She had protested meanwhile, but the man had repeated the order curtly enough, and she had had unwillingly to submit, resigning herself to postponing to a later date any explanation of his conduct.

Sura had put out the lamp, had gone to bed, and now slept by the side of Strul.

The woman was right. Leiba was really ill.

Night had fallen. For a long time Leiba had been sitting, listening by the doorway which gave onto the passage.

What is that?

Indistinct sounds came from the distance—horses trotting, the noise of heavy blows, mysterious and agitated conversations. The effort of listening intently in the solitude of the night sharpens the sense of hearing: when the eye is disarmed and powerless, the ear seems to struggle to assert its power.

But it was not imagination. From the road leading hither from the main road came the sound of approaching horses. Leiba rose, and tried to get nearer to the big door in the passage. The door was firmly shut by a heavy bar of wood across it, the ends of which ran into holes in the wall. At his first step the sand scrunching under his slippers made an indiscreet noise. He drew his feet from the slippers, and waited in the corner. Then, without a sound that could be heard by an unexpectant ear, he went to the door in the corridor, just as the riders passed in front of it at a walking pace. They were speaking very low to each other, but not so low but that Leiba could quite well catch these words:

"He has gone to bed early."

"Supposing he has gone away?"

"His turn will come; but I should have liked—"

No more was intelligible; the men were already some distance away.

To whom did these words refer? Who had gone to bed or gone away? Whose turn would come another time? Who would have liked something? And what was it he wanted? What did they want on that by-road—a road only used by anyone wishing to find the inn?

An overwhelming sense of fatigue seemed to overcome Leiba.

Could it be Gheorghe?

Leiba felt as if his strength was giving way, and he sat down by the door. Eager thoughts chased each other through his head, he could not think clearly or come to any decision.

Terrified, he reëntered the inn, struck a match, and lighted a small petroleum lamp.

It was an apology for a light; the wick was turned so low as to conceal the flame in the brass receiver; only by means of the opening round the receiver could some of the vertical shafts of light penetrate into a gloom that was like the darkness of death—all the same it was sufficient to enable him to see well into the familiar corners of the inn. Ah! How much less is the difference between the sun and the tiniest spark of light than between the latter and the gloom of blindness.

The clock on the wall ticked audibly. The monotonous sound irritated Leiba. He put his hand over the swinging pendulum, and stayed its movement.

His throat was parched. He was thirsty. He washed a small glass in a three-legged tub by the side of the bar and tried to pour some good brandy out of a decanter; but the mouth of the decanter began to clink loudly on the edge of the glass. This noise was still more irritating. A second attempt, in spite of his efforts to conquer his weakness, met with no greater success.

Then, giving up the idea of the glass, he let it fall gently into the water, and drank several times out of the decanter. After that he pushed the decanter back into its place; as it touched the shelf it made an alarming clatter. For a moment he waited, appalled by such a catastrophe. Then he took the lamp, and placed it in the niche of the window which lighted the passage: the door, the pavement, and the wall which ran at right angles to the passage, were illuminated by almost imperceptible streaks of light.

He seated himself near the doorway and listened intently.

From the hill came the sound of bells ringing in the Resurrection morning. It meant that midnight was past, day was approaching. Ah! If only the rest of this long night might pass as had the first half!

The sound of sand trodden underfoot! But he was sitting in the corner, and had not stirred; a second noise, followed by many such. There could be no doubt someone was outside, here, quite near. Leiba rose, pressing his hand to his heart, and trying to swallow a suspicious lump in his throat.

There were several people outside—and Gheorghe! Yes, he was there; yes, the bells on the hill had rung the Resurrection.

They spoke softly:

"I tell you he is asleep. I saw when the lights went out."

"Good, we will take the whole nest."

"I will undo the door, I understand how it works. We must cut an opening—the beam runs along here."

He seemed to feel the touch of the men outside as they measured the distance on the wood. A big gimlet could be heard boring its way through the dry bark of the old oak. Leiba felt the need of support; he steadied himself against the door with his left hand while he covered his eyes with the right.

Then, through some inexplicable play of the senses, he heard, from within, quite loud and clear:

"Leiba! Here comes the coach."

It was surely Sura's voice. A warm ray of hope! A moment of joy!

It was just another dream! But Leiba drew his left hand quickly back; the point of the tool, piercing the wood at that spot, had pricked the palm of his hand.

Was there any chance of escape? Absurd! In his burning brain the image of the gimlet took inconceivable dimensions. The instrument, turning continually, grew indefinitely, and the opening became larger and larger, large enough at last to enable the monster to step through the round aperture without having to bend. All that surged through such a brain transcends the thoughts of man; life rose to such a pitch of exaltation that everything seen, heard, felt, appeared to be enormous, the sense of proportion became chaotic.

The work outside was continued with method and perseverance. Four times in succession Leiba had seen the sharp steel tooth pierce through to his side and draw back again.

"Now give me the saw," said Gheorghe.

The narrow end of a saw appeared through the first hole, and started to work with quick regular movements. The plan was easy to understand; four holes in four corners of one panel; the saw made cuts between them; the gimlet was driven well home in the center of the panel; when the piece became totally separated from the main body of the wood it was pulled out; through the opening thus made a strong hand inserted itself, seized the bar, pushed it to one side and—Gentiles are in Leiba's house.

In a few moments, this same gimlet would cause the destruction of Leiba and his domestic hearth. The two executioners would hold the victim prostrate on the ground, and Gheorghe, with heel upon his body, would slowly bore the gimlet into the bone of the living breast as he had done into the dead wood, deeper and deeper, till it reached the heart, silencing its wild beatings and pinning it to the spot.

Leiba broke into a cold sweat; the man was overcome by his own imagination, and sank softly to his knees as though life were ebbing from him under the weight of this last horror, overwhelmed by the thought that he must abandon now all hope of saving himself.

"Yes! Pinned to the spot," he said, despairingly. "Yes! Pinned to the spot."

He stayed a moment, staring at the light by the window. For some moments he stood aghast, as though in some other world, then he repeated with quivering eyelids:

"Yes! Pinned to the spot."

Suddenly a strange change took place in him, a complete revulsion of feeling; he ceased to tremble, his despair disappeared, and his face, so discomposed by the prolonged crisis, assumed an air of strange serenity. He straightened himself with the decision of a strong and healthy man who makes for an easy goal.

The line between the two upper punctures of the panel was finished. Leiba went up, curious to see the working of the tool. His confidence became more pronounced. He nodded his head as though to say: "I still have time."

The saw cut the last fiber near the hole toward which it was working, and began to saw between the lower holes.

"There are still three," thought Leiba, and with the caution of the most experienced burglar he softly entered the inn. He searched under the bar, picked up something, and went out again as he entered, hiding the object he had in his hand as though he feared somehow the walls might betray him, and went back on tiptoe to the door.

Something terrible had happened; the work outside had ceased— there was nothing to be heard.

"What is the matter? Has he gone? What has happened?" flashed through the mind of the man inside. He bit his lower lip at such a thought, full of bitter disappointment.

"Ha, ha!" It was an imaginary deception; the work began again, and he followed it with the keenest interest, his heart beating fast. His decision was taken, he was tormented by an incredible desire to see the thing finished.

"Quicker!" he thought, with impatience. "Quicker!"

Again the sound of bells ringing on the hill.

"Hurry up, old fellow, the daylight will catch us!" said a voice outside, as thought impelled by the will of the man within.

The work was pushed on rapidly. Only a few more movements and all the punctures in the panel would be united.

At last!

Gently the drill carried out the four-sided piece of wood. A large and supple hand was thrust in; but before it reached the bars it sought two screams were heard, while, with great force, Leiba enclosed it with the free end of the noose, which was round a block fixed to the cellar door.

The trap was ingeniously contrived: a long rope fastened round a block of wood; lengthwise, at the place where the sawn panel had disappeared, was a spring-ring which Leiba held open with his left hand, while at the same time his right hand held the other end taut. At the psychological moment he sprang the ring, and rapidly seizing the free end of the rope with both hands he pulled the whole arm inside by a supreme effort.

In a second the operation was complete. It was accompanied by two cries, one of despair, the other of triumph: the hand is "pinned to the spot." Footsteps were heard retreating rapidly: Gheorghe's companions were abandoning to Leiba the prey so cleverly caught.

The Jew hurried into the inn, took the lamp and with a decided movement turned up the wick as high as it would go: the light concealed by the metal receiver rose gay and victorious, restoring definite outlines to the nebulous forms around.

Zibal went into the passage with the lamp. The burglar groaned terribly; it was obvious from the stiffening of his arm that he had given up the useless struggle. The hand was swollen, the fingers were curved as though they would seize something. The Jew placed the lamp near it—a shudder, the fever is returning. He moved the light quite close, until, trembling, he touched the burglar's hand with the burning chimney; a violent convulsion of the fingers was followed by a dull groan. Leiba was startled at the sight of this phenomenon.

Leiba trembled—his eyes betrayed a strange exaltation. He burst into a shout of laughter which shook the empty corridor and resounded in the inn.

Day was breaking.

Sura woke up suddenly—in her sleep she seemed to hear a terrible moaning. Leiba was not in the room. All that had happened previously returned to her mind. Something terrible had taken place. She jumped out of bed and lighted the candle. Leiba's bed had not been disturbed. He had not been to bed at all.

Where was he? The woman glanced out of the window; on the hill in front shone a little group of small bright lights, they flared and jumped, now they died away, now, once more, soared upwards. They told of the Resurrection. Sura undid the window; then she could hear groans from down by the door. Terrified, she hurried down the stairs. The corridor was lighted up. As she emerged through the doorway, the woman was astonished by a horrible sight.

Upon a wooden chair, his elbows on his knees, his beard in his hand, sat Leiba. Like a scientist, who, by mixing various elements, hopes to surprise one of nature's subtle secrets which has long escaped and worried him, Leiba kept his eyes fixed upon some hanging object, black and shapeless, under which, upon another chair of convenient height, there burnt a big torch. He watched, without turning a hair, the process of decomposition of the hand which most certainly would not have spared him. He did not hear the groans of the unhappy being outside: he was more interested, at present, in watching than in listening.

He followed with eagerness each contortion, every strange convulsion of the fingers till one by one they became powerless. They were like the legs of a beetle which contract and stretch, waving in agitated movement, vigorously, then slower and slower until they lie paralyzed by the play of some cruel child.

It was over. The roasted hand swelled slowly and remained motionless. Sura gave a cry.

"Leiba!"

He made a sign to her not to disturb him. A greasy smell of burnt flesh pervaded the passage: a crackling and small explosions were heard.

"Leiba! What is it?" repeated the woman.

It was broad day. Sura stretched forward and withdrew the bar. The door opened outwards, dragging with it Gheorghe's body, suspended by the right arm. A crowd of villagers, all carrying lighted torches, invaded the premises.

"What is it? What is it?"

They soon understood what had happened. Leiba, who up to now had remained motionless, rose gravely to his feet. He made room for himself to pass, quietly pushing the crowd to one side.

"How did it happen, Jew?" asked someone.

"Leiba Zibal," said the innkeeper in a loud voice, and with a lofty gesture, "goes to Jassy to tell the Rabbi that Leiba Zibal is a Jew no longer. Leiba Zibal is a Christian—for Leiba Zibal has lighted a torch for Christ."

And the man moved slowly up the hill, toward the sunrise, like the prudent traveler who knows that the long journey is not achieved with hasty steps.

ANGEL
KARALITCHEFF

The Little Coin

Angel Karalitcheff, the Bulgarian short story writer, was born in 1902 in Straz-higga. His first book was published in 1924, and he has written several books for children. Until 1939 he was with the Agricultural Cooperative Society in Sofia. [From *Best European Short Stories, 1928.*]

"TELL MY FORTUNE."

Two burning black eyes waited to catch the secret which Grandpa Gheno was about to reveal. Grandpa Gheno sees through the years, through the clouds and the mountains, beyond unknown seas. He can tell you where your road is going and how you will travel along it —whether on a fiery horse or a limping donkey.

Two young eyes implored him.

The fire began to flame up, yellow sparks flew about, and the branches of the old willow, which had bent its trunk out over the gushing spring, trembled in alarm. Black leaves began to rock about in the clear water of the stone trough.

Evening had fallen upon the plain of Belin. Above the place where the sun had gone down there appeared a yellow star, resembling a little coin dropped from the necklace of Jesus' mother. Little crickets began to chirp over the drooping wheat heads. Along the great road which led toward the level land of Dobroudga a white head cloth was seen and a bright-colored baby's hammock, a child's voice was heard, a little black head showed itself and two eyes popped wide open. The upright slats on the sides of a heavy hay rack rattled, and the backs of a pair of big water buffaloes rose and fell. In a little while, all these and the broad white road sank beneath the warm waves of the grain fields. The blackened peaks of the Balkan mountains began to fall away. The woods and hills tucked themselves out of sight somewhere or other. The trees, scattered throughout the fields, lay down to sleep on the soft blanket of ripening wheat. Nothing was left but the silent green mist over the plain. In the midst of the plain was the willow tree bending over the trough filled with scum-covered water and the little grass plot lighted up by a vigorous fire. Beside the fire a group of girl harvesters had lain down, worn out by their long journey. They were all sound asleep, as if they had just taken a bath. Only two of them looked up at the evening star making its way across the black sky, and as they listened to the whispering of the wheat stalks a sweet sadness melted in their eyes. They asked the wakeful star to drop low over the village camping grounds when the secret trysting hour was passing above their village beyond the mountain, where "the Huts" are. That's the place where the black-eyed horse boys sleep. The girls wanted the star to creep along the thick capes of the sleepers and to say: "Greetings from the harvester girls."

Old Grandpa Gheno, the girls' supervisor, smoked as he sat half reclining by the fire with his heavy, much-decorated coat thrown about him. On her knees before him was Vella, the youngest of the harvesters. She had never been to unknown parts before and was so wild that she couldn't get her fill of looking at things she had heard about; nor was she able to go far enough to suit her or to sleep when the night came. She ran before the others with bare feet and flowing hair like a wild goat. She scampered up all the hills which had stood along the road since time immemorial—so as to find a high enough place from which to look out over the great fields and the villages submerged in the yellow laughter of summer time. Her joy knew no bounds of a morning when she came across a white stork as it was slowly walking along the stones and bending its head over the broad river. No stork ever came down to her village.

This evening Grandpa Gheno was telling her fortune. With her hand outstretched she waited, like a lamb on its first St. George's day when the shepherd fixes his gaze upon it as he opens the little gate of the fold early in the morning. The white lamb waits and wonders whether the master will throw it over his shoulder and carry it off to serve as a holiday feast or whether he will turn it out to frolic over the broad plain.

Vella held her breath while the old man bit his walnut pipe, elevated his right brow, squinted his eyes, touched the extended brown arm and, wrapped in thought, read the girl's fortune.

"Tell me what's written."

"Wait."

"Just see what an awful man you are, don't torment me that way."

"Don't outrun your fortune teller, little chicky. Let me take a good look. It's not just words that I have to read, but your fate. Hold on now, don't pout or I'll not tell you a single thing. Here, let me see your eyes! That's right. Black. Awfully black and full of fire," softly whispered the old man to himself. Then he grew silent, gave himself up to thought for a moment and went on:

"There's no getting away from that. In the end everything comes down to a little coin."

"What kind of a little coin, Uncle?"

"A little piece of white, silver money."

"Where is it?"

"On your neck, little Vella. It contains your fortune. You were born on a lucky hour, you've got the little coin and it'll bring you the best of everything. Who put it on your necklace, your mother?"

"Yes, do you remember her?"

"Do I remember her? Yes, I do, how could I help it? Why she and I, who . . ."

"What?"

"Nothing. Your mother once wore the little coin. One fall my grandfather—Lord, have mercy on his soul—dug it up as he was plowing at Beliabreg. The little silver kostadinka glistened in the furrow. He took it to the priest, Petko—you don't remember him—that was in Turkish times, and after he looked at it he said to grandfather, 'Hang onto that, old fellow, you've found good luck.' My grandmother wore it and when she died she gave it to mamma. Since we didn't have any sister, mamma gave it to our youngest brother, Kolyou, your daddy."

The night grew darker and darker and bright dewdrops began to glisten on the ends of the tiny wheat beards, drooping over the girls' heads.

"Have they gone to sleep?"

"They are asleep."

Like a watchful chieftain, the old man looked over the girls stretched on the ground; before the break of dawn he would start off with them on the way to Dobroudga in order to harvest its wheat. The girls from "the Huts" were warm as they slept with half opened, blistered lips. The soft yellow light of the fire bathed their dark faces and their hard chemises of village homespun which creaked from their deep breathing.

"Why aren't you asleep?"

"I'm not sleepy. Say, are there many little coins like mine?"

"No. Yours is the only one on earth and lucky is the person who wears it."

"Why?"

"Because it wasn't mine."

Vella laid her head on his knee.

"Was mamma an unusual girl?"

"The most unusual that ever was!"

Grandpa Gheno swallowed hard and his eyes grew lively. Something from long ago began to burn in them. Something that had passed and would never come back. For the bent willow will never grow young again.

"Do I look like her?" asked Vella.

"Like your mother?"

The old man leaned over and felt the warm breath of a young life with beating wings. A shudder went over him; the same. An image of her mother, as if she and the girl were two drops of water.

"Vellie—"

He felt like telling her here on the very spot.

"Listen, child, I have gone over the hill. Your mother passed away long ago. Didn't she ever tell you about me?"

"No, Uncle."

"No? That was right. That was like your mother, she always kept things to herself. She kept that to herself, too. What a lot of water has passed under the bridge, what great rocks have been overturned; but that night, how well I remember it, as though it had just happened yesterday."

"What?"

"Why, that. There at that very water trough. You must remember that trough. You're young. Maybe you'll pass here again sometime. It was here that I lost everything. Under this same old willow. Hey, look how it's back's broken. It's so old it's forgotten its age. But it was young then. Its branches were tender and soft. They were singing songs. All around the Belin plain was burning with yellow wheat. It always seems to me that the wheat was bigger then. If you rubbed a head out in your hand, it had grains as big as hazel-nuts. All along the pathways between the fields heavy blackberries hung down, each one like a bunch of grapes. You could gather as many as you liked."

He became silent.

"When you come back past this place may you never be forgiven if you don't stop and say, 'God, have mercy on him.'"

"On who?"

"On me."

"What do you mean by that?"

"Nothing. Go to sleep."

The old man stroked her on the forehead and lost himself in his *nothing*.

That evening he and Kolyou had taken out the two black horses. The animals stood before them with backs shining like tar. The two young brothers got on them. The older boy was happy, burning with joy. The younger one knew nothing about what they were going to do. And before they had given the first lash to their horses the younger one's began to paw with its left foot. That's not a good sign. If your horse takes to pawing with its left foot, turn around and go back home.

Gheno and Kolyou sailed across the fields. The moon sailed over them, stars fell into the wheat.

Kolyou asked him, "Where you going, brother?"

"We're going to steal a girl from Cherkeuvee village."

"Which girl?"

"Guess."

"Which house does she live in?"

"In the big house across from the church."

"Rada Vulyouva?"

"Yes."

Kolyou at once reined up his horse and turned around.

"Stop, brother, let's go back."

Gheno laughed at him derisively.

"Did little Kolyou lose his nerve? All right, let him wait outside the village. I'll do the job myself. Don't stop me for the night'll soon be over."

And he turned round to look at his brother. The younger boy's eyes were like two glowing coals, like the eyes of a wolf. His right hand was plucking hair from his horse's mane. "Are you coming along?"

Gheno started off by himself, but he had hardly gone a hundred steps when the youngster flew past him like a cyclone, shouting, "Come on-n-n!"

"That's the stuff."

The fire began to go out. The little plot of grass grew dark. The willow got black and the dark faces of the girls got black. For a long time Grandpa Gheno poked about in the fire with a half burnt stick. The girl had closed her eyes, she had gone to sleep. The old man wanted to tell her the rest in a whisper but didn't dare. He bent over until he almost touched her forehead and looked at her for a long time. What was she dreaming about?

The willow began to rustle. Another memory stirred.

When they came back she was thrown over the horse in front of him—Vella's mother. They stopped here on this grassy plot. Their horses were trembling, all covered with foam. They turned them loose to graze. Kolyou went along after them in the moonlight, he disappeared and the two were left by themselves, he and she. He remembers her as all ashudder that first night. Her neart was in a flutter and so were her eyes in which the stars bathed themselves. He sat down beside her and caressed her forehead with his hand. Her head was hot. It was baked as though by a fire which had just been stirred up. The young willow had thrown a heavy shadow over them and enshrouded them. Gheno didn't know what to talk to her about. She was just about to become his bride but the fellow didn't know how to start a conversation with her. He slowly put his arms about her and bent his head down upon her breast. He felt a cold disk on his forehead. He ran his fingers over her necklace and found it to be of black beads with a little coin in the middle. He looked at it and started—it was his mother's. Something in his breast gave way.

"Where did you get it?" he asked.

There was no answer.

"Tell me, who gave it to you?"

Instead of answering him, she threw herself wildly on his neck, embraced him, poured her warm breath over him, intoxicated him. Oblivion seized upon him, he sank away. Never had he felt such a burning within him. And somehow or other, he went to sleep.

When he awoke and sought her with his hands she was not there. He jumped up and looked around. On every side desolation. The shadow of the willow had revolved to another place. The water gushed from the spring with an alarmed murmur. What had happened? He couldn't get his bearings. His horse raised its head, looked about and snorted. Kolyou's horse was gone, and so was Kolyou, and so was she.

They had run away.

He looked around like a wild man. On the white water trough he saw a bunch of blackberry twigs, heavy with fruit. Someone had picked them and forgotten them.

He reared like an ox enraged at the sight of the blood of a butchered comrade. He roared until he split the heavens in two. He put his hand on his knife, drew it out, waved it about and threw it in the middle of the road. He stooped down over it. The sharpened blade glistened. The moon rushed glinting along it and his whirling head rushed too. He fell upon his face and began to burrow in the ground with fingers stiffened into a claw. He bit the earth. He ate dirt.

He came to himself after the gray heavens had become red. His eyes were warmed as though he had made a visit to his mother's grave. Before him the wheat stalks were bathing, the fields were all aflame, behind them, over toward "the Huts" a little cloud of blue smoke was rising. He didn't start for "the Huts" but mounted his horse and struck across the field through the tall wheat toward the Danube. By evening he reached the city of Rouschouk (on the Bulgarian shore of the river), sold his horse and crossed over into Rumania.

The old man sighed. Before his eyes filed a long line of years during which he was a hired laborer in a strange land. He began to burrow with his fingers in the dust heap of the past, hoping to find at least two warm eyes. Nine years he had met no one there. No one! His heart had turned within him.

At the end of nine years he went back to "the Huts." When he opened the gate of his father's yard an old dog vociferously barked at him. It sprang at him, then recognized him and stopped with wide open eyes. Under the mulberry tree he saw a little black-eyed girl with tousled hair. She was gathering little stones in her little skirt and gazing at him with open mouth.

"It was you, little Vellie."

Her uncle kissed her hand and forgave everything. Was it possible not to forgive his own brother?

Uncle Gheno once more leaned over Vella, who was breathing sweetly; then he wrapped her in his big coat and lay down beside her.

The black sky above weighed heavily upon him. A little coin, fallen from the most precious of all necklaces, was creeping toward an unknown land.

LILIKA NAKOS

Maternity

Lilika Nakos was born in Athens in 1903. Her first story was printed in the French magazine, *Europa*. One of her best known novels is *Lost Soul*. [From *Heart of Europe*; copyright 1943 by L. B. Fischer Publishing Corp.; used by permission of A. A. Wyn, Inc., and Klaus Mann.]

IT WAS MORE THAN A MONTH since they were at Marseilles and the camp of Armenian refugees on the outskirts of the town already looked like a small village. They had settled down in any way they could: the richest under tents; the others in the ruined sheds; but the majority of the refugees, having found nothing better, were sheltered under carpets held up at the four corners by sticks. They thought themselves lucky if they could find a sheet to hang up at the sides and wall them from peering eyes. Then they felt almost at home. The men found work—no matter what—so that in any case they were not racked with hunger and their children had something to eat.

Of all of them, Mikali alone could do nothing. He ate the bread which his neighbors cared to offer and it weighed on him. For he was a big lad of fourteen, healthy and robust. But how could he think of looking for work when he literally bore on his back the burden of a new-born babe? Since its birth, which had caused his mother's death, it had wailed its famine from morn till night. Who would have accepted Mikali's services when his own compatriots had chased him from their quarters because they were unable to bear the uninterrupted howls which kept them awake at night. Mikali himself was dazed by these cries; his head was empty and he wandered about like a lost soul, dying from lack of sleep and weariness, always dragging about with him the deafening burden that had been born for his misfortune—and its own—and that had so badly chosen the moment to appear on this earth. Everybody listened to it with irritation—they had so many troubles of their own—and they all pitifully wished it would die. But that did not happen for the new-born child sought desperately to live and cry louder its famine. The distracted women stuffed their ears and Mikali went hither and yon like a drunken man. He hadn't a penny in his pocket to buy the infant milk and not one woman in the camp was in a position to give it the breast. Enough to drive one mad!

One day, unable to bear it further, Mikali went to the other side of the place where the Anatolians were: they also had fled from the Turkish massacres in Asia Minor. Mikali had been told that there was a nursing mother there who might take pity on his baby. So there he went full of hope. Their camp was like his—the same misery. Old women were crouched on pallets on the ground; barefooted children played about in pools of dirty water. As he approached, several old women rose to ask what he wanted. But he walked on and stopped only at the opening of a tent where an Ikon of the Holy Virgin was hanging; from the interior of the tent came the sound of a wailing infant.

734

"In the name of the Most Holy Virgin whose Ikon you show," he said in Greek, "have pity on this poor orphan and give him a little milk. I am a poor Armenian . . ."

At his appeal, a lovely, dark woman appeared. She held in her arms an infant blissfully sucking the maternal breast, its eyes half-closed.

"Let's see the kid. Is't a boy or a girl?"

Mikali's heart trembled with joy. Several neighbors had come closer to see and they helped him to take from his shoulders the sack where the baby brother was held; with curiosity they leaned over. He drew back the cover. The women gave vent to various cries of horror. The child had no longer anything human about it. It was a monster! The head had become enormous and the body, of an incredible thinness, was all shriveled up. As until then it had sucked only its thumb, it was all swollen and could no longer enter the mouth. It was dreadful to see! Mikali himself drew back in fright.

"Holy Mother!" said one of the old women, "but it's a vampire; a real vampire, that child! Even if I had milk I still wouldn't have the courage to feed it."

"A true Anti-Christ!" said another, crossing herself. "A true son of the Turk!"

An old crone came up. "Hou! Hou!" she screamed, seeing the new-born child. "It's the devil himself!" Then turning to Mikali she yelled: "Get out of here, son of mischance, and never set foot again. You'll bring us bad luck!"

And all of them together chased him away, threatening. His eyes filled with tears, he went off, bearing the little child still wailing its hunger.

There was nothing to be done. The child was condemned to die of hunger. Mikali felt himself immensely alone and lost. A chill ran up his spine at the thought that he was carrying such a monster. He slumped down in the shadow of a shed. It was still very warm. The country spread out before him in arid, waste land, covered with refuse. Noon rang out somewhere. The sound reminded him that he had eaten nothing since the day before. He would have to go sneaking about the streets, round café terraces, filching some half-eaten roll left on a plate; or else rake about in the garbage for what a dog would not have eaten. Suddenly life seemed to him so full of horrors that he covered his face with his hands and began to sob desperately.

When he raised his head a man stood before him gazing down upon him. Mikali recognized the Chinaman who often came to the camp to sell paper knick-knacks and charms which no one ever bought from him anyway. Often they mocked him because of his color and his squint eyes; and the children hounded him, shouting: "Lee Link, the stinkin' Chink!"

Mikali saw that he was looking gently down at him and moving his lips as though to speak. Finally the Chinaman said: "You mustn't cry, boy. . . ." Then, timidly: "Come with me. . . ."

Mikali's only answer was to shake his head negatively; he longed to flee. He had heard so many horrors about the cruelty of the Orientals! At the camp they even went so far as to say that they had the habit— like the Jews—of stealing Christian children in order to kill them and drink their blood!

Yet the man remained there and did not budge. So, being in great distress, Mikali followed him. What more awful thing could happen to him? As they walked along he stumbled weakly and almost fell with the child. The Chinaman came to him and taking the baby in his arms, tenderly pressed it to him.

They crossed several empty lots and then the man took a little lane that led them to a sort of wooden cabin surrounded by a very small garden. He stopped before the door and clapped his hands twice. A few light steps inside and a tiny person came to open the door. Seeing the men her face reddened and then a happy smile lit it up. She made a brief curtsy to them. As Mikali remained there, hesitatingly rooted to the threshold, the Chinaman said to him: "Come in, then; do not be afraid. This is my wife."

Mikali went into the room, rather large it seemed, separated in the middle by a colored paper screen. It was all so clean and neat, though very poor looking. In the corner he noticed a wicker cradle.

"That is my baby," said the young woman cocking her head graciously to one side and smiling to him. "He is very tiny and very beautiful; come and see."

Mikali went up closer and silently admired it. A chubby baby, but lately out of the darkness of the maternal body, slept peacefully, covered with a gold-brocade cloth, like a little king.

Then the husband called his wife over, bade her sit on a straw mat, and without a word set down on her lap the little famished one, bowing deeply before her. The woman leaned over with astonishment and drew back the covering in which the child was wrapped. It appeared to her in all its skeletonic horror. She gave a cry—a cry of immense pity —then pressed the babe to her heart, giving it the breast. Then with a gesture of modesty she brought forward a flap of her robe over the milk-swollen breast and the poor, gluttonous infant suckling there.

ASIAN SECTION

Introduction

What Can the American Artist of Tomorrow Learn from the Eastern Attitude Toward Nature?

The Eastern attitude toward nature is very different from that of the West; as different as white from black. Westerners do not like passivity, drifting with the dark forces, becoming will-less, listening to the world's will—they fear it. They must retain the self, and the self's integrity even to the last gasp on the threshold of death. Even when they say "giving up the self," they are not really giving up. To live for others or with reference to others is one thing, but to *be* another, to *be* others, that is like sin against the Holy Ghost. Westerners, I should think, would not dare, if they could, to give themselves up to the mood of the Chinese landscape painters, for that would be to become re-incarnated forces, ancestor-ghosts, and water—no more a respectable solid and mold. To lose control over nature is, to the soul of the West, *sin*. It is to renounce responsibility, to cease to be the statesman, the scientist, the critic, the artist—the Hamlet and the Prospero. In the West, Nature and God are unalterably opposed.

To treat adequately these differences in Western and Eastern attitude would require volumes of metaphysics. One would need to probe anthropology, comparative religions, modern psychology—perhaps even the unanswerable question: What is life?

But briefly, in the healthy indigenous art of the East, we pass back and away from the Western distinction between outer and inner nature. As a child first sees its mother—somebody in him, not outside (for it is only later that she becomes the retreating Other, one of the forces he is perhaps in conflict with) so is nature to the Eastern painter. The painter is in the landscape as a child is in the mother; the landscape is in him as the mother is in the child.

Let us look at it another way. It would be difficult for a true Western artist to draw a human mother and child devoid of all Western thought on the subject, even though he felt himself completely free of creed or symbol. He will inevitably use inherited religious atmosphere in the concept of that picture. And that picture will have to an Eastern mind, unbeknownst, unplanned by the artist, all the connotations of a Western cultural past.

So it is with the East. You will find the Chinese landscape painting also saturated with a religious atmosphere. It is a religion different, almost opposite to your own, for it is that of nature-worship—nature-acceptance, the desire to melt into nature with harmonious dissolution. A great painting from that thought-world, properly understood, would seem to the Westerner almost incomprehensible, and alien with a soul-destroying mysticism. Fortunately, Westerners are nearly immune to this other, this fundamental meaning of Chinese art. What they get mainly from a Chinese landscape is form, decorative beauty, universality of subject, austere absence of human emotion as the West understands human emotion. Yet these are really only externals—for Western art has always been keyed, not to the Self, but to the Other; not to personal distinction, but to resolving self in the different; not toward defining with boundary, but to issuing on the boundless. Chinese landscapes lack perspective and they have their own logic for this. Space, they say, cannot be measured. If so, it limits the imagination.

Nature is within the Chinese artist, but he never draws from nature as the Westerner draws from nature, and however sound the West's policy is in the West, I think that some change toward their conceptions of nature is needed in both East and West. For cultures are profoundly conditioned by their thoughts toward nature. Has not the West been thrown into a deep-seated trouble and conflict over its own view? One of the greatest factors in shaping the last century or more of world thought has been the clash of Darwin's outer nature, enormously enlarged and explored, with the Christian inner nature of the West. They seemed incompatible and yet they both seemed real. Already men were faced with "God's duplicity," as Emily Dickinson has said. All this, before inner Christian nature had been invaded by another dragon-thought—Freud and his pleasure-principle. It seems to me that both natures, inner and outer, so real and so vital, have been torn and wracked by possibly wrong conceptions.

Where is survival of the fittest—or the pleasure-principle either—to be seen in that wolf story I read about not long ago in the papers? I refer to the she-wolf who twice stole human children, and kept one for eight hours in a cave with male wolves and a succession of wolf cubs, and who died defending her mixed brood in front of the cave, snarling? This is more nature as the Chinese have seen it—cruel, filled with horrors, but never mechanical, neither bad nor good, always unpredictable, enormous, boundless and ever-vital. There is grandeur in that wolf, not to be found in a lamb led to slaughter or in the meteorite cast down by chance. There is a grandeur not human, but one we can thrill to. It is not as alien as a world of dust.

I think there is something very profound and more ancient than primitive in the open-mindedness or rather open-heartedness of the Chinese toward nature. In think the Chinese artist in the future ought to retain something of that, to unite it with his new interest in change and in fit survival. On the other hand, perhaps the most scientific nation of Europe has made a *reductio ad absurdum* of the concept of the survival of the fittest, since it curtailed scientific free-thought, individual integrity and the last intact value of Western logic—thought's honesty, itself. Here in America, in a land built upon so many races and creeds, where man and woman are seen as equal citizens, may we not hope that we can learn Otherness before it is too late, that we may reach those great unities which come out of boundaries broken down, not through dogma or force, but through going out to others' Otherness.

CHINA

The art of the short story is something new to China. It has followed upon the introduction of Western ideas, and seems to have sprung up with an intensified critical consciousness. Previously the Chinese had written many short stories, but these were always despised by the scholars and by all the men who knew what art was for. For instance, if you had never read any short stories, novels, or plays, this was to your credit, never to your shame. A scholar sometimes pretended not to have read them when he really had. They were called "Petty Talk," "Small Conversation." Their arrangement was purely anecdotal. They were almost always anonymous. This fact had its own advantage, such as the opportunity to satirize political conditions, or to disclose one's own crimes. The books written like this really were innumerable. *The Strange Stories of Old and New* is a good example of the archaic Chinese short story. They are amusing in relating incidents but are without any consciousness of the material of art.

The new Chinese short story—written in the "plain language, and hence accessible to thousands more than the small educated class—is somewhat different. The characters are real, and have a past and a future. They are set in a definite geographical place and an historical time. Even the characteristic moral aim or earnestness of the old Chinese literature is not lacking in this new kind of story, although the moral has become different. Many of these short stories are attempting to point a new way or to say that an old way is no good. All are realistic.

The most important modern short story writer in China is Lu Hsun (1881–1936), the leader of the All China League of Left Wing Writers. Whether or not one agrees with the path he had chosen, that of communism, he was in every respect the most striking and original writer in modern China, and had walked alone for over ten years, far in advance of his followers. The Literary Revolution began with Hu Shih and Chen Tu-Siu, but the actual creator of the new literature was preeminently Lu Hsun.

He began writing short stories in 1918 with one called "A Mad Man's Diary." This was incorporated in his first volume, entitled very appropriately *The War Cry*. In this he attacked the traditional customs, superstitions and corruptions of the Chinese people in vehement but not hard-hearted satire. He announced himself plainly an enemy of Confucian and Buddhistic culture. His inspiration has been from the Russian writers Chekhov, Dostoevsky and Tolstoy. In technique he most resembles Chekhov, but he is of a more virile personality, and treats most sympathetically the peasants.

Several of the stories in *The War Cry* deal with the superstitions of old-fashioned medical practice in China. These he was very competent to observe, having been trained as a doctor, before turning to the still more vital question of remaking the mind of China. "Medicine" revolves around the Chinese medical beliefs that human blood taken warm is a cure for anything. "Guaranteed, assured, eaten warm like this—a roll of cake with human blood—sure to heal any kind of consumption." It ends: "But the silence of Death only there was. They stood in withered grass, gazing up at the black crow, with its head tucked in, sitting on his branch as though cast in iron."

Mao Tun's real name is Shen Yenping (1896–). He edited *Short Story Monthly* with Cheng Chento and Keng Chichih in the early twenties. He is a great student of Western literature and one of the best known Chinese novelists today. He was very active in politics, but retired to write when Kuomintang became conservative. Chang T'ien-i's (1907–) volumes of short stories are very popular among Chinese intellectuals. He has taken his characters from his friends, relatives, and those with whom he has had frequent contact, and he makes these people speak directly and dramatically in the almost exclusive use of dialogue. Sun Hsi-chen (1906–) is one of the most talented story-writers of rural China. His satires are bitter and ironic, and he is best known for his trilogy: the *Field of War, War,* and *After War.* Wang Hsi-yen is a popular writer, most of whose stories have grown out of his own experience in the War. Lin Yutang, editor of the *Analects,* and humorous essayist, needs no introduction to the American readers.

KOREA

The Koreans have a very high regard for literature. Even the illiterate will not step on a piece of paper upon which characters are written; picking it up, they will place it in some high place, such as on a tree. This symbolizes the sacredness of written words. The oldest printed book in the world, now in the British museum, is a Korean book, showing that printing from movable type was invented in Korea first. While there are volumes of scientific works on agriculture, philosophy, astronomy, geography, medicine, law, military, strategy and mathematics, the bulk of the literature consists of *belles lettres* and history, aphorisms and moral essays.

At present, an intellectual and artistic ferment goes on in Korea. It is probably sharper and more desperate and more vital here than in either China or Japan, because Korea is in the throes of a death-birth. If she is more closely knit and harmonized at present, it is by national agony and the loss of her racial heritage under Japanese domination. Any people who go through suffering and struggle, if they survive, produce something that lasts long after the epoch-making political movements and social changes.

Yet, except for the best known novelists (Lee Taichun, Kim Namchun, Sul Chungsik and Park Chongwha), these Korean writers cannot support themselves as authors. They are all miserably paid. The average rate is from 75 yen to 100 yen per short story, although Mr. Sul gets as much as 2500 yen a short story and 500 yen per poem. This is very little when a small bowl of soup costs 30 yen and a pair of shoes about 2000 yen in Korea today. Newspapers and magazines cannot print much because of paper shortage. Formerly, one third or one fourth of a newspaper was devoted to literature and art; today only a few of the fifteen leading papers of Seoul carry a poem or a short story. Therefore, what they write is for quality, not quantity, and never merely journalistic. They write in order to free themselves from their emotional burden; they create for the inner necessity.

JAPAN

The art of writing in Japan was introduced from Korea, when Wangin went there with the Confucian Analects and One Thousand Characters, the beginner's classic of China. After the introduction of Buddhism in 522 A.D., Chinese literature became popular. Ever since, the Japanese have shown themselves remarkably proficient in borrowing a literature, a culture, without losing a sense of their own spirit.

Since the opening of Japan hardly anything of real significance or quality has been produced, as one can readily see by reading popular authors. However, quantity is not lacking, and many books appear— literary criticism, historical essays, poems, dramas, and novels. Modern literature began with the Restoration of 1868, and was marked by an importation of Anglo-Saxon literature, followed by French, German and Russian.

During the war the Japanese government—with its customary thoroughness—regimented the Japanese writers to feed the fever of the Japanese mind. From these Japanese writings, therefore, we can gain a valuable insight into the diseased psychology of the Japanese. The Japanese reading public was fed on war literature of this sort to the total exclusion of genuine creative writing. There was no longer any room for the high standards of art achieved by Japanese writers in the first decade of this century, when such books as *Death of a Believer*, by Ryunosuke Akutagawa, and *I Am a Cat*, with its independent irony and playful, relaxed humor, appeared.

To understand this, we must go back and examine what *has* been suppressed in Japanese literature. Surveying the dark trend in Japanese writing from the Russo-Japanese War to the present time, we see over and over again the suicide motif—suicide stemming from despair. This is not quite the same thing as the suicide spirit we speak of in the Japanese soldier; but perhaps it is related. Suicide was the avenue of escape chosen by many of the heroes of Japanese fiction between 1914 and 1927—from Natsume Soseki's *Kokoro (The Mind)* to the works of Ryunosuke Akutagawa, who killed not only his protagonist but himself. Loneliness has been the great theme of modern Japanese literature, together with a constant preoccupation with new unsolved relations between men and women and between the guilt-oppressed individual and his environment.

By 1933 one might say that the guilt-complex had at last been defined. In Kamura Isota's short story, *Marriage Before the Altar,* individualism stands out quite clearly as the source of evil. Thus we note the swiftly mounting sense of futility in the independent thinker—a futility which grows sooner or later to a frenzy of self-immolation. And ever present, even for the most isolated and daring of artists, is the mystic shadow of the emperor, on whose behalf suicide is the traditionally "holy" thing.

Japan's war-era began in the early nineteen-thirties. One of the first conscious elaborations of a new kind of martial spirit was the novel, *Japan Arises,* by Naoki Misogo, published in 1932. In this novel all problems are purported to be solved by this new view of national destiny, "grappling with the realities." The "Holy War" had begun.

The new assumption was that the Japanese are in no way responsible for their own neuroses, which are ascribed to false Western ideas of individual freedom. The great enemy was not their own emperor-image, demanding suicide when private problems loomed too large. The Japanese instead resolved their profound guilt complex by total submersion of the individual ego in the mystic concept of national destiny, and their suicide urge now found release on the battlefields.

Akutagawa, mentioned above, whose *Handkerchief* is in this volume, was born in 1892. He wrote many *haiku poems.* He was a great student of William Morris and Natsume. Skeptical and nervous, he killed himself in 1927.

India

Sanskrit has served the Hindus as a literary language for 2000 years. It was a language of cultivation and perfected composition. The uncultivated used the Prakrit, which sprang from Sanskrit and was contemporary with it. The ancestors of the Aryan, the Greek, Roman, and the English once lived with those of the Hindu in India, and used the same language, and prayed to the same gods. The languages of Europe and those of India are only different forms of the same original Aryan speech. The Hindui, written in Sanskrit characters, is the language of the pure Hindu, while the Hindustani, written in Arabic letters, is the language of the Mohammedan Hindus.

The literature of the modern languages of India consists chiefly of importations and translations from the Sanskrit, Arabic, and other Western languages. There are, however, a number of original writers today in India. There are a dozen major languages and 225 dialects spoken by the 388,800,000 people of India. No one language is understood by all; Urdu, the Moghul "camp language" is in use in the North, while English is used in the South by the educated—only a small section of the population. The most widely spoken language is Hindustani, and in this many books are written. Sir Rabindranath Tagore (1861–

1941) was talented in music, literature and painting. He wrote a great deal in Bengali, receiving the Nobel prize for literature in 1913. In 1901 he had founded a school in Bengal, which became an international institute. Critics who looked for major poetry were disappointed by the somewhat mystic rhetoric of those poems which were translated into English. He published several volumes of stories, from one of which *My Lord, the Baby* was taken.

The other Indian story in this collection, *Drought* by S. Raja Ratnam, gives a vivid picture of present conditions in India. Mr. Ratnam is a Jaffnese by birth, but he spent his childhood in Malaya. He is at present on the staff of the London Office of the Free Press of India.

IRAN (PERSIA)

Persian literature has grown continuously for 2700 years, but with much greater development in verse than in prose. The ancient Iranian, up to the third century, consists largely of inscriptions on the monuments of kings, and the religious writings of Zoroaster. The originals were destroyed when Alexander caused the palace at Persepolis to be burned in the 4th century B.C., and other copies were lost when the Greeks conquered. From the 3rd to the 10th century A.D., during the Zoroasterian revival, the copies of the original translations into other languages were re-translated into Persian. There is no evidence of creative writing of the period, but we may still unearth some in archaeological excavations. Persia was conquered by the Arabs in 641, thus producing Muslim literature (inspired by Arabic models from the 10th century to the present). Matthew Arnold drew "Sohrab and Rustum" from the historical romance of Firdausi's (940?–1920?) great epic, *Shah Nanah* (the *Book of Kings*). Omar Khayyam's (?–1123) *Rubaiyat* is popular in English through Edward Fitzgerald's translation. The *Arabian Nights*, an adaptation of a Persian version of an Indian original, is well-known.

In modern times, sincere efforts have been made to produce the national novel. Little of Iranian literature, however, has been translated into English.

SAUDI ARABIA

In Arabia, because of the barren land and the scattered people, there has been no single national epic, but many tales told by the Bedouin professional tale tellers. Antar is the popular hero—with his beautiful horse and famous sword and mighty deeds. *The Thousand and One Nights* is well known in English.

The novel in Arabia stems from Western influence, as the traditional romances had little artistic value. The most outstanding novelist today is Tawfiq Al-Hakim, who has written *Yawmiyat Na'ib Fi'l Rif (Journals of a Country Deputy)*. I have included one piece by him from a recent translation, *Images from the Arabic World*.

ARMENIA

The Armenians, through all the political disasters amidst revolutions, have faithfully preserved national tradition and have exhibited an ardent love for a national literature.

The language belongs to the Indo-European group, and particularly to the Iranian variety. It has gone through many changes, because of contact with the Turks and others. Its modern dialect today is spoken in Southern Russia, around the sea of Azof, in Turkey, Galicia and Hungary. The ancient Armenian, used down to the 12th century, produced many books and is still used in their best works.

Until the beginning of the 4th century A.D. all songs and ballads were influenced by the philosophy of Zoroaster. In 319 Christianity was introduced and its influence was felt very much in Armenian literature. The golden age of this literature belongs to the 6th and 10th centuries A.D., and contains a strong religious impulse. When the Arabians invaded, it suffered a temporary decline under Arab persecution for refusal to abjure Christianity. Later, the Armenians fell under the Greek influence until the 14th century. In 1375 the Turks occupied the country, and the Armenians became wandering exiles, yet they never lost their desire to sustain a national literature.

TURKEY

The literature of Turkey is very rich, but contains little that is original. However, it is a good imitation of Arabic or Persian. During the 16th century both Fasli, an erotic poet, and Balsi, a lyric poet, attained a very high reputation. This was the most flourishing period, under the reign of Solyman the Magnificent and his son Selim.

The press was introduced into Constantinople early in the 18th century, and the most important books in Persian, Arabic, and Turkish were published.

BURMA

The Burmese literature has not become widely known outside its borders, although Burma's literary heritage is rich. The language is tonal and monosyllabic, like Tibetan, in sounds and structure, but written characters are different from Chinese. The written language is based upon an alphabet of ten vowels and thirty-two consonants, rather than the picture language of China. Buddhism is a universal religion among the Burmese, and it has greatly influenced life and literature. More than half of the Burmese books are novels, and many of these depict the tortures of sinners in *ngayai* (hell) and the rewards of saints in *neikban* (heaven) with startling vividness.

Since 1915, the short story has been based upon Western models. One outstanding writer, U Tin Hla, had published more than one hundred novels, under the *nom de plume* of Tet Tun, before he died in 1937 at the age of 28.

THAILAND (SIAM)

Siamese belongs to the Tai group of the Siamese-Chinese family of languages. It is influenced by the Chinese, Combodian, Sanskrit, Malay, and Laos languages. Most of the words are monosyllabic and are pronounced, as in Chinese, with different intonations or inflexions of the voice. There are five of these vocal accents, which are indicated by signs. Thus the same word has five different meanings when pronounced in five different tones. Although there are some Mohammedans, Buddism is the prevailing religion of Siam. Some of the priests are learned scholars in the Buddhistic monasteries, and Siamese life is closely connected with religious ceremonies. Siam is rich in historical, mythological and animal stories. *Phum hon,* a popular story, deals with a young lady loved by an elephant. *Prang tong* is a tale of a princess who was prenatally betrothed to a giant. The maxims of *Phra Ruang,* who was the national hero-king, are read by young people, as offering the high ideal of manhood. *My Thai Cat,* by Pratoomratha Zeng, which I have included in this book, is traditional (*niti*) and Buddhistic in spirit.

THE PHILIPPINES

The Philippine Islands number more than 7,000, with a total area of 114,000 square miles. Eighty-seven distinct native dialects are spoken by the 16 million population. The three most important are: Tagalog, Visayan, and Ilokano. The Moros in the south use the Arabic system of writing. These different peoples with their diversity of language, custom, and religion are wedded into an independent nation, and the United States has given a common medium of communication by the American system of free education in English.

So, Asia begins the written record of the world. There are narratives concerning Yao, Shun, Yu, T'ang, Wen Wu, Chou Kung, Tangoon, Kicha, Noah, Abraham, Joseph, Moses, David, Daniel and many others. There are rich imagery and balanced phrases of ancient songs, such as those of Shu Ching and Solomon. The stories of Chuang Tsu and the Books of Ruth and Esther are harbingers of the modern short stories.

H. G. Wells once said: "The biggest thing I have learned in writing the 'Outline' is the importance of Central Asia and China. They have been, and they are now still, the center of human destiny."

When the East is put upon the world's intellectual and spiritual map—as I believe will happen in this generation—it will have, among other values, one that is unique. Eastern civilization, if it can survive, will dramatize for mankind one long continuous process.

YOUNGHILL KANG

LU HSUN

Medicine

Lu Hsun (1881–1936) was a native of Chekiang Province. His family was poor, and he educated himself, studying mining and attending the Japanese Sendai Medical School. In 1917 he became the principal of the high school in his native town, and later, professor of Chinese at Peking National University. In 1926 he became the Dean of Amay University. He has published three volumes of stories: *The War Cry, Wandering* and *Wild Grass*. [From *Living China;* used by permission of Edgar Snow; translated by Yao Hsin-nang.]

IT IS AUTUMN, and late at night, so that the moon has already gone. The sky is a sheet of darkling blue. Everything still sleeps, except those who wander in the night, and Hua Lao-shuan. He sits up suddenly in his bed; leaning over, he rubs a match and touches it to a lamp which is covered with grease. A pale greenish light flickers and reveals the two rooms of a tea house.

"Father of Hsiao-shuan, are you leaving?" queries the voice of a woman. There is a series of tearing coughs in the small room in the rear.

"M-m." Lao-shuan, listening for a moment, fastens his garments and then stretches forth a hand toward the woman. "Give it," he says.

Hua Ta-ma fumbles beneath her pillow and drags forth a small packet of silver dollars, which she hands to him. Nervously he thrusts it into his pocket, then pats it twice, to reassure himself. He lights a paper lantern and blows out the oil lamp. Carrying the lantern, he goes into the small rear room. There is a rustle, and then more coughing. When it is quiet again, Lao-shuan calls out, in an undertone: "Hsiao-shuan—don't bother getting up. The shop—your mother will see to that."

His son does not answer him, and Lao-shuan, thinking he will sleep undisturbed, goes through the low door into the street. In the blackness nothing is at first visible save a gray ribbon of path. The lantern illumines only his two feet, which move rhythmically. Dogs appear here and there, then sidle off again. None even barks. Outside, the air is cold, and it refreshes Lao-shuan, so that it seems to him he is all at once a youth, and possesses the miraculous power of touching men into life. He takes longer strides. Gradually the sky brightens, till the road is more clearly marked.

Absorbed in his walking, Lao-shuan is startled when, almost in front of him, he sees a crossroad. He stops, and then withdraws a few steps, to stand under the eaves of a shop, in front of its closed door. After a long wait, his bones are chilled.

"Uhn, an old fellow?"

"High-spirited, up so early . . ."

Opening his eyes, Lao-shuan sees several people passing near him. One of them turns back and looks at him intently. He cannot distinguish the features clearly, but the man's eyes are bright with a cold, lusting gleam, eyes of famishment suddenly coming upon something edible. Looking at his lantern, Lao-shuan sees that it has gone out. He feels quickly at his pocket; the hard substance is still there. Then he peers out, and on either side of him are numerous strange people, loitering and looking oddly like ghosts in the dim light. Then he gazes fixedly at them, and gradually they do not seem unusual at all.

He discerns several soldiers among the crowd. On their coats they wear, both in front and behind, the large white circle of cloth of the government troops, which can be seen for some distance. As one draws nearer, the wine-colored border of their uniforms is also evident. There is a trampling of many feet, and a large number of people gathers, little groups here and there merging swiftly into one crush that advances like the ocean's tide. Reaching the crossroad, they halt and form a semicircle, with their backs toward Lao-shuan.

Necks stretch forth from collars and incline toward the same point, as if, like so many ducks, they are held by some invisible hand. For a moment all is still. Lao-shuan seems to hear a sound from somewhere beyond the necks. A stir sweeps through the onlookers. With a sudden movement, they abruptly disperse. People jostle one another hurriedly, and some, pushing past Lao-shuan, almost tumble him to the ground in their haste.

"*Hai!* One hand gives the money, another hand gives the goods!" screams a man clad entirely in black, who halts before Lao-shuan. In his eyes is a metallic glitter. They resemble the bright luster of a pair of swords. They stab into Lao-shuan's soul, and his body seems to shrivel to half its normal size. The dark man thrusts one huge, empty paw at him, while in the other he offers a steamed roll, stained with a fresh and still warm red substance, drops of which trickle to the earth.

Hurriedly, Lao-shuan fumbles for his dollars. He attempts to hand them over to the black-garbed man, from whose hand slowly depend the drops of red, but somehow he cannot embolden himself to receive the saturated roll.

"What's afraid of? Why not take it?" the fellow demands, brusque and impatient. Lao-shuan continues to hesitate until the other roughly snatches his lantern, tears off its paper shade and uses it to wrap up the roll. Then he thrusts this package into Lao-shuan's hand, and at the same time seizes the silver and gives it a cursory feel. As he turns away he murmurs, "That old fool . . ."

"And to cure what person?" Lao-shuan seems to hear someone ask him. He does not reply. His attention is centered upon the package, and he embraces it as if it were the only child descended from a house of ten generations. Nothing else in the world matters, now that he is about to transplant into his own home the robust life which he holds in his hands. He hopes, thereby, to reap much happiness.

The sun lifts over the horizon. Before him, the long street leads straight into his tea house. Behind him, the light of day caresses a worn tablet at the crossroad, on which are four characters limned in faint gold: "Ancient—Pavilion—"

Lao-shuan, reaching home, finds the tea house swept clean, with the rows of tables smooth and glistening but as yet serving no customers. Only Hsiao-shuan sits alone at a table by the wall and eats his food. Large drops of sweat drip down his forehead, and his little lined coat sticks against his sunken spine. His shoulder blades project sharply, from under his coat, so that there appears on his back, as though embossed, the character 丿 乀, *pa*. Seeing it causes Lao-shuan to pinch his brow together. He wife emerges hastily from the kitchen, her mouth open, her lips quivering.

"Do you have it?" she asks.

"Yes, I have it."

The pair disappear into the kitchen for a time, where they consult. Then Hua Ta-ma comes hurriedly forth, goes out and in a moment returns with a dried lotus leaf, which she spreads on the table. Lao-shuan unwraps the crimson-stained roll and neatly repacks it in the sheet of lotus. Meanwhile, Hsiao-shuan has finished his meal, and his mother warns him: "Sit still, Little Door-latch. Don't come here yet."

When the fire burns briskly in the mud stove, the father thrusts his little green and red parcel into the oven. There is a red and black flame. A strange odor permeates the rooms.

"*Hao.* It smells good, but is it? What are you eating?" demands Camel-Back Fifth, who arrives at this moment and sniffs the air questioningly. He is one of those who pass their days in tea houses, the first to come in the morning, the last to leave at night. Now, tumbling to a table by the lane, he sits down to make idle inquiry.

"Could it be baked rice *congee?*"

Nobody replies. Lao-shuan silently serves him boiled tea.

"Come in, Hsiao-shuan," Hua Ta-ma calls from the inner room, in the center of which she has placed a stool. The Little Door-latch sits, and his mother, saying in a low voice, "Eat it, and your sickness will vanish," hands him a plate on which is a round object, black in color.

Hsiao-shuan picks it up. For a moment he gazes at it curiously, as if he might somehow hold his own life in his hand. His heart is unspeakably moved with wonder. Very carefully, he splits the object. A jet of white vapor gushes forth, and immediately dissolves in the air. Now Hsiao-shuan sees that it is a white flour roll, broken in half. Soon it has entered his stomach, so that even the taste of it cannot be clearly remembered. In front of him there is the empty dish; on one side stands his father and, on the opposite side, his mother. Their eyes are potent with a strange look, as if they desire to pour something into him, yet at the same time draw something forth. It is exciting. It is too much for Hsiao-shuan's little heart, which throbs furiously. He presses his hands against his chest and begins to cough.

"Sleep a little; you'll be well."

So Hsiao-shuan coughs himself to sleep, obeying the advice of his mother. Having waited patiently till he is quiet, she drapes over him a lined quilt, which consists mostly of patches.

In the tea house are many customers, and Lao-shuan is kept engaged in his enterprise. He darts from one table to another, pouring hot water and tea, and seemingly intent on his tasks. But under his eyes are dark hollows.

"Lao-shuan," inquires a man with whiskers streaked with white, "are you not a little unwell?"

"No."

"No? But I already see that it's unlikely. Your smile now—" The bearded one contradicts himself.

"Lao-shuan is always busy. Of course if his son were—" begins Camel-Back Fifth. His remark is interrupted by the arrival of a man whose face is massive, with distorted muscles. He wears a black cotton shirt, unbuttoned and pulled together carelessly around the waist with a broad black cloth girdle [the apparel of an executioner]. As he enters, he shouts to Lao-shuan:

"Eaten, eh? Is he well already? Lao-shuan, luck is with you! Indeed lucky! If it were not that I get news quickly—"

With the kettle in one hand and the other hanging straight beside him in an attitude of respect, Lao-shuan listens and smiles. All the guests listen with deference, and Hua Ta-ma, her eyes dark and sleepless, also comes forth and smiles, serving the new arrival some tea leaves, with the added flourish of a green olive. Lao-shuan himself fills the cup with boiling water.

"It is a guaranteed cure! Different from all others! Think of it, brought back while still warm, eaten while warm!" shouts the gentleman with the coarse face.

"Truly, were it not for Big Uncle Kan's services, how could it be—" Hua Ta-ma thanks him, in deep gratitude.

"Guaranteed cure! Guaranteed cure! Eaten up like that while still warm. A roll with human blood is an absolute cure for any kind of consumption!"

Mention of the word "consumption" seems to disconcert Hua Ta-ma; for her face suddenly turns pallid, though the smile quickly creeps back. She manages to withdraw so inconspicuously that Big Uncle Kan still shouts with the full vigor of his lungs and does not notice that she is gone till from the inner room, where Hsiao-shuan sleeps, there comes the sound of dry, raucous coughing.

"So, it is true Hsiao-shuan has come upon friendly luck. That sickness will unquestionably be cured utterly. There's no surprise in Laoshuan's constant smiling." Thus speaks the whiskered old man, who walks toward Big Uncle Kan. "I hear," he says to the latter in a suppressed voice, "that the criminal executed today is a son of the Hsia family. Now, whose son is he? And, in fact, executed for what?"

"Whose?" demands Big Uncle. "Can he be other than the son of the fourth daughter-in-law of the Hsias? That little *tung-hsi!*" Observing that he has an alert audience, Big Uncle expands, his facial muscles become unusually active and he raises his voice to heroic heights, shouting: "The little thing did not want to live! He simply did not want life, that's all."

"And I got what from the execution this time? Not the merest profit! Even the clothes stripped from him were seized by Red Eye Ah Yi, the jailer. Our Uncle Lao-shuan was the luckiest. Second comes the Third Father of the Hsia family. He actually pocketed the reward —twenty-five ounces of silver!—all alone. He gave not so much as a single cash to anyone!"

Hsiao-shuan walks slowly from the little room, his hands pressed to his chest, and coughing without respite. He enters the kitchen, fills a bowl with cold rice and sits down at once to eat. Hua Ta-ma goes to him and inquires softly: "Hsiao-shuan, are you better? Still as hungry as ever?"

"Guaranteed cure, guaranteed!" Big Uncle Kan casts a glance at the lad but quickly turns back to the crowd and declares: "Third Father of Hsia is clever. Had he not been the first to report the matter to the official, his whole house would have been beheaded, and all their property confiscated. But instead? Silver!

"That little tung-hsi was an altogether rotten egg. He even attempted to induce the head jailer to join the rebellion!"

"*Ai-ya!* If it were actually done, think of it!" indignantly comments a youth in his twenties, sitting at a back table.

"You should know that Red Eye Ah Yi was anxious to gather some details; so he entered into conversation. 'The realm of *Ta Ching* Dynasty really belongs to us all,' he told Red Eye. Now, what do you make of that? Is it possible that such talk is actually human?

"Red Eye knew that there was only a mother in his home, but he could not believe that he was so poor that 'not a drop of oil and water' could be squeezed from him. His rage already had burst his abdomen, yet the boy attempted to 'scratch the tiger's head'! Ah Yi gave him several smacks on the face."

"Ah Yi knows his boxing. His blows must have done the wretch good!" exults Camel-Back Fifth, from a corner table.

"No! Would you believe it? His worthless bones were unafraid. The fellow actually said, what is more, that it was a pity!"

Black-and-White Whiskers snorted, "What is it? How could pity be shown in beating a thing like that?"

"You've not listened well," sneers Big Uncle contemptuously. "The little tung-hsi meant to say that Ah Yi himself was to be pitied!"

The listeners' eyes suddenly dull, and there is a pause in the conversation. Hsiao-shuan, perspiring copiously, has finished his rice. His head seems to be steaming.

"So he said Red Eye should be pitied! How, that is pure insanity!" Black-and-White Whiskers feels proudly that he has logically solved the whole matter. "Obviously, he had gone mad!" . . .

"Gone mad," approvingly echoes the youth who spoke earlier. He too feels like a discoverer.

Equanimity is restored to the other tea house visitors. They renew their laughing and talking. Hsiao-shuan, under cover of the confusion of sounds, seizes the opportunity to cough hoarsely, with all his emaciated strength.

Big Uncle Kan moves over to pat the child's shoulder, repeating, "Guaranteed cure, Hsiao-shuan. You mustn't cough like that. Guaranteed cure!"

"Gone mad," says Camel-Back Fifth, nodding his head.

Originally, the land adjacent to the city wall beyond the West Gate was public property. The narrow path that now cavorts through it was first made by feet seeking a short cut, which in time came to be a natural boundary line. On the left of it, as one goes out from the gate, are buried those who have been executed or have starved to death in prison. On the right are grouped the graves of the paupers. All of these graves are so numerous and closely arranged that they remind one of the sweet buns laid out in a rich man's home for a birthday celebration.

The Clear and Bright Day, when graves are visited, has dawned unusually cold, and willows have just issued new buds about the size of a half-grain of rice. Hua Ta-ma has laid out four dishes and a bowl of rice in front of a new grave on the right side, has left tears over it and has burned imitation money. Now she sits dazedly on the ground, as if waiting for something, but nothing which she herself could explain. A light breeze sweeps by, and her short hair flutters. It is much grayer than last year.

Down the narrow path comes another woman, gray also, and in torn rags. She carries a worn round basket, lacquered red, with a string of paper ingots hanging from it. Now and then she halts her slow walk. Finally she notices Hua Ta-ma gazing at her, and she hesitates, embarrassed. A look of confused shame crosses her pale, melancholy face. Then, emboldening herself, she walks to a grave on the left of the path and lays down her lacquered basket.

It so happens that the grave is directly opposite Hsiao-shuan's, with only the narrow path between them. Hua Ta-ma watches mechanically as the woman lays out four dishes and a bowl of rice; burns paper money and weeps. It occurs to her that in that grave also there is a woman's son. She watches curiously as the woman moves about absently and stares vacantly into space. Suddenly she sees her begin to tremble and stagger backward, as if in stupor.

Hua Ta-ma is touched. "She may be mad with sorrow," she fears. She rises and, stepping across the path, speaks to her quietly: "Old Mother, don't grieve any more. Let us both go home." The woman nods stupidly, her eyes still staring. Suddenly she utters an exclamation, "Look! What is that?"

Looking along the woman's pointing finger, Hua Ta-ma's eyes take in the grave before them, which is unkempt and has ugly patches of yellow earth on it. Looking more closely she is startled to see, at the top of the little mound, a circlet of scarlet and white flowers.

For many years neither of them has seen clearly, and yet now both see these fresh blossoms. They are not many, but they are neatly arranged; they are not very splendid, but they are comely in an orderly way. Hua Ta-ma looks quickly at her son's grave, and at the others, but only here and there are a few scattered blossoms of blue and white that have braved the cold; there are no others of scarlet. She experiences a nameless emptiness of heart, as if in need, but of what she does not wish to know. The other walks nearer and examines the flowers closely. "What could be the explanation?" she muses.

Tears stream from her face, and she cries out: "Yü, my son! You have been wronged, but you do not forget. Is it that your heart is still full of pain, and you choose this day and this method of telling me?" She gazes around, but, seeing only a black crow brooding in a leafless tree, she continues: "Yü, Yü, my son! It was a trap; you were 'buried alive'. Yet Heaven knows! Rest your eyes in peace, but give me a sign. If you are here in the grave, if you are listening to me, cause the crow to fly here and alight on your grave. Let me know!"

There is no more breeze, and everywhere the dry grass stands erect, like bristles of copper. A faint sound hangs in the air and vibrates, growing less and less audible, till finally it ceases entirely. Then everything becomes as quiet as death. The two old women stand motionless in the midst of the dry grass, intently watching the crow. Among the straight limbs of the tree, its head drawn in, the crow sits immobile and as if cast in iron.

Much time passes. Those who come to visit graves begin to increase in numbers. To Hua Ta-ma it seems that gradually a heavy burden lifts from her, and to the other she says, "Come, let us go."

The old woman sighs dejectedly and gathers up her offertory dishes. She lingers for still another moment, then at length walks away slowly, murmuring, "What could it have been?"

When they have walked only some thirty paces they suddenly hear a sharp cry from above. "Yah-h-h." Turning round with a shudder they see the crow brace itself on a limb and then push forth, spreading its broad wings and flying like an arrow toward the far horizon.

MAO TUN

*Spring
Silkworms*

Mao Tun, whose real name is Shen Yen-ping, was born in 1896. A leader of modern Chinese literature, he edited *Short Story Monthly* in the early twenties. He is a student of Western literature and was very active in politics until the Kuomintang became conservative, when he retired to devote all his time to writing. [From *Contemporary Chinese Stories;* copyright 1944 by Columbia University Press; translated by Chi-chen Wang.]

TUNG PAO SAT ON A ROCK along the bank of the canal with his back to the sun, his long-stemmed pipe leaning against his side. The sun was already strong, though the period of Clear Bright had just set in, and felt as warm as a brazier of fire. It made him hotter than ever to see the Shaohing trackers pulling hard at their lines, large drops of sweat falling from their brows in spite of their open cotton shirts. Tung Pao was still wearing his winter coat; he had not foreseen the sudden warm spell and had not thought of redeeming his lighter garment from the pawnshop.

"Even the weather is not what it used to be!" muttered Tung Pao, spitting into the canal.

There were not many passing boats, and the occasional ripples and eddies that broke the mirrorlike surface of the greenish water and blurred the placid reflections of the mud banks and neat rows of mulberry trees never lasted long. Presently one could make out the trees again, swaying from side to side at first like drunken men and then becoming motionless and clear and distinct as before, their fistlike buds already giving forth tiny, tender leaves. The fields were still cracked and dry, but the mulberry trees had already come into their own. There seemed to be no end to the rows along the banks and there was another extensive grove back of Tung Pao. They seemed to thrive on the sunlit warmth, their tender leaves growing visibly each second.

Not far from where Tung Pao sat there was a gray white building, used by the cocoon buyers during the season but now quite deserted. There were rumors that the buyers would not come at all this year because the Shanghai factories had been made idle by the war, but Tung Pao would not believe this. He had lived sixty years and had yet to see the time when mulberry leaves would be allowed to wither on the trees or be used for fodder, unless of course if the eggs should not hatch, as has sometimes happened according to the unpredictable whims of Heaven.

"How warm it is for this time of the year!" Tung Pao thought again, hopefully, because it was just after a warm spring like this almost two score years ago that there occurred one of the best silk crops ever known. He remembered it well: it was also the year of his marriage. His family

754

fortune was then on the upward swing. His father worked like a faithful old ox, knew and did everything; his grandfather, who had been a Taiping captive in his time, was still vigorous in spite of his great age. At that time too, the house of Chen had not yet begun its decline, for though the old squire had already died, the young squire had not yet taken to opium smoking. Tung Pao had a vague feeling that the fortunes of the Chens and that of his own family were somehow intertwined, though one was about the richest family in town while his was only well-to-do as peasants went.

Both his grandfather and the old squire had been captives of the Taiping rebels and had both escaped before the rebellion was suppressed. Local legend had it that the old squire had made off with a considerable amount of Taiping gold and that it was this gold which enabled him to go into the silk business and amass a huge fortune. During that time Tung Pao's family flourished too. Year after year the silk crops had been good and in ten years his family had been able to acquire twenty mou of rice land and more than ten mou of mulberry trees. They were the most prosperous family in the village, just as the Chens were the richest in the town.

But gradually both families had declined. Tung Pao no longer had any rice land left and was more than three hundred dollars in debt besides. As for the Chen family, it was long ago "finished." It was said that the reason for their rapid decline was that the ghosts of the Taiping rebels had sued in the courts of the nether world and had been warranted by King Yenlo to collect. Tung Pao was inclined to think that there was something to this notion, otherwise why should the young squire suddenly acquire the opium habit? He could not, however, figure out why the fortunes of his own family should have declined at the same time. He was certain that his grandfather did not make away with any Taiping gold. It was true that his grandfather had to kill a Taiping sentinel in making his escape, but had not his family atoned for this by holding services for the dead rebel as long as he could remember? He did not know much about his grandfather, but he knew his father as an honest and hardworking man and could not think of anything he himself had done that should merit the misfortunes that had befallen him. His older son Ah Ssu and his wife were both industrious and thrifty, and his younger son Ah Dou was not a bad sort, though he was flighty at times as all young people were inclined to be.

Tung Pao sadly lifted his brown, wrinkled face and surveyed the scene before him. The canal, the boats, and the mulberry groves on both sides of the canal—everything was much the same as it was two score years ago. But the world had changed: often they lived on nothing but pumpkins, and he was more than three hundred dollars in debt.

Several blasts from a steam whistle suddenly came from around a bend in the canal. Soon a tug swept majestically into view with a string of three boats in tow. The smaller crafts on the canal scurried out of the way of the puffing monster, but soon they were engulfed in the wide wake of the tug and its train and seesawed up and down as the air became filled with the sound of the engine and the odor of oil. Tung Pao watched the tug with hatred in his eyes as it disappeared around the next bend. He had always entertained a deep enmity against such foreign deviltry as steam boats and the like. He had never seen a foreigner himself, but his father told him that the old squire had seen some, that they had red hair and green eyes and walked with straight knees. The old squire had no use for foreigners either and used to say that it was they that had made off with all the money and made everyone poor. Tung Pao had no doubt that the old squire was right. He knew from his own experience that since foreign yarn and cloth and kerosene appeared in town and the steamer in the river, he got less and less for the things that he produced with his own labor and had to pay more and more for the things that he had to buy. It was thus that he became poorer and poorer until now he had none of his rice land that his father had left him and was in debt besides. He did not hate the foreigners without reason! Even among the villagers he was remarkable for the vehemence of his anti-foreign sentiments.

Five years back someone told him that there had been another change in government and that it was the aim of the new government to rescue the people from foreign oppression. Tung Pao did not believe it, for he had noticed on his trips to town that the youngsters who shouted "Down with the foreigners" all wore foreign clothes. He had a suspicion that these youths were secretly in league with the foreigners and only pretended to be their enemies in order to fool honest people like himself. He was even more convinced that he was right when the slogan "Down with the foreigners" was dropped and things became dearer and dearer and the taxes heavier and heavier. Tung Pao was sure that the foreigners had a hand in these things.

The last straw for Tung Pao was that cocoons hatched from foreign eggs should actually sell for ten dollars more a picul. He had always been on friendly terms with his daughter-in-law, but they quarreled on this score. She had wanted to use foreign eggs the year before. His younger son Ah Dou sided with her, and her husband was of the same mind though he did not say much about it. Unable to withstand their pressure, Tung Pao had to compromise at last and allow them to use one sheet of foreign eggs out of three that they decided to hatch this year.

"The world is becoming worse and worse," he said to himself. "After a few years even the mulberry leaves will have to be foreign! I am sick of it all!"

The weather continued warm and the fingerlike tender leaves were now the size of small hands. The trees around the village itself seemed to be even better. As the trees grew so did the hope in the hearts of the peasants. The entire village was mobilized in preparation for the silk-worms. The utensils used in the rearing were taken out from the fuel sheds to be washed and repaired, and the women and children engaged in these tasks lined the brook that passed through the village.

None of the women and children were very healthy looking. From the beginning of spring they had to cut down on their meager food, and their garments were all old and worn. They looked little better than beggars. They were not, however, dispirited; they were sustained by their great endurance and their great hope. In their simple minds they felt sure that so long as nothing happened to their silkworms everything would come out all right. When they thought how in a month's time the glossy green leaves would turn into snow white cocoons and how the cocoons would turn into jingling silver dollars, their hearts were filled with laughter though their stomachs gurgled with hunger.

Among the women was Tung Pao's daughter-in-law Ssu-da-niang with her twelve-year-old boy Hsiao Pao. They had finished washing the feeding trays and the hatching baskets and were wiping their brows with the flap of their coats.

"Ssu-sao, are you using foreign eggs this year?" one of the women asked Ssu-da-niang.

"Don't ask me!" Ssu-da-niang answered with passion, as if ready for a quarrel. "Pa is the one that decides. Hsiao Pao's pa did what he could to persuade the old man, but in the end we are hatching only one sheet of foreign eggs. The doddering old fool hates everything foreign as it were his sworn foe, yet he doesn't seem to mind at all when it comes to 'foreign money.' " [1]

The gibe provoked a gale of laughter.

A man walked across the husking field on the other side of the brook. As he stepped on the log bridge, Ssu-da-niang called to him:

"Brother Dou, come and help me take these things home. These trays are as heavy as dead dogs when they are wet."

Ah Dou lifted the pile of trays and carried them on his head and walked off swinging his hands like oars. He was a good-natured young man and was always willing to lend a hand to the women when they had anything heavy to be moved or to be rescued from the brook. The trays looked like an oversize bamboo hat on him. There was another gale of laughter when he wriggled his waist in the manner of city women.

"Ah Dou! Come back here and carry something home for me too," said Lotus, wife of Li Keng-sheng, Tung Pao's immediate neighbor, laughing with the rest.

"Call me something nicer if you want me to carry your things for you," answered Ah Dou without stopping.

---

[1] That is, the dollar coin. So called because the Chinese dollar is based on the Mexican peso, brought to China by European traders.

"Then let me call you godson!" Lotus said with a loud laugh. She was unlike the rest of the women because of her unusually white complexion, but her face was very flat and her eyes were mere slits. She had been a slave girl in some family in town and was already notorious for her habit of flirting with the men folk though she had been married to the taciturn Li Keng-sheng only half a year.

"The shameless thing!" someone muttered on the other side of the brook. Thereupon Lotus's pig-like eyes popped open as she shouted:

"Whom are you speaking of? Come out and say it in the open if you dare!"

"It is none of your business! She who is without shame knows best whom I'm speaking of, for 'Even the man who lies dead knows who's kicked his coffin with his toes.' Why should you care?"

They splashed water at each other. Some of the women joined the exchange of words, while the children laughed and hooted. Ssu-da-niang, not wishing to be involved, picked up the remaining baskets and went home with Hsiao Pao. Ah Dou had set down the trays on the porch and was watching the fun.

Tung Pao came out of the room with the tray stands that he had to repair. His face darkened when he caught Ah Dou standing there idle, watching the women. He never approved of Ah Dou's exchanging banter with the women of the village, particularly with Lotus, whom he regarded as an evil thing that brought bad luck to anyone who had anything to do with her.

"Are you enjoying the scenery, Ah Dou?" he shouted at his son. "Ah Ssu is making cocoon trees in the back; go and help him!" He did not take his disapproving eyes off his son until the latter had gone. Then he set to work examining the worm holes on the stands and repaired them wherever necessary. He had done a great deal of carpentering in his time, but his fingers were now stiff with age. After a while he had to rest his aching fingers and as he did so he looked up at the three sheets of eggs hanging from a bamboo pole in the room.

Ssu-da-niang sat under the eaves pasting paper over the hatching baskets. To save a few coppers they had used old newspapers the year before. The silkworms had not been healthy, and Tung Pao had said that it was because it was sacrilegious to use paper with characters on it. In order to buy regular paper for the purpose this year they had all gone without a meal.

"Ssu-da-niang, the twenty-loads of leaves we bought has used up all the thirty dollars that we borrowed through your father. What are we going to do after our rice is gone? What we have will last only two more days." Tung Pao raised his head from his work, breathing hard as he spoke to his daughter-in-law. The money was borrowed at $2\frac{1}{2}$ percent monthly interest. This was considered low, and it was only because Ssu-da-niang's father was an old tenant of the creditor that they had been able to get such a favorable rate.

"It was not such a good idea to put all the money in leaves," complained Ssu-da-niang, setting out the baskets to dry. "We may not be able to use all of them as was the case last year."

"What are you talking about! You would bring ill luck on us before we even got started. Do you expect it to be like last year always? We can only gather a little over ten loads from our own trees. How can that be enough for three sheets of eggs?"

"Yes, yes, you are always right. All I know is that you can cook rice only when there is some to cook and when there isn't you have to go hungry!"

Ssu-da-niang answered with some passion, for she had not yet forgiven her father-in-law for their arguments over the relative merit of foreign and domestic eggs. Tung Pao's face darkened and he said no more.

As the hatching days approached, the entire village of about thirty families became tense with hope and anxiety, forgetting it seemed, even their gnawing hunger. They borrowed and sought credit wherever they could and ate whatever they could get, often nothing but pumpkins and potatoes. None of them had more than a handful of rice stored away. The harvest had been good the year before but what with the landlord, creditors, regular taxes, and special assessments, they had long ago exhausted their store. Their only hope now lay in the silkworms; all their loans were secured by the promise that they would be paid after the "harvest."

As the period of Germinating Rains drew near, the "cloth" in every family began to take on a green hue. This became the only topic of conversation wherever women met.

"Lotus says they will be warming the cloth tomorrow. I don't see how it can be so soon."

"Huang Tao-shih went to the fortune teller. The character he drew indicated that leaves will reach four dollars per picul this year!"

Ssu-da-niang was worried because she could not detect any green on their own three sheets of eggs. Ah Ssu could not find any either when he took the sheets to the light and examined them carefully. Fortunately their anxiety did not last long, for spots of green began to show the following day. Ssu-da-niang immediately put the precious things against her breast to warm, sitting quietly as if feeding an infant. At night she slept with them, hardly daring to stir though the tiny eggs against her flesh made her itch. She was as happy, and as fearful, as before the birth of her first child!

The room for the silkworms had been made ready some days before. On the second day of "warming" Tung Pao smeared a head of garlic with mud and put it in a corner of the room. It was believed that the more leaves there were on the garlic on the day that silkworms were hatched, the better would be the harvest. The entire village was now engaged in this warming of the cloths. There were few signs of women along the brooks or on the husking grounds. An undeclared state of emergency seemed to exist: even the best of friends and the most intimate of neighbors refrained from visiting one another, for it was no joking matter to disturb the shy and sensitive goddess who protected the silkworms. They talked briefly in whispers when they met outside. It was a sacred season.

The atmosphere was even tenser when the "black ladies" began to emerge from the eggs. This generally happened perilously close to the day that ushered in the period of Germinating Rains and it was imperative to time the hatching so that it would not be necessary to gather them on that particular day. In Tung Pao's house, the first grubs appeared just before the tabooed day, but they were able to avoid disaster by transferring the cloths from the warm breast of Ssu-da-niang to the silkworms' room. Tung Pao stole a glance at the garlic and his heart almost stopped beating, for only one or two cloves had sprouted. He did not dare to take another look but only prayed for the best.

The day for harvesting the "black ladies" finally came. Ssu-da-niang was restless and excited, continually watching the rising steam from the pot, for the right moment to start operations was when the steam rose straight up in the air. Tung Pao lit the incense and candles and reverently set them before the kitchen god. Ah Ssu and Ah Dou went out to the fields to gather wild flowers, while Hsiao Pao cut up lamp-wick grass into fine shreds for the mixture used in gathering the newly hatched worms. Toward noon everything was ready for the big moment. When the pot began to boil vigorously and steam to rise straight up into the air, Ssu-da-niang jumped up, stuck in her hair a paper flower dedicated to the silkworms and a pair of goose feathers and went into the room, accompanied by Tung Pao with a steelyard beam and her husband with the prepared mixture of wild flowers and lampwick grass. Ssu-da-niang separated the two layers of cloth and sprinkled the mixture on them. Then taking the beam from Tung Pao she laid the cloths across it, took a goose feather and began to brush the "black ladies" off gently into the papered baskets. The same procedure was followed with the second sheet, but the last, which contained the foreign eggs was brushed off into separate baskets. When all was done, Ssu-da-niang took the paper flower and the feathers and stuck them on the edge of one of the baskets.

It was solemn ceremony, one that had been observed for hundreds and hundreds of years. It was as solemn an occasion as the sacrifice before a military campaign, for it was to inaugurate a month of relentless struggle against bad weather and ill luck during which there would be no rest day or night. The "black ladies" looked healthy as they crawled about in the small baskets; their color was as it should be. Tung Pao and Ssu-da-niang both breathed sighs of relief, though the former's face clouded whenever he stole a glance at the head of garlic, for the sprouts had not grown noticeably. Could it be that it was going to be like last year again?

Fortunately the prognostications of the garlic did not prove very accurate this time. Though it was rainy during the first and second molting and the weather colder than around Clear Bright, the "precious things" were all very healthy. It was the same with the "precious things" all over the village. An atmosphere of happiness prevailed, even the brook seemed to gurgle with laughter. The only exception was the household of Lotus, for their worms weighed only twenty pounds at the third "sleep," and just before the fourth Lotus's husband was seen in the act of emptying three baskets into the brooks. This circumstance made the villagers redouble their vigilance against the contamination of the unfortunate woman. They would not even pass by her house and went out of their way to avoid her and her taciturn husband. They did not want to catch a single glance of her or exchange a single word with her for fear that they might catch her family's misfortune. Tung Pao warned Ah Dou not to be seen with Lotus. "I'll lay a charge against you before the magistrate if I catch you talking to that woman," he shouted at his son loud enough for Lotus to hear. Ah Dou said nothing; he alone did not take much stock in these superstitions. Besides, he was too busy to talk to anyone.

Tung Pao's silkworms weighed three hundred pounds after the "great sleep." For two days and two nights no one, not even Hsiao Pao, had a chance to close his eyes. The worms were in rare condition; in Tung Pao's memory only twice had he known anything equal to it—once when he was married and the other time when Ah Ssu was born. They consumed seven loads of leaves the first day, and it did not take much calculation to know how much more leaf would be needed before the worms were ready to climb up the "mountain."

"The squire has nothing to lend," Tung Pao said to Ah Ssu. "We'll have to ask your father-in-law to try his employers again."

"We still have about ten loads on our own trees, enough for another day," Ah Ssu said, hardly able to keep his eyes open.

"What nonsense," Tung Pao said impatiently. "They have started eating only two days ago. They'll be eating for another three days without counting tomorrow. We need another thirty loads, thirty loads."

The price of leaves had gone up to four dollars a load as predicted by the fortune teller, which meant that it would cost one hundred and twenty dollars to buy enough leaves to see them through. There was nothing to do but borrow the required amount on the only remaining mulberry land that they had. Tung Pao took some comfort in the thought that he would harvest at least five hundred pounds of cocoons and that at fifty dollars a hundred pounds he would get more than enough to pay his debts.

When the first consignment of leaves arrived, the "precious things" had already been without food for more than half an hour and it was heartbreaking to see them raise their heads and swing them hither and yon in search of leaves. A crunching sound filled the room as soon as the leaves were spread on the beds, so loud that those in the room had difficulty in hearing one another. Almost in no time the leaves had disappeared and the beds were again white with the voracious worms. It took the whole family to keep the beds covered with leaves. But this was the last five minutes of the battle; in two more days the "precious things" would be ready to "climb up the mountain" and perform their appointed task.

One night Ah Dou was alone on watch in the room, so that Tung Pao and Ah Ssu could have a little rest. It was a moonlit night and there was a small fire in the room for the silkworms. Around the second watch he spread a new layer of leaves on the beds and then squatted by the fire to wait for the next round. His eyes grew heavy and he gradually dozed off. He was awakened by what he thought was a noise at the door, but he was too sleepy to investigate and dozed off again, though subconsciously he detected an unusual rustling sound amidst the familiar crunching of leaves. Suddenly he awoke with a jerk of his drooping head just in time to catch the swishing of the reed screen against the door and a glimpse of someone gliding away. Ah Dou jumped up and ran out. Through the open gate he could see the intruder walking rapidly toward the brook. Ah Dou flew after him and in another moment he had flung him to the ground.

"Ah Dou, kill me if you want to but don't tell anyone!"

It was Lotus's voice, and it made Ah Dou shudder. Her piggish eyes were fixed on his but he could not detect any trace of fear in them.

"What have you stolen?" Ah Dou asked.

"Your precious things!"

"Where have you put them?"

"I have thrown them into the brook!"

Ah Dou's face grew harsh as he realized her wicked intention.

"How wicked you are! What have we done to you?"

"What have you done? Plenty! It was not my fault that our precious things did not live. Since I did you no harm and your precious things have flourished, why should you look upon me like the star of evil and avoid me like the plague? You have all treated me as if I were not a human being at all!"

Lotus had got up as she spoke, her face distorted with hatred. Ah Dou looked at her for a moment and then said:

"I am not going to hurt you; you can go now!"

Ah Dou went back to the room, no longer sleepy in the least. Nothing untoward happened during the rest of the night. The "precious things" were as healthy and strong as ever and kept on devouring leaves as if possessed. At dawn Tung Pao and Ssu-da-niang came to relieve Ah Dou. They picked up the silkworms that had gradually turned from white to pink and held them against the light to see if they had become translucent. Their hearts overflowed with happiness. When Ssu-da-niang went to the brook to draw water, however, Liu Pao, one of their neighbors, approached her and said to her in a low voice:

"Last night between the Second and Third Watch I saw that woman come out of your house, followed by Ah Dou. They stood close together and talked a long time. Ssu-da-niang, how can you let such things go on in your house?"

Ssu-da-niang rushed home and told her husband and then Tung Pao what had happened. Ah Dou, when summoned, denied everything and said that Liu Pao must have been dreaming. Tung Pao took some consolation in the fact that so far there had been no sign of the curse on the silkworms themselves, but there was Liu Pao's unshakable evidence and she could not have made up the whole story. He only hoped that the unlucky woman did not actually step into the room but had only met Ah Dou outside.

Tung Pao became full of misgivings about the future. He knew well that it was possible for everything to go well all along the way only to have the worms die on the trees. But he did not dare to think of that possibility, for just to think of it was enough to bring ill luck.

The silkworms had at last mounted the trees but the anxieties of the growers were by no means over, for there was as yet no assurance that their labor and investment would be rewarded. They did not, however, let these doubts stop them from their work. Fires were placed under the "mountains" in order to force the silkworms to climb up. The whole family squatted around the trees and listened to the rustling of the straws as the silkworms crawled among them, each trying to find a corner to spin its chamber of silk. They would smile broadly or their hearts would sink according to whether they could hear the reassuring sound or not. If they happened to look up and catch a drop of water from above, they did not mind at all, for that meant that there was at least one silkworm ready to get to work at that moment.

Three days later the fires were withdrawn. No longer able to endure the suspense, Ssu-da-niang drew aside one corner of the surrounding reed screens and took a peep. Her heart leaped with joy, for the entire "mountain" was covered with a snowy mass of cocoons! She had never seen a crop like this in all her life! Joy and laughter filled the household. Their anxieties were over at last. The "precious things" were fair and had not devoured leaves at four dollars a load without doing something to show for it, and they themselves had not gone with practically no food or sleep for nothing; Heaven had rewarded them.

The same sound of joy and laughter rose everywhere in the village. The Goddess of Silkworms had been good to them. Everyone of the twenty or thirty families would gather at least a seventy or eighty percent capacity crop. As for Tung Pao's family they expected a hundred-and-twenty or even a hundred-and-thirty percent crop.

Women and children were again seen on the husking fields and along the brook. They were thinner than a month ago, their eyes more sunken and their voices more hoarse, but they were in high spirits. They talked about their struggles and dreamed of piles of bright silver dollars; some of them looked forward to redeeming their summer garments from the pawnshop, while others watered at the mouth in anticipation of the head of fish that they might treat themselves to at the Dragon Boat Festival.

The actual harvesting of the cocoons followed the next day, attended by visits from friends and relatives bringing presents and their good wishes. Chang Tsai-fa, Ssu-da-niang's father, came to congratulate Tung Pao and brought with him cakes, fruits and salted fish. Hsiao Pao was as happy as a pup frolicking in the snow.

"Tung Pao, are you going to sell your cocoons or reel them yourself?" Chang asked, as the two sat under a willow tree along the brook.

"I'll sell them, of course."

"But the factories are not buying this year," Chang said, standing up and pointing in the direction of the buildings used by the buyers.

Tung Pao would not believe him but when he went to see for himself he found that the buyers' buildings were indeed still closed. For the moment Tung Pao was panic-stricken, but when he went home and saw the basket upon basket of fine, firm cocoons that he had harvested he forgot his worries. He could not believe it that such fine cocoons would find no market.

Gradually, however, the atmosphere of the village changed from one of joy and laughter to one of despair, as news began to arrive that none of the factories in the region were going to open for the season. Instead of the scouts for the cocoon buyers who in other years used to march up and down the village during this season, the village was now crowded with creditors and tax collectors. And none of them would accept cocoons in payment.

Curses and sighs of despair echoed through the entire village. It never occurred to the villagers even in their dreams that the extraordinarily fine crop of cocoons would increase their difficulties. But it did not help to complain and say that the world had changed. The cocoons would not keep and it was necessary to reel them at home if they could not sell them to the factories. Already some of the families had got out their long neglected spinning wheels.

"We'll reel the silk ourselves," Tung Pao said to his daughter-in-law. "We had always done that anyway until the foreigners started this factory business."

"But we have over five hundred pounds of cocoons! How many spinning wheels do you plan to use?"

Ssu-da-niang was right. It was impossible for them to reel all the cocoons themselves and they could not afford to hire help. Ah Ssu agreed with his wife and bitterly reproached his father, saying:

"If you had only listened to us and hatched only one sheet of eggs, we would have had enough leaves from our own land."

Tung Pao had nothing to say to this.

Presently a ray of hope came to them. Huang Tao-shih, one of Tung Pao's cronies, learned from somewhere that the factories at Wusih were buying cocoons as usual. After a family conference it was decided that they would borrow a boat and undertake the journey of around three hundred li in order to dispose of their crop.

Five days later they returned with one basket of cocoons still unsold. The Wusih factory was unusually severe in their selection and paid only thirty dollars a hundred pounds of cocoons from foreign eggs and twelve dollars for the native variety. Though Tung Pao's cocoons were of the finest quality, they rejected almost a hundred pounds of the lot. Tung Pao got one hundred and eleven dollars in all and had only an even hundred left after expenses of the journey, not enough to pay off the debts they contracted in order to buy leaves. Tung Pao was so mortified that he fell sick on the way and had to be carried home.

Ssu-da-niang borrowed a spinning wheel from Liu Pao's house and set to work reeling the rejected cocoons. It took her six days to finish the work. As they were again without rice, she sent Ah Ssu to the town to sell the silk. There was no market for it at all and even the pawnshop would not loan anything against it. After a great deal of begging and wheedling, he was allowed to use it to redeem the picul of rice that they had pawned before Clear Bright.

And so it happened that everyone in Tung Pao's village got deeper into debt because of their spring silkworm crop. Because Tung Pao had hatched three sheets of eggs and reaped an exceptional harvest, he lost as a consequence a piece of land that produced fifteen loads of mulberry leaves and thirty dollars besides, to say nothing of a whole month of short rations and loss of sleep!

CHANG T'IEN-I

Mr. Hua Wei

Chang T'ien-i is considered one of China's outstanding progressive writers. Very few of his numerous works have been translated into English. [From *Asia Magazine*, October, 1941; used by permission of *United Nations World*; translated by M. Q. Ho and Clarence Moy.]

IF ONE CALCULATES BY devious twists and turns, he may be considered to be a relative of mine. I called him "Mr. Hua Wei." He felt this manner of address not very appropriate.

"Elder Brother T'ien-I, you are really . . . !" he said. "Why must you use 'Mister'? You should call me 'Younger Brother Wei.' If not that, then call me 'Ah Wei.' "

After dealing with this piece of business he immediately put on his hat.

"Elder Brother T'ien-I, shall we talk again some other day? I always want to have a pleasant conversation with you—*ai*, but I never find the time. Today, Director Lau drafted a plan for the district magistrates' after-hour work. He insisted I contribute my opinion and told me to revise the plan for him."

At this point he shook his head and could not help laughing ruefully. He asserted that he would never be afraid of eating bitterness. During a war of resistance, all of us should suffer a bit. But still—there must be enough time to apportion. "And committee-member Wang has sent three wires insisting that I go to Hankow. How can I run off? My heavens!"

Then he hurriedly shook hands and stepped into his private ricksha.

He always clasped under his arm his brief case. And he always carried his heavy, shiny black stick. On his left-hand ring finger he wore his wedding ring. When holding a cigar, he bade this ring finger coil slightly and raised high his little finger to form a shape like an orchid.

In this city few people cared to ride in the rickshas, which were pulled step by step very deliberately like a man taking a thousand steps after a meal. But the private rickshas were exceptions: Ding dang, ding, dang, ding dang!—and in an instant they would rush to the front. The *huangpaoche,* the common rickshas, immediately would have to give way and turn off to the left. The wheelbarrows would speedily have to be rolled aside. The peddlers, shouldering their loads, quickly would shy away. The pedestrians would hurriedly escape into the stores on either side. And, according to the calculations of some of the higher class patriots, the swiftest private ricksha was that of Mr. Hua Wei.

His time was very important. He said: "I regret that the system of sleeping at night cannot be abolished. And I wish that one day were not just twenty-four short hours. Indeed, there is too much patriotic work to be done."

Following this, he drew out his watch for a look; the plump flesh on his face immediately became tense. Knitting his brows and puckering up his lips as if he were concentrating all his energy in his face, he left: he had to go to a meeting of the Refugee Relief Association.

As usual, all the people at the meeting had assembled and seated themselves and were awaiting him. As was always his habit, when he got off the ricksha at the door, he gave one incidental stamp on the foot-bell: ding!

The comrades looked at one another: Hmn, Mr. Hua Wei had arrived. Some sighed deeply. Some drew long faces and looked at the door. One of them even seemed to want to prepare for combat—with fists clenched and eyes glaring.

Walking into the hall with easy steps, Mr. Hua Wei's attitude was very serious, his previous hurry seemingly erased by his own earnestness. At the door he stopped for a moment to let everyone have a good look at him, as if to awaken in his comrades a confidence in him, as if to give them a kind of assurance—there was no need to worry about any difficult and important undertaking now. And he nodded his head. His eyes did not take in anyone but looked only at the ceiling. He was greeting the whole group.

"I cannot be the chairman," he gestured with his cigar. "The Directory Division of the Workers' National Salvation Committee is holding a regular meeting today. The meeting for studying popular literature is also today. Later I have to go to the Wounded Soldiers' Work Group, too. You know that I do not have enough time to apportion: it allows me only ten minutes for discussion here. I should like to nominate Comrade Lau for chairman."

When the chairman was making his report, Mr. Hua Wei continuously scratched matches to light his cigar. He placed his watch before him and perpetually looked at it.

"I make a motion!" he shouted. "Our time is very valuable: I wish that the chairman would try his utmost to report briefly. I wish that the chairman would finish his report in two minutes."

After scratching matches for two minutes, he stood up with a bound and waved his hand at the chairman, who was speaking.

"Enough, enough. Although the chairman is not through with his report, I already understand it. And now I have to go to another meeting; let me give my opinion."

There was a pause. He inhaled twice on his cigar and swept the listeners with his eyes.

"My idea is very simple. It has only two points." He licked his lips. "The first point is this—no worker should neglect his obligations. On the contrary, he should intensify his work. I need not say too much on this point. You are all very hard-working youths, and you are enthusiastic over what you have to do: I am very grateful to you. But there is still another point—you must never forget it; it is the second point I wish to speak about."

He again drew twice on his cigar, but what he blew out of his mouth was only hot air. So he again scratched a match.

"The second point is this: the young workers should recognize a center of leadership. You have only to put yourselves under the guidance of this center of leadership and become consolidated and united. It is also under the guidance of this center of leadership that patriotic work can then be developed. Youths are hard-working; they are enthusiastic; but, because their comprehension is not sufficient and their experience is not enough, it is always easy for them to commit errors. If there is no center of leadership over them, nothing will ever be accomplished."

He glanced at the expressions on the faces before him. The flesh on his own face quivered a bit, assuming a slight smile. He continued: "You are all young comrades, so I am speaking very frankly, very informally. All of us are doing patriotic work. There is no need to be formal. I think all of you young comrades will surely accept my ideas. I am very grateful to you. Well, I am very sorry; I must go."

He put on his hat, clasped his brief case under his arm, nodded with his eyes to the ceiling and, jutting out his stomach, walked out.

Reaching the door, he thought of something else. He drew aside his comrade, the chairman, and whispered a few words.

"Your work—do you have any difficulty or not?" he asked.

"In my report just now, I have referred to this point. We—"

Mr. Hua Wei extended his index finger and touched the chairman's chest.

"Mn, mn, mn. I know, *wo chih tao*. I do not have very much more time to talk about this thing. After this, whenever you think of any work plans, you can come to my home to find me for council."

The long-haired youth sitting next to the chairman was looking attentively at them. Now he could not hold back and interrupted, "On Wednesday we went to Mr. Hua's home three times, but Mr. Hua was not home."

Mr. Hua coldly gave him a glance and snorted. "Mn, I had other affairs," and he turned to whisper to the chairman again.

"If I am not home, you can just as well see Miss Wong." Miss Wong was none other than his wife. He always referred to her thus.

After these instructions, he actually left. Then he went to the Popular Literature Research Club meeting place, where he found others were already holding the meeting and where someone was in the act of speaking his mind. He sat down and lighted his cigar and clapped his hands three times with displeasure.

"Chairman!" he shouted. "I have another meeting to attend today, and I cannot wait for the end of this meeting. Now I have some ideas and should like to submit them first."

Then he mentioned two points. First, he told the group—all those seated here were local men of culture; the work of men of culture was very important and should be intensively carried on. Second, men of culture should recognize clearly a center of leadership. Under the guidance of the local center of leadership, let the men of culture consolidate and unite.

At five forty-five he arrived at the meeting hall of the Directory Division of the Workers' National Salvation Committee.

This time his face was covered with a smile, and he even nodded to someone.

"Very sorry; *tui pu chu tê hêng.* Three-quarters of an hour late."

The chairman smiled slightly at him. Mr. Hua Wei laughed, and, as if he had brought on some misfortune and was afraid of being scolded for it, thrust out the tip of his tongue. He looked all around to observe the atmosphere and, seeking out a lightly bearded man, sat down.

He put on a secretive and serious expression. In a low tone he asked the lightly bearded one, "Last night, did you get drunk or not?"

"Not so bad, but my head was a little dizzy. And you?"

"I?—I should not have drunk those three cups of strong wine," he said solemnly. "Especially the Fen wine, I cannot drink much. Director Lau forced me to drink bottoms up—hai! as soon as I reached home I fell asleep. Miss Wong said she had to go to settle the score with

Director Lau! Had to question him why he made me drunk. You see!"

As soon as this conversation was over, he hurriedly opened his brief case and took out a piece of paper; writing a few words on it, he handed it to the chairman.

"Please wait just a moment," the chairman stopped a speaker. "Mr. Hua Wei has some other business and has to go. Now he has some ideas which he wishes to be allowed to express first."

Mr. Hua Wei, nodding his head, stood up. He asserted: this directory division was an organ of leadership; this directory division should incessantly exercise its function as the center of leadership. The masses are complex—especially today; their elements are very complex. If we cannot exercise the function of leadership, then it is very dangerous, very dangerous. In fact, the various aspects of work in this region cannot be without a center of leadership. Our burden is really too heavy, but we are not afraid of suffering and we must lift up this burden.

He repeatedly explained the importance of the function of a center of leadership. Then he put on his hat to go to a dinner.

Every day he was busy like this. He had to go to Director Lau's to attend to affairs. He had to go to the various organizations for meetings. And each day—if it was not someone inviting him to dinner, then he invited others.

Every time Mrs. Hua Wei met me, she spoke for Mr. Hua Wei of his hardships. "Ai, he really is suffering to death. The work is so much that there is not even any time for him to eat."

"Can he not attend to a little less and concentrate on one certain kind of work?" I asked.

"How can that be? A great deal of work needs his leadership."

But once Mr. Hua Wei was actually very much frightened. Some members of the women's circle organized a war-time nursery for children and did not seek him out!

He began to look for information and to investigate. He found a way of getting one of the responsible persons to come to him.

"I know that your committee has already been selected. I think that it can be increased by several members."

He saw the person opposite him there hesitate. He lowered his chin.

"The question is on this point: can or cannot your committee members really lead in this work? Can or can you not guarantee me that within your committee there are no undesirable members? Can you or can you not guarantee me that hereafter your work will not be erroneously done, that you will not neglect your obligations? Can you or can you not guarantee? Can you or can you not? If you can guarantee, then I must ask you to write it down for me. If there is one chance in ten thousand—if your work should show some failing, then you must assume the responsibility."

Following this he asserted that this was not at all his own idea: he was only the one who was carrying out the idea. Here he pointed his index finger at the other person's breast.

"If you cannot do what I have just mentioned, then is not your organization illegal?"

After a second dose of this kind of discussion, Mr. Hua Wei became a member of the war-time nursery for children. Thus, when the committee held a meeting, Mr. Hua Wei went with his brief case clasped under his arm and sat for five minutes and, after expressing a bit of his opinion, stepped into his ricksha.

One day he asked me to dinner, because, he said, a piece of cured meat had been sent from his village. When I arrived at his home, there he was, showing his temper to two persons who looked like students.

"Why didn't you go yesterday? *Wei shih mo pu chu?*" he roared. "I asked you to get several persons to go. But when I went on the platform to speak and had a look—even you had not gone to listen! I really don't understand what you did!"

"Yesterday—I went to a newly organized refugee reading club."

Mr. Hua Wei sprang up fiercely.

"What! *Shih mo!* A newly organized refugee reading club? Why didn't I know about it?"

"All of us had just decided on it that day. I came to look for Mr. Hua, but Mr. Hua wasn't home—"

"*Hao ah,* you are moving secretly!" He glowered. "You tell me honestly—what background does this reading club really have, you tell me honestly!"

One of the persons opposite seemed to have become inflamed.

"What is the background? It is that of the Chinese nation! There is no secret at all. Mr. Hua, when we hold a meeting, you do not come; when you come, you do not stay to the end; when we come to look for you, we cannot find you. Anyway, we cannot stop our work—"

Mr. Hua Wei threw down his cigar and, with the strength of a lifetime, struck his fist on the table—bang!

"Get out!" He bit on his teeth and his lips quivered. "You be careful— You! Heng! You! You!—" He fell on the sofa, and his mouth twisted painfully: "*Ma-tê! chê-k̂ê, chê-k̂ê*—you young fellows!"

After five minutes, he raised his head and, as if afraid, looked all around. Those two visitors had already gone. He heaved a long sigh: "Ai, you see, you see! Elder Brother T'ien-I, you see! Today's youth —what is to be done with them? Today's youth!"

That evening, without regard for life, he drank much wine. Muttering in his mouth, he swore at those youngsters. He broke to pieces a teacup. After Miss Wong helped him into bed, he shivered suddenly and said, "Tomorrow at twelve o'clock there is a meeting."

SUN HSI-CHEN

Ah Ao

Sun Hsi-chen was born in 1906 in Che-kiang Province and began writing as a child. His novels are widely popular with Chinese youth, who praise him for his stories of rural life. His best known works are *Beaten Gold, The Ring of Flowers, Woman of the Night,* and his war trilogy, *The Field of War, War,* and *After War.* [From *Living China;* used by permission of the translator, Edgar Snow.]

THROUGHOUT THE DAY, from early dawn, Ah Ao had remained hidden under a bed in the small dark room, her head bent, her body still, scarcely daring to breathe.

At the foot of the Purple-Red Mountain, down which spilled a dense growth of fragrant pines and other trees, a small stream ran into the open cornfields, and beside it stood a row of seven houses, most of them old and dilapidated. This place was known as Tao Village, although none of the inhabitants was named Tao. In four of the seven houses lived the family Chen, the house on the western end was a family temple reserved for the spirits, while in the center of the row stood a comparatively new and handsome residence (some eighteen years old) which was owned by Chin the Rich.

It was in the seventh house, poorest of all, consisting of five little rooms, where the Wang family dwelt, that Ah Ao lay hidden. Half of this house was in fact mortgaged to Chin the Rich who, two years before, when old Wang died, had lent his widow forty thousand cash to pay for the funeral feast and obsequies. Consequently she now lived with her son, Small One Brother, and her daughter, Ah Ao, in only the nether part of the little hut, which did not belong to Chin the Rich. In the room next to the kitchen—or rather in one corner of the kitchen itself, since the bed was separated from it only by a few thin planks— Ah Ao, in secret dread, trembled and stifled her lungs all day.

Some grindstones and empty bamboo baskets leaned against the wall of the kitchen, which was just now very noisy. There were four square wooden tables, with long benches ranged on each side, and these, with their occupants, completely choked up the little room. Altogether one could count more than thirty men, including not only the male population of Tao Village but also guests from the neighboring villages of Yu and Red Wall. They sat drinking and feasting in exuberant mood. Most of them wore blue or white cotton shirts and trousers and were in their bare feet. Chin the Rich, Wu the Merchant, who could read and write, and the Hairy-Headed Village Elder, respected for his age, wore long gowns, however, made of linen. Only on rare occasions did these long-gown men visit such a lowly establishment, and it was plain that they were now quite aware of the extraordinary dignity their appearance lent to the feast.

771

The food seemed simple enough, with but four big bowls of meat, fish, turnips and soup, spread on each table, but they were refilled again and again, and each time emptied almost as soon as replenished. Later on, besides, the women of the village would have to be fed. Everybody gorged, helping himself to great hunks of meat and full bowls of wine without any pretense at etiquette; their presence at the feast was not in the interest of good will, but a punitive measure against the mother of a shameless daughter. Never mind the financial burden to Widow Wang! It was the way of justice.

The fact was that only by mortgaging the other half of her house had the unhappy woman managed to get together the money to finance this strange banquet. A sentimental person might have observed that what the guests clipped between the blades of chopsticks was actually Widow Wang's flesh and blood; for the feast meant utter ruin to her. By this sacrifice, however, she was saving the life of her daughter, who was, no one could deny it, guilty of that crime. Now, although a crime of such a nature necessarily required two to commit it, the unwritten but powerful law of custom nevertheless made her alone responsible, and gave any villager the right to attack, insult, abuse or kill her, as he saw fit. By what other means, then, could the child's life be saved, than through this, an expensive banquet in honor of the offended villagers, with the especial aim of winning mercy from Chin the Rich, Wu the Merchant and the Hairy-Headed Village Elder? Even though it meant her own death in the end, still the Widow would have gone through with it.

Two days before, in the afternoon, she had sent her son to Chin. He had bowed, begged mercy and requested the loan of thirty thousand cash, pledging the rest of the Wang House as security. Then with this money the boy had, again at his mother's instruction, gone to the market where he bought thirty pounds of meat, more than twenty pounds of fish, fully a bushel of turnips and some other ingredients of the feast. Since early in the morning of the previous day she had busied herself with cleaning and making ready this food, preparing rice wine and attending to other duties, so that she had not once had a moment to rest.

With the arrival of the guests she had become even busier. All alone, she worked ceaselessly, serving everybody, keeping all the bowls filled with food, pouring forth the warm wine that was like emptying the vessels of her own body, but all the same managing to smile and give the appearance of enjoying her duties immensely.

"Brother Lucky Root," shouted one coarse fellow, "don't hesitate! This isn't an occasion for ceremony, but a free feed. See, you don't have to give anything in return; so eat up! Fill yourself to the brim!"

"You are quite right," agreed Lucky Root. "Why be slow about it, eh? Let's eat; for such opportunities as this are rare indeed. As a matter of fact this girl, now, Ah Ao; shameless, but still rather good-looking. How many girls around compare with her? Actually—?"

"The more girls like Ah Ao the more free feasts," yelled a third. "Personally I hope we'll have others."

"Ai-ya, Old Fa! Always boasting. You, the hungry devil with women! But don't forget the facts in this case; the girl right under your nose chooses instead a fellow from a neighboring village, not you!"

"Old Fa, ha, ha!"

"Ho, what an—Old Fa!"

The Widow Wang did not appear to understand these remarks, but bent her attention on the tasks of service and of maintaining the smile on her face. She did not once frown. But Ah Ao heard and trembled and crawled still farther toward the wall. She did not know whether the feeling she experienced was humiliation or terror or indignation or merely a heavy sadness, but something like a great stone seemed to be crushing her down, and her heart burned as if pierced by a shaft of red-hot iron. A few days ago she had boldly resigned herself to whatever fate might bring, but now she wanted only to crawl, crawl, crawl.

The Hairy-Headed Elder at last came to the issue. "To be precise," he began slowly, "this is perhaps after all not so serious a matter. It is natural for a grown girl to want marriage, isn't it so? But to make love—to a young man—in secret, you know, and without anybody's knowledge—without the usual formalities—who can excuse it?"

"Exactly!" exclaimed Wu the Merchant. "Widow Wang, this is something that can come to a mother only as punishment for her own sins in the past. Such a daughter, just consider, is not only a disgrace to your own family name but to the whole Tao Village as well. You very well know that according to age-old custom this crime merits nothing less than death. Recall, now, the case of the Chao girl—it happened three or four years ago in Stone Gate Village—who was beaten to death for the very same offense. Do you remember, she was buried without even a coffin? Nobody could call it cruelty, but only justice; for she had violated the laws of right conduct. Moreover, the worst of it is that even after their death such girls continue to dishonor the good name of the community. Ending life does not end their sin—no, indeed, and, as everyone knows, death doesn't begin to make up for it!"

"What you have just said is undeniably true. Death doesn't cover up the crime at all. But, on the other hand, it's not altogether the girl's fault. The mother is to blame also—a certain laxness, a waning of discipline. Again, in this case it may be that the mother was not herself very virtuous in some previous incarnation. Widow Wang, let me advise you to take care—in this life you had better be more strict."

The Village Elder was the donor of this speech, which oddly did not seem to anger the Widow, but on the contrary encouraged her to speak. She moved forward timidly, her hands pulling nervously on the edge of her worn dress. She spoke, in a very low voice, and smiled painfully:

"Yes, Honored Elder—that is correct. If she did wrong it was really my fault. I don't know what unpardonable sin I have back of me in some previous existence, but it must be as you say. And this terrible crime of my daughter, you're quite right, death would only be the punishment deserved. Still—" she broke suddenly into tears. "But I can't speak, I haven't 'face' to say—only I ask—*mercy!* Spare her life at least."

This was a reckless demand, an extraordinary request indeed, and were it not that the villagers were at that moment eating her food she would never have escaped ridicule by them. They believed in enforcing justice and morality to the letter, and ordinarily would stand no non-sense. Yet it seemed generally understood that because they had ap-peared, and had eaten, and had enjoyed themselves, and had some of them even come on their own invitation, they would not be altogether adamant. But their decision rested upon the opinions voiced by Chin the Rich, Wu the Merchant and the Hairy-Headed. Everybody re-mained silent until Chin finally gave the verdict.

"Wu has, I agree, spoken very wisely, and very much to the point. 'Death doesn't begin to cover up the crime.' Precisely! Then, perhaps, or so it seems to me, little is to be gained by taking her life now. The guilt has been admitted, and the Widow Wang, asking mercy, has begged us also to give 'face' to her late husband. She wants us to spare her daughter's life, and everything considered that is perhaps possible, but at the same time we cannot permit such an altogether immoral woman to continue to besmirch the village good name. She must leave at once!"

The Elder shared this view. "What is done is done; though totally without honor, still it's no use, now, to kill her. Better, as you say, expel her—move her out immediately."

These two having rendered a judgment, the rest of the guests, who considered themselves a kind of "jury," reined in their tongues. The decision was unanimously approved. The pale, weary face of the Widow Wang broke out suddenly into a genuine smile; she bowed low to the three wise men and obsequiously thanked the members of the self-appointed jury. But, back in the darkness, the hidden Ah Ao heard and yet curiously did not feel happy at all at this reprieve. She understood well enough that life had been miraculously restored to her, but although the prospect of death had been terrifying she was after all too young to have a deep fear of it, whereas to be banished from the village, to leave and never again to see her mother, to bid farewell to her brother, to plunge into an unknown, uncertain future—that was something which she knew to be worse than death. Grief shook her body, seemed to break, to shatter it, so that it was no longer whole, but a heap of something that mysteriously still trembled with life.

It had happened two months before, in early April, on a day filled with an ineffable softness, an unbearable languor and gladness that made men dreamy-eyed, drowsy and as if drunk with some wonderful wine.

Ah Ao, on her way home in the afternoon from the near-by Yu Village, thought that she had never known such a glorious day. There was a new warmth in her body, a strange vigor in her as if she had just begun to live. The fields bordering the road were touched from a withered yellow into a lush new green, the trees were coming to life, and in their budding limbs birds had appeared and were joyously chattering. The whole world, as far as she could see, was young, fresh, growing, awakened, expectant. She felt in harmony with all that she saw, and expectant too. Of what? She did not know, but somehow she found herself walking more slowly. Her face burned as from some inner fire, and she became all at once conscious of her body, vibrant and warm against the fabric of her garments.

"Ah Ao—" a voice called from somewhere.

Surprised and a little afraid, she stopped, looked around, peered over the fields into the clustered pines and through the rocky pass, but saw no one. Above her head a pair of eagles circled. She blushed, rubbed her burning face and walked on.

"Ah Ao—" someone cried again, but this time much nearer. She stopped, more puzzled, but saw no one, and started to go on, when once more she heard the same voice, now quite close, speak out, "Ah Ao, it's me!" Turning round quickly, she saw, protruding from the bushes and greenery, a head. Then slowly a young man in a long linen gown gave her a full-lenth view of himself, including his handsome red-buttoned cap. He was perhaps twenty years old, not a bad-looking fellow, and he wore on his face a pleased look. Ah Ao recognized him. He was the son of Li, a shop-owner in the neighboring village. His name, she knew as Ah Hsian.

"*Ai-ya!* so it's you," said Ah Ao. "You frightened me almost to death. Where did you come from?" Nevertheless, she seemed not altogether dissatisfied that he had appeared.

"I?" he demanded. "I? I just happened to be coming from town, saw you in the distance and hid myself to have some fun with you."

"You impudent rascal!" she shouted gaily, raising her hand as if to slap him. "Frightening a person to death!"

"I apologize, Ah Ao, with all my heart. The truth is I have something very important to tell you."

"For example?"

But the youth suddenly became weak or timid. He kept murmuring "I—I—I—" Then he seized her hand.

"What is this?" Ah Ao started back quickly, but for some reason her legs refused to move. Her body quivered, as from some shock, and again she felt her flesh warm beneath her garments. All the strength seemed to run out of her. He put his arms around her, pulled her toward him, and then led her into the forest. She could not summon up any resistance, her mind did not seem to work as usual, she was hardly conscious that they moved at all, and she did not utter a sound. She only knew that within she felt intolerably buoyant and enlarged.

They sat down under the leafy arm of a tree, her head resting upon his shoulder. Her eyes closed and she breathed rapidly. She felt his hand close softly over her breast, over her beating heart. She felt his lips upon hers, and suddenly she knew a bodily glow that she had never felt before.

"Caw-w-w," a magpie, circling overhead, startled her, and for a moment recalled to her that the world existed. She trembled. "Ah Hsian! No, no! Don't, please! Mother will beat me to death!"

"Don't, you must not worry. Trust me, believe in me; everything will be wonderful, like this always."

His voice shook too, and some strange vibrancy of it, some summons which she had never heard before, and which would not be denied, completely overpowered her. He caressed her arms, her face, her throat. She ceased to resist.

"What is the matter with you, Ah Ao?" Widow Wang asked her daughter when, very much agitated, she returned home late that afternoon. "Fever?" She touched her forehead, which was covered with a short fringe of hair. "Have you caught a cold?"

"Nothing at all. I—I simply don't feel very well—" Ah Ao murmured, half to herself. She went to the bed and lay down and for a long time she did not stir. She knew very well the risks, the danger, the fate opening up ahead of her, but just as well she knew that she would meet Ah Hsian again, whenever he asked, yes, even tomorrow!

She expected something dreadful to happen; she prepared herself for it. In the future, after each interval with him, she waited dully for the exposure of their crime, and each time was rather surprised when no one came to denounce her. Nevertheless, she resigned herself to ultimate discovery, but found comfort in the thought that her lover would come to her defense, take punishment as pronounced; and she imagined herself, in his moment of disgrace, going proudly to his side, sharing whatever fate imposed upon him. And what she constantly feared did happen at last, but its consequences were nothing like what she had romantically foreseen. It was just three days before the Widow Wang offered the villagers such a splendid banquet.

Behind Purple-Red Mountain there was a small hill, the name of which had long been forgotten. Halfway up its flank, nearly buried in the foliage, was a temple to the mountain god. The surrounding forests were owned by one of the great landlords, and few ventured to trespass through the leafy lanes. The place was pervaded by a ghostly stillness, but it was gentle shelter for young lovers.

On this day Lao Teh, the Spotted Face, a woodcutter, had stealthily crept into the forest to steal wood. He had gathered a load and was prepared to leave just as the setting sun splashed ruddily against the wall behind the mountain temple. The sight invited him, and he sat down on the threshold of the enclosure, sighed, lighted his pipe and gazed at the sky.

But was that not a sound? Thrusting the pipe into his girdle, he seized his ax and stood ready to combat with any wild animal that might rush forth. He waited for several minutes, tense and excited. He thought of running away but reconsidered, remembering that "an offensive is the best defensive." Picking up a stone as big as a goose egg, he threw it with all his strength into the thickest part of the forest.

To his astonishment it was not a wild beast but a man that burst from the trees. He did not stop or even look in Lao Teh's direction, but vanished like a devil. Lao Teh nevertheless saw enough of him to recognize Ah Hsian. Somewhat perplexed, he advanced toward the spot whence he had emerged.

Then, in a moment he came upon Ah Ao, languidly spread out, with her dress loosened, her dark hair starred with bits of green leaves, and altogether wearing a look of abandon. The spectacle somehow aroused in Lao Teh, the Spotted Face, an intense fury. He stared with wide-open eyes, and then he bent down and severely struck her.

"Ha! Ah Ao! The devil! You've done a fine thing!" She did not speak, but lifted up eyes that implored and eloquently begged pity. "Scandalous and shameless one! To come here in secret and lie with him!"

Later on, this scene and the subsequent abuse flung upon her by the infuriated Lao Teh remained rather obscure in Ah Ao's mind. She could not remember how, under his guidance, she returned home in disgrace, nor how news of her love spread throughout the village in a few minutes. Only afterward all the eyes she looked into were full of wrath, cold-gleaming eyes of hate. Even her mother gazed at her with anger and bitterness, yet deeper, deep down in those eyes, was a look of poignant sadness that troubled her heart. But the blows of bamboo sticks, the beatings that came in rapid succession, the curses hurled at her, not one of these caused her any pain, nor any shame, nor even the least regret.

She had expected all this, and now it had come. It was no accident, but had all along been in the certainty of fate, and she was prepared for everything that happened. The single unforeseen development that dismayed and depressed her was that her lover suffered none of the consequences and did not appear to be in the least interested in her any longer.

Even before the men guests had finished sipping the last of their wine, the women began to come for their share, and during all this time Ah Ao continued to press closely against the wall, hovering in her hiding place, hungry and shivering, not because it was cold, not because she felt any longer the fear of death, but from some nameless malady that had seized her inmost being. The women ate no more lightly than their menfolk, and like the men they dropped cynical, sardonic remarks meant to stab mother and daughter cruelly.

The air seemed charged with heightened drama when Mrs. Li, the fat mother of Ah Hsian, unexpectedly appeared at the feast. She had come, it was soon apparent, not to apologize for the part her son had taken in the affair, but on the contrary to curse the Widow Wang for permitting her daughter to induce him to commit adultery. At sight of the unhappy mother, she pointed fixedly at her and began loudly to revile her: "Miserable woman! Where there is such a daughter, there is such a mother also! And you have the 'face' to come to meet me? Actually? My son is pure, chaste, good; he has made the genuflections before the image of Confucius; he has understood well the teachings of the great sage. Yet you, shameless mother and immoral daughter, attempt to seduce and ruin him! I am resolved to die with you this instant!"

And, saying this, she did indeed rush toward the Widow Wang and appeared to be determined to dash her brains out against her. Other woman guests grouped round them, forming a little circle, not without experiencing an inner satisfaction at the scene, and comforting and soothing the wrath of the offended Mrs. Li. The fat woman in fact so far forgot her original intention that she partook heartily of the feast and in the end contented herself with muttering now and then, "She abused my son, seduced him—from now on he will be unable to raise his head above others!"

When the last guest had gone, the old widow stepped slowly into the little dark enclosure, carrying an oil lamp in her hand. She called to Ah Ao to come out and eat, and the girl dragged herself forth, but she had scarcely strength enough to stand erect. A moment ago she had thought herself famished; now she could not swallow a morsel.

Midnight. Widow Wang was not yet in bed. She moved about in the little room, picking up articles from here and there, busily arranging them in the baggage which Ah Ao must take with her when she left at tomorrow's dawn. Finally she fastened the bag.

Spring nights are brief; in a very short time the cocks began to crow. The widow awoke her son and daughter, lighted a lantern, gave them their morning food and then accompanied Ah Ao almost at once to the barrow which stood beside the door.

"Understand, daughter, it's not I who wants to desert you—you have spoiled yourself—" But the stooped figure shook with sudden tears. She seemed to brace herself against the air, and continued, managing to smile very gently: "Just be careful, Ah Ao. From now on stand firmly on your own feet, and I shall have no more cause for worry. As for me, daughter, well just think that I am dead, no longer in this world. If we can't meet here again, then perhaps after death; anyway, let's hope!"

She sat beside Ah Ao on the barrow pushed by her son, until they reached the great oak, at the main road, half a mile from her home. She alighted there, bade a last farewell to her daughter and stood watching the receding lantern till, like the last flutter of life in a great void of death, its dim spark crept into utter darkness.

WANG HSI-YEN

Growth of Hate

Wang Hsi-yen's stories about the war and Chinese soldiers are based on his own first-hand experiences during the war in China. Many of his stories have appeared in the popular Chinese magazine *Battlefront of Literature.* [From *Asia Magazine,* August, 1943; used by permission of *United Nations World;* translated by M. Q. Ho and Clarence Moy.]

AFTER BREAKING THROUGH the enemy lines and marching rapidly for a night and a day, our troops arrived at a "peaceful area" west of Woyang. It was black night again. Woyang had been in flames from enemy bombing, but twenty *li* farther on we came to a quiet little village. Dead tired from the fatigue of the past fortnight, we crawled indiscriminately into the millet sheds and fell asleep on the wheat stalks. "*Wei,* Lao Ch'en, this won't do! This wheat stalk stinks!" I muttered. But I did not have the strength to move.

When I awoke, my eyelids were sticky, and felt painful. I thrust my head out of the shed and looked around me. Wheat stalks! So, after all, it was a pile of half-dry donkey dung!

"Lao Ch'en, look—what sleepy devils we are! What kind of wheat stalk is this!"

Lao Ch'en uttered an oath and spat and stamped his feet.

At this point a hunchbacked farmer dashed out from a squatty house opposite. Humbly and apologetically he said to me: "*Tse tse!* It is all donkey dung. I was drying it for fuel. *Lao tsung,* you are really—. And you didn't say a word. There is an empty place in my house."

I thanked him and looked him over. This man's wrinkled temple showed clearly that his heart was virtuous. When he spoke, he showed the farmer's characteristic shyness and timidity. A pipe for which he seemed to have no place was now in his mouth, now in his hands. A dirty tobacco pouch swung continuously from his pipe.

"I'll dip out some water for you to wash in."

"Never mind, the river is more convenient."

When we returned from washing ourselves, the farmer again came up to us.

"Lao tsung, I have boiled water for you."

This term "lao tsung," literally, "old chief," is used by the common people to show their respect in addressing a soldier. Oh, how warm and deep was the sentiment shown us by the simple villagers all along the road! Whenever we stopped to rest or to camp, they would welcome

us with boiled water, congee, millet cake and noodles, and those particularly concerned looks and simple questions, as if welcoming their own
sons or husbands just returning home wearily from the fields. Almost
all of them were simple and kind. In their minds, they kept unhappy
memories about these fellows who carried arms; their village saying
was "Fear only soldiers; do not fear bandits." But all of them knew
that now it was not the same. These guests from far away were their
own people and shared their fate.

Bending low, we entered the farmer's dark squatty little house. A
huge earthen stove left very little space for anything else. The roof,
made of strips of millet stalk, was already in disrepair, and the broken
stalks that hung down would from time to time hit your head and
spread a layer of dust over you. On the stove, a pot was puffing out
steam. Another pot, in which there was probably left some sort of
wheat congee, had become a battleground for flies.

At this point, a thin woman, with protruding yellow teeth, stood up
in front of the stove door. She did not say a word, but carefully and
shyly took off for us the pot-cover woven of millet stalk, suddenly releasing a lot of steam.

The farmer outside the door was still calling to other brothers, "Lao
tsung, there is boiled water here!" As soon as he said "boiled water," a
group of our men crowded in like a drove of ants that had discovered
something tasty. More than ten tin cups were thrust into the pot at
the same time, making clashing sounds and splashing water flowers.
This situation caused the woman to laugh out. She wiped away the
perspiration from her face and repeated over and over: "Not enough?
Boil some more. Boil another big pot!"

Before half the tin cups were filled, the pot was dry. Some took back
their cups empty. Some tried to get the few pitiful drops left in the
bottom, making a scraping sound. Still others called anxiously from
without, "Wei, let us all be a little more polite!"

The farmer stood beside the door and uneasily rubbed and twisted
his hands. Laughing unnaturally, he said: "Old chief, just bear it a
while. I will go right away to fetch water." Putting down his pipe, he
hurriedly looked for his wooden bucket and murmured to the woman,
"I told you to boil a big pot, a big pot."

When you entered this squatty little house, you saw nothing clearly;
but you soon became accustomed to the darkness. Now I noticed
crouching before the stove, like toads hiding in some dark ditch, two
little children, their bodies shrunken up, their eyes rolling, timidly staring at the rough intruders. When they saw me looking at them, these
two youngsters, in sudden fright, pulled and tugged at each other and
scurried behind the woman.

The farmer quickly returned with two buckets of water. With a dried
gourd shell he laded it into the pot. His slightly hunched body bent
even more, and he coughed.

"Wei, old villager, what is your name?"

"I am called Hunched Chang Erh," he answered, laughing in embarrassment. "The younger people—they like to call me Uncle Hunched Chang Erh."

"Are those two your children?"

"You mean those two girls? *He he*—yes, two mouths that know only how to eat!"

The lovable thing about these farmers is in this! Their hearts are like a folded paper fan. When folded, they are very close and tight and do not let through a breath of wind; but, as soon as they are open, they show everything before your eyes. He revealed all his sorrow and hate at the same time, without selection, without consideration. He talked of everything from the lack of land and the scantiness of crops to the many heavy taxes and duties.

"Old chief, our crops are taken for tribute, and on each village taxes are levied ten times over. They have so many different names that you cannot even remember what they are. Ah, it is not easy. Oil can be omitted, but salt is hard to do without. And it has risen to such a price you are lucky if you have any!"

He paused and sighed. The bitter things of life had saturated his heart. He took out his pipe, his only comforter, and lit it, releasing a thread of smoke that coiled up into his sad face.

"Are not the devils wanting to attack here?"

The pipe left his bearded mouth, and he sighed heavily again.

"I heard they are only forty or fifty li from Woyang," interrupted his woman in front of the stove. "Old chief, is that true? Forty or fifty li is not even a day's journey. Bald-headed Lao Wu says that, whenever the devil's foreign guns open fire, they can shoot eighty li away!"

"Not so fast," I answered casually, purposely making my voice very soft and indistinct.

For seven or eight days we had not put into our mouths a complete meal. Sour peaches and mulberries had been our only food, and muddy, yellow creek water had become very precious liquid. Thinking to comfort our ill-treated stomachs a bit, a large group of us discussed having an "abundant" meal. But where could we get rice and meat? In the village, the families of any importance had already left their homes, and only a few families who ate wheat congee were left. Hunched Chang Erh told us that to get rice or meat one had to go to a big market more than ten li away. "Old chief," he said, "you have only to trust me, Hunched Chang Erh. I would not cheat lao tsung half a cash!"

Not trust him? We did not even think of this. We gave him money and explained what we needed.

After a while he returned, panting, with a heavy load suspended from the pole on his shoulder. He reported in detail the cost and weight of the rice, vegetables, meat. Then, taking off his patch-covered jacket, he wiped the perspiration from his head, smiling as if he had just completed some important affair of his own concern.

"Really, it is dangerous!" he said in an exaggerated and excited tone.

Spiritedly, he went on to tell us of being inspected along the road by entries of another troop. Several soldiers on horseback had blocked his way, pointing with bayonets at his chest and ordering him to leave his rice and meat. He had steadfastly refused, explaining his mission, and had been released after receiving several blows from rifle butts. And at another place, near the outskirts of his village, a guard ordered him to halt. He did not hear, so *pa!*—a rifle sounded, and a bullet flew by near his ear. He had almost lost his life!

When we wanted to give him a bit of reward for his trouble, he was bewildered and could not speak for half the day. He could only wave his hands continuously, his face reddening and his hump seeming to grow in size. "Old chief, you—this, this, this—I, Hunched Chang Erh, am not, not—this, this, this sort of person!"

"You take it. This is the rule in our army. It is impossible not to take it!"

"Do not pretend—really!" another brother mumbled.

"No, it is not so." He protested uneasily. "I heard one old chief say that you had been broken up at the front by the devils. All of you have suffered a great deal. I do not want money!"

When the meal was cooked, each of us filled our tin cup with hot, steaming rice, breaking off millet stalks for chopsticks. Those who were too late in getting millet stalks used their fingers.

"Really tasty. But it lacks a little salt!"

At the same time as our meal, that buck-toothed woman had cooked, in a small pot, some wheat congee, a rough, thick yellow soup. The two skinny little girls had joined their father and mother to eat it. Opening and closing their bloodless, thin lips, they stole glances at us.

We called out to Hunched Chang Erh: "Old villager, we have caused you much trouble, and you do not want money. Come, eat with us— you and Elder Sister-in-law and the two little ladies."

"No, what words do you speak? For many days you have not comfortably eaten a meal. You have many men and should eat it yourselves. I can eat wheat congee. Don't be so formal."

He hunched his body and left us.

The airplanes were coming! The frightening sound of the motors came closer and closer. The enemy were mad and bold, flying low in the air. Vaguely, we could see the killers in the planes on their way to drop down several tons of heavy bombs in a small near-by village. Great explosive sounds swept across half the sky, and the earth began to tremble.

This frightened Hunched Chang Erh badly. He was as confused as a weasel pursued by a hunting dog; and to escape this threat of death he crouched under a large willow tree by the river, embracing the tree trunk with both hands. The color of his face had changed completely. After the sound of the planes had disappeared, he was still crouched in the water, tightly holding to a root of the tree, as if he had lost his senses.

Someone made fun of him and called: "Wei, old villager, the thing is over. Come up."

"Anyhow those bombs fell far off, at least five li. Don't be afraid!"

"Don't be afraid?" He looked at us perplexedly. "Cannot one bomb bomb twenty or thirty li? I heard one bomb can kill more than a hundred men."

Now his woman had come out. She, likewise, was stupefied with terror and cursed stammeringly: "Those men up there! One bomb— makes, makes, makes evils—evils!"

The two little girls pulled tightly at the corner of their mother's clothes, frightened without understanding what had happened.

The talking turned to other things. Someone spoke of the ways the devils killed people, saying that, when they caught the men, they tied them under the cinches of horses. Five or ten men were tied to five or ten horses and then they were led outside of the stockade. A shot was fired, and the devil soldiers on the backs of the horses would kick their spurs recklessly.

"And when they catch the women?"

"You listen to me," the same fellow began describing boastfully. "The devils' hearts are black! When they catch the women, they pick out the ones with good-looking faces and take them under the trees. What do you say would happen now? The devils sit stiff and upright like a board, holding their bayonets in their hands, their mustaches bristling. They force the women to take off their jackets and trousers, and if they hesitate a little they kick their bottoms with the points of their shoes. Under the blue sky and the white sun, it is like this. When one is finished, another comes up."

"Tse, tse, tse . . . makes evils!"

After the sky darkened, orders came for us to prepare to depart so that we could catch up with our main forces ahead of us. Just then, Hunched Chang Erh found me. "Corporal—old chief—" he called confusedly.

"Ah, Uncle! What is it?"

"It is impossible to sleep on that pile of donkey dung there! That bed of mine can hold two persons. I and the little girls and their mother can sleep in front of the stove. That pile of donkey dung is damp!"

"Old villager, it is not necessary. We will be leaving soon."

"Leaving?" To him this was not a small matter. "Old chief, why are you leaving? Are you leaving so quickly?"

He was so excited—this Hunched Chang Erh—that I told him the truth.

"We stopped only a moment to rest our legs and to restore our spirits. The main force has already gone ahead, and we are to catch up with them to avoid losing our connections. Behind, the devil soldiers are pursuing us closely. Our munitions and supply have not been entirely received. Our weapons, also, are incomplete. We must hurry to catch up with the main force."

After these words were spoken, I felt I had been too careless. Hurriedly, I then added: "But we still have troops behind us who are withstanding the devil soldiers."

"What?" he asked anxiously. "The devil soldiers are coming, and you are running away! Leaving us farmers who cannot go. Letting the devil soldiers come to devastate, to drag men tied to the cinches of horses, to make evil on women. And letting the devil soldiers drop bombs, bombs which can kill more than a hundred people apiece—which are so loud, they sound like thunder!"

He was just like a dog which had swallowed some poison and gone mad.

Suddenly that buck-toothed woman also stood before me, like a crazy woman.

"What? The devil soldiers are coming? What shall we do? How can you go away?"

"Lao tsung, you cannot." Hunched Chang Erh was as terrified as if the black hand of death had already clutched him. "You cannot go. If you go, I will go with you, lao tsung! Mother of our little girls, you hurry pack up!"

"Go with them? What of these two little girls? What of the wheat in the fields?"

"You won't go? When the devil soldiers arrive, will you go or not?"

He turned around very quickly, and in the dark there immediately came from the squatty house the banging of furniture, the low sound of deliberation and sounds of shouting.

All this seemed to frighten the neighbors.

"Uncle Hunched Erh, what is happening?"

"Take—take refuge! Devils are coming. It is hard to escape with your life! The lao tsung do not look after us, so I am going with them."

"What about your house? And your wheat?"

"There is nothing to be done. The devil soldiers' hearts are black!"

But we could not wait! The horses at the outskirt of the village neighed anxiously in a low tone, and in the village there arose a short, mild disturbance. Thus we left. Nor did we see Hunched Chang Erh come after us.

By the time we arrived at the town of X—and had caught up with the main forces, three days had gone by. Our troop was stationed at a small stockade five or six li south of the town.

This time, we were ordered to withstand the pursuing enemy here.

When a plan was decided upon, we found a house under the shade of a tree outside the west end of the stockade. In disorderly fashion, we lay in the pile of wheat stalks. Some of the soldiers were busy washing their feet, changing their clothes or singing "This is the critical moment for sacrifice." Some brought back from a small provisions store a bottle of wine and fought and yelled over it. After a while, shots rang out from the east end of the stockade. The special service lieutenant blew sharply on his whistle, and many brothers ran over with their arms.

"What's the matter?"

"A spy! Pretended to be a *lao pai hsing*. He hunched his back and made up very well. A sentry called at him to halt, but he spread his legs and ran back. Pa, one shot. Hit him just right."

What? Spy? So all of us rushed over.

The spy had already been caught and was being escorted into the stockade by several brothers. Half his front lapel was running with blood, and his legs were spotted with red. His face a deathly gray, he walked along, his body shivering, a pipe hanging from the back of his neck.

"Uncle Hunched Erh, is it you. You?"

As soon as he saw me, his eyes brightened, and he wept aloud.

"Corporal! You save—save my life!"

I looked at him doubtfully:

"How is it? You?"

"Corporal, is it not?" he began. By this time he had been deposited under a large poplar tree. Painfully his face puckered up. Now pausing, now continuing, he tried with all his strength to speak, but he could not make his words coherent: "That evening was the evening—of the seventh. Lao tsung had already set out. I did not want to let those black-hearted devil soldiers. . . . My woman said: 'What of the wheat in the fields? And what of this tumble-down house?' I said: 'You won't go? When the devil soldiers arrive, will you go or not?' I shouldered the two little girls by a pole—the little nuisances—and with their mother ran after you lao tsung in the night. The night was too dark. I followed the highway—but, no matter how, I could not catch up with you. My woman could not run fast, and the pair of nuisances hindered us. The next day, the—the eighth, that day—we had just arrived at X—market. I said, 'Move quickly, catch up with them.' My woman refused stubbornly to do this. 'No life. I want to rest my feet here, drink a little water.' It was really so, and the little girls had cholera. I could do nothing, and I ran by myself out of the market to the bank of a stream to wash my face."

He paused a moment. Then his speaking became more urgent.

"Ah, the airplanes came. Everybody—ran away. I hurried back to the market—to find the mother and children. The airplanes dropped their bombs. *Hung—hung*—I could only run away from the market. Afterward the airplanes flew away, and I went back to the market—to look for the mother and children. They—in a heap—dead. Died so —so terribly—terribly!"

He wept inarticulately.

"I could only—run with empty hands. I could only—follow lao tsung. I—I—"

He rolled his eyes and painfully tried to push himself up with both hands. His voice was pitiful and hoarse.

"I do not hate lao tsung. I hate the black-hearted devils! I will not—will not die—"

A red light seemed to flash forth from his face, and he stretched out
a hand appealingly.

"Give me a gun!"

Again he rolled his eyes. He had fainted away.

LIN YUTANG

The Dog-Meat General

Lin Yutang, born in 1895 in Changchow,
went to St. John's, a missionary school in
Shanghai, graduating in 1916. He studied
at Harvard and received a doctorate degree
at Leipzig. He joined the staff of Peking
National University in 1923, and edited
two popular magazines which contributed
much toward the development of art and
humor in Chinese literature. He is best
known for his book *My Country and My
People,* which depicts the decay of Chinese
feudal civilization. [From *With Love and
Irony* by Lin Yutang; copyright 1940 by
Lin Yutang; used by permission of the
John Day Co., Inc.]

SO GENERAL CHANG TSUNG-CHANG, the "Dog-meat Gen-
eral," has been killed, according to this morning's report. I am sorry
for him, and I am sorry for his mother, and I am sorry for the sixteen
concubines he has left behind him and the four times sixteen that had
left him before he died. As I intend to specialize in writing "in memo-
riams" for the bewildering generals of this bewildering generation, I
am going to begin with the Dog-meat General first.

So our Dog-meat General is dead! What an event! It is full of
mystic significance for me and for China and us poor folk who do not
wear boots and carry bayonets! Such a thing could not happen every
day, and if it could there would be an end to all China's sorrows. In
such an eventuality you could abolish all the five Yuan, tear up the will
of Dr. Sun Yat-sen, dismiss the hundred odd members of the Central
Executive Committee of the Kuomintang, close up all the schools and
universities of China, and you wouldn't have to bother your head about
Communism, Fascism, and Democracy, and universal suffrage, and
emancipation of women, and we poor folk would still be able to live
in peace and prosperity.

So one more of the colorful, legendary figures of medieval China has
passed into eternity. And yet Dog-meat General's death has a special
significance for me, because he was the most colorful, legendary, medieval, and unashamed ruler of modern China. He was a born ruler
such as modern China wants. He was six feet tall, a towering giant,
with a pair of squint eyes and a pair of abnormally massive hands. He
was direct, forceful, terribly efficient at times: obstinate and gifted with

moderate intelligence. He was patriotic according to his lights, and he was anti-communist, which made up for his being anti-Kuomintang. All his critics must allow that he wasn't anti-Kuomintang from convictions, but by accident. He didn't want to fight the Kuomintang: it was the Kuomintang that wanted to fight him and grab his territory, and, being an honest man, he fought rather than turn tail. Given a chance, and if the Kuomintang would return him his Shantung, he would join the Kuomintang, because he said that the Sanmin doctrine can't do any harm.

He could drink, and he was awfully fond of "dog-meat," and he could swear all he wanted to and as much as he wanted to, irrespective of his official superiors and inferiors. He made no pretense to being a gentleman, and didn't affect to send nice-sounding circular telegrams, like the rest of them. He was ruthlessly honest, and this honesty made him much loved by all his close associates. If he loved women he said so, and he could see foreign consuls while he had a Russian girl sitting on his knee. If he made orgies he didn't try to conceal them from his friends and foes. If he coveted his subordinate's wife he told him openly, and wrote no psalm of repentance about it like King David. And he always played square. If he took his subordinate's wife he made her husband the chief of police of Tsinan. And he took good care of other people's morals. He forbade girl students from entering parks in Tsinan, and protected them from the men-gorillas who stood at every corner and nook to devour them. And he was pious, and he kept a harem. He believed in polyandry as well as polygamy, and he openly allowed his concubines to make love with other men, provided he didn't want them at the time. He respected Confucius. And he was patriotic. He was reported to be overjoyed to find a bed-bug in a Japanese bed in Beppo, and he never tired of telling people of the consequent superiority of Chinese civilization. He was very fond of his executioner, and he was thoroughly devoted to his mother.

Many legends have been told about Dog-meat's ruthless honesty. He loved a Russian prostitute and his Russian prostitute loved a poodle, and he made a whole regiment pass in review before the poodle to show that he loved the prostitute that loved the poodle. Once he appointed a man magistrate in a certain district in Shantung, and another day he appointed another man to the same office and started a quarrel. Both claimed that they had been personally appointed by General Dog-meat. It was agreed, therefore, that they should go and see the General to clear up the difficulty. When they arrived it was evening, and General Chang was in bed in the midst of his orgies. "Come in," he said, with his usual candor.

The two magistrates then explained that they had both been appointed by him to the same district.

"You fools!" he said, "can't you settle such a little thing between yourselves, but must come to bother me about it?"

Like the heroes of the great Chinese novel *Shui Hu,* and like all

Chinese robbers, he was an honest man. He never forgot a kindness, and he was obstinately loyal to those who had helped him. His trousers-pockets were always stuffed with money, and when people came to him for help he would pull out a bank-roll and give a handful to those that asked. He distributed hundred-dollar notes as Rockefeller distributed dimes.

Because of his honesty and his generosity he was beyond the hatred of his fellow-men.

This morning as I entered my office and informed my colleagues of the great news everyone smiled, which shows that everyone was friendly toward him. No one hated him, and no one could hate him.

China is still being ruled by men like him, who haven't got his honesty, generosity, and loyalty. He was a born ruler, such as modern China wants, and he was the best of them all.

YOUNGHILL KANG

Doomsday

Younghill Kang was born in a Korean village at the turn of the century. He was educated at Seoul, the cultural capital of Korea, and in Tokyo. When he was eighteen he came to Canada, where he also studied, then going to Boston and New York. Ultimately, he taught at New York University and is now on an educational mission for the United States Government. He has written *The Grass Roof* and *East Goes West*. [From *The Grass Roof* by Younghill Kang; copyright 1931 by Charles Scribner's Sons; used by permission of the publishers.]

IN THE LATE SPRING when I was almost ten I came home from the village school, sick, and under that pretense, I refused to go there any longer. My grandmother was worried about my stomach-ache. She called in a witch. Ordinarily my grandmother seemed to be a Confucian, and had raised her children by the ethical codes of that sage. Temperamentally, of course, she was a Buddhist, loving to meditate to herself, or to tell the stories of Buddha and its legends. Also she had her idea of God as the supreme ruler of the Universe: she was a monotheist like many Koreans. But when somebody was sick or anything went wrong in her life which required some practical measure, she called in a fortune-teller.

This witch, or fortune-teller, was an old woman of the lowest class, bent over, dressed in dirty mud-colored clothes, and walking by a wrinkled cane. I have always thought that when a woman is very very old, she must be very beautiful, for there is the record of many true and sincere moments on her face. On the other hand, if she has spent her life in ugliness and tricky ways, there are few objects more vile to see than the furrows telling of her past. I always thought the women I saw in Song-Dune-Chi had good-looking faces, even my fat aunt, until I saw this woman, who pretended to be friends with the spirits of sickness and ill-will and destruction; she bargained to put them favorable to you, if you gave her something for the service.

She often came around our house, for two reasons. If my grandmother accepted her, the other women in the village would too, for my grandmother was a criterion. Then my grandmother was so emotional that she almost lost her mind when anyone she loved was endangered. This time the fortune-teller advised that the shoes, socks, coats and trousers I had worn when I got sick, be given away at once; and then she took them home with her for her own son.

Yes, she was always very shrewd. She was careful to speak with my grandmother alone, when nobody else was near, for my grandmother was the only one she could deceive. None of the men in our house believed in these spirits, but they did not contradict my grandmother any more than a gentleman in the West contradicts his mother when she wants to believe in the Fundamental Doctrine. If she desired to send up a wish to the village ghosts, my crazy-poet uncle would write it for her in elegant verses, but with no enthusiasm; and all he would say was once in a while, "O Sug!"—inside. Now my grandmother was not exactly superstitious, and seemed to have plenty of commonsense when nobody was sick, or needed anything badly. Still, it is a fact, she always listened to the fortune-teller, and when told to destroy my clothes, she reasoned:

"It couldn't do any harm to Chung-Pa's stomach-ache. It couldn't possibly make him any sicker. So why not do it and feel more comfortable? If he grew worse, and I had not done everything possible, how bad I should feel!"

But my stomach-ache did not go away, because I did not intend to return to Co-Mool's school. So the old witch came back. I saw her come in at the bamboo gate, and enter the kitchen door. I was very angry, because she had taken my clothes. I went running into the kitchen to show I was not sick, just as she was trying to make my grandmother give my best long ribbon over to her. She said the evil spirits wanted that, in addition to the rest.

"Get out!" I cried. "Get out! You dirty Devil-woman. I am not sick. Where do you get your stuff? Go to hell, you fake!"

She seemed to be really frightened, and cleared out, not saying a word. But she came back one day when I had gone fishing. She told my grandmother that I would surely bring the ruin on my family, if I were not sent off to study the doctrines of Buddha at once. This seemed to my grandmother a very good idea. My father, though he had no affiliations with the Buddha, did not object. Buddhism when compared with Western civilization was at least honored and ancient. Besides, though my father was the theoretical boss, my grandmother, in matters like this, was the practical boss.

The week on which we set out to make our Pilgrimage had been very hot and still, in our village, as if in the heat of Summer. No one felt like doing any work. Everybody sat in chronological groups, discussing the political situation. All this discussion just made my father angry, and he alone kept right on working. My crazy-poet uncle sat under the broad-leafed Odong tree, and drank wine, and looked worried, but said, "No—O no! Japan will not take Korea. In spite of all her new ways, she respects the ancient culture too much, and besides she has promised not to."

Before setting out, my grandmother and I had each a complete baptism in the bathtub. This was a round wooden tub, painted bright red, a nice place to sit, but sometimes too hot on these occasions. Our complete cleansing of every hair was symbolic, and the water was boiled first, to make it holy and pure. We started, before the sun got up, for the journey was thirty miles and we must walk steadily all day in order to do that amount on foot. The air was sweet and hushed and ghost-colored, so that it too seemed purified for the journey. My grandmother's eyes were shining; she was very happy to be going away, leaving all family and national troubles behind, for a while. Her mood was that of the old Korean poem:

> I take up my green budding rod,
> I turn up the rocky path-way,
> To three or four heavenly vales
> With halos of clouds.
> I shake off the world's dust today,
> To gather the pine's scarlet cones.

(The pine to the oriental is the symbol of immortality.)

My grandmother had her cane, and I my little bundle of clothes with paper and pens. Behind us my grandmother's servant followed with the food. This was a little girl of fourteen or fifteen who was named Keum-Soon, or child-of-gold, the daughter of a poor widow. There was not much to do in her house, so she came to us for food and clothes and to help my grandmother and her daughters do all the work of washing and of sweeping and of ironing clothes with the laundry stick. That old woman who owned the apricot tree and thought that the best thing in life was a good chicken was an excellent helper at an ancestor festival, or for any feast of food, but was not much good for everyday at our house.

The morning grew only more calm. Ten miles below the monastery we entered no-man's land. Here was no house, nor any human. No horse could be used here. We traveled along a narrow walk of stone-slabs, with silent greenery on every side, stretching for miles, always upward. Some of the stone slabs were carved with Chinese characters and my grandmother and I read them aloud to each other. Once in a while we saw a squirrel being caught by an eagle, or a big bird having a bath in the stream. Late in the afternoon a monk parted some bushes and passed us on his way to the heights. He took no notice of us, but walked in silence like the monk in the poem about:

> A shadow is made in the water.
> On the bridge a monk is passing.
> Stop . . . O monk, talk with me,
> Which is your way?
> But his hand points to the white clouds . . .
> He goes stilly by. . . .

All the way up, my grandmother talked of Buddha.

"You know," she said to me, "Buddha was a very very great man. You should do what he says, and follow in his footsteps."

"Why, Grandmother?"

"A great man always does what he says he will do. When he makes a resolution, he follows it to the straight, through floods, fires, mountains and every danger."

She told me a tale about Buddha. She believed it was actually a fact.

"Buddha was born a great prince, in an aristocratic family, where he had honor and servants and wealth. But he was not satisfied, because he wanted to understand about life. One day he heard a baby crying and he asked his guardian:

"'Guardian, why is that baby crying?'

"'Why, Master, it is being born, and that is the beginning of sorrow.'

"And Buddha thought, 'This is strange. Why is the baby crying? Where did *he* come from?'

"He went under a willow tree, and he saw an old man, gray-headed and wrinkled and ghost-like. He asked his guardian:

"'Guardian, why is the old man ugly like that?'

"'All men, Master, must grow old, in this life. It is the way of sorrow.'

"And Buddha thought, 'I wouldn't like to be old like him. That would be Hell.' (This is the nearest translation to my grandmother's and the Buddha's expression.)

"Then Buddha came on a man who was groaning with pain. And Buddha asked his guardian:

"'Guardian, what is the matter with that man?'

"'Master, he is in pain. Every man must know pain at some time or other in this life. There is much much sorrow here.'

"Then Buddha thought, 'I want to avoid *that*!'

"Presently he found people crying in front of a house.

"'Guardian, why do the people cry?'

"'Master, there is a man dead in there. At last he has gone away from this earth for good. It is the end.'

"And Buddha thought: 'Where did he go to? Why did this man die?'

"So Buddha thought and thought: 'What is it all about?' and all he wanted was to solve the problem. Finally he gave up his beautiful wife, his beautiful baby, his beautiful home, and he went up to the great Snow

Mountain, still trying to solve the problem. After many many years he was enlightened. He saw how every living creature was making a pilgrimage to reach the no-life again and every soul that did wrong had to go back and begin all over again. After Buddha had solved the problem, he resolved never to do two things: He would not tell a lie, and he would kill no living thing, for everything he saw was his brother.—This," said my grandmother, "is why the good monk, Kim, never eats chicken when he comes to our house, you know."

"But the monk, Pak, did, Grandmother."

"Well, there are true monks, and false monks," explained my grandmother, "like everything else in this world."—And she went on with the story.

"And you know when you decide to be a great man, God always sends you a messenger to examine you. So after Buddha came down from the mountain and had made his two vows, God sent his messenger to examine Buddha, and his messenger was a deer.

"As Buddha was walking along, the deer ran out of the forest, and he cried to Buddha:

" 'O save me, save me, Buddha! A hunter is trying to kill me!'

"So Buddha thought, 'If I am to keep my resolution, I must save this deer.' He dug a hole in the ground and put the deer down there and covered it with oak leaves and told it to lie still.

"By and by a hunter came along.

" 'Tell me, did you see a deer? Where did he go? I am going to kill that deer right now.'

"What was Buddha to do? If he said no, he would be telling a lie, if he said yes, he would betray the deer, and the murder would be upon his soul. So he said nothing.

"The hunter kicked him on this side, then kicked him on that. But Buddha stood very firm on his rocky foundation. The hunter cut off his right arm and then his left. Still, Buddha said nothing. Then the hunter fell down and worshiped Buddha.

" 'Ah! Here is a great man!' he cried.

"And he became Buddha's convert, because Buddha had met the test and stuck to the resolution."

So the time passed delightfully with my grandmother until the sun went down and the mountains became soft and shadowy, with white mist here and there, like the Bodhisattvas, or future Buddhas, waiting to receive us. We did not reach the monastery until almost dark; so it was generally with pilgrims, for the monasteries were far away from the villages and had little to do with them.

It is a beautiful experience to come upon an old Buddhist monastery by twilight. There are many poems in the native literature of my country about this.

> From the boom of the drums that temple
> Must be close though they say it is far—

Far over the green mountains,
Away at the foot of the clouds. . . . .
But I cannot see;
Thick mists obscure the way. . . .

At one time many centuries ago, they were a very powerful factor in the state, and even the king was compelled to put on monk's dress, as a sign that he was only an official of abbots. But by and by the country became corrupt under the rule of the abbots. A certain platform on which pretty young women worshiped would fall through the floor by a miracle. Far down underground these women got betrayed by monks. At last the monasteries were exiled to remote mountain sites where they could not work any more miracles. But those whose mystical natures could not be satisfied by the practical ethics of Confucius, like my grandmother, still made pilgrimage once or twice a year, and confided their prayers to the monks.

Up here in the Yellow Dusk the antique monastery seemed to melt into the summit of the green mountain, bounded everywhere with stone tigers and marble lions, singing streams and holy groves. These statues of fantastic shapes had been fashioned I suppose by the hand of man, but nothing here looked artificial; it seemed as if all must have sprung out of the ground. The rich dim colors of the shrines bathing in sun and rain, wind and storm of the mountain for countless centuries—all natural, natural the gray of the steps, natural the deep red of the pillars, all in tune with the natural rocks and natural trees, bound together it seemed, by invisible, indivisible unity. The song of the evening bird grew imperceptibly out of the sound of the running brook, and vanished again in the long sobbing of the pines. But somehow it was all ethereal and unreal like a mystic's dream.

In a series of cloud-like pictures, I recall my three months' sojourn at this monastery which belonged to the Meditation School of the Buddha—the darkness of the mountain hollows by dawn and by twilight, the hushed, almost buried stillness of everything by day, the mysterious greeting which the monks all gave one another, and which I soon learned to say: "Nam moo ah mi to pool" (I honor you and resort to you, Amitabha), or the prayer "Po che choong saing" (for the salvation of all living things), the cool silent ghost-chamber where I studied, with walls gorgeously painted with the heroes and sages who had lived in the past, the Buddhistic scriptures of the library in which I read and read, and the gray abbot, my teacher, in his mournful, mud-colored robes, and his transparent face free from all wordly care or desires.

He tried to teach me the way of Nirvana, which means a "blowing out," like a candle. We sat in his large empty room with pillars which held the engravings:

Make no evil deed,
All good obediently do.

Purge the mind of self,
This is all Buddha's teaching.

When I went out in the beautiful gardens I was rebuked for slapping the gnat to death which landed on my ear or my nose.

"Even gnats," said the monk, Kim, "may have within them Buddha. They too may attain to Nirvana, and the state of never being born again. Endeavor to be more calm, do not become the evil fate of any living thing."

So I was taught how Buddhists kill neither mouse, louse, nor cows.

When I returned to my home during the last week in August, I found a shocking contrast to the mystic world I had just left. . . .

It may seem strange to the reader unfamiliar with Far-Eastern politics that Korea, an independent nation for over forty-two centuries, should have been so helpless those first ten years of the twentieth century before the stealthy but persistent encroaching of New Japan. But Japan's strength in the East is due to rapid Westernization, especially in regard to armament. That alone, perhaps, she thoroughly learned, since the time of Perry's entrance, and is thoroughly competent to proselyte. With the vigor of a younger nation, engaged already in enormous changing, inherently imitative, it is easy for her to slough one borrowed culture and to absorb another in its place. Yes, comparatively easy, as it was not for the older nations, China and Korea. Clinging closely to the old Confucian culture, and each in an exhausted era of their history, they were truly stunned for those first decades of world-wide intercourse.

That little Japan won over the million millions of wise deep China, first. After her victory, she began to make her demands upon Korea, during the Russo-Japanese war. She must be allowed passage for her troops through Korea, and she signed a treaty stating that she had no designs upon the Korean state as a whole. These troops were never withdrawn. They remained to shelter the swarms of low-class Japanese adventurers who followed, and to uphold them in all they mis-did. Japan moved deliberately step by step. She first seized the silent control of the incompetent and bewildered government at Seoul, in 1907: hemmed in by spies and Japanese generals, the old emperor was made to abdicate to a minor son; then at last Japan spoke plainly, the 29th of August, 1910, when all treaties were annulled and Korea was publicly declared annexed. . . .

When the news reached the grass roof in Song-Dune-Chi, my father turned a dark red, and could not even open his mouth. My uncle *pak-sa* became suddenly very old, and he shrivelled and fainted in his own room. My crazy-poet uncle sat staring straight ahead of him until far into the night. My first thought was a selfish and immature one.

"Now I cannot be a *pak-sa* or the prime minister of Korea."

I burst into tears. But my elders did not cry, not yet. So I ran crying out of the house. I looked up at the sky, to see if there were really a black doom up there. Were a final thunderstorm and a flood about to come which would wipe us all out? But the sky was blue and serene, and the river had only a sunny crystal foam as it whirled past. Children were standing around with scared blank faces. The village was quiet. Nobody spoke. Later on, in the afternoon, there was a general weeping, everywhere the sound of mourning, as if each house in the village were wailing for somebody dead. Some men began to drink and drink, shouting:

"The doomsday has come! We have all gone to the Hell!"

My father lurched out of the house, although he had had nothing to drink, and nothing to eat since morning.

"My poor poor children!" he cried out, and tears now streamed from his eyes. He held out his hands to us, as if we were all his eldest sons. "Now all are going to die in the ruined starvation. The time of the unending famine has come down upon us. Who knows when we may be happy again?"

And with tears running over his face, and mingling with his beard, he put up the Korean flag over our gateway and bowed down to it.

There was no supper that night. My grandmother sat up by candle-light, in the same dress she had worn in the morning. Again and again she took a cup of rice tea to my father, but he lay heavily on the mats, and he would not accept it.

In the morning, it was found that several of the young men who had been among those drunk the night before had committed suicide. Their bodies lay along the banks of the stream where the women usually did washing on this day.

A Japanese policeman came to our village, at the head of a band of pale-blue-coated Japanese, each armed with a long sword. Of course they knocked at our gate, and asked why we did not have the sun flag of Japan instead of the red and white flag of Korea betokening the male and female realm, and in accordance with the Confucian philosophy of the Book of Changes, sun and moon and all the elements used in geo-mancy. My father shrugged his shoulders and pretended not to under-stand. The small Jap policeman then flew at my father, kicking and striking him, with menace of the sword. My grandmother saw from the window, and ran out, without even stopping to put her coat over her head and screen her face from vulgar eyes.

"Don't you touch my son!" she screamed, stepping between, "because he has had nothing to eat for these two days and doesn't know what he is doing."

As soon as she came between them the policeman knocked her down. He kicked her fiercely with his Western boot. Her sons seeing it, gasped. In the eyes of Koreans to touch an old woman, the mother of sons, was a crime punishable by death. Even criminals were safe behind her skirts. My father would have strangled him, but saw that my grandmother had fainted with pain. He at once lifted her on his back and started off toward the market-place where there was a fairly good doctor. But her ankle was broken and she was sick for many weeks.

That night I went into my crazy-poet uncle's studio and lay down on the mat, crying miserably. By and by I heard the crazy-poet walking around and muttering in the next room. With my wet finger I made a hole in the paper door and looked through. He stood at the outer door and just shook his fist in the face of the sky.

"Oh, stars and moon, how have you the heart to shine? Why not drop down by thunderstorm and cover all things up? And mountains, with your soul shining and rustling in the green leaves and trees and grass, can't you understand that it is over now? This national career of the people who have lived with you all these many ages, who have slept in your bosoms, whose blood you have drunk, whose muse you have been for the countless years? You spirits of water, you ghosts of the hollows, don't you see how death has just come to this people established among you for the 4,000 years since the first king Tan-Koon appeared on the white-headed mountain by the side of the Sacred Tree? Don't you know the soul of Korea is gone, is passing away this night, and has left us behind like the old clothes?"

I knew that my crazy-poet uncle was as if saying good-by to a ghost, just as the tall doctor had given the farewell to my grandfather's spirit on top the grass roof. . . . Was Korea ended then? A pristine country, contemporary of Homeric times and of the Golden Ages—far, far removed from the spirit of the Roman Empire and all later modernity until this day. . . . I cried and cried myself to sleep. Outside all night I heard an unnatural day-sound—the jingle-jangle of cows which had not been put up for the night, and their astonished moos.

RYUNOSUKE
AKUTAGAWA
The
Handkerchief

Ryunosuke Akutagawa lived in Japan during an interlude between two storms—the Meiji Revolution and the Showa Restoration. His ailing health, his heritage of insanity and his pessimism were advanced as the causes of his suicide on July 24, 1927. [From *Asia Magazine,* May, 1943; used by permission of *United Nations World;* translated by Kiyoshi Morikubo.]

PROFESSOR KINZO HASEGAWA of the Tokyo Imperial University Law School, seated on a cane chair on his veranda, was reading Strindberg's "Dramaturgy."

The Professor's specialty, we all know, is the study of colonial administration. Perhaps the reader finds it strange that he was reading a book of dramatic criticism. But the Professor is known as an educator as well as a scholar, and it has been his policy to look over any book, in or out of his field, that has any influence on the thought or emotion of modern students. For instance, he has read Oscar Wilde's *De Profundis* and *Intentions* for the simple reason that they were widely read among the pupils of a special college of which he is the dean. Therefore, there is nothing strange in finding the Professor perusing a book which treats of the drama and acting of modern Europe. For among the numerous students of the Professor are not only some who write criticism of Ibsen, Strindberg and Maeterlinck, but others who intend to follow in the footsteps of these modern dramatists and make playwriting their life-work.

At the close of each of its witty chapters the Professor would drop the yellow, cloth-bound book on his lap and vaguely look over to the Gifu lantern hanging from the ceiling. Immediately his mind left Strindberg behind. Instead he would be thinking of his wife who had gone with him to buy the lantern. The Professor had married in America, where he was studying. His wife, therefore, is an American. But in the love of Japan and the Japanese she is no different from the Professor. In particular, the intricate art work of Japan has been Mrs. Hasegawa's passion. The Gifu lantern on the veranda is more an expression of Madam's taste than due to the wishes of the Professor.

Whenever he dropped the book the Professor thought of his wife, and the Gifu lantern, and the civilization represented by that lantern. The Professor believes that Japanese civilization has made great progress materially in the past fifty years, but spiritually has remained stagnant: in fact, in some phases, it has retrogressed. What are the means by which contemporary thinkers may help erase this retrogression? The Professor argues that the means must be found in Japan's own *Bushido*. Bushido should not be regarded merely as the narrow morality of an island nation. In fact, it has many elements that correspond to the Christian spirit of the western nations. If a forward impetus were to be given Japanese thinking by the revival of Bushido, it would not only contribute to the spiritual civilization of Japan but would lead to a better understanding between Japan and the western countries. It might even contribute to international peace. The Professor has always wished, in this sense, to become a bridge connecting East and West. That being the case, it was not unpleasant to this man to find in his consciousness the presence of the harmonious trio: his wife, the lantern and the civilization represented by that lantern.

The Professor at last realized that this self-satisfied reverie was keeping him from fully understanding Strindberg. He shook his head irritably and again began patiently to scan the fine print before him. The first thing he read was this:

"When an actor finds a suitable, expressive technique for any common emotional state and wins success by this technique, he will have a tendency to resort to this technique regardless of its suitability to the material at hand, partly because it is easy, partly because it has been successful before: this is mannerism."

The arts, especially the stage, have been a *terra incognita* to the Professor. He could count on the fingers of one hand the number of times he has seen plays in Japan. One of his students once wrote a novel in which the name "Baiko" appeared. The name meant nothing to the Professor's encyclopedic mind. The next time he met the student he put the question:

"Eh, this Baiko, what is that?"

"Baiko, sir? Baiko is an actor attached to the Imperial Theater, and is now appearing as Misao in the tenth play of the Taikoki," answered the student very politely.

The Professor, therefore, had absolutely no critical opinion of his own about the various techniques of theatrical production so provocatively discussed by Strindberg. It kept up a slight interest in him by reminding him of certain plays he had seen abroad. His reading of Strindberg, in fact, was not much different from the reading of Bernard Shaw's plays by a teacher of English in a secondary school in order to collect a few new idioms. However negligible, interest is, nevertheless, an interest.

An unlit Gifu lantern hanging from the ceiling of the veranda and, on the cane chair underneath, Professor Kinzo Hasegawa reading Strindberg's "Dramaturgy"—this is enough to show the reader that this was a long afternoon of a day in early summer. But do not think the Professor was being tormented by boredom. If anybody insists on such a cynical interpretation I can only say he is mistaken. For even the Strindberg the Professor had to abandon. A maid announcing a caller interrupted his pleasant leisure. The world was insistent that the Professor must be kept busy even on such a long summer day.

He put down his book and looked at the small card that the maid had just brought him. On the ivory paper was printed in small letters, "Mrs. Atsuko Nishiyama." The name struck no chord of recognition. As he left the chair, he made a quick roll call of his extensive acquaintance. But no face was remembered that matched the name. Leaving the book on the chair with the card as a marker, the Professor tidied his appearance a little and took another look at the lantern. Often the host keeping a guest waiting is more impatient for the meeting than the waiting guest. It is not necessary to add here, to those who know him, that the Professor's impatience was not on account of the sex of the unknown caller.

Soon the Professor opened the door to the drawing room. Almost at the same time a woman in her forties got up from a chair. The caller was dressed in tasteful, iron-blue kimono, over which she wore a *haori* of black silk gauze, leaving the cool, diamond-shaped *obi*-brooch of nephrite exposed near the breast. That she wore her hair in a sort of round chignon peculiar to married women, even the Professor, who is careless about these trifles, recognized. She was clearly a "wise mother" type, with the round face and amber-colored skin characteristic of the

Japanese. One glance convinced the Professor that he had seen this face before.

"How do you do; I am Hasegawa," he said and bowed amiably, thinking that with that greeting she would have to answer where and when she had met him before.

"I am the mother of Kenichiro Nishiyama," she said in a clear voice and bowed courteously.

Kenichiro Nishiyama was a name quite familiar to the Professor. He was one of those very students who often wrote criticism of Ibsen and Strindberg, though his specialty at the University was German law. He frequented the Professor's home, always full of ideological problems. This spring he had been taken with peritonitis, and the Professor had visited him once or twice at the University Hospital. No wonder I felt I had seen this woman before, the Professor thought. That lively young man with his dark eyebrows and this woman resembled each other amazingly; like two melons, as the Japanese commonly say.

"Oh, Mr. Nishiyama's—yes, of course."

The Professor nodded to himself as he pointed to the chair on the other side of the small table. "Please sit down."

The woman apologized for her sudden call and bowed courteously again before she sat down. As she took the chair she drew out something white from her long sleeve. Recognizing a handkerchief, the Professor recommended the use of the Korean fans on the table and took the chair facing hers.

"This is indeed a beautiful room," she said rather artificially and looked about the room.

"Well, it's large, but we hardly bother with it."

Quite used to these preliminary conversations, the Professor placed the cup of tea, just brought in by the maid, before her and shifted the topic toward the caller.

"How is Mr. Nishiyama? I hope he is better now."

"Well," she stopped for a moment as she modestly folded her hands on her lap, then went on in the same smooth voice. "My visit to you today is really for his sake. I am sorry to say he was not able to pull through; and since he was such a bother to you while he was alive—"

Seeing that the woman did not touch her tea, and interpreting this as her reserve, the Professor had just taken up his teacup. He wanted to put her at ease by setting the example. But before the cup reached his soft mustache the woman's words threatened his ears unexpectedly. Should I drink this or shouldn't I? For one moment this question monopolized the Professor's mind to the complete exclusion of the young man's death. He knew he shouldn't keep the cup in the air for ever. So, with one quick gulp, he drank the tea, and was barely able to bring out in a choking voice, "No, really?"

"He spoke of you so often while in the hospital," she went on. "I presumed to call today, though I know how occupied you are, to offer our thanks as well as to let you know—"

"Oh, not at all."

The Professor deposited the cup and took up a fan with a blue wax finish, while his voice went on thoughtfully:

"I had no idea his condition was so critical. And he was just at the age when we could have expected great things in a few years, too. I neglected the hospital for a while, and so believed that he was quite well by now. Just exactly when was he—?"

"It would be a week ago yesterday."

"Eh—at the hospital, was it?"

"Yes, at the hospital."

"Well, this is most unexpected," he said.

"We should console ourselves," she replied, "knowing all the excellent care he had, but still it is easy to cry over spilt milk when one thinks of all that might have been."

In the course of the conversation the Professor became aware of something surprising. There was no trace in this woman's attitude or manner of the fact that she was talking of her son's death. There were no tears. The voice was calm. There was even a trace of a smile in the corner of her mouth. Anyone seeing her without hearing her words would have thought she was speaking of some ordinary daily happening. This was strange to the Professor.

A long time ago, when the Professor was studying in Berlin, the old Kaiser, Wilhelm I, died. He heard of the death at a café he frequented, but his sense of loss was naturally quite slight. So he returned to his pension at his usual lively gait, his cane under his arm. As soon as he opened the outer door, the two children of the concierge rushed up to him, weeping loudly—the girl of twelve, in her brown jacket, the nine-year-old boy clad in short blue pants. Always very fond of children, the Professor bent down, patting their tow heads, earnestly asking, "Why, what's the matter, what's the matter?" Finally he made out what they were saying through their tears: "Grandpapa Emperor died. Grandpapa Emperor died!"

It had been strange to him to find the death of the head of a state so affecting to children. Not only did it make him think of such a question as Royalty and the People; the Westerner's impulsive expression of emotion, which he had so often noted before, renewed the sense of wonder in the Professor, a Japanese and a believer in Bushido. He could never forget the curious, uncomprehending sympathy which he felt on that occasion. Now he was surprised to an equal degree in the opposite direction by the fact that this woman was dry-eyed.

But the first discovery was soon succeeded by a second.

The conversation was proceeding from reminiscences of the deceased to the details of his daily life, back again to general reminiscences. The Professor accidentally dropped the fan on the parquet floor. The conversation, of course, was not so pressing that he could not interrupt it by reaching under the table to pick up the fan, which was lying near the woman's neat, white *tabis,* partly hidden in her slippers.

The Professor's eyes took in the woman's lap, and the folded hands resting on it. That in itself would not be a discovery. But he saw that the hands were trembling violently and, in the effort to suppress the shaking, they clutched the handkerchief so tightly as to nearly tear it. And, finally, he saw that the wrinkled silk handkerchief within her delicate fingers communicated the trembling of her hands, for its embroidered edges were shaking as if fanned by a breeze. The woman had been laughing with her face but weeping with her whole body.

When he picked up the fan and straightened himself, there was a new expression on the Professor's face. A kind of pious sense of guilt that he had seen something he was not supposed to, and a certain satisfaction coming from the consciousness of that feeling, both exaggerated into a slight theatricality—it was a very complex expression.

"No, even a childless person like me can imagine what a terrible loss this has been to you," said the Professor in a low voice, full of emotion, and his eyes looked as if they were gazing at something dazzlingly bright.

"Thank you very much," she said. "But, after all, this is something we cannot bring back."

She made a slight bow; her untroubled face still supporting a gracious smile.

Two hours later, the Professor had had his bath, finished his supper, eaten some cherries for dessert and was again seated luxuriously in the cane chair on the veranda.

The summer's long twilight was still some way off from the oncoming night in this broad, open veranda. The Professor sat in this pleasant afterglow, his knees crossed, his head pressed back on the chair, his eyes placidly contemplating the red tassel on the Gifu lantern. The Strindberg was in his hand, but he hadn't turned a page since his return, for his mind was full of the gallant demeanor of Mrs. Atsuko Nishiyama.

During supper he had told his wife of the encounter, praising the other's conduct as the expression of the Japanese woman's Bushido. Mrs. Hasegawa, who loved Japan and the Japanese, was naturally sympathetic. The Professor was pleased to find in his wife an enthusiastic listener. The three—his wife, the other woman and the Gifu lantern—had been occupying his consciousness with a certain ethical implication.

For a long time he was immersed in this happy reverie. It presently came to him that he had been requested by a magazine to contribute an article. The magazine was collecting general opinions on morals by various eminent personages under the tile of "The Book Addressed to Contemporary Youth." "I could send them an impression based on today's incident," thought the Professor and scratched his head.

The hand with which he scratched his head was the hand that had held the book. The Professor realized he had been neglecting the book and opened it to the page in which the calling card was inserted as a marker. The maid had lit the lantern above his head, which gave him

enough light to pick through the fine print of the book. He idly scanned
the page, not particularly anxious for the content. Says Strindberg:
"When I was young, the people talked about Mme. Heiberg's Parisian
handkerchief. It was a double acting in which, with her face smiling,
the hands tear the handkerchief in two. We now call it mannerism."
The Professor lowered the book. It was still open, with the card of
Mrs. Atsuko Nishiyama left on the page. But that woman was no
longer in the Professor's mind. Neither were Mrs. Hasegawa nor the
civilization of Japan. What was left was some indefinable thing that
attempted to break the peaceful harmony of the trio. Of course, problems in practical morality are different from the production technique
pointed out by Strindberg. But there was something in the hint he had
received from the passage that was disturbing to the hitherto comfortably assured mind of the Professor. Bushido, and its mannerism—
The Professor shook his head once or twice as though to drive away
the unpleasant thought, then again looked up at the newly lit lantern.

RABINDRANATH TAGORE

My Lord, the Baby

Rabindranath Tagore (1861–1941), Hindu
poet and musician, was born in Calcutta
of a distinguished family. He was educated in Europe and returned to India to
found a university at Bengal. He won the
Nobel Prize in 1913 and was knighted by
King George in 1915. He achieved an
international reputation as a philosopher,
educator and poet. [From *The Hungry
Stones and Other Stories* by Rabindranath
Tagore; used by permission of The Macmillan Co., publishers; translated by C. F.
Andrews.]

RAICHARAN WAS TWELVE YEARS OLD when he came as a
servant to his master's house. He belonged to the same caste as his
master, and was given his master's little son to nurse. As time went on
the boy left Raicharan's arms to go to school. From school he went on
to college, and after college he entered the judicial service. Always,
until he married, Raicharan was his sole attendant.

But, when a mistress came into the house, Raicharan found two
masters instead of one. All his former influence passed to the new
mistress. This was compensated for by a fresh arrival. Anukul had a
son born to him, and Raicharan by his unsparing attentions soon got a
complete hold over the child. He used to toss him up in his arms, call
to him in absurd baby language, put his face close to the baby's and
draw it away again with a grin.

Presently the child was able to crawl and cross the doorway. When
Raicharan went to catch him, he would scream with mischievous

laughter and make for safety. Raicharan was amazed at the profound skill and exact judgment the baby showed when pursued. He would say to his mistress with a look of awe and mystery: "Your son will be a judge some day."

New wonders came in their turn. When the baby began to toddle, that was to Raicharan an epoch in human history. When he called his father Ba-ba and his mother Ma-ma and Raicharan Chan-na, then Raicharan's ecstasy knew no bounds. He went out to tell the news to all the world.

After a while Raicharan was asked to show his ingenuity in other ways. He had, for instance, to play the part of a horse, holding the reins between his teeth and prancing with his feet. He had also to wrestle with his little charge, and if he could not, by a wrestler's trick, fall on his back defeated at the end, a great outcry was certain.

About this time Anukul was transferred to a district on the banks of the Padma. On his way through Calcutta he bought his son a little go-cart. He bought him also a yellow satin waistcoat, a gold-laced cap, and some gold bracelets and anklets. Raicharan was wont to take these out, and put them on his little charge with ceremonial pride, whenever they went for a walk.

Then came the rainy season, and day after day the rain poured down in torrents. The hungry river, like an enormous serpent, swallowed down terraces, villages, cornfields, and covered with its flood the tall grasses and wild casuarinas on the sandbanks. From time to time there was a deep thud, as the river-banks crumbled. The unceasing roar of the main current could be heard from far away. Masses of foam, carried swiftly past, proved to the eye the swiftness of the stream.

One afternoon the rain cleared. It was cloudy, but cool and bright. Raicharan's little despot did not want to stay in on such a fine afternoon. His lordship climbed into the go-cart. Raicharan, between the shafts, dragged him slowly along till he reached the rice-fields on the banks of the river. There was no one in the fields, and no boat on the stream. Across the water, on the farther side, the clouds were rifted in the west. The silent ceremonial of the setting sun was revealed in all its glowing splendor. In the midst of that stillness the child, all of a sudden, pointed with his finger in front of him and cried: "Chan-na! Pitty fow."

Close by on a mud-flat stood a large *Kadamba* tree in full flower. My lord, the baby, looked at it with greedy eyes, and Raicharan knew his meaning. Only a short time before he had made, out of these very flower balls, a small go-cart; and the child had been so entirely happy dragging it about with a string, that for the whole day Raicharan was not made to put on the reins at all. He was promoted from a horse into a groom.

But Raicharan had no wish that evening to go splashing knee-deep through the mud to reach the flowers. So he quickly pointed his finger in the opposite direction, calling out: "Oh, look, baby, look! Look at the bird." And with all sorts of curious noises he pushed the go-cart rapidly away from the tree.

But a child, destined to be a judge, cannot be put off so easily. And besides, there was at the time nothing to attract his eyes. And you cannot keep up for ever the pretense of an imaginary bird.

The little Master's mind was made up, and Raicharan was at his wits' end. "Very well, baby," he said at last, "you sit still in the cart, and I'll go and get you the pretty flower. Only mind you don't go near the water."

As he said this, he made his legs bare to the knee, and waded through the oozing mud toward the tree.

The moment Raicharan had gone, his little Master went off at racing speed to the forbidden water. The baby saw the river rushing by, splashing and gurgling as it went. It seemed as though the disobedient wavelets themselves were running away from some greater Raicharan with the laughter of a thousand children. At the sight of their mischief, the heart of the human child grew excited and restless. He got down stealthily from the go-cart and toddled off toward the river. On his way he picked up a small stick, and leant over the bank of the stream pretending to fish. The michievous fairies of the river with their mysterious voices seemed inviting him into their play-house.

Raicharan had plucked a handful of flowers from the tree, and was carrying them back in the end of his cloth, with his face wreathed in smiles. But when he reached the go-cart, there was no one there. He looked on all sides and there was no one there. He looked back at the cart and there was no one there.

In that first terrible moment his blood froze within him. Before his eyes the whole universe swam round like a dark mist. From the depth of his broken heart he gave one piercing cry: "Master, Master, little Master."

But no voice answered "Chan-na." No child laughed michievously back; no scream of baby delight welcomed his return. Only the river ran on, with its splashing, gurgling noise as before—as though it knew nothing at all, and had no time to attend to such a tiny human event as the death of a child.

As the evening passed by Raicharan's mistress became very anxious She sent men out on all sides to search. They went with lanterns in their hands, and reached at last the banks of the Padma. There they found Raicharan rushing up and down the fields, like a stormy wind, shouting the cry of despair: "Master, Master, little Master!"

When they got Raicharan home at last, he fell prostrate at his mistress's feet. They shook him, and questioned him, and asked him repeatedly where he had left the child; but all he could say was, that he knew nothing.

Though everyone held the opinion that the Padma had swallowed the child, there was a lurking doubt left in the mind. For a band of gypsies had been noticed outside the village that afternoon, and some suspicion rested on them. The mother went so far in her wild grief as to think it possible that Raicharan himself had stolen the child. She called him aside with piteous entreaty and said: "Raicharan, give me back my baby. Oh! give me back my child. Take from me any money you ask, but give me back my child!"

Anukul tried to reason his wife out of this wholly unjust suspicion: "Why on earth," he said, "should he commit such a crime as that?"

The mother only replied: "The baby had gold ornaments on his body. Who knows?"

It was impossible to reason with her after that.

Raicharan went back to his own village. Up to this time he had had no son, and there was no hope that any child would now be born to him. But it came about before the end of a year that his wife gave birth to a son and died.

An overwhelming resentment at first grew up in Raicharan's heart at the sight of this new baby. At the back of his mind was resentful suspicion that it had come as a usurper in place of the little Master. He also thought it would be a grave offense to be happy with a son of his own after what had happened to his master's little child. Indeed, if it had not been for a widowed sister, who mothered the new baby, it would not have lived long.

But a change gradually came over Raicharan's mind. A wonderful thing happened. This new baby in turn began to crawl about, and cross the doorway with michief in its face. It also showed an amusing cleverness in making its escape to safety. Its voice, its sounds of laughter and tears, its gestures, were those of the little Master. On some days, when Raicharan listened to its crying, his heart suddenly began thumping wildly against his ribs, and it seemed to him that his former little Master was crying somewhere in the unknown land of death because he had lost his Chan-na.

Phailna (for that was the name Raicharan's sister gave to the new baby) soon began to talk. It learnt to say Ba-ba and Ma-ma with a baby accent. When Raicharan heard those familiar sounds the mystery suddenly became clear. The little Master could not cast off the spell of his Chan-na, and therefore he had been reborn in his own house.

The arguments in favor of this were, to Raicharan, altogether beyond dispute:

(i.) The new baby was born soon after his little Master's death.

(ii.) His wife could never have accumulated such merit as to give birth to a son in middle age.

(iii.) The new baby walked with a toddle and called out Ba-ba and Ma-ma. There was no sign lacking which marked out the future judge.

Then suddenly Raicharan remembered that terrible accusation of the mother. "Ah," he said to himself with amazement, "the mother's heart was right. She knew I had stolen her child." When once he had come to this conclusion, he was filled with remorse for his past neglect.

He now gave himself over, body and soul, to the new baby, and became its devoted attendant. He began to bring it up, as if it were the son of a rich man. He bought a go-cart, a yellow satin waistcoat, and a gold-embroidered cap. He melted down the ornaments of his dead wife, and made gold bangles and anklets. He refused to let the little child play with anyone of the neighborhood, and became himself its sole companion day and night. As the baby grew up to boyhood, he was so petted and spoilt and clad in such finery that the village children would call him "Your Lordship," and jeer at him; and older people regarded Raicharan as unaccountably crazy about the child.

At last the time came for the boy to go to school. Raicharan sold his small piece of land, and went to Calcutta. There he got employment with great difficulty as a servant, and sent Phailna to school. He spared no pains to give him the best education, the best clothes, the best food. Meanwhile he lived himself on a mere handful of rice, and would say in secret: "Ah! my little Master, my dear little Master, you loved me so much that you came back to my house. You shall never suffer from any neglect of mine."

Twelve years passed away in this manner. The boy was able to read and write well. He was bright and healthy and good-looking. He paid a great deal of attention to his personal appearance, and was specially careful in parting his hair. He was inclined to extravagance and finery, and spent money freely. He could never quite look on Raicharan as a father, because, though fatherly in affection, he had the manner of a servant. A further fault was this, that Raicharan kept secret from everyone that himself was the father of the child.

The students of the hostel, where Phailna was a boarder, were greatly amused by Raicharan's country manners, and I have to confess that behind his father's back Phailna joined in their fun. But, in the bottom of their hearts, all the students loved the innocent and tender-hearted old man, and Phailna was very fond of him also. But, as I have said before, he loved him with a kind of condescension.

Raicharan grew older and older, and his employer was continually finding fault with him for his incompetent work. He had been starving himself for the boy's sake. So he had grown physically weak, and no longer up to his work. He would forget things, and his mind became dull and stupid. But his employer expected a full servant's work out of him, and would not brook excuses. The money that Raicharan had brought with him from the sale of his land was exhausted. The boy was continually grumbling about his clothes, and asking for more money.

Raicharan made up his mind. He gave up the situation where he was working as a servant, and left some money with Phailna and said: "I have some business to do at home in my village, and shall be back soon."

He went off at once to Baraset where Anukul was magistrate.

Anukul's wife was still broken down with grief. She had had no other child.

One day Anukul was resting after a long and weary day in court. His wife was buying, at an exorbitant price, an herb from a mendicant quack, which was said to insure the birth of a child. A voice of greeting was heard in the courtyard. Anukul went out to see who was there. It was Raicharan. Anukul's heart was softened when he saw his old servant. He asked him many questions, and offered to take him back into service.

Raicharan smiled faintly, and said in reply: "I want to make obeisance to my mistress."

Anukul went with Raicharan into the house, where the mistress did not receive him as warmly as his old master. Raicharan took no notice of this, but folded his hands, and said: "It was not the Padma that stole your baby. It was I."

Anukul exclaimed: "Great God! Eh! What! Where is he?"

Raicharan replied: "He is with me. I will bring him the day after tomorrow."

It was Sunday. There was no magistrate's court sitting. Both husband and wife were looking expectantly along the road, waiting from early morning for Raicharan's appearance. At ten o'clock he came, leading Phailna by the hand.

Anukul's wife, without question, took the boy into her lap, and was wild with excitement, sometimes laughing, sometimes weeping, touching him, kissing his hair and his forehead, and gazing into his face with hungry, eager eyes. The boy was very good-looking and dressed like a gentleman's son. The heart of Anukul brimmed over with a sudden rush of affection.

Nevertheless the magistrate in him asked: "Have you any proofs?"

Raicharan said: "How could there be any proof of such a deed? God alone knows that I stole your boy, and no one else in the world."

When Anukul saw how eagerly his wife was clinging to the boy, he realized the futility of asking for proofs. It would be wiser to believe. And then—where could an old man like Raicharan get such a boy from? And why should his faithful servant deceive him for nothing?

"But," he added severely, "Raicharan, you must not stay here."

"Where shall I go, Master?" said Raicharan, in a choking voice, folding his hands; "I am old. Who will take an old man as a servant?"

The mistress said: "Let him stay. My child will be pleased. I forgive him."

But Anukul's magisterial conscience would not allow him. "No," he said, "he cannot be forgiven for what he has done."

Raicharan bowed to the ground, and clasped Anukul's feet. "Master," he cried, "let me stay. It was not I who did it. It was God."

Anukul's conscience was worse stricken than ever, when Raicharan tried to put the blame on God's shoulders.

"No," he said, "I could not allow it. I cannot trust you any more. You have done an act of treachery."

Raicharan rose to his feet and said: "It was not I who did it."

"Who was it then?" asked Anukul.

Raicharan replied: "It was my fate."

But no educated man could take this for an excuse. Anukul remained obdurate.

When Phailna saw that he was the wealthy magistrate's son, and not Raicharan's, he was angry at first, thinking that he had been cheated all this time of his birthright. But seeing Raicharan in distress, he generously said to his father: "Father, forgive him. Even if you don't let him live with us, let him have a small monthly pension."

After hearing this, Raicharan did not utter another word. He looked for the last time on the face of his son; he made obeisance to his old master and mistress. Then he went out, and was mingled with the numberless people of the world.

At the end of the month Anukul sent him some money to his village. But the money came back. There was no one there of the name of Raicharan.

S. RAJA RATNAM

Drought

S. Raja Ratnam, a Singhalese, has for the past several years been studying law in England. During the war, he wrote fiction between air raids. [From *Asia Magazine*, September, 1941; used by permission of *United Nations World*.]

THE EXHAUSTED EARTH groaned and quivered under the monotonous glare of the sun. Spirals of heat rose from the ground as if from molten lava. A panting lizard crawled painfully over the fevered rock in search of a shady crevice. Cattle and dogs cringed under the scanty shade of the trees and waited for the rain to deliver them from the heat and thirst. Instead the heat grew more intense and oppressive each day, singeing and stifling all living things with an invisible sheet of fire, which only the rain could put out.

The drought had persisted for over a month. Each day the farmers anxiously scanned the sky only to notice that even the ghostly wisps of cloud were being drained off it. Their hearts were filled with a foreboding which showed itself in the grim expressions on their faces. Their crops of paddy had not been gathered in and were slowly shriveling up in the fields. But, above all, if the drought persisted, their cattle would die of thirst.

Some of the villagers had made futile attempts to dig for water. Neither above the earth nor under it was water to be had. What water there was, was in the two village tanks. But now even this supply had run low and they had been informed that there was to be no more water for their cattle.

There was, however, one other tank that could provide the cattle with water for some time, and that was the private tank of Vela Mudaliar. But he had refused to let the villagers water their cattle in his tank. They offered to pay for it. They resorted to threats. But the Mudaliar was stubborn in his refusal. He saw in their present plight an opportunity to enrich himself. He countered their demands with an offer. He said he was prepared to buy their cattle for a price that was ridiculously low. When the farmers rejected his unscrupulous offer, he pointed out with a certain amount of exacerbation that, if they preferred to hand over their dead cattle to the tanner's knife, they were at liberty to do so. After holding out for a while the farmers gave in to the Mudaliar. That is, everyone except old Kathar.

Old Kathar was ill with a slight fever. He lay on a mat outside his hut under the shade of the jutting palm-roof. Though past fifty, he still looked strong. By some freak of heredity he had escaped the cruel lot that fell to farmers of his age, and this fact had engendered in him a conviction of his own superiority and unquenchable strength. Ever since he could remember, his life had been dedicated to the task of retaining the land that had belonged to his fathers. And this task he had performed to his satisfaction. He had done his duty by his fathers. When he was gone his two sons would carry on.

He looked at Rasu, his elder son. Rasu was a giant of a man, and it was sheer delight to watch his muscles ripple like sea-waves as he toiled in the fields. He was clumsy, patient and good-natured, so that even his wife Sarasvati chaffed him with impunity. He was a good son though, for even if he lacked an alert mind his strength would stand him in good stead.

Suriar, however, was a problem. Physically he was lean, and his fragile constitution had made him a prey to frequent illness. He stooped like a consumptive when he walked. He was inclined to be taciturn and moody. He read a lot and whenever he did talk it was with a passion and vigor incredible in so frail a person. His ideas as they emerged frightened most of the farmers, for he flouted and ridiculed their traditional beliefs with a mocking logic that they could not answer. He talked about rights and justice for the oppressed. In his heart he bore a profound hatred for men like the Mudaliar which passed the understanding of the farmers. Much to their consternation, he called upon them to unite and fight their oppressors.

It was Suriar who had been set against selling their bull, Achi, to the Mudaliar. All the arguments of Kathar and Rasu had only made him angrier. He would rather see the bull dead than make a deal with a thief. He even threatened to do violence to the Mudaliar and, lest he should make good his threats, Kathar had temporarily acceded to his son's wishes.

Kathar lay on his mat, which was greasy with sweat, and looked at Suriar, wondering how to bring up the question of Achi. His son was apparently immersed in a book, as he usually was when he had nothing better to do. Beside him sat Rasu, squatting on his heels and feeling hot and uncomfortable. He fingered his hot perspiring belly as the sweat ran down it. On the mud wall behind him were dark, sweaty patches that had been sucked in from his moist back. Every now and then Rasu turned to look at his wife, busy inside.

A profound silence filled the air for a while till Suriar shut his book abruptly.

"Will there be no end to this heat!"

"Om! Om!" agreed Rasu, his whole body hot and flaming, "I burn as if on fire. Even these dung walls breathe out a hot vapor. Mercy on me! It will not be long before I am reduced to ashes."

"I shall suffocate in this heat," cried Suriar, wiping his face with his shawl. "If only the rain would come! I shouldn't care even if it would rain a flood. Rather be drowned in a flood than be roasted alive or die of thirst. Look at them all! So meek and resigned to their fate. Dumb. Dumb. All of them."

Rasu smiled good-humoredly at Suriar's outburst. His brother was queer but he loved him all the same. Suriar had relapsed into silence, exhausted by his emotion. He saw Achi walk weakly up to a palmyra tree. A dry rasping sound reached him as the bull hopefully licked the tree for something to allay its thirst. Then it looked in the direction of the hut and turned slowly away to pasture. It lifted up its dry swollen lips and tore at the withered grass.

"Poor Achi," said Rasu, shaking his head slowly. "He will die of thirst soon." Then he clicked his tongue sympathetically.

Suriar turned suddenly on his brother.

"Why don't you give him some water then, instead of groaning about poor Achi. Even a little."

"That's easy to say, little brother," protested Rasu, "but where is the water to come from? As it is, there is not enough water for the household. They tell me that we are to get even less from the tank in the future." Then he continued pleasantly: "I did take Achi some water this morning and what do you think happened? I held out a coconut-shellful of water to him. The poor thing was so thirsty that the sight of water made him crazy with greed. He gave one toss— and knocked the water out of my hand. And then the foolish thing had to be content with what he could lick off the ground. Poor Achi!"

He shook his big head. Suriar was staring ahead of him.

Kathar broke into the silence, his voice weak because of the fever.

"Suri, why not let us sell Achi to the Mudaliar. It is no use keeping him back and watching him die. At least he will not die of thirst if we sell him."

Rasu nodded his head in agreement.

"Father is right, Suri. It would do nobody any good to let Achi die. Poor Achi! He cannot even tell us of his sufferings."

Suriar looked at them both, his lips parted and quivering.

"What are you both saying! Have you no pride? Fine. Fine. Sell Achi to a rogue and admit we are beaten? A very nice sight it will be when we crawl humbly back to the Mudaliar."

"But, Suri," said the old man quietly, "if we refuse to sell Achi we are not going to hurt anybody but ourselves. One bull will make no difference either way to the Mudaliar. He is too rich for that. As for pride, we should have saved it if we had sold him long ago without any fuss."

Suriar interrupted.

"Don't you both understand what I mean? Father, it is time for us to stand up to people like the Mudaliar and show them that they cannot have everything as they wish. We should show that we poor folks are not the slaves of the Mudaliar's wishes."

"But, my son, you are fighting against thin air. What weapon can you use against the Mudaliar? He has everything on his side and you only the fire of youth."

Suriar shivered as a torrent of emotions filled his being. "At the worst I can kill a pig and feed his flesh to the dogs. With my own hands I will kill him and be glad to rid the world of such a swine."

"Suri! Suri!" cried his father, "you don't know what you are saying. Promise me, my poor unhappy son, that you will never do anything rash. It's all futile. Men like the Mudaliar cannot be tamed by individual violence. They are too many and too powerful. Only God can destroy them."

Suriar made as if to interrupt. But Kathar continued.

"Besides you have seen how Achi is suffering. He's a dumb creature, Suri. You have no right to torture him so. If he dies, the sin will be upon our own head."

Suriar looked glumly first at his father and then at Rasu. His lips quivered and set thin.

"All right, Father," he said, rising to his feet. "Do as you wish. After all, it's your bull. Should you like me to take Achi to the Mudaliar?"

"I'd rather Rasu took him to the Mudaliar," said his father kindly.

Suriar turned on his heels and entered the hut. He felt thirsty. He dipped a cup into the earthen jar.

"Be careful of the water, Suri," Sarasvati called out. "There is very little in the jar."

He took a few sips and replaced the cup.

Then, wrapping a shawl around his head, he walked out of the house. The earth burned under his feet and the blinding glare of the sun hurt his eyes. The landscape quivered as if viewed through a wet glass. He turned into a dusty lane and made in the direction of his friend Nathan's house.

The sun was falling fast into the orange-tinged horizon when
Suriar made his way home. Though the stifling heat of the day had
gone, a parched, dry feeling still clung uncomfortably to the air.
Around him there lay a drowsy calmness running into the distance.
As he walked, he kicked up puffs of fine dust which clung to his bare
feet and the hem of his garment. The whole country seemed so calm
and gentle now. Perhaps tomorrow the clouds would roll sluggishly,
lusciously, under the skies and squeeze out their moisture. Then all
creation below would sit wondering at the goodness of God.

Suriar, however, had a better reason to feel satisfied. A smile
flickered about his face as he thought of what he had done to the
Mudaliar.

Tomorrow, perhaps even before the night set in, every one of the
Mudaliar's cattle would be stone dead. Nathan had given him the
poison and had assured him that it had enough potency to poison the
Mudaliar's tank. It had been a risky task to crawl up to the tank and
empty the poison into it, for the Mudaliar had prudently set a watchman to guard it. But somehow Suriar had managed to evade the
vigilance of the watchman and pour the poison. Soon the cattle would
drink of the water and be dead.

He had avenged a crime. The Mudaliar deserved what was coming to him and none would be sorry for him. Even if the perpetrator
of the deed were discovered, Suriar would have the sympathy and
support of the villagers. He would, however, not let anyone know
what he had done. As far as he knew, no one had seen him poison
the tank, except Nathan. He could trust Nathan to keep it a secret.

He hummed softly and quickened his pace. The sense of victory
brought a sparkle to his eyes.

He pushed open the gate of his house and heard the sound of
weeping come from within. He stopped and felt his body turn chill.
His first thought was that someone had seen him poison the well
and had come to get him. His legs trembled. He listened. Sarasvati's
voice rose high above the others. He discerned, too, the voices of men.
Slowly it dawned on him that he was listening to the cry of mourners.
His heart and stomach turned sick. Someone had died in his house
and he knew for certain who it was.

He hurried into the house. People stood aside as he made his way
toward the dead body of his father. Sarasvati flung her arms about
him and wept. Suriar's eyes had no tears. They were fixed on his
father—horrified.

Rasu, his eyes red with weeping, put his arm comfortingly around
his brother.

"How? I cannot believe it. He was quite well when I left him,"
said Suriar.

Rasu broke into loud sobs all of a sudden.

"Tell me, how? What happened?"

Suriar gripped his brother's arms.

"It was horrible, Suri. The way he died. There was no peace. Look at his face, twisted in pain. He did not die the way he should have. He was in terrible agonies before he died."

Rasu broke into uncontrollable sobs.

"That's impossible. What happened?"

"Father and I were talking about you," said Rasu amidst his sobs. "There was nothing wrong with him then. But he felt thirsty and I gave him a cup of water. Soon after I heard him cry out in pain. There he was turning and twisting and kicking. Oh, Suri!"

Suriar felt as if a knife were being pushed through his spine. A cold, cold blade that sent an agony of pain through him.

"Water? Water?" he repeated, a hoarseness in his voice. "Rasu, where did you get that water? Answer me. Where?"

Rasu's sobs stopped as he saw the urgent expression on his brother's face. He could feel Suriar tremble all over.

"From the pitcher," stammered Rasu.

"Yes, I know. But where? From where?"

"From the Mudaliar's tank. There was not enough water and so, when I went to sell Achi, I asked him for some water."

"You fool. You fool, poor fool," cried Suriar, his hands moving wildly in the air. "It was poisoned. I poisoned it. Let me go."

He shot away from Rasu's grasp, a wild look on his face.

"Suri! Suri!" cried out Rasu in alarm. But Suriar seized the pitcher and ran out of the house. Then, sobbing and hysterical, he lifted it high above his head and dashed it to the ground.

A dark stain of water spread on the ground and caressed its parched surface with its cold, moving fingers. The thirsty earth drank the water greedily, greedily.

HELEN DAVIDIAN

The Jealous Wife

Helen Davidian was born in Teheran, Iran, as was her father. Her mother was a native of Van, Turkey. An Armenian, Miss Davidian was educated at the American Missionary High School in Teheran. She came to the United States in 1937.
[From *Asia Magazine*, August, 1943; used by permission of *United Nations World*; translated by P. Noorigian.]

WITH THE HELP of her Negro maid Zobayda disguised herself as a Persian gypsy. She put on a blue blouse flowered with yellow roses, a dark red skirt reaching to her knees, black satin trousers and a tight-fitting green jacket.

Tall and slender, she looked shorter in her gypsy costume. She covered her head with a large white kerchief pinned tightly under her chin, and put on a necklace and a bracelet of colorful beads. She sat down upon a cushion facing a large mirror and glanced at herself, but turned her face quickly away from the mirror. In her heart she repeated some terrible curses and aloud she muttered: "He deserves it, the unbeliever! He has not come home these three days!"

Her Negro maid brought a large box of cosmetics and took out a dark red, sticky powder and painted Zobayda's face and hands, then broadened the fine arcs of her brows and dyed her eyelashes dark blue. Again Zobayda stared into the mirror. She hated her disguise, but she was satisfied with it. In the mirror her eyes looked as dark as night and full of fury. She took courage and rose and hastily picked up a bag filled with raisins and walnuts and thrust a small package in it. Then she placed two large sieves upon her shoulder, covered herself with a heavy colorful veil and stepped out of the back door.

When Zobayda found herself in the street, her heart was seized with a shiver and she said to herself: "What am I doing? If I fail to disguise my voice properly and if I am discovered, I shall have made myself ridiculous. And what am I to do if my husband really happens to be there?"

The big clock on top of the British Legation struck ten. "I must hurry," thought Zobayda. "If he stayed there last night, he must return to his clinic at eleven."

Splashing her way through the mud, her bare heels wet and cold, she came to Shah-Abad and stopped in front of a door. She put her bundles down and blew on her cold fingers. In her heart she cursed herself and all seven of her past generations. A few more curses meant for her husband came to her tongue, but she smothered them. She adjusted her costume and held an eye against a crack in the closed door. Then she cleared her throat and, holding her lips against the crack, called in a shrill gypsy tone, "*Khanum,* I have raisins, walnuts, dry mulberries! I can tell your fortune! Aye, dear khanum!"

She paused and listened. Then she muttered, "I shall cry my wares until that daughter of a bitch calls me in."

She began to call again, "Aye, khanum, I sell sieves for sifting flour, I sell talismans for good luck!"

A maid suddenly opened the door, shouting: "What is all this? You shameless unbeliever! Why do you go around the town pestering people with your stinking mouth? Come in, my khanum wants you!"

Zobayda walked in, banging her sieves against the door.

"Be careful, you big mare!" cried the maid, "and don't scrape the door."

"Upon my eye," said Zobayda. "But tell me, sister, is there any stranger in the house?"

"Do not ask about things that do not concern you, fool! Follow me, and look beneath your feet," grumbled the maid, as she latched the door.

Biting her lips, and her heart beating feverishly, Zobayda followed the maid through the yard and up a short flight of stairs. By the door on top of the stairs she took off her slippers and stepped into the living room.

"Peace be with you, khanum," she said in a cracked voice.

The khanum sat by the *kursi,* her fat body expanding in the warmth, lazily smoking a water-pipe.

"Peace be with you," answered the khanum, after she had inhaled the smoke from her water-pipe and blown it slowly out of her nostrils, while she measured Zobayda from head to foot with her large cold eyes.

Zobayda looked at the khanum's face, so small and plump, set over a short neck and shining with paint, and thought, "You look like one of those pictures upon the walls of a public bath house!" but she said in a soft voice, "Beautiful khanum, what would you wish?"

"Wait! Don't you see I am smoking? How did you wait inside your mother for nine months?"

Zobayda stood, her glance wandering around the spacious room. The doors and windows were hung with heavy dark brown curtains. Clean white cloths with embroidered edges lined the niches in the walls. In one of the niches were a pair of the khanum's black shoes and a pair of stockings, in another, a mirror, a ball of white silk thread and a cosmetic box with its cover ajar. Suddenly in another niche she saw a man's hat. She lowered her eyes, and below the niche she saw a cane with a silver handle, which she well knew belonged to her husband. Her knees began to shake with fear and anger. She thought she saw her husband's eyes glaring at her from behind every curtain. It seemed to her as if even the cane could recognize her.

To avoid betraying herself, she turned toward the wall and put the sieves down, and placed the bags in them.

"Why do you fumble with those sacks?" shouted the khanum. "No one here wants to buy raisins or mulberries. I want you to tell my fortune."

Zobayda lowered her eyes and knelt upon the rug in front of the khanum and said with a feigned smile: "Let me see your hand, fair khanum! Your moonlike face tells me that you have enemies. A beautiful lady like you must have many rivals."

The fat khanum smiled broadly, extending her left hand. Zobayda stroked the hand gently down to the finger tips, then turned it over in her palm, gazed at it for a moment and let it drop. Out of her pocket she took a pair of copper dice, shook them in her hand and glanced at them.

"I was correct, lovely lady," she said, "you have many enemies around you, but you take them for friends. One of them is a short, fat woman and another is a red-haired girl. The wheel of your fate is turning fast, but you do not realize it. But wait! What do I see? The wheel of your fortune is beginning to slow down!"

Casting the dice once more, Zobayda declared, "There is someone

who loves you!" The khanum listened anxiously, her small head leaning toward Zobayda.

"Yes, and it is a gentleman with a fine complexion and large, dark
eyes."

"Aye, Doctor!" the khanum called loudly, "did you hear what this
daughter of a bitch said?" Come out here and listen to what she says!"

"Let the dust fall upon my head! Why didn't you tell me there is a
man in this house?" exclaimed Zobayda, pulling her veil hastily over
her head.

"Don't be nervous, woman," said the khanum. "The gentleman is
not going to eat you and, besides, he is a doctor." Then she cackled
loudly, "Come out of there, Doctor, I must have your fortune told too.
I will not let you get away until I learn the secrets of your heart."

Zobayda's knees shuddered as she cast the dice again: "May your
enemies go blind, khanum, they are trying to harm you, especially the
well-shaped woman with the soft eyes of a doe, the one who sings like
a nightingale and is as beautiful as the moon of the fourteenth night.
Beware of her! She pretends to be a friend, but she is your worst
enemy."

A smile froze upon the khanum's lips. She knitted her brows and
called: "Doctor, do you realize now that I am not lying? Your wife is
my enemy! I am sure she has been setting a trap for me."

"Choke yourself!" came the Doctor's angry voice from behind one
of the heavy curtains. "My wife does not even know I call upon you."

"You men are so stupid," shouted the khanum. "You think she does
not know! Aye, is there anything we women don't know about you
men? You poor fool!"

Upon hearing her husband's voice Zobayda was seized with terror.
She stood up, pulled her veil up and covered her face and went to her
bundles, her face toward the wall, cursing inwardly: "This stinking
woman! A leftover from a thousand men! So she is the one you chose!
You worthless dog!"

Aloud she said beseechingly, "Khanum, will you please pay me and
let me go?"

"What is your hurry, woman! Wait until the Doctor comes out and
you may tell his fortune too."

"Yes, let her wait," cried the Doctor from the next room. "I shall
come as soon as I put my shoes on."

But the khanum, inhaling smoke from her water-pipe and frowning,
made a sign to the maid to pay the gypsy woman and send her away.

Zobayda did not even glance at the silver coins. She wrapped them
hastily in a corner of her handkerchief and rushed out of the room.

When she was alone in the street, she let loose the sobs she had
choked in her throat, and the tears streamed down her cheeks. She hurried into a ruined house at the end of the street, where behind a wall
she threw the sieves aside in the mud. Then she took out of her bag

the bundle of her everyday clothes and changed her costume, rolling up and tossing away the gypsy garments.

On her way home she stopped at a small store.

"*Agha,* let me have sixteen grains of opium," she said, covering her face carefully. The merchant stared at her with sharp eyes and twirled his mustache.

"Hurry, agha, I have much to do," she said, thrusting a piece of silver into his hand. As he took it he patted her soft hand with his finger tips. She pulled her hand back angrily.

"Khanum," he said, "this does not look like the hand of a maid. Please uncover your lovely face and let me see it."

Zobayda swung her arm and slapped the man's face. "Oh, khanum," he cried, "that was good! Let me have one more, my soul, one more," and turned his other cheek. She spat upon the ground and went away, without even taking her money back, saying in her heart: "Men are worse than street dogs! Fools!" Why were people moving back and forth in the street, chattering carelessly or laughing or even singing? "Why do they buy food instead of opium?" she thought. "My grandmother took opium and put an end to her miserable life. She was the wisest woman I ever knew."

At length, with some difficulty, she bought sixteen grains of opium. Holding it tightly in her hand, wrapped in a piece of paper, she mechanically began to walk toward home.

Khadijeh, her Negro maid, was squatting outside the door, waiting for her. The maid undressed her and washed the paint off her face, as her mistress sat motionless.

"Poor Khadijeh," thought Zobayda, "You do not know that this will be the last time you will have to undress me and wash my face." She rose to her feet and put on a small black coat and covered herself with a pink silk *chadir.* "Listen, Khadijeh," she said, "I don't want to be disturbed today. Even if the Doctor comes tell him I am not in. Now bring me a glass of water, quickly."

With the glass of water in her hand she entered her husband's office and locked the door behind her. The office windows opened upon a garden with a pool in the middle, fringed with flowering plants and fruit trees and weeping willows.

"This is a bad omen," said the maid to herself. "I never saw my khanum in such a joyless mood, she who always sang like a nightingale. She is white like chalk and her eyes are red and swollen. I wish the day had never come when the Doctor with his evil step entered this house!"

She wrapped herself in her veil and sat down before the locked door, her legs folded under her. She said, "I shall stay at this door until this evil hour blows away."

Inside Zobayda drew the curtains at the window and door. Then she went to her husband's desk and rummaged the papers and books lying upon it. She took up some of the papers, without even glancing at them, and tore them up and threw the pieces into the waste basket.

She tore the covers off the books, and then she took all the papers out
of the drawers one by one and scattered them on the floor.

Outside the door Khadijeh thought, "It is good, she is at least clearing her husband's desk." She stood up and peered through a crack in
the door. Through that crack she had often watched the Doctor with
his patients. "Curses be upon you, evil Satan, she has even drawn the
door curtains," she said to herself, and sat back, her ear close to the door.

In one of the desk drawers Zobayda discovered a small box. "These
must be her letters," she thought. She flung the box to the floor and
broke it open under her foot. Out fell a package of letters tied with
pink ribbon, which she cut with her teeth. She scattered the letters all
over the room. A small picture flew out of the packet and landed on
the green blotter upon the desk. "Now the culprit need not think that
I know nothing about his affair," she thought. She threw herself in
the chair and closed her eyes.

The odor of the opium in her pocket rose into her nostrils and
brought her to her senses. When she opened her eyes she saw the picture lying upon the green desk blotter. The smiling face was her own.
She laughed bitterly, "No! This is not my picture! This is the happy
Zobayda of the past." She tore it up and threw the pieces in the waste
basket. Now she took the opium out of her pocket and held it in her
hand, "But no, not yet," she said to herself, and placed the opium on
the desk beside the glass of water. "People must not think I went mad
and killed myself. I must write a letter first." She took a sheet of paper
and began to write. Her thoughts flowed so fast that her pen could not
keep pace with them.

"Sefieh, do you wish to hear the story of my life? I shall tell it to
you. When you read this letter, leaning against soft cushions, side by
side with the Doctor, rejoice, for there will be no more Zobayda. But
I beg one thing of you. Do not dare to attend my funeral. If you do,
I would curse you even from the grave . . . You know well that the
feverish season of my youth was already over when I married the
Doctor two years ago. You became intimate with me soon after we first
met, because you loved my husband."

Tears began to drip upon the letter; she wiped her eyes with her sleeve
and wrote on.

"I was the spoiled child of a rich family, the only daughter of my
parents. Even my smallest wish was promptly done. When I sat down
for dinner, the Negro maids of my mother were all at my service. They
were like toys in my hands. One of them played a tambourine for me,
another danced, a third placed the choicest morsels of food in my mouth,
while a fourth stood at the door, waiting upon my whim. I lack nothing in the world. But when I became of age, I was disgusted with
that sort of life. I would not obey anyone. I looked upon everything as
my own. Like a bird in a cage I only ate and sang. But I had a strong
desire for freedom. And I decided to get out of that prison, because I
was not born for a harem. I did get out. I devoted my life to singing,

the art I loved. My parents and relatives considered me dead, but I did not care, for I was free and happy.

"My garden seemed a real paradise to me. My servants moved about me busy as ants, and my maid Khadijeh followed me like my own shadow . . ." ("Oh, my poor Khadijeh," thought Zobayda, "I wonder if your old age will be able to bear the grief.")

"I did not want to get married. I hated all men. During the long winter nights when Teheran was covered with a thick blanket of snow, and the breath froze upon men's beards, many men came to my door. They all loved to hear me sing. My visitors fell upon their knees begging for a glance of love from me, but my heart was hard as stone and my spirit soared high in the air.

"And why do I write you all these details? But have patience, Sefieh! I want to enjoy once more, and for the last time, the memory of the irrevocable joy of my past.

"Now what did I write down?" asked Zobayda to herself. Knitting her brows, she read the word she had just written—"Irrevocable . . ." "But why?" She felt within her the sudden rise of a dim hope, which she tried to ignore.

"I enjoyed my freedom and happiness for years. Then came a cool spring night—Oh, why did not the world come to an end that night? A pale moon lighted my porch and the fragrance of honeysuckle was spread over the garden. Half dressed, leaning against soft cushions, I watched the moon. I loved to feel the caress of moonlight on my skin. I would not let any visitors come that night. And later I slept all through the spring night, half-naked, without any covering. The following day I was stricken with pneumonia.

"Then the Doctor came and saved my life, he who was later to rob me of everything I valued. My soul was weak within my frail body. With the magnetism of his eyes he conquered me. He knew well that I was a virgin in soul as well as in body. I could not understand how he could forsake the house he had built and give up his wife and children to devote himself to me. But I believed him."

Zobayda's heart beat faster, but she held the pen firmly and went on writing:

"So I do not blame you, Sefieh. I think of the sufferings you must go through. Whoever loves him is compelled by some power. But when you too are discarded, and when you suffer, remember me . . ."

Within her suddenly she felt the sagging of her will. She could not hate her husband. It was all my own fault, she thought. She saw before her eyes the lewd face of Sefieh, and thought she heard the sickening sound of her shrill laughter. She dropped the pen and jumped to her feet and nervously paced the floor . . . "He will come back!" she thought, "I am sure he will come back. It is Sefieh who must suffer!"

She went to the window and looked out. The rain had ceased and a spring sun spread its bright mantle over the pool where small gold fish played and gleamed. A powerful passion for life gripped her heart, slowly, firmly.

She saw the gardener pruning rosebushes with his great shears. She saw a sparrow with a worm in its beak on the edge of a nest in the wall.

The warm sun streamed over her cold hands. Among the green bushes in the garden below violets bloomed. The air was teeming with life and fragrant with the breath of spring.

From the depths of her heart a voice spoke: "He may come back. He may not. But you must live, if only for your music, and you will be happy as you were before."

She recalled her favorite song and began to sing it softly:

> My eyes are wet, and in my breast
> There is a furnace full of fire,
> My cup of pleasure brims again
> With Blood from out of my beating heart.

She smiled. It seemed to her as if many years had passed since the last time she had smiled, many, many years.

TAWFIQ AL-HAKIM

A Deserted Street

Tawfiq Al-Hakim has written many plays, and is the best known dramatist in the Arabic. His masterpiece, *Journals of a Country Deputy*, probably would interest Western readers more than any other modern Arabic novel. [From *Images from the Arabic World* by Tawfiq Al-Hakim; used by permission of the Pilot Press, Ltd.; translated by Herbert Howarth and Ibrahim Shukrallah.]

[*A deserted street. Only one house, a lamp burning at the gate. Music from the distance comes in snatches on the wind. The night is moonless.*

The Magician comes forward, bringing a slave-girl back to the house.

He is questioning her.]

THE MAGICIAN: That negro slave from abroad, what was he saying to you?

THE SLAVE-GIRL: He was asking the reason of the celebrations in the city, and I told him it was the gala our virgins are giving in honor of the Queen Shahrazad.

THE MAGICIAN: Then why is your body trembling?

THE SLAVE-GIRL (*in a whisper*): I don't know.

THE MAGICIAN: Time and again I've warned you. Keep away from that old slave. I see debauchery in his eyes.

THE SLAVE-GIRL (*whispering*): He's not old.

THE MAGICIAN: You mutter as if the devil possessed you. Give me your hand, and come inside. Perhaps it's his ugliness that's made you frightened.

THE SLAVE-GIRL (*whispering*): He's not ugly.

[*They go into the house. The negro appears, following the girl with his eyes.*]

THE NEGRO: The loveliest of virgins! Her body is like a man's shelter.

A VOICE (*just behind him*): Or the devil's! Or my sword's!

THE NEGRO (*turning round*): It's you, is it?

THE EXECUTIONER: You recognize me easily.

THE NEGRO: Where have you left your sword, executioner?

THE EXECUTIONER: I sold it in exchange for dreams.

THE NEGRO: Now I understand your extravagance yesterday at the tavern. The smoke of perfumed hemp still lingers and proves how generously you spent on me.

THE EXECUTIONER: We like to do what's right with our guests from abroad.

THE NEGRO: And what are you doing at present for your employer in the palace?

THE EXECUTIONER: I've lost my job. I'm no longer the King's swordsman.

THE NEGRO: Ah, I see.

THE EXECUTIONER: What do you see?

THE NEGRO: Aren't the virgins holding a feast today?

THE EXECUTIONER: That's it. The King doesn't need a swordsman any more.

THE NEGRO (*admiringly*): And the body of Shahrazad did that!

THE EXECUTIONER: No. The King loves Shahrazad, but that wasn't what stopped him killing virgins.

THE NEGRO (*suddenly listening*): Listen to the singing. Beautiful and strange! Whose is this house?

THE EXECUTIONER (*furtively*): The magician's. The King comes here secretly to consult him.

THE NEGRO: The magician! Is he that slave-girl's father?

THE EXECUTIONER: They say so.

THE NEGRO (*listening to the music again*): A singing-bird safe from your blade!

THE EXECUTIONER (*turning to go*): Anything I miss goes to the devil.

THE NEGRO: Here, don't go. You've nothing to hurry for, I think.

THE EXECUTIONER: I think I have. My intuition tells me of something red.

THE NEGRO: No, it's black if you look. Your intuition's color-
                    blind.

[*At that moment a weird moan, long drawn-out, comes from a
window of the house.*]

THE EXECUTIONER: Did you hear that?

THE NEGRO: Hear what?

THE EXECUTIONER: A sound like an owl hooting.

THE NEGRO: Owl. I see no owl. Don't fill the world with bad
                    omens, you unemployed swordsman.

THE EXECUTIONER (*moving away*): Well, God help the deaf, I say.

THE NEGRO: Wait a minute. Don't go till you've told me about
                    the beautiful Shahrazad.

THE EXECUTIONER: What more do you want to know about her. I told
                    you everything yesterday. Anyone would think you
                    had traveled thousands of miles to this city for no
                    reason but her.

THE NEGRO (*pointing to the distance and shouting excitedly*): Look at
                    the bright bursts over there. Like an explosion, or
                    a fountain of light.

THE EXECUTIONER: That's the King's chamber.

THE NEGRO: And the Queen's too?

THE EXECUTIONER: No, the Queen has her suite on the other side of
                    the palace.

THE NEGRO: Strange. The King no longer needs the Queen to
                    tell him stories till she sees the sunrise and stops the
                    tale at the exact moment.

THE EXECUTIONER (*whispering*): The King is going mad.

THE NEGRO: But it's the madness of her love.

THE EXECUTIONER: No. A true madness.

THE NEGRO: Miserable is the man condemned to wander in the
                    darkness.

[*The strange moan comes from the window, a prolonged "Ah."*]

THE NEGRO (*starting*): Who is it?

THE VOICE FROM
  THE WINDOW: Somebody who sees you and sees the glimmer in
                    your eyes.

THE NEGRO: Someone who knows me?

THE VOICE: Yes: and knows that you came before your time,
                    in desperate longing for the light of the sun.

THE NEGRO: Has not the hour struck yet to see her who is the
                    sun?

THE VOICE: If you desire life, escape in the darkness and try not
                    to be overtaken by the morning.

THE NEGRO: Why is that, my virgin?

THE VOICE: The man to be is still a child, who has not yet
                    learned to spare the black man when he sees him.

THE NEGRO: Is my life in danger?

THE VOICE:	Go, before the King's eyes fall on you. The King still remembers that one day he saw his wife in the arms of a negro slave. Escape, slave. Disappear. Return to the darkness.
THE NEGRO:	Allow me one word.
THE VOICE:	Be quick with it.
THE NEGRO:	I want to see her.
THE VOICE:	Did you come because of her?
THE NEGRO:	Yes, and I must know what she is.
THE VOICE:	She is everything, and nothing is known about her.
THE NEGRO:	And you? Don't you know?
THE VOICE:	I do not. They kept questioning me about her. They implored me to answer. But I know nothing. They may cut my head off and ask it—perhaps it will tell them. Now go.
THE NEGRO:	One word more.
THE VOICE:	Go. I said go.
THE NEGRO:	Are you alone in this house?
THE VOICE:	With me is a man who has been soaking in a jug of sesame fat for forty days. The magician has fed him on nothing but figs and walnuts, until now all his flesh has gone, and he is left with only his veins and the concerns of his head. Tonight the magician will bring him out of the jug and let him stand in the air to dry.
THE NEGRO:	Why has he done this?
THE VOICE:	So that he will answer everything he is asked.
THE NEGRO:	And who will ask the questions?
THE VOICE:	The King.
THE NEGRO:	And what does the King want to know?
THE VOICE:	Away, slave. Be off from this place. They are coming to put out the lamp.
THE NEGRO:	But your father has already put it out.

[*The virgin again moans her long drawn-out "Ah."*]

THE NEGRO:	Why are you always making that queer sound?
THE VOICE:	If a green cloud passes you in the darkness, remember Zahida the mad.

ARREPH
EL-KHOURY

Hillbred

Arreph El-Khoury is a young Syrian now living in Kefier. He traveled abroad for twelve years. [From *Asia Magazine,* December, 1936; used by permission of *United Nations World.*]

HASBAYA IS A NICE little city—"The Biggest Little City Between Mount Hermon and the Mediterranean," as it is called by its inhabitants. Squatting on its two slopes around the banks of its river, its gray and white stone houses with their flat or pyramidal roofs among the trees give the appearance of bas-relief on emerald-green, deep-sea majolica. The most noticeable building in Hasbaya, next to the ancient crusaders' castle, is the courthouse, which was built by the Turks, to be inherited by the Arabs when His Majesty King Faisal was the head of the Syrian government after the World War, and most recently by the Lebanese government after the French had added Hasbaya to Mount Lebanon.

On a warm and sunny spring day in which the glorious Syrian sun was bathing in a sea of jade and the warm wind was racing over the purple and blue hills, a young man by the name of Kasid and a girl by the name of Hind were seen entering the high archway gate of the courthouse, in front of which a Lebanese soldier with a fixed bayonet stood motionless as if carved of rock.

They were dressed in homespun clothes and wore native shoes, black and hobnailed. A black *ighal* of coiled goat's hair encircled Kasid's white muslin headkerchief. Under the tight-fitting red *aba* which reached to his knees, he wore an embroidered jacket and vest of black cloth and a shirt of effulgent white. A peach-colored silk sash around his waist held a curved dagger. His trousers were voluminous and indigo-dyed. As for Hind, her gentle, brown eyes were heavily loaded with kohl and her fingertips dyed red with henna. The white muslin *mandil* over her head fell in folds to her ankles, partially obscuring her blue dress and black coat.

The eyes of this young pair were scrutinizing every object around them as they proceeded forward. Silently they advanced toward the inner courtyard where a number of soldiers were basking in the sun. They turned their eyes away from the soldiers as if these were gray *jin* of evil and looked to the left, knowing not what to do. On the wall they saw a number of bulletins on blackboards. Kasid advanced toward the bulletins, read a while, turned his head away from them and came back to Hind. He motioned her to follow him. She obeyed, and they walked to the end of the corridor, glanced to the left and right. Kasid, seeing a few doors at their right, motioned Hind to follow him a second time, walked toward these doors and began to read the signs on them. He read the sign on the first, the second, the third, and, seeing that none of these doors was that of the office he sought, he advanced to the foot of a winding stairway which led to the second story.

Kasid looked at the grim, ghastly walls and the disconsolate steps and paused for a moment. Finally he told Hind to follow him and began to climb the stairs with the uncertain, suspicious step of the hillbred who reckons with the inequalities of the land. Hind followed him in silence. Sometimes he was looking at the walls, at other times glancing over his shoulder at Hind behind him, and with added mistrust at the higher steps. Finally they reached a door at their left with the Clerk's sign on it. Here they stood firm—their eyes like those of a cat confronted by a mastiff.

"Enter," Kasid ordered Hind with a motion of his head.

"You enter—you who are armed with a dagger!" retorted Hind.

Kasid stood his ground. Hind looked at him. He grinned childishly. She turned her head away from him and stared at the wall. Kasid drew his head close to her. She turned facing him. She was the first to speak. "What shall we do?"

"I do not know, by Allah!" replied Kasid with an awkward shrug of his broad shoulders. They looked at each other helplessly. Kasid ventured a step forward toward the door of the Clerk's office. Hind followed him with her eyes as her red lips opened with a sardonic smile. Suddenly he stopped, pondered a while and as suddenly sat down on the steps. Hind came and sat beside him as if they were on the steps of their respective houses.

"Why don't you enter?" asked Kasid.

"Why don't you enter first and bring it?" she snapped at him.

Kasid shook his head disapprovingly.

At that moment they heard footsteps coming toward them from the higher part of the steps and in unison they looked over their shoulders. A man, dressed in European clothes, came down toward them. They turned their heads away from him. The man continued to descend until he was two steps from them.

"What are you doing here?" the man asked. They did not answer but smiled. "What are you doing here—what do you want?" he asked impatiently.

They stood up. "We want to enter this room," Kasid said, pointing to the door of the Clerk's office.

"Come on," said the man, smiling, "I am the Clerk." He walked to the door and pushed it open. He entered. Kasid and Hind followed him inside with a shambling gait.

The Clerk went inside his office and faced them across a wide desk. He sat on a chair. "Now," he said, business-like, "what can we do for you?"

"We want a marriage license," announced Kasid, his face flushing darkly. Hind giggled.

The Clerk smiled broadly, opened a drawer and produced a sheet of paper which he handed to Kasid across the table, saying, "Fill it in."

Kasid took the sheet of paper with a shaky hand, looked at Hind, motioned her to follow him and went to another desk in the room and sat down on a chair. There were penholders, inkwells and blotters on the desk. Kasid began to read and write without asking Hind a question. She stood looking at him and smiling sarcastically. Finally, he stood up, breathed contentedly, motioned Hind to follow him and came toward the Clerk. He handed him the sheet of paper. The Clerk began to read what Kasid had written in an exceptionally poor penmanship; he read their names, ages, conditions, birthplaces, the names of their parents, their occupations, their addresses and the date. Glancing at the sheet of paper for a second time, the Clerk smiled and shook his head.

"My lad," said the Clerk sympathetically, "you are not old enough nor is she!"

"*Allahu Akbar!* (God is Greater)" Kasid and Hind exclaimed in unison. "How old do we have to be?" asked Kasid with a dark frown on his highly hawkish face.

The Clerk told him the age required by the law.

"But we are not that and we want to marry each other," argued Kasid, vehemently.

"It is necessary, then, to have your parents sign this sheet of paper before we can issue a license for you," the Clerk informed him as he handed him the sheet of paper.

"We are orphans. Our parents were killed by the French in the last uprising against them," pronounced Kasid with a pain in his heart.

"It is regrettable; you have to wait until you are old enough!" said the Clerk.

Kasid made a wry face. He looked at Hind beside him and suddenly his face became haggard, passionate and tragic. Quickly he returned the sheet of paper to the Clerk, and, with his right hand on the haft of his dagger and his left grasping Hind by the arm, he went out of the room, whispering in her ears, "Allah did not say so in the Book!"

CONSTANT ZARIAN

The Pig

Constant Zarian, Armenian poet, was born in the Caucasus. He studied at the University of Brussels, published a review in Constantinople, and settled in Italy after the First World War. He returned to the Armenian republic to teach in 1922, but is now living in Italy again. [From *Asia Magazine*, August, 1929; used by permission of *United Nations World*.]

IT WAS ON A DAY in autumn that the pig made his entry into the capital of the republic. At the extremity of the vast plain stood

Ararat, Biblical and majestic, its summit capped by blue and pink clouds. Silence hung about the yellowed trees. The listening town heard the dry cold sweeping its roofs. Small and stunted, under the shelter of the copper-colored rocks, it spread out its streets, like a dead spider's legs, around its half-ruined houses, with their roofs fallen in and their windows damaged.

The political régime and poverty had filled the dusty ways with dull melancholy, tattered rags and black care. The Dictatorship had torn into shreds the citizens' footwear, made their heads vacant and their bellies empty and filled their eyes with a strange light, where some read a feeling of fear and others, despair.

They were a God-fearing people and were for the most part dull in their cups. And, while the days succeeded one another as uninterestingly as the pages of an old calendar that has done duty for several years, these people focused their souls, like a light that had been diffused, on anything which might hold a trace of novelty or a suggestion of joy.

Hence, when one fine morning a broad-shouldered newcomer, with a small head, an imperial on his firm chin, and powerful arms, was seen to give out bills announcing the arrival of a circus, it was a genuine event.

"We have had enough of the State Theater. We are going to have some fun."

"A circus!"

"And it will bring back a little of the good old times when—"

"Be careful! There are ears everywhere."

It was the talk at every street corner. All were discussing it. All were gladdened.

A circus! A great event!

Crowds thronged the streets. Many women and many children. Women of the people, for the most part, with wide-open eyes, simple and amazed about the event. And street children: young birds fallen from the nest, barefoot, ragged and laughing, undisciplined chatterboxes withal.

The circus made its triumphal entry into the town. And, since a legend had been circulated about the pig—an artist of incomparable talent—nearly all the inhabitants were collected on the broken pavements of the main street. Dejected members of the Cheka, with bright eyes and attentive ears, crept in everywhere. The militia were on the watch. It seemed for all the world like a national holiday.

When the pig slid down a plank and found himself on the platform of a small station, dazed and tottering, he still felt the continuous sensation, as of rhythmic hammer-blows on his belly, which unsettled his insides. Then he made an effort, pulled himself together and sniffed the air. There was a smell of coal, manure and sweat. He dug his nose into the ground and, besides mud, ate up rotten straw, worms and other things that are the delights of the poultry-yard and of the neighborhood round about small provincial towns.

Almost immediately after leaving the station, he walked into a yellow pond of water, full of thick and complex things. But he was not allowed to stay there. Huge, heavy with fat and muscle, lowering his long head, somewhat weak on his legs, he proceeded slowly with a nervous movement of the ears.

But, when he heard the drum beat and the bugle call, he drew himself up. Fatigue disappeared as by magic, and through his skin ran that thrill which is felt by artists and great orators on solemn show occasions. What a crowd! What an uproar! He had never had such a reception. He realized it was in his honor.

The crowd followed the circus—athletes, gymnasts, clowns—making a noise, clapping their hands, shouting and passing remarks full of fun. So many people were massed together at the corner of the main street that the pig was held up; new spectators were coming up from the side streets.

There reigned a smell of boots, sweat and poverty. The pig grunted. No one ever knew whether it was for joy or from weariness.

Meanwhile the state telephones were sounding the alarm. The Central Committee was constantly jarring the ear-drums of the Executive Committee; the latter clamored for the Cheka, then for the Commissar of the Interior, then for the militia. All the telephone handles turned feverishly.

"Damn it all! Damn it all! Can't you see what's happening?"

"It's a scandal!"

"You are allowing the people to get enthusiastic over a pig? What next? Communism—making a profit out of the people—"

"Prohibit! prohibit! prohibit!"

From all sides militia came running up and, rifle in hand, drove off the people and stopped the procession.

The pig understood nothing of all this. He was taken into the circus, a wooden structure just put up by a group of speculators.

A dry wind was blowing from the surrounding hills. Everybody was cold.

The pig became something of a hero. The Soviet citizens, bowed down by a life of shame and misfortune, had found neutral ground on which to raise a Babel of illusions. Sapped by poverty, bruised and dispirited by boredom, chained down by the Dictatorship, these simple souls looked upon this sight as something recalling life as it used to be, as a foretaste of that freedom which was so long in coming, as a pretext for useless, hearty and spontaneous pleasure.

Sometimes the presence in a prison of a single fly stirs into life a thousand illusions.

It was the talk of everyone.

"What about the pig? What?"

"Wonderful, old man, a real artist!"

"He seems to understand everything—"

"Nowadays animals understand more than men."

Behind the circus there was a tiny room, which had been set apart for the pig. Humble and solitary—like a Dominican friar in his cell— this artist spent the greater part of the day in sitting on his haunches with his gaze lost in dreamy vacancy.

A practiced eye could have discerned in his snout a certain melancholy, that special and strange form of melancholy to which thinkers and creative geniuses are subject.

In this new country were a sour smell of manure and an unpleasant odor of tanned skin, acrid and oppressively heavy. Besides, it was cold. Through the holes entered an almost ice-cold wind, nipping his flesh, beating on his back and making his nose tingle. In spite of this, he was well-behaved and resigned to his lot. Who can fathom a pig's soul? Undoubtedly this particular pig was conscious of his important mission. He seemed to perform, with philosophic calm and a simple and honest religious faith, the duty assigned to him by Providence. He knew, he felt, that everything he did brought a little joy, illusion and forgetfulness to a weary and grieving public. To dull and hardened faces he brought the innocent smile of childhood.

He was also conscious that his master was pleased. The latter was a large, stout man with a long neck capped by a tiny, emaciated head, with drawn features, a weak mouth and a low, somewhat overhanging forehead. His eyes were blue—the cold blue of steel. He was as a rule gentle to the pig and, if, during a performance, he stuck a needle into him to make him grunt, it was for art's sake.

Yes, art is pain, but it is also joy. Deep down within himself the pig felt a pleasant sensation. He had the impression of having had a fill of good acorns.

And then there was the question of popularity! People were constantly coming and going around his little room. Like a lot of distracted bees, the children set upon the boards. They climbed up on all sides, got on the roof, made holes in it to look eagerly through, shouting for very joy. There was no lack of older people besides. Women of the people, peasants come to market, old, doddering nuns, soldiers from the Red army, all went out of their way, stopped in front of the circus, related to one another the extraordinary things the pig could do and carried the news to the most distant parts of the country.

"We are told," said an old woman, "that, when the end of the world comes, animals will speak."

"Extraordinary things happen these days," added an old peasant, "Saint Carapet preserve us!"

"So be it!"

In fact, the pig was feeling tired, but, like operatic tenors and actors of lovers' parts on the stage, he could not have lived without that popularity. His dignity and pride had become used to this sweet poison.

In the evening, when the time came for the show to begin, there was not a single unoccupied place in the hall. Poor, rich, Communists, non-Communists, the dwellers in the center of town and those in the suburbs, all hurried to the circus. The performers strutted about proudly, heads held high, chests expanded, self-confident, their insides well filled and warm. At eight o'clock the band began to play. Thin, twangy notes made trills and then swelled into a march tune piercing the ear-drums like a gimlet.

The show began. Shouts, exclamations, howling of babies, whistles of joy. There was a great noise of feet on the boards, a clapping of hands; and, when the difficult numbers took place, all gazed in silence, holding their breath, their eyes wide-open with fear.

A heavy cloud of smoke, laden with various odors, hung over the heads of the audience, packed close together. With their red, burning cheeks, they all seemed a prey to fever, and on their flushed faces the same smile was to be seen.

"Good God! Good God!"

"He's going to get a crack on the head. Now he is sure to fall."

"Bravo! bravo! bravo!"

Excitement brought out perspiration all over their faces.

Toward the end the nimble orchestra played a dance tune wherein mingled freakishly a kind of jig, a Moorish dance melody and a cake-walk. Then entered the clown, astride the pig. The hall became an agitated hive. Eyes kindled, giving forth electric sparks, hearts beat fast and faces relaxed into an indulgent and admiring smile.

Like a true artist, the pig felt that *rapport* which must exist between the performer and his audience. The acrid and sickening odor, which may be unpleasant to human beings, tickled his nostrils pleasantly and elated him. He had the impression of being near a pond, with good black mire, on a day of baking sunshine. He got on a cask and rolled it along carefully; he raised his head and answered by a grunt the amusing questions his master asked; he sprang through a hoop, did a little dance and bowed to the audience.

A burst of applause filled the hall; there was a great stir and the building all but collapsed under the noisy stamping of the audience. The three speculators who had advanced the money for the business were drinking spirits at the bar and rubbing their hands with pleasure.

The same thing took place every evening.

And every evening the State Theater—the pride of the régime and the center of propaganda—was empty. At first little heed was paid to this. The circus was a novelty, and the people are children. They would get tired of it in the long run.

However, when one evening the prima donna, the lady love of one of the commissars, came on in one of her best parts and saw four persons in the hall, she could scarcely get to the end of the act, and, before the curtain fell, she fainted, shrieking, "The pig! The pig!" Everyone was upset.

A new revolutionary play was advertised. Large posters, publicity of all kinds, articles in the newspapers. The state exchequer paid all expenses.

On the night of the first performance, ten wretched spectators constantly put their hands to their mouths and yawned secretly. There was a full house at the circus, and people were being turned away at the doors.

"What is the meaning of this? Art is being sacrificed. The pig—"

The manager, who had welcomed the circus as a sign of progress, closed "the window open to civilization" and vindictively uttered that word which ever has a telling effect—"counter-revolutionary."

What about the state budget? What will the proletariat say? And what will Moscow say?

Moscow? Hidden away mysteriously in dark rooms to which no one was admitted but whence everything could be seen, the Cheka raised its head. What is this? One hand pushed another, one eye focused upon another eye, signs in red ink were placed on delation sheets, electric bells rang in the passages, setting silent-footed people in motion.

The circus! Why, it was but a blind. Those noisy gatherings of the lower middle class about a pig merely cloaked a counter-revolution. Karl Marx's plaster statue frowned.

Meetings. Resolutions. Decrees. Close the circus.

That evening the buildings made of boards placed one above the other lay in darkness. Fearful of being taken for counter-revolutionaries, people dared not pass in front of the circus.

"The pig? Don't you know anything about it?"

"I at the circus? Never saw it."

The three spectators, large and fat, with reddened faces and wicked eyes, agreement in hand, threatened the poor, dumfounded, bruised and pallid athletes.

The circus became a danger spot. On the main door, boards had been nailed up in the form of a cross. But from time to time one of the side doors would open, and there would come out one of the artists, with bowed head, a spiritless look in his eyes and pale, dull lips.

In sad plight, these people rushed from the court to the commissar's office, from the Cheka to the trade-union, documents and vouchers in hand and words of misery on their trembling lips. They were hungry, they were cold. The officials received them with hatred and murmurs but, seeing their poverty, out of sheer pity made them vague promises.

"Come again next week; we shall try to do something for you."

And the next week it was the same story.

The tradesmen demanded their money for goods supplied in connection with the building and attached all the circus property, including the pig. The pig? Why, the pig was not a commodity, a piece of property—he was one of the artists! Alas, he was brought down to his commercial value. He was sounded, weighed and had his teeth examined to tell his age.

And, besides, he was hungry. Accustomed as he was to triumphs, in vain for the first few days he waited to be fetched. He rose at his usual hour, listened for a sign of life from the outside and, hearing nothing, no music, no noise, hammered at the door with his head. The silence oppressed him. He turned round nervously and, being used to daily exercise, performed a few steps, stopped, waited a long while. Still nothing. Sometimes his master would enter, look at him sadly, say a few endearing words and go away with tears in his eyes.

The pig was getting thinner every day. He had become very sensitive to the cold. He swept the ground with his snout, blew on the boards, sniffed the air, found nothing. Then in silence and in all humility, as if inspired by a supreme wisdom, he would lie down on his side and with half-closed eyes dream of the acorn eaten in his childhood in the forest of the North.

No one ever came to see him now. Even the children were afraid. He felt most unhappy.

One day, toward evening, as he was lying on his side, his head between his feet, suddenly curious lights began to play before his eyes. A pleasant warmth crept over him. Then the lights got larger and larger, just like the electric lamps which illumined the circus on showdays. He saw his master come forward dressed as a clown, with an enormous white mouth and thin red lips. Then much noise, shouts, exclamations; then the vast deep forest, a continual murmur, a wind that leaped from branch to branch—acorns. He raised his head, opened his eyes—it was a dream.

His nature became embittered through hunger. That was the cause of his unsociable and vindictive temper. He began to grunt and would strike his head with rage against the walls and door, trying to escape. He had eaten up all the bits of paper, all the wood shavings and all the filth lying about; he had tried to chew an empty sardine-box, to make a hole in the hardened earth, to lick the walls and bite his own feet. He was hungry and cold, cold, cold.

Those who passed near the circus at night-time heard the pig's cries, grasped what was the matter, cursed life and went on their way in sadness and disgust.

The clown knocked at all the doors, shouting: "Kill him or give him food, kill him."

"Call again next week."

In the morning the court passed a resolution.

In the evening the door was opened. The pig, who had been lying down, sprang from his place, no one knows how, recovered all the untamed strength of his ancestors, charged furiously, head lowered, into the strangers, upset someone and bolted. His eyes were wild, his brow was hardened, his legs were tipsy. People gave chase. "The pig, the circus pig!" The children were convulsed with laughter and ran behind with noisy, ironical cheers. Passers-by stopped. A crowd collected. But it was a hateful, hostile crowd, which took pleasure in tracking down the animal, making sport of him and seeing him powerless. He was captured near a pond and, with a rope round his neck, was dragged through those very streets that had been the scene of his triumph.

At the far end of a dark and dirty yard he was given food. That quieted him. A little while after, when the sound of knives and iron reached his ears, he felt almost happy: this was assuredly another circus. Near by a graphophone twanged out a tune. He listened. When the door opened, his strength returned. He entered cheerfully, hopping about a little as he used to do at show-time.

No sooner was he inside than he was overthrown, and, before he could grasp what was happening, they had cut his throat.

On the following day, headless, cleaned out and disemboweled, with its flesh too red from grief, his huge body was crucified above the door of a shop in the main street. No one would buy his flesh. It was sent to Tiflis to be made up into sausages.

REFIK HALID

The Gray Donkey

Refik Halid is a contemporary popular Turkish writer and humorist. He supported the Sultanate in opposition to Ataturk and escaped into voluntary exile when his arrest was ordered. Later, when amnesty was granted to many political prisoners, he returned to Turkey. [From *Asia Magazine,* August, 1943; used by permission of *United Nations World;* translated by Eleanor Bisbee.]

THE CHILDREN WHO CARRIED WATER from the river brought news of an old man lying on the mountain trail and of a gray donkey wandering around loose.

"Let us go and see," said Hüsmen Hoja.

It was nearly evening. Heavy fumes and an odor from unhusked rice spread over the fever-ridden land, the ditches and this swamp where two streams met. The sun shone behind willows, five or ten years old, with lifeless, broken, charred trunks, and it sparkled here and there on the still waters of the drainage canal which gave back a muddy light. This light in fragments in the middle of an ash-colored damp plain resembled cracks in a cloudy sky. Gradually it became less clear and finally it went out.

Three peasants, one behind the other, passed slowly and laboriously up the steep, hilly trail. One of them coughed badly like a sick horse. They saw the gray donkey first. The donkey had found a dusty, bare place among the bushes, perhaps he had pawed it up and he had lain down and rolled over. Now he approached them with a contented air, then stopped, and indifferently watched the setting sun.

The Hoja (Koranic teacher) called, "*Haydi,* where are you, traveler?"

Beyond, a feeble old man, panting for breath, leaning his back against a wild-pear tree, looked with dull eyes at the newcomers and made a gesture pointing to his chest with his hands. To the questions, "What is it, what has happened, uncle?" he gave unintelligible replies in a groaning rattle which was more breath than voice and which sounded like asthma. The peasants, supposing that he was dying, sat down and waited. But he got better and came to life.

He was an old man with a patriarchal beard, and he was garbed in rags of the poor, in a yellow-striped turban and a violet-colored cloak. The part of his face which his rough gray beard left exposed was in wrinkles and creases, and it was tanned by the sun of the hot plain. His tiny light blue eyes, almost white under sagging fat lids, looked straight at one with a childish stare. Very slowly color came into this face and brightness into these eyes. In the same position, leaning his back against the pear tree, he said some things in a muffled tone and very likely explained that he had come from afar and was going far.

At Hüsmen Hoja's offer, "Bring him to the community guest-room, let him lie down," the men helped him up and got him mounted on the donkey. Supporting him on both sides, they descended with a thousand difficulties over sliding stones and earth.

The sun had gone; the waters that were behind them had stopped sparkling. The steep peaked mountains which shut them in on all sides had long since fallen asleep, leaning their huge, smoky, cloud-wrapped heads together. The village, buried in the shadows of the rock ledges, with neither a light in the window nor a sound on the roads, waited in the darkness.

At the noise of the arrivals occasional faces were thrust out of the doors. The cows lowed in the barns. Hüsmen shouted, "Where are you? Come out," and gave the news, "a guest has come." Now various people in white canvas undergarments came from all sides carrying flaming pine torches in their hands. In a halo composed of smoke and light, as the flicker of their torches fell into dark corners and played in patches on manure heaps, they came, utterly amazed, straight to the guest room.

Here, at two days' distance from the nearest town of any size, was a barren, trackless, tumble-down village of Anatolia. If the weather was very dry, and if there were fords across the Kizil Irmak, travelers without wagons who were on their way to other parts of the province left the paved highway and saved two days' journey by calling at this village as a short cut. Thus, in the course of a year, five or ten people with this excuse, five or ten penniless men, would come tired and weary at such a gloomy hour and knock on the doors. Then the mayor, Hüsmen, would send word to the villager whose turn it was to provide for the guest, and Hüsmen, in person, would escort the visitor to the community guest room where pine logs burned in the fireplace winter and summer without ever going out. The community learned of world affairs through the unfounded, erroneous reports which were brought by these ignorant transients.

The sick man became quiet. "My chest," he said, "it gets this way every now and then."

One of the villagers hung a copper kettle on the crane in the fireplace. The resinous flames reflected on it, and its contents foamed up in multi-colored bubbles like soap suds. They took it off and gave the old man a cupful. Blowing on it, he drank with relish. He had barely finished the milk when he had an attack of persistent hiccoughs. His whole body shook. At every quiver he said, *"Elhamdülillah."* The peasants sat facing him with their legs crossed and waited impatiently, seeking a chance to talk. The young men lined up before the door and could not understand a thing about this sick, silent guest whose eyes, craving sleep, were becoming hollow.

The hiccoughs did not cease; on the contrary they became more frequent and violent. The sick man gestured once with his hands. "Come, come close." Hüsmen stepped forward and the other elders took places behind him. The young men, very curious but lacking courage to draw nearer, stayed by the door. Perhaps the traveler by an effort was explaining his business. Maybe he was making a will. They heard Hüsmen saying now and then, "Don't worry. Let your heart rejoice. We'll attend to it." Suddenly the elders leaned over the cot. Then they rose silently.

Hüsmen murmured, "He has joined his God." In the fireplace one of the logs broke, pouring a glow of light over the face of the one who had died, and then it went out. Outside a cow mooed long.

The traveler had had time to explain his final wish. He had made a pious bequest to Hejaz of the eight gold pieces sewed up in his girdle and of the gray donkey on which he had been riding.

On their return from the cemetery, the peasants gathered together under the trellis, chatting and speculating on how to carry out this command and what they should do with the donkey and the liras which remained in their hands. At last they decided that someone should go to the district capital and consult the judge. In a week Hüsmen should make the trip, leading the donkey.

The animal acquired importance; they stacked corn stalks and quantities of food before him. This was done at regular hours in uncomplaining duty as if it were a religious obligation. The peasants reminded one another very often, saying, "Did you take water to the gray donkey? Have you given him his barley?"

One morning as colors were emerging from the darkness of night, everyone escorted Hüsmen Hoja as far as the front of the mill and saw him off. The gray donkey, tied to the Hoja's donkey, went along behind, unladen, and freely switching his tail. The newly risen, gold-streaked sun made the faded felt of the pack-saddle shine like velvet.

What a boring, long trail this was. The whole length of the quiet stream was invisible behind green borders of lush rice and corn stalks, and the road continued for two days over barren, level ground without coming to a single village, to a single mill or to a spring shaded even by as much as two weeping willows. Then a terrifying pass and a steep, rocky hill were traversed, and, on reaching the top, a pleasant view and a cool breeze began. Amidst quince and apple orchards, very green and lush, a narrow stream, glistening like the flat side of a short sword, smiled into one's eyes. A white, smooth paved highway lined with telegraph poles turned and twisted, climbing to the mountains. Hüsmen spent the night at an inn and took the road to the district capital early in the morning.

This little capital owned a huge mansion which resembled a casino with a tower and a balcony, but it had not been possible to complete it. The unplastered, unbaked brick walls had openings here and there which furnished nests for the turtle doves. The ground floor remained boarded up without windows and without plaster. In a corner a shed, left from when the laborers operated a very large lime kiln a little to one side of it, still stood in its original state. The main kiln building had long since been destroyed.

A coatless, hatless sergeant of gendarmes asked what the Hoja wanted. Starting from the beginning, Hüsmen began to relate how the children who brought water from the river had come and given the news. Before he had half finished his story, the man opposite him turned away, tossed bread to the ducks in the stream and said to a turbanned man smoking his nargile in a corner of the balcony, "What do you say, Hadji Effendi? Are you taking your morning recreation?"

Hüsmen, learning that the judge had gone on leave to Istanbul, sought a single chance to explain his business to the district director, the kaymakam. Leaving his shoes at the door, with his feet in holey socks which left his toes exposed, he stepped in timidly, his hands folded tight across his stomach, and began his story.

The kaymakam was a nasal-voiced, toothless man with a dyed mustache, who had a linen jacket of splotched, faded indigo on his back. Not displaying patience enough to hear the story to the end, he commanded, "Call the sergeant."

For five days Hüsmen Hoja wandered around the little capital telling his troubles to anyone he met. The gendarme sergeant neither accepted the donkey nor allowed the Hoja to take him away. At last someone who took pity on the Hoja made an appeal, saying: "Let him go. Let him come two weeks from now. Let us leave the matter to the judge."

Now the judge there was famous; he was called the Pumpkin Judge. He managed all affairs and he unsnarled all untieable knots. He had a fashion of passing through the market with his red umbrella, wearing an orange-colored cloak on his back, and he had a way of laughing at trifling things while holding his fat sides, so that people adored him.

The two, man and donkey, returned by the same route and in the same status; the gray donkey was still bound as a legacy. At the capital, where feed cake and barley were expensive, it had cost much to supply Hüsmen and the donkey, and the latter must necessarily be well fed. The villagers, convoking a council, did not consider this excessive, for they said, "He is dedicated to a holy place. His care is our obligation." Hüsmen brought no complaints of weariness, and his effort to do right had made him forget the tribulations of the journey.

The week of the second trip, however, he had to return home with the donkey again behind him. The judge had not come back, and the sergeant of gendarmes, on encountering the Hoja, had scolded, saying, "Stupid fellow, what's the hurry?" The peasants were in doubt whether an animal left as a pious bequest should be put to any use, so they did not disturb the donkey.

The return from the third journey was again the same, with the donkey following behind. One peasant with far-seeing eyes spied from afar the gray donkey again coming back and spread the news through the village. The people, astounded, waited now with curiosity. Hüsmen, without dismounting, explained in a joyful voice the outcome of this attempt, "What have we done? We should have taken a witness."

A witness—how had they not thought of that! No harm had been done, however; the judge would accept the donkey, he would write out a certificate; indeed next week, three people would go and, if need be, would pledge their oath.

The gray donkey, eating and eating the abundant food set before him to prepare for these trips made at intervals and without any load, had grown fat. He ran after the females when they were taken to water, and he became ill-tempered. Thus two and one-half months passed.

At last everything was ready for the final trip. While the villagers saw them off from in front of the mill, the new-risen sun shone on the dust raised by this little procession. As it climbed the hill in a gilded cloud, it seemed to those who remained behind to be mounting to the sky.

The gray donkey did not come back any more. The villagers, seeing the certificate which had been made out and the seals which had been stamped on it, believed that the creature would travel to Hejaz

slowly, unladen, without suffering, and receiving due homage everywhere, and that there he would carry the holy water of the well of
Mecca. Hüsmen one night in a dream saw the donkey's saddle covered
with the sacred green velvet, and that reenforced the belief.

Now everyone often talked of the donkey with a joy born of doing
their duty, and, seeming to forget that he had run with the females,
they recounted and persuaded one another that while remaining alone
in the stable the donkey, as he turned his head from side to side, had
begun to invoke the name of God.

On the anniversary of the affair, however, Hüsmen, who went to
the district capital to sell rice, returned as if he had been struck dumb.
At a time when the market place was completely crowded, he had
heard from a distance the cry to clear the road for a pack animal,
"Make room, don't touch!" The people parted to the sides and the
Pumpkin Judge passed. On his back was the well-known orange
cloak, and under him was the gray donkey; he was dispensing salaams
on all sides in a fashion that shook his fat body.

SAW TUN

Tales of a Burmese Soothsayer

Saw Tun is a native of Burma who is
studying chemical engineering at Yale
University. He also is a student of Bur-
mese literature. [From *Asia Magazine*,
March, 1946; used by permission of *United
Nations World*.]

THE BURMAN is a great believer in omens, portents and signs.
Hardly a thing happens before he begins to interpret it either as good
or bad. Many a time was I warned by my mother to be careful on my
way to school: her right upper eyelid had involuntarily twitched that
morning. In my native town, back in Burma, whenever the band
played to announce the coming of a new movie my aunt began repeating a little limerick to the effect that all this music in the streets
heralded the destruction of Arakan. Only in 1939 I made fun of her
and her prophecy. Today, knowing that there is hardly anything left
of my native town and many towns near by, I slowly stroke my chin
and wonder. I remember clearly in 1940, just before I left Burma for
the United States, there was quite a stir because "O's" were supposed
to have appeared on the pagodas, on the statues of Buddha and on
the sacred banyan trees. The Burmans interpreted this as a sign of
approaching freedom from British domination.

It is difficult to knock this trait out of the Burmese people. I have met many Burmans brought up in England, with high academic degrees from Oxford and Cambridge, so thoroughly Anglicized that they can hardly speak the Burmese language on their return to their motherland, who visit fortune-tellers and ask them to interpret certain signs that heralded their birth. Yes, it would be well-nigh impossible to get the Burman out of this habit. He has been born with it, and it has grown with him. He practices it every day, and if things do not come true, it is not the signs but his interpretations that were wrong. For did not his master the learned monk tell him that all events, either great or small, are heralded by signs?

The words of a child or a mad man, some striking feature of one's surroundings, the words of a popular song, some age-old prophecy, the appearance of a comet—all these can be used to foretell coming events. We just have to go back a few hundred years in Burmese history to see how many decisions of great political significance were influenced by omens and signs. Every Burmese King had his own soothsayer. And any evening, if you happen to sit with a few Burmans around a pot of tea and a bowl of salted peanuts, you will hear tales of the great soothsayers and how their interpretations of the various omens turned out to be true.

The greatest of them all was Ahyoudawmingala, who served King Bodawphya in the eighteenth century. My intention is to relate some of the incidents which have made his name immortal in Burma.

THE BRASS LIME-BOX

It was on a Thursday afternoon, in the month of July, 1782, that the ear-boring ceremony of the second son of King Bodawphya (also known as King Bawashinmintaya) took place. Many people from all over the country came to attend this ceremony. In one of the pandals, or booths, erected for the occasion, the ministers of the court and the wise men of the country congregated and began discussing literature and history.

Ahyoudawmingala, still in his teens, joined in the discussion of the graybeards. It was not long before everyone present recognized how well read he was and what vast information he had gathered. He was loudly applauded by all and particularly by U Pye, a leading adviser to His Majesty the King, who lavishly praised him but, like all elders, wound up by delivering a sermon. "My son," said he, "though you be young, an old head rests on your shoulders. Great must have been the merit you achieved in past existence. But take care that fame does not get into your head."

At this juncture, the Minister of the Royal Stables joined in and said, "My Lord, there is no need of praising this young boy any further. Everyone who is connected with the Chamber of Justice and the courts knows his abilities, his great learning and his intelligence. But there

are many amongst us today who have known him by mere hearsay.
Now that I have a chance I should like to test his abilities, that is if
he doesn't mind, so that I may in future be able to tell of him and his
greatness from personal experience."

"Dear uncle," replied Ahyoudawmingala, "please do not hesitate to
ask your questions; I shall try to answer them to the best of my
ability."

On getting this reply, the Minister of the Royal Stables took out the
brass box which held his lime for betel-chewing and said, "I would like
you to tell us the weight of this box without touching it."

It was a difficult question, and many said that it was an unfair one
too. Ahyoudawmingala looked around for an *ateik*—that is, a visible
sign that might give him a clue. Nothing striking caught his eye except a piece of broken bamboo in the matting used to roof the pandal.

With this as a lead he argued, "When two of our most revered monks
of history met to test each other's learning, one asked the other for
ta-bin and *hnit-pin* (that is, one and two). The second monk, reasoning that one and two make *thon-bin*, or three, and that thon-bin with
the vowels reversed is *thin-bon*, which means slate, gave him a slate.
Again, when the second monk was asked for *ta-gyauk-eik*, he reasoned
that ta-gyauk-eik is like *ta-jeik-auk*, which means *ko-yauk*, or nine
persons, and ko-yauk with the vowels reversed is *kauk-yo*, or straw. So
he handed him some straw. Now, when I look around, this broken
bamboo matting or *kut-kyo* is the only thing that strikes my attention
and kut-kyo with the vowels reversed is *ko-kyut*, nine ticals [about six
ounces]. So it stands to reason this lime box weighs nine ticals."

The lad then told his guess, and when the Honorable Minister admitted it was correct and presented him with a new lacquer box, the
others followed suit and showered presents upon him in appreciation
of his rare ability.

THE WHITE MICE

Three days later, at the same festival, thirty-two novices were ordained into monkhood and the leading ministers met again to distribute various articles of clothing, food and money in charity. When
the business of the day was over, they sat down to talk and happened on
the subject of signs and omens.

Since their arguments led them nowhere, the Minister of Personal
Affairs sent for Ahyoudawmingala, who answered all their questions
and cleared up their doubts by quoting the Buddhistic Scriptures and
illustrating from ancient writings. But this only roused their desire to
test him. So they quietly sent a servant after the white mouse which
was on show at the public museum and, covering it up with a betel
box, asked the lad what creature was under the box.

Ahyoudawmingala then thought to himself: "This morning, when
I came into the palace grounds, I noticed a sow with its litter near the

compound of His Majesty's right-hand man U Paw U. Now, the elephant and the mouse are the only creatures which resemble the pig. Elephants are too big to get under a betel box, so obviously this must be mice." He told the ministers so. Then they wanted to know how many. Since he had seen the pig with two little ones, he replied, "Three." At this guess, the Minister of the Eastern Gate smiled and, uncovering the mouse, sardonically said, "Here you sign expert—take one." But to everyone's amazement there were three mice as predicted. While confined under the betel box, the mouse had given birth to two little ones.

Presents were showered upon Ahyoudawmingala, while the Minister of the Eastern Gate promised that he would personally report the matter to His Majesty the King.

Foretelling a Flood

One day, Ahyoudawmingala, together with a small group of friends, decided to take a holiday and visit various places. As they approached a village a few miles west of the Royal City of Ava, a madman came toward them with a bundle of nursery plants in his right hand and a bundle of corn in his left. Recognizing this as a *nameik*, or sign by which a coming event can be foretold, and wishing to warn the villagers of approaching danger, Ahyoudawmingala turned to the village headman and said, addressing him with a complimentary term common in Burma, "Builder of Monasteries, in this ever-changing world of ours events good and bad are forever taking place, and these events are always heralded by signs and omens. Now, take this madman leaving your village with nursery plants and corn. These are substances included in the category of things related to the day Thursday. So also is rain. We know very well the old prophecy. 'In five days times three, due to excess water, everything shall be destroyed.' The sign shows that the time is now ripe and after fifteen days there will be a great downpour of rain from the heavens and all the towns along the river banks will be destroyed. So the people must leave their homes and shift to safer places." (Corn in Burmese is *pyaung,* which also means shift.)

Those who believed the prediction quickly left their homes, while the skeptics remained behind. As foretold, on the sixteenth day, due to heavy rains in northern Burma, the Irrawaddy River overflowed its banks, causing much death and destruction.

When the King heard of all this he made Ahyoudawmingala Lord of Sataungmyo and created for him the post of Royal Adviser.

The King Disregards the Omens

Bodawphya had ascended to the throne in March, 1782. He was entire master of the Irrawaddy River basin. The chiefs in the districts east of the Salween as far as the Mekong acknowledged his supremacy. The seacoast, as far south as the port of Tenasserim, was subject to his government. In October, 1784, he attacked Arakan, and conquered it within three months. Ambitious of military glory, Bodawphya determined to subdue Siam. Informing the ministers of his intentions, he asked his Royal Adviser the outcome.

Ahyoudawmingala then reported, "Your Majesty, last night as I returned home, a boy coming out of the Siamese Market was singing:

> Cast away your sense of superiority;
> March not forth,
> And you shall be the king of kings.
> Tathagi, the Zamaree,
> Lead your forces
> And you shall live to regret your action.

"The first part of this song means it is not worthy of Your Majesty to attack such a weakling as the King of Siam. And if Your Majesty would only allow things to remain as they are, before long, the time would come when the King of Siam would have to pay homage to Your Majesty annually. In the rest of the song, the word 'tathagi' refers to the descendants of Lord Buddha. According to history, King Kanyazagyi, a direct descendant of Our Lord Buddha, came to Burma and in time his descendants spread far and wide and established small kingdoms all over Burma. Your Majesty belongs to that great family of Thagiwins, so the word tathagi definitely refers to Your Majesty. The word 'Zamaree,' which literally means the king of beasts, also refers to Your Majesty. The rest of the sentence is quite plain. Should Your Majesty, the Lord of all creatures, attack Siam, the Burmese Army will meet with defeat and disaster and Your Majesty will suffer mental agony and regret. In short, if we don't attack, we shall remain on top, otherwise, we shall live to regret it."

It hurt the Burmese King's pride to be told he would fail to conquer Siam. So, disregarding the advice given by his faithful servant, he prepared for the great invasion.

The preliminary steps were taken early in 1785. Leaving his eldest son to rule over the country, the King himself led the attack in 1786. The Burmese forces suffered defeat over and over until the King, fearing for his safety, left the army in the hands of his ministers and returned to Martaban. There he sent for the royal family, but before they arrived, he proceeded to Hanthawaddy and rebuilt the famous Shwe Mawdaw Pagoda, which was in ruins. He then went down to Rangoon to meet his family. Together they worshiped at the Schwe Dagon Pagoda and then returned to the Royal City of Ava. From the capital, reenforcements were sent. But news soon arrived that the Burmese army had been ambushed and practically annihilated. What remained ran back helter-skelter to Martaban.

The news greatly disturbed the King, and, calling his ministers together, he said to them: "When I first comtemplated invading Siam, Ahyoudawmingala advised against such a step. But, not seeing any reason why I should not be able to conquer that small and weak country, I disregarded his advice. Now we have met with disaster, and it is all because I don't have a single one amongst you wise and able enough to lead us to victory. When occasion arises, all the ministers and the wise men of the state are practically useless."

Hearing this note of dejection and dissent in the King's voice, U Paw U, the chief Minister of Personal Affairs and a favorite of the King, said, "Your Majesty, in this world there are four great islands, the East, the West, the North and the South, and ours is the southern one, which according to our books is especially noted for signs and omens, as is indicated by the clockwise twining of plants. One can notice that in general in this island, plants twine round from right to left or clockwise. When they do twine counterclockwise, from left to right, then these plants possess specific medicinal properties. Therefore, here in this southern island where this peculiar plant phenomenon occurs, we make the best use of the signs before us. Now, because Your Majesty did not like Ahyoudawmingala's interpretation of the *tabaung*, or song that heralded a future event, and disregarded this sign, we have suffered loss in men and resources.

"This is not the first time that things have happened thus. During the time of Your Majesty's great grandfather, we went to war with the King of Hanthawaddy. The astrologers warned the heir apparent to refrain from attacking the enemy forces, but the rash prince disregarded their advice and failed hopelessly.

"Similarly, King Ahnuruda, the great grandfather of our Lord Buddha, while riding out in his royal chariot, heard the strange and loud voice of a frog, which the astrologers reported was a female frog weeping and wailing over the death of its mate. When the ground was dug, the dead and live frogs were found exactly as predicted. The King demanded the interpretation of this sign, and the astrologers replied that he should remain within the palace grounds to avoid mishap. Not heeding the warning, the King ventured forth and fell a prey to the attack of a wild buffalo.

"Also, in the Jataka stories we find that when the time was ripe Mahajanaka obtained the throne without even asking for it. In this same tale, our Lord Buddha said that at times, without planning or exerting, one may achieve things, and at times, even with planning and exertions, one may achieve nothing. That is why, Your Majesty, time and opportunity are more important than planning. Moreover, the winning of a war does not depend wholly upon bravery and numbers; the terrain, the climate and adequate supplies also play a very important role. For this reason, though Your Majesty, who is an embryo Buddha, has suffered defeat like King Mahajanaka, when the time arrives the King of Siam shall meet with destruction only to leave the kingdom in Your Majesty's golden hands."

The King was greatly consoled and rewarded U Paw U and Ahyoudawmingala each with a ruby ring and twelve pounds of silver.

THE ENGLISHMAN COMES TO BURMA

A century and a half ago, thanks to the East India Company, the British Empire was expanding rapidly. Consequently the demand for ships increased a great deal. The forests of England were already depleted, but little Burma was full of teak forests. Good hard wood, teak was, an ideal wood to build the ships for the British Navy. Indeed, Burmese teak is still used in the British Navy's best ships. But the Burmese King was not going to give away his teak free. He imposed an export duty. And the Company did not want to pay. Why should they anyway! The Burmans were not using the teak. Anyhow there was so much surplus stuff that a little exploitation did harm to no one. In fact wasn't it a favor to these Burmese people to clear their snake-infested jungles? Imposing a tax, what cheek! This saucy Burmese King must be taught a lesson. So in the year 1795 or thereabouts a courteous little note was sent to the Burmese King. "Give up the area around Bassein or . . ." (Sometimes I feel that if we had not any teak we might have remained a free nation right up to this very day!)

The Burmese King was very upset. He did not know what to do. Hastily, he sent for Ahyoudawmingala and the other ministers. Waving the note frantically before the ministers' faces, he asked for advice. "What shall I do?" he asked. "Should I give them the whole of Bassein District, or should I send my troops?"

"Your Majesty," Ahyoudawmingala replied, while coming through the central gate, I came across a group of children having a stage show. And the song they sang was:

" 'Sonny boy, when you meet your opponent, don't be rash. The gray matter in your head will tell you that the big bellied *Nga-see-bu* will run away only when hit by a silver bullet.'

"The first portion of this song simply means that should an opponent appear, one should not fight but use one's brains and achieve one's purpose. '*Nga see bu*' (literally, a kind of fish with a big, round belly) here refers to people associated with the sea, especially those going about from place to place by sea routes. 'Big-bellied' refers to the English people who are never satisfied with fighting and conquering other people's homes and countries. Their desire for other countries is as big as this fish's belly, which can never be filled to the brim. Such an enemy will turn around and leave only if they are hit with the silver weapon."

Hearing Ahyoudawmingala's interpretation of the tabaung, the

King handed over a sum of one hundred thousand silver coins to the English, who quietly took the money and went away.

A couple of years later, about 1797, the English sent an envoy to the Burmese court. This time they brought not an ultimatum but an offer of friendship. In furtherance of the existing friendship between the two kingdoms, Burma and England, Her Majesty's representative requested a piece of land for the establishment of an English court in the Royal City of Ava. Together with this request, the English sent many presents.

When Ahyoudawmingala heard of this he said: "Your Majesty, this morning, I met Honorable U Paw U at a street crossing and stood chatting for a few minutes. During that time, the boys from the Monastery who had come out with the monks to beg for the morning meal went by, singing a song which U Paw U told me I should note, for it seemed like a tabaung. It went like this: 'Your ladyship, should the lordship come smiling and entice you with some sugar candy, don't fall for it.'"

The King smiled and remarked that the tabaung required no special interpretation. So the British envoy returned home very much disappointed.

It is hard to tell whether it was Ahyoudawmingala's interpretations or the Burmese King's own good judgment that influenced his decisions. An English writer has summed him up in the following words, "Notwithstanding his cruelty he was a man of ability and except in the great folly of heading an invasion of Siam, carried out his plans, for what he considered the glory of the kingdom, with prudence and perseverance." And, to judge from the kind of stories we hear and read about him, it seems as if this author was right.

TAO KIM HAI

The Cock

Tao Kim Hai, an Annamese, is well known in the literary life of France as a journalist, short story writer and the author of two books on French Indo-China. The Cock is the first of his works to be published in English. Mr. Hai came to the United States in 1945 as a French Government delegate to the Conference on Pacific Relations, and remained to head the San Francisco branch of the Colonial section of the French Information Service. [From Asia Magazine, March, 1946; used by permission of United Nations World; translated by Ruth Barber.]

YOU'RE QUITE RIGHT; he has certainly outlived his usefulness, and we should kill him. But my husband would never agree to it, and neither would I. Help yourself to betel again, honored sister, and I will tell you why.

Yes, he's getting quite old for a rooster, and he doesn't perform his conjugal duties as he should. But there's no question of killing him, nor even of giving his harem to a younger cock. In the first place, he'd fight until his crop was torn open rather than be deposed. He comes of fighting stock—see how long and sharp his spurs are, and how they curve. And in spite of his age, he's still fast enough on his feet to defend his rights. His feet are his most aristocratic feature; notice how the scales grow in two straight lines like the Chinese mottoes on either side of a door, with not a sign of a feather between them. His mother was only an ordinary Cochin-China hen, but his sire was a real Cambodian fighting cock with I've no idea how many fights to his credit. But that's neither here nor there; it's not for his fighting blood that I value him. The truth is that he did me a great service five years ago. It's thanks to my poor old rooster that I married the man I love.

Five years ago, my husband lived next door to my parents. We were neighbors, but the distance between us was immeasurable, unbridgeable. He had neither father nor mother; my father was the *ly-truong* (mayor) of the community. His house was a little hut built on date-palm posts, walled with bamboo and thatched with water-palm leaves; my house had four rows of carved teakwood columns, walls of whitewashed brick and a red-tiled roof. My father had twenty oxen and ten buffaloes, and a thousand acres of rice fields; *he* hadn't even a patch of ground, and raised only a few chickens. To tell the truth, he was our *ta-diên* (tenant farmer).

Tenant or no, he was the handsomest young man, the best monochord player and the fastest rice planter of the whole district. You should have heard him play the monochord in those days; it was enough to bring a goddess down from heaven. I've made him give up playing since we've been married, although I love music myself. It wasn't all because I was jealous of his monochord; I was afraid for his eyesight, too. Everybody says the monochord causes blindness, and the better the musician, the greater the danger.

He was eighteen, and I was two years younger. We were in love, and our love was all the stronger because it was hopeless. An irresistible attraction drew me to him, in spite of his rough farm clothes and his unkempt hair.

In his poultry yard a young cock with green and gold plumage and a blood-red comb lorded it over the admiring hens. He fought all the other cocks in the village, and gallantly refused the paddy and broken rice thrown to his little flock until his wives had eaten their fill. He was brave, and he was not at all bashful, either with the hens or before me. You would have said he took a wicked delight in making love to them in my presence. Then he would cock a glittering eye at me, and crow.

One day his master and I were talking behind the bamboo hut, where we were safe from all indiscreet eyes. Suddenly we heard a loud "Ha, ha, ha!" We turned around in alarm; it was only the cock. My suitor threw a stick at him. He saw it coming and made a magnificent leap to one side, so that the stick only grazed his tail. Then with an indignant "Kut-kut-kut" he stalked off to rejoin his hens, looking for all the world like an insulted sovereign. From the safety of the poultry yard he looked back at us, and, like a practical joker who has just pulled off a good one, he crowed, "Ha, ha, ha, ha-a-a-!"

Another day we had found a trysting-place at the foot of a big straw-stack, from which we could look out over the endless reaches of my father's rice fields, the obstacle to our marriage. That accursed cock came and perched on top of the straw-stack, discovered us and, beating his wings in the air as if to call the whole world to witness, he let out a scandalized "Oh-oh-oh-rooo!"

In trying to chase the old tattle-tale away, we lost all sense of caution, and he was not the only one to see us together that time. Soon the village was buzzing with gossip about us; the cock had set tongues wagging. Jealous girls, and young men too, whispered that I had lost my virtue, and the old *bagia* shook their heads and began to speculate on the date when my figure would show the results of my fall. And of course the rumors did not fail to reach my parents' ears.

The cock joined the other gossips. No longer satisfied to crow all day, he started to crow in the evening, too, after the lamps were lit. His competitors, a thousand times outcrowed but still ambitious, replied from all the henhouses of the village. You never heard such a racket.

Do you believe here in your province, honorable elder sister, that the crowing of a cock in the evening is the sign of an extramarital pregnancy? In our district everybody believed it, even my mother. My poor mother is superstitious. In spite of my tears and my denials, she took me for a lost virgin who dared not acknowledge her fall. No need for *me* to admit it; the cocks were there to proclaim it far and wide.

My grandparents were summoned, and my aunts and uncles on my mother's side and on my father's. They shut me up in my little room and held a family caucus in the living room before the altar of our ancestors. I thought my last hour was come, and I waited for them to bring me the lethal cup, the saber and the red silk cord. Which death should I choose—poisoning, bleeding or hanging? Would they shave my head like a nun's before they forced me to commit suicide? Suicide it certainly must be, for the family of a mayor must never lose face.

But I was an only child, and my mother was already old. No matter what the sacrifice, the family must have another generation to carry on the cult of the ancestors. If I were to die without issue, my mother would be forced to choose a concubine for my father and to admit her to the marriage bed, to cherish the concubine's children as her own. Then, too, I suspect that my father was beginning to be influenced by European ideas. Above all, he loved me a great deal, although the traditional reserve that a father must observe toward his daughter kept him from showing it. Whatever the reason, the family council decided to do nothing worse than to marry me off in all haste. And to whom, God in Heaven? To my seducer, no less. I agreed without a murmur.

The six preliminary marriage ceremonies were gotten through with before two weeks had passed, and we were married in the strictest privacy. The formal proposal was without pomp and palaver; the betel ceremony was reduced to little more than a tête-a-tête in everyday clothes. As for the suitor's period of probation in the house of his future wife, which usually lasts from six months to two years, we simply omitted it. No invitations on scarlet paper with gold script, no official delegation from the town council, no gift of ring-necked ducks on a brass platter, no open-air banquet lasting far into the night. But there were also none of those more or less annoying jokes which most young couples have to resign themselves to—the drinking party in the bridal chamber, the bed that rocks, the bridegroom who is kidnapped. We had only to prostrate ourselves, I in a wide-sleeved red dress and he in a black tunic and turban, before the altars of our ancestors and before my parents, less to ask their benediction than to make honorable amends.

It was a bad match, and a scandalous one; the less said the better.

It had been agreed that we should leave our native village immediately and make our home in some distant province where we were not known. On our wedding night we set out on the long journey, in a big barge that my parents had loaded with rice, salt fish, and *piastres*. We were accompanied by two faithful servants and the cock, who followed us into exile with all his little harem.

We've been here for five years now, honorable sister, in your rich and peaceful province, and as you know, we haven't yet had a child. My poor mother writes me that she spends her days running to the pagodas having prayers said and sacrifices made, in the hope of becoming a grandmother before she goes to join her ancestors at the Golden Spring. The poor old cock has been proved a liar. But thanks to his lies I'm a happy woman, and he shall have all the white rice he can eat to the end of his days.

PRATOOMRATHA ZENG

My Thai Cat

Pratoomratha Zeng was born in Ubol, a northern district of Siam, in 1918. Educated in Bankok, Siam, and at New York University, he has worked for the Siamese Government. During the war, he was a translator for the United States Army.

SII SWARD was our Thai or Siamese cat in my home town Muang, a northern village in Thailand. She was a gift from my father's friend to me when I was five years old. She had piercing blue eyes and delicate dark brown fur which she constantly cleaned with her tongue. I was completely devoted to her. She was also very popular with my entire family, and later was to be well known in the whole district.

During the drought in 1925, our Sii Sward was a heroine; she had the great honor of being elected the Rain Queen.

We had been without rain for three months that summer. It was hot and dry. Our public well was reduced to mud; the river was at its lowest ebb. The grass and the trees were dry as tinder. Many of the buffaloes and farm animals on our farms died of heat, so we took the remainder to be fed far away on the bank of the river Moon in the north. It seemed as if farming that year would be impossible. We were on the verge of chaos and famine. Already there were reports of forest fires in the other districts. Families from other villages had migrated southwest seeking for new places for farming.

Every day the villagers gathered in the village Buddhist temple praying for the rain. All day long the Buddhist priests chanted the sacred ritual for water from the sky. All the farmers were worried and thought only of rain, rain, rain.

Then someone suggested that we perform the old Brahmo-Buddhist rain ceremony called the Nang Maaw, the queen of the cats. This ceremony has been performed by the peasants since time immemorial.

No exact date can be given when the ceremony asking for the rain started. In Brahmanism, Varuna, or the god of rain, must be pleased. Varuna was the god or guardian spirit of the sea, water or rain. He was one of the oldest Vedic deities, a personification of the all investing sky, the maker and upholder of heaven and earth. It is said that once Varuna who was very militaristic appeared in the form of a female cat to fight a demon. He won the battle and thus continued to give to the world rain and prosperity.

Whether the Thai farmers knew the story of Varuna I do not know. All they thought during that time might be only to please Varuna, the god of rain.

One day, an old lady and her friends came to my father and begged him to help in the rain ceremony.

That day my father approached me and my cat seriously. He patted Sii Sward's head gently and said to me, "Ai Noo (my little mouse), the villagers have asked us to help in the ceremony asking for the rain. I promised them to use our cat—your Sii Sward."

I was stunned. How could they use my cat to get rain? I thought of those chickens that the Chinese killed and boiled during their annual Trut-Chine, the Chinese ritual days for sacrificing to and honoring the memory of their ancestors. To have my cat killed and boiled like a chicken! Oh, no.

I almost shouted to protest, "Oh, no, father, I cannot let anyone kill my Sii Sward. Rain or no rain, I don't care."

In the Thai family, the father is the sole absolute authority of the house; to deny his wish is sinful and inexcusable. My father, however, was a very understanding man. He looked at me coldly and said calmly, "Son, no one is going to kill Sii Sward. Instead of doing that, and because our cat is the most beautiful and cleanest of all the cats in the village, she was elected by the people to be the Rain Queen of our district. This is a great honor to her and to our family."

I was reluctant to consent until father said, "We can take Sii Sward back home as soon as the ceremony is over."

That evening there was an announcement from the temple ground by the old leader of the village that there would be a Nang Maaw ceremony starting in the afternoon of the following day.

Next morning everyone in the village went to the temple ground. The women were dressed in their bright blue skirts, Pha Sin, and white blouses, and the men in their white trousers and the Kui-Heng shirts. Children of all ages put on their new clean clothes; they walked along with their parents. Two artists built up a big bamboo cage and the people fastened flowers and leaves to it and dressed it up until it looked like a miniature castle.

At noon time, my cat Sii Sward had her usual lunch of dry mudfish and rice, then my father gave me the great honor of carrying her to the temple ground. Some old ladies brushed and sprayed sweet native perfume upon her proud head. Sii Sward protested vehemently; she struggled to get away, and I had to put her into the adorned cage. However, once inside the cage, she became calm and serene as befitted her role and soon curled up in silent slumber. Buddhist priests came to sprinkle sacred water on her, but Sii Sward slept on.

In spite of the heat and the sun, that day people packed into the monastery to see Sii Sward, the Rain Queen, and to pray for rain. They carried the cage into the big Vihara, our best and most beautiful temple; and then the priests chanted a sacred prayer in front of the image of Lord Buddha, Pra Kantharaj (the image of Lord Buddha asking for rain). Sacred water was sprinkled onto poor Sii Sward as a high priest lit a candle near the cage and chanted long moaning prayers in the sacred Pali tongue.

In mid-afternoon the sun was so hot that the villagers took refuge under the shade of the big mangoes and Po trees on the temple ground. A group of people began to chant the Nang Maaw song, softly at

first, then louder and louder until everyone seemed to shout. Long
native drums, Taphone, began to beat in chorus. People started to
dance while chanting the song:

> Oh, mother cat, please give us rain from the sky
> So that we can make sacred water
> We need silver for the mother cat
> We need fish and we need honey
> If we do not get it, we will be ruined.
> Don't let the widow down to sell her children.
> Let them have all white rice
> To have pleasure, we need gold and silver
> We want to buy bananas
> We need provisions for the priests and the people
> Let us see the lightning and let us have rains
> Oh, let us have rain.

It was a most impressive ceremony and made me feel warm and
confident of the queen's powers.

Sii Sward still slept peacefully in her adorned cage. Cool as a
cucumber, she ignored the noise and the chanting until two men came
to her miniature castle and lifted it to their shoulders, and then led the
people out of the temple. A procession was formed; two drummers
with Taphone drums led the crowd. They beat the drums incessantly
as the people chanted and made a lot of noise. After the drummers
there were a group of dancers dressed in the Thai theatrical style.
They danced in front of the cage as if to perform the show for the
Queen of Rain.

The procession moved toward the market place. There was a
huge crowd following the procession; all of them chanted the Nang
Maaw. On the narrow street people laid cakes and water which the
pedestrians ate after Sii Sward passed. Some people gave the two men
who carried the Rain Queen some rice wine. Both of them toasted the
queen and drank the wine happily. These foods and drinks were to
impress the Queen of Rain that ours was the land of plenty, and that
the goddess of rain must give us water so that abundance of life
would be preserved.

Sii Sward slept all the way; she was not impressed by the demonstra-
tion. Before we entered the open market place there was so much
noise; someone fired many big fire crackers. A few women who were
traders in powder and perfumes approached the cage and poured cups
of sweet-smelling perfume and flowers onto the poor Rain Queen.
At this moment, the noise of frantic shouting, of chanting, of fire
crackers, and that perfumed water proved to be too much for the
poor Sii Sward. More water and perfume were poured and splashed
into the cage. Sii Sward stood up, her blue eyes staring at the culprits.
Her brown and smooth hair was soaking wet. She began to cry and
tried to find the way to escape in vain.

Seeing the whole condition going from bad to worse, I was almost crying asking father to rescue the poor cat. However, father said that everything would be all right. After a while, everyone seemed to be satisfied giving the Rain Queen perfumes; they stopped the noises completely as if to listen to the tormented noise of the Rain Queen. At that moment Sii Sward stopped crying, too. She was soaking wet and trembling with fear.

People chanted softly as they led the procession back to the monastery, even the drummers and the two men who ten minutes ago were chanting frantically now calmed down. Sii Sward continued crying on the way back to the temple as if her heart would break. I was helpless, but I followed the procession closely to the monastery.

When we reached the Vihara, the men placed the cage in front of the temple, and then all of them went into the Vihara to pray for the rain goddess again. At this moment, I saw the opportunity to help my poor Sii Sward. Having seen the last person enter the temple, I took Sii Sward out of the cage and ran home with her.

At nine o'clock that same night, it was pitch dark. Sii Sward now calmed herself down and seemed to forget the whole event in the day time. She lay down under my bed and slept soundly. My parents were not yet returned from the temple ground; they joined the neighbors praying for rain in the monastery. I still wondered about the whole procession in the day time, but I was too tired and did not know when I went fast asleep.

When my people came back from the temple ground at eleven o'clock, there was still no sign of rain. Someone came into my room to see Sii Sward, but seeing us asleep they went out quietly. It must have been about three o'clock in the morning, a sound like a train running and a big hurricane was heard. Later there was a strong sound of thunder over the mountains, and a few minutes later, a shower, a real tropical shower, came down. Everyone in the village got up from his bed. We were happy. The farmers started at once to their farms. It rained for three days, and three nights, and it seemed as if the showers would never stop until the water in the sky would be gone. Our crops were saved.

But Sii Sward ignored the whole rain. She slept happily the whole three days. Farmers and their families dropped down to see her afterward. The patted her delicate fur and left dry fish and meat for her, her favorite food. That year the farmers thought that Sii Sward saved their crops and their families. Sii Sward was a heroine.

MANUEL
BUAKEN

The Horse of
the Sword

Manuel Buaken was born in the Philippines and educated in American universities. In 1943 he joined the First Filipino Infantry, U.S. Army, and was stationed at Camp Beale, California. [From *Asia Magazine*, August, 1943; used by permission of *United Nations World*.]

"BOY, GET RID OF THAT HORSE," said one of the wise old men from Abra where the racing horses thrive on the good Bermuda grass of Luzon uplands. "That's a bandit's horse. See that Sign of Evil on him. Something tragic will happen to you if you keep him."

But another one of the old horse traders who had gathered at that auction declared: "That's a good omen. The Sword he bears on his shoulder means leadership and power. He's a true mount for a chieftain. He's a free man's fighting horse."

As for me, I knew this gray colt was a wonder horse the moment I saw him. These other people were blind. They only saw that this gray, shaggy horse bore the marks of many whips, that his ribs almost stuck through his mangy hide, that his great eyes rolled in defiance and fear as the auctioneer approached him. They couldn't see the meaning of that Sword he bore—a marking not in the color, which was a uniform gray, but in the way that the hair had arranged itself permanently: it was parted to form an outline of a sword that was broad on his neck and tapered to a fine point on his shoulder.

Father, too, was blind against this horse. He argued with me and scolded: "Maning, when I promised you a pony as a reward for good work in high school English, I thought you'd use good judgment in choosing. It is true, this horse has good blood, for he came from the Santiago stables—they have raised many fine racers, but this colt has always been worthless. He is bad-tempered, would never allow himself to be bathed and curried, and no one has ever been able to ride him. Now, that black over there is well trained—"

"Father, you promised I could choose for myself," I insisted. "I choose this horse. None of them can tame him, but I can. He's wild because his mouth is very tender—see how it is bled. That's his terrible secret."

My father always kept his promises, so he paid the few *pesos* they asked for this outlaw colt and made arrangements to have the animal driven, herded, up to our summer home in the hills.

"I used to play, but now I have work to do," I told Father. "I'll show you and everybody else what a mistake you made about my horse."

Father agreed with me solemnly, and smiled over my head at Mother, but she wasn't agreeing at all. "Don't you go near that bad horse your father foolishly let you buy. You know he has kicked so many people."

It hurt me to disobey Mother, and I consoled myself with the thought she'd change her mind when I had tamed my Horse of the Sword.

But could I win where all others, smart grown men, had failed? I could, if I was right. So early in the morning I slipped off to the meadow. The Horse of the Sword was cropping the grass industriously, but defiantly, alert for any whips. He snorted a warning at me, and backed away skittishly as I approached. "What a body you have," I said, talking to accustom him to my voice and to assure him of my peaceful intentions. "Wide between the shoulders—that's for strength and endurance. Long legs for speed, and a proud arched neck, that's some Arabian aristocracy you have in you, Sword Horse."

I kept walking slowly toward him and talking softly, until he stopped backing away. He neighed defiance at me, and his eyes rolled angrily, those big eyes that were so human in their dare and their appeal. He didn't move now as I inched closer, but I could see his muscles twitch. Very softly and gently I put my hand on his shoulder. He jumped away. I spoke softly and again put my hand on the Sword of his shoulder. This time he stood. I kept my hand on his shaggy shoulder. Then slowly I slipped it up to his head, then down again to his shoulder, down his legs to his fetlocks. It was a major victory.

That very day I began grooming him, currying his coat, getting out the collection of insects that had burrowed into his skin. He sometimes jumped away, but he never kicked at me. And next day I was able to lead my gray horse across the meadow to the spring, with my hand on his mane as his only guide—this "untamable outlaw" responded to my light touch. It was the simple truth—his mouth was too tender for a jerking bridle bit. The pain just drove him wild; that's all that had made him an outlaw. Gentle handling, no loud shouts, no jerks on his tender mouth, good food and a cleaned skin—these spelled health and contentment. Kindness had conquered. In a few days the gaunt hollows filled out with firm flesh to give the gray horse beauty. Reckless spirit he always had.

Every morning I slipped off to the meadow—Mother was anxious to have the house quiet so Father could write his pamphlet on the language and Christianization of the Tinggians, so I had a free hand. It didn't take more than a month to change my find from a raging outlaw to a miracle of glossy horseflesh. But was his taming complete? Could I ride him? Was he an outlaw at heart?

In the cool of a late afternoon, I mounted to his back. If he threw me I should be alone in my defeat and my fall would be cushioned by the grass. He trembled a little as I leaped to his back. But he stood quiet. He turned his head, his big eyes questioning me. Then, obedient to my "Kiph"—"Go"—he trotted slowly away.

I knew a thrill then, the thrill of mastery and of fleet motion on the back of this steed whose stride was so smooth, so much like flying. He ran about the meadow eagerly, and I turned him into the mountain lane. "I know how a butterfly feels as he skims along," I crowed delightedly. Down the lane where the trees made dappled shade around our high-roofed bungalow we flew along. Mother stood beside her cherished flame tree, watching sister Dominga as she pounded the rice.

The Horse of the Sword pranced into the yard. Mother gasped in amazement. "Mother, I disobeyed you," I blurted out quickly. "I'm sorry, but I had to show you, and you were wrong, everybody was wrong about this horse."

Mother tried to be severe with me, but soon her smile warmed me, and she said, "Yes, I was wrong, Maning. What have you named your new horse?"

"A new name for a new horse, that's a good idea. Mother, you must name him."

Mother's imagination was always alive. It gave her the name at once. "Glory, that's his name. *MoroGlorioso*. Gray Glory." So MoroGlory it was.

Too soon, vacation was over and I had to go back to school. But MoroGlory went with me. "You take better care of that horse than you do of yourself," Father complained. "If you don't stop neglecting your lessons, I'll have the horse taken up to the mountain pasture again."

"Oh, no, Father, you can't do that," I exclaimed. "MoroGlory must be here for his lessons too. Every day I teach him and give him practice so that next spring, at the Feria, he is going to show his heels to all those fine horses they boast about so much."

Father knew what I meant. Those boasts had been mosquito bites in his mind too; for our barrio was known to be horse-crazy.

For instance, it was almost a scandal the way the Priest, Father Anastacio, petted his horse Tango. Tango ate food that was better than the priest's, they said. He was a beauty, nobody denied that, but the good Father's boasts were a little hard to take, especially for the Presidente.

The Presidente had said in public, "My Bandirado Boyo is a horse whose blood lines are known back to an Arabian stallion imported by the Conquistadores—these others are mere plow animals."

But the horse that really set the tongues wagging in Santa Lucia and in Candon was Allahsan, a gleaming sorrel who belonged to Bishop Aglipay and was said to share the Bishop's magic power. There were magic wings on his hooves, it was said, that let him carry the Bishop from Manila to Candon in one flying night.

Another boaster was the Municipal Treasurer—the Tesero, who had recently acquired a silver-white horse, Purao, the horse with the speed and power of the foam-capped waves.

The Chief of Police hung his head in shame now. His Castano had once been the pride of Santa Lucia, had beaten Katarman—the black satin horse from the near-by barrio of Katarman who had so often humbled Santa Lucia's pride. Much as the horses of Santa Lucia set their owners to boasting against one another, all united against Katarman. Katarman, so the tale went, was so enraged if another horse challenged him that he ran until the muscles of his broad withers parted and blood spattered from him upon his rider, but he never faltered till his race was won.

These were the boasts and boasters I had set out to dust with defeat.

Winter was soon gone, the rice harvested and the sugar cane milled. Graduation from high school approached. At last came the Feria day, and people gathered, the ladies in sheer flowing gowns of many colors, the men in loose flowing shirts over cool white trousers. Excitement was a wild thing in the wind at the Feria, for the news of the challenge of the wonder horse MoroGlory had spread. I could hear many people shouting "Caballo a Bintuangin—The Horse of the Sword." These people were glad to see the once despised outlaw colt turn by magic change into the barrio's pride. They were cheering for my horse, but the riders of the other horses weren't cheering. I was a boy, riding an untried and yet feared horse. They didn't want me there, so they raised the entrance fee. But Father had fighting blood also, and he borrowed the money for the extra fee.

As we paraded past the laughing, shouting crowds in the Plaza, the peddlers who shouted "Sinuman—Delicious Cascarones" stopped selling these coconut sweets and began to shout the praises of their favorite. I heard them calling: "Allahsan for me. Allahsan has magic hooves." The people of Katarman's village were very loud. They cried out: "Katarman will win. Katarman has the muscles of the carabao. Katarman has the speed of the deer."

The race was to be a long-distance trial of speed and endurance— run on the Provincial Road for a racetrack. A mile down to the river, then back to the Judge's stand in the Plaza.

MoroGlory looked them over, all the big-name horses. I think he measured his speed against them and knew they didn't have enough. I looked them over too. I was so excited, yet I knew I must be on guard as the man who walks where the big snakes hide. These riders were experienced; so were their horses. MoroGlory had my teaching only. I had run him this same course many times. MoroGlory must not spend his strength on the first mile; he must save his speed for a sprint. In the high school, I had made the track team. An American coach had taught me, and I held this teaching in my head now.

The starter gave his signal and the race began. Allahsan led out at a furious pace; the other horses set themselves to overtake him. It hurt my pride to eat the dust of all the others—all the way out the first mile. I knew it must be done. "Oomh, Easy," I commanded, and MoroGlory obeyed me as always. We were last, but MoroGlory ran that mile feather-light on his feet.

At the river's bank all the horses turned quickly to begin the fateful last mile. The Flagman said, "Too late, Boy," but I knew MoroGlory.

I loosened the grip I held and he spurted ahead in flying leaps. In a few space-eating strides he overtook the tiring Allahsan. The pacesetter was breathing in great gasps. "Where are your magic wings?" I jeered as we passed.

"Kiph," I urged MoroGlory. I had no whip. I spoke to my horse and knew he would do his best. I saw the other riders lashing their mounts. Only MoroGlory ran as he willed.

Oh, it was a thrill, the way MoroGlory sped along, flew along, his hooves hardly seeming to touch the ground. The wind whipped at my face and I yelled just for pleasure. MoroGlory thought I was commanding more speed and he gave it. He flattened himself closer to the ground as his long legs reached forward for more and more. Up, and up. Past the strong horses from Abra, past the bright Tango. Bandirado Boyo was next in line. "How the Presidente's daughter will cry to see her Bandirado Boyo come trailing home, his banner tail in the dust," I said to myself as MoroGlory surged past him. The Tesero's Purao yielded his place without a struggle.

Now there was only Katarman, the black thunder horse ahead, but several lengths ahead. Could MoroGlory make up this handicap in this short distance, for we were at the Big Mango tree—this was the final quarter.

"Here it is, MoroGlory. This is the big test." I shouted. "Show Katarman how your Sword conquers him."

Oh, yes, MoroGlory could do it. And he did. He ran shoulder to shoulder with Katarman.

I saw that Katarman's rider was swinging his whip wide. I saw it came near to MoroGlory's head. I shouted to the man and the wind brought his answering curse at me. I must decide now—decide between MoroGlory's danger and the winning of the race. That whip might blind him. I knew no winning was worth that. I pulled against him, giving up the race.

MoroGlory had always obeyed me. He always responded to my lightest touch. But this time my sharp pull at his bridle brought no response. He had the bit between his teeth. Whip or no whip, he would not break his stride. And so he pulled ahead of Katarman.

"MoroGlory—The Horse of the Sword," the crowd cheered as the gray horse swept past the judges, a winner by two lengths.

I leaped from his back and caught his head. Blood streamed down the side of his head, but his eyes were unharmed. The Sword on his shoulder was touched with a few drops of his own blood.

Men also leaped at Katarman, dragged his rider off and punished him before the Judges could interfere. The winner's wreath and bright ribbon went to MoroGlory, and we paraded in great glory. I was so proud. The Horse of the Sword had run free, without a whip, without spurs. He had proved his leadership and power. He had proved himself a "true mount for a chieftain, a free man's fighting horse," as the old Wise Man had said.

Golden days followed for MoroGlorioso. Again and again we raced, —in Vigan, in Abra, and always MoroGlory won.

Then came the day when my Father said, "The time has come for you, my son, to prove your Sword, as MoroGlory proved his. You must learn to be a leader," Father said.

And so I sailed away to America, to let the world know my will. As MoroGlory had proved himself, so must I.

LATIN AMERICAN SECTION

Introduction

The Spanish word "cuento" does not exactly correspond to what we call the short story. It has covered anecdotes, legends, folklore, pictures of customs. Lately, however, it has become more often identified with brief prose narrative. An example of a great earlier writer limiting himself to recounting historical or traditional tales is Ricardo Palma, who began to publish his *Tradiciones peruanas* in 1872 and continued till 1910, filling ten volumes with folklorish material about colonial Peru. Later writers, such as the Venezuelan Díaz Rodriguez and the Mexicans Gutierrez Nájera and Amado Nervo, introduced symbolic and fantastic elements not generally associated with simple narrative.

The more modern trend of the short story, with its impact of realism and social import, can be dated from 1898 and the Spanish-American War. Authors were jolted away from the poetic dreaminess to which they were naturally inclined. From Mexico to Argentina, they began to scrutinize and report the world about them. They saw squalor as it is pictured in José de la Cuadra's *Valley Heat,* or the gay adventurous frontier as recounted in Jesus del Corral's *Cross Over, Sawyer!* This reversion to reality was strengthened by the threat of Yankee power, the impending social revolutions, and the steady stream of influence from French, Spanish, and Russian realists or naturalists.

While European authors were widely read (Tolstoy, Turgenev, Dostoevsky, Gorky, Dickens, Kipling, Lagerlöf, and the whole gamut of Frenchmen beginning with Zola, Daudet, Maupassant and France), these models were not crudely imitated. They furnished the starting inspiration for bold native originality. Poe and Whitman are widely known in Latin America, but the preponderance of French influence has always been a constant factor and can be only partly explained by the popularity of Rubén Darío's *Azul,* which in 1888 revealed the power of such models as Hugo and Verlaine. Yet Darío by his own poetic universality added his name to the great masters and started the long process of making South American writing a part of world literature.

Gradually prose assumed its true place as an artistic medium, and the short story and novel, focused on the native heath, eliminated European trends. The Latin-American heritage moved into the foreground, particularly with such authors as López Albújar, in his picture of Indian mores in *Adultery.* The Negro and Negro-white relations began to claim attention: witness the striking story, *The Lottery Ticket* by García Calderón. Authors like Proust, Joyce and Romains, had wide influence, but by now Latin American writers maintained steadily their connection with their own time and locale. How completely this separation from European influence is established can be measured by looking at the stories of Benito Lynch, a descendant of Irish and French ancestry, whose moving tale of *The Sorrel Colt* is a pure indigenous product. Hernández-Catá does connect his story of *The Servant Girl* with the old world, but only to show the wickedness and treachery of the decadent continent, and by contrast the kindliness of the new one. It would be foolish to exaggerate this separatism, since, even in North America, we are transplanted Europeans for the most part. Even an original painter like Diego Rivera lived some twenty years in Paris and knew his Marx as well as his Giotto and Botticelli.

But Latin American literature of today is undeniably an independent force, conscious of its own achievement and promise, and seething with energy and creative power sufficient to warrant the statement that no world perspective of great writing can ignore it. The fine authors present in this collection of stories are bound to awaken appreciative echoes in the future. Already an author like Quiroga with his delightful jungle tales holds first rank among the connoisseurs. A shrinking world will bring such writers closer, and their sterling qualities, till lately unknown, will give them their rightful place in world literature.

With some of our stories, it will be useful to review a few historic events. Beside the fateful date of 1898 and its impact on literature, subsequent political movements have exerted their influence upon creative artists interpreting their native background. Foremost of these is the six year Mexican Revolution following the fall of the Díaz regime, May 25, 1911. The whirlwind released by this event and involving the poor and the humble blows fitfully in the story by Jorge Ferretis, *The Failure*. The progressive social and economic reforms of Uruguay (1911–1927) also produced a new awareness in the other, less radical republics. It would be difficult to find a stronger Robin Hood protest against the static forces of law and order than Urbaneja Achelpohl's *Ovejón*.

Finally, and inevitably, came the repercussions of the hemispheric policies of the United States, and of the two World Wars. The Pan-American Conferences, our inauguration of the Good Neighbor policy, various inter-American agreements—these tendencies toward cohesion gradually counteracted our dollar and military diplomacy of the early 1900s. It is good to remember that we actually helped patch up the terrible Chaco War between Paraguay and Bolivia (1932–38), brilliantly pictured in Cespedés' *The Well*. It is probable that the second world conflagration has forced the Anglo-Saxon and the Latin Americas into a more consistently unified relation.

Writers living in such a ferment would inevitably be aroused to sympathy with the little people kicked around by so many mighty pressures. The masses deprived of education, the Negro and Indian barely subsisting, industrialization grouping large numbers of underpaid workers in cities—these are the materials that will enter into fiction. The dreary landscapes and their starving denizens are powerfully sketched everywhere, consummately for example by Mariano Latorre in his *Woman of Mystery*.

Unlike their northern brethren, these writers who translate into
stories the life of their countries do not work for money; literature has
rarely afforded a living to its creators in Latin Amerca. Writing is a
secondary occupation, after time has been given to earning a livelihood.
This has its bright side, since our authors do not work to attract publishers. They think of their art as a way of serving their country and
of portraying, along with its stark needs, its true greatness—which re-
sides essentially in high character and noble independence, such as we
meet in the rider in Castro Z.'s *Lucero*. Such a point of view toward
their craft makes their stories fewer than ours, but often more effective
and meaningful.

There are two literary cores or orbits in Hispano-America, one the
Mexico-Peru tradition, where quick conquest of gold and Indians for
agriculture developed a type of civilization different from that of the
Argentine-Uruguay regions, where soil was untilled and savage tribes
scattered. On this historical basis we may separate the writers of Ecuador,
Colombia, Peru, Venezuela, Mexico, from those of Chile, Uruguay,
Argentina.

In the former group, the historical tale predominated until the social
ferment made authors contemporaries again. In the latter, the story
has been marked by the frontier episode, the gaucho and his lasso—
aspects that will subsist until the land has been fenced in. That is why
Argentine stories often have what we might call here a "western" tinge.
Still, it must be remembered that Argentine has the second biggest
Latin city in the world, Buenos Aires with its 2,600,000 people. Hence
urban living is bound to emerge more and more in literary expression
as time goes on. This tendency is revealed by stories like that of the
city slicker so comically sketched by Quiroga in *Three Letters and a
Footnote*.

By contrast, while Mexico City has 1,800,000 people, the country itself
is much more primitive—as pictured in Ferretis' *The Failure*. Many of
the South American republics, with large native elements in their populations, naturally turn to Mexico, similarly illiterate but on the move,
rather than to Argentina with its high predominance of European immigration and its streamlined modern capital city. Our own United
States diplomatic policy is more consistent in its dealings with Mexico
than with Argentina. Mexico seems somehow more dependable because
it is more indigenous, less European.

In both Mexico and Argentina, the novel will be the preferred
medium for literary expression, because it affords room for picturing of
vast movements of social forces. The short story will not fare so well in
these countries placed at the political crossroads. It is Chile, more than
any other Latin American land, that has distinguished herself in the
short narrative—both in terms of the number of her authors and of the
quality of their product. While in other countries it is the novelists
who on occasion try the short story, in Chile the opposite is the case.

The most notable predecessor of the Chilean authors included here was Alberto Blest Gana (1831-1920), and he seems to have directed the trend in Chilean fiction toward objectivity amidst the wondrous Andean landscape. After him, the authors here given come as a natural development. The Chilean "cuento," while it makes use of psychology and inner consciousness to add interest, is nevertheless more pronouncedly non-lyrical and unsentimental than that of other countries, and also more self-conscious as a literary form. Special encouragement has been given to it by the foundation of the publishers, *Zig-Zag,* in 1905, whereby numerous young authors were summoned to try the "cuento," first in magazines, and later with an assured re-publication in collections of all sorts. Thus a place, both temporary and permanent, was offered to ambitious writers of the short story, and an emphasis which is distinctively Chilean given to this literary genre. In the United States there is perhaps no more perishable literary type than the story in the weekly magazine. In Chile, by intensive cultivation, this product has been raised to a special place of honor.

The literary situation in Brazil merits a short comment. This great country, whose extent and future can well stir the imagination, should have been by its very size, population, wealth, and variety, the leader among the Latin-American republics in artistic creation. But linguistically, it is caught on the historical accident of Portuguese exploration. Hence the chasm between it and the other countries, where Spanish is spoken. World War II has enhanced the significance of Brazil, and her creative artists, musicians, painters, sculptors, have become better known. Less so her writers—for whom their unique language in this hemisphere is a distinct disadvantage, frankly regretted at times by young Brazilians who feel the true power of their extraordinary country and its potential place as a leader in Latin America.

Recommended reading in this connection is the little book, *Brazil, An Interpretation,* by Gilberto Freyre (Knopf, 1945). The tendency of Brazilian writers is toward realism with a sprinkling of fantasy, perfectly illustrated in Monteiro Lobato's *The Funny-Man Who Repented.* Other names connected with objective prose narrative could be listed: José Lins do Rego, Vitorino Carneiro da Cunha, Jorge Amado, Roquel de Queriroz, Amando Fontes, Vianna Moog, Erico Veríssimo, Graça Aranha, Mario de Andrade, Nachada de Assiz, Luis Jardim.

One final caution that cannot be too often repeated. We have so comfortably appropriated the term America for the United States that it comes to us as something of a shock to discover that we have millions of fellow Americans outside our borders who use the same name for their native land. The time may come when the simple word "American" will be accepted naturally as universally applicable to any citizen of this hemisphere. For the present, we of the United States might learn to substitute the designation North American for ourselves, for that is what we are to our brothers, whom we call South Americans.

HARRY KURZ

MARIANO LATORRE

A Woman of Mystery

Mariano Latorre was born in Cobequecura, Chile, in 1896. He studied at Valparaiso and Santiago and devoted his life to education. He is at present Professor of Spanish Literature at the Institute Peda gógico of Santiago. He has written many short stories portraying the Chilean mountain landscape of which *A Woman of Mystery* is one. His main works are *Cuentos del Maule, Cuna de Cóndores, Ully y Otres Cuentos* and *Chilenos del Mar.* [Translated by Harry Kurz.]

THE HIGHLANDER, A BIG FELLOW who looked as if he had been hacked out of old native woods by deft strokes of the axe, kept busy untangling the harness gear of his mountain wagon without answering the question put to him by the young man standing near-by. The latter was an emaciated youth, poorly dressed. His gray, restless, moist eyes followed every movement of the driver who was now fastening the yoke to the shaft between the oxen. The face of the questioner showed weariness and his grimy fingers kept twisting as if they suddenly possessed a life independent of his will. He was obviously afraid that the wagoner would start off without answering his request on which, at that moment, his whole being hung in suspense. When the driver let the oxen move ahead a few yards in order to test the dependability of all the fastenings, the young man also stepped forward in the belief that the wagon was beginning its journey. Then he repeated his entreaty in a trembling voice.

"What do you say, sir? Will you take me to Recinto? I beg of you for the sake of what you hold most dear . . ."

This time the man spoken to raised his huge rough head showing his face lined with deep wrinkles like the bark of the *coigüe* tree, and answered with a certain mocking indifference, "The wagon is rather small, Master, and what is more, the oxen haven't had enough to eat in this arid country-land."

Helplessness and fear were revealed in the tearful eyes of the young man who betrayed an utter fatigue. His hands traveled unconsciously, nervously, rubbing his face, red with anxiety. He stepped even closer to the driver, unaware of the humor of his action as he followed him in all his movements around the oxen. His voice betrayed the humble insistence and entreaty of a beggar.

"I can't give you more than ten pesos. I have only fifteen in my pocket and I need five for the train out of Recinto. I lost all my money. I haven't any more."

The driver pointed to the narrow rectangular form of his vehicle, a thick board mounted on rough wheels, the traditional sturdy wagon that wins through in crossing the highlands. The top of rough *colihue* staves fashioned for this trip was covered with old faded quilts and mantles, and from the rear peeped the edge of a mattress.

"Don't you see she's nothing, and besides my mistress is traveling inside. There's no room for you."

The young man looked at the darkened opening through which nothing was visible. The argument of the driver seemed to convince him. His trembling hand brushed a few drops of sweat from his forehead. In a faltering voice he made the last attempt.

"I could go with you in front."

The wagoner, feeling himself master of the situation, smiled pityingly and said, "There's barely room for me on the cross-beam." Then, instead of alms, he threw out a generous bit of advice. "Tomorrow Bustamante's wagon will go this way bound for Veguillas. His is bigger than this one."

The young man answered, now subdued, "Thanks, very much." There echoed in these few words of courtesy a tone of bitterness and of resignation at what couldn't be helped. The back of his right hand was held trembling against his chin trying to hide his grimace of despair. Nevertheless, he didn't budge. He had his back turned to the driver, and faced the volcano whose shadowed pyramid dominated the heights, outlined in strong relief against the limpid summer sky, and watched the rose-colored tuft of vapor that the crater expelled at that instant with a distant rumbling, blending like the final notes of a prodigious crescendo into the near-by murmur of the river.

A woman's voice, with a masculine note of roughness, gave the order from inside. "Cachi, tell the gentleman he can go in the wagon."

Humbly the driver repeated the order of his traveling mistress. "You can go inside the wagon, says the lady."

The young man's face was radiant. He took off his soiled cap in a respectful gesture, although the lady of the wagon did not reveal herself within her retreat of quilts and cloaks.

"Madam, God will reward you. You can't know how much I thank you."

"Don't mention it," was the response, raspingly uttered. "You may get in."

"No, madam, after the climb. I can go afoot so that the oxen may have it easier." He was surprised at the gentle tone of his own voice in which there was mingled the grateful humility of the outcast.

Nothing more happened. His benefactress did not deign to show her face to him. He barely succeeded in noting the sole of a sharp pointed shoe as it was withdrawn in a movement for greater comfort in the inside of the covered wagon; an old country shoe, of thick reed which disclosed the fat ankle of some village woman.

The wagon started off with a great creaking of heavy wood at the cry of the driver who, with his long goad brandished above his head, urged on his team.

"Nifty! Shaver!"

And the young man trotted after. For a moment he thought about returning to the filthy little corner where he had lived for a month. There he had left behind a pair of old shoes, a worn-out toothbrush, and a fragment of soap; but he didn't do it. He felt a loathing for that shanty of boards where at night as many as ten people piled in. He didn't want to see again the red nose of Romualdo Soto, the card shark, always wrapped up in blood-stained strips that hid his festering sores. He found repulsive that perverse society among which he had lived in a settlement built of worm-eaten boardings, swarming with grubs. The concession-holder had nailed it together roughly on a slope in the hollow of a ravine in order not to interfere with the view from the chalets of the Baths. Up there, however, there was another crowd congregated, driven by the same passions and rotting with the same vices. Between the swaggerers who shuffled their cards by the light of a sputtering candle and those aristocrats who were grouped around the gaming tables, there was no other difference than the size of the banknotes taken in by the roulette-spinner or the tips that kept the backs of the attendants bowed at an abased angle.

This February afternoon draped in its roseate tranquillity the twisting walls of hills with their sudden juts and deep-cut torrent beds. In all this harsh rocky landscape one tone dominated, the gray glisten of volcanic ash, the porous dullness of hardened lava.

The wagon had by now entered the path along the reddish cleft which cut a deep glen into the enormous sandy hill. The young man, forgetting everything else, sank his feet with a voluptuous pleasure into the softness of the ground. He felt himself lighter, purer, freed from former ideas. He didn't have more than fifteen pesos in his pocket, but his basic problem was solved. Now he would be able to get to Chillán where he had friends to help him.

He looked with affection at the little mountain cart, enveloped in a cloud of dust that the sunlight colored red. The peaceful gait of the oxen as they covered the leagues left the track of their cloven-hooves between the parallel lines of the wheels. He even enjoyed the shouts of the driver who seemed irritated by one of the faithful animals. "Shaver! Shaver!" His mind kept up a playful dialogue with himself. "Why has he given that name to that spotted little ox, stained like a laborer's old jacket?" And he was overjoyed to discover the reason for this fanciful country nickname. Obviously it was because the white spots on the ox's flanks made them seem like cheeks dripping with dirty water.

A quarter of an hour later this mountain corner with its temporary structures, the ugly white cabins of the Baths stuck on the hot slopes, and the dirty churning of the brook, had all disappeared behind the uneven outlines of the old hill plateau. Now, beyond the immense angle of a hollow, the mass of the volcano stood out solitarily, looking

like a Titanic heap of shining rocks whose jagged stone cuspid pointed
the way to the void of the smoking mouth of the crater.

The afternoon was passing. Little by little its bright rosiness was
paling, observable especially in the smoky plume of the volcano which
at intervals swelled its extent to the accompaniment of a tidal rever-
beration that also echoed from the valleys by some distant magic. The
rough crests and the snow patches shining like old enamel seemed to
melt softly into the thin liquid atmosphere. The moon, like a globe
of polished crystal, sketched its outlines above the summits.

The wagon was entering a wood of *coigüe* trees with large leaves
and twisted trunks. A sapling uprooted by the avalanches was now
held up within the fork of another tree in its lingering death. Within
this grove were traces of a melancholy destructive ruthlessness, left by
primitive cataclysms. In the background, with the roseate hue of its
plume of smoke and its rhythmic beat, the volcano resembled an
Indian chieftain who had intimidated his tribe with the tyranny of
his power.

By now the wagon was dropping into the last turn of the descent.
It stopped before entering the thick woods at this point about level
with the floor board. The foliage of the *coigüe* trees and the beeches
hid the mountain summits, and above the treetops there floated a ruddy
haze. The babble of the river drifted toward the other end of the little
valley, alongside the bald mountains.

The driver adjusted the lashings and straightened above the shaft
the laurel yoke-pads of the oxen. Then he invited the young man to
get into the cart.

Hesitantly, the traveler walked up to the rear of the wagon and
said, "Madam, if you permit me?"

From the inside there came forth an inarticulate mumble that
sounded like acquiescence. Setting his knees up on the edge, he
gradually slipped into the cavity, taking all manner of precaution not
to loosen the quilt. He had to stretch and relax at full length with
care so as not to bump against his companion. There was no ease
possible under the arched structure of the wagon-top because the
woman at his side was stout and took up most of the space. Fortunately,
a soft country mattress covered the floor of the cart and his head could
rest on a wide bolster like that of a marriagebed. Like an offended
bride, the woman had turned her back on him, and all he saw of her
was the dim curve of her hips and the angle of her shoulder. The
wagoner closed the semi-circle of the aperture, fastening a box between
the end of the cart and the side rods. Not without a pang did the
young man realize that he was going to spend the whole night inside
that rolling receptacle of hard Chilean planks now advancing into
the heart of the sierra with steady jolts. Only one flap had remained
unfastened and here the summer sky glowed blue and an occasional
end of a branch waved for a second. Above his head a thrush uttered
two sweet notes solid as two seeds of the Chilean *boldo* nightplant.

Presently he began to drowse off. His recollections became indistinct.
Inside the little cart he beheld a new world about him. This mysterious
woman who lay hunched up close to the side-rods holding up the
wagontop and who had shown toward him without any explanation
an impulse of generosity rarely seen among country folk; then the
dull loud knocks of the heavy wheels against the rocks and the sinking
counter blow when they fell into the hollow ruts of the road; finally
the odor of forest woods emanating from the driver's jacket as he
sat perched on the cross-beam an inch away from his head, and his
voice when he broke the twilight silence every little while, "Shaver,
uaaa!"

It was a primitive shout that the young man enjoyed interpreting.
It was aimed at the animal as if it were a comrade to whom one has
patiently taught to do his job and who, because of some unforgivable
neglect, forgot the most elementary rules concerned with cart-pulling;
it was an admonition to exert the same effort as his yoked companion.
For this reason, in the shout there was entreaty as well as annoyance.
And the small ox surely understood, for each time the ropes of the
yoke groaned with renewed effort as the powerful square forehead
tugged on.

Inside the heat was suffocating. It lingered in the ravine between
the high hills. The fringe of sky that the flapping quilt revealed
began little by little to ease its color and turn dark. At times the
golden glimmer of a star seemed to sniff its way inside the cart.

The breeze that started from the icy stretches and cooled off the
land and the forests was now beginning its whispering murmurs. The
crystal globe of the moon was assuming a thick golden flush that
spread the mystery of its peaceful glimmer over the woods. The
wild life among the trees woke beneath the light as if it were early
dawn, and the cry of a hunting fox echoed once in the masses of the
thickets.

The young man had closed his eyes. The dimness within the
covered wagon wooed him to slumber. But a sharp hatred stirred
within him against the woman who was dozing at his side and
whose noisy breathing, to his disgust, was just plain and simple
respiration. Who could this lump of a woman be? An invalid suffering from a contagious malady and who was ashamed to show her
face? Why didn't she talk to him?

She was, perhaps, some town woman who bathed only for medical
reasons, one of those rheumatics who emigrated each year to the
Baths from all the corners of the valley as if they were going to the
feast of Saint Sebastian, seeking some miraculous relief for the strange
and tragic afflictions that usually attack people in the solitudes of
rural life. Or she was a landowner, one of those who lived in big
houses with long balconies giving on sad town squares, held prisoner
by ancestral inheritance dating from better times. Was she showing

her contempt for his beggarly appearance or for the supplicating tone of his request?

At a jolt of the cart these notions jumbled and disappeared as if they were shaken out. But presently his mind returned to its listless, subconscious round. He remembered keenly the anguished hours of temptation at the roulette wheel surrounded by a multitude of strangers whose gaze, concentrated by a strange fascination, eagerly followed the dizzy turning of the small wheels or the movements of the multi-colored heaps of the chips on the varnished tables; his transfer to the rough shelter of Romualdo Soto when his last bank notes were raked in by the croupier's pole; and during this time of anguish in which reality faded away, the little wheels continuing their mad whirl on their steel axis; then finally his humiliation before the chip changers who took in the rest of his money. Then he recollected the sudden awakening of his conscience as if he were coming out of a nightmare, and the depths of his loathing for his shoes open at the toes, for his soiled shirt and his finger-nails, long, like those of a sick patient.

At the remembrance of these scenes of his ruin, a cold trickle of sweat formed down his skin and his heart beat with sharp jerks. Finally his memories faded and an immense stupor lulled his body. But his mind was still awake and received fragments of confused impressions; the loud fidgeting noise of the oxen chewing the cud from their bellies; at intervals the vague rumble of the volcano. Suddenly he was completely aroused. He didn't hear any noise as he lay wrapped in a gentle immobility. The wagon had stopped.

Gradually he became aware of the woman at his side, like the unpleasantness of an opposing force taking shape in the dark. He felt her moving about restlessly. The shiftings of her body were now so obvious that in the depths of his being was aroused also that ancient urge that awakens and calls every time a man and a woman are close to each other; then he sensed the smell of clean flesh perspiring, and this impelled him beyond measure; moreover, during the unconscious movements of sleep, the woman had drawn much closer toward him and her thigh and shoulder were in contact with his knees and side.

A smile came to his lips at the thought that took shape in his mind. "This graceless woman is a bad sleeper!" He was surprised to note that the person who said these words almost aloud seemed to be com-pletely outside himself. With extreme precautions, now entirely aroused, and in order not to awaken the stranger, he raised the quilt which shut away the view, and the breeze from the woods that was wafted into the small opening together with the fresh scents, calmed the burning in his cheeks.

This lasted just a moment. Then he turned back to the warm silence of his corner.

"What's wrong, Cachi?"

"Nothing, just a lashing of the yoke that broke. I've fixed it."

Once more, the cart resumed its journey. The driver, completely awake, was muttering in a twangy voice snatches of song with amusing monotony. Perhaps the warm night laden with fragrant mildness had lit in his soul in bondage some spark of poetry. Little by little the words became more distinct and the young man heard bits of verse, simple stanzas nostalgic of better days, the good old patriarchal times when the wagoner, stretched on the floor of his rough vehicle urged on his team, overcoming the lonely roads and the straying paths of the forest.

Now the beginning of the song came out clearly:

> *A rancher received in dower*
> *Many colored oxen with bride.*

And the rest of the stanza was lost in the whining uncertain tones:

> *And as in a g . . . flower*
> *In them he took m . . . . . ide.*

Something unexpected made the young man forget all about the toneless voice of the driver. The body of the woman who was drowsing at his side was drawing closer to him by degrees. He realized clearly that this was not the unintentional pressure of a body accustomed to plenty of room and which, in the unawareness of slumber, is unmindful of another resting at its side. His heart told him as its beats increased that the quiet shifting of the unknown woman meant something more. Soon he became aware of a warm breath close to him, full of desire, and lips that sought his with that groping that only death or birth imparts to the movements of human beings.

And in that cart which rolled along with its reptilian heaviness through the mountains, the world seemed to pause for a moment in its eternal trajectory through space, as were joined the lips of two human beings unknown to each other till then.

The wagoner on his perch under the moon was still muttering his nostalgic verses:

> *And as in a garden a flower*
> *In them he took much pride.*

The young man felt himself suddenly released. It seemed as if his worry had been carried off by the warm surge of blood that was now quivering in his veins with the rhythmic beat of health. He hummed in a low voice some tune that came to his mind just then without his knowing why. He tried to get her to talk, that woman who so unexpectedly had given herself to him. He attempted to summon her features, the masculine resonance of her voice, and her figure, as if she were standing before him; and from the details he had been able to glimpse or imagine, he got nothing concrete. Deprived of her material qualities she seemed something vague, abstract, that he couldn't picture. At times the recollection of some woman he had met before intervened, and then a photograph glimpsed in a show-window display or in magazines. He tried to recall the taste of those frantic kisses which had descended on his mouth like a rain of fire. But all he could do was to be certain that she was a corpulent woman, hard and rough-skinned, of ample bosom and thick hair that he imagined dark, and giving off a slight odor of moisture. Then he remembered the dirty shoe that he had seen the day before as they left the Baths and smiled. Now there passed before his mind objects of ordinary living, images of peasant women in starched percale dresses, with their straggling locks of hair. He smiled condescendingly; and presently fell asleep, with no memories, no anxiety, into an animal lethargy disturbed by one question at the threshold of his consciousness.

"Who can that woman be?"

A rough push awoke him with a start. The wagoner had slipped his hand through the quilts and was rudely jabbing his guest.

"Eh! What's up?"

"Get up, boss, we're reached Recinto."

The question emerged from the interior of the cart into the open air and the answer of the driver drifted in, laden with the fresh gray atmosphere of dawn. He slipped down the mattress toward the opening with caution so as not to awaken his companion. A queer bashfulness checked him. He would have begun to tremble if the woman had spoken a word to him or had suddenly revealed herself. He felt a vague shame at having played the feminine role in this adventure. Nevertheless, the sluggish indifference of this strange woman again aroused in him the same indignant irritation he had felt the day before. He was hurt in his self-respect as a man, almost insulted in his masculine pride. The contemptuous questions of yesterday passed again through his mind. He decided to put a halt to it all.

Dawn was coming. In the near-by trees, nodding sleepily at the side of the road, some sparrows were tearing apart the vapors of the morning with their short wild chirpings. He spoke to the driver with a hoarse voice.

"Here are the ten pesos."

The man was about to stretch out his hand with the respectful gesture that bumpkins always made on receiving money. But his movement was stopped abruptly by the decisive "No!" uttered by the woman's voice inside the cart.

The young man shrugged his shoulders.

"That's better," he muttered.

At a shout from the wagoner, the oxen gave a vigorous tug, and the cart slid along quietly upon the reddish spongy ground.

The young man did not move from the middle of the road, his eyes riveted upon the mountain wagon, poor and dilapidated as a hovel, but in which he had lived a singular moment of his life. Its outline was already fading in the dimness of early daybreak. It was returning into the unknown from which it had emerged the day before and was bearing with it a secret. In his memory was left the burning impress of a mouth eager for his kisses and the shapeless toe of a village woman's shoe.

He waited hoping that perhaps a hand would come forth out of the wagon-cover with a romantic gesture bidding him farewell. But the unlifted quilt which draped the entry to the cart like a curtain, afforded no sign of movement.

The little settlement of Recinto was clustered in the ravine, among the trees. Through the white dawn came the crow of a cock; a surge of wind suddenly brought close the babbling of the river.

The young man slowly walked toward the station.

OSCAR CASTRO Z.

Lucero

Oscar Castro Z. was born in Rancagua, Chile, in 1910, where he has spent most of his life. He has been a teacher, journalist, poet and novelist. Despite his short literary career, he has achieved unusual acclaim. His two short story collections are *Hellas en la Tierre*, from which we take *Lucero*, and *La Sombra de las Cumbres*. [Translated by Harry Kurz.]

OUTLINED ONE AGAINST THE OTHER, the crests of the mountain chain seemed shuffled like a deck of stony cards as far as Ruben Olmos' eyes could travel. Dazzling white peaks, bluish dips, dentillated escarpments, upjutting points arose before his gaze, constantly shifting, more inaccessible as the traveler mounted. Before starting on an abrupt and tiring declivity, he decided to give a rest to his mount panting like bellows. During the pause, he crossed his left leg over the saddle and let his eyes wander down toward the valley. The first thing that attracted his gaze was the mirror-like glitter of the river stretching with reluctance its capricious windings among pastures and filled fields. Then his view shifted over beyond some rectangular enclosures, and sought the village he had left that morning. There it was framed in the distance like the toys in a shop window with its tiny houses and the dim ravines of its streets. A few zinc plate roofs darted back the sun's brilliance, cutting the air with streaks of violent silvery radiance.

With a flutter of his eyelids Ruben Olmos rubbed out the picture of the valley and now examined his mount, whose damp flanks rose and fell in rhythmical movement.

"So you're getting old, Lucero?" he asked in an affectionate tone.

And the animal, as if it understood, turned toward him its face, black with a white star on its forehead.

"Well, it's a sure thing that you have worked plenty, but you have many years of travel ahead of you yet. At least, while there are still some mountains around here."

He turned to gaze at the Andean massiveness, familiar and friendly to him and Lucero. They hadn't crossed and recrossed it for nothing during these eleven years. Ruben Olmos, a bit dazzled by the white blaze of the sun on the snow, thought of his travel comrades and of the lead they had over him. But he didn't pay much attention to this detail, for he was certain he would overtake them before nightfall.

"So long as you go along with me, we won't have to spend the night alone," he declared to his horse, finishing his thought.

Ruben Olmos was an experienced mountain guide. He had learned his difficult art from his father who had taken him along even as a child over these precipices and ravines in spite of his unwillingness and the mistrust that the mountains at first had roused in him. When the old man had died, peacefully in his bed, the ranch owner had appointed the young man as successor. He had crossed at least a hundred times this mountain barrier which, in his young days, had seemed to him impassible, and had led over numerous herds of cattle from Cuyó, always with good luck on his side.

He chose Lucero when the animal was still a frisking colt and had broken him in himself. After that the rider had never been willing to use another mount although his boss had presented him with two other horses apparently more powerful and from better breeds. Lucero had become for him a mascot to which he clung with a sort of superstition induced by a hazardous life.

The guide, accustomed to the epic struggle against the elements, loved danger more than women. With instinctive wisdom he centered his devotion on a beast, perhaps with the feeling that from it he need expect no rebuff or treason. If some day he were asked to choose between losing his brother or Lucero, he would hesitate before making up his mind, because this creature, more than a mere conveyance, inspired in him from the beginning the feeling of a friend. He was in a sense an extension of his own being, as if the push of his muscles flowed into the tendons of Lucero.

Ruben Olmos was born with flesh fashioned out of hard substance. He felt life in a rush of tides throbbing along the passages of his being. On horseback he was always the leader, not one to be led. And this energy needed space to exert itself; no place could seem more favorable or more adapted to his talents than the tumultuous heights of the Andes.

If observed superficially, the guide looked like an ordinary fellow. At the best, he gave the impression of self-confidence. His coppery skin and flattened nose evoked the Indian in his ancestry. His smile had no brightness, it was dimmed by his eyes, at most it gleamed momentarily at the edge of his teeth. A herdsman amidst solitudes, he had learned from them silence and penetration. He had a deeper tie with Lucero than with human beings. It must have been because the horse did not answer, or because he always said "yes" with his loving moist eyes. There was no telling.

"Fine, now we must be moving."

Setting his iron shoes into the cracks, the horse ascended toward heaven. The rider, bent forward, moved with the rhythmic sway of each step. Pebbles rolled down into the depths and the rings on the reins tinkled. And Lucero—toc, toc, toc—was finally there on the crest after toiling upwards for a quarter-hour.

Upon the heights the wind flowed more constant, bearing more cold moisture. It glided over the face of the guide. It sought some opening in his cloak, in order to grasp it with its teeth. However, long practice made this man safe from its attack, and although the blast persisted, it did not succeed in altering his course.

With several crests of mountains crossed, the valley was no longer visible. There were hills ahead, toward which the eye looked. And above stretched a thin sky, pure, more blue than the cold of the wind, hardly speckled by the flashing flight of an eagle, sole possessor of this unattainable space.

The loneliness of the heights was so immense, so clearly desolate, that the traveler sometimes had the swift impression of drowning in the wind, as if he were swirling in the depths of treacherous waters. But this man did not have time to admire the magnificent stretches of the landscape. The atmosphere, like a transparent bubble, the deep orchestral tones of the verdure, the symphony of birds and insects which mounted upwards in delicate surges—none of these things found an echo in his spirit, formed as it was out of the dark substances of struggle and decision.

From a rise which gave a clear view of the near-by heights, Ruben Olmos scanned the path in the hope of seeing those who had gone ahead of him. But he perceived nothing but emptiness during this exploration. The man pursed his lips. The four companions who had left the ranch an hour ahead of him had gained quite a lead. He would have to press his horse.

On he went past the familiar landmarks, the Lion's Cave, the Condor's Perch, the Black Gap. "My comrades must be waiting for me in the Muleteer Shelter," he thought, and sank his spurs into Lucero's ribs.

The path was hardly more than a vague track from whose line other eyes less experienced than his might stray. But Ruben Olmos couldn't go wrong. This slight rut over which he was traveling was, for him, a wide and spacious thoroughfare leading to one goal: the pueblo of Cuyó.

As he reached higher land, vegetation became tougher and more twisted to resist the attacks of the storms. Hawthorn, rosemary, sharp-edged cactus loomed up like dark splashes of a painter's brush against the pale snow. The solitudes began to get whiter and deeper, clothed with a dignified serenity. Ruben Olmos imagined that it was five o'clock in the afternoon. The sun, already slipping into the West, was struggling to sift its warmth through the wind.

The setting suddenly changed as the horse of the guide emerged into an immense stadium of stone. Two enormous mountains framed it, each with its half parenthesis circling a crevice whose depths could not be plumbed. It seemed as if an immense cataclysm had severed the mountain chain at a blow.

The rider stopped Lucero. The Vulture Pass exerted a strange fascination on his mind. When he was fifteen and had crossed it for the first time, he had had a whim to look down into it in spite of his father's warning, and after a moment he had noticed that the ravine began to whirl around like a blue funnel. Something like an invisible claw was pulling him into the abyss and he was letting himself go. Fortunately his father had observed the danger and shouted, "Turn your head around, you fool!" From that time on, in spite of all his calm control, he had not dared to let his gaze wander down that unfathomable depth.

Moreover, the Vulture's Pass had its legends. No herd of cattle could cross it on Good Friday, without some terrible misfortune. It was his father who had given him this information, illustrating with stories of various incidents when cattle or horses had been swallowed up in some mysterious way by this chasm.

In fact, this pass was one of the most impressive in the mountain chain. The path at that point was only eighty centimeters wide, just enough to let an animal get by between the stone wall and the abrupt drop. One false step . . . and that would be the end till Judgment Day.

Before venturing along that shelf suspended who knew how many feet above the depth, Ruben Olmos complied scrupulously with the agreement established among those who crossed the mountains: he took his pistol out of his holster and fired two shots into the air to give warning to any possible traveler that the route was being used and that he was to wait. The explosions sent their waves into the clear air. They rebounded against the rocks and returned multiplied to the ears of the guide. After a little pause, the rider decided to resume his journey. Lucero, carefully setting his iron shoes on the rocky road was apparently unaware of any change in the aspect of the route. "Splendid horse!" mused the rider, summing up in these words all his affection for the animal.

Ruben Olmos will never be able to forget what was about to happen. Upon emerging from an abrupt turn, his heart gave one wild leap in his breast. From the opposite direction, less than twenty paces away, appeared a man mounted on a dark sorrel-colored nag. Amazement, frustration, and anger flashed across the faces of the travelers. Both, with an instinctive pull, reined in their horses. The first to break the anguished silence was the rider on the sorrel. After a growling curse, he shouted, "And how did you ever presume to start on this way without giving warning?"

Ruben Olmos knew that mere words would not help. He kept on advancing till the heads of the two horses almost touched. Then, in a quiet firm voice that seemed to come from way down in his chest, he said, "It was you, my friend, who didn't give the signal shots."

The other draw his revolver and Ruben did likewise, with a promptness unsuspected in him. They looked at each other fixedly for a moment, with a spark of defiance in their eyes. The stranger had steely cold eyes and features that betrayed will-power and decisiveness. In his aspect, his assurance, he revealed that he was a mountaineer accustomed to danger. Both realized that they were worthy adversaries.

Ruben Olmos finally decided to prove that he was in the right. Grasping his weapon with the barrel pointed to the abyss so as not to arouse distrust, he drew out the bullets, presenting a pair of empty cartridges.

"Here are my two shots," he declared.

The stranger imitated him, likewise offering as proof two leadless shells.

"Tough luck, my friend; we fired at the same time," declared the guide.

"That's how it was, comrade. And now what are we going to do?"

"As for going back, it just can't be done."

"Well then, one of us will have to get along on foot."

"Yes, that's so, but which one of us?"

"Luck will have to decide that."

And without any other comment the sorrel rider took a coin out of his pocket, and put it between his two hands without looking.

"You say which," he said.

There was a terrible hesitation in Ruben's mind. Those two clamped hands which he beheld hid the secret of an unalterable verdict. They represented more power than all the laws written by men. Fate would speak through them in its inexorable, impartial voice. And, as Ruben Olmos never defied the decrees of uncertain Fate, he pronounced the word that someone whispered in his brain.

"Heads!"

The other then slowly uncovered the coin and the oblique afternoon sun lit up a laurel wreath circling a sickle and hammer: Ruben had lost. He did not betray by the slightest gesture his inner dismay. His eyes turned softly and slowly toward the head and neck of Lucero. Presently, his hand gestured the caress that burst from his heart. And finally, as if to free himself from the fatality bearing down on him, he let himself drop to the path over the shining croup of his horse. He untied the gun and the provision-bag attached to the saddle. Then he slipped off the blanket roll resting on the animal's haunch. And all this slowly created between the two men a silence more dreadful than the Andean solitude.

During these preparations, the stranger seemed to suffer as much as the loser. Pretending to see nothing, he was busy braiding and unbraiding the thongs of his whip. Ruben Olmos was deeply grateful to him for this feigned indifference. When his painful work was done, he said to the other in a voice which preserved an inexpressibly desperate firmness, "Did you happen to meet four herdsmen with two mules on the way?"

"Yes, they're resting at the Refuge. Are they your companions?"

"Yes, it happens they are."

Lucero, perhaps surprised to be freed from the saddle in such an inappropriate spot, turned his head, and Ruben gazed for a moment upon his eyes, gentle as dark pools. The star on his forehead. His ears erect. His nostrils quivering. To gather his determination, Ruben uttered into the air in a voice laden with secret sorrow, "Keep a close rein on your beast, friend."

The other pulled in the reins, turning the head of his sorrel toward the rocky wall.

Only then Ruben Olmos, his heart dissolved in agony, lightly patted Lucero's neck once more, and with an immense shove sent him rolling into the abyss.

JOSE DE LA CUADRA

Valley Heat

José de la Cuadra was born at Guayaquil, Ecuador, in 1903. Active in education, he was President of the Federation of Ecuadorian Students, and representative of his country at the Hispano-American educational conferences. Among his notable stories are *El Amor Que Dormía, Repisas, Horno* and *La Vuelta de la Locura*. [Translated by Harry Kurz.]

JOE TIBERIADES TURNED OVER ON HIS COT, under the awning roof of flowered Ruán cotton cloth, whose sagging length almost touched his face.

"Mama!"

The old woman answered from her vermin infested coverlet. "What?"

Joe Tiberíades replied in a spiteful tone, "I can't fall asleep."

"Ah!"

"It's the heat and the mosquitoes."

"Have they gotten under the netting?"

"No, it's their buzzing, Mama . . . how they buzz . . . and the heat . . . I haven't a stitch on me, really, Mama . . . *gee,* it's hot!"

"Aha!"

Refugio, his sister, who was stretched out in the same bed with her mother, shouted, "Let's sleep! The night isn't meant for conversation."

There was a moment of silence in the room. All that could be heard was the hum of mosquitoes. A deep panting seemed to rise from the valley. The forest was breathing with a sort of sigh, muffled, distant, like a great beast in fatigue.

"Mama!"

"Ah?"

"What time. can it be?"

"Midnight."

Joe Tiberíades insisted. "Mama!"

"What?"

"It must be dawn, it's quite light."

"No, son, it's the moonlight."

"Ah!"

"Sleep . . ."

"I can't. It's so hot, Mama . . . and the mosquitoes."

The sister again shouted angrily, "Shut up!"

But a moment later Joe Tiberíades called again. "Mama!"

"What?"

"I'm going to get up. I don't know what is the matter but I'm suffocating shut up in this room . . . I'll stretch out on the hammock in the yard . . . There will be a breeze . . ."

"Better not go out."

"Why?"

"There's a moon. You'll see spirits running around."

"Are there really such things as spirits?"

"Of course. Your dead father ran across one long ago, right there by the *caimito* grove. It was a white shape. It looked like a woman. It was calling to him, stretching out its arms."

"And was it a woman?"

"Yes."

"And who was she, Mama?"

"Death."

"Ah! But listen, Mama, I'm not afraid of spirits . . . I'm hot, really, Mama, I'm burning up inside as if I had a fever . . . Gee, it's hot . . . Out there it will be cool . . . I'll close my eyes so that I won't see the spirits . . . and I'll rock myself to sleep in the hammock . . ."

Joe Tiberíades got up. He slipped on his trousers, leaving his chest bare. He went out.

"Silly boy! Make the sign of the Cross at least."

"All right."

He crossed himself while from her bed the old woman blessed him.

Joe Tiberíades went out to the yard. It could be entered from one side of the hovel. It was fenced in with sharply pointed stakes, because there were times when they had to defend themselves. Attacks by animals and men were in the realm of probability, especially by men when they were the enemies of the landowner Jiménez. And the attack was easy if directed against the only exposed side of the building: the yard. The pointed poles, sharpened at the end, tall as a man's thigh, thick as a woman's, presented an obstacle to any assault.

The stove and the hammock were set up in the yard. Also the coop for setting hens, and the water conduit, and finally a rectangle of brambles that served as a perch for the *toucan* bird with his formidable bill.

Joe Tiberíades lay rocking in the hammock and listened to its gentle squeak. "Tac, tac; tac, tac . . ." He wasn't afraid. Quite the contrary. He kept his eyes wide open and looked all around, at the field, at the sky.

It seemed to him as if he were in the bottom of a hollow. The sky was low, misty, milky because of the full moon. The mountains shut him in on all sides, permanently, with the house set in the middle on a little terrace cleared by *machetes* in the very heart of the woods. He thought that he would never be able to get out from there, from his deep hollow.

Still, that wasn't so. He knew that behind those solid masses of trees there would be a path which led after a day's journey to Bejucal, the ranch of the boss Jiménez, way yonder, close by the river. Each time he traveled it, he covered it without a halt. When his father was alive, he as a little boy used to go along with him.

Now he went alone. He used to call on the ranch owner in his office, receive the money that Jiménez paid his family simply because they lived where they were. He would buy in the ranch store the articles of food and clothing that his mother, Na Nicolosa, wanted. The next morning he would start on his way back. He took this precaution so that he wouldn't be caught by darkness on the mountain, and could get back by daylight.

He had never gone to the mountain at night, but he knew that it was a fearful thing to do. The jaguars lay in wait, and the big monkeys. Besides, and this was very real to him, all sorts of witches, goblins and ghosts might jump out at him from the tangled footpaths. On the ground snakes slithered around. And above in the air fluttered birds of ill omen.

Here at home things were different. To be sure, you could hear the howling of monkeys and the hoarse growling of tigers. There were times when these beasts came up to the circle of the clearing and the phosphorescent glare of their eyes could be seen. But there was safety behind the stockade around the yard, and there was the gun always loaded, and in addition there was the siring bull, Zapote, who drowsed down below with his three cows and the calves. When Zapote bellowed, the tigers made off as if they had heard the devil howl,

Joe Tiberíades was amused at all this. "Tigers are womanish," he used to say. In his vocabulary that word meant the same as cowardly. He got the idea from his mother. One day when he went in bathing naked with some other boys, sons of some laborers on the ranch, Cañarte, the witch-doctor, happened to pass. He looked at the boy and then said to him, laughing, "You're womanish, Joe Tiberíades, although you're grown up!" When he went home, Joe asked his mother eagerly what he meant.

"He meant to tell you that you were lazy and soft. Were you afraid of going in the water?"

"No, I know how to swim. I learned . . ."

"Ah!"

"Listen, Mama, why did he say I was grown-up? Of course I'm not a boy any more. How old am I?"

Na Nicolosa counted on her fingers and answered, "Sixteen."

"Ah! . . . And sis, how old is Refugio, Mama?"

The old woman started counting once more. "Fourteen."

"Eh!"

This had happened a year ago. It was on the day when their landlord Jiménez had increased their monthly pay. Ah! their boss Jiménez who was so generous that he gave them money and a home just that they might stay there in that corner of the forest! (It is true that some declared the rancher would become in a few years the owner of an enormous section around the mountain just by having them live where they were as his hired hands. It was also stated that Jiménez had been Na Nicolosa's husband and that she was now rearing the young girl Refugio for him to bed with. But this was mere gossip.)

But just now Joe Tiberíades wasn't thinking about these matters at all, nor was he scared by any phantoms. He was in a bad mood, that's all. Something queer was the matter with him. Heat. Yes, that was it, heat. A fire was raging inside of him, all over. In his chest, in his belly. His head was in a whirl. It seemed to him as if he had a swarm of stinging insects inside his ears. At times he quieted down, and then felt as if he were going to faint. But a bit later, his turmoil started up again. He had a wild urge to bite, bite, twist and turn, tussle—yes, tussle body to body as Zapote did with his cows . . . To play around, like that, to play around! . . .

He called out, "Sister, make me some coffee!"

Refugio answered from the room in an ill humor. "I don't feel like it. I'm sleeping."

The boy begged, "Don't be mean, Sis. Get up! When I go again to Bejucal I'll bring you back a roll of ribbon, pretty, green, to fasten up your hair."

"I don't want it."

Na Nicolosa interrupted. "Just a minute, son. I'll make you some coffee."

"No, not you, Mama. You're sick. Let Refugio do it."

At length Refugio gave in. "Don't think that I'm doing it for your sake or for the ribbon. It's just to keep Mama from getting up."

She slipped on a wrapper over her thin undergarment and came out. Then she pushed some chips into the stove, got a wick, lit it, and began to blow with her breath. After a little the firebox began to glow. She set the stewpan with water to boil and began to quicken the blaze with a fan made of leaves. The ash box of the stove was loose. Refugio dropped her wrapper to crouch down and adjust it.

She was visible in the moonlight, and outlined against the gleam from the stove. She was revealed as if she were naked. Her clean young lines showed up sharply. Her tight round curves seemed modeled, her small breasts, her wide hips, her thin shapely legs. Joe Tiberíades kept watching her.

"Aren't you warm, Sis?"

"No, I'm cold."

"So'm I . . . I feel cold all of a sudden . . . I don't know . . ." Then he added, "Let the water boil by itself, Sis, and come over here to the hammock, and we won't feel the cold."

"Aha!"

They lay stretched out side by side, with their heads together, their bodies touching.

"Sis!"

"Nothing."

Joe Tiberíades caressed his sister's face. Then he kissed her.

Refugio asked, "Why do you kiss me?"

He didn't answer but she returned his kisses. Finally she said, "Let me alone now."

She could hardly speak. Joe Tiberíades was squeezing her so tightly in his arms that it hurt. She found it difficult to catch her breath. She was almost suffocating.

"What are you doing?" she finally murmured.

"I don't know . . . it's nothing . . . we're just playing . . ."

"Leave me alone . . ."

But Joe Tiberíades didn't speak any more. His eyes were frenzied and his gaze distracted.

Refugio uttered a sharp cry. "Oh, my God! Mama! Mama! Oh, my God!"

Na Nicolosa hurried out fast.

From the doorway she caught sight of her two children . . . "Curses on you!" she cried and ran toward them. She stumbled and fell forward against the stakes of the yard. A sharp pole, standing out from the rest, sank deep into her abdomen. The old woman rolled to the ground. With both hands she tried in vain to cover the gaping wound from which her life was ebbing.

Lying face up, quivering, dying, she managed to stammer, "God

has punished me . . . He has punished me in the way I have sinned
. . . I'm to blame. . . . I bore these unnatural children . . . Forgive
me! . . ."

Her children didn't see or hear . . . They lay there prostrate . . .
swooning . . . as if asleep.

Far down in the mountain a cluster of coconuts broke loose from
a palm and fell with a thud, like the sound made by a coffin when
it drops to the bottom of the grave.

The forest kept on heaving languidly. The valley was breathing in
a low murmur, prolonged, like that of a weary animal. . . .

AUGUSTO

CESPEDES

The Well

Augusto Cespedes, born in Cochabamba,
Bolivia in 1904, studied law, became a
journalist, founded two newspapers and
served as a Lieutenant in the Chaco War,
and as a Congressman. He has written
two novels, *Sangre de Mestizos* (scenes
from the Chaco War, one of which is used
here) and *Metal del Diablo,* chosen to represent Bolivian literature in the contest
for the best Latin American novel. [Trans-
lated by Harry Kurz.]

I AM A BOLIVIAN LIEUTENANT, Miguel Majaya by name, and
I happen to be just now in the Tairairí Hospital, where I have been
confined for fifty days with beriberi. This illness was not serious
enough to bring about my evacuation to La Paz, my native city and
the ideal place for me. I have been in active military service for two
and a half years, but neither the bullet wound that I got last year in
my side nor this first-class vitamin deficiency disease from which I
am suffering could get me my discharge from the army.

So, in the meantime, I'm bored, wandering among the numerous
ghosts in shorts who are the patients in this hospital. Since I have
nothing to read during the hot hours of this inferno, I read and reread
to myself my Diary. Putting down page after page of distant experience, I have managed to relate in the Diary the story of a well which
right now is in the possession of the Paraguayans.

But for me, this well is still ours, it is Bolivian, perhaps because of
the awful suffering it brought us. Near it and in its depths, there
was enacted a terrible drama in two parts; the first during the digging,
and the second at its bottom. My Diary tells the story.

15 Jan. (1933)

A summer without water. In this region of the Chaco, north of
Platanillas, it scarcely rains and the little rain we had had evaporated.
To the north and south, left or right, wherever one looks or wanders

into the almost unreal bareness of the woods consisting of leaden uprights that are really tree trunks, stretching up like unburied skeletons condemned to remain erect on arid sand, nowhere is there a drop of water. This does not prevent men from living here at war. We exist, feeble, miserable, prematurely aged, the trees with more branches than leaves, and the men with more thirst than hate.

I command some twenty men. We are a section of a regiment of sappers stationed here a week ago in the vicinity of Fort Loa, and assigned to the task of hacking out a road. The mountain is thorny, covered with thick pale growth. There is no water.

In front of us our regiment has seized the mountain and defends the region.

21 Jan.

Toward evening, amidst clouds of dust, the water-truck arrives, its mudguards battered, without windshield and one of its lights covered; this old truck trundling its black barrels looks as if it had come out of an earthquake. It is driven by a chauffeur glistening with sweat, his moist chest revealed by his shirt opened to his midriff.

"The pond is drying up," he announced today, "and the water ration for the regiment will have to be cut." He also informed me that in Platanillas they are planning to send our Division further ahead. This news aroused comments among the soldiers. One of them, Chacón, who comes from Potosí, a short, hard fellow, black as a hammer, uttered the unanimous question, "Will there be water?"

"Less than here," was the answer.

"Less than here? Are we going to live on air like desert plants?"

Unscrewing the cap of one of the barrels, the chauffeur fills two gasoline cans with water, one for cooking and the other for drinking, and then drives off. Always a few drops of water drip to the ground, wetting it, and swarms of white butterflies flutter about seeking this moisture. Sometimes I splash a handful of water over the back of my neck, and some bees, I don't know how they exist here, come to get tangled in my hair.

21 Jan.

Last night it rained. During the day the heat shut us in like a garment of warm rubber. The reflection of the sun on the sand tormented us with its white blaze. But at six it rained. We stripped and got soaked, feeling the warm mud under our soles and between our toes.

25 Jan.

Again the heat. Once more that invisible glare, dry, beating on our bodies. I think that somewhere a window should be opened to let the air in. The sky is an enormous slab of stone under which the sun has become stranded.

We keep on living, axe and shovel in our hands. Our guns are stacked half-buried in the dust under our tents, and we are just road workers cutting into the mountain in a straight line, opening a way, we don't know why, straight through the tangled underbrush which also is shriveled with heat. The sun burns up everything. A meadow, yesterday morning yellow, has become gray today and parched and flattened merely because the sun has walked over it.

From eleven in the morning to three in the afternoon, work is impossible in this mountain forge. During these hours, after seeking vainly for a solid mass of shadow, I stretch out under any tree with its imaginary shelter of dry branches.

The soil, without the firmness given by moisture, floats up like a white death, wrapping the tree trunks in dusty embrace. The sun's rays send magnetic vibrations over the surface of the adjoining pasture, stretched prone and pallid like a corpse.

Prostrate, swollen, we stay there overcome by the listlessness of the daily fever, sunk in a warm stupor that is penetrated only by the chirping of locusts endless as time. The heat seems to snore through the clamor of the locusts that people the whole forest amidst a noise that deafens the atmosphere for leagues around.

We, placed in the middle of this maddening concert, live on empty of words, without thought, hour after hour, watching in the colorless sky the slow soaring of the vultures that, to my eyes, seem outlined like stylized birds printed on an infinite stretch of wallpaper. In the distance, occasional firing can be heard from time to time.
1 Feb.

The heat has taken possession of our bodies, making them part of the inorganic stillness of mother earth, reducing them to dust, soft, feverish, present to our awareness only by the torment they convey to us from the sweating torch of furnace-like kilns upon our skin. Only at night do we manage to reclaim ourselves. Night finally comes with its longing for sleep, nevertheless harassed by the annoyance of oft-repeated cries of animals: whistles, chirps, cackles, a whole range of voices unfamiliar to us who come from the uplands and mountains.

Night, then day. We are silent during the day, but the words of my soldiers start up during the nights. Some of them are real veterans, like Nicolás Pedraza, a Vallegrandino who has been in the Chaco since 1930. He is ridden with malaria, yellow and dried up like a hollow reed.

"They say those Paraguys have advanced toward our clearing," declared Chacón.

"There's certainly no water around here," Pedraza stated with authority.

"But the Paraguys always find it. They know the mountain better than anyone," objected Joe Trusta, a man from La Paz, a rough fellow with sharp cheekbones and slanting eyes.

Then a soldier from Cocpabamba whom they have nicknamed Smoky, answered, "Yah, that's what they say, I know . . . But how about that Paraguy trooper we found dead of thirst at Sicte not far away from a water pond, Lieutenant?"

"Yes, that's so," I agreed. "And there was another in front of Campas whom we found poisoned by the prickly pears he had eaten."

"People don't die of hunger. Thirst can certainly kill them. I have seen some of our men in the Sicte grassland sucking mud after the battle on the tenth of November."

So deeds and words pile up without effect. They pass like the breeze over a meadow that is not even rippled by it.

6 Feb.

It has rained. The trees look revived. We got water in the puddles, but we are without bread and sugar, because the supply truck got stuck in the mud.

10 Feb.

They are advancing us some twenty kilometers. The road we have cleared won't be used and we are ordered to start another.

18 Feb.

The shirtless chauffeur brought us the bad news. "Our water pond is dried up. We have to fetch our water now from La China."

26 Feb.

Yesterday there wasn't any water. The supply system is breaking down because of the distance the trucks have to cover. Yesterday, after hacking away all day in the mountain, we were expecting along our road the arrival of the truck, and the last rays of the sun now rose-colored lit up the dusty faces of my detachment without bringing through the dust of the clearing the familiar rumble.

This morning the water truck finally came and around the can there was a tumult of hands, pitchers and canteens clashing eagerly in rivalry. There was a fight and I had to intervene.

1 March.

A short, blond, bewhiskered lieutenant came to our outpost. He spoke to me asking how many men I could spare.

"On the front we have no water," he said. "Three days ago three of my men had sunstroke. We were supposed to look for wells."

"They say that wells have been dug in La China."

"And did they strike water?"

"Yes, they found some."

"It is a matter of luck."

"Around here also, near Loa, they tried to dig some wells."

It was then that Pedraza, who was listening, declared that about five kilometers from here there was indeed an excavation dug years and years ago, a few meters deep, abandoned probably because those who were seeking water had given up the undertaking. Pedraza thought we might dig a bit deeper.

2 March.

We have explored the region mentioned by Pedraza. There is indeed a hollow covered by underbrush near a tall tree. The blond lieutenant stated that he would inform Headquarters and this afternoon we have been given the order to continue the excavation until we found water. I have selected eight sappers for this job, Pedraza, Trusta, Chacón, Smoky, and four Indians besides.

3 March.

The pit is about five meters in diameter and the same in depth. The ground is hard, like cement. We have cleared a path to the spot and camped in the vicinity. We are going to dig all day because the heat has diminished somewhat.

The soldiers, naked to the waist, glisten like fish. Rivulets of sweat like snakes writhing earthy heads run down their torsos. They send the pickaxe flying to sink it into the loosened sand and then slip down into the hole by means of a leathern strap. Its cheering color gives an impression of fresh novelty around the edges of the hollow.

10 March.

Twelve meters. It looks as if we're going to strike water. The earth we bring up is more and more moist. We have inserted wooden steps on one side of the well and I have ordered the installation of a ladder and windlass to get the earth out with the aid of a pulley. The soldiers take turns regularly and Pedraza is certain we are going to strike water within a week.

22 March.

I've gone down into the well. As you get into it, you have the sensation of a body penetrating a solid. Lost to the light of the sun, you feel contact with a peculiar air which is the smell of the earth. As I sink into the dark depth and touch the smooth earth with my bare feet, I am surrounded by a great coolness. I am approximately at a depth of eighteen meters. I raise my eyes and the perspective of a black tube stretches above me till it stops at the mouth flooded by the light at the surface. On the floor at the bottom there is mud and the wall crumbles easily in the hand. I emerged muddy and was attacked by mosquitoes till I had swollen feet.

30 March.

Strange things are going on. Ten days ago we were getting pasty mud out of the well, but now again only dry soil. I went down once more into the well. The odor of earth compresses one's lungs down there. As I touch the wall I can feel the moisture but when I reach bottom, I realize that we have cut through a layer of dampness. I give the order to cease digging to see if in a few days water can collect by filtration.

12 April.

After a week the bottom of the well continued to stay dry. Thereafter the digging went on and today I went down to a depth of twenty-four meters. Down there, all is dark. Earth, earth, the solid earth that clenches its fists at your throat with a silent shaking firmness. The soil brought up has, somehow, left in the hollow beneath the feel of its weight and when I strike the wall with my pickaxe, I get an answering knock, echoless, that reverberates within my heart.

28 April.

I guess we have failed in our search for water. Yesterday we reached thirty meters without obtaining anything but dust. We ought to stop this fruitless work and with this in view I have forwarded a petition to battalion headquarters, where I am commanded to appear tomorrow.
29 April.

"Captain," I said to my superior, "we have reached thirty meters and it appears impossible for us to find water."

"But we need water at all costs," he answered.

"Let them try in some other spot then, Captain."

"No, no, keep right on digging where you've begun. Two borings of thirty meters each will not give us water. One of forty might."

"Very well, Captain."

"Besides, perhaps you are about to strike it."

"Very well, Captain."

"Good, just a bit more effort. Our men are dying of thirst."

Well, we are not exactly dying, just being tortured daily. It is a ceaseless anguish, maintained by one jug of water per man. My soldiers suffer more thirst inside the excavation than outside, with all the dust and work, but the digging must go on.

I transmitted this order to them and they expressed an impatient protest which I tried to mitigate by offering them, in the name of the commanding officer, a bigger ration of *coca* plant and water.
9 May.

The work is going on. This hole is acquiring among us a fearful personality, real and destructive, turning into a boss, an unknown master of the sapper. They follow that ghostly route, that vertical cavern, yielding to a gloomy pull, an implacable command which condemns them to live withdrawn from light, reversing the meaning of their existence as human beings. Each time I look at them, they give me the feeling that they are no longer made up of living cells, but of molecules of dust, with earth in their ears, on their eyelids, their eyebrows, in their nostrils, their hair white with it, earth in their eyes, their souls so stuffed with Chaco earth.
24 May.

We have gone a few meters deeper. The work is slow. One soldier digs deep down, another outside runs the pulley, and the soil comes up in a bucket improvised out of a gasoline can. The soldiers are complaining of lack of air. When they dig, the atmosphere crushes in their bodies. Under their feet and all around them and all the way above, beneath, stretches like night. Pitiless, somber, shadowy, saturated with a heavy silence, motionless, and choking, a mass with the weight of lead piles up above the digger, burying him in darkness like a worm hidden away during some geologic epoch, many centuries distant from the earth's crust.

He drinks the warm thickish liquid of his canteen and it gives out quickly because the ration, in spite of being doubled for the diggers, evaporates in their gullets beset with unspeakable thirst. He seeks with bare feet in the wearisome dust the familiar freshness of the furrows he used to trace in the irrigated lands of his distant farm valleys, the memory of which persists in his touch.

And now he strikes, strikes with his pickaxe, while the earth falls away, covering his feet, without ever revealing the water for which we are all panting.

5 June.

We are approaching forty meters. To encourage my soldiers, I went down into the hole to do some digging myself. I felt myself slipping as if in a dream into an endless drop. Here below I seem separated forever from the rest of mankind, the war far off, carried by my solitude into a fate marked for destruction by strangulation at the incorporeal hands of nothingness. There is no glimmer of light, and the air's heaviness presses down on all the surfaces of my body. The column of darkness falls vertically upon me and buries me far from the hearing of men.

I have tried to dig, striking furiously with my pick, hoping by vigorous effort to hasten the passing of time. But in these precincts, time is fixed and invariable. When the passing of the hours is no longer revealed by changes in the light, time becomes stagnant in this sub-soil with its black uniformity of a dark room. Here is where light dies, here are the roots of that enormous tree that shoots up in the night and shuts out the heavens, casting earth into mourning.

16 June.

Queer things are going on. The dark room enclosed within the well bottom seems to be developing pictures of water through the chemical reagent of our dreams. Our obsession with water keeps on creating a peculiar and fantastic world that took its stand at forty-one meters, revealing itself in a curious event that occurred at that depth.

Smoky told me about it. Yesterday he had fallen asleep at the bottom of the shaft when he saw the gleam of a silvery serpent. He grabbed it and it vanished in his hands, but others appeared on the floor of the well forming a spring of white sonorous bubbles that spread, imparting life to the shaft of dark till it seemed a magic serpent, no longer rigid, but flexible like a column of water, on the surface of which Smoky was floated up until he emerged into the dazzling light of day. To his amazement, he found the whole camp transformed by the water. Each tree had become a fountain. The meadow was gone; instead it was a green lake, where our soldiers were bathing under the shade of the willows. He was not surprised to find our enemy firing machine guns from the opposite shore, and to see our soldiers diving in to catch the bullets amidst shouts and bursts of laughter. All he wanted to do was to drink. He drank at the fountain in the lake, slipping into numerous liquid depths that washed against his body, while the fountains spattered his head. He drank and drank, but his thirst was not slaked by this water, unreal and abundant as a mirage.

Last night Smoky had a fever. I have arranged to have him transferred to the first-aid station of our regiment.

24 June.

The C.O. of the Division ordered his car stopped on his way through here. He spoke to me, finding it hard to believe that we have dug to nearly forty-five meters, using a bucket and pulley to bring up the earth. I told him, "We have to shout, Colonel, to get the soldier out when he has finished his round."

Later, together with a fresh supply of *coca* plant and cigarettes, the Colonel sent us a bugle. And so we are stuck to this well. We just keep it up. Or rather, we are receding to the innermost part of the planet, toward a geologic age where shadows dwell. It is a pursuit of water through an impenetrable mass. More alone each time, more gloomy, overshadowed as their thoughts and their fate, my men dig and dig, spade up atmosphere, earth, life with the slow monotonous excavating of gnomes.

4 July.

Is there such a thing really as water? Since Smoky's dream, all of us see it. Pedraza has told us that he was drowning in a sudden flood of water that swelled up over his head. Trusta reports that his pick struck blocks of ice, and Chacón yesterday emerged chattering about a grotto all lit up with the fleeting reflections of waves from an underground lake.

Does this gushing of water sources come from so much suffering, so much seeking, so much eagerness, so much thirst in our spirits?

16 July.

My men are falling sick. They refuse to go down in the hole. I have to insist. They have requested me to get them transferred to the front. I went down once more and came out stunned and filled with fear. We're practically at fifty meters. The atmosphere gets blacker and blacker, and encloses the body within a disquieting torment. The embrace of this subsoil chokes the men who can't stay more than an hour in the abyss. It has become a nightmare. This Chaco earth has something extraordinary, accursed.

25 July.

The bugle presented by the C.O. was blown at the mouth of the shaft to summon the digger at the end of each hour. The blast from the bugle must have seemed, down in the depths, like a bolt of lightning. But that afternoon, in spite of the bugle, no one came up.

"Who's down there?" I asked.

It was Pedraza. They called down and the bugle kept on blowing. "Tarariii! Pedrazaaa!"

"He must have fallen asleep."

"Or dead," I added, and gave the order for someone to go down and investigate.

A soldier went down and after a long wait, in the midst of the circle we made around the well-mouth, tied to the strap, raised by the windlass and pushed by the soldier, the body of Pedraza emerged, half-suffocated.

29 July.

Today Chacón fainted and during the sullen hoisting up of his body, he resembled a hanged man.

4 Sept.

Will this business never end? The digging continues, but no longer in the hope of finding water, just to fulfill a fatal destiny, some blind, inscrutable purpose.

Up here this well has taken on the aspect of something inevitable, endless and overwhelming like war. The heaped-up earth has hardened into mounds over which pass lizards and redbirds. When the sapper appears at the mouth of the well, dripping sweat and dirt, his eyelids and hair white, he seems to come from some remote Plutonian region, he resembles a prehistoric monster emerging after a flood. Sometimes, just to say something, I ask him, "Anything?"

"Nothing, still nothing, Lieutenant."

Nothing, just nothing, like our war. This nothing will never have an end.

1 Oct.

The order has come to stop digging. Despite seven months of excavating, we have not struck water.

During that time, this outpost has changed a lot. Some cabins have been put up and a battalion command station established. We are now going to clear a road toward the east, but our camp will remain situated at this same place.

The well also remains, abandoned, with its silent mouth and its hopeless depth. This sinister hole is in our midst, a sort of intruder, a stupid but dreaded enemy, beyond the pale of our hatred like a scar. It is useless.

7 Dec. (Platanillos Hospital)

Yes, that cursed well proved useful after all! My recollections are still fresh because the attack occurred on the 4th, and on the 5th they brought me here shivering with malaria.

Surely some prisoner captured at the front where the existence of our well had become a legend, must have told the Paraguys that behind the Bolivian position there was a well. Beset with thirst, the Guarani Indians decided to visit us by assault.

At six A.M. the mountain started crumbling, bitten by machine guns. We realized that our front line trenches must have been taken when we noted two hundred meters before us the shots of the Paraguys. Two Stokes bombs landed behind our tents.

I armed my sappers with their dirty guns and deployed them in sharpshooting formation. At that moment one of our officers arrived on double quick with a detachment of soldiers with one machine gun. He arranged them on a line extending to the left of the well while our line held the right. Some got protection behind the earth-mounds. Making sounds like machetes cutting, the bullets lopped off branches. Two prolonged bursts of machine gun fire cut swaths in a big tree. The gunfire of the Paraguys came closer and their wild shouts could be heard mingled with the explosions as they centered the fury of their attack on the well. But we didn't give way a single meter, defending it as if it really had water in it.

The cannon shot gouged out the earth, machine gun bullets tore into skulls and chests, but we did not abandon that well during the five hours that the combat lasted.

At noon there was an echoing lull. The enemy had retreated. We then picked up the dead. The Paraguys had left five behind and among our eight were Smoky, Pedraza, Trusta and Chacón, their breasts bare, their open mouths revealing teeth still covered with dirt.

The heat, like a transparent ghost, lay prone over the mountain, making the earth crack. To avoid the labor of digging graves, I thought of the well.

The thirteen corpses were dragged over to the edge, then were slowly pushed into the void, where they seemed in obedience to gravity to flatten slowly before disappearing, swallowed up by the dark.

"That's all there are."

Then we threw in earth, a lot of earth. But even so, this shaft is still the deepest in the entire Chaco.

JESUS DEL CORRAL

Cross Over, Sawyer!

Jesus del Corral (1871–1931) was born in Antioquia, Colombia. He led an active political life, and was at one time Minister of Agriculture. He collaborated with a Rockefeller mission to fight tropical diseases, and was responsible for the wide development of plantations in the interior of Colombia. His stories were published in reviews like La Brisa and El Ciriri, and other periodicals of Bogotá. [Translated by Harry Kurz.]

I WAS OPENING UP A plantation on the banks of the river Cauca, between Antioquia and Sopetrán. As superintendent I took along Simón Perez, a prince of a fellow, now thirty years old, twenty of which he had lived in a constant and relentless fight with nature, without ever suffering any real defeat.

For him obstacles just didn't exist and whenever I proposed that he do something tough he had never tried before, his regular answer was the cheerful statement, "Sure, I'll tend to it."

One Saturday evening after we'd paid off the ranch hands, Simón and I lingered around chatting on the veranda and discussing plans for next week's undertakings. I remarked that we should need twenty boards to set up gutters in the drainage ditch but that we didn't have any sawyers on the job. Whereupon he replied, "Oh, I can saw those up for you one of these days."

"What?" was my answer. "Are you an expert at sawing lumber?"

"First class. I'm what you might call a sawyer with a diploma, and perhaps the highest paid lumberman who ever pulled a saw. Where did I learn? I'll tell you the story, it's quite funny."

And he told me the following tale which I consider truly amusing.

In the civil war of '85, I was drafted and stationed on the coast. Soon I decided to desert along with an Indian. One night when we were on duty as sentinels, we beat it, following a brook, and without bothering to leave our regards for the General.

By the following day we were deep in the mountains ten leagues away from our illustrious ex-commander. For four days we kept on hoofing it in the forests, without food and our feet pretty well torn by the thorns, since we were really making our way through wild territory, breaking a trail like a pair of strayed cows.

I had heard about a mining outfit operated by Count de Nadal on the Nus River, and I resolved to head for that direction, groping our way and following along one side of a ravine which opened out on that river, according to reports I'd heard. And indeed, on the morning of our seventh day, the Indian and I finally emerged from our gully into the clear. We were overjoyed when we spied a workman, because we were almost dead of hunger and it was a sure thing that he would give us something to eat.

"Hey, friend," I shouted to him, "what's the name of this place? Is the Nus mine far from here?"

"This is it. I'm in charge of the rope bridge but my orders are not to send the basket over for any passengers because the mine doesn't need workers. The only labor we're accepting now is lumbermen and sawyers."

I didn't hesitate a moment with my reply. "That's what I'd heard and that's why I've come. I'm a lumberjack. Send the basket over this way."

"How about the other man?" he asked, pointing to my companion.

The big chump didn't hesitate either with his quick reply. "I don't know anything about that job. I'm just a worker."

He didn't give me a chance to prompt him, to tell him that the essential thing for us was to get some food at all costs, even if on the following day they kicked us out like stray dogs, or even to point out the danger of dying if he had to keep on tramping along and depending on chance, as settlements were widely scattered in these regions. There was also the risk, even if he did manage to strike some town before the end of a month, of being beaten up as a deserter. It was no use. He didn't give me the time to wink an eye at him, for he repeated his statement even though he wasn't asked a second time.

There wasn't a thing I could do. The man in charge of the rope bridge sent the basket to our side of the river after shouting, "Cross over, sawyer!"

I took leave of the poor Indian and was pulled over.

Ten minutes later I was in the presence of the Count with whom I had this conversation:

"What do you ask for your work?"

"What's the scale of pay around here?"

"I had two first class lumberjacks, but two weeks ago one of them died. I paid them eight reals a day."

"Well, Count, I can't work for less than twelve reals. That's what I've been getting at all the companies where I've been. Besides, the climate here is bad; here even the quinine gets the fever."

"That's fair enough, if you're a master sawyer. Besides we need you badly and a monkey will eat prickly pears if he has nothing else. So we'll take you on and we'll pay you your price. You had better report to the peon quarters and get something to eat. Monday, you start on the job."

God be praised! They were really going to give me something to eat! It was Saturday, and next day also I was going to get free grub, I, who could hardly speak without holding on to the wall. I was practically walking backwards through weakness from starvation.

I went into the kitchen and even gobbled up the peels of the bananas. The kitchen dog watched me in amazement, presumably saying to himself, "To the devil with this master craftsman; if he stays a week in this place, the cat and I will be dead of hunger!"

At seven o'clock that night I walked over to the Count's house, where he lived with his wife and two children.

A peon gave me some tobacco and lent me a guitar. I got busy puffing and singing a popular mountain ballad. The poor lady of the Count, who had been living there more bored than a monkey, was considerably cheered by my song, and she begged me to stay on the veranda that evening and entertain her and the children.

"Here's your chance, Simón," I softly whispered to myself. "We might as well win these nice people over to my side in case this business of sawing wood turns out badly."

So I sang to them all the ballads I knew. The fact was, I'll admit, I didn't know a thing about a lumberman's job but when it came to popular songs, I was an old hand at it.

The upshot of it was that the lady of the manor was delighted and invited me to come over in the morning to entertain the children, for she was at her wit's end to keep them interested on Sundays. And she gave me lots of crackers with ham and guava jelly!

The boys spent the next day with the renowned master sawyer. We went bathing in the river, ate prunes and drank red wines of the best European brands.

Monday came and the boys wouldn't let the sawman report for his work, because he had promised to take them to a guava tree grove to catch orioles with snares. And the Count laughingly permitted his new lumberjack to earn his twelve reals in that most agreeable occupation.

Finally on Tuesday, I really began to tackle my job. I was introduced to the other sawyer so that we might plan our work together. I made up my mind to be high-handed with him from the start.

In the hearing of the Count who was standing near-by I said to him, "Friend, I like to do things in their proper order. First let's settle on what's needed most urgently—boards, planks or posts?"

"Well, we need five thousand laurel-wood boards for the irrigation ditches, three thousand planks for building jobs and about ten thousand posts."

I nearly fell over: here was work enough to last two years . . . and paid at twelve reals a day . . . and with good board and lodging . . . and no danger of being arrested as a deserter because the mine was considered "private territory" outside of military jurisdiction.

"Very well then, let's proceed according to some plan. The first thing we have to do is to concentrate on marking the laurel trees on the mountain that are fine and straight and thick enough to furnish us with plenty of boards. In that way we won't waste any time. After that we'll fell them and last of all, we'll start sawing them up. Everything according to plan, yes siree, if we don't do things in order, they won't come out right."

"That's the way I like it too," said the Count. "I can see you are a practical man. You go ahead and arrange the work as you think best."

That's how I became the master planner. The other fellow, a poor simple-minded chap, realized he would have to play second fiddle to this strutting, improvised lumberjack. And soon afterward we sallied out in the mountain to mark our trees. Just as we were about to enter into the timber tract, I said to my companion, "Let's not waste any time by walking along together. You work your way toward the top while I select trees down below in the ravine. Then in the afternoon we can meet here. But be very careful not to mark any crooked trees."

And so I dropped down into the ravine in search of the river. There, on its bank, I spent the whole day, smoking and washing the clothing that I had brought from the General's barracks.

In the afternoon, in the appointed place, I found my fellow lumberman and asked him, "Let's see now. How many trees did you mark?"

"Just two hundred and twenty, but they're good ones."

"You practically wasted your day; I marked three hundred and fifty, all first class."

I had to keep the upper hand on him.

That night the Count's lady sent for me and requested that I bring the guitar, as they had a meal all set out. The boys were most eager to have me tell them the tale of Sebastian de las Gracias, and then the one about Uncle Rabbit and Friend Armadillo, also the one about John the Fearless which is so exciting. This program was carried out exactly. Funny stories and songs, appropriate jokes, dinner on salmon because it was the eve of a fast day, cigars with a golden band on them, and a nip of brandy for the poor Count's jack who had worked so hard all that day and needed something comforting to keep up his energy. Ah, and I also put in some winks at a good looking servant girl who brought his chocolate to the master sawyer and who was enraptured when she heard him singing, "Like a lovesick turtledove whose plaintive coo is heard in the mountain . . ."

Boy, did I saw wood that evening! I even sawed the Count into little pieces, I was that good. And all this clowning was intermingled for me with the fear that the lumber business wouldn't turn out too well. I told the Count that I had noticed certain extravagances in the kitchen of the peons' quarters and quite a lot of confusion in the storeroom service. I mentioned to him a famous remedy for lameness (thought up by me, to be sure) and I promised to gather for him in the mountain a certain medicinal herb that worked wonders in curing disorders of the stomach. (I can still remember the gorgeous-like name I gave it: Life-Restorer!)

Yes, all of them, the man and his whole family, were enchanted with the master craftsman Simón. I spent the week in the mountains marking trees with my fellow workman, or to be more accurate, not with but far away from him since I always sent him off in a different direction from the one I chose for myself. But I must confess to you that since I didn't know what a laurel tree looked like, I had to first walk around and examine the trees that the real lumberjack had marked.

When we had selected about a thousand, we started to fell them with the aid of five laborers. On this job in which I played the role of supervisor, we spent more than two weeks.

And every evening I went to the Count's house and ate divinely. On Sundays I lunched and dined there because the boys had to be entertained—and the servant girl also.

I became the mainspring of the mine. My advice was the deciding factor and nothing was done without consulting me.

Everything was sailing along fine when the fearful day finally dawned on which the sawbuck was to be put in place. The platform for it was all set up. To be sure when we constructed it there were difficulties because my fellow craftsman asked me, "At what height do we set it up?"

"What's the usual practice around here?"

"Three meters."

"Give it three twenty, which is the generally accepted height among good sawyers." (If it works at three meters, what difference would twenty centimeters more make?)

Everything was now ready: the log athwart the platform and the markings on it made by my companion (for all I did was to give orders)—all was in place as the nuptial song relates:

"The lamp lit and the bridal veil at the altar."

The solemn moment came and one morning we sallied forth on our way to the trestle, our long sawing blades on our shoulders. This was the first time I had ever looked right into the face of one of those wood-devourers.

At the foot of the platform, the sawyer asked me, "Are you operating below or above?"

To settle such a serious matter I bent down, pretending to scratch an itch in my leg and quickly thought, "If I take the upper part, it is probable this fellow will send me flying into the air with that saw blade of his." So that when I straightened up, I answered, "I'll stay below; you go on up."

He climbed upon the platform, set the blade on the traced marking and . . . we began to saw wood.

Well, sir, the queerest thing was happening. A regular jet of sawdust kept spurting all over me, and I twisted from side to side without being able to get out of the way. It was getting into my nostrils, my ears, my eyes, ran down inside my shirt . . . Holy Mother! And I who had had a notion that pulling a gang-saw was a simple matter.

"Friend," my companion shouted to me, "the saw is not cutting true on the line."

"Why, devil take it, man! That's why you're up there. Steady now and watch it as you should!"

The poor fellow couldn't keep us from sawing awry. How could he prevent a deflection when I was flopping all over the place like a fish caught on a hook!

I was suffocating in the midst of all those clouds of sawdust, and I shouted to my companion, "You come down, and I'll get up there to control the direction of the saw."

We swapped places. I took my post at the edge of the scaffold, seized the saw and cried out, "Up she goes: one . . . two . . ."

The man pulled the blade down to get set for the upstroke just when I was about to say "three," and I was pulled off my feet and landed right on top of my companion. We were both bowled over, he with his nose banged up and I with some teeth knocked out and one bruised eye looking like an egg-plant.

The surprise of the lumberjack was far greater than the shock of the blow I gave him. He looked as stunned as if a meteorite had fallen at his feet.

"Why, master!" he exclaimed, "why, master!"

"Master craftsman my eye! Do you want to know the truth? This is the first time in my life that I have held the horn of one of those gang-saws in my hand. And you pulled down with such force! See what you've done to me"—(and I showed him my injured eye).

"And see what a fix I'm in"—(and he showed me his banged-up nose).

Then followed the inevitable explanations in relating which I pulled a real Victor Hugo stunt. I told him my story and I almost made him weep when I described the pangs I suffered in the mountain when I deserted. I finally ended up with this speech.

"Don't you say a word of what's happened because I'll have you fired from the mine. So keep a watch on your tongue and show me how to handle a saw. In return I promise to give you every day for three months two reals out of the twelve I earn. Light up this little cigar (I offered him one) and explain to me how to manage this mastodon of a saw."

As money talks, and he knew of my pull at our employers' house, he accepted my proposition and the sawing lessons started. You were supposed to take such a position when you were above, and like this when you were below; and to avoid the annoyance of the sawdust, you covered your nose with a handkerchief . . . a few insignificant hints which I learned in half an hour.

And I kept on for a whole year working in that mine as head sawyer, at twelve reals daily, when the peons got barely four. The house I now own in Sopetrán I bought with money I earned up there. And the fifteen oxen I have here all branded with a saw-mark, they too came out of my money earned as a sawyer. . . . And that young son of mine who is already helping me with the mule-driving is also the son of that servant girl of the Count and god-son of the Countess. . . .

When Simón ended his tale, he blew out a mouthful of smoke, looked up at the ceiling, and then added, "And that poor Indian died of hunger . . . just because he didn't know enough to become a sawyer!"

JORGE

FERRETIS

The Failure

Jorge Ferretis was born in San Luis Potosi, Mexico, in 1902. He devoted his life to literature and is generally ranked as one of the most significant younger authors. His work deals with the Mexican Revolution. His collections include *Tierra Caliente, Quando Engorda el Quijote, El Sur que Quema* (from which our story is taken), *San Automóvil* and *Hombres en Tempestad*. [Translated by Harry Kurz.]

I

The Locomotive

"DON PONCIANO, YOUR 'DARKY' is out here waiting for you."

"Well, that's where I'm going. I'll be right with her."

"Hello, Don Ponciano, how's your 'darky'?"

"As pretty as ever, Don Camilo! Good-by!"

He looked like an ordinary sort. A simple fellow who, besides bearing the name of Ponciano, was fat and pot-bellied. He limped a little and his soot-colored face showed slight pock-marks. As for the rest, he was like anyone else. Don Ponciano had no talent, nor was he ambitious. He was unlucky with women. He had had a sweetheart but when he was about to propose she left him because another man had convinced her she was pretty. Even a very talkative parrot that he kept in his home and of which he was getting to be fond flew off while he was out. Some neighbors thought it had been stolen, another that it had escaped, and a third that perhaps some dog . . .

Don Ponciano was the only one who hadn't taken the trouble to invent an explanation. Those who disappeared out of his life didn't worry him much.

But, as has been remarked, he was like any other human being. Therefore, at some time or other, he was bound to fall in love. General ideas were not in his line; convictions made him uneasy because he had no sympathy with obstinate people. When he was a child, his mother had told him not to be stubborn. And he didn't see any difference between a conviction and an obsession.

It was inevitable that he should fall in love. So he fell in love. In the town, all his acquaintances maintained that he had fallen in love with his "darky" as he called her. In her he finally found obedience and unselfishness. Of course he was aware of the fact that those who inquired about her were poking fun at him; his "darky" had ended by becoming a popular topic. And since he was a kindly good-natured soul, he could hear at intervals on every street, upon the lips of people smiling at him, remarks of this sort: "Regards to your 'darky,' Don Ponciano."

He was a railroad engineer. For some years he had run a train on

898

a little branch line, and little by little, as the days sped on as well as his locomotive, he began to realize that the latter was the only creature that had never fooled him, the only one always obedient to his wish. Always. It was so pleasant for him to be sure of someone! He understood appreciatively all her virtues.

Once he was cleaning one of her pistons with a rag in his fingers. And it seemed to him that his hand acted gently and that the oily rag was making the gesture of a caress.

"Caramba!" he said to himself wiping away the sweat. "Can it be that we have hands, really, for the purpose of petting?"

He nodded his head and with more energy rubbed the shining steel block. After all, his locomotive was the best thing he had. They knew each other perfectly and got along well. She was glad to work for him. And since there was no obstacle, he ended by falling in love with her. From then on he began to call her "my darky."

When for some reason the locomotive had to make a run when he was not on duty, he always tried to be at the station when she came back. That was one of his greatest joys! When he saw her coming along, he beheld her so proud and disdainful! God, how graceful a locomotive can be! She moves ahead, advancing at such a haughty pace, her tresses of smoke always blowing, those tresses that impertinent little winds try to fondle! But how his "darky" scorned them as she waved her plumes with solid dignity.

One morning she went out with another man. It happened to be one of those rare occasions when Don Ponciano was not on duty.

What a little bit of dynamite it takes to reduce a train to splinters! A band of hungry rebels were being pursued in the mountains. For a month they had not been able to get near enough to any settlement to obtain supplies. The only stuff they had left besides their guns and a small quantity of cartridges was twenty-one pounds of dynamite. That was plenty.

On the rails, in a second, the locomotive was smashed into a heap of smoking metal. The boiler was still giving out rumbles, but nothing usable was left.

When the news reached the town, all commented on the good luck of Don Ponciano who by a miracle had not taken out the locomotive on that trip. But he said nothing. The only thing they saw him do was to shake his head.

As he walked along, people jokingly remarked, "So you've become a widower, Don Ponciano?"

"Yes, my friend; I'm in mourning," he answered, smiling in response.

But if it was night and there was no danger of people seeing, his eyes became moist.

Although those were times of confusion when Mexico was plunged into revolution, everyone thought Ponciano would wait around till he got another locomotive when communications were re-established.

But he did nothing of the sort. He felt that in all due decency, he shouldn't work as an engineer any more. He also nursed a deep grievance against the rebels who had caused the destruction of his "darky." Perhaps it wasn't hatred that he felt, but it was pretty close to it. And because he could find nothing else to do, he enlisted as a soldier to fight bandits.

"Is it because you were scared, Ponciano, at seeing how men get killed in their engines?"

Ponciano smiled and said nothing. It is true that the other engineer must have been horribly mangled. When she got to the place of the catastrophe with some troops, his wife could find only one of her husband's shoes with his foot still in it. But the powers above knew that if his locomotive had been spared, Ponciano would have kept on as an engineer.

That's how it came about that people began to see him on the streets with a gun on his shoulder. At times when they told him that he was a fool to identify himself with the brutes to whose ranks he now belonged, he smiled, he just smiled.

Among the recruits he stood out and was liked. He began to be trusted with orders and commissions of some importance. He could read. He was unruffled and serene, more so than anyone else. He was called in as umpire in almost all disputes. At the beginning, he put all his good will into his work as pacifier; but on seeing in most cases, in spite of his decision and his reasons, that one of the disputants ended by killing the other, he refused to intervene in any of the quarrels.

His commanding officers esteemed him highly.

And so the day came when, with some distinction and many friends among the Revolutionists, he found himself in Mexico City, now that the weakened country could fight no longer. Exhaustion settled on the land, or as we call it allegorically, Peace. He never lost his good humor, nor had he conceived any ambition. It was his lot to keep on being stout and cheerful.

Concerning his engine, after the passing of fifteen years, his feeling was no longer poignant. Presumably he would have gone back to the job of engineer, if they had taken him on. The pay was desirable. But unemployment was beginning to spread. Things were different now. Even the Bible had to be brought up to date. According to the Good Book, work was a curse. But in modern times, there could be no curse of more terrible import than the two tragic words: "No jobs." If we spoke Biblically, we should have to say today: "Thou shalt not earn thy bread, not even by the sweat of thy brow."

But after all, Don Ponciano had lots of friends among the higher-ups. And they did not go back on him. His record as an old dependable veteran who, according to the popular phrase, "did his full duty as a soldier of the Revolution," brought him for the time being a job "that would improve with time."

He began a new existence now, that of a hireling.

II

Among the Big Shots

He had hired out in a way all his life, but this was different. He considered that between an ordinary laborer and a government employee there was more or less the same difference as exists between service and servitude. Any worker gets paid for the labor of his arms and hands, but in public employment, you are rewarded for your flatteries and smiles and other attitudes not natural to Ponciano. His conscience was the cleanest thing he had but it was at times a bothersome, unpractical luxury. A pair of good-looking legs have always been more profitable.

And so the old Revolutionist realized he was being punished and demoted in a relentless scale of descent. They finally set him up in a gloomy ugly room where the public applying at the offices never penetrated, just because the Chief thought that that man presented a disagreeable appearance. Moreover, the poor fellow had had the misfortune of walking into the Chief's office at the moment when he was presenting a box of silk stockings to his pretty stenographer.

Ponciano used to talk things over with another employee like himself in temperament, who had also soldiered in the Revolution; but this fellow had been driven to it by his ideals. For this comrade, having an ideal was like fuming at the mouth. When he talked about his convictions, he almost shook all over. He joined up with the Revolution because on the farm he had learned to hate the whole breed of land proprietors. The owners! The owners! That accursed race was the reason why men are driven to behave like devils.

This man's name was Nicholas and he swore there was a time when he was well-disposed toward everyone. But the proprietors! The mere recollection of them drove him crazy. From the good sort he swore he had been, he was changed by the working and effect of the Revolution into a kind of cursing centaur who would have been happy to abandon all imaginable pleasures in return for running wild with a torch in his right hand, setting fire to barns, buildings, or anything! The mere remembrance of such deeds seemed to make his eyes smolder. They became bloodshot and his veins swelled up in his enormous hairy hands. He related how one time he got a bullet in his head and while he lay abed with fever, he dreamed he was setting things ablaze. And perhaps he would continue to have this dream to his dying day.

"But all that is over," said Nicholas afterward, as they were walking together along the street. "What is going on now is even worse."

"What is going on now?"

"Sure, friend Ponciano. Don't you see it?"

"What?"

'The proprietors! They're back with us right here."

"No, Nicholas. Here there's no such thing as proprietors."

"But I'm not crazy, nor a fool. I'm not suffering from delusions. I'm talking about our office. There, yes, even there, the proprietors have slunk in on us. Those who never knew them hardly realize it. But we who have always been under their heel, we'll recognize them even if they come disguised as stuffed turkeys."

"You're exaggerating, Nicholas. Some of them are pretty fair."

"I exaggerate! But all they've done is to change their name! Formerly they were called land owners, today they bear the title of Department Head, or Top Official, or Governor, or Minister. But they are all of the same composition with this difference, that the landowners after all had faith in themselves whereas our government officials put their faith only in those who give them their jobs."

Don Ponciano, after such conversations, realized it was better not to quarrel with his companion who became excited when discussing his favorite topic. Perhaps the wound he had received in his head would land him in time in a straitjacket, for his emphatic declarations became continually more and more alarming.

Among the few who associated with Don Ponciano, mention should be made also of Suarez, as the office Chief called him, or Suaritos, the name by which his fellow workers addressed him.

Suaritos had a spirit addicted to flattery. He had been working for the Government for so many years! Some faces turn into masks and that of Suaritos was a sample. A smiling mask! When his superiors were merely of the lower ranks, Suaritos turned out to be rather useful to them because of his deference; he gradually gave them all notions of their own importance. When they were inflated to just the right amount, Suaritos being a model of prudence, would return to his own corner.

He was of limited intelligence but had extraordinary resistance. When the emergency arose, he could swallow insults, accept vexations, even drunken abuse, and his stoic smile was scarcely altered. There could be no doubt of it: Suaritos was extraordinary in this respect. The only thing that made him lose sleep was when there was a wave of dismissals which produced in him as well as the others a veritable panic. And secondly, demotions in rank. For the political wire-pulling of the bosses which brought about such misfortunes was not at all rare.

Nevertheless, you ought to behold Suaritos at home. And above all, you ought to hear him talking to his wife.

Men do not like it when their wives don't admire them, although of their own initiative, they make little effort to be people worthy of admiration. Suaritos avoided inviting to his home any of his office comrades. Don Ponciano happened to meet his wife by accident. And who could have imagined it! Senor Suarez at home was an ogre! His wife, his children, and even some of the neighbors, found him impressive. When he got off the streetcar on his corner, not one of his office colleagues would have recognized him. His bearing was lordly, harsh, aggressive. His poor wife did all she could to be submissive, seeing to it that dinner was ready and that the children should not make a noise. Her husband was such a domineering nature! And she didn't say that by way of complaint; no, it was proper in his case, that is the way men ought to be. Her husband in his office was surely at a disadvantage because of his haughtiness, since his Chiefs must be somewhat uneasy in his presence. It was probably galling for them to observe such superiority in a subordinate. Oh, what answers he presumably flung at them!

During the evening meal when he was somewhat good-natured, he would recount to his wife terrific tales.

"That poor Chief who has just been appointed had the cheek to say to me, 'Suarez, I expect my subordinates to carry out my orders.' And I replied, emphasizing his name. 'Perez, I expect my Chiefs not to address me in the tone of overseers.'"

The woman felt something like an inner tingling. If her husband were not so imposing, she would have thrown herself about his neck like a weak little fawning kitten. But before her Titan she restrained herself, feeling only a vague desire to weep tears of admiration. And she attributed her moist eyes to having swallowed a spoonful of hot broth. The children kept more quiet than in church; not one of them dared to jest in the presence of that father who seemed like an ancient God, austere and severe.

When he was by himself, he understood how his attitudes were false and clownish. But, there they were, all fixed. Besides, he had his children to consider. Even with the effort to maintain a fictitious double personality, he felt it was better for them to learn to admire a strong spirit. All this was the reaction from the despicable deeds he regularly committed, often unnecessarily, urged on by terror at not being able to feed seven pale mouths.

However, he really relished this state of affairs. To inspire fear! To observe how all held their breath when he spoke in anger! That is what the Gods of antiquity must have felt while cringing human beings trembled at their feet! And Senor Suarez began to think that after all, his life might be considered a model for intelligent living.

His wife, although she could leave her mean little home only rarely, and had to keep her children neat (if you can call the results she achieved neatness), and also cook, and see to it that the older ones swept the floors, and in addition had to mend the trousers of her Olympian husband, herself aware that she went about in rags and smelt of garlic—in spite of all this she was happy. Some evenings she even could be heard singing.

In the office, Nicholas' spasms became more and more frequent. He would suddenly get up from his seat and, taking a stand before the desk of his apparently busy colleagues, he would thunder, "They had convinced me that we would get rid of our bosses by shooting them! What nonsense! There will always be men cut out to serve, and consequently others to order them around. It isn't the masters who make the servants, but exactly the opposite is true. The happiest nation will be the one which has the largest number of men taking orders only from themselves! Let no one slave for us, and let us not impose servitude on anybody!"

His office comrades collectively began to laugh at his outbursts, leading him on in his discourses till his poor mind began to totter.

There was one office-head who was stout and phlegmatic. In his public career he had steered his way with a discerning eye. He always knew how to detach himself from a bad Ministry, that is a ministry (spelled with a small letter) about to fall. He was classified as a man who would arrive. And in his private life he used his keen eye also. Just now he was concerned about a great woman, a poetess, no less, whose intellectual qualities the public refused to recognize. The first evening they dined together, the Chief was so touched by a poem she recited to him that he promised to find her some post in his office.

Next morning this official stepped out of his car, still impressed. That woman might turn out to be the greatest poetess of America, the glory of her country. It was his duty to extend a helping hand.

"Lopez, bring me a list of our personnel."

He was rather irritated by the idea that for the present he would be obliged to offer that woman a position paying very little. But "soon this would increase."

A cross with his pencil and that was all.

"Don Ponciano, the Chief asks me to inform you that he is very sorry, but by order from the Ministry, you are to be discharged on the 30th."

"On the 30th? You mean that in ten days I'll be without my job?"

But the Chief after his consultation with the higher-ups came out quite exasperated. It seemed that the Ministry of that time did not wish to fire employees without a stated cause. Humbug! As if the personnel were not used to it. In spite of his preference, he would have to be more formal about it. And so a cause was found to persuade the higher-ups to sign the order.

Don Ponciano protested, but in vain.

"Yes sir, certainly it was I who went to pay that money but I did it at the order of the Purchasing Agent. Whether or not his transactions were fraudulent was no concern of mine."

Such are the arguments that all those who protest their innocence will never fail to advance! The Minister considered him, Ponciano Cruz, implicated in a shady transaction. Because of pity, he wasn't going to bring him before a court, but he was dismissing him "for the good of the service." By that process, as a result of ministerial generosity, Ponciano was left not only without a job but also discredited And in the world around him, hunger was increasing.

III

Lead

However, not all those who had fought for the Revolution with Ponciano Cruz were as yet being fired from their public jobs. Thus, once more, because of his past record as a man who had carried arms, he got a new post, a better one in fact.

It was as a Customs Collector in a forgotten port town on the Pacific. To be sure, among customs jobs, this was about the worst; it was of the lowest rank, but such as it was, he was going to be the Chief.

He arrived. There were three employees under him and that was more than enough. This promised to turn out like living in a hammock, with time for idle fancies and dreams.

And our hero who had always lived a haphazard existence, never worrying about the future, began to feel it a great stroke of luck for him that circumstances had removed him from the Capital.

Yes, he had been in danger of changing into one of those unfortunate city dwellers. Country folk in the big town are like wretched puppets, without purpose, will, or integrity. The Capital acts like a big machine in whose belly stones and pebbles are whirled around. The machine turns faster and faster, and the pebbles keep on getting rounder by friction, until they become smooth, all alike, without rough edges. That is how characters lose their identity.

Our Customs Chief had had a narrow escape.

Then something extraordinary came up.

In that forgotten port where nothing important ever happened, some contraband was discovered. The export of gold was forbidden. Yet, thanks to the thoroughness and zeal of the Customs Inspector, he was able to confiscate a consignment of the fabulous metal. He sent the report to Headquarters by telegraph. And the next day, the residents of the town made acquaintance with an airplane. Never had such a thing landed in that vicinity. Three men stepped down under the simple pretext of taking dips in the ocean in a port that was so beautiful and off the beaten track. They invited the Customs Inspector to dine with them.

Of course they never did any ocean bathing! And the queer thing was that they were in possession of his telegram, although they were not government officers. Ponciano Cruz soon caught on to the situation.

That night when he reached his home, he found the lock on his bedroom broken. But nothing was missing; on the contrary, when he lit the candle by the bed, he saw that an unpainted wooden table, usually standing in the middle, had been moved to a corner, and was bending under a load of twelve sacks of silver pesos.

Ponciano Cruz, with his hands behind his back, left the bedroom and began to walk up and down on his porch in the dark. And when it was very late in the night, he went to bed. He was smiling as he whispered to himself, "The only decent thing I can call mine is my conscience."

With twelve thousand pesos, he could be his own master, and he wouldn't need a job any more. This was surely the great opportunity of his life.

But he didn't accept. He refused to forget about this matter. Then they offered him thirty thousand pesos.

They argued that integrity was just nonsense, that only fools let such considerations hamper them. Yes, the strangers were certainly right! But he was going to hang on to the contraband and report it once more.

From all directions he was assailed by a voice that seemed to come out of his own being but yet wasn't his own: "Don't be a fool, Ponciano. Don't you see clearly that in this transaction some powerful person is involved? Don't you realize that they'll make you shut up somehow? After all, it was you yourself who invented a wise proverb, when you said, 'If you don't seize an opportunity the first time it comes within your grasp, the second time it comes along it will give you a kick!' And you're not going to have another like it the rest of your life!"

Ponciano Cruz kept on smiling.

But the outcome of this business didn't depend merely on his choice. The fact was that those gentlemen were disposed to take any measure in order to rescue their shipment. Ponciano listened to their threats.

"Since you haven't been willing to behave like a human being, we're going to treat you like an animal, you old mule! Can't you get it through your head that this matter will go through in spite of you? Perhaps you will begin to understand when you're rotting away in the cemetery."

And Ponciano answered, "We'll see . . ."

His situation was that of a man entirely alone, abandoned to his own devices. Should he notify the municipal authorities? But he was aware that all doors would be shut against him! Was it better to steal away secretly from the town? But that treasure was in his keeping! Should he try to get in touch again with the Central Customs office? How could he when his messages were delivered into the hands of those three men! Only one recourse was open to him: the Press. In the telegraph office an Inspector had arrived suddenly and Ponciano knew that any message would be intercepted. So, on the preceding day, he had sent off his office boy in a boat, a lad in whom he placed most trust. From the neighboring town he would be able to dispatch the written messages that he was bearing.

As for him, Ponciano, perhaps that night they were going to kill him.

He didn't go back home. At dusk he had dismissed his subordinates and shut himself up in the dark Customs building. He himself made sure of the bolts. And he locked himself into the watchman's quarters, having sent him away also. In a corner was a cot. On the table he had set a bundle. About nine o'clock at night he undid it: some pieces of bread, a bottle of coffee and milk, and a pistol. Thus he ate his supper, seated at the table by the light of an oil lamp, drinking straight out of the bottle. As he had nothing to do, he spent some time picking up all the crumbs from the newspaper in which he had wrapped up the bread. Now he was no longer hungry; but still he had nothing special to do.

Thereupon he went out on the porch and with quiet steps walked up and down from one end to the other. On that night it didn't matter to him that he was bitten up by mosquitoes in the dark and the heat. He went back to his room; he picked up the lamp to examine the cot and see if a scorpion hadn't dropped on it from the ceiling. Then, with the netting draped over him, he fell asleep.

Some hours later he woke up. Were they really going to kill him that night? He spent a long time musing idly. It must have been about three in the morning when there was a knock on the gate. Then a pause. They knocked again and again; the blows were increasing. Perhaps they were striking with stones, for by now the thumps were resounding with force. They were really furious whacks.

Don Ponciano on hearing such an uproar, smiled, thinking, "Imbeciles! If they had provided themselves with a ladder and climbed quietly over the wall, all would have been simpler. The way things are going now, in spite of the late hour, they will arouse people, and perhaps they won't dare to beat the gate down with hatchets before a crowd. They don't take into account that in a place like this, the slightest disturbance wakes up the whole town."

His conjectures were accurate, for a few moments later voices were heard outside. Two policemen had arrived on the scene. Later some fishermen came up and a few women; presently, some of the neighbors. The policemen, disregarding the assertions and threats of the strangers, refused to leave. At such a time, the sole authority present was symbolized by those two timid oil lanterns held by the civil guards.

Dawn came. Don Ponciano was alive and smiling.

The newspapers in the Capital had received his messages. They did not give them the publicity that might be expected. But after all, they did call public attention to this affair. So the three airplane men received instructions not to commit any violence. Testimony was taken. An Inspector was dispatched to make inquiries, and the Customs were ordered to deliver to the Court the appropriate documents and the bars, ingots of lead filled in the middle with gold coins.

This was done. The investigation was about to begin when it was discovered that there was none of the aforementioned gold, since the bars were all plain solid lead, as was stated on the bill of lading. All

argument was useless. In the presence of the local Customs Inspecto,·
and of fifty witnesses besides, and the experts, one by one, all the bars
were broken. Solid lead!

In the space of one morning, they had been transmuted into pure
lead.

Don Ponciano when he had held up the shipment (because he
became suspicious at seeing a consignment of lead going abroad at
high freight rates), had taken the stuff to the only jeweler in the port.
They had drilled into some of the ingots and gotten out gold. He was
still carrying in his pocket a paper containing some of the metal
dust. He showed it to the investigators; but one of the experts, smiling
pityingly, before the spectators, patted him on the shoulder and said,
"My friend, you thought that anything yellow is gold. You must
beware of that kind of thinking. It is usual to find in lead ingots
certain impurities, bronze, for example. You are surely still reading
tales for children and so in a most routine affair you are led to invent
fantastic adventures."

Saying this, he threw the scrap of paper and its contents out of a
window.

The investigators before leaving town advised the Customs Inspector
to cut down on his drinking, because one can reach a point where one
takes for real the things one imagines when drunk.

But he never took a drop!

"Come now, Mr. Inspector! There is nothing to worry over! We are
your superiors in rank, and away from our job we like our little liba-
tions. Come along with us and we'll show you. Come."

And they got him into a tavern where they poked fun at him.
He drank, laughed boisterously, and said nothing.

The affair blew over. Sometimes he ran across the old jeweler on the
street. The latter would approach him and say, "There was gold, it
was gold all right . . ."

Two months later in the Capital, taking into account his ineptitude
and lack of experience, they sent his discharge to the Customs Inspector.
And two weeks later, for reasons of economy, his office boy was also
dismissed. Don Ponciano expected this. "Fine," he said, "who knows,
perhaps they are doing me a favor . . ."

Almost all his acquaintances in the port tried to incite him to do
something. If he went to the Capital, he could stir up an enormous
scandal. He could give to the Press various statements signed by three
hundred or more people who were ready to testify, so that this affair
wouldn't end without some fireworks. They would make declarations
about the landing of an airplane, the attempt to beat down the door,
the bags of silver (which subsequently, before he could send them on to
Mexico City as palpable proof of attempted bribery, had been taken
back). And at least to make him keep quiet, they would offer him a
better post. He owed this effort to his own reputation.

Yes, it was all well thought out. They were right. That was an intelligent plan. It certainly was.

But Don Ponciano did not return to the Capital.

IV

The Ideal Woman

He wanted to lead an easy existence, routine, quiet. So he returned to the village where everybody knew him by that amusing legend concerning his "darky."

He had with him some pesos he had saved. And he also kept another little bundle, a small package containing filings and rough fragments of yellow metal. This last wouldn't be of any use to him, but he wanted to preserve it as a souvenir.

He was going to buy some farmland and open up a little vegetable stand. Yes, he, in spite of having so many friends in the government! The opportunities he had missed! He was nothing more than a poor barbarian! Poor fellow! Condemned to selling onions after having rubbed elbows with so many important people!

His old neighbors saw him return with his smile. He was just the same, except that some graying locks showed vividly against the mass of his black hair. But that didn't mean anything. He bought his land and opened a little store. And smelling of heat and neglect, he sat down to let the days pass.

In the evenings, an old tamale woman used to take her place on a stone at the corner, with her enormous earthern pot in front of her. During one or two hours she would patiently sell her wares, taking in penny after penny. That odor from her tamales was appetizing. Don Ponciano began to report to her stand for purely business purposes.

The woman had accepted the idea with resignation that her mission in life was just that: to make tamales. At her age and with her face, she no longer felt that she was meant for love.

Nevertheless she began to go to Don Ponciano's store to prepare his meals. Then later they arranged to have her do his wash since he was living alone. Still later, she found it more convenient to cook her tamales right there. Finally one day, the idea came to them that they might get married.

A few months afterward our graying hero realized that for the first time his life was assuming some importance to him. He found it out one night on passing in front of a saloon, when he saw two drunkards come out shouting insults at each other. In a twinkling, they had drawn their pistols and begun firing as they crouched in the darkness.

And Ponciano Cruz, in an awful hurry, had wedged himself into a doorway, making himself as small as he could, and holding his breath. He was trembling! What a queer thing for him!

The two men emptied their pistols, and when their firing stopped, others came out of the saloon and took their weapons away. As happens in such cases, the disputants had not received a single scratch. But two blocks away a woman was leading by the hand a pale little girl of seven. The woman thought that the bare little feet had stumbled against a cobble, but a bullet had entered her body near her stomach. At first the woman could find nothing wrong with her child, and thought that perhaps she had fainted in her fright at the shooting. A few people about her gave her some light with matches, and then she saw that one of her hands groping over the warm little body was red. She couldn't even weep as she knelt on the ground, stupefied. Then, without saying a word, she got up, raised the little body in her long arms, and with a firm and rapid step she disappeared into the darkness, her throat quivering with sobs. A few people stayed on the spot in the middle of the street, speechless.

Ponciano Cruz went into his house thinking of death. What a strange thing for him! He had never felt fear before. He had been a man whose life seemed of no value. People speak of scorning death. That's a foolish notion, for it is life that they scorn.

What he had experienced was perfectly clear to him; for the first time he had been scared.

Perhaps he had never loved life. Perhaps, before that night, he had never felt like a man of twenty. One is twenty on the day one wants to have a child.

He went to bed but remained awake for a long time. On her cot in the dark, his wife was snoring close by. But he felt happy just thinking of her asleep. Ponciano Cruz, drowsy, patted her tenderly, just as, rag in hand, he had caressed his locomotive long ago. But on this occasion he was a different person; he wanted to live.

He had plenty of gray streaks in his hair; but taking it easy he could still live many years. He would live longer than a lot of young men. Yes, you celebrated your twentieth birthday on the day when you crave for your first child.

He would have plenty of time to teach his son many things. He would tell him that the world was crazy and that men's civilization is too much for them, that they don't know what they want. Or rather, that poor humans are no longer capable of desiring anything because their purposes have become colorless and their hope overcast.

During the mornings, his wife was still able to look after the shop although she moved about with difficulty. That is why he had plenty of time to take long walks afoot, for no visible purpose so far as people could judge. He used to follow at dawn the loneliest road that led to the mountain.

His lameness did not prevent him from covering long distances. For hours on a stretch he would lurch along the dusty way, smiling. Some drivers reported they saw him talking all alone.

That was not so. They didn't notice that his right hand hung down always clenched. Because Ponciano Cruz, sensible and plain fellow though he was, was borrowing on his imagination. And inspiration never refuses to be generous to children and to simple souls. Ponciano Cruz felt within his own hand the trusting little fist of his own son about to be born. They always went out together on those roads. Obviously the drivers couldn't hear the innocent little voice, but he heard, "Daddy, what are kings like?"

The lame man remained silent for a few moments and then answered, "They are men so haughty that they think they are the owners of all other men, and so they can never live in peace."

"Why not?"

"Because being master over a nation involves a lot of work, plenty of distrust, and many troubles."

"Papa, I should like to be a king."

"Would you want to suffer a great deal?"

"No, because kings can do what they like. And if they don't like it, they needn't suffer."

Ponciano Cruz remained silent for a long distance, since he didn't know how to answer so that his son would understand. On approaching the outskirts of the pueblo, he shook his head. As if returning to reality over those muddy streets, he reached his shop where his wife was singing, her face radiating light.

"Tacha, is lunch ready?"

"Yes, Ponciano, sit down."

He patted her and then sat down on his wooden bench. The woman pushed toward him the box they used as a table, and a moment later, with his earthenware plate in his hands, the man smiled. That was real living! He wouldn't swap that woman of his for any queen. Now would he exchange his farm and store for any empire.

By some strange chance he had extricated himself from the whirlpools of straining and trembling men; he had been in danger of becoming like them; but no, his smile had become clouded. To live at peace, in quiet, with her! And soon with a chubby boy, full of health and questions.

Don Ponciano was sure now that no harm could come to him from anyone or anything. He didn't possess the words to express it, but he felt that the ideal situation is the one where no harm can come to us from anyone or anything, where we cannot give occasion for pity or envy. To be envied is to carry around in oneself something misleading, something that doesn't belong to us. But the poor dwellers in cities have lost track of the distinction between envy and admiration.

Even if he could have gone back to his job as an engineer, even if his "darky" had appeared before him by magic, beckoning to him, he would not have gone to her now. His Kingdom was the one and only one in the world, and he had no intention of abdicating.

While his wife, seated in the shade, kept an eye on the store and knitted woolen garments, he was busy measuring the spaces between four walls to see where he should suspend the baby's hammock. Or, he would have to go to the stores in the shopping district to buy balls of yarn, or he would return with a big basket full of articles to sell. Or, he would go to his farm to read children's stories, because when his boy became inquisitive, he would have to know many things to tell him.

No, he wouldn't like to have his son be a King. He would be satisfied if the child were not born with the soul of a hireling. He certainly did not want that. He would never wish to see his son as he himself had been once, living discontentedly amidst men at the beck and call of masters.

It was night. Don Ponciano was waiting outside his shop, trembling between anxiety and joy, thinking of the son who would soon disturb the neighborhood with his bellows. Inside, moans, voices of women, suggestions, running around, jostling. Suddenly the moans stopped. The voices of the women became hushed. Their breathing was almost audible. And then, without warning, a wail! That plaintive cry which he felt under his dirty shirt like a flash of lightning.

And Ponciano Cruz bent his head in the shadow, and smiled in silence, more jubilant than ever before in his whole life.

VENTURA GARCIA CALDERON

The Lottery Ticket

Ventura García Calderón was born in Lima, Peru, in 1881. Son of a former Peruvian president, he has lived mainly in Paris, trying to interpret abroad South American culture. He has published in many magazines, but chiefly in *La Prensa* of Buenos Aires. His important works are *Frívolamente, Bajo el Clamor de las Sirenas,* and *La Venganza del Condor.* In Paris he published a well-known anthology of Hispano-American stories. [Used by permission of the translator, Richard Phibbs; first published in English by The Golden Cockerel Press, London.]

YOU HAVE HEARD THIS STORY BEFORE? No matter, I will tell it again because it points to a moral, and, better than that, to a state of mind. Also it is not without present-day interest.

The dancer, whom we will call Cielito, was the loveliest Spanish "bailadora" of about fifteen years ago, though not in the fashion of Madrid, where the taste in women at that time was Turkish—for fat all over. She was the Medici Venus, not the Milo—which measures three feet eleven inches round the hips.

You remember Cielito's version of the rumba, with a pink-tipped finger pointing to Heaven; and how the public used to roar for one more look; and how she allowed it, just for one second, smiling like an angel fallen in the worst Gomorrah? If you have not seen Cielito dance the rumba, you do not know tropical love. In her dancing she played instinctively the cruel game of rousing lust and leaving it. Like the Persian butterfly, she was always playing with fire without ever getting burnt.

Cielito learned to dance in the West Indies, where this story takes place. The "danse du ventre" is a bourgeois family spectacle beside this swinging of the breasts. Breasts fit to be molded into beautiful cups, or like coupled doves to be caressed. The impish wanton shawl follows the swinging game, and at last, for a too brief unforgettable instant, is thrown aside.

One loses one's head when one speaks of Cielito; which would hardly surprise her, for there is not a woman in the world who knows more about men than she does.

Once when she was touring in Cuba she drove the men so mad that they had to have a lottery for her. Yes, a singular idea, but not really so strange in South America, where we leave everything to chance, even the pretty women. Well, in this distant town of the island of sugar cane and honey, the spectators were able one night to buy with their theater tickets the chance of taking Cielito away with them after the performance. Only one spectator could win of course, but in the crowds at the booking-office every man was Don Juan looking with hatred at his possible rival, the neighbor who was also buying the right to be the happiest of men.

Even Cielito was a little moved when the evening came, and there was something almost chaste in her languorous glances at the audience who riotously refused any other music-hall items. They only wanted Cielito with her shuffling false-negro steps and very soft creole words "arza columpiate." But there were no passionate encores, no one asked Cielito to carry her perversity any further. Everyone was in too great a hurry for the draw, which was very correctly carried out, like a family lottery, on the stage itself.

A top hat was filled with numbered place-slips, and the draw was presided over by the theater manager; rather pale and nervous, for any suspicion of trickery would have been punished on the spot, and there's no knowing what may happen when a lot of violent men are after the same girl. Believe me it was more than mere lust for a beautiful woman; you have no idea how much magic and romance is attached to any European actress by South Americans dreaming of Montmartre and Andalusia. A Frenchwoman is all Paris to them, a Spaniard is Seville or Granada with the chirrup of grasshoppers in the sunshine. These phantasies are a sort of feverish mental stimulant to our people, and a beautiful body does not help to lessen the fever.

At exactly midnight the winning number, 213, was called by a man in evening dress who had turned his back on the hat and unhesitatingly drawn a slip of paper.

The whole room looked for the winner, some mocking voices called for him to go up on the stage so that everyone could see him before he went into the wings with Cielito.

No one answered, and there was an expectant silence. A spectator who had come very near success jogged the elbow of his neighbor in seat 213, almost forcing him to rise.

He was a fine looking negro, "a bit of ebony" the conquistadores would have called him; "black as sin" the old women say even now. He rose slowly with the charming comic solemnity of the colored people, whose vain smile fitly answers the amused glances of the crowd. With deliberate slowness he looked through his note-case for the ticket, found it at last in a greasy envelope, and tore it up into very small pieces which he threw in the air like confetti before the astounded audience.

That ample gesture ought to have made his refusal clear enough. But the people could not believe he was rejecting Cielito, the finest flower of Spain. So he shook his head, looking grave and sulky, but enjoying very much the displeasure he was causing.

All the bitterness of the subject races was in him, all the misery of his ancestors who had died as slaves among the sugar cane. The hot joy of revenge burned on his obstinate coal black face as he disdained what so many white men had dreamed about with longing. Then with a shrug of his shoulders, very dignified and sure of his importance, he prepared to leave the theater, while from the stage Cielito with her hands on her hips in a truly Spanish fury spat out at him her shame and her disgust.

But there was no need of a word from her. The whole audience rushed on the black man and began to beat him. So he did not want the flower of Spain—he was disgusted with the darling of Andalusia— they would show him—they would finish him.

It was a most unlooked for lynching, unknown no doubt in the United States where they don't yet punish the abstemious negro who refuses to "outrage" a white woman.

Half an hour afterwards they sent the dying man to hospital; and, as they have given up drawing lots for Cielito, I will not bother you with the address of the theater.

ENRIQUE LOPEZ ALBUJAR

Adultery

Enrique López Albújar was born in Piura, Peru, in 1875. He became a lawyer, and is now a judge at Tacna, through whose court many cases involving Indian natives pass. The Peruvian sierra and their indigenous dwellers are the landscapes and types he pictures effectively, as in the story here given. His two main collections are *Cuentos Andinos* and *Nuevos Cuentos Andinos*. [Translated by Harry Kurz.]

AFTER HIS RETURN FROM TACNA, Carmelo Maquera noticed something queer about his wife. He had left her a woman willing to work hard and now he discovered she was lazy. The spindle didn't turn in her hands as usual, and the meat stew which she prepared for him every morning after his chores, didn't have the spicy relish of former times. She sighed a great deal and frequently remained plunged within herself and without paying attention to what he was saying. She was doing a poor and slow job in her help with the shearing, and was apparently indifferent to the promise made by Carmelo to deliver the wool promptly in order to pay off a loan that was overdue.

What was the matter with Isidora? And this wasn't the only thing that had the Indian worried, but also the refusal of his wife to spread her quilt of skins beside his own when it was time to go to bed. She had been carrying on like this since the very eve of his return, barring the door and refusing to open it to him despite his threat that he would beat it down. This was the really serious element in the situation.

During the three years of their married life, the skins they used for beds had never lain separate, not even after a quarrel or because of illness. No; the blessing of the priest was not intended to have them sleep apart, but rather to make them lie down together, always together, especially at night, since that was what marriage was for.

Why, then, did Isidora refuse to sleep with him? Why did she prefer to keep him outside, suffering from the harshness of the cold as he lay hunched up within the flea-infested circle of his dogs? This matter required some talking over; perhaps he ought to go to Tarata to lay it all before the priest who had married them or before his godfather, Callata, in whom he could confide easily.

Could it be that the "sparrow-hawk" was fluttering above his hut? Or was it some fox sniffing after his dish, the one the church had provided for him alone and for which he had paid plenty of good silver "soleo"? Or was the fox already nibbling in it?

And these many questions didn't let him tend his flocks properly nor pasture them for their good. Seized by a sudden fit of anger one day, not waiting for dusk to herd his animals and close them in the folds, he abandoned the fields and all and returned to his hut to find his wife sniffling and wiping her eyes on her petticoat.

915

"You were crying! . . . What ugly thing have you seen to bring the mist to your eyes? Has someone died for whom you mourn more than for me?"

"It's the smoke from the pot. It smokes a lot."

"Never before have I seen you weep because of that. Perhaps you're getting delicate like the young ladies in the cities below. Is something troubling you?"

"Maybe."

"Can I cure it . . . ?"

"Never! It isn't a cut of the knife, nor a blow from a stone or a hand."

"What then is it?"

"If I dared to tell you, Carmelo . . ."

"Is the fox hanging around here?"

"Worse than that. He met me on the road."

"And what did you do?"

"I couldn't do a thing; I was alone. And I couldn't prevent being unfaithful to you."

The Indian snapped his mouth shut and throwing to the floor the bundle he held on his shoulder, his face contorted by an angry grimace, he went over to his wife until his nose almost touched hers and finally stuttered the words, "Adultery, you? With whom?"

"I'll tell you everything."

And the woman, as if the menacing looks of her husband inspired courage in her rather than fear, began to relate the whole story of what happened to darken their lives.

It happened in their isolated farm section, the Capujo, on the Sunday afternoon before Carmelo's return. Dusk was falling as she was piling up a dike in the irrigation ditch. Suddenly she felt on her back something disagreeable which made her turn around. There among the cornstalks she saw two evil eyes spying on her. They belonged to their neighbor, Leoncio Quelopana. She was afraid and wanted to throw down her shovel and run. But she was ashamed, and even though she was a woman, she couldn't bring herself to act scared like a rabbit when it sees people.

So she smiled to hide her agitation and finally inquired after Leoncio's wife. Then the fellow, coming out of the cornfield and moving to the edge of the furrow in which she was crouching, without saying even a word to her, pounced on her like a panther. He grabbed her hands. Then came a struggle with him, two or three bites to make him let go, and shouts that no one could hear because not a soul was near-by. The sun, the only witness, hastened to set so as not to behold the crime of that bad man. What had to happen, happened. But it was against her will. She could swear to that. She still felt outraged by what he had done to her that afternoon, that accursed Leoncio whom the devil ought to carry off to punish him for his misdeed.

She ended her tale with these words. "When he left me, I thought of running to godfather Callata to tell him everything, but I was afraid that Leoncio would overtake me and do it again. For that reason I didn't go. Instead I went back home and I put up the bars on the door in case that man got the notion to come during the night. There all alone I begged God to send you back soon. And He heard me, Carmelo, because you did come back the same week."

Her story could not be more definite, nor the truth more harsh and painful. Yet this Aymara Indian, reared in the mountains and completely unsophisticated, was not satisfied. Hadn't Isidora somehow given some encouragement to Leoncio? When she was so robust at her work and so ready with the shovel, why hadn't she been able to defend herself? He, her husband, had never managed to do what that Indian attacker of women had done. Whenever he tried it, he always came out rebuffed and put to shame.

A cold fury put out the flame that was lit for a moment in his eye by his wounded sense of dignity as a man and a husband. After casting a furtive glance at the knife that hung on the clay wall, he brought himself to say, "So it was my sister's husband who stole my honor? That's even worse, for I'll have to stain my knife with his blood two times, and stab that scoundrel twice in the heart."

"No, Carmelo. You're not going to murder him. If you do it, I'll have to stay here, a woman alone, forsaken, and then there will be more adulteries. That's why I didn't want to tell you. It's all I can do to bear it now."

"If I don t do it, Leoncio is going to think I'm afraid. He will have no respect for me and he won't let you alone either and I shan't be able to go very far to sell the crops or the wool."

"You mustn't believe that, Carmelo. If he ever comes back, I'll be the one to stick a knife into him. Have you noticed your knife hanging up there? Take it down and you will see that I have sharpened the edge, to take it along whenever I go out alone."

The Indian seemed to calm down after this confession. But an inner voice warned him that although his wife had told him the whole truth, there remained something for him to do: collect damages or kill. If he didn't act, he would have to submit to living the rest of his life feigning ignorance of a deed perhaps known to the whole village of Cairani.

How could he leave things as they were? In dealing with the whites, one can pretend, indeed it is a duty to pretend, because ruse is the best weapon the Indian has to use in his fight against them. That is a law of the race. But in dealing with another Indian, an equal, dissimulation is just unspeakable cowardice, a moral disease of infection that doesn't let the sufferer breathe. And then, among Indians, full retribution must be insisted on. Yes, fool the white, cheat him, lie to him, trick him as much as possible, but not a brother Indian, no.

Payment for debts and offenses must be collected promptly, from equal to equal, as man to man, without favoritism.

Why then didn't he go to Leoncio to demand satisfaction for the harm done to his honor during his absence? He who commits damage should be ready to make amends. From his childhood he had always heard again and again this principle, which is one of the props of the ethical, economic, and social edifice of the Ayllo Indians. It had been confirmed by the shyster lawyers and the pettifogging clerks every time he had had to resort to legal papers to defend his rights from unjust intruders.

Hadn't Quelopana robbed him of his honor? Well then, he should pay for it. The idea seemed to him appropriate as a desirable vengeance. Why should he wound the other in his body when he could make him suffer in his purse, where it would be most painful, and all without a disagreeable sequel to himself? By that means he would not run the risk of ending up in prison or becoming a runaway homeless Indian.

And the covetous imagination of Carmelo began to get excited. He could see himself before the judge making his complaint; then his antagonist confessing his crime, cringing before the declarations and tears of Isidora. Then the document was drawn up in which all this was set down, vouched for by the judge and the witnesses, and finally the compensating punishment. The retribution! A goodly sum of money, some amount that Leoncio was not going to be able to pay right away. After that would come the attachment on his property, and they would seize his farmland, his llamas and alpacas, his alfalfa fields, in fact everything he called his . . . For he, Carmelo, was not going to be satisfied with whatever Quelopana might be ready to pay willingly. If that came about, he had plenty of friends in Cairani and Tarata who would stand up for him and take his side. And if he had to carry his case to Tacna, well then, he would. God had given him the means to plead his cause.

Convinced by all these reflections, yet at the same time held in bondage by the chains of century old traditions, he decided to try out first the means of impartial arbitration. He would summon Quelopana before a court of his neighbors, for in such matters it was the business of him who sought justice to arrange for the meeting and the hearing.

In the prescribed manner, he began by going first to the house of his sponsor in marriage and godfather, Callata, who would be selected to preside at the trial. There, after two or three drinks of brandy, which he himself brought along for the purpose, Maquera repeated the whole confession of his wife without omitting a detail, all with due solemnity, since the ceremonial visit did not permit any informality. He even became grandiloquent. He was ready to swear that when Isidora told her story to him, his knife quivered as it listened, and even, it seemed, begged him to draw it out of its sheath. But he preferred to let it remain where it was till his godfather decided on the best line of action.

Callata scratched his head, asked for one more glassful, swished the gulp around in his throat, and, after throwing at the ceiling a wizard's profound glance, he spat out noisily a mouthful of the glistening liquid.

"Fine! I have listened to you with interest, since our custom requires that a godchild should be heard when he comes to tell us of the injury suffered and asks for advice. You have done right in not obeying the summons of your knife. The offense done to you by Leoncio is still lacking in one element."

Maquera, jolted by this remark, loudly banged the table with his bottle, and full of amazement he interrupted the discourse of his marriage sponsor.

"How's that? How can anything be lacking?"

"I insist, the wrong was not complete, for Quelopana alone committed it without the consent of Isidora. And as she did not contribute the adultery, the offense was only half done. If she didn't prevent it, s because she couldn't. What resistance can a hen offer when the x takes her unaware and seizes her by the neck while her rooster is asleep or crowing in another yard? The whites have a saying: Opportunity makes the thief, and that seems to me true. Don't forget, godson Carmelo, that you've got to keep money and wife always in your belt, so that a thief may not come and snatch them, unless it is by superior force. Why didn't you take Isidora along with you to Tacna?"

"I didn't have anyone to leave on the farm to look after the alfalfa and the herds of llamas."

"Yes, true that the farm and the llamas are worth a lot, sometimes more than a wife; but yours has greater value than all your flocks. You shouldn't have left her alone. I'm beginning to think, Carmelo, that Isidora may be in your way when you go to Tacna. I've heard tell that one can find there nice little hens for all sorts of foxes and at different prices. Is that true?"

Maquera, in spite of the gravity of the situation, smiled cunningly and said, "You know a lot, godfather Callata. Advise me how to arrange matters with Leoncio, since neither you nor Isidora want me to settle accounts by the knife."

"It will be enough if he pays plenty for the harm to your honor. What more should one expect? Would you accept from him two hundred soles . . . ?"

"That's too little. Isidora is not an old woman. Leoncio has fine herds. Why not five hundred?"

"Are you crazy, Maquera? Where is that skirt-chaser going to get such a sum? Well then, you go ahead and visit the others who are to be present at the agreement tonight and leave the rest to me. I'll see to it that Quelopana and his wife will not be missing."

It can be taken for granted that nobody stayed away from the meeting, in spite of the lateness of the hour and the blustering night. It was called for four in the morning. This had to be done to comply with Ayllo rules. Matters of this sort have to be dealt with before the crack of dawn so that those who are not there won't find out about the arrangement, and the sun will not be shocked by it. The sun doesn't like things of this nature. He becomes angry, and so do the highlands, and the crops come out damaged. The settlement has to be made before the sun wakes up and begins to reach over the uplands near the crests.

Callata, clothed with importance and solemnity, cast a look all around him, in order to make sure that all those summoned were present. The council was complete. There, forming a circle about him, stifling their yawns and modestly crushing their lice between their fingers, were Manuel Mamani, Inocencio Cahuana, Narciso López, Tomás Condori, and of course the parents-in-law of the offended party, and the latter as well as Quelopana with their respective spouses, Isidora and Carlota, sister to Maquera. Quelopana thus happened to be Carmelo's brother-in-law and this fact added to the seriousness of the "case at hand," as they say in juridical parlance. The offended had not been restrained by his awareness of this.

This relationship had profoundly shocked Callata's ideas of morality and it was surely going to stir up the indignation of all those present. It was an aggravating circumstance and Callata had every intention of using it to the advantage of his godson and for the successful outcome of what he was going to propose.

When they were all on their knees in a perfect circle around him, and felt penitent as they do at the mass in church, Callata, addressing Isidora, exclaimed, "Isidora Coahila, wife of Carmelo Maquera, do your duty."

At once the Coahila woman began to distribute handfuls of *coca* leaves which she drew out of a sack concealed till then under her cloak. Beginning with Callata, she begged them all to accept the *coca*, adding as she faced each one, "Forgive me, also, for the adultery, for it is the first time . . ."

Then the spectator Cahuana, because he was the oldest present, asked, "Leoncio Quelopana, does Isidora speak the truth?"

The man questioned, after a long silence, his head hanging down like that of a criminal facing the guillotine, answered, "It is the truth! It is the truth! Forgive me for the adultery the first time!"

"Have you nothing more to say?" chided Callata.

"Let Carmelo decide what price he wants for his honor."

He whose name was thus mentioned then spoke. "It has already cost me more than a hundred soles to go back and forth to Tarata. My attorney Calisaya asks a good price for his services. Let Quelopana pay me five hundred soles."

"That's too much, I believe. The titles to my land are all mortgaged, my llamas and alpacas are dying; the harvest has brought me no profit this year and Carlota has had to sell her rings, her ear-rings, and all the jewelry she owned in order to pay the priest his due at the feast-day of our patron saint. Where am I going to get so much money?"

Callata thought it opportune to intervene.

"Leoncio, he who does harm should pay for it, and when the wrong committed is as great as yours, it is no time to tighten the knot on your purse. Who asked you to drink water belonging to another? You have polluted it and must render it clean again, as its owner requires."

"Do you consider three hundred enough, papa Callata?"

Callata could not suppress a gesture of surprise, but it was so slight that only Carmelo, who didn't take his eyes off him, could detect it. Both looked at each other fixedly and in silent approval.

"It is well!" said Callata in a pompous voice. "Go at once and fetch them."

"I couldn't, papa Callata, because I don't have them. Tomorrow morning I'll go to Tarata to find someone from whom I can borrow the money."

"That isn't necessary. I'll lend you the sum. Let Cahuana make out a receipt for you to sign."

Quelopana, caught in his own trap, could do nothing else but accept and sign while his wife, deeply grieved by this settlement, groaned, "That's too much, much too much for an adultery!" The others, still kneeling, asked mutual forgiveness of one another.

The ceremony completed, everyone clinked a glass with Carmelo and received another fistful of *coca* from the hands of the Maquera woman. The latter was already smiling and had even dared to let her eyes rest on Leoncio. Then each man took leave, not without saying first to the woman, "You have a fine husband, Isidora. Beware of another rape." To Quelopana each repeated, "Don't take it into your head, you sinful, disreputable Indian, to try any monkey business with my wife. I've got a first-class knife in my house as well as an excellent musket."

When the time had come for the Maqueras to retire also, Callata, leaving aside all his oracular grandiloquence, gave each one of them a tight hug, and remarked, emphasizing his meaning with a smile, "The settlement came out fine. What's going to be my share?"

"Whatever you say, godfather."

"What do you think of fifty soles?"

"That's all right. Take them and give me the rest."

Now in the open country on their way to their farm, Carmelo, half intoxicated by the joy of holding so many banknotes in his hand, an event that hadn't happened to him in a long time, stopped short and said to his wife, indulgently, "Listen, Isidora, with an adultery like that each month, we would soon be rich enough to buy up all the land around Cairani."

"So you don't want me to take along a knife when you go off alone
to Copaja. . . ."

BENITO LYNCH

The Sorrel

Colt

Benito Lynch was born in Buenos Aires in
1885, of Irish-French ancestry. Possessing
private wealth, he has led a secluded
bachelor life in the university town of La
Plata. The story here given is from *De los
Campos Porteños*. His other main works
include *Plata Dorada, Raquela, El Inglés
de los Güesos, Romance de un Gaucho*
and *Palo Verde y Otras Novelas Cortas*.
[Translated by Harry Kurz.]

MARIO WAS TIRED OF "Tiger," a game of his own invention,
played by pursuing through the tree-tops his brother Leo who was
supposed to defend himself bravely by using green figs as projectiles.
So Mario strolled to the backyard gate behind the vegetable and
flower garden. Under the noon sun, leaning against one of the old
posts, he looked up and down the street, waiting patiently in the
hope that his little brother, still eager to continue the fight up there
on the highest branch of the fig-tree, would get tired in his turn of
taunting him with shouts of "stupid carrot" and "obstinate mule."
Suddenly an unexpected sight filled him with happy surprise.

Turning the corner of the garden, a man was entering the lane
and slowly approaching. He was mounted on a big-bellied mare
which was followed by a tiny colt.

"Say!"

And Mario, his eyes wide open and his face flushed, walked over
to the edge of the path to get a better view of the procession.

A colt! To understand his emotion, one must figure out what a
colt meant to Mario at this time in his life, what it meant to have a
colt of his own, that is to say a real horse proportioned to his size.

It was his hobby, his passion, his constant dream. But unfortunately,
he knew from experience that his parents didn't want animals in the
garden because they ate plants and scraped the bark off the trees.

Way off on the Ranch, they said he could have anything he wanted,
that is to say, some docile little pony, but here in the garden, back
of the house, no animals were permitted!

That's why Mario was going to be a good boy, as usual, just watching with suppressed desire the passing of that little miracle. But unexpectedly something extraordinary happened.

When he reached Mario, without stopping his trotting mare and
hardly turning his head, the strapping rider with sullen face under his
red beret let fly at Mario a stupendous offer.

"Say, kid! If you want this colt, you can have it! I'm taking it to the field to kill it!"

As he listened, Mario felt the ground heaving under his feet. His eyes grew misty, all his blood rushed to his head. But alas! He knew all the laws of his home with such finality that he didn't hesitate a second. Red as a tomato, he refused, shame-faced.

"No! Thanks! No!"

The robust young fellow shrugged his shoulders slightly and without adding a word continued along under the sunlight that filled the street. He whisked away with him, following the weary pace of the mare, that gem of a sorrel colt which trotted gracefully after. With its fluffy light-colored tail it flicked the flies off as if it were a big horse.

"Mama!"

Mario rushed headlong toward the house like a colt, without speaking to his brother who, unaware of anything new and still mounted on his fig-tree, took advantage of his brother's hasty passing to pelt him with some figs. Mario arrived under the arbor, blurting out, "Oh, Mama! Oh, Mama!"

The mother, busy at her sewing, seated in an armchair under the young vines, got up startled.

"Holy Virgin! What's the matter, son?"

"Nothing, Mama, nothing—just that a man—"

"Well what, son, what is it?"

"A man passed with a wonderful little colt and he wanted to give it to me!"

"What a scare you gave me!" The mother smiled with relief; but he, excited, continued without listening to her.

"A wonderful colt, Mama, a sorrel colt, small, this high—and the man said he was going to kill him, Mama!"

And now another amazing thing happened. Contrary to all logic and to what would seem normal, Mario heard his mother say to him in a grieved tone, "Really? Good Heavens! Why didn't you accept? Silly boy! We shall soon be going to the Ranch!"

In the face of that extraordinary, unexpected and astounding remark, the boy opened his mouth wide. But he was so crazy about the colt that he didn't stop for questions. With an "I'll call him, then!"—as excited and resonant as a neigh, the boy darted for the door.

"Be careful, son!" shouted the mother.

Careful my eye! Mario was running so fast that his brother couldn't hit him with a single fig as he flashed by.

When he dashed out into the street, the glare of the sun dazzled him. No colt, no mare, no man to be seen anywhere! But presently his straining eyes made out over there in the distance the red beret dancing to the rhythm of a trot in the midst of a cloud of dust.

The clods of dry mud made him stumble and fall several times, his emotion almost choked him, the hateful yapping dogs of the laundress got in his way, but nothing mattered. Nothing, nobody could stop Mario in his mad race.

Before he had covered a few hundred yards, he managed to reach with his voice the ears of that supreme master of his joy, who was going along dejectedly on his humble big-bellied mare.

"Ss! Ss!—Man! Man!"

On hearing him, the strapping young fellow stopped his nag and waited for Mario, frowning.

"Well, what do you want?"

"The colt!—I want the colt," blurted Mario almost choking, and at the same time he stretched out both arms toward the animal as if he expected them to receive it like a store package.

The man's face wore an uncertain expression.

"Fine," he said, "lead him off, then." And he added quickly, looking at the boy's hands, "Didn't you bring a halter, or anything?"

Once more Mario flushed.

"No, I didn't."

And puzzled, he gazed all around him as if he expected to find halters hidden among the weeds.

"Well, you sure are dumb as a sausage!"

The man dismounted and twisted off a bit of wire that happened to be swinging free by the thorn-hedge. In the meantime, the child watched him in excitement but without any regret, for if a great king once offered his kingdom for a horse, certainly Mario could, without loss of face, accept an insult in exchange for a colt.

Only Mario could realize what this sorrel colt meant to him, although he did damage plants, he bit, he kicked, and he refused to go when it suited him. Once he even yanked a lock of hair from the boy's head with one bite, thinking no doubt that it was hay. But how nicely he ate sugar out of his hand and neighed when he saw him in the distance!

This colt was his love, his worry, his aim in life, his light of the spirit—so much so that his parents had acquired the habit of using the animal as a means of controlling the youngster and making him behave.

"If you don't do your lessons, you can't go out this afternoon on the colt. If you act like that, we'll take away your colt. If you do this or if you fail to do that . . ."

Always the colt standing watch over the misconduct of Mario like the flaming banner of an invincible army in the midst of battle! But at the same time the colt was a delight, so gentle, so fond, so cunning!

The horse-breaker of the Ranch, a skillful leather braider, had made him a marvelous halter. Little by little, the other ranch hands, because they were fond of Mario or wanted to outrival one another, had made all the other equipment, till now the boy had a pretty riding outfit that aroused everyone's admiration.

For Mario, he was the finest of all colts and the handsomest creature in the whole world who some day would be a great race horse. His conviction of this was so firm that when his brother Leo joked and called the sorrel "little donkey" and other complimentary names of the sort, these sounded like true blasphemies to Mario.

On the other hand, when the Ranch foreman said, after squinting at the colt, "In my opinion, he is going to grow up into a beauty," Mario found the foreman the most understanding and intelligent man around.

Mario's father had decided to plant a garden in the grounds near the house. But it happened that this "hateful colt"—that is what some were calling him now, even Mama, perhaps because he stepped on some new chicks—this creature seemed opposed to the idea of a garden. This could be gathered from the determination with which he attacked tender little plants each time he was let loose, so that Mario had been officially notified that it was a rule never to leave him untethered at night. Still Mario forgot, had, in fact, forgotten a number of times, so that finally, one morning, his exasperated father said to him, shaking his index finger a lot and emphasizing by that rhythm the gravity of his warning, "The first day that darned colt ever again damages a single plant, that same day we'll turn him loose in the open country."

"Oh! Oh!" In the open country! Turn him loose! Could Mario's father possibly know what such a threat meant to his boy?

One would have to be eight years old like him, think the way he does and love his sorrel colt just as he loved him, to estimate the enormity of such a menace.

The open country! Turn him loose! The open country was for Mario something infinite, unfathomable; and to send his colt out into that vastness seemed as atrocious and inhuman as throwing a new born babe into the sea.

It was not surprising therefore that Mario had stopped being careless, and a whole long week now had passed without the infliction by the colt of the slightest hurt to the tiniest flower.

Outside, a radiant February morning was dawning. Mario, lying across his bed with his feet against the wall, was confiding to his brother Leo some of his plans for the brilliant future of his sorrel colt. Unexpectedly his mother came into the bedroom.

"Now you're in for it!" she said very excitedly. "Yes, you'll catch it now! Have you seen your colt?"

Mario turned red, then pale.

"What's wrong? What's happened, Mama?"

"Your colt is running loose in the garden and he has damaged lots of things!"

The whole world was tumbling down on Mario.

"But how can that be?" he managed to say. "How?"

"I don't know how," his mother answered, "but you can't say I didn't warn you till I was blue in the face! Now your father . . ."

"But I tied him up! I tied him up!"

And while he hastily put on some clothes with trembling hands, everything about him seemed murky as if the room had filled with smoke.

It was an awful disaster. Never before had the colt managed to create so much devastation. This time he had not only trampled the lawn but had even carried his mischief to the flower-bed. Here, apparently scraping with his hoof, he had torn up by the roots a number of the rare carnations set out carefully in a graceful diamond pattern.

"My goodness, what you've done! What you've done, baby!"

And as in a dream and not knowing what he was doing, Mario knelt down on the moist earth and started feverishly to set the carnations upright, while "Baby" or "The Rascal" stood by motionless, his head lowered, the halter slipped off his muzzle, and an expression of cynical indifference in his whole attitude.

Like a sleep-walker, as if he were stepping in a soft wool-stuffed mattress, Mario led the colt by the halter along the wide way with its border of poplars. At its end yonder was the large cattle gate with its white posts, and outside extended the terrible open country in its desolate immensity.

The poor boy's head throbbed with the rush of blood to his brain and he saw things hazily through a cloud. He still heard ringing in his ears the catastrophic admonition of his father.

"Take that colt and turn him loose in the open!"

Mario did not weep because he couldn't shed tears. But he walked along like a mechanical toy; he walked in such a very queer way that his mother watched anxiously from the garden.

The fact was that for Mario, the other side of that cattle gate with its white posts was the end of everything. It was the vortex into which, in a few more seconds, all his being was going to tumble, his very existence swallowed up with his sorrel colt.

When Mario had covered half the distance, his mother could not bear it any longer and she moaned, nervously pressing the father's arm, "That's enough, John! That's enough!"

"All right! Call him back!"

But just then Leo rushed off quickly, the mother uttered a piercing scream and the father ran desperately in Mario's direction.

There, close to the cattle gate, Mario in his canvas smock had collapsed on the turf like a bird winged by a bullet.

A few days later when Mario could finally sit up in his bed, his parents, smiling, but with eyelids red and faces pale with so much anxious wakefulness, forced the sorrel colt into the bedroom, one tugging at the halter and the other pushing hard behind his rump.

ALFONSO HERNANDEZ-CATA

The Servant Girl

Alfonso Hernández-Catá (1885–1940) was born in Santiago, Cuba. He entered the Cuban diplomatic service, held posts in Europe, and from 1937 to 1940 was minister to Brazil. Collections of his short stories are *Los Frutos Acidos, Los Siete Pecados Capitales, Cuentos Passionales, La Voluntad de Dios* and *Piedras Preciosas,* from which is taken the characteristic story included here. [Translated by Harry Kurz.]

THE DOCTOR, A KINDLY INTELLIGENT MAN who had to remind himself at times of the social responsibility of his position as immigration official in order not to give way to pity at individual unfortunate cases, spotted her just as he was stepping onto the lower deck. Her face expressed her anxiety not to attract attention and contrasted oddly with the eager looks of the rest of the group as they pressed forward to land and made up for the ten days of crowding and vibration that they had borne on the ship's journey from Coruña to Havana.

While he went through the formalities of checking the vaccination certificates or occasionally pressing a suspicious looking eyelid, there swirled around the vessel all sorts of tugs, launches, small craft and rowboats, all waiting for the yellow flag to be lowered as a signal for them to make contact. The sea sparkled and the shores extending from the wharf seemed to project into the city huddled behind the docks a terrific blast of sunny heat. The sides of the big vessel rang with the calling of ordinary names shouted inquiringly, and questions as to whether some Juan Lopez or Pedro Perez had already shown his landing card. These calls echoed along the vessel's tall plates and reverberated till they died away into the near-by port.

On the first-class deck brightly colored frocks flitted by, and the eagerness to land showed the futility of those promises of eternal friendship made during the sea trip, no doubt inspired by the constant restlessness of the waves. The inspection of the immigrants was practically over. Only two persons remained, a man, and the young girl with the frightened eyes whom the government physician had spotted trying to avoid him. The ship doctor said, pointing her out to his medical colleague, "She's a brave little Galician girl. She comes here to find work and doesn't know a soul. Don't bother to inspect her. She's as strong as an ox."

"But she doesn't know a thing about the country. What sort of job does she want?"

The girl from Galicia summoned her courage.

"I can work as a servant. I'd heard people talking about Cuba as a good place. I've got a willing pair of arms and can be useful with children."

There was in her face a gentleness which her urgent tone could not lessen. The doctor was touched by it and asked, "And have you got the thirty pesos required by our immigration laws before you can land?"

"When I went aboard at Coruña I didn't have a cent, but I have earned the money on the ship." Her eagerness to make that money had prevailed over the poverty of her travel companions and even over her seasickness. A determined little heroine!

The doctor took another look at her, very much impressed. She couldn't have been more than twenty-four years old. In the pupils of her innocent young eyes there lingered some of the lush green of her fertile pastures. She was robust, but slender. He remembered hearing his wife complain of one of her servants. He suddenly made up his mind.

"Do you want to work in my house? I don't know what your wages will be, but they won't be any less than in any other place. In my household there are three of us, my wife, my sister-in-law, and myself. There are no children."

The Galician girl accepted amidst the congratulations of the ship's doctor, who insisted that she had had a great stroke of luck. And so they landed. On their way to El Vedado she hardly turned her face to observe the sights of the new city. Apparently she was entirely absorbed by some inner vision. In the house she was gladly welcomed, and her new mistress gently explained to her the things she was supposed to do; clean, help her and her unmarried sister with their clothes, take telephone messages when they were out, and lend a hand in the kitchen whenever it was necessary. The girl nodded her agreement without speaking. "The wages will be twenty pesos to start, twenty-five when you know your way about."

"Twenty pesos? Is that the same as twenty duros, our money?"

"Yes, twenty duros, a bit more really because the peso is worth more than the duro."

In her timid eyes two tears started, but on her lips there was a smile, as she answered, "Why of course, I'll learn what there is to do. I want to do my best and give satisfaction. And then, you can see if I'm worth more."

And indeed her master and mistress found out the amazing power of two tireless arms and a tenacity of purpose that could not be distracted. The floor tiles shone, not a speck of dust marred the luster of the furniture from the day she arrived. The cook left things for her to do and never uttered a single complaint. And as if the hours of work could stretch into incredible length because of her activity, she asked that they stop sending their personal linen to the laundry, but took it on herself to wash and iron and fold. The mistress and her sister were torn between fear and joy. Wasn't all this industriousness merely a flood of energy while she was new at the job? A new broom sweeps clean! But such was not the case. The days piled up into weeks, the weeks became months, and her eagerness for work never diminished. Even on Sundays she was unwilling to go out on the streets. For a walk? She? Why? Certainly not. Yet, in spite of everything, they could not manage to become truly fond of her.

Between her and the talkative informality of the house something stood in the way, something composed of timidity, distance, mystery, and silence. When they tried to fathom the reason for this unfriendliness, they finally discovered the cause: she was economical, almost avaricious. To make her discard her ragged things, they had to offer her their castoff clothing. Rather than spend a single cent on herself, she would have given up the shy modesty that made her avoid like the devil the neat workman who almost from her arrival began to lay siege to her. She saved her pennies with the single-mindedness of a magpie. One afternoon, after many pauses and turns in the vicinity of the doctor, she finally blurted out in a voice trembling with fear, "Now, sir, please, I should like you to send this money for me to Spain, to Puebla de Trives, in the name of Santiago Pazos. Will you do that?"

And she spread on the table the thirty duros she had earned aboard ship, the seventy-five she had received in the house, and two more a month that she got from the cook because she remained in the house on her days off, releasing the cook on holidays. All this money, she had saved, and was now placing on the table.

As if the stifling strand of a collar that choked her into silence had suddenly loosened a bit, that noon, during the lull of the siesta, she gave vent to some *confidencia* to her mistress's sister, for she would not have dared to confide in that way to her mistress. She begged the sister to read her several letters that had come for her up to that time. She carried them around in her bosom, perhaps hoping their message that she could not read herself would somehow register in her mind by contact, so she would make out what they told her about her child, her precious little boy.

The sister was deeply moved. How easy it is to make false judgments before knowing the truth. This beast of burden, this penny-pinching miser who had never yielded to the blandishments of a fine young man or to the attractions of any entertainment, was not saving her money because of selfishness, but on the contrary, because of love. She had just given to her listener a lesson in self-sacrifice. The letters, insisting, demanding, revealed the whole story. The little Galician girl had been kicked out of her home as punishment for the one unforgivable sin of a young defenseless woman, and forced to pay for it with the sweat, not only of her brow but also of her whole body, and even worse, with the sufferings of her poor soul. One August afternoon, after a rain that had summoned from the earth intoxicating odors, the mingled scent of flowers and poverty, she had fallen amidst the ripe grain flattened by a man. Nine months later a bit of wailing humanity came forth from her womb. And now honor was used as a mask for avarice.

The angry authority of her father had exploded over her, and there were even harsh blows to extract submission from her. Shame rather than old age was now going to drive them to the grave. She must go away, if not for her own sake, then for the baby, as they didn't have a bowl of broth to keep him alive. They knew that in Havana one could earn good money. The father would keep the sinful brat, and she could send him money from there. Despised and scorned, what else could she do but submit? That was her usual way. This habit of obedience had led to her fall that rainy afternoon amidst the wheat fields, with no love in her heart. Her father's command drowned out the infant's squeal not yet a voice, and she embarked in third class amidst the poor drove of filthy and covetous human beings all kept alive mainly by hunger and dreams. During the sea voyage and now in the city where she seemed bewildered, one single idea dominated her being. It was simply that she must earn money for her son! However, this was not punishment. It was the joy of her life. It was what her heart prompted her to do!

When her secret was revealed in the house where she toiled, what was formerly queer stingy behavior on the part of the girl now assumed aspects of heroism. And her frugality became henceforth the basic guide to the household economy. If there was any small change from a bill paid, if they got a discount on anything, the unanimous cry sounded: "This goes to the Galician girl." These gifts mounted up so rapidly that the doctor decided one day to divide them into two parts: one to pay for her monthly money order sent overseas; the other to be saved up till, slowly, there would be enough to permit the mother to cross the ocean to claim her child. When she was informed of this scheme, her astonished eyes were covered for a minute with a tearful mist in her effort to take it in. She could go? She? That was too much to expect. Then the tears came with a light flashing deep within her eyes like happy rays in a sun-shower. She doubled her gratefulness and her energy at work. As if she were eager to efface the days that still separated her from that distant time when she could start off to join forever the two parts of her being, she buried herself in her work without venturing across the outer threshold except to scrub the tiles; without paying the slightest heed to the undismayed suitor who, with the humble tenacity of his race, watched her from the sidewalk with that deep velvety look, as soft and melancholy as his voice.

And time now urged along by hope, began to move on with that uneven pace that mocks the fixed divisions of calendars and clocks, sometimes monotonously, and then again swiftly. Intervals were marked by the arrival each month, from Spain, of the same sort of letter asking for money. It would seem that as the baby grew, it required more and more for it used up the milk of a cow and the medicines of a whole drugstore. His little body, shown in a photo so faded and crumpled that the photographer's name was illegible, must have developed into incredible dimensions to justify the demand for so many yards of cloth to clothe it. Measles extracted from the Galician mother a veritable flood of money, and the first tooth of this prodigious infant must have been of gold. But it mattered naught to her. All the better if the expenses kept mounting so strangely. That was what gave her strength and that was why the Saints had cast her lot in the best home in the world. Eagerly, like the prow of a vessel plunging on to get to port sooner, she thrust herself into her work to arrive at the end of her wait. The only time she betrayed uneasiness was when the letters from abroad were expected, the corkscrew letters as the mistress's sister called them.

But suddenly, her energy, which had continued untiring for almost three years, began to show signs of exhaustion. There were new neighbors in the house opposite and they had a child. He was blond and pale, and so fragile that it seemed as if any sudden movement might fracture him. The Galician girl used to stop with her broom or her dustcloth in her hand to watch him with an anxious absorption. Her suitor, who seeing her gaze out into the street, entertained the notion that his pertinacity had finally overcome her long shyness, lost her completely, without however giving up his quest. The house mistress, her sister, and the doctor did realize fully what was passing in her mind and held a family council. They would have to send her back home or she would fall sick on their hands. Couldn't the doctor with all the influence he had at the port secure a free passage for her? In that way her savings would be useful to her on the way, and once over there, to shut up greedy mouths, pay the ransom for her son, and assure her return! "I'll contribute the two gold coins that I have in my piggy-bank," said the sister. "And I'll add the money that god-father gave me for his godchild and that the good Lord has not let me bear," the mistress said, her eyes glistening. The doctor approved and the trip was arranged.

Two days before the boat sailed they abruptly announced their plan to the servant, smilingly, attempting to speak of it as if it were a simple matter of no importance. At first she remained rigid, swallowed up in a long moment of stupor. Then she began to sway as if about to faint, recovering however rapidly in her eager pursuit of hands and feet to kiss.

And two days later they went to see her off as if she were a relative. Through the intervention of the doctor, she had been given a passage in second-class. The sea was sparkling, and the thousand noises of harbor activity reached them slightly hushed far out in the port. When the vessel groped its way along the canal, they lost from view her handkerchief waving from the deck.

"How promptly she has gone to her cabin!"

"It's because she can't see us any longer."

"There she is—there she is," said the doctor, who was looking through his field-glasses.

And they spied her way over on the prow, no longer deigning to look back, leaning forward as if her eyes could distinguish over the surging surface of the waves the road that was to take her back to her youngster.

Like the gradually increasing space between the hulk of the vessel and its pier as the boat vanished into distance, so time interposed its obliterating stretch between the departure of the Galician servant girl and the present day. She was remembered affectionately and her name cropped up occasionally in their conversation. Would she come back? No, she would certainly remain in Spain, perhaps opening up a little shop with the aid of her savings. No letter from her ever came. "Who the dickens could write for her in her tiny village?" Recollections of her became more and more vague, and after three months, her name was not mentioned for several days in succession. And then, one night, unexpectedly, feeble and in tatters, they saw her leaning, almost clinging to the garden rail, not daring to enter. At first, because of the dusk of twilight, they took her for a beggar.

"God help you, sister. We have nothing for you."

"Wait, give her a half peso. Here."

"Why, it's our Galician girl!"

"Come in, come in, woman!"

And they had to help her in as if she were paralyzed. She was famished, weak almost to the point of fainting, and it took some time to revive her. She looked around gradually, making an effort to let her eyes rest on this happy oasis of her past. But to all questions she opposed a stubborn silence, and her final answer was a throbbing fit of weeping released by the pressure of a sob emerging from the depths of her being.

"Come now—take it easy. Did you arrive today? Why didn't you let us know? And your son?"

"Stop asking her questions. Don't think of anything, my girl. Just drink this glass of sherry—then go to bed and we'll take you some broth. What you need now is sleep. We can talk later. Come now."

She let them help her to bed where she fell for hours into that leaden slumber which envelops those who have borne great sorrow. When she awoke, the sister of the lady of the house was at her side and received her story. They had fooled her! For more than two and a half years her boy lay buried in the ground and they had kept it from her to get more money out of her. The hateful photo they sent her was of some other child—some other child! And again she relapsed into a stupor interrupted presently by paroxysms of anger and hopelessness. From time to time she muttered fragments of revealing words that broke her panting silence. At the beginning she had wanted to murder—yes, her father—just as he had done to her mother, perhaps to her child also. Then she wanted to run away, and everything went black, pitch dark so that she could not see her way. One thought alone remained clear in all that blackness; she knew she must see them again before she died, for they had been so good to her. She couldn't remember how she got onto the boat, thrown like a bundle. In the depths of the water she could see two little arms summoning her; but the ship's priest guessed what she was contemplating, and as she was leaning over the deck rail to answer the call, he grabbed her and led her to the chapel and made her swear before the image of Saint Iago. And then he talked to her of God, and of those good people in Havana who would help her to start life anew. Moreover, he had added, her little boy was up there, in Heaven, and if she cast herself into the ocean, she would go to Hell and she would never see him again—and that was what he was trying to say to her!

They gave her loving care, tended her body and soul, with that gentle hospitality which is the gracious gift of Cuba. The entire block inquired for days about her illness, and followed her improvement, her convalescence. Presently, her robust constitution restored strength to her blood and her muscles. Finally one day, as if urged by instinct, she found herself walking to the front door with her broom and cloths in her hand.

"What, you are going to do work already? Let it go woman, not yet," they said to her.

"But if it takes my mind off—I should like to do it! It will help me not to think and that's better for me."

She resumed her tasks with her former youthful eagerness, even smiled, hummed the sad old tunes of her native heath without however expressing in their plaintiveness anything beyond the collective melancholy of her race. One afternoon, when the lady and her sister returned from a walk, they found her, to their immense surprise, talking at the rail with that stubborn suitor to whom she had not even given a single glance during three long years. Filled with mysterious wonder, they went into the house to tell the doctor about it.

"She acts now as if that awful thing . . . ! And anyway I'm glad of it. By talking with her Galician compatriot and his mustachios . . ."

"Who could have believed it possible!"

"You can't be sure of anything in this world. If anyone had told me that—why, it seems impossible!"

The doctor raised his kindly and intelligent face from the book he was reading.

"You can't pass judgment lightly," said he. "The one sure thing set by Nature into her mind, primitive as that of an animal, is the maternal instinct. Through her maternity we have observed her become splendid, admirable. The truth is that there is no change in her, she is merely seeking out the way to her son, another son to love and to make sacrifices for. Don't you understand that?"

HORACIO QUIROGA

Three Letters...

and a Footnote

Horacio Quiroga (1878–1937) was born in Salto, Uruguay. He lived in Buenos Aires for a time and then moved to the northern Argentine Paraná jungle, where he spent many years. Here he wrote nearly 100 stories, many dealing with the life of the jungle for animals and men. The best collections of his work are *Cuentos de Amor, de Locura, de Muerto, Cuentos de la Selva* (for children), *El Salvaje, El Desierto, Los Desterrados* and *Más Allá*. [Translated by Harry Kurz.]

Sir:

I am taking the liberty of sending you these lines, hoping you will be good enough to publish them under your own name. I make this request of you because I am informed that no newspaper would accept these pages if I sign them myself. If you think it wiser, you may alter my impressions by giving them a few masculine touches, which indeed may improve them.

My work makes it necessary for me to take the streetcar twice a day, and for five years I have been making the same trip. Sometimes, on the return ride, I travel in the company of some of my girl friends, but on the way to work I always go alone. I am twenty years old, tall, not too thin, and not at all dark-complexioned. My mouth is somewhat large but not pale. My impression is that my eyes are not small. These outward features which I've estimated modestly, as you have observed, are nevertheless all I need to help me form an opinion of many men, in fact so many that I'm tempted to say all men.

You know also that you men have the habit before you board a streetcar of looking rapidly at its occupants through the windows. In that way you examine all the faces (of the women, of course, since they are the only ones that have any interest for you). After that little ceremony, you enter and sit down.

Very well then; as soon as a man leaves the sidewalks, walks over to the car and looks inside, I know perfectly what sort of fellow he is, and I never make a mistake. I know if he is serious, or if he merely intends to invest the ten cents of his fare in finding an easy pick-up. I quickly distinguish between those who like to ride at their ease, and those who prefer less room at the side of some girl.

When the place beside me is unoccupied, I recognize accurately, according to the glance through the window, which men are indifferent and will sit down anywhere; which are only half-interested and will turn their heads in order to give us the once-over slowly, after they have sat down; and finally, which are the enterprising fellows who will pass by seven empty places so as to perch uncomfortably at my side, way back in the rear of the vehicle.

Presumably, these fellows are the most interesting. Quite contrary to the regular habit of girls who travel alone, instead of getting up and offering the inside place to the newcomer, I simply move over toward the window to leave plenty of room for the enterprising arrival.

Plenty of room! That's a meaningless phrase. Never will the three-quarters of a bench abandoned by a girl to her neighbor be sufficient. After moving and shifting at will, he seems suddenly overcome by a surprising motionlessness, to the point where he seems paralyzed. But that is mere appearance, for if anyone watches with suspicion this lack of movement, he will note that the body of the gentleman, imperceptibly, and with a slyness that does honor to his absent-minded look, is slipping little by little down an imaginary inclined plane toward the window, where the girl happens to be, although he isn't looking at her and apparently has no interest in her at all.

That's the way such men are: one could swear that they're thinking about the moon. However, all this time, the right foot (or the left) continues slipping delicately down the aforementioned plane.

I'll admit that while this is going on, I'm very far from being bored. With a mere glance as I shift toward the window, I have taken the measure of my gallant. I know whether he is a spirited fellow who yields to his first impulse or whether he is really someone brazen enough to give me cause for a little worry. I know whether he is a courteous young man or just a vulgar one, whether a hardened criminal or a tenderfoot pickpocket, whether he is really a seductive Beau Brummel (the *séduisant* and not the *séducteur* of the Frenchy) or a mere petty masher.

At first view it might seem that only one kind of man would perform the act of letting his foot slip slyly over while his face wears a hypocritical mask, namely the thief. However that is not so, and there isn't a girl that hasn't made this observation. For each different type she must have ready a special defense. But very often, especially if the man is quite young or poorly dressed, he is likely to be a pickpocket.

The tactics followed by the man never vary. First of all the sudden rigidity and the air of thinking about the moon. The next step is a fleeting glimpse at our person which seems to linger slightly over our face, but whose sole purpose is to estimate the distance that intervenes between his foot and ours. This information acquired, now the conquest begins.

I think there are few things funnier than that maneuver you men execute, when you move your foot along in gradual shifts of toe and heel alternately. Obviously you men can't see the joke; but this pretty cat and mouse game played with a size eleven shoe at one end, and at the other, up above, near the roof, a simpering idiotic face (doubtless because of emotion), bears no comparison so far as absurdity is concerned with anything else you men do.

I said before that I was not bored with these performances. And

my entertainment is based upon the following fact: from the moment
the charmer has calculated with perfect precision the distance he has
to cover with his foot, he rarely lets his gaze wander down again. He
is certain of his measurement and he has no desire to put us on our
guard by repeated glances. You will clearly realize that the attraction
for him lies in making contact, and not in merely looking.

Very well then: when this amiable neighbor has gone about half-
way, I start the same maneuver that he is executing, and I do it
with equal slyness and the same semblance of absent-minded preoccupation with, let us say, my doll. Only, the movement of my foot
is away from his. Not much; a few inches are enough.

It's a treat to behold, presently, my neighbor's surprise when, upon
arriving finally at the calculated spot, he contacts absolutely nothing.
Nothing! His size eleven shoe is entirely alone. This is too much for
him; first he takes a look at the floor, and then at my face. My
thought is still wandering a thousand leagues away, playing with my
doll; but the fellow begins to understand.

Fifteen out of seventeen times (I mention these figures after long
experience), the annoying gentleman gives up the enterprise. In the
two remaining cases I am forced to resort to a warning look. It isn't
necessary for this look to indicate by its expression a feeling of insult,
or contempt, or anger: it is enough to make a movement of the head
in his direction, toward him but without looking straight at him. In
these cases it is better always to avoid crossing glances with a man who
by chance has been really and deeply attracted to us. There may be
in any pickpocket the makings of a dangerous thief. This fact is
well known to the cashiers who guard large amounts of money and
also to young women, not thin, not dark, with mouths not little
and eyes not small, as is the case with yours truly,

                                        M. R.

Dear Miss:
Deeply grateful for your kindness. I'll sign my name with much
pleasure to the article on your impressions, as you request. Nevertheless, it would interest me very much and purely as your collaborator
to know your answer to the following question. Aside from the seventeen concrete cases you mention, haven't you ever felt the slightest
attraction toward some neighbor, tall or short, blond or dark, stout
or lean? Haven't you ever felt the vaguest temptation to yield, ever
so vague, which made the withdrawing of your own foot disagreeable
and troublesome?

                                        H. Q.

Sir:
To be frank, yes, once, once in my life, I felt that temptation to
yield to someone, or more accurately. that lack of energy in my foot

to which you refer. That person was *you*. But you didn't have the sense to take advantage of it.

M. R.

LUIS MANUEL URBANEJA ACHELPOHL

Ovejon

Luis Manuel Urbaneja Achelpohl (1872–1937) was born in Venezuela. He spent many years there writing highly praised stories of Creole life. He sketched the Venezuelan landscapes and types in realistic, humorous or satirical tales printed in reviews or newspapers of Caracas. Of his published novels, the chief ones are *En Este País, El Tuerto Miguel, El Gaucho y el Llanero* and *La Casa de las Cuatro Pencas*. [Translated by Harry Kurz.]

NEAR THE INTERSECTIONS of the highroad, groups of inquiring people were repeating in alarm, "Ovejón! Can it be Ovejón?"

But on the road nothing was visible, just the sun turning the rising dust into gold.

No one had caught a glimpse of him, yet the armed band that had come in hot pursuit all the way from Zuata, scattering people as they passed, had insisted it was he. Now the alarm was spread. With such a visitor loose, this was no time to sleep with doors ajar in the good old neighborly fashion of the town.

Ovejón, as usual, had vanished in full view of his pursuers, at the very moment, fatal for him, when they were taking good aim and were expecting that a mere pressure on their triggers would bowl him over with his chest full of holes like a sieve. But the bandit somehow had shaken out before them a blinding cloud and had gotten away. Ovejón knew a lot of magic.

The inquisitive crowds were now returning to their homes and discussing what had happened. It was the same old story, pursuits and alarms, with Ovejón up to his old tricks. By now, he must be far indeed from the vicinity.

In the vast sky, twilight was gathering, a silky, even twilight. The whole countryside was solemn and peaceful. Upon the spire of the church, a reddish glow showed hazily. Down by the river ford the water glided cool and clear with a pleasant murmur, and little sparkles of light glimmered in the canebrake and the underbrush.

A ragged filthy beggar with bloated face, thick lips and yellow skin was painfully dragging himself along despite a shapeless swollen foot. He was making an effort to cross the ford by stepping on flat stones, green and glistening in the water. He leaned on a tall stick.

and his coarse beggar's knapsack was flapping empty at his side, with not even an ember-brown pancake to give it the slightest bulge.

The beggar was making progress, feeling out with his stick the unsteadiness of the stone slabs and setting down his misshapen foot with great precaution. To keep an even balance was difficult and uncertain, the light was blinding. The beggar suddenly fell headlong on the stones.

At his pitiful groans, a man thrust aside the underbrush near-by. He was of medium height and his eyes were very brilliant. He seemed uneasy, but about the hard lines of his mouth there played a kindly and gentle smile.

The man sprang to the river and, as if the beggar were a mere child, he lifted him up in his arms and very gently carried him up the sloping bank. The beggar w˙s groaning and lamenting. There seemed to be no way of treating the bruised, festering flesh of his foot. The swollen ankle was bleeding. Thick tears clung to the edges of his puffy eyelids.

The stranger raised his eyes and gazed all around. His look was deliberate and careful. All was plunged in calm and shadow in the peace of dusk. He then drew near the beggar, examined the wound, and began to wash it with water from the river, as a mother might tend her young child. The flow of blood did not stop; it was not violent but steady. The man went off a short distance. Bent over the ground, he was groping among the weeds. He stood up. Between his strong fingers he was now crushing some green stalks into a wad. This he placed upon the wound, and since the beggar didn't possess a rag clean enough for a bandage, he unfastened his ample muleteer's shirt, covering him from his neck down to his calves, and drew forth a kerchief, one of those gaudy affairs of pure silk that people coming from the Canary Isles used to slip through the customs as gifts.

The beggar watched the man without saying a word, and the stranger paid attention only to the wound. When the trickle of blood ceased, the man applied the bandage. Not the slightest stain of red came through onto the whiteness of the silk. A smile of satisfaction showed on the man's lips.

The beggar murmured, "Thank you. I'm healed."

The man: "Don't worry. This herb will close your wound."

The beggar made an effort to get up. The man stretched out both arms solicitously, and helped him to stand up. The wretched man's clothes were wringing wet and stuck to his body. The stranger took off his muleteer's shirt and gave it to him.

Astonished, the beggar looked at him; under his coarse shirt this man had been wearing a fine white linen suit. And while he was slipping on the shirt, the beggar examined him carefully. Two details became fixed in his mind: the man's flashing eyes which were very brilliant, and his hair, which was curly and the color of taffy.

The man then handed over to the beggar the stick to lean on **and** he also picked up the knapsack from the ground. Seeing that it was empty, he loosened his wide belt in which were stuck a dagger and a revolver of large caliber, and drew out one after another a number of silver coins. Mixed with these was one golden venezolano dollar. The man looked at it for an instant, but threw it together with the other coins into the knapsack, saying, "It must be meant for you since it came out by itself."

The beggar tried to kiss his hands. This money was a treasure he had never imagined. He uttered thanks and blessings as he hobbled along, overflowing with gratefulness for his benefactor. The man turned around and said, "Today it's my turn to help you. Tomorrow it will be yours to help me."

The sun no longer dazzled the beggar's eyes. The town was far away. A gentle light was still illuminating that long autumn afternoon. The beggar started off alone, cheerfully, without paying much attention to his deformed foot.

The lamplighter had not yet started out on his usual round. His ladder was still leaning against the wall under the lantern with which he always began. Inside, in the tavern, amidst the rounds of drinks, comments could be heard on the most recent exploits of Ovejón. At Zuata he had robbed a rancher and killed a man with his dagger.

Through the doorway of the tavern the beggar's bloated face peered in. When they saw his shapeless foot all fell silent, expecting to hear his plaintive voice imploring charity as his wretched hand held out his dirty hat to receive any gifts. Instead the beggar hobbled to the counter and ordered a drink. Under his shirt he felt the dampness of his clothes, and he was hungry and cold. He sipped the old cane-sweetened liquor and patiently began to chew a hard beggarly crust.

The others stopped looking at him and resumed their conversation. The lamplighter was saying, "As far as his magic powers are concerned, I'll say he has plenty."

The tavern-keeper, incredulous, rejoined, "If I ever have a chance to get a shot at him with my double-barreled gun, it will be all up with his magic!"

A big, strapping half-breed added, "I'd like to know what Ovejón looks like and win the five-hundred pesos reward for his head. They're offering five-hundred pesos to anyone who brings him back dead or alive."

An oily negro spoke. "That's very simple. He's a great big blond fellow with eyes that flash like two bright coins and hair the color of well-beaten taffy. Now go ahead and seek him out in the mountain. When you bring him back, you can pay for my drink."

The lamplighter remarked, "That's the drink I'm swallowing right now. The brandy passed around at wakes tastes the best."

The beggar was trying to soften in his mouth his starchy pancake, but he was thinking, "The man by the river was Ovejón. Five-hundred pesos for anyone who aids in his capture, dead or alive. That wizard Ovejón has sold his soul to the devil. If I betrayed him, I shouldn't have to beg any more. My days of dragging myself along these roads would be over. I could get a doctor to heal my leg. Five-hundred pesos! If I had that money, I could get well."

The beggar slipped his hand into his knapsack for another piece of the pancake and his fingers struck the coins. Then he felt the golden venezolano. His thoughts went on. "Ovejón must have plenty of these. He parts with them easily enough. He is a generous fellow and I wonder if that is why he's a robber. It's because he likes to give charity. These men in the tavern feel repugnance for me and would never have washed my foot. Why did he alone show pity for me when he's a highwayman?" And he remembered the flashing eyes and the light hair, the hard lines of the mouth and the kindly smile.

In the street the quick regular beat of a horse's hooves was heard. The beggar stepped out to look.

A piebald horse was carrying a rider wearing long boots. A sheepskin blanket was draped over the pommel of the saddle. As he rode past the tavern at full gallop, the man on horseback turned his face and the beggar's eyes met those of the rider. The beggar's jaw dropped, but promptly he snapped his mouth shut.

The tavern-keeper also stuck out his head to look around, but the mounted man had gone past. The tavern-keeper remarked, "That sounds like a splendid horse."

The beggar to himself: "It's he, Ovejón. I saw his eyes shining like two bright coins. Their look stabbed into me like two daggers."

The lamplighter: "I'm going to light the lanterns."

The greasy negro poking fun at the Indian: "Well, why haven't you gone off to look for Ovejón? Beware lest you find him tonight asleep in your hammock. Go on and make the rounds of the pueblo. This is the right time for patrol duty. But look out for Ovejón."

The beggar to himself: "It was he, it was he. He's fleeing. He has killed someone, or he has robbed. I wonder whom?"

Along the street four armed men came running along. They burst into the tavern. "Did anyone see him pass?"

"Who? Whom?"

"Ovejón! Ovejón!"

All looked at one another in amazement. "Ovejón! Ovejón!" they repeated.

The armed men: "The piebald mare has been stolen, and the general's saddle, and his boots, too."

All dumbfounded echo, "The piebald mare, the saddle and the boots of the general!"

The men: "Did anyone see him pass?"

The tavern-keeper: "Somebody rode by."

The men: "On the black and white mare?"

The tavern-keeper turning toward the beggar: "See here, you looked out when he passed. Was it a piebald horse?"

The beggar: "I couldn't see it."

The tavern-keeper: "Turn her foal loose. The creature will follow the trail of its mother."

The Indian: "That's right, turn the foal loose and we'll get our five-hundred pesos."

The beggar slipped out like a shadow. Along the street he went limping as fast as he could. The lamplighter was busy with his wick at the street lanterns. The armed men had loosed the foal and were following it. By that time the beggar had left behind the last house of the town and was far ahead on the highroad. At a turn, where the road narrowed to a dangerous pass, he stopped and crouched against the slope.

Soon he heard the quick trot of the foal, a newly-born animal. In the distance men could be heard shouting, trying to get volunteers to join the posse. They were drawing closer. There came the foal along the turn in the road. The beggar raised his stick with both hands and brought it down with all his might on the animal's head. The creature stopped in its tracks, stunned. One more blow sent it headlong into the ravine.

The beggar groped his way toward the dark coffee groves as he whispered softly to himself, "Today it's my turn to help you out, tomorrow it will be yours."

And the planet Venus, as it set, glowed like a golden venezolano.

MONTEIRO LOBATO

The Funny-Man Who Repented

Monteiro Lobato was born in Taubaté, Brazil, in 1886. He has had a great influence upon younger writers. His first collection of tales was *Urupés*, his two best collections, *Contos Pesados*, from which our tragi-comic story is taken, and *Contos Leves*. [Used by permission of the author; translated by Harry Kurz.]

FRANCISCO TEIXERA DE SOUZA PONTES, illegitimate scion of a Souza Pontes who owned some large Barreiro plantations, began to think seriously on life only when he reached his thirty-second birthday.

A natural clown, he had used his comic gifts until then to make his way and provide him with home, food, clothing, and the rest. The currency he used in payment consisted of funny-faces, jokes, stories about the English, and everything calculated to produce an effect on the facial muscles of the laughing animal commonly called man, by summoning him to chortle or break into guffaws.

He knew by heart the *Encyclopedia of Laughter and Merriment* by Fuao Pechincha, the most insipid author God ever let into this world; but Pontes' art was so fine that the most pointless tales received, when recounted by him, a special tang, enough to make his listeners froth at the mouth with pure joy.

He was a genius at imitating people or animals. The entire gamut of canine noises, from the baying at the wild boar, to the howling at the moon, and the rest, all these were molded in his mouth with such perfection that he could fool the dogs themselves—and even the moon.

He could also grunt like a pig, cackle like a hen, croak like a toad, scold like an old woman, whimper like a crybaby, call for silence like a congressman in power, or harangue like a patriot on the balcony. When he had before him a favorable audience, what cry of biped or quadruped could he not imitate to perfection?

On other occasions, he would hark back to pre-historic times. As he had received some education, when his listeners were not ignorant he would reconstruct for them the paleontological roar of extinct monsters—snarls of mastodons or the bellows made by colossal creatures at their first glimpse of hairy, ape-like men lolling on tree ferns— a performance that would have added fun and popularity to the lectures on fossils by our famous Barros Barreto.

On the street, if he ran across a group of friends standing on the corner, he would steal up behind and—bing!—he would deliver a slap with his wrist on the calf of the handiest leg. It was fun to witness the frightened leap and the startled exclamation of the unsuspecting victim, and, after that, the continuous laughter of the others, and of Pontes who guffawed in a manner all his own, a combination of the boisterous and musical as in Offenbach's operas. Pontes' laugh was a parody on the normal spontaneous laughter of a human being, presumably the only creature that could make that sound except a drunken fox; but he would suddenly stop, without being gradual about it, falling abruptly into a seriousness that was irresistibly funny.

In all his gestures and ways, in walking, reading, eating, in the most insignificant doings of life, this devilish fellow was different from all the others because he made them seem terribly ridiculous to one another. This reached such a point that merely to open his mouth or begin a gesture was sufficient to send all around him into spasms. Just his being present was enough. They hardly spied him before their faces were creased in smiles; if he made a move, ripples of laughter spread; if he opened his mouth, some roared, others loosened their belts, still others unbuttoned their vests. If he merely half opened his snout, Holy Mother! what outbursts, horselaughs,

screams, chokings, snorts, and terrifying efforts to catch one's breath.
"That fellow Pontes is unbeatable!"

"Stop, man, you're killing me!"

The joker however wore an air of innocence on his idiotic face.
"But I'm not doing anything. I didn't even open my mouth."

"Ha! Ha! Ha!" the whole company shouted open-mouthed, tears
streaming down their cheeks as they shook in spasms of uncontrollable
laughter.

With the passing of time the mere mention of his name was enough
to kindle boisterous merriment. If anybody uttered the word "Pontes,"
the round of snorting hilarity was set going, the noise by which man
rises superior to the animals that don't laugh.

In this manner Pontes lived along into his early thirties in the
midst of a smiling parabola, as it were, himself laughing and making
others laugh, and never thinking of anything serious—the life of a
sponger who exchanges funny grimaces for his meals and pays his
small debts with a currency of excellent jokes.

A merchant to whom he owed some money said to him one day
amidst sputters of laughter, "You at least are amusing, not like Major
Sourpuss, who lets his bills go unpaid with a frown."

This left-handed compliment vexed our joker, more or less; but his
debt amounted to fifteen milreis, and it seemed better to swallow the
taunt. However, the memory of that prick stuck in his mind like a
pin in the cushion of his self-respect. Later on he felt the pins stick
into him more and more, some just lightly, others right up to their
heads.

In the end, he couldn't take it any longer. Fed up with the life he
was leading, our playboy began to reflect on the pleasure of being
taken seriously, of speaking and being heard without the exertion of
facial muscles, of gesturing without breaking down the composure of
friends, of walking along a street without hearing on his trail a chorus
of, "Here comes Pontes!" shouted in tones of people doubled up in
bursts of merriment or all prepared to let out huge belly-laughs.

Reacting to this situation, Pontes tried to be serious.

Catastrophe.

Pontes, now harping on a sober string, naturally fell into the English
style of humor. Whereas before he had figured as a diverting clown,
now he was considered even more amusing as Gloomy Gus.

The resounding success of what everybody imagined to be a new
facet of his comic gifts, made more morose the soul of our repentant
joker. Was it then fated that he would never be able to strike out
afresh on a road different from the one he had followed and which
he now hated? Laugh, clown, laugh, that is thy destiny.

But the life of an adult has its solemn requirements, calling for
gravity and dignity not so essential in the immature years. The most
modest position in an office, the job of simple town-selectman, demands the facial steadiness of at least some idiot who doesn't laugh.

One just can't imagine a boisterous city-father. Rabelais' dictum has one exception: laughter is common to all the human species except to city aldermen.

With accumulating years, his judgment matured, his self-respect steadied, and parasitic meals began to taste sour. His currency of tricks seemed harder to coin; he could no longer cast it with wonted freshness, for he was using it now for a livelihood and not for idle relaxation as formerly. In his mind he compared himself to a circus clown, old and ailing, whom poverty forces to make funny faces out of his rheumatic pains because the paying public enjoys them.

He began to avoid people, and spent several months studying the changes necessary in him for the attainment of an honest job. He thought of being a counter salesman, or working in some factory, or being foreman of a plantation, or possibly opening up a bar—for anything at all seemed preferable to the comic foolishness of his life till then.

One day, his plans well advanced, he decided to change his way of living. He went to a business friend and earnestly explained his wish to mend his ways, ending by asking him for a job in his firm, even if only as sweeper. Hardly had he finished his statement when his Portuguese friend and those who were watching them near-by waiting for the point of the joke, all broke out into loud guffaws as if someone were tickling them.

"That's a good one! It's the best he has pulled off! Ha! Ha! Ha! So that now . . . Ha! Ha! Ha! You're killing me, man! If you're thinking of what you owe me for tobacco, forget it, for I've got my money's worth. That Pontes is full of tricks."

And the clerks, the customers, the idlers at the counters and even the passers-by halted on the sidewalk in front to enjoy the joke, and made the air quiver with their roars like the beat of a rattle, till their diaphragms ached.

Perturbed and insistently solemn, Pontes tried to make them understand they were wrong.

"I'm speaking seriously and you don't have the right to laugh at me. For the love of God, don't make sport of a poor man who is begging you for a job and who doesn't want your laughs."

The merchant loosened the belt of his trousers.

"He's speaking seriously, pff! Ha! Ha! Ha! Look, Pontes, you . . ."

Pontes walked out on him in the middle of his sentence and went off, his soul torn between despair and anger. This was too much. So society was rejecting him? Was he condemned to remain frozen forever in his comic mold?

He visited other firms, explained as best he could, implored. But his act was judged by unanimous agreement as one of the neatest tricks of an incorrigible joker. Many persons repeated the usual comment: "That devil of a fellow refuses to change his ways! And yet, he is no longer a child . . ."

Thwarted in his commercial quest, he turned toward agriculture. He sought out a ranch owner who had discharged his foreman and explained his situation to him.

After listening attentively to his statements, followed by the request to get the foreman's place, the Colonel exploded in a hilarious burst, "Pontes the foreman! Sh! Sh! Sh!"

"But . . ."

"Let me laugh, man, for I don't get a chance often to do so here in the back woods. Sh! Sh! Sh! That's a good one! I've always said that for making jokes, Pontes, old boy, there's no one your equal!"

And bellowing into the house, "Maricota, come out here and listen to this new one of Pontes. It's a scream! Sh! Sh! Sh!"

On that day our unhappy joker wept. He finally understood that one cannot destroy in a twinkling what it has taken years to build. His reputation as the unexcelled life of the party and as a joker unequaled and monumental, was built of lime too good and cement too hard to be overthrown suddenly.

Yet he felt impelled to change his way of living. Pontes now turned his consideration toward a political job, for government is an accommodating employer, perhaps the only one approachable under the circumstances; it is impersonal, it has nothing to do with laughter and doesn't even know intimately the separate units that make it up. Such an employer alone would take him seriously—yes, the road to salvation led that way.

He examined the possibility of serving in the postoffice, or the department of justice, or with the tax collector and all the rest. Weighing the pros and cons carefully, with all the trumps in the deck, he fixed his choice upon the federal internal revenue office, whose head, Major Bentes, would probably not last long because of his age and a heart ailment. There was public gossip about his aneurism or tumor in an artery that might burst any time.

Pontes' ace card was a relative in Rio, a wealthy fellow able to exert political pressure if certain changes in the government took place. Pontes followed him around and did so much to win him over to his idea that his relative finally dismissed him with a formal promise.

"Don't worry, for if I get the break I expect in the government and your collector's artery explodes opportunely, nobody is ever going to laugh at you again. Now get along, and let me hear from you when your man dies, and don't wait for his corpse to get cold."

Pontes returned home radiant with hope and patiently awaited the movement of events, one eye on politics and the other on the tumor that was to provide his salvation.

The political crisis came first, ministers fell, others replaced them, and among the latter a party big-shot who was associated with Pontes' relative. The road now was half traveled. Just the second part remained.

Unfortunately, the Major's health seemed steady, affording no evident signs of an early decline. In the opinion of the doctors who killed patients allopathically, the tumor was a dangerous thing that might burst under the slightest strain. But the surly old tax collector, thus warned, was in no hurry to depart for a better world, leaving behind a life for which the fates had provided plenty of comfort and ease. He did his best therefore to doublecross his incurable malady by following a rigidly methodical regimen. If some violent effort was to kill him, they needn't worry, he just wouldn't make such an effort.

Naturally, Pontes, already mentally the occupant of that sinecure, became impatient with this unsettling stalemate to his projects. How was he going to remove this obstacle from his path? He studied up in the Chernoviz medical volumes the chapters on tumors, in fact memorized them; he went about investigating all that was said or written on the subject; he began to know more about it than Dr. Iodope, the local physician, of whom it may be reported here confidentially that he never knew anything at all in his whole life.

Having thus bitten into this tempting apple of science, Pontes was gradually led to the notion that he might hurry the man's death by helping him to burst. Any exertion would kill him? Very well then, Souza Pontes would bring him to make that exertion.

"A burst of laughter is an exertion," he reflected satanically to himself. "A sudden guffaw could kill. Well, I'm an expert at making people laugh . . ."

Pontes passed many days in seclusion, holding a mental dialogue with the serpent of his temptation.

"Is it a crime? No! According to what code is it criminal to cause laughter? If a man should die of it, the blame should fall on his weak aorta."

The mind of our evil doer became a battlefield where his plan fought a duel against all the objections sent against it by his conscience. His embittered ambition served as judge and God knows how many times said judge prevaricated, influenced by scandalous partiality for one of the contending parties.

As was to be expected, the serpent won and Pontes emerged once more into society a bit more lean, with hollows under his eyes, yet with a queer light of victorious resolution shining in them. Also noticeable to those who looked at him with penetration was the nervousness of his manner—but penetration was not an abundant virtue among his fellow citizens, and morever the state of mind of a Pontes was a matter of no significance, because Pontes . . .

"As for Pontes . . ."

The future office-holder now began to forge careful plans for his campaign. First it was necessary to make contact with the Major, a man who lived a retired life and was very little given to idle conversation; then to insinuate himself into his intimacy; study his whims and hobbies until he found in what part of his anatomy was located his heel of Achilles.

He began to frequent regularly the collector's office under various pretexts, now for stamps on documents, again for information concerning taxes, anything that served as an opportunity for a bit of clever skillful conversation intended to undermine the old man's hostility.

He even went there on the business of other people, to pay excise taxes, obtain permits, and errands of the sort; he made himself very useful to friends who had dealings with the Treasury.

The Major was astonished at the frequency of his visits and told him so but Pontes parried this remark by inventing masterful pretexts and persisted in his well-calculated plan of letting time take its course in wearing down the sharp angles of his acquaintance of the weak heart.

By the end of two months Bentes had become accustomed to that lively "chipmunk" as he nicknamed Pontes, who after all seemed to him a kind-hearted fellow, eager to be of service and quite inoffensive. It was only a step from that point to the time when he asked Pontes to help him out on a day when the work had piled up, and again after that, and even once more. This development finally made Pontes a sort of an associate in his department. For certain services, there was no one like him. What industry! What subtlety! What tact! On scolding one of his clerks once, the Major held up Pontes' diplomacy as an example and a reprimand.

"You big idiot! Learn from Pontes who is skillful in everything and witty into the bargain."

On that same day he invited him to dinner. Great was the exultation in the heart of Pontes! The fortress was opening its doors to him.

That meal marked the beginning of a series of movements in which the "chipmunk," now an indispensable factotum, had a free field for his tactics.

Yet Major Bentes appeared invulnerable. He never laughed, but limited his manifestations of hilarity to ironic smiles. A jest that forced other table companions to get up from their chairs and stuff their napkins in their mouths, hardly did more than bring a curl to the Major's lips. And if the humor was not of extraordinary keenness, he used to humble the narrator without pity.

"That's an old joke, Pontes. You'll find it in the Laemmer almanac for 1850; I remember reading it."

Pontes smiled meekly, but within himself he took comfort with the reflection that if he hadn't caught him that time, he would catch him some other time.

All his sagacity was focused now on the single goal of sounding out the weakness of the Major. Every man has some preference for a certain type of humor or satire. One is fond of licentious tales about fat friars. Another dotes on good-humored jests connected with

German folk-songs. Another would sell his life for a tale with Gallic
spice. The Brazilian adores satire which exposes the boorish stupidity
of the natives of Portugal or the Azores.

But the Major? Well, he didn't laugh at humor served English
fashion, nor German, nor French, nor even Brazilian. What was his
type?

A systematic exploration, with the exclusion of humorous types
proven ineffective, brought Pontes to the realization of the special
weakness of his tough adversary; the Major licked his fingers for
tales about Englishmen and friars. However, it was necessary for
these to be worked in together. Separately, they missed fire. Such are
the peculiarities of an old man. Whenever in the same story, beef-
eating, ruddy Englishmen, in checkered suits, with cork helmets,
formidable boots, with a pipe in their mouths, figured together with
chubby friars, addicted to pipes and to feminine flesh, there and then
the Major would actually open his mouth and interrupt the process
of chewing, like a child who is being enticed with coconut candy.
And when the point of the joke was sprung, he would laugh with
pleasure, frankly, although without any abandonment endangering his
state of health.

With infinite patience, Pontes banked on this sole type of humor
and never left it for any other. He increased his repertory, regulated
the dosage of wit and malice, and systematically bombarded the
Major's aorta with the products of a skillful combination.

When the story was lengthy because the narrator embellished it
to delay and conceal the ending or heighten its effect, the old man
showed his quickened interest and during the cleverly placed pauses
he would ask for clarification or for the rest of the story.

"Well, how about that rascal of a beef-eater? What happened then?
Did Mister John whistle?"

Although the fatal guffaw was slow in coming, the future tax-
collector did not despair, trusting in the fable about the pitcher that
went to the water so often that it finally cracked. His plan was really
not too bad. Psychology was working for him—and also Lent.

On a certain occasion toward the end of the Carnival, the Major
gathered his friends around an enormous stuffed fish presented to
him by one of his colleagues. The Carnival sports had enlivened the
spirits of his table companions as well as those of their host, who on
that day was contented with himself and the world, as if he had beheld
some extraordinary marvel. The odors of cooking coming from the
kitchen took the place of liquid appetizers and called forth upon all
faces an expression of gastronomic anticipation.

When the fish was brought in the Major's eyes sparkled. He doted
on excellent fish, all the more when cooked by his faithful Gertrude.
And at that banquet Gertrude surpassed herself in the seasoning
which excelled the limits of the culinary art and rose to lyrical heights.
What a fish! Vata would have signed it himself with the pen of his

helplessness moistened in the ink of envy, one of the clerks remarked, an observation read in Brillat-Savarin and in other artists of the palate.

Amidst swallows of strong but inferior wine, the fish was gradually being inserted into stomachs with appreciative fervor. No one dared to break the silence of this alimentary blissfulness.

Pontes felt that this was the opportune moment for his final blow. He had prepared a story about an Englishman, his wife, and two Franciscan friars, an anecdote that he had elaborated by the effort of the best gray matter in his brain, perfecting it during long nights of insomnia. For a number of days he had his trap all set, always awaiting the right occasion when everything would cooperate to obtain for him the maximum result.

This was the final hope of our villain, his last cartridge. If it misfired, he was resolved to put two bullets into his own brain. He realized it was impossible to contrive a more ingenious explosive than this story. If the sick artery resisted this shock, then the so-called tumor was a fake, the aorta a figment of the imagination, the Chernoviz medical disquisition a stream of nonsense, medicine a failure, Doctor Iodope an ass, and he, Pontes, the most complete simpleton ever warmed by the sun—and therefore unfit to live.

Thus Pontes meditated, gazing appealingly with the eyes of psychology, on his intended victim, when the Major met him half-way; he blinked his left eye, a sign that he was all set to listen.

"Here goes now," thought our bandit; and with peerless naturalness, picking up as if by chance a bottle of sauce, he began to read the label.

"Perrins: Lea and Perrins. I wonder if he can be a relative of that Lord Perrins who tricked two Franciscan friars?"

Intoxicated by the delicious fish, the Major's eyes sparkled with a lustful light of greediness for a spicy story.

"Two friars and a Lord! This story must be A 1. Tell it to us, chipmunk."

And chewing unconsciously, he became absorbed in the fateful tale.

The anecdote ran along craftily, combining the usual threads of events until the denouement was near. It was related with a masterly art, clear and precise, in a strategic development full of genius. Half way toward the end, the plot had the old man so spellbound that it held him in suspense, his mouth half-open, an olive stuck on his fork stopped in mid-ar. A readiness to burst out laughing—now held in check but eager to explode—a roaring laugh about to erupt, illuminated his face.

Pontes hesitated. He foresaw the bursting of the artery. For an instant his conscience put a brake on his tongue, but Pontes kicked it aside and with a steady voice pulled the trigger.

Major Antonio Pereira da Silva Bentes let forth the first guffaw in his life, a loud resounding roar that could be heard to the end of the street, a bellow like that of Carlyle's Teufelsdröckh facing Jean Paul Richter. It was his first, to be sure, but also his last, for in the midst of it his astounded companions saw him slump face down over his plate, at the same time that a jet of blood reddened the tablecloth.

The assassin rose, hallucinated. Taking advantage of the confusion, he slipped out into the street like a second Cain. He hid himself in his house, bolted the door of his room, his teeth chattered all night long, his perspiration ran cold. The slightest noises filled him with terror. Could it be the police?

It took weeks for that agitation of his soul to begin to calm down. Everybody attributed his indisposition to his sorrow over the death of his friend. Nevertheless, his eyes constantly beheld the same vision: the collector slumped over his plate, his mouth spurting blood, while in the air there echoed that shriek of his last laughter.

While he was in this depressed frame of mind, he received a letter from his Rio relative. Among other things, this influential person wrote: "As you didn't notify me in time according to our understanding, it was only through the newspapers that I found out about the death of Bentes. I went to the Minister but it was too late, the name of a successor had already been selected. Your carelessness made you lose the best chance in your life. Keep in mind for your guidance this Latin dictum: *'tarde venientibus ossa,* whoever arrives late finds only bones'—and be more alert in the future."

One month later he was found hanging from a beam, stiff, his tongue out.

He had strangled himself with the leg of a pair of drawers.

When the news spread in the city, everyone was amused by this detail. The Portuguese department store owner passed this comment before his clerks:

"What a funny fellow he was! Even at his death he thinks up a prank. To hang oneself on one's drawers! That's a trick that only Pontes could pull off."

And the group around him echoed in chorus a half dozen "Ha! Ha!'s"—the sole epitaph granted by society to poor Pontes.